AFRIKAANS/ENGLISH-ENGLISH/AFRIKAANS

Happy birthday, Schnicklepooper!
Use this for the forces of good, not
evil ...

                    wederom!
                      ~ Dafna

AFRIKAANS/ENGLISH ENGLISH/AFRIKAANS DICTIONARY

M. S. B. KRITZINGER
JAN KROMHOUT

HIPPOCRENE BOOKS
New York

Originally published by J.L. Van Schaik Publishers,
Pretoria, South Africa.

Copyright © 1988 J.L. Van Schaik (Pty), Ltd.
Published under license.

ISBN 0-7818-0052-8

For information, address:
Hippocrene Books, Inc.
171 Madison Ave.
New York, NY 10016

Printed in the United States of America.

AFRIKAANS – ENGELS

AFKORTINGS

b	=	byvoeglike naamwoord
bw	=	bywoord
mv	=	meervoud
s	=	selfstandige naamwoord
telw	=	telwoord
tw	=	tussenwerpsel
verklw	=	verkleinwoord
vgw	=	voegwoord
vnw	=	voornaamwoord
vs	=	voorsetsel
w	=	werkwoord

TEKENS

Verboë vorme van woorde word tussen hakies aangegee en in vet letter direk na die woord gedruk. Uitdrukkings is kursief gedruk.

1 **Tilde of slangetjie: ~ :**

Die tilde vervang die woord soos hy staan:
a) **nippertjie:** *op die ~,* beteken: *op die nippertjie*
b) **aand: ~ete, ~kerk** beteken: **aandete; aandkerk**

2 **Koppelteken (-):**

a) Na selfstandige naamwoorde beteken dit: voeg die letter(s) by die woord vir die meervoud: **eend (-e) = eend, eende; dame (-s) = dame, dames; kind (-ers) = kind, kinders**

b) Twee letters of lettergrepe voorafgegaan deur strepies beteken die woord het twee meervoude: **leeu (-e, -s) ↗ leeu, leeue, leeus; kas (-se, -te) = kas, kasse, kaste**

c) Na byvoeglike naamwoorde en bywoorde gee dit te kenne: voeg die letters by vir die trappe van vergelyking: **lelik (-e; -er, -ste) = lelik, lelike, leliker, lelikste**

d) Na werkwoorde beteken dit: voeg, vir die verlede deelwoord, ge- voor die woord: **loop (ge-) = loop, geloop;** voeg -ge- tussen die dele van die woord: **weggaan (-ge-) = weggaan, weggegaan**

e) Aan die end van 'n reël dui die koppelteken aan dat die betrokke samevoeging met 'n koppelteken geskryf word.

3 **Afbreekteken: =.** Die afbreekteken = aan die end van 'n reël dui in hierdie publikasie aan dat daardie woord aanmekaar geskryf word

4 **Kolletjies: ..** Oral waar die spelling van verboë vorme verander, word sulke veranderings voorafgegaan deur twee kolletjies: **orgaan (..gane) = orgaan, organe; musikaal (..kale; ..kaler, -ste) = musikale; musikaler, musikaalste**

5 **Ronde hakies: ( ).** Ronde hakies om 'n letter of letters in 'n woord beteken dat die woord met of sonder daardie letter(s) gespel word: **gestrem(d) = gestremd of gestrem**

6 **Die klemteken: ′.** Dié verskyn net ná die letter of lettergreep wat die hoofklem het in 'n woord: **kin′ders, hobbelag′tig, aristokrasie′, mu′sici**

7 **Die gelykteken: =.** In die geval van dubbelvorme verwys hierdie teken na die vorm waaraan die samesteller die voorkeur gee: **a′lewee = aalwyn**

8 **Die balk: /.** Keuse/keur beteken die student het 'n keuse tussen die twee.

A

aak'lig (-e; -er, -ste) horrible, nasty, awful; *'n ~e gesig,* a horrible sight
aal'moes (-e) alms, charity, dole
aal'wee (-s), **aal'wyn** (-e) aloe
aam'beeld (-e) anvil; *altyd op dieselfde ~ slaan,* keep on harping on the same string
aam'bei (-e) piles, haemorrhoids
aambors'tig (e-; -er, -ste) asthmatic
aan¹ (b, bw) on, in, upon; *ek wil weet waar ek ~ of af is,* I want to know where I stand
aan² (vs) at, near, next to, upon; *~ die gang,* on the go; *~ die grens,* on the border; *~ tafel,* at table; *~ tering sterf,* die of consumption
aan'beveel recommend; *aanbevole prys,* recommended price, *ook* **rigprys**
aan'beveling (-e, -s) recommendation; *op ~ van,* on the recommendation of
aanbid' (~) adore, worship, idolise
aan'bieding (-e, -s) offer, tender, presenta= tion
aan'bied (-ge-) offer; present; volunteer; tender
aan'blik (s) sight; view, look: *by die eerste ~,* at first sight
aan'bly (-ge-) continue, remain; hold on; *bly asseblief aan,* please hold the line
aan'bod (..biedinge, ..biedings) offer, proposal; supply; *vraag en ~,* demand and supply
aan'bou (w) (-ge-) build on; **~ing** (-s) addi= tion (to building)
aan'brand (-ge-) burn (food)
aan'breek (-ge-) dawn; come; *die dag sal ~,* the day will come
aand (-e) evening, eve
aanda'dig (-e) accessory, instrumental to
aan'dag attention, devotion; *die ~ vestig op,* draw attention to
aandag'tig (-e; -er, -ste) attentive
aan'deel (..dele) share; portion, part; *~ hê in,* have a share in; **~houer** (-s) share= holder
aan'dele: ~bewys (-e) share certificate; (pl) scrip; **~kapitaal** share capital
aan'denking (-e, -es) remembrance, keep= sake, souvenir, memento
aand: ~ete (-s) supper; **~kerk** evening ser=

vice; **~klas** (-se) evening/night class; **~klokreëling** curfew
aan'doen (-ge-) call at (port); cause, affect, move; *smart, leed ~,* cause grief/sorrow; *~ lik* (-e; -er, -ste) touching, pathetic
aand'pak (-ke) dress suit
aan'dra (-ge-) bring to, carry to; tell, inform
aan'draai (-ge-) screw tighter, turn on
aan'dring (-ge-) urge, press on, insist on; *op 'n saak ~,* insist on a matter
aand'rok (-ke) evening dress (lady)
aand: ~sitting (-s) evening/night session; **~skool** (..skole) night school
aan'dui (-ge-) indicate, point out
aan'duiding (-e, -s) indication, designation
aan'durf (-ge-) dare; *'n taak ~,* tackle a job
aaneen' together, connected, consecutively; *tien dae ~,* ten days on end
aaneen'skakel (-geskakel) link together; connect consecutively
aan'gaan (-ge-) concern, begin; proceed, continue; *koste ~,* incur expenses; *'n ooreenkoms ~,* conclude (enter into) an agreement; *wat my ~,* as far as I am con= cerned.
aangaan'de as for, concerning, as regards
aan'gaap (-ge-) stare/gape at
aan'gee (s) (..geë) pass (rugby); (w) (-ge-) hand on, pass; *die pas ~,* set the pace
aan'geklaagde (-s) accused, defendant
aan'geklam (-de) tipsy
aan'geleentheid (..hede) affair, concern, incident, matter
aan'genaam (..name; ..namer, -ste) plea= sant, agreeable, comfortable, enjoyable; *~!, ..name kennismaking,* how do you do? pleased to meet you
aan'genome (b) accepted; adopted; *'n ~ kind,* an adopted child
aan'gesien because, as, considering, since
aan'gesig (-te) countenance, face
aan'geteken (-de) noted; registered; *~de pos,* registered post
aan'gewese obvious, right, proper; *die ~ persoon,* the right person
aangren'send (-e) adjacent, bordering on, adjoining; *~e binneland,* adjacent inter= ior

aan'gryp (-ge-) seize, catch hold of; attack; *'n geleentheid ~*, grasp/seize an opportunity

aangry'pend (-e; -er, -ste) touching, moving, gripping

aan'haak (-ge-) hook on, fasten; hitch on

aan'haal (-ge-) quote, cite; *~ .. afhaal,* quote .. unquote; *bewyse ~,* produce proof/evidence; *~tekens* quotation marks

aan'haling (-e, -s) quotation, quoted passage

aan'hang (s) following; adherents, party; *~er* follower; fan

aan'hangsel (-s) supplement, appendix, annexure

aan'hef (s) beginning, preamble; *die ~ van 'n brief,* the beginning/salutation of a letter

aan'heg (-ge-) affix, annex, attach; *die aangehegte kwitansie,* the attached receipt

aan'help (-ge-) help on with

aan'hits (-ge-) instigate, incite, egg on

aan'hoor (-ge-) listen to; *~der* (-s) listener

aan'hou (-ge-) continue, insist, persevere; keep (servant); keep on (clothes); detain, arrest; *in ~ding,* detained, in custody; *aangehoudene,* detainee

aanhou'dend (-e) continual, incessant; *~e droogte,* prolonged drought

aan'houer (-s) perseverer; *~ wen,* perseverance will be rewarded

aan'kla (-ge-) accuse, charge with

aan'klaer (-s) prosecutor

aan'klag (-te) accusation, charge; *~kantoor* charge office (police)

aan'kleef, aan'klewe (-ge-) stick/adhere to

aan'klop (-ge-) knock, beat (at the door); *om hulp ~,* ask for help

aan'knoop (-ge-) fasten; enter into (conversation); tie on to

aan'kom (-ge-) arrive, get at; acquire, obtain; drop in; *betyds ~,* arrive in time

aan'komeling (-e) newcomer, beginner

aan'koms arrival

aan'kondig (-ge-) announce, publish, inform, advertise; *~er* (-s) announcer; *~ing* (-e, -s) announcement, notification

aan'koop (s, w) purchase; *verkry deur ~,* acquired through purchase

aan'kweek (-ge-) cultivate, grow, rear; *'n goeie gewoonte ~,* cultivate a good habit

aan'kyk (-ge-) look at; *iem. skeef ~,* look askance/doubtingly at someone

aan'las (-ge-) join, attach, dovetail

aan'lê (-ge-) aim at; apply; plan, build, lay out; court; *~ met 'n geweer,* take aim; *by 'n nooi ~,* court a girl

aan'leer (-ge-) learn, acquire

aan'leg (-te) plan, arrangement, talent; disposition; installation; *~ en masjinerie,* plant and machinery; *~toets* (-e) aptitude test

aan'leiding (-e, -s) cause, reason, motive; *na ~ van,* with reference to, concerning

aanlok'lik (-e; -er, -ste) attractive, charming, inviting

aan'loop (s) patronage; takeoff; (w) (-ge-) go on walking; walk faster; call in passing; *agter meisies ~,* run after girls; *~baan (..bane)* runway, *ook* stygbaan

aan'maak (-ge-) prepare, mix

aan'maan (-ge-) warn, admonish; remind

aan'maning (-e, -s) warning, reminder; relapse (disease)

aan'matigend (-e; -er, -ste) presumptuous, arrogant; *~e houding,* arrogant bearing/attitude

aan'mekaar together, connected; consecutively, continuously; *die twee is ~,* the two of them are fighting

aan'meld (-ge-) announce, report; *~bare siekte,* notifiable disease; *jy moet jou môre ~,* you must report tomorrow

aan'merking (-e, -s) remark, criticism; observation; *'n beledigende ~,* an insulting remark; *in ~ kom vir,* qualify for; *in ~ neem,* take into consideration

aanmerk'lik (-e; -er, -ste) considerable, notable, appreciable; *'n ~e verbetering,* a remarkable improvement

aan'moedig (-ge-) encourage; *~ing* encouragement

aan'neem (-ge-) accept, adopt; assume, admit; confirm; *'n vriendelik houding ~,* adopt a friendly attitude; *'n uitnodiging ~,* accept an invitation

aanneem'lik (-e; -er, -ste) acceptable, credible, reasonable

aan'nemer (-s) contractor, undertaker

aan'neming acceptance; adoption; confirmation

aan'pak (-ge-) seize, take hold of; tackle

aan'pas (-ge-) try on, fit; adapt, adjust; *by omstandighede* ~, adapt to circumstances; ~**ser** (-s) adapter (electricity); ~**sing** (-e, -s) adjustment; ~(**sings**)**vermoë** adaptability

aan'plak (-ge-) post up (bills), stick; ~**bord** (-e) notice board

aan'por (-ge-) prod, rouse, urge, instigate

aan'prys (-ge-) commend, extol

aan'raai (-ge-) advise, suggest, recommend

aan'raak (-ge-) touch

aan'raking (-e, -s) touch, contact; *in* ~ *kom met*, get in touch with

aan'rand (-ge-) assault, attack; ~**ing** (-s) assault, attack; *onsedelike* ~**ing**, indecent assault

aan'rig (-ge-) cause, commit, do; *skade* ~, cause damage

aan'roer (-ge-) touch upon, broach, mention; stir up; hasten; *'n saak* ~, broach a subject/matter

aan'rye, aan'ryg (-ge-) string (beads); lace up (boots); baste

aan'sê (-ge-) announce, inform; instruct

aan'sien (s) appearance, respect, esteem; *hoog in* ~ *wees*, be highly respected

aansien'lik (-e; -er, -ste) respectable; considerable, notable; handsome

aan'sit (-ge-) sit down at table; put on; instigate; start (motor); ~**kabel** jumper lead; ~**ter** (-s) starter (motor)

aan'skaf (-ge-) procure, buy, secure

aanskou' (~) see, look at, contemplate, view, behold; *die lewenslig* ~, be born; ~**ingsonderwys** visual education

aan'skryf, aan'skrywe (-ge-) notify; send a letter of demand, sue

aan'skrywing (-e, -s) notification, letter of demand; summons

aan'slaan (-ge-) touch, strike, assume (a tone); assess, salute; knock on (rugby); *die regte toon* ~, strike the right note

aan'slag (..slae) stroke; attempt; touch (music); assessment (income tax); *'n* ~ *op sy lewe*, an attempt on his life

aan'sluit (-ge-) join, follow; enlist, enrol; connect; *by die leër* ~, join the army

aan'soek (-e) application, request, proposal; ~ *doen om 'n betrekking*, apply for a position; *'n* ~ *rig*, apply; ~**er** (-s) applicant

aan'spoor (-ge-) spur on, urge on, encourage; ~**bonus** incentive bonus

aan'sporing stimulation, incentive

aan'spraak (..sprake) address; claim, title; ~ *maak op iets*, lay claim to something; ~**maker** contender (for a title)

aan'spreek (-ge-) address, speak to; accost

aanspreek'lik (-e; -er, -ste) responsible, answerable, liable; ~ *hou vir die koste*, hold responsible for the cost; ~**heid** liability

aan'staan (-ge-) please, like, suit; *hy staan my glad nie aan nie*, I don't like him at all

aanstaan'de (s) (-s) intended, fiance(e); (b) next; prospective; forthcoming

aan'staar (-ge-) stare at, gaze at

aan'stalte (-s) preparation; ~ *maak*, getting ready

aan'stap (-ge-) walk on; walk briskly

aan'steek (-ge-) infect; light, kindle; pin on

aansteek'lik (-e; -er, -ste) infectious, contagious

aan'stel (-ge-) appoint; pretend; sham, put on; *moenie jou so* ~ *nie*, do not put on such airs

aan'stellerig (-e; -er, -ste) affected, conceited

aan'stelling (-e, -s) appoinment

aan'sterk (-ge-) recuperate, convalesce; ~**verlof** convalescent leave

aan'stip (-ge-) jot down, touch on, hint at

aan'stons presently, directly, anon

aan'stoot (s) (..stote) offence; ~ *gee of neem*, give or take offence

aanstoot'lik (-e; -er, -ste) offensive, indecent, objectionable

aan'stryk (-ge-) walk on; brush over

aan'stuur (-ge-) send on, despatch

aan'suiwer (-ge-) settle; adjust; *'n tekort* ~, make up a deficit; ~**ings** adjustments (bookkeeping)

aan'sukkel (-ge-) struggle/trudge along

aan'syn existence, presence

aan'tal (-le) number; *'n hele* ~ *foute*, quite a few mistakes

aan'tas (-ge-) touch; attack, affect; *sy gesondheid was aangetas*, his health was impaired

aan'teel (w) (-ge-) breed, increase

aan'teken (-ge-) note down, record; register; score; *'n brief* ~, register a letter; *'n drie* ~, score a try (rugby); *protes* ~, lodge a protest; ~ing (-e) note; record; registration; ~ingboek (-e) notebook

aan'tog approach, advance

aan'toon (-ge-) show, demonstrate; indicate

aan'tref (-ge-) meet, find; 'n vreemde plant ~, come across a strange plant

aan'trek (-ge-) dress; draw tighter; attract

aan'trekking attraction; ~s'krag gravitation (of earth)

aantrek'lik (-e; -er, -ste) attractive; sensitive

aan'tyging (-e, -s) imputation, accusation

aanvaar' (~) accept, assume

aanvaar'ding assumption; acceptance

aan'val (s) (-le) attack, charge; fit; 'n ~ afslaan, repel an attack; 'n ~ van beroerte, an apoplectic stroke; (w) (-ge-) attack, assail, charge

aan'valler (-s) assailant, attacker

aanval'lig (-e; -er, -ste) lovely, amiable, charming

aan'vang (s) beginning, start; (w) (-ge-) begin, commence; wat het jy aangevang? what have you been up to? ~stadium initial stage

aanveg'baar (..bare; -der, -ste) open to attack, debatable

aan'vly (-ge-) nestle against

aan'voer (w) (-ge-) supply; allege; advance; lead; ~der (-s) commander, leader

aan'voor (-ge-) begin, commence; 'n saak ~, take the first steps

aan'vra (-ge-) apply for, request

aan'vraag (..vrae) application, demand, request, requisition; daar is 'n groot ~ vir hierdie artikel, there is a great demand for this article

aan'vul (-ge-) fill up, replenish, supplement; ~(lings)eksamen supplementary examination

aan'wakker (-ge-) encourage; fan (hatred); belangstelling ~, rouse interest

aan'was (s) growth, increase; (w) (-ge-) grow, increase

aan'wend (-ge-) use, employ, apply; appropriate; ~ing van fondse, application of funds (bookkeeping); 'n poging ~, make an attempt

aan'wensel (-s) (bad) habit

aan'werk (-ge-) sew on

aanwe'sig (-e) present; veertien leerlinge is ~, fourteen pupils are present

aan'wins gain, profit, acquisition, asset

aan'wys (-ge-) show, point out, indicate; allocate

aan'wyser (-s) pointer, indicator; ekonomiese ~, economic indicator

aan'wysing (-e, -s) indication, hint; direction; allocation

aap (ape) ape; monkey; fool; die ~ kom uit die mou, the cat is out of the bag; ~stert (-e) monkeytail; sjambok

aap'stuipe: hy kan die ~ kry, he is beside himself

aar[1] (are) ear (of corn)

aar[2] (are) vein; underground watercourse; core (electr.)

aar'bei (-e) strawberry; ~konfyt strawberry jam

aard[1] (s) nature, kind, temper; niks van die ~ nie, nothing of the kind; 'n ~jie na sy vaartjie, like father, like son; (w) (ge-) take after; thrive

aard[2] (w) (ge-) earth (elec.)

aard: ~be'wing (-e, -s) earthquake; ~bol globe

aar'de earth; hemel en ~ beweeg, leave no stone unturned; moeder ~, mother earth

aar'dig (a) (-e; -er, -ste) nice, agreeable; unpleasant, queer; 'n ~e sommetjie geld, a considerable sum of money

aard: ~kors crust of the earth; ~kunde geology; ~rykskunde geography

aardrykskun'dig (-e) geographical; ~e (-s) geographer

aards (-e) worldly, mundane

aard: ~skok (-ke), ~skudding (-e) earth tremor

aar'sel (ge-) hesitate, waver

aart'appel (-s) potato; ~moer (-e) seed potato; ~skyfie (potato) chip, ook ertappel

aarts: ~biskop (-pe) archbishop; ~engel (-e) archangel; ~vader (-s) patriarch; ~vyand (-e) archenemy

aar'verkalking arteriosclerosis

aas[1] (s) carrion; bait; (w) (ge-) feed on, prey on; scrounge

aas[2] (s) (ase) ace

aas'voël (-s) vulture; glutton

ab (-te) abbot

abattoir' (-s) abattoir; municipal slaughterhouse

ab'ba (ge-) carry on one's back (baby); ~hart (-e) piggy-back heart; ~skip (..skepe) aircraft carrier

abdis' (-se) abbess

abdy' (-e) abbey, monastery

abnormaal' (..male; ..maler, -ste) abnormal

abor'sie (-s) abortion, *ook* vrugafdrywing

absent' absent; ~isme absenteeism

abses' (-se) abscess, ulcer

absoluut' (b) (..lute) absolute; (bw) absoslutely

absorbeer' (~, ge-) absorb

abstrak' (-te) abstract

absurd' (-e) absurd, preposterous; ~e *teaster*, theatre of the absurd

abuis' mistake, error; *per* ~, by mistake

a'dams: ~appel (-s) Adam's apple; ~kosstuum in nature's garb, nude; ~vy (-e) Adam's fig

ad'der (-s) adder, viper; ~gebroedsel (-s) breed of vipers; vermin

addisioneel' (..nele) additional

a'del nobility

a'delaar (-s) eagle

a'delbors marine cadet; midshipman

a'del: ~lik (-e) noble, high-born; *hy is van ~like afkoms*, he is of noble birth; ~stand nobility, peerage

a'dem (s) (-s) breath; (w) (ge-) breathe (fig.); ~lose stilte, breathless silence

adjektief' (..tiewe) adjective

adjudant' (-e) adjutant, aide-de-camp

adjunk' (-te) deputy, assistant; ~-minister deputy minister

administra'sie administration

administrateur' (-s) administrator; ~-geseneraal (administrateurs-generaal) adminstrator-general

admiraal' (-s) admiral

admis'sie admission; ~-eksamen (-s) entrance examination (mostly theology)

adolessen'sie adolescence

adoons' monkey; ugly fellow

adrenalien' adrenalin(e)

adres' (-se) address

adresseer' (~ ge-) address, direct

adverbiaal' (..biale) adverbial

adverteer' (~ ge-) advertise

adverten'sie (-s) advertisement

advies' advice; *op ~ van*, on the advice of; *van ~ (be)dien*, advise; ~raad advisory council

adviseer' (~ ge-) advise

adviseur' (-s) adviser

advokaat'[1] (..kate) advocate, barrister-at-law, lawyer; *hy praat/pleit soos 'n ~*, he has the gift of the gab

advokaat'[2] egg flip

af off, down, from; *van sy jeug ~*, since his (early) youth; *~ en toe*, now and then

af'baken (-ge-) divide; beacon off, mark out; ~ing delimitation, demarcation; (job) reservation

af'beeld (-ge-) picture, portray, depict; ~ing (-e, -s) picture, portrait, illustration

af'been cripple(d)

af'betaal (~) pay off, settle

af'betaling (-e, -s) payment, settlement; *op ~ koop*, buy on instalment system, on terms

af'bly (-ge-) leave alone, keep off

af'brand (-ge-) burn down

af'breek (-ge-) pull down, demolish; destroy; break off

af'breuk damage; *~ doen aan*, injure, prejudice

af'bring (-ge-) bring down, reduce; come off

af'byt (-ge-) bite off; *die spit ~*, bear the brunt

af'dak (-ke) shed, lean-to; penthouse; **motor~** carport

af'dank (-ge-) disband, dismiss, discharge; cast off

af'deling (-e, -s) division, section, department; detachment; *'n ~ soldate*, a squad of soldiers

af'doen (-ge-, afgedaan) finish, complete; take off; expedite; ~*de bewys*, clear proof

af'draai (-ge-) turn off, twist off, branch off

af'draand (s) (-e, -es, -s) af'draande (-s) slope, declivity, descent; *hy is op die ~*, he is going down-hill

af'dreig (-ge-) blackmail; extort; ~ing (s) blackmail; extortion

af'druk (s) (-ke) imprint; copy, impression, reproduction

af'dwaal (-ge-) stray, deviate, digress, err, wander

af'dwing (-ge-) extort, force from; enforce

affê're (-s) affair, thing, matter

affilia'sie affiliation

affilieer' (ge-, ~) affiliate
affodil' (-le) daffodil
af'gaan (-ge-) go down, descend; wear off
afgedank'ste confounded; *'n ~ loesing (pak slae),* a severe thrashing
af'gee (-ge-) deliver, hand over; come off, give off; *onenigheid ~,* cause dissen= sion
af'gelas (~) call off; *die polisie gelas die soektog af,* the police are calling off the search
af'geleë (meer ~, mees ~) remote, distant
af'geleef (-de) worn with age, decrepit
af'gemat (-te; -ter, -ste) tired, weary, ex= hausted
af'gesaag (-de; -der, -ste) hackneyed, stale; *'n ~de grap,* a stale joke
af'gesant (-e) messenger; envoy, emissary
af'gesien: ~ *van,* notwithstanding, apart from
af'gesonder (-de) isolated, retired, lonely
af'gestorwene (-s) (the) deceased, (the) dear departed
af'getrokke (meer ~, mees ~) absent= minded; abstract; *die ~ professor,* the absent-minded professor
af'gevaardigde (-s) deputy, delegate
af'god (-e) idol; *geld tot 'n ~ maak,* idolise money
af'gooi (-ge-) throw down; cast off
af'grond (-e) precipice, abyss
afgrys'lik (-e; -er, -ste) horrible, hideous, dreadful, ghastly
af'guns envy, jealousy, spite
afguns'tig (-e; -er, -ste) envious, jealous
af'haak (-ge-) unhook, detach; let go, let loose; deliver a blow; *wanneer gaan julle ~?,* when are you getting married?
af'haal (-ge-) take down, fetch down; call for; unquote
af'handel (-ge-) settle, terminate, conclude
af'hang (-ge-) hang down; depend (up)on; *alles hang van jou af,* everything depends on you
afhank'lik (-e; -er, -ste) dependent; (s) ~e (-s) dependant
af'jak (s) (-ke) rating, rebuff; snub; (w) (-ge-) rate, scold, chide, snub
af'kam (-ge-) comb off; run down (by cri= ticism)
af'kap (-ge-) cut off, chop off; apostroph= ise; ~teken, ~pingsteken (-s) apostrophe

af'keer[1] (s) aversion, dislike; *'n ~ hê van,* have a dislike of
af'keer[2] (w) (-ge-) avert, ward off
afke'rig: ~ *van,* averse to
af'keur (-ge-) disapprove, condemn; reject
af'keuring disapproval, censure; *sy ~ uit= spreek,* express his disapproval
af'klim (-ge-) climb down, descend; *van sy perdjie ~,* come down a notch or two
af'klop (-ge-) beat, thrash; peg out, die
af'knou (-ge-) hurt, bully; ~er (s) bully
af'koel (-ge-) cool down
af'kom (-ge-) come down, descend; *met 'n boete daarvan ~,* get off with a fine; *die rivier sal ~,* the river will be in flood; ~e'ling (-e) descendant; ~s descent, derivation, extraction, origin; *van hoë ~s wees,* be of noble birth
afkoms'tig derived from, descended from; ~ *van die Karoo,* hailing from the Karoo
af'kondig (-ge-) proclaim, declare, prom= ulgate, publish; *gebooie ~,* publish the banns
af'konkel (-ge-) coax away; alienate
af'koop (w) (-ge-) surrender (insurance policy); redeem; ~boete spotfine
af'kort (-ge-) shorten, abbreviate, abridge; ~ing (-e, -s) abbreviation, abridgment
af'kyk (-ge-) copy, crib; look down; spy
af'laai (-ge-) unload, discharge
af'lê (-ge-) lay down, part with; lay out; take (oath); pass (examination); give (evidence); pay (visit); *'n besoek ~,* pay a visit; *'n eed ~,* take an oath; *eksamen ~,* take/pass an examination; *getuienis ~,* give evidence
af'leer (-ge-) unlearn, forget
af'lees (-ge-) read out, call out
af'lei (-ge-) deduce, infer, derive; divert; ~ding (-e, -s) derivation, deduction; di= version, distraction, recreation; ~er (-s) (lightning) conductor; ~kunde etymology
af'lewer (-ge-) deliver; ~ing (-e, -s) deliv= ery
af'loer (-ge-) spy, watch
af'loop (s) end, result, issue; expiration; run= off; *na ~ van die vergadering,* after the meeting
af'los (-ge-) relieve, redeem, discharge; *mekaar ~,* take turns; ~baar (..bare) redeemable; ~wedloop (..lope) relay race
af'luister (-ge-) overhear; eavesdrop

af'maak (-ge-) kill, finish

af'mat (-ge-) tire, fatigue, exhaust; **~tend** (-e; -er, -ste) tiresome, fatiguing; **~ting** weariness, fatigue, exhaustion

af'merk (-ge-) tick off, mark; mark down

af'meting (-e, -s) measurement, measure, dimension

af'neem (-ge-) take away, deprive; decrease, shrink; take a photo, photograph; *'n eed ~*, take an oath; *'n eksamen ~*, examine; *sy kragte neem vinnig af*, his strength is rapidly declining

af'nemer (-s) photographer

af'paar (-ge-) pair off

af'pak (-ge-) unload, unpack

af'pen (-ge-) pegg off (claim)

af'pers (-ge-) extort, exact from; blackmail; **~er** (-s) blackmailer, racketeer; **~ing** extortion, exaction; blackmail

af'plat level off, slow down (economy)

af'pluk (-ge-) pick off, gather

af'praat (-ge-) arrange, agree upon

af'raai (-ge-) dissuade from

af'rammel (-ge-) rattle off; prattle; *die voordrag ~*, rattle off the recitation

af'ransel (-ge-) trash, flog

af'reken (-ge-) settle, get even with

af'rig (-ge-) train, coach (sport); **~ter** (-s) trainer, coach; **~ting** training, coaching

A'frika Africa

Afrikaan' (..kane) African

Afrikaans' (s) Afrikaans; (b) (-e) Afrikaans

Afrika'ner[1] (-s) Afrikaner

afrika'ner[2] (-s) marigold

Afrika'nerbees (-te) (..bul, ..koei, ..os) Afrikaner, Africaner

af'rit (-te) offramp, exit (traffic)

Af'ro-Asia'ties (-e) Afro-Asian

af'rokkel (-ge-) coax away, wheedle away

af'rond (-ge-) round off, finish off; **~ing** rounding off; finish; **~(ing)skool** (..skole) finishing school

af'room (-ge-) skim (milk)

af'saag, af'sae (-ge-) saw off; *afgesaagde grap*, stale joke

af'sê (-ge-) sack; countermand; *die nooi het hom afgesê*, the girl gave him the sack (broke the engagement)

af'send (-ge-) send off, forward, consign; **~er** (-s) sender, consignor

af'set turnover, sales; **~gebied** (-e) market, sales area

af'setter (-s) swindler, cheat

af'sien (-ge-) give up, abandon; see off; *van 'n plan ~*, give up a plan

afsig'telik (-e; -er, -ste) ugly, hideous

af'sit (-ge-) put down; dismiss; dethrone (a king); **~ter** (-s) starter (sport)

af'skaf (-ge-) abolish, abrogate, repeal; **~fer** (-s) abstainer, teetotaller

af'skeep (-ge-) do work in a slip-shod manner, treat shabbily; *jou werk ~*, neglect your work

af'skeer (-ge-) shear, shave

af'skei (-ge-) separate; sever from; secrete

af'skeid parting, departure, farewell; **~toewuif**, wave farewell; **~s'geskenk** farewell gift/present; **~s'maal** (..male) farewell dinner; **~s'preek** (..preke) farewell/valedictory sermon

af'skil (-ge-) peel, rind

af'skilder (-ge-) depict, paint, describe

af'skilfer (-ge-) scale, peel off

af'skop (w) (-ge-) kick off

af'skort (-ge-) partition off; **~ing** (-s) partition

af'skrif (-te) copy, duplicate; *gewaarmerkte ~*, certified copy

af'skrik (w) (-ge-) frighten, scare away, discourage; **~middel** (-s) deterrent

afskrikwek'kend (-e; -er, -ste) terrifying

af'skryf, af'skrywe (-ge-) copy, crib; cancel, write off; *R5 van 'n rekening ~*, write off R5 from an account

af'sku abomination, horror, abhorrence

af'skud (-ge-) shake off

afsku'welik (-e; -er, -ste) abominable, horrible, detestable

af'slaan (-ge-) decline, refuse (an invitation); repulse, beat off (the enemy); serve, service (tennis); *'n aanbod ~*, refuse an offer

af'slaer (-s) auctioneer

af'slag[1] (s) reduction, rebate, discount

af'slag[2] (w) (-ge-) flay, skin

af'slagwinkel (-s) discount store

af'sloof, (-ge-) drudge, toil; flog oneself

af'sluit (-ge-) close, shut off; fence in; seclude; *jou ~*, seclude oneself; *rekenings ~ aan die einde van die boekjaar*, close off accounts at the end of the financial year

af'slyt (-ge-) wear out, waste

af'smeer (-ge-) palm off on; *hy het daardie ou fiets aan my afgesmeer,* he palmed off that old bicycle on me

af'smyt (-ge-) throw off, fling off

af'snou (-ge-) speak harshly to, snub

af'sny (-ge-) cut off, curtail, lop off

af'sonder (-ge-) isolate, separate; **~ing** seclusion, retirement; **~ingshospitaal (..tale)** isolation hospital

afson'derlik (b) (-e) separate, isolated; *~e gevalle,* isolated cases; *~e ontwikkeling,* separate development; (bw) separately

af'spraak (..sprake) agreement; appointment; *~ met tandarts,* appointment with dentist; **~oproep (-e)** fixed time (trunk) call

af'spreek (-ge-) agree upon, arrange

af'spring (-ge-) jump off, alight; **~plek (-ke)** springboard (for attacks)

af'staan (-ge-) give up, yield, surrender

af'stam (-ge-) descend, spring from; **~meling (-e, -s)** descendant

af'stand abdication, cession; (-e) distance; **~(s)beheer** remote control; **~(s)onderrig** teletuition

af'steek (-ge-) contrast with; deliver (speech); cut off; mark off; *iem. die loef ~,* outdo someone

af'stof (-ge-) dust

af'stoot (-ge-) push off; repel; *jy stoot al jou vriende van jou af,* you alienate all your friends

af'studeer (v) (-ge-) complete studies

af'sweer (-ge-) abjure, swear off, renounce; *hy het alle aardse genietinge afgesweer,* he renounced all worldly pleasures

af'takel (-ge-) unrig (ship); dismantle; thrash; *hy takel vinnig af,* he is getting weak and decrepit

af'teken (-ge-) mark; draw; sign off; *die berge staan afgeteken teen die lug,* the mountains are silhouetted against the sky

af'tel¹ (-ge-) lift off

af'tel ² (-ge-) count out; count down; **~ling** count off; countdown (space launch)

af'tog retreat; *die ~ blaas,* sound the retreat

af'trap (-ge-) wear out (heels); break by treading; *'n lelike stel ~,* have a nasty experience

af'trede, af'treding resignation, retirement

af'tree¹ (-ge-) pace, measure

af'tree² (-ge-) resign; retire; **~-annuïteit** retirement annuity

af'trek (s) sale, demand; subtraction; *die boek kry baie ~,* the book is much in demand; **~som (-me)** subtraction sum

af'vaardig (-ge-) delegate, return, depute; **~ing (-e, -s)** deputation, delegation

af'val (s) head and trotters of a sheep; offal; refuse, trash, waste; (w) (-ge-) fall off, tumble down; forsake; *~ herwin/hersikleer,* recycle refuse/trash

afval'lig (-e; -er, -ste) faithless, apostate; disagreeing, dissident; **~e (-s)** dissident

af'val: **~produk (-te)** byproduct

af'vee(g) (-ge-) wipe off, dry, polish

af'voer (w) (-ge-) lead away, carry off; **~pyp (-e)** waste/overflow pipe; downpipe (gutter)

af'vra (-ge-) ask, request; *die boer die kuns ~,* fish for information

af'vry (-ge-) oust (in courting), cut out

af'vryf, af'vrywe (-ge-) rub off

af'wag (-ge-) await, abide; *sy beurt ~,* take his turn; **~rekening (-e)** suspense account

af'water (w) (-ge-) drain, pour off; *afgewaterde teks,* watered-down text/version; (s) effluent

af'weer (-ge-) ward off, prevent, avert

af'wend (-ge-) turn aside, divert; *die gevaar ~,* avert the danger

af'werk (-ge-) complete, finish; put finishing touches to; **~ing** finish; workmanship

af'werp (-ge-) throw off, shake off

afwe'sig (-e) absent; **~heid** absence

af'wissel (-ge-) change, alternate; take turns; vary; **~end (b) (-e; -er, -ste)** alternative, diversified; *~ende kleure,* varying colours

af'wyk (-ge-) deviate, depart from, differ from; deflect; *van die waarheid ~,* swerve from the truth

af'wys (-ge-) reject, refuse, decline

ag¹ (s) attention, care; *in ~ neem,* take into consideration; *~ slaan op,* pay attention to; (w) (ge-) esteem, value; *iets nodig ~,* consider something necessary

ag/agt² (telw) eight

ag³ (tw) alas! oh!

ag'baar (..bare) respectable, venerable, honourable; *agbare voorsitter (voorsitster),* Mr Chairman (Madam Chair)

ageer' (ge-, ~) act (for someone), deputise

agen'da (-s) agenda, *ook sakelys*

agent' (-e) agent; **~skap** (-pe) agency
aggressief' (..slewe; ..siewer, -ste) aggressive
a'gie (-s) quidnunc, Paul Pry; *nuuskierige ~s hoort in die wolwehok,* curiosity killed the cat
agita'tor (-s) agitator; demagogue
agiteer' (~ ge-) agitate
ag(t) eight; *oor 'n dag of ~,* within a week
agte(r)lo'sig (-e; -er, -ste) careless; perfunctory; **~heid** carelessness
ag'ter behind, after; late; *my oorlosie is ~,* my watch is slow; *~ die tralies,* in goal
ag'teraan behind, at the back
ag'teraf out-of-the-way; backward; secretly; *~ mense,* uncultured/backward people
agterbaks' (-e; -er, -ste) sly, underhand
ag'terbanker (-s) backbencher
ag'terbeen (..bene) hind leg
ag'terbly (-ge-) remain behind, straggle
ag'terbuurt (-e), **ag'terbuurte** (-s) backstreet, slum(s)
ag'terdeur (-e) backdoor; *'n ~ oophou,* keep a loophole open
ag'terdog suspicion; *~ koester,* harbour suspicion
agterdog'tig (-e; -er, -ste) suspicious
agtereenvol'gens successively, consecutively
ag'terent hind part, rear, backside
ag'tergrond background
ag'terhoede (-s) rearguard; back line
ag'terin at the back (of)
ag'terkant (-e) back, back part, reverse side
ag'terkleinkind (-ers) great-grandchild
ag'terkom (-) discover, find out
ag'terlaat (-ge-) leave behind; *sy vrou onversorg ~,* leave his wife unprovided for
ag'terlig (-te) tail light
ag'terlik (-e; -er, -ste) backward, mentally deficient, (mentally) retarded
ag'terlyf (..lywe) hind quarters; abdomen (insect)
agtermekaar' in order, orderly; spick and span, neat; *'n ~ kêrel,* a fine/smart fellow
agtermid'dag (..middae) afternoon
agterna' after, later, subsequently
ag'ternaam (..name) second name, surname
ag'terom round the back
agteroor' backward(s), supinely
agterop'skop (-geskop) frisk, kick up the heels; be unmanageable

ag'teros (-se) hind ox; *~ kom ook in die kraal,* slow but sure
ag'terpant (-e) back panel/gore (skirt)
ag'terpoot (..pote) hind foot; *gou op die ..pote wees,* be quick-tempered
ag'terplaas (..plase) backyard
ag'terryer (-s) attendant on horseback; henchman
ag'tersaal, (-s) pillion
ag'terspeler (-s) back (football)
ag'terstaan (-ge-) be behind; *by niemand ~ nie,* be inferior to nobody
agterstal'lig (-e) in arrear, overdue; *sy rekening is drie maande ~,* his account is three months overdue
ag'terstand arrears; backward position; backlog
ag'terste last, hindmost
ag'terstel (s) (-le) rear part (chassis)
agterstevoor' hind part foremost; topsyturvy
ag'terstewe (-ns) stern; backside (of a person)
ag'tertoe astern; towards the back; *staan asseblief ~,* please stand back
agteruit' backwards; *die pasiënt gaan ~,* the patient is getting worse
agteruit'gang retrogression, deterioration, decline
ag'tervoegsel (-s) suffix
agtervolg' (~) follow, pursue; **~ing** pursuit, persecution; **~ingswaan** persecution mania/complex
agterwe'ë aside, behind; *~ bly,* fail to appear; remain in abeyance
ag'terwiel (-e) back/rear wheel
ag(t)'hoek (-e) octagon
ag'ting regard, esteem, respect, *ook* eerbied, respek
ag(t)'ste (-s) eighth
agt'(t)ien eighteen; **~de** (-s) eighteenth
agt'uur eight o'clock; breakfast; *~ werkdag,* eight-hour working day
akade'mie (-s) academy; studies
akade'mies (-e) academic(al); **~e opleiding,** academic training
aka'sia (-s) acacia
akkedis' (-se) lizard
ak'ker¹ (-s) field; acre; *Gods water oor Gods ~ laat loop,* let matters take their own course

ak'ker² (-s) acorn; ~boom (..bome) oak (tree) *kyk* eikeboom; ~boon (..bone) cowpea; ~hout oak, *kyk* eikehout
ak'kertjie (-s) garden/flower bed
akklimatiseer' (ge-) acclimatise
akkommoda'sie accommodation
akkoord' (-e) agreement, harmony; chord (music); ~ gaan met, agree with
akkordeer' (ge-, ~) agree
akkor'deon (-s) accordion
akkuraat' (..rate; ..rater, -ste) accurate
akkusatief' (..tiewe) accusative
ak'nee acné, facial pimples, *ook* puisies
akoestiek' acoustics
akrobaat' (..bate) acrobat
aksent' (-e) accent
aksep'bank (-e) merchant bank
aksepteer' (ge-) accept; 'n wissel ~, accept a bill (of exchange)
ak'sie (-s) action, suit; tiny bit; 'n ~ hê teen iem., have a bone to pick with someone
aksyns' excise; ~belasting (-s) excise duty
ak'te (-s) deed; certificate; ~ van oprigting, memorandum of association (of company); ~tas (-se) briefcase
akteur' (-s) actor
aktief' (..tiewe; ..tiewer, -ste) active; ..tiewe vulkaan, active volcano
aktivis' (-te) activist
aktiwiteit' (-e) activity
aktri'se (-s) actress
aktualiteit' (-e) actuality; topicality
aktua'ris (-se) actuary
aktueel' (..tuele) actual, real, topical; vital
akuut' (akute) acute
akwa'rium (-s) acquarium
al¹ (b, telw) all, every; ~ om die ander week, every other week; ~ drie, all three; in ~le geval, in any case
al² (bw) already; continually; ~ hoe meer, more and more
al³ (vgw) though, even if; ~ is hy nog so arm, however poor he may be
alaba'ma (-s) puggree
alarm' (-s) alarm; ~ blaas, sound the alarm
albas'ter (-s) marble (game); alabaster
al'batros (-se) albatross
al'bei both; hulle is ~ siek, both of them are ill
albi'no (-'s) albino
al'bum (-s) album

al'dag all day, every day; nie ~ se kêrel nie, an outstanding fellow
aldus' thus, so
al'ewig (-e) continual, incessant; ~ laat wees, be continually late
al'fa alpha; die ~ en die omega, the beginning and the end
al'fabet (-te) alphabet
alfabe'ties (-e) alphabetic(al)
al'gar all, everybody, *ook* almal
al'ge algae
al'gebra algebra
al'geheel (..hele) total(ly), entire(ly), overall; algehele wenner, overall winner
algemeen' (..mene; ..mener, -ste) general(ly), universal(ly), common(ly); algemene jaarvergadering, annual general meeting; oor (in) die ~, in general; algemene praktisyn, general practitioner; algemene (ver)koopbelasting, general sales tax
alhoewel' (al)though
a'lias (s) (-se) alias; (bw) alias, otherwise
a'libi (-'s) alibi; sy ~ bewys, establish one's alibi
a'likreukel (-s) periwinkle (snail)
alka'li (-ë, -'s) alkali
al'kant all sides; ~ selfkant, six of the one and half-a-dozen of the other
al'kante on all sides
al'kohol alcohol
alkoholis' (-te) alcoholic (person); ~me alcoholism
al'ko: ~meter alcometer; ~toetser breathalyser
alledaags' (-e) commonplace, ordinary, trivial
alleen' alone, single, lonely; sole; ~handel monopoly; ~lik only; ~opsluiting solitary confinement; ~spraak (..sprake) monologue, soliloquy; ~verspreider (-s) sole distributor
allegaar'tjie (-s) mixed grill; chow-chow, jumble, medley, hodge-podge
allegorie' (-ë) allegory
al'lemansvriend hail-fellow-well-met, everybody's friend
alle'nig alone, lonely
allerbes'te very best
allereers'(te) very first
al'lerhande all sorts, all kinds, sundry
Allerhoog'ste the Supreme Being, God
allerlaas'te very last, ultimate

al'lerlei all kinds of, miscellaneous
allermins'(te) very least, least of all
al'lerweë everywhere, in all respects, on all sides
al'les all, everything; ~ op sy tyd, there is a time for everything; ~ en nog wat, one thing and another
al'lesbehalwe anything but, not at all
al'leswinkel (-s) hypermarket
allitera'sie alliteration
allooi' alloy, standard, quality; van die suiwerste ~, of the finest quality
alluviaal' (..viale) alluvial
al'mag omnipotence
almag'tig (-e) almighty, omnipotent; die A ~e God, the Almighty
al'mal all, everybody; ons ~, all of us
almanak' (-ke) almanac
almaskie', almiskie' still, nevertheless, notwithstanding; dis nie ~ nie, it is quite certain
al'melewe always, the whole time; ~ laat wees, be continually late
alom' everywhere; ~ bekend, known by all
alomteenwoor'dig (-e) omnipresent
alomvat'tend (-e) all-embracing
alreeds' already, ook reeds
alsien'de all-seeing; ~ oog, all-seeing eye
alsy'dig (-e) versatile, allround, many-sided ook veelsydig
alt (-e) contralto, alto
al'taar, altaar' (altare) altar
altans' at least, anyway, at any rate
al'te very; too; ek voel nie ~ wel nie, I don't feel too well
altemit(s)' perhaps, maybe
alternatief' (..tiewe) alternative
al'tesaam, al'tesame altogether, together
al'tyd always, ever
aluin' (-e) alum
alumi'nium aluminium
alum'nus (..ni, -se) alumnus, old student
alvo'rens before, until; ~ hy aangestel word, moet hy..., before he is appointed he should...
alweer' once again, ook al weer
alwe'tend (-e) all-knowing, omniscient
amalgama'sie amalgamation, ook samesmelting
aman'del (-s) almond
amaril' emery
amaso'ne (-s) amazon

amateur' (-s) amateur
am'bag (s) (-te) trade, profession, handicraft, business; twaalf ~te, dertien ongelukke, Jack of all trades, master of none; ~skool (..skole) trade/industrial school; ~(s)man (..lui, -ne) artisan, workman
ambassa'de (-s) embassy
ambassadeur' (-s) ambassador
am'ber amber
ambi'sie ambition
ambisieus' (-e; -er, -ste) ambitious
ambulans' (-e) ambulance
a'men (-s) amen; op alles ja en ~ sê, agree to everything
amendement' (-e) amendment
Ame'rika America
Amerikaans' (-e) American
Amerika'ner (-s) American
ametis' (-te) amethyst
ameublement' (-e) set of furniture
amfibie' (-ë) amphibious animal, amphibian
amfi'bies (-e) amphibious
amfitea'ter (-s) amphitheatre
ammoniak' ammonia
ammuni'sie ammunition
amnes'tie amnesty; ~ verleen, grant a pardon
amok' amok; ~ maak, run amok
amoreus' (-e) amorous
amp (-te) office, employment; charge; duty, function; 'n ~ beklee, hold an office; ~bekleder, ~bekleër office bearer, incumbent (of post)
am'per, am'pertjies nearly, almost; amper maar nog nie stamper nie, a miss is as good as a mile
am'perbroekie (-s) scanty-panty, scanties
ampè're (-s) ampere
amp'genoot (..note) colleague, official counterpart
amps: ~bekleër holder of office, incumbent; ~gewaad robes of office; ~halwe officially, ex officio, in attendance (meetings); ~motor (-s) official car; ~termyn term of office
amp: ~telik (-e) official(ly); ~tenaar (..nare) official, officer, functionary
amusant' (-e; -er, -ste) amusing, entertaining
amuseer' (~, ge-) amuse, entertain

anachronis'me (-s) anachronism

analfabeet' (..bete) analphabete, illiterate (person)

anali'se (-s) analysis, *ook* ontleding

anali'ties (-e) analytic

analogie' (-ë) analogy

anapes' (-te) anapaest

anargie' anarchy

anargis' (-te) anarchist; ~me anarchism

anatomie' anatomy

an'der other, another; *aan die ~ kant,* on the other hand; *met ~ woorde,* in other words; ~half (..halwe) one and a half; ~kant across, on the other side; ~kleu-'rig (b) differently coloured; (s) (-e, mv -es) person of a different colour/race

an'ders otherwise, else, different; failing which; *~ as sy familie,* not like his relations; *heeltemal iets ~,* something totally different; *maak gou, ~ is jy laat,* hurry up, else you'll be late

andersden'kend (-e) dissenting, of a different opinion

an'dersins otherwise

an'dersom the other way about; *dis net ~,* just the reverse

an'derste = anders

andy'vie (-s) endive

anekdo'te (-s) anecdote

ane'mies (-e) anaemic

anemoon' (..mone) anemone

an'gel (-s) sting (of a bee)

angelier' (-e) carnation

Anglikaans' (-e) Anglican

angliseer' (ge-) Anglicise

Anglisis'me (-s) Anglicism

Anglo-Boe'reoorlog Anglo-Boer War; South African War

angs (-te) anxiety, fear, agony; *met ~ en bewing,* in fear and trembling; *dodelike ~ uitstaan,* be in mortal fear; ~kreet (.. krete) cry of distress; ~sweet cold perspiration

ang'stig (-e; -er, -ste) afraid, terrified; *~e oomblikke,* anxious moments

angswek'kend (-e; -er, -ste) alarming, fearsome

an'ker (s) (-s) anchor; *êrens ~ gooi,* go courting somewhere ; *voor ~ lê,* lie/ride at anchor

anna'le annals

anneks' (-e) annex

anneksa'sie (-s) annexation

annekseer' (ge-, ~) annex

annuiteit' annuity

anomalie' (-ë) anomaly

anoniem' (-e) anonymous

ansjo'vis anchovy

antagonis'me antagonism

anten'ne (-s) aerial (wire), *ook* lugdraad

antibio'ties (b) (-e) antibiotic

antibio'tikum (s) (-s, ..tika) antibiotic

an'tichris antichrist

antiek' (-e) antique; ~winkel antique shop

an'tiklimaks anticlimax

an'tiloop (..lope) antelope

antipatie' (-ë) antipathy

an'tirevolusionêr, an'tirewolusionêr (s) (-e) anti-revolutionist, pacifist, Calvinist; (b) (-e) anti-revolutionary

an'ti-Semiet (-e) anti-Semite

antisep'ties (-e) antiseptic

antite'se antithesis

antitoksien' (-e), antitoksi'ne (-s) antitoxin

An'tjie: *~ Somers,* bogeyman; *~ taterat,* gossip, chatterbox

antrasiet' anthracite

antropologie' anthropology

antropoloog' (..loë) anthropologist

ant'woord (s) (-e) answer, reply; *'n gevatte ~,* (good) repartee; *in ~ op,* in reply to; (w) (ge-) answer, reply; *bevestigend (ont-kennend) ~,* reply in the affirmative (negative); ~koevert reply-paid envelope

anys' anise (plant); ~saad aniseed

apart' (-e) apart, separate; ~heid separateness; apartheid (racial theory)

apatie' apathy

apokopee' (-s) apocope

apokrief' (..kriewe) apocryphal; *Apokriewe Boeke,* Apochrypha

apologie' (-ë) apology; *~ aanteken,* make/lodge an apology

apos'tel (-s) apostle

aposto'lies (-e) apostolic

apostroof' (..strowe) apostrophe

apparaat' (..rate) apparatus

apparatuur' computer hardware

ap'pel (-s) apple; pupil (eye); *die ~ val nie ver van die boom nie,* like father like son; *vir 'n ~ en 'n ei,* for a mere song

appèl' (-le) appeal; *~ aanteken,* give notice of appeal; ~hof court of appeal appelkoos' (..kose) apricot; ~konfyt apricot preserve, apricot jam; ~siekte diarrhoea

appelleer' (ge-, ~) appeal

appellie'fie (-s) Cape gooseberry

ap'pelwyn cider

appendisi'tis appendicitis, ook blindedermontsteking

applikant' (-e) applicant, ook aansoeker

applika'sie (-s) application (for a post); 'n ~ besorg/indien, submit an application

appliseer' (ge-) apply

applous' applause

appresia'sie appreciation

appresieer' (ge-, ~) appreciate

apteek' (..teke) chemist's shop, pharmacy

apte'ker (-s) chemist, druggist

aptyt' appetite

Ara'bië Arabia

Arabier' (-e) Arab

Ara'bies (s) Arabian; (b) (-e) Arabian

ar'bei (ge-) work, labour, toil

ar'beid work, labour, toil; ~ adel, labour ennobles; geskoolde ~, skilled labour; ~er (-s) labourer, workman, worker; ~intensief labour intensive

ar'beid(s); ~betrekkinge labour relations, industrial relations; ~terapie occupational therapy; ~veld sphere of action, field of activity; ~verhoudinge industrial/labour relations

arbi'ter (-s) arbiter, arbitrator

arbitra'sie arbitration

arbitrêr (-e) arbitrary

a'rea (-s) area

are'na (-s) arena

a'rend (-e) eagle

argaïs'ties (e) archaic, obsolete

Argenti'nië Argentina

Argentyn' (-e) (an) Argentinean; ~s (b) Argentine

argeologie' archaeology

argeoloog' (..loë) archaeologist

argief' (argiewe) archives

argipel' (-le) archipelago

argitek' (-te) architect

argitektuur' architecture

argiva'ris (-se) archivist

argument' (-e) argument, plea

argumenteer' (ge-, ~) argue

arg'waan suspicion, mistrust

a'ria (-s) air, tune, song, aria

aristokraat' (..krate) aristocrat

aristokra'ties (-e) aristocratic

ark (-e) ark; uit die ~ se dae, from time immemorial; saam met Noag in die ~ gewees, as old as the hills; ~mark petshop

arka'de (-s) arcade, ook deurloop

arm¹ (s) (-s) arm

arm² (b) (-e; -er, -ste) poor, indigent, needy

arm'band (-e) bracelet, bangle

ar'mesorg care of the poor

arm'holte (-s) armpit

armlas'tig (-e; -er, -ste) chargeable to the parish; (s) ~e (-s) pauper

ar'moede poverty, want

armoe'dig (-e; -er, -ste) poor, needy, indigent, shabby; 'n ~e huisie, a shanty house

armsa'lig (-e; -er, -ste) pitiful, miserable

arm'stoel (-e) easy chair, armchair

aro'ma (-s) aroma, fragrance

a'ronskelk (-e) arum lily

arres', arresta'sie arrest, custody, ook aanhouding

arresteer' (ge-, ~) arrest, take prisoner

arseen' arsenic; ~vergiftiging arsenic poisoning

arsenaal' (..nale) arsenal

arte'sies (-e) artesian; ~e bron/put, artesian well

arties' (-te) artist

arti'kel (-s) article, clause; commodity

artikula'sie articulation

artillerie' artillery

artisjok' (-ke) artichoke

artistiek' (-e; -er, -ste) artistic, tasteful; die ~e gehalte, the artistic quality

arts (-e) physician, doctor

artseny' medicine, medicament; ~kunde pharmacology

as¹ (s) ashes; ~ is verbrande hout, if ifs and ans were pots and pans; in die ~ sit, repent

as² (s) (-se) axle, axis

as³ (bw, vgw) as, like; than; when, if; so nimmer ~ te nooit, never

asa'lea (-s) azalea

as: ~baan dirt track, cinder track; ~bakkie (-s) ash tray

asbes' asbestos; ~sement asbestos cement

a'sem (s) (-s) breath; die laaste ~ uitblaas, expire; (w) (ge-) breathe; ~haal (-ge-) breathe; ~haling (-e, -s) breathing, respiration; *kunsmatige ~haling,* artificial respiration

asetileen' acetylene

as'falt asphalt

asgaai' (-e) assegai

as'hoop (..hope) ash heap, scrap heap, rubbish dump

Asiaat' (Asiate) Asiatic

Asia'ties (-e) Asiatic

A'sië Asia; **~r** (-s) Asian; South African Indian

asiel' (-e) asylum, place of refuge, sanctuary

as'jas (-se) rascal; joker (cards)

as'koek (-e) ashcake; ne'er-do-well; **~ slaan,** dance a reel

as'ma asthma

aspaai' I spy (hide-and-seek game)

aspek' (-te) aspect

asper'sie (-s) asparagus

aspirant' (-e) aspirant, applicant; **~-onderwyser** teacher in training, teacher trainee

as'poestertjie (-s) cinderella

aspres' *kyk* **ekspres**

asseblief' please, if you please; **~ tog!** do please!; *bly ~ aan,* please hold the line

assegaai' = **asgaai**

asses'sor (-s, -e) assessor, co-opted member

assimila'sie assimilation

assistent' (-e) assistant; **~-rekenmeester** assistant accountant

assosiaat' (..ate) associate (of a society)

assosia'sie association

assuran'sie insurance, assurance; **~agent** (-e) insurance agent: **~maatskappy** (-e) insurance company

as'ter (-s) aster, chrysanthemum; girl, girl friend

astrant' (-e; -er, -ste) cheeky, impudent, bold

astrologie' astrology

astroloog' (..loë) astrologer

astrono'mies (-e) astronomic(al); **~e koste** astronomic/huge costs

astronoom' (..nome) astronomer

as'tronout (-e) astronaut, spaceman

asuur' azure

as'vaal ashen pale; *jou ~ skrik,* become pale with fright

asyn' vinegar

atavis'me atavism, reversion

ateïs' (-te) atheist; **~me** atheism; **~ties** (-e) atheistic

ateljee' (-s) studio, workshop

ateljee'orkes (-te) studio orchestra

at'jar pickles

Atlan'ties (-e) Atlantic

at'las (-se) atlas

atleet' (atlete) athlete

atletiek' athletics **~baan** athletic track; **~byeenkoms** (-te) athletic meeting

atle'ties (-e) athletic; **~e figuur,** built like an athlete

atmosfeer' (..sfere) atmosphere

atmosfe'ries (-e) atmospheric(al)

atoom' (atome) atom; **~bom** (-me) atom bomb; **~fusie** atomic fusion; **~oorlog** (..loë) atomic war; **~splitsing, ~splyting** splitting of the atom, atomic fission

attaché (-s) attaché

attent' (-e; -er, -ste) attentive; *iem. op iets ~ maak,* draw someone's attention to

attributief' (..tiewe) attributive

attribuut' (..bute) attribute

Augus'tus August

Austra'lië Australia; **~r** (-s) Australian

Austra'lies (-e) Australian

avoka'do (-'s), **avoka'dopeer** (..pere) avocado pear

avonturier' (-s) adventurer; fortune hunter

avontuur' (..ture) adventure; **~lik** (-e; -er, -ste) adventurous; **~verhaal** (..verhale) adventure story

a'wend (-e) evening, night (poetic)

A'wendmaal the Lord's Supper

a'weregs (-e) wrong; purl (knitting)

a'wery average (at sea); **~klousule** average clause (insurance)

B

ba! bah! pshaw! *nie boe of ~ sê nie,* not say boo to a goose

baad'jie (-s) coat, jacket

baai[1] (s) (-e) bay

baai[2] (w) (ge-) bathe; **~er** (-s) bather

baal (s) (bale) bale; (w) (ge-) bale

baan (s) (bane) course, way; orbit (of a planet); court (tennis); lane (traffic)

baan: ~**breker** (-s) pioneer; ~**tjie** (-s) employment, job; ~**tjies vir boeties,** jobs for pals

baar (b) (-der, -ste) uncivilised, unskilled

baard (-e) beard

baar'moeder (-s) womb, uterus

baars (-e) bass; perch (fish)

baas (base) master, boss; crack, ace; ~**bakleier** (-s) champion fighter; ~**raak** (-ge-) overcome, master

baat (s) profit, gain; (bate) assets; *ten bate van,* in aid of

ba'ba (-s), **ba'batjie** (-s) baby; ~**wagter** (-s) babysitter, *ook* **kroostrooster**

ba'balaas (**ba'belas**) hangover

bab'bel (ge-) tattle, chatter; ~**aar** (-s) tattler, chatterer; ~**bek** (-ke), ~**kous** (-e) chatterbox

ba'ber (-s) barbel

baccalau'reus (..**rei**, -**se**): *B~ Artium,* Bachelor of Arts

bad (s) (-de, -dens) bath; (swimming) bath; (**baaie**) (mineral) bath, hot spring; (w) (ge-) take a bath, bathe; ~**kamer** (-s) bathroom; ~**kostuum** (-s) bathing costume

baga'sie baggage, luggage; ~**bak** (-ke) boot

bag'ger (ge-) dredge; ~**boot** (..**ote**), ~**masjien** (-e) dredger, dredging machine

bai'e (**meer, meeste**) very, much, many; ~ *dankie,* thank you very much; ~**maal** many a time, frequently, often

bajonet' (-te) bayonet

bak[1] (s) (-ke) basin, trough, bowl; body (of a car(t)); (b, bw), baggy; cupped

bak[2] (w) (ge-) bake, fry, roast; ~ *en brou,* muddle; *'n poets* ~, play a trick on someone

bak[3] (b) fine, first-rate, decent; *hy is 'n ~ ou,* he is a first-rate chap

bakatel' (-le) trifle, bagatelle

bak'boord larboard, port (side); *iem. van ~ na stuurboord stuur,* send someone from pillar to post

ba'ken (-s) beacon, buoy

bak'gat (b, tw) excellent; swanky

bak'ker (-s) baker; ~**y** (-e) bakery

bak'kie (-s) small dish (tray, basin, bowl); pickup van, bakkie; punnet

bak'kies (-e) face, phiz, mug, dial (idiom)

bak'kopslang (-e) ringed cobra

baklei' (~, **ge-**) fight, scrap, quarrel; ~**ery** fighting, scrap

bak'maat capacity, content (of a dam)

bak'oond (-e) (Dutch) oven

bak'oor (..**ore**) large prominent ear

bak'sel (-s) batch, baking; *'n ~ brode,* loaves in (out of) the oven

bak'steen (..**stene**) brick

bakte'rie (-ë, -s) bacterium

bak'vis (-se), **bak'vissie** (-s) flapper, teenager

bal[1] (s) (-le) ball (e.g. tennis); (w) (ge-) clench (the fist)

bal[2] (s) (-s) ball (dance); *gemaskerde ~, maskerbal,* fancy dress ball

balans' (-e) balance

balanseer' (~, **ge-**) balance, poise

balans'staat (..**state**) balance sheet

balda'dig (-e; -er, -ste) mischievous; boisterous

balho'rig (-e; -er, -ste) unruly, intractable

ba'lie[1] (-s) bar; *tot die ~ toegelaat word,* to be admitted to the bar

ba'lie[2] (-s) tub

baljaar' (~, **ge-**) play noisily, gambol, frolic

balju' (-'s) messenger of the court, bailiff, sheriff

balk[1] (s) (-e) beam, rafter; stave, bar (music)

balk[2] (w) (ge-) bray

balkon' (-ne, -s) balcony

balla'de (-s) ballad

ballas' ballast; ~**mandjie** (-s) large bushel basket

ballet' (-te) ballet; ~**danser** (-s), ~**danseres** (-se) ballet dancer

bal'ling (-e) exile; outcast; ~**skap** exile, banishment

ballon' (-ne, -s) balloon

bal'sem (s) (-s) balm, balsam, ointment; (w) (ge-) embalm

bamboes' (-e) bamboo

ban (s) excommunication, banishment; *in die ~ doen,* ban; excommunicate; (w) (ge-) banish, exile

banaal' (..**nale**; ..**naler, -ste**) banal, vulgar

bana'na (-s) banana, *ook* **piesang**

band (-e) band (for clothes); ribbon (for hair); tape, cord; girdle; tyre (for car)

bandelier' (-e, -s) bandoleer

bandiet' (-e) prisoner, convict, bandit

band: ~opname tape recording; ~masjien (-e), ~opnemer (-s) tape recorder; ~oteek (..teke) tape library; ~skyfiereeks tape= slide sequence, *ook* klankskyfiereeks

bang (-e); -er, -ste) afraid, frightened; *liewer ~ Jan as dooie Jan,* better a living dog than a dead lion; ~broek (-e) coward; funk(y)

bang'erig (-e) rather afraid; nervous, skit= tish

banier' (-e) banner, standard

ban'jo (-'s) banjo

bank¹ (s) (-e) bench, form, desk; pew (church); *deur die ~,* on the average; throughout

bank² (s) (-e) bank; (w) (ge-) bank; ~be= stuurder (-s) bank manager

banket' confectionery; (-te) banquet; ~bak= ker (-s) confectioner

bankier' (-s) banker

bank: ~klerk (-e) bank clerk; ~kommissie bank exchange; ~noot (..note) banknote; ~rekening (-e, -s) bank(ing) account

bankrot' (s) (-te) bankruptcy; *~ speel,* go bankrupt

bank: ~staat (..state) bank statement; ~wissel (-s) bank draft

ban'neling (-e) exile, outcast, *ook* balling

ban'tamhoendertjie (-s) bantam fowl

Ban'toe Bantu; ~kunde Bantu studies; ~taal (..ale) African/Bantu language, ethnic language

Bantoelo'gies (-e) pertaining to Bantu stu= dies

barak' (-ke) barracks

barbaar' (..bare) barbarian, savage

barbaars' (-e; -er, -ste) barbarous, barba= rian

barbier' (-s) barber

baret' (-te) beret; birette

ba'riton (-s) baritone

barmhar'tig (-e; -er, -ste) merciful, com= passionate; *'n ~e Samaritaan,* a good Samaritan

ba'rometer (-s) barometer

baron' (-ne, -s) baron

barones' (-se) baroness

bars¹ (s) (-te) burst, crack; (w) (ge-) burst, crack; *buig of ~,* bend or break

bars² (b, bw) (-e); -er, -ste) harsh, rough; *veg dat dit ~,* fight like mad

bas¹ (-se) bass (singer)

bas² (-te) bark, rind; body; *sy ~ red,* save his skin; *tussen die boom en die ~,* be= twixt and between

basaar' (-s) bazaar

baseer' (~, ge-) base, ground

ba'sies (-e) basic

ba'sis (-se) basis, base; foothold; *militêre ~,* military base

basket'bal basketball (men)

Basoe'to (-'s) Basuto

bas'stem (-me) bass (voice)

bas'ta! enough! stop! *~ nou met jou lol= lery!* stop bothering me!

bas'ter¹ (s) (-s) bastard, halfcaste; hybrid; (w) (ge-) hybridise

bas'ter² (bw) rather, somewhat; *ek voel ~ naar,* I am feeling a little sick

bas'ter: ~mielies hybrid maize; ~taal barbarism (language), mixed jargon

bataljon' (-ne, -s) battalion

ba'te asset; credit; *~s en laste,* assets and liabilities

ba'tig: ~e saldo credit balance

battery' (-e) battery; *'n ~ laai,* charge a battery

beaam' (~) assent to, concur, approve

beamp'te (-s) employee; (honorary) official

beangs' (-te) anxious, afraid, uneasy

beant'woord (~) answer, reply; *aan die doel ~,* meet the purpose

bebloed' (-e) bloodstained, bloody

beboet' (~) fine; mulct; *iem. met R10 ~,* fine someone R10

bebou' (~) cultivate, till; ~de gebied built-up area

bed (-de, -dens) bed

bedaar' (~) quiet, appease; subside, abate; ~middel (-s) tranquilliser, *ook* kal= meermiddel

bedaard' (-e; -er, -ste) calm, sedate

bedags' during the day

bedag'saam (..same; ..samer, -ste) thought= ful, circumspect, considerate

bedank' (~) thank; decline, refuse; resign; *as lid ~,* resign one's membership; *~ uit 'n komitee,* resign from a committee; ~ing (-e, -s) refusal, resignation; expres= sion of gratitude; *die ~ing doen/uit= spreek,* propose a vote of thanks

bed'degoed bedding, bedclothes

be'de (-s) prayer, petition; entreaty; ~vaart pilgrimage

bedees' (-de; -der, -ste) timid, bashful

bedek' (w) (~) cover up, conceal, hide; (b) (-te) hidden, covered; ~*te seën*, blessing in disguise

be'del (ge-) beg, ask alms; ~**aar** (-s) beggar, mendicant

bede'ling (-e, -s) endowment, supply; *'n nuwe* ~, a new dispensation/deal

beden'king (-e, -s) consideration, reflection, remark; ~*e teen iets hê*, have doubts about something

bedenk'lik (-e; -er, -ste) critical, dangerous; serious; *hy lê in 'n* ~*e toestand*, he is in a critical condition

bederf' (s) corruption, depravity; decay; (w) (~) spoil, corrupt, deprave, ruin; ~*bare goedere*, perishable goods

bedien' (~) serve, attend, wait upon; administer; ~**de** (-s) servant, attendant; ~**er** operator (of machine)

bedink' (~) consider, reflect, contrive

bed: ~**kussing** (-s) pillow; ~**laken** (-s) (bed)sheet; ~**lêend** (-e) bedridden, confined to bed

bedoel' (~) mean; intend; purpose; *ek het dit nie so* ~ *nie*, this is not what I meant; ~**ing** (-e, -s) meaning, intention, aim, purpose; *met goeie* ~*ings*, with the best of intentions

bedom'pig (-e; -er, -ste) suffocating, close; stuffy, sultry

bedor'we spoiled; depraved

bedra' (~) amount to: *die rekening* ~ *R5*, the account amounts to R5

bedrag' (bedrae) amount

bedreig' (~) threaten, menace; ~**ing** (-e, -s) threat, menace

bedrem'meld (-e) confused, perplexed, puzzled

bedre'we (meer ~, mees ~) skilled, experienced, versed

bedrieër (-s) fraud, deceiver, cheat

bedrieg' (~) cheat, deceive, defraud; ~**lik** (-e; -er, -ste) deceptive, fraudulent, deceitful

bedro'ë deceived

bedroef' (w) (~) grieve, afflict; (b) (-de; -der, -ste) sorrowful, sad, grieved; ~ *min*, precious little; ~ *wees oor*, grieve at

bedroe'wend (-e) distressing, saddening

bedrog' (bedrieërye) deceit, deception, fraud; cheating; ~ *pleeg*, commit fraud

bedruk' (-te; -ter, -ste) oppressed, dejected, downhearted

bedryf' (s) (bedrywe) (branch of) industry; (line of) business; profession, trade; act (play); *'n* ~ *beoefen*, practise a trade; *in* ~ *kom*, start operations; (w) (~) commit, perpetrate; ~**s'bates** current assets; ~**sielkunde** industrial psychology; ~**s'** = **kapitaal** working capital; ~**s'kennis** industrial art(s); ~**s'koste** working expenses; ~**s'laste** current liabilities; ~**s'leier** executive; ~**s'verhoudinge** labour/industrial relations

bedry'wig (-e; -er, -ste) active, busy, bustling

bedug' (meer ~, mees ~) afraid, apprehensive

bedui'dend significant, meaningful

bedui'e (~) signify, mean, imply; point out, direct; *iem. die pad/rigting* ~, explain the road/direction to someone

bedui'wel (~) make crazy, spoil; *hy het die hele saak* ~, he has bungled the whole affair

bedwelm' (w) (~) stun, stupefy; drug; (b) (-de) benumbed, stunned, drugged; ~**ing** daze, stunned state; ~**middel** (-s) drug, *kyk* **dwelms**

bedwing' (~) curb, check, suppress, restrain; *hy kon hom nie* ~ *nie*, he could not restrain himself

beë'dig (w) (~) swear to; put upon oath; *die burgemeester is* ~, the mayor was sworn in; (b) (-de) sworn; ~*de verklaring*, sworn affidavit

beef (ge-) tremble, shiver; quiver; ~ *soos 'n riet*, tremble like an aspenleaf

beëin'dig (~) finish off, terminate

beeld (-e) image, likeness, picture, statue

beeld'hou (ge-) sculpture, carve; ~**er** (-s) sculptor; ~**kuns** sculpture

beeld: ~**radio** television; ~**saai**, ~**send** televise; ~**skoon** (..skone) beautiful as a picture; ~**spraak** figurative/metaphorical language

been (bene) bone; leg; *harde bene kou*, suffer hardships; *deur murg en* ~, to the marrow of one's bones; ~**af** in love

beer (bere) bear (wild animal); boar (male pig)

bees (-te) beast; bovine (animal); (mv) cattle

bees: ~vleis beef; ~wagter (-s) cattle herd

beet[1] (bete) beetroot

beet[2] (bete) bite; hold, grip; ~kry (-ge-) get hold of, seize; ~neem (-ge-) take hold of; deceive

befoe'ter (~) spoil, bedevil; ~d (b) cantankerous, contrary, unreasonable

begaaf' (-de) talented, gifted; 'n ~de kind, a gifted child

begaan'[1] (w) (~) commit, perpetrate; 'n fout ~, make a mistake

begaan'[2] (b) beaten, trodden; upset, worried; ~ oor die uitslag, worried about the result

begeer' (~) desire, wish for, covet; ~lik (-e; -er, -ste) desirable; ~te (-s) desire, wish

begelei' (~) accompany, escort; ~de toer, guided/conducted tour; ~ding accompaniment

begena'dig (~) pardon, condone, reprieve

bege'rig (-e; -er, -ste) desirous; eager

bege'we (~) abandon, forsake; proceed to; sy kragte ~ hom, his strength fails him

begin' (s) beginning, start, outset, commencement

begin'ner (-s) beginner, novice

begin'sel (-s) principle, rudiment

begin'voorraad opening stock

begraaf' (~) bury, inter; ~plaas (..plase) graveyard, cemetery

begraf'nis (-se) burial, funeral; ~stoet (-e) funeral procession

begra'we (~) bury, inter

begrip' (-pe) idea, notion, conception; concept; traag van ~, slow to understand, slow on the uptake

begroet' (~) greet, welcome

begroot' (~) estimate

begro'ting (-s) estimate, budget

begryp' (~) understand, comprehend

behaal' (~) obtain, get, win, gain, score; hy het sy graad ~, he obtained his degree

beha'e delight, pleasure; ~ skep in, delight in

behal'we except, save, besides; alles ~, anything but

behan'del (~) treat; handle; manage; ~ing (-e, -s) treatment

behar'tig (~) have at heart; take care of; hy ~ die geldsake, he looks after the finances

beheer' (s) management, direction, control; (w) administer, control, manage

beheers' (~) rule, govern, manage, control

behels' (~) embrace; contain

behen'dig (-e; -er, -ste) dexterous, handy

behoed' (~) preserve, guard, protect

behoed'saam (..same; ..samer, -ste) cautious, circumspect, wary

behoef' (~) want, need, require; ~te (-s) want, need, necessity; ~tig (-e; -er, -ste) poor, needy

behoe'we on behalf of, in aid of; die kollekte is ten ~ van die armes, the collection is in aid of the poor

behoor'lik (b) (-e) proper, fit, becoming

behoor(t)' (~) belong to; behove, ought; be proper; die boek ~ aan my, the book belongs to me; hy ~ tot/aan daardie kerk, he is a member of that church

beho're: na ~, as it should be

behou' (~) keep, retain, preserve, save

behou'e safe and well

behou'ering containerisation

behui'sing housing; house; ~skema (-s) housing scheme

behulp' aid, help, shift; met ~ van, with the aid of

bei'de both; geen van ~, neither of the two

beïnvloed (~) influence, affect, bias

bei'tel (s) (-s) chisel; (w) (ge-) chisel

bejaard' (-e) aged, old, elderly; tehuis vir ~es, old-aged home

bejaar'desorg care of the aged

bejam'mer (~) deplore, lament, bewail; ek ~ jou, you have my sympathy

beje'ën (~) treat, act towards; met minagting ~, treat with contempt

bek (-ke) beak (bird); snout (animal); muzzle (of firearm); mouth (animal); 'n dik hê, sulk; hou jou ~! shut up! met 'n ~ vol tande, without saying a word

bekaaid': ~ daarvan afkom, come away with a flea in one's ear

bek: ~af downhearted, down in the dumps; ~drywer (-s) backseat driver

bekeer' (~) convert, proselytise

beken' (~) confess, acknowledge

bekend' (-e; -er, -ste) known, conversant with, noted, familiar

bek-en-klou'seer foot and mouth disease

be'ker (-s) cup, jug, bowl, mug; sports trophy

beke'ring conversion

bek'ken (-s) pelvis, basin; catchment area

bekleed'sel (-s) covering, upholstery

beklem'toon (~) emphasise, stress

beklink' (~) arrange, settle; 'n saak ~, close a deal

beknop' (-te; -ter, -ste) succinct, concise, abridged; 'n ~te uitgawe van die boek, a condensed version of the book

bekom' (~) obtain; agree (with the stomach); recover from (fright)

bekom'mer (~) trouble, worry; ek ~ my daaroor, I am worried about it; ~nis (-se) uneasiness, worry, anxiety

bekon'kel (~) plot, scheme, concoct

bekoor' (~) charm, enchant, fascinate, tempt; ~lik (-e; -er, -ste) charming, fascinating

beko'ring charm, fascination

bekos'tig (~) defray, pay; afford; ek kan dit nie ~ nie, I cannot afford it

bek'praatjies boasting, bragging

bekrag'tig (~) confirm, sanction, ratify

bekrom'pe narrow-minded

bekro'ning crowning; reward of merit; award

bekroon' (~) crown; award; met die eerste prys ~, awarded the first prize

bekruip' (~) creep upon, steal upon, stalk

bekwaam' (w) (~) qualify; enable; train; (b) (bekwame; bekwamer, -ste) able, capable, clever, efficient; ~heid (..hede) ability, capability, capacity

bekyk' (~) look at, view, inspect

bel (s) (-le) bell; wattle (bird); (w) (ge-) ring, 'phone

belaai' (~) load, burden

belag'lik (-e; -er, -ste) ridiculous

beland' (~) land; get to; arrive

belang' (-e) importance; interest; concern; in jou eie ~, in your own interest

belang'rik (-e; -er, -ste) important, considerable; ~heid importance

belang'stel (-ge-), belang stel (belang ge-) take an interest in, be interested in

belas' (~) burden; tax; rate; assess; ~ en belade, heavily laden; ~te wins, profits after tax; ~baar (..bare) taxable

belas'ting (-s) tax(ation); load; rate, duty; ~ hef, levy tax on; ~aanslag (..slae) assessment; ~betaler (-s) taxpayer; ratepayer; ~gaarder tax collector, receiver of

revenue (state income); ~pligtige (-s) taxpayer; ~vry tax-free

belê' (~) convene, call (meeting); invest (money)

bele'dig (~) insult, offend, injure; ~ing (-e, -s) insult

beleef'[1] (w) (~) experience, witness, live to see

beleef'[2] (b) (-de; -der, -ste) polite, civil, courteous

beleefd'heid civility, politeness, courtesy

bele'ër (~) besiege, lay siege to

bele'ëring (-e, -s) siege

beleg' (beleëringe, beleërings) siege; staat van ~, state of siege; ~ger (-s) investor (of money)

beleg'ging (-e, -s) investment

beleid' (~e, beleidrigtings) policy; ~maker policy maker

belem'mer (~) hamper, obstruct; die uitsig is ~, the view is obstructed

bele'se (meer ~, mees ~) well-read, widely read

belet' (~) prohibit, forbid

bele'we (~) experience, witness, live to see

bel'hamel (-s) bellwether; ringleader

belig' (~) lighten up; illuminate; expose

belig'ting exposure; illumination, lighting

belof'te (-s) promise; 'n ~ nakom, keep one's promise

belo'ning (-e, -s) reward; 'n ~ uitloof, offer a reward

beloof' (~) promise

beloon' (~) reward, remunerate, recompense

bely' (~) confess, avow; ~denis (-se) confession; avowal

bemaak' (~) bequeath

beman' (~) man, equip; ~ning (-s) crew; manning (staff provision)

bemark (w) market; ~ing marketing

bemees'ter (~) overpower; master

bemerk' (~) observe, notice, perceive

bemid'delaar (-s) mediator, go-between

bemid'deld (-e) well-to-do, wealthy, rich

bemin' (~) love, be fond of; ~d' (-e; -er, -ste) loved, beloved; ~de (-s) loved one, lover

bemoei' (~) meddle, interfere; ~ jou met jou eie sake, mind your own business; ~siek (-e) meddlesome, officious

bemors' (~) soil, stain, begrime

bena'deel (~) harm; hurt, injure

benader (~) approach, approximate, estimate; ~ing (-e, -s) approximation, rough estimate; by ~ing, approximately

bena'ming (-e, -s) name, title, term

benard' (-e, -er, -ste) distressed, trying; embarrassed; in ~e omstandighede, in straitened circumstances

benat'baar wettable (powder)

ben'de (-s) band, troop, gang; ~leier gangleader

bene'de below, beneath, under, downstairs; dis ~ my waardigheid, it is beneath my dignity

beneuk' (w) (~) damage, spoil, mar; (b) (-te) mad, daft, cantankerous, unmanageable

bene'wel (~) cloud, darken, obscure

bene'wel(d) (-de) foggy, misty, hazy

bene'wens besides, in addition to

benoem' (~) nominate, appoint; ~ing (-e, -s) appointment, nomination

benoud' (-e; -er, -ste) anxious, oppressed; stifling; ~heid (..hede) anxiety; closeness

bensien', bensi'ne benzine

benul' notion, idea; geen ~ nie, not the slightest notion

benut' (~) utilise, avail oneself of

beny' (~) envy, grudge; ek ~ hom sy gesondheid, I envy him for his health

beoe'fen (~) study; practise; cultivate, exercise; geduld ~, exercise patience

beoog' (~) aim at, have in view; ~de uitbreidings, planned extensions

beoor'deel (~) judge, criticise, adjudicate; review

beoor'delaar (-s) adjudicator, judge; reviewer, critic

beoor'deling (-e, -s) criticism, review; appreciation; adjudication

bepaal' (~) determine (date); define; stipulate

bepaald' (b) (-e) fixed, positive, definite

bepa'ling (-e, -s) stipulation, determination; provision; fixture (sport)

beperk' (w) (~) limit, confine, restrict; ~ tot, restricted to; (b) (-te) limited, restricted; ~ing (-e, -s) limitation, restriction

beplan' (w) plan; ~ning planning

beplant' (~) plant

bepleit' (~) plead, advocate

beproe'wing (-e, -s) trial, tribulation

beraad' deliberation, talk(s); ~slaag (~) deliberate, consult; ~slaging (-e, -s) deliberation, consultation

beraam' (~) plan, contrive; frame, estimate; 'n plan ~, make a plan

bera'deling (-e) counsellee

bera'der (-s) counsellor (psychology)

bera'ding (s) counselling

bera'ming (-e, -s) estimate; specification

bê're (ge-) store, save, put aside

bered'der (~) administrate, wind up (estate)

bere'de mounted; ~ polisie, mounted police

beredeneer' (~) discuss, reason

berei' (~) prepare; dress; 'n maaltyd ~, prepare a meal

bereid' ready, prepared, willing; ~heid readiness

bereidwil'lig (-e) ready, willing

bereik' (s, w) reach

bere'ken (~) calculate; compute; charge; ~ing (-e, -s) calculation

bê'rekoop lay-by

bê'replek (-ke) storage space/room

berg¹ (s) (-e) mountain, mount; van 'n molshoop 'n ~ maak, make a mountain out of a molehill

berg² (w) (ge-) salvage; store, kyk opberg

bergag'tig (-e) mountainous

berg: ~e'nier mountaineer; ~hang (-e) mountain slope

ber'ging salvage, salvaging (a ship); storing of; stowage (mealies), kyk opberging; ~skip salvage vessel

berg: ~ketting (-s) mountain range; ~klimmer (-s) mountaineer, ook bergenier; ~pas (-se) mountain pass; B~rede Sermon on the Mount; ~skool (..skole) initiation school

berig' (s) (-te) intelligence, news, report

beroemd' (-e; -er, -ste) famous, renowned, celebrated; ~heid fame, renown

beroep' (s) (-e) profession; calling, vocation; trade; appeal; 'n ~ beoefen, follow a profession; 'n ~ doen op, appeal to; (w) (~) call, nominate; appeal to; ~s'halwe by virtue of one's profession; ~siekte (-s) occupational disease; ~s'keuse choice of profession; ~s'leier (-s) careers adviser; ~s'leiding career/vocational guidance/counselling; ~s'man (beroepslui) professional (person); **~s'opleiding** vocational training; **~sokker** professional soccer; **~speler (-s)** professional (player); **~stoei** professional wrestling; **~s'voorligting** careers/vocational guidance; **~wedder** bookie

beroerd' (-e; -er, -ste) rotten, miserable

beroe'ring (-e, -s) commotion, disturbance

beroer'te apoplexy, palsy; stroke

berok'ken (~) cause, create; *skade* ~, cause damage

beroof' (~) deprive. bereave, rob

berou' (s) repentance, regret, remorse; (w) repent, regret

berug' (-te; -er, -ste) notorious, infamous

berus' (~) rest upon, depend upon; acquiesce; *in die onvermydelike* ~, resign oneself to the inevitable

bes (s) best, utmost; quite; *sy uiterste* ~ *doen,* do his utmost

besaai' (~) strew, overspread

besa'dig (-de) composed, sedate, calm

beseer (~) hurt, injure (in accident)

besef' (s) idea, realisation; *tot die* ~ *kom,* realise; (w) (~) realise, comprehend

be'sem (-s) broom

besen'ding (-e, -s) consignment

bese'ring (-e, -s) injury

beset' (~) occupy (a place); engage; *die telefoon is* ~, the telephone is engaged

bese'tene (-s) one possessed, maniac; *hy gaan te kere soos 'n* ~, he carries on like a maniac

beset'ting (-e, -s) occupation, garrison

besiel' (~) animate, inspire

besie'ling inspiration, animation

besienswaar'dig (-e) worth seeing, remarkable; **~heid** (..hede) tourist attraction; curiosity

be'sig (w) (ge-) use, employ (words); (b) (-te; -er, -ste) busy, engaged; **~heid** (..hede) business, occupation, employment

besig'tig (~) examine, inspect

besin' (~) reflect, come to one's senses; ~ *voor jy begin,* look before you leap

besit' (s) possession; assets; *in* ~ *neem,* take possession of; (w) (~) own, possess, have; **~lik** (-e) possessive; **~reg** right of ownership; title; **~ting** (-e, -s) possession, property, estate

beskaaf' (w) (~) cultivate, civilise; (b) (-de; -der, -ste) cultured, civilised

beska'dig (~) damage, harm, injure

beska'wing (-e, -s) civilisation, culture

beskei'e (meer ~, mees ~) discreet, modest; *na my* ~ *mening,* in my humble opinion

beskerm' (~) protect; shelter; guard; **~(e)'ling** (-e) protégé; **~engel** (-e) guardian angel; **~er** (-s) protector, patron; **~heer** (..here) patron; **~heilige** (-s) patron saint

besker'ming protection; patronage; auspices; *onder* ~ *van die nag,* under cover of the night

beskik' (~) manage; arrange; dispose; *die mens wik, God* ~, man proposes, God disposes; **~baar** (..bare) available; **~king** disposal, arrangement; *tot sy* **~king** *hê,* have at his disposal

beskon'ke intoxicated, tipsy, drunk

besko're granted to, allotted; *dit was my nie* ~ *nie,* I was not destined to . . .

beskou' (~) view, look at, behold; consider

beskryf', **beskry'we** (~) describe, depict; draw up (in writing)

beskry'wing (-e, -s) description; **~s'punt** (-e) point/item for discussion (on the agenda)

beskuit' (-e) rusk

beskul'dig (~) accuse, charge with; ~ *van,* accuse of; **~de** (-s) accused, defendant; **~ing** (-e, -s) accusation, charge

beskut' (~) protect, shelter; **~te beroep/ werk,** sheltered occupation

beslaan (w) (~) occupy, fill; cover (area)

besleg' (~) decide, settle; *hulle het die geskil* ~, they settled the argument

beslis' (w) (~) decide; (b) (-te; -ter, -ste) decided, positive; (bw) decidedly, positively; **~send** (-e) decisive, final, conclusive; **~sende stem,** casting vote; **~sing** (-e, -s) decision, ruling, resolution

beslom'mering (-e, -s) **beslom'mernis** (-se) vexation, trouble, cares (of office)

besluit' (s) (-e) resolution; decision; (w) (~) resolve, decide; **~e'loos** (..lose) irresolute, wavering

besmeer' (~) soil, smear; grease

besmet' (~) infect, contaminate, pollute

besmet'lik (-e; -er, -ste) contagious, infectious

besmet'ting infection, contagion

besne'de cut, chiselled; circumcised

besnoei' (~) curtail, retrench; cut; *uitga=*
wes ~, cut down on expenses
besny' (~) circumcise; **~denis** circumci=
sion
besoe'del (~) stain, contaminate, pollute;
~ing contamination, pollution
besoek' (s) (-e) visit, call; *'n ~ aflê, ~*
bring, pay a visit; (w) (~) visit, call on;
try, afflict; **~er** (-s) visitor, guest; **~ing**
(-e, -s) visitation, affliction, trial
besol'dig (~) pay, remunerate, give salary;
~ing pay, wages, salary, remuneration
beson'der (s): *in die ~*, particularly; (b)
(-e) particular, special, peculiar; (bw) ex=
ceptionally, particularly; **~heid** (..hede)
detail, particular; *meer/nadere beson=*
derhede, further details
beso'pe drunk, fuddled (with drink)
besorg' (w) (~) deliver (goods); procure;
furnish (details); (b) (-de) anxious, con=
cerned, uneasy; **~d'heid** anxiety, care,
worry
bespaar' (~) economise; save; *~ jou die*
moeite, save yourself the trouble; *geld ~*,
save costs/spending
bespa'ring saving
bespied' (~) spy, watch; **~er** (-s) spy
bespie'gel (w) (~) speculate, contemplate
bespoe'dig (~) accelerate; hasten; expedite
bespot' (~) mock, laugh at, ridicule; **~lik**
(-e; -er, -ste) ridiculous; *hom ~lik maak*,
make an ass of himself; **~ting** mockery,
derision, ridicule
bespreek' (~) discuss, talk over/about;
review (books); reserve, book (seats); *sit=*
plekke ~, book seats
bespre'king (-e, -s) discussion; conference;
booking, reservation; review; **~(s)groep**
(-e) discussion group
besproei' (~) irrigate, water
besproei'ing irrigation
bes'sie (-s) berry; **~sap** currant juice
bestaan' (s) existence, livelihood; (w) (~)
exist, live, consist (of); *~ uit*, consist of;
~ van, live on
bestand' proof (against), equal to; **~deel**
(..dele) ingredient, component (part)
bes'te best, excellent; dear; *my (ou) ~*, my
better half; *sy ~ vertoning nog*, his best
performance ever
beste'ding expenditure

bestee' (~) spend; use; expend; *aandag ~*
aan, give attention to
besteel' (~) rob
bestek' (-ke) compass; range; specification
bestel' (w) (~) order, arrange, appoint
bestel'ling (-e, -s) order, delivery; appoint=
ment; *'n ~ plaas*, place an order; *'n ~*
uitvoer, execute an order
bestel'vorm (-s) order form
bestel'wa (..waens) delivery van; bakkie
bestem' (~) destine, fix, apportion; **~ming**
destination, destiny
bestem'pel (~) stamp; name, call (names);
designate as
besten'dig (w) (~) confirm; perpetuate; (b)
(-e) constant; consistent, stable; *'n ~e*
speler, a safe/consistent player
bestier' (s) guidance; dispensation; **~ing** act
of Providence
bestook' (~) harass; batter, bombard; *met*
vrae ~, bombard with questions
bestorm' (~) storm, assail, attack
bestor'we deadly pale, livid; deceased; *~*
boedel, deceased estate
bestraf' (~) rebuke, reprove, punish
bestrooi' (~) strew, sprinkle
bestry' (~) combat, contest; dispute
bestudeer' (~) study; investigate
bestuif', bestui'we (~) cover with dust;
pollinate
bestuur' (s) (..sture) management; direc=
tion; directorate, board of control; (w)
(~) govern, rule, manage, direct; drive,
steer; *besturende direkteur*, managing
director; **~der** (-s) manager, director;
driver (car); **~derslisensie** driver's licen=
ce, *ook* **rybewys**
bestuurs': **~hoof**, **~leier** an executive;
~komitee management committee; **~lid**
(..lede) board member
bestuur'skool (..skole) driving school; school
of management
bestuur'stel (-le) executive suite
bestuurs'vergadering (-e, -s) board meeting
besui'nig (~) economise, retrench
beswaar' (s) (besware) objection, grievance,
scruple; *besware maak/opper*, raise ob=
jections
beswad'der (~) calumniate, slander
besweer' (~) swear; conjure; entreat; charm
(snake)
bes'wil: *vir jou eie ~*, for your own good

beswyk' (~) succumb; yield; die; *aan 'n siekte ~*, die of a disease

beswym' (~) faint, swoon; ~**ing** swoon, fainting fit; trance

betaal' (~) pay, settle; *haal-en-~*, cash-and-carry; *vooruit ~*, pay in advance

betaam' (~) become, befit, behove; *dit ~ jou nie*, it is not for you to

beta'kel dirty, besmear

beta'ling (-e, -s) payment

betas' (~) finger, touch, feel; fondle

bete'ken (~) mean, signify, imply; spell, portend; serve; *dagvaarding ~ aan*, serve summons on

bete'kenis (-se) meaning; sense, significance, importance; *manne van ~*, men of note; ~**vol** (-le) significant, meaningful

be'ter better, superior; ~**skap** improvement, recovery; ~**weter** (-s) pedant, wiseacre

beteu'el (~) restrain, check, bridle, curb

beteu'ter(d) (-de) perplexed, puzzled

beto'ger (-s) demonstrator

beto'ging (-e, -s) demonstration (public)

beton' concrete; *gewapende ~*, reinforced concrete

betoog' (s) (..toë) argument(ation); (w) (~) demonstrate, argue, prove

beto'wer (~) enchant, charm, fascinate

beto'wer'end (-e) charming, fascinating, glamorous

betrap' (~) catch; surprise; trap; detect; *iem. heter daad op diefstal ~*, catch a thief redhanded

betree' (~) tread upon, enter, set foot upon; *onregmatige betreding*, trespassing

betref' (~) concern, relate to, touch, affect; *wat my ~*, as for me; ~**fende** concerning, regarding

betrek' (~) occupy; involve; ~**king** (-e, -s) relation; situation, job; *met ~king tot*, with reference to

betreur' (~) regret, lament, deplore

betrok'ke cloudy, overcast; gloomy; *die ~ amptenaar*, the official concerned

betrou' (~) trust; ~**baar** (..bare; -der, -ste) trustworthy, reliable; ~**baarheid** reliability

betuig' (~) testify; declare; assure; show; express (thanks); *sy dank ~*, express his thanks

betwis' (~) dispute; contest; *'n setel ~*, contest a seat

betwy'fel (~) doubt, question, query

betyds' in time

beu'el (-s) bugle, trumpet

beul, (-e, -s) hangman, executioner

beur (ge-) pull with force, strain at

beurs (-e) purse; bursary, scholarship; stock exchange; ~**notering** (-e, -s) stock exchange listing

beur'sievryer (-s) sugardaddy

beurt (-e) turn; over (cricket); ~**e'lings** by turns, alternately, in rotation

beval'ling (-e, -s) confinement, delivery (of a child)

bevan'ge seized; foundered; *van skrik ~*, seized with fear

beva're: *~ seeman*, able seaman

bevat' (~) contain, comprise, hold; comprehend

beveel' (w) (~) order, command, enjoin

beveg' (~) combat, fight (against)

bevei'lig (~) shelter, protect, safeguard

bevel' (-e) order, command; mandate; ~**voerder** (-s) commander; ~**voerend** (-e) commanding; ~**voerende offisier**, commanding officer

beves'tig (~) confirm, corroborate, bear out; ~**end** (-e) affirmative; ~**ing** confirmation, affirmation

bevind' (w) (~) find, experience; ~**ing** (-e, -s) finding

bevlek' (~) stain, defile, pollute

bevlie'ging (-e, -s) caprice, sudden fancy, whim; *'n ~ kry*, act on a sudden impulse

bevoeg' (-de) competent, qualified, able; ~**d'heid** (..hede) competence, qualification; power

bevoel' (~) feel; finger; touch

bevolk' (~) people, populate; *dig ~*, densely populated; ~**ing** (-e, -s) population; ~**ingsontploffing** population explosion

bevoor'deel (~) favour, promote, advance

bevoor'oordeel(d) (-de) biased, prejudiced

bevoor'reg (~) privilege, favour

bevor'der (~) promote, advance; ~**ing** promotion, rise

bevraag'teken (~) query, doubt, question

bevre'dig (~) satisfy, appease, gratify; ~**end** (-e) satisfactory; ~**ende diens**, satisfactory service

bevrees' (~) afraid, anxious

bevriend', **bevrind'** (-e) friendly, on good terms; ~*e land,* friendly country
bevries' (~) freeze, congeal
bevro're frozen; ~ *hoender,* dressed chicken
bevrug' (~) impregnate, fecundate; ~**ting** conception, impregnation; *kunsmatige* ~*ting/inseminasie,* artificial insemination
bevry' (~) free, deliver, liberate
bewaak' (~) watch, guard
bewaar' (~) keep, preserve; ~**der** (-s) keeper, warder; ~**kas** (-te) locker
bewa'pen (~) arm, provide with arms; ~**ing** armament
bewa'ring keeping; custody; conservation
be'we (ge-) tremble, shiver, quiver, *ook* **beef**
beweeg' (~) move, stir; persuade; ~**lik** (-e; -er, -ste) movable, mobile; vivacious; ~ **rede** (-s) motive
beween' (~) weep over, mourn
beweer' (~) assert, contend, allege
bewe'ging (-e, -s) movement, motion
be'wer (-s) beaver
bewera'sie trembling fit, shivering
be'werig (-e; -er, -ste) shaking, trembling, quivering; tremulous, shaky
bewe'ring (-e, -s) assertion, contention, statement, allegation
bewerkstel'lig (~) effect, cause, bring about
bewil'lig (w) grant, consent; *geld* ~, vote money/funds
bewim'pel (~) disguise, palliate
bewind' government, rule, administration; *aan die* ~ *kom,* come to power; *die* ~*hebbende party,* the ruling party; ~**hebber** governor, ruler
bewo'ë moved, affected; agitated
bewolk' (-te) cloudy, overcast
bewon'der (~) admire; ~**aar** (-s) admirer, fan; ~**aars'pos** fan mail; ~**ing** admiration
bewo'ner (-s) inhabitant; occupier; ~ *van 'n huis,* occupant of a house
bewoon' (~) occupy, inhabit
bewoord' (~) word, express (in words); ~**ing** (-e, -s) wording, expression
bewus' (-te) aware, conscious; in question; ~**syn** consciousness
bewus'teloos (..lose) unconscious
bewys' (s) (-e) proof, evidence; (w) (~) prove, demonstrate; show; do (a favour)

bey'wer (~) endeavour, apply oneself; *hom* ~ *vir,* work/strive for
bib'ber (ge-) shiver, tremble
bibliograaf' (..grawe) bibliographer
bibliografie' (-ë) bibliography
biblioteek' (..teke) library
bibliotekares'se (-s) lady librarian
biblioteka'ris (-se) librarian
bid (ge-) pray, beseech, ask a blessing, say grace; ~**sprinkaan** (..ane) (praying) mantis; ~**stond** (-e) prayer meeting
bie (ge-) bid; tender
bied (ge-) offer, present; *teenstand* ~, offer resistance
bie'der, **bie'ër** (-s) bidder
bief'stuk beefsteak
bieg (s) confession; (w) (ge-) confess; ~**poë-sie** confessional poetry
bie'lie (-s) stalwart; whopper; *jy is darem 'n* ~! you're a brick!
bier beer; ~**brouer** (-s) brewer; ~**brouery** brewery; ~**saal** (..sale) beerhall; ~**vat** (-e) beercask, beer barrel
bies beestings, colostrum; ~**bruilof** non-alcoholic wedding reception
bie'sie (-s) rush, reed; ~**pol** (-le) tussock of rush; peach of a girl
bie'tjie (s) a little bit; a moment; *alle* ~*s help,* every little helps; (b) few; little; (bw) rather, slightly; *'n* ~ *baie,* rather much; *gee 'n* ~ *pad,* just stand clear; *help* ~, please give me a hand
bifokaal' bifocal; ..*kale bril,* bifocal spec-tacles; (mv) bifocals
bigamis' (-te) bigamist
bilhar'zia bilharzia, *ook* **rooiwater**
biljart' (s) billiards
biljoen' (-e) billion
bil'lik (w) (ge-) approve of; (b) (-e; -er, -ste) reasonable, fair, just, equitable; *nie meer as* ~ *nie,* only fair
bil'likheid equity, justice, fairness
bil'tong (-e) biltong (dried meat); ~ *sny voor die bees geslag is,* count one's chickens before they are hatched
bind (ge-) tie, bind, fasten; ~**geld** retaining fee, retainer; commitment fee
bin'ne in, within, into, inward, inside; ~ *'n paar dae,* within a few days; *B~landse Sake,* Interior; *te* ~ *skiet,* flash into one's mind; ~**aarse voeding,** intravenous feed-ing; ~**band** (-e) tube; ~**brandmotor** in-

ternal combustion engine; **~goed** intes-
ines, entrails; *meer bek as ~goed,* all talk;
~-in inside, within; **~kant** inside;
~kort' shortly, soon, before long; **~land**
interior; **~lands (-e)** inland, home, in the
interior; **~landse verbruik,** domestic consumption
bin'nens: ~huis indoors, in the house;
~huise versiering, interior decorating
bin'ne(n)ste innermost; ~ *buite,* inside out
bin'ne: ~pasiënt (-e) in-patient; **~versie-
ring** interior decorating
biografie' (-ë) biography
biologie' biology
biolo'gies (-e) biological; *~e navorsing,*
biological research
bioskoop' (..skope) bioscope, cinema
bis'kop (-pe) bishop
bits, bit'sig (-e; -er, -ste) harsh, sharp, biting
bit'ter ([-e]; -der, -ste) bitter, grievous; ~
min, precious little; *in ~e nood verkeer,*
be in sore distress; **~einder (-s)** diehard,
persister; **~heid** bitterness; acerbity;.
~lemoen (-e) grapefruit, *ook* pomelo
blaad'jie (-s) leaflet
blaai (ge-) turn over pages; ~ *om (b.o.),*
please turn over (p.t.o.)
blaam blame, blemish
blaar[1] (blare) blister, bleb
blaar[2] (blare) leaf (of a plant)
blaas[1] (s) (blase) bladder
blaas[2] (s) (blase) bubble; (w) **(ge-)** blow,
puff; **~balk (-e)** bellows; **~gom** bub-
blegum; **~kaak** (..kake) gasbag, braggart;
~kans, ~ **tyd** break, time for a breather;
~oppie (-s) toby (fish)
blaas'orkes (-te) brass band
blaas'pyp (-e) blowgun, blowpipe
blad (blaaie) leaf (of a book); newspaper;
blade (spring); shoulder (animal)
blad: ~sak (-ke) knapsack; **~skrif** leaflet,
hand-out; **~sy (-e)** page; **~wyser (-s)**
bookmark, index
blaf (s) (blawwe) bark; (w) **(ge-)** bark;
kommandeer jou eie honde en ~ self, do
your own dirty work
bla'ker (-s) candlestick
blameer' (ge-, ~) blame, slander
Blan'ke (-s) white man; White (member of
group or race)
blan'ko blank; *'n ~ tjek,* a blank cheque
blaps mistake, blunder, slip-up

blas (-ser, -ste) sallow, darkbrown
blat'jang chutney; relish, ketchup
bleek (w) (ge-) bleach; (b) **(bleker, -ste)** pale,
pallid, colourless
bleik (ge-) bleach; **~poeier (-s)** bleaching
powder
blêr (ge-) bleat; **~fliek** talkie film; **~kas
(-te)** jukebox
bles (-se) blaze; bald head; **~bok (-ke)** bles-
buck; **~hoender (-s)** whitefaced coot,
moorhen; **~perd (-e)** horse with a glaze
blie'per (-s) bleeper (apparatus)
blik[1] (s) (-ke) glance, view; *in een ~,* at a
glance; (w) **(ge-)** glance, look; *sonder om
te ~ of te bloos,* without a blush
blik[2] (s) (-ke) tin; **~brein** computer (idiom.);
~kiesdorp (-e) shantytown; slum; **~kies-
kos** tinned foodstuffs; **~kiesmelk** con-
densed/tinned milk
Blik'oor (..ore) nickname for Freestater
blik'sem (s) (-s) lightning; scoundrel; (w)
(ge-) flash, lighten; **~afleier (-s)** lightning conductor; **~straal** (..strale) flash of
lightning
blik: ~skêr (-e) plate shears; tin opener;
~skottel! silly ass! rascal! **~slaer (-s)**
tinsmith; rascal; **~snyer (-s)** tin opener
blind (-e) blind; *~e hoogte,* blind rise; *so
~ soos 'n mol,* as blind as a bat; *~e vertroue,* implicit faith; **~doek (s) (-e)** eye
bandage; (w) **~doek (ge-)** blindfold
blin'dederm (-s) appendix; **~ontsteking**
appendicitis
blin'de-instituut (..tute) institute for the
blind
blinde: ~lings blindly, implicitly; **~molle-
tjie** blind man's buff (a game)
blin'der[1] (-s) window blind
blin'der[2] (-s) stymie (golf)
blin'de: ~skool (..skole) school for the
blind; **~vlieg** (..vlieë) stingfly
blin'ding (-s) window blind
blind: ~tik touch typing; **~tikster (-s)**
touch typist
blink (w) (ge-) shine, glitter; (b) **(-er, -ste)**
shining, glittering; *'n ~ gedagte,* a brain-
wave
blits (s) (-e) lightning flash; *hy loop soos die
~,* he runs like lightning; (w) **(ge-)** flash;
~aanval (-le) blitz, lightning attack;
~debat snap debate; **~motor** (flying)

squad car; **~patrollie** flying squad; **~verkoper** bestseller; **~vinnig** like a flash

bloed blood; strain; *goed en ~ opoffer*, offer life and property; *sy ~ kook*, he is furious; **~armoede** anaemia, chlorosis; **~bad (-de(ns))** bloodbath; massacre, slaughter

bloeddors'tig (-e; -er, -ste) blood-thirsty

bloed: ~druk blood pressure; **~druppel (-s)** drop of blood; **~e'rig (-e)** bloody; *'n ~erige stuk vleis*, meat dripping with blood; **~hond (-e)** bloodhound; **~ig (-e; -er, -ste)** sanguinary, bloody, scorching; *'n ~ige geveg*, a bloody fight; **~ing** bleeding, haemorrhage; **~jong, ~jonk** very young; **~min** precious little; **~rooi** bloodred; **~skande** incest; **~skenker (-s)** blood donor

bloeds'omloop circulation of the blood

bloed: ~oortapping blood transfusion; **~suier (-s)** leech, bloodsucker; extortioner; **~vergieting** bloodshed; **~vergiftiging** blood poisoning; **~verwant (-e)** relative, kinsman; **~vete (-s)** blood grudge/feud

blood'vint (-e) boil, furuncle

bloed: ~vlek (-ke) bloodstain; **~weinig** precious little

bloei¹ (s) bloom, flourishing condition; *in die ~ van sy jare*, in the prime of his life; **(w) (ge-)** bloom (flowers); blossom (trees); flourish

bloei² (w) (ge-) bleed

bloei'sel (-s) blossom

bloe'kom bluegum

bloemis' (-te) florist

bloem'lesing (-s) anthology, selected writings

bloes (-e), bloe'se (-s) blouse

bloe'sem (-s) blossom, bloom

blok¹ (s) (-ke) block, log; clog; **~bespreking (-s)** block booking; **~fluit (-e)** recorder

blok² (w) (ge-) grind at, cram, swot

blok'huis (-e) blockhouse

blokka'de (-s) blockade; block (road)

blokkeer' (ge-) blockade; block

blok'kies: ~raaisel (-s) crossword puzzle; **~vloer (-e)** parquet floor(ing)

blok'man (-ne) blockman

blom (s) (-me) flower, blossom; flour; **~kool** cauliflower

blom'merangskikking (-s) flower arrangement

blom'meskou (-e), blom'metentoonstelling (-s) flower show

blom: ~pot (-te) flowerpot; **~ryk (-e; -er, -ste)** flowery; florid; **~tjom** flowerchild; **~tuin (-e)** flower garden

blond (-e; -er, -ste) fair, light

blondi'ne (-s) blonde, fair woman

bloos (ge-) blush, colour; *~ tot agter die ore*, blush to the roots of one's hair

bloot (blote) naked, bare; mere; *die blote feite*, the bald facts; *met die blote oog*, with the naked eye

bloots bareback(ed)

bloot'stel (-ge-) expose; *hom ~ aan gevaar*, expose himself to danger

blos (-se) blush, bloom

blo'send (-e; -er, -ste) blushing, flushed; rosy, ruddy

blou (-er, -ste) blue; *bont en ~ slaan*, beat black and blue

blou-blou: ~ laat, let the matter rest

blou: ~druk (-ke) blueprint; **~kopkoggelmander (-s)** blueheaded lizard; **~kous (-e)** bluestocking, literary woman; **~oog** blue-eyed; **~reën** wistaria; **~sel** (washing) blue; **~skimmel (-s)** bluish grey horse; **~tjie:** *'n ~tjie loop*, unsuccessful; refused by a girl; **~wildebees (-te)** blue wildebees, brindled gnu

bluf bluff

blus (s): *sy ~ is uit*, he is done for; **(w) (ge-)** extinguish, quench, put out; slake (lime)

bly¹ (w) (ge-) stay, remain, live; *~ aan*, hold the line

bly² (b) (-e; -er, -ste) glad, joyful, cheerful; *~ u te kenne*, how do you do, pleased to meet you

blyd'skap joy, happiness

blyk (s) (-e) proof, mark, token, sign; *~ van waardering*, token/mark of appreciation; **(w) (ge-)** appear, seem, be evident; *dit sal gou ~*, we shall soon see

blyk'baar apparently, obviously, evidently

bly'kens according to; *~ koerantberigte*, judging from newspaper reports

blymoe'dig (-e; -er, -ste) joyful, glad, cheerful; joyous

bly'spel (-e) comedy

bly'wend (-e) lasting, permanent; fast; *~e vrede*, lasting peace

bo above; upstairs; up, upon; over; ~ *en behalwe*, over and above; ~ *alle verwagting*, beyond all expectations

bo: ~**aan** at the top, at the head; ~*aan die klas staan*, be at the top of the class; ~**baas** topdog

bobbejaan' (..jane) monkey; baboon; *die ~ agter die bult gaan haal*, meet your troubles halfway; ~**boud** (-e) old-fashioned musket; ~**spinnekop** (-pe) tarantula, baboon spider; ~**stuipe** hysterics, fits

bobo'tie curried hash, bobotie

bod (botte) offer, bid

bo'de (-s) messenger

bo'dem (-s) bottom; soil; *op vaderlandse ~*, on native soil

boe (tw) bo(h); *hy kan nie ~ of ba sê nie*, he can't say boo to a goose

Boeddhis' (-te) Buddhist; ~**me** Buddhism; ~**ties** (-e) Buddhistic

boe'del (-s) estate; ~ *oorgee*, go bankrupt; ~**belasting** estate duty; ~**beredderaar** (-s) executor, administrator (of an estate)

boef (boewe) rogue, villain, knave

boeg (boeë) bow, prow; ~**lam** tired out, fatigued, deadbeat

boe'goe buchu; ~**brandewyn** buchu brandy

boei (s) (-e) shackle; handcuff, fetter; (w) (ge-) handcuff, chain, fetter, fascinate, captivate; ~**end** (-e; -er, -ste) captivating, fascinating, interesting; *'n ~ende verhaal*, a gripping story

boek (s) (-e) book; *anderman se ~e is duister om te lees*, the lives of others are a closed book; *te ~ stel*, record; put on paper; (w) (ge-) book, enter

boekanier' (-s) buccaneer

boek: ~**beoordelaar** (-s) reviewer, critic; ~**deel** (..dele) volume, part; *dit spreek ~dele*, it speaks volumes; ~**drukkuns** printing art, typography; ~**(e)kas** (-te) bookcase; ~**ery** (-e) library (private)

boeket' (-te) bouquet

boe'kevat (-ge-) observe divine service at home

boek'handel booktrade; bookshop; ~**aar** (-s) bookseller, stationer

boek'hou (s) bookkeeping; (w) (-ge-) keep books, keep accounts; ~**er** (-s) bookkeeper

boe'kie (-s) small book, booklet; bookmaker (colloquial)

boek'jaar (..jare) financial year

boek: ~**rak** (-ke) bookshelf, bookcase; ~**sak** (-ke) schoolbag, case, satchel; ~**staaf** (ge-) put on record, commit to paper; ~**winkel** (-s) bookshop; ~**wurm** (-s) bookworm

boel crowd, lot, a great many

boeljon' beef tea, broth

boe'mel (ge-) booze, spree; ~**aar** (-s) tramp, loafer; reveller; ~**trein** (-e) slow hobo, train

boe'merang boomerang

boen'der (ge-) scrub, rub, polish; bundle away

bo'-ent (-e) topside; upper half

boe'pens (-e) paunch; potbelly, corporation

Boer (-e) Boer (member of former group or race); *die ~ met sy roer*, the Boer and his (faithful) gun

boer (s) (-e) farmer, peasant; jack, knave (cards); *die ~ die kuns afvra*, try to find out a secret; (w) (ge-) farm; stay; frequent; *hy ~ by daardie nooi*, he is always off to that girl; *agteruit ~*, go downhill; ~**dery** (-e) farm; farming; ~**(e)beskuit** (-e) rusk; ~**boontjie** (-s) broadbean; ~**e'ma triek** confirmation (church); ~**e'musiek** popular music; ~**e-orkes** (-te) traditional rural orchestra; ~**pot** jackpot

boer: ~**e'raat** home remedy; ~**e'troos** coffee (idiom); ~**e'verneuker** (-s) confidence man; cheat; quack; ~**(e)wors** boerewors; ~**kool** borecole, kale

boe'sel (-s) bushel

boe'sem (-s) bosom, breast; *die hand in eie ~ steek*, search one's own heart; ~**vri(e)nd** (-e) chum, bosom friend

Boes'man (-s) Bushman; ~**tekening** (-e, -s) Bushman drawing

boet[1] (s) brother; *baantjies vir ~ies*, jobs for pals; ~*ie~ie speel*, be hand and glove together

boet[2] (w) (ge-) atone, expiate; *vir sy sondes ~*, pay for his sins

boe'ta (-s) brother; old chap; *ek sal jou wys, ~!* I'll show you, old chap!

boe'te (-s) fine; penalty; penance; ~ *doen*, do penance; ~ *oplê*, impose a fine; ~**bessie** metermaid; ~**bossie** (-s) burweed

boetiek' boutique

boetseer' *(~,* ge-) model; **~kuns** (art of) modelling

boe'we: ~streek (..streke) villainy, roguery; ~tronie (-s) hangdog face

bof¹ (s) tee (golf); base (baseball); home (games)

bof² (w) (ge-) be lucky, have more success than expected

bof'bal baseball

bog (s) trash, tripe; (-te) blighter; fool; *jou klein ~,* you little fool; *dis pure ~,* it's all bunkum

bo'gemiddeld above average

bog'gel (-s) hump, hunch; ~tjie (-s) ~rug hunchback

bog: ~rympie (-s) limerick; ~praatjies twaddle, trash, piffle

bohaai' fuss, hubbub, noise

boi'kot (s) boycott; (w) (ge-) boycott

bok¹ (-ke) goat, antelope, buck; trestle; *'n ou ~ is ook lus vir 'n groen blaartjie,* old men like tender chickens

bok² (-ke) blunder; *'n ~ skiet,* make a blunder

bok'baard billy goat (beard)

bok-bok-staan-styf' high cockalorum

bok: ~haar mohair; ~hael buckshot; ~kapater (-s) castrated goat

bok'kem, bokkom (-s) (dried) Cape herring; bloater

bok'kesprong (-e) caper, antic

bok'kie¹ (-s) kid

bok'kie² (-s) buggy

bokmakie'rie (-s) bush shrike

bok: ~melk goat's milk; ~ooi (-e) she-goat; ~ram (-me) he-goat

bo'koste overhead costs, overheads

boks (ge-) box

bok'seil (-e) bucksail, tarpaulin

bok'ser (-s) boxer

boks'handskoen boxing glove

bok'spring (s) (-e) caper, antic; (w) (ge-) caper

bok'veld goat pasture; *hy is ~ toe,* he has gone west, has joined his forefathers

bok: ~vet goat suet; ~wa (-ens) buck-wagon; ~wiet buckwheat

bo: ~laag (..lae) upper layer; topdressing (lawn)

bol (-le) (s) ball; bulb; globe; (w) (ge-) bulge; (b) convex, round

Bo'land Western Province Boland; ~er (-s) inhabitant of the Western Province

bo: ~leer upper leather, uppers; ~lig (-te) skylight, fanlight

bol'la (-s) chignon, bun (hair)

bollemakie'sie, bolmakie'sie head over heels, somersault; *~ slaan,* loop the loop

bol: ~puntpen (-ne) ballpoint pen; ~rond (-e) convex, spherical

bol: ~werk (s) (-e) bulwark, rampart; (w) (ge-) fortify; manage; ~wurm (-s) boll-worm

bo'lyf (..lywe) body above the hips; ~ie (-s) bodice

bom (-me) bomb, shell: *die ~ het gebars,* the fat is in the fire

bombardement' (-e) bombardment

bombas'ties (-e; -er, -ste) bombastic

bom: ~skok (-ke) shellshock; ~werper (-s) bomber

bo'natuurlik (-e) supernatural

bond (-e) confederation, association, union, league

bon'del (-s) parcel, bundle; ~draer (-s) pedlar, tramp; ~transaksie package deal, *ook* pakketakkoord

bond'genoot (..note) ally, confederate; ~skap alliance, confederacy

bon'dig (-e; -er, -ste) brief, terse, succinct, concise; *kort en ~,* short and to the point

bons (s) (-e) bump, bang, thud; (w) (ge-) beat, palpitate, bounce (ball)

bont¹ (s) fur; ~jas (-se) fur coat, *ook* pels-jas

bont² (b) (-er, -ste) odd-coloured, varie-gated, motley; *sy ~ varkie is weg,* he has a screw loose; ~e'bok (-ke) nunni, pied antelope, bontebok; ~kwagga (-s) Bur-chell's zebra; ~loper (-s) jaywalker; ~lopery jaywalking; ~rokkie (-s) stone-chat

bo'nus (-se) bonus; ~obligasie (-s) bonus bond

bood'skap (s) (-pe) message, errand; *die blye ~,* the glad tidings/gospel; ~per (-s) messenger

boog (boë) bow; curve, arch, arc; *pyl en ~,* bow and arrow; ~skiet archery; ~skutter (-s) archer

boom¹ (bome) bottom

boom² (bome) tree; bar, beam; *tussen die ~ en die bas,* betwixt and between

boom: ~**singertjie** (-s) cicada, scissor grin=
der; ~**skilpadjie** (-s) ladybird
boom'skraap finished; empty; rock-bottom
boon (bone) bean; **grond** ~, peanut
boon'op moreover, besides
boon'ste top uppermost, highest
boon'tjie (-s) bean; ~ *kry sy loontjie,* every
dog has his day
boon'toe to the top, up(wards)
bo'-oor over the top, right over
bo'-op on top, atop of
boor (s) (bore) bore, drill; gimlet; (w) (ge-)
bore, drill
boord¹ (-e) orchard
boord² border, edge, brim; board (ship);
aan ~ gaan, to go aboard; *oor~ gooi,*
throw to the winds
boord'jie (-s) collar
boor: ~**gat** (~**e**) borehole; ~**ling** (-e): *'n
~ling v.d. Pêrel,* born in Paarl; ~**man**
driller; ~**masjien** drilling machine
boor'suur boracic acid
boor'tjie (-s) gimlet
boor'toring (-s) (oil) rig
boos ([bose]; **boser, -ste**) angry, wicked,
evil; *bose kringloop,* vicious circle
boos: ~**doener** (-s) evildoer, villain, crim=
inal; ~**wig** (-te) villain, criminal
boot (bote) boat
bo'raks borax
bord (-e) plate, board
bordeel' (..dele) brothel, house of ill-fame
bord'jie (-s) small plate; notice board; *die
~s is verhang,* the tables are turned
bord'papier cardboard, paste board, mill=
board
borduur' (ge-) embroider
borg (-e) surety, security, guarantee, bail;
guarantor; sponsor; ~ *staan,* become
surety; stand bail; ~**skap** suretyship;
sponsorship; *op ~tog uit,* admitted to
bail; *hy ~ die byeenkoms,* he is sponsor=
ing the event
bor'rel (s) (-s) bubble; drop, tot; (w) (ge-)
bubble; tipple; ~**siekte** air embolism;
bends (diving)
bor'rie turmeric, curcuma
bors (-te) breast; chest; thorax; *dit stuit my
teen die ~,* it goes against the grain;
~**beeld** (-e) bust
bor'sel (s) (-s) brush; bristle; (w) (ge-) brush

bors: ~**hemp** (..hemde) dress shirt; ~**lap**
(-pe) breastpiece; bib; ~**plaat** fudge;
~**speld** (-e) brooch; ~**suiker** sugarstick,
lollipop; ~**rok** (-ke) corset; foundation
garment
bos¹ (-se) bundle, bunch
bos² (-se) forest, wood; shrub, bush; shock
(hair); *om die ~ lei,* lead by the nose;
~**aap** (..ape) thick-tailed lemur; ~**apie**
(-s) bushbaby; ~**bou** forestry, affores=
tation
bosga'sie, boska'sie (-s) copsewood, thick=
et; unkempt hair
bos: ~**lanser** (-s) unkempt country cousin;
coward; ~**luis** (-e) bushtick
bos'ryk (-e) woody, wooded
bos'sie (-s) shrub, copse; *geld soos ~s,*
plenty of money
bo'staande above(-mentioned)
bos'tamboer grape vine (idiom)
bos'vark (-e) bushpig
Bos'veld Bushveld
bos: ~**wagter** (-s) ranger, gamekeeper
bot¹(s) (-te) fluke; flounder (fish); bid
(auction), *kyk* **bod**
bot² (s) (-te) sprout, bud; (w) (ge-) bud,
sprout
bot³ (b) (-te; -ter, -ste) blunt, dull, abrupt
bota'nies (-e) botanic(al)
bota'nikus (-se, ..ici) botanist
bo'tol (w, s) topspin (ball games)
bo'toon overtone; *die ~ voer,* boss the
show
bots (s) shock, collision; (w) (ge-) collide,
clash; ~**ing** (-e, -s) collision, smash, clash
bot'stil quite still, very quiet
bot'tel (s) (-s) bottle, flask; *al bars die ~,*
come what may; (w) (ge-) bottle
bottelier' (-s) butler (bottle bearer)
bot'ter butter; ~ *aan die galg smeer,* pour
water on a duck's back; *dis ~ op 'n warm
klip,* it serves no purpose; *met die neus in
die ~ val,* be lucky; ~**broodjie** (-s) scone,
kyk skon; ~**peer** (..pere) avocado pear;
~**pot** (-te) butterdish
bou (s) construction; build; structure; (w)
(ge-) build, construct; ~**aannemer** (-s)
building contractor; ~**bedryf** building
industry/trade
boud¹ (s) (-e) buttock, leg
boud² (b) bold
bou'er (-s) builder

bou'kontrakteur (-s) building contractor
bou'kunde, bou'kuns architecture
boul (w) bowl; ~beurt over; leë ~beurt, maiden over; ~er (-s) bowler
bou'rekenaar (-s) quantity surveyor
bout (-e) bolt, pin
bouval'lig (-e; -er, -ste) dilapidated, decayed, tottering, ramshackle
bou'vereniging (-s) building society
bo'we above; upon; over; upstairs
bowenal' above all (things)
bowendien' moreover, besides
bra rather, really, actually; (s) bra; *hy is maar ~ dom,* he is rather stupid; *dit kan nie ~ anders nie,* it can hardly be different
braaf (brawe; brawer, -ste) honest, good, upright
braai (ge-) roast, fry, grill; scorch; ~gereg (-te) grill; *gemengde ~gereg,* mixed grill, *kyk* allegaartjie; ~hoek (-e) barbecue; ~hoender, ~kuiken (-s) broiler; ~huis, ~restourant steakhouse; ~ribbetjie (-s) roast(ed) rib; ~vleis roasted meat, roast; ~vleisaand braaivleis social, barbecue, *kyk* vleisbraai
braais = braai'huis
braak[1] (w) (ge-) vomit
braak[2] (w) (ge-) break up; fallow
braam (brame) bramble
brab'bel (ge-) jabber, mutter
brak[1] (s) (-ke) dog; cur, mongrel
brak[2] (b) (-ker, -ste) brackish, briny; ~water brack water
brak'kie (-s) small dog; small mongrel
brand (s) (-e) fire, conflagration; mildew, blight; *aan die ~!,* on the go!; *aan die ~ steek,* set on fire; (w) (ge-) burn, scald, blaze, scorch, cauterise; brand (cattle); ~alarm (-s) fire alarm; ~arm indigent, destitute; ~assuransie fire insurance; ~baar (..bare) combustible; (in)flammable; ~bestryding fire fighting; ~blusser (-s) fire extinguisher; ~bom (-me) incendiary bomb
bran'der (-s) large wave, breaker; (mv) surf; ~plank surfboard; ~ski surf skiing
bran'dewyn brandy
bran'ding surge, surf, breakers
brand: ~kas (-te) safe, strongbox; ~maer skinny, scraggy, as lean as a rake; ~merk (s) (-e) brand, stigma; (w) (ge-) brand,

stigmatise; ~polis (-se) fire policy; ~punt focus; ~slaner (-s) firefighter; ~solder (-s) fireproof ceiling; ~spiritus methylated spirits; ~spuit (-e) fire hose/hydrant; ~stapel (-s) stake, pile; pyre
brand'stigting arson
brand: ~stof fuel; ~stofbesparing fuel economy/saving; ~stof'inspuiting fuel injection; ~stofverbruik fuel consumption; ~trap fire escape; ~versekering fire insurance; ~wag (-te) guard, outpost; sentry, picket
brand'weer fire brigade
bras (ge-) carouse, booze
brava'de bravado, boast
bre'die stew (vegetables and meat), ragout
breed (breë, breër, -ste) broad, wide
breed'te (-s) breadth, width
breedvoe'rig (-e; -er, -ste) circumstantial, detailed, exhaustive
breek (ge-) break, smash, crush, snap, fracture; *maak en ~,* make and mar; ~baar (..bare) breakable, fragile; ~goed, ~ware crockery
brei[1] (ge-) knit
brei[2] (ge-) prepare skins; coach, train
brei'er (-s) coach (sports); knitter
brein brain; intellect; ~floute black-out
brei'naald (-e) knitting needle
brein'spoeling brainwashing
brek'fis (s) breakfast
breuk (-e) rupture, hernia; breach (peace); fracture; fraction
brief (briewe) letter, epistle; *aangehegte ~,* attached letter; *begeleidende ~,* covering letter; *bygaande ~,* accompanying letter; ~kaart (-e) postcard; ~wisseling correspondence
bries[1] (s) (-e) breeze
bries[2] (w) (ge-) snort, fret; ~end (b) (-e) snorting, furious, wild with rage
brie'we: ~besteller (-s) postman; ~boek (-e) letterwriter; ~bus(-se) posting box; ~sak(-ke) letterbag, postbag, mailbag
briga'de (-s) brigade
brigadier' (-s) brigadier
briket' (-te) brikett
bril (s) (-le) pair of spectacles; (w) (ge-) wear spectacles; ~huisie (-s) spectacle case
briljant' (s) (-e) cut diamond; (b) (-e; -er, -ste) brilliant
bril'maker (-s) optician

bring (ge-) bring, take, carry, convey; *te berde* ~, broach a matter; *iem. om die lewe* ~, kill a person

Brit (-te) Briton, Britisher; ~**s** (-e) British **Brittan'je** Britain

broe'der (-s) brother; ~**liefde** brotherly love; ~**lik** (-e) brotherly, fraternal; ~**moord** fratricide; ~**skap** brotherhood, fraternity

broei (ge-) brood, hatch; ~**masjien** (-e) incubator

broeis broody

broei'sel (-s) brood; clutch

broek (-e) (pair of) trousers, breeches; drawers, bloomers; ~**pak** slacksuit; ~**sak** (-ke) trouser pocket

broe'kiekouse pantihose

broer (-s) brother; ~**s'kind** (-ers) nephew, niece

brok (-ke) piece, fragment; *stukkies en* ~*kies,* odds and ends

brom (ge-) grumble, mutter, growl

brom: ~**mer** (-s) grouser, grumbler; bluebottle, blowfly; ~**ponie** (-s) (motor) scooter; ~**pot** (-te) growler, grouser, grumbler; ~**voël** (-s) ground hornbill

bron (-ne) spring; source, origin; ~ *(herkoms) en aanwending/besteding van fondse,* source and application of funds

brongi'tis bronchitis

brons[1] (s) bronze, brass

brons[2] (s) rut, heat; ~**tig** (-e) ruttish, in/on heat

brood (**brode**) bread; loaf; *die een se dood is die ander se* ~, one man's meat is another man's poison; ~**boom** (..bome) breadfruit tree, cycad; ~**lyn:** *onder die* ~*lyn leef,* live under the breadline; ~**mes** (-se) bread knife; ~**mielie** (-s) variety of early mielies; ~**skrywer** (-s) penny-a-liner; ~**winner** (-s) breadwinner; ~**wortel** cassava

brosju're (-s) brochure, pamphlet

brou (ge-) brew; bungle, botch; ~**ery** (-e) brewery

brug[1] bridge (cards)

brug[2] (-ge, brûe(ns)) bridge; parallel bars; *'n* ~ *slaan oor,* bridge; ~**hoof** (-de) bridgehead

bruid (-e) bride; ~**e'gom** (-s) bridegroom; ~**skat** dowry

bruids: ~**koek** (-e) wedding cake; ~**kombuis:** ~*kombuis hou,* give a kitchen tea; ~**paar** (..pare) bridal couple; ~**uitset** (-te) trousseau

bruik'baar (..bare; -der, -ste) serviceable, useful

bruik'huur leasing; lease; *ek het die (motor)kar op* ~, I am leasing this car

bruik'leen loan (for use); lease-lend; *in* ~ *afstaan,* make a loan of (for use)

brui'lof (-te) wedding; *goue* ~, golden wedding; ~**s'gas** (-te) wedding guest; ~**s'plegtigheid** (..hede) marriage ceremony

bruin (-er, -ste) brown; bay

bruin: ~**kapel** (-le) brown cobra; **B**~**mense** Coloured people, Coloureds

bruis (ge-) foam, froth, effervesce; ~**melk** milkshake; ~**poeier** (-s) fruitsalts; ~**suiker** sorbit; ~**wyn** (-e) sparkling wine, champagne

brul (s) (-le) roar; (w) (ge-) roar; ~**padda** (-s) bullfrog

brunet' (-te) brunette

brutaal' (..tale; ..taler, -ste) cheeky, impudent, insolent

bru'to gross; ~ **gewig/massa** gross weight/mass; ~ **wins** gross profit

bry (ge-) roll the ''r'', speak with a burr

buf'fel (-s) buffalo; rude fellow

buf'fer (-s) buffer; bumper

buffet' (-te) sideboard; bar; ~**ete** (-s) buffet lunch/supper

bui (e) shower; whim, mood

bui'e, buig (ge-) bend, bow, stoop; curve

buig'baar (..bare; -er, -ste) bendable; *daardie yster is* ~, you can bend that piece of iron

buig'saam (..same; ..samer, -ste) flexible, pliable; yielding (person); *'n* ..*same rottang,* a flexible cane

buik (-e) stomach, belly; abdomen; ~**spraak** ventriloquy; ~**spreker** (-s) ventriloquist; ~**vliesontsteking** peritonitis; ~**vol** fed up

buil (-e) boil; swelling; ~**e'pes** bubonic plague

buis (-e) tube, pipe, duct; ~**lig** (-te) fluorescent light (tube)

buit (s) booty, loot, plunder; (w) (ge-) rob, loot

bui'te outside; out of doors; *van ~ ken,* know by heart; *~ geveg stel,* disable; **~band** (-e) tyre; **~egteiik** (-e) out of wedlock, illegitimate (child); **~baan** off-course (totalisator); **~kans** unexpected advantage, windfall; **~kant** (s) outside, exterior; (bw) outside; **~klub** (-s) country club; **~land** foreign country; **~lander** foreigner; **~lands** (-e) foreign; exotic; *B~landse Sake,* Foreign Affairs; **~lug** open air; **~muurs** (-e) extramural
bui'ten besides, except, beyond
buitendien' moreover, besides
bui'tengewoon (..wone) extraordinary, peculiar
bui'tenshuis out of doors
buitenspo'rig (-e; -er, -ste) extravagant, excessive; *~e wins,* exorbitant profit
bui'tenste outermost, exterior
bui'te: ~pasiënt (-e) outpatient; **~perd** (-e) outsider; **~pos** (-te) outpost, outstation; **~sintuiglike waarneming** extrasensory perception; **~staander** (-s) outsider; **~stedelik** (-e) peri-urban; **~verkoop** off-sales
buit'maak (-ge-) seize, capture, carry off
buk (-ge-) stoop, bend, bow
buk'sie (-s) saloon rifle; smallish person
bul (-le) bull, steer
bul'der (ge-) roar, rage, boom
bulk (ge-) low, bellow, moo
bul'kalf (..kalwers) bullcalf
bulle'bak (-ke) bully; surly person; lout
bulletin' (-s) notice, bulletin
bul'sak (-ke) bolster, featherbed
bult (-e) hillock, ridge, rising ground; hump, bump; *ons is amper oor die ~,* the worst is nearly over
bun'del (s) (-s) volume (book); bundle
burg (-e) gelded pig, barrow
bur'gemeester (-s) mayor; **~es** (-se) lady mayor; **~s'vrou** (-e, -ens) mayoress
bur'ger (-s) citizen, civilian, burgess; burgher; **~bandradio** citizen-band radio; **~blinde** (-s) civilian blind; **~klere** civilian clothes, civvies; *in ~drag, in ~klere,* in plain clothes, in mufti; **~kunde** civics; **~like** (-s) civilian (person); **~like beskerming** civil defence; **~lugvaart** civil aviation; **~oorlog** (..loë) civil war; **~sentrum** civic centre; **~wag** (-te) civic guard
buro' (-'s) office; desk; bureau

burokraat' (..krate) bureaucrat
bus[1] (-se) box, tin; bush (of a wheel)
bus[2] (-se) (omni)bus; **~diens** (-te) bus service; **~drywer** bus driver; **~kaartjie** (-s) bus ticket
bus'kruit gunpowder
buur (bure) neighbour; **~man** (bure) neighbour
buurt (-e), **buur'te** (-s) neighbourhood, area, quarter, vicinity
buur'vrou (-e, -ens) neighbour's wife
buus'te (-s) bust; **~lyfie,** bra
by[1] (s) (-e) bee
by[2] (vs) at, near, by, with
by'bedoeling (-e, -s) ulterior aim/motive
by'behore accessories
By'bel (-s) Bible; **~kennis** scriptural knowledge; **~s** (-e) biblical, scriptural; **~verklaring** (-e, -s) exegesis; **~teks** (-te) text from Scriptures
byderhand' close by; handy
byderwets' with-it, trendy, modern in outlook
by'dra (-ge-) contribute; **~e** (-s) contribution
byeen' together; **~roep** call together, convene (a meeting); **~roepende kennisgewing,** notice calling the meeting
byeen'kom (-ge-) meet, gather, assemble; (s) **~s** (-te) gathering, meeting, event (sport), assembly
by'e: ~korf (..korwe) beehive; **~was** beeswax
by'gaande accompanying, enclosed; *~ brief,* the accompanying letter
by'gebou (-e) annex; outhouse
by'geloof (..lowe) superstition
bygelo'wig (-e; -er, -ste) superstitious
by'kans nearly, almost
by'klank (-e) sound effect(s)
by'kom (-ge-) come up with; recover (from a faint); reach
by'komende additional, incidental; *~ inligting,* additional/further information
bykoms'tig (-e) accessory, minor, incidental; *~e nalatigheid,* contributory negligence; **~hede** accessories; minor matters
byl (-e) axe, hatchet
by'lae (-s) appendix, annexure, supplement
by'lyn (-e) extension (telephone)
bymekaar' together
by'na nearly, almost; *~ nooit,* hardly ever

by'naam (..name) nickname
by'nes (-te) beehive
by'saak (..sake) side issue, secondary matter
bysien'de short-sighted, myopic
by'sin (-ne) dependent/subordinate sentence
by'sit (w) (-ge-) add to; inter; help; *hand* ~, lend a hand
by'smaak (..smake) aftertaste, peculiar flavour, tinge
by'staan (-ge-) assist, help, back up
by'stand assistance, aid, support; *op* ~, on standby; ~ *verleen,* render assistance
bys'ter: *die spoor* ~ *wees,* be on the wrong track
by'syn presence
byt (s) (-e) bite; (w) (ge-) bite, snap at

byt'soda caustic soda
by'vak (-ke) ancillary subject
by'val[1] (s) applause, approval, approbation; ~ *vind,* meet with approval
by'val[2] (w) (-ge-) come into (one's mind); remember
by'verdienste sideline, extra income
by'voeg (-ge-) add, annex, append; ~'lik (-e) adjectival; ~*like naamwoord,* adjective
byvoor'beeld for example
by'voordeel (..dele) fringe benefit, perk
by'werk revise, update, bring up to date
by'woner (-s) subfarmer; squatter
by'woon (-ge-) be present at, attend
by'woord (-e) adverb
by'wyf (bywywe) concubine, mistress

C

Calvinis' (-te) Calvinist; ~me Calvinism; ~ties (-e) Calvinistic
camoufla'ge camouflage, *kyk* kamoeflage
cha'os chaos
chao'ties (-e) chaotic; ~*e toestande,* chaotic conditions
chauffeur' (-s) chauffeur
chauvinis' (-te) chauvinist; ~me chauvinism; ~ties (-e) chauvinistic
chemie' chemistry
che'mies (-e) chemical; ~*e onkruidbeheer,* chemical weed control
chemika'lieë chemicals
chev'ronteken (-s) chevron sign
Chi'na China
Chinees' (..nese) Chinese
chiropraktisyn' (-s) chiropractor
chirurg' (-e) surgeon; ~ie surgery; ~ies (-e) surgical; *plastiese* ~*ie,* plastic surgery

chloor chlorine
chlo'roform chloroform
cho'lera cholera
choreograaf' (..awe) choreographer
Chris'telik (-e) Christian(like); *die* ~*e jaartelling,* the Christian era
Chris'ten (-e) Christian; ~dom Christianity
Christin' (-ne) Christian (woman)
Chris'tus Christ; *na* ~, Anno Domini (AD); *voor* ~, before Christ (BC)
chro'nies (-e) chronic; ~*e siekte,* chronic illness
chronolo'gies (-e) chronological, in order of time
chroom chromium
cochenil'le cochineal (dye, insect)
cum: ~ *laude,* with distinction

D

daad (dade) deed, action; *op heter* ~ *betrap,* catch in the act
daag (ge-) summon; dawn; ~liks (-e) daily, every day
daal (ge-) descend; sink; fall

Daan'tjie: *tot by oom* ~ *in die kalwerhok,* to the limit
daar (bw) there; (vwg) since, as, because; ~agter behind that (it); ~benewens besides, in addition; ~by thereto, besides,

in addition; **~deur** thereby, by that means; through (there); **~die** that; those

daarente'ë, daarenteen' on the other hand; *Piet is slim, Jan ~ is 'n bietjie dom,* Peter is a clever boy, John on the other hand is not so bright, *kyk* **inteendeel**

daar: ~heen thither, there, to that place; **~in** therein, in that; **~mee** therewith, with that; **~na** after that, afterwards; **~naas** next to that

daar'om therefore, thus, for that reason

daar: ~onder under that, down there, by that; **~oor** about that; therefore; **~op** thereupon, upon that; **~so** there, yonder

daar: ~teë, ~teen against that; **~uit** thence, out of that; **~van** of that, about that, thereof; **~vandaan** from there, thence; **~voor** for that, therefore

da'del (-s) date (fruit)

da'delik immediately, at once, directly

dag (dae) day; **~bestuur** executive/management committee; **~boek** diary; **~breek** daybreak

dag'ga dagga, Cape hemp, hashish, marijuana

da'gha clay (bricklaying), mortar

dag'lig daylight; **~besparing** daylight saving

dag: ~loner (-s) daylabourer; **~pak (-ke)** lounge suit; **~sê (-ge-)** greet, say good day (goodbye); **~skolier (-e)** day scholar; **~skool (..skole)** day school; **~taak (..take)** daily task; *sy ~taak is afgedaan,* he has finished his day's work

dag'vaar (ge-) summon, subpoena; **~ding (-e, -s)** summons, warrant; *'n ~ding beteken/bestel aan,* serve a summons

dak (-ke) roof; **~fees: ~fees vier,** wet the roof; **~geut (-e)** gutter; **~pan (-ne)** tile; **~stel (-le)** penthouse suite

dak: ~tuin (-e) roofgarden; **~vink (-e)** roofclutcher (motorist); **~woning (-s) ~woonstel (-le)** penthouse

dal (-e) valley, dale, dell

da'ling descent; fall, drop, slump

dalk perhaps, maybe

dal'kies by and by, presently; maybe

dam (s) (-me) dam, reservoir; **(w) (ge-)** dam up

dam'bord (-e) draught board

da'me (-s) lady; **~s en here!** ladies and gentlemen!

damp (s) (-e) vapour, steam, fume

dan¹ (bw) then

dan² (vgw) than; *al ~ nie,* whether or not

da'nig (b) (-e) (bw) much, awfully; over-friendly; *nie te ~ goed nie,* not too wonderful; *hom ~ hou,* give himself airs

dank (s) thanks, gratitude; **~ betuig,** express thanks; *stank vir ~,* get small thanks; *teen wil en ~,* in spite of; **(w) (ge-)** thank, give thanks; say grace; *te ~e aan,* due to, thanks to; **~baar (..bare; -der, -ste)** thankful, grateful

dan'kie! thank you! thanks! *jy kan ~bly wees,* you can thank your lucky stars

dank: ~offer (-s) thanks offering; **~segging** thanksgiving; **~sy** thanks to; **~sy** *Piet het ons dit oorleef,* thanks to Peter we survived

dans (s) (-e) dance; **(w) (ge-)** dance; *die poppe is aan die ~,* the fat is in the fire

dan'ser (-s) dancer

danseres' (-se) dancer (female)

dans: ~les (-se) dancing lesson; **~party (-e)** ball, dance; **~skoen (-e)** dancing shoe, pump

dap'per (-der, -ste) brave, valiant, plucky, valorous, gallant; *met ~ en stapper reis,* ride shanks's mare

da'rem though, all the same; after all; surely; *hy is ~ nie te sleg nie,* after all he is not too bad

das¹ (-se) rockrabbit, dassie

das² (-se) tie (for the neck)

das'sie (-s) rockrabbit

das'speld (-e) tie pin, scarf pin

dat that, so that, in order that

da'ta data, facts; **~verwerking** data processing

dateer' (~, ge-) date (from)

da'tum (-s) date

Dawid David; *weet waar ~ die wortels graaf/grawe,* know what is what

dê! (w, imp.) take! here you are! **~, vat hier,** here, take this

dê! (tw) now! see!

debat' (-te) debate

debet', debiet' debit; ~nota (-s) debit note; **~pos (-te)** debit entry; **~saldo (-'s)** debit balance

debiet' sale, market; debit

debiteer' (ge-) debit, charge with

debiteur' (-e, -s) debtor

debutant' (-e) débutant; ~e (-s) débutante (fem.)

debuut' first appearance; debut, *ook* **buiging**

deeg dough

deeg'lik (-e; -er, -ste) solid, thorough, sterling, sound

deel (s) (dele) part, portion; share; division, section; *ten dele,* partly; (w) (ge-) divide; participate; share

deel: ~neem (-ge) participate in, partake, take part in; ~neem aan, participate in; ~neemverband (-e) participation bond; ~nemer (-s) participant, contestant; ~neming participation; sympathy; ~neming betuig, express sympathy

deels partly, in part

deel: ~som (-me) division sum; ~teken (-s) diaeresis; division sign; ~titel sectional title; ~woord (-e) participle; *verlede ~woord,* past participle; ~tyds en heeltyds, part-time and fulltime

deemoe'dig (-e; -er, -ste) humble, meek

deer'nis compassion; commiseration, pity

defek' (s) (-te) defect; (b) defective

defini'sie (-s) definition

definitief' (..tiewe) definite, decisive

def'tig (-e; -er, -ste) stately, grave, dignified, exclusive (suburb)

dein (ge-) heave, surge, swell; ~ing (-e, -s) heave, swell

deins (ge-) shrink (back), recoil; retreat

dek (s) (-ke) deck; (w) (ge-) cover, clothe; be at stud, cover (horse); thatch (house); *die aftog ~,* cover the retreat; *tafel ~,* lay the table

dekaan' (..kane) dean (university)

deka'de (-s) decade, ten (years)

dekadent' (-e) decadent, deteriorating

de'ken[1] (-s) counterpane, quilt, coverlet

de'ken[2] (-s) dean (church); doyen (ambassadors)

dek: ~gras thatch (grass); ~king cover, shelter; coverage (news); guard

dek'mantel (-s) cloak; excuse, pretext; *onder die ~ van,* under the cloak of

de'kor, dekor' decor, (stage) scenery

dekora'sie (-s) decoration; order of knighthood

dekreet' (dekrete) decree, edict

dek'sel (-s) cover, lid

dek'sels (b) (-e) blessed, confounded; *'n ~e gelol,* a darned nuisance; (bw) confounded, darned; ~ hard, dashed hard

dek: ~spaan (..spane) thatch spade; ~stoel (-e) deck chair

dek'verband (-e) covering bond

delegeer' (ge-) delegate

de'ler (-s) divider; divisor; *grootste gemene ~,* greatest common factor

delf, del'we (ge-) dig, mine

delf'stof (..stowwe) mineral

delg (ge-) discharge, pay off, redeem; *jou skuld ~,* discharge one's debt

del'ging discharge, redemption, amortisement: ~(s)fonds (-e) sinking fund, redemption fund

delikaat' (..kate; ..kater, -ste) delicate

delikates'se (-s) delicacy, savoury bit

de'ling division; *lang ~,* long division

deli'ries (-e) delirious

del'ta (-s) delta

del'wer (-s) digger; ~y, diggings

demobilisa'sie demobilisation

demobiliseer' (ge-) demobilise

demokraat' (..krate) democrat

demokrasie' democracy

demokra'ties (-e) democratic

demonstreer' (ge-, ~) demonstrate

demoralise'rend (-e) demoralising

demp (ge-) fill up with earth; quell (riot); quench (fire); dim (light); mute (sound)

den (-ne) fir (tree), pine (tree)

denk'baar (..bare) imaginable, conceivable

denk'beeld (-e) idea, notion

denkbeel'dig (-e) imaginary

den'ke thought, (act of) thinking; ~r (-s) thinker

denk: ~vermoë intellectual capacity; ~wyse (-s) way of thinking, opinion

den'ne: ~bol (-le) fircone; ~boom (..bome) fir, pine; ~bos (-se) pine forest; ~hout pinewood; firwood

denomina'sie denomination

deo'dorant deodorant, *ook* **reukweerder**

departement' (-e) department, office

departementeel' (..tele) departmental

deponeer' (ge-, ~) deposit, lodge

deporteer' (ge-) deport

deposant' (-e) depositor (bank)

depo'sito (-'s) deposit

depot' (-s) depot

depresia'sie depreciation, *ook* waardever-
mindering
depresieer' (ge-, ~) depreciate
depres'sie (-s) depression
deputa'sie (-s) deputation, *ook* afvaardiging
der'de (-s) third; *ten* ~, in the third place;
~dekking third-party cover (insurance);
~magswortel cube root; ~mannetjie:
~*mannetjie speel*, play gooseberry; play
two's and three's; ~ vloer/vlak third
floor; ~rangs (-e) third-rate
der'gelik (-e) such, the like, similar
der'halwe therefore, so, consequently, thus
derm (-s) intestine, gut; (mv) bowels, entrails
derm: ~ontsteking enteritis; ~snaar (..
snare) catgut
der'tien thirteen; ~de (-s) thirteenth
der'tig thirty; ~ste thirtieth
des: ~ *te beter*, so much the better; *'n kind
~ doods*, a dead man
de'se: *na* ~, after this
Desem'ber (-s) December
desentralisa'sie decentralisation
desentraliseer' (ge-) decentralise
de'ser: *die tiende* ~, the 10th instant
de'sibel (-s) decibel (unit of sound)
desimaal' (..male) decimal; *..male breuk*,
decimal fraction; ~komma (-s) decimal
comma; ~stelsel decimal system
deskun'dig (-e) expert; ~*e getuienis*, expert
evidence; (s) ~e (-s) expert
des'nieteenstaande in spite of, notwithstanding
desnoods' if need be, in case of need
des'ondanks nevertheless
desperaat' (..rate) desperate
despoot' (..pote) despot, tyrant
despo'ties (-e) despotic, tyrannic(al)
destabiliseer' (~, ge-) destabilise
des'tyds at that time, then
deten'sie detention
déten'te détente
deug (s) (-de) virtue, excellence; *liewe* ~!
good gracious! (w) (ge-) be good for, serve
a purpose, be of use; *potlood sal* ~, pencil will do; ~niet (-e) rascal, good-for-
nothing
deun'tjie (-s) air, tune, ditty
deur[1] (s) (-e) door, gate; *met die* ~ *in die
huis val*, plunge into a matter

deur[2] (b) passed; (vs) through, by, throughout; ~ *die bank*, all, without exception
deurboor' (~) pierce, stab, transfix
deur'braak breach, burst, rupture; break-
through
deur'bring (-ge-) pass; spend, squander;
~er (-s) spendthrift
deurdag' (-te) well-thought-out; *'n* ~*te
betoog*, a well-reasoned submission
deur'dat because, as
deurdring' (~) permeate, pervade, impress;
die stank ~ *die huis*, the bad smell fills the
house
deur'dring (-ge-) penetrate, permeate, pierce;
die waarheid het tot hom deurgedring, the
truth dawned upon him
deurdrin'gend (-e) shrill, penetrating; searching
deur'druk (-ge-) press through; persist
deur en deur thoroughly, out and out
deur'entyd all the time
deur'gaan (-ge-) pass, go through
deur'gaans usually, invariably
deur'gang (-e) passage
deur'gestoke: ~ *kaart*, prearranged matter
deur: ~glip (-ge-) slip through; ~grawing
(-e, -s) cutting; ~grendel (-s) doorbolt
deurgrond' (~) fathom, penetrate, understand
deur'haal (-ge-) delete; fetch/pull through
deur'hak (-ge-) cut through; solve; *die
knoop* ~, cut the knot
deur'knop (-pe) doorknob
deur'kom (-ge-) get through; pass; survive;
hy het net-net deurgekom, he just man-
aged to pass
deur'kosyn (-e) doorframe
deurkruis' (~) traverse, intersect
deur'kyk (-ge-) look over, skim, peruse;
sum up
deur'laat (-ge-) let through, allow to pass
deurleef', deurle'we (~) live through
deur'lees (-ge-) read through, peruse
deur'loop[1] (s) (..lope) arcade
deur'loop[2] (w) (-ge-) move on; walk
through; peruse; punish; *die stout seuns het
almal deurgeloop*, the naughty boys all had
their punishment
deurlo'pend (-e) continuous, uninterrupted
deurlug'tig (-e) illustrious
deur'maak (-ge-) go through, experience
deur'mat (-te) doormat

deurmekaar' (-der, -ste) in confusion; 'n
~spul, a mix-up

deur: ~pad (..paaie) freeway (rural),
motorway, throughway (urban); ~paneel
(..nele) doorpanel

deur'reis¹ (s) passage; through journey; (w)
(-ge-) travel, pass through

deurreis'² (~) travel all over

deur'settingsvermoë persistence, perseverance

deursig'tig (-e) transparent, lucid

deur'sit¹ (-ge-) sit oneself sore

deur'sit² (-ge-) have one's will, persist; put
through (a deal)

deur'skemer (-ge-) glimmer through; laat
~, hint at

deursko'te interleaved, interfoliate

deursky'nend (-e) transparent, translucent

deur'slaan¹ (-ge-) strike/hit through; punch

deur'slaan² (-ge-) tip; turn; die skaal laat
~, tip the scale

deur'slag moist soil, boggy ground; decisive
factor; (..slae) punch; ~papier (-e) carbon paper

deur: ~slot (-te) doorlock; ~sluip (-ge-)
steal/sneak through; ~smokkel (ge-)
smuggle through

deur'snede (-s) deur'snee (..sneë) section;
diameter; average

deur'sneeprys average price

deur'snit (-te) cross section

deur'snuffel (-ge-) hunt through, rummage,
ransack

deur'soek (-ge-) examine, search, explore

deurspek' (~) interlard; intersperse; sy
proefskrif is ~ met aanhalings, his thesis
is riddled with quotations

deurstaan' (~) endure, suffer, bear; stand

deurstraal' (~) illuminate, irradiate

deurstren'gel (~) intertwine

deur: ~styl (-e) doorpost; ~sukkel (-ge-)
struggle through; ~syfer (-ge-) trickle
through; ~syg (-ge-) filter; ~sypel (-ge-)
ooze through

deurtas'tend (-e) energetic, decisive, resolute, vigorous, thorough

deur'tog passage; march through

deurtrap' (-te) sly, crafty, cunning; 'n ~te
skelm, a confounded rascal

deurtrek'¹ (~) pervade, permeate, imbue;
~ van bedrog, filled with deceit

deur'trek² (-ge-) pass through, pull through;
~ker (-s) spendthrift; pullthrough (rifle);
loincloth; G-string

deur'voer (-ge-) carry out; follow out;
planne ~, carry out/execute plans

deur'waarder, ..wagter (-s) porter, janitor,
doorkeeper, commissionaire

deurweek' (~) soak, moisten; ~ van die
reën, drenched with rain

deur'weg (..weë) throughway

deur'werk (-ge-) work through, mix; inter-
lace

devalueer' (ge-, ~) devaluate

diabe'tes diabetes, ook suikersiekte

diabo'lies (-e) diabolic(al), devilish

diagno'se (-s) diagnosis

diagnoseer' (ge-) diagnose

diagonaal' (..nale) diagonal

diagram' (-me) diagram

dia'ken (-s) deacon

diakones' (-se) deaconess

dialek' (-te) dialect

dialoog' (..loë) dialogue

diamant' (-e) diamond; sparkler; onwettige
~handel, illicit diamond buying (IDB);
~slyper (-s) diamond cutter

didak'ties (-e) didactic

die (lw) the

dié (vnw) this; these

die'derik (-e, -s) golden cuckoo

dieet' (diëte) diet; ~kundige (-s) dietician

dief (diewe) thief

dief'alarm burglar alarm

dief'stal (-le) theft, robbery; larceny; skuldig aan ~ van geld, guilty of theft of
money

dief'wering burglar proofing; burglar guard

die'gene those

dien (ge-) serve, wait on; attend to; suit;
van advies ~, advise; tot bewys ~, serve
as proof; hy ~ in die stadsraad, he serves
on the City Council

die'naar (-s; ..nare) servant, valet; werkgewer en ~, master and servant

dien'der (-s) policeman, constable

dien'lik (-e; -er, -ste) serviceable

dien'ooreenkomstig accordingly

diens (-te) service; function, duty; 'n ~ bewys, do a good turn; in ~ neem, engage;
op (aan) ~, on duty; tot u ~, at your service; van ~ af, off duty; ~bode (-s) servant, domestic; ~bus (-se), ~bussie (-s)

service bus, courtesy bus; **~heffing** service charge; **~ingang** (-e) tradesman's entrance; **~jaar** (..jare) official year; year of service; **~meisie** (-s) maid, servant girl; **~plig** compulsory (military) service, conscription; **~pligtige** (s) (-s) national serviceman; **~reg** law of employment; **~termyn** (-e), **~tyd** (..tye) term of office

diens'voorwaardes conditions of service

diens'weieraar (-s) conscientious objector

dienswil'lig (-e; -er, -ste) assiduous, ready to serve; obedient

dien'tafel (-s) dinner wagon

dien'tengevolge accordingly

diep (-er, -ste) deep; profound; **~ in gedagte**, deep in thought; **~ ongelukkig**, extremely unhappy; **~gaande** profound, deep, thorough; **'n ~gaande ondersoek**, a searching enquiry

diepsin'nig (-e; -er, -ste) profound, abstruse

diep'te (-s) depth; profundity; **~bom** (-me) depth charge; **~studie** (-s) in-depth study

dier (-e) animal; brute

diera'sie (-s) monster; vixen, (she)devil

dier'baar (..bare; -der, -ste) dear, beloved

dier'bare (-s) loved one, beloved

die're: **~beskerming** animal protection; **D~beskermingvereniging**, Society for the Prevention of Cruelty to Animals (SPCA); **~kliniek** (-e) veterinary clinic; **~ryk** animal kingdom; **~sorg** animal care; **~tuin** (-e) zoological gardens, zoo; **~winkel** (-s) petshop, *kyk* arkmark

die'sel diesel; **~pomp** diesel pump

dieself'de the same; *presies ~*, exactly the same

diesul'ke such

die'we: **~bende** (-s) gang/pack of thieves; **~sleutel** (-s) picklock, skeleton key; master key; **~taal** thieves Latin, argot

differensieer' (ge-) differentiate

dig[1] (w) (ge-) write poetry, compose, versify

dig[2] (b) (-te; -ter, -ste) tight; close, near; dense, compact; dull, stupid; **~bevolk** densely populated

dig'by (digterby, digsteby) nearby, close; **~-opname** (-s) close-up (photography)

dig: **~kuns** poetry, poetic art; **~maat** (..mate) metre, poetic measure

dig'ter (-s) poet

digteres' (-se) poetess

dig'terlik (-e; -er, -ste) poetic(al); **~e vryheid**, poetic licence

digt'heid density, denseness

dik (-ker, -ste) thick; bulky; stout, corpulent; satiated; **~ vir**, fed-up with; **hulle is ~ vriende**, they are close friends; **~bek** (s) (-ke) sulk, sulky (person); pouter; (b) fed-up (slang); **~melk** curdled milk; **~sak** (-ke) stout person, fatty

dik'sie diction

diktafoon' (-s) dictaphone

dikta'tor (-s) dictator

dik'te (-s) thickness, swollenness

diktee' (-s) dictation

dikteer' (ge-, ~) dictate; **~masjien** (-e) dictating machine, dictaphone

dik'wels often, frequently

dilem'ma (-s) dilemma, predicament

dilettant' (-e) dilettante, amateur

dina'mies (-e) dynamic

dinamiet' dynamite

dinee' (-s) dinner

ding[1] (s) (-e) thing, object, affair, matter

ding[2] (w) (ge-) try for, compete

din'ges what-do-you-call-it, thingumajig

dink (ge-) think, consider, ponder; **aan iets ~**, think of something; **daar val nie aan te ~ nie**, it is out of the question; **~skrum** thinktank

Dins'dag (..dae) Tuesday

dip (s) (-pe) dip; (w) (ge-) dip

diplo'ma (-s) diploma, certificate; **~plegtigheid** (..hede) graduation ceremony

diplomaat' (..mate) diplomat, diplomatist

diploma'ties (-e) diplomatic

direk' (b) (-te) direct, straight

direk'sie (-s) direction; board of directors

direkteur' (-e, -s) director, manager; **~-generaal** (direkteure-generaal) director-general

direktri'se (-s) directress, manageress

dirigeer' (ge-) conduct (music); **~stok** (-ke) baton

dirigent' (-e) (music) conductor

dis it is; **~ te sê**, that is (to say)

diskonteer' (ge-, ~) discount

diskon'to discount, *ook* afslag, korting

diskoteek' (..teke) record library; discothéque, disco

dis'krediet discredit; **in ~ bring**, bring discredit on

diskre'sie discretion, *ook* goeddunke

diskrimina'sie discrimination
dis'kus (·se) disc(us)
diskusseer' (ge-) discuss
diskus'sie (-s) discussion, argument; ~groep (-e) discussion group
diskwalifika'sie (-s) disqualification
diskwalifiseer' (ge-, ~) disqualify
dislek'sie dyslexia, reading impediment
dis'nis: ~ loop, beat thoroughly, outdis- tance; run/knock someone flat
disputeer' (..pute) dispute, controversy, ar- gument
dis'sel (-s) adze
dis'selboom (..bome) shaft, thill, beam (of wagon); pole (of cart)
disserta'sie (-s) dissertation, thesis
dissi'pel (-s) disciple
dissipli'ne discipline; strenge ~ handhaaf, maintain rigid discipline
dissiplineer' (ge-) discipline
dissiplinêr' (-e) disciplinary; ~e stappe neem/doen, take disciplinary action
dis'tel (-s) thistle
distilla'sie distillation
distilleer' (ge-) distil
distribu'sie distribution
distrik' (-te) district; ~s'geneesheer (..here) district surgeon
dit this; it
divan' (-s) divan, sofa; ottoman
diver'se sundries; incidental expenses; ~ uitgawes, sundry/miscellaneous expenses
diversifeer' (ge-, ~) diversify
dividend' (-e) dividend; 'n ~ uitkeer/uit- betaal, pay a dividend; tussentydse ~, interim dividend; 'n ~ verklaar, declare a dividend
divi'sie (-s) division; ligte ~, mobile divi- sion (army)
dob'bel gamble, play at dice; ~aar (-s) gambler; ~masjien (-e) gambling ma- chine, armed bandit; ~steen (..stene) dice, cube; ~wiel roulette
dob'ber (s) (-s) float, buoy; (w) (ge-) bob up and down, float, fluctuate
do'de: ~dans (-e) death dance; ~lik (-e) deadly, mortal, fatal; 'n ~like wond, a fatal wound; ~mars (-e) funeral march; ~ryk realm of death; ~tal number of deaths; ~tol death toll
doea'ne (-s) custom house; customs

doe'del (ge-) play the bagpipe; ~sak (-ke) bagpipe
doe'die (-s) girl, young woman; foon~ switchboard operator
doe'doe (ge-) sing to sleep; go to sleep; dormy (golf)
doek (-e) cloth; napkin (baby); canvas, painting
doel (s) (-eindes) purpose, aim, object; (-e) goal; sy ~ bereik, attain one's goal/ob- ject; die ~ heilig die middele, the end justifies the means; ~einde (-s) purpose, end, aim, goal; ~gebou custom made; customised; ~loos (..lose; ..loser, -ste) aimless, useless; ~lyn (-e) goal line
doelma'tig (-e; -er, -ste) efficacious, effi- cient, appropriate
doel: ~paal (..pale) goalpost; ~punt (-e) goal; ~skop (-pe) goalkick, conversion
doeltref'fend (-e; -er, -ste) effective, effi- cient, effectual; ~heid effectiveness, ef- ficacy, efficiency
doel: ~wagter (-s) goalkeeper; ~wit (-te) aim, view, goal; ~witbestuur manage- ment by objectives
doem (ge-) doom, condemn; ~profeet prophet of doom
doemdoem'pie (-s) small variety of gnat
doen¹ (s): ons ~ en late, our goings out and comings in
doen² (w) (ge-) do, make, effect, perform; daar is niks aan te ~ nie, there is no help for it; ~lik (-e) feasible, practical; ~lik- heidstudie feasibility study
doe'pa love potion, charm
dof (dowwe; dowwer, -ste) dull, faint, dim, indistinct; lack-lustre (eyes)
dog but, still, however, yet; hy is siek, ~ hy kom skool toe, he is ill, but he comes to school
dog'ma (-s) dogma
dogma'ties (-e) dogmatic(al)
dog'ter (-s) daughter; girl
doi'lie (-s) doily
dok (-ke) dock; ~geld dock duties/dues
dok'ter (s) (-s) doctor, physician; (w) (ge-) doctor, nurse; ~es (-se) female doctor; ~s'geld(e) medical fees; ~s'hande: onder ~s'hande wees, receive medical treatment
dok'tor (-e, -s) doctor (of literature, law, etc.)

doktoraal' (..rale) doctorial; *doktorale ek=
samen,* examination for the degree of
doctor

doktoraat' (..rate) doctorate

dok'torsgraad (..grade) doctor's degree

dokument' (-e) document; **~asie** docu=
mentation

dokumenteer' (ge-, ~) document

dokumentêr' (-e) documentary; *~e film,*
documentary (film)

dol (-ler, -ste) mad, crazy, frantic, ridicu=
lous; *in ~le vaart,* in headlong career

dolf, dolwe (ge-) dig deep

dolfyn' (-e) dolphin

dol: **~graag** very keen; ever so much;
~heid madness; **~huis** (-e) bedlam

dolk (-e) dagger, poniard

dol'lar (-s) dollar

dol'leeg (..leë) absolutely empty

dolomiet' dolomite

dol'os (-se) ball of anklejoint, astragulus,
knucklebone; *~ gooi,* throw the bones
(witchcraft)

dol'verlief (-de) madly in love

dom[1] (s) (-me) dome, cathedral

dom[2] (b) (-mer, -ste) stupid, fatuous; dull;
nie so ~ as hy lyk nie, not as green as he is
cabbage-looking

domastrant' (-e; -er, -ste) impudent, cheeky

dom'heid stupidity, dullness

do'minee (-s) clergyman, minister, parson

domineer (ge-) predominate, domineer

dom: **~kop** (-pe) blockhead, stupid, clot,
dud; **~krag** (-te) jackscrew, jack; *die kar
opdomkrag,* jack up the car

dom'migheid stupidity

dom'oor (..ore) dunce, blockhead

domp (ge-) dim (lights)

dom'pel (ge-) plunge, dive, dip, immerse;
in ellende ~, plunge into misery

dom'per (-s) extinguisher, quencher

donateur' (-s) contributor, patron; donor

don'der (s) (-s) thunder; *jou ~!,* you
scoundrel! (w) (ge-) thunder, boom, ful=
minate; **~bui** (-e) thunderstorm

Don'derdag (..dae) Thursday

don'der: **~slag** (..slae) thunderclap; **~=
storm** (-s) thunderstorm; **~weer** thundery
weather; **~wolk** (-e) thundercloud

don'ga (-s) donga, gully

don'ker (s) darkness; *in die ~ tas,* grope in
the dark; (b) (-der, -ste) dark, dusky;

deep; gloomy, obscure; **~blou** dark blue;
~bruin dark brown; dun; **~heid** dark=
ness, obscurity; **~te** darkness; **~vat** lucky
dip; **~werk:** *~werk is konkelwerk,*
bunglers work in the dark

don'kie (-s) donkey, ass; **~long** (-e) con=
certina (idiom.)

dons (-e) down, fluff; **~agtig, ~erig, ~ig**
(-e) fluffy, downy; **~hael** fine shot, dust;
~kombers (-e) (eiderdown) quilt

dood (s) death, decease; *~ moet 'n oorsaak
hê,* there is an excuse for everything; (w)
(ge-) kill; (b) **(dooie)** dead, deceased, de=
funct; *liewer bang Jan as dooi(e) Jan,*
discretion is the better part of valour; *op
sy dooie gemak,* very leisurely; *so ~ soos
'n mossie,* as dead as a doornail; **~berig**
(-te) death notice; **~bloei** (ge-) bleed to
death; **~druk** (ge-) squeeze to death;
squash, silence; **~eenvoudig** (-e) quite
simple, plain sailing; **~eerlik** (-e) quite
honest; **~gaan** (-ge-) die; **~gebore**
stillborn; **~gerus** (-te) perfectly calm,
quite unconcerned; **~gewoon** (..wone)
very simple, very common; **~goed**
(..goeie) very kind; **~grawer** (-s) grave=
digger; **~kis** (-te) coffin; **~lag** (-ge-) laugh
to death; **~loop** (-ge-) tire oneself out by
walking; come to a dead end; peter out;
~luiters free and easy; **~maak** (-ge-) kill;
~mak quite tame; **~maklik** (-e) very easy;
~martel (-ge-) torture to death; **~moeg**
(..moeë) deadbeat, deadtired; **~ongeluk=
kig** (-e) utterly miserable; **~ry** (-ge-) ride
to death; override, kill

doods (-e) desolate, dreary, deathlike; *'n ~e
stilte,* a deadly silence; **~angs** agony, mor=
tal fear; **~berig** (-te) death notice; **~bleek**
(..bleke) ghastly/deadly pale; livid;
~engel angel of death; **~gevaar** peril of
death

dood: **~siek** dangerously ill; **~skiet** (-ge-)
shoot dead

doods: **~kleed** (..klede) shroud; **~klok**
(-ke) deathbell, knell

doods'kop[1] (n) (-pe) death's head, skull

dood'skop[2] (w) (-ge-) kick to death

dood: **~skrik** (-ge-) be frightened to death;
~slag manslaughter, homicide; **~snik**
(-ke) last gasp

doods'nood imminent danger; agony of
death

dood: ~**sonde** (-s) deadly sin; ~**steek** (s) (..**steke**) deathblow, coup de grace; *sy ~steek,* his pet aversion; (w) (**ge-**) stab to death; ~**still** very still, quiet as a mouse; ~**straf** capital punishment

doods'vyand (-e) mortal enemy

dood: ~**sweet** cold sweat of death; ~**swyg** (**ge-**) ignore; ~**tevrede** quite content; ~**verlief** (-**de**) love-sick; ~**verwonderd** (-e) quite astonished; ~**vonnis** (-se) death sentence

doof[1] (w) (**ge-**) extinguish, put out

doof[2] (b) (**dowe; dower, -ste**) deaf; *so ~ soos 'n kwartel,* as deaf as a post; ~**blind** deaf and blind; ~**middel** (-s) anaesthetic, drug(s), *kyk* **dwelmmiddel**

doof'stom deafmute, deaf and dumb; ~**me** (-s) deafmute

dooi (**ge-**) thaw (ice, snow)

dooi'e (-s) the dead, the deceased

dooi'(e)mansdeur: *voor ~ kom,* find nobody at home

dooi'epunt (-e) deadlock; stalemate; *op die ~,* deadlock reached

dooi'er (-s) yolk (of egg)

dooi'erig (-e; -er, -ste) lifeless, listness

dooi'eskuld bad debts

dool (**ge-**) wander, roam; ~**hof** (..**howe**) maze, labyrinth

doop (s) christening, baptism; (w) (**ge-**) christen, baptise; dunk, dip; *sy pen in gal ~,* dip one's pen in gall; ~**formulier** baptismal formulary; ~**gelofte** (-s) baptismal vow; ~**naam** (..**name**) Christian name; ~**plegtigheid** (..**hede**) christening ceremony; ~**register** (-s) church register; ~**seel** (-s) baptismal certificate

Doops'gesind (-e) Baptist

doop: ~**vont** (-e) baptismal font, baptistry

doos (**dose**) box, case; *uit die ou ~,* old-fashioned, antiquated

dop (s) (-**pe**) shell (eggs); peel, husk (seed); drink; *'n halwe eier is beter as 'n leë ~,* a bird in the hand is better than two in the bush; *'n ~ steek,* have/take a drink; (w) (**ge-**) shell, peel; fail (examination); ~**-ertjie** (-s) green pea

dop'hou (-**ge-**) keep an eye on

Dop'per (-s) Dopper, Calvinist-Reformed

dop'pie (-s) percussion cap; shell; tot; *sy ~ het geklap,* he has had his chips

dor (-[**re**]; -**der, -ste**) dry, barren, withered

do'ring (-s) thorn, prickle, spine; topper; ~**draad,** barbed wire

dorp (-e) village, town

dor'peling (-e), **dor'penaar** (-s; ..**nare**) villager

dorps: ~**bewoner** (-s) villager; ~**japie** (-s) ignorant/stupid chap from the town

dorps: ~**lewe** village/town life; ~**ontwikkelaar** (-s) town developer

dors[1] (s) thirst; *die ~ les,* quench the thirst; (w) (**ge-**) thirst; (b) thirsty

dors[2] (w) (**ge-**) thresh

dors'masjien (-e) threshing machine

dos (s) attire, array, raiment; (w) (**ge-**) attire, deck out; *spoggerig uitgedos,* dressed to kill

doseer'[1] (~, **ge-**) teach, lecture

doseer'[2] (~, **ge-**) dose (animals)

dosent' (-e) teacher, lecturer

dosen'te (-s) lady teacher, lady lecturer

do'sie (-s) little box; *'n ~ vuurhoutjies,* a box of matches

do'sis (-se) dose; *te groot ~ (oordosis),* overdose; *skraag~* booster dose

dossier' (-s) dossier, (personal) docket

dosyn' (-e) dozen

dot'jie (-s) little dear; dot; brimless hat

dou (s) dew; (w) (**ge-**) dew; ~**trapper** early bird (for a person); ~**voordag** very early in the morning

do'werig (-e) somewhat deaf

do'yen doyen, senior member

dra (**ge-**) carry; wear; bear

draad (**drade**) wire; thread, fibre; grain; filament; fence; *kort van ~,* short-tempered; ~**loos** (..**lose**) wireless; ~**loosstasie** (-s) broadcasting station; ~**sitter** (-s) temporiser; ~**tang** (-e) wire pliers; ~**trekker** (-s) wirepuller; ~**trekkery** wirepulling, intrigue; ~**werk** wire grate, filigree work; wiring; nonsense; *vol ~werk wees,* be full of fads and fancies

draag'baar[1] (s) (..**bare**) bier, litter; stretcher

draag'baar[2] (b) (..**bare; -der, -ste**) portable, wearable; bearable; *'n ..bare tikmasjien,* a portable typewriter

draag: ~**lik** (-e; -er, -ste) bearable, tolerable; ~**rak** (-**ke**) carrier (on motorcar); ~**wydte** range; import

draai (s) (-e) turn, twist; corner, bend; whorl (shell); *'n Kaapse ~,* a sudden sharp turn; *'n slap ~,* a slight turn; (w) (**ge-**) turn;

writhe; revolve, twist, wind; tarry, linger; *stokkies ~*, play truant; **~bank** (-e) lathe; **~boek** (-e) scenario, script (film); **~hek** (-ke) turnstile; **~jakkals** (-e) long-eared fox; **~kolk** (-e) whirlpool; **~kous** (-e) loiterer; **~orrel** (-s) barrel organ; **~potlood** (..lode) propelling pencil; **~tafel** (-s) turntable

draak (drake) dragon; *met iem. die ~ steek*, poke fun at somebody

draal (ge-) tarry, linger, dawdle

dra'er (-s) carrier, bearer

draf (s) trot; (w) (ge-) trot; jog; **~broekie** (-s) running shorts; **~karretjie** (-s) sulky

drag (-te) load, burden; dress, fashion; crop; *'n ~ slae*, a sound thrashing

drag'tig (-e) pregnant, with young

dra'ma (-s) drama; playwriting

drama'ties (-e) dramatic

dramatiseer' (ge-) dramatise

dramatise'ring dramatisation

dramaturg' (-e) dramatist

drang (-e) urge, urgency, pressure

drank (-e) strong drink, liquor; beverage; potion; *'n ~kie maak*, have/take a drink; *sterk ~*, alcoholic liquor, *aan die ~ verslaaf wees*, be addicted to alcohol; **~bestryding** temperance movement; **~lisensie** (-s) liquor licence; **~verbod** prohibition; **~verslaaf** alcoholic

drapeer' (ge-) drape

dras'ties (-e) drastic

dra'wieg (-e) (..wieë), **dra'wiegie** (-s) carrycot

draw'wer (-s) trotter; jogger, *ook* pretdrawwer

draw'wertjie (-s) trotter, courser (bird)

dreef: *op ~ kom*, get into one's stride

dreig (ge-) threaten, menace

dreigement' (-e) threat, menace

drei'gend (-e) threatening, impending

dreineer' (~, ge-) drain

dreine'ring drainage

drek muck, dirt, dung

drel (-le) indecent woman; good-for-nothing; slowcoach

drem'pel (-s) threshold (fig.), *kyk* **drum'pel**

drenk (ge-) drench, soak; allow to drink; **~e'ling** (-e) drowned/drowning person

dren'tel (ge-) saunter, loiter

dresseer' (ge-) train, coach; drill, dress

dreun (s) rumble, roar, thud, shock; (w) (ge-) rumble, roar, roll, boom; **~strook** (..stroke) rumble strip (on road)

drib'bel (ge-) dribble

drie (-ë) three, try (rugby)

Drie-een'heid Trinity

drie'ërlei of three kinds

drie'hoek (-e) triangle; **~ig** (-e) triangular; **~(s)meting** trigonometry

drie: **~klank** (-e) triphthong; **~kuns** hattrick; **~kwart** (-e) three fourths; threequarter (rugby); **~lettergrepig** (-e) trisyllabic; **~ling** (-e) triplets; **~maandeliks** (-e) quarterly; **~manskap** triumvirate; **~master** (-s) threemaster; **~poot** (..pote) tripod; **~sprong** (-e) junction of three roads; **~sydig** (-e) three-sided, trilateral; **~voet** (-e) tripod, trivet; **~voud** treble; triple; *'n verklaring in ~voud*, a statement in triplicate; **~wiel** (-e), **~wieler** (-s) tricycle

drif¹ (driwwe) ford, drif(t)

drif² (-te) anger, hot temper, passion; *sy ~ beteuel*, keep one's temper; **~tig** (-e; -er, -ste) passionate, hasty, quick-tempered

dril (ge-) bore; drill, exercise, train, coach

dring (ge-) press, urge, throng, push; **~end** (e-; -er, -ste) urgent, pressing

drink (ge-) drink; **~beker** (-s) goblet, beaker

dro'ë (s) dry land; *sy skapies op die ~ hê*, have made one's pile; (w) dry, make dry; **~bek:** *~bek sit*, wait in vain (for refreshments); be disappointed

droef (droewe) sad, dejected

droefgees'tig (-e; -er, -ste) melancholy, dejected, gloomy

droef'nis sadness, sorrow, affliction

droe'wig (-e; -er, -ste) sad, dismal, gloomy, sorrowful; *'n ~e afloop*, a sorry end

drom (s) (-me) metal drum/container; (w) troop, crowd, throng; *die mense ~ saam*, the people are flocking together

dro'merig (-e; -er, -ste) dreamy

drom'mel (-s) deuce, devil; wretch; *arme ~*, poor wretch; *wat de/die ~ doen hy*, what on earth is he doing

dronk (b) (-er, -ste) drunk(en), intoxicated; **~aard** (-s) drunkard; **~bestuur** drunken driving; **~en'skap** drunkenness, inebriety; **~lap** (-pe) drunkard; **~slaan** (ge-) flabbergast, beat one's apprehension; *dit* *slaan my* ~, it gets me beat; **~verdriet** intoxicated self-pity

droog (w) (ge-) dry, make dry; (b) (**droë; droër, -ste**) parched, arid; *nie ~ agter die ore wees nie,* be a greenhorn; **~dok (-ke)** dry (graving) dock; **~reiniger (-s), ~skoonmaker (-s)** drycleaner; **~te (-s)** drought

droom (s) (**drome**) dream; (w) (ge-) dream; **~uitlêer (-s)** interpreter of dreams

drop liquorice, *ook* **soethout**

dros (ge-) run away, abscond, desert

drosdy' (-e) magistrate's residence, residency

dros'ter (-s) runaway, absconder, deserter

druif (**druiwe**) grape; **~luis (-e)** phylloxera

druip (ge-) drip, trickle, fall in drops; fail (in examination); **~e'ling (-e)** failure (in examination); **~nat** dripping wet, soaked; **~steen** stalactite, stalagmite; **~stert** sneaking; *~stert weggaan,* slink off; **~syfer** failure rate (of students); **~vet** dripping

druis (ge-) roar, swirl

drui'we- **~prieel (..priële)** vinebower; **~sap** grapejuice; **~stok (-ke)** vine; **~tros (-se)** bunch of grapes

druk (s) pressure, weight; print; (-ke) edition; (w) (ge-) press, print; squeeze, push; (b) (**-ker, -ste**) busy, fussy, lively; **~fout (-e)** printer's error, erratum; **~groep (-e)** pressure group; **~kastrol (-le)** pressure cooker

druk'ker (-s) printer; **~s'duiwel** printer's devil, literal, *ook* **setsatan**; **~y (-e)** printing works

druk- **~knoptelefoon** pushbutton/pressbutton telephone; **~kuns** art of printing; typography; **~pers (-e)** printing press; **~proef (..proewe)** proofsheet, printer's proof; **~skrif** typescript, print; **~te** stir, bustle, fuss, ado; *'n ~te maak,* make a fuss

drum'pel (-s) threshold

drup (s) eaves; drip (medical); (w) (ge-) drip, drop

drup'pel (-s) drop; *'n ~ in 'n emmer,* a drop in the ocean; (w) (ge-) drop, trickle

dryf (ge-) float; swim; impel, drive, conduct: *handel ~,* trade; *die spot ~,* mock; **~krag** motive power, force; drive; **~sand** driftsand, quicksand

dryf'veer (..vere) motive

dry'wer (-s) driver, wagon driver; fanatic

dub'bel (-de) double; twice; *~ en dwars verdien,* deserve over and over again

dub'beldoor (..dore) double-yolked egg

dub'belganger (-s) double, second self, alter ego

dub'bel: **~loop (..lope)** double-barrel (gun); **~mediumskool (..skole)** double medium school; **~punt (-e)** colon

dubbelsin'nig (-e; -er, -ste) ambiguous

dub'beltjie (-s) devil's thorn; *loop voor die pad vol ~s is,* be quick about it

duet' (-te) duet

dui'delik (-e; -er, -ste) clear, distinct, obvious; legible

duif (duiwe) pigeon, dove

duik[1] (s) (-e) dent; (w) (ge-) dent

duik[2] (w) (ge-) dive, plunge; **~bomwerper (-s)** divebomber; **~boot (..bote)** submarine, U-boat; **~er (-s)** diver; culvert; duiker (antelope); cormorant (bird); **~long** aqualung; **~plank (-e)** springboard; **~weg (..weë)** subway

duim (-e) thumb; inch; *iets uit die ~ suig,* trump up a story; **~gooi (-ge-)** hitchhike; **~gooier (-s)** hitchhiker; **~pie (-s)** little thumb; *Klein D~pie,* Tom Thumb; **~ry (-ge-)** hitchhike; **~ryer (-s)** hitchhiker; **~spyker(tjie) (-s)** drawing pin; **~stok (-ke)** inch measure, footrule

duin (-e) dune

dui'nebesie (-s) beachbuggy

dui'sel (ge-) grow giddy/dizzy, reel; **~ig (-e)** giddy, dizzy; **~ig** *word,* grow giddy

dui'send (-e) thousand; **~jarig (-e)** millennial; *~jarige ryk,* millennium; **~poot (..pote)** millipede; **~voudig (-e)** thousandfold

duis'ter (s) dark(ness); (b) (-der, -ste) dark, dusky, obscure; **~(e) poësie,** obscure poetry

duit (-e) farthing; *geen blou ~ werd nie,* not worth a brass button

Duits (s) German; (b) (-e) German; **~er (-s)** German; **~land** Germany

dui'wehok (-ke) pigeon house, dovecot

dui'wel (-s) devil; *dank jou die ~!* well I never; *so bang soos die ~ vir 'n slypsteen,* be as scared as the devil is of holy water;

~s'kunstenaar (-s) sorcerer, magician; **~spiraal** vicious circle

duld (ge-) bear, tolerate, endure

dun (-ner, -ste) thin, rarefied; sparse; slender; washy

duplikaat' (**..kate**), **du'plo (-'s)** duplicate

durf (s) pluck, daring, guts

dus thus, so, therefore

dus'kant on this side of

dut'jie (-s) nap, snooze; *'n ~ doen,* nap

duur¹ (s) duration; (w) **(ge-)** last, continue; *dit ~ tien dae,* it lasts ten days

duur² (b) (**[dure]**; **-der, -ste**) dear, expensive; *'n dure eed sweer,* vow a solemn oath

duur'saam (**..same**; **..samer, -ste**) durable, lasting; wearing well

duur'te dearness; expensiveness; **~toeslag** cost of living allowance

dwaal (ge-) err; wander, roam; **~gees (-te)** wandering spirit; **~lig (-te)** will-o'-the-wisp; **~spoor** (**..spore**) false track

dwaas (s) (**dwase**) fool, silly fellow; (b) (**dwase**; **dwaser, -ste**) foolish, silly; **~heid** folly, stupidity

dwa'ling (-e, -s) error, misconception

dwang compulsion, coercion, force, constraint; **~arbeid** hard labour; penal servitude; **~buis (-e)** straitjacket

dwar'rel (ge-) whirl; **~wind (-e)** whirlwind

dwars across, athwart; contrary; **~boom (ge-)** thwart, obstruct; **~lêer (-s)** sleeper (railway); **~skop (-pe)** crosskick; **~straat** (**..strate**) cross-street; **~trekker (-s)** squabbler, thwarter

dweep (ge-) rave about; **~pos** fan mail

dwelm: ~middel, dwelms non-medical drug(s); **~misbruik** drug abuse; **~slaaf** drug addict; **~smous** drug pedlar/pusher; **~toer (-e)** trip; **~verslawing** drug addiction

dwe'per (-s) fanatic, bigot

dwerg (-e) dwarf, pygmy, midget

dwing (ge-) force, compel, constrain; **~e'land (-e)** tyrant

dwingelandy' tyranny

dy¹ (s) (-e) thigh

dy² (w) (ge-) thrive, prosper

dyk (-e) dike, bank

dyn: *myn en ~,* mine and thine

dyn'serig (-e; -er, -ste) misty, hazy

dyn'sig (-e; -er, -ste) misty, hazy

dy'spier (-e) hamstring

E

eb (s) ebb; *~ en vloed,* ebb and flow

eb'behout ebony wood

e'del (-e; -er, -ste) noble, generous; precious; *Sy Edele,* His Honour; *Sy Edele die Eerste Minister,* the Honourable the Prime Minister

edelag'baar (**..bare**) honourable; *Your/His Worship; Sy Edelagbare die Burgemeester,* His Worship the Mayor

e'delman (-ne, edelliede) nobleman

edelmoe'dig (-e; -er, -ste) generous, magnanimous

e'delsteen (**..stene**) precious stone, gem

e'dik¹ vinegar

edik'² (-te) edict, decree

ê'e (geêe) harrow

eed (ede) oath

eek'horinkie (-s) squirrel

eelt (s) (-e) horny skin, callus

een one, someone, a certain; *op ~ na,* all but one; **~akter (-s), ~bedryf** (**..drywe**) one-act play

eend (-e) duck

een'dag once, one day

een'dekker (-s) monoplane

een'ders similar, alike; *presies ~ lyk,* look exactly alike

een'drag concord, union, unity, harmony; *~ maak mag,* union is strength

eend: ~stert (-e) ducktail; **~voël (-s)** wild duck; *jy sal jou ma vir 'n ~voël aansien,* you will find yourself in Queer Street

een: ~heid (**..hede**) unity; **~horing (-s)** unicorn; **~kant** on one side, apart

een: ~kleurig (-e) monochrome; **~lettergrepig (-e)** monosyllabic; **~lopend (-e)** unmarried, single; **~maal** once, one day

een'oog one-eye, one-eyed person

eenpa'rig (-e) unanimous; ~e besluit/be= slissing, unanimous decision

een'persoonsbed (-dens) single bed

een'rigtingstraat one-way street

eens once, even; unanimous, of the same opinion; ek is dit ~ met jou, I agree with you

een'saam (..same; ..samer, -ste) solitary, lonely, desolate; eensame opsluiting, sol= itary confinement; ~heid solitude, lone= liness, seclusion

eens'klaps suddenly, all of a sudden

eenstem'mig (-e) for one voice; unanimous; ~e liedere, unison songs

eensy'dig (-e; -er, -ste) onesided, unilateral; partial; ~heid onesidedness, partiality; ~e onafhanklikverklaring, unilateral declaration of independence (UDI)

een'talig (-e) unilingual

een'tjie one; op sy ~, all by himself

eento'nig (-e; -er, -ste) monotonous, te= dious; ~heid monotony, tedium

een'vloeiklep (-pe) non-return valve

eenvor'mig (-e) uniform

een'voud simplicity

eenvou'dig (-e; -er, -ste) simple, homely; singular

eer[1] (s) honour, repute, credit; in ere hou, hold in esteem; die laaste ~ bewys, render the last (funeral) honours, pay the last respects; (w) (geëer) honour, respect

eer[2] (vgw) before

eer[3] (bw) sooner, rather

eer'baar (..bare; der-, -ste) virtuous, chase, honest; worthy

eer'betoon, eer'bewys (-e) homage, mark of honour

eer'bied respect, regard, reverence; uit ~ vir, in deference to

eerbie'dig (w) (geëer-, ~) respect, revere; obey; die verkeersreëls ~, obey the traffic rules

eer'der sooner, rather; hoe ~ hoe beter, the sooner the better

eer'gevoel sense of honour

eer'gister the day before yesterday

eerlang', eerlank' before long, erelong

eer'lik (-e; -er, -ste) honest, upright, fair; ~heid honesty

eers first; formerly; only; even; nie ~ 'n sent nie, not even a cent

eers'daags, eer'daags soon, shortly

eers'geboortereg birthright

eers'genoemde the former

eer'skennis defamation

eers'komende next, following

eer'ste first; die ~ die beste boek, the first book at hand; ten ~, in the first place; ~hands (-e) firsthand; ~hulp first aid; ~klas first class, first rate; ~ling (-e) firstling, firstborn; ~ns firstly; ~rangs (-e) first rate

eersug'tig (-e; -er, -ste) ambitious

eer'tyds (-e) former(ly)

eer'vol (-le) honourable; ~le vermelding, honourable mention

eerwaar'de reverend

eet (geëet) eat; ~kamer (-s) dining room; ~lepel (-s) tablespoon; ~lus appetite; ~luswekker(tjie) (-s) appetiser; ~maal (..male) meal; banquet; ~servies (-e) dinner service; ~staking hunger strike

eeu (-e) century

eeu'e-oud (..oue) age-old, age-long

eeu'fees (-te) centenary

ef'fe even, level, flat, smooth; plain

effek[1] (-te) effect, result

effek'te securities, stocks; ~beurs (-e) stock exchange; ~makelaar (-s) stockbroker

effektief' (..tiewe) effective

ef'fens, ef'fentjies slightly; a moment; a little; just; wag ~, half a mo(ment)

eg[1] (s) marriage, wedlock; in die ~ tree, enter into matrimony

eg[2] (s) (ëe, egge) harrow

eg[3] (b) (-te; -ter, -ste) authentic, real, thor= ough, genuine; legitimate; ~te diamante, genuine diamonds

ega'lig (-e; -er, -ste) level, smooth, even

eg'genoot (..note) spouse, husband

eg'genote (-s) spouse, wife

eg'go (-'s) echo

Egip'te Egypt; ~naar (-s, ..nare) Egyptian

e'go ego, self; jou ~ streel, boost one's ego

egoïs' (-te) egoist; ~me egotism

eg'skeiding (-e, -s) divorce

eg'ter however; yet, notwithstanding; die meeste leerlinge het geslaag, heelparty het ~ gedruip, most pupils passed, quite a few however failed

ei'e own; natural; peculiar, specific; famil= iar; ~ aan, peculiar to; uit ~ beweging, of one's own accord; ~belang self-inte= rest

eiegereg'tig (-e; -er, -ste) self-righteous
eiehan'dig (-e) with one's own hand
ei'en (geëien) recognise; appropriate, own
ei'enaar (-s, ..nare) proprietor, owner
eienaar'dig (-e; -er, -ste) peculiar, singular
eienares' (-se) owner, proprietress
ei'endom (-me) property, estate, belongings, possession; *vaste* ~, real estate, fixed property; *die* ~ *word van,* become the property of; ~ontwikkelaar property developer
ei'endoms proprietary; ~agent (-e) real estate agent; ~reg (-te) right of possession
ei'enskap (-pe) quality, property, attribute
ei'er (-s) egg; *'n halwe* ~ *is beter as 'n leë dop,* half a loaf is better than no bread at all; ~dop (-pe) eggshell; ~kelkie (-s) eggcup; ~kokertjie (-s) eggboiler, sandglass, hourglass; ~stok (-ke) ovary; ~vrug brinjal
eiesin'nig (-e; -er, -ste) wilful, obstinate
ei'etyds (-e) contemporary, with-it
ei'ewaan self-conceit, conceitedness
eiewys' (-er, -ste) conceited, headstrong
ei'ke: ~boom (..bome) oaktree
ei'land (-e) island, isle
ei'na (b, bw) poor, weak; painful; small; *sy kennis van Grieks is maar* ~, his knowledge of Greek is scanty; (tw) auch, oh! ow! ~broekie (-s) minipants; scantypanty
ein'de (-s) end, conclusion, termination
eind'eksamen (-s) final examination
ein'delik at last, finally, at length
ein'deloos (..lose) endless, infinite
ein'dig (geëindig) end, conclude, terminate; *boekjaar* ~*ende 31 Maart,* financial year ending 31 March
eind: ~punt terminus, end; ~ronde final
ein'ste same; *die* ~ *man,* the very same man
eint'lik (b) proper, real, actual; (bw) properly, really, actually; *nie* ~ *nie,* not exactly
eis (s) (-e) demand, claim, requirement, exigency; *aan die* ~*e voldoen,* come up to requirements; (w) (geëis) demand, claim
ei'ser (-s) plaintiff, claimant
eistedd'fod (-au, -s) eisteddfod
ei'wit albumen; ~stof protein
ek, I; ~ *en my vriend,* my friend and I
ek'ke I (with stress); ~rig (-e; -er, -ste) egotistic, self-centred

eklips' (-e) eclipse
ekologie' ecology
ekonomie' economy; economics
ekono'mies (-e; -er, -ste) economic(al)
ekonoom' (..nome) economist
ekosisteem' ecosystem
eksak' (-te) exact; *die* ~*te wetenskappe,* the exact sciences
eksa'men (-s) examination; ~ *aflê (doen, skryf),* sit for an examination; *sy* ~ *sak (dop, druip),* fail his examination; *(in) sy* ~ *slaag,* pass his examination; ~vraag (..vrae) examination question; ~vraestel (-le) examination paper
eksamina'tor (-e, -s) examiner
eksamineer' (~, geëks-) examine
ekseem' eczema
eksekuteur' (-e, -s) executor (of an estate)
eksekutri'se (-s) executrix
eksellen'sie (-s) excellency
eksemplaar' (..plare) specimen, copy
eksentriek' (-e; -er, -ste) eccentric, odd
ek'sie-perfek'sie perfect, very particular
eksklusief' (..siewe; ..siewer, -ste) exclusive
ekskur'sie (-s) excursion, outing
ekskuseer' (geëks-) excuse, pardon
ekskuus' (..kuse) excuse, pardon; ~ *maak,* apologise, *kyk* verskoning
ekskuus'! pardon me! sorry!
ek'sodus exodus
ekso'ties (-e) exotic, foreign
ekspedi'sie (-s) expedition
eksperiment' (-e) experiment; ~eel (..tele) experimental; ~eer' (geëks-) experiment
ekspres' expressly, on purpose, intentionally, deliberately, by design
ekspres'sie (-s) expression; ~f' expressive
eksta'se ecstasy; *in* ~ *raak,* go into raptures
eksta'ties (-e) ecstatic
ekstern' (-e) extern; ~*e studie,* external study
ek'stra extra
ekstrak' (-te) extract
ekstremis' (-te) extremist
ekume'nies (b) (-e) ecumenical, universal
ekwa'tor equator; ..*riale stiltegordel,* doldrums
ekwitei'te equities (shares)
ekwivalent' (-e) equivalent
el (-le) ell; *'n ellelang verduideliking,* too long an explanation

e'land (-e) eland (SA); elk (Europe); moose (America)

elastiek' (-e) elastic, *kyk* **rubber**

elas'ties (b) (-e) elastic; flexible

elastisiteit' elasticity; ~ *van vraag en aanbod*, elasticity of demand and supply

el'ders elsewhere

elegant' (-e; -er, -ste) elegant

elegie' (-ë) elegy

ele'gies (-e) elegiac

elek'tries (-e) electric(al); ~*e stoel*, electric chair; ~*e, elektrotegniese ingenieur*, electrical engineer

elektrifiseer' (~, geël-) electrify

elektrisiën' (-s) electrician

elektrisiteit' electricity

elek'trokardiogram (EKG) electrocardiogram (ECG), *kyk* **kardiograaf**

elektro'nies (b) electronic; ~*e beheer*, electronic control; ~*rekenaar*, computer

elektro'nika electronics

element' (-e) element; ~**êr'** (-e; -der, -ste) elementary

elf¹ (s) (elwe) elf, fairy

elf² (s) (elwe) chad (fish)

elf³ (s) (-e, -s) eleven; *ter* ~*der ure*, at the eleventh hour; ~**de** (-s) eleventh; ~**tal** (-le) team (cricket)

elimineer' (~, geël-) eliminate

elk (-e) each, every; ~**een** everybody, everyone

el'lelang (-e), **el'lelank** longdrawn

ellen'de of misery, wretchedness, distress

ellen'dig (-e; -er, -ste) wretched, miserable

elm'boog (..boë) elbow

eloku'sie elocution

emal'je enamel; ~**verf** enamel paint

emansipa'sie emancipation

embar'go (-'s) embargo, prohibition

embleem' (..bleme) emblem

em'brio (-'s) embryo

emeritaat' (..tate) clergyman's pension, superannuation

emigrant' (-e) emigrant

em'mer (-s) pail, bucket

emo'sie (-s) emotion

emosioneel' (..nele) emotional

empi'ries (-e) empiric(al); ~*e navorsing*, empirical research

en and; *èn . . . èn*, both . . . and

end (ente) end; termination; extremity

ende'mies (-e) endemic

end'jie (-s) short length, *kyk* **ent²**

endosseer' (~, geën-) endorse

endossement' (-e) endorsement

e'ne one, a certain; ~ *mnr. X*, a certain Mr X

energie' energy; ~**besparing** energy saving/conservation

eng (-er, -ste) narrow, tight

en'gel (-e) angel

En'geland England

en'gelebak (-ke) upper gallery, gods (theatre)

En'gels (s) English; *suiwer* ~, good English; the King's English; (b) (-e) English; ~*e siekte*, rickets (idiom); ~*e sout*, Epsom salt (idiom)

En'gelsman (Engelse) Englishman

eng'te (-s) strait, defile, isthmus; difficulty; ~**vrees** claustrophobia

e'nig (-e) only, sole, any; unique; ~ *in sy soort*, unique; the only of its kind

e'nigsins somewhat; *as dit* ~ *kan*, if at all possible

e'nigste only, sole

enjambement' (-e) enjambment

en'jin (-s) engine; *die* ~ *slaan/skop terug*, engine backfires; ~**drywer** engine driver

en'kel¹ (s) (-s) ankle

en'kel² (b) (-e) single; ~*e reis*, single journey; ~**kwartiere** single quarters

en'kel³ (bw) solely, merely, only

en'kel: ~**bed** (-de, -dens) single bed; ~**geslag** unisex; ~**ing** (-e) individual; ~**spel** (-e) singles, single game; ~**voud** singular; ~**vou'dig** (-e) singular; ~*voudige rente*, simple interest

enorm' (-e) enormous

ensiklopedie' (-ë) encyclopaedia

ent¹ (s) (-e) graft; (w) (geënt) graft

ent² (s) distance, length; end; *dis 'n hele* ~ *hiervandaan*, it is quite a distance from here

ent'jie (-s) end; length; short distance

entoesias' (-te) enthusiast, fan

entomoloog' (..loë) entomologist

ent'stof (..stowwe) serum, vaccine

epide'mie (-s) epidemic

epide'mies (-e) epidemic; *die kinderverlamming het 'n ~e afmetings aangeneem*, infantile paralysis (poliomyelitis) has assumed epidemic proportions

e'pies (-e) epic

epigram' (-me) epigram

epilep'sle epilepsy, *ook* vallende siekte

episo'de (-s) episode

e'pos (-se) epic, epopee

erbarm' (~) have pity; *jou ~ oor,* have pity on

er'de: ~skottel (-s) earthenware basin; ~ware ceramics, *kyk* keramiek; ~werk earthenware, pottery

erd: ~vark (-e) ant eater; ~wurm (-s) earthworm

e're honour; *ter ~ van,* in honour of; ~burgerskap freedom of the town/city; ~diens (-te) divine service; ~graad (..grade) honorary degree; ~lid (..lede) honorary member

è'rens somewhere

e're: ~sekretaris (-se) honorary secretary; ~wag (-te) guard of honour; ~woord word of honour

erf¹ (s) (erwe) plot, stand

erf² (w) (geërf) inherit; ~(e)nis inheritance, heritage; ~geld inherited money; *~geld is swerfgeld,* lightly come, lightly go; ~genaam (..name) heir; ~porsie (-s) inheritance, share of inheritance; ~stuk (-ke) heirloom

erg (w) (geërg) give offence, annoy, be vexed; (b) (-er, -ste) bad, evil, ill; (bw) badly, severely, extremely; *wat te ~ is, is te ~,* this is really too bad

er'gernis (-se) annoyance, vexation, nuisance; *al die ~,* all the annoyance/hassles

erg'ste worst; *op die ~ voorberei,* prepare for the worst

erken' (~) acknowledge, own up, admit; ~ning acknowledgement, admission

erkent'lik (-e; -er, -ste) grateful, thankful

erns earnest(ness), seriousness, gravity

ern'stig (-e; -er, -ste) serious, grave; earnest; *iets ~ opneem,* take a serious view of

ero'sie erosion

ero'ties (-e) erotic

er'tappel (-s) potato; ~repie, ~skyfie (potato) chip, *ook* aartappel

er'tjie (-s) pea; ~so(e)p peasoup

erts (-e) ore; ~afsetting ore deposit

erudi'sie erudition, learning

ervaar' (~) experience, undergo

erva're (meer ~, mees ~) experienced, skilled

erva'ring (-e, -s) experience; *~ opdoen,* gain experience

e'sel (-s) ass, donkey; mule; easel; blockhead

eska'der (-s) squadron (navy, airforce)

eskadron' (-ne, -s) squadron (cavalry)

eskaleer' (w) (~) escalate, increasing progressively

essensieel' (..siële) essential

este'ties (-e) aesthetic(al)

e'tanol, etielalkohol ethanol

e'te (-s) meal, dinner; food

e'ter¹ (-s) eater

e'ter² ether, upper air; ~golf ether wave

ete'ries (-e) ethereal

e'ties (-e) ethical

etiket'¹ etiquette

etiket'² (-te) label; ~jie (-s) ticket, label

etimologie' (-ë) etymology

et'maal 24 hours, full day; ~diens 24-hours service

et'nies ethnic; *~e tale,* African/ethnic languages

ets (s) (-e) etching; (w) (geëts) etch; ~naald (-e) etching needle

et'ter (s) matter, pus

eufemis'me euphemism, *ook* versagting

euforie' euphoria, elation

Eu'romark Euromart

Euro'pa Europe

Europeaan' (..peane), Europe'ër (-s) European

Europees' (..pese) European

eu'wel (-s) evil, defect

evalueer' (~, geëv-) evaluate, assess

evange'lie (-s) gospel, evangel

evangelis' (-te) evangelist

evolu'sie, ewolusie evolution

e'we just as, even, equally; ~groot, of the same size

e'we: ~beeld likeness, image, counterpart; ~kansig random; ~knie equal, match; peer; ~mens fellowman

e'wemin no more than, just a little

e'wenaar¹ (s) equator, line; (-s) differential (car)

ewenaar'² (w) (geëw-) equal, rival; *niemand kan hom ~ nie,* no one can match/rival him

e'weneens similarly, in the same manner, likewise

ewere'dig (-e) proportional, pro rata

e'wewig equilibrium, balance, poise

ewewy'dig (-e) parallel, equidistant

e'wig (-e) eternal, everlasting, perpetual

e'wigheid eternity

F

faal (ge-) fail, be unsuccessful

fa'bel (-s) fable; legend, fiction

fabriek' (-e) factory

fabrieks': ~**afval** factory waste/effluent; ~**arbeider** (-s) factory hand; ~**geheim** (-e) trick(s) of the trade; ~**werker** (-s) factory worker; ~**wet** factories act

fabrikaat' (..kate) fabric, manufacture, brand; *'n nuwe ~ motor,* a new make of car

fabrikant' (-e) manufacturer, *ook vervaar=diger*

fagot' (-te) bassoon

fak'kel (-s) torch; ~**loop** (..lope), ~**optog** (-te) torchlight procession

fakto'tum (-s) factotum, handyman

faktuur' (..ture) invoice; bill

fakulteit' (-e) faculty

fami'lie (-s) family; relations, relatives; *aangetroude ~,* relations by marriage; *ver langs ~,* distantly related; ~**kring** (-e) family circle; ~**kwaal** (..kwale) hereditary malady; ~**lid** (..lede) member of a family; ~**wapen** (-s) family coat of arms

fanatiek' (-e) fanatic(al)

fantasie' (-ë) imagination, phantasy, fancy; ~**kostuum** (-s) fancy dress

fantas'ties (-e; -er, -ste) fantastic

farise'ër (-s) pharisee, hypocrite

farmaseu'ties (-e) pharmaceutical

fa'se (-s) phase, stage

faset' (-te) facet (of a diamond); ~**ryk** multi-facetted, versatile

fasiliteit' (-e) facility; comfort, convenience; ~*e vir alle volksgroepe,* facilities for all population groups

fat (-te) dandy, swell

fatalis' (-te) fatalist; ~**me** fatalism

fatsoen' (-e) shape, form; fashion, manners, good form

fatsoen'lik (-e; -er, -ste) decent, proper

Fe'bruarie (-s) February

federa'sie (-s) federation

fee (feë) fairy

feeks (-e) vixen, virago, shrew

fe'ë: ~**ryk** fairyland; ~**verhale** fairy tales

fees (s) (-te) feast, festival, fête; *nasionale ~,* national festival; *'n ~ vir die oë,* a

treat for the eyes; *'n ~ vier,* celebrate a feast; (w) (ge-) feast; ~**lied** (-ere) festive song; ~**maal** (..male) banquet; ~**rede** (-s) speech of the day; inaugural speech

fees'telik (-e) festive; ~ *onthaal,* entertain lavishly

fees'vier (-ge-) feast, celebrate; ~**ing** (-e, -s) festival, feast; celebration

feil'baar (..bare) fallible

feil'loos (..lose) faultless

feit (-e) fact; *deur ~e gestaaf,* supported by facts

fei'te: ~**kennis** knowledge of facts; ~**ma=teriaal** body of facts; ~**sending** (-s) fact-finding mission

feit'lik factual(ly); really, actually, practi=cally, as a matter of fact, indeed, truly; ~*e gegewens,* factual details; *hy het ~ geen familie nie,* he has practically/vir=tually no relatives

fel (-le; -ler, -ste) fierce, sharp, severe

feodaal' (..dale) feudal

ferm (-e; -er, -ste) firm, solid, strong

fermenta'sie fermentation

ferweel' corduroy; ~**broek** (-e) corduroy trousers, *kyk* **fluweel**

fe'tisj (-e) fetish

fias'ko (-'s) fiasco, washout

fie'mies capriciousness, freakishness; non=sense; *vol ~ wees,* finicky, fussy, faddish

fier (-e; -der, -ste) proud, bold

fieterja'sies superfluous ornaments

fiets (s) (-e) bicycle; (w) (ge-) cycle; ~**ryer, -er** (-s) cyclist, biker

figuur' (figure) shape, figure; *'n droewige ~ slaan,* cut a sorry figure; ~**lik** (-e) figurative(ly)

fiks (-e; -er, -ste) healthy, robust, fit; *die rugbyspeler is nou weer ~,* the rugby player is fit again; ~**heidtoets** fitness test

fikseer' (ge-) fix; stare at

fik'sie (-s) fiction; **wetenskap~** science fic=tion (sci-fi)

fiktief' (..tiewe) fictitious, imaginary

filantroop' (..trope) philanthropist

filet' (-te) fillet (meat, fish)

filharmo'nies (-e) philharmonic

filatelie' philately

filiaal' (s) (**filiale**) subsidiary; branch office; (b) (**filiale**) filial; **~maatskappy** subsidiary company

fillok'sera phylloxera

film (s) (-s) film; (w) (ge-) film; **~er** (-s) film producer; **~oteek'** (..teke) film library; **~ster** (-re) film star

filosofie' philosophy

filoso'fies (-e) philosophic(al); *hy is nogal ~ aangelê,* he is philosophically inclined

filosoof' (..sowe) philosopher, *ook* wysgeer

fil'ter (-s) filter, percolator

filtreer' (ge-) filter; **~koffie** filter(ed) coffee

finaal' (**finale**) final, total

fina'le (-s) finale; final (match)

finaliteit' finality

finansieel' (..siële) financial, monetary

finansier' (s) (-s) financier, banker; (w) (ge-) finance; *'n projek ~,* finance a project

finan'sies finances

finans'komitee (-s) finance committee

fineer' (s, w) veneer

fir'ma (-s) firm, house; *die ~ Brits en Bell,* Messrs Brits and Bell; **~blad** (..blaaie) house journal/magazine; **~motor** (-s) company car

firmament' firmament, sky

fisant' (-e) pheasant

fisiek' (s) physique; (b) (-e) physical; *sy ~e toestand,* his physical/bodily condition

fi'sies (-e) physical; *~e aardrykskunde,* physical geography

fi'sika physics

fisiologie' physiology

fisioterapie' physiotherapy

fiskaal' (s) (..kale) fiscal; bailiff; butcherbird; (b) (..kale) fiscal; *..kale beleid,* fiscal/taxation policy

flad'der (ge-) flutter, flit, flap

flamink' (-e) flamingo

flank (-e) flank, side; **~aanval** (-le) flank attack

flankeer' (~, ge-) flank; gad about; *met die nooiens ~,* flirt with the girls

flap (s) (-pe) widowbird, sakabula; flap; iris (flower); (w) (ge-) flap

flap'pertjie (-s) crumpet

flap'teks (-te) blurb (of a book)

flap'uit (-e) chatterbox, blabber

flard (-e) rag, tatter; *aan ~e skeur,* tear to pieces

fla'ter (-s) blunder, mistake, slip-up; *'n ~ begaan,* make a blunder

fleksiel' flexible

fleksiteit' flexibility

flen'nie flannel; **~bord** flannel graph

flen'ter (s) (-s) rag, tatter; *g'n ~ omgee nie,* not care a snap of the fingers

flen'ters in tatters; *iets fyn en ~ slaan,* smash to smithereens

fler'rie (-s) flirt

fles (-se) bottle, flask

flets (-e) faded, pale, dim

fleur prime, bloom; *in die ~ van sy lewe,* in the prime of life

fliek (s) (-e) bioscope; (w) (ge-) go to the bio; *kom ons gaan ~,* let's go to the bioscope/movies

flik'flooi (ge-) coax, fawn, flatter, cajole

flik'ker (ge-) glitter, sparkle, twinkle; **~gram** brain scan; **~lig** (-te) flickerlight, flashlight

flik'kers leaps (dancing), pranks; *~ maak/gooi by 'n nooi,* dance attendance on a girl

flink (b) (-e; -er, -ste) robust; energetic; thorough; brisk, spirited, vigorous; (bw) soundly, vigorously, firmly

flits (s) (-e) (lightning) flash; (w) (ge-) flash; **~berig** (-te) news flash (radio); **~lig** (-te) flashlight, torch

flon'ker (ge-) sparkle; **~ing** sparkling

flo'ra flora, plant life

floreer' (~, ge-) flourish, thrive

flore'rend (-e; -er, -ste) flourishing, thriving (business)

flou (-e; -er, -ste) faint, weak, dead-tired; insipid; dim; *geen ~e benul hê nie van,* not have the vaguest idea of; *~ val,* have a fainting fit

flous (ge-) cheat, deceive

flou'te (-s) swoon, fainting fit, blackout, *ook* breinfloute

fluister (ge-) whisper

fluit (s) (-e) flute, whistle; (w) (ge-) whistle, play on the flute; zip (of bullets); make water; **~-fluit** easily; *hy het ~-~ (in) sy eksamen geslaag,* he passed his examination without effort

fluks (-e; -er, -ste) hardworking

fluweel' velvet; *so sag soos ~,* velvety soft/smooth

foe'lie tin(foil)

foe'ter (ge-) bother, trouble; beat, thrash, wallop

fo'kus (-se) focus

folk'lore folklore

fol'ter (ge-) torture, torment; **~kamer** torture chamber

fondament' (-e) foundation, bottom

fonds (-e) fund; **~insameling** fund(s) raising effort, *ook* **geldinsameling**

fonetiek' phonetics

fone'ties (-e) phonetic

fontein' (-e) fountain, spring

fooi (s) (-e) tip; (w) **(ge-)** tip

foon (fone) phone; **~doedie (-s)** telephonist, switchboard operator; **~flerrie (-s), ~snol (-le)** callgirl

fop (ge-) hoax, cheat, fool, spoof; **~myn (-e)** booby trap; **~-oproep (-e)** hoax (telephone) call

fop'speen (..spene) baby's dummy, comforter

forel' (-le) trout

formaat' (..mate) size, shape; format

formaliteit' (-e) formality, matter of form

forma'sie (-s) formation

formeel' (..mele) formal

formu'le (-s) formula

formuleer' (ge-) formulate

fors (-e; -er, -ste) robust, strong, powerful, vigorous; **~ gebou,** sturdily built

forseer' (~, ge-) force, compel

fort (-e) fortress, fort

fortuin' luck, fortune; wealth; **~hou (-e)** hole-in-one (golf); **~soeker (-s)** adventurer; *vreemde ~soekers,* foreign adventurers; **~verteller (-s)** fortuneteller, soothsayer; clairvoyant

fosfaat' (..fate) phosphate

fos'for phosphor(us)

fossiel' (-e) fossil

fo'to (-'s) photo(graph); **~album (-s)** photo(graph) album; **~beslissing (-s)** photo finish (races); **~ge'nies (-e)** photogenic

fotograaf' (..grawe) photographer

fotografeer' (ge-) photograph, take a photo; *jou laat ~,* have one's photo taken

fotografie' photography

fotogra'fies (-e) photographic

fout (s) (-e) mistake, error, fault

fouteer' (~, ge-) err, make a mistake

foutief' (..tiewe) faulty, erroneous

fout'speurder (-s) troubleshooter

fraai (-e; -er, -ste) fine, handsome, becoming

fragment' (-e) fragment, piece

frai'ing (-s) fringe, tassel

framboos' (..bose) raspberry

Frank'ryk France

Frans (-e) French

Frans'man (Franse) Frenchman

fra'se (-s) phrase

fraseer' (~, ge-) phrase

frats (-e) freak, caprice, whim; *vol ~e wees,* be mischievous; **~ongeluk** freak accident

fregat' (-te) frigate

frekwen'sie frequency; **~modulasie** frequency modulation (FM)

frekwentatief' (..tiewe) frequentative

fres'ko (-'s) fresco, mural (painting)

fret (-te) ferret (animal)

frie'mel (ge-) fumble, fidget, *ook* **wriemel**

frikkadel' (-le) minced-meat ball, rissole, fricadel; *~ maak van iets,* smash something to atoms; **~broodjie** hamburger

fris (-[se]; -ser, -ste) fresh, cool; strong, stout, healthy; *~ gebou,* well-built

from'mel (ge-) fumble, crease, rumple

frons (s) (-e) frown; (w) **(ge-)** frown

front (-e) front; **~aanval (-le)** frontal attack

frustra'sie (-s) frustration

frustreer' (~, ge-) frustrate

fu'ga (-s) fugue

fuif (s) (fuiwe) spree, carousal; (w) **(ge-)** carouse, spree; **~party** drinking party

fundamenteel' (..tele) fundamental; *..tele verskille,* fundamental/basic differences

fungeer' (~, ge-) act, officiate, perform duties; *die fungerende voorsitter,* the chairman for the time being

funk'sie (-s) function

funksioneel' (..nele) functional

fusilleer' (ge-) execute, shoot, fusillade

fut mettle, dash, vim, zip; *sy ~ is uit,* he has lost his spirit

futiel' (-e) futile

futuris' (-te) futurist; **~me** futurism; **~ties (-e)** futuristic

fyn (-e; -er, -ste) fine, delicate; refined, subtle, swell; *~ en flenters breek,* smash completely; *~ oplet,* pay careful attention

fyngevoe'lig (-e; -er, -ste) sensitive

fyn: ~kam (ge-) search thoroughly; **~proewer (-s)** connoisseur, epicure, gourmet; **~stop** invisible mending

fyt (-e) whitlow

G

gaaf (gawe; gawer, -ste) good, nice, excellent; undamaged; *'n gawe kêrel*, a fine fellow, a decent chap/guy

gaan (ge-) go; move; walk; *hoe ~ dit?* how do you do?

gaan'deweg gradually, by degrees

gaap (s) (gape) yawn; (w) (ge-) yawn; gape; *so warm dat die kraaie ~* very hot

gaar sufficiently cooked; done; dressed

gaas gauze, netting

ga'de (-s) spouse, consort

ga'deslaan (-ge-) observe, watch

gaf'fel (-s) pitchfork, prong

gaip (-e) lubber, churl, boor

gal gall, bile

ga'la (-s) gala, festive show

gal'agtig, gal'lerig (-e) bilious

gal: ~bitter bitter as gall; ~blaas (..blase) gallbladder

galery' (-e) gallery

galg (-e) gallows, gibbet; *so slim soos die houtjie van die ~*, as sharp as a needle; ~e'maal last parting meal

galm (s) (-e, -s) peal, clangour; (w) (ge-) sound, resound

galop' (s) gallop

gal: ~siekte gall sickness; ~steen (..stene) gallstone, biliary calculus

gang (s) (-e) gait, walk; pace (horse); course; passage, corridor (in a house)

gang: ~baar (..bare) passable, current; feasible; *in die gangbare sin van die woord*, in the accepted sence of the word; ~baarheidstudie feasibility study, *ook* uitvoerbaarheidstudie

gangreen' gangrene, *ook* kouevuur

gans¹ (s) (-e) goose; *~e aanja*, be tipsy

gans² (b) (-e) whole, entire, all; *~ anders*, totally different

gans'loper (-s) jaywalker

ga'ping (-e, -s) gap, hiatus; *die ~ vernou*, narrow the gap

gara'ge (-s) garage

garan'sie (-s) guarantee, security

gar'de (-s) guard, bodyguard; *die ou ~*, the old schoolguard

garde'nia (-s) gardenia

ga're, ga'ring thread, yarn; *'n tolletjie ~*, a reel of cotton

garnaal' (..nale) shrimp; steur~ prawn

garnisoen' (-e) garrison

gars barley; ~koffie barley coffee

gas¹ (-te) guest

gas² (-se) gas; *op ~ kook*, cook by gas

gaset' (-te) gazette

gas'heer (..here) host; *ons is ~ vir die geleentheid*, we are hosting the event

gas: ~koeldrank (-e) carbonated soft drink; ~lamp (-e) gaslamp

gas'masker (-s) gasmask, respirator

gas'spreker (-s) guest speaker, *ook* geleentheidspreker

gaste'huis (-e) guest house

gas: ~vrou (-e, -ens) hostess; ~vryheid hospitality

gat¹ (-e) hole, gap

gat² (-te) anus

gatsome'ter (-s) gatsometer

ga'we (-s) gift, donation; talent; *dis 'n ~ Gods*, it is a gift of God; *van gunste en ~s leef*, live on charity

geag' (-te) respected; esteemed; *Geagte Heer*, Dear Sir; *Geagte Heer/Dame*, Dear Sir/Madam; *Geagte mev De Kock*, Dear Mrs de Kock

gebaar' (..bare) gesture; gesticulation

gebab'bel babble, prattle, gossip

gebak' pastry, cake; *met sy ~te pere bly sit*, be left holding the baby

geba'ker: *kort ~ wees*, be short-tempered

gebal' (-de) clenched; *~de vuis*, clenched fist

gebed' (-e) prayer; *'n ~ doen*, say/offer a prayer

gebed'(s)roeper (-s) muezzin

gebeur' (~) happen, occur, come to pass; *wat ook al ~*, come what may; ~likheid (..hede) possibility, eventuality; contingency; ~tenis (-se) event, occurrence; *ryk aan ~tenisse*, eventful

gebied'¹ (s) (-e) territory, area, domain, sphere

gebied² (w) (~) command, order, direct; *iem. hiet en ~*, order someone around

gebie'dend (-e) imperious, imperative

gebit' (-te) set of teeth; bit (bridle)

gebod' (..booie) commandment; command, order, decree; *iem. die tien gebooie voorlees*, bring someone to book

gebooi'e marriage banns

geboor'te (-s) birth; **~beperking** birth control; **~dag** (..dae) birthday; **~syfer** birthrate

gebo're born; née; ~ *en getoë,* born and bred

gebou' (-e) building

gebrek' (-e) defect, fault; lack, want, dearth; *by* ~ *aan,* lacking; ~ *ly,* suffer want; **~kig** (-e; -er, -ste) defective, faulty; *sy kennis van Engels is ~kig,* his English is poor; **~lik** (-e) disabled, decrepit; infirm; **~like** kind, crippled/deformed child

gebroe'ders brothers; *die* ~ *Jones,* Jones Bros

gebro'ke broken; ~ *gesin/huis,* broken home

gebruik' (s) (-e) use; usage; practice, habit, custom; *in* ~ *neem,* put into service; (w) (~) use, employ, take, enjoy; **~s'aanwysing** (-e, -s) directions for use

gedaan' (..dane) done, finished; exhausted; *gedane sake het geen keer nie,* it is no use crying over spilt milk

gedaan'te (-s) shape, form, aspect; **~(ver)wisseling** (-e, -s) metamorphosis

gedag'te (-s) thought, idea, notion, opinion; **~s** *wissel oor,* exchange views on; **~nis** remembrance, memory; keepsake; *ter* **~nis** *aan,* in memory of

gedeel'te (-s) part, section, portion, share, instalment; **~lik** partly, partially

gedek' (-te) covered (head); pregnant (animal); secured (debts)

gedemp' (-te) filled up; dim; *op* **~te** *toon,* in a muffled voice

gedenk' (~) remember, commemorate; *ons* ~ *sy geboorte,* we commemorate his birth; **~boek** (-e) memorial volume, album; **~naald** (-e) obelisk; **~penning** (-s) medal(lion); **~plaat** (..plate) plaque; **~skool** (..skole) memorial school; **~skrif** (-te) memoir; **~teken** (-s) monument, memorial

gedenkwaar'dig (-e; -er, -ste) memorable; *'n* ~ *e dag,* a memorable day

gedig' (-te) poem

geding' (-e) lawsuit, case; action, quarrel

gedissiplineer' (-de) disciplined

gedoen'te (-s) fuss, noise, business

gedo'riewaar really, upon my word

gedra' (~) behave, conduct, act; *hy* ~ *hom goed,* he behaves well

gedrag' behaviour, conduct; *'n bewys van goeie* ~, testimonial (of good behaviour); **~s'kode** code of ethics; **~sielkunde** behavioural psychology; **~s'lyn** line of conduct, course

gedrang' crowd, throng

gedrog' (-te) monster

gedug' (-te) formidable, tremendous, severe; *'n* **~te** *span,* a formidable team

geduld' patience, forbearance; *my* ~ *is op,* my patience is exhausted; **~ig** (-e; -er, -ste) patient

gedu'rende during

gedu'rig (b) (-e) constant, continual, incessant; (bw) constantly, continually

gedwee' (..dweë) submissive, pliant, tractable

gee (ge-) give, confer, present with, yield; *dit gewonne* ~, yield the point; *te kenne* ~, notify, intimate

geëer' (-de) honoured

geel (geler, -ste) yellow; **~bek** (-ke) Cape salmon; **~slang** (-e) yellow cobra; **~sug** jaundice; **~vink** (-e) yellow finch; **~wortel** (-s) carrot

geen none; no; ~ *van beide,* neither of the two

geeneen' no one, not one

geen'sins by no means, not at all

ge'ër (-s) giver, donor

gees (-te) spirit, ghost; mind, wit, intellect; *voor die* ~ *bring,* call to mind; *die* ~ *is gewillig maar die vlees is swak,* the spirit is willing but the flesh is weak; *teenwoordigheid van* ~, presence of mind; **~drif** enthusiasm

geesdrif'tig (-e; -er, -ste) enthusiastic, zealous

gees'telik (-e) spiritual; intellectual; religious; **~e** (-s) clergyman, minister, parson

gees'te: **~s'gesteldheid** state of mind, mentality; **~s'wetenskappe** human sciences

gees'tig (-e; -er, -ste) witty, bright, smart

gege'we given; *op 'n* ~ *uur,* at a given hour

gege'wens data, information; *nadere/meer* ~, further details

gegig'gel giggling, tittering

gegradueer'de (-s) graduate

gegroet'! greeted! hail!

gegrond' (-e) well-founded; ~e redes, sound reasons

gehak'kel stammering

gehal'te quality, standard; van hoë ~, of high standard; ~beheer quality control

gehard' (-e) hardened, hardy

gehar'war bickering, wrangling

geha'wend (-e) battered, dilapidated

geheel' (s) whole; entireness, entirety; oor die ~, on the whole; (b) (gehele) whole, entire, complete; (adv) all, entirely; quite; ~ en al, completely; ~onthouer (-s) teetotaller, good templar

geheg' (-te) attached, fond; ~t'heid fond-ness, attachment

geheim' (s) (-e) secret; 'n ~ verklap, let the cat out of the bag; (b) (-e) secret; ~hou-ding secrecy, concealment

geheimsin'nig (-e; -er, -ste) mysterious

geheu'e (-s) memory; ~verlies loss of memory

gehoor' hearing; (..hore) audience; ~ gee aan 'n versoek, comply with a request; die ~ toespreek, address the audience/con-gregation; ~buis (-e) receiver (tel.), ook hoorstuk

gehoor'saam (w) (~) obey, submit; (b) (..same; ..samer, -ste) obedient, submissive, docile; ~heid obedience

gehoor'vlies (-e) tympanum

geho'rig (-e) sounding, resounding, noisy

gehug' (-te) hamlet

gehuud' (gehude) married; ongehude moe-der, unmarried mother

gei'gerteller (-s) geiger counter

geil (-er, -ste) rank; rich, fertile; lush

geïllustreer' (-de) illustrated

geïnteresseer' (-de) interested

gei'ser (-s) geyser

geit'jie (-s) small lizard; shrew, virago

geju'bel cheering, rejoicing

gejuig' rejoicing, cheering, applause

gek (s) (-ke) fool, madman, guy; vir ~ hou, play the fool; vir die ~ hou, make a fool of; die ~ skeer, poke fun at; (b) ([-ke]; -ker, -ste) foolish, mad, queer, crazy

gek'heid folly, foolishness, madness; alle ~ op 'n stokkie, all joking aside

gekib'bel bickering, squabbling

gek'ke: ~getal fool's number, number ele-ven; ~paradys (-e) fool's paradise

geklets' tattle, twaddle

gekleur'de (-s) coloured; Coloured person

geknoei' messing, botching; plotting, scheming

geknor' grunting, grumbling

gekompliseer' (-de) complicated

gekonfyt': ~ wees in, be well versed in

gekon'kel botching; intriguing

gekruis' (-te) crossed; ~te tjek, crossed cheque

gek'skeer (-ge-) jest, joke, fool; hy laat nie met hom ~ nie, he is not to be trifled with

gekwalifiseer' (-de) qualified, certificated

gekwes' (-te) wounded; disabled; ~te bok, wounded buck

gekwets' (-te) hurt, offended; ~te gevoe-lens, hurt feelings

gekwis'pel (tail) wagging

gelaat' (gelate) face, countenance, mien; ~s'kleur complexion; ~s'trek (-ke) (fa-cial) feature

gelag'[1] laughter, laughing

gelag'[2] score, bill; die ~ betaal, pay the piper

gelang': na ~ van, according to, in pro-portion to

gelas' (~) order, instruct, command; ~ die soektog af, call off the search

gelatien' gelatine

geld[1] (s) (-e) money, cash; ~soos bossies, money like dirt; ~ wat stom is, maak reg wat krom is, money works wonders

geld[2] (w) (ge-) be in force, obtain, be valid, concern, apply to; die koepons ~ net vir een maand, the coupons are valid for one month only

gel'delik (-e) monetary, financial, pecuni-ary; ~e verknorsing, financial dilemma

geldige'rig (-e; -er, -ste) covetous, miserly

gel'dig (-e) legal, valid, binding; ~e redes, valid/acceptable reasons

geld: ~insameling fund raising; ~skieter (-s) moneylender; ~stuk (-ke) coin; ~trommel (-s) moneybox; ~wolf (..wol-we) moneygrubber, miser

gele'de ago, past; (b) articulated (vehicle); vyftig jaar ~, fifty years ago; tot kort ~, until recently

gele'ë situated; convenient; ter geleëner tyd, in due course; veraf ~, distantly situated

geleent'heid (..hede) opportunity; occasion; ~spreker guest speaker; ~(s)werk casual labour geleer' (-de) learned, scholarly, bookish; trained; ~de (-s) scholar, learned person

geleerd'heid learning, erudition

gelei' (s) jelly (meat, fruit), ook sjelei'

gelei'delik gradual(ly), by degrees

gelid' (geledere) rank, file

gelief' (-de) dear, beloved; ~de (-s) beloved one, dearest, sweetheart

gelief'koosde favourite, kyk gunsteling

gelie'we please; ~ kennis te neem van 'n vergadering . . ., notice is hereby given of a meeting . . .; ~ my te laat weet, please let me know

gelof'te (-s) vow, solemn promise

Gelof'tedag Day of the Vow

geloof' (s) credit, credence; trust, faith; (.. lowe) belief, creed

geloofs': ~belydenis (-se) credo, confession of faith; ~briewe credentials, letters of credence; ~geneser faith healer; ~vryheid freedom of faith/worship

geloofwaar'dig (-e; -er, -ste) trustworthy, credible, authentic; ~heid credibility

gelo'wig (-e; -er, -ste) believing, faithful, pious; ~e (-s) true believer

geluid' (-e) sound, noise

geluk' (s) (-ke) joy, happiness; good luck; fortune; op goeie ~ af, at a venture; veels ~, hearty congratulations; (w) (~) succeed; dit het my ~, I succeeded in doing it; ~bringer (-s) mascot

geluk'kig (-e; -er, -ste) happy, fortunate, lucky

geluk': ~skoot (..skote) windfall, fluke; ~soeker (-s) adventurer, fortune hunter; ~s'pakkie (-s) lucky packet

geluk'wens (s) (-e) congratulation; (w) (-ge-) congratulate; ~ing (-e, -s) congratulation

gelyk' (b) (-e; -er, -ste) equal, even, similar; deuce (tennis)

gely'ke (-s) equal, like, peer, match; ~nis (-se) resemblance, likeness; parable

gelyk'heid equality; similarity, evenness

gelyk'maak (-ge-) level; assimilate, raze; equalise

gelykma'tig (-e) equable, uniform, regular

gelyk'op equally, fifty-fifty; ~ speel, play a draw/tie; ~ verdeel, divide equally

gelykstaan (gelykge-) be equal; ~de aan, equal to

gelykty'dig (-e) simultaneous, concurrent

gelykvor'mig (-e) uniform, of like form; ~heid uniformity, conformity

gemaak' (-te) affected, forced; so ~ en so laat staan, beyond redemption; ~t'heid affectation, pretence

gemaal' (..male, -s) husband, consort

gemak' (-ke) ease, convenience, comfort, leisure; op sy (dooie) ~, at ease; ~huisie (-s) toilet, loo; convenience; ~lik (-e; -er, -ste) easy, convenient, comfortable; ~s'halwe for convenience sake

gemalin' (-ne) wife, consort, spouse

gemas'ker (-de) masked; ~de bal, masked (fancy dress) ball, ook maskerbal

gema'tig (-de) moderate, temperate

gemeen' (..mene; ..mener, -ste) common; mean, vulgar, niks ~ hê nie, have nothing in common; gemene spel, foul play; ~plaas (..plase) commonplace; platitude; ~skap community; intercourse; met ~skap van goed, in community of property

gemeenskap'lik (-e) common, joint, mutual

gemeen'skap: ~s'bou community development; ~s'diens community service; ~sentrum (-s) community centre

gemeen'te (-s) community; congregation, parish

geme'nereg common law

gemeng' (-de) mixed, miscellaneous

gemeubeleer', gemeubileer' (-de) furnished

gemid'deld (b) (-e) average, mean; ~e temperatuur, mean temperature

gem'mer ginger; ~bier ginger beer; ~lim(onade) ginger ale

gemoed' (-ere) mind, heart; sy ~ lug, vent one's feelings

gemoe'delik (-e; -er, -ste) kind-hearted, genial

gemoed': ~stemming (-e, -s) mood, humour, frame of mind; ~s'toestand state of mind, mental condition

gemoeid' concerned, at stake; baie geld is daarmee ~, a big sum is involved

gemom'pel muttering, grumbling

gemors' mess, waste; hash

gems'bok (-ke) gazelle, roebuck (Bible); gemsbuck, oryx

genaak' (~) approach, come near; ~baar (..bare) accessible, approachable

gena'de mercy, grace, clemency; ~ betoon, pardon; ~brood bread of charity; ~dood euthanasia; ~slag final stroke, death-blow, coup de grâce

gena'dig (-e; -er, -ste) merciful, lenient

gene'ë (meer ~, mees ~) inclined, disposed

genees' (~) cure, heal, recover; *iem. ~ van,* cure a person of; ~heer (..here) physician, doctor, medical practitioner

genees'kunde medical science, medicine

geneeskun'dig (-e) medical; ~*e ondersoek,* medical examination; ~e (-s) physician

genees': ~lik (-e) curable, remediable; ~middel (-s) remedy, medicine, drug

geneig' inclined, prone; ~ *tot die verkeer-de,* prone to wrong

ge'ner: *van nul en ~ waarde,* null and void

generaal' (s) (-s) general; (b) (..rale) algemeen; *generale repetisie,* dress rehearsal, *kyk* kleedrepetisie

generaal'-majoor (generaals-majoor) major-general

genera'sie (-s) generation; ~gaping generation gap

gene'sing recovery, restoration to health

ge'nesis genesis

gene'ties (-e) genetic

genie' (-ë) genius

geniep'sig (-e; -er, -ste) sly, underhand; false, purposely hurting, bullying

genië'ring engineering (process)

geniet' (~) enjoy, possess; *ek het die aand ~,* I enjoyed the evening

ge'nitief (..tiewe) genitive

genoe'ë (-ns) pleasure, delight; joy; *dit doen my ~,* it gives me pleasure

genoeg' enough, sufficient

genoot' (..genote) fellow (of a society); ~skap (-pe) society, company, association

genot' (genietinge, genietings) enjoyment, pleasure; ~vol (-le; -ler, -ste) delightful, enjoyable

genug'tig: *my ~!* goodness me! good gracious!

geoe'fen (-de) trained, exercised, expert

geografie' geography, *ook* aardrykskunde

geologie' geology, *ook* aardkunde

geometrie' geometry, *ook* meetkunde

geoor'loof (-de) allowed, permissible

gepaard' (-e) coupled, in pairs; ~ *gaan met,* coupled/attended with

gepas' (-te) becoming, suitable, seemly

gepensioeneer' (-de) pensioned; ~de (-s) pensioner

gepeu'pel mob, populace, rabble

geraam'te (-s) skeleton, carcass; framework

geraas' (gerase) noise, din; ~bestryding noise abatement

gera'de advisable; *dit nie ~ ag nie,* not think it advisable

geraffineer' (-de) refined; consummate; ~de suiker refined sugar

gereed' ready, prepared; ~skap (-pe) tools, implements, utensils

gere'ël (-de) arranged, adjusted; *alles is ~,* everything has been arranged

gereeld' (-e; -er, -ste) regular, orderly; ~*e diens,* scheduled service; *hy kom ~ laat,* he is always late

gereformeerd' (-de) reformed

gereg'¹ (-te) dish, course, meal

gereg'² justice, court; *voor die ~ verskyn,* appear before court; ~s'bode (-s) messenger of the court; beadle; sheriff; ~telik (-e) judicial, legal; ~*telike bestuur,* judicial management

gereg'tig (-de) entitled, qualified; ~held justice; ~ *op,* entitled to

gerei': eet~ cutlery; hengel~ fishing tackle; huis~ household appliances; skryf~ stationery, *ook* skryfware

gerf (gerwe) sheaf

gerief' (..riewe) comfort, convenience; facility; closet; ~lik (-e) convenient, comfortable, commodious; ~s'halwe for the sake of convenience

gering' (-e; -er, -ste) small, slight, trifling; *weg van die ~ste weerstand,* line of least resistance

gering'ag (-ge-), gering'skat (-ge-) slight, hold cheap, underestimate

gerit'sel rustling, rustle, frou-frou

gerog'gel rattling (in throat), death rattle

geroos'ter (-de) roasted, toasted; ~de brood, toast, *ook* roosterbrood

gerug' (-te) rumour, report; ~*te versprei,* spread rumours; ~steun assisted, backed up, supported

gerui'me: *'n ~ tyd,* a considerable time

geruis' (-e) rustling, murmur, tingling

gerus' (b) (-te) quiet, calm, peaceful; (bw) safely, really; *jy kan dit ~ doen,* you can safely do it; *kom ~,* do come

gerus'stel (-ge-) reassure, soothe, relieve

gesaal'de (-s) crop, *kyk* gewas

der (-s) commander
gesa'mentlik (b) (-e) total (amount); collec=
tive; united (forces); joint (owners)
gesang' (-e) song, hymn
gesant' (-e) ambassador; minister plenipo=
tentiary; envoy, emissary; legate; deputy
gesant'skap (-pe) embassy; legation
gese'ën (-de) blessed, fortunate
geseg'de (-s) saying, expression; predicate
(gram.)
gesel'¹ (s) (-le) mate, companion, fellow
ge'sel² (s) (-s) scourge, whip; (w) (ge-)
scourge, whip; flagellate
gesel'lig (-e; -er, -ste) sociable, homelike,
cosy; ~heid sociability; (..hede) social,
party
gesels' (~) chat, talk
gesel'skap (-pe) company; party; in ver=
keerde ~ raak, fall into bad company;
~(s)dame (-s) hostess
geset' (-te) stout, corpulent
gesien': 'n ~e man, an esteemed man
gesig' (-te) face, sight, view; vision; eye=
sight; ~gie (-s) little face; pansy
gesig'(s): ~bedrog optical illusion; ~einder
horizon; ~kuur (..kure) facelift; ~punt
(-e) viewpoint; aspect; ~snesie facial tis=
sue
gesin' (-ne) household, family
gesind' (-e) disposed, minded; iem. gunstig
~ wees, be favourably disposed to; ~heid
attitude, disposition, inclination
gesins'beplanning family planning
Gesins'dag Family Day
geska'ter burst of laughter, peals of laugh=
ter
geskenk' (-e) present, gift
geskied' (~) happen, occur, take place; U
wil ~, Thy will be done
geskie'denis (-se) history
geskiedkun'dig (-e) historical
geskied'skrywer (-s), geskied'vorser (-s)
historian
geskik' (-te; -ter, -ste) fit, suitable, proper;
capable, appropriate
geskil' (-le) quarrel, difference, dispute; 'n
~ besleg/bylê, settle a dispute
geskoei' (-de) shod; op dieselfde lees ~,
organised on the same lines
geskool' (-de) trained, schooled, skilled;
~de arbeiders, skilled labourers

geskree(u)' shouting, crying, shrieking; veel
~ en weinig wol, much ado about nothing
geskrif' (-te) writing, document
geskut' cannon, artillery
geslag¹ (s) (-te) gender, sex; lineage, race,
generation; species; die skone ~, the fair
sex; ~siekte (-s) venereal disease
geslag'² (b) (-te) slaughtered; butchered
geslags': ~drang, ~drif sex drive/urge;
~onderrig sex education; ~organe sexual
organs; ~register genealogical table/
register
geslag'telik (-e) sexual
gesle'pe (-ner, -nste; meer ~, mees ~) sly,
cunning, cute
geslo'te closed, shut; reticent; agter ~
deure, privately, in camera; ~ geledere,
closed shop (trade unions)
gesneu'welde (-s) casualty, dead
gesofistikeer(d) sophisticated
gesog' (-te) forced, far-fetched; in demand
gesond' (-e; -er, -ste) healthy, sound;
wholesome; sane; ~e verstand, com=
monsense; ~heid health, soundness;
~heid! cheers! op iem. se ~heid drink,
drink to someone's health
gesout' (-e) salted; seasoned; immune (horse)
gespan'ne tense, strained
ges'pe(r) (s) (-s) buckle, clasp; (w) (ge-)
buckle, clasp
gespesifiseer' (-de) specified
gespier' (-de) muscular
gespik'kel, gesprik'kel (-de) speckled,
spotted
gesprek' (-ke) conversation, discourse
gespuis' rabble, scum, riffraff
gestal'te (-s) build; stature, figure; size
gestand': sy woord ~ doen, keep one's
word
gestel' (s) body, system; (vgw) supposing,
assuming
geste'wel (-de) booted; ~ en gespoor, ready,
booted and spurred
gestig' (-te) institution, establishment
gestrem'de (-s) (s) disabled/handicapped
person
gesuk'kel botheration; trouble; small pro=
gress; pottering
geswel' (-le) swelling, tumour, growth
geswoeg' drudging, toiling
getal' (-le) number
getalm' lingering, loitering

getjank' yelping, whining

getor'ring teasing, nagging; worry

getroos' (~) submit; bear, resign to; *hom baie moeite* ~, spare no pains

getrou' (-e; -er, -ste) faithful; true, reliable, trusty

getroud' (-e) married; *kwartiere vir* ~*es*, married quarters

getrou'heid fidelity, faithfulness

getui'e (s) (-s) witness; ~*nis* evidence, testimony; ~*nis aflê*, give evidence

getuig' (~) testify, bear witness; give evidence; ~**skrif** (-te) testimonial, reference

getwis' quarrelling, wrangling

gety' (-e) tide; *as die* ~ *verloop, versit 'n mens die bakens,* one must set one's sails to the wind

gety'poel (-e) tidal pool

geur (s) (-e) fragrance; savour; scent, odour, perfume, aroma, essence, flavour

geu'rig (-e; -er, -ste) fragrant, odorous

geur'sel (-s) flavouring, essence

geut (-e) gutter; sewer, drain; duct

gevaar' (gevare) danger, peril, risk; *buite* ~, out of danger (patient); ~**lik** (-e; -er, -ste) dangerous, perilous; ~**te** (-s) colossus, monster

geval' (s) (-le) case, event, matter; *in alle* ~, in any case; (w) (~) please, suit; *jou iets laat* ~, put up with something; ~**le'stu die** (-s) case history

gevan'gene (s) prisoner, captive

gevan'genis (-se) prison, goal

gevan'ge(n)skap imprisonment, captivity

gevat' (-te; -ter, -ste) shrewd, clever, smart, quick; ~*te antwoord,* witty reply/retort

geveg' (-te) fight, battle, combat; *buite* ~ *stel,* put out of action

geveins' (-de) feigned, dissembling, hypocritical

gevoel' (-e, -ens) feeling, sentiment, sense, sensation, emotion

gevoe'lig (-e; -er, -ste) tender, sensitive; *'n* ~*e slag,* a severe blow

gevolg' (-e) consequence, result; retinue, followers; suite; *ten* ~*e van,* as a result of; ~**lik** consequently, hence

gevolg'trekking (-e, -s) conclusion; deduction, inference; *oorhaaste* ~ *maak,* jump to conclusions

gevolmag'tigde (-s) plenipotentiary; proxy

gevor'der (-de) advanced; *op* ~*de leeftyd,* at an advanced age

gevreet' gnawing pain; gorging; (..**vrete**) face, mug, phiz

gewaag (b) (-de) risky, dangerous, bold, hazardous; *'n* ~*de stap,* a bold decision

gewaar'merk (-te) hallmarked; certified; ~*te afskrif,* certified copy

gewaar'word (-ge-) become aware of, perceive, notice; ~**ing** (-e, -s) sensation, perception, experience

gewa'pen (-de) armed, prepared

gewas' (-se) crop(s); harvest; growth, tumor

geween' weeping, wailing

geweer' (-s, ..**were**) rifle, firearm, gun; *presenteer* ~*!* present arms!

ge'wel (-s) gable

geweld' force, violence

gewelda'dig (-e) violent; *'n* ~*e dood,* a violent death

gewel'dig (b) (-e; -er, -ste) violent, severe; (bw) dreadfully, awfully; ~ *duur,* extremely expensive

geweld'pleging violence

ge'wer (-s) giver, donor

gewer'skaf bustle, to-do

gewe'se late, former; ex-; *die* ~ *koning,* the former king

gewe'te (-ns) conscience; *sy* ~ *kwel hom,* his conscience pricks him

gewe'tens: ~**beswaar** (..**sware**) conscientious scruple/objection; ~**wroeging** (-e, -s) qualms of conscience

gewig' (-te) weight/mass; importance, moment; *soortlike* ~, specific gravity

gewild' (-e) wished-for, popular, in demand, favoured

gewil'lig (-e; -er, -ste) willing, ready

gewis' (b) (-se) sure, certain; ~*se dood,* certain death; (bw) certainly, surely

gewoel' bustle, tumult, stir, crowd

gewon'ne won; *dit* ~ *gee,* yield the point

gewoon' (gewone) common, ordinary, usual; ~**d** accustomed, used; ~**lik** usually, ordinarily; ~**te** (-s) habit, custom, practice; *ouder* ~*te,* according to custom; ~**te'misdadiger** (-s) habitual criminal

gewrig' (-te) joint, wrist

gewyd' (-e) sanctified, consecrated, sacred; *'n* ~*e oomblik,* a sacred moment

ghan'tang (-s) suitor, lover
ghitaar' (-s, ..tare) guitar, *ook* kitaar
ghoen (-e, -s) shooting (big) marble
gholf golf; ~baan (..bane) golf course;
golf links; ~joggie (-s) caddie; ~stok (-ke)
golf club
ghong (-s) gong
ghries grease
ghwa'no guano
ghwar (-re) uncouth person, lout
gids (-e) guide; directory; ~aanleg (-te) pilot
plant; ~hond (-e) guide dog
gier (s) (-e) fancy, whim, caprice; *die ~ kry,*
get a sudden fancy
gie'rig (-e; -er, -ste) avaricious, miserly;
~aard (-s) miser
giet (ge-) pour; cast, found; *reën dat dit ~,*
come down in sheets (rain); ~er (-s)
watering can
gif[1] (-stowwe, giwwe) poison, venom
gif[2] (-te) present, gift, donation
gif: ~klier (-e) poison gland; ~stof poison;
~tand (-e) poison fang; ~tig (-e; -er, -ste)
poisonous, venomous
gig'gel (ge-) giggle
gil (s) (-le) yell, scream, shriek; (w) (ge-) yell,
scream
gil'de (-s) guild
gimnas' (-te) gymnast
gimna'sium (-s) gymnasium
gimnastiek' gymnastics; ~vertoning (-s)
gymnastics display
ginekoloog' (..loë) gynaecologist
gips gypsum, plaster of Paris
giraf' (-fe, -s) giraffe
gis[1] (s) yeast; (w) ferment, rise
gis[2] (s) guess; (w) (ge-) guess, conjecture;
~sing (-e, -s) conjecture, supposition
gis'ter yesterday; *nie ~ se kind nie,* no
chicken
gisteraand' yesterday evening, last night
gistermô're, gistermo're, gisterog'gend
yesterday morning
gits! *o ~ !* oh dear! oh my!
git'swart jet-black
gla(a)s'oog (..oë) artificial eye
glad (b) (-de; -der, -ste) smooth, slippery,
sleek; *so ~ soos seep,* very slippery; (bw)
quite, altogether; even; *~ nie,* not at all
glans (s) gloss, lustre; brilliancy; (w) (ge-)
shine, gleam, glisten; ~punt (-e) acme;

crowning feature; star turn; ~ryk (-e; -er,
-ste) glorious, brilliant; ~verf (..verwe)
gloss/enamel paint
glas (-e) glass, tumbler; *geslypte ~,* cut
glass; ~blaser (-s) glassblower
gla'serig (-e) glassy; glazed
glas'helder clear as crystal
glasuur' enamel (teeth); glazing (pottery);
icing (cake)
glet'ser (-s) glacier
gleuf (gleuwe) groove; slot; slit
glib'berig (-e; -er, -ste) slippery, slimy
glim'lag (s) (-te) smile; (w) (ge-) smile
glim'verf luminous paint
glim'wurm (-s) glowworm, firefly
glin'ster (ge-) glitter, glisten, sparkle
glip (ge-) slip, slide; *die ~pe,* the slips
(cricket)
glips (-e) slip, mistake
glip'weg (..weë) slipway, filter (traffic)
gliserien', gliseri'ne glycerine
glo (w) (ge-) believe, credit, trust; *iem. glo,*
believe somebody; *~ in God,* believe in
God
gloed glow, heat; ardour, fervour, passion
gloei (ge-) glow, be red-hot; ~end (-e; -er,
-ste) glowing; scorching; ~lamp (-e)
(electric) bulb
glo'rie glory, lustre, fame
gly (ge-) glide, slide, slip; ~erig (-e; -er, -ste)
slippery; ~skaal sliding scale
g'n no; not
God God; *~ sy dank,* thank God; *as ~ wil,*
God willing
god (-e) idol, god
god: ~dank thank God; ~delik (-e) divine,
sublime, glorious
goddeloos' (..lose; ..loser, -ste) godless,
wicked, impious
godin' (-ne) goddess
godlo'ënaar (-s) atheist
gods'diens (-te) divine worship, religion,
faith; ~onderrig religious instruction
godsdiens'tig (-e; -er, -ste) religious, pious;
devout
godslas'ter: ~aar (-s) blasphemer; ~lik
(-e; -er, -ste) blasphemous
gods'naam: *in ~,* for Heaven's sake
godvre'send (-e; -er, -ste) God-fearing;
pious
goed[1] (s) (-ere) goods, stuff, property,
things; *~ en bloed,* life and property; *in*

gemeenskap van ~, in community of property

goed² (b) (**goeie; beter, beste**) good, kind, well, proper; *iets* ~*s*, something good

goed: ~**doen** (-ge-) do good; cheer up; ~**dunke** opinion, discretion; *na* ~*dunke,* at will/discretion

goe'dere: ~**loods** (-e) goods shed; ~**trein** (-e) goods train

goedertie're merciful, clement

goed: ~**guns'tig** (-e) well-disposed; ~**har'tig** (-e; -er, -ste) kind-hearted; ~**heid** kindness, goodness

goe'dig (-e) good-natured, kind

goed'keur (-ge-) approve, confirm, consent; ~**ing** approval, consent; *sy* ~*ing wegdra,* meet with his approval

goed: ~**koop** (..**koper, -ste**) cheap, inexpensive; ~*koop is duurkoop,* a bad bargain is dear at a farthing

goed'vind (-ge-) think fit, approve of

goeienaand' good evening

goeie: ~**middag!** good afternoon! ~**môre!** ~**mo're!** good morning! ~**nag!** good night!

goei'en: ~**dag!** good day! ~**dag sê** (**goeiendag ge-**) greet; say good day

Goeie Vry'dag Good Friday

goei'ste: *my* ~*!* dear me! ~ *weet!* goodness knows!

go'ël (ge-) juggle, conjure

goe'ters things, small fry

goewerment' (-e) government

goewernan'te (-s) governess

goewerneur' (-s) governor

goewerneur-generaal' (**goewerneurs-generaal**) governor-general

gog'ga (-s) insect, vermin; bogey

goi'ingsak (-ke) gunny bag; hessian

golf¹ (s) (**golwe**) bay, gulf

golf² (s) (**golwe**) wave, billow; (w) (**ge-**) wave; ~**lengte** (-s) wavelength

gom gum, glue

gomlastiek' Indiarubber, elastic

gom'papier gummed paper

gom'pou (-e) kori bustard

gom'tor (-re) clodhopper, uncouth person, lout, churl

gon'del (-s) gondola

gon'na: ~*!* oh my!

gons (ge-) buzz, hum, drone; *leer dat dit* ~, study very hard; ~**er** buzzer

gooi (ge-) throw, cast, fling

goor (-der, -ste) dirty; nasty; rancid

gord, gort (s) (**gorte**) band, girdle, belt; (w) (**ge-**) gird; ~ *vas!* belt/buckle up!

gor'del (-s) belt, girdle; zone; ~**roos** shingles

gordyn' (-e) curtain, blind; *die* ~ *gaan op,* the curtain rises; ~**kap** (-pe) pelmet

gor'rel (s) (-s) throat; (w) (**ge-**) gargle, gurgle; waffle (in exam.)

gort groats, grits; barley

gou (-er, -ste) quick, rapid, soon

goud gold

gou'dief (..**diewe**) pickpocket, sneak thief, *ook* **grypdief, sakkeroller**

goud: ~**myn** (-e) goldmine; ~**prys** gold price; ~**rif** (..**riwwe**) gold reef; ~**smid** (..**smede**) goldsmith; ~**snee** gilt edge (of book); ~**vis** (-se) goldfish

gou'e golden, gold; ~ *bruilof,* golden wedding

gou'-gou very soon, in a moment, quickly, in a trice

gous'blom (-me) calendula

graad (**grade**) degree; stage, grade; class (potatoes); *'n* ~ *behaal,* obtain a (university) degree

graaf¹ (s) (**grawe**) spade; (w) (**ge-**) dig, burrow

graaf² (s) (-s) earl (England); count; ~**skap** (-pe) county, shire; earldom

graag (**liewer; liefste** [**graagste**]) gladly, readily, willingly; *ek wil* ~ *weet,* I should like to know

graan (**grane**) grain, corn

graan: ~**korrel** (-s) grain seed; ~**silo** (..**silo's**) grain elevator; ~**skuur** (..**skure**), ~**solder** (-s) granary; ~**sorghum** (grain) sorghum; ~**suier** (-s) (grain) elevator

graat (**grate**) fishbone

graat'tjiemeerkat (-te) true meercat; suricat

gra'de: ~**dag** (..**dae**) honours day: ~**plegtigheid** (..**hede**) graduation ceremony

grade'ring (-e, -s) grading, graduation

gradueer' (-ge-) graduate (at university)

graf (-te) grave, tomb

grafiek' (-e) graph

gra'fies (-e) graphic; in the form of a graph

grafiet' graphite

graf: ~**kelder** (-s) vault; ~**skrif** (-te) epitaph; ~**steen** (..**stene**) gravestone, tombstone

grag (-te) canal, ditch
gram (-me) gram
gramadoe'las rough country, inhospitable country, bundu
gramma'tika (-s) grammar
grammofoon' (..fone) gramophone; ~**plaat** (..plate) gramophone record
granaat' (..nate) pomegranate (fruit); grenade, shrapnel; garnet (gem)
granadil'la, grenadel'la (-s) grenadilla
graniet' granite
grap (-pe) joke, jest, fun; ~**pig** (-e; -er, -ste) funny, comic(al), droll; ~**pigheid** drollery, fun
gras (-se) grass
gra'sie grace, favour; *by die* ~ *Gods*, by the grace of God
grasieus' (-e; -er, -ste) graceful, elegant
gras: ~**perk** (-e) lawn, green, grassy plot; ~**snyer** (-s) lawnmower; ~**weduwee** (-s) grass widow
gra'tis gratis, free; ~ *monster,* free sample
graveer' (~, ge-) engrave
gravin' (-ne) countess
greep (grepe) grasp, grip; hilt; *'n ~ uit die geskiedenis,* a dip into history
grein (-e) grain
grein'hout white pinewood
grein'tjie (-s) grain; particle; *geen ~ nie,* not an atom
grenadel'la, granadil'la (-s) grenadilla
grenadier' (-s) grenadier
gren'del (s) (-s) bolt, bar; (w) (ge-) bolt, bar
grens[1] (s) (-e) boundary, border, limit, frontier; *aan die ~,* on the border; *geen ~e ken nie,* know no bounds
grens[2] (w) (ge-) cry; ~**balie** (-s) crybaby
grens: ~**(e)loos** (..lose) boundless, infinite; ~**nywerheid** (..hede) border industry; ~**oorlog** (..loë) frontier war; ~**voordele** fringe benefits, *kyk* **byvoordele**
gre'tig (-e; -er, -ste) eager, desirous
grief (s) (griewe) grievance
griep influenza, flu
grie'selig (-e; -er, -ste) creepy, gruesome, nasty
grie'seltjie (-s) particle, bit
grif'fel, grif'fie (-s) slate pencil
griffier' (-s) registrar, recorder
gril[1] (-le) caprice, whim, freak
gril[2] (w) (ge-) shudder; ~**lig** (-e; -er, -ste) fantastic, whimsical, fanciful

grimeer' (~, ge-) make up
grimeer'sel, grime'ring makeup
grin'nik (ge-) sneer, mock, grin, snigger
groef (s) (groewe) groove, flute
groei (s) growth; (w) (ge-) grow; ~**fonds** (-e) growth fund; ~**koers** growth rate
groen (-er, -ste) green, verdant; unripe
groen'te (-s) vegetables, greens
groen'tjie (-s) fresher, freshette, freshman; novice
groen'voer fresh fodder
groep (s) (-e) group; ~**dinamika** group dinamics
groepeer' (~, ge-) group, form groups
groepe'ring (-e, -s) grouping
groet (s) (-e) salute, greeting; (w) (ge-) greet, salute, shake hands, say goodbye; ~**e,** ~**nis** regards, greetings, compliments; *groete van huis tot huis, die groete tuis,* love to all at home
grof (growwe; growwer, -ste) coarse; rough; rude, gruff; ~**geskut** heavy ordnance; heavy guns
grom (ge-) grumble, growl, grouse
grond (s) (-e) ground, soil; reason; *te ~e gaan,* be ruined; *op ~ van,* by virtue of; (w) (ge-) found, ground, base; ~ *hulle mening op,* base their opinion on; ~**belasting** (-s) land tax; ~**boontjie** (-s) peanut, monkeynut
gron'dig (-e; -er, -ste) thorough, profound, well-founded; searching; ~*e ondersoek,* thorough investigation, *kyk* **gegronde redes**
grond: ~**laag** (..lae) bottom layer; first coat (paint); ~**legging** foundation; ~**reëls** constitution (of an association/club); ~**slag** (..slae) foundation, basis; *die beginsels wat daaraan ten ~slag lê,* the underlying principles; ~**stof** (..stowwe) element, raw material; ~**tot-lug missiel** (-e) ground-to-air missile
grond'waardin (-ne) ground hostess
grond'wet (written) constitution, fundamental law (of a country)
grondwet'tig (-e), **grondwet'lik** (-e) constitutional
groot (groter, -ste) great, large, big, tall; vast; grown-up, adult; important; *grote genugtig!* good gracious! ~ *kokkedoor,* big shot (person); *die ~ publiek,* the general public; *soos 'n ~ speld verdwyn,*

disappear on the sly; **~baas (..base)** master, chief; **~bek (-ke)** braggart; **~boek (-e)** ledger

Groot-Brittan'je Great Britain

groot'handel wholesale trade; **~aar (-s)** wholesale merchant, wholesaler

groothar'tig (-e; -er, -ste) magnanimous

groot'heid greatness, magnitude; grandeur; quantity (maths.); *die ~ van Napoleon,* the greatness of Napoleon; **~(s)waan** megalomania

groot'jie (-s) great grandmother (≈father), granny; *loop na jou ~,* go to Jericho

groot: ~liks greatly, to a great extent, in a high degree; **~maak (-ge-)** rear, bring up; **~man:** *jou ~man hou,* pretend, show off; **~mens (-e)** adult, grown-up (person); *eers ~mense, dan langore,* first adults, then children; **~moeder (-s)** grandmother; **~moe'dig (-e; -er, -ste)** magnanimous; **~oë:** *~oë maak,* show dissapproval; **~ouers** grandparents; **~pad (..paaie)** highroad, main road; **~praat (-ge-)** brag, boast

groot: ~skaals (-e) on a large scale; **~skeeps (-e)** grand, copious, elegant; on a large/grand scale

groot'te (-s) size, extent; *die ~ van die kamer,* the size of the room

groot: ~vader (-s) grandfather; **~wild** big game

gros gross; majority

grot (-te) cave, grotto; **~bewoner (-s)** cave dweller; **~kunde** speleology

gro'tendeels for the greater part, chiefly

gru (ge-) shudder

gruis gravel; roughly-ground meal; crushed mealies

gru'saam (..same) gruesome, horrible

gru'wel (-s) horror, abomination, crime; **~daad (..dade)** crime, atrocity, outrage; **~grot** chamber of horrors

gru'welik (-e. -er, -ste) horrible

gryns (s) (-e) grin, sneer; **(w) (ge-)** grin, sneer; **~lag** grin, sneer

gryp (ge-) seize. snatch, grab, clutch; **~dief (..diewe)** snatch and grab thief

grys ([-e]; -er, -ste) grey; *die ~e verlede,* hoary antiquity, dim past; **~aard (-s)** old man, greybeard

guerril'la (-s) guerrilla

guilloti'ne (-s) guillotine

gul'de (b) golden; *'n ~ geleentheid,* a golden opportunity; *die ~ middeweg,* the golden mean

gul'den (s) (-s) (Dutch) guilder

gulp (-e) fly (of trousers)

gul'sig (-e; -er, -ste) gluttonous, greedy

gun (ge-) grant, allow; not grudge; *ek ~ jou dit,* you are welcome to it

guns (-te) favour, goodwill; *'n ~ bewys,* do a favour; *leef van ~te en gawes,* live on charity; *ten ~te van,* in favour of; **~loon** kick-back, unofficial commission; **~te= ling (-e)** favourite; *my gunstelingskrywer,* my favourite author; **~tig (-e; -er, -ste)** favourable, advantageous, propitious; *'n ~tige ligging,* a favourable site/situation

guur (-der, -ste) bleak, cold, harsh, inclement; *gure weer,* inclement/rough weather

gy'selaar (-s) hostage; *vrylating van ~s,* release of hostages

H

haai¹ (s) (-e) shark

haai² (tw) heigh! I say!

haai³ bleak, barren; *die ~ Karoo,* the bare Karoo

haak (s) (hake) hook, hasp, bracket; *in die ~ bring,* square, arrange, settle; **(w) (ge-)** hook; heel (ball)

haaks (-e) right-angled, square; *hulle is al= tyd ~,* they are continually at loggerheads

haak'speld (-e) safety pin

haal (s) (hale) stroke, lash; **(w) (ge-)** fetch, reach, catch; *die trein ~,* catch the train;

~-en-betaal cash-and-carry, *ook* **koop-en-loop**

haan (hane) cock, rooster; *geen ~ sal daar= na kraai nie,* nobody will be the wiser

haar¹ (s) (hare) hair; *hare kloof,* split hairs

haar² (vnw) her

haar³ (b) right; *hot en ~,* left and right

haard (-e) hearth, fireside

haar: ~fyn as fine as hair; in detail; **~kap= per (-s)** barber, hairdresser; **~knipper (-s)** (pair of) hairclippers; hairdresser; **~lint (-e)** hair ribbon; **~lok (-ke)** lock of hair;

~**middel** (-s) hair restorer; ~**naald** (-e) hairpin

haar'olie (-s) hair oil

haar: ~**snyer** (-s) hairdresser; ~**sproei** hairspray

haas[1] (s) haste, hurry; *hoe meer* ~ *hoe minder spoed*, more haste, less speed

haas[2] (s) (**hase**) hare

haas[3] (bw) almost, nearly; *hy is* ~ *daar*, he must have nearly arrived

haas: ~**bek** harelip; with a tooth missing; ~**lip** (-pe) harelip

haas'tig (-e; -er, -ste) hasty, hurried

haat (s) hatred; (w) (ge-) hate, detest

haat'draend (-e; -er, -ste) revengeful, resentful, rancorous

haat'lik (-e; -er, -ste) hateful, malicious

ha'el (s) hail; shot; (w) (ge-) hail; ~**geweer** (-s, ..**were**) shotgun; ~**korrel** (-s) grain of shot; hailstone; ~**steen** (..**stene**) hailstone; ~**versekering** hail insurance/cover

hag'lik (-e; -er, -ste) critical, risky, perilous, precarious

hak[1] (s) (-ke) heel; hock (animal)

hak[2] (w) (ge-) cut; mince; ~ *die knoop deur*, cut the (Gordian) knot

ha'ker (-s) hooker (rugby)

ha'kie (-s) bracket; little hook; *tussen* ~*s*, in brackets, in parenthesis; by the way

hak'kejag hot pursuit (military)

hak'kel (ge-) stammer, stutter; ~**aar** (-s, ..**lare**) stammerer

hak'skeen (..**skene**) heel

hal (-le) hall

half (**halwe**) half; *daar slaan dit* ~, the half-hour is striking

halfag(t) half past seven

halfe'del (-) semiprecious; ~**stene** semiprecious stones

half'eindronde (-s) semifinal

halfmaan' (..**mane**) crescent, semicircle

halfne'ë, **halfne'ge** half past eight

half'-om-half fifty-fifty, half and half

half: ~**stok** halfmast; ~**uur** (..**ure**) half an hour; ~**vol** half-full

halfwas' half-grown, medium

half'weekliks (-e) bi-weekly, twice weekly

hallelu'ja (-s) hallelujah

hallusina'sie (-s) hallucination

hals (-e) neck; *jou iets op die* ~ *haal*, bring trouble on oneself; ~**band** (-e) collar (dog); ~**doek** (-e) neckcloth; ~**ketting** (-s)

necklace, neckchain; ~**misdaad** capital crime/offence; ~**oorkop** head over heels; hurry-skurry; ~**oorlosie** (-s) pendant watch; ⇸**snoer** (-e) necklace

halsstar'rig (-e; -er, -ste) obstinate, headstrong, stubborn

halt! halt!

hal'te (-s) halt; siding

hal'ter (-s) halter

halveer' (~, ge-) halve, divide into halves

ham (-me) ham

ha'mel (-s) wether

ha'mer (s) (-s) hammer; (w) (ge-) hammer; *altyd op dieselfde aambeeld* ~, keep on harping on the same string

ham'burger (-s) hamburger

hand (-e) hand; *iets aan die* ~ *gee (doen)*, suggest something; *die* ~*e uit die mou steek*, put the shoulder to the wheel; ~ *in die as slaan*, oust; ~**boeie** handcuffs; ~**boek** (-e) manual, handbook, textbook

hand: ~**doek** (-e) towel; ~**druk** (-ke) handshake, handclasp

han'dearbeid manual labour

han'del (s) trade, commerce, business, traffic; ~ *dryf (drywe)*, carry on a trade; ~ *en wandel*, conduct in life; (w) (ge-) act; deal, carry on a business; ~**aar** (-s) merchant, dealer; ~**ing** (-e, -s) action, conduct, handling

han'dels: ~**agent** (-e) commercial agent; ~**artikel** (-s) commodity; ~**balans** balance of trade; ~**bank** (-e) commercial bank; ~**bedryf** (..**drywe**) branch of trade; ~**belange** commercial interests; ~**betrekking** (-e, -s) commercial relation, trade connection

han'delsender (-s) commercial transmitter (broadcasting)

han'delsfirma (-s) trading firm

han'del: ~**skip** (..**skepe**) merchantman; ~**skool** (..**skole**) commercial school

han'dels: ~**korting** trade discount; ~**kunstenaar** (-s) commercial artist; ~**merk** (-e) trademark; ~**onderneming** commercial firm; commercial undertaking/venture; ~**reg** mercantile/commercial law; ~**reisiger** (-s) commercial traveller; ~**rekene**, ~**rekenkunde** commercial arithmetic

han'delwyse procedure, method, course of action

hande-vier'voet on all fours

hand'gekeur handpicked; ~de personeel, handpicked staff

hand'gemeen (s) (..mene) hand-to-hand fighting; (bw): ~ raak, come to blows

hand: ~granaat (..nate) hand grenade; ~haaf (ge-) maintain, uphold; jou ~ haaf teen, hold one's own against; standaarde ~haaf, maintain standards

han'dig (-e; -er, -ste) useful; clever, skilful, adroit

hand: ~kykery palmistry; ~langer (-s) helper, handyman; ~leiding (-e, -s) textbook, manual (of instruction), handbook; ~perd (-e) led-horse; mistress; ~pop (-pe) puppet; ~rug backhand (tennis); ~(s) manual(ly); ~skoen (-e) glove; met die ~skoen trou, marry by proxy; ~skrif (-te) handwriting; manuscript

hand: ~tekening (-e, -s) signature; ~ves (-te) charter; ~wapen (-s) handgun; ~werksman (-ne, ..liede, ..lui) artisan, workman, labourer; ~woordeboek (-e) pocket dictionary

ha'ne: ~geveg, (-te), cockfight; ~spoor (..spore) cock's spur; ~treetjie (-s) short distance, stone's throw

hang (s) (-e) slope; (w) (ge-) hang, suspend

han'gar (-s) hangar

hang'brug (..brûe, -ge) suspension bridge

han'gende pending; hanging

hang: ~kas (-te) wardrobe; ~lamp (-e) hanging lamp; ~mat (-te) hammock; ~slot (-te) padlock; ~sweef hanggliding; ~swewer (-s) hangglider

hans orphan; die lam is ~, it is an orphan lamb; ~ grootmaak, bottle rearing

hans'lam (-mers) pet lamb, orphan lamb

hans'wors (-te) clown

hanteer' (~, ge-) handle, manage, operate

hap (s) (-pe) bite, piece; (w) (ge-) bite, snap

ha'per (ge-) ail, be impeded, falter; waar ~ dit? where is the hitch?

haraki'ri harakiri; happy despatch (suicide)

hard (-e; -er, -ste) hard; loud; stern

har'depad hard labour

har'der (-s) Cape herring; mullet

har'deware hardware goods

hardhan'dig (-e; -er, -ste) rough, rude, hard-handed

hard'heid hardness, sternness

hardhoof'dig (-e; -er, -ste) stubborn, obstinate

hardho'rig (-e; -er, -ste) hard of hearing, deaf

hardkop'pig (-e; -er, -ste) obstinate, stubborn

hard'loop (ge-) run, hurry, make haste

hardly'wig (-e) constipated, costive

hard'op aloud, in a clear voice; ~ lees, read aloud

hardvog'tig (-e, -er, -ste) hard-hearted, heartless

hardwer'kend (-e) hardworking, industrious

ha'rem (-s) harem

ha'ring (-s) herring; gerookte ~, kippered herring

hark (s) (-e) rake; (w) (ge-) rake

harlekyn' (-e) buffoon, harlequin, clown

harmonie' (-ë) harmony

harmo'nika (-s) harmonica, concertina

har'nas (-se) armour, cuirass; iem. in die ~ ja, antagonise someone

harp (-e) harp

harpoen' (-e) harpoon

harpuis' resin, rosin (from fir trees)

hars resin, rosin

har'sing: ~s cerebrum, brains; die ~s inslaan, dash out the brains; ~skudding concussion of the brain; ~vliesontsteking meningitis

hart (-e) heart, mind; core; courage; ~aanval heart attack

hart'bees (-te) hartebees (antelope); ~huis (-e) wattle-and-daub house

hartbre'kend (-e) heart-rending

har'te: ~lus heart's desire; na ~lus, to one's heart's content; ~(n)aas ace of hearts; ~(n)boer knave of hearts

har'tens hearts (cards)

har'tewens fondest wish

hart: ~jie (-s) little heart; darling; in die ~tjie van die winter, in midwinter; ~kloppings palpitations; ~lam darling, dearest

hart'lik (-e; -er, -ste) hearty, sincere, cordial; ~e groete tuis, sincere greetings to all (at home)

hart: ~oorplanting (-s) heart transplant; ~-pasaangeër (-s) heart pacemaker; ~roe'rend (-e; -er, -ste) touching, pathetic; ~'seer (s) grief, sorrow; (b) heartsore, sad

harts'tog (-te) passion
hartstog'telik (-e; -er; -ste) passionate
hartversa'king cardiac/heart failure
hartverskeu'rend (-e) heartrending
ha'sepad: *die ~ kies,* take to one's heels
ha'we¹ goods, property, stock; *lewende ~,* livestock
ha'we² (-ns) port, harbour
ha'wer oats
ha'werklap: *om die ~,* on the slightest provocation, for every trifle
hê (had, gehad) have, possess
hè! oh! my!; not so! *jy kom bedel weer, ~,* you are begging again, you ..!
heb'sug covetousness, greed, greediness
he'de¹ (s) the present, this day; *die ~ en die verlede,* the present and the past; (bw) today, at present
he'de!² (tw) *o ~!* oh my! oh heavens! oh goodness!
he'dendaags (-e) modern, presentday, nowadays
heel¹ (w) (ge-) heal
heel² (w) (ge-) receive (stolen property); *die heler is so goed as die steler,* the receiver (of stolen goods) is as bad as the thief
heel³ (b) (hele; heler, -ste) whole, entire
heel⁴ (bw) very, quite; *~ in die begin,* at the very outset; *~ eenvoudig,* quite simple; *~ waarskynlik,* most probably
heelal' universe
heel: *~dag* the whole day, always, frequently; *~huids* unscathed; *daar ~huids van afkom,* get off unscathed
heel'temal quite, altogether, entirely, severely; *~ alleen,* all alone
heel'tyds fulltime
heel'wat quite a lot, a good deal
heen away, thither, thence; *~ en weer,* to and fro
heen-en-weer'tjie (-s) moment, very short time
heen: *~gaan* (-ge-) go away, depart; die; *~kome* refuge, escape; *êrens 'n ~kome vind,* find a refuge somewhere
Heer¹ the Lord, God
heer² (here) gentleman; lord, master; *die ~ des huises,* master of the house; *Geagte Heer/heer,* Dear Sir
heer³ (here) host, army

heer'lik (-e; -er, -ste) glorious, delightful, delicious
heers (ge-) reign, govern, rule; prevail; *~ende pryse,* ruling prices; *~er* (-s) ruler
heerseres' (-se) ruler (woman)
heerskappy' (-e) power, reign, authority
heerssug'tig (-e; -er, -ste) imperious, ambitious
hees (heser, -ste) hoarse, husky
heet¹ (w) (ge-) be called; name; *hy ~ na sy pa,* he is called after his father; *hy ~ hom welkom,* he welcomes him
heet² (b) (hete; heter, -ste) hot, burning; torrid
heet: *~heid* heat, warmth; *~hoof* (-de) hothead
hef¹ (s) (-te, hewwe) handle; *die ~ in hande hê,* control a situation
hef² (w) (ge-) raise, lift; levy, impose; *belastings ~,* impose taxes
hef'boom (..bome) lever
hef'fing (-e, -s) levy; surtax
hef'tig (-e; -er, -ste) violent, vehement
heg (w) (ge-) fasten, attach; *geen waarde ~ nie aan,* attach no value to; (b) (-te; -ter, -ste) firm, solid, strong
heg: *~pleister* (-s) sticking plaster; *~tenis* custody; detention; *in ~tenis neem,* arrest (a person)
hei'den (-e, -s) heathen, pagan
heil welfare, good, prosperity; *alle ~ en seën!* best wishes!
Hei'land Saviour
heil'dronk (-e) toast; *die ~ instel,* propose the toast
hei'lig (w) (ge-) sanctify, consecrate, hallow; (b) (-e; -er, -ste) holy, sacred; *~dom* (-me) sanctuary, holy shrine
hei'lige (-s) saint
hei'lig: *~skennis* blasphemy, sacrilege; *~verklaring* canonisation
Heils'leër Salvation Army
Heil'soldaat (..date) Salvationist
heil'wens (-e) congratulation, good wish(es)
heim'wee homesickness, longing
hein'de: *~ en ver,* far and wide
hei'ning (-s) fence, hedge, enclosure
hei: *~paal* (..pale) pile; *~werk* piling
hek (-ke) gate; railing; hurdle; turnpike
he'kel¹ (s) dislike, hatred; *'n ~ aan iem. hê,* dislike someone intensely

he'kel[2] (w) (ge-) heckle; crochet; satirise; ~digter (-s) satirist; ~werk crochet work

hek'geld gate money; admission

hek'kiesloop (s) (..lope) hurdle race; (w) (-geloop) hurdle

heks (-e) witch, hag, vixen

hek'sluiter (-s) lastcomer; youngest child, kyk laatlammetjie

hek'stormer (-s) gatecrasher

hektaar' (..tare) hectare

hek'to~gram (-me) hectogram; ~liter (s) hectolitre; ~meter (-s) hectometre

hek'wagter (-s) gatekeeper

hel[1] (s) hell; gehenna

hel[2] (w) (ge-) lean, slant, slope; incline

helaas'! alas! alack

held (-e) hero

hel'de: ~akker hero's acre; ~daad (..dade) heroic deed; ~dig (-te) heroic poem; ~dood hero's death; ~moed heroic courage

hel'der ([-e]; -der, -ste) clear, bright, serene; sonorous; so ~ soos kristal, as clear as crystal

heldersiend'heid clairvoyance

hel'de: ~stryd heroic struggle; ~verering hero worship

heldhaf'tig (-e; -er, -ste) heroic, brave

heldin' (-ne) heroine

he'ler[1] (-s) receiver (of stolen property)

he'ler[2] (-s) healer

helf'te (-s) half; die ~ minder, less by half

he'liblad helipad

helikop'ter (-s) helicopter; ~blad (..blaaie) heliport, helipad

heliograaf' (..grawe) heliograph

he'lihawe (-ns) heliport

hel'lebaard (-e) halberd; battle-axe

hel'levaart descent into hell

hel'leveeg (..veë) hellcat, termagant, shrew

hel'ling (-e, .-s) slope, incline, declivity; gradient (of a road)

helm (-s) caul; helmet; met die ~ gebore wees, born with a caul, kyk valhelm

hel'met (-s) helmet (against sun)

help (ge-) help, assist, aid; alle bietjies ~, many a mickle makes a muckle; ~er (-s) helper; ~-my-krap-winkel junk shop

hels (-e) hellish, devilish, infernal; 'n ~e lawaai, a hell of a noise

he'mel (-e) heaven, sky; (-s) canopy (of throne)

he'mel: ~liggaam (..game) heavenly/celestial body; ~poort gate of heaven; ~ruim sky; outer space

he'mels (-e) heavenly, celestial

he'melswil: om ~, for goodness' sake

He'melvaart Ascension; ~dag Ascension Day

hemp (hemde) shirt; die ~ is nader as die rok, charity begins at home

hen (-ne) hen

hends'op, hens'op (ge-) put up one's hands, surrender

hen'gel: ~aar(-s) angler, fisherman; ~gerei fishing tackle; ~stok fishing rod

hen'nep hemp

her: ~ en derwaarts, hither and thither

heraldiek' heraldry

her'berg (s) (-e) inn, hotel, tavern; (w) (ge-) shelter, lodge, accommodate

herbergier' (-s) innkeeper, host

her'bevestig reaffirm

herbo're reborn, regenerate

herdenk' (~) commemorate, remember; ~ing commemoration, remembrance, kyk gedenk

her'der (-s) shepherd, herd; clergyman

her'der: ~s'hond (-e) shepherd's dog; ~spel (-e) pastoral play

herdoop' (~) re-baptise, rename

her'druk (s) (-ke) reprint; new edition; (w) (~) reprint

He're the Lord, God

he'rehuis (-e) mansion

her'eksamen (-s) re-examination

here'nig (~) reunite

he'reregte transfer duty/dues

herfs (-te) autumn; ~nagewening autumn equinox; ~tint (-e) autumnal tint

herhaal' (~) repeat, recapitulate; ~delik repeatedly, over and over

herha'ling (-e, -s) repetition

herin'ner (~) remember, remind; ~ aan, remind of; vir sover ek my kan ~, as far as my memory serves me; ~ing (-e, -s) memory; remembrance, recollection; aangename ~ings, pleasant memories; ter ~ing aan, in memory of

herkies' (~) re-elect; ~baar (..bare) eligible for re-election; hy is en stel hom ~baar, being eligible he offers himself for re-election

her'koms origin, descent, extraction

herkou' (~) chew the cud, ruminate; repeat; *'n saak* ~, ponder over a matter
herlei' (~) reduce; convert; simplify
hermafrodiet' (-e) hermaphrodite
hermelyn' ermine
herme'ties (-e) hermetic; *die tenk is* ~ *ge-
sluit*, the tank is hermetically sealed
hermita'ge, hermityk' hermitage
herneu'termes (-se) big hunter's knife,
bowieknife, jackknife
hernieu', hernu'we, hernu' (~) renew, renovate
hernu'wing renewal, renovation; **~kennis-
gewing** (-s) renewal notice
hero'ïes (-e) heroic; *~e stryd*, heroic struggle
her'oorweeg (w) (~) reconsider
her'open reopen
herout' (-e) herald
herpetoloog' herpetologist, snake expert
her'rie confusion, noise, rumpus, row; *iem.
op sy* ~ *gee*, thrash someone
herroep' (~) revoke, repeal, rescind, annul,
recall, retract; *die ordonnansie is* ~, the
ordinance has been repealed
her'senskim (-me) figment of the imagination; phantasm, chimera; hallucination
her'senskudding concussion of the brain
hersien' (~) revise, update; reconsider;
~ing revision, review
hersikleer' (~) recycle
herskep' (~, herskape) re-create, regenerate, transform
her'soneer (~) rezone
herstel' (s) reparation; repair; redress; recovery; (w) (~) recover, rectify, restore;
repair, mend; **~ling** (-e, -s) recovery,
restoration; **~oord** (-e) convalescent
home
hert (-e) stag
her'tog (hertoë) duke
hertogin' (-ne) duchess
hervat' (~) resume, repeat, begin again; *sy
werk* ~, resume his work
her'vestig resettle; **~ing** resettlement
hervorm' (~) reform, reshape; **~(d)' (-de)**
reformed; *die H~de Kerk*, the Reformed
Church; **~ing** (-e, -s) reformation; reform
hervul'ling refill
her'waarts hither, this way
herwin' (~) regain, recover; recycle; *sy be-*

wussyn ~, recover his consciousness;
~ning recovery, recycling
he'serig (-e) slightly hoarse, husky
heterogeen' (..gene) heterogeneous
hetsy' either; whether; ~ *warm of koud*,
either hot or cold
heug (s): *teen* ~ *en meug*, against one's will;
(w) (ge-): *dit* ~ *my*, I remember; *'n ~like
dag*, a memorable day
heu'ning honey; ~ *om die mond smeer*,
softsoap a person
heu'wel (-s) hill
he'wel (s) (-s) siphon; (w) (ge-) siphon;
petrol uit die tenk ~, siphon petrol out of
the tank
he'wig (-e; -er, -ste) severe, violent, fierce,
vehement; ~ *ontstel*, violently upset
hlasint' (-e) hyacinth
hiberneer' (~, ge-) hibernate
hibri'dies (-e) hybrid
hidrou'lies (-e) hydraulic
hiel (-e) heel; bead(s) (of tyre)
hië'na (-s) hyena
hiep! hip! (hip, hip, hurrah!)
hier here; ~ *te lande*, in this country
hiërargie' hierarchy
hier: **~benewens** besides this, in addition
to; **~by** herewith; enclosed; included;
~die this, these; **~deur** through this
(means), by this; **~heen** this way, to this
side; **~in** in this, herein
hier'jy! (s) lout; (tw) hallo! I say!
hier: **~mee** with this, herewith; **~na** after
this, hereafter
hierna'maals hereafter, in the beyond
hier'natoe this way
hiëroglief' (..gliewe) hieroglyph
hier: **~oor** about this, over this; **~op** upon
this, after this; hereupon; **~so** here, at
this place; *kom ~so!* come here; **~teen**
against this; **~teenoor** opposite; against
this; **~uit** from this, out of this, hence;
~van herefrom, of this, about this; *~van
en daarvan praat*, talk about this, that and
the other thing; **~vandaan** from here;
~voor for this, in return (for this)
hiet (ge-) order; *iem.* ~ *en gebied*, order
someone about
higië'ne hygiene
higië'nies (-e) hygienic
hik (s) (-ke) hiccough; (w) (ge-) hiccough
him'ne (-s) hymn

hin'der (s) trouble, impediment, hindrance, obstacle; (w) (ge-) hinder, annoy, hamper; **~laag** (..lae) ambush; **~lik** (-e; -er, -ste) annoying, troublesome; inconvenient, cumbersome; **~nis** (-se) obstacle, impediment; **~niswedloop** (..lope) obstacle race

hings (-te) stallion, stud horse

hing'sel (-s) handle, hinge

hink (ge-) limp; halt, vacillate; *op twee gedagtes ~*, halt between two opinions

hiperbo'lies (-e) hyperbolic, exaggerated

hiperbool' (..bole) hyperbole, exaggeration; hyperbola

hi'perintelligent hyperintelligent

hi'permark (-te) hypermarket

hiperten'sie hypertension, high blood pressure

hipno'se hypnosis

hipochon'dries (-e) hypochondriac(al), *ook* **ipekondries**

hipokon'ders whims, caprices; imaginary ailments; *hy is 'n regte hipokonder/ipekonder*, he is a real hypochondriac

hipoteek' (..teke) bond, mortgage

hip'pie (-s) hippie

histerektomie' hysterectomy, removal of womb

histe'ries (-e) hysterical

histo'ries (-e) historic(al)

histo'rikus (..rici, -se) historian

hit'sig (-e; -er, -ste) hot, lewd, in heat

hit'te heat; *in die ~ van die stryd*, in the heat of battle; **~golf** (..golwe) heatwave; **~graad** (..grade) temperature

hit'tete: *so ~!* nearly, touch and go

hit'te-uitputting heat exhaustion

hit'tig (-e; -er, -ste) ruttish, heated

hob'bel (ge-) rock, go seesaw; (s) hump (speedbreaker)

ho'bo (-'s) hautboy, oboe

hoe how; what; *~ eerder ~ beter*, the sooner the better; *~ dit ook sy*, be that as it may

hoed[1] (s) (-e) hat, bonnet

hoed[2] (w) (ge-) guard, protect, tend

hoeda'nig (-e) how, what kind of; **~heid** (..hede) quality, capacity; *in die ~heid van*, in the capacity of

hoe'de guard, care, protection

hoëdigt'heidsbehuising high-density housing

hoef[1] (s) (hoewe) hoof

hoef[2] (w) need; *jy ~ nie te kom nie*, you need not come; *jy ~ nie te gekom het nie*, you need not have come

hoef: **~smid** (..smede, -s) farrier; **~yster** (-s) horseshoe

hoe'genaamd: *~ niks*, nothing whatever; *~ geen voorraad nie*, no stocks at all/ whatever

hoek (-e) corner, angle; hook

hoe'ka: *van ~ se tyd af*, from time immemorial, *ook* **toeka**

hoe'kie (-s) little corner, nook; bar (shop); *uit alle ~s en gaatjies*, from every nook and corner

hoe'kig (-e) angular, rugged

hoe'kom why, for what reason

ho'ë kommissaris (-se) High Commissioner

hoek'steen (..stene) corner/foundation stone: **~legging** laying of the foundation/ corner stone

hoe lank how long, till when

hoen'der (-s) fowl; chicken; *die ~s in wees*, be furious; *mal Jan onder die ~s*, a thorn among the roses; **~kop** drunk, tipsy; **~spoor** (..spore) broad arrow; *die ~spoor dra*, be blind bars; **~vel** gooseflesh; *ek kry ~vel daarvan*, it gives me gooseflesh; **~vleis** chicken; goose flesh/pimples

hoe'pel (-s) hoop

ho'ëpriester (-s) high priest

ho'ër higher; **~ onderwys** higher/tertiary education; **~ seunskool/meisieskool** boys'/ girls' high school

hoer (-e) prostitute, harlot, whore

hoera'! **hoerê!** hurrah!

Hoërhand: *van ~*, from God

Ho'ërhuis (-e) Upper house, Senate; House of Lords (England)

ho'ërskool (..skole), **hoër skool** (hoër skole) high/secondary school

ho'ërskoolleerling (-e) high school pupil

hoes (s) cough; (w) (ge-) cough

ho'ëskool (..skole) university, academy

ho'ëtrou high fidelity

hoeveel' how much/many; **~heid** (..hede) quantity, amount

hoe'veelste: *die ~ van die maand?* what day of the month? what is the date?

Ho'ëveld Highveld

hoever', **hoever're:** *in ~*, to what extent, (as to) how far

hoe'we (-s) smallholding; plot
hoewel' though, although
hof (howe) court; ~ van appèl, court of appeal; 'n meisie die ~ maak, court a girl
hof: ~kapelaan (..lane) court chaplain; ~leweransier (-s) purveyor (by royal appointment)
hof'lik (-e; -er, -ste) courteous, obliging, polite; ~heidsbesoek courtesy visit
hof: ~meester (s) steward, purser; ~nar (-re) court fool, jester; ~saak (..sake) court case, lawsuit
hok (s) (-ke) pen (fowl); shed (cattle); kennel (dog); sty (pig); hutch (rabbit); cage (bird); (w) (ge-) enclose, shut in; gate (scholars); die meisies is ge~, the girls have been gated
hok'kie[1] hockey
hok'kie[2] (-s) small shed, cubicle; pigeonhole
hol[1] (s) (-e) cave, den; (-le) anus; (b) (-le; -ler, -ste) hollow, empty
hol[2] (s): die kop op ~ maak, make someone's head turn; (w) (ge-) run, rush, bolt
holderstebol'der topsy-turvy, head over heels, pell-mell
holis'me holism
hom (vnw) him, it
hom(e)opaat' (..pate) hom(o)eopath
hom(e)opa'ties (-e) hom(o)eopathic
homogeen' (..gene) homogeneous, of the same kind/level
homoniem' (s) (-e) homonym; (b) (-e) homonymous
homoseksueel' (s, b) (..ele) homosexual; gay
hond (-e) dog, hound
hon'de: ~herberg kennel; ~hotel kennel, ook woefietuiste; ~lewe wretched life
hon'derd (-e) hundred; ~ en een moeilikhede, a thousand and one troubles; ~jarig (-e) centennial, centenary; ~ste (-s) hundredth; ~tal a hundred
hon'de: ~siekte dog disease, distemper; ~weer beastly weather
hon'djie (-s) pup(py); nie so erg vir die ~ as vir die halsbandjie nie, not as disinterested as it would appear
honds (-e) brutal, churlish, cynic; ~dolheid rabies, hydrophobia
hon'ger (s) hunger; ~ ly, starve; sy ~ stil, appease one's hunger; (w) (ge-) hunger; (b) (der, -ste) hungry; ~loon (..lone) star-

vation wage; ~s'nood famine, dearth; ~staking (-s) hunger strike, kyk eetstaking
honneurs' honours; ~eksamen honours examination; ~graad (..grade) honours degree
honora'rium (..ria, -s) honorarium, fee, royalty
honoreer' (ge-) honour (a bill)
hoof (-de) head; chief, leader; principal (school); die ~ van die gesin, die ~ des huises, the head of the family; iets oor die ~ sien, overlook something; ~artikel (-s) leader, editorial; ~bestuurder (-s) general manager; ~bestuursleier (-s) chief executive; ~brekens, ~brekings brainracking; ~doel main object
hoof: ~kantoor (..tore) head office; ~kwartier (-e) headquarters; ~letter (-s) capital letter; ~lyn (-e) main line, trunk line; ~onderwyser (-s) headmaster, principal; ~pyn headache; ~redakteur (-s) editor in chief; ~regter (-s) chief justice; ~rekene, ~rekenkunde mental arithmetic; ~rol (-le) leading role/part
hoof'saak main point, chief matter
hoofsaak'lik chiefly, mainly, principally
hoof: ~sekretaris (-se) general secretary; ~sin (-ne) principal sentence/clause; ~stad (..stede) capital, metropolis; ~stuk (-ke) chapter; ~vak (-ke) main/ major subject
hoog (hoë, hoër, -ste) high, tall, lofty; hoë bloeddruk, high blood pressure, hypertension; ewe ~ en droog sit, be quite unconcerned; dit is ~ nodig, it is absolutely necessary; ~ag (-ge-) esteem highly, respect; ~agtend die uwe, yours faithfully
hoogdra'wend (-e; -er, -ste) bombastic, pompous, stilted, highflown
hooge'dele right honourable
hoogeerwaar'de right reverend
hoog'geregshof (..howe) supreme court
hooghar'tig (-e; -er, -ste) proud, haughty
hoog'heid highness; Sy H~, His Highness
Hoog'hollands (-e) (S.A.) High Dutch
hoog: ~land (-e) highland, plateau; ~leraar (-s) professor
Hoog'lied Song of Solomon, Canticles
hoogmoe'dig (-e; -er, -ste) proud, haughty
hoog: ~nodig (-e) most necessary, urgently needed; ~oond (-e) blast furnace; ~sei-

soen high season; ~**spanning** high tension; ~**ste** highest, senior; *op sy* ~*ste,* at the most; ~**stens** at most, at best, at the outside

hoogs waarskynlik most probably

hoog'te (-s) height, altitude; hill; ~**punt** (-e) acme, zenith; pinnacle; ~**vrees** acrophobia, fear of heights

hoogty: ~ *vier,* reign supreme

hoog: ~**verraad** high treason; ~**waardigheidsbekleër** (-s) dignitary; VIP

hooi hay; *te veel* ~ *op sy vurk neem,* too many irons in the fire; ~**koors** hay fever

hool (hole) hovel, unsavoury dwelling

hoop[1] (s) (**verwagtings**) hope; *dis te hope dat,* it is to be hoped that; ~ *koester,* cherish hope

hoop[2] (s) (**hope**) heap; crowd

hoop'vol (-le; -ler, -ste) hopeful, sanguine

hoor (s): *'n lawaai dat* ~ *en sien vergaan,* a deafening noise; (w) (**ge-**) hear, listen, heed, learn; *horende doof wees,* sham deafness; ~**baar** (..**bare**) audible; ~**beeld** feature programme (radio)

hoor'spel (..**ele**) radio play/drama

hoor'stuk (-ke) receiver (tel.)

hoort (**ge-**) belong, be proper, ought; *dit* ~ *nie hierby nie,* it does not belong here

ho'peloos (..**lose;** ..**loser,** -**ste**) hopeless

ho'ring (-s) horn; *die huis op* ~**s** *neem,* create an uproar

ho'rinkie (-s) little horn; (icecream) cone

ho'rison (-ne, -te) horizon

horisontaal' (..**tale**) horizontal, level; ..*tale kommunikasie,* horizontal communication

horlo'sie (-s) watch; clock, *ook* **oorlosie**

hor'relvoet (-e) clubfoot, *ook* **klompvoet**

hor'ries delirium tremens

hor'tjie (-s) wire blind, shutter; ~**blinder** (-s), ~**blinding** (-s) (Venetian) blind

hospitaal' (..**tale**) hospital

hospitalisa'sie hospitalisation

hostel' (-le) (mine) hostel

hot left (team of animals); ~ *en haar stuur,* send from pillar to post; *dit* ~*agter kry,* have a difficult time

hotel' (-le, -s) hotel; ~**houer** (-s), ~**ier'** (-s) hotelkeeper; ~**joggie** (-s) page boy

hot'klou southpaw (lefthander)

hot'tentotsgot (-te) praying mantis

hou[1] (s) (-e) blow, cut, stroke, lash; (w) (**ge-**) cut, hack; strike

hou[2] (w) (**ge-**) keep, hold; contain; lash; fulfil; *links* ~, keep left; ~ *van,* like; ~**ding** (-e, -s) conduct, bearing, attitude, deportment, pose; *'n* ~*ding aanneem,* strike a pose; ~**er** (-s) container; ~**er'diens** container service; ~**er'maatskappy** (-e) holding company; ~**er'skip** container vessel

hout (-e) wood, timber

hout'jie (-s) bit of wood; *iets op eie* ~ *doen,* do something off one's own bat

houts'kool charcoal

hout'snee (..**sneë**) woodcut; ~**kuns, hout'snykuns** art of wood engraving

hou'vas hold, handle, hold fast, foothold; ~ *hê op iem.,* have a hold on someone

hu (**ge-**) marry, wed; ~**baar** (..**bare**) marriageable

huid (-e) hide, skin

hui'dige present, modern, recent; *die* ~ *lewensduurte,* the present cost of living

hui'gel (**ge-**) dissemble, feign, sham; ~**aar** (-s) hypocrite

huigelary' hypocrisy, dissimulation, cant

huil (**ge-**) cry; weep; howl; *dis om van te* ~, it is enough to make one weep

huis (-e) house, dwelling, household; ~ *en haard,* hearth and home; *die* ~ *op horings neem,* turn the house upside down; *elke* ~ *het sy kruis,* there is a skeleton in every cupboard; ~ *toe,* home(wards); ~**braak** housebreaking, burglary; ~**breker** (-s) burglar; ~**dier** (-e) domestic animal; ~**dokter** (-s) family doctor; ~**genoot** (..**note**) house mate; inmate (of the same house); ~**gesin** (-ne) family, household

huishou'delik (-e) economical, domestic; *'n* ~*e aangeleentheid,* a domestic/internal affair

huis: ~**houding** (-s) household; housekeeping; ~**houdkunde** domestic science, home economics; ~**houdskool** (..**skole**) school for domestic science; ~**huur** (..**hure**) house rent; ~**inwyding** (-s) housewarming

huis'lik (-e, -er, -ste) domestic, homely; ~*e pligte,* household duties/chores

huis'ves (**ge-**) house, lodge, give boarding; ~*ting verskaf,* provide boarding/shelter

huis: ~**vlyt** home craft, home industry; ~**vrou** (-e, -ens) wife, housewife; ~**werk** homework, *kyk* **tuiswerk**

hui'wer (ge-) shiver, tremble

hul (pers. vnw) they, them; (besit; vnw) their, *ook* **hulle**

hul'de homage; ~ *betuig/bring aan,* do homage to; ~**blyk** (-e) mark of respect, tribute

hul'dig (ge-) do homage, honour

hul'le they; their, them; *Jan-~,* John and his party

hulp help, aid, support; assistant; *eerste~,* first aid; ~ *verleen,* render assistance

hul'peloos (..lose; ..loser, -ste) helpless

hulp: ~**middel** (-e, -s) aid, means, makeshift, expedient; ~**troepe** auxiliary troops

hulpvaar'dig (ge-; -er, -ste) helpful

hulp'werkwoord (-e) auxiliary verb

humeur' (-e) temper, mood, humour; *uit sy ~ wees,* be in a bad temper

humeu'rig (-e; -er, -ste) bad tempered, moody

hu'mor humour; ~**sin** sense of humour

humoris' (-te) humorist; ~**ties** (-e) humorous, humoristic

hun'ker (ge-) long for, hanker for

hup'pel (ge-) skip, hop, frolic

hups (-e) lively, pretty, fine

hup'stootjie (-s) a last push/shove

hurk (ge-) squat

hur'ke haunches; *op sy ~ sit,* squat

hus'se: *dis ~ met lang ore,* curiosity killed the cat

hut (-te) hut, cottage; cabin; hovel

huur (s) (hure) rent, hire, lease, tenancy; *die ~ opsê,* give notice; (w) (ge-) hire, rent, engage, charter; *te ~,* to let; ~**der** (-s) tenant, lessee; ~**geld** (-e) rental, rent; ~**koop** hire purchase; ~**moordenaar** hitman; ~**motor** hired car, rent-a-car; ~**pag** occupational lease; ~**soldaat** (..date) mercenary; ~**tol** (-le) royalty, *kyk* **vrugreg;** ~**vliegtuig** (..uie) chartered plane

hu'welik (-e) marriage, wedding, wedlock; *in die ~ tree,* enter into matrimony

hu'weliks: ~**berader** (-s) marriage counsellor; ~**bootjie** (-s) boat of hymen; *in die ~bootjie stap,* get married

hu'weliks: ~**gebooie** banns; ~**onthaal** (..hale) wedding reception; ~**reis** (-e) honeymoon trip; ~**voorwaarde(s)** antenuptial contract

hy he; it

hyg (ge-) pant, gasp for breath

hys (ge-) hoist; ~**bak** (-ke) skip, lift, elevator; ~**er**, (-s) lift, elevator, ~**ertrap** (-pe) escalator, *kyk* **roltrap;** ~**kraan** (..krane) crane

I

i (-'s) i; *die puntjies op die i's sit,* dot one's i's

ideaal' (ideale) ideal

idealis': ~**me** idealism; ~**ties** (-e) idealistic

idee' (ideë, -s) idea, notion

iden'ties (-e) identical

identifika'sie identification

identifiseer' (~, geïd-) identify; *die probleme ~,* identify the problems

identiteit' identity

idil'le (-s) idyll

idioma'ties (-e) idiomatic

idioom' (idiome) idiom

idioot' (idiote) idiot, imbecile

ie'der (-e) each, every one, every; ~**een,** everybody, everyone

ie'mand someone, somebody

iesegrim'mig (-e; -er, -ste) surly, grumbling

ietermago' (-'s), **ietermagô'** (-'s), **ietermagog'** (-ge, -s) pangolin, scaly anteater

iets something, anything; ~ *moois,* something beautiful

ie'wers somewhere

ignoreer' (~, geïg-) ignore

illustra'sie (-s) illustration

imbesiel' (-e) imbecile

im'mer every, always; ~**groen** evergreen

im'mers yet, but, indeed, though; *hy behoort ~ beter te weet,* he should, after all, know better

immigrant' (-e) immigrant

immigra'sie immigration

immoraliteit' immorality

immoreel' (..rele) immoral
immuun' (**immune**) immune
imperatief' (..tiewe) imperative
imperialis' (-te) imperialist; **~me** impe‑
rialism; **~ties** (-e) imperialistic
im'pie (-s) impi
implement' (-e) (s), (farm) machinery,
tools
implementeer' (**~**, **geïm-**) (w) implement
implika'sie (-s) implication
imponeer' (**geïm-**) impress forcibly, awe
improvisa'sie (-s) improvisation
improviseer' (**geïm-**) improvise
impuls' (-e) impulse
impulsief' (..siewe) impulsive
in¹ (w) (**geïn**) gather, collect; *belastings* **~**,
collect taxes
in² (vs) in, into, within, during; **~** *die ses‑
tig*, turned sixty
in ag neem (**in ag ge-**) observe, consider,
take account of
in'asem (**-ge-**) inhale, breathe in; *rook* **~**,
inhale smoke
in'begrepe included; *alles* **~**, everything
included, all found
in'begrip inclusion; *met* **~** *van,* including
in'boesem (**-ge-**) inspire, fill, strike (fear)
into
in'boet (**-ge-**) plant in between; lose; *die
lewe* **~**, pay with one's life
in'boorling (-e) native, aborigine
in'bors character, nature, temper
in'bou (**-ge-**) build in; *ingeboude kaste*,
built-in wardrobes
in'braak (**inbrake**) housebreaking, burg‑
lary
in'breek (**-ge-**) break into, burgle
in'breker (**-ge-**) housebreaker, burglar
in'breuk infringement, transgression; **~**
maak op, encroach upon
in'deel (**-ge-**) divide, classify
in'deks (-e) index
in'deling (-e -s) division, classification
indemniteit' indemnity, indemnification
inderdaad' indeed, really, in fact
inderhaas' hurriedly, in haste
indertyd' at the time, formerly
Indiaan' (**Indiane**) Red Indian; **~s'**, (-e)
Red Indian
in'dien¹ (w) (**-ge-**) hand in, lodge, tender,
present, submit; *'n klag* **~**, lay a com‑
plaint

indien'² (vgw) if, in case; *hy sal kom* **~** *dit
nie reën nie,* he will come if it isn't raining
indiens': **~nemer** employer; **~neming** em‑
ployment; **~opleiding** in-service/in-com‑
pany training; **~plasing** job placement
in-die-oog'-lopend (-e) salient, obvious
In'diër (-s) Indian, *kyk* **Asiër**; **~sake** In‑
dian Affairs
In'dies (-e) Indian; **~e** *rys*, Indian rice
in'direk (-te) indirect
individu', **indiwidu'** (-e, -'s) individual
individualis' (-te) individualist; **~me** in‑
dividualism; **~ties** (-e) individualistic
indoe'na (-s) induna, tribal councillor
indoktrina'sie indoktrine'ring indoctri‑
nation
in'dring (**-ge-**) penetrate, intrude, force in;
~er (-s) intruder; gatecrasher
in'druk (s) (**-ke**) impression; *onder die* **~**
verkeer, be under the impression; *die* **~**
wek, create the impression
indrukwek'kend (-e; -er, -ste) impressive
industrieel' (..riële) industrial
ineens' at once, at the same moment
ineen'stort (**-gestort**) fall in, collapse, *kyk*
instort
in'ent (**ingeënt**) inoculate, vaccinate; **~ing**
vaccination, inoculation
infaam' (**infame**) infamous, shameful; *'n
infame leuen,* an outrageous lie
infanterie' infantry
infanteris' (-te) infantryman, foot soldier
infek'sie infection
infinitief' (..tiewe) infinitive
inflamma'sie inflammation
infla'sie inflation; **~spiraal** (..ale) infla‑
tion(ary) spiral
influen'sa influenza, *ook* **griep**
informant' (-e) informer
informa'sie information, *ook* **inligting**
informa'tika information studies
informeel' (..mele) informal; ..mele *drag*
informal attire/dress
in'gaan (**-ge-**) enter; go in for; take effect;
~ *op iets,* consider/study/examine some‑
thing
in'gang (-e) entrance, entry; doorway; *met*
~ *5 Junie,* with effect from 5 June
in'gebore inborn, innate
in'gebou (**-de**): **~de** *vermoë/bekwaamheid,*
built-in ability

ingedag'te absent-minded, absorbed in thought

in'gee (-ge-) give in, inspire, administer; stop; yield, surrender

in'gelê (ingelegde) inlaid; canned, preserved, furnished; *ingelegde/ingemaakte perskes*, canned peaches

in'gelyf (-de) incorporated, embodied

in'gemaak (-te) canned

ingenieur' (-s) engineer; *raadgewende ~*, consulting engineer; *~s'wese* engineering (subject), *kyk* **geniëring**

in'genome pleased, charmed, taken up with; *met jouself ~ wees*, be pleased with oneself

in'gerig (-te) arranged, prepared, organised, furnished; *hy het sy kantoor pragtig ~*, he has equipped his office beautifully

in'geskrewe enrolled; registered; conscript; *~ student*, registered student; *~ klerk*, articled clerk, *kyk* **leerklerk**

in'getoë modest, discreet, sedate

in'geval in case; *~ dit gebeur*, if it should happen

ingevol'ge in terms of, in pursuance of, as a result, in consequence of

in'gewande bowels, intestines, entrails

in'gewikkel(d) (-de) complicated, intricate

in'gewing (-e, -s) inspiration; suggestion; *skielike ~*, sudden (bright) idea

in'gewy (-de) initiated, inaugurated

in'gryp (-ge-) intervene, step in; encroach

in'haal (-ge-) overtake, catch up with; receive in state; make up for

inha'lig (-e, -er, -ste) greedy, covetous, niggardly

in'ham (-me) inlet, creek, bay

inheems' (-e) native, home, indigenous; endemic; *~e bosse*, indigenous forests

inhibi'sie inhibition, hang-up, phobia

in'hou (-ge-) restraint, keep in check; contain; retain; *jou ~*, control one's temper

in'houd contents; capacity, purport; *~(s)maat* cubic measure; *~(s)opgawe* index, table of contents

in'huldig (-ge-) inaugurate, install (mayor)

inisiatief' initiative

ink (-te) ink; *skryf met ~*, write in ink

in'keep (-ge-) notch, indent (paragraph)

in'keer repentance; *tot ~ kom*, repent

inken'nig (-e; -er, -ste) shy, timid

in'klaar (-ge-) clear in, clear (goods)

in'klim (-ge-), climb into; rebuke

inkluis' included

inklusief' (..siewe) inclusive; *AVB ~*, GST inclusive

in'kom (-ge-) come in(to), enter

in'komste (soms -s) income, earnings, receipts; *~ en uitgawes*, revenue and expenditure; *~belasting* income tax

in'koop (s) (..kope) purchase(s); buying; (w) **(-ge-)** buy, purchase; *~prys (-e)* cost price

in'kopie (-s) small purchase; *~s doen*, go shopping

inkorpora'sie incorporation

inkorporeer' (geïnkor-) incorporate, *kyk* **inlyf**

ink: ~vis (-se) cuttlefish, sepia, squid; *~vlek (-ke)* inkstain (blot)

in'laat (s) (inlate) inlet, intake; (w) **(-ge-)** let in, admit; *jou ~ met*, have dealings with

in'lae (-s) enclosure (document); deposit (money)

in'lander (-s) native

in'lê (-ge-) can; deposit, invest; inlay

in'leg: ~geld (-e) stakes; entrance money; investment; *~strokie (-s)* deposit slip

in'lei (-ge-) introduce, preface; usher in; *~ding (-e, -s)* introduction, preface

in'lewer (-ge-) deliver up, send in, hand in; submit; *die taak ~*, hand in the assignment

in'lig (-ge-) inform, enlighten

in'ligting (-e, -s) information, intelligence; *~ inwin*, obtain information; *meer/nader(e) ~*, further information

in'lyf, in'lywe (-ge-) incorporate; *ingelyfde vereniging sonder winsoogmerk*, incorporated association not for gain

in'lywing incorporation

in'maak (-ge-) can, preserve; *~fabriek (-e)* cannery

inmekaar' into each other

in'meng (-ge-) meddle, interfere; *jou in 'n ander se sake ~*, meddle with another's business

inmid'dels meanwhile, in the meantime

in'name capture, taking; collection

in'neem (-ge-) take, take in; conquer

inne'mend (-e; -er; -ste) captivating, fascinating, attractive

in'nerlik (-e) inner; internal, intrinsic

in'nig (-e; -er, -ste) cordial, sincere, fervent, fond; intrinsic; ~e meegevoel/simpatie, sincere sympathy

in'pak (-ge-) pack; jou koffers ~, pack one's suitcases

in'palm (-ge-) haul in; get possession of, appropriate

in'pas (-ge-) fit in

in'perk (-ge-) restrict, ban

in'plof (w) implode; ~fing implosion

in'pomp (-ge-) pump in; cram

in'prent (-ge-) imprint, impress, inculcate; hom allerlei bogstories ~, stuff his head with all kinds of nonsense

in'rig (-ge-) arrange, organise; fit up, equip

in'rigting (-e, -s) arrangement; establishment, institution

in'roep (-ge-) call in

in'ruil (-ge-) exchange, barter; ~waarde trade-in value (car)

in'ry (-ge-) ride/drive in; ~teater (-s) drive-in theatre, ook veldfliek

in'sae inspection, perusal; ter ~, for perusal

in'samel (-ge-) gather, collect; ~ing (-e, -s) collection; ~ing(s)veldtog fund raising campaign/drive

in'sek (-te) insect; ~doder insecticide, pesticide

in'sekte: ~kunde entomology; ~kundige (-s) entomologist

insemina'sie insemination; kunsmatige ~ (K.I.), artificial insemination (A.I.)

in'send (-ge-) send in, contribute; ~ing (-e, -s) contribution, exhibit

in'set (-te) stakes (gambling); pool; input; boerdery verg hoë ~te, farming requires/demands high inputs

ins'gelyks likewise, in the same way

in'sien (-ge-) look into; understand, realise

in'sig (-te) insight, view, opinion; iem. met ~, a man of discernment

in'sink (-ge-) sink in, sag, subside; ~ing subsidence, collapse; relapse

insinueer' (~, geïn-) insinuate, hint indirectly

in'sit (-ge-) strike up; begin (song); install; put in; set in; be inside

in'skakel (-ge-) switch on (light); tune in (radio); insert; connect up; put into gear

in'skeep (-ge-) ship, take on board

in'skep (-ge-) ladle into; dish up

in'skerp (-ge-) inculcate, impress; reinforce; die oefening ~, repeat/drill the exercise

in'skiet (-ge-) shoot into; sy lewe ~ by, lose his life in

inskik'lik (-e; -er, -ste) complying, yielding, willing, affable

in'skink (-ge-) pour in

inskrip'sie (-s) inscription

in'skryf, in'skrywe (-ge-) inscribe; subscribe; enrol, enlist, enter; tender; jou laat ~, enter, sign on; ~geld (-e) entrance fee; ~vorm (-s) entry form

in'skrywing (-e, -s) subscription, enrolment, registration, entry, tender

in'slaan (-ge-) drive in, smash, strike; swallow (drink); ~ by die publiek, catch the popular fancy

in'slag woof; skering en ~, warp and woof

in'sleep (-ge-) drag in(to); tow; ~diens breakdown service; tow-away service; ~wa breakdown van/lorry

in'sleutel (w) (-ge-) feed (computer)

in'sluimer (-ge-) doze off, fall asleep

in'sluit (-ge-) enclose; include, shut in, contain, embrace; hierby ingesluit, enclosed herewith

in'sluk (-ge-) swallow

in'smokkel (-ge-) smuggle in

insolvent' insolvent, bankrupt

inson'derheid especially

inson'derheid especially

in'span (-ge-) exert; inspan; jou ~, exert oneself; ~ning exertion, strain, effort

inspek'sie (-s) inspection

inspekteer' (~, geïn-) inspect

inspekteur' (-s) inspector

inspira'sie inspiration

inspireer' (~, geïn-) inspire

in'spraak dictate(s) (of one's heart); joint consultation, participation; hulle leiers wil ~ hê in landsake, their leaders want a say in national issues

in'spring (-ge-) jump in(to); indent (lines)

in'spuit (-ge-) inject; ~ing (-e, -s) injection; skraag~ing booster injection

in'staan (-ge-) guarantee, warrant, vouch for; vir die waarheid ~, vouch for the truth

installa'sie (-s) installation, kyk aanleg

installeer' (geïn-) install; inaugurate

in stand hou (in stand ge-) maintain, keep up
instand' houding maintenance, upkeep
instand' houkoste maintenance costs
instan' sie instance, place; body, person (in power); *in eerste ~*, in the first place; *verwys na ander ~s*, refer to other bodies/parties
in'stel (-ge-) institute, establish, introduce; *ondersoek ~*, make investigations; **~ling** (-e, -s) institution, establishment
in'stem (-ge-) agree, concur; tune in; **~mer** (-s) tuner (radio); **~ming** agreement, accord; assent; *met algemene ~ming*, by common consent
in'stink (-te) instinct
instinkma'tig (-e) instinctive
instinktief' (..tiewe) instinctive
instituut' (..tute) institute
in'stort (-ge-) collapse, tumble down; relapse; **~ing** relapse; collapse
in'stroom (-ge-) stream in(to), flock in(to); **~beheer** influx control
instruk'sie (-s) instruction, direction
instrukteur' (-s) instructor
instrument' (-e) instrument, tool, implement; **~paneel (..nele)** dashboard
in'studeer (-ge-) study; practise (songs)
in'sypel (-ge-) infiltrate; **~aar (-s)** infiltrator; **~ing** infiltration
inteen' deel on the contrary; *hulle is nie arm nie; ~, hulle is skatryk;* they are not poor; on the contrary, they are very well-off, *kyk* **daarenteen**
integra'sie integration, combination of parts
integre'rend (-e) integral, integrating; *~e deel van*, integral part of
integriteit' integrity
in'teken (-ge-) subscribe; *op 'n maandblad ~*, subscribe to a monthly (magazine); **~aar (-s, ..nare)** subscriber; **~geld (-e)** subscription; **~ing (-e, -s)** subscription; **~lys (-te)** subscription list
inteliek' (-te) intellect
intellektueel' (..tuele) intellectual
intelligen'sie intelligence; **~diens** intelligence service; **~kwosiënt** intelligence quotient
intelligent' (-e; -er, -ste) intelligent, bright
intens' (-e) intense
intensief' (..siewe; ..siewer, -ste) intensive; *(intensiewe) sorgeenheid, waakeenheid*, intensive care unit

interessant' (-e; -er, -ste) interesting
interesseer' (geïn-) interest, be interested in; *hy is geïnteresseer in tuinmaak*, he is interested in gardening
intermediêr' (-e) intermediate
intern' (-e) intern, internal; *~e beheer*, internal control; *~e eksamen*, internal examination; *~e kontrole*, internal check
internasionaal' (..nale) international
internis' (-te) specialist physician
interplanetêr' (-e) interplanetary; *~e vlugte*, interplanetary flights
interpreta'sie (-s) interpretation, *kyk* **vertolking**
interprovinsiaal' (..siale) interprovincial
interpunk'sie interpunction, punctuation
intiem' (-e; -er, -ste) intimate
intona'sie (-s) intonation
in'trede entry, entrance
in'tree (w) (-ge-) enter, go in; *hiermee het 'n nuwe tydperk ingetree*, this marks a new era; **~geld** admission/entrance fee; **~preek (..preke)** induction sermon; **~rede (-s)** inaugural address; maiden speech (parliament)
in'trek (s) abode, residence; *sy ~ neem*, settle, come to live; (w) (-ge-) go in, move in (house); draw in (smoke); repeal (an act); cancel (leave); revoke (an edict); *nuwe ~kers*, new occupants/neighbours
intri'ge (-s) intrigue, plot, scheme
introduk'sie (-s) introduction
intuï'sie intuition
intuïtief' (..tiewe) intuitive
intus'sen meanwhile, in the meantime
in'val (s) (-le) idea, thought; raid, invasion; (w) (-ge-) collapse; occur; join in
invali'de (-s) invalid
inventa'ris (-se) inventory; *die ~ opmaak*, take stock
in'vlie(g) (-ge-) fly in(to); rebuke
in'vloed (-e) influence; **~ryk (-e; -er, -ste)** influential; **~werwing** canvassing (for a job)
in'vloei (-ge-) flow in(to)
in'voeg (-ge-) put in, insert
in'voer (s) import(ation); (w) (-ge-) import; **~der (-s)** importer (of)
in'vorder (-ge-) collect (taxes); demand (payment)

in'vul (-ge-) fill in, fill up; *'n vorm ~,* complete a form
in'wendig (-e) internal, inner; *nie vir ~e gebruik nie,* not to be taken
in'willig (-ge-) grant, consent, agree
in'win (-ge-) obtain (information)
in'wissel (-ge-) exchange, cash
in'woner (-s) inhabitant, resident
in'woning (board and) lodging
in'woon (-ge-) board, lodge

in'wy (-ge-) open, initiate, ordain, conse=crate; ~ding (-e, -s) opening, inaugura=tion, initiation
ipekon'ders whims, caprices; imaginary ailments, *ook* hipokonders
i'ris (-se) iris
ironie' irony
iro'nies (-e) ironical
isola'sie isolation
ivoor' ivory

J

ja yes; *op alles ~ en amen sê,* agree to everything
ja(ag) (ge-) chase, pursue; race; *iem. die skrik op die lyf ~,* give someone a terrible fright.
jaag: ~duiwel (-s) helldriver
jaar (jare) year; *~ in en ~ uit,* from one year to another; ~einde year-end; ~geld (-e) annuity; ~gety (-e) season; ~liks (-e) yearly, annual; ~syfer (-s) year mark, record
jaart (-s) yard
jaar: ~tal (-le) date; ~telling (-e, -ste) era; ~vergadering (-s) annual (general) meeting
jaar'verslag (..slae) annual report
ja'broer (-s) yes-man
jag¹ (s) (-te) yacht
jag² (-te) hunt, chase (of game); *die ~ na rykdom,* the pursuit of wealth; (w) (ge-) hunt; ~geselskap (-pe) hunting party
jags (-e) ruttish, in heat
jag'ter (-s) hunter, huntsman
jakaran'da (-s) jacaranda
jak'kals (-e) jackal; sly person; *~ prys sy eie stert,* he blows his own trumpet
Ja'kob: *die ware ~,* Mr Right, the right man
jakopreg'op (-pe, -s) zinnia (flower)
jakope'weroë protruding eyes
jaloers' (-e; -er, -ste) jealous, envious; ~heid jealousy, envy
jaloesie' jealousy, envy
jam'be (-s) iambus
jam'bies (-e) iambic
jam'mer (s) pity; misery; (b) (-der, -ste) sorry; *hoe ~!* what a pity!

jam'mer: ~lappie (-s) damp cloth for wip=ing hands/mouth; ~lik (-e) miser=able, pitiable; ~te sorrow; *iets uit ~te doen* do something out of pity
Jan John; *~ burger,* John Citizen; *~ rap en sy maat,* rag-tag and bobtail; *~ salie,* a nonentity, stick-in-the-mud; *~ Taks* Receiver of Revenue; *~ Tuisbly: met ~ Tuisbly se karretjie ry,* have to stay at home
ja-nee'! sure! indeed!
janfiskaal' (..kale, -s) butcherbird, fiscal shrike
janfre'derik (-e, -s) Cape redbreast, robin=chat
jangroen'tjie (-s) malachite sunbird
janmaat' (-s) jack tar
jan'na (-s) jeans
Jan'tjie, Jannetjie Johnnie; *~ wees,* be jealous
Janua'rie (-s) January
ja'pie (-s) johnny; bumpkin, clodhopper
japsnoet' (-e) inquisitive/impertinent child; wise-acre, know-all
jap'trap: *in 'n ~,* in a jiffy, in no time
ja'relange long-continued; *ons ~ vriend=skap,* friendship of many years standing
jare lank for years (on end)
jas (-se) coat, greatcoat
jasmyn' jasmine
ja'vel (-s) lout, bumpkin, *ook* gomtor
ja'woord consent, permission, promise; *die ~ kry,* be accepted (as lover)
jeens to, towards, by
jelei'boontjie (-s) jelly bean
jel'lie (-s) jelly
jene'wer gin
jeremia'de (-s) jeremiad, woeful tale

Je'sus Jesus

jeug youth; *in sy prille ~*, in his early youth

jeug'dig (-e) young, youthful; ~e (-s) juvenile

jeug: ~herberg (-e) youth hostel; **~klub** (-s) youth club; **~misdaad** (..dade) juvenile crime; **~misdadigheid, ~wangedrag** juvenile delinquency; **~weerbaarheid** youth preparedness

jeuk (ge-) itch

jig gout

jo'del (ge-) yodel

jo'dium iodine

joernaal' (..nale) journal, newspaper; logbook; **~inskrywing** (-s) journal entry

joernalis' (-te) journalist, pressman

joernalistiek' journalism

jog'gie (-s) caddie (golf)

jog'hurt yoghurt

jok (ge-) lie, tell stories

jok'kie (-s) jockey

jol (ge-) make merry, make fun

jo'lig (-e) jolly, merry

jolyt' merry-making, revelry

jong (s) (-es) young (animal): (w) (ge-) bring forth young; (b, attributive) (-er, -ste) young; *van ~s af*, from an early age; *die ~ste berigte*, the latest news/intelligence

jon'geling (-e) youth, young man

jon'genskool (..skole), boys' school; *hoër ~*, boys' high school, *kyk* **hoër seunskool**

jong'getroude (-s) newly married person; *~ paar*, newly married couple

jong: ~kêrel (-s) bachelor, young man; **~leur** (-s) juggler; **~meisie** (-s) young girl, lass; **~span** young people

jonk[1] (s) (-e) junk (sailing vessel)

jonk[2] (b, predicative) (**jonger, jongste**) young

jon'ker (-s) squire; *hoe kaler ~, hoe groter pronker*, great boast, small roast

jool (jole) (students') rag, fun, jollification; **~blad** (..blaaie) rag magazine; **~koningin** (-ne) rag queen; **~optog** (-te) rag procession

joos: *dit mag ~ weet*, goodness knows

jou[1] (w) (ge-) boo

jou[2] (pers. vnw), you; (besit. vnw) yours

jou'e, jou'ne yours; *dis ~*, it is yours

joviaal' (..viale; ..vialer, -ste) jovial, jolly

ju'bel (s) rejoicing, cheering; (w) (ge-) rejoice, cheer, exult

jubile'um (-s) jubilee

juf'frou (-e, -ens) miss, young lady; (lady) teacher

juig (ge-) rejoice, exult

juis (b) (-te; -ter, -ste) exact, correct; (bw) exactly, precisely; *~ wat nodig is*, just exactly what is needed; *~ter gesê*, to be more precise

juistement' exactly, certainly

juist'heid correctness, exactitude

juk'skei (-e) yokepin, yokeskey; *'n orige ~*, a fifth wheel to the coach; **~laer** (-s) jukskei league

Ju'lie (-s) July

jul'le (pers. vnw) you; (besit. vnw) your

Ju'nie (-s) June

ju'nior (s) (-s) junior; (b) junior

ju'rie (-s) jury

justi'sie justice; *die Minister van J~*, the Minister of Justice

ju'te jute

juweel' (juwele) jewel, precious stone, gem

juwelier' (-s) jeweller; **~s'ware** jewellery

jy you; *~ kan nooit weet nie*, one never knows

K

kaai (-e) wharf, quay

kaai'man (-ne, -s) alligator, cayman

kaak[1] (kake) jaw

kaak[2] (kake) pillory; *aan die ~ stel*, expose to public contempt

kaal (kale; kaler, -ste) bald, bare, naked; *daar ~ van afkom*, come off second best; **~bas** (-se) nudist; **~(bas)swemmer** nude bather; **~hol** streak; **~holler** streaker; **~kop** (-pe) baldpate, baldhead; *iem. ~kop die waarheid sê*, go for a person baldheaded; **~perske** (-s) nectarine; **~voet** barefoot

Kaap[1] Cape; Cape Town

kaap[2] (s) (**kape**) cape, promontory

kaap[3] (w) (ge-) practise piracy, hijack, steal

Kaap: ~land, ~provinsie Cape Province

Kaaps (-e) Cape; *die ~se dokter*, the south-easter; *~e draaie maak*, take sharp turns; *so oud soos die ~e wapad*, as old as the hills

Kaap'stad Cape Town

kaart (-e) map, chart; card; ticket; *'n deur- gestoke ~*, a pre-arranged affair; *~ en transport*, title deed

kaar'tjie (-s) ticket; card

kaart: ~mannetjie (-s) jack-in-the-box; ~speel (-ge-) play cards

kaas (kase) cheese; ~-en-wynonthaal cheese and wine reception; ~burger (-s) cheese-burger

kaat'jie: ~ *van die baan wees*, be cock of the walk

Kaat'jie: ~ Kekkelbek chatterbox

kaats (ge-) play (at) ball; ~er (-s) reflector

kabaai' (-e) loose gown

kabaal' noise, hubbub, clamour; *~ maak/ opskop*, raise Cain

kabaret' (-te) cabaret; ~liedjie (-s) cabaret song

kab'bel (ge-) babble, ripple

ka'bel (s) (-s) cable; *'n kink in die ~*, a hitch; (w) (ge-) cable; ~gram (-me) cable-gram

kabeljou' (-e) cod (fish); Cape salmon

ka'bel: ~spoor cableway; ~televisie closed-circuit television

kabinet' (-te) cabinet, case; ministry, cabinet

kabou'ter (-s) gnome, elf, imp; ~mannetjie hobgoblin, elf

ka'der (-s) frame, framework; skeleton

kadet' (-te) cadet

kaf chaff; nonsense, tommyrot; *~ verkoop*, talk nonsense; *iemand ~ loop*, knock spots off someone

kafee' (-s) café

kafete'ria (-s) cafeteria

kag'gel (-s) fireplace; range

kai'ing (-s) greave(s), browsel(s)

kajuit' (-e) cabin; ~raad council of war

kak (s, w) shit; (s) dung

kaka'o cocoa

ka'kebeen (..bene) jaw, jawbone; ~wa Voortrekker oxwagon

ka'kie (-s) khaki; tommy; ~bos (-se) kha-kibos

kak'kerlak (-ke) cockroach

kak'tus (-se) cactus

kalan'der (-s) weevil

kalant' (-e) rogue, scamp; old hand, sly fox; *ou ~, lank in die land*, someone who knows the ropes

kalbas' (-se) calabash, gourd

kalbas'sies orchitis

kalen'der (-s) calendar, almanac

kalf (s) (kalwers) calf; (w) (ge-) calve

kalfs'vleis veal

kali'ber calibre

kalk lime; *gebluste ~*, slaked lime

kalkoen' (-e) turkey; *hy is nie onder 'n ~ uitgebroei nie*, he is not as green as he looks

kalm (-e; -er, -ste) calm, quiet

kalmeer' (ge-) calm, soothe, allay; ~middel (-s) sedative, tranquilliser

kalme'rend (-e) calming, soothing

kalorie' (-ë) heat unit, calorie

kal'wer: ~hok (-ke) kraal for calves; *tot by oom Daantjie in die ~hok*, go the whole hog; ~liefde boy-and-girl-love, calflove, puppy love

kam (s) (-me) comb; crest; *almal oor die- selfde ~ skeer*, treat all alike; (w) (ge-) comb; card

kamas' (-te) gaiter, legging

kameel' (kamele) camel; giraffe; ~doring (-s) camelthorn; ~perd (-e) giraffe

kame'lia (-s) camelia

ka'mer (-s) room, chamber; *K~ van Koop- handel*, Chamber of Commerce; *K~ van Mynwese*, Chamber of Mines; *K~ van Nywerhede*, Chamber of Industries

ka'mera (-s) camera

kameraad' (..rade) comrade, companion, mate; ~skap companionship, comrade-ship

ka'mer: ~jas (-se) dressing gown; ~musiek chamber music

kam'ma, kammakas'tig, kammalie'lies quasi, so-called, as if (it were); bogus; *hy het ~ geleer*, he pretended to study

kam'mahortjie (-s) mock shutter

kam'makreef mock lobster

kamoefleer' (w) camouflage

kamp[1] (s) (-e) camp, encampment; (w) (ge-) camp; encamp

kamp[2] (s) (-e) fight, struggle; (w) (ge-) fight

kamp'bed (-dens) stretcher, *ook* **voukatel**

kampeer' (~, ge-) encamp; **~wa** (-ens) caravan

kampioen' (-e) champion; **~skap** (-pe) championship

kam'pus (-se) campus

kamp'vegter (-s) fighter (for a cause), champion; **~ vir vryheid** champion/advocate of liberty

kam'rat (-te) cogwheel

kam'tag, kam'tig = kamma

kan¹ (s) (-ne) can, jug; *die wysheid is in die ~,* be tipsy

kan² (w) (kon) be able, can

kana'rie (-s) canary

kandidaat' (..date) candidate, applicant

kandy' candy; **~suiker** sugar candy

kaneel' cinnamon

kan'fer camphor

kanferfoe'lie honeysuckle

kan'ferolie camphorated oil

kangaroe' (-s) kangaroo

kan'ker cancer, canker

kan'netjie (-s) small boy, kid, nipper; small jug, cannikin

kannibaal' (..bale) cannibal

kan'niedood (s) diehard; persister; variegated aloe; *hy is 'n regte ~,* he is everlasting; (b) indestructible

kano' (-'s) canoe

kanon'¹ (-ne) (big) gun; cannon (obsolete)

ka'non² canon (music)

kano'resies, kano'wedvaart canoe race

kano'vaarder (-s) canoeist

kans (-e) chance, opportunity, prospect; *'n ~ waag,* take a chance

kan'sel (-s) pulpit; chancery

kanselier' (-s) chancellor

kanselleer' (~, ge-) cancel

kant¹ (s) lace (fabric)

kant² (s) (-e) side, edge, brink; margin; *jou ~ bring,* do one's share; *~ kies,* side with; *~ en klaar,* quite ready; *aan ~ maak,* tidy

kanta'te (-s) cantata

kan'tel (ge-) topple, fall, capsize, tilt; **~demper** anti-roll bar

kantien' (-e) canteen, bar, pub; tin can

kant'lyn (-e) margin line; sideline

kantoor' (..tore) office

kant':~ruimte (-s) margin; **~strokie** counterfoil; **~tekening** (-e, -s) marginal note

kant'werk lacework, lace

kap¹ (s) (-pe) shade; cart hood; principal of roof; hatch

kap² (s) cut, chop (with axe); (w) **(ge-)** fell, cut wood, chop; paw (horse)

kap³ (w) (ge-) cut, dress (hair)

kapa'bel (-e) capable, in a fit state

kapasiteit' (-e) capacity, *kyk* **vermoë**

kapa'ter (s) (-s) castrated goat, cut he-goat; (w) castrate

kapel'¹ (-le) chapel

kapel'² (-le) cobra, *kyk* **koperkapel**

kapelaan' (-s) chaplain

ka'per (-s) hijacker, privateer, pirate, freebooter

kapitaal' (s) (..tale) capital; *~ en rente,* principal and interest; (b) (..tale) capital, splendid; **~delging** capital redemption; **~uitbreiding** capital expansion

kapitalis'me capitalism

kapitalis'ties (-e) capitalistic(al); *~e stelsel,* capitalist system

kapit'tel¹ (s) (-s) chapter; *vers en ~,* chapter and verse

kapit'tel² (w) (~, ge-) lecture, rebuke

kapituleer' (ge-) capitulate

kapok' (-) snow; wadding; capoc; (w) **(ge-)** snow; **~haantjie** (-s) bantam cock; cheeky fellow; **~hoender** (-s) bantam fowl

kapot' (-ter, -ste) broken; exhausted, tired

kap'per (-s) hairdresser

kap'pertjie (-s) nasturtium

kap'pie (-s) sun bonnet; canopy (of a bakkie); circumflex; **~kommando** (-'s) petticoat army

kap'sel (-s) hairdress, coiffure; **~parade** hairstyle parade

kap'sie: *~ maak teen/op,* raise (captious) objections

kap:~stewel (-s) topboot, jackboot; **~stok** (-ke) hall stand, hat rack

kapsu'le (-s) capsule

kaptein' (-s) captain, chief

kar (-re) cart; (motor)car

karaat' (karate) carat

karabyn' (-e) carbine; **~katryn** (-e) female soldier (idiom)

karak'ter (-s) character, nature

karakteristiek' (s) (-e) characteristic; feature; (b) (-e) characteristic(al)

karak'ter: ~trek (-ke) characteristic trait; **~(uit)beelding** portrayal of character

karavaan' (..vane) caravan

karba' (-'s) wicker bottle, demijohn

kardinaal' (s) (..nale) cardinal; (b) (..nale) cardinal, chief

kardiograaf' (..grawe) cardiograph (apparatus)

kardiogram' (-me) cardiogram (recorded tracing)

kardoes' (-e) paperbag; cartridge; ~broek (-e) plusfours

karee'boom (..bome) karee tree

ka'rig (-e; -er, -ste) sparing, niggardly, scanty, frugal; *'n ~e maaltyd*, a scanty meal

kariljon' (-s) carillon, chimes

karkas' (-se) carcass

karkat'jie (-s) sty (on the eye)

karmenaad'jie (-s) choice piece of meat

karnal'lie (-s) rogue, scamp, rascal

karnaval' (-s) carnival

karnuf'fel (ge-) hug, fondle, cuddle; bully, manhandle

karos' (-se) skin rug, kaross

karp' (-e) carp

kar'ring (s) (-s) churn; (w) (ge-) churn; ~melk buttermilk

karton' cardboard, pasteboard; carton; ~doos (..dose) cardboard box

karwats' (-e) riding whip

karwei' (ge-) ride transport, cart; ~er (-s) transport rider; cartage/removals contractor; carrier, haulier

kas[1] (s) (-te) box; case; cupboard, chest, cabinet

kas[2] (s) (-te) socket (eye); cashbox, treasury; coffer; (w) (ge-) deposit, bank

kasarm' (-s) rambling house; *die hele ~*, the whole lot

kas'boek (-e) cash book

kaser'ne (-s) barracks, (army) camp

kaska'de (-s) cascade

kaskena'de (-s) prank, mischievous trick

kas'register (-s) cash register/till

kassa'we cassava, *kyk* broodwortel; manioc

kasset'speler (-s) cassette player

kassier' (-s) cashier

kastai'ing (-s) chestnut

kas'te (-s) caste

kasteel' (kastele) castle

kas'terolie castor oil

kas'tig = kamma

kastra'sie castration

kastreer' (~, ge-) castrate, geld

kastrol' (-le) stewpan, saucepan

kasty' (ge-) castigate, chastise, punish

kat (-te) cat; *die ~ uit die boom kyk*, wait and see which way the cat jumps; *die ~ in die donker knyp*, do things on the sly

kata'logus (-se) catalogue

katar' catarrh

katarak' (-te) cataract

katastro'fe (-s) catastrophe

katedraal' (..drale) cathedral

kategorie' (-ë) category

ka'tel (-s) bedstead

katjiepie'ring (-s) gardenia

katkisant' (-e) candidate for confirmation

katkisa'sie catechism (class)

kat'lagter (-s) babbler (bird)

katoen' cotton

katoe'ter (-s) gadget

Katoliek' (-e) Roman Catholic

kat'oog (..oë) cat's eye; reflectorised stud (on roads)

katrol' (-le) pulley; ~tou (-e) pulley rope

kats (s) (-e) cat-o'-nine-tails; (w) (ge-) thrash, lash, whip

kats'wink unconscious, dazed, in a swoon; *slaan iem. ~*, knock someone unconscious

kat'te: ~bak (-ke) dickey seat, rumble seat; ~kwaad mischief, naughtiness, tricks; ~kwaad doen/aanvang, be up to mischief; ~ry (-e) cattery (cat kennels)

kavalier' (-s) cavalier

kaviaar' caviare

keel (kele) throat; *sy eie ~ afsny*, cut one's own throat

ke'ël (-s) cone; skittle; icicle; ~spel skittles; ~vormig (-e) conical, *kyk* kegel

keep (s) (kepe) notch, indentation, nick; tally; (w) (ge-) notch

keer (s) (kere) turn; time; *drie ~*, three times; *te kere gaan*, make a fuss; rave; ~ *op ~*, time after time; (w) (ge-) turn; prevent; ~dag return day/date; ~kring (-e) tropic (line); ~punt turning point; ~sy other/reverse side; ~tyd return day/date; ~weer (..were) cul-de-sac, blind alley

kees (kese) monkey; *dis klaar met ~*, he is a goner

kef (ge-) yelp, yap

ke'gel (-s) cone; skittle, pin; ~baan pin alley; ~vormig conical

kei'ser (-s) emperor

keiserin' (-ne) empress

kei'ser: ~**ryk** (-e) empire; ~**snee** Caesarian operation

kek'kel (ge-) cackle; ~**bek** (-ke) chatterbox, slanderer

kel'der (s) (-s) cellar; bottom of the sea; *na die ~ gaan*, go to Davy Jones' locker; (w) (ge-) sink; ~**kamer** (-s) basement room; ~**verdieping** (-s) basement

kelk (-e) chalice, calyx

kel'kie (-s) wineglass

kelkiewyn' (-e) Namaqua sandgrouse

kel'ner (-s) waiter, steward

kelnerin' (-ne) waitress

ken¹ (s) (-ne) chin

ken² (w) (ge-) know; recognise; understand; *van buite ~*, know by heart; *te ~ne gee*, give to understand

ken: ~**letter(s)** designatory initials/title; ~**merk** (s) (-e) characteristic; feature; (w) ~**merk (ge-)** characterise; ~**merkend** (-e) characteristic

ken'netjie (-s) tipcat (game)

ken'nis knowledge, consciousness; intima= tion; (-se) acquaintance; ~ *gee*, give no= tice; ~ *maak met*, make acquaintance with; *in ~ stel*, notify; ~**gewing** (-e, -s) notice, announcement

ken: ~**strokie** (-s) name tag (at conferences); ~**teken** (-s) characteristic, distinctive mark; badge

ken'ter (ge-) change; turn upside down; ~**ing** turn; change; *'n ~ing in die oorlog*, a change of fortunes of war

ken'wysie (-s) theme/signature tune

ke'per (s) twill; *op die ~ beskou*, examine/ consider closely

keramiek' ceramics

ke're: *te ~ gaan*, make a fuss; carry on, rave

kê'rel (-s) fellow, chap; bloke, guy; *'n gawe ~*, a decent/fine chap; *haar ~*, her suit= or/boyfriend; *hulle is ~ en nooi*, they are on courting terms

ke'rende: *per ~ pos*, by return of post

kerf (s) (kerwe) notch, incision; (w)·(ge-) notch, carve; cut (tobacco); ~**stok** (-ke) nickstick

kerk (-e) church, chapel; congregation; *die koeël is deur die ~*, the die is cast

ker'ker (-s) dungeon

kerk'hof (..howe) churchyard, cemetery

kerk: ~**klok** (-ke) church bell; ~**muis** (-e) church mouse; *so arms soos 'n ~muis*, as poor as a church mouse; ~**plein** (-e) church square

kerm (ge-) lament, groan, whine

ker'mis (-se) fair, fête; *van 'n koue ~ tuis kom*, come away with a flea in your ear

kern (-s) kernel; core, pith; gist; nucleus; *die ~ van die saak*, the gist of the matter; ~**aangedrewe** nuclear powered; ~**afval** atomic waste

kernag'tig (-e; -er, -ste) pithy, terse

kern: ~**-as** nuclear fallout; ~**fisika** nuclear physics; ~**fusie** fusion of atom, nuclear fusion

kern: ~**krag** nuclear power; ~**reaktor** nu= clear reactor, cyclotron; ~**sillabus** (-se) core syllabus; ~**splyting** splitting of atom; ~**tyd** core time

ker'rie curry; ~**kos** curry food

kers (-e) candle

Kers: ~**aand** Christmas evening/Eve, *kyk* **Oukersaand;** ~**boom** (..bome) Christmas tree; ~**dag** Christmas Day; ~**fees** Christmas; ~**geskenk** (-e) Christmas box/ present

ker'sie (-s) cherry

Kers: ~**lied** (-ere) Christmas carol; ~**pastei** (-e) mince pie

kers'ten (ge-) christianise

Kers'vakansie Christmas holidays/vacation

ke'tel (-s) kettle; boiler (of engine)

ket'ter (-s) heretic, unbeliever; *vloek soos 'n ~*, swear like a trooper; ~**y** heresy

ket'ting (-s) chain; ~**reaksie** (-s) chain re= action

keur (s) choice, selection; (-e) charter, by= law; *te kus en te ~*, for the choosing; (w) (ge-) test, try, judge; seed (sport); *die eer= ste ge~de*, the first seed; assay (minerals); ~**der** (-s) selector (sport); ~**graad** choice grade (butter)

keu'rig (-e; -er, -ste) fine, exquisite, nice

keu'ring selection; ~**toets** (-e) efficiency/ aptitude test, *kyk* **aanlegtoets**

keur: ~**koop** bargain; ~**merk** hallmark; ~**raad** selection board

keurs'lyf (..lywe) bodice, corset

keu'se (-s) choice, selection; *volgens ~*, as you like; *uit vrye ~*, of one's own free will

ke'wer (-s) beetle

kiaat'hout teak (wood)

kib'bel (ge-) quarrel, squabble, bicker

kie'kie (-s) snap, snapshot

kiel (-e) keel (of a ship); **~haal (ge-)** keel=haul, careen

kiel'houer (-s) pickaxe

kie'lie (ge-) tickle

kiem (s) (-e) germ; embryo; *in die ~ smoor,* nip in the bud; (w) **(ge-)** germinate

kie'persolboom (..bome) umbrella tree

kie'piemielie (-s) popcorn

kie'rie (-s) stick, walking stick; **~wisselaar** floorshift (car) `

kies¹ (s) (-e, -te) cheek pouch; molar (tooth), grinder

kies² (w) (ge-) choose, elect, pick; *sy woorde ~,* pick one's words carefully

kies³ (b) (-e; -er, -ste) delicate, dainty

kies: ~afdeling (-s) electoral division; con=stituency; **~baar (..bare)** eligible; **~distrik (-te)** constituency

kie'ser (-s) voter, elector; **~s'lys (-te)** vo=ters' roll

kieskeu'rig (-e; -er, -ste) particular, fasti=dious

kieskollége (-s) college of electors

kies'tand (-e) molar (tooth), grinder

kiet(s) quits, equal; *ons is ~,* we are quits

kiet'siesorg (s) cattery, *ook* **kattery**

kieu (-e, kuwe) gill

kie'wiet (-e) lapwing, noisy plover

kik (s) (-ke) scarcely audible sound; *g'n ~ nie,* keep mum

kikoe'joegras kikuyu grass

kil (-le; -ler, -ste) chilly, cold; *'n ~(le) ont=vangs,* a chilly reception

ki'lo (-'s) kilo; **~gram (-me)** kilogram; **~liter (-s)** kilolitre; **~meter (-s)** kilometre; **~watt (-s)** kilowatt

kind (-ers) child; infant, baby; *'n ~ des doods,* a doomed man; *~ nòg kraai hê,* have neither kith nor kin; *geremde ~,* backward child; *gestremde ~,* handicap=ped child; *vertraagde ~,* retarded child

kinderag'tig (-e; -er, -ste) childish, silly

kin'der: ~arts (-e) paediatrician; **~hawe (-s)** crèche; **~jare** childhood; **~lik (-e; -er, -ste)** childlike, innocent, filial; **~rym=pie (-s)** nursery rhyme; **~sorg** child wel=fare; **~speletjies** child's play; *dis nie ~speletjies nie,* it is no child's play; **~sterftesyfer** infant mortality rate; **~tuin (-e)** kindergarten; **~verlamming** infantile paralysis, poliomyelitis; **~waentjie (-s)** perambulator

kinds (-e) in one's dotage, senile; *hy is al ~,* he is in his second childhood

kink (s) (-e) twist, knot, hitch; *daar is 'n ~ in die kabel,* there is a hitch somewhere

kin'kel (-s) knot, twist

kink'hoes (w)(w)hooping cough

kiosk' (-e) kiosk

kis (s) (-te) box, case, trunk; coffer; coffin; (w) **(ge-)** coffin; **~hou (-e)** winning shot, ace (sport); **~klere** Sunday best

kitaar' (-s; ..tare) guitar, *ook* **ghitaar**

kits moment, trifle; *in 'n ~,* in the twink=ling of an eye; **~klaar** ready in an instant; **~koffie** instant coffee; **~rekenaar** ready reckoner (replaced by calculator)

kla, klae (ge-) complain; *ek kan nie ~ nie,* things are not too bad

klaag: ~lied (-ere) lamentation, dirge; **~muur** wailing wall; **~stem (-me)** plain=tive voice

klaar ready, finished; clear

klaarblyk'lik (-e) evident, obvious

klaar: ~kom (-ge-) get finished; get along, manage; *ek sal darem ~ kom,* I'll be able to manage; **~maak (-ge-)** get ready, fin=ish; prepare

Klaas Vaak', Klaas Va'kie Willie Winkie, the dustman, the sandman

klad¹ (s) (-de) blot, stain; (w) **(ge-)** blot

klad² (s) rough draft; *in ~,* in draft; **~werk** rough work

kla'er (-s) plaintiff, complainant

klag (-te), klag'te (-s) complaint; *'n ~ in=dien,* lodge a complaint

klam (-mer, -ste) damp, moist

klamp (s) (-e) clamp; (w) **(ge-)** clamp

klandi'sie customers, patronage; clientele, custom; **~waarde** goodwill

klank (-e) sound, tone; **~baan** sound track; **~bord (-e)** sound(ing) board; **~demper (-s)** silencer (car); **~dig** soundproof; **~film (-s)** talkie, soundfilm; **~getrou=heid** fidelity; *hoë ~getrouheid,* high fidelity, *kyk* **hoëtrou**; **~grens** sound bar=rier; **~nabootsing (-e, -s)** onomatopoeia; **~skyfiereeks** tapeslide sequence; **~ver=springing** metathesis; **~versterker (-s)** amplifier

klant (-e) customer

klap (s) (-pe) slap, blow, crack; flap; (w) (ge-) smack, clap; crack
klap'per¹ (-s) cracker, explosive (sound)
klap'per² (-s) coconut
klap'roos (..rose) corn poppy
kla'ring clearing; ~(s)agent (-e) clearing agent; ~(s)bank (-e) clearing bank
klarinet' (-te) clarionet
klas (-se) class, form; grade; category; eerste ~, first class; ~kamer (-s) classroom; ~kaptein (-s) class captain; ~onderwyser (-s) class teacher
klassiek' (-e) classic(al); ~e musiek, classical music
klassifiseer' (ge-) classify
klassikaal' (..kale) class; klassikale onderwys, teaching by groups (classes)
klavier' (-e) piano
kla'wer¹ (-s) key (piano)
kla'wer² (-s) clover, shamrock
kle'ding clothing, apparel; dressmaking; ~stuk (-ke) garment, (article of) dress
klee(d) (w) (ge-) clothe, dress
kleed (s) (klede) garment, garb; carpet; ~kamer (-s) dressing room, cloakroom; ~repetisie (-s) dress/fulldress rehearsal
kleef (ge-) cling, stick, adhere; ~band sticking tape; ~myn (-e) limpet mine
klei clay; ~ trap, flounder
klein (-er, -ste) small, little; petty; ~ begin, aanhou win, perseverance will be rewarded; 'n ~ bietjie, a tiny/little bit
klein'dogter (-s) granddaughter
Klein Duim'pie Tom Thumb
kleineer' (~, ge-) belittle, minimise
kleingees'tig (-e; -er, -ste) narrow-minded
klein'geld small cash, change; van iem. ~ maak, make mincemeat of someone
klein'goed small ones, children, kids
klein'handel retail trade; ~aar, (-s) retail dealer; ~prys, (-e) retail price
klei'nigheid trifle, small thing
klein: ~kind (-ers) grandchild; ~kas, petty cash; ~kry, understand, grasp; ek kan dit nie ~kry nie, I cannot understand/fathom it; ~lik (-e) petty, narrow-minded
klei'nood (..node) jewel, treasure, gem
kleinse'rig (-e; -er, -ste) delicate, touchy, sensitive, easily hurt
klein'seun (-s) grandson
kleinsie'lig (-e; -er, -ste) narrow-minded

klein: ~span little ones, youngsters, kids; ~tjie (-s) small/little one; ~tongetjie (-s) uvula; ~vee small livestock; ~wild small game
klem (s) stress, accent; (-me) cramp, binding screw; ~ in die kake, lockjaw, tetanus; ~ lê op, stress; (w) (ge-) clench, clasp, jam; ~tang vicegrip (pliers)
klep (s) (-pe) flap; valve
kle'pel (-s) tongue (of a bell)
kleptomaan' (..mane) kleptomaniac
klera'sie clothing
kle're clothes, clothing; ~drag fashion, dress, clothing; ~kas (-te) wardrobe; ~maker (-s) tailor
klerikaal' (..kale) of clergy; ..kale drag, clerical garb
klerk (-e) clerk; ~lik (-e) clerical; ~like werk, clerical work
klets (ge-) chatter, talk, yap; ~kous (-e) gossiper, chatterbox
klet'ter (ge-) clatter, patter, clash, clang; die hael ~ op die dak, the hail beats on the roof
kleur (s) (-e) colour; ~ beken, follow suit (cards); (w) (ge-) colour, stain; tone; blush; ~baadjie (-s) blazer
Kleur'ling (-e) Coloured; (pl) Coloured people; ~betrekkinge Coloured Relations; ~gemeenskap (-pe) Coloured community
kleur: ~loos (..lose) colourless, drab; ~serp (-e) academic hood; ~skyfie (-s) colour slide; ~stof pigment, dye
kleu'ter (-s) toddler; ~skool nursery school
kle'werig (-e; -er, -ste) sticky; viscous
kliek (s) (-e, -s) clique, set; (w) (ge-) form a clique/set
kliënt' (-e) client; ~betrekkinge client relations; ~(e)lokker (-s) tout
klier (-e) gland
klik (s) (-ke) click (with tongue); (w) (ge-) tell tales; click; bug; ~bek (-ke), ~spaan (..spane) telltale, talebearer; ~ker (-s) (electronic) bug; my kantoor is geklik, my office is bugged, kyk luistervlooi
klim (ge-) climb, ascend, rise; die jare ~, the years are advancing
klimaat' climate
kli'maks (-e) climax

klim: ~**baan** (..bane) climbing lane; ~**op** ivy; creeper; ~**plant** (-e) creeper, climber (plant); ~**tol** (-le) yo-yo

kliniek' (-e) clinic

kli'n/es clinical; ~*e ondersoek*, clinical examination

klink[1] (ge-) rivet, clinch

klink[2] (ge-) sound, ring; touch glasses; ~**er** (-s) vowel; army biscuit

klink'nael (-s) rivet; ~**broek** (-e) studded jeans

klip (-pe, -pers) stone, rock, pebble; *hy slaap soos 'n* ~, he sleeps like a top; *stadig oor die* ~ *pe*, go carefully; ~**hard** (-e) very hard

klits[1] (s) (-e) bur, burdock

klits[2] (w) (ge-) beat (eggs); whip (cream)

kloek (w) (ge-) cluck

klok (-ke) clock, bell; *aan die groot* ~ *hang*, proclaim from the housetops; (w) *'n toespraak* ~, time a speech; ~**ke'spel** chimes; carillon; ~**reël** curfew; ~**slag** (s) striking of the clock; (bw) exactly, sharp; ~**slag eenuur**, one o'clock sharp

klomp[1] (-e) crowd, number, lot; lump; ~**voet** (-e) club foot

klomp[2] (-e) wooden shoe, clog

klont (-e) lump (sugar); clod (earth); clot (blood)

kloof (s) (klowe) ravine, cleft, chasm; (w) (ge-) cleave, split; *hare* ~, split hairs; ~**paal** split pole

kloos'ter (-s) monastery, nunnery, cloister, convent; ~**skool** (..skole) convent school

klop (s) (-pe) knock; beat; tap, rap; throb; (w) (ge-) knock; beat; throb, tap; balance, tally; defeat, lick; *dit gaan* ~**disselboom**, everything is in top gear; ~**jag** (-te) public raid, round-up

klos (-se) bobbin, spool, reel; coil (electr.)

klots (ge-) beat, clash (water)

klou (s) (-e) claw, paw

klousu'le (-s) clause, paragraph; *ingevolge/ kragtens* ~ *6*, in terms of clause 6

klou'tang (-e) vicegrip (pliers)

klou'ter (ge-) climb, clamber; ~**dief** (..diewe) cat burglar

klou'tjie (-s) hoof; *nie die* ~ *by die oor bring nie*, unable to make a tale sound plausible

klub (-s) club

klug (-te) farce; joke, scream

kluif (s) (kluiwe) bone (to pick); (w) (ge-) pick, gnaw

kluis (-e) hermitage, cell, hut; strongroom; ~**e'naar** (-s) hermit, recluse

kluis'ter (w) (ge-) fetter, shackle, confine

kluit (-e) clod, lump

klui'tjie (-s) dumpling; lie; *iem. met 'n* ~ *in die riet stuur*, put someone off with fair words

kluts: *die* ~ *kwyt raak*, be at sea

knaag (ge-) gnaw; ~**dier** (-e) rodent (animal)

knaap (knape) lad, boy; chap

knab'bel (ge-) nibble

knae'end (-e) gnawing; nagging, boring

knak (s) (-ke) crack; (w) crack, snap; impair (health); ~**breuk** greenstick fracture

knal (s) (-le) report (of gun); clap, crack; (w) (ge-) clap, crash; explode; ~**demper** (-s) exhaust box, muffler, silencer; ~**dop** (-pe), ~**doppie** (-s) detonator

knap[1] (b) (-per, -ste) clever, able, brainy; handsome, good-looking

knap[2] (b, bw) (-per, -ste) tight, close-fitting; only just

kna'pie[1] (-s) small fellow

kna'pie[2] (-s) small pulpit, lectern

knap'sak (-ke) knapsack

knap'sakkerwel, knap'sekerwel (-s) blackjack, beggar tick, sweetheart

knee (ge-) knead, *kyk* **knie**[2]

kneg (-te) servant, slave

knel (s) (-le) pinch, difficulty; *in die* ~ *sit*, be in a predicament; (w) (ge-) pinch; squeeze; press tightly; get jammed; ~**punt** bottleneck; issue

kners (ge-) gnash, grind; ~**ing** gnashing

knet'ter (ge-) crackle (fire)

kneu'kel (-s) knuckle

kneus (ge-) bruise, contuse; ~**ing** (-e, -s) bruise, contusion

kne'wel (-s) moustache; whopper, bouncer; *'n* ~ *van 'n leeu*, a huge lion

knib'bel (ge-) haggle, higgle

knie[1] (s) (-ë) knee; *sy knieë dra*, hurry away

knie[2] (w) (ge-) knead

knie: ~**broek** (-e) knickers, knee breeches; bloomers (for women); ~**buiging** (-e, -s) genuflexion; curtsy; ~**diep** knee-deep; ~*diep in die moeilikheid*, in real trouble; ~**halter** (ge-) kneehalter

kniel (ge-) kneel

knik (s) (-ke) nod; rut (in a road); (w) (ge-) nod

knip (s) (-pe) bolt, clasp; clip; wink; (w) (ge-) cut; clip; wink; ~**mes** (-se) pocket knife; *so gou as jy ~mes kan sê*, before you can say Jack Robinson; ~**oog** (ge-) wink, blink; ~**pie** (-s) pinch (of salt); ~**sel** cutting, clipping; ~**seldiens** (press) cutting service; ~**speld** (-e) safety pin

knoei (ge-) botch, blunder, bungle; intrigue; *aan iets ~*, meddle with

knof'fel garlic

knol (-le) nag, hack; tuber, bulb; ~**skrywer** (-s) hackwriter

knoop (s, w) (knope) button; knot, tie; curse, oath; *die ~ deurhak*, cut the Gordian knot; *daar sit die ~*, there's the rub; (w) (ge-) tie, knot, swear; *iets in jou oor ~*, make a mental note of; ~**'s'gat** (-e) buttonhole

knop (-pe) knob, pommel; bud; *'n ~ in die keel*, a lump in the throat; ~**kierie** (-s) knobkerrie, club

knor (s) (-re) grunt, growl; (w) (ge-) grumble, growl, grunt; ~**tjor** (-re) go-cart

knou (s) (-e) gnaw, snap, bite; injury; *'n ~ gee*, impair (health); (w) (ge-) hurt

knup'pel (s) (-s) club, cudgel; ~**dik** gorged; ~**stormloop** baton charge

knut'sel (ge-) trifle, be employed in trifles

knyp (s) (-e) pinch; *in die ~ sit*, be in a fix; (w) (ge-) pinch, squeeze; ~**tang** (-e) (pair of) pliers/pincers

ko'bra (-s) cobra

kod'dig (-e; -er, -ste) funny, comic, odd

ko'de (-s) code

koe'doe (-s) kudu

koëd'skool (..skole) co-educational school

koëduka'sie co-education

koe'ël (s) (-s) bullet (rifle); pellet (airgun); ball; ~**vaste baadjie**, bulletproof vest/jacket; *die ~ is deur die kerk*, the die is cast

koei (-e) cow; *oor ~tjies en kalfies praat*, indulge in small talk; *ou ~e uit die sloot haal*, rake up old stories

koeja'wel (-s) guava; *'n harde ~*, a hard nut (person)

koek (s) (-e) cake; (w) (ge-) knot, cluster

koekeloer' (ge-) peep, leer, spy

koekoek' (-s) cuckoo

koek: ~**pan** (-ne) baking pan; ~**poeding** (-s), ~**struif** trifle

koel (w) (ge-) cool; vent; (b) (-e; -er, -ste) cool, cold, fresh; ~*bly in gevaar*, keep a level head in danger

koelbloe'dig (-e; -er, -ste) cold-blooded

koel: ~**drank** cooldrink, soft drink; ~**te** light breeze, shade; ~**toring** cooling tower; ~**trok** (-ke) refrigerator truck

koem'kwat (-te) cumquat (fruit)

koepee' (-s) coupé

koe'pel (-s) dome, cupola

koeplet' (-te) couplet, verse, stanza

koepon' (-s) coupon

koer (ge-) coo

koerant' (-e) newspaper, *ook* **nuusblad**

koers (-e) course, direction; exchange rate

koes (ge-) dodge, duck down

koesis'ter, koeksis'ter (-s) cruller

koes'ter[1] (s) (-s) pipit (South African lark)

koes'ter[2] (w) (ge-) cherish, pamper, nurse; *'n wrok ~*, bear a grudge

koes'tertjie (-s) pipit

koets[1] (s) (-e) coach, carriage; sedan car

koets[2] (w) (ge-) dodge, duck down, *ook* **koes**

koetsier' (-s) coachman

koevert' (-e) envelope; ~**flap** (-pe) back flap of envelope

koe'voet (-e) crowbar

kof'fer (-s) trunk, travelling box, coffer; ~**dam** (-me) coffer dam

kof'fie coffee

kog'gel (ge-) mimic, mock; ~**aar** (-s), mocking bird; mimic, ape

koggelman'der (-s) black agama, lizard

kok (-ke, -s) cook; *te veel ~s bederwe die bry*, too many cooks spoil the broth

koket' (s) (-te) coquette; (b) (ter, -ste) coquettish

kokkatiel' (-s) cockatiel (bird)

kok'kedoor (..dore) big wig

kokkewiet' (-e) bush shrike

kokon' (-s) cocoon

ko'kosboom (..bome) cocoanut tree

kol (-le) star (of a horse); bull's eye; spot

kolf (s) (kolwe) butt-end (rifle); bat (cricket); (w) (ge-) bat; ~**beurt** (-e) innings; ~**blad**, (..blaaie) pitch; ~**kampie** (-s) crease

kol'hou (-e) hole in one (golf)

koliek' colic

koljan'der coriander; *dis vinkel en* ~, six of the one and half a dozen of the other

kolk (-e) abyss; whirlpool, eddy

kollateraal' (..rale) collateral; *..rale seku= riteit*, collateral security

kolle'ga (-s) colleague

kol'lege (-s) college; *op/aan* ~, at college

kollektant' (-e) collector

kollek'te (-s) collection (church, street)

kollekteer' (ge-) collect; ~**oproep** (-e) collect call (telephone)

kollektief' (..tiewe) collective; *..iewe be= dinging*, collective bargaining

kol'lig (-te) spotlight

kolom' (-me) column

kolonel' (-s) colonel

koloniaal' (..niale) colonial

kolo'nie (-s) colony, settlement

kolonis' (-te) colonist

kolonisa'sie colonisation

kolon'ne (-s) (army) column; *vyfde* ~, fifth column

kolossaal' (..sale) colossal, gigantic

kolporteur' (-s) colporteur, vendor of reli= gious books

kol'skoot bull's eye

kol'toets (-e) spot check, *kyk* **steekproef**

kom¹ (s) (-me) basin, bowl; dale, vale

kom² (w) (ge-) come, arrive

komaan'! come on!

kombers (-e) blanket

kombina'sie (-s) combination

kombuis' (-e) kitchen

komediant' (-e) comedian, actor

kome'die (-s) comedy, farce, *ook* **blyspel**

komeet' (komete) comet

ko'mies (-e; -er, -ste) comic(al)

komitee' (-s) committee; *hy dien in/op 'n* ~, he serves on a committee; *uitvoerende* ~, executive committee

komkom'mer (-s) cucumber

kom'ma (-s) comma

kommandant' (-e) commandant, com= mander

kommandant'-generaal (kommandante= generaal) commandant-general

kommandeer' (~, ge-) command, com= mandeer; ~ *jou eie honde en blaf self*, do your own dirty work

kommandeur' (-s) commander

komman'do (-'s) commando; ~**wurm** (-s) army worm

kom'mapunt (-e) semicolon

kommentaar' (..tare) commentary, com= ment; ~ *lewer op (maak oor)*, comment upon

kommenta'tor (-e, -s) commentator

kom'mer trouble, distress, care, anxiety, sorrow; *die toestand wek* ~, the situation is causing concern; ~**krale** worry beads; ~**nis** (-se) worry, care, anxiety

kommersieel' (..siële) commercial; *..iële reg*, commercial law

kommissariaat' commissariat

kommissa'ris (-se) commissioner; *K~ van Ede*, Commissioner of Oaths; ~**-generaal** (**kommissarisse-generaal**) commissioner-general

kommis'sie (-s) commission; *K~ vir Staatsadministrasie*, Commission for State Administration

kommoditeit' (-e) commodity, consumer article

kommu'ne (-s) commune

kommu'nie holy communion

kommunika'sie (-s) communication; ~**= kunde**, ~**leer** communication (subject)

Kommunis' (-te) Communist; ~**me** Communism; ~**ties** (-e) Communistic

komp (w) computerise

kompanjie' (-s) company

komparatief' (..tiewe) comparative

kompartement' (-e) compartment

kompas' (-se) compass

kom'per (s) computer; ~**druk** (-ke) com= puter print-out; ~**kunde** computer science; ~**staat** computer print-out; ~**ter= minaal** (..ale) computer terminal

kompeteer' (~, ge-) compete, *ook* **wed= ywer**

kompeti'sie (-s) competition

kompleet' (..plete) complete

kompleks' (-e) complex

komplement' (-e) complement

komplementêr' (-e) complementary; ~**e kleure**, complementary colours

komplika'sie (-s) complication

kompliment' (-e) compliment; *iem. 'n* ~ *maak*, pay someone a compliment

komplimenteer' (~, ge-) compliment

komplimentêr' (-e) complimentary; ~**e kaartjie**, complimentary ticket

komplot' (-te) plot, intrigue, conspiracy; *'n* ~ *smee*, hatch a plot

komponeer' (ge-) compose
komponis' (-te) composer
komposi'sie (-s) composition
kom'pos compost
koms arrival, coming, advent
kondensa'sie condensation
kondi'sie (-s) condition; state
kondoleer' (ge-) condole
kondukteur' (-s) conductor, guard
konfedera'sie (-s) confederation
konferen'sie (-s) conference; **~ganger** (-s)
  conference delegate
konfes'sie (-s) confession
konfidensieel' (..siële) confidential; *kon=
  fidensiële inligting,* confidential informa=
  tion, *ook* **vertroulik**
konfiskeer' (ge-) confiscate
konflik' (-te) conflict
konfronta'sie confrontation
konfronteer' (~, ge-) confront
konfyt'[1] (s) (-e) jam; preserve
konfyt'[2] (w): *in iets ge~ wees,* be well versed
  in
kongres' (-se) congress
ko'ning (-s) king
koningin' (-ne) queen
ko'ninklik (-e) royal, regal, kingly; *van ~e
  afkoms,* of royal descent
ko'ninkryk (-e) kingdom, empire
konjunktuur' (..ture) conjuncture; eco=
  nomic cycle
kon'ka (-s) empty (petrol) tin, drum, bra=
  zier; fire tin
kon'kel (ge-) plot, scheme, intrigue; botch
kon'kelwerk muddling, botching; *don=
  kerwerk is ~,* a bungler works in the dark
konklu'sie (-s) conclusion
konkreet' (..krete) concrete
konkurren'sie competition, rivalry; *straw=
  we ~,* stiff competition (in business)
konkurrent' (-e) competitor, rival
konnek'sie (-s) connection
konnekteer' (ge-) connect
konsekwent' (-e) consistent; *~ optree,* act
  consistently
konsensieus' (-e) conscientious, *ook* **pligs=
  getrou**
konsen'sus consensus, agreement, accord
konsentra'sie concentration; **~kamp** (-e)
  concentration camp
konsen'tries (-e) concentric

konsep' (-te) draft, concept; **~ordonnan=
  sie** (-s) draft ordinance; **~wetgewing** draft
  legislation; **~wetsontwerp** draft bill
konsert' (-e) concert
konserti'na (-s) concertina, squash-box;
  ~hek concertina (folding, collapsible)
  gate
konservato'rium (-s) conservatoire, con=
  servatory
konserwatief' (..tiewe) conservative
konses'sie (-s) concession; **~kaartjie** (-s)
  concession ticket
konsisto'rie (-s) consistory, vestry
konskrip'sie conscription
konsolida'sie consolidation
konsonant' (-e) consonant
konsool' (..ole) console
konsta'bel (-s) constable
konstant' (-e) constant
konstateer' (~ ge-) state, prove, declare
konstella'sie (-s) constellation; *~ van state,*
  constellation of states
konsterna'sie consternation
konstitu'sie (-s) constitution
konstitusioneel' (..nele) constitutional
konstrueer' (ge-) construe, construct
konstruk'sie (-s) construction
konsuis' quasi, as if (it were)
kon'sul (-s) consul
konsulaat' (..late) consulate
konsul-generaal' (konsuls-generaal) con=
  sul-general
konsult' (-e) consultation; **~-ingenieur** (-s)
  consulting engineer
konsulta'sie (-s) consultation
konsulteer' (ge-) consult
kontak' (s) (-te) contact; *in ~ bly met,* keep
  in touch with; **~lens** (-e) contact lens; (w)
  contact (a person)
kontamineer' (ge-) contaminate
kontant' (s) (-e); *~ by aflewering,* cash on
  delivery; **~strokie** cash slip
kontinent' (-e) continent, *ook* **vasteland**
kontinentaal' (..tale) continental
kontinuïteit' continuity
kontoer' (-e) contour
kontrak' (te) contract; *'n ~ sluit/aan=
  gaan,* make (enter into) a contract
kontrakteer' (w) contract; *uit~,* contract
  out
kontrakteur' (-s) contractor
kontras' (-te) contrast

kontrasteer' (ge-) contrast
kontrei' (-e) region, area, (platteland) dis=
trict
kontro'le control
kontroleer' (~, ge-) control
kontroleur' (-s) controller, supervisor
konvensioneel' (..nele) conventional
konvoka'sie convocation (of a university)
konvooi' (-e) convoy
konyn' (-e) rabbit
kooi (-e) bed; cage; ~ toe gaan, go to bed
kook (ge-) boil, cook; do the cooking; my
bloed ~, my blood is up
kool¹ cabbage; die ~ is die sous nie werd
nie, the game is not worth the candle
kool² (kole) coal; op hete kole sit, be on
pins and needles
kool'stof carbon
koop (s) purchase, bargain; met iets te ~
loop, show off; op die ~ toe, into the
bargain; (w) (ge-) buy, purchase; ~brief
(..briewe) deed of sale; ~-en-loop cash-
and-carry; ~-en-loophappies take-aways
koöpera'sie (-s) co-operative society (co-
op)
koop: Kamer van K~handel, Chamber of
Commerce; ~kontrak (-te) contract of
sale; ~krag purchasing/buying power;
~prys cost price, purchase price
koöpteer' (ge-) co-opt
koopvaardy' commercial navigation, mer=
cantile marine; ~skip (..skepe) mer=
chantman
koor (kore) choir (of singers); chorus (of a
song)
koord (-e) cord, rope; ~danser (-s) rope
dancer; tightrope walker
koördina'sie co-ordination
koors (-e) fever; ~agtig (-e) feverish;
hectic, frenzied
hoor'sang (-e) choral song; choral singing
koors: ~blaar (..blare) blister; ~boom
(..bome) fever tree; ~(er)ig (-e) feverish;
~pennetjie (-s) clinical thermometer
kop¹ (s) (-pe) cob, ear (mealie); (w) (ge-)
form a cob (mealie); form a head (cab=
bage)
kop² (-pe) head; mountain peak, summit;
~ in een mus, be hand in glove (together);
op die ~ sesuur, exactly six o'clock
ko'per¹ (-s) buyer

ko'per² copper; ~draad copper wire;
~kapel (-le) yellow cobra
ko'pie¹ (-s) bargain, kyk winskopie
kopie'² (-ë) copy
kopieer' (ge-) copy, transcribe
kopie'reg copyright
kop'pel (w) (ge-) couple, tie, connect; hy=
phenate; ~aar (-s) coupler; match maker;
pimp; clutch (motor); ~teken (-s) hyphen
kop'penent (-e) head (of a bed)
kop'pesneller (-s) headhunter, scalphunter
kop'pie (-s) cup; hill, koppie
kop'pig (-e; -er, -ste) obstinate, stubborn;
~heid obstinacy, stubbornness
koraal'¹ (..rale) chorale
koraal'² (..rale) coral (reef); ~boom
(..bome) coral tree, cork tree
kordaat' (..dater, -ste) brave, undaunted,
bold; Jan K~, brave fellow
kordon' (-ne, -s) cordon; 'n ~ span/trek
om 'n gebied, cordon off an area
korf (korwe) hive; ~bal basketball (wo=
men); ~behuising cluster housing
ko'ring wheat; ook groen ~ op die land hê,
have fledglings of one's own
koronê're trombo'se coronary thrombosis
korporaal' (-s) corporal
korpora'sie (-s) corporation
korps (-e) corps
korrek' (-te) correct, right; ~sie (-s) cor=
rection; ~t'heid correctness
kor'rel (s) (-s) grain; sight (rifle); bead;
met 'n ~ tjie sout neem, take with a pinch
of salt; (w) (ge-) aim; pick off (grapes)
korrespondeer' (~, ge-) correspond
korresponden'sie correspondence; ~kol=
lege (-s) correspondence college
korrespondent' (-e) correspondent
korrigeer' (ge-) correct
korro'sie corrosion
korrup' (-te) corrupt; ~sie corruption
kors (-te) crust; ~breker (-s) subsoiler
(farming)
korset' (-te) corset, stays, foundation gar=
ment
kors'sie crust (of bread)
kors'wel (s) jest, joke; (w) (ge-) jest, joke;
ek ~ sommer, I'm only joking
kort (w) (ge-) shorten; (b, bw) ([-e]; -er,
-ste) short, brief; ~ en kragtig, short and
sweet; te ~ skiet, fail, fall short; ~af
(-fer, -ste) abrupt, blunt; ~asem short of

breath; **~golfstasie** (-s) short wave station; **~ing** (-e, -s) discount, reduction; **~kuns** (modern) short prose; **~liks** in short, briefly; **~om** in a word

kortsig'tig (-e; -er, -ste) short-sighted

kort'sluiting short circuit

kortston'dig (-e; -er, -ste) short, short-lived, transitory; **~e vrede**, short-lived peace

kort: **~verhaal** (..hale) shortstory; **~wiek** (ge-) clip the wings; thwart

kos[1] (s) (-se) food; **~ en inwoning**, board and lodging

kos[2] (w) (ge-) cost; **dit ~ niks**, no charge

kos: **~baar** (..bare; -der, -ste) precious, dear; expensive; **..bare juwele**, expensive jewels; **~ganger** (-s) boarder, lodger; **~huis** (-e) boarding house; **~leerling** (-e) boarder (at school)

kosme'ties: **~e verandering**, cosmetic/superficial change

kos'mies (-e) cosmic; **~e strale**, cosmic rays

kosmopoliet' (-e) cosmopolitan, **ook wêreldburger**

kosmopoli'ties (-e) cosmopolitan

kos'mos cosmos

kos: **~skool** (..skole) boarding school; **~te**, expenses, costs; **ten ~te van**, at the cost of; **~telik** (-e; -er, -ste) precious, fine, excellent; **'n ~telike grap**, a priceless joke; **~teloos** (..lose) free, gratis

kos'ter (-s) churchwarden, beadle, sexton

kostuum' (-s, ..tume) costume; **~bal** (-s) fancy-dress ball

kosyn' (-e) frame, sill; doorpost

kot'huis (-e) cottage

kots (ge-) vomit

kou[1] (s) (-e) cage

kou[2] (s) cold

kou[3] (w) (ge-) chew, masticate; **harde bene om te ~**, have a tough job

koud ([koue]; kouer, -ste) cold, chilly

kou'e cold, chill; **~ vat**, catch a chill; **~vuur** gangrene, **ook gangreen**

kou'gom chewing gum

kou'kus (-se) caucus (of political party); (v) confer, deliberate

kou'lik (-e; -er, -ste) sensitive to cold

kous (-e) stocking, sock; **die ~ op die kop kry**, come away with a flea in one's ear

kraag (krae) collar

kraai (s) (-e) crow; **so maer soos 'n ~**, as thin as a lath; (w) (ge-) crow

kraak (s) (krake) crack; **~been** cartilage

kraal[1] (krale) pen, kraal, fold; tribal village; **dis so in sy ~**, that is food and drink to him

kraal[2] (krale), **~tjie**, (-s) bead

kraam[1] (krame) purpose; booth, stall

kraam[2] childbed; labour (childbirth); **~inrigting** (-e, -s) maternity home

kraan (krane) tap, stopcock; crane

kraan'voël (-s) crane

krab'bel (w) (ge-) scratch, scrawl, scribble

krab'betjie (-s) earring

kraf'fie (-s) waterbottle, decanter

krag (-te) strength, power, force, vigour; **al sy ~te inspan**, exert one's strength; **van ~ word**, come into force; **~boot** (..bote) power boat

krag: **~fiets** (-e) buzz-bike, moped; **~mas** (-te) pylon; **~meting** (-s) match; contest; **~remme** power brakes

krag'sentrale (-s) power station

krag'tens by virtue of, in consequence of; **~ die ordonnansie**, under the ordinance

krag'tig (-e; -er, -ste) powerful, strong

krag: **~voer** concentrates; **~woord** (-e) expletive, strong exclamation

kra'letjie (-s) bead

kram (s) (-me) clamp, cramp; staple: (w) (ge-) clamp, cramp, staple; **~drukker** (-s) stapler

kram'mer (-s) stapling machine, stapler

kram'metjie (-s) (wire) staple

kramp (-e) cramp, spasm, convulsion

krampag'tig (-e) convulsive, spasmodic

kranksin'nig (-e) insane, mad, crazy, lunatic; **~e** (-s) lunatic; **~e'gestig** (-te) lunatic asylum

krans[1] (s) (-e) wreath; (w) (ge-) festoon

krans[2] (s) (-e) rocky ridge, krans

krans[3] (s) (-e) (children's) circle

krap[1] (s) (-pe) crab

krap[2] (s) (-pe) scratch; (w) (ge-) scratch

kras[1] (w) (ge-) screech; scrape; croak

kras[2] (b) (-ser, -ste) vigorous; drastic: **~ optree teen**, take drastic steps against

krat (-te) crate

kra'ter (-s) crater

krediet' credit; **~geriewe** credit facilities; **~kaart** (-e) credit card

kre'dit (-s) credit (item)

krediteer' (ge-) credit; *iem. ~ met*, credit a person's account with

krediteur' (-e, -s) creditor, *kyk* **skuldeiser**

krediet'/kre'dit: **~nota** (-s) credit note; **~saldo** (-'s) credit balance

kreef (krewe) lobster; crayfish, crawfish

Kreefs'keerkring Tropic of Cancer

kreet (s) (krete) cry, scream, shriek

kremato'rium (-s) crematorium

kremetart' cream of tartar; **~boom** (..bome) baobab tree

krenk (ge-) offend, hurt, mortify

kreu'kel (s) (-s) crease, fold, ruck; (w) (ge-) crease, fold; **~traag** (..trae) crease resistant; **~vry** (-e) non-creasing

kreun (s) (-e) groan, moan; (w) (ge-) groan, moan

kreu'pel lame, crippled, limping

kre'wel (-s) prawn, *ook* **steurgarnaal**

kriek (-e) cricket (insect)

krie'ket cricket (game); **~bal** (-le) cricket ball; **~kolf** (..kolwe) cricket bat; **~speler** (-s) cricketer

krie'wel (ge-) tickle, itch; fidget; **~rig** (-e) itchy, ticklish; fussy

krimineel' (..nele) criminal; *'n kriminele aanklag*, a criminal charge

krimp (ge-) shrink, diminish; *~ van die pyn*, writhe with pain; **~vry** (-e) un-shrinkable; **~ystervark** small hedgehog

kring (-e) circle; ring; circuit, orbit; *in sekere ~e*, in certain quarters; **~loop** circular course; cycle; *bose ~loop*, vicious circle/spiral; **~televisie** closed-circuit television

krin'kel (s) (-s) crinkle; (w) (ge-) crinkle

krioel' (ge-) swarm, abound/teem with; *dit ~ hier van die muise*, the place is overrun with mice

krip (-pe) manger; *aan die ~ staan*, have a plush occupation

krip'ties cryptic(al); obscure, hidden

krisant' (-e) chrysanthemum

kri'sis (-se) crisis

Kris'mis Christmas, *kyk* **Kersfees**

kristal' (-le) crystal; *so helder soos ~*, as clear as crystal

krite'rium (-s) criterion, *ook* **maatstaf**

kritiek' (s) criticism, critique; (-e) review

kri'ties (-e) critical

kri'tikus (-se, kritici) critic

kritiseer' (ge-) criticise, slam

kroeg (kroeë) public house, pub, tavern; **~baas** (..base) barkeeper; **~meisie, ~doedie** (-s) barmaid

kroes (-er, -ste) curly, frizzy, crisp

krokodil' (-le) crocodile

krom (-mer, -ste) crooked, curved, bent; *~ van die lag*, splitting one's sides with laughter; *~ Afrikaans praat*, speak faulty Afrikaans; **~houtsap** wine; **~me** (-s) curve (mathematics); **~ming** (-e, -s) curve; turn, bend; curvature

kroniek' (-e) chronicle

kro'ning coronation

kron'kel (w) (ge-) wind, twist, twirl, coil; meander

kroon (s) (krone) crown; (w) (ge-) crown; **~getuie** (-s) crown witness; **~juwele** crown jewels; **~prins** (-e) crown prince

kroos offspring, descendants; **~trooster** (-s) babysitter; *ons gaan vanaand ~troos*, we will be babysitting tonight

krop (s) (-pe) crop, gizzard; *dwars in die ~ steek*, go against the grain; (w) (ge-) cram, bottle up

krot (-te) hovel, den, shanty; **~buurt** (-e) slum

kru (b) crude

krul (w) (ge-) spice, season

kruid (kruie) herb, spice

kruidenier' (-s) grocer; **~s'ware** groceries

kruidjie-roer'-my-nie (-s) touch-me-not, sensitive plant; touchy fellow

krui'e (s) spice; **~kundige** (-s) herbalist

krui'er (-s) porter

krui'e: (s) **~stel(letjie)** cruet stand; **~ry** condiment(s)

kruik (-e) pitcher, jug

kruin (-e) top, crown, summit

kruip (ge-) creep, crawl, cringe; **~trekker** caterpillar tractor

kruis (s) (-e) cross; affliction; sharp (music); crux; *elke huis het sy ~*, there is a skeleton in every cupboard; *~ of munt*, heads or tails; (w) (ge-) cross; cruise; crucify; intersect; interbreed; *ge~te tjek*, crossed cheque; (ge-) (pair of) braces; **~boog** (..boë) crossbow

kruisement' mint

krui'ser (-s) cruiser

krui'sig (ge-) crucify; **~ing** crucifixion

krui'sing (-e, -s) crossbreed(ing); crossing, intersection kruis: ~pad (..paaie) crossroad; ~ridder (-s) crusader; ~tog (-te) crusade; ~verhoor cross examination; ~verwy= sing (-e) cross reference; ~vra (ge-) cross examine

kruit gunpowder; ~bad mineral baths

krui'wa (-ens) wheelbarrow

kruk (-ke) crutch; stool; crank; ~kerlys (-te) casualty list

krul (s) (-le) curl; scroll; (w) (ge-) curl; wave (hair); ~hare curly hair; ~kop (-pe) curly-head; ~kopklonkie (-s) curly-headed (Coloured) boy

krum'mel (s) (-s) crumb; bit

krup'pel (-er, -ste) lame, cripple(d)

kry (ge-) get, obtain, acquire, receive

krygs: ~gevangene (-s) prisoner of war; ~raad (..rade) court martial; ~tuig munitions

krygs'wet martial law

krys (ge-) croak, scream, screech

kryt¹ ring (for boxing), arena

kryt² chalk, crayon

kubiek' (-e) cubic; ~wortel cube root

kud'de (-s) herd, flock

kui'er (s) outing, visit, call; (w) (ge-) visit, call; walk; hy het 'n maand lank by sy oom ge~, he stayed with his uncle for a month; ~gas (-te) guest

kuif (kuiwe) crest, tuft

kui'ken (-s) chick, young chicken

kuil¹ (s) (-e) pool, dam; dimple; bunker (golf)

kuil² (w) (ge-) ensile

kuil'tjie (-s) dimple

kuip (s) (-e) coop, tub; pit (motor racing); (w) (ge-) cooper

kui'per (-s) cooper

kuis (-e; -er, -ste) chaste, pure, virtuous

kuit (-e) calf; - been (..bene) fibula

kul (ge-) cheat, deceive

kul'tivar (-s) cultivar

kultureel' (..rele) cultural

kul'tus cult, creed

kultuur' (..ture) culture, civilisation; cul= tivation; ~histories (-e) sosio-historical

kun'dig (b) able, competent, skilful; ~heid skill, ability, expertise, knowhow

kuns (-te) art, skill; knack; trick; die beel= dende ~te, the plastic arts; die skone ~te, the fine arts; die ~ verfyn, perfect the art; ~aas artificial bait, dummy; ~galery (-e)

art museum, picture gallery; ~gebit (-te) denture, set of artificial teeth; ~hars (-e) plastics; ~ledemate artificial limbs

kunsma'tig (-e) artificial; ~e inseminasie, (K.I), artificial insemination

kuns: ~mis fertiliser, artificial manure; ~skilder (-s) artist, painter; ~stop invi= sible mending, ~stuk (-ke) work of art; clever feat; ~tenaar (-s, . .nare) artist; ~tig (-e; -er; -ste) ingenious, clever, art= ful

kuns: ~vlyt, arts and crafts; ~wedstryd (-e) eisteddfod; ~werk (-e) work of art

kurk (-e) cork; ~droog (. .droë) dry as a bone; ~(e)trekker (-s) corkscrew

kur'per (-s) kurper, tilapia

kursief' (..siewe) italic, in italics

kur'sus (-se) course; 'n ~ loop/volg, attend a course

kur'we (-s) curve

kus¹ (s) (-te) coast, shore

kus² (s) (-se) kiss; (w) (ge-) kiss

kus³ (s): te ~ en te keur, for picking and choosing

kus'sing (-s) pillow, cushion; ~sloop (. .slope) pillow case; ~tuig (. .tuie) hovercraft, kyk skeertuig

kuur (kure) cure

kwaad (s) evil, mischief, wrong

kwaadaar'dig (-e; -er, -ste) malignant; malicious, vicious; ~e groeisel/gewas, malignant growth/tumour

kwaad: ~doener (-s) evildoer; ~geld mis= chief; vir ~geld rondloop, gad about

kwaai (-er; -ste) vicious, wild; hot-tempered; 'n ~ hond, a vicious dog

kwaaivri(e)n'de bad friends

kwaak (ge-) croak, quack

kwaal (kwale) ailment, complaint, malady

kwadraat' square, quadratic

kwa'drupleeg (. .pleë) quadruplegic

kwag'ga (-s) quagga; zebra

kwa'jong (-ens) mischievous boy, urchin; ~streek (. .streke) monkey trick, prank

kwak'salwe (ge-) play the quack; ~r (-s) quack, charlatan, mountebank

kwalifika'sie (-s) qualification

kwalifiseer' (~, ge-) qualify

kwa'lik ill, amiss; hardly, scarcely; hy kon ~ loop, he could hardly walk

kwaliteit' (-e) quality

kwan'sel (ge-) haggle, bargain, barter

kwansuis' quasi, as if (it were); so-called

kwantiteit' (-e) quantity

kwarantyn' quarantine; *onder ~ plaas,* put in quarantine

kwart (-e) quart; quarter; *~ voor agt,* a quarter to eight

kwartaal' (. .tale) quarter, term

kwar'tel (-s) quail; *so doof soos 'n ~,* stone deaf, as deaf as a post

kwartet' (-te) quartet

kwartier' (-e) quarter (of an hour, of the moon, battle); district

kwarts quartz; *~oorlosie* quartz watch

kwas[1] squash

kwas[2] (-te) brush; tuft; knot; tassel

kwa'sie quasi, as if

kwa'sjiorkor kwashiorkor

kweek[1] (s) couch/quick grass

kweek[2] (w) (ge-) cultivate, train; grow; *vrugtebome ~,* grow fruit trees

kweek: *~huis* hothouse; *~pêrel* (-s) cultured pearl; *~skool* training school; seminary

kweel (ge-) warble

kwe'keling (-e) pupil teacher; cadet; trainee

kwe'kery (-e) nursery

kwel (ge-) worry, trouble, harass, torment

kwe'per (-s) quince; *~lat* (-te) quince stick, cane

kwes (ge-) wound, injure; *'n bok ~,* wound a buck; *~baar* vulnerable

kwes'sie (-s) question, matter; issue; *buite die ~,* out of the question

kwets grieve, offend; *iem. se gevoelens ~,* hurt someone's feelings

kwik'silwer mercury, quicksilver

kwik'stertjie (-s) wagtail, Willie Wagtail

kwink'slag (. .slae) witticism, funny saying

kwintet' (-te) quintet

kwis'pel (ge-) wag the tail

kwis'tig (-e; -er, -ste) lavish, prodigal

kwitan'sie (-s) receipt (for money paid)

kwo'rum (-s) quorum; *geen ~ aanwesig nie,* no quorum present

kwo'ta (-s) quota

kwota'sie (-s) quotation

kwoteer' (~, ge-) quote, estimate

kwyl (s) slaver, drivel; (w) (ge-) slaver, drivel

kwyn (ge-) languish, pine away, wilt

kwyt (ge-) discharge; acquit oneself

kyf (ge-) quarrel, dispute

kyk (s) (-e) look, view; (w) (ge-) look, see, view; pry; *op sy neus ~,* look foolish; *~er* (-s) eye; looker-on; viewer (TV); *~gat* (-e) peephole; *~kas(sie)* (-s) television set

kys: *hy is my ~,* he is my (steady) boyfriend; *ons is ge~,* we are going steady

L

laaf, la'we (ge-) refresh; help one to recover from a swoon; *~nis* refreshment; relief

laag[1] (s) (lae) layer, stratum; coating; course (bricks)

laag[2] (b) (lae; laer, -ste) mean; low; vulgar; *lae profiel,* low profile; *teen 'n lae prys,* at a low price

laaghar'tig (-e) base, vile, mean

laag'te (-s) valley, dale, dell, dip

laag'water low tide

laai[1] (s) (-e) drawer, till

laai[2] (s) (-e) trick, dodge; *dis sy ou ~,* that's his old trick

laai[3] (w) (ge-) load; charge; *~graaf* (..awe) front-end loader; *~kas* (-te) chest of drawers, tallboy; container

laai'meester (-s) checker (railways)

laan (lane) avenue, lane, alley

laas last; *~genoemde* the latter, last-named; *~lede* last, ultimo; *~te* last; *die ~te (leste) een van julle,* all of you; *ten ~te,* at last; *~tens* lastly

laat[1] (w) (ge-) let, allow, refrain from (doing); make (one) do; *~ staan dit!* leave it alone! *in die steek ~,* leave in the lurch

laat[2] (b) (late; later, laatste) late

laat'lammetjie afterthought, late arrival

laborato'rium (..ria, -s) laboratory

la'ding (-e, -s) cargo, load, shipment

la'er[1] (s) bearing

la'er[2] (s) (-s) camp, lager

la'er[3] (b, comp. of **laag**) lower, inferior

La'erhuis Lower House, House of Assembly; House of Commons (England)

la'erskool (..skole) primary school, *ook* **primêre skool**

laf (lawwe; lawwer, -ste) insipid, flat; cowardly, silly; *'n lawwe grap,* a silly joke

laf: ~**aard** (-s) coward

lafhar'tig (-e; -er, -ste) cowardly

lag (s) laugh, laughter; *ek kon my* ~ *nie hou nie,* I could not help laughing; *skater van die* ~, shake with laughter; (w) (ge-) laugh; *in die vuis* ~, laugh up one's sleeve

lagu'ne (-s) lagoon, *ook* strandmeer

lagwek'kend (-e; er, -ste), ludicrous

lak[1] (s) seal, sealing wax, lacquer; (w) (ge-) seal; japan; ~**vernisser** (-s) French polisher

lak[2] (w) (ge-) tackle (rugby)

lakei' (-e) footman, lackey

la'ken (-s) cloth, sheet

laks (-e; er, -ste) lax, indolent, slack

lakseer' (ge-) purge, open (the bowels); ~**middel** (-s) laxative, purgative

laks'heid laxity, looseness, indolence

laks'man (-ne) hangman; butcherbird, fiscal shrike

lam[1] (s) (-mers) lamb; (w) (ge-) lamb

lam[2] (b) lame, paralysed; ~**geskrik,** paralysed with fright

lamel'hout laminated wood

lamlen'dig (-e; -er, -ste) lazy, indolent, miserable

lam'mer: ~**ooi** (-e) ewe with lamb (at foot); ~**vanger** (-s) golden eagle, lammergeyer; school attendance officer

lam'metjie (-s, **lammertjies**) little lamb

lamp (-e) lamp

lamp: ~**kap** (-pe) lampshade; ~**olie** paraffin (oil)

lam'sak (-ke) lazybones, weakling, shirker

lams'boud (-e) leg of lamb

lam: ~**siekte** lameness, paralysis; botulism; ~**slaan** (-ge-) paralyse; *dit het my lamgeslaan,* it knocked me sideways

land (s) (-e) land; country; field; *oor* ~, by road; ~ *en sand (see) aanmekaar praat,* talk without stopping; *hier te* ~*e,* in this country; (w) (ge-) disembark, arrive, land

land-af off-shore

land'bou agriculture; *Departement (van) L*~ *en Visserye,* Department of Agriculture and Fisheries

landboukun'dig (-e) agricultural

land: ~**dros** (-te) landdrost; magistrate; ~**elik** (-e) rustic, rural; ~*elike omgewing,* rural environment; ~**engte** (-s) isthmus;

~**genoot** (..note) countryman, compatriot; ~**goed** (-ere) estate, country seat

lan'ding (-e, -s) landing

land: ~**kaart** (-e) map; ~**loop** (..lope) crosscountry race; ~**loper** (-s) vagrant, tramp, vagabond; ~**meter** (-s) (land) surveyor

land: ~**myn** (-e) landmine; ~**skap** landscape

lands: ~**reën,** ~**reent** general rain; ~**taal** vernacular, language of the country

land: ~**streek** (. .streke) region, district; ~**verraaier** (-s) traitor; ~**wyd** nationwide, countrywide; *'n landwye veldtog,* a national campaign

lan'fer crape (crêpe)

lang (attributive) (-er, -ste) long, tall

langdra'dig (-e; -er, -ste) long-winded, wordy, prolix

langdu'rig (-e; -er, -ste) long-lasting, protracted; ~*e droogte,* prolonged drought

lang'saam (. .same; . .samer, -ste) slow, tardy

lang'samerhand gradually

lang: ~**speelplaat,** ~**speler** LP record

langwer'pig (-e) oblong, rectangular

la'ning (-s) hedge, grove; avenue

lank (predicative) (**langer, langste**) long, tall ~**al** long ago, for a long while already

lankmoe'dig (-e; -er, -ste) patient, clement

lans (-e) lance, spear

lanseer' (~, ge-) launch (torpedo, spacecraft); start; lance, pierce (tumour); ~**blad** launch(ing) pad

lanterfan'ter (s) (-s) loiterer, lazybones; (w) (ge-) idle, laze, loiter

lantern' (-s) lantern

lap (s) (-pe) patch; cloth; rag; *op die* ~*pe bring,* bring to light; (w) (ge-) mend, patch; *'n ge*~*te broek,* patched trousers

lapel' (-le) lapel; ~**wapen** (-s) lapel badge

lar'we (-s) larva

las[1] (s) (-se) seam, joint, weld; (w) (ge-) join, weld; pool funds

las[2] (s) (-te) burden, freight; charge, order; nuisance; *bates en* ~*te,* assets and liabilities; *op* ~, by order

la'ser laser; ~**straal** (..ale) laser beam

las'pos (-te) nuisance, toublesome person

las'ter (s) slander, defamation, libel; (w) (ge-) slander; curse, blaspheme

las'tig (-e; -er, -ste) troublesome, burden=
some, annoying, difficult

lat (-te) lath; stick, cane; batten

latent' (-e) latent

la'ter later; *hoe ~ hoe kwater,* the longer it
lasts, the worse it becomes

Latyn' Latin

laven'tel lavender, scent; **~haan** dandy

la'wa lava

lawaai' (s) noise; hubbub, tumult

law'wigheid insipidity, foolishness, tom=
myrot

lê (ge-) place, put; lay (eggs); *dit ~ voor die
hand,* it goes without saying; *op sterwe ~,*
be dying

le'de *kyk* lid; *'n siekte onder ~ hê,* have an
illness coming on, be sickening for

le'degeld (-e) subscription, membership fee

le'de: **~lys** (-te) list of members; **~mate**
(net in mv) limbs, parts of the body;
~stand composition of members; **~tal**
number of members

le'dig (w) (ge-) empty; (b) (-e) idle; with=
out employment

le'digheid idleness; emptiness; *~ is die
duiwel se oorkussing,* Satan finds some
mischief for idle hands to do

leed pain, sorrow, grief

leef (ge-) live, exist, subsist; *volgens jou
oortuiging ~,* live up to one's convic=
tions; **~tyd** lifetime; time of life, age; *op
middelbare ~tyd,* in middle life; **~wyse**
manner of living (life), lifestyle

leeg (leë, leër, -ste) empty, void; vacant

leek (leke) layman; novice

leem'te (-s) defect, gap, blank, lacuna; *'n
~ aanvul,* fill (up) a gap

leen, (s) fief, feudal tenure; (w) (ge-) lend;
borrow; *ek ~ van hom en hy ~ aan my,*
I borrow from him and he lends to me

leer¹ (s) leather; (b) leather

leer² (s) (lere) ladder

leer³ (leerstellinge) doctrine; apprenticeship;
(w) (ge-) learn, study; teach; *van buite ~,*
learn by heart

le'ër (s) (-s) army; lair, bed (animal); (w)
(ge-) encamp

lê'er (-s) layer (hen); register; leaguer (for
wine); sleeper (railway); file (for papers)

leer: **~der** learner; **~gang** (-e) course of
study, curriculum; **~geld** (-e) tuition fees;
duur ~geld betaal, pay heavily for one's
experience

leergie'rig (-e; -er, -ste) studious

leer: **~jare** apprenticeship; **~klerk** (-e) ar=
ticled clerk; **~krag** (-te) teacher; **~ling** (-e)
scholar, pupil; learner; **~lingrybewys**
learner driver's licence

leer'looier (-s) tanner; **~y** (-e) tannery

le'ërmag (-te) army, *ook* weermag

leer: **~meester** (-s) teacher, tutor, precep=
tor; **~plan** (-ne) syllabus, scheme of work;
~plig compulsory education; **~saam**
(. .same; . .samer, -ste) instructive, in=
formative

leer'skap articles (accountant, attorney)

leer'skool practice/demonstration school;
die ~ van die lewe, the school of life

leer: **~stoel** (-e) chair (university); **~stuk**
(-ke) dogma, tenet; **~vak** (-ke) subject (of
study)

leer'werk¹ leatherwork

leer'werk² studies; things to be learnt

lees¹ (s) (-te) last; figure, waist; *op dieselfde
~ geskoei,* cast in the same mould

lees² (w) (ge-) read; **~baar** (. .bare) legible,
readable; **~boek** (-e) reader, reading
book; **~gebrek** (e) dyslexia; **~les** (-se)
reading lesson; **~stof** reading matter;
~teken (-s) punctuation mark

leeu (-s) lion; **~bekkie** (-s) snapdragon, an=
tirrhinum; **~e-aandeel** lion's share

leeu'emoed great courage

leeu: **~hok** (-ke) lion's cage; **~kuil** (-e)
lions' den; **~mannetjie** (-s) lion

leeu'rik (-ke) skylark, *kyk* lewerik

leeu: **~temmer** (-s) lion tamer; **~wyfie** (-s)
lioness

legaat' (legate) legacy

lê'geld dock dues; demurrage

legenda'ries (-e) legendary; *'n ~e figuur,* a
legendary figure

legen'de (-s) legend

le'gio legion

legioen' (-e) legion

leg'kaart (-e) jigsaw puzzle

lê'hen (-ne) laying hen

lei¹ (s) (-e) slate; *~ en griffel,* slate and
pencil

lei² (w) (ge-) lead, conduct, guide; preside

lei'dak (-ke) slate roof

lei'ding direction, management, guidance,
leadership; conduit

lei'draad (. .drade) guide(line), clue, lead

lei: ~er (-s) leader, guide; *'n gebore* ~er, a born leader; ~ersberaad summit talks; ~erskap leadership

lei'klip slate (stone)

lei'sel (-s) rein; *die* ~ *in hande neem,* take charge

lek[1] (s) (-ke) leak(age), puncture; (w) (ge-) leak

lek[2] (s) (-ke) lick; (w) lick

le'keprediker (-s) lay preacher

lek'ker[1] (s) (-s) sweet

lek'ker[2] (b) (-der, -ste) dainty, nice, sweet, palatable, savoury; tipsy; ~bek (-ke) epicure, sweet tooth

lek'kergoed, lek'kers sweets, confectionery

lek'kerlyf tipsy

lekkerny' (-e) titbit, delicacy

lek'sikon (-s) lexicon, dictionary

lek'tor (-e, -s) lecturer

lektoraat' (. .rate) lectureship

lektri'se (-s) (lady) lecturer

lektuur' reading matter

lel (-le) lobe (of the ear); wattle (bird)

le'lie (-s) lily; ~wit lily-white

le'lik (-e; -er, -ste) ugly, unsightly, deformed; *so* ~ *soos die nag,* as ugly as sin

lem (-me) blade (of a knife)

lem'metjie[1] (-s) lime (fruit)

lem'metjie[2] (-s) (razor) blade; small blade

lemoen' (-e) orange; ~konfyt orange jam, preserve; ~sap orange juice

len'de (-ne, -s) loin; *die* ~ne *omgord,* gird one's loins

len'delam (-mer, -ste) hipshot, rickety; ~ *tafel,* rickety table

le'ner (-s) borrower; lender

leng'te (-s) length; longitude

le'nig (b) lithe, supple, agile

le'ning (-e, -s) loan

lens (-e) lens

len'sie (-s) lentil; ~so(e)p lentil soup

len'te (-s) spring

le'pel (-s) spoon; ~ *in die dak steek,* give up the ghost

le'raar (-s) minister (of religion), parson

les[1] (s) (-se) lesson; *lelik* ~ *moet opsê,* have a most difficult time

les[2] (w) (ge-) quench, slake; *jou dors* ~, quench one's thirst

les[3] (b): ~ *bes,* last but not least

les'biër (s) (-s) lesbian

le'ser (-s) reader

leseres' (-se) reader (lady)

le'sing (-s) lecture, reading

les'senaar (-s) desk

let (ge-) heed, mind; *sonder om op die gevaar te* ~, heedless of the danger; ~ *wel,* mind, note, N.B.

let'sel (-s) hurt, damage, injury; *sonder* ~, unscathed, *kyk* ongedeerd

let'ter (s) (-s) letter; (w) (ge-) mark: ~dief (. .diewe) plagiarist

let'terdiefstal plagiarism; cribbing; ~ *pleeg,* plagiarise

let'tere literature; *fakulteit (van)* ~, faculty of arts

let'ter: ~greep (. .grepe) syllable; ~kunde (-s) literature

letterkun'dig (-e) literary; pertaining to literature; ~e (-s) man of letters

let'ter: ~lik (-e) literal(ly); *hulle is* ~*lik afgemaai,* they were literally decimated; ~naam (. .name) acronym, name compounded from initials (e.g. UNO, ISCOR); ~raaisel (-s) letter riddle, puzzle

leu'en (-s) lie, falsehood; *al is die* ~ *nog so snel, die waarheid agterhaal hom wel,* a lie has short wings; ~aar (-s) liar

leu'en: ~taal falsehood, untruth; ~verklikker (-s) lie detector

leukemie' leukemia, *ook* bloedkanker

leun (ge-) lean; ~stoel arm chair

leu'ning (-s) support; back of a chair; rail

leus (-e), **leu'se** (-s) motto, device, slogan

Leviet' (-e) Levite; *iem. die L*~*e voorlees,* rebuke a person

le'we (s) (-ns) life; *sy* ~ *lank,* all his life; *die* ~ *skenk aan,* give birth to; (w) (ge-) live, exist, subsist

le'wend (-e) living, alive; ~e hawe, livestock; *in* ~e *lywe,* in the flesh; ~e uitsending, live broadcast

le'wendig (-e; -er, -ste) living (person); alive (animal); quick, lively (person); vivid (description); vivacious (animal)

le'wens: ~beskouing (-e, -s) view of life; ~beskrywing (-e, -s) biography; ~geskiedenis (-se) life story; ~gevaarlik (-e) very dangerous; ~groot life-size; full length

le'wenskets (-e) biography

le'wens: ~krag (-te) vital power, vitality; ~kwaliteit quality of life; ~lang (-e),

~lank liefelong; indeterminate; ~lange erelidmaatskap, honorary life member= ship; ~lig light of life; *die ~lig aanskou,* be born; ~loop career, course of life

le'wens: ~lus energy, vivacity; ~nood= saaklik vital; ~redder (-s) liefesaver, *kyk* strandwag

lewensvat'baar (. .bare) viable, capable of life; ~heidstudie viability study, *kyk* gangbaar(heid)studie

le'wensversekering life insurance; ~(s)= maatskappy (-e) life insurance company

le'wens: ~verwagting life expectancy; ~wyse way/manner of life, lifestyle, *ook* leefwyse

le'wer[1] (s) (-s) liver; *wat het oor jou ~ ge= loop?* what is eating you?

le'wer[2] (w) (ge-) furnish, supply; deliver

leweransier' (-s) furnisher, supplier

le'werik (-e), le'werkie (-s) (sky)lark

le'wer: ~traan cod-liver oil; ~wors liver sausage

liasseer' (~, ge-) file; ~kabinet (-te) filing cabinet

liberalis'me liberalism

libertyn' (-e) libertine, *kyk* vrydenker

lid (lede) member; limb; ~ *word van,* be= come a member of

lid'maat (. .mate) member (of a church); ~skap membership

lid'woord article

lied (-ere) song

lie'derlik (-e; -er, -ste) filthy, dirty, de= bauched, dissolute

lied'jie (-s) song, ballad, ditty; *altyd die= selfde ~ sing,* harp on the same string

lief (s): *in ~ en leed,* come rain, come shine; *vir ~ neem,* make shift; make do; (b) (liewe; liewer, -ste) dear, beloved, ami= able; lovely, sweet; *'n liewe meisie,* a sweet girl

liefda'dig (-e) charitable, benevolent; ~heid charity, benevolence

lief'de love; charity; *geloof, hoop en ~,* faith, hope and charity; *ou ~ roes nie,* true love never grows old; ~groete: ~groete van, yours with love

lief'des: ~gedig (-te) love poem; ~ge= skiedenis (-se) love story, love affair; ~naam: *in ~naam,* for heaven's sake; ~verhaal (. .hale) love story; ~wil: *om ~wil,* for heaven's sake

lief'hê (. .gehad) love, care for

liefheb'bend (-e) loving, affectionate; *u ~e niggie,* your loving niece

lief'hebbery (-e) hobby, favourite pursuit

lie'fie (-s) dear, darling, sweetheart

lie'fies lovely, nicely, sweetly

lief: ~koos (ge-) caress, fondle, stroke; *my ge~koosde boek,* my favourite book

lief'ling, (-e) darling, pet, favourite; ~s'boek (-e) favourite book; ~s'vak (-ke) favourite subject

liefs preferably, rather; *ek sal ~ nie gaan nie,* I'd rather not go

lief'ste (s) (-s) sweetheart, dearest, darling; (b) dearest

lieftal'lig (-e; -er, -ste) sweet, attractive

lieg (ge-) lie, tell lies

lier (-e) lyre

lies (-te) groin

liet'sjie (-s) litchi

lie'wer(s) rather, preferably; *ek wil ~ hier= die een hê,* I'd prefer this one

lig[1] (s) (-te) light, give a light; (b) (te; -ter, -ste) light

lig[2] (w) (ge-) lift; *~ op die klip!* pick up that stone!

lig[3] (b) (-te; -ter, -ste) easy; mild; slight; *te ~ in die broek wees,* not equal to the task

li'ga (-s) league

lig'gaam (..game) body; *met ~ en siel,* body and soul

liggaam'lik (-e) bodily; physical (educa= tion); corporal (punishment); corporeal

lig'gaams: ~bou build of body, stature; ~oefening (-e) physical exercise; ~op= voeding physical education; ~taal body language

liggelo'wig (-e; -er, -ste) credulous

liggeraak' (-te) touchy, sensitive

lig'ging (-e, -s) site, position, situation

lig'koeël (-s) light ball, fireball; tracer bul= let

lig: ~spoor(patroon) tracer; ~straal (..strale) ray of light

lig'telaaie: *in ~,* ablaze, in a blaze

likeur' (-e, -s) liqueur

likied' liquid; ~e bates, liquid assets

likkewaan' (..wane) iguana, leguan

likwida'sie liquidation

likwideer' (~, ge-) liquidate

limona'de lemonade

lin'de (-s) lime; ~boom (..bome) lime tree

linguis' (-te) linguist
liniaal' (liniale) ruler
linieer' (ge-) rule (lines)
lin'ker left; ~**arm** (-s) left arm; ~**kant** (-e) left side; ~**stuur** left-hand drive
links left-handed; to (on) the left; ~ *af*, to the left; *iets* ~ *laat lê*, leave something undone; ~ *om*, to the left; left turn; ~**gesind** leftwing (students, workers)
lin'ne linen; ~**goed** linen
lint (-e) ribbon, riband; ~**wurm** (-s) tapeworm, taenia
lip (-pe) lip; ~**pe'diens** lip service; ~**stiffie** (-s) lipstick
liriek' lyric poetry
lirie'ke lyrics
liriek'skrywer (-s) lyricist
li'ries (-e) lyric(al)
lis[1] (-te) trick, ruse, artifice
lis[2] (-se) noose, loop; frog (on uniform)
lisensiaat' licentiate
lisen'sie (-s) licence, *ook* **liksens**
lis'tig (-e; -er, -ste) cunning, artful, wily
lit (-te) joint; internode; *uit* ~, out of joint
li'ter (-s) litre; *twee* ~ *melk*, two litres of milk
litera'tor (-e, -s) literator, man of letters
literatuur' (..ture) literature; ~**geskiedenis** history of literature
literêr' (-e) literary
litografie' lithography
lit'teken (-s) scar
loei (ge-) low, bellow, moo; roar
lo'ën (ge-) deny
loer (ge-) spy, watch, lurk; *op die* ~ *lê*, lie in wait
loe'rie (-s) lourie
loer: ~**koop** window shopping; ~**kyker** (-s) seeing eye; ~**vink** Peeping Tom
loe'sing (-s) thrashing, hiding; *iem. 'n afgedankste* ~ *gee,* give someone a sound thrashing
lof praise, eulogy; *met* ~ *slaag*, pass with honours/distinction; *groot* ~ *toeswaai,* give high praise to; ~**rede** (-s) panegyric, eulogy; ~**sang** (-e) song of thanksgiving, ode; ~**waardig** (-e) praiseworthy
logarit'me (-s) logarithm
lo'gies (-e) logical
lo'gika logic
lojaal' (lojale) loyal

lojaliteit' loyalty
lok[1] (s) (-ke) curl, lock
lok[2] (w) (ge-) decoy, entice; ~ *hom weg!* draw him away!
lokaal' (s) (lokale) hall, room; (b) (lokale) local
lok'aas (..ase) bait, allurement, decoy
loket' (-te) ticket window, box office; ~**treffer** box office success
lok'film trailer
lokomotief' (..tiewe) locomotive, engine
lok'val (-le) ambush, trap
lok'vink (-e) police trap
lok'voël (-s) decoy
lol (ge-) bother, trouble; *moenie heeldag met my* ~ *nie*, don't pester me always
lomp (-e; -er, -ste) clumsy, awkward
long (-e) lung; ~**ontsteking** inflammation of the lungs, pneumonia; *dubbele* ~*ontsteking*, double pneumonia; ~**tering** pulmonary consumption, phthisis
lont (-e) fuse; ~ *ruik,* smell a rat
lood lead; plumb, plummet; *onder die* ~ *steek*, pepper; ~**gieter** (-s) plumber; ~**reg** (-te) perpendicular, vertical
loods[1] (s) (-e) shed
loods[2] (s) (-e) pilot (harbour); (w) (ge-) pilot
loof (w) (ge-) praise, extol
looi (ge-) tan; beat; ~**bas** tanning bark, wattle bark; ~**ery** (-e) tannery
loom (lomer, -ste) heavy, languid, drowsy
loon (s) (lone) reward; pay; wages; *boontjie kry sy (kom om) sy* ~*tjie*, chickens come home to roost; *hy kry sy verdiende* ~, it serves him right; (w) (ge-) pay, reward; *dit sal die moeite* ~, it will be worth the trouble; ~**gaping** wage gap; ~**verhoging** wage increase
loon'trekker (-s) wage earner
loop (s) (lope) course, run; walk; stream; barrel (gun); (w) (ge-) walk; go; ~**baan** (..bane) career, course; ~**baanuitstalling** (-s) careers exhibition; ~**dop** last drink, one for the road; (w) (ge-) pay, reward; ~**graaf** (..grawe) trench; ~**plank** (-e) gangway, footboard; ~**ring** (-e) walking ring (for child)
loops (-e) ruttish
loop: ~**tyd** duration, currency; ~**vlak** (-ke) tread
loot[1] (s) (lote) shoot; descendant

loot² (w) (ge-) draw lots, raffle; ~**jie** (-s) lottery ticket; *die ~ wen*, win the toss (sport)

lo'pend (-e) current, present, running; ~*e belastingstelsel (LBS)*, Pay As You Earn (PAYE); ~*e rekening*, current account

lo'per¹ (-s) runner, staircarpet; walker; masterkey

lo'per² (-s) big shot, buckshot

lo'pie (-s) little stream; run (cricket)

lor'rie (-s) lorry; ~**drywer** (-s) lorry driver

los (w) (ge-) loosen; fire; redeem; let go; *laat my ~!* let me go! (b) (-ser, -ste) loose, free

losban'dig (-e; -er, -ste) dissolute, licentious

los'bars (-ge-) burst/break loose, explode

los'bol (-le) rake, libertine, playboy

los'brand (-ge-) discharge, fire off

los'breek (-ge-) break loose/away

loseer' (~, ge-) lodge, board, stay at; ~**der** (-s) lodger

los'geld ransom

los'goed movable property

lo'sie (-s) lodge (Freemason)

losies' lodging, boarding; *vry ~ hê*, be in goal; ~**huis** (-e) boarding house

loskruitpatroon' (..trone) blank cartridge

los'loop (-ge-) run loose, be at large; **los-loperhond** stray dog

los'lootjie (-s) bye (in a draw)

los'pitperske (-s) freestone peach

los'prys ransom, *kyk* **losgeld**

lot¹ fate, destiny; *hom aan sy ~ oorlaat*, leave him to his fate

lot² (-te) lot (at sale)

lot³ lot; *die ~ laat beslis*, decide by casting lots

lo'tery (-e) lottery, raffle

lo'ting draw, drawing of lots

lot'jie *van ~ getik*, mad, crazy (person)

lou (-er, -ste) lukewarm, tepid

lou'ere laurels; *op sy ~ rus*, rest on one's laurels

lourier' (-e) laurel, bay; ~**krans** (-e) laurel wreath

lo'wer foliage; ~**groen** quite (very) green

lug (s) (-te) air, sky; smell; *die blou ~*, the blue sky; *~ skep*, take an airing; (w) (ge-) air, ventilate; *sy gevoelens ~*, vent one's feeling; ~**aanval** (-le) air attack; ~**alarm** (-s) aircraft alarm; ~**bombardement** air raid; ~**(buite)band** (-e) tubeless tyre; ~**bus**

(-se) monorail; ~**diens** (-te) airways; ~**dig** (-te) airtight; ~**draad** (..drade) aerial; ~**druk** atmospheric pressure; ~**filter** (-s) air filter; ~**foto** (-'s) aerial photograph

lughar'tig (-e; -er, -ste) light-hearted

lug: ~**hawe** (-ns) airport; ~**ledig** (-e) airless, void of air; *'n ~leë ruimte*, a vacuum; ~**mag** (-te) air force; ~**pos** airmail; ~**re-dery** (-e) airline; ~**ruim** atmosphere; ~**skip** (..skepe) airship, dirigible; ~**spieëling** mirage; fata morgana; ~**spoor** (..spore) aerial railway; ~**suiweraar** (-s) air filter

lug'tig (-e) airy, lightly, light-hearted; afraid; *hy is maar ~ vir my*, he takes no liberties with me

lug: ~**vaart** aviation, aeronautics; ~**ver-frisser** air freshener; ~**versorging** air-conditioning; *die winkel is lugversorg*, these premises are air-conditioned; ~**waardin'** (-ne) air hostess; ~**werk-tuigkundige** (-s) air mechanic

lui¹ (w) (ge-) sound, ring, toll, peal; *hoe ~ die brief?* how does the letter go?

lui² (b) (-e; -ste) lazy, idle; slothful; ~**aard** (-s) sluggard, lazybones, laggard, slacker

luid'keels at the top of one's voice

luid'lees reading aloud

luid'roeper (-s) loudhailer

luidrug'tig (-e; -er, -ste) noisy, clamorous

luid'spreker (-s) loudspeaker; ~**stelsel** (-s) public address system

lui'er¹ (s) (-s) swaddling cloth, napkin (baby); ~**diens** napkin service

lui'er² (w) (ge-) be lazy, laze about; idle (motor)

lui'er: ~**ig** (-e) rather lazy, idle; ~**spoed** idling (motor) speed

luik (s) (-e) shutter; manhole; trapdoor; hatch (ship); ~**rug** (..rûe) hatchback (car)

lui'lak (s) (-ke) sluggard, lazybones

luilek'kerland (land of) Cocagne, fool's paradise, happy valley

lui'perd (-s) leopard

luis (-e) louse, vermin; *jou lae ~!* you cad!

lui'slang (-e) python, boa constrictor

lui'ster¹ (s) lustre, glory

luis'ter² (w) (ge-) listen, hear; obey; *na goeie raad ~*, follow good advice; ~**liedjie** (-s) light modern song; ~**aar** (-s) listener (radio)

luis'tervink (-e) eavesdropper

luis'tervlooi (-e) electronic bug
luit (-e) lute
luitenant' (-e, -s) lieutenant
lukwart' (-e) loquat
lum'mel (-s) simpleton, boor, lout, lubber, stupid fellow
luns (-e) linchpin; ~riem (-e) axle-pin strap; dirty fellow
lus (s) (-te) desire, appetite, inclination
lusern' lucerne
lus: ~hof (..howe) pleasure garden; ~te-loos (..lose) listless, dull
luuk'se luxury; nie gewoond aan sulke ~s nie, not used to such luxuries; ~artikel (-s) luxury article; ~bus (-se) luxury bus
ly (ge-) suffer, bear, endure; skipbreuk ~, be wrecked; dit ~ geen twyfel nie, there is no doubt
ly'delik(-e) passive, submissive; ~e verset passive resistance
ly'dend (-e) suffering, passive; ~e vorm passive voice
ly'ding suffering; 'n dier uit sy ~ verlos, put an animal out of its pains
ly'er (-s) sufferer, patient
lyf (lywe) body

lyf: ~rente (-s) annuity, gratuity; ~straf corporal punishment; ~straf oplê/toe-dien, impose/inflict corporal punishment; ~taal body language; ~wag (-te) body-guard
lyk¹ (s) (-e) corpse, cadaver
lyk² (w) (ge-) resemble, appear, look, seem to be; baie na mekaar ~, resemble each other closely
lyk: ~besorger (-s) undertaker; ~skouing (-s) autopsy, inquest, post-mortem (examination); ~stasie (-s), ~stoet (-e) funeral procession; ~verbranding cremation, ook verassing; ~wa (-ens) hearse, ook roukoets
lym (s) glue; (w) (ge-) glue
lyn (-e) rope, line, string; track (railway)
lyn: ~olie linseed oil; ~reg (-te) straight, perpendicular; ~regter linesman, line judge; ~staan line-out (rugby)
lys (-te) list, catalogue; frame, rail; ledge; 'n ge~te Kommunis, a listed Communist; ~ jou vrae, list your questions
lys'ter (-s) thrush
ly'wig (-e; -er, -ste) corpulent, fat, thick; bulky, voluminous; 'n ~e verhandeling, a comprehensive thesis/dissertation

M

ma (-'s) ma, mother; jy sal jou ~ vir 'n eendvoël aansien, you will find yourself in Queer Street
maag (mae, mage) stomach; jou oë is groter as jou ~, you ask for more than you can eat
maagd (-e) virgin, maiden
maag: ~kanker cancer in the stomach; ~koors gastric fever; ~pyn stomach ache; dit gee 'n mens ~pyn, it turns one's stomach; ~seer (..sere) gastric/duodenal ulcer
maai (w) (ge-) mow, reap; hy ~ waar hy nie gesaai het nie, reap where you have not sown
maak (s) make; (w) (ge-) make, do, shape; alles wil ~ en breek, try to force the issue; dit ~ geen saak nie, it doesn't matter
maal¹ (s) (male) time; drie ~ vier, three times four

maal² (s) (male) meal; mosterd na die ~, mustard after meat
maal³ (w) (ge-) grind; paint; circle round and round; ~stroom (..strome) whirl-pool, maelstrom
maal'tyd (..tye) meal, repast
maan (s) (mane) moon
maand (-e) month; die ~ Maart, the month of March
Maan'dag (..dae) Monday; blou ~, blue Monday
maand: ~blad (..blaaie) monthly magazine; ~e'liks (-e) monthly; ~stonde men-struation
maan: ~landing (-s) moon landing; ~lig moonlight; ~s'verduistering (-e, -s) eclipse of the moon
maar but, merely, only, yet, just; toe ~! right-o! don't mention it
maar'skalk (-e) marshal

maat¹ (mate) measure; dimension, size; *die ~ hou,* beat time

maat² (-s, maters) mate, comrade, partner; *Jan Rap en sy ~,* ragtag and bobtail

maat'reël (-s) measure

maatskap'lik (-e) social; *~e werker/werk= ster,* social worker

maatskappy' (-e) society; company

maat'staf (..stawwe) criterion, standard

ma'deliefie (-s) daisy

ma'er (-der, -ste) lean, thin; meagre; *so ~ soos 'n kraai,* as thin as a lath

mag¹ (s) (-te) power, might, strength, con= trol

mag² (w) (mog) may

magasyn' (-e) shop, warehouse; magazine

ma'gies (-e) magic(al)

magis'ter (-s) master's degree

magistraat' (..strate) magistrate, landdrost

magneet' (..nete) magnet

magne'ties (-e) magnetic

mags: ~de'ling power sharing; ~vertoon show of force/strength

mag'teloos (..lose) powerless, helpless

mag'tig (w) (ge-) authorise, warrant, em= power; (b) (-e; -er, -ste) powerful, mighty

ma'-hulle mother and the rest, mum and co(mpany)

ma'jesteit (-e) majesty; splendour

majestueus' (-e) majestic, august

majoor' (-s) major

mak (-ker, -ste) tame, docile, gentle; *so ~ soos 'n lam(metjie),* as gentle as a lamb

makeer' (~, ge-) ail, lack, matter; be wanting; *wat ~ jou?* what are you suf= fering from? *wat ~ jy?* what has come over you, what are you up to?

ma'kelaar (-s) broker

ma'ker (-s) maker

makie'tie, mokie'tie (-s) feast, festivity, celebration

mak'lik (-e; -er, -ste) easy

mak'rostraler (-s) jumbo jet

mak'simum (-s) maximum

mal (-ler, -ste) mad, foolish, silly

mala'ria malaria

Malei'er (-s) Malay

mal: ~heid madness, nonsense, foolish= ness; ~huis (-e) lunatic asylum

mal'jan: *~ onder die hoenders,* a thorn among the roses

mal: ~kop (-pe) madcap, tomboy; *~kop wees,* act like a lunatic; ~le'meule (-s) merry-go-round

mals (-e; -er, -ste) soft, juicy, tender

mal'va (-s) geranium

mama' (-'s) mamma

mam'ba (-s) mamba

mam'ma (-s) mamma

mam'mie (-s) mummy (mother)

mampar'ra (-s) ass, fool; raw labourer

mampoer' peach brandy, *kyk* perske= brandewyn, witblits

Mams, Mum (mother)

man (-ne, -s) man, husband; *'n ~ van aan= sien,* a man of standing; *aan die ~ bring,* sell, dispose of; *met ~ en muis vergaan,* lost with all hands on board

mandaat' (..date) mandate, power to act

mand'jie (-s) basket, hamper

manel' (-le) dress coat, frock coat; *so waar soos padda ~ dra,* as true as faith

maneu'ver (-s) manoeuvre

manewa'le (-s) antics, capers

man'gel (-s) tonsil

manhaf'tig (-e; -er, -ste) brave, courageous

maniak', ma'niak (-ke) maniac

manie', ma'nie (-s) mania, craze, rage

manier' (-e) manner, fashion, way; *op hierdie ~,* in this way; *geen ~e ken nie,* be ill-mannered

manifes' (-te) manifest(o)

manipuleer' (~, ge-) manipulate

mank, (-er, -ste) limping, lame, crippled

man'lik (-e) manly; masculine; *alle ~e af= stammelinge,* all male descendants

manmoe'dig (-e; -er, -ste) brave, manly, courageous

man'na manna

man'nekrag manpower, labour force; ~benutting manpower utilisation; ~na= vorsing manpower research

mannekyn' (-e) mannequin

mans'hemp (..hemde) man's shirt

mansjet' (-te) cuff

man: ~skap (-pe) crew; man, soldier; ~slag manslaughter, homicide

mans'mens (-e), mans'persoon (..sone) man, male

man'tel (-s) mantle, cloak, cape; ~draaier (-s) turncoat, chameleon; ~pak (-ke) coat and skirt (costume)

manuskrip' (-te) manuscript

mari'ne navy; ~versekering marine insurance

marionet' (-te) puppet

mark (-te) market; ~aanwyser market indicator

markeer' (~, ge-) mark; *die pas* ~, mark time

markee'tent (-e) marquee (tent)

mark: ~navorsing market research; ~plein (-e) market square

marmela'de marmelade

mar'mer marble

marmot'jie (-s) guinea-pig

mars (-e) march

mars'banker (-s) horse mackerel, bastard mackerel

mars(j)eer' (~, ge-) march

mar'tel (ge-) torment, torture, rack; ~aar (-s; ..lare) martyr

martelares' (-se) martyr (woman)

mar'tel: ~dood death by torture; ~kamer (-s) torture chamber

Mar'tjie: ~ *Louw*, Martial Law, *kyk* krygswet

mas (-te) mast, pole; *sien om die* ~ *op te kom*; fend for oneself

mas'banker (-s) horse mackerel

ma'sels measles; *Duitse* ~, German measles

masjien' (-e) machine; engine

masjinerie' (-ë) machinery

masjinis' (-te) machinist; mechanic; engineer; engine driver

mas'ker (s) (-s) mask, disguise; *onder die* ~ *van vroomheid*, under the cloak of piety; (w) (ge-) mask; ~bal (-s) fancydress ball

mas'sa (-s) mass, crowd; bulk, lump; mass/weight

mas'samedia, mas'samediums mass media

massa: ~produksie mass production; ~versending bulk posting

masseer' (~, ge-) massage; ~salon massage parlour, *ook* streelperseel

massief' (..siewe) massive, solid

mas'tig! gracious!

masur'ka (-s) mazurka

mat[1] (s) (-e) (door)mat; (chair) bottom; *deur die* ~ *val*, take a tumble; (w) (ge-) mat

mat[2] (b) (-te; -ter, -ste) lack-lustre, dull; exhausted, tired

ma'te measure, degree, extent; *in 'n groot* ~, to a large extent

matema'tikus (-se) mathematician

materiaal' (..riale) material

materialis' (-te) materialist; ~me materialism; ~ties (-e) materialistic

ma'ters companions, chums, friends

mate'sis mathematics, *ook* wiskunde

mat'glas frosted glass

ma'tig (w) (ge-) moderate, mitigate, restrain; (b) (-e; -er, -ste) moderate, temperate; sober; *iets* ~ *gebruik*, use/consume in moderation

matinee' (-s) matinee

ma''tjie (-s) small mother, mummy

mat'jie (-s) rug, little mat

mat'jiesgoed rushes

matras' (-se) mattress

Matriek' Matriculation, Matric

Matrikula'sie Matriculation; ~-eksamen Matriculation examination

matrikuleer' (~, ge-) matriculate

matro'ne (-s) matron, housemother

matroos' (..trose) sailor; *vloek soos 'n* ~, swear like a trooper

me'bos dried and sugared apricots, mebos

medal'je (-s) medal

medaljon' (-s) medallion; locket

me'de (together) with, co-; ~burger (-s) fellow citizen

mededeel'saam (..same) liberal, charitable

me'de: ~deling (-e, -s) communication; ~dinger (-s) competitor, rival

me'de: ~eienaar (-s) joint owner; part owner; ~klinker (-s) consonant

medely'(d)e compassion, pity, commiseration; ~ *hê met*, sympathise with

medeplig'tig (-e) accessory to, concerned in; ~e (-s) accomplice, accessory

me'de: ~werking co-operation, collaboration; ~wete knowledge; *sonder die* ~wete van A, without A's knowledge

me'dia (s) (mv) media; ~gebruiker (-s) media user; ~sentrum (-s) media centre

me'dies (-e) medical; ~e keuring (ondersoek), medical examination (inspection)

me'dikus (-se, ..dici) physician, doctor, medical practitioner

medisy'ne medicine

me'dium (..dia, -s) medium

mee with, together; also, likewise; comee'deel (-ge-) inform, communicate, impart

mee'ding (-ge-) compete

meegaan'de sympathetic, tolerant

mee'gevoel sympathy

meel meal; flour; ~blom flour

mee'luister (-ge-) listen together; monitor; tap (telephone); ~apparaat bugging device

meen (ge-) mean, intend, think; ~ *jy dit regtig?* do you really mean it?

meent'huis (-e) townhouse

meer¹ (s) (mere) lake

meer² (b) moor, tie up (boat)

meer³ (b) more; *niks ~ as billik nie,* only fair; ~dere (-s) superior

meer'derheid majority, superiority; ~(s)*regering majority government

meerderja'rig (-e) major, of age; ~e (-s) major

meer'graad multigrade (oil)

meer'kat (-te, ..kaaie) meercat

meer'min (-ne) mermaid

meer'voud (-e) plural

mees (b) most; (bw) mostly; *hy is die ~ verleë persoon wat ek ken,* he is the most bashful person I know

mees'(t)al generally, as a rule, mostly

mees'te most, greatest; *die ~ mense,* most people

mees'ter (-s) master; teacher; *hom ~ maak van,* capture; *hy is ~ van sy vak,* he knows his trade/profession thoroughly

mees'terbrein mastermind

mees'ter: ~lik (-e, -er, -ste) excellent, masterly; *hy het hom ~lik van sy taak gekwyt,* he made an excellent job of it; ~stuk (-ke) masterpiece

meet (w) (ge-) measure, gauge

meet: ~band (-e) tape measure; ~kunde geometry

meeu (-e) seagull

mee'val (-ge-) cause surprise, succeed (beyond expectation); ~ler(tjie) (-s) windfall, stroke of luck, bonanza

meewa'rig (-e; -er, -ste) rueful, sympathetic

mee'werk (-ge-) co-operate, collaborate

mega'nies (-e) mechanical

mega'nikus (-se, ..nici) mechanic

meganis'me mechanism

Mei May

mein'eed perjury; ~ *pleeg,* commit perjury

mei'sie (-s) girl, maiden

mei'sieskool (..skole) girls' school; *Hoër Meisieskool Boksburg,* Boksburg Girls High School

mei'siestem (-me) girl's voice; girlish voice

mejuf'frou (-e) miss

mekaar' each other, one another; *na ~,* one after the other

melaats' (-e) leprous; ~heid leprosy

melancho'lies (-e; -er, -ste) melancholic

meld (ge-) mention, inform, communicate; ~ *jou môre aan,* report tomorrow; *in antwoord ~ asseblief...,* in reply please quote...

mel'ding mention; ~ *maak van,* make mention of

melk (s) milk; (w) (ge-) milk

melk: ~baard down (on the chin), soft beard; ~ery (-e) dairy, dairy farm; milking; ~koei (-e) milch cow; ~tert (-e) milk tart; M~weg Milky Way

melodie' (-ë) melody

melodieus' (-e) melodious

memoran'dum (..da, -s) memorandum; minute

memoriseer' (~, ge-) commit to memory, memorise

mena'sie (-s) mess (club for soldiers/sailors)

meneer' (menere) sir, mister; gentleman

meng (ge-) mix, blend; mingle; ~ *jou met semels, dan vreet die varke jou op,* touch pitch and you will be defiled

men'gel (ge-) mingle, mix

meng'sel (-s) mixture, blend

me'nige many, several

me'nig: ~een many, several, many a one; ~maal often; ~te (-s) multitude, crowd

me'ning (-e, -s) opinion, belief, view; *'n ~ huldig,* hold a belief; *na my ~,* in my opinion; *die openbare ~,* public opinion; ~(s)opname (-s) opinion poll, survey; ~vormer opinion former

me'ningsverskil (-le) difference of opinion

me'nopouse menopause, change of life

mens (s) (-e) human being, person; *die ~ wik, maar God beskik,* man proposes, God disposes; (vnw) one, you; ~dom humanity, mankind

men'se: ~hater (-s) misanthrope; ~heugenis living memory; ~kennis knowledge of men; ~materiaal human resources; ~regte human rights

men'severhoudinge human relations
menslie'wend (-e; -er, -ste) humane, phi=
  lanthropic(al)
mens'lik (-e) human
mens'likheid humanity, human nature
menstrua'sie menstruation
mens: ~vreter (-s) cannibal, man-eater;
  ~waardig worthy of a human being
mentaliteit' mentality
menuet' (-te) minuet
me'rendeel majority; ~s mostly, for the
  greater part
meridiaan' (..diane) meridian
merie'te merits; *op die ~ van die saak in=*
  gaan, go into the merits of the case
merk (s) (-e) mark; sign; token; brand; (w)
  (ge-) mark; observe, notice
merk: ~artikel brand(ed) article/goods;
  ~baar (..bare) perceptible, noticeable
merkwaar'dig (-e; -er, -ste) remarkable
mer'rie (-s) mare
mes (-se) knife; *onder die ~ kry,* operate;
  voor jy ~ kon sê, before you could say
  Jack Robinson
mes'sel (ge-) lay bricks, build; ~aar (-s)
  bricklayer, mason
met with; ~ *geweld,* by force; ~ *sak en*
  pak, with bag and baggage; ~ *vakansie*
  (sake), on holiday (business); *iem.* ~
  vrede laat, leave someone in peace
metaal' (metale) metal; ~verklikker (-s)
  metal detector; ~verswakking metal
  fatigue
metafoor' (..fore) metaphor
metallurgie' metallurgy
meteen' at the same time
meteens' all of a sudden, all at once, sud=
  denly
meteoor' (meteore) meteor
me'ter (-s) meter, gauge; metre
met'gesel (-le) companion, mate
me'ting (-e, -s) measuring, reading
meto'de (-s) method, manner; *te werk gaan*
  volgens 'n ~, follow a method
metodiek' method(ics)
meto'dies (-e) methodical
metriek' (b) (-e) metric; ~*e stelstel,* metric
  system
metrise'ring metrification
metronoom' (..nome) metronome

metropolitaan' (..tane) metropolitan; ~s
  (-e) metropolitan; ~*se desentralisasie,*
  metropolitan decentralisation
me'trum (-s, ..tra) metre
mettertyd' in course of time
meu'bel (-s) piece of furniture
meubileer', meubeleer' (ge-) furnish; ~der
  (-s) furnisher
meul (-e), **meu'le** (-(n)s) mill; *water op sy ~,*
  grist to his mill; ~*e'naar* (-s) miller
mevrou' (-e, -ens) madam, my lady, mis=
  tress; *is ~ tuis?* is your wife (the madam)
  at home?
mid'dae in the afternoon
mid'dag (..dae) midday, noon; *'n vry ~,* an
  afternoon off; ~ete (-s) lunch, luncheon;
  (midday) dinner; ~vertoning (-s) matinee
mid'de middle, midst; *te ~ van gevaar,* in
  the midst of danger
mid'del[1] (-s) waist; centre, middle
mid'del[2] (-e, -s) means, instrument, remedy;
  product; *deur ~ van,* by means of; *'n ~*
  tot 'n doel, a means to an end
mid'delbaar (..bare) secondary; average,
  moderate, middle; *van ..bare leeftyd,*
  middle-aged; *..bare onderwys,* secondary
  education
middeldeur' (b) in two, asunder
Mid'deleeue Middle Ages
mid'del: ~lyn (-e) diameter; equator; half=
  way line; ~man (-ne) middleman;
  ~mannetjie (-s) hog's back
middelma'tig (-e) middling; mediocre; only
  average
middelpuntsoe'kend (-e) centripetal
middelpuntvlie'dend (-e) centrifugal
mid'de(l)weg middle course; the golden
  mean
mid'delvinger (-s) middle finger
mid'dernag midnight; *lank na ~,* long past
  midnight; ~son midnight sun
mied (-e, -ens) pile, heap; stack (hay)
mie'lie (-s) mealie, maize; ~boer (-e) maize
  farmer; ~meel mealie meal; ~pap mealie
  porridge; ~pit (-te) mealie grain, kernel
mier (-e) ant; ~*e hê,* be fidgety
mier(s)'hoop (..hope) antheap
mik (s) (-ke) forked stick; gibbet; (w) (ge-)
  aim
mik'punt aim, mark, target; objective
mikrochirurgie' microsurgery
mi'krofilm microfilm

mikrofoon' (..fone) microphone

mi'krogolf (..golwe) microwave

mi'krokomper, mi'kromper (-s) microcomputer, micromputer

mikroskoop' (..skope) microscope

mi'kroskyfie, mi'krovlokkie (-s) microchip

mi'kroverwerker microprocessor

mik'stok (-ke) forked stick

mild (-e; -er, -ste) generous, liberal, soft

militant' (-e; -er, -ste) militant

militaris' (-te) militarist; ~ties (-e) militaristic

militêr' (s) (-e) military man; (b) (-e) military; ~e attaché, military attache; ~e diens, military service, national service

miljard' (-e) milliard

miljoen' (-e) million

miljoenêr' (-s) millionaire

mil'li: ~gram (-me) milligram; ~liter (-s) millilitre; ~meter (-s) millimetre

milt (-e) spleen, milt; ~siekte anthrax (in cattle); splenic fever

mimiek' mimicry

min¹ (s) love; (w) (ge-) love

min² (b) (-der, -ste) little, few; (bw) minus, less; ~ of meer, more or less; drie rand te ~, three rand(s) short

min'ag (ge-) disdain, slight; undervalue; ~ting disdain, disrespect; ~ting van die hof, contempt of court

min'der less, fewer, inferior

min'dere (-s) inferior; rating

min'derheid minority; inferiority

min'derjarig (-e) under age, minor

minderwaar'dig (-e) inferior; geestelik ~, mentally deficient; ~heid(s)kompleks inferiority complex

mineraal' (s) (..rale) mineral; (b) (..rale) mineral; ..rale bad/bron, mineral baths, ook kruitbad

mineur' minor (music)

mi'ni (s) (-'s) mini; mi'ni- (b) mini-

miniatuur' (..ture) miniature; toy

minimaal' (..male) minimal

mi'nimum (..ma, -s) minimum

mi'nirok (-ke), mi'niromp (-e) minidress; miniskirt

minis'ter (-s) minister

ministe'rie (-s) ministry, cabinet

min'naar (-s) lover

minnares' (-se) ladylove, paramour, mistress

min'ne: in der ~ skik, settle amicably; ~brief (..briewe) love letter; ~dig (-te) love poem; ~digter (-s) amatory/erotic poet; ~lied (-ere) love song; ~sanger (-s) minstrel

min'saam (..same, ..samer, -ste) kind, affable

min'ste least, smallest; op sy ~, (at) the least; ten ~, at least

min'stens not less than, at least; sy is ~ veertig, she is forty if she is a day; dit weeg ~ tien kilogram, it weighs at least ten kilograms

mi'nus minus

minuut' (..nute) minute; ~wys(t)er (-s) minute hand

mira'kel (-s) miracle, wonder

mis¹ (s) (-se) mass

mis² (s) (-te) mist, fog

mis³ (s) manure

mis⁴ (w) (ge-) miss; (b, bw) amiss, wrong

mis'bruik (s) (-e) abuse, misuse; ~ maak van, take advantage of

misbruik' (w) (~) abuse, misuse

mis'daad (..dade) crime, offence, misdeed; 'n ~ begaan/pleeg, commit a crime; ~voorkoming crime prevention

misda'dig (-e) criminal, felonious; ~er (-s) criminal, evildoer

mis'dryf (s) (..drywe) crime, offence, misdemeanour

mishan'del (~) ill-use, maltreat, abuse

misken' (~) misjudge, fail to appreciate; 'n ~de genie, a neglected/disregarded genius

miskien' perhaps, perchance

mis'kol (-le) fog patch

mis'kraam (..krame) miscarriage, abortion

mis'kruier (-s) tumble bug, dung beetle

mis'lik (-e; -er, -ste) sick, qualmish, nauseous; disgusting; ~heid sickness, nausea

misluk' (~) fail, miscarry; dit het hom ~, he dit not succeed; ~te poging, vain attempt; ~keling (-e) misfit; dropout; ~king (-e, -s) failure, miscarriage

mismaak' (w) (~) deform, disfigure; (b) (-te) deformed

mismoe'dig (-e) discouraged, dejected

misnoe'ë discontent, displeasure; sy ~ te kenne gee, express his displeasure

misre'ken (~) be mistaken, meet with disappointment; hy het hom ~, he backed the wrong horse

missiel' (..e) missile

mis: ~slaan (-ge-) miss (when hitting); ~stap (-pe) false step, wrong step; *'n ~stap begaan/doen*, make a false step

mis'stof (..stowwe) manure, fertiliser

mis'tel[1] (s) (-s) mistletoe

mis'tel[2] (w) (-ge-) count wrongly, miscount

miste'rie (-ë, -s) mystery

mis'tig (-e) foggy, misty

mis'verstaan (~) misunderstand

mis'verstand (-e) misunderstanding, error

misvorm' (w) (~) disfigure; shape wrongly; (b) (-de) deformed, disfigured

mi'te (-s) myth

mitologie' mythology

mits provided (that); on condition (that); *ek sal jou help, ~ jy my vertrou*, I shall help you if you trust me

mobiel' (-e) mobile

mod'der mud, mire, sludge; ~ig (-e) muddy; ~skerm (-s) mudguard, fender

mo'de (-s) fashion, mode, vogue; *in die ~*, in vogue; *uit die ~ raak*, go out of fashion

model' (-le) pattern, example, model

mo'de: ~ontwerper (-s) fashion designer; ~pop (-pe) fop, dandy; dressy woman; dressmodel

modereer' (~, ge-) moderate; ~komitee (-s) committee/panel of moderators

modern' (-e; -er, -ste) modern, fashionable

moderniseer' (~, ge-) modernise

mo'deskou (-e) fashion show

modieus' (-e) fashionable

modis'te (-s) milliner, dressmaker, modiste

moed courage, heart, spirit; *hou goeie ~*, never say die! be of good cheer!

moe'deloos (..lose; ..loser, -ste) dejected, disheartened, crestfallen

moe'der (-s) mother; ~liefde motherly/maternal love; ~maatskappy (-e) holding company, *ook houermaatskappy*; ~sielalleen quite alone; ~skap motherhood; maternity; ~taal mother tongue/language, vernacular

moe'dig (-e; -er, -ste) brave, courageous

moedswil'lig (b) (-e; -er, -ste) wilful, mischievous, petulant

moeg (moeë; moeër, -ste) tired, weary

moei'lik (-e; -er, -ste) difficult, hard, arduous, hard to handle; *veels te ~*, far too difficult; ~heid (..hede) difficulty, trouble; *jy soek ~heid*, you are looking for trouble

moei'te trouble, difficulty, pains, hassle; *jou baie ~ getroos*, spare no pains; *nie die ~ werd nie*, not worth while

moe'nie! don't!

moer (-e) nut (with bolt)

moeras' (-se) marsh, morass, swamp

moer'bei (-e) mulberry

moe'sie (-s) mole; beauty spot

moet (w) (moes) must, ought, be obliged, have to; *ek moes lag*, I couldn't help laughing; *sy ~ dit sien*, she is bound (ought) to see it

mof'fie (-s) mitten; gay (homosexual)

mo'ker (ge-) strike, beat, hammer

mol[1] (-le) flat (music)

mol[2] (-le) mole; *so blind soos 'n ~*, as blind as a bat

moleku'le (-s) molecule

moles' (-te) trouble, harm; rumpus; *~ maak*, cause trouble, harm

molesteer' (~, ge-) molest

mol'lig (-e; -er, -ste) soft, plump, chubby

mols'hoop (..hope) molehill

mol'trein (-e) tube, underground train

mom (-me) mask; ~bakkies (-e) mask

moment' (-e) moment

mom'pel (ge-) mutter, mumble, grumble

monarg' (-e) monarch

monargie' (-ë) monarchy

mond (-e) mouth; estuary; *by ~e van*, as cited/stated by, through/by the mouth of; *nie op sy ~ (bek) geval wees nie*, have a ready tongue; *hou jou ~!* shut up!

mon'delik, mon'deling(s) (b) (-e) verbal, oral; *'n mondelinge eksamen*, an oral examination

monde'ring (-e, -s) equipment; uniform, outfit

mond'fluitjie (-s) mouth organ

mon'dig (-e) of age, major; ~wording coming of age

mond'jievol (mondjiesvol) tiny bit; smattering; *hy ken 'n ~ Engels*, he knows a little English

monetêr' (-e) monetary; *internasionale ~e fonds (IMF)*, international monetary fund (IFM)

moniteer' (w) (~, ge-) monitor

mo'nitor (s) (-s) monitor

mon'nik (-e) monk, friar

mono'kel (-s) monocle
monoloog' (..loë) monologue, soliloquy, ook alleenspraak
monopolie' (-ë, -s) monopoly
mon'ster[1] (s) monstrous creature
mon'ster[2] (s) (-s) sample; 'n volledige stel ~s, a complete range of samples; (w) (ge-) compare; muster (army)
mon'steragtig (-e) monstrous
mon'ster: ~neming sampling; ~vergade= ring (-e, -s) mass meeting
monta'siebou prefab. building process
monteer' (~, ge-) mount, assemble, set; fit out; ~baan (..bane) assembly line; ~huis (-e) prefabricated house
monument' (-e) monument
monumentaal' (..tale) monumental
mooi (-er, -ste) handsome, nice, fine, pret= ty; ~ broodjies bak, eat humble pie; dis 'n ~ grap! well, I never! 'n ~ meisie, a pretty girl; ~praatjies flattery, softsoap= ing; ~weersvriend (-e) no friend in need
moond'heid (..hede) power, state; die groot ..hede, the big powers
moont'lik (-e) possible; ~heid (..hede) possibility
moor (w) (ge-) maltreat; jouself ~, flog oneself
moord (-e) murder, slaughter; ~ en brand skree, cry murder
moor'denaar (-s) murderer
moordenares' (-se) murderess
moord: ~poging (-e) attempted murder; ~toneel (..nele) scene of a murder
moraal' moral; hierdie storie hou 'n ~ in, this story has a moral/lesson
moraliteit' morality
mô're, mo're (s) (-s) morning, morrow; ~ is ook 'n dag, tomorrow is another day; (bw) tomorrow; ~aand tomorrow even= ing
moreel' (s) morale; (b) (..rele) moral; sy soldate se ~ verstewig, improve the mor= ale of his soldiers; jou morele plig, one's moral duty; ~kikker morale booster
mo're=, môreog'gend tomorrow morning
mo're=, mô'repraatjies: sy aand- en môre= praatjies kom nie ooreen nie, his word is unreliable
morfien', morfi'ne morphia, morphine
moroon' (..one) moron, mentally deficient person

mors (ge-) dirty, make a mess, waste, spill; ~dood stone-dead
mor'sig (-e; -er, -ste) dirty, filthy, grimy
mors: ~jors (-e) litterbug, ook rommel= strooier; ~pot (-te) dirty person, messer
mortier' (-e) mortar
mos[1] (s) (-se) moss
mos[2] (v) must
mos[3] (bw) indeed, at least; ek het ~ gesê hulle sal verloor, didn't I say they would lose?
mosaïek' mosaic
mo'ses match, superior; sy ~ teëkom, meet one's match
mo'sie (-s) motion, vote; 'n ~ van wan= troue, a motion of no confidence
moskee' (-s, ..keë) mosque
mos'konfyt moskonfyt, grape syrup
mos'sel (-s) mussel
mos'sie (-s) Cape sparrow
mos'terd mustard; ~ na die maal, too late
mot (-te) moth
motel' (-le, -s) motel
motief' (..tiewe) motive, motive force
motiveer' (ge-) give reasons for, motivate
mo'tocross motocross (motorbike off-road racing)
mo'tor (s) (-e, -s) motor, motorcar; en= gine; ~bestuurder (-s) car driver, chauf= feur; ~fiets (-e) motor cycle; ~hawe (-s) garage; ~huis (-e) garage (private); ~is (-te) motorist; ~skuiling (-s) carport; ~voertuig (..tuie) motor vehicle
mot'reën, ..reent drizzle
mou (-e) sleeve; die hande uit die ~ steek, put the shoulder to the wheel
muf (muwwe; muwwer, -ste) musty, fusty
mug'gie (-s) gnat, midge; van 'n ~ 'n oli= fant maak, make a mountain of a mole= hill
muil[1] (-e) mule
muil[2] (-e) mouth (animal); ~band (s) (-e) muzzle; (w) (ge-) muzzle
muis (-e) mouse; ball (thumb); fetlock (of horse); klein ~ies het groot ore, little pitchers have long ears; so stil soos 'n ~, as quiet as a mouse; ~hond (-e) skunk, polecat; mongoose; ~nes (-te) mousenest; (mv) musings; die kop vol ~neste hê, have a mind full of cobwebs (when in love)
muit (ge-) mutiny, revolt, rebel; ~ery (-e) mutiny, sedition

mum'mie (-s) mummy (embalmed body)
muni'sie munition
munisipaal' (..pale) municipal; ..ale veror=
deninge, municipal by-laws
munisipaliteit' (-e) municipality
munt (s) (-e) mint, coin; met dieselfde ~
betaal, pay someone back in his own coin;
hy slaan daar ~ uit, he makes capital out
of this; (w) (ge-) mint, coin; ~kunde
numismatics; ~stuk (-ke) coin
mura'sie (-s) old walls, ruins (of a house)
murg marrow; deur ~ en been gaan, pene=
trate to the marrow
mur'mel (ge-) murmer, babble; gurgle
murmureer' (ge-) grumble, grouse
mus (-se) cap; nightcap; teacosy
muse'um (s) museum
musiek' music; ~ van die meesters, klas=
sieke ~, classical music; ~blyspel (-e) a
musical; ~instrument (-e) musical in=
strument; ~sentrum (-s) music centre;
~stuk (-ke) piece of music, musical com=
position
musikaal' (..kale) musical; 'n musikale ge=
hoor hê, have an ear for music

musikant' (-e) member of a band
mu'sikus (-se, ..ci) musician
muskaat' nutmeg
muskadel' muscadel
muskeljaat'kat, musseljaat'kat (-te) genet
muskiet' (-e) mosquito
muur (mure) wall; oor die ~ wees, be done
for; tussen vier mure sit, be behind bars
my (pers, vnw) me; dis vir ~ te duur, I can't
afford it; ek het ~ vergis, I was mistaken;
(besit. vnw) my, mine
myl (-e) mile
my'mer (ge-) ponder, meditate, muse
myn¹ (s) (-e) mine; (w) (ge-) mine (mil.)
myn² (vnw): ~ en dyn, mine and thine
my'ne mine
myn: ~bou mining (industry); ~er (-s)
miner, ook mynwerker; ~ingenieur (-s)
mining engineer; ~skag (-te) shaft; ~te=
ring miner's phthisis, pneumoconiosis;
~werkersbond miners' union; ~wese
mining, mines; Kamer van Mynwese,
Chamber of Mines
myself' myself; ek praat net vir ~, I speak
only on my own behalf

N

'n a, an; ~ mens, one, you
na¹ (b, bw) (nader, naaste) close, near
na² (voors) after; to; according to; on; op
een ~ die laaste, the last but one; ~ my
mening, in my opinion; ~ skool, after
school(hours)
na'-aap (-ge-) ape, imitate, mimic
naaf (nawe) nave, hub; ~dop (-pe) hub cap
naai (ge-) sew; ~masjien (-e) sewing mach=
ine
naak (-te; -ter, -ste) naked, nude; ~loper
(-s) nudist; ~lopery nudism
naakt'heid nudity, nakedness
naald (-e) needle; spire, obelisk; ~ en ga=
ring, needle and cotton; 'n mens kan hom
deur 'n ~ trek, he is as smart as a new
pin; ~e'koker (-s) needlecase; dragon fly;
~werk needlework
naam (name) name, appellation; ~bord (-e)
signboard; ~kaartjie (-s) visiting card
naam'lik namely, to wit
naam'loos (..lose) nameless, anonymous

naam'strokie (-s) name tag, ook kenstrokie
naam'tekening signature, ook handteke=
ning
naam'val (-le) case
naam'woord (-e) nomen (noun, pronoun,
or adjective); byvoeglike ~, adjective;
selfstandige ~, noun
naand! good evening!
na'-aper (-s) imitator
naar (b) (nare; -der, -ste) sick, dreary, sad
naas next to, beside, alongside of, besides;
~bestaande (-s) next of kin, nearest rela=
tive; ~eergister three days ago; ~oor=
môre, ~oormore three days hence
naas'te (s) (-s) neighbour, fellow-man; (b)
nearest
naas'te(n)by approximately, more or less
naas'teliefde love of one's fellow-men
naas'wenner (-s) runner-up
naas'wit off-white
naat (nate) seam; joint; suture, op die ~
van jou rug lê, lie flat on your back

na'boots (-ge-) imitate, mimic; simulate, copy; ~**er** (-s) simulator
na'by (nader, naaste) near, close to; *van ~ bekyk,* inspect at close quarters; *~ die dood omdraai,* have been at death's door
naby'geleë adjacent, neighbouring
na'dat after, when
na'deel (nadele) disadvantage; loss, injury
nade'lig (-e; -er, -ste) detrimental, disad= vantageous; *~e saldo,* debit balance
na'demaal whereas
na'der (w) (ge-) approach, come nearer; (b, bw) nearer; *~e (meer) besonderhede,* further particulars; *~ kennis maak,* make closer acquaintance
na'dink (-ge-) reflect, consider
na'doods after death; posthumous
na'draai after effects, sequel, aftermath
na'druk emphasis, stress; *~ lê op,* empha= sise
na'el[1] (s) (-s) nail; *sy ~s byt,* bite one's nails
na'el[2] (s) (-s) navel
na'el[3] (w) (ge-) nail; sprint; *hy het laat ~,* he took to his heels
na'el: ~**ren** (-ne), ~**ry** cycle race/sprint; ~**skraap** by the skin of the teeth; *dit het ~skraap gegaan,* it was touch and go; ~**string** (-e) umbilical cord
na'eltjies cloves; ~**olie** oil of cloves
na'elwedloop (..lope) sprint (sport)
nag (-te) night; *so lelik soos die ~,* as ugly as sin
na'gaan (-ge-) trace, check; follow, run over (with the eye); *die inskrywings ~,* check the entries
nag: ~**aap** (..ape) bushbaby; ~**adder** (-s) night adder
na'gedagtenis memory, remembrance; *ter ~ aan,* in memory of
na'gemaak (-te) forged, false, imitated
na'genoeg almost, pretty near
na'gereg (-te) dessert (course)
na'geslag (-te) posterity, descendants, off= spring
Nag'maal Holy Communion
nag: ~**merrie** (-s) nightmare; ~**skof** (-te) night shift
na'graads (-e) post-graduate
nag'tegaal (..gale) nightingale
nag: ~**telik** (-e) nocturnal, nightly; ~**wag** (-te) night watchman

naïef' (naïewe; naïewer, -ste) naive/naïve, simple, artless
na'jaar autumn
na'kend (-e) naked, nude
na'kom (-ge-) fulfil; carry out; perform; meet (obligation); *beloftes ~,* keep promises
na'komeling (-e) descendant
na'kyk (-ge-) look after; examine, revise, check, correct, mark; eye
na'laat (-ge-) bequeath (an inheritance); leave off; neglect; omit; *sy oom het hom R1 000 nagelaat,* he inherited R1 000 from his uncle
nala'tenskap inheritance, heritage
nala'tig (-e; -er, -ste) negligent, careless
na'maak (-ge-) imitate, copy; ~**sel** (-s) im= itation, counterfeit
nama'te as, in proportion to; *~ hy aan= sterk, eet hy beter,* as he improves/recup= erates he has a better appetite
na'meloos: *namelose ellende,* inexpressible misery
na'mens in the name of, on behalf of, for
Nami'bië Namibia; *Namibiese ekonomie,* Namibian economy
Namibiër Namibian
na'middag (..dae) afternoon
nar (-re) fool, jester, buffoon
narcis'me, narcissis'me narcissism
narko'se narcosis
narko'tikaburo narcotics bureau
narkotiseur' (-s) anaesthetist, narcotist
nar'tjie (-s) mandarin (orange), tangerine, nartjie
nasaal' (nasale) nasal
na'saat (nasate) descendant
nasale'ring nasalisation
na'sie (-s) nation; *Verenigde N~s,* United Nations
na'sien (-ge-) correct; mark; examine, look over, revise, check; ~**er** (-s) marker (of scripts)
nasionaal' (..nale) national; *..nale diens= pligtige,* national serviceman; *..nale pad,* national road
nasionalis' (-te) nationalist; ~**me** nation= alism
nasionaliteit' (-e) nationality
na'skrif (-te) postscript
na'slaan (-ge-) look up, consult (a book); *maklik om na te slaan,* easy to refer to;

~biblioteek (..teke) reference library; **~werk** (-e) reference book/work

na'sleep (s) consequence, result, after-effects; *die ~ van die oorlog,* the aftermath of the war

na'smaak aftertaste

na'sorg aftercare, follow-up

nat (-ter, -ste) wet, moist; *so ~ soos 'n kat,* wet through

nat: **~heid** moistness, wetness; **~maak** (-ge-) water (garden); wet

natu'ra: *in ~,* in kind (income)

naturalisa'sie naturalisation

naturel'[1] natural (music)

Naturel'[2] (-le) former expression for South African Black

naturel'[3] (-le) native, original inhabitant

naturis' (-te) naturist (nudism)

natuur' (nature) nature; temper, temperament; *van nature,* by nature; **~- en skeikunde,** physical science; **~bewaring** nature conservation; **~bronne** natural resources; **~frats** (-e) freak of nature; **~geneser** (-s) naturopath; **~lewevereniging** wildlife society

natuur'lik (b) (-e; -er, -ste) natural; *'n ~e aanleg,* a natural bent; (bw) of course, naturally; *hy sal ~ kom,* of course he will come

natuur': **~oord** (-e) nature resort; **~skoon** (natural) scenery; **~verskynsel** (-s) phenomenon of nature

natuurwetenskap'lik (-e) scientific, pertaining to natural science

na'volg (-ge-) follow, imitate

na'vors (-ge-) research; **~er** (-s) researcher; **~(ings)werk** research work

na'vraag (navrae) enquiry; query; *~ doen (na 'n persoon),* seek information (about a person)

na'week (naweke) weekend

na'wel (-s) navel

nè? is it not? isn't it? yes? *dink 'n bietjie, ~!* just fancy!

ne'derig (-e; -er, -ste) humble, modest

Ne'derland: **~er** Dutchman, Hollander

ne'dersetter (-s) settler

ne'dersetting (-e, -s) settlement, colony

nee no; *~ sê,* say no; refuse

neef (-s) (male) cousin; nephew

neem (ge-) take, receive, accept

neer down, downwards; *op en ~,* up and down

neerbui'gend (b) condescending

neer'kom (-ge-) come down, fall on; *dit kom alles op dieselfde neer,* it works out to the same thing

neer'laag (..lae) defeat, reverse; *die ~ ly,* suffer defeat

neer'lê (-ge-) lay down, abdicate, resign

neer'sien (-ge-) look down (upon); *minagtend ~ op,* hold in contempt

neerslag'tig (-e; -er, -ste) dejected, despondent, melancholy

neer'stryk (-ge-) touch down (aircraft)

neer'vly (-ge-) lay down; lie down; *~ op die rusbank,* make (himself) comfortable on the couch

nef'fens next to, alongside of

negatief' (s) (..tiewe) negative; (b) (..tiewe) negative

ne'ge nine; *~ maal ~,* nine times nine; *~ keer,* nine times

ne'gentien, ne'ëntien nineteen

neig (ge-) bend, incline; *mense is ge~ om,* people are apt to

nei'ging (-e, -s) inclination, bent; tendency

nek (-ke) neck; mountain pass; *op iem. se ~ lê,* abuse someone's hospitality

neologis'me (-s) neologism, *ook* **nuutskepping**

nê'rens nowhere; *~ voor deug nie,* serve no earthly purpose

nerf (s) (nerwe) grain (of leather); outer skin, cuticle; nerviture

nes[1] (s) (-te) nest

nes[2] (bw) just as, just like; *~ hy kom, sluit ons die deur,* as soon as he arrives we'll lock the door

net[1] (s) (-te) net; *agter die ~ visvang,* turn up too late

net[2] (b) (-te; -ter, -ste) neat, clean

net[3] (bw) only, just; *~ genoeg,* just enough

ne'telig (-e; -er, -ste) knotty, critical, thorny; *'n ~e kwessie,* a tricky/thorny issue

net: **~heid** tidiness, neatness; **~tjies** (b) (-e; -er, -ste) neat, tidy, clean, trim; (bw) neatly, nicely; *jou werk ~jies doen,* produce tidy work; **~nou** just now, in a moment

net'to net; *~ gewig/massa,* net weight/mass

neuk (ge-) hit; bother, trouble; **~ery** botheration, fine how-do-you-do

neul (ge-) nag, bother, trouble, annoy; **~kous** (-e) grumbler, naggard

neu'rie (ge-) hum, croon

neus (s) (-e) nose; *met sy ~ in die botter val,* strike oil; *be in clover; ~ in die lug,* conceited; haughty

neut (-e) nut; nutmeg; **~kraker** (-s) pair of nutcrackers

neutraal' (..trale) neutral

ne'wel (-e) mist, fog

ne'weproduk (-te) byproduct

nie not; *so ~,* if not, else, failing which; *dis ~ so ~,* it isn't true; **~-aanvalsver= drag** (..verdrae) non-aggression pact; **~-betaling** non-payment

nie'-fiksie non-fiction, factual books, faction

nie'mand nobody, none, no one; *~ anders nie as,* no other than

nie'-amptelik (-e) unofficial

nie'-oordraagbaar not transferable

nier (-e) kidney

nies (s) (-e) sneeze; (w) (ge-) sneeze

niet nothing, nought; *te ~ doen,* declare null and void; undo; do away with

nie'teenstaande notwithstanding

nie'temin nonetheless

nie'tig (-e; -er, -ste) insignificant; void

nig (-te), **nig'gie** (-s) (female) cousin; niece

nikotien', nikoti'ne nicotine

niks nothing; **~nuts** (-e) good-for-nothing; **~werd** worth nothing, worthless

nimf (-e) nymph; **~omaan** (..ane) nymphomaniac, highly-sexed female

nim'mer never

nip (w) sip

nip'pel (-s) nipple

nip'pertjie: *op die ~,* in the nick of time

no'ag: ~kar, ~motor vintage/veteran car

no'dig (-e;·-er, -ste) necessary

noem (ge-) call, name, mention

noe'mer (-s) denominator

noen noon; **~maal** luncheon

nog[1] (b, bw) still, yet; *~ iets?* anything else? *~ 'n keer,* once again

nog[2] (bw) now; *tot ~ toe,* up till now

nòg .. nòg (vgw) neither . . . nor; *nòg die een, nòg die ander,* neither the one, nor the other

nog: ~maals once more; **~maals hartlik bedank,** once again many thanks; **~tans** however, yet, nevertheless

nok (-ke) ridge (of the roof); cam (of wheel); **~as** (-se) camshaft

nomina'sie (-s) nomination

nomineer' (~, ge-) nominate

nom'mer (s) (-s) number; copy (paper); size (shoe); **~pas** perfect fit; **~plaat** (..plate) number plate; (w) (ge-) number

non (-ne) nun

nood need, want; distress; danger; *in geval van ~,* in case of emergency; *~ leer bid,* necessity is the mother of invention; **~berig** (-te) emergency/distress message; **~deur** (-e) emergency door, fire escape

nood: ~hulp first aid; makeshift; **~leni= ging(s)fonds** (-e) relief fund; **~leuen** (-s) white lie; **~lot** fate, destiny

noodlot'tig (-e; -er, -ste) fatal, ill-fated

nood: ~maatreël (-s) emergency measure; **~oproep** (-e) emergency/distress call

noodsaak'lik (b) (-e) necessary, imperative

nood'toestand state of emergency

nood'weer self-defence

nood'wiel (-e) spare wheel

nooi[1] (s) (-ens) young lady; sweetheart; *by 'n ~ vlerksleep,* court a girl

nooi[2] (w) (ge-) invite; *ek ~ jou vir Saterdag,* I am inviting you for Saturday

nooi: ~ens'toespraak (..ake) maiden speech (parliament), *kyk* **nuwelingtoespraak;** **~ens'van** (-ne) maiden name

nooit never; *so ~ as te nimmer!* never!

noord north

noor'de north; *ten ~ van,* north of

noor'der: ~breedte northern latitude; **~lig** aurora borealis

noor'dewind north wind

Noord'pool North Pole

noordwes' north-west; **~te** north-west; **~tewind** north-west wind

Noor'man (-ne) Norman, Norseman

noot (note) note

nop nap (clothes; putting green)

nop'pies: *in sy ~,* as pleased as Punch

normaal' (..male) normal; **~skool** (..skole) normal college

nors ([-e]; -er, -ste) surly, peevish

nos'sel (s) (-s) nozzle, *ook* **spuitkop**

noteer' (~, ge-) jot down; quote (prices)

note'ring (-e, -s) quotation; *~ op die beurs,* stock exchange listing

noti'sie (-s) notice; *~ neem,* take notice of

no'tule, notu'le (-s) minutes; *die ~ lees en goedkeur,* read and approve the minutes
notuleer (ge-) record; minute; take down
nou¹ (b) ([-e]; -er, -ste) narrow, tight
nou² (bw) now
nou'geset (-te; -ter, -ste) conscientious, painstaking
noukeur'rig (-e; -er, -ste) exact, accurate, precise
nou'liks scarcely, hardly
nou'-nou just now, in a moment
nousien'de particular
nou'strop: ~ trek, be under pressure
nou'te (-s) narrowness; narrow pass; *in die ~ dryf,* corner; ~vrees claustrophobia
novel'le (-s) short novel, novelette
nudis' (-te) nudist, naturist; ~me nudism
nug'ter ([-e]; -der, -ste) sober, clearheaded; *op sy ~ maag,* on an empty stomach
nuk (-ke) freak, whim, caprice, mood; ~kerig (-e; -er, -ste) moody, capricious
nul (-le) nil, zero, nought, cipher; *van ~ en gener waarde,* null and void
numeriek' (-e) numerical; ~e volgorde, numerical order

nut use, benefit, avail
nut'(s)korporasie (-s) utility corporation
nut'teloos (..lose. ..loser, -ste) useless
nut'tig¹ (w) (ge-) partake (meal)
nut'tig² (b) (-e; -er, -ste) useful, serviceable
nuus news, tidings; *die jongste ~,* the latest news; ~beeldsending newscast (TV); ~berig newsitem; ~blad newspaper
nuuskie'rig (-e; -er, -ste) inquisitive, curious; ~e agie, a bumptious child; ~heid inquisitiveness, curiosity
nuus'uitsending (-s) news broadcast, newscast (radio)
nuut (nuwe; nuwer, -ste) new, recent; ~skepping (-s) neologism
Nuwejaars': ~dag New Year's Day; ~voorneme (-ns) New Year's resolution
nuwerwets' (-e) modern, new-fangled; with-it, *kyk byderwets*
nu'wigheid (..hede) novelty
nyd envy, jealousy; ~ig (-e; -er, -ste) angry, cross
ny'wer (-e) industrious; ~aar (-s) industrialist
ny'werheid (..hede) industry, *ook bedryf*

O

oa'se (-s) oasis
obelisk' (-e) obelisk
objektief' (..tiewe) objective
oblie'tjie (-s) (rolled) wafer
obliga'sie (-s) debenture (of a company); obligation; bond
obseen' (obsene) obscene
observa'sie (-s) observation; ~pos (-te) observation post
obses'sie obsession; *hy het 'n ~ oor/vir,* he has an obsession about/for
obstruk'sie (-s) obstruction
o'de (-s) ode
oe'fen (w) exercise, practise; train, coach; ~baan (..bane) practice court/track; ~ing (-e, -s) exercise, practice, training; ~ing baar kuns, practice makes perfect; ~lopie (-s) trial run; ~sessie (-s) practice session; ~skrif (-te) exercise book
o'ënskou: *in ~ neem,* inspect; survey
oënskyn'lik (b) (-e) apparent, ostensible; (bw) apparently, seemingly

oer: ~mens (-e) first/primeval man; ~woud (-e) native/virgin forest; jungle
oes¹ (s) (-te) harvest, crop; yield; (w) (ge-) harvest, reap
oes² (b) bad, off-colour, out of sorts; *'n ~ affère,* a feeble affair
oes'ter (-s) oyster
o'ëverblindery make-believe, magic, optic delusion
oe'wer (-s) riverbank; ~bewoner (-s) riparian (dweller)
of or; but, if, whether; *min ~ meer,* more or less; *'n stuk ~ drie,* about three; *ek weet nie ~ dit waar is nie,* I don't know whether it is true
òf .. òf either .. or; ~ Jan ~ Piet, either John or Peter
offensief' (s) (..siewe) offensive
of'fer (s) (-s) sacrifice, offering; (w) (ge-) devote, sacrifice
of'ferande (-s) offering, sacrifice
offisier' (-e, -s) (military or naval) officer

ofskoon' although, though

of'te: *nooit ~ nimmer,* never, on no condition

og'gend (-e) morning; **~blad (..blaaie)** morning paper; **~ete (-s)** breakfast, morning meal

o'gie (-s) eyelet; **~s maak,** wink, give the glad eye, ogle

o'giesdraad wire netting

oka'pi (-'s) okapi

o'ker ochre, red clay

okkerneut' (-e) walnut

okkupeer' (~, ge-) occupy

oksida'sie oxidation

oktaaf' (..tawe) octave

okta'vo (-'s) octavo (8vo)

oktrooi' (-e) charter, patent

oktrooieer' (ge-) charter, patent; *geoktrooieerde rekenmeester,* chartered accountant

o'lie (s) (-s) oil; (w) **(ge-)** oil; **~bak (-ke)** sump; **~boortoring (-s)** oil rig

o'lie: **~kan (-ne)** oilcan; **~kleedjie (-s)** oilskin cover

olien'hout wild olive

o'lie: **~pypleiding (-s)** oil pipeline; **~slik** oil slick; **~verbruik** oil consumption; **~verfskildery (-e)** oil painting

o'lifant (-e) elephant

o'lifant(s)tand (-e) elephant's tusk; ivory

o'lik (-e; -er, -ste) bad, unwell, seedy, out of sorts; **~heid** seediness; *na vrolikheid kom ~heid,* after laughter come tears

olimpia'de (-s) olympiad (maths, science)

olm (-s) elm

olyf' (olywe) olive

om (bw) out; round; over, up; *~ en ~,* round and round; (voors) at, about, round; *~ agtuur,* at eight o'clock; *~ en by vyftig,* about fifty; *~ die hoek,* round the corner

om'blaai (-ge-) turn over (leaves of a book)

om'dat because, since, as

om'draai (-ge-) turn round, turn back; reverse (a car); twist; revolve; *nie doekies ~ nie,* not mince matters

omelet' (-te) omelet

om'gaan (-ge-) mix with, associate; go round

om'gang intercourse, association

om'gangstaal colloquial language, common way of speaking

om'gee (-ge-) care; *nie ~ nie,* not care, not mind

om'gekeerd (b) (-e) turned upside down, reversed; *in ~e verhouding,* in inverse proportion

omge'wing (-e, -s) surroundings, environment, vicinity, precincts; *aanpassing by die ~,* adaptation to the environment; **~sake** environmental affairs; **~s'bewaring** environmental conservation; **~s'leer** ecology; environmental studies

omgord' (~) gird on; *die lendene ~,* gird up one's loins

omhein' (~) fence in; **~ing (-s)** fence

omhels' (~) embrace

om'kom (-ge-) die, perish; come round; *in 'n ongeluk ~,* die in an accident

om'koop (-ge-) bribe, corrupt; *'n getuie ~,* bribe a witness; **~geld** bribe (money)

om'krap (-ge-) bring in disorder, upset; *omgekrap voel,* be upset

om'kyk (-ge-) look back, look around; attend to

om'leiding (-s) by-pass (heart operation)

omlig'gende surrounding, neighbouring; *die ~ plase,* the neighbouring/adjacent farms

om'loop (s) circulation; **(omlope)** ringworm, cutaneous disease

om'mekeer (s) sudden change; *'n hele ~,* quite a big change

om'mesientjie: *in 'n ~,* in a trice/jiffy

om'pad (ompaaie) round-about way, detour

om'praat (-ge-) persuade, dissuade, prevail upon

omring' (~) surround, encircle

om'roep (-e) broadcasting station; **~er (-s)** (town)crier; announcer (radio)

om'ruil (-ge-) exchange, swap/swop

om'ry (-ge-) drive down; drive/ride round; knock down, run over

om'sendbrief (..briewe) circular (letter)

om'set turnover; *jaarlikse ~,* annual turnover (sales)

omsin'gel (~) surround, enclose, encircle; *hulle het die laer ~,* they surrounded the laager

om'skep (-ge-) change, convert; *die tennisbaan word in 'n tuin omgeskep,* the tennis court is being changed into a garden

omskep' (~) transform, recreate; *dit het*

hom ~ tot 'n nuwe mens, it transformed him into a new person

omskry'wing (-e, -s) description, definition

om'slag (..slae) hem, border, cuff; wrap= per; fold-over; brace

omslag'tig (-e; -er, -ste) wordy, circum= stantial, digressive, prolix

om'stander (-s) bystander, onlooker

omstan'dig (-e; -er, -ste) detailed, circum= stantial, in detail; *~ vertel*, give a detailed account

omstan'digheid (..hede) circumstance; *on= der geen ..hede nie*, in/under no circum= stances; *versagtende ..hede*, extenuating circumstances

omstre'de controversial, contentious, dis= puted; *~ boek*, controversial book

om'streeks about

om'streke (mv) vicinity, neighbourhood

om'trek (s) (-ke) outline, circumference; vicinity; *in ~*, in circumference; *in die ~*, in the neighbourhood

omtrent' about, almost, nearly; *dis ~ tyd*, it is just about time

om'val (-ge-) fall over/down, topple over; *~ van die lag*, split one's side with laugh= ter

om'vang extent; circumference; size

omvat' (~) embrace, enclose, include, comprise; *~tende versekering*, compre= hensive insurance

om'vou (-ge-) fold down, turn (down)

om'wenteling (-e, -s) revolution, rotation; *'n ~ teweegbring*, revolutionise; *dertig ~e per minuut*, thirty revolutions a minute

onaan'genaam (..name; ..namer, -ste) un= pleasant, disagreeable

onaantrek'lik (-e) unattractive

onaanveg'baar (..bare) indisputable

onaar'dig (-e) unpleasant; *nie ~ nie*, rather attractive; not so bad

onaf'gebroke uninterrupted, continuous; *~ vlug*, non-stop flight

onafhank'lik (-e) independent; *~ wees van*, be independent of; *~heid* independence; *~verklaring* declaration of independence

onafskei(d)'baar (..bare), **onafskei'delik** (-e) inseparable

onbaatsug'tig (-e; -er, -ste) unselfish; dis= interested

onbarmhar'tig (-e; -er, -ste) merciless, un= merciful

onbeant'woord (-e) unanswered, unreturn= ed (love)

onbedag'saam (..same) thoughtless, in= considerate

onbedui'dend (-e; -er, -ste) insignificant, of small importance

onbegaan'baar (..bare) impassable

onbegon'ne impossible; *'n ~ taak*, an im= possible task

onbegryp'lik (-e; -er, -ste) inconceivable, incomprehensible

onbehol'pe awkward, clumsy, helpless

onbehoor'lik (-e) improper, indecent

onbekend' (-e) unknown; unacquainted; unfamiliar; *~ maak onbemind*, unknown, unloved

onbekom'merd (-e) unconcerned, careless

onbekwaam' (..kwame; ..kwamer, -ste) in= capable, unable, incompetent; unfit

onbelang'rik (-e) unimportant, immaterial

onbeleef' (-de; -der, -ste) impolite, uncouth, uncivil; *~d'heid* (..hede) incivility, im= politeness, rudeness

onbelem'mer (-de) unhindered, unimpeded, free; *~de uitsig*, unrestricted/unobscured view

onbenul'lig (-e) fatuous; dull-witted; trif= ling; *dis 'n ~heid*, it is of no importance

onbepaald' (-e) indefinite, unlimited; *vir 'n ~e tyd*, indefinitely

onbeperk' (-te) unlimited, boundless

onbere'kenbaar (..bare) incalculable; *..bare skade*, incalculable harm/damage

onberis'pelik (-e) faultless, blameless; irre= proachable; *~e gedrag*, exemplary be= haviour

onbeskaaf' (-de; -der, -ste) rude, uncivil= ised, uncouth, ill-bred

onbeskof' (-te.; -er, -ste) insolent, ill-man= nered, rude, impudent

onbeskre'we blank

onbeskryf'lik (-e) beyond description; *~e ellende*, indescribable suffering

onbeskut' (-te) unprotected

onbeslis' (-te) undecided, uncertain; pend= ing; sub judice (suit); drawn (game); *die wedstryd het ~ geëindig*, the match was drawn

onbeson'ne thoughtless, inconsiderate, foolish; *'n ~ daad*, a rash deed

onbespro'ke irreproachable; *van ~ karak= ter*, of high integrity onbestel'baar (..bare) undeliverable; *'n ..bare brief*, a dead letter

onbestre'de undisputed, unopposed; ~ *setel*, unopposed seat

onbeswaar(d)' (-de) unencumbered; *~de eiendom*, unbonded property

onbetaal(d)' (-de) unpaid; *~e rekening*, unpaid/arrear account

onbetrou'baar (..bare, -der, -ste) unreliable, untrustworthy

onbetwis' (-te) undisputed

onbevlek' (-te) undefiled, untainted; innocent; *die ~te ontvangenis*, the immaculate conception

onbevoeg' (-de) incompetent, unqualified

onbevoor'oordeeld (-e) unbiased

onbevre'digend (-e; -er, -ste) unsatisfactory; *~e toestand*, unsatisfactory state of affairs

onbewoon' (-de) uninhabited, desolate

onbewus' (-te) ignorant, unaware, unwitting; unconscious; ~ *van die gevare*, unaware of the dangers

onbil'lik (-e; -er, -ste) unfair, unjust

onchris'telik (-e) unchristian

on'dank ingratitude, thanklessness; ~ *is wêreldsloon*, the world pays with ingratitude

ondank'baar (..bare) ungrateful

on'danks in spite of, notwithstanding; ~ *al sy pogings*, in spite of all his efforts

on'der under; down; among; below; ~ *andere*, inter alia; ~ *vier oë*, in private; *~aan*, at the foot, at the bottom

onderaards' (-e) subterranean

on'der: ~afdeling (-s) subdivision; ~baadjie (-s) waistcoat; ~beklemtoning understatement

on'derbelig (~) underexpose

on'derbewus (-te) subconscious; *die ~te*, the subconscious; ~syn subconsciousness

onderbreek' (~) interrupt

onderbre'king (-e, -s) interruption, break

on'derbroek (-e) pair of pants/drawers

onderbro'ke interrupted; ~ *reis*, broken journey

on'derdaan (..dane) subject (of a country)

onderdak' house, shelter; ~ *vra*, ask for shelter

onderda'nig (-e; -er, -ste) submissive, obedient, humble

on'derdeel (..dele) subdivision; spare part

on'derdompel (-ge-) immerse

on'derdruk[1] (-ge-) press down or under

onderdruk'[2] (~) oppress (a nation); suppress (feelings); repress; quell (riot)

onderduims' (-e) underhand, cunning

on'derent (-e) bottom/lower end

ondergaan'[1] (~) undergo, suffer; *behandeling ~*, receive treatment

on'dergaan[2] (-ge-) go under; set (sun); be ruined; perish; ~ *in die stryd*, perish in the struggle

on'dergeskik (-te) subordinate, inferior; *van ~te belang*, of minor importance; *jou ~tes*, your subordinates

on'dergetekende (-s) undersigned

ondergronds' (-e) underground, subterranean; *~e spoorweg*, underground railway, tube, *kyk moltrein*

onderhan'del (~) negotiate, bargain; ~aar (-s) negotiator; ~ing (-e, -s) negotiation; *~inge aanknoop*, open negotiations; *salaris ~baar/reëlbaar*, salary negotiable

on'derhemp (..hemde) vest, undershirt, singlet; chemise (women's)

onderhe'wig liable to, subject to, open to; ~ *aan twyfel*, open to doubt

on'derhoof (-de) vice-principal

onderho'rig (-e) dependent, inferior; *sy ~es*, his subordinates

onderhou'[1] (~) support, maintain; feed

on'derhou[2] (-ge-) hold down or under

on'derhoud[1] maintenance, support, upkeep; *betaal ~ vir kind*, pay maintenance for child

on'derhoud[2] (-e) interview; *'n ~ hê/voer met iem.*, interview someone; ~voering interviewing

on'derklere underclothing

on'derkomitee (-s) subcommittee

on'derlaag (..lae) bottom layer, substratum; undercoat (paint)

on'derling (-e) mutual; *tot ~e voordeel*, to mutual advantage/gain

on'derlip (-pe) underlip

ondermaans' (-e) mundane, sublunary

ondermyn' (~) undermine, sap

onderne'mend (-e) enterprising, daring

onderne'mer (-s) undertaker, originator, entrepreneur

onderne'ming (-e, -s) enterprise, undertaking, venture; *vrye ondernemerskap*, free enterprise; **~s'gees** spirit of enterprise; **~s'vryheid** free enterprise

on'deroffisier (-e, -s) non-commissioned officer, petty officer

on'derpand (-e) pledge, guarantee; *byko= mende* **~**, collateral security

on'derpresteerder under-achiever

on'derrig (s) instruction, tuition

onderrig' (w) (~), instruct, teach

onderskat' (~) undervalue, underestimate

onderskei' (~) distinguish, differentiate; discern; **~vermoë** power of distinction

on'derskeid difference, distinction; **~ maak tussen,** distinguish between

onderskei'delik respectively

onderskei'ding (-e, -s) distinction

onderskei'e various, different; respective

on'dersoek (s) examination, inquiry, inves= tigation, probe; research; **~ instel,** in= quire into; *by nader* **~,** on closer ex= amination

ondersoek' (w) (~) examine; scrutinise; inquire, investigate, probe

on'derspit: *die* **~** *delf,* come off second best

on'derstaande subjoined, following; **~ paragraaf,** the paragraph below

on'derste (s) (-s) bottom; (b) lowermost, lowest

onderstebo' upside-down, higgledy-pigg= ledy; upset; *hy sit kop* **~,** he feels depressed

on'derstel (s) (-le) undercarriage (railway truck); chassis (motorcar)

ondersteun' (~) support, succour, assist, back up; **~er** (-s) supporter; **~ing** sup= port, relief

onderte'ken (~) sign, undersign; *'n brief* **~,** sign a letter; **~aar** (-s) signatory (of document); subscriber; **~ing** signature, *ook* **handtekening**

on'dertoe lower down, to the bottom

ondertus'sen meanwhile, in the meantime

on'derverhuur (~) sublet

ondervind' (~) experience; **~ing** (-e, -s) experience; **~ing** *is die beste leermeester,* experience is the best teacher

ondervoed' (w) (~) underfeed; (b) (-e) underfed; **~ing** malnutrition, under= feeding

on'dervoorsitter (-s) vice-chairman

ondervra' (~) interrogate, question, ex=

amine; *aangehou vir* **~ging,** detained for questioning

onderweg' on the way; in transit

on'derwerp[1] (s) (-e) subject, topic, theme

onderwerp'[2] (w) (~) subdue, subject; *hom aan Gods wil* **~,** resign oneself to God's will

onderwor'pe subject to; submissive; **~ aan goedkeuring,** subject to approval

onderwyl' meanwhile, while

onderwys' (w) (~) teach, instruct, inform

on'derwys (s) education, tuition. instruc= tion; **~ buite skoolverband,** adult educa= tion; **~ gee,** teach; **hoër ~,** higher (university) education; *middelbare (se= kondêre)* **~,** secondary education; **~ vir volwassenes,** adult education; *voortgesette* **~,** continuing education; **~departement** (-e) department of education

onderwy'ser (-s) teacher

onderwyseres' (-se) teacher (lady)

on'derwys: ~kollege (-s) college of educa= tion; **~personeel** (..nele) teaching staff; **~stelsel** (-s) educational system

on'deug (-de) vice, mischief, depravity; imp, bounder; *'n klein* **~,** a little boun= der

ondeund' (-e; -er, -ste) mischievous, naughty

ondeursky'nend (-e) opaque

on'dier (-e) monster, brute

on'ding undesirable thing; absurdity, non= sense, monstrosity

ondraag'baar (..bare) too heavy to be car= ried; unwearable

ondraag'lik (-e) intolerable, unbearable; **~e pyne,** excruciating pains

ondubbelsin'nig (-e) unambiguous

ondui'delik (-e; -er, -ste) indistinct; not clear (meaning); illegible (handwriting)

one'del (-e) ignoble, mean; base; **~e metale,** base metals

oneerbie'dig (-e; -er, -ste) disrespectful

oneer'lik (-e; -er, -ste) dishonest, unfair, fraudulent; **~e praktyke,** sharp practices; **~heid** dishonesty, bad faith

oneg' (-te) falsified, spurious; **~te diamant,** imitation diamond

onein'dig (-e) infinite, endless; **~ dank= baar,** extremely grateful; *tot in die* **~e,** ad infinitum; **~heid** infinity one'nig at variance, discordant; ~heid disagreement, discord; ~heid kry, quarrel

onerva're (-ner, -nste) inexperienced

one'we unequal, uneven; ~ getal, odd number

onewere'dig (-e) disproportionate

onfatsoen'lik (-e) indecent, improper

onfeil'baar (..bare) infallible

ongeag' (-te) unesteemed, unnoticed; irrespective of; ~ die koste, regardless of expense

ongedeerd' (-e) unhurt, uninjured; unharmed, unscathed, safe; daar ~ afkom, escape unhurt

ongedier'te (-s) vermin, wild animals

ongedul'dig (-e; -er, -ste) impatient

ongeërg (-de) without creating a fuss; imperturbed, calm, nonchalant; ~de houding, don't care attitude

ongeëwenaard' (-e) unequalled, unparalleled

ongegrond' (-e) false, unfounded; ~e aantygings/bewerings, unbased accusations/statements

ongehoor'saam (..same; ..samer, -ste) disobedient; ~heid disobedience

ongehuud' (..hude) unmarried; ongehude moeder, unmarried mother

on'gekeur not selected; unseeded; ~de speler, unseeded player

ongel'dig (-e) invalid, null and void; ~ verklaar, declare null and void

ongeleer(d)' (-de; -der, -ste) uneducated, illiterate; not broken in (horse)

ongelet'ter(d) (-de) illiterate

ongeloof'lik (-e; -er, -ste) incredible

ongelo'wig (-e; -er, -ste) unbelieving, sceptical, incredulous; ~e (-s) unbeliever

on'geluk (-ke) accident, mishap, misfortune; per ~, by accident/mistake

ongeluk'kig (-er; -er, -ste) unhappy, unfortunate, unlucky

ongelyk' (b) (-e) unequal, uneven

on'gemak (-ke) inconvenience, hardship, discomfort; ~syfer humiture (climate)

ongemak'lik (-e; -er, -ste) uncomfortable; ill at ease; uneasy, inconvenient

ongemanierd' (-e) rude, uncivil, ill-mannered

ongenaak'baar (..bare) unapproachable, inaccessible

on'genade disfavour, disgrace

ongena'dig (-e) merciless, cruel

ongene'ë disinclined; unwilling; sy is hom nie ~ nie, she rather likes him

ongenees'lik (-e) incurable (illness)

ongenooi' (-de) uninvited, unbidden; ~de gaste, uninvited/unwelcome visitors

ongeoor'loof (-de) unpermitted, forbidden

ongepoets' (-te; -ter, -ste) uncouth

ongereeld' (-e; -er, -ste) irregular, disorderly; op ~e tye, at odd times

on'gerief (..riewe) inconvenience, discomfort; ~ veroorsaak, inconvenience

ongerus' (-te; -ter, -ste) uneasy, anxious; ~ oor iem., anxious, worried about a person

ongerymd' (-e) absurd

ongeskik' (-te; -ter, -ste) unsuitable, unfit

ongeskon'de uninjured, intact

ongeskool' (-de) untrained, unskilled; ~de arbeid, unskilled labour

ongesond' (-e; -er, -ste) unhealthy, injurious to health; unwholesome, unsound

ongetroud' (-e) unmarried, single; kwartiere vir ~es, single quarters

ongetwy'feld undoubtedly, doubtless

on'geval (-le) accident, mishap, casualty; ~le'versekering accident insurance

on'geveer roughly, approximately, about

ongevraag' (-de) uncalled for; ~de advies, unasked for advice

ongewa'pen(d) (-de) unarmed; unprepared

ongewens' (-te) undesired, undesirable; ~te publikasie, undesirable publication

ongewoon' (..wone; ..woner, -ste) unusual, uncommon; iets ~s, something out of the ordinary; ~d' (-e) unaccustomed

ongrondwet'lik (-e) unconstitutional

on'guns disfavour, disgrace; in ~ raak, fall into disfavour

onguns'tig (-e; -er, -ste) unfavourable; ~e rapport, unfavourable report

onguur' (ongure) rough, coarse, repulsive; 'n ..gure vent, an unsavoury fellow

onheilspel'lend (-e; -er, -ste) ominous

onherberg'saam (..same) inhospitable; barren

onherroep'lik (-e) irrevocable

onherstel'baar (..bare) irreparable, irretrievable; ..bare verlies, irreparable loss

o'niks (-e) onyx

on'juis (-te) incorrect, erroneous

on'kant off-side (sport)

on'klaar out of order, defective; ~ raak, break down (car)

on'koste expenses, charges; na aftrek van ~, all charges deducted

onkreuk'baar (..bare) unimpeachable

on'kruid (-e) weeds; ~ vergaan nie, ill weeds grow apace; ~doder weedkiller, herbicide

onkuis' (-e) unchaste, impure

on'kunde ignorance; sy ~ openbaar, display his ignorance

on'langs (b) (-e) recent

on'lus dislike, listlessness; (-te), disturbance, riot; ~eenheid riot squad/unit

onmens'lik (-e) inhuman, cruel, brutal

onmid'dellik (-e) immediate(ly), direct(ly)

on'min disagreement, discord

onmis'baar (..bare) indispensable, essential

onmoont'lik (-e; -er, -ste) impossible

onnatuur'lik (-e; -er, -ste) unnatural

onno'dig (-e) unnecessary

onno'sel (-e) innocent; silly; stupid; ~e vent, simpleton, Simple Simon

onnut'sig (-e; -er, -ste) naughty, mischievous

onomatopee' (..peë) onomatopoeia, ook klanknabootsing

onontbeer'lik (-e) indispensable

onop'gevoed (-e) uneducated, rude, ill-bred

onophou'delik (-e) incessant, continuous

onoplet'tend (-e; -er, -ste) inattentive; ~e leerling, inattentive pupil

onopset'lik (-e) unintentional

on'paar odd, unmatched; ~ kouse, odd stockings

onparty'dig (-e; -er, -ste) impartial, unbiassed; ~heid impartiality

onplesie'rig (-e; -er, -ste) unpleasant, disagreeable

on'raad danger, trouble; ~ merk, smell a rat, scent danger

onre'delik (-e; -er, -ste) unreasonable, unfair

onreëlmatig (-e) irregular

on'reg wrong, injustice; 'n skreiende ~, a glaring injustice

on'regstreeks (-e) indirect(ly)

onregver'dig (-e; -er, -ste) unjust, unfair, unequitable; ~heid injustice, iniquity

onroe'rend (-e) immovable; ~e goed(ere), immovable property, kyk vasgoed

on'rus unrest, anxiety; disquiet, disturbance, commotion; ~ baar, create alarm

onrusba'rend (-e; -er, -ste) disquieting, alarming

on'russtoker (-s) mischief maker; agitator

onrus'tig (-e; -er, -ste) restless, uneasy, anxious; turbulent; ~ slaap, sleep uneasily

ons[1] (s) (-e) ounce

ons[2] (pers. vnw, mv), we, us

onse'ker (-e) uncertain, unsafe, insecure

onsig'baar (..bare) invisible, unseen

on'sin nonsense; ~ uitkraam, talk rubbish

onska'delik (-e) harmless, innocuous; ~ maak/stel, render harmless

onskat'baar (..bare) invaluable, inestimable; van ..bare waarde, of inestimable value

onskei(d)'baar (..bare) inseparable

on'skuld innocence

onskul'dig (-e; -er, -ste) innocent, harmless

onsterf'lik (-e) immortal; ~heid immortality; ~e roem, immortal/lasting fame

onstui'mig (-e; -er, -ste) turbulent, wild, boisterous; rough (weather); ~e vergadering, unruly meeting

onsy'dig (-e) impartial; neuter (gender)

ontbied' (~) send for, summon; call in

ontbind' (~) dissolve; decay, untie, undo; 'n vennootskap ~, dissolve a partnership

ontbloot' (w) (~) strip, deprive; lay bare; (b) (..blote) deprived, devoid; uncovered; met onblote hoof, bareheaded; ~ van alle waarheid, devoid of all truth

ontbreek' (~) be wanting, be missing

ontbyt' (s) (-e) breakfast; ~ nuttig, have breakfast; (w) (~) have breakfast

ontdek' (~) discover, find out; ~king (-e, -s) discovery; ~kingsreisiger (-s) explorer

ontdooi' (~) thaw

ontduik' (~) shirk, evade, dodge; escape; die wet ~, evade the law

ontevre'de (-ner, -nste of meer ~, mees ~) discontented, dissatisfied

ontgroen' (~) initiate; ~ing initiation; induction

onthaal' (s) (..hale) reception; treat, regale; (w) (~) entertain; gaste ~, entertain guests

onthef' (~) exempt, exonerate

onthei'lig (~) desecrate, profane

onthoof' (~) behead, decapitate

onthou' (~) remember, recall, bear in mind; retain; abstain, refrain; *help my ~,* remind me, please; **~er (-s)** abstainer, teetotaller

onthul' (~) unveil; reveal; disclose

ontken' (~) deny; **~nend (-e)** negative; *~nend antwoord,* reply in the negative

ontken'ning (-e, -s) denial; *die dubbele ~,* the double negative

ontklee' (~) undress; **~dans (-e)** striptease (act); **~danseres (-se)** stripper, striptease dancer

ontle'ding (-e, -s) analysis; dissection

ontlont' (w) (~) defuse (crisis)

ontluik' (~) open, unfold; **~ende talent,** budding talent

ontman' (~) castrate, emasculate

ontmas'ker (~) expose, unmask

ontmoet' (~) meet, encounter

ontnug'ter (~) disillusion, disenchant

ontplof' (~) explode, detonate, pop off; **~fing (-e, -s)** explosion, blast, detonation; **~fingstof** (..stowwe) explosive, *kyk* **plofstof**

ontplooi' (~) unfurl, unfold; deploy (troops)

ontrim'peling facelift

ontroer' (~) move, touch, affect; **~ende tonele,** stirring/moving scenes

ont'rond (~) unround (a vowel)

ontrou' (b) (-e; -er, -ste) disloyal, faithless

ontruim' (~) evacuate; vacate; *die gebou ~,* evacuate (the people in) the building

ontsag' awe, respect; *~ inboesem,* stand in awe of; command respect

ontset' (w) (~) perplex; appal; (b) (-te) appalled, aghast; **~tend (-e; -er, -ste)** terrible, awful, appalling

ontsien' (~) respect, stand in awe of; *~ sy grys hare,* have respect for his grey hair; *geen moeite ~ nie,* spare no pains

ontslaan' (~) dismiss, discharge; sack; *iem. uit sy betrekking ~,* dismiss someone

ontsla'e discharged; rid; *~ raak van,* get rid of

ontslag' release; acquittal, dismissal, discharge

ontsla'pe dead, deceased

ontsluit' (~) open, unlock; develop (mining); *inligting ~,* retrieve information

ontsmet' (~) disinfect; **~ting** disinfection;

~(tings)middel (-s) disinfectant

ontsnap' escape; **~ping** escape; gaolbreak, jailbreak

ontsout' (w) (~) desalinate, desalt

ontspan' (~) relax, divert; unbend; *tyd om te ~,* time to relax; **~geriewe** recreational facilities/amenities

ontspoor' (~) derail

ontstaan' (s) origin, beginning; (w) (~) begin, originate, arise; *hoe het die rusie ~?* what was the cause of the argument?

ontstel' (~) startle, upset, disconcert, disturb; **~lende gebrek aan kennis,** alarming lack of knowledge

onttrek' (~) withdraw; *jou ~ aan,* withdraw from; **~king'simptoom** withdrawal symptom

on'tug prostitution, fornication, immorality; **~wet** immorality act

on'tuis ill at ease; *~ voel,* be ill at ease

ontvang' (~) receive; conceive; **~er** recipient, receiver; tax gatherer; **~er van inkomste,** receiver of revenue; **~s' (-te)** receipt; reception; takings, returns; *in ~s neem,* take delivery of; **~s'dame (-s)** receptionist

ontvoer' (~) abduct, kidnap; **~der (-s)** kidnapper, *kyk* **kaper/skaker**

ontvolk' (~) depopulate

ontwa'pen (~) disarm; **~ing** disarmament

ontwa'semer (-s) demister

ontwa'ter (~) dehydrate

ontwerp' (s) (-e) draft, sketch, design; project; (w) (~) project, plan, design; draft

ontwik'kel (~) develop, evolve; **~d (-e)** developed; educated; **~ende lande,** developing countries; **~aar (-s)** developer

ontwik'keling development, evolution; *algemene ~,* general education; **~s'gang** evolution, course of development

ontwil' sake; *om my ~,* for my sake

ontwrig' (~) dislocate; disrupt; *die klas ~,* disrupt the class

ontwyk' (~) evade, shun, escape; *'n vraag ~,* evade a question; **~end (-e)** evasive

onuitput'lik (-e) inexhaustible

onuitspreek'lik (-e) inexpressible

o'nus onus, obligation

onvanpas' out of place, unsuitable

onverantwoor'delik (-e; -er, -ste) irresponsible, inexcusable

onverbe'terlik (-e) incorrigible

onverbid'delik (-e) inexorable, relentless

onverdraag'saam (..same; ..samer, -ste) intolerant; ~heid intolerance

onvergank'lik (-e) imperishable, undying, everlasting; ~e roem, immortal fame

onvergeef'lik (-e) unpardonable

onvergeet'lik (-e) never to be forgotten, memorable, unforgettable

onverhoeds' unexpectedly, unawares; ~ betrap, caught unawares

onverkry(g)'baar (..bare) unobtainable

on'vermoë impotence; inability

onvermy'delik (-e) unavoidable; inevitable

on'verrigter sake without having effected a purpose, unsuccessfully; ~ tuis kom, come home without any success

onversig'tig (-e; -er, -ste) imprudent, incautious; ~heid imprudence

onverskil'lig (-e; -er, -ste) indifferent; rash, reckless, heedless; ~ ry, drive recklessly

onverskrok'ke intrepid, bold, undaunted; 'n ~ jagter, a fearless hunter

on'versoet unsweetened

onverstaan'baar (..bare) incomprehensible, unintelligible

onverstan'dig (-e; -er, -ste) unwise, foolish

onverwag' (-te) unexpected; ~s' unexpectedly, unawares, suddenly

onvoldoen'de insufficient, inadequate; 'n blote kennisgewing is ~, a mere notice will not meet the case

onvoltooi' (-de) imperfect, incomplete; ~de simfonie, unfinished symphony

onvoorsiens' unawares; dit het heeltemal ~ gebeur, it happended quite unexpectedly

onvoorwaar'delik (-e) unconditional; ~e oorgawe, unconditional surrender

on'vrede discord, feud; in ~ lewe, lead a cat-and-dog life

onvri(e)n'delik (-e; -er, -ste) unkind, unfriendly; ~heid unkindness

onvrug'baar (..bare, -der, -ste) sterile, barren, unfertile

onwaar' (..ware) untrue

onwaarskyn'lik (-e; -er, -ste) improbable

on'weer thunderstorm; bad weather

onweerstaan'baar (..bare) irresistible

onwerk'lik (-e) uncanny, unreal

onwet'tig (-e) unlawful, illegal; naughty

onwillekeu'rig (b) (-e) involuntary; (bw) involuntarily; ek moes ~ lag, I could not help laughing

onwil'lig (-e) unwilling, loth

oog (oë) eye; fountain, source; noose; met die blote ~, with the naked eye; uit die ~, uit die hart, out of sight, out of mind; ~appel (-s) eyeball; darling; ~arts (-e) eye specialist, oculist, ophthalmic surgeon; ~getuie (-s) eyewitness; ~haar (..hare) eyelash; nie ~hare hê vir, not fancy someone/something; ~knip wink; ~kun'dige (-s) optometrist; ~lid (..lede) eyelid; ~lopend (-e) salient, obvious

ooglui'kend stealthily, on the sly; close an eye to; ~ toelaat, connive at

oog: ~merk (-e) aim, intention; ~opslag glance; met 'n ~opslag, at a glance; ~punt (-e) point of view; ~tand (-e) eyetooth; ~wink moment, wink; ~wimper (-s) eyelash

ooi (-e) ewe

ooi'evaar (-s, ..vare) stork; ~s'drag maternity wear

ooit ever, at any time

ook also, too

oom (-s) uncle; Liewe ~ Piet, Dear uncle Peter

oom'blik (-ke) moment, instant

oomblik'lik (-e) instantaneous(ly), immediate(ly), direct(ly), instantly

oond (-e) oven, furnace

oop open; vacant

oop'staan (-ge-) be open (door)

oop'stel (-ge-) throw open; geriewe ~ vir almal, open (the) facilites for all

oor¹ (s) (ore) ear; iem. ore aansit, outdo someone; in die ~ knoop, make sure not to forget

oor² (bw) over, past; left; ~ en weer, to and fro, mutually; (vs) over, via, beyond, across; ~ die geheel, on the whole

oor³ (vgw) because; hy vorder ~ hy werk, he makes progress because he works

oor: ~beklemtoning overstatement; ~bel (-le) earring; earlobe

oorbie'tjie (-s) oribi antelope

oorbluf' (~) disconcert, strike dumb, put out of countenance; heeltemal ~ wees, be completely dumbfounded

oorbo'dig (-e) superfluous, excessive

oorbrug' (~) bridge (over); probleme ~, solve (the) problems

oord (-e) region, locality, place

oor'daad excess, extravagance; *in ~ lewe,* live extravagantly

oordag' during the day

oor'deel (s) (..dele) judgment; verdict; opinion; *~ vel,* pass judgment/sentence; (w) (ge-) judge

oordeelkun'dig (-e) judicious

oor'deels: *~dag* judgment day, doomsday; *~fout* (-e) error of judgment

oorden'king meditation, epilogue

oordraag'baar (..bare) transferable

oor'drag transfer, cession

oordre'we exaggerated; overdone

oordryf', oordry'we (~) exaggerate, overdo

ooreen' in agreement; *hulle kom ~,* they agree

ooreen'koms (-te) resemblance, conformity; agreement, contract, treaty; *'n ~ aangaan/sluit/tref,* enter into an agreement

ooreenkoms'tig (-e) corresponding; in accordance with

ooreen'stem (-gestem) agree, concur, correspond; *~ming* agreement

oorerf'lik (-e) hereditary

oor'gang transition, passing across; (-e) crossing, passage

oorgank'lik (-e) transitive

oor'gawe (-s) surrender; transfer, cession

oor'gee (-ge-) surrender, yield, hand over, deliver up; *hom ~ aan,* surrender himself to, become a slave to

oor: *~genoeg* more than enough; *~gerus* overconfident; *~gevoelig* (-e) oversensitive, hypersensitive; *~gewig* overweight; obese/obesity; excess weight

oor'groot: *~moeder* (-s) great-grandmother; *~ouers* great-grandparents; *~vader* (-s) great-grandfather

oor'haal (-ge-) fetch across; persuade; cock (rifle); induce; *ek het hom oorgehaal,* I have persuaded him

oorhan'dig (~) hand over, deliver; present; *~ing* handing over, delivery, presentation (of prizes)

oorheers' (~) dominate, domineer; *die ~ende vraag,* the all-important question; *~ing* domination

oor'hou (-ge-) save, have left

oor'kant (s) other/opposite side; *(aan die)*

~ (van) die straat, on the opposite side of the street

oor'klank (-ge-) dub; *~ing* dubbing

oor'klere overall(s)

oorkoe'pel (~) cover, vault, arch; *~ende organisasie,* umbrella organisation

oor'kussing pillow; *ledigheid is die duiwel se ~,* Satan finds mischief for idle hands to do

oor'kyk (-ge-) peruse, look over; correct

oorlaai' [1] (~) overload, overcharge, overburden, glut; *hy is met presente ~,* presents were heaped upon him

oor'laai [2] (-ge-) reload; transship

oor'laat (-ge-) leave over, leave (to others); *aan sy lot ~,* leave to his fate

oorlams' (-e) clever, handy; cunning, crafty, wily, shrewd; trained

oor'las nuisance, trouble

oor'le, oorle'de, oorlee' deceased, late; *~ Jan,* the late John

oorle'dene (-s) the deceased, the departed

oorleef' (~) outlive, survive

oor'lees (-ge-) read through, peruse

oorleg' deliberation, counsel, consideration, judgment; *~komitee* liaison committee, *ook skakelkomitee*; *~pleging* (-e, -s) consultation, talks

oor'lel (-le) lobe of the ear

oorle'wing survival; *~ van die sterkste,* survival of the fittest; *~(s)kursus* (-se) survival course

oor'log (..loë) war; *~ verklaar,* declare war; *~ voer,* wage war

oor'logverklaring (-e, -s) declaration of war

oor'loop (s) overflow; (..lope) spillway; (w) (-ge-) desert; overflow (dam); defect; *na die vyand ~,* defect/desert to the enemy

oorlo'sie (-s) watch, clock; *my ~ is agter,* my watch is slow; *my ~ is voor,* my watch is fast

oormees'ter (~) overpower; master

oormekaar' the one over/across the other

oor'môre day after tomorrow; *môre, ~,* one of these days

oornag' (w) (~) stay overnight; (b, bw) overnight

oor'name (s) (-s) takeover

oor'neem (-ge-) take over (management); assume; copy; borrow

oor'pak (-ke) overall

oor'plaas (-ge-) transfer, shift, remove
oor'plant (-ge-) transplant
oor'pyn earache
oorreed' (~) persuade, prevail on
oorrom'pel (~) surprise, fall upon
oor'saak (..sake) cause, reason; ~ *en ge=*
volg, cause and effect
oorsees' (..sese) oversea(s), transmarine;
oorsese handel, overseas/foreign trade
oor'sig (-te) view; digest; survey; review,
summary
oor'sit (-ge-) put over; translate; move up
(pupils)
oorskat' (~) overestimate, overrate
oor'skiet (s) remains; rest; remnant; (w)
(-ge-) remain; be left over; ~**kos** (-se)
left-overs
oor'skot (-te) remainder, residue; remnant;
surplus; *die stoflike* ~, the mortal re=
mains; ~**waarde** scrap value
oorskry' (~) exceed, surpass
oor'slaan (-ge-) omit, pass, miss out
oorspan'ne overstrung; ~ *senuwees,* over=
wrought nerves
oor'sprong origin, cause, root, source
oorspronk'lik (-e) original, primary, prim=
ordial; ~**heid** originality
oor'steek (-ge-) cross (a street)
oorstroom' (~) overflow, inundate
oortol'lig (-e) superfluous, redundant
oortre'der (-s) trespasser, transgressor; de=
linquent, offender; *-s word vervolg,*
trespassers will be prosecuted
oortref' (~) surpass, excel; ~**fend** (-e)
superlative
oortrek' (w) (~) overdraw; ~**king** overdraft
(bank account)
oor'trektrui (-e) pull-over, sweater
oortuig' (~) convince; *daarvan* ~, satisfied
with
oortui'ging conviction; *tot die* ~ *kom,*
come to the conclusion
oor'tyd overtime; ~**betaling** (-s) overtime
pay
oor'vloed abundance, plenty
oorvra' (~) overcharge, surcharge
oorweeg' (~) consider, deliberate; pre=
ponderate; *'n voorstel* ~, consider a pro=
posal/suggestion
oor'weg (..weë) level crossing; crossroad
oorwe'ging (-e, -s) consideration, delibera=
tion

oorwel'dig (~) overpower, overwhelm;
~**end** (-e) overpowering, overwhelming
oorwin' (~) conquer, overcome; ~**naar**
(-s) conqueror, victor
oorwin'ning (-e, -s) victory, conquest; *die*
~ *behaal,* gain the victory
oor'wins surplus profit; ~**belasting** (-s)
excess profit duty; supertax
oorwin'ter (~) winter, hibernate
oorwo'ë considered; contemplated; ~ *me=*
ning, considered opinion
oos east; ~ *wes, tuis bes,* there is no place
like home
Oos'te Orient, the East; *die Verre* ~, the
Far East
oos'tewind (-e) east wind
op (b) finished; (bw) up, on; (vs) on, upon;
at, in; *almal* ~ *een na,* all but one; ~ *'n*
manier, in a manner, after a fashion; ~
skool, at school; ~ *tyd,* on time, *ook*
betyds
opaal' (opale) opal
op'bel (-ge-) ring up, phone
op'berg (-ge-) store, stock; stockpile
op'beur (-ge-) cheer up
op'blaas (-ge-) inflate, blow up
op'bou (w) (-ge-) build up; ~**end** (-e) con=
structive, edifying; ~**ende kritiek,** con=
structive criticism
op'brengs (-te) output, yield, proceeds
op'daag (-ge-) turn up, arrive
op'doen (-ge-) get, gain, acquire, obtain;
overhaul, recondition; *kennis* ~, acquire
knowledge
op'dok (-ge-) pay, foot the bill
op'domkrag (opge-) jack up
op'dons (-ge-) do carelessly; spoil; treat
severely; *iem. goed* ~, give someone a
drubbing
op'draand (s) (-e), **op'draande** (-s, **op=**
draans) rise, slope, uphill, rising ground;
upgrade; acclivity
op'drag (-te) instruction, order; commis=
sion; terms of reference; dedication; *in* ~
van die bestuur, by order of management
o'pe open; vacant; blank (line); *dis nog 'n*
ope vraag, it remains a moot point; ~ **dag**
open day
opeen'hoop (-gehoop) accumulate, heap up
opeens' all of a sudden, suddenly
opeen'volg (-gevolg) follow each other;

~end (-e) successive, consecutive; *vir tien ~ende dae*, for ten consecutive days
op'eet (opgeëet) eat up, finish; *alles vir soetkoek ~*, believe everything
o'pelug open-air; **~museum** (-s) open-air museum; **~teater** (-s) open-air theatre
opelyf' evacuation of the bowels
o'pen (ge-) open; *~ met gebed*, open with prayer
openbaar' (s) public; *in die ~*, in public; (w) (ge-) make public, disclose, reveal
openba're = **betrekkinge** public relations; *~ skakelamptenaar* public relations official/officer
openba'ring (-e, -s) revelation, apocalypse
openhar'tig (-e) open-hearted, frank
o'pening (-e, -s) opening, aperture, gap
o'penlik (-e) openly, publicly
o'pera (-s) opera
opera'sie (-s) operation; *'n ~ ondergaan*, undergo an operation; *operasionele gebied*, operational area
operateur' (-s) operator
opereer' (~, ge-) operate (on)
operet'te (-s) operetta
op'gaan (-ge-) go up, ascend, rise
op'gawe (-s) task, assignment, brief; statement, return (income)
op'geblase (-ner, -ste) puffed up, inflated
op'geruimd (-e; -er, -ste) cheerful, gay
op'geskeep (-te) saddled (with); at a loss
op'geskort (-e) suspended (sentence)
op'gewasse equal (to); *nie ~ teen iem.*, no match for; *nie ~ vir die taak nie*, not equal to the task
op'gewek (-te, -ter, -ste) lively, cheerful, bright; *~te musiek*, bright/light music
op'gewonde excited; *~n'heid* excitement
op'gooi (-ge-) throw up; chuck up; vomit; *tou ~*, throw up the sponge
ophan'de approaching, at hand, near
op'hang (-ge-) hang; suspend
op'hef (s) fuss; *'n groot ~ maak van*, fuss about; (w) (ge-) abolish, waive
op'hoop (-ge-) pile up, accumulate, heap up; *opgehoopte verliese*, accumulated losses
op'hou (-ge-) keep up, support; keep on; uphold; cease, stop; *die reën sal nou ~*, it will cease raining now; *hou op!* stop it!
opi'nie (-s) opinion; **~peiling** opinion poll

op'kikker (-ge-) cheer up; pep up; **~tablet** (-te) pep pill
op'klaar (-ge-) brighten, clear (up)
op'knap (-ge-) tidy up, smarten up; recondition; renovate; **~per(tjie)** pick-me-up; **~kursus** (-se) refresher course
op'kom (-ge-) come up, rise; occur; crop up; **~s** rise; attendance
op'kommandeer (-ge-) commandeer, requisition
op'laag (..lae) edition, impression (of a book)
op'laai (-ge-) give a lift
oplaas' at last, finally
op'lê (-ge-) apply, impose, charge
op'lei (-ge-) instruct, educate, train; **~deling** (-e) trainee; **~er** (-s) trainer; **~kursus** (-se) training course
op'leiding education, training
op'let (-ge-) pay attention, attend, take notice
oplet'tend (-e; -er, -ste) attentive
op'lewing revival; *~ van die ekonomie*, revival of the economy
op'loop (w) (ge-) accumulate, accrue, increase; *opgeloopte rente*, accrued interest
op'los (-ge-) dissolve; solve, puzzle out
op'lossing (-e, -s) solution; explanation
op'meet (-ge-) survey, measure
op'merk (-ge-) notice; observe; remark
op'merking (-e, -s) remark, observation
opmerk'lik (-e; -er, -ste) remarkable
opmerk'saam (..same) attentive, observant
op'meter (-s) mine surveyor
op'name (-s) taking up; admission; survey
op'neem (-ge-) take up; receive, shelter; *die voorraad ~*, take stock
opnuut' again, once more, anew
op'offering (-e, -s) sacrifice; *jou ~e getroos*, make sacrifices
op'onthoud delay, stoppage
op'pas (-ge-) be careful, beware, mind; attend to, care for, nurse; *pas op!* be careful! look out!
op'passer (-s) caretaker, attendant, nurse
op'per (w) (ge-) suggest, moot; *besware ~*, raise objections
op'perbevel high/supreme command
op'perhoof (-de) chief, chieftain
op'perste uppermost, highest; *'n ~ vabond*, an archscoundrel

op'**pervlak** surface; *die swemmer verdwyn onder die* ~, the swimmer disappears under the surface

oppervlak'kig (-e; -er, -ste) superficial, shallow; *~e kennis,* a nodding acquaintance; superficial knowledge

op'**pervlakte** (-s) area; *die wandellaan beslaan 'n ~ van 3 hektaar,* the mall covers an area of 3 hectares

Op'perwese Supreme Being, God

opportunis' (-te) opportunist

opposi'sie opposition

op'**pot** (w) (-ge-) hoard (gold)

opreg' (-te; -ter, -ste) sincere, genuine

op'**rig** (-ge-) erect; found; raise; establish; *'n maatskappy ~,* form/float a company

op'**rit** (-te) onramp (traffic)

op'**roep** (s) (-e) summons; (telephone) call; (w) (-ge-) convoke; call up, commandeer

op'**roer** (-e) revolt, insurrection, riot

op'**roermaker** (-s) rioter, insurgent

op'**ruim** (-ge-) clear away, tidy; clear off

op'**sê** (-ge-) recite, say; dismiss, give notice; *die huur ~,* give notice

op'**set** plan, set-up, purpose, intention; *met ~,* on purpose; *met die ~ om,* with intent to

opset'lik (-e) on purpose, deliberate(ly)

op'**sie** (-s) option

op'**siener** (-s) overseer, supervisor, invigilator, commissioner

op'**sig** (-te) supervision; respect; *in alle ~te,* in all respects; *in dié ~,* in this respect; *~ter* (-s) overseer, supervisor; caretaker

op'**skeep** (-ge-) saddle with

op'**skop**[1] (-ge-) kick up; *'n lawaai ~,* make a fuss

op'**skop**[2] (s) (-pe) informal dance

op'**skort** (-ge-) suspend (a sentence)

op'**skrif** (-te) inscription, title, heading

op'**skudding** agitation, sensation, alarm

op'**slaan** (-ge-) raise, put up (prices); pitch (tent); lift (eyes); **~huis** préfabricated house

op'**slag** (opslae) rise; glance; voluntary plants; bounce; **~koeël** (-s) ricochet shot; **~plek** (-ke) supply dump

op'**som** (-ge-) summarise, sum up; **~ming** (-e, -s) summary, résumé

op'**spoor** (-ge-) track, trace

op'**spraak** sensation, commotion; *~ verwek,* flutter the dovecotes

op: **~staan** (-ge-) stand up, rise, get up; revolt; **~stal** (-le) buildings, premises (farm), homestead

op'**stand** (-e) revolt, insurrection; *in ~ kom,* revolt

opstan'deling (-e) insurgent, rebel

op'**standing** resurrection

op'**steek** (-ge-) raise, put up; light; incite; prick up; *stem per/met ~ van hande,* vote by show of hands

op'**stel** (s) (-le) essay, composition; (w) (-ge-) plan; compose; draft; compile

op'**stoker** (-s) inciter, instigator, agitator

op'**stop** (-ge-) fill up; stuff, mount; **~per** (-s) blow, smack; stuffer, taxidermist

op'**styg** (-ge-) rise, ascend; **~ing** ascent, rising; lift-off (spacecraft)

op'**sweep** (-ge-) whip up, drive up, incite; *die gemoedere ~,* rouse the feelings/passions

op'**swel** (-ge-) swell, inflate

op'**tel** (-ge-) enumerate; add; lift, raise; **~som** (-me) addition sum

op'**ties** (-e) optic(al)

optimis' (-te) optimist; **~me** optimism

op'**tog** (-te) procession; *'n historiese ~,* historical pageant

op'**tree** (-ge-) appear, take action/steps; *as voorsitter ~,* act as chairman

opval'lend (-e; -er, -ste) conspicuous, noticeable, striking

op'**vang** (-ge-) intercept, catch up, overhear; **~gebied** catchment area

op'**varende** (-s) passenger (on ship)

op'**vat** (-ge-) understand, take up; *iets ernstig ~,* regard something seriously; **~ting** (-e, -s) idea, opinion, conception, view

op'**veil** (-ge-) sell by auction

opvlie'ënd (-e) quick-tempered, irascible

op'**voed** (-ge-) educate, rear, bring up; **~e'ling** (-e) educant; **~er** (-s) educator, educationist; **~ing** education; **~kunde** pedagogy

opvoedkun'dig pedagogic, educative, educational; **~e** (-s) educationist

op'**voer** (-ge-) lead up to; perform, act; **~ing** (-e, -s) performance (dramatic)

op'**volg** (-ge-) follow, succeed; **~aanval** hot pursuit, ook hakkejag

op'**vra** (-ge-) call in, demand back; withdraw; **~ging** (-s) withdrawal (money)

op'**vreet** (-ge-) devour (animal)

op'wek (-ge-) awake, stimulate, rouse; generate (electricity; steam)

o'ral(s) everywhere

orang-oe'tang (-s) orang-outang

oran'je orange (colour)

Oranje-Vry'staat Orange Free State

or'de order, arrangement

or'delik (-e; -er, -ste) orderly

ordent'lik (-e; -er, -ste) decent, reasonable

or'der (-s) command, order; *aan die ~ van A.*, to the order of A

ordinan'sie (-s) ordinance (Church ruling/ritual)

ordonnan'sie (-s) ordinance (of a province)

orent' upright, straight up

orgaan' (organe) organ

orga'nies (-e) organic

organisa'sie (-s) organisation

organiseer' (~, ge-) organise; ~der (-s) organiser, promoter

orgidee' (..deë) orchid

orgie' (-ë) orgy, debauching

oriënta'sie, oriënte'ring orientation; in-duction (students, staff)

o'rig (-e; -er, -ste) superfluous; meddlesome

orkaan' (orkane) hurricane

orkes' (-te) orchestra, band; ~begeleiding orchestral accompaniment; ~leier (-s) bandleader

ornament' (-e) ornament, *ook* sieraad, ver-siering

ornitologie' ornithology, science of birds

or'rel (-s) organ

orrelis' (-te) organist; ~te (-s) lady organist

ortodontis' (-te) orthodontist

ortopeed' (..pede), ortopedis' (-te) ortho-paedist

os (-se) ox

os'braai (-e) ox-braai

oseaan' (oseane) ocean

ot'jie (-s) young pig; grunter (fish)

ot'ter (-s) otter

ot'tery (-e) piggery

ou (s) (-ens) chap, fellow, guy; *ek het nie ooghare vir daardie ~ nie,* I do not fancy that guy

ou'boet (-e), ou'boeta (-s), ou'boetie (-s) eldest brother

oud-[1] ex; former; retired

oud[2] (b) (ou[e], -ouer, -ste) old, aged; *~ maar nog nie koud nie,* there is still a kick left in the old horse; *so ~ soos Metusalem (die berge, die Kaapse wapad),* as old as Methuselah

ou'der: *~ gewoonte,* as usual

ou'derdom (-me) age; ~gaping generation gap, *ook* generasiegaping

ou'derling (-e, -s) elder

ouderwets' (-e) old-fashioned; forward, precocious (child)

oud'gediende (-s) veteran, ex-serviceman

oud'heid oldness; antiquity

oudheidkun'dige (-s) antiquarian

oudiën'sie audience; *~ verleen,* grant an audience

oudiovisueel' (b) audio-visual; *..visuele hulpmiddels,* audio-visual aids

oudi'sie audition

ou'dit (s) (w) audit

ouditeer' (ge-) audit

oudedeur' (-e, -s) auditor

ouditeurs'verslag, ou'ditverslag (..slae) auditor's report

ou'ditkunde (science of) auditing

oud-leerling (-e) ex-pupil, old boy/girl (of a school)

oud'ste (-s) eldest, oldest, doyen

oud'-student (-e) ex-student, alumnus

ou'e (-s) old one; chap; *die ~s van dae,* the aged; *haai, julle ~(n)s!* I say, chaps!

ou'er (-s) parent; ~komitee (-s) parents-teachers committee

ou'etehuis (-e) old-aged home, home for senior citizens

Ou'jaar Old Year's Day; ~s'aand, ~s'-dagnag, ~s'nag New Year's Eve, Old Year's Night; ~s'dag Old Year's Day

ou'jong: ~kêrel (-s) (old) bachelor; ~nôi, ~nooi (-ens) spinster, old maid

Ou'kersaand (-e) Christmas Eve

ou'laas: *vir ~,* for the last time

ou'lik (-e; -er, -ste) precocious; tricky, nice; sharp, smart, cute; *'n ~e kêreltjie,* a smart little chap

ou'ma (-s) grandmother; ~grootjie (-s) great-grandmother

ou'pa (-s) grandfather; ~grootjie (-s) great-grandfather

outentiek' authentic, *ook* eg

outeur' (-s) author

ou'tjie (-s) (old) fellow, chum, chap, chap‑pie; *die klein ~s,* the tiny tots
outobiografie' (-ë) autobiography
outoma'ties (-e) automatic; *~e telefoon,* automatic telephone
outonomie' autonomy
ou'tyds (-e) old-fashioned, old-fangled
ou'volk spiny-tailed lizard

ou'vrou-onder-die-kombers toad-in-the-hole
ovaal' (ovale) oval
o'werheid (..hede) authority; ~besteding public/state expenditure/spending; ~‑sektor public sector
o'werspel adultery
o'werste (-s) chief, head

P

pa (-'s) pa, dad
paad'jie (-s) footpath, small path
paai (ge-) appease, coax, soothe; ~boelie (-s) bugbear, golliwog, bogey; ~pappie (-s) sugardaddy, *ook* vroetelvader
paaiement' (-e) instalment
paal (pale) pole, stake, standard; *die ~ nie haal nie,* unable to make the grade
paar (s) (pare) couple, pair; a few; (w) (ge-) match, mate; copulate; pair off
paar'tyd mating season
Paas: ~fees Easter; Passover; ~maandag Easter Monday, *kyk* Gesinsdag; ~skou (-e) Easter show
pad (paaie) path, road; way; *iem. in die ~ steek,* send someone packing; ~blokkade (-s) roadblock; ~buffel roadhog
pad'da (-s) frog, toad; *so waar as ~ manel dra,* truly; ~man (-ne) frogman; ~slag‑ter (-s) blunt knife; ~stoel (-e) toadstool; mushroom
pad: ~kafee (-s) roadhouse; ~kos provi‑sions (for a journey)
pad'langs straight
pad: ~loop (..lope) roadrace; ~skraper grader; ~vaardig (-e) ready for the road; ~vark (-e) roadhog (motorist); ~veilig‑heid road safety; ~verlegging (-s) devia‑tion (of road); ~versperring (-s) roadblock; ~vinder (-s) boy scout; pathfinder; ~waardig (-e) roadworthy
pa'-hulle father and the rest, dad and co(mpany)
paja'ma (-s) pyjamas
pak (s) (-ke) suit (of clothes); pack, bundle; thrashing, licking; *'n ~ klere,* a suit of clothes; *met ~ en sak,* with bag and bag‑gage; *'n ~ slae,* a thrashing; (w) (ge-) pack up; seize, grasp

pak'kend (-e; -er, -ste) gripping, stirring
pakket' (-te) parcel, packet; package; ~akkoord package deal, *ook* bondel‑transaksie; ~pos parcel post
pak'kie (-s) parcel, packet
pak: ~stapper backpacker; ~stuk (-ke) gasket (engine)
paleis' (-e) palace
pa'ling (-s) eel
paljas' (s) (-se) charm, spell; (w) (ge-) be‑witch
palm (-s) palm; ~boom (..bome) palm(tree)
palmiet' bulrush
pamflet' (-te) pamphlet; brochure, hand-out
pampelmoes' (-e) shaddock; ~ie (-s) gooseberry
pampoen' (-e) pumpkin; *vir koue ~ skrik,* afraid of one's own shadow; ~tjies mumps, parotitis
pan (-ne) pan; tile; small lake
pand (-e) pledge, pawn, forfeit
pan'dak (-ke) tiled roof
pand: ~jies'baas (..base) pawnbroker; ~jieswinkel (-s) pawnshop
paneel' (panele) panel; *die ~ beoordelaars,* the panel of adjudicators; ~kassie (-s) cubbyhole; ~klopper (-s) panelbeater; ~wa (..ens) panel van
paniek' (-e) panic, stampede; ~bevange, ~erig (-e) panic-stricken, panicky
pan'nekoek (-e) pancake
pan'ter (-s) panther
pantof'fel (-s) slipper
pap¹ (s) porridge; (-pe) poultice; (w) (ge-) poultice
pap² (b) (-per, -ste) soft, weak; deflated; *'n ~ band,* a deflated tyre
papa' (-'s) papa
papa'ja (-s) papaw

papa'wer (-s) poppy
pap'broek (-e) milksop, coward
papegaai' (-e) parrot, polly; popinjay
papier' (-e) paper
pap'nat dripping wet
pap'pa (-s) papa
pap'pie (-s) daddy
paraat' (b) (parate) ready, prepared; ~heid
preparedness (soldiers)
para'de (-s) review, parade
paradoks' (-e) paradox
paradys' (-e) paradise
parafeer' (~, ge-) initial; ~ elke bladsy,
initial every page
paraffien' paraffin oil
parafra'se (-s) paraphrase
paragraaf' (..grawe) paragraph
pa'ralans paralans (intensive care ambu=
lance)
parallel' (-le) parallel
parame'dies paramedical
parapleeg' (..pleë) paraplegic
parasiet' (-e) parasite; sponger
parente'se parenthesis
parfumier' (-s) perfumer
parfuum' (-s) scent, perfume
pa'ri par; onder ~, below par
park (-e) park; ~ade parkade
parkeer' (~, ge-) park; ~meter (-s) park=
ing meter
parkiet', parakiet' (-e) parakeet; ~tjie (-s)
budgerigar (budgie)
parlement' (-e) parliament
parman'tig (-e; -er, -ste) impudent, imper=
tinent, cheeky
parodie' (-ë) parody, travesty
parool' (-s) parole, watchword
part (-e) part, portion, share
party'¹ (s) (-e) party; faction; ~ kies, take
sides
party'² (b) some, a few
party'dig (-e; -er, -ste) partial, biassed
party'keer(s), party'maal sometimes
Parys' Paris (France); Parys (SA)
pas¹ (s) (-se) pass; passage; step, gait; die
~ aangee, set the pace; ~aangeër (-s)
pacemaker (heart)
pas² (s) place; fit; (w) (ge-) fit, suit, try on,
measure; be proper; nie bymekaar ~ nie,
not match; ~geweer custom made gun/
rifle

pas³ (bw) just, only; hardly; ~ aangestelde
hoof, newly appointed head/principal
Pa'se Easter
pasiënt' (-e) patient
pasifis' (-te) pacifist; ~me pacifism
pas'klaar ready for fitting on; ready-made
pas'lik (-e) fitting, suitable, becoming
pas'poort (-e) passport
passaat' (..sate) passage; ~wind (-e) trade
wind
passa'sie (-s) passage; ~ uit 'n roman,
fragment/passage from a novel
passasier' (-s) passenger; blinde ~, stow=
away, ook verstekeling; ~straler (-s) air=
liner
pas'send (-e) fitting; proper, appropriate;
daarby ~e skoene, shoes to match
pas'ser (-s) pair of compasses; ~ en draaier,
fitter and turner
pas'sie passion, craze
passief' (..siewe; ..siewer, -ste) passive
pas'siespel passion play
pas'stuk (-ke) adaptor, kyk aanpasser
pas'ta (-s) paste
pastei' (-e) pie, pastry
pastel' (-le) crayon, pastel
pasteuriseer' (~, ge-) pasteurise, sterilise
pastoor' (-s, ..tore) pastor; priest
pas'tor (-s) clergyman, pastor (Protestant)
pastorie' (-ë) parsonage, vicarage, rectory
patat'(ta) (-ë) sweet potato
patent' (s) (-e) patent
patent'reg patent right
pate'ties (-e; -er, -ste) pathetic
pa''tjie (-s) little father, daddy
patrio'ties (-e) patriotic
patrol'lie (-s) patrol
patroon'¹ (patrone) model, design, pattern
patroon'² (patrone) cartridge; ~dop (-pe)
cartridge case
patrys' (-e) partridge; ~poort (-e) porthole;
scuttle port
paviljoen' (-e), pawiljoen' (-e) pavilion
pê tired, worn out; hy kan nie ~ sê nie, he
cannot say boo to a goose
pedaal' (pedale) pedal
pedagogie(k)' pedagogics, education
pedan'ties (-e; -er, -ste) pedantic
peer (pere) pear; met die gebakte pere bly
sit, be saddled with something
pees (pese) tendon, sinew

peet (pete) sponsor, godparent; **~tjie:** *loop na jou ~jie,* go to the devil; **~kind** (-ers) godchild; **~ouers** godparents

peil (s) mark, gauge, standard, level; (w) (ge-) sound, fathom, gauge, plumb

peins (ge-) meditate

pe'kel (s) brine; difficulty

pel'grim (-s) pilgrim

pelikaan' (..kane) pelican

peloton' (-s) squad, platoon

pels (-e) fur, skin; **~er** (-s) pilchard; **~jas** (-se) fur coat

pen (s) (-ne) pen, nib, quill

pena'rie difficulty, predicament, fix

pen'del (w) (ge-) commute; **~aar** (-s) commuter; **~diens** shuttle service; **~tuig** (..tuie) space shuttle

pendu'le (-se) pendulum

pen'kop (-pe) young fellow, inexperienced youth

pen'(ne)lekker (-s) clerk, penpusher

pen'ning (-s) medal, penny; **~meester** (-s) treasurer

pen: **~punt** (-e) nib; **~orent** erect, straight up, upright; **~regop** perpendicular

pens (-e) belly, stomach, paunch (animal); **~ en pootjies,** bodily

penseel' (..sele) brush (artist)

pensioen' (-e) pension; retiring pay; *met ~ aftree,* retire on pension; **~aris** (-se) pensioner

pensioen': **~fonds** (-e) pension fund; **~trekker** (-s) pensioner

pens: **~klavier** (-e) accordion; **~winkeltjie** (-s) pedlar's tray

pen'tameter (-s) pentameter; *jambiese ~ / vyfvoetige jambe,* iambic pentameter

pe'per (s) pepper; **~duur** sinfully dear; **~korreltjies** short woolly hair

peperment' (-e) peppermint

per by, via, per; **~ abuis,** by mistake; **~ adres,** care of; **~ geluk,** luckily; **~ kerende pos,** by return of post

perd (-e) horse

per'de: **~by** (-e) wasp; hornet; **~krag** horsepower; **~ruiter** (-s) horseman, equestrian; **~sport** show jumping, horseriding

perd: **~fris** hale and hearty; **~gerus** without suspecting anything; **~jie** (-s) small horse, pony; *gou op sy ~jie wees,* to be touchy

pê'rel (-s) pearl; *~s voor die swyne werp/ gooi,* cast pearls before swine; *gekweekte ~,* cultured pearl

perfek' (-te) perfect; **~sie** perfection

perio'de (-s) period, *ook* **tydperk**

periodiek' (-e) periodic(al), from time to time

perk (-e) limit; **~tyd** deadline, *ook* **spertyd**

perlemoen', perlemoer' mother of pearl

permanent' (-e) permanent

permissiwiteit' permissiveness

permit' (-te) permit, pass

perron' platform (railway), *ook* **platform**

pers (b) purple

perseel' (..sele) lot; plot; premises

persent' percent; *'n 10 ~ styging,* a 10 percent increase

persenta'sie (-s) percentage

pers'ke (-s) peach; **~brandewyn, ~snaps** peach brandy

personeel' (..nele) staff, personnel

personifika'sie (-s) personification

persoon' (..sone) person; *die aangewese ~,* the right person; **~lik** (-e) personal; **~likheid** (..hede) personality, individuality; *gesplete ~likheid,* split personality

pers: **~verklaring** press release; **~vryheid** freedom of the press

pervert' (s) pervert; (a) perverted

pes (s) (-te) pest, plague

pessimis' (-te) pessimist; **~me** pessimism; **~ties** (-e; -er, -ste) pessimistic

pestilen'sie pestilence

pet (-te) cap

peti'sie (-s) petition

pe'trol petrol; **~joggie** (-s) pump attendant

pe'trol: **~pomp** (-e) petrol pump, bowser; **~tenk** (-e, -s) petrol tank

peul (s) (-e) pod, husk, shell

peu'sel (ge-) nibble, pick; piffle; **~happie** (-s) snack; **~kroeg** (..kroeë) snackbar; **~werkie** (-s) odd job

pianis' (-te) pianist; **~te** (-s) lady pianist

pia'no (-'s) piano; **~begeleiding** piano accompaniment

piou'ter pewter

piek (-e) peak

piek'fyn spick-and-span; grand

piek'niek (-s) picnic

pienk (b) pink (colour)

piep'erig (-e; -er, -ste) sickly, weak, thin, squeaky

pie'pie (ge-) make water (nursery term), piddle
piep'jong, piep'jonk very young, tender
piekanien' (-s) piccanin
pie'rewaaier (-s) playboy, goodtimer
pie'ring (-s) saucer, **~skiet** clay pigeon shooting
pie'sang (-s) banana
pieterse'lie, pietersie'lie parsley
piet-my-vrou' (-e) red-chested cuckoo
piets (ge-) whip lightly, flick
pigmee' (..meë) pygmy
pik'donker pitch dark
pikkewyn' (-e) penguin
pik'swart black as pitch, pitch black
pil (-le) pill; *die ~ verguld,* sugar a pill
pilaar' (pilare) pillar, column
Pila'tus Pilate; *van Pontius na ~,* from pillar to post
pim'pel: ~ *en pers,* black and blue
pin'kie (-s) little finger
Pink'ster: **~fees** Whitsuntide, Pentecost; **~week** Whitsunweek
pinset' (-te) forceps, tweezers
pint (-e) pint
pion' (-ne) pawn (chess)
pionier' (-e, -s) pioneer
pirami'de (-s) pyramid
pis (s) piss, urine; (w) (ge-) maké water, urinate
pistool' (pistole) pistol
pit (-te) kernel (nut); core (tree); stone (peach); pip (orange); wick (lamp)
pit'tig (-e; -er, -ste) pithy; terse
pla (w) (ge-) tease, annoy, vex, worry
plaag (s) (plae) plague, pest; affliction; vexation; **~beheer** pest control; **~doder** (-s) pesticide, insecticide, herbicide; **~gees** (-te) tease, tormenting fiend; **~siek** (-e) fond of teasing
plaak plaque (teeth)
plaas (s) (plase) place; farm; (w) (ge-) put, place, locate; insert; **~japie** (-s) (country) bumpkin, yokel; **~kiosk** farm stall; **~lik** (-e) local; **~like bestuur,** local government; **~like inhoud,** local content; **~like owerheid,** local authority; **~vervanger** (-s) substitute, deputy; proxy
plaat (plate) plate; slab; sheet; plateau, stretch; stake (races); **~kompetisie** plate event (sport)

plafon' (-ne, -s) ceiling
plagiaat' plagiarism
plak[1] (s) (-ke) ferule; slab; *'n ~ sjokola(de),* a slab of chocolate
plak[2] (w) (ge-) paste, paper, stick; **~boek** (-e) scrapbook
plakkaat' (..kate) placard, poster
plak: **~ker** (-s) paster, paper hanger; stick- er; squatter; **~papier** wallpaper; **~kery** squatting
plan (-ne) plan, scheme, project, intention
planeet' (..nete) planet
planeta'rium (-s) planetarium
plank (-e) plank, board, deal; *~e saag,* snore stertorously; *~e'koors, ~e'vrees* stage fright
plant (s) (-e) plant; (w) (ge-) plant
planta'sie (-s) plantation
plant: **~e'groei** vegetation; **~etend** (-e) herbivorous; **~kunde** botany
plantkun'dig (-e) botanical; **~e** (-s) botanist
plas (s) (-se) pool, puddle; (w) (ge-) paddle, splash; **~poel** (-e) paddling pool
plas'ma plasm(a)
plastiek' plastic art; **~beker** plastic mug
plas'ties (-e) plastic; *~e snykunde, ~e chirurgie,* plastic/cosmetic surgery
plat (-ter, -ste) flat, level, even; low
plataan' (platane) plane tree
platan'na (-s) spur-toed frog, platanna
pla'tejoggie (-s) disc jockey
pla'temusiek recorded music
plat'form (-s) platform
pla'tina platinum
plat'jie (-s) rogue, scamp; mischievous fel- low
plato' (-s) plateau
plato'nies (-e) platonic
plato'rand (-e) escarpment
plat'riem (-e) ferule, strap; *iem. met die ~ gee,* apply the strap
plat'sak hard up, broke, penniless
plat'tegrond groundplan, sketch
plat'teland country, rural districts
plat'voet (-e) flat foot
plavei' (ge-) pave; **~sel** pavement
pleeg (ge-) commit, perpetrate; *selfmoord ~,* commit suicide; **~ouers** foster parents
pleg'tig (-e; -er, -ste) solemn, ceremonious
pleidooi' (-e) plea, argument, defence
plein (-e) square
pleis'ter[1] (s) (-s) poultice

pleis'ter² (s) (-s) plaster; (w) (ge-) plaster, stucco; ~kalk lime plaster

pleit (s) plea; (w) (ge-) plead; intercede

plek (-ke) place; spot; room, space; position; ~ *bespreek,* book a seat, make a reservation; *op die ~ rus!* stand at ease!

pleks instead of

plesier' (-e) pleasure, enjoyment, fun

plesie'rig (b) (-e; -er, -ste) pleasant, happy; merry, jolly

plesier': ~oord (-e) pleasure resort; ~tog (-te) excursion, pleasure trip

plig (-te) duty, obligation

ploeg (s) (ploeë) plough; gang, shift

ploe'ter (ge-) drudge, toil, plod

plof (s) (plowwe) thud, thump; (w) (ge-) flop down

plof'stof (..stowwe) explosives; ~deskundige (-s) explosives expert

plomp stout, awkward, clumsy

plons (s) (-e) splash; (w) (ge) splash

plooi (s) (-e) fold, wrinkle, crease, pleat; (w) (ge-) fold

plot'seling (b) sudden, abrupt; (bw) suddenly, all of a sudden

pluim (-e) plume, feather; ~bal badminton; ~pie (-s) plumelet; compliment; *'n ~pie kry,* be complimented; ~vee poultry

pluis all right, in order

pluis: ~ie (-s) plug, wad, fluff, plush; ~keil (-e) top hat

pluk (ge-) pick, gather; ~sel (-s) lint; crop (of feathers)

plun'der (ge-) plunder, ransack, loot

plura'le: ~ *gemeenskap,* plural society

plus plus; ~minus about, more or less

poe'del (-s) poodle; P~hond (-e) poodle; ~naak (-te), ~nakend (-e) stark-naked; ~prys (-e) booby prize

poe'ding (-s) pudding

poei'er (-s) powder; (w) (ge-) powder

poel (-e) pool, puddle

poelpetaan' (..tane), poelpetaat' (..tate), poelpeta'ter (-s) guinea fowl

poe'ma (-s) puma

poens'kop (-pe) hornless animal, poll

poësie' poetry; ~waardering poetry appreciation

poë'ties (-e) poetic(al)

poets¹ (s) (-e) trick, prank; *iem. 'n ~ bak,* play a trick on someone

poets² (w) (ge-) polish, rub; ~katoen cotton waste

pof: ~adder (-s) puff adder; ~broek (-e) plus fours; ~fertjie (-s) fritter, puffcake

po'ging (-e, -s) effort, attempt, endeavour; *'n ~ aanwend,* make an attempt

pok'ke, pokkies smallpox

pol (-le) tuft of grass

po'lis (-se) insurance policy

poli'sie police; *geheime ~,* secret police; *die ~ ontbied,* call the police; ~hond (-e) police dog; ~kantoor (..tore) charge office; ~man (-ne) policeman, constable; ~-ondersoek (-e) police investigation

politiek' (s) politics; (b) political; politic

poli'tikus (-se, ..tici) politician

politoer' (s) (-e) polish; (w) (ge-) polish

po'lo polo

pols (s) (-e) pulse; (w) (ge-) feel the pulse; sound; *iem. ~,* sound someone; ~horlosie, ~oorlosie (-s) wristwatch

polys' (ge-) polish, burnish, civilise

pome'lo (-'s) pomelo, grapefruit

pomp (s) (-e) pump; (w) (ge-) pump; ~joggie (-s) pump attendant

pond (-e) pound, sovereign

pondok' (-ke) hovel, hut, shanty

po'nie (-s) pony

pons punch

pont (-e) ferryboat, pontoon, punt

Pon'tius Pontius; *iem. van ~ na Pilatus stuur,* send someone from pillar to post

poog (ge-) try, attempt

pooi'er (-s) pimp (middleman for prostitutes)

pook (s) (poke) poker; (w) (ge-) poke

pool (pole) pole; *negatiewe ~,* cathode; *positiewe ~,* anode

poort (-e) gate, gateway; poort, defile

poos (pose) while, pause

poot (pote) foot, leg, paw; *op eie pote staan,* be independent

poot'jie (w) (ge-) trip

poot'uit down, done for; ~ *raak,* become dead-tired

pop (-pe) doll; puppet; *die ~pe is aan die dans,* the fat is in the fire

pop'pekas (-te) puppet show, Punch and Judy show

populariteit' popularity

populêr' (-e; -(d)er, -ste) popular

populier' (-e), populier'boom (..bome) poplar; ~hout poplar (wood)

por (w) (ge-) poke, jab; urge, egg on

po'rie (-ë) pore

pornogra'fies (-e) pornographic

porselein' (real) china, porcelain

por'sie (-s) portion, share; helping (of food)

portaal' (..tale) porch, lobby, hall

portefeul'je (-s) portfolio; wallet; 'n ~ aandele, share(s) portfolio

portier' (-e, -s) porter

portret' (-te) portrait, photo(graph)

portuur' (porture) match, equal, peer; ~groep peer group

pos¹ (s) (-te) post (office); (w) (ge-) post; 'n brief ~, post a letter

pos² (s) (-te) entry; (w) (ge-) enter; in die grootboek ~, enter in ledger

pos³ (s) (-te) job, post, position

pos: ~beskrywing job description; ~besteller (-s) postman; ~bus (-se) Post Office box; letterbox

pos'duif (..duiwe) homing pigeon, carrier pigeon

po'se (-s) pose

poseer' (~, ge-) pose

pos: ~evaluering job evaluation; ~geld postage; ~gids (-e) postal guide

posi'sie (-s) position

positief' (..tiewe) positive

positie'we senses; by sy ~ kom, regain consciousness

pos: ~kantoor (..tore) post office; ~meester (-s) postmaster; ~order (-s) postal order

pos'seël (-s) postage stamp; ~versamelaar (-s) philatelist

pos: ~spaarbank (-e) post office savings bank; ~terye all postal services

postuur' (..ture) posture, figure; ~drag foundation garment, ook vormdrag

pot (-te) pot; jar; game (tennis); die ~ aan die kook hou, be able to make ends meet

pot'as potash

pot: ~dig (-te) perfectly closed, airtight; very reserved; ~doof (..dowe) stone-deaf

potensiaal' (..siale) potential

pot'loodskerpmaker (-s) pencil sharpener

potsier'lik (-e; -er, -ste) farcical, droll

pot'tebakker (-s) potter, ceramist; ~y (-e) pottery

pot'yster cast iron, ook gietyster

pou (-e) peacock

pous (-e) pope; ~dom papacy

pou'se (-s) interval, pause, break, recess

pouseer' (~, ge-) pause, have an interval

po'wer (-e) poor, miserable

praal (s) pomp, magnificence; (w) (ge-) boast, make a display of; ~graf (-te) mausoleum; ~koets (-e) state coach

praat (ge-) talk, chat, converse

prag splendour, magnificence

prag: ~tig (-e; -er, -ste) beautiful, magnificent; ~werk (-e) thing of beauty, masterpiece

prakseer' (~, ge-) think, consider, plan

prak'ties (b) (-e; -er, -ste) practical; (bw) practically, virtually

praktiseer' (~, ge-) practise

praktisyn' (-s) practitioner; algemene ~, general practitioner (doctor)

praktyk' (-e) practice

predikant' (-e) minister, parson

predikatief' (..tiewe) predicative

pre'diker (-s) preacher

preek (s) (preke) sermon; (w) (ge-) preach; ~stoel (-e) pulpit

prefek' (-te) prefect

pre'histories (-e) prehistoric(al)

preliminêr' (-e) preliminary

pre'mie (-s) premium; bounty; bonus

premier' (-s) premier, prime minister

premiè're première, first performance

prent (-e) picture; engraving; ~e'boek (-e) picturebook; ~strokies, ~verhale comic strips

presedent' (-e) precedent

presen'sie presence, attendance; ~lys (-te) attendance roll/register

present' (s) (-e) present, gift

presenteer' (ge-) offer, present; ~ geweer! present arms!

president' (-e) president; ~s'raad president's council

presies' (b) (-e; -er, -ste) exact, precise; particular; (bw) exactly, precisely; punctual

presta'sie (-s) performance, achievement; dis 'n groot ~, it is a great achievement; ~meting (-s) performance appraisal

presteer' (~, ge-) achieve, perform, be worth; ~der (-s) achiever

presti'ge prestige, influence

pret pleasure, fun; **~bederwer** (-s) spoil‑sport, killjoy

pret: **~draf** jogging; **~park** (-e) amusement park

preuts (-e; -er, -ste) coy, prudish, pert

pre'wel (ge-) mutter

prieel' (priële) summerhouse, arbour, bower, trellised vine, pergola

priem (s) (-e) bodkin, awl, bradawl

pries'ter (-s) priest

prik (s) (-ke) prick, stab; puncture; (w) (ge-) prick

prik'kel (s) (-s) spur, stimulus; (w) (ge-) prick, irritate, excite; stimulate; **~baar** (..bare, -der, -ste) irritable; **~end** (-e) pricking, irritating, stimulating; **~pop** (-pe) glamour girl, pin-up

pri'ma prime, first-rate; ~ *sekuriteit*, gilt‑edged security; ~ *uitleenkoers*, prime lending rate

primêr' (-e) primary; **~e onderwys**, primary education

primitief' (..tiewe; ..tiewer, -ste) primitive

prins (-e) prince

prinses' (-se) princess

prinsipaal' (..pale) principal, head(master)

prioriteit' priority; **top~** top priority

pris'ma (-s) prism

prisonier' (-s) prisoner, *kyk gevangene*

privaat¹ (s) (..vate) lavatory

privaat² (b) (~, ..vate) private; **~sektor** (-e) private sector; **~skool** (..skole) private school

priva'te inisiatief' private initiative, free enterprise

probeer' (~, ge-) try, attempt; ~ *is die beste geweer*, there is nothing like trying

probleem' (..bleme) problem

produk' (-te) product, produce, outcome; **~sie** production, output; **~te'handelaar** (-s) produce dealer

produktiwiteit' productivity

produsent' (-e) producer

proe (ge-) taste, sample; *hy ~ die wyn en dit smaak lekker*, he tastes the wine and it tastes nice

proef (proewe) experiment, test, trial; speci‑men, proof, sample; **~arts** (-e) houseman; **~balans** (-e) trial balance; **~beampte** (-s) probation officer; **~buisbaba** (-s) test‑tube baby; **~neming** (-e, -s) experiment; **~konyn** (-e) experimental guinea pig

proef: **~onderwys** practical teaching; **~skrif** (-te) dissertation, thesis

proes (ge-) sneeze aloud, snort

profeet' (..fete) prophet

profesie' (-ë) prophecy

profes'sie (-s) profession, *ook beroep*

professioneel' (..nele) professional

profes'sor (-e, -s) professor

profe'ties (-e) prophetic

profiel' (-e) profile, side face

profyt' (-e) profit, gain, *ook wins*

program' (-me) programme; **~matuur'** computer software; **~meer'der** (-s) pro‑grammer (computer)

progressief' (..siewe) progressive

projek' (-te) project

projekteer' (ge-) project, plan

proklama'sie (-s) proclamation

prokura'sie (-s) power of attorney

prokureur' (-s) solicitor, attorney

promes'se (-s) promissory note, IOU

promo'sie (-s) promotion; graduation

promo'ter (-s) promotor; presenter

pronk (s) splendour, show; (w) (ge-) show off, display; **~doedie** (-s) show/chorus girl; **~ertjie** (-s) sweet pea

pront (-er, -ste) exact, pure, prompt

prooi (-e) prey; *ten ~ val*, fall prey to

prop (-pe) stopper, plug, cork, gag, wad

propagan'da propaganda

proporsioneel' (..nele) proportional

pro'sa prose

prosaïs' (-te), **pro'saskrywer** (-s) prose writer

prosedu're (-s) procedure

proses' (-se) process; **~sie** (-s) procession

prospekteer' (ge-) prospect; **~der** (-s) pros‑pector

prospek'tus (-se) prospectus

prostituut' (..tute) prostitute

proteïen', **proteï'ne** protein

protes' (-te) protest

protes'vergadering (-e, -s) protest meeting

provinsiaal' (..siale) provincial; *Provinsiale Raad,* Provincial Council

provin'sie (-s) province

pruik (-e) wig, peruke

pruil (ge-) pout, be sulke, sulk

pruim¹ (s) (-e) plum; prune

pruim² (s) (-e) chew, quid; (w) (ge-) chew (tobacco)

pruim'boom (..bome) plumtree

pruimedant' (-e) prune

prul (-le) trifle, trash, rubbish; **~kos** junk food

prut'kis(sie) haybox

pryk (ge-) shine, look fine, show off

prys[1] (s) (-e) price, value; *tot elke ~,* at all costs; *op ~ stel,* esteem, value; (w) (ge-) price; **~beheer** price control

prys[2] (s) (-e) prize, award

prys[3] (s) praise; (w) (ge-) praise

prysenswaar'dig (-e; -er, -ste) praiseworthy

prys: ~fees sale (for shoppers); **~gee** (ge-) abandon, give up; **~geld** prize money

prys: ~lys (-te) pricelist; **~opgawe** (-s) quotation of prices, estimate

prys: ~skiet bisley; **~styging** (-s) price increase; **~uitdeling** (-e, -s) prize giving, awards ceremony

psalm (-s) psalm

psigia'ter (-s) psychiatrist

psigoanali'se psycho-analysis

psigologie' psychology, *ook* **sielkunde**

psigopaat' (..pate) psychopath

puberteit' puberty; **~s'jare** age of puberty

publiek' (s) public; (b) (-e) public

publika'sie (-s) publication

publiseer' (~, ge-) publish

publisiteit' publicity; **~ gee aan,** make public; **~s'buro** (-'s) publicity bureau

puf (w) (ge-) puff

puik (-er, -ste) excellent, splendid, choice

puil (ge-) protrude, bulge

puim'steen pumice

puin ruins, debris

puis (-te) pimple, pustule; **~ie** (-s) pimple

pulp pulp

punt[1] (-e) point, tip; *~e aanteken,* score points; *hoë ~e in die eksamen,* good marks in the examination; *iets op die ~e van sy vingers ken,* know something thoroughly

punt[2] (-e) stop, fullstop

pun'telys (-te) marksheet; log

puntene'rig, punteneu'rig (-e; -er, -ste) touchy, easily offended, particular

pun'tetelling score

pupil' (-le) pupil (of eye)

purgeer' (ge-) purge; **~middel** (-s) purgative, laxative

puris' (-te) purist; **~me** purism

pur'per purple; **~winde** morning glory (flower)

put (s) (-te) well; pit; cesspool; (w) (ge-) draw

puur (pure; -der, -ste) pure, excellent; *pure onsin,* sheer/absolute nonsense

pyl (-e) arrow, dart; *soos 'n ~ uit die boog,* fly like an arrow from a bow; (w) (ge-) dart, go straight; **~reguit** straight as an arrow; **~tjie** (-s) dart (game); **~vak** (-ke) home stretch; straight (athletics)

pyn[1] (s) (-e) pine tree, fir tree

pyn[2] (s) (-e) pain, ache; *ineenkrimp van ~,* writhe with pain; (w) (ge-) ache, smart

pyn'appel (-s) pineapple

pyn'doder (-s) painkiller, *ook* **pynstiller**

py'nig (ge-) torture, torment; **~ing** torture

pyn: ~lik (-e; -er, -ste) painful; distressing; **~stiller** (-s) analgesic

pyp (-e) pipe; leg (of trousers); *na iem. se ~e dans,* dance to someone's tune; **~kan** (s) (-ne) feeding bottle; (w) (ge-) cheat, fool; (sell a) dummy (rugby); **~leiding** (-s) pipeline; **~steel** (..stele) pipe stem; panhandle (street)

Q

quidproquo' something for something, counter-performance, quid pro quo

quis'ling (-s) quisling, traitor

R

raad[1] (rade) council, board; **~(s)kamer** (-s) boardroom

raad[2] (-gewinge, -gewings) advice, counsel; *met ~ en daad,* with words and deeds; *ten einde ~ wees,* be at one's wits' end; **~gewend** (-e) advisory; consulting (engineer);

~-op at one's wits' end; ~pleeg (ge-) consult, take counsel with; *die dokter ~pleeg*, consult the doctor

raad'saal (..sale) council chamber

raad: ~s'besluit (-e) decision/resolution of the council; ~s'lid (..lede) councillor

raaf (rawe) raven

raai (ge-) guess; advise; spot (a question)

raai'sel (-s) riddle, puzzle, enigma

raak (w) (ge-) hit; touch; concern

raam¹ (s) (rame) window frame; (w) (ge-) frame

raam² (w) (ge-) estimate, calculate; *hy ~ die koste op*, he estimates the cost at

raap¹ (s) (rape) turnip

raap² (w) (ge-) gather, pick up

raar ([rare]; -der, -ste) funny, strange, odd, queer; ~ *maar waar*, believe it or not

raas (ge-) make a noise, scold; rave

raat (rate) (traditional) remedy; means, advice; (honey)comb

rabar'ber rhubarb

rabat' allowance, rebate, discount

rabbedoe' (-ë, -s) rough/careless person; tomboy, tomboy/play

rab'bi (-'s), rabbyn' (-e) rabbi

ra'dar radar, radio location

ra'dio (-'s) radio, wireless; broadcasting; ~aktief (..tiewe) radio-active; ~drama (-s) radio drama/play

radioloog' (..loë) radiologist

ra'dio: ~-omroeper (-s) announcer; ~program (-me) radio programme

radys' (-e) radish

ra'fel (s) (-s) fray, ravel; (w) (ge-) ravel

raf'fia raffia

raffinadery', raffina'dery (-e) refinery (sugar, oil), *ook* raffineerdery

ragi'tis rickets

rak (-ke) rack, shelf; web

raket' (-te) racket (tennis)

rak'ker (-s) little bounder, rascal

rak'leeftyd (s) shelf life (fruit)

ram (-me) ram

ramenas' (-se) black radish

ra'ming (-e, -s) estimate, forecast

ram'mel (ge-) rattle, clatter, clank

ramp (-e) disaster, calamity, catastrophe

ram'party (-e) stag party

rampok'ker (-s) gangster, gunman; racketeer

rampsa'lig (-e; -er, -ste) wretched, miserable

rand¹ (s) rand (monetary unit); *dit kos twaalf ~*, it costs twelve rand(s)

rand² (s) (-e) brim (hat); edge, margin; verge (disaster); (w) (ge-) border; ~eier (-s) outer egg; outsider; ~steen (..stene) kerb, kerbstone

rang (-e) rank, class, grade

rangeer' (~, ge-) shunt; ~der (-s) shunter; ~terrein (-e) shunting yard

rang'skik (ge-) arrange, tabulate, classify; ~king arrangement, classification

rang'telwoord (-e) ordinal number

rank (s) (-e) tendril, clasper; twig, shoot, sprout; (w) (ge-) sprout trail, shoot tendrils; reach high (rugby)

ranon'kel (-s) ranunculus

rant' (-e) hill, ridge; reef

rantsoen' (-e) ration, allowance; ransom

rapport' (-e) report, statement, account, dispatch; (w) (ge-) *lewer*, give account of

rapport'ryer (-s) dispatch rider

raps (s) (-e) blow, flick, cut; (w) (ge-) strike, hit, flick

rap'sie (-s) a little, a bit; slight blow/cut

rapsodie' (-ë) rhapsody

rariteit' (-e) curiosity, rarity

ras (s) (-se) race; breed; *van suiwer ~*, thoroughbred

ras'eg (-te) pure bred, thoroughbred

ra'send (-e) furious, raving

raserny' (-e) madness, rage, fury, frenzy

ra'sieleier (-s) cheerleader

ras'se: ~haat race hatred, racialism; ~hater (-s) racialist

ras: ~sis' (-te) racist; ~sis'me racism

rat (-te) gear; (cog)wheel

ra'tel¹ (s) (-s) rattle; (w) (ge-) rattle

ra'tel² (s) (-s) Cape (honey) badger

ra'telslang (-e) rattlesnake

rat'kas (-se) gearbox

rats (-er, -ste) nimble, swift, quick, agile

ravyn' (-e) gorge, canyon

reageer' (~, ge-) react

reak'sie (-s) reaction

realis' (-te) realist

realis'ties (-e) realistic

rebel' (-le) rebel

rebels' (-e; -er, -ste) rebellious

red (ge-) save, rescue; *iem. uit die nood ~*, help one out of distress

redak'sie (-s) editorial staff; wording

redakteur' (-s) editor

red'dings: ~boei (-e) lifebuoy; ~boot (..bote) lifeboat; ~vlot (-te) liferaft

re'de (-s) sense; speech; address, oration; reason, cause; *direkte* ~, direct speech; *sonder (enige)* ~, without any reason; *iem. in die* ~ *val*, interrupt someone

re'dedeel (..dele) part of speech

re'dekawel (ge-) argue, reason

re'delik (-e; -er, -ste) tolerable, fair, reasonable

re'denaar (-s) orator

redeneer' (~, ge-) reason, argue

re'der (-s) shipowner; ~y (-e) shipping/airline/transport firm; airline

red'gordel (-s) safety belt; lifebelt

red'poging (-s) rescue attempt

reduplika'sie reduplication

reeds already; ~ *jare gelede*, many years ago

reëel (reële) real, genuine; *reële groei*, real growth

reeks (-e) series, row, sequence

re'ël (s) (-s) rule; line; custom; *'n gulde* ~, a golden rule; *tussen die* ~*s lees*, read between the lines; (w) (ge-) regulate, arrange, settle; ~**aar** governor (engine); ~**baar** negotiable (salary)

re'ëling (-e, -s) regulation, adjustment, arrangement; ~(**s)komitee** (-s) organising/steering committee

reëlma'tig (-e; -er, -ste) regular

re'ën (s) (-s) rain; (w) (ge-) rain; *dit* ~ *dat dit giet*, it is raining cats and dogs; ~**boog** (..boë) rainbow; ~**bui** (-e) shower (of rain); ~**jas** (-se) mackintosh; ~**meter** (-s) rain gauge

reent = reën

reep (repe) string, strip; *'n* ~ *sjokola(de)*, a slab of chocolate

referaat' (..rate) lecture, paper, treatise

referent' (-e) reporter, informer; lecturer; referee (for testimonial)

refleks' (-e) reflex; ~**beweging** (-e, -s) reflex action

refrein' (-e) chorus, refrain

reg[1] (-te) right, title; claim; law, justice; duty; *sy* ~*te laat geld*, assert one's rights; *in die* ~*te studeer*, study law

reg[2] (b) (-te) right, correct; straight

reg'bank (-e) court of justice, tribunal, bench

regeer' (~, ge-) rule, govern, reign; ~**der** (-s) ruler

rege'ring (-e, -s) government, reign, rule

reghoe'kig (-e) rectangular

regie' stage management; *onder die* ~ *van*, produced by

regiment' (-e) regiment

regisseur' (-s) stage manager; producer (of a play, film)

regis'ter (-s) register, record, index

registra'sie registration

registrateur' (-s) registrar

registreer' (~, ge-) register

reglement' (-e) rules, regulations, by-laws; ~ *van orde*, standing orders

reg'maak (-ge-) correct, put right; square up; pay; repair, mend; castrate (male animal); spay (female animal); neuter (cat)

reg'makertjie (-s) a pick-me-up

regma'tig (-e) rightful, lawful, fair; ~**e** *eienaar*, rightful/legal owner

reg'op erect, perpendicular, straight (up)

regs (b) right-handed; of the right; (bw) to the right

regs: ~**advies** legal advice; ~**geleerde** (-s) jurist, lawyer

regska'pe righteous, honest

reg'soewereiniteit rule of law

regs: ~**persoonlikheid** body corporate; incorporation; ~**pleging** administration of justice

reg'stel (w) rectify, amend, adjust; ~**ling** correction

regs: ~**praktyk** legal practice; ~**term** (-s) law/legal term

reg'streeks (b) (-e) direct; *'n* ~*e bewys*, direct evidence; ~ *en onregstreeks*, direct(ly) and indirect(ly)

reg'te[1] (s) rights, law; *in die* ~ *studeer*, study/read law

reg'te[2] (bw) truly, quite so, really; *na* ~, really, by right(s)

reg'ter[1] (s) (-s) judge, justice

reg'ter[2] (b) right; ~**hand** (-e) right hand; ~**kant** right side

reg'tig (b) (-e) real, true; (bw) really

reg'uit (b) straight, honest, candid; (bw) straight, openly, candidly

regula'sie (-s) regulation

regver'dig (w) (ge-) justify; (b) (-e; -er, -ste) just, fair, righteous

reg voor right in front
rehabiliteer' (~, ge-) rehabilitate, discharge
rei (-e) chorus, choir, song
rei'er (-s) heron
reik (ge-) reach, extend to; *iem. die hand ~,*
lend someone a helping hand
rein (s): *in die ~e bring,* put right; (b) (-e;
-er, -ste) pure, clean, chaste; *die ~e
waarheid,* the gospel truth
rei'nig (ge-) purify, cleanse; **~ing** purifi=
cation, cleaning, cleansing; **~ingsdiens**
sanitary department, street cleaning
reïnkarna'sie reincarnation
reis (s) journey, trip, voyage; (w) (ge-)
travel; *~ en verblyf,* transport and sub=
sistence; **~agentskap** (-pe), **~buro** (-'s)
travel agency; **~beskrywing** (-e, -s) ac=
count of a journey, travelogue; **~deken**
(-s) (travelling) rug; **~gids** (-e) traveller's
guide, timetable
re(i)'sies races; **~baan** (..bane) racecourse;
~perd (-e) racehorse, *kyk* renperd
rei'siger (-s) traveller, tourist
reis: ~indrukke impressions of travel;
~tjek (-s) traveller's cheque
reis'verhaal (..hale) account of (one's) tra=
vels; travelogue
rek (s) elasticity; (-ke) catapult, elastic; (w)
(ge-) stretch, extend, protract
re'ken (ge-) calculate, cipher, compute;
reckon; do sums; **~aar** (-s) arithmetician;
computer; reckoner; **~aarstudie, ~aar=
wetenskap** computer science; **~ariseer** (w)
computerise
re'kene arithmetic, *kyk* rekenkunde
re'kening (-e, -s) calculation; bill, account;
statement; *buite ~ laat,* leave out of ac=
count; *lopende ~,* current account;
~kunde accounting, accountancy; **~kun=
dige** (-s) accountant, *kyk* rekenmeester;
~kundige beleid, accounting policy
re'kenkunde arithmetic
re'ken: ~meester (-s) accountant; **~skap**
account; **~skap gee van,** account for
rek'ker (-s) stretcher; elastic, catapult;
garter
rekla'me advertising, boosting; **~agentskap**
(-pe) advertising agency/firm; **~koste**
advertising costs
rekonsilia'sie reconciliation
rekonstrueer' (ge-) reconstruct

re'kord (-s) record; *die ~ slaan/verbeter,*
beat/break the record (sport); **~houding**
keeping of records; **~s** office records/
documents
rekruteer' (ge-) recruit
rekruut' (rekrute) recruit
rek'stok (-ke) horizontal bar; catapult's
handle
rek'tor (-e, -s) rector
rekwisi'sie (-s) requisition
relatiwiteit' relativity; **~s'teorie** theory of
relativity
reliëf' (-s) relief; **~kaart** (-e) relief map
religieus' (-e) religious
re'ling (-s) railing
rel'letjie (-s) scandal, row, squabble
rem (s) (-me) brake; (w) (ge-) apply a brake,
brake; **~pedaal** (..dale) brake pedal
remedië'rend remedial; *~e onderwys,* re=
medial education
ren (ge-) race, run
ren: ~baan (..bane) racecourse, racetrack;
speedway; **~bode** (-s) courier
ren'dier (-e) reindeer
renegaat' (..gate) renegade, apostate
ren'jaer (-s) racing driver
ren'motor (-s) racing car
renos'ter (-s) rhinoceros
ren'perd (-e) racehorse
rens sour, rancid
ren'stel (-le) dragster; **~jaery** drag racing,
kyk versnelrenne
ren'te (-s) interest; **~draend** (-e) bearing
interest; **~koers** (-e) rate of interest
reorganisa'sie (-s) reorganisation
rep (s) commotion; *in ~ en roer,* in com=
motion; (w) (ge-) hurry up; mention
repara'sie (-s) repair; **~koste** cost of repair
repeteer' (ge-) repeat, recur, rehearse;
~geweer (-s, ..were) repeating rifle
repeti'sie (-s) repetition; rehearsal
reproduk'sie (-s) reproduction
reptiel' (-e) reptile
republiek' (-e) republic
republikein' (-e) republican
reputa'sie (-s) reputation; *'n firma van ge=
vestigde ~,* a firm of established reputa=
tion; *'n slegte ~ hê,* stand in bad repute
rê'rig really, truly
res (s) (-te) rest, remainder
resensent' (-e) reviewer, critic
resen'sie (-s) review (books, plays)

resep' (-te, -pe) recipe, prescription; **~te-boek** (-e) recipe book
reservis' (-te) reservist
reservoir' (-s) reservoir
reser'we (-s) reserve
reser'wefonds (-e) reserve fund
reses' (-se) recess; **termyn~,** mid-term break
reses'sie (-s) recession, economic slump
re'sies = **reisies**
resita'sie (-s) recitation; ~ *opsê,* recite
resiteer' (~, ge-) recite
respek' respect, esteem, regard
respekta'bel (-e, -er, -ste) respectable
respekteer' (~, ge-) respect, hold in respect
respyt' respite, grace; **~dae** days of grace
restant' (-e) remainder, remains
restourant' (-e, -s) restaurant, *ook* **restau-rant**
restoura'sie restoration
resultaat' (..tate) result, outcome; *sonder* ~, to no purpose
reten'siegeld (-e) retainer, *kyk* **bindgeld; lien**
retoer' (-e) return; **~kaartjie** (-s) return ticket; **~reis** (-e) return journey
reto'ries (-e) rhetorical
reuk (-e) scent, smell, odour; **~orgaan** (.. gane) olfactory organ; **~weerder deodo-rant**
reun (-e, -s) gelding (horse); male dog
reü'nie (-s) reunion
reus (-e) giant
reusag'tig (-e; -er, -ste) gigantic
reu'se: **~gebou** (-e) huge building; **~krag** strength of a giant
reu'sel (-s) lard, suet
reu'se: **~skrede** (-s) giant stride; *met* **~skredes vooruitgaan,** progress by leaps and bounds; **~taak** gigantic task
revolu'sie, rewolu'sie (-s) revolution
rewol'wer (-s) revolver
rib (-bes) rib; **~be'been** (..bene) rib; **~be'kas** (-te) thorax, thoracic skele-ton; **~betjie** rib, rafter (ship); cutlet
rid'der (-s) knight, chevalier; *tot ~ slaan,* knight; **~orde** (-s) order of knighthood; **~spoor** (..spore) larkspur; **~verhaal** (..hale) tale of chivalry
riel (-e) reel, old-fashioned dance
riem[1] (-e) oar (rowing)
riem[2] (-e) ream (paper)

riem[3] (-e) strap, thong; riem; belt; *die ~ bêre,* take to one's heels; *'n ~ onder die hart steek,* put fresh heart into someone; *hy het sy ~e styfgeloop,* he has come to the end of his tether; he has met his Waterloo; **~spring** (-ge-) skip; *iem. laat ~spring,* give someone a hiding; **~tele-gram** (-me) mere/unfounded rumour
riet (-e) reed, rush; cane; thatch; **~blits** cane spirits; **~dak** (-ke) thatched roof; **~skraal** very thin, as thin as a rake; **~stoel** (-e) wicker chair
rif (riwwe) reef
rif'fel (s) (-s) ripple, wrinkle; corrugation (road); (w) (ge-) wrinkle; corrugate; **~strook** (..stroke) jiggle bar (on road)
rif'rug ridgeback (dog)
rig (ge-) direct, address; aim; *die woord ~ tot,* address
rig: **~lyn** guideline; **~prys** recommended price; **~snoer** rule of conduct, guide (line); **~ting** (-e, -s) direction; trend; *in noordelike ~ting,* in a northerly direction
ril (ge-) shiver, shudder; **~ler** (-s) thriller (book, film)
rim'pel (s) (-s) wrinkle, fold, crease, furrow, ruffle; (w) (ge-) wrinkle, ripple
ring (-e) ring; circle; church district
ring: **~kop** (-pe) (Zulu) veteran; **~muur** (..mure) circular wall; **~vinger** (-s) ring-finger
rin'kel (ge-) jingle, tinkle
rink'halsslang (-e) ringed cobra, rinkhals (snake)
rinkink' (ge-) tinkle, jingle, rattle, row; gambol, make merry
rinneweer' (~, ge-) ruin, destroy
riole'ring sewerage, drainage
riool' (riole) drain, sewer; **~slyk** sludge; **~stelsel** (-s) sew(er)age system
ri'siko (-'s) risk; *op jou ~,* at your risk
ris'sie (-s) cayenne pepper, chilli
rit (-te) ride, drive, spin
rit'mies (-e) rhythmic(al)
rits (-e) string, series; zip fastener
rit'sel (ge-) rustle, crackle; **~ing** (-e, -s) rustling, rustle
rits'sluiter (-s) zip fastener
rit'tel (ge-) shake, shiver, tremble, quiver; **~dans** (s) (-e) jive session
ritteltit': *die ~(s) kry,* go into hysterics
ritueel' (rituele) ritual

rivier' (-e) river; ~bedding (-e, -s) river bed; ~mond (-e) estuary, river mouth

rob (-be) seal

robbedoe' (-ë, -s) rough/careless person; tomboy, don't care, *ook* rabbedoe

ro'bot (-s) robot, mechanical man

robyn' (-e) ruby

roe'de (-s) rod, birch; verge, rood; *wie die ~ spaar, bederf die kind,* spare the rod and spoil the child

roei (w) (ge-) row; ~ *met die rieme wat jy het,* manage with the tools at one's disposal; ~bootjie (-s) rowing boat; ~er (-s) rower; ~spaan (..spane) oar; ~wedstryd (-e) boatrace, regatta

roe'keloos (..lose, ..loser, -ste) reckless, rash, dare-devilish; *roekelose bestuurder,* reckless driver

roem (s) glory, renown, fame; (w) (ge-) praise, extol, laud

roem'ryk (-e; -er, -ste) glorious, famous

roep (ge-) call, cry, shout; *om hulp ~,* cry for help; ~baar on call

roe'per (-s) loud-hailer, megaphone

roe'ping (-e, -s) calling, vocation

roep'soek (w) page (someone)

roer[1] (s) (-s) gun, rifle

roer[2] (w) (ge-) stir, move; ~ *jou (riete),* get a move on; ~eiers scrambled eggs; ~end (-e; -er, -ste) touching; movable; *'n ~ende verhaal,* a moving/poignant story; (bw) quite; *hulle is dit ~end eens,* they agree in all respects

roer'loos (..lose) motionless

roes[1] (s) rust; blight; (w) (ge-) rust; *ou liefde ~ nie,* first love never dies

roes[2] (s) drunken fit; ecstasy, frenzy

roes: ~vlek (-ke) rust stain; ~vry rustproof, stainless

roet soot

roe'te (-s) route, road

roeti'ne routine; ~taak (..take) chore(s)

rof'stoei (s) all-in wrestling; (w) (ge-) wrestle (professionally); ~er (-s) all-in wrestler

rog rye; ~brood rye bread

rog'gel (s) (-s) ruckle, rattle, phlegm; (w) (ge-) rattle (in the throat); ruckle

rog'meel rye meal

rojaal' (rojale; rojaler, -ste) royal, generous, lavish; ~ *lewe,* live extravagantly

rojalis' (-te) royalist

rok (-ke) skirt, costume, dress; *die hemp is nader as die ~,* charity begins at home

ro'ker (-s) smoker

rol (s) (-le) roll, list; roller; part, role; scroll; *van die ~ skrap,* strike off the roll; *'n ~ speel,* play/act a part; (w) (ge-) roll

rol: ~baan (..bane) runway; ~bal bowls; ~besetting cast (of a play); ~ler (-s) roller; ~prent (-e) film, motion picture, movie; ~prentster (-re) film star; ~saag (..sae) circular saw; ~skaats (-e) roller skate; ~tabak rolled tobacco; ~trap (-pe) escalator; ~verdeling (-e, -s) cast

roman' (-s) novel

roman': ~se (-s) romance; ~skrywer (-s) novelist

roman'ties (-e) romantic

roman'tikus (-se) romantic novelist, romanticist

Romein' (-e) Roman; ~s' (-e) Roman; *Romeins-Hollandse Reg,* Roman-Dutch Law; ~se syfers, Roman numerals

ro'mery (-e) creamery

rom'mel[1] (s) lumber; rubbish, junk, litter

rom'mel[2] (w) (ge-) rumble

rom'mel: ~strooier litterbug, *ook* morsjors; ~veldtog (-te) anti-littering campaign; ~verkoping (-s) jumble sale

romp (-e) trunk, torso; hull; fuselage; skirt; *bloese en ~,* blouse and skirt

romp'slomp red tape

rond (-e; -er, -ste) round; *'n ~e jaar,* a full year; *'n ~e som,* a lump sum; round figures

ronda'wel (-s) round hut, rondavel

ron'de (-s) round; tour; *in die derde ~,* in the third round (boxing); *die gerug doen die ~,* there is a rumour abroad

rond'gaan (ge-) go about; ~de hof, circuit court

rond: ~kyk (ge-) look about; ~loop (ge-) stroll, loaf, gad about; ~loperhond (-e) stray dog

rond'om all round, on every side

rondomta'lie round about, in a circle; round robin (sport)

rond'reis (s) (-e) tour; (w) (ge-) travel about, tour

rond: ~strooi (ge-) scatter/strew about; ~swerf, ~swerwe (ge-) roam/wander about

rond'te (-s) round; circumference; lap (motor sport); *die ~ van Vader Cloete doen,* do the rounds; *in die ~,* in a circle
rond'trek (-ge-) move/journey about; pull about
rond'vaar (-ge-) cruise; ~t (s) (-e) cruise
roof (s) plunder, booty; (w) (ge-) rob, loot; ~bou overcropping; ~dier (-e) beast of prey
roof: ~onderdeel (..dele) pirate part (motor trade); ~taxi (-'s) pirate taxi; ~tog (-te) marauding/looting expedition; ~voël (-s) bird of prey
rooi (-er, -ste) red; ~baadjie (-s) redcoat (English soldier) in SA War; hopper (lo= cust); ~bekkie (-s) waxbill; ~bok (-ke) impala; ~borsie (-s) robin redbreast; ~bostee redbush/rooibos tea, *kyk* rooi= tee
Rooi'huid (-e) Red Indian
rooi: ~jakkals (-e) red jackal; ~mier (-e) red ant
Rooi'nek (-ke) Englishman (nickname from SA War)
Rooi'taal English; *hy gooi die ~ goed,* he speaks English like a native (idiom)
rooi: ~tee rooibos tea; ~vonk scarlatina, scarlet fever; ~water redwater (cattle); bilharzia (humans)
rook (s) smoke; ~mis smog; ~skerm (-s) smokescreen; ~wors (-e, -te) smoked sausage
room cream; *die ~ afskep van,* skim the cream; ~afskeier (-s) (cream) separator; ~kan (-ne) cream can; ~kleurig (-e) cream (-coloured)
Rooms-Katoliek' (-e) Roman Catholic
room: ~tert (-e) cream tart; ~ys ice cream
roos¹ erysipelas, eczema
roos² (rose) rose; *'n ~ tussen die dorings,* a rose among thorns
roos: ~kleurig (-e) rose-coloured; *'n ~kleurige toekoms,* a bright future; ~knop (-pe) rosebud
roos'ter (-s) gridiron, grate, griller; time= table; ~brood toast; ~brood met kaas= sous, rarebit; ~vlug (-te) scheduled flight
roos'tuin (-e) rose garden
ro'sekrans (-e) rosary
roset' (-te) rosette
ros'kam (w) (ge-) currycomb; criticise sev= erely

rosyn' (-e) raisin
rot¹ (-te) rat; *so kaal soos 'n ~,* as poor as a church mouse
rot² (bw): *iem. ~ en kaal steel,* strip some= one bare
Rota'riër (-s) Rotarian
rota'sie rotation; ~gewys by/in rotation
roteer' (~, ge-) rotate
rot'ren (s) (-ne) ratrace
rots (-e) rock, cliff; ~storting rockfall
rotsag'tig (-e; -er, -ste) rocky
rots: ~tuin (-e) rockery; ~vas (-te) firm as a rock
rot'tang (-s) cane, rattan
rot'te: ~kruid arsenic, ratsbane; ~plaag rat pest
rot'(te)vanger (-s) rat catcher; rodent era= dicator
rou¹ (s) mourning; *in die ~ wees,* be in mourning; (w) (ge-) mourn; ~beklaer (-s) mourner
rou² (b) (-er, -ste) raw; hoarse
rou: ~brief (..briewe) death notice; mourn= ing letter; ~dig (-te) elegy
rou: ~koets (-e) hearse; ~koevert (-e) mourning envelope
rou'koop forfeit money; rue bargain
ro'wer (-s) robber, pirate, highwayman; ~bende (-s) band of robbers
ru (-we; -wer, -uste) rough, rude, crude
rub'ber rubber; ~bootjie (-s) dinghy
rubriek' (-e) rubric, category, column; ~skrywer (-s) columnist
rug (-ge, rûe, rûens) back; *dis gelukkig agter die ~,* fortunately that is over
rug'by rugby; ~speler (-s) rugby player; ~wedstryd (-e) rugby match
rug'graat (..grate) backbone, spine
rug: ~pyn backache; ~sak (-ke) rucksack; ~steun (s, w) support; back (up)
ruig (ruie; ruier, -ste) bushy, shrubby, dense; ~ryp hoarfrost; ~te (-s) undergrowth, copse, jungle
ruik (s) = reuk; (w) (ge-) smell, scent; *sterk ~ na drank,* smell strongly of liquor; *lont ~,* smell a rat
rui'ker (-s) nosegay; bouquet; posy; ~tjie (-s) nosegay, buttonhole
ruil (w) (ge-) barter, exchange
ruim (s) (-e) hold (ship); (b, bw) (-e; -er, -ste) ample, wide, spacious; *'n ~e keuse,* a

wide choice; ~ *van opvatting,* broad-
minded
ruim'te (-s) room; scope; space; ~**man (-s),**
~**reisiger (-s)** spaceman, astronaut, cos=
monaut; ~**rommel** space debris; ~**tuig**
(..tuie) spacecraft; ~**vaarder (-s)** astro=
naut, cosmonaut; ~**vaart** space travel
rui'ne (-s) ruins
ruis (ge-) rustle, murmur
ruit (-e) (window)pane; rhombus
rui'tens diamonds (cards)
rui'ter (-s) horseman, horserider, eques=
trian; ~**lik (-e)** frank, straight out, chival=
rous; ~**sport** showjumping, (horse) riding
competition; ~**standbeeld (-e)** equestrian
statue; ~**y** cavalry
ruit'koevert (-e) window envelope
ruit'veër (-s) windscreen wiper
ruk (s) (-ke) pull, tug, jerk; while, time;
(w) (ge-) pull, tug, jerk; ~**stopgordel (-s)**
inertia reel safety belt; ~**wind (-e)** squall,
gust
rum rum
rumatiek' rheumatism
rumoer' (s) (-e) uproar, noise; **(w) (ge-)**
make a noise, be rowdy
run'nik (ge-) neigh
ru'olie (-s) crude oil
rus (s) rest, repose; calm; safety catch; rest
(music); *geen ~ of duur hê nie,* have no
moment's peace; ~ *roes,* to rest is to rust;
(w) (ge-) rest, repose
ru'sie (-s) quarrel, dispute, brawl; ~**maker**
(-s) brawler, quarrelsome person; ~**soe=**
ker (-s) bully, meddler, troublemaker
rus'kamp (-e) rest camp

rus'pe(r) (-s) caterpillar; ~**trekker (-s)**
caterpillar tractor
rus'teloos (..lose; ..loser, -ste) restless
rus'tend (-e) retired; ~*e vennoot,* retired/
inactive partner
rus: ~**tig (-e; -er, -ste)** calm, placid; ~**tyd**
holiday; time of rest; interval, halftime
ru'yster pig iron
ry¹ (s) (-e) row, series; *almal in 'n ~,* all in
a row
ry² (w) (ge-) ride, drive; ~**bewys (-e)** driver's
licence
ryk¹ (s) (-e) empire, kingdom, realm; *die*
~ van die verbeelding, the realm of fancy
ryk² (b) (-e; -er, -ste) rich, wealthy; ~ *en*
arm, rich and poor; ~**dom (-me)** wealth,
riches; profusion
ry: ~**laan (..lane)** drive; ~**loop (ge-)** hitch=
hike; ~**loper (-s)** hitchhiker
rym (s) (-e) rhyme; **(w) (ge-)** rhyme; tally,
agree; *dit ~ nie met die feite nie,* this does
not tally with the facts; ~**dwang** forcing
the rhyme
ryp¹ (s) (hoar)frost; **(w) (ge-)** frost
ryp² (b) (-e; -er, -ste) ripe, mature
ry'perd (s) (-e) riding horse, saddle horse;
(tw) splendid!
ry'plank (-e) scooter; surfboard
rys¹ (s) rice
rys² (w) (ge-) rise; ferment
ry'skool (..skole) riding school
rys: ~**korrel (-s)** grain of rice; ~**kultuur**
rice culture
rys'mier (s) (-e) white ant, termite; **(w) (ge-)**
undermine, infiltrate
ry'stoel (-e) rocking chair
ry: ~**tuig (..tuie)** (railway) coach, vehicle,
carriage; ~**wiel (-e)** bike, bicycle

S

sa! catch him! tally-ho!
saad semen (human); sperm (animals);
progeny, offspring; germ; **(sade)** seed
(plants)
saag (s) (sae) saw; **(w) (ge-)** saw, cut; *balke*
~, snore loudly; ~**meul (-e, -e(n)s),**
~**meule (-ns, -s)** sawmill; ~**sel** sawdust
saai¹ (w) (ge-) sow, scatter; *wat jy ~, sal jy*
maai, as you sow, so shall you reap
saai² (b) (-e; -er, -ste) dull, tedious, drab

saak (sake) affair, thing, matter, business,
concern; action, case; *bemoei jou met jou*
eie sake, mind your own business; *dit*
maak geen ~ nie, it does not matter
saak'lik (-e; -er, -ste) matter-of-fact, busi=
nesslike, precise, ad rem, succinct
saal¹ (sale) hall; *vol sale trek,* draw full
houses
saal² (-s) saddle; *iem. uit die ~ lig,* usurp
someone's position

saam together, (con)jointly, between them
saam'gaan (-ge-) go together, go with, agree, accompany
saam'gesteld (-e) compound; complex; *~e rente*, compound interest
saam'hoort (-ge-) belong together
saamho'righeid solidarity, coherence
saam'roeper (-s) convener
saam'ryklub (-s) liftclub
saam: ~**smelt** (-ge-) merge, amalgamate; ~'**span** (-ge-) conspire, plot together; unite; ~'**stel** (-ge-) put together, compose, compile; ~'**stem** (-ge-) agree, concur
saam'trek (s) (-ke) rally; gathering
saam: ~**val** (-ge-) happen simultaneously, synchronise; ~'**werk** (-ge-) cooperate, join hands, work in concert
saans in the evening, at night
Sab'bat (-te) Sabbath; *die ~ ontheilig,* desecrate the Sabbath
sa'bel[1] (-s) sword, sabre
sa'bel[2] (-s) sable (animal); ~**bont** sabeline
sabota'sie sabotage
saboteur' (-s) saboteur
sadis'me sadism
safa'ri (-'s) safari, hunting trip
saffier' (-e) sapphire
sag (-te; -ter, -ste) soft, low; mild; sweet
sa'ga (-s) saga (Scandinavian epic tale of heroism)
sa'ge (-s) legend, myth, fairy tale; romantic folktale
sag'geaard (-e) gentle, kind, meek
sag'gies gently, softly, quietly
sagmoe'dig (-e; -er, -ste) sweet, mild
sa'go sago; ~**meel** sago flour
sag'tebal softball (game)
sag'teware soft goods
sagt'heid softness, smoothness, gentleness
sajet' sayette; woollen yarn
sak[1] (s) (-ke) bag, sack; pocket; pouch; *sy hand in sy ~ steek,* bear the expense; *met ~ en pak,* with bag and baggage; *~, Sarel!* less exaggeration, please!
sak[2] (w) (-ge-) sink, subside; fail (in examination); go flat
sak: ~**almanak** (-ke) pocket calendar; ~**boek** (-e) pocket book; ~**doek** (-e) handkerchief, hanky
sa'ke: *ter ~,* to the point, relevant; ~**brief** (..briewe) business letter; ~**kamer** (-s)

(Afr.) chamber of commerce; ~**kennis** business knowledge; business acquaintance; ~**kern** central business area/district; ~**lui** business men (pl); ~**lys** (-te) agenda; ~**man** (-ne, ..lui) businessman; ~**vernuf** expertise, know-how
sak: ~**ke'roller** (-s) pickpocket; ~**komper(tjie)** calculator; ~**mes** (-se) pocket knife, penknife; ~**oorlosie** (-s) pocket watch
sakrament' (-e) sacrament; *die heilige ~e,* the holy sacraments
sak'rekenaar (-s) calculator
sal (sou) shall, will; *hy sou dit agterlaat,* he was to have left it behind
sala'ris (-se) salary; ~**kerf** (..kerwe) salary notch; ~**skaal** (..skale) salary scale
saldeer' (w) (~) balance books (of a firm)
sal'do (-'s) balance
salf (s) (salwe) ointment, salve, unguent
sa'lie salvia, sage
sa'lig (-e; -er, -ste) blessed, blissful
Sa'ligmaker Saviour
salm (-s) salmon; *die neusie van die ~,* a titbit
salon' (-s, -ne) drawing room, saloon
salot' (-te), **salot'ui** (-e) shallot
salpe'ter (s) salpetre; ~**suur** nitric acid
salueer' (~, ge-) salute
saluut' (s) (salute) salute
sal'vo (-'s) salute, volley
sambok' (-ke) sjambok
sambreel' (..brele) umbrella
samehan'gend (-e) connected, coherent
sa'me: ~**koms** (-te) gathering, meeting; ~**lewing** society, community
sa'meloop concourse, junction; *'n ongelukkige ~ van omstandighede,* an unfortunate coincidence
sa'me: ~**roeper** (-s) convener; ~**smelting** (-e, -s) fusion, union, amalgamation; ~**spraak** (..sprake) dialogue
sa'mespreking (-e, -s) interview, talk(s), conference, discussion; *~ (s) voer,* confer, deliberate, discuss
sa'meswering (-e, -s) conspiracy, plot
sa'me: ~**vatting** (-e, -s) resumé, summary; ~**vloeiing** (-e, -s) confluence, concourse; ~**voeging** (-e, -s) union, junction, bond; ~**werking** cooperation, collaboration
sampioen' (-e) champignon, mushroom
sanato'rium (-s, ..ria) sanatorium

sand sand
sandaal' (..dale) sandal
san'derig (-e) sandy
sand: ~hoop (..hope) heap of sand, dump
(mine); ~korrel (-s) grain of sand; ~lo=
pertjie (-s) hourglass, egg glass; ~suiker
crystallised sugar
sang (-e) song, tune, singing; canto
san'ger (-s) singer, vocalist
sangeres' (-se) singer, vocalist (lady)
sang: ~kuns art of singing; ~les (-se) sing=
ing lesson; ~onderwyseres (-se) singing
mistress; ~speletjie (-s) action song;
~stuk (-ke) song; ~vereniging (-e, -s)
choral society
sa'nik (ge-) worry, bother; nag
sap (-pe) juice, sap
sappeur' (-s) sapper
sardien'(tjie) (-s) sardine
sar'dyn (-e) pilchard
sarkas'ties (-e; -er, -ste) sarcastic
sar'sie (-s) volley (of shots)
sat (-ter, -ste) sick, satiated
sata'nies (-e) satanic(al), diabolical
satelliet' (-e) satellite; ~foto (-'s) satellite
photograph
sa'ter (-s) satyr
Sa'terdag (..dae) Saturday
sati're (-s) satire
sati'ries (-e) satirical
satyn' satin
saxofoon' (..fone) saxophone
s'-draai (-e) hairpin bend
se 's, of; pa ~ hoed, father's hat
sê (s) say; (w) (ge-) say, speak, tell, order,
state; so ge~, so gedaan (gedoen), no
sooner said than done; dis nie te ~ nie, it
does not necessarily follow
sean'ce (-s) seance
se'bra (-s) zebra; ~oorgang zebra crossing
se'de (-s) habit, custom, morals, manners;
~bewaker (-s) guardian of morals
sedeer' (~, ge-) cede
se'der (-s) cedar; ~boom (..bome) cedar
se'dert since; ~ verlede maand, since last
month
se'dig (-e; -er, -ste) demure, prim, coy; so
~ soos 'n predikant, as pious as a priest
see (seë) sea, ocean; reg deur ~ gaan, steer
a straight course; oor~ gaan, go abroad
see: ~-eend (-e) sea duck; yellowbill;
~geveg (-te) naval battle, seafight; ~juf=

fer (-s) Swan (fleet); ~kaptein (-s) sea cap=
tain; ~kat (-te) octopus
see'koei (-e) hippopotamus; ~gat (-e) hippo
pool; ~koei (-e) hippopotamus cow
see: ~kus coast, seashore; ~kwal (-le) jel=
lyfish
seel (-s) certificate
se'ël (s) (-s) seal, stamp; sy ~ op iets sit/
druk, set his seal to something; sanction;
(w) (ge-) seal; ~belasting (-s) stamp duty
see'leeu (-s) seal, sea lion
se'ël: ~lak sealing wax; ~reg (-te) stamp
duty; ~ring (-e) signet ring
see: ~man (..liede, ..lui) sailor, marine(r);
~meeu (-e) seagull
seem(s)'leer shammy, chamois leather
see'myl (-e) nautical mile
se'ën (s) (-ings, -inge) benediction, blessing;
bedekte ~, blessing in disguise; sanction; die ~
uitspreek, pronounce the benediction; (w)
(ge-) bless; ~wens (-e) blessing, good
wishes
seep soap
seer (s) (sere) sore, wound; (b) (-der, -ste)
painful, sore
seer'keel sore throat
see'rower (-s) pirate
see: ~siek seasick; ~skilpad (..paaie) sea
turtle; ~skulp (-e) sea shell; ~slag (..slae)
naval battle; ~soldaat (..date) marine;
~spieël sea level; ~strand beach, fore=
shore; seashore
see: ~vaarder (-s) navigator; ~versekering
marine insurance
se'ëvier (ge-) triumph
see: ~vlak sea level; ~wier seaweed
se'fier (-e, -s) zephyr
se'ge victory, triumph
seg'genskap say, authority; ~ hê in die
saak, have a say in the matter
seg'gingskrag expressiveness, power of ex=
pression
segment' (-e) segment
segrega'sie segregation
segregeer' (ge-) segregate
segs'man (-ne, ..liede, ..lui) spokesman
segs'wyse (-s) standing phrase, set expres=
sion, saying
seil (s) (-e) tarpaulin, sail, canvas; ~e hys,
hoist sails; ~e stryk, strike sails; (w) (ge-)
sail; ~boot (..bote) sailing boat; ~jag
(-te) (sailing) yacht; ~plankry windsurf=

ing; ~skip (..skepe) sailing vessel; wind=
jammer; ~skoen (-e) tackie
sein (s) (-e) signal; (w) (ge-) telegraph, signal;
~fakkel (-s) flare
seis (-e) scythe
seismograaf' (..grawe) seismograph
seisoen' (-e) season; *buite die ~*, out of
season; ~aal (b) seasonal; ~kaartjie (-s)
season ticket
se'kel (-s) sickle
se'ker (b) *([-e]; -der, -ste)* certain; sure,
positive; (bw) certainly, surely; probably;
(w) make safe; ~ *die pistool*, put the
pistol on safety
se'kerheid certainty, surety; ~s'personeel
security personnel/staff
se'kering (-e, -s) safety (cut-out) fuse; *die
~ het gesmelt*, the fuse has blown;
~s'draad fuse wire
se'kerlik certainly, decidedly
sekondant' (-e) second(er)
sekon'de (-s) second
sekondeer' (ge-) second
sekondêr' (-e) secondary
sekon'dewyser (-s) second hand (watch)
sekretaresse'se (-s) lady secretary
sekreta'ris (-se) secretary; ~-generaal
(sekretarisse-generaal) secretary-general;
~voël (-s) secretary bird
seks (s) sex; sensuality; (w) (ge-) sex; ~=
ka(a)tjie (-s) sex kitten; ~straling, ~trek
sex appeal
sek'sie (-s) section
seksueel' (..suele) sexual
sek'te (-s) sect
sek'tor (-s) sector
sekuriteit' (-e) security; *kollaterale ~*, col=
lateral security; ~s'wag security guard
sekuur' ([..kure]; -der, -ste) secure, accu=
rate
sel (-le) cell
sel'de (minder, minste) seldom, rarely; ~ *of
(n)ooit*, hardly ever
seld'saam (..same; ..samer, -ste) rare,
scarce; *..same versameling*, rare collection
selery celery
self self; ~aansitter (-s) self-starter
self'bediening self-service
self'(be)dienwinkel (-s) self-service shop,
supermarket
self'beskikking self-determination; ~(s)reg
right of self-determination

self: ~bestuur self-government, home rule;
~bewus (-te) self-assuring; self-conscious
self'dien self-service; ~winkel self-service
shop
self'kant selvedge/selvage; *alkant ~*, it is all
the same
self'moord (-e) suicide; ~ *pleeg*, commit
suicide
self: ~opoffering self-sacrifice; ~respek
self-respect
selfs even; ~ *as dit waar was*, even if it were
true; ~ *Piet het geslaag*, even Peter passed
selfstan'dig (-e; -er, -ste) independent, self-
supporting, unaided; ~*e naamwoord*,
noun, substantive; ~heid independence
selfsug'tig (-e; -er, -ste) selfish, egotistic
self: ~verdediging self-defence; ~vertroue
self-confidence
se'mel: ~agtig (-e) full of bran, branny;
~s bran; *meng jou met ~s, dan vreet die
varke jou*, touch pitch and you will be
defiled
sement' cement
semes'ter (-s) semester, halfyear; ~kursus
(-se) semester course
semifinaal' (..ale) semifinal (game), *ook
halfeindronde*
senaat' (senate) senate
sena'tor (-e, -s) senator
send (ge-) send; ~brief (..briewe) letter,
epistle; ~e'ling (-e, -s) missionary; ~er
(-s) sender; transmitter (person; radio)
sen'ding consignment; mission; ~genoot=
skap (-pe) missionary society; ~stasie (-s)
mission station
send'stasie (-s) transmitting station
se'ning (-s) sinew
se'nior (-es, -s) senior; ~ *burger*, senior
citizen
sensa'sie (-s) sensation
sensasioneel' (..nele) sensational
sensitief' (..tiewe) sensitive
sen'sor censor
sen'sus (-se) census; ~opgawe (-s) census
return
sensuur' censure; censorship; ~raad (..ra=
de) censureship board
sent (-e) cent
sentiment' (-e) sentiment
sentimenteel' (..tele; ..teler, -ste) senti=
mental
sen'timeter (-s) centimetre

sent'meester (-s) treasurer, *ook* penning-meester

sentraal' (..trale) central; *sentrale verwarming*, central heating

sentra'le (-s) power station, generating plant; (telephone) exchange

sentralisa'sie centralisation

sen'trum (-s) centre

se'nuaanval (-le) nervous attack

se'nu: ~lyer (-s) nervous sufferer, neurotic; ~siekte neurosis, nerve disease; ~stelsel nervous system; ~tergend nerve-racking

se'nuwee (-s) nerve; *op sy ~s kry*, be all nerves; *aan die ~s ly*, suffer from nerves; ~aanval (-le) nervous attack

senuweeag'tig (-e; -er, -ste) nervous

sep'ter (-s) sceptre; *die ~ swaai*, rule

serebraal' (..brale) cerebral; ~verlam cerebral palsied

seremo'nie (-s) ceremony

seremo'niemeester (-s) master of ceremonies, *ook* tafelheer

serena'de (-s) serenade

serfyn' (-e) harmonium

se'rie (-s) series; ~nommer (-s) serial number

sering' (-e) lilac; ~boom (..bome) lilac tree

serp (-e) muffler, scarf, sash

sersant' (-e) sergeant; ~-majoor (-s) sergeant-major

sertifikaat' (..kate) certificate

se'rum (-s) serum

servet' (-te) serviette, napkin; ~ring (-e) serviette ring

servies' (-e) service, set

serwituut' (..tute) claim, servitude

ses (-se) six

ses'de (-s) sixth

ses: ~hoekig (-e) hexagonal; ~kantig (-e) six sided; ~maandeliks (-e) halfyearly

sessie (-s) cession; sitting, session

sestet' (-te) sestet (part of a sonnet)

ses'tien (-e) sixteen; ~de (-s) sixteenth

ses'tig (-s) sixty; ~ste (-s) sixtieth; *op sy ~ste verjaar(s)dag*, on his sixtieth birthday

ses: ~uur six o'clock; ~voud multiple of six

set (s) (-te) move; push, trick; putt (golf); (w) (ge-) set up (in type); putt (golf)

se'tel (s) (-s) seat (government); chair

set'laar (-s) settler

set: ~perk (-e) (putting) green (golf); ~satan printer's devil; ~ter (-s) compositor; putter (golf)

seun (-s) son, boy

se'we (-s) seven; ~dubbeld (-e) sevenfold

se'wende (-s) seventh; *in die ~ hemel van geluk*, be in one's seventh heaven

se'wentien (-e) seventeen; ~de (-s) seventeenth

se'wentig (-s) seventy; ~ste (-s) seventieth

se'wevoud multiple of seven

sfeer (sfere) sphere

sfinks (-e) sphinx

sianied' cyanide

sid'der (ge-) shudder, tremble

siedaar'! see! behold!

siek (-er, -ste) ill, sick, diseased; *so ~ soos 'n hond*, as sick as a dog; *jou ~ lag*, rock with laughter; ~bed (-de, -dens) sickbed; illness

sie'ke (-s) patient, invalid; *die ~ dra die gesonde*, the halt and the lame have to care for the healthy; ~boeg sickbay; ~fonds (-e) sick fund

siek'lik (-e; -er, -ste) ailing, sickly

siek'te (-s) illness, malady, sickness, disease; *'n aansteeklike ~*, an infectious disease; *'n besmetlike ~*, a contagious disease; ~verlof sick leave; *met ~verlof*, on sick leave; ~versekering insurance against sickness

siel (-e) soul; mind, spirit

siel'kunde psychology

sielkun'dig (-e) psychological; *~e oorlogvoering*, psychological warfare; ~e (-s) psychologist

siel'siek mentally deranged, psychopathic; ~e (-s) mental patient, psychopath; ~e'hospitaal (..tale) mental hospital

siem'bamba simbamba (picnic dance)

sien (ge-) see, look, view, observe; interview; ~de blind, eyes and no eyes; *oor die hoof ~*, overlook mistakes

sie'ner (-s) seer, prophet; ~s'blik, ~s'oog prophetic eye

siens: *tot ~!* so long!

siens'wyse (-s) opinion, view

sie'raad (..rade) trinket, ornament

sier: ~boom (..bome) ornamental tree/shrub; ~duik display diving

sier'lik (-e; -er, -ste) ornamental; elegant, neat, graceful

sier: ~**rooster** (-s) (ornamental) grid (car); ~**steen** (..stene) facebrick; ~**struik** (-e) ornamental shrub; ~**wa** (..waens) float (rag)

sie(s)! fy! for shame! bah! pooh! **sies tog!** shame! what a pity! *ook* **foei tog**

sif (s) (siwwe) sieve; (w) (ge-) sift; ~**draad** wire netting, gauze

si'filis syphilis

sig (s) sight, visibility

sigaar' (..gare) cigar; ~**koker** (-s) cigar case

sigaret' (-te) cigarette

sig'baar (..bare) visible; ~**heid** visibility

Sigeu'ner (-s) gipsy

sigorei' chicory

sig'sag zig-zag

sig: ~waarde face value; ~**wissel** (-s) sight draft/bill

sikadee' (sikadeë) cycad, *ook* **broodboom**

sik'kel (-s) shekel

sikloon' (siklone) cyclone

si'klus (-se) cycle

silhoeët (-te) silhouette

silin'der (-s) cylinder

silla'be (-s) syllable, *ook* **lettergreep**

silla'bus (-se) syllabus

si'lo (-'s) silo, *ook* **graansuier**

sil'wer silver; ~**bruilof** (-te) silver wedding; ~**doek** (cinema) screen; ~**kollekte** (-s) silver collection; ~**smid** (..smede, -s) silversmith

simbaal' (..bale) cymbal

simbo'lies (-e) symbolic(al)

simbool' (..bole) symbol

simfonie' (-ë) symphony

simme'tries (-e) symmetric(al)

simpatie' (-ë) sympathy; ~ *met jou verlies,* sincere sympathy

sim'pel (-e; -er, -ste) simple, silly; plain

simptoom' (..tome) symptom

simuleer' (~, ge-) copy, simulate; pretend

sin[1] (s) (-ne) sense, mind; inclination; meaning; taste, fancy; *in figuurlike* ~, in a figurative sense; ~ *vir humor,* sense of humour

sin[2] (s) (-ne) sentence

sinago'ge (-s) synagogue

sin'delik (-e; -er, -ste) clean, tidy; housetrained (animal)

sindikaat' (..kate) syndicate

sindroom' syndrome (disease symptoms)

sinds since

sing (ge-) sing; twitter, warble

sin'gel (-s) crescent; moat

sin'ger (-s) warbler; singer

si'nies (-e) cynic(al)

sinjaal' (..jale) signal

sink[1] (s) zinc; sheet iron, galvanised/corrugated iron

sink[2] (w) (ge-) sink; *sy moed* ~, his courage ebbs; ~**dal** (-e) rift valley, *ook* **slenkdal**; ~**gat** (-e) sinkhole

sin'kings rheumatic pains, neuralgia; ~**koors** rheumatic fever

sinkopeer' (~, ge-) syncopate

sink'plaat (..plate) sheet of galvanised iron

sin'nigheid liking, inclination

sino'de (-s) synod

sinoniem' (s) (-e) synonym; (b) (-e) synonymous

sinop'ties (-e) synoptic; ~*e kaart,* synoptic chart

sins'bou construction of a sentence; syntax

sins'ontleding analysis (sentence)

sint (-e) saint

sintak'sis syntax

sin'tel (-s) cinder

Sinterklaas' Santa Claus; Christmas Father

sinte'ties (-e) synthetic(al); ~*e rubber,* synthetic rubber

sin'tuig (..tuie) sense organ

sin'vol (-le; -ler, -ste) meaningful

sipier' (-e, -s) gaoler, turnkey

sipres' (-se) cypress

sire'ne (-s) siren; ~**sang** (-e) siren's song

sir'kel (-s) circle; ~**gang** circular course; circuit; ~**saag** (..sae) circular saw

sirkoon' (..kone) zircon, near diamond

sirkula'sie circulation; *in* ~ *bring,* bring/put into circulation

sirkuleer' (ge-) circulate

sirkulê're (-s) circular, *ook* **omsendbrief**

sir'kumfleks (-e) circumflex, *ook* **kappie**

sir'kus (-se) circus

sistema'ties (-e) systematic

sit[1] (ge-) sit; *dit* ~ *in sy bloed,* it runs in his blood; *aan tafel* ~, sit at table

sit[2] (ge-) put, place; *op loop* ~, chase away

sit[3] (s) sitting down; *kry jou* ~*!* do sit down now!

si'ter (-s) zither

sit: ~kamer (-s) lounge; ~**kierie** (-s) shooting stick

sit'plek (-ke) seat, place

si'trus citrus

sit-'sit' sitting; sitting for a while; ~ *slaap*, sleep in a sitting posture

sit'ting (-e, -s) session, sitting; seat

situa'sie (-s) situation

siviel' (-e) civil; *in* ~, in mufti; ~*e inge= nieur*, civil engineer

sjaal (-s) shawl

sjabloon' (..blone) stencil

sjampan'je champagne

sjampoe' shampoo

sjarmant' (-e; -er, -ste) charming

sjar'me (s) charm; ~*skool* charm/finishing school

sjebeen' (-s) shebeen, *ook* **smokkelkroeg**

sjef (-s) chief, chef

sjeik (-s) sheikh

sjelei', selei' meat jelly

sjer'rie (-s) sherry

sjiek (-er, -ste) chic, smart

sjimpansee' (-s) chimpanzee

sjoe'broekie (-s) scanty-panty; scanty pants, minipants

sjokola'de (-s) chocolate

skaad (ge-) damage, harm

skaaf (s) (skawe) plane; (w) (ge-) plane; chafe; scrape

skaak[1] (s) chess; *'n potjie* ~, a game of chess; ~ *sit*, check

skaak[2] (w) (ge-) kidnap, carry off, *kyk* **kaap**; elope

skaak: ~*bord* (-e) chessboard; ~*mat* checkmate; ~*toernooi* (-e), ~*wedstryd* (-e) chess tournament

skaal (skale) scale, balance

skaam (w) (ge-) be ashamed; ~ *jy jou nie?* are you not ashamed of yourself? ~*jou!* fie! shame on you! (b) (skamer, -ste) shy, bashful, timid

skaam'te shame, modesty

skaap (skape) sheep; ~*boud* (-e) leg of mutton; ~*skêr* (-e) (pair of) shears

skaaps'klere *(wolf) in* ~, in sheep's cloth= ing

skaap: ~*vel* (-le) sheepskin; ~*wagter* (-s) shepherd; ~*wagtertjie* (-s) capped wheat= ear (bird)

skaars (b) (-er, -ste) scarce, scanty; (bw) hardly, scarcely

skaats (s) (-e) skate; (w) (ge-) skate, rink; ~*baan* (..bane) skating rink; ~*bord*, ~*plank* (-e) skateboard

skade (-s) damage, loss; ~ *aanrig (be= rokken)*, cause damage; *deur* ~ *en skande wys word*, experience makes fools wise; ~*lik* (-e; -er, -ste) harmful, injurious, noxious; ~*loosstelling* compensation, indemnification; ~*vergoeding* compen= sation

ska'du (-'s) shadow, shade; ~*personeel* skeleton staff

ska'du: ~*ryk* (-e; -er, -ste) shady, shadowy; ~*sy* dark side, unpleasant part

ska'duwee (-s) shade, shadow

skag (-te) shaft; ~*delwing* shaft sinking; ~*grawer* (-s) shaft sinker

ska'kel (-s) link; shackle; (w) (ge-) dial (telephone); link; connect; liaise; switch (elec.); ~*aar* (-s) switch; ~*amptenaar* public relations (liaison) officer; ~*bord* (-e) switchboard; ~*huis* (-e) semidetached house; ~*komitee* (-s) liaison committee

ska'ker[1] (-s) chess player

ska'ker[2] (-s) seducer, kidnapper

skake'ring (-e, -s) tint, shade, variegation

skandaal' (..dale) scandal, disgrace

skan'de (-s) shame, disgrace, dishonour

skan'delik (-e; -er, -ste) shameful, dis= graceful

skande'ring scansion

skans (-e) bulwark, trench

ska're (-s) crowd, multitude, host; mob

skarla'ken scarlet; ~*koors* scarlatina, scarlet fever; ~*rooi* scarlet

skarnier' (-e) hinge; (w) hinge

skar'rel (ge-) rummage, search, ransack

skat[1] (s) (-te) treasure; darling, dearest

skat[2] (w) (ge-) estimate; esteem, appraise; *die waarde te hoog/laag* ~, overestimate/ underestimate the value

ska'ter (ge-) burst out laughing; ~*lag* (s) loud laugh; (w) (ge-) laugh heartily

skat: ~*kis* (-te) treasury, exchequer; ~*ryk* very rich

skat'tebol: *my* ~, my darling/heartbeat/ sweetie(pie)

skat'tejag (-te) treasure hunt

skat'ting (-e, -s) tax, estimate, estimation; *'n globale* ~, a rough estimate; *volgens* ~, approximately

skavot' (-te) scaffold

ske'de (-s) sheath, scabbard

ske'del (-s) skull, cranium; ~*breuk* (-e) cranial fracture, fracture of the skull

skeef (skewe; skewer, -ste) crooked, wry, slanting; distorted

skeel[1] (w) (ge-) matter, lack, ail, be wanting; *wat kan dit my ~?* what does it matter to me?

skeel[2] (b) (skeler, -ste) squinting; *so ~ soos 'n skaap,* cock-eyed; **~hoofpyn** (-e) migraine

skeen (skene) shin

skeeps: **~bemanning** (-s) crew; **~kaptein** (-s) skipper, ship's captain; **~lading** (-e, -s) shipload, cargo; **~redery** (-e) shipping line; **~ruim** ship's hold; **~werf** (..werwe) dockyard

skeep'vaart navigation, shipping

skeer (ge-) shave, shear, trim, cut; **~boot** (..bote) hydrofoil/jetfoil craft; **~kwas** (-te) shaving brush; **~mes** (-se) razor

skeer'tuig (..tuie) hovercraft, *kyk* skeerboot

skeet (skete) imaginary ailment; whim, caprice; *vol skete,* have all kinds of ailments

skei (w) (ge-) part, separate; divide, sever, disconnect; divorce; *van tafel en bed ~,* be separated/divorced from bed and board

skeids: **~muur** (..mure) partition wall; **~regter** (-s) arbitrator, umpire, referee

skei'kunde chemistry

skeld'woord (-e) invective, abusive word

skelm (s) (-s) rogue, knave, rascal, crook; (b) (-er, -ste) knavish, furtive, astute

skel'vis (-se) haddock

ske'ma (-s) scheme; sketch, outline; **~huis** (-e) subsidised house (of housing scheme)

ske'mer (s) twilight, dusk; (w) (ge-) grow dusk, glimmer; **~kelkie** (-s) sundowner, cocktail; **~party** (-e) cocktail party

skend (ge-) violate, desecrate; mutilate

skenk (ge-) give, endow, present, grant

skenk: **~er** (-s) donor; **~ing** (-e, -s) endowment, grant, donation

skep[1] (w) (ge-) scoop; spoonful; spadeful; (w) (ge-) dip out, scoop

skep[2] (w) (geskape) create

skep'doel (-e) dropgoal

Skep'per Creator

skep'ping creation

skep'rat (-te) paddle (wheel)

skep'sel (-s) creature, human being, man

skep'skop (-pe) dropkick (rugby)

skep'ties (-e) sceptical

skêr (-e) (pair of) scissors; (pair of) shears

skerf (skerwe) shard, morsel, bit

skerm[1] (s) (-s) protection; curtain, screen; *agter die ~s,* behind the scenes

skerm[2] (w) (ge-) fence, spar, parry; *hy ~ vir homself,* he is defending his own interests; **~kuns** (art of) fencing; **~maat** (-s) sparring partner (boxing)

skermut'sel (ge-) skirmish; **~ing** (-e, -s) skirmish, brush

skerp (-er, -ste) sharp, keen, acute, severe

skerpioen' (-e) scorpion

skerpsin'nig (-e; -er, -ste) sagacious, acute

skerp'skutter (-s) sniper, sharpshooter

skerts (s) fun, joke; legpulling

skets (s) (-e) sketch, draft; (w) (ge-) sketch, draw roughly; *in breë trekke ~,* sketch in broad outline; **~boek** (-e) sketchbook

skeur (s) (-e) tear, rent; crack, fissure; (w) (ge-) tear, rend; *die wêreld ~,* run away very quickly; **~buik** scurvy; **~ing** (-e, -s) division; split; **~kalender** (-s) tear-off calendar; **~strokie** (-s) tear-off slip

skeut (-e) shoot, sprig; dash (of brandy)

ske'webek wry face; *~ trek,* pull faces

ski (-'s) ski; **~boot** (..bote) skiboat; **ski'ër** (-s) skier

skie'lik (-e; -er, -ste) sudden(ly), quick(ly), unexpected(ly)

skier'eiland (-e) peninsula

skiet[1] (s): *~ gee,* give more rope

skiet[2] (w) (ge-) shoot, fire, snipe; dart; blast; bag (game); invite; *te kort ~,* shoot short of the mark; *met spek ~,* tell tall stories

skiet: **~baan** (..bane) rifle range; **~geveg** (-te) shootout, *ook* skietery

skiet: **~staking, ~stilstand** ceasefire; **~vereniging** (-e, -s) rifle club

skik[1] (s) liking; pleasure; *in sy ~ wees,* be delighted

skik[2] (w) (ge-) arrange, order, settle, yield; *jou ~ na omstandighede,* adapt oneself to circumstances

skik: **~king** (-e, -s) arrangement, agreement, settlement; **~plan** settlement plan; **~tyd** flextime, staggered hours

skil (s) (-le) peel, skin, shell, rind; (w) (ge-) peel, skin; *'n appeltjie met iem. ~,* pick a bone with someone

skild (-e) shield, buckler; aegis

skil'der (s) (-s) painter (artist); (w) (ge-) paint

skilderag'tig (-e; -er, -ste) picturesque
skil'der: ~kuns (art of) painting; ~kwas (-te) paint brush; ~(s)esel (-s) painter's easel; ~stuk (-ke) picture, painting
skildery' (-e) picture, painting
skild: ~vel (-le) rawhide shield; ~wag (-te) sentry, sentinel; *op* ~*wag staan,* stand sentry
skil'fer (s) (-s) dandruff, scale; (w) (ge-) give off scales
skil'pad (skilpaaie) tortoise (on land); turtle (in water)
skim (-me) shadow; apparition, ghost
skim'mel (s) mildew; (w) (ge-) mould, grow musty
skim'patrollie (-s) ghost squad (police)
skimp (s) (-e) taunt, mockery, gibe, jeer, scoff; (w) (ge-) mock, jeer, scoff
skin'der (ge-) gossip, slander, backbite; ~bek (-ke) gossiper, slanderer; ~praat= jies gossip, slanderous talk
skink (ge-) pour in; *koffie* ~, pour coffee; ~bord (-e) tray, salver; ~juffrou (-e), ~juffer, ~juffie (-s) barmaid
skip (skepe) ship, vessel, boat; skip (mining); ~breuk shipwreck; ~*breuk ly,* be wrecked; ~breukeling (-e) shipwrecked person; castaway
skip'per (s) (-e) captain, skipper
ski'roei paddle skiing; ~er (-s) paddle skier
skit'ter (ge-) glitter, shine, sparkle; ~ *deur sy afwesigheid,* be conspicuous by his absence; ~end (-e; -er, -ste) brilliant, sparkling, radiant
skob'bejak (-ke) rascal, scamp, rogue
skoei (ge-) shoe; tread (tyre); *op dieselfde lees* ~, cast in the same mould; ~sel footwear
skoen (-e) shoe, boot; (my) footwear; *wie die* ~ *pas, kan dit (hom) aantrek,* if the cap fits, you may wear it; *die stoute* ~*e aantrek,* screw up one's courage to do something
skoen'lapper (-s) butterfly
skoen: ~lees (-te) (boot)last; ~maker (-s) cobbler, shoemaker; ~*maker, hou jou by jou lees,* cobbler, stick to your last; ~riem (-e) shoe lace, shoe string; ~smeer boot polish; ~veter (-s) shoe lace; ~waks boot polish
skof[1] (skowwe) shoulder (ox), withers

skof[2] (-te) distance covered in one trek; hop (aero.); stage; shift
skof'baas (-te) shiftboss
skof'fel (s) (-s) hoe; (w) (ge-) clear (weeds), hoe; dance; ~ploeg (..ploeë) cultivator
skok (s) (-ke) shock; fright; (w) (ge-) shock, frighten; ~demper (-s) shock absorber
skok'kend (-e; -er, -ste) shocking
skok'troepe shock troops
skolier' (-e) scholar, pupil; ~patrollie (-s) scholar patrol
skol'lie (-s) ragamuffin, street arab, hooligan; skollie
skom'mel (ge-) rock, shake, swing, wobble; fluctuate
skon (-s) scone, *ook* botterbroodjie
skool[1] (s) (skole) school; *die* ~ *sluit,* the school breaks up; *op* ~, at school; (w) (ge-) train; *ge*~*de arbeid,* skilled labour
skool[2] (s) (skole) shoal; *'n* ~ *visse,* a shoal of fish; (w) (ge-) flock together
skool: ~besoekbeampte (-s) (school) attendance officer; ~biblioteek (..teke) school library; ~blad (..blaaie) school magazine
skooleind'sertifikaateksamen (-s) school= leaving certificate examination
skool: ~hoof (-de) school principal; ~hou (-ge-) teach; ~kind (-ers) schoolchild, pupil
skoolmeesterag'tig (-e) pedantic, conceited
skool'raad (..rade) school board
skool: ~tug school discipline; ~verlater (-s) school leaver
skoon[1] (s) the beautiful; ~ *vergaan, maar deug bly staan,* beauty is but skindeep; (b) (skone; skoner, -ste) clean, beautiful; *die skone geslag,* the fair(er) sex; ~ *stelle,* straight sets (tennis)
skoon[2] (bw) quite, altogether; ~ *vergeet,* forget completely
skoon'dogter (-s) daughter-in-law
skoon'heid (..hede) beauty
skoon'heids: ~deskundige (-s) beautician; ~leer aesthetics
skoon: ~maak (-ge-) clean; ~maker (-s) cleaner; ~moeder (-s) mother-in-law; ~ouers parents-in-law
skoon'vader (-s) father-in-law
skoon'vang (-e) mark (rugby)
skoon'veld (s) fairway (golf); (b) clean gone, out of sight

skoor (s): ~ *soek,* look for trouble; **~soe‹ker** troublemaker

skoor'steen (..stene) chimney, stack, fun‹nel, flue; **~mantel** (-s) mantlepiece; **~veër** (-s) chimney sweep

skoot[1] **(skote)** shot, report; turn

skoot[2] **(skote)** lap, bosom; fold; *met die hande in die* ~, with folded arms

skoot'hondjie (-s) lapdog

skop (s) (-pe) kick; (w) (ge-) kick; recoil (rifle)

skop'graaf (..grawe) shovel

skoppelmaai' (-e), **..maai'er** (-s) swing

skop'pens spades (playing cards)

skorriemor'rie rabble, riff-raff, hooligans

skors (w) (ge-) suspend (from school, membership); **~ing** suspension

skort (w) (ge-) postpone; hinder; ail, lack, be wanting; *wat — daar?* what is the matter there?

sko'tig (-e) gradually sloping; *'n ~e op‹draand,* a gradually steeper slope/incline

skots (b): ~ *en skeef,* topsy-turvy

skot'tel (-s) dish, basin; **~goed** dishes, crockery; **~ploeg** (..ploeë) disc plough

skot'vry unpunished, untouched, scot-free

skou (-e) show, exhibition; (w) (ge-) exhibit, put on show

skou'burg (-e) theatre, cinema; **stad‹** civic theatre

skou'er (-s) shoulder

skou: ~huis show house; **~put** (-te) man‹hole; **~spel** spectacle, sight

skouspelag'tig (-e) spectacular

skraag (ge-) prop, support, buttress up; **~dosis** booster dose; **~inspuiting** boos‹ster injection

skraal (skraler, -ste) meagre, thin, scanty

skraap (s) **(skrape)** scratch; (w) (ge-) scrape, scratch; *raap en* ~, pinch and scrape

skrams grazingly; *hy is* ~ *geraak,* he re‹ceived a glancing wound

skram'skoot (..skote), **skram'skot** (-e) grazing shot; graze

skran'der (-der, -ste) intelligent, shrewd, clever; *'n ~ leerling,* a bright pupil

skrap (ge-) erase, strike off, scratch out; *van die lys* ~, remove from the list; ~ *waar nodig,* delete which is not applicable; **~nel** shrapnel

skraps (-er, -ste) poorly, scarcely, narrowly

skre'de (-s) step, tread, stride, pace; *met rasse* ~, with rapid strides

skreeu (s) (-e) **(skreeue)** shout, scream, cry; (w) (ge-) scream, cry, shout; *moord en brand* ~ *oor,* cry murder; ~ *soos 'n maer vark,* squeal like a pig; **~balie** (-s) crybaby

skreeu: ~lelik (s) (-s) bawler, crybaby; (b) very ugly; **~snaaks** hilariously funny

skre'fie (-s) little opening, slit; *die deur staan op 'n* ~, the door stands ajar

skrei (ge-) weep, cry; *'n ~ende skande,* a crying shame

skri'ba (-s) secretary of the church council

Skrif: *die Heilige* ~, the Scriptures, Holy Writ

skrif handwriting; **(-te)** exercise book; **~geleerd** (-e) educated; cunning; **~ge‹leerd wees,** be a sly fox; **~geleerde** (-s) scribe; **~lesing** (-e, -s) prayers; reading of the lesson; **~telik** (-e) written, in writing; *'n ~telike eksamen,* a written examina‹tion

skrik (s) fright, terror; *die ~ op die lyf ja,* give someone a fright; (w) (ge-) be star‹tled, be frightened; *hy het groot ge~,* he got a big fright

skrik: ~beeld (-e) scarecrow, bugbear, bogey; **~bewind** (-e) reign of terror

skrik'keljaar (..jare) leap year

skrikwek'kend (-e; -er, -ste) alarming, ter‹rifying

skril (-le; -ler, -ste) shrill, piercing; glaring

skrobbe'ring (-e, -s) scolding, telling off, lecture, dressing down

skroef (s) **(skroewe)** screw, vice; propeller (aero.); **~sleutel** (-s) shifting spanner

skroei (ge-) scorch, burn, singe, sear

skroe'wedraaier (-s) screwdriver

skroom (s) timidity, modesty, diffidence; (w) (ge-) hesitate, be shy

skroot grapeshot; scrap, scrap iron; **~han‹delaar** scrap dealer; **~magasyn** (-e), **~werf** (..werwe), **~winkel** (-s) scrapyard

skrop (s) (-pe) dam scraper; (w) (ge-) scrub; scrape (dam); scratch (poultry); work (odd/casual jobs); **~borsel** (-s) scrubbing brush

skrum (s) (-s) scrum; (w) (ge-) scrum; **~skakel** (-s) scrumhalf

skryf (ge-) write; *met ink* ~, write in ink; **~behoeftes** stationery, *kyk* **skryfware;** **~blok** (-ke) writing pad; **~boek** (-e) ex‹

skry'we 149 slag

ercise book; writing pad; ~goed station=
ery; ~ster (-s) author (lady); ~tafel (-s)
writing table, desk; ~ware stationery
skry'we (s) letter, minute; *u ~ van 3 deser,*
your letter of 3 instant; (w) (ge-) write
skry'wer (-s) writer, author
sku (w) (ge-) shun; (b) (-(w)er, -uste) shy,
timid
skud (ge-) shake; shuffle; *hy ~ soos hy lag,*
he is convulsed with laughter; *kaarte ~,*
shuffle the cards; ~ding shaking; tremor;
concussion
skug'ter (-der, -ste) shy, timid, coy
skuif (s) (skuiwe) slide, bolt; move; puff
(pipe); (w) (ge-) shove, move, push;
~deur (-e) sliding door
skui'fel (ge-) shuffle, slide
skuif: ~leer (..lere) extension ladder;
~meul(e) noughts and crosses (game);
pretext, excuse; *hy het altyd 'n ~meul(e),*
he always has an excuse; ~raam (..rame)
sash window; ~speld (-e) paperclip;
~trompet (-te) trombone, sliding trumpet
skuil (ge-) hide, take shelter; *daar ~ iets
agter,* there is more to it than meets the
eye; ~kelder (-s) air raid shelter; ~naam
(..name) pseudonym; ~plek (-ke) hiding
place, hide-out, retreat
skuim (s) foam, scum, froth; *die ~ staan op
sy mond,* he is foaming at the mouth; *die
~ van die volk,* the rabble; (w) (ge-)
foam; ~rubber foam rubber; ~wyn
sparkling wine
skuins (-er, -ste) sloping, slanting, oblique
skuit (-e) boat
skui'wergat (-e) drainhole; loophole
skuld (-e) debt; fault; guilt; *agterstallige ~,*
arrears; *dis jou eie ~,* you have only
yourself to blame; *oninbare (dooie) ~,*
bad debts; (w) (ge-) owe; ~bekentenis
confession of guilt; ~bewys (-e) note of
hand; iou; ~brief (..briewe) debenture;
~delging debt redemption; ~eiser (-s)
creditor; ~e'naar (-s, ..nare) debtor;
~erkenning admission of guilt
skul'dig (-e) guilty; culpable; indebted; *~
bevind aan,* found guilty of; *~ pleit,*
plead guilty; ~e (-s) guilty person; culprit,
offender
skulp (-e) shell, conch
skurf (skurwe; skurwer, -ste) scabby; rough;
chapped (hands); dirty (joke)

skurk (-e) rascal, rogue, scoundrel
skut¹ (s) (-s) shot, marksman
skut² (s) (-te) protection; guard; pad
(cricket); (w) protect
skut³ (s) (-s) (-te) (animal) pound; (w)
(ge-) impound
skut'blad (..blaaie) flyleaf
skut: ~geld (-e) poundage; ~meester (-s)
poundkeeper
skut'ter (-s) rifleman; marksman
skut'verkoping (-e, -s) pound sale
skuur¹ (s) (skure) barn, shed
skuur² (w) (ge-) polish, rub, scour; ~papier
sand paper, glass paper, emery paper
skyf (skywe) slice, disc, quoit; target; quar=
ter (of an orange); puff (pipe); ~ie (-s)
film slide; disc (sticker); ~letsel (-s) slip=
ped disc; ~skiet (-ge-) shoot at targets
skyn (s) light, glow; appearance, pretence;
(w) (ge-) shine; seem, appear; ~aanval
(-le) mock attack; ~baar (..bare) ap=
parent(ly); ~geveg (-te) sham fight, mock
fight
skynhei'lig (-e; -er, -ste) sanctimonious;
hypocritical
slaaf (s) (slawe) slave; (w) (ge-) slave,
drudge, toil
slaafs (-e; -er,-ste) slavish, servile
slaag (ge-) succeed; pass; *ek het daarin ge~,*
I succeeded in . . .
slaags fighting, engaged; *~ raak,* come to
blows
slaai salad; lettuce; *in 'n mens se ~ krap,*
meddle with someone else's girl
slaak (ge-) heave, utter, breathe; *'n sug (van
verligting) ~,* heave a sigh (of relief)
slaan (ge-) beat, strike; *'n slag ~,* make a
bargain; *op die vlug ~,* take to flight
slaap¹ (s) (slape) temple
slaap² (s) sleep; *aan die ~ raak,* fall asleep;
(w) (ge-) sleep; ~drank (-e) narcotic;
~kamer (-s) bedroom; ~klere pyjamas;
~saal (..sale) dormitory; ~sak (-ke) sleep=
ing bag; ~siekte sleeping sickness;
lethargy; ~wandelaar (-s) somnambulist
sla'e thrashing, hiding; *'n pak ~,* a
thrashing
slag¹ (s) (slae) battle; loss; slap (with hand);
beat (pulse); clap (thunder); blow, stroke;
op ~ dood, killed instantly; *'n swaar ~,* a
severe blow

slag[2] (w) (ge-) slaughter, kill; ~aar (..are) artery

slag: ~gat (-e) pothole; ~huis (-e) butchery; ~offer (-s) victim; ~orkes (-te) percussion band

slag: ~pale slaughtering place; ~plaas (..plase) abattoir; ~room whipped cream; ~spreuk (-e) slogan

slag: ~tand (-e) tusk (elephant); fang; eye tooth; ~ter (-s) butcher

slag: ~vee slaughter animals; ~veld (-e) battlefield; ~yster (-s) spring trap

slak (-ke) snail; slag (ore smelting waste)

Slamai'er (-s) Malay (person)

slampam'per (w) (ge-) revel; stroll; ~lied=jie (-s) carousal song; vagrant song

Slams (-e) former expression for Malay, Mohammedan

slang (-e) snake, serpent; hosepipe

slank (-er, -ste) slender, fragile, slim

slap (-per, -ste) loose; slack, dull; supple

sla'per (-s) sleeper, dreamer

slap'gat (-te) spineless fellow; (b) spineless

slap'verkeer off-peak traffic

slavin' (-ne) female slave

slawerny' slavery

slee (sleë) sledge, sleigh

sleep (s) (slepe) retinue, train; boy/girl friend; (w) (ge-) drag, trail; tow; 'n slepende siekte, a lingering disease; ~boot (..bote) tug; ~ren (-ne) drag racing; ~tou (-e) towing rope; op ~tou neem, take in tow; ~wa (-ens) trailer

sleg (b, bw) (-te; -er, -ste) bad, evil, base

slegs only, merely; ~ volwassenes, adults only

Slenk'dal Rift Valley

slen'ter (s) trick, bluff, ploy; (w) (ge-) saunter; ~broek (-e) slacks; ~drag casual dress/wear

slet (-te) slut, bitch (woman)

sleur (s) habit, humdrum way, rut, routine; (w) (ge-) drag; ~faktor drag factor (aerodynamics); ~werk routine work

sleu'tel (-s) key (door); clef (music); register; wrench, spanner; ~been (..bene) collarbone

slik silt, mire, slime

slim (-mer, -ste) clever, intelligent; crafty, sly; ~praatjies, ~stories stories, claptrap, evasive talk

slin'ger (s) (-s) pendulum (clock); sling; handle; crank (motorcar); (w) (ge-) sling; oscillate, reel; ~vel (-le) sling(shot)

slinks (-e; -er, -ste) clandestine, treacherous; artful; underhand

sloer (ge-) loiter, linger, dawdle, drag (on); lank met 'n saak ~, keep on postponing a matter

sloer'staking (-s) go-slow strike

sloof (ge-) drudge, toil

sloop[1] (s) (slope) pillowcase

sloop[2] (w) (ge-) raze, demolish; undermine (one's health), drain; break up (a ship)

sloot (slote) ditch, furrow, trench

slor'dig (-e; -er, -ste) careless, untidy

slot[1] (-te) lock; clasp; agter ~ en grendel, under lock and key

slot[2] end(ing), conclusion; per ~ van rekening, after all; ten ~te, in conclusion

slot[3] (-te) castle, citadel

slot'maker (-s) locksmith

slot: ~sang (-e) final song/hymn; ~som result, conclusion

slu (-we; -(w)er, -uste) sly, cunning, artful, astute, wily; ~heid cunning, slyness

slui'er (s) (-s) veil, mask

sluik: ~handel black market; ~werk moonlighting, double-jobbing

slui'mer (s) slumber; (w) (ge-) slumber

sluip (ge-) steal along, sneak away; ~moord (-e) assassination; ~moordenaar (-s) assassin; ~slaper (-s) yard sneaker, yard snooper, sly lodger

sluis (-e) sluice, lock, floodgate

sluit (ge-) lock, close, shut; conclude; die skole ~, the schools are breaking up; vrede ~, conclude/make peace; ~datum closing date

sluk (s) (-ke) epiglottis; gulp, swallow; (w) (ge-) swallow, gulp; ~derm (-s) gullet, esophagus

slum (-s) slum

slurp (w) (ge-) sip, lap, gobble

slyk mud, mire, ooze, sludge

slym slime, phlegm, mucus

slyp (ge-) sharpen, whet, grind; polish; sy tande vir iets ~, look forward to with keen anticipation; ~steen (..stene) whetstone, grindstone, hone

slyt (ge-) wear away, diminish

slyta'sie wear, wastage; billike ~, fair wear and tear

smaak (s) (smake) taste, relish, flavour; liking; *na my ~*, to my liking; (w) (ge-) taste, savour; appear; *dit ~ goed*, it tastes nice

smaak'lik (-e; -er, -ste) tasty, palatable; *'n ~e ete*, a tasty meal

smaak'vol (-le) tasteful, elegant; *sy is ~ aangetrek*, she is dressed elegantly

smal (-ler, -ste) narrow, thin

sma'lend (-e) sneering, railing

smarag' (-de) emerald

smart (s) (-e) pain; grief, sorrow; *gedeelde ~ is halwe ~*, company in distress makes sorrow less

smee(d) (ge-) weld, forge, coin, devise; *'n komplot ~*, hatch a plot

smeek (ge-) pray, beg, beseech, entreat, implore; *om genade ~*, plead for mercy; ~bede (-s) petition, prayer

smeer (ge-) grease, smear, oil, lubricate; ~veldtog smear campaign

smee'-yster wrought iron

smelt (ge-) melt, dissolve; fuse (wire); ~oond (-e) furnace

sme'rig (-e; -er, -ste) greasy, squalid, dirty

smet (-te) blot, stain, blemish

smeul (ge-) smoulder; ~stoof (..stowe) slow-combustion stove

smid (smede, -s), smit (-te) smith

smid'dags in the afternoon (midday)

smok'kel (s) smuggling; (w) (ge-) smuggle; ~aar (-s) smuggler; bootlegger; ~kroeg (..kroeë) shebeen

smoor (w) (ge-) suffocate, smother; ~dronk dead drunk; ~klep (-pe) choke (engine); ~verlief (-de) head over heels in love

smo'rens, smô'rens in the morning

smous (s) (-e) hawker, pedlar; (w) (ge-) barter; hawk

smuk: ~spieëltjie vanity mirror; ~tassie vanity case, *ook* tooitassie

smul (ge-) feast, junket, banquet; ~paap (..pape) gastronome, gourmand; belly worshipper; ~party (-e) carousal, feast

smyt (ge-) throw, fling, hurl

s'n 's, of; *hulle ~*, theirs; *pa ~*, father's

snaaks (-e; -er, -ste) droll, funny, queer, strange, comical

snaar (snare) string, cord; chap, guy; lover

snags during the night, by night

snap (ge-) understand, comprehend, catch

snaps (-e) drop, drink, tot

sna'ter (s) (-s) mouth, mug, snout (vulgar-ism); beak; *hou jou ~!* shut up! (w) (ge-) chatter, jibber

sna'wel (-s) beak, bill

snees'papier(tjie) (-s) tissue(-paper), *ook* snesie

sneeu (s) snow; (w) (ge-) snow; ~vlokkie (-s) snowflake; ~wit snow white

snel (w) (ge-) rush, hurry; (b) (-le; -ler, -ste) rapid, quick, fleet, swift; ~heid velocity; ~heidsgrens (snelperk) speed limit

snel'ler (-s) trigger; sprinter

snel: ~perk speed limit; ~rat overdrive; ~sêer (-s) tongue twister

snel'skrif shorthand, stenography; ~tikster (-s) shorthand typist

snel: ~strik (-ke) speed trap; ~trein (-e) express train, fast train; ~vuur rapid fire; ~weg (..weë) freeway (rural), highway (Am.); speedway, expressway

sner'pend (-e) painful, biting, smarting; *~e koue*, biting cold

snert small talk, trash

sne'sie (-s) tissue; *kry 'n ~ en snuit jou neus*, get a tissue and blow your nose

sneu'wel (ge-) perish, be slain, fall (in battle)

snik (s) (-ke) sob; (w) (ge-) sob, sniffle; ~sanger (-s) crooner, sobsinger

snip'per: ~jag (-te) paperchase; ~mandjie (-s) wastepaper basket

snit (-te) cut, fashion

snob (-s) snob

snobis'me snobbery

snoei (ge-) prune, clip, lop; ~skêr (-e) garden/pruning shears, pruner

snoek (-e) snoek; barracuda; sea pike

snoep (w) (ge-) eat dainties secretly; with-hold; (b) (-er, -ste) tight-fisted; epicurean; ~erye snacks, dainties; ~hoekie (-s) snackbar; ~winkel(tjie) (-s) tuckshop

snoer (s) (-e) string, cord; *'n ~ pêrels*, a string of pearls; (w) (ge-) silence, close

snoet (-e) snout, muzzle

snor (s) (-re) moustache

snork (s) (-e) snore; (w) (ge-) snore, snort

snot mucus, snot; ~neus (-e) snotty nose; brat, little minx

snou (w) (ge-) snarl, rebuke

snuf'fel (ge-) sniff, sniffle, smell (out), fer-ret (out); search, investigate

snuif (s) (**snuiwe**) snuff; (w) (**ge-**) take snuff, sniff; **~doos** (**..dose**) snuff box

snuis'tery (**-e**) novelty, trinket, bric-a-brac

snuit (**-e**) snout, nose, nozzle; (w) (**ge-**) blow the nose; **~er** (**-s**) little fellow, youngster; snuffer(s)

sny (s) (**-e**) slice; cut, gash; (w) (**ge-**) cut; castrate, geld; operate; spring; **~dokter** (**-s**) surgeon; **~kunde** surgery; *plastiese* **~kunde**, plastic/cosmetic surgery

so so, thus, like this

so'ber ([**-e**]; **-der, -ste**) sober, temperate

soda'nig (**-e**) such, such like; *die toestand is* **~** *dat,* the position is such that

so'dat so that, in order that

so'doende thus, in that manner

sodra' as soon as; the moment that

soe'bat (**ge-**) beg, entreat, plead, implore

soek (s): *op* **~** *na,* in search of; (v) (**ge-**) seek, look for, search; **~geselskap** (**-pe**) search party

soen (s) (**-e**) kiss; (w) (**ge-**) kiss

soep = **sop**

soe'pel (**-er, -ste**) supple; flexible

soet (s) the sweet; *die* **~** *en suur van die lewe,* the ups and downs of life; (b) (**-er, -ste**) sweet; well-behaved, good; fresh

soetema'ling tuberose

soet: ~igheid sweetness, sweets; **~jies** gently, unnoticed, noiselessly; **~koek** sweet cake; *alles vir* **~koek** *opeet,* swallow everything you are told; **~lief** sweetheart

soewenier' (**-s**) souvenir

soewerein' (b) (**-e**) sovereign, supreme

so'fa (**-'s**) sofa

sog (**-ge, sôe**) sow

so'genaamd, so'genoemd (b) (**-e**) so-called; (bw) in name, ostensibly

sog'gens in the morning

so'heen thither, there; **~toe** thither, that way, *kyk* **soontoe**

so'jaboon(tjie) (**-s**) soybean

sok'kervoetbal association/soccer football

sok'kie (**-s**) sock

solank' for the time being, meanwhile

soldaat' (**..date**) soldier

soldeer' (**~, ge-**) solder; **~bout** (**-e**) soldering iron

sol'der (**-s**) garret, loft

soldoe'die, sol'liedollie (**-s**) woman soldier

soldy' soldier's pay, wages

solidariteit' solidarity

solied' (**-e; -er, -ste**) solid; reliable

solis' (**-te**) soloist, solo vocalist

so'lo (**-'s**) solo; **~sanger** (**-s**) soloist

so'lus-se'we seven-single (gram. record)

som (**-me**) sum, amount; problem; *hy is goed in* **~me,** he is good at sums

som'ber (**-der, -ste**) sombre, gloomy

so'mer (**-s**) summer; *in die* **~,** in/during summer; **~vakansie** (**-s**) summer holidays

som'mer just, for no reason; at a glance, without further ado; *ag* **~**! oh, just because; **~** *huil,* cry for no reason

sommerso' nothing particular, in a way, after a fashion; *ek laat my nie* **~** *fop nie,* I am not to be fooled that easily

som'mige some

soms, som'tyds sometimes

son (**-ne**) sun; *die* **~** *kom op (gaan onder),* the sun rises/sets

sona'te (**-s**) sonata

son: ~besie (**-s**) cricket (cicada); **~bruin** (s) tan; (w) (**ge-**) tan

son'daar (**-s, ..dare**) sinner

Son'dag (**..dae**) Sunday; **~** *oor agt dae,* next Sunday week

Son'dagskool (**..skole**) Sunday school

sondares' (**-se**) sinner (woman)

son'de (**-s**) sin, trespass; probe; **~bok** (**-ke**) scapegoat, guiltless person; whipping boy

son'der without; **~** *tuiste,* of no fixed abode; **~** *twyfel waar,* no doubt true; **~** *winsoogmerk/winsbejag,* not for gain/profit

sond'vloed deluge, great flood

so'ne (**-s**) zone

son: ~lig sunlight; **~ne'blom** (**-me**) sunflower

sonnet' (**-te**) sonnet

son'onder (s) sunset; (bw) at sunset

sonoor' (**sonore**) sonorous

son'op (s) sunrise; (bw) at sunrise

son: ~steek sunstroke; **~straal** (**..strale**) sunbeam

sons'verduistering (**-e, -s**) solar eclipse

son: ~verhitting solar heating; **~verwarmer** solar heater; **~vlek** (**-ke**) sunspot, solar spot; **~wyser** (**-s**) sundial

soog (**ge-**) suckle, give suck, nurse; **~dier** (**-e**) mammal; **~vrou** (**-e**) wet nurse

sooi (**-e**) sod; **~brand** heartburn; **~merk** (**-e**) divot (golf)

sool (**sole**) sole; **~leer** sole leather

soölogie' zoology

soom (s) (**some**) seam, hem; edge, border

soon'toe thither, that way

soort (-e) kind, sort; *enig in sy ~,* the only one of its kind; *~ soek ~,* birds of a feather flock together; **~gelyk** (-e) similar, suchlike; **~lik** (-e) specific; **~like gewig,** specific gravity

soos as, like; *so siek ~ 'n hond,* very ill/miserable; *~ volg,* as follows

sop soup

so'pie (-s) glass of liquor, drink, tot

sopraan' (**soprane**) soprano

sorg (s) (-e) care, charge; trouble, anxiety; *~ dra,* take care; (w) (ge-) care for, look after, provide for; *~ vir die oudag,* provide for one's old age; **~eenheid** intensive care unit, *ook* **waakeenheid**

sor'ghum (grain) sorghum

sorgvul'dig (-e; -er, -ste) careful, thorough

sorgwek'kend (-e) alarming

sorteer' (~, ge-) sort, assort, select, grade

sosa'tie (-s) sosatie, grilled curried meat

sosiaal' (**sosiale**) social

sosialiet' (-e) socialite

sosialis' (-te) socialist; **~me** socialism

so'sio-ekonomies socio-economic

sosiologie' sociology

sot (s) (-te) fool; (b) (-ter, -ste) foolish; **~heid** (..hede) folly, stupidity

sous (s) (-e) sauce, gravy

sout (s) (-e) salt; *'n sak ~ saam opeet,* know someone intimately; (w) (ge-) salt, cure; initiate; (b) (-er, -ste) briny, salt; **~happies** savouries

so'veel so much, so many; **~ste** umpteenth

sover' so far; *~ ek weet,* as far as I know

so'ver so far, thus far; *tot ~,* as far as this

sowaar' truly; indeed, really

so'wat about; *~ vyftig rand,* fifty rands odd

sowel' both...and; as well (as); *~ as,* as well as; *~ hy as sy,* both he and she

spaan (s) (**spane**) skimmer; oar; racket

spaan'der (s) (-s) chip of wood; (w) (ge-) run away; *laat ~,* take to one's heels; **~bord,** **~hout** chipboard

spaar (ge-) save, economise; spare; **~bank** (-e) savings bank; **~bankboekie** (-s) deposit book

spaar'saam (..same; ..samer, -ste) thrifty

spalk (s) (-e) splint; (w) (ge-) splint; set (leg or arm)

span (s) (-ne) span, team; *'n ~ arbeiders,* a team of labourers; (w) (ge-) stretch; brace; hobble; cock (gun)

spanda'bel (-e; -er, -ste) spendthrift, extravagant

spandeer' (~, ge-) spend

span'doek (-e) wide banner/streamer (across building, etc.)

span'gees team spirit, esprit de corps

span'nend (-e; -er, -ste) tight; exciting, thrilling; *~e oomblikke,* tense moments

span'ning tension, suspense; voltage

spanspek' (-ke) musk melon, spanspek

spar'tel (ge-) gambol; sprawl, twitch

spa'sie (-s) space, opening

spasië'ring spacing

spat (ge-) splash, spatter

spea'ker (-s) speaker (of parliament)

speek (**speke**) spoke

speek'sel spittle, saliva

speel (ge-) play; trifle with; perform, act; *ek ~ maar,* I am only joking; *jy ~ met vuur,* you are playing with fire; **~ding** (..goed) toy; **~goed** toys

speels (-e; -er, -ste) playful

speel: **~tyd** (..tye) playtime; recess, interval; **~vak** (-ke) season, run (theatre)

speen (s) (**spene**) teat; (w) (ge-) wean; *ge~ wees van,* be weaned from; **~vark** (-e) sucking pig

speer (**spere**) spear

spei (w) spay (a bitch), neuter (a cat)

spek bacon; pork; *vir ~ en boontjies,* for the fun of a thing; *met ~ skiet,* draw the long bow

spekta'kel (-s) scene; row; sight

spekula'sie (-s) speculation; flutter

spekuleer' (ge-) speculate, stag (stock exchange)

spek: **~vark** (-e) porker; **~vet** very fat

spel[1] (s) (-e) game, play; *daar is baie op die ~,* there is much at stake; *oneerlike ~,* foul play

spel[2] (w) (ge-) spell; foretell

spel: **~bederwer,** **~breker** (-s) killjoy, spoilsport

speld (s) (-e) pin

spe'ler (-s) player, actor

spe'letjie (-s) game, fun

spel'fout (-e) spelling mistake

spe'ling play, scope, range
spel'letjie (-s) game; *'n ~ kaart,* a game of cards
spel'ling (-e, -s) spelling, orthography
spelonk' (-e) cave, cavern
spens (-e) pantry
sper'streep (..strepe) barrier (solid white) line
sper'tyd (..tye) deadline, *ook* **perktyd**
spesery' (-e) spice; **~handel** spice trade
spesiaal' (..siale) special
spesialis' (-te) specialist (medicine, etc.)
spesialiseer' (~, ge-) specialise
spesialiteit' (-e) speciality; *brei is haar ~,* she excels in knitting
spesifiek' (-e) specific
spesifika'sie (-s) specification
spesmaas' idea, notion, feeling, inkling; *ek het 'n ~ dat..,* I have an idea/feeling that...
speur (ge-) track, trace, spy, ferret out; **~der** (-s) detective; **~hond** (-e) sleuth hound, bloodhound, police dog; **~verhaal** (..hale) detective story
spie'ël (s) (-s) mirror, looking glass; *so glad soos 'n ~,* deadlevel; (w) (ge-) mirror
spier (-e) muscle; *geen ~ vertrek nie,* without batting an eyelid; **~bouer** bodybuilder
spier: ~krag muscular force; **~wit** snowwhite, lily-white
spies (-e) spear, lance; **~hengel** spearfishing
spik'kel (-s) spot, speck
spik'splinternuut (..nuwe) brand new, spick-and-span
spil[1] (s) (-le) pivot, axis; spindle
spil[2] (w) (ge-) waste, spill
spin (ge-) spin; purr (cat)
spina'sie spinach
spin'nekop (-pe) spider
spin'ne: ~rak (-ke) cobweb
spioen' (s) (-e) spy; (w) (ge-) spy
spioena'sie espionage, spying
spioeneer' (ge-) spy, pry
spiraal' (..rale) spiral
spiritis' (-te) spiritualist
spiritua'lieë spirits (alcoholic), spirituous liquors
spi'ritus spirit(s), alcohol
spit[1] (s) lumbago; *~ in die rug,* lumbago
spit[2] (s) (-te) spadeful; spade depth; *die ~ afbyt,* bear the brunt; (w) (ge-) dig

spit[3] (s) (-te) spit (for roasting)
spits (s) (-e) pint, top, tip, peak, spire, pinnacle; (w) (ge-) point; *die ore ~,* prick up the ears; (b) (-er, -ste) pointed, sharp; **~beraad** summit talks; **~tyd** peak period; **~uur** (..ure) peak hour/period, rush hour; **~verkeer** peak traffic
spitsvon'dig (-e; -er, -ste) subtle, quibbling, quick-witted
spleet (splete) crevice, slit, fissure, chink
splin'ter (s) (-s) splinter; (w) (ge-) splinter; **~nuut** (..nuwe) brand-new; **~vry** shatterproof
split (s) (-te) slit, vent; (w) (ge-) split, divide; **~pen** (-ne) split pin
splits (ge-) split, divide; splice
splyt (ge-) cleave, split; *gesplete lip,* hare lip; **~ing** splitting (atom)
spoed (s) (snelhede) speed, progress, haste; *hoe meer haas hoe minder ~,* the more haste the less speed; (w) (ge-) speed, hasten; **~bestelling** (-e, -s) express order; **~hobbel** (-s) speed hump; **~ig** (-e; -er, -ste) soon, speedy/speedily, quick(ly)
spoed: ~rat (-te) overdrive; **~waggel** speed wobble
spoeg (s) spittle, saliva; (w) (ge-) spit, expectorate
spoel[1] (s) (-e) shuttle, spool
spoel[2] (w) (ge-) rinse, wash; flow; **~bak** (-ke) washtub; cistern; **~diamant** (-e) alluvial diamond
spog (ge-) boast, show off, brag
spons (s) (ge-) sponge; (w) (ge-) sponge; **~rubber** foam rubber
spontaan' (..tane) spontaneous
spook (s) (spoke) ghost, apparition, spectre; (w) (ge-) be very active, struggle, fight; haunt; **~asem** candyfloss; **~storie** (-s) ghost story
spoor[1] (s) (spore) track, footprint; trail; scent; vestige; rail(way); spore; *die ~ kwyt raak (byster raak),* be on the wrong track; *per ~,* by rail; (w) (ge-) align (wheels), *kyk* **wielspoor**
spoor[2] (s) (spore) spur; (w) (ge-) spur; page; *gestewel en ge~,* booted and spurred
spoor: ~brug (-ge, ..brûe(ns)) railway bridge; **~loos** (b) (..lose) trackless; (bw) completely; **~loos verdwyn,** vanish into space; **~lyn** (-e) railway line
spoor'snyer (-s) tracker

spoor'weg (..weë), railway; **~kaartjie** (-s) railway ticket; **~tarief** (..riewe) railway rate/tariff

spora'dies (-e) sporadic

spo'ring alignment of wheels

sport[1] (-e) rundle, step, rung

sport[2] (-e, -soorte) sport; **~baadjie** (-s) sports jacket

sportief' (..tiewe) sportive

sport: ~klub (-s) sports club; **~manskap** sportsmanship

spot (s) scorn, mockery; (w) (ge-) jest, deride, mock, jeer; **~goedkoop, ~koop** dirt-cheap; **~prent** (-e) caricature, cartoon

spraak speech, language, tongue; **~gebrek** (-e) speech defect; **~orgaan** (..gane) organ of speech

spra'ke rumour, talk; *ter ~ bring*, broach a subject; *geen ~ van*, no question about it; **~loos** (..lose) speechless, dumb

sprank (-e) spark; *geen ~ie hoop*, beyond any hope

spran'kel (ge-) spark(le)

spreek (ge-) speak, talk, converse; *kan ek die hoof ~?* may I see the principal? *dit ~ vanself*, it goes without saying; **~kamer** (-s) consulting room; **~woord** (-e) proverb, saying, adage

spreekwoor'delik (-e) proverbial

spreeu (-s) starling

sprei[1] (s) (-e) counterpane, bedspread, quilt

sprei[2] (w) (ge-) scatter, spread out; **~lig** (-te) floodlight

spre'kend (-e) speaking; lifelike; *'n ~e ge-lykenis*, an exact/striking likeness

spre'ker (-s) speaker

spreuk (-e) proverb, aphorism, maxim

spriet (-e) blade (grass); feeler (insect)

spring (s) (-e) leap, jump, hop; (w) (ge-) jump, leap, bound; **~bok** (-ke) springbok

spring: ~jurk (-e) gym, gymnastic costume; tunic; **~lewendig** (-e) very much alive, sprightly; **~mat** (-te) trampoline, *ook* **wipmat; ~mes** (-se) flick-knife; **~mielies** popcorn; **~plank** (-e) springboard; **~stof** (..stowwe) explosive(s); **~tou** (-e) skipping rope; **~werke** blasting operations

sprin'kaan (..kane) locust, grasshopper; **~voël** (-s) locust bird; stork (large)

sprin'kel (ge-) sprinkle; **~besproeiing** spray/sprinkler irrigation

sproei (w) (ge-) spray, irrigate; (s) **~er** (-s) sprayer; jet

sproet (-e) freckle; **~gesig** (-te) freckled face

spro'kie (-s) fairytale, fable

sprong (-e) jump, leap, bound, caper, hop

spruit (s) (-e) shoot; offshoot; brook, stream(let); (w) (ge-) sprout; arise

spuit (s) (-e) syringe; squirt; sprayer; (w) (ge-) inject; spout, spray, squirt; **~kan-(netjie)** spray can, aerosol can; **~stof** (..stowwe) vaccine; spraying mixture; **~verf** (..verwe) spray paint; **~water** sodawater

spul affair, case; lot; *die hele ~*, the whole lot

spy'ker (-s) nail; brad, tack; **~skoen** (-e) (mv) spikes (athletics); **~tafel** pintable

spys (-e) food, viands, victuals; **~e'nier** (-s) caterer; **~e'neer** (w) cater; **~e'nering** catering

spys: ~kaart (-e) menu, bill of fare; **~ver-tering** digestion

spyt (s) regret, sorrow; *ten ~e van*, in spite of; (w) (ge-) regret, be sorry; *dit ~ my*, I am sorry

staaf[1] (s) (stawe) bar, rod, stave

staaf[2] (w) (ge-) confirm; ratify; prove, support; *~ u antwoord met*, support your answer with

staaf'goud bar gold, bullion

staak (ge-) strike, cease work; discontinue; stall (car); **~wag** (-te) picket

staal steel; *jou ~ toon*, show one's mettle; **~draad** steel wire

staal'tjie (-s) yarn, yoke; anecdote

staan (ge-) stand; *duur te ~ kom*, pay dearly for; **~de** standing; upright

staan'der (-s) standard

staan'spoor start, beginning; *uit die ~ uit, van die ~ af*, from the outset

staar (ge-) gaze, stare

staat[1] (state) statement; return

staat[2] condition; *in ~ wees*, be able

staat[3] (state) state; **~huishoudkunde** political economy

staat'kunde politics, statemanship

staat: ~maak (-ge-) rely (up)on; **~maker** (-s) mainstay, stalwart, reliable person

staats: ~aanklaer (-s) public prosecutor; **~amptenaar** (-s, ..nare) civil servant; **~diens** civil service; **~greep** (..grepe) coup (d'état)

staat'sie pomp, state; *in ~ lê*, lie in state

staats'koerant (-e) government gazette

staats: ~leer political science; ~lotery (-e) state lottery; ~man (-ne, ..liede) statesman, diplomat

stabiel' (-e) solid, firm, stable

stabiliseer' (ge-) stabilise

stad (stede) city

stad'huis (-e) town hall, city hall, municipal complex

sta'dig (-e; -er, -ste) slow

sta'dion (-s) stadium; ~ Boland, Boland stadium

sta'dium (-s, ..dia) stage, phase; in hierdie ~, at this stage; op hierdie ~, at this point, kyk tydstip

stad'saal (..sale) town hall, city hall

stads: ~huis (-e) house in town; ~kalant (-e) city slicker; ~klerk (-e) town clerk

stad'skouburg (-e) civic theatre

stads: ~raad (..rade) town council, municipality; ~wapen (-s) coat-of-arms (of a town)

staf (stawe) staff; mace (parliament); baton (marshall); crozier (bishop)

stagna'sie stagnation

sta'ker (-s) striker; ~(s)wag picket

sta'king (-e, -s) strike; suspension, cessation; die ~ afgelas, countermand/call off the strike; ~ van stemme, equality of votes

stal (-le) stable; (w) stable; park (off-street)

stal'letjie (-s) (display) stall; booth

stam (s) (-me) trunk, stem; tribe, clan; (w) descend

stam'boom (..bome) genealogical tree, family tree, pedigree

sta'mel (ge-) falter; stammer

stam: ~geveg (-te) faction fight; ~oorlog (..loë) tribal war

stamp (s) (-e) knock, stamp, bump; met ~e en stote, by fits and starts; (w) (ge-) pound, stamp, bump; ~motor (-s) stock car; ~vol (-le) chockful, packed (hall)

stand (-e) standing, position; rank; stance

standaard' (-e, -s) standard, criterium; ~werk (-e) standard work

stand'beeld (-e) statue

stan'derd (-s) standard (class in school)

stan'dertjie (-s) cruet stand

stand'plaas (..plase) stand, erf

stand'punt (-e) standpoint; point of view

standvas'tig (-e) firm, constant, steadfast

stang (-e) bit (of bridle); bar

stank (-e) stench, bad smell, stink; ~ vir dank kry, not to get as much as a "thank you"

stan'sa (-s) stanza, kyk strofe

stap (s) (-pe) step, pace, stride; move; ~pe doen, take action; (w) (ge-) walk; step, stride; hike; 'n entjie gaan ~, go for a walk

sta'pel (s) (-s) pile, heap, stack; die skema van ~ laat loop, to launch the scheme; (w) (ge-) heap up, pile, stack; ~gek insane, raving mad, stark mad; ~kos staple food

stap: ~per (-s) walker, hiker; met dapper en ~per, on foot; ~toer (-e) hiking trip

sta'sie (-s) station

stat (-te) tribal village, kraal

sta'tebond federation of states; commonwealth

sta'ties (-e) static

sta'tig (-e; -er, -ste) stately, elegant

statistiek' (-e) statistics

statis'tikus (-se) statistician

statuut' (statute) statute

ste'de stead; in ~ van, instead of; ~lik (-e) urban, municipal; ~like bevolking, urban population; ~like Swartmense, urban Blacks; ~like terrorisme, urban terrorism; ~ling (-e) townsman, city dweller

steeds (bw) constantly, always; ~ kouer, colder and colder

steeg (stege) lane, alley

steek (s) (steke) prick (pin); stitch (needle); sting (bee); bite, stab, thrust; in die ~ laat, leave in the lurch; (w) (ge-) prick; sting; stab; daar ~ iets agter, there is a catch in it; ~proef (..proewe) test sample

steeks (-e; -er, -ste) obstinate, restive

steel[1] (s) (stele) handle; stalk (flower); stem (pipe); shaft

steel[2] (w) (ge-) steal, thieve

steel'kant blind side (rugby)

steen (stene) brick; stone; bar (soap)

Steen'bokskeerkring Tropic of Capricorn

steen: ~groef (..groewe) quarry; ~kool (..kole) coal

steg (w) (ge-) take cuttings; ~gie (-s) cutting

stei'er[1] (s) (-s) scaffold(ing)

stei'er[2] (w) (ge-) stagger, prance, rear

steil (-e, -ste) steep, precipitous, sheer; bluff; ~te (-s) gradient, rise, steepness

stel[1] (s) (-le) set (tennis); (dinner) service; suite (of rooms)

stel[2] (w) (ge-) fix; draw up; adjust; put, set; compose; *gestel dat*, supposing that

stel'ling (-e, -s) doctrine, system, thesis, theorem; statement; *bespreek hierdie ~*, discuss this statement/assertion

stel'sel (-s) system; *metrieke (tiendelige) ~*, metric system

stelselma'tig (-e, -s) systematic(al)

stel'skop (-pe) placekick

stelt (-e) stilt; *~loper* (-s) stilt walker

stem (s) (-me) voice; vote; *~me uitbring*, cast votes; poll; *die ~ verhef*, raise the voice; (w) (ge-) tune; vote; *~band* (-e) vocal chord; *~brief(ie)* (-s) ballot paper; *~buiging* (-e, -s) modulation, intonation; *~bus* (-se) ballot box; *~mig* (-e; -er, -ste) serious, sedate, sober, quiet

stem'ming (-e, -s) ballot, election, voting, poll, mood; *in 'n goeie ~ bring*, put in a good mood; *tot ~ oorgaan/bring*, proceed/put to the vote

stem'opnemer (-s) polling officer, returning officer, scrutineer

stem'pel (-s) seal, stamp

stem: *~reg* franchise; right to vote; *die ~reg uitoefen*, exercise the vote; *~vurk* (-e) tuning fork

ste'nig (ge-) stone

ster (-re) star; luminary

stereofo'nies (b) (-e) stereophonic

stereotiep (-e) stereotype

sterf (ge-) die, expire; *~geval* (-le) death; *~lik* (-e) mortal; *~ling* (-e) mortal (being); *geen ~ling nie*, not a living soul; *~te'syfer* (-s) death rate

steriel' (-e) sterile

sterilisa'sie sterilisation

sterk (w) (ge-) strengthen; *iem. in sy kwaad ~*, encourage a person in wrongdoing; (b) (-er, -ste) strong, powerful; numerous; *~te* strength; *~te!* good luck to you!

ster're: *~beeld* (-e) constellation; *~kunde* astronomy

sterrekun'dig (-e) astronomical; *~e* (-s) astronomer

ster're: *~tjie* (-s) little star; asterisk; *~wag* (-te) observatory; *~wiggelaar* (-s) astrologer

stert (-e) tail

ster'we (ge-) die, expire

stetoskoop' (..skope) stethoscope

steun[1] (s) (-e) groan, moan; (w) (ge-) groan

steun[2] (s) support, aid; (w) (ge-) support, aid, stay; *geldelik ~*, finance; *~pilaar* (..lare) pillar of support; *~sool* (..sole) arch support

steur[1] (s) (-s) sturgeon; *~garnaal* (..ale) prawn, *kyk* **garnaal**

steur[2] (w) (ge-) disturb, trouble; care for, mind; *moenie jou daaraan ~ nie*, don't mind that; *~ing* inconvenience, intrusion; *atmosferiese ~ings*, atmospherics

ste'we (-ns) prow, stem, bow

ste'wel (-s) boot; *vier ~s in die lug lê*, lie flat on the back

ste'wig (-e; -er, -ste) firm; thorough; solid

stie'beuel (-s) stirrup

stief step; *~broer* (-s) stepbrother; *~moeder* (-s) stepmother

stier (-e) bull; *~geveg* (-te) bullfight

stig (ge-) found, establish, raise; form (a company); edify; *brand ~*, raise a fire; *'n fonds ~*, establish a fund

stig'gie (-s) cutting

stig'ma (-s) stigma, brand

stig'telik (-e) edifying, ennobling

stig: *~ter* (-s) founder; *~ters'lid* (..lede) founder member; *~ting* (-e -s) foundation, founding; home, institution

Stig'tingsdag Founders' Day

stik[1] (ge-) embroider, stitch

stik[2] (ge-) choke, suffocate; *~sienig* short-sighted, myopic; *~stof* nitrogen

stil (w) (ge-) calm, soothe, allay, satisfy; *honger ~*, appease hunger; (b, bw) ([-le] -ler, -ste) quiet, calm, peaceful; *~bly* (-ge-) remain silent, keep quiet

stil'hou (-ge-) stop, pull up

stil: *~letjies* quietly, on the sly, secretly; *~lewe* (-ns) still life; *~stand* truce, cessation, standstill; *tot ~stand kom*, come to a stop; *~swye*, silence; *die ~swye bewaar*, keep silent

stilswy'end (-e) quiet, silent

stil'te quietness, calm, silence; *die ~ voor die storm*, the lull before the storm

stimuleer' (ge-) stimulate

sting'el (-s) stalk, stem

stink (w) (ge-) stink, reek; (b) stinking

stip[1] (s) (-pe) spot, dot, speck

stip[2] (b, bw) (-te; -ter, -ste) strict; punctual; *~te betaling*, prompt payment

stip'pel (s) (-s) spot, dot, speck; (w) (ge-) spot, dot; **~streep** (..strepe) dotted/broken line (traffic)

stip'telik (-e) punctually, promptly

stoei (ge-) wrestle; romp; **~er** (-s) wrestler; **~kryt** (-e) wrestling ring; wrestling arena; **~promotor** (-s) wrestling promotor

stoel (s) (-e) chair, seat, stool

stoep (-e) stoep; patio

stoer (-e) powerful, brave, sturdy, staunch

stoet[1] (-e) procession; retinue, train

stoet[2] (-e) stud; **~beeste** stud/pedigree cattle; **~ery** (-e) stud farm

stof[1] (stowwe) material, matter, stuff

stof[2] (stowwe) dust, powder; *loop dat die ~ staan/trek,* run like the wind

stoffeer' (~, ge-) furnish, upholster; **~der** (-s) upholsterer

stof'fer (-s) duster

stof: **~lik** (-e) mortal, material; *~like oorskot,* mortal remains; **~suier** (-s) vacuum cleaner

stok (-ke) stick, cane, staff; **~doof** (..dowe) stone-deaf

sto'ker (-s) stoker, fireman; distiller

stok: **~kie** (-s) little stick; **~kies draai,** play truant; *'n ~kie voor iets steek,* put an end to something; **~kie'lekker** (-s) lollipop; **~kiesdraaier** (-s) truant; **~oud** (..oue) very old, hoary with age; **~perdjie** (-s) hobby; fad; **~sielalleen** all alone; **~styf** (..stywe) stiff as a poker

stol (ge-) congeal, coagulate; freeze (TV image)

stolp (-e) bell glass

stom [-me] dumb, mute; stupid; *die ~me diere,* the poor animals; *~ van verbasing,* in blank amazement

stommiteit' (-e) stupid thing, blunder

stomp (b) (-er, -ste) blunt, dull, obtuse

stom'pie (-s) cigarette end, fag-end, stub

stonk (ge-) stump (cricket)

stoof (s) (stowe) stove, range; (w) (ge-) warm, stew, braise, simmer

stook (ge-) stoke, distil; pick (teeth); *kwaad ~,* stir up strife; instigate; **~ketel** (-s) still

stoom (s) steam; (w) (ge-) steam; **~boot** (..bote) steamship; **~ketel** (-s) boiler

stoor (w) (ge-) disturb, interrupt; store (away); **~nis = steurnis;** (s) (store) storeroom

stoot (s) (stote) stab; gore, poke; push; (w) (ge-) poke, butt; push; thrust, jostle; **~karretjie** (-s) handcart, pushcart; **~skraper** bulldozer

stop[1] (s) (-pe) pipe-fill; (w) (ge-) darn; fill; *iem. 'n fooitjie in die hand ~,* slip a tip into someone's hand

stop[2] (w) (ge-) stop, halt

stop'horlosie, stop'oorlosie (-s) stopwatch

stop'pel (-s) stubble

stop'sel (-s) filling (pipe; tooth)

stop'straat (..strate) stop street

stop: **~verf** putty; **~woord** (-e) expletive

sto'rie (-s) story, tale

storm (s) (-s) storm, tempest; (w) (ge-) attack, storm

stormag'tig (-e; -er, -ste) stormy, tempestuous, tumultuous

storm: **~jaer** (-s) dumpling; doughnut; assailant; **~loop** (s) (..lope) rush, onslaught; (w) (ge-) attack, rush at; **~wind** (-e) gale, hurricane

stort (ge-) pour, spill, shed; deposit; (take a) shower; *trane ~,* shed tears; *in die verderf ~,* dash to ruin; **~bad** (..baddens) shower bath; **~ing** (-e, -s) payment, deposit; shedding; *geen ~ing,* no dumping; **~reën** (s) (-s) heavy shower, downpour; (w) (ge-) come down in torrents

stot'ter (ge-) stutter

stout ([-e]; -er, -ste) naughty; bold, brave; *die ~e skoene aantrek,* take a bold step

stow'werig (-e; -er, -ste) dusty

straal (s) (strale) beam, ray; radius (circle); jet, spurt (water); (w) (ge-) beam, radiate; **~draal** jetlag; **~jaer** (-s), **~vegter** (-s) jet fighter; **~jakker** (-s) jetsetter; **~laag** radial ply (tyres); **~tam** (suffering from) jetlag; **~vliegtuig** (..tuie) jet aircraft/plane

straat (s) (strate) street; strait; (w) (ge-) pave; **~boewery** hooliganism, gangsterism; **~geweld** (street) violence; **~vlinder** (-s) streetwalker (prostitute); streetgirl; **~vrou** (-e) prostitute

straf[1] (s) (strawwe) punishment, penalty; (w) (ge-) punish

straf[2] (b) (strawwe; strawwer, -ste) severe, sharp, rigid, stern; *strawwe droogte,* severe drought straf: ~baar (..bare) punishable; ~bare manslag, culpable homicide, manslaughter; ~skop (-pe) penalty kick, free kick; ~werk punishment, detention work

strak ([-ke]; -ker, -ste) tight, taut, stiff, set

straks perhaps

strak'kies presently

stra'lend (-e) beaming, radiant; ~ van geluk, radiant with happiness

stra'ler (-s) jet (of engine); jet (plane); jetliner; ~jakker (-s) jetsetter; ~kliek jetset

stram (-mer, -ste) stiff, hard, rigid

strand (-e) beach, shore, seaside; (w) (ge-) strand, run ashore

strand'jut (-te) brown hyena; beachcomber (fig.)

strand: ~meer (..mere) lagoon; ~oord (-e) seaside resort; ~wag (-te) lifesaver, lifeguard

strategie' strategy

streef, strewe (ge-) strive, endeavour

streek (streke) district, region; line; tract; artifice, trick; ~nuus regional news; ~spraak (..sprake) dialect

streel (ge-) caress, stroke; flatter

streep (s) (strepe) line, stroke; dash; (w) (ge-) streak, line; hit; ~suiker thrashing, strap oil

strek (ge-) stretch, extend, reach; dit ~ jou tot eer, it does you credit; ~king (-e, -s) tendency, tenor, drift; moral

stre'lend (-e) pleasant, soothing; flattering

strem (ge-) congeal, curdle; inhibit, hinder

streng ([-e]; -er, -ste) strict, stern, rigorous

strignien', strigni'ne strychnine

strik[1] (s) (-ke) bow

strik[2] (s) (-ke) trap, snare

strik[3] (b) (-te; -ter, -ste) strict; accurate, exact

strik'das (-se) bow tie

strik'vraag (..vrae) tricky question, twister, poser

string (-e) string; trace, skein, strand

stroef (stroewe; stroewer, -ste) gruff, harsh

stro'fe (-s) stanza, verse; strophe

stro'kies: ~film (-s) strip film; ~prent (-e), ~verhaal (..hale) comic (strip)

strom'pel (ge-) stumble along, hobble

stronk (-e) stalk; cob (mealie)

stront shit, dung; rotter

strooi[1] (s) straw

strooi[2] (w) (ge-) distribute, scatter; strew

strooi'biljet (-te) handbill; pamphlet

strooi: ~dakhuis (-e) house with thatched roof

strooi: ~jonker (-s) bestman; ~meisie (-s) bridesmaid

strooihuis (-e) straw hut

strook (s) (stroke) strip; flounce, fillet; band; (w) (ge-) agree, tally

stroom (s) (strome) stream, current; (w) (ge-) flow, stream

stroop[1] (s) syrup; treacle, molasses

stroop[2] (s) love (in tennis)

stroop[3] (w) (ge-) pillage, plunder; rustle (cattle); ~tog (-te) raid, invasion

strop (s) (-pe) strap, halter, rope; strop

stro'per (-s) poacher (of game); plunderer; harvester, combine

strot (-te) throat; ~te'hoof (-de) larynx

struik (-e) bush, shrub

strui'kel (ge-) stumble; ~blok (-ke) stumbling block, obstacle

struik: ~gewas (-se) shrubs, shrubbery, undergrowth; brush; ~rower (-s) highwayman

stru'weling (-e, -s) dispute, wrangle

stry (ge-) dispute, contradict, argue

stryd fight, strife, struggle, conflict, combat; ~byl hatchet; die ~byl begrawe, bury the hatchet, make peace; ~dag (..dae) party rally

stry'der (-s) warrior, fighter, combatant

stryd'kreet (..krete) warcry, slogan

stryd'vraag (..vrae) question at issue, point in dispute, moot point

stryk[1] (s) stroke; pace (of horse); op ~ kom, get into form; van ~ wees, be out of form; (w) walk, stride; ~er (-s) fiddler; streaker

stryk[2] (ge-) iron (clothes); smooth; stroke; strike (flag)

stryk: ~orkes (-te) stringed orchestra; ~stok (-ke) fiddle stick; bow

stryk'yster (-s) flat iron

stu (ge-) push, propel; prop, stow; ~dam (-me) weir, barrage

studeer' (~, ge-) study; ~ vir onderwyser, study to become a teacher; ~kamer (-s) study

student' (-e) student

studen'te: ~**blad** (..**blaaie**) students' magazine; ~**raad** (..**rade**) students' (representative) council

stu'die (-s) study; ~**beurs** (-e) scholarship, bursary; ~**fonds** (-e) scholarship fund

stug ([-ge]; -**ger**, -**ste**) stubborn, surly, sullen, obstinate

stuif (**stuiwe**) (ge-) make dust; drizzle; ~**meel** pollen; ~**sand** drift sand

stui'pe convulsions; *die ~ kry*, be violently upset, become livid with anger

stuit (ge-) stop, check; offend

stui'tjie (-s) rump, tailbone; pope's nose (fowl)

stuk (-ke) piece, fragment, oddment; document; play, part

stuk'kend (-e; -er, -ste) broken, torn

stuk'kie (-s) small piece, bit, morsel

stut (s) (-te) support, prop; shore; sprag, truss; (w) (ge-) support, prop; ~**muur** (..**mure**) retaining wall; ~**prys** support price

stuur (s) (**sture**) steering gear, rudder, helm (ship); handle; (w) (ge-) send; steer; *in die war ~ (bring)*, throw into confusion; ~**boord** starboard; ~**kajuit** (-e) cockpit; ~**man** (-ne, ..**lui**) helmsman, chief mate; pilot; ~**outomaat** (..**mate**) automatic pilot

stuurs ([-e]; -**er**, -**ste**) surly, sulky, sullen

stuur'wiel (-e) steering wheel

stuwadoor' (-s, ..**dore**) stevedoor

styf (w) (ge-) = **stywe**; (b) (**stywe**; **stywer**, -**ste**) stiff, tight; rigid, formal

styfkop'pig (-e; -er, -ste) obstinate, headstrong

styg (ge-) ascend, mount, climb, rise; ~**baan** (..**bane**) runway, *ook* **aanloopbaan**; ~**ing** (-e, -s) rise; increase; ascension; ~**spekulant** (-e) bull (stock exchange)

styl style, manner; (-e) doorpost, bedpost

sty'sel starch

subjektief' (..**tiewe**) subjective

subjunktief' (..**tiewe**) subjunctive

sub'komitee (-s) subcommittee

subliem' (-e; -er, -ste) sublime

subsi'die (-s) subsidy, grant-in-aid

subskrip'sie (-s) subscription

subtiel' (-e; -er, -ste) subtle

sub'tropies (-e) subtropical

suf (w) (ge-) dote; (b) ([**suwwe**] **suwwer**, -**ste**) dull, stupid, beef-witted

sug (s) (-te) sigh; passion, lust; *'n ~ slaak (van verligting)*, heave a sigh (of relief); (w) (ge-) sigh

sugges'tie (-s) suggestion

suid south

Suid-A'frika South Africa (SA)

sui'de south; *na die ~*, to(wards) the south; *ten ~ van*, south of; ~**lik** (-e) southern, southerly; ~*like halfrond*, Southern hemisphere

Sui'der-A'frika Southern Africa

sui'derbreedte south latitude

Sui'derkruis Southern Cross

sui'dewind (-e) south wind

suid'kus (-te) south coast

suidoos' (te) south-east

Suidwes'-Afrika South West Africa (SWA)

suidwes'telik (-e) south-westerly

sui'er (-s) piston; sucker; off-shoot, sprout

suig (ge-) absorb; suck, suckle

sui'ker (s) (-s) sugar; (w) (ge-) sugar, sweeten; ~**bedryf** sugar industry; ~**klontjie** (-s) lump of sugar; ~**oompie** sugardaddy; ~**riet** (-e) sugar cane; ~**siekte** diabetes

suil (-e) column, pillar, obelisk

sui'nig (-e; -er, -ste) sparing, stingy; frugal

suip (ge-) drink (animals); booze, tope; ~**lap** (-pe) toper, tippler; boozer

suis (ge-) rustle, buzz, sough

sui'te (uitspr. *swiete*), suite (rooms, offices)

sui'wel butter and cheese, dairy products

sui'wer (w) (ge-) purify, refine, cleanse; purge; (b) (-der, -ste) pure (gold); clean (hands), sheer (nonsense)

suk'kel (ge-) progress poorly; languish; trudge along; annoy someone; *hy ~ met sy gesondheid*, he is in indifferent health; ~-~, struggling all along; ~**aar** (-s) bungler, stick-in-the-mud

sukses' (-se) success; *ek wens jou ~!* good luck to you!; ~**jag** ratrace

sukses'vol (-le; -ler, -ste) successful

sulfaat' (..**fate**) sulphate

sul'ke such; *~ domkoppe!* such fools!

sult brawn

summier' (-e) summary, without formalities; *~e ontslag*, summary/instant dismissal

superintendent' (-e) superintendent

superlatief' (..**tiewe**) superlative

su'permark (-te) supermarket

superso'nies (-e) supersonic

su'ring sorrel

sur'plus (-se) surplus, excess, *ook* **oorskot**

sus (w) (ge-) hush, quiet (a child); pacify; soothe; *sy gewete ~,* silence/salve his conscience

suspi'sie suspicion, *ook* **agterdog**

sus'sie (-s) little sister

sus'ter (-s) sister; **~lik** (-e) sisterly

suur (s) (sure) acid; (b) (-der, -ste) sour, acid, acetous, tart; **~deeg** yeast, leaven; **~knol** (-le) sourpuss; **~lemoensap** lemon juice; *daar loop ~lemoensap deur,* there is something fishy about it; **~stof** oxygen

suut'jies = soetjies

swaai (s) (-e) swing; (w) (ge-) swing; wave

swaan (swane) swan

swaap (swape) blockhead, fool, clot, idiot

swaar (-der, -ste) heavy, ponderous; difficult, arduous

swaard (-e) sword, rapier

swaar'gewig heavyweight (boxer)

swaarly'wig (-e; -er, -ste) corpulent, obese

swaarmoe'dig (-e; -er, -ste) melancholy, dejected, depressed

swaar'te weight, heaviness; **~krag** gravitation, gravity; **~punt** centre of gravity

swa'el[1] (s) sulphur

swa'el[2] (s) (-s) swallow (bird)

swa'el[3] (w) (ge-) drink, booze; *hy was lekker ge~,* he had one too many

swa'elsuur, swa'welsuur sulphuric acid

swa'eltjie (-s) swallow

swa'er (-s) brother-in-law

swak (s) weakness; (b) (-ker, -ste) weak, infirm, delicate, feeble, faint; **~ke'ling** (-e) weakling

swaksin'nig (-e) mentally deficient, feebleminded; **~e** (-s) mentally deficient person, imbecile

swak'te weakness, feebleness

swam (-me) fungus, agaric

swa'nesang (-e) swan song, death song

swang vogue; *in ~ wees,* be in fashion

swan'ger pregnant; **~skap** pregnancy

swart (s) black; (b) (-er, -ste) black

swartgal'lig (-e; -er, -ste) melancholy, morose; **~heid** melancholy, moroseness

swartwit'pens (-e) sable antelope

swa'(w)el = swael; **~suur** sulphuric acid

sweef, swe'we (ge-) hover, float, soar, glide; **~stok** trapeze; **~tuig** (..tuie) glider

sweem semblance, shadow, trace; *sonder 'n ~ (sweempie) van angs,* without the least trace of anxiety

sweep (swepe) whip, lash

sweer[1] (s) (swere) abscess, sore, boil; ulcer, *kyk* **maagseer;** (w) (ge-) fester, ulcerate

sweer[2] (w) (ge-) vow; swear, take an oath; *hoog en laag ~,* swear by all that is holy; *vals ~,* commit perjury

sweet (s) perspiration; (w) (ge-) perspire, sweat; **~pak** (-ke) tracksuit

sweis (ge-) weld; **~er** (-s) welder

swel (ge-) swell, expand

swelg (ge-) swallow, gorge, swill

swem (ge-) swim; *gaan ~,* go for a swim; **~bad** (-dens) swimming bath; pool; **~duik** skindiving, findiving; **~mer** (-s) swimmer; **~pak** (-ke) swimming costume

swen'del (s) gross fraud, swindling; (w) (ge-) swindle; **~aar** (-s) swindler, racketeer

swenk (ge-) swerve, wheel; *regs !* right wheel!

swerf, swerwe (ge-) roam, wander, rove

swerm (-s) swarm, flock, throng; (w) (ge-) swarm, cluster

swer'noot (..note) rascal, rogue

swer'wer (-s) wanderer, vagabond, rover, tramp; **~s'drang** (-e) wanderlust, roaming spirit

swets (ge-) brag, boast, swear

swetterjoel' (-e) crowd, caboodle, lot

swier (s) elegance, gracefulness; swagger; (w) (ge-) loaf, be on the spree; **~bol** (-le) rake, wild spark; playboy, *ook* **pierewaaier**

swig (ge-) yield, give in

swik (ge-) sprain, twist

swoeg (ge-) drudge, toil and moil

swoel (-er, -ste) sultry, close, oppressive

swoerd crackling

swyg (w) (ge-) be silent, keep quiet/mum

swyn (-e) hog, pig, swine; *pêrels voor die ~e werp/gooi,* cast pearls before (the) swine

sy[1] (s) silk; *~ dra ~,* she wears silk

sy[2] (s) (-e) side; *met die hande in die ~e,* with arms akimbo; *~ ~ is seer,* his side is aching

sy³ (pers. vnw) she; (besit. vnw) its, his
sy'fer¹ (s) (-s) figure, number; par, bogey (golf); **~oorlosie** (-s) digital watch
sy'fer² (w) (ge-) ooze (through); **~put** (-te) French drain
syg (ge-) strain, percolate, filter
syn being

sy'ne his, 's; *dis Piet ~ (s'n)*, that is Peter's; *dis ~*, that is his
sy'paadjie (-s) sidewalk, pavement
sy'pel (ge-) seep, drain; **~put** (-te), **~riool** (..riole), **~tenk** (-e) French drain
sy'sie (-s) seed eater, siskin
sy'wurm (-s) silkworm

T

't: *aan ~ speel,* playing; *as ~ ware (as= ware),* as it were
T-aansluiting T-junction
taai (-e; -er, -ste) tough, wiry, stringy; sticky; *so ~ soos 'n ratel,* as tough as nails; *~ wedstryd,* hard/tough match; **~pitperske** (-s) clingstone peach
taak (take) task, job, duty; assignment; **~= mag** (-te) task force
taal (tale) language, speech; **~kunde** grammar; linguistics
taalkun'dig (-e) grammatical, linguistic; **~e** (-s) linguist, philologist
taal: **~laboratorium** (-s) language labora= tory; **~onderwyser** (-s) language teacher; **~skat** vocabulary (of a language)
taam'lik (b) (-e) fair, tolerable; (bw) rather, fairly; *~ goed,* fairly good
taan tan (colour)
tabak' tobacco; **~boetiek** (-e) tobacconist's shop, smoker's emporium; **~sak** (-ke) tobacco pouch
tab'berd (-s) gown, dress, frock
tabel' (-le) table; index
taberna'kel (-s) tabernacle
tablet' (-te) tablet, lozenge
tablo' (-s) tableau
taboe' taboo
tabuleer', tabelleer' (ge-) tabulate
ta'fel (-s) table; index
ta'fel: **~geld** service charge (restaurant); **~heer** master of ceremonies; **~rede** (-s) after-dinner speech; **~tennis** ping-pong, table tennis
tafereel' (..rele) scene, picture, description
tag'tig eighty; *die jare T~,* the Eighties; *~er jare,* in/during the eighties
tag'tigjarige (-s) octogenarian
tag'tigste (-s) eightieth
tak (-ke) branch, bough; tine (antler); *van die hak op die ~ spring,* jump from one

subject to another; *hoog in die ~ke wees,* be three sheets in the wind
ta'kel (s) (-s) tackle; (w) (ge-) maul; rig; knock about, confront; **~aar** (-s) rigger
tak'haar (..hare) backvelder
tak'kantoor (..tore) branch office
taks estimate, rate, share; *Jan Taks,* Re= ceiver of Revenue
takseer' (~, ge-) estimate, value, appraise
takt tact; *~ gebruik,* exercise tact
taktiek' tactics
takt'vol (-le; -ler, -ste) tactful, judicious, discreet
tal (-le) number
talent' (-e) talent, natural gift, ability; *met sy ~e woeker,* not bury one's light be= neath a bushel; **~vol** (-le; -ler, -ste) talented, gifted
talm (ge-) linger, loiter, dawdle; **~lont** (-e) delayed-action fuse
tal'ryk (-e; -er, -ste) numerous
tam (-mer, -ste) tired, exhausted
tamaai' (-er, -ste) huge, colossal, giant, enormous
tama'tie (-s) tomato; **~pruim** (-e) persim= mon; **~slaai** tomato salad
tamboer' (e) drum, tambour; **~nooi** (-ens) drum majorette, *ook* **trompoppie**
tand (-e) tooth; cog; tine; **~arts** (-e) dentist, dental surgeon
tan'de: **~borsel** (-s) toothbrush; **~pasta** toothpaste; **~vlos** dental floss, *ook* **tandegare**
tand: **~rat** (-te) cogwheel; **~vleis** gum; **~ vulling** (-e, -s) stopping, filling, plugging
tang (-e) (pair of) tongs, pincers, forceps, pliers; virago, shrew; low-class fellow
tan'nie (-s) auntie
tans now, at present; *~ van Pretoria,* pre= sently living in Pretoria

tant aunt (when followed by proper name); *Liewe ~ Hester,* Dear aunt Hester

tan'te (-s) aunt

tap (s) (-pe) tap (of a barrel); tenon (mor= tise); bung, spigot (hole); (w) (ge-) tap, draw

tapisserie' tapestry

tap'per (-s) barman; ~y (-e) beerhall, can= teen; pub

taps tapered; ~*e groef,* tapered groove

tap'toe tattoo (mil.); last post

tapyt' (-e) carpet, tapestry

tarentaal' (..tale) guinea fowl

tarief' (tariewe) tariff

tar'ra tare (weight)

tart (ge-) taunt, provoke, challenge, defy

tas[1] (s) (-se) bag; pouch; wallet

tas[2] (w) (ge-) feel, touch, grope; *in die duister ~,* grope in the dark

tas'baar (..bare; -der, -ste) tangible, tactual, palpable; *tasbare bewys,* tangible token/ proof

ta'ter (-s) scoundrel, villian

tatoeëer' (ge-) tat(t)oo

ta'xi (-'s) taxi

te (bw) too; ~ *sleg,* too bad; (vs) to, at, on, in; ~ *huur,* to let; ~ *perd,* on horseback; ~ *alle tye,* at all times

tea'ter (-s) theatre

tech'nikon (-ne, -s) technikon

tee tea

te'ë against; tired of

teef (tewe) bitch

te'ëhanger (-s) contrast, match, counter= part, opposite number

te'ël (-s) tile

teel (ge-) breed, rear, raise (animals); beget

tee'lepel (-s) teaspoon

teen against, to, towards, versus

teen': ~**aanval** (-le) counterattack; ~**deel** contrary; *die ~deel is waar,* the contrary is true; ~**insurgensie,** ~**inspeling** count= erinsurgence/infiltration; ~**maatreël** (-s) countermeasure; ~**middel** (-s) antidote, remedy; ~**offensief** counteroffensive

teenoor'gestel(d) (-de) opposite, contrary

teen: ~**produktief** counterproductive; ~ ~ **reaksie** backlash; ~**spoed** (-e) adversity, ill-fortune, ill-luck; breakdown; ~**spoed= wa** breakdown van

teen: ~**staan** (-ge-) resist, withstand; ~ ~ **stand** resistance, opposition; ~**stand bied,**

offer resistance; ~**stander** (-s) adversary, opponent

teen'stelling (-e, -s) contrast, set-off; *in ~ met sy broer,* unlike his brother

teen: ~**stem** (-ge-) vote against; (s) dissent= ing/negative vote; ~**stribbel** (-ge-) kick against, resent

teenstry'dig (-e) contradictory, conflicting

teenswoor'dig (-e) nowadays, at present; *kos is ~ baie duur,* food these days is most expensive

teen'verkeer approaching/oncoming traffic

teenwoor'dig (-e) present; *veertien lede is ~ (aanwesig),* there are fourteen members present; ~*e tyd,* present tense; ~**heid** presence; ~**heid van gees,** presence of mind

te'ëpraat (-ge-) contradict

teer[1] (s) tar; (w) (ge-) tar; *iem. ~ en veer,* tar and feather someone

teer[2] (w) (ge-) consume, live on, sponge on; *op sy roem ~,* rest on his laurels

teer[3] (b) (-der, -ste) tender; slender; delicate; *'n ~ punt,* a sore point

teer: ~**pad** (..paaie) tarred road; ~**straat** (..strate) tarred/asphalt street

tee: ~**servies** (-e) tea service; ~**siffie** (-s) tea strainer

te'ësin aversion, dislike; ~ *hê in,* have an aversion to

te'ëspoed = teenspoed

te'ëvoeter (-s) antipode; opposite (of)

tef teff

tegelyk' together, at the same time; *almal ~,* all together; ~**ertyd** simultaneously, concurrently

tegemoet'kom (-gekom) meet halfway; ~**ing** (-e, -s) meeting halfway; partial compensation; willingness to accom= modate

tegniek' technique

teg'nies (-e) technical; ~*e benaminge/ter= me,* technical terms

teg'nikus (-se) technician

tegnologie' technology

tegnolo'gies (-e) technologic(al)

tehuis' (-e) hostel, home; ~ *vir bejaardes,* old-aged home, home for senior citizens

tei'ken (-s) target

teis'ter (ge-) afflict, ravage, scourge

te'ken (s) (-s) sign; token; signal; mark; symptom; (w) (ge-) sign; draw; ~**aar** (-s) draftsman, designer; **~ing** (-e, -s) signature; drawing, sketch

tek'kie (-s) (pair of) tackies

tekort' (-s) deficit, shortage; *'n ~ aan mielies,* a shortage of maize; **~koming** (-e, -s) shortcoming, imperfection

teks (-te) text, context, book

tekstiel': **~goedere** soft goods; **~nywerheid, ~bedryf** textile industry

teks'verwerker (-s) word processor

tel (s) count; **~bord** (-e) scoreboard

telefoneer' (~, ge-) telephone

telefonis' (-te) telephone operator

telefoon' (..fone) telephone; **~gids** (-e) telephone directory; **~nommer** (-s) telephone number; **~oproep** (-e) telephone call; **~sentrale** (-s) telephone exchange

telegraaf' (..grawe) telegraph

telegrafeer' (ge-) wire, telegraph

telegram' (..me) telegram, wire

telekommunika'sie telecommunication

te'leks (s) (-e) telex, ticker; (w) (ge-) teleks

telepatie' telepathy

teleskoop' (..skope) telescope

teleur'gestel(d) (-de) disappointed

teleur'stel (-gestel) disappoint, baffle; **~ling** (-e, -s) disappointment

televi'sie television

tel'kens every time, ever and anon; ~ *as,* whenever

tel'ler (-s) counter; scorer; teller (bank); numerator

tel'ling (-e, -s) census; numeration, counting; score (games)

tel'raam (..rame) abacus, ball frame

tel'woord (-e) numeral

tem (ge-) tame, break in, subdue

te'ma (-s) theme, subject

tem'pel (-s) temple

temperament' (-e) temperament, temper; **~eel** (..ele) temperamental

temperatuur' (..ture) temperature

tem'po (-'s) tempo, pace, rate; *die ~ versnel,* quicken the pace

ten at, in; ~ *behoewe van,* in aid of; ~ *einde (aflewering te bespoedig),* in order to (expedite delivery); ~ *opsigte van,* with respect to; ~ *spyte van,* in spite of

ten'der (s) (-s) tender; (w) (ge-) tender

tenk (-e, -s) tank

ten'nis tennis; **~baan** (..bane) tennis court; **~bal** (-le) tennis ball; **~speler** (-s) tennis player

tenoor' (tenore) tenor

tensy' unless

tent (-e) tent; hood; ~ *opslaan,* pitch tent

tentoon'stelling (-s) show, exhibition, *ook* skou

teolo'gies (-e) theological; *~e skool,* theological seminary

teore'ties (-e) theoretical

teorie' (-ë) theory

te'pel (-s) nipple, teat

ter at, to, in; ~ *sake,* to the point; ~ *wille van,* for the sake of

teraar'debestelling (-e, -s) interment, burial

terapie' therapy

terapeut' (-e) therapist

terde'ë thoroughly, duly

tereg' rightly, justly, in good reason; **~stel** (-ge-) execute; **~stelling** execution

ter'g(e) (ge-) tease, annoy, nag

terg: **~gees** (-te) nagging fellow, tormentor, tease: **~siek** (-e) fond of teasing

te'ring consumption (phthisis, tuberculosis, pneumoconiosis, silicosis)

terloops' (s) (-e) casual, incidental; (bw) by the way, incidentally; ~, *wat doen ons môre?* by the way, what are our plans for tomorrow?

term (-e) term; *nuwe ~e vir,* new terms/ names for

termiet' (-e) termite

terminaal' (..ale) terminal; *..ale pasiënte,* terminal patients

terminologie' nomenclature, terminology

ter'minus (-se, ..ni) terminus

ter'mometer (-s) thermometer

termyn' (-e) term, time, period; *binne die vasgestelde ~,* within the appointed time; **~reses** midterm break

terneer'druk (-ge-) depress

ternou'erdood scarcely, hardly

terpentyn' turpentine, oil of terebinth

terras' (-se) terrace

terrein' (-e) building site; ground; sphere, domain; area

terreur' terrorism

terroris' (-te) terrorist

terroris'me terrorism

terset' (-te) terzetto (mus.)

tersiêr (-e) tertiary; ~*e onderwys,* tertiary education

tersi'ne (-s) tercet, terza rima

tert (-e) tart; ~**pan** (-ne) tart pan

terug' back, backwards; *heen en* ~, there and back

terug: ~**gaan** (-ge-) go back, retrace; ~**gee** (-ge-) return, restore, give back

terug: ~**keer** (s) return; (w) (-ge-) return; ~**kom** (-ge-) come back; return; *op 'n saak* ~*kom,* revert to a matter; ~**reis** (s) return journey

terug'slag (..slae) recoil; setback, reverse

terug: ~**trek** (-ge-) retreat, withdraw, retract, pull back; ~**voer(ing)** feedback; ~**werkend** (-e): ~*werkend van,* retrospective from

terwyl' while, as

tes (-se) earthern firepot; chafing dish

tesaam', tesa'me together

te'sis (-se) thesis

tesourie' treasury; ~**r'** (-e, -s) treasurer

testament' (-e) testament, will

testateur' (-e, -s) testator

testatri'se (-s) testatrix

te'tanus tetanus

teu'el (-s) bridle, rein

tevergeefs' in vain

tevo're before, previously

tevre'de (-ner, -nste; meer ~, mees~) satisfied, content(ed); ~ *stel,* satisfy, please; ~*n'heid* contentment, satisfaction

tie'mie thyme

tien (-e) ten; ~**de** (-s) tenth; ~*des betaal,* pay tithes; ~**delig** (-e) decimal; ~**er** (-s), ~**derjarige** (-s) teenager; ~**er'drag** teenage dress/clothes; ~**kamp** decathlon; ~**kegelbaan** ten-pin (bowling) alley; ~**tal** (-le) ten, decade; ~**uur** ten o'clock; ~**voud** tenfold

tier[1] (s) (-e, -s) tiger; SA leopard

tier[2] (w) (-ge-) thrive, flourish; rage

tierlantyn'tjie (-s) flourish, trifle, knickknack

tier: ~**melk** strong drink; *hy het* ~*melk gedrink, hy is ge*~, he is intoxicated; ~**wyfie** (-s) tigress; *so kwaai soos 'n* ~*wyfie,* a veritable shrew

tifoon' (tifone) typhoon

ti'fus typhus fever, camp fever

tik (s) (-ke) pat, touch, rap; (w) (-ge-) tap, rap; type; *van lotjie ge*~ *wees,* have a

screw loose; *op die vingers* ~, reprimand; ~**masjien** (-e) typewriter; ~**skrif** typing, typewritng; ~**poel** typing pool; ~**ster** (-s) lady typist

tim'mer (ge-) build, construct

tim'mer: ~**hout** timber; ~**man** (-ne, -s) carpenter

tin tin, pewter; ~**erts** tin ore

tin'gel (ge-) tinkle, jingle

tin'ger (-der, -ste) slender, frail, delicate

tinktin'kie (-s) (Cape) wren warbler

tint (-e) tinge, hue, tint

tin'tel (ge-) twinkle, sparkle; ~**ing** (-e, -s) twinkling, sparkling

tip (-pe) tip, point

ti'pe (-s) type, character

tipeer' (~, ge-) typify

ti'pies (-e) typical

tiran' (-ne) tyrant

ti'tel (-s) title, heading; ~**rol** (-le) title role; title part

tja'lie (-s) shawl, wrap

tjank (ge-) yelp, howl; ~**balie** (-s) crybaby

tjek (-s) cheque; *gekruiste* ~, crossed cheque; ~**boek** (-e) cheque book

tjel'lo (-'s) (violin) cello

tjienkerientjee' (-s) chinkerinchee

tjoep'stil very quiet, absolutely silent

tjok'ker(tjie) young chappie

tjom, tjommie chum, pal

tjops chops (meat)

tjop-tjop in no time, in a jiffy

tjor(rie) jalopy, old/dated motorcar

tjor'lapper (-s) backyard mechanic

toe[1] (b) closed; dumb, stupid; *die winkels is* ~, the shops are closed; *hy is darem* ~, isn't he stupid?

toe[2] (bw) then; in those days; *van* ~ *af,* since then

toe[3] (bw) to, towards; *sleg daaraan* ~ *wees,* be badly off

toe[4] (vgw) when; while; *hy het eers gewerk,* ~ *het hy gaan swem,* first he worked, then he went for a swim; ~ *ek daar kom, was hy in die bed,* when I got there he was in bed

toe[5] (tw) do! please! ~ *maar!* never mind! *help my,* ~? won't you please help me?

toe'behore (s) belongings, accessories; adjuncts, fittings

toe: ~**'broodjie** (-s) sandwich; ~**'doen** assistance, aid; *buite my* ~*doen,* through no fault of mine; **~draaipapier** wrapping paper

toe'drag particulars, circumstances; *ware ~ van die sake,* the ins and outs of the affair

toe'gang entrance, admission, access

toegank'lik (-e; -er, -ste) accessible

toe'geeteken (-s) yield sign

toe'geneë (meer ~, mees ~) kindly disposed, affectionate; *jou ~ vriend,* yours sincerely/affectionately

toe'gepas (-te) applied; *~te wiskunde,* applied mathematics

toe'gewing concession

toe'gif (-te) extra, bonus, additional allowances; encore

toe'hoorder (-s) hearer

toe'juig (-ge-) cheer, applaud, approve; **~ing** applause, cheer

toe'ka very remote; *van ~ se dae (af),* from time immemorial; **~motor, ~kar** vintage/veteran car

toe'keer turn to; *iem. die rug ~,* turn one's back upon someone

toe'ken (-ge-) award; allot; **~ning** (-e, -s) grant, award; allotment

toeko'mend (-e) next, future; *~e tyd,* future tense

toe'koms future; *in die ~,* in future

toekoms'tig (-e) future

toe'kring-TV closed-circuit TV, *kyk* **kringtelevisie**

toe: **~laag** (..lae), **~lae** (-s) gratification, subsidy, bonus, allowance; **~laat** (-ge-) admit, permit, allow

toe'lating admission, admittance, permission; **~(s)eksamen** (-s) entrance examination

toe'lig (-ge-) illustrate, elucidate, explain; *iets nader ~,* explain something more fully

toe'nader (-ge-) approach, strive to reconcile; **~ing** friendly advance, rapprochement; *~ing soek,* make friendly overtures

toe'name increase

toe'neem (-ge-) increase, progress; become worse; *toenemende belangstelling,* growing interest

toen'tertyd then

toe'pas (-ge-) apply to, put into practice

toepas'lik (-e; -er, -ste) suitable, appropriate, fitting, applicable

toer (s) (-e) tour, excursion, walk; trick; (ge-) tour, travel; **~bus** (-se) motor coach

toe'reteller (-s) rev(olutions) counter

toeris' (-te) tourist; **~me** tourism

toernooi' (-e) tournament

toe'rus (-ge-) equip, fit out; **~ting** equipment, outfit

toe'sig supervision; surveillance; care; *~ hou,* supervise; invigilate; **~houer** (-s) invigilator (exam.), supervisor (factory)

toe: **~skouer** (-s) spectator, onlooker; **~skryf, ~skrywe** (-ge-) ascribe to, attribute; **~sluit** (-ge-) lock up, close

toe'spits: *~ op,* concentrate on

toe'spraak (..sprake) address, speech; *'n ~ lewer/hou,* deliver a speech; *'n ~ klok,* time someone's speech

toe: **~spreek** (-ge-) address; **~staan** (-ge-) allow, permit, grant

toe'stand (-e) state, condition, circumstances

toe'stel (-le) apparatus, appliance, device

toe'stem (-ge-) grant, consent, agree; **~ming** consent, permission, approval

toet (w) (ge-) blow a horn, hoot

toe'ter (s) (-s) horn, hooter; (w) (ge-) hoot

toets (s) (-e) key (piano); test; trial; assay (minerals); *'n ~ deurstaan,* stand the test; (w) (ge-) test, try; **~ling** (-e) testee; **~rit** (-te) trial run; **~saak** (..sake) test case; **~steen** (..stene) touchstone; **~vlug** (-te) test flight; **~wedstryd** (-e) test match

toe'val[1] (s) accident, chance, coincidence; *blote ~,* (mere) coincidence; *by ~,* by chance

toe'val[2] (s) (-le) fainting fit

toe'val[3] (w) (-ge-) fall to the lot of; become closed by falling; cave in

toe'val[4] (w) (-ge-) accrue to

toeval'lig (b) (-e; -er, -est) casual, accidental; (bw) accidentally, by chance

toe'vertrou (~), entrust

toe'vlug refuge, recourse; *~ tot 'n vriend neem,* seek a friend's aid; **~(s)oord** (-e) refuge, sanctuary

toe'voeg (-ge-) add, join to; **~ing** (-e, -s) addition

toe'voer (s) supply; (w) (-ge-) supply; **~diens** feeder service; **~pad** access road

toe'wy (-ge-) dedicate, consecrate, devote; **~dingsformulier** act of dedication

tog[1] (s) (-te) draught, current of air; expedition, journey, trip

tog[2] (bw) yet, still, all the same; *as jy ~ daarlangs gaan,* if you do call there; *hy is siek, ~ kom hy skool toe,* he is ill, yet he comes to school

to'ga (-s) gown, robe, toga

tog'snelheid (..hede) cruising speed

toi'ings rags, tatters

toilet' (-te) toilet

tok'kel (ge-) touch (string of a musical instrument), strum, twang; **~klavier** honkytonk piano

tokkelok' (-ke) theological student

toktok'kie (-s) tapping beetle; tick-tock

tol[1] (-le) top; (w) spin, turn; *so dronk soos 'n ~,* very dizzy; **~droër** (-s) spindrier

tol[2] tribute, customs; toll; **~beampte** (-s) customs officer; **~geld** (-e) toll, customs; **~hek** (-ke) tollgate

tolk (s) (-e) interpreter; (w) (ge-) interpret

tol'lenaar (-s, ..nare) publican

tol'letjie (-s) reel, bobbin

tom'be (-s) tomb

ton (-ne) cask, tub; ton (weight); *~ne geld,* tons of money

toneel' (tonele) scene, stage; **~geselskap,** **~groep** (-e) theatrical company, performing group; **~inkleding** decor

toneel': **~opvoering** (-s) dramatic performance; **~skrywer** (-s) dramatist; **~speler** (-s) actor; player; **~stuk** (-ke) play

tong (-e) tongue; sole (fish); **~knoper** (-s) tongue twister, *kyk snelsêer;* **~val** (-le) dialect, vernacular; **~vis** (-se) sole

ton'nel (s) (-s) tunnel; (w) (ge-) tunnel

ton'nemaat tonnage

tonsilli'tis tonsillitis, *ook* **mangelontsteking**

ton'tel tinder; **~doos** (..dose) tinderbox

tonyn' (-e) tunny

tooi (s) ornament, finery; (w) (ge-) adorn, decorate, array, trim; **~tassie** vanity case

toom (-s, tome) bridle

toon[1] (s) (tone) toe; *van kop tot ~,* from head to foot

toon[2] (s) (tone) pitch (of voice); tone

toon[3] (s): *ten ~ stel,* exhibit; (w) (ge-) show, indicate, demonstrate

toon'bank (-e) counter

toon'beeld (-e) model, example

toon'der (-s) bearer; **~sertifikaat** (..kate) bearer certificate

toon'kas (-te) display case/cabinet

toon'ladder (-s) scale, gamut

toon'leer tonology

toon'lokaal (..kale) showroom

toon'set (ge-) put to music, compose; **~ting** (-e, -s) (musical) composition

toon'venster (-s) display window

toor (ge-) conjure, practise witchcraft; **~dokter** (-s) witch doctor; **~kuns** sorcery, magic, witchcraft

toorn anger, wrath

toorts (-e) torch (flame)

top[1] (s) (-pe) summit, peak, top, tip

top[2] (w) (ge-) top, trim

top'bestuur top management

top'punt (-e) summit, peak; zenith; apex

top'swaar (-der, -ste) top-heavy

tor (-re) beetle; clodhopper

to'ring (-s) tower, steeple

torna'do (-'s) tornado, whirlwind

tornyn' toothed whale

torpe'do (-'s) torpedo

tor'ring (ge-) rip up, unpick

tor'sie torsion

tor'telduif (..duiwe) turtle dove

tos'sel (-s) tassel

tot to, until, till; *~ die dood veroordeel,* sentence to death; *~ en met,* up to and including; *~ siens!* so long!

totaal' (s) (totale) total amount; (bw) altogether, totally; *..tale aanslag,* total onslaught

totalisa'tor (-s) totalisator

tot'dat until, till

to'tempaal (..pale) totem pole

tou[1] (s) (-e) string, twine, cord; rope

tou[2] (s) (-e) queue; (w) (ge-) straggle after; walk in tandem, queue up

tou: **~spring** (-ge-) skip; **~staan** (-ge-) form a queue

toutologie' tautology

tou'trek (s) tug-of-war; (w) (-ge-) pull at tug-of-war

tou'wys: *iem. ~ maak,* show someone the ropes

to'wenaar (-s) sorcerer, magician

to'wer (ge-) enchant, charm; **~goed =** **toorgoed;** **~heks** (-e) witch; **~kuns =** **toorkuns;** **~staf** (..stawwe) magic wand

traag (trae; traer, -ste) slow, indolent, inert, dull; **~gang**, **~tempo** slowmotion

traak touch, concern; *dit ~ my nie*, I do not care

traan[1] (s) fish oil, blubber

traan[2] (s) (trane) tear; *trane stort*, shed tears; *trane met tuite huil*, weep bitterly; (w) (ge-) water (eyes)

traan'rook tear smoke

tradi'sie (-s) tradition

tra'gies (-e; -er, -ste) tragic

trajek' (-te) trajectory, stretch, stage

trak'sie traction

traktaat' (..tate) treaty, tract

trakteer' (~, ge-) treat, entertain, regale; *iem. op 'n drankie ~*, stand someone a drink

traktement' (-e) salary, emolument (minister of religion)

tra'lie (-s) trellis, lattice; *agter die ~s sit*, be behind bars

trampolien' (-s) trampoline, *ook* wipmat

tra'ne: ~dal vale of tears; **~trekker** tearjerker (film, book)

transak'sie (-s) transaction, deal

transforma'sie (-s) transformation

transport' (-e) transport; **~akte** (-s) deed of transfer, title deed

trant manner, way, style; *op die ou ~*, as usual

trap[1] (s) (-pe) trample, kick; (w) (ge-) kick, tread; flee, go away, scoot; thresh

trap[2] (s) (-pe) staircase; step; degree; pedal; *stellende, vergrotende en oortreffende ~*, positive, comparative and superlative degree

trap: ~fiets (-e) pushbike; **~kar** (-re) pedal car; **~leer** (..lere) stepladder

trapsoe'tjies, trapsuut'jies (-e) chameleon; slowcoach

tras'sie (-s) hermaphrodite, freemartin

trau'ma trauma; *'n ~tiese ondervinding*, a traumatic experience

tred (ge-) pace, tread, step; *(gelyke) ~ hou met*, keep step with, keep abreast of

tree (s) (treë) pace, step; (w) (ge-) pace, tread, step; *in diens ~*, enter service; *in die huwelik ~*, marry

tref (ge-) hit, strike; fall in with, chance, come across; *maatreëls ~*, take steps; **~afstand** effective range; *binne ~afstand*, within range; **~-en-trapvoorval** hit and run case; **~fend** (-e; -er, -ste) striking, stirring, touching, salient; **~fer(boek)** bestseller; **~ferparade** hit parade (radio)

treg'ter (-s) funnel

treil (ge-) tow; **~er** (-s) trawler, *ook* vistreiler

trein (-e) train; *die ~ haal*, catch the train; *die ~ mis/verpas*, miss the train; **~drywer** (-s) train driver

trei'ter (ge-) tease, torment, nag

trek (s) (-ke) pull; migration; stage (bus); draught; *in breë ~ke*, in broad outline; (w) (ge-) pull, draw, haul; move; migrate; be draughty; *in twyfel ~*, doubt; **~arbeid** migrant labour; **~ker** (-s) puller; trekker; emigrant; tractor

trek: ~klavier (-e) accordion; **~pas** dismissal; *die ~pas kry*, be discharged/sacked; **~pleister** (-s) drawing plaster; lover; **~skaal(tjie)** spring balance; **~sluiter** (-s) zip fastener; **~voël** (-s) bird of passage

trem (-me, -s) tram; **~bus** trolleybus

treur (ge-) mourn, grieve for; **~ig** (-e; -er, -ste) sad, mournful, sorrowful, gloomy; *'n ~ige vertoning*, a miserable performance; **~mars** (-e) funeral march; **~sang** (-e) elegy, dirge; **~spel** (-e) tragedy, **~wilg** (e) **~wilgerboom, ~wilkerboom** (..bome) weeping willow

tries'tig (-e; -er, -ste) gloomy, sad

triet'serig (-e; -er, -ste) weak, feeble, frail

tril (ge-) tremble, shiver, vibrate

tril'ling (-e, -s) vibration; tremor

trilogie' (-ë) trilogy

trim'park (-e) trimpark

triomf' (-e) triumph, victory

triplikaat' (..kate) triplicate

tri'plo (-'s) triplicate, *ook* **drievoud**

trip'pel (ge-) trip along; tripple (horse)

troebadoer' (-s) troubadour

troe'bel (-er, -ste) muddy, turbid

troef (s) (troewe) trump; (w) (ge-) trump

troep (-e) troop, group; troupe (actors)

troe'pe troops, forces; **~draer** (-s) troop carrier; **~mag** (-te) military force

troe'tel (ge-) pet, fondle, caress, coddle, pamper; **~dier** (-e) pet animal; **~dierwinkel** (-s) pet shop, *ook* **arkmark**

trofee' (trofeë) trophy

trof'fel (-s) trowel

trog (trôe, -ge) trough

trogee' (trogeë, -s) trochee

troglodiet' (-e) cavedweller, troglodyte

trok (-ke) truck

trol'lie (-s) trolley

trom (-me) drum

trombo'se thrombosis

trom'mel (-s) drum; trunk; canister; tympanum, eardrum; **~dik** quite filled

trompet' (-te) trumpet

trom'pie (-s) mouth harp

tromp'op point-blank; close; *iem. ~ loop*, rebuke someone unceremoniously

trom'poppie (-s) drum majorette

tronk (-e) prison, gaol; *van nuuskierigheid is die ~ vol*, curiosity killed the cat; **~bewaarder** (-s) prison warder; **~voël** (-s) gaolbird; habitual criminal

troon (s) (trone) throne; (w) (ge-) reign; **~ opvolger** (-s) heir to the throne

troos (s) comfort, consolation, solace; (w) (ge-) console, comfort; **~prys** (-e) consolation/booby prize

trop (-pe) flock (sheep); troop (baboons); covey (partridges); drove (cattle); pride (lions)

tro'pies (-e) tropical

trop'sluitertjie (-s) youngest child

tros (s) (-se) bunch, cluster; (w) (ge-) cluster

trots (s) pride, haughtiness; (b) (-e; -er, -ste) proud, haughty

trotseer' (~, ge-) go against, defy, withstand, challenge, brave; *~ alle aanslae*, withstand all onslaughts

trou[1] (s) fidelity, faith; *te goeder ~*, in good faith; *~ sweer aan*, swear allegiance to; (b) ([-e]; -er, -ste) faithful

trou[2] (w) (ge-) marry, wed; *met iem. ~*, marry someone; *die pasgetroude paartjie*, the newly-wed couple

trou'ens besides, indeed, really; *daar is ~ nog niks gedaan nie*, nothing, in fact, has yet been done

trous'seau (-x) trousseau, *kyk* **bruidsuitset**

tru'beeld (-e) replay (TV)

trui (-e) jersey

tru: **~kaatser** reflector; **~projektor** overhead projector; **~rat** (-te), **~versnelling** (-s) reverse gear; **~spieël(tjie)** rearview mirror

trust (-e) trust, ring, pool; **~ee** (-s) trustee

tru'tol backspin

truuk (-s) trick, gimmick

tsaar (tsare) czar

tsari'na (-s) czarina

tset'sevlieg (..vlieë) tsetse fly

tug (s) discipline, punishment; (w) (ge-) punish; **~komitee** (-s) disciplinary committee; **~maatreël** disciplinary measure; **~meester** (-s) disciplinarian

tuig (tuie) harness; rigging

tui'mel (ge-) tumble, topple over; **~droër** tumble drier

tuin (-e) garden; **~beplanner** (-s) landscape gardener; **~bou** horticulture

tuinier (-e, -s) gardener

tuin'slang (-e) garden hose

tuis at home; **~karteling** (-e, -s) home perm; **~land** homeland; **~nywerheid** (..hede) home industry; **~werk** (school) homework

tuit[1] (s) (-e) spout, nozzle

tuit[2] (w) (ge-) tingle

tul'band (-e) turban

tulp (-e) tulip; **~bol** (-le) tulip bulb

turbi'ne (-s) turbine

turf peat, turf

turksvy' (-e) prickly pear

tus'sen among, between; *~ die reëls lees*, read between the lines

tus'senganger (-s) (inter)mediator, go-between

tussenin' in between, in among

tus'sen: **~poos** (..pose) interval, pause; **~tyds** (-e) meantime, interim; **~tydse dividend**, interim dividend; **~verkiesing** (-e, -s) by-election; **~werpsel** (-s) interjection

twaalf twelve; **~de** (-s) twelfth; **~uur** twelve o'clock; dinner time

twak tobacco; nonsense; piffle

twee (tweë, -s) two; *~ maal/keer*, twice; **~daags** (-e) of two days

twee'de second; *T~ Kersdag* (Welwillendheidsdag) Day of Goodwill (Boxing Day); *~ vloer/vlak*, second floor; **~hands** (-e) secondhand; **~ns** secondly, in the second place; **~rangs** (-e) secondrate

twee: **~drag** discord; *~drag saai*, sow the seeds of discord; **~geveg** (-te) duel; **~klank** (-e) diphthong

twee: **~lettergrepig** (-e) disyllabic; **~ling** (-e) twin

twee'ërlei of two kinds

twee'romper (-s) catamaran (sailing boat)

twee: ~sprong (-e) crossroad, fork; ~stryd indecision; inward conflict

tweeta'lig (-e) bilingual

twee: ~uur two o'clock; ~voud, multiple of two; in ~voud, in duplicate

twin'tig twenty; ~ste (-s) twentieth

twis (s) (-te) quarrel, dispute, row; (w) (ge-) dispute, quarrel; ~appel (-s) apple of discord

twis'siek (-e; -er, -ste) intolerant, quarrelsome

twy'fel (s) doubt; (w) (ge-) doubt

twyfelag'tig (-e; -er, -ste) dubious, doubtful

tyd (tye) time; tense; ~-en-bewegingstudie, time and motion study; te eniger ~, at any time; ten tye/tyde van, at the time of;

~(s)berekening timing; ~bom (-me) time bomb; ~deling time sharing

ty'delik (-e) temporary; temporal (affairs)

ty'dens during

tyd: ~gees spirit of the age; ~genoot (..note) (s) contemporary; ~gleuf time slot

ty'dig (-e; -er, -ste) seasonable, timely, betimes; ~ en ontydig, in season and out (of season)

ty'ding (-e, -s) news, tidings

tyd: ~perk (-e) period; ~rei. (-ne) rally (cars)

tydro'wend (-e) taking up much time

tyd: ~skrif (-te) periodical; ~stip (-pe) point (of time); period, epoch; op hierdie ~stip, now; at this point in time; ~tafel (-s) timetable; ~verdryf (..drywe) pastime

U

u (pers. vnw) you; (besit vnw) your (singular and plural); ek waardeer ~ hulp, I appreciate your help

ui (-e) onion

ui'er (-s) udder

uil (-e) owl; soos 'n ~ op 'n kluit, alone and perplexed; 'n ~tjie knyp (knip), take a nap; ~s'kuiken (-s) dunce, stupid, numskull

uil'spieël (-s) rogue; clown, wag

uin'tjie (-s) nut grass, uintjie

uit (w) (ge-) utter, voice; (b, bw) over, out, off; (vs) out, out of, from

uit-a'sem (b, bw) out of breath

uit'bars (-ge-) burst out; explode; erupt (volcano); ~ting (-e, -s) eruption

uit'beeld (-ge-) sketch, draw, depict, delineate

uit'betaal (~), pay out, disburse; 'n dividend ~, pay a dividend

uit'blaas (-ge-) blow out

uit'blaker (-ge-) blurt out

uit'blink (-ge-) outshine, surpass, excel; ~er ace, crack, topdog

uit'breek (-ge-) break out, erupt, burst out

uit'brei (-ge-) extend, enlarge; spread; ~ op, elaborate on; ~ding (-e, -s) extension, enlargement

uit'broei (-ge-) hatch

uit'buit (-ge-) exploit, overwork; take advantage of; ~ing (-e, -s) exploitation

uitbun'dig (-e; -er, -ste) exceeding, excessive; clamerous; ~e vreugde, hilarious joy

uit'daag (-ge-) challenge, defy; ~beker (-s) challenge cup

uit'daging (-e, -s) challenge

uit'deel (-ge-) distribute, mete out, portion

uit: ~delg (-ge-) exterminate, extirpate; ~dos (-ge-) trim out, deck out

uit'draai (-ge-) turn aside; evade; turn out; ~pad (..paaie) turn-off

uit'druk (-ge-) express; squeeze out; ~king (-e, -s) expression

uitdruk'lik (-e) (-e) emphatic, explicit; (bw) emphatically, explicitly

uit'dun (-ge-) thin out; eliminate; cull (animals); ~ronde (-s) elimination round/bout; ~wedloop (..lope) heat (athletics)

uiteen' asunder, apart; ~lopend (-e) divergent, different; ~setting (-e, -s) explanation; ~sit (-ge-) explain, expound

uitein'delik finally, at last, ultimately

ui'ter (ge-) utter, voice

uiteraard' naturally, by nature, from the nature of the case

ui'terlik (s) outward appearance, exterior; (b, bw) (-e) outward(ly), external(ly); ~ 30 Mei, not later than 30 May/May 30th

ui'ters exceedingly, extremely; dis ~ jammer, it is a great pity ui'terste (s) (-s) death; extreme limit; (b) extreme, utmost, last; *jou ~ bes doen,* do one's utmost

uit'faseer (~), phase out

uit'gaan (-ge-) go out; end in; emanate from

uit'gang (-e) exit, way out; ending; ~ s'punt starting point

uit'gawe (-s) expenditure, expenses, cost; edition, issue, impression

uit'gelate (meer ~, mees ~) exuberant, wanton, boisterous

uit'gelese choice, picked; ~ geselskap, select/distinguished company

uit: ~geslape sly, cunning, wide awake; ~gesonderd except, excluding, save; ~gewekene (-s) refugee, fugitive; expatriate

uit'gewer (-s) publisher

uit'gif (-te) hand-out; aandele-uitgifte shares issue

uit'grawing (-e, -s) excavation, exhumation; dug-out; cutting

uit'haler (s) (-s) ace; showy person; (b) smart, showy; first-rate, crack; ~speler (-s) a crack player

uitheems' (-e) foreign, exotic

uit'hou (-ge-) bear, stand, endure; ~vermoë endurance; ~wedren endurance race

uithui'sig (-e; -er, -ste) fond of being away from home, gad-about

ui'ting (-e, -s) saying, utterance

uit: ~jou (-ge-) hoot, boo, hiss at; ~kamp (-ge-) camp out, go under canvas

uit'keer (-ge-) pay out, pay back, pay (dividend); drive aside; ~polis (-se) endowment policy

uit'ken recognise, identify; ~parade identification parade

uit'klaar (-ge-) check out (of army)

uit'kyk (s) lookout; *op die ~,* on the lookout; (w) (-ge-) look out

uit'laat (s) (..late) outlet; exhaust (engine); (w) (-ge-) omit, skip, leave out; let out; express; ~pyp (-e) exhaust pipe

uit: ~lander (-s) outlander, foreigner, alien; ~lating (-e, -s) omission; utterance

uit'leen (-ge-) lend (out); ~koers lending rate

uit'leg₂ lay-out, plan

uit'leg² explanation; *teks en ~ gee,* give a full explanation

uit'lewer (-ge-) deliver, hand over, surrender, extradite; ~ing (-e, -s) surrender, delivery, extradition

uit'lok (-ge-) tempt, allure, solicit; decoy; elicit; *baie kritiek ~,* arouse a great deal of criticism

uit'loof (-ge-) offer, institute/promise a prize

uit'loop (s) (..lope) spillway; (w) (-ge-) walk out; result in; bud (plant)

uit: ~loot (-ge-) release bonds by drawings, draw; raffle; ~loper (-s) sucker, offshoot; foothill

uit'maak (-ge-) make out, settle; break off

uit: ~mond (-ge-) disembogue/debouch into; flow; ~mond in die oseaan, flow/ discharge into the ocean (river); ~moor (-ge-) massacre, butcher; ~munt (-ge-) excel, shine out, surpass

uitmun'tend (-e; -er, -ste) excellent

uitne'mend (-e; -er, -ste) excellent; ~heid excellence; *by ~heid,* par excellence

uit'nodiging (-e, -s) invitation

uit'nooi (-ge-) invite, *kyk* nooi (w)

uit'oefen (-ge-) practise, exercise; discharge (duties); exert, *kyk* beoefen

uit'oorlê (~) outmanoeuvre, get the better of, outwit, bluff

uit'peul (-ge-) protrude, be protuberant

uit: ~plant (-ge-) bed out, plant out; transplant; ~pluis (-ge-) pick out, sift, ferret out; unravel

uit'put (-ge-) exhaust, deplete; ~ting exhaustion; ~(tings)oorlog (..oorloë) war of attrition

uit'reik (-ge-) hand out, issue; *sertifikate ~,* issue certificates

uit'roei (-ge-) uproot; exterminate, eradicate; *met die wortel en tak ~,* destroy something altogether

uit'roep (s) (-e) exclamation, cry; (w) (-ge-) call out, exclaim; *'n staking ~,* call a strike; ~(ings)teken (-s) exclamation mark

uit: ~ruil (-ge-) exchange; ~ruilstudent (-e) exchange student

uit'rus¹ (-ge-) repose

uit'rus² (-ge-) equip, fit out; ~ter (-s) outfitter; ~ting outfit; equipment

uit'saai (-ge-) broadcast; ~stasie (-s) broadcasting/radio station

uit'sak (-ge-) bulge out; fall (rain); lag behind; ~ker (-s) dropout (student)

uit'set (-te) marriage outfit, trousseau; output, yield; ~ting (-e, -s) expulsion;

eviction; expansion; **~koëffisiënt (-e)** coefficient of expansion

uit'sien (-ge-) look out for, look forward to

uit'sig (-te) view; prospect; *'n onbelem= merde ~,* an unobstructed view; *met ~ op die see,* facing the sea

uit'sit (-ge-) invest (money); expand, dilate; eject; evict, expel; *iem. by sy nooi ~,* oust a rival; **~voeg (..voeë)** expansion joint

uit'skakel (-ge-) cut out, disconnect, switch off (current); eliminate

uit'skei¹ (-ge-) cease, stop; *met/teen ~tyd,* at the close of play (cricket)

uit'skei² (-ge-) separate; excrete, discharge

uit'skietstoel ejection seat (aircraft)

uit'skot rejects; rabble, riff-raff

uit'slag¹ eruption (skin), rash

uit'slag² (..slae) result, issue; *die ~ van die eksamen,* the examination results

uitslui'tend exclusive(ly)

uitsluit'lik exclusively, solely

uit'smyt (-ge-) eject, chuck out; **~er (-s)** chucker-out

uit: **~soek (-ge-)** select, choose, have one's pick; **~sonder (-ge-)** except, exclude

uit'sondering (-e, -s) exception; *met ~ van,* with the exception of; *'n ~ op die reël,* an exception to the rule

uit'span (-ge-) unharness, outspan, un= yoke; **~ning (-e, -s)** outspan

uit'spansel firmament, sky

uitspat'tend (-e) dissipated; gaudy

uit'spraak (..sprake) pronunciation; sent= ence, verdict; award; *~ voorbehou,* re= serve judgment

uit: **~spreek (-ge-)** pronounce, express; *~ =* **spring (-ge-)** jump out; project; bail out (from aircraft)

uit'staan (-ge-) endure, bear, withstand; stand out; bulge out; *ek kan hom nie ~ nie,* I cannot bear him; **~de** outstanding (debts); projecting (rock)

uit'stal (-ge-) put out for sale, display, ex= hibit; **~ling (-e, -s)** display, exhibit

uit'stap (-ge-) get out, alight, step out; *~ =* **drag,** step-outs; **~pie (-s)** excursion, trip, outing

uitste'dig (-e) out of town

uit'stek: *by ~,* par excellence, pre-emi= nently

uitste'kend (-e) excellent

uit'stel (s) delay; postponement; *van ~ kom afstel,* procrastination is the thief of time; *~ gee,* grant an extension of time; (w) **(-ge-)** delay, postpone

uit'sterf, uit'sterwe (-ge-) become extinct, die out

uit: **~straling (-e, -s)** radiation, emission; **~stryk (-ge-)** iron out; **~tart (-ge-)** pro= voke, defy; **~teer (-ge-)** pine away, emaciate

uit'tog departure, exodus

uit'trede, uit'treding retirement

uit'tree (-ge-) retire (as chairman); withdraw

uit'trek (-ge-) undress; march out (soldiers); extract, pull out (tooth)

uit'treksel (-s) extract; epitome

uit'vaagsel scum, riff-raff

uit'vaardig (-ge-) issue, proclaim, enact

uit'val (s) (-le) sally; sortie; clash, outburst; (w) **(-ge-)** fall out

uit: **~veër (-s)** eraser, rubber; **~verkiesing** predestination

uit'verkoop (..kope) (s) clearance sale; (w) **(~),** sell out; *dit is ~,* it is sold out

uit'verkoping (-e, -s) (clearance) sale

uit'verkore elect, select; *die ~ volk,* the chosen people; **~ne (-s)** favourite, elect

uit'vind (-ge-) invent, find out; **~ing (-e, -s)** invention; **~sel (-s)** invention, contri= vance, device

uit'vloei (-ge-) flow out; **~sel (-s)** result, outcome

uit'vlug (s) (-te) excuse, evasion, pretext

uit'voer (s) export; *ten ~ bring,* carry into effect; (w) **(-ge-)** export; execute; imple= ment; perform; **~artikel (-s)** export article

uitvoer'baar (..bare) feasible, practicable; exportable; **~heidstudie** feasibility study

uit'voerend (-e) executive; *U~e komitee,* Executive Committee; **~e kunste,** per= forming arts

uit'waarts outward; **~e beleid,** outward policy

uit'weg (..weë) outlet, escape, way out

uit'wei (-ge-) expatiate, digress, expand

uitwen'dig (-e) external, outward; *vir ~e gebruik,* not to be taken (medicine)

uit'woed (-ge-) spend itself, cease raging

uit'wyk (-ge-) turn aside, dodge; go into exile; **~spoor (..ore)** loop (railway)

u'nie (-s) union

uniek' (-e) unique

u'niform (s) (-s) uniform; (b) (-e) uniform, *kyk* eenvormig

universeel' (..sele) universal, general

universiteit' (-e) university; *op/aan* ~, at university; ~s'kursus (-se) university course

universitêr (b) (-e) university, academic; ~*e opleiding*, university training

uraan' uranium; ~verryking uranium enrichment

urinaal' (urinale) urinal

uri'ne urine

urn (-s) urn

uto'pies (-e) utopian

uur (ure) hour; *om vyf* ~, at five o'clock; *ter elfder ure*, at the eleventh hour; ~werk (-e) timepiece, clock; ~wyser (-s) hour hand

u'we yours; *die* ~, yours faithfully

V

vaag (vae; vaer, -ste) vague

vaak (b) (vaker, -ste) sleepy, drowsy; ~ *hê/ word*, be sleepy; *Klaas Vakie*, Willie Winkie, sandman

vaal (valer, -ste) tawny; pale, sallow; drab

vaal'pens (-e) nickname for Transvaler

vaan'del (-s) standard, flag, banner

vaar (w) (ge-) sail, navigate

vaar'dig (-e; -er, -ste) skilled, handy, clever, dexterous

vaart (-e) cruise, voyage, navigation; haste; leap; speed; ~belyn (-de) streamlined

vaar'tjie: *'n aardjie na sy* ~, like father like son

vaar'tuig (..tuie) vessel; (mv) watercraft

vaarwel' farewell, goodbye; ~ *sê*, ~ *toeroep*, say goodbye

vaas (vase) vase, flowerpot

vaat'jie (-s) barrel, tub, vat, cask

va'bond (-e) vagabond; rogue; (little) rascal

va'dem (-s) fathom

va'der (-s) father; sire (animal)

va'derland (-e) native country, fatherland; ~er (-s) patriot; ~s'liefde patriotism

va'der: ~lik (-e) paternal, fatherly; ~s'naam: *om* ~*s'naam*, for God's sake

va'doek (-e) dishcloth

va'evuur, va'gevuur purgatory

vag (-te) fleece, pelt, fell

vak (-ke) subject; compartment, partition, pigeon hole; vocation, trade

vakan'sie (-s) holiday(s), vacation; ~ *hou*, be on holiday; *in die* ~, during the holidays; *met (op)* ~, on holiday

vakant' (-e) vacant, empty; ~*e pos*, vacancy

vakatu're (-s) vacancy

vak'bond (-e) trade union

vak: ~kennis vocational/technical knowledge; ~leerling (-e) apprentice; ~man (-ne) expert, professional man, specialist; artisan; ~manskap workmanship; ~onderwys technical/vocational education/instruction; ~praatjies shop talk

vaksineer' (ge-) vaccinate

vakuum' (-s) vacuum

val¹ (s) (-le) trap; *in die* ~ *sit*, be caught in a trap

val² (s) (-le) fall; downfall; gradient; (w) (ge-) fall, drop, succumb; *in die oog* ~, catch one's eye; *in die rede* ~, interrupt; ~byl (-e) guillotine; ~bylpot (-te) tiebraker game (tennis)

val: ~hek (-ke) boom; ~helm (-s) crash helmet

valk (-e) falcon, hawk

vallei' (-e) valley, dale, vale

vall'end (-e) falling; ~*e siekte*, epilepsy

vall'luik (-e) trapdoor; drop (gallows)

val'reep (..repe) manrope; gangway

vals ([-e]; -er, -ste) false, treacherous; spurious, forged, artificial

val'skerm (-s) parachute; ~troepe para(chute) troops, parabats; ~springer (-s) parachutist

val'strik (-ke) trap, snare, pitfall

valueer' (~, ge-) valuate, value

valu'ta (foreign) currency; ~beheer exchange control

vampier' (-e, -s) vampire, bloodsucker

van¹ (s) (-ne) surname, family name

van² (vs) of, from, with, by, for

vanaand' this evening, tonight

vanaf' from

vandaal' (..dale) vandal

vandaan' from

vandaar' hence, thence, that is why
vandag' today
vandalis'me vandalism
vandees'jaar this year
vandees'maand this month
vandees'week this week
vandi'sie (-s) auction sale/mart, *ook* **vendusie**
vang (ge-) catch, seize, capture, trap; **~s** (-te) catch, haul; **~wa** (..waens) pick-up van (police)
vanjaar' this year
vanmekaar' to pieces, asunder, separated
vanmele'we formerly, in earlier times, in days of yore
vanmo're, vanmôre this morning
vannag' tonight; last night; *dit was ~ koud,* it was cold last night
vanself' of its own accord; **~sprekend (-e)** obvious, self-evident, implied
vantevo're previous(ly), before
vanwe'ë on account of, because of, owing to
va'ria miscellany; **~konsert (-e)** variety concert
varia'sie (-s) variation
varieer' (~, ge-) vary, change
variété' (-s) variety theatre
va'ring (-s) fern
vark (-e) pig, hog, swine; **~oor** (..ore) pig's ear; arum lily; **~sog (-ge, ..sôe)** sow; **~vleis** pork
vars (-er, -ste) fresh; *~ eiers,* new-laid eggs
vas¹ (w) (ge-) abstain from food, fast
vas² (b) (-te; -ter, -ste) firm, fixed; engaged; stationary; permanent; compact; **~te** *eiendom,* immovable property; *my ~te oortuiging,* my firm conviction; (bw) firmly; soundly
vas'berade (meer ~, mees ~) resolute
vas: **~beslote** determined; **~brand (-ge-)** run dry, seize; get into difficulty
vas'goed immovable/landed property
vas'golf permanent wave; *sy laat haar hare ~,* she is going to have a perm
vas'keer (-ge-) corner, drive into a corner
vas: **~klou** cling to; **~lê** steal, pinch; **~maak** fasten, tie
vas'pen (-ge-) control, peg; *pryse ~,* peg prices
vas'stel (-ge-) fix, establish, ascertain, determine, stipulate; *die skade ~,* assess the damage

vas'teland continent
vas'trap (s) popular folk dance; (w) (-ge-) stand firm, persevere; cane; **~plek (-ke)** footing; stepping stone
vas'vra (-ge-) corner, quiz; **~wedstryd (-e)** quiz
vat¹ (-e) tub, barrel; vessel; vat; cask
vat² (s) grip, hold; (w) (ge-) grip, take, catch, seize; grasp, understand; *koue ~,* catch a chill; *vlam ~,* catch fire
vee¹ (s) livestock
vee² (w) (ge-) sweep, wipe
vee'arts (-e) veterinary surgeon
vee'boer (-e) stock farmer, cattle farmer, sheep farmer; **~dery** stock farming
vee'dief (..diewe) cattle thief, stock thief
veeg (s) (veë) wipe; (w) (ge-) sweep, whisk; wipe
veel (b, bw) (meer, meeste) much, many, often, frequently; *te ~,* too much; *~ eerder,* much sooner
veel'belowend (-e) promising, hopeful
veel'betekenend (-e) significant
veel'eisend (-e) demanding, exacting
veelkeu'sig multiple choice; **~e** *vrae,* multiple choice questions
veelras'sig (-e) multiracial
veels: **~** *geluk,* hearty congratulations; **~** *te veel,* altogether too much
veelsy'dig (-e) many-sided; all-round
veelvol'kig multinational, multiracial
veel'voud (-e) multiple; *kleinste gemene ~,* least common multiple
veel'wywery polygamy
veer¹ (s) (vere) ferry
veer² (s) (vere) spring; (w) (ge-) spring
veer³ (s) (vere) feather; (w) (ge-) feather; **~gewig** featherweight; **~kombers (-e)** eiderdown, down quilt
veerkrag'tig (-e) elastic, resilient
veer'pyltjie (-s) dart(s) (game)
veert'tien (-e) fourteen; *~ dae,* a fortnight; **~daags (-e)** lasting a fortnight; **~de (-s)** fourteenth
veer'tig (-s) forty; **~ste (-s)** fortieth; **~tal** forty
vee: **~teelt** stock breeding; **~veiling (-s)** cattle auction
veg (ge-) fight, contend
vegeta'riër (-s) vegetarian
veg'knoper (-s) promotor (boxing, wrestling), *ook* **vegventer**

veglus'tig (-e; -er, -ste) pugnacious

veg'vliegtuig (..tuie) fighter plane

veg'ter (-s) fighter, combatant; **~s'baas** (..base) bully, fire-eater

veg'tuig (..tuie) combat vehicle

veg'venter (-s) promotor (boxing, wrestling), *ook* **vegknoper**

veil (w) (ge-) sell by auction

vei'lig (-e; -er, -ste) safe, secure

vei'ligheid safety, security; **~s'gordel** safety belt; **~s'halwe** for safety's sake; **~skeermes** (-se) safety razor; **~s'polisie** security police; **~s'raad** Security Council (UN); **~s'wag** (-te) security guard

vei'ling (-e, -s) auction, sale

veins (ge-) feign, sham, pretend

vel[1] (s) (-le) skin, hide; sheet

vel[2] (w) (ge-) pass (sentence); fell, cut down; *met gevelde bajonet,* with fixed bayonets; *vonnis ~,* pass sentence

veld (-e) field, plain; **~beampte** (-s) extension officer; **~fiets** (-e) scrambler (bike); **~fliek** (-e) drive-in theatre; **~party** (-e) picnic; **~renne** scrambling; off-road racing (cars); **~skool** (..skole) veld school; **~slag** (..slae) battle; **~stoel** (-e) folding stool, campstool; **~tog** (-te) campaign

vel'ling (-s) felly, rim

vel'skoen (-e) homemade shoe

vendu': **~afslaer** (-s) auctioneer

vendu'sie (-s) auction, sale, *ook* **vandisie**

vene'ries (-e) venereal

vennoot' (..note) partner; **~skap** (..pe) partnership; *die ~skap ontbind,* dissolve the partnership

ven'ster (-s) window; **~bank** (-e) window sill; **~koevert** (-e) window envelope, *kyk* **ruitkoevert**; **~kykery** window shopping, *kyk* **loerkoop**

vent[1] (s) (-e) fellow, chap, guy, bloke; *'n gawe ~,* a decent chap; *'n snaakse ~,* a funny guy/bloke

vent[2] (w) (ge-) carry about for sale, hawk, peddle

ven'ter (-s) pedlar, hawker

ventiel' (-e) valve; ventil (organ)

ventila'sie ventilation

venyn' venom, poison

ver (-re; -der, -ste) far, remote, distant

ver'af far away, remote; **~ geleë,** remote

veraf'sku (~) abhor, loathe, detest

verag' (~) despise, disdain

veral' especially; **~ hy,** he of all people

veran'der (~) change, alter, modify; **~ing** (-e, -s) change, alteration

verantwoor'delik (-e) responsible, accountable; *'n ~e posisie,* a position of trust; **~heid** responsibility

veras' (~) cremate; **~sing** (-e, -s) cremation

verbaal' (verbale) verbal; *verbale kommunikasie,* verbal communication

verbaas' (w) (~) astonish, amaze; *hom ~ oor,* be astonished at; (b) (-de) astonished, amazed

verban' (~) banish, exile, expel

verband'[1] (-e) bandage (for an arm), sling

verband'[2] (s) (-e) bond, mortgage; *eerste ~,* first mortgage bond; (w) (~) bond; (b) bond; *die ~e eiendom,* the bonded property; **~gewer** (-s) mortgagor; **~houer** (-s) mortgagee

verband'[3] connection, context; *in ~ met,* in connection with

verba'sing astonishment, amazement

verbas'ter (~) degenerate; hybridise

verbeel' (~) imagine; represent; be proud, fancy; *hy ~ hom baie,* he is very conceited; **~ jou!** just fancy!

verbeel'ding (-e, -s) fancy, imagination

verbe'ter (~) correct, improve, mend, rectify; **~skool** reformatory

verbe'tering (-e, -s) improvement, correction; **~(s)gestig** (-te) reformatory

verbeur' (~) forfeit; *jy sal punte ~,* you will lose marks

verbeurd' (-e) confiscated, forfeited; **~ verklaar,** confiscate, seize

verbied' (~) prohibit, forbid; *'n boek ~,* ban a book; *rook ~,* no smoking; *ten strengste ~,* strictly forbidden

verbind' (~) join; connect; combine; commit; bandage; **~ tot verandering,** committed to change

verbin'ding (-e, -s) connection, junction, combination; communication

verbin'tenis (-se) union, promise, contract, agreement; **~student** (-e) agreement/contract student

verbit'ter (~) embitter, exasperate

verbleik' (~) fade, fade out

verblind' (w) (~) dazzle, blind

verbloem' (~) disguise, hide, conceal

verbluf' (~) dumbfound, nonplus, baffle

verbly' (~) gladden, please, cheer; **~dend** (-e) joyful, joyous, gladdening; *'n ~den= de teken,* a hopeful sign

verblyf' (..blywe) residence, abode, so= journ; **~permit** (-te) resident's permit; *reis en ~,* transport and subsistence

verbod' (..botte, ..booie) prohibition; ban (on books); embargo (on imports); ban= ning; suppression

verbo'de prohibited, forbidden; *~ boek,* banned book

verbo'ë declined, inflected

verbond' (-e) treaty, league, covenant

verbon'de connected, linked, allied

verbouereerd' (-e) embarrassed, amazed, confused, flabbergasted

verbrand' (w) (~) burn; cremate (corpse); *sy mond ~,* put his foot into it; (b) (-e) burnt, charred; sunburnt, tanned

verbrands'! hang it all! confound it!

verbreek' (~) break, burst; violate; *'n ver= lowing ~,* break off an engagement

verbrok'kel (~) disrupt, crumble to pieces

verbrou' (~) spoil, muddle, make a mess

verbruik' (s) consumption; (w) (~) use up, consume

verbrui'ker (-s) consumer; **~sake** consumer affairs; **~(s)besteding** consumer spend= ing; **~(s)prysindeks** consumer price index

verbruiks'artikel (-s) consumer article

verbui'ging (-e, -s) declension, flexion

verby' past, beyond; *dis alles ~,* it is all over

verby'gaan (-ge-) pass, go past; neglect

verby'pad (..paaie) bypass

verby'praat (-ge-): *sy mond ~,* let the cat out of the bag

verby'steek overtake (a car), (by)pass

verby'ster (~) perplex, bewilder

verdaag' (~) adjourn (a meeting); post= pone, prorogue

verdag' (-te) suspicious, suspected; *'n ~te persoon,* a suspect

verda'ging (-e, -s) adjournment, proroga= tion

verdamp' (~) evaporate; **~ing** (-e, -s) evaporation

verde'dig (~) defend, stand up for; **~er** (-s) defender; counsel for the defence

verde'diging defence; *Departement (van) V~,* Department of Defence; **~s'mag** defence force

verdeel' (~) divide, distribute; apportion

verdeeld' (-e) divided; **~heid** discord, strife

verden'king suspicion; mistrust; *in/onder ~,* under suspicion

ver'der father, further; again

verderf' (s) ruin, destruction; perdition

verdien' (~) earn; deserve, merit

verdien(d)' (-de) deserved; *dis jou ~de loon,* that serves you right

verdien'ste desert, merit; wages, earnings; *na ~,* according to one's deserts; *sertifi= kaat van ~,* certificate of merit; **~lik** (-e; -er, -ste) meritorious, deserving

verdiep' (~) deepen; **~ing** (-e, -s) storey, floor; deepening; *onderste ~ing,* ground floor; *die tweede ~ing,* second floor, *kyk* **tweede vloer**

verdink' (~) suspect; distrust

verdiskonteer' (~) discount; *wissels ~,* discount bills (of exchange)

verdoel' (~) convert a try (rugby)

verdoem' (~) reject, curse, damn, slam

verdof' (~) dim; *jou ligte ~,* dim one's lights, *kyk* **domp**

verdor' (w) (~) wither; (b) (-e) shrivelled up, parched, withered

verdo'wing stupor, numbness; anaesthesia; **~s'middel** (-s) narcotic; anaesthetic; *verslaaf aan ~(s)middels/dwelms,* ad= dicted to drugs

verdra' (~) bear, endure, tolerate, suffer; *ek kan hom nie ~ nie,* I can't bear him

verdraag'saam (..same; ..samer -ste) tole= rant, patient

verdraai' (~) twist, distort, contort

verdrag' (..drae) treaty, convention, pact

verdriet' grief, affliction, sadness

verdring' (~) push aside; supplant, oust

verdrink' (~) drown; be drowned

verdruk' (~) oppress

verdub'bel (~) double; redouble; *jou winste ~,* double your profits

verdui'delik (~) elucidate, explain; **~ing** (-e, -s) clarification, explanation

verduis'ter (~) eclipse (sun); obscure, dim; embezzle, peculate, defalcate (money); **~ing** (-e, -s) eclipse

verdui'wels confounded, darned

verdwaal' (~) go astray, lose the way, get lost; *ek het ~,* I got lost

verdwyn' (~) disappear, vanish; *alle vrees laat ~,* dispel all fear(s)

vereensel'wig (~) identify (with)

vereenvou'dig (~) simplify

vereer' (~) honour, respect, adore, revere

veref'fen (~) settle; adjust; pay

vereis' (~) require, demand; ~**te** (-s) requirement, requisite; *aan alle ~tes voldoen,* satisfy all the requirements

vere'nig (~) unite; reconcile; merge, amalgamate; joint; *V~de Nasies,* United Nations (UN); *V~de State van Amerika,* United States of America; ~**ing** (-e, -s) union, society, association; combination

vererg' (w) (~) grow angry; *ek ~ my vir hom,* he annoys me; (b) (-**de**) angry

verf (s) (**verwe**) paint, dye; (w) (**ge-**) paint; dye; ~**kwas** (-**te**) paint brush

verfris' (~) refresh; ~**send** (-**e**) refreshing

verfyn' (~) refine

verg (**ge-**) require, demand; *dit ~ nadere ondersoek,* this requires closer examination

vergaan' (~) perish, decay; be wrecked (ship), founder

vergaap' (~): *hom ~ aan,* stare in wonderment

vergaar' (~) collect, gather

verga'der (~) meet, gather; assemble; ~**ing** (-e, -s) meeting, assembly; gathering; *'n ~ing (af)sluit,* close a meeting; *'n ~ing belê,* convene/call a meeting; *openbare ~ing,* public meeting; *'n ~ing verdaag,* adjourn a meeting

vergank'lik (-e; -er, -ste) transitory, transient, fleeting, mortal

vergas'ser (-s) carburettor

vergeef' = **vergewe**[1]; ~**lik** (-e) pardonable

vergeefs' (b) (-e) futile; idle; *'n ~e poging,* an abortive attempt; (bw) in vain

vergeet' (~) forget; *ek het skoon ~,* I quite forgot; ~**agtig** (-e; -er, -ste) forgetful

vergel'ding requital, retaliation, retribution, recompense; ~**s'oorlog** (..loë) war of retribution

vergele'ke compared; ~ *met,* in comparison with

vergelyk' (s) (-e) compromise; arrangement, agreement; (w) (~) compare; ~**end** (-e) comparative

vergely'king (-e, -s) comparison, equation

vergesel' (~) accompany, attend

ver'gesig (-te) view, prospect, vista

ver'gesog (-te) far-sought, far-fetched

verge'telheid oblivion

verge'we[1] (~) forgive, forgave; ~ *en vergeet,* forgive and forget

verge'we[2] (~) poison, *kyk* **vergiftig**

vergif' (-te) poison, venom, *kyk* **gif**

vergif'nis pardon, forgiveness, indulgence

vergif'tig (~) poison; ~**ing** poisoning

vergis' (~) mistake, be mistaken; ~**sing** (-e, -s) mistake, error, slip

vergoed' (w) (~) defray, compensate; indemnify, reimburse; *skade ~,* compensate; ~**ing** compensation, indemnification, reimbursement, amends

vergroot' (~) enlarge, magnify, increase; *vergrotende trap,* comparative degree; ~**glas** (-e) magnifying glass

vergro'ting (-e, -s) enlargement, increase

vergun'ning (-e, -s) permission, allowance; concession, licence; *met vriendelike ~ van,* by/with kind permission of

verhaal' (s) (..hale) narrative, story, account; (w) (~) narrate, tell, relate; recover (a debt)

verhan'del (~) discuss, debate; transact, deal, negotiate

verhef' (~) raise, elevate; pride oneself

verhe'melte (-s) palate; *gesplete ~,* cleft palate; *harde/sagte ~,* hard/soft palate

verheug' (w) (~) rejoice, please, delight; *hom ~ oor,* rejoice at; (b) (-**de**) delighted

verhe'we exalted, sublime

verhin'der (~) prevent, hinder

verhit' (w) (~) heat; (b) (-**te**) heated, hot; ~**ting** heating, calefaction

verhoed' (~) prevent, ward off

verho'ging (-e, -s) elevation, promotion; increment, increase, rise (in salary)

verhoog' (s) (..hoë) platform; (w) (~) raise, elevate, promote, enhance

verhoor' (s) (..hore) examination; hearing, trail; (w) (~) hear, interrogate, examine; *sy gebed is ~,* his prayer was answered

verhou'ding (-e, -s) relation, proportion, ratio; (love) affair

verhuis' (~) move; die; ~**ing** (-e, -s) removal; migration; ~**wa** pantechnicon, removals van

verhuur' (~) let, hire; ~**der** (-s) landlord, lessor

verifika'sie (-s) verification

verjaar' (~) celebrate one's birthday; prescribe (a debt); ~(s)'dag (..dae) birthday; ~s'geskenk, ~s'present (-e) birthday present

verjong' (~) rejuvenate, make young again; ~ing(s)kuur (..kure) facelift

verkeer' (s) traffic; communication; (w) (~) have intercourse; keep company with; ~beheer traffic control

verkeerd' (-e; -er, -ste) wrong

verkeers': ~beampte (-s) traffic officer; ~boete (-s) traffic fine; ~knoop (..knope) traffic jam; ~konstabel (-s) traffic constable; ~lig (-te) traffic light, robot; ~teken (-s) traffic sign/signal; ~wisselaar (-s) traffic interchange

verken' (~) reconnoitre, spy; ~ner (-s) scout

verken'ningstog reconnaissance expedition

verkies' (~) elect; choose, prefer; *tot die raad ~,* elected to council; *tot voorsitter ~,* elected as chairman; ~baar (..bare) eligible; ~ing (-e, -s) election; ~lik (-e; -er, -ste) preferable, desirable

verklaar' (~) explain, clarify; declare

verklap' (~) tell tales, tell a secret

verkla'ring (-e, -s) explanation, statement; evidence; declaration; *'n ~ aflê,* make a statement; *'n beëdigde ~,* an affidavit

verklee(d)' (~) change (clothes)

verkleineer' (~) belittle, humiliate

verklein'woord (-e) diminutive

verkleur' (~) fade, lose colour; change colour; discolour; ~mannetjie (-s) chameleon; turncoat

verklik' (~) disclose, give away (secret)

verkluim (~) grow stiff/numb with cold

verknoei' (~) spoil, make a mess, muddle

verknor'sing fix, sorry plight

verkoel' (~) cool, refrigerate; ~er (-s) radiator

verkon'dig (~) announce, proclaim

verkool' carbonise, char

verkoop' (s) sale; ~belasting sales tax; ~bestuurder sales manager; ~kuns salesmanship; ~lokaal (..kale) auction mart; ~prys (e) selling price

verko'per (-s) seller, vendor, salesman

verko'ping (-e, -s) sale, auction

verkort' (w) (~) shorten, abridge, abbreviate; (b) (-e) abridged

verko'se returned, elected; *~ president,* president-elect

verkou'e (-s) cold, chill; *'n ~ kry,* catch a cold; *~ wees,* have a cold

verkrag' (~) infringe, violate; ravish, rape

verkramp' unenlightened, over-conservative

verkry' (~) obtain, acquire; ~(g)'baar (..bare) obtainable

verkwik' (~) refresh; ~kend refreshing

verkwis' (~) waste, squander, dissipate

verkyk' (~) stare in amazement

ver'kyker (-s) (pair of) fieldglasses, telescope, binoculars

verlaat' (~) leave, abandon, forsake

verlam' (~) paralyse; lame, cripple; ~ming paralysis; crippling, lameness

verlang' (~) desire, long for; *vurig ~ na,* yearn for; ~e (-ns), ~ste (-s) desire, wish, longing

verla'te (meer ~, mees ~) abandoned, lonely, forsaken

verle'de (s) past; *die grys(e) ~,* the distant past; *die ~, hede en toekoms,* the past, present and future; (b) past; last; *~ deelwoord,* past participle; *~ maand,* last month

verle'ë timid; perplexed, embarrassed

verleen' (~) grant, give, confer, bestow

verleent'heid embarrassment, quandary

verleg'ging shifting, deviation; detour

verlei' (~) seduce, tempt; mislead

verleng' (~) lengthen, prolong, extend

verlep' (w) (~) fade, wilt, wither; (b) (-te) withered

verlief' (-de) in love, fond of, sweet on; amorous; *~ raak op,* fall in love with

verlief'de (-s) person in love

verlies' (-e) loss; defeat; bereavement

verlig'[1] (w) (~) relieve; (b) (-te) relieved

verlig'[2] (w) (~) illuminate; (b) (-te) enlightened; lit up; *die ~te eeu,* the enlightened age; ~ting lighting, illumination

verlof' leave, permission

verloof' (~) become engaged/betrothed; *~ raak aan,* become engaged to; ~de (-s) fiance (man), fiancee (woman)

verloop' (s) course, lapse, sequel; progress

verloor' (~) lose

verlo're lost, forlorn

verlos' (~) deliver; release, liberate; save, redeem; ~kunde midwifery, obstetrics, *ook* obstetrie

Verlos'ser Redeemer, Saviour

verlos'sing deliverance; redemption

verlo'wing (-e, -s) engagement, betrothal

vermaak' (s) (..make) pleasure, delight, amusement, entertainment; (w) (~) enjoy, amuse

vermaak'lik (-e; -er, -ste) enjoyable, pleasurable, amusing, entertaining; ~heid (..hede) amusement, diversion, entertainment

vermaan' (~) admonish, warn, exhort

vermaard' (-e) celebrated, famous

vermeen'de alleged, supposed, reputed

vermeer'der (~) increase, enlarge, augment; ~ing (-e, -s) increase

vermeng' (~) mix, blend, mingle

vermenigvul'dig (~) multiply; ~ met, multiply by; ~ing multiplication

verme'tel (-e; -er, -ste) audacious, daring

vermin'der (~) lessen, diminish, decrease; slacken (speed); *die pryse ~*, reduce the prices; ~ing (-e, -s) rebate, reduction, decrease

vermink' (~) mutilate, maim

vermis' (~) miss; *as ~ aangegee*, reported missing

vermoed' (~) suspect, presume, suppose

vermoe'de (-ns) suspicion, presumption

vermo'ë (-ns) fortune, wealth; ability

vermoei' (~) tire, weary, fatigue; ~end (-e; -er, -ste) tiring, wearisome

vermom' (~) disguise, mask

vermoor' (~) murder, kill

vermors' (~) squander, spend, spill

vermy' (~) avoid, shun, evade

vernaam' (b) (..name; ..namer, -ste) important, prominent, distinguished; (bw) especially; ~lik especially, mainly

verne'der (~) humiliate, degrade, humble; ~end (-e) humiliating; ~ing (-e, -s) humiliation, degradation

verneem' (~) understand, learn; enquire

verneuk' (~) cheat, defraud, swindle

verniel' (~) destroy, wreck

verniet' in vain; gratis; unnecessarily

vernie'tig (~) annihilate, crush, destroy

vernieu' (~) renew, *kyk hernu*; renovate

vernis' (s) (-s) varnish; (w) (~) varnish

vernou' (~) grow narrower, narrow; *die loongaping ~*, narrow the wage gap

vernuf' (-te) intelligence, talent, expertise, genius, intellect; ~tig (-e; -er, -ste) ingenious, intelligent

vernu'wing (-e, -s) renewal; renovation

veron(t)ag'saam (~) neglect, slight, ignore, disregard

veronderstel' (~) suppose, assume; ~ling (-e, -s) assumption, supposition

veron'geluk (~) fail, miscarry; lose one's life in an accident; jeopardise (one's chances)

verontskul'dig (~) excuse; ~ing (-e, -s) excuse, apology; justification; ~inge aanbied, offer apologies

verontwaar'dig (-de) indignant, grieved

veroor'deel (~) condemn, sentence; *ter dood ~, tot die dood ~*, condemn to death

veroor'loof (~) permit, give leave

veroor'saak (~) cause, bring about, occasion; *moeite ~*, cause/give trouble

veror'den (~) order, enact, decree; ~ing (-e, -s) (municipal) by-law; decree, ordinance, statute

verou'der (~) grow old, become obsolete

vero'wer (~) conquer, capture

verpand' (~) pawn; pledge, mortgage

verpas' (Germ.) (~) miss (train)

verplaas' (~) remove, displace; transfer (to another post/town)

verpla'sing (-e, -s) transfer, displacement, removal

verpleeg' (~) nurse, tend; ~kunde nursing; ~personeel nursing staff; ~ster (-s) nurse; ~suster (-s) nursing sister

verple'ër (-s), verple'ger (-s) male nurse

verple'ging nursing

verplet'ter (~) crush, smash

verplig' (w) (~) oblige, compel; (b, bw) (-te) obliged, bound; compulsory; ~te onderwys, compulsory education; *wetlik ~ wees om*, be legally bound to; ~tend (-e) compulsory, obligatory; ~ting (-e, -s) obligation; liability; *sonder ~ting*, without obligation

verraad' treason, treachery

verraai' (~) betray, disclose; ~er (-s) traitor, betrayer

verras' (~) surprise, startle; ~send (-e) surprising; ~sing (-e, -s) surprise

ver'regaande outrageous, scandalous

ver'reikend (-e) far-reaching; ~e gevolge, far-reaching consequences

ver'reweg by far; ~ *die beste plan*, by far the better plan

verrig' (~) do, perform, execute; **~tinge** proceedings (at a meeting)
verroer' (~) stir, move, budge
verroes' (~) rust, get rusty
verrot' (w) (~) decay, putrefy, decompose; (b) (-te; -ter, -ste) rotten, decayed
verryk' (~) enrich; *sy kennis ~*, increase one's knowledge; *~te uraan*, enriched uranium; **~ing** enrichment
vers¹ (-e) heifer
vers² (-e) stanza, verse; *met ~ en kapittel bewys*, quote chapter and verse
versa'dig (~) satisfy, appease, saturate
versag' (~) soften, relieve, mollify, mitigate; **~tend** (-e) extenuating, mitigating; *~tende omstandighede*, extenuating circumstances; **~ting** alleviation, mitigation, relief
versa'mel (~) collect, gather, amass; *moed ~*, muster up courage; **~ing** (-e, -s) collection; compilation; gathering
versap'per (-s) liquidiser
verse'ël (~) seal; **~ing** sealing
verseg' (~) refuse pointblank
verseil': *~ raak onder*, get mixed up with
verse'ker (w) (~) insure, assure; affirm; (b) (-de) assured, insured; *wees daarvan ~*, rest assured about that
verse'kering assurance, insurance; *~ teen brand*, fire insurance; *ek gee julle die ~*, I give you the assurance; **~maatskappy** (-e) insurance company; **~polis** (-se) insurance policy
versend' (~) dispatch, consign, forward
ver'sene: *die ~ teen die prikkels slaan*, kick against the pricks
verset' (s) resistance; *lydelike ~*, passive resistance; (w) (~) resist
versien' (~) service; **~ing** (-s) service (of a car)
ver'siende long-sighted; far-seeing
versier' (~) adorn, decorate; **~ing** (-e, -s) decoration, ornament; **~suiker** icing sugar, *ook* **siersuiker**
versig'tig (-e; -er, -ste) careful, prudent
verskaf' (~) supply, furnish, provide; **~er** (-s) supplier
verskei'denheid variety, assortment, diversity; **~s'konsert** (-e) variety concert, *ook* **variakonsert**
verskei'e several, sundry, various

verskerp' (~) sharpen, intensify; *~te aanval/aanslag*, intensified attack/assault
verskeur' (~) tear to pieces, lacerate
verskil' (s) (-le) difference, disparity, discrepancy; *~ van mening*, difference of opinion; (w) (~) differ, vary; **~lend** (-e) different, various; unlike
versko'ning (-e, -s) excuse, apology
verskoon' (~) excuse, pardon; *~ my*, pardon/excuse me
verskrik' (~) terrify, horrify; **~king** (-e, -s) horror, terror; **~lik** (b) (-e; -er, -ste) terrible, horrible, dreadful
verskroei' (~) scorch, singe
verskul'dig (-de) due, indebted, owing
verskyn' (~) appear; be published; **~ing** (-e, -s) appearance; publication
verslaaf' (w) (~) enslave; *~ raak aan*, become addicted to; (b) (-de) enslaved, addicted; **~middel** (-s) habit-forming drug
verslaan' (~) defeat, conquer
verslaap' (~) oversleep (oneself)
versla'e (meer ~, mees ~) dismayed
verslag' (..slae) report, account; *~ doen/lewer*, give an account; (submit a) report; **~gewer** (-s) reporter
verslank' (w) slim; **~ing** slimming
versleg' (~) deteriorate, grow worse
versmaai' (~) scorn, despise, slight; *dis nie te ~ nie*, it is not to be scorned/sneezed at
versmoor' (~) suffocate, stifle
versna'pering (-e, -s) delicacy, dainty titbit, light refreshment; **~s** snacks
versnel' (~) accelerate, quicken
versnel'ling (-e, -s) acceleration; speed; gear (of motor)
versnel'renne drag racing, *ook* **sleeprenne**
versoek' (s) (-e) request, petition; (w) (~) request, ask, invite
versoe'king (-e, -s) temptation
versoek'skrif (-te) petition
versoen' (~) reconcile, conciliate, placate
versoet' (~) sweeten; (s) **-er** (-s) sweetener
versool' (~) resole (shoe); retread, recap (tyre)
versorg' (~) care for, attend to
versor'ging maintenance, care
versper' (~) block, obstruct, bar, barricade; *~ die uitsig*, obscure the view; **~ring** (-e, -s) barricade, entanglement, roadblock

verspied' (~) reconnoitre, spy, scout; **~er** (-s) scout, spy

verspil' (~) squander, waste

verspoel' (~) wash away; **~ing** (-s) wash away, flood

verspot' (-te; -ter, -ste) ridiculous, silly

verspreek' (~): *jou* ~, make a slip of the tongue, commit oneself

versprei' (~) spread, disperse, scatter

ver'spring (s) long jump; (w) (-ge-) do the long jump

verstaan' (~) understand, comprehend; *rede* ~, listen to reason; **~baar** (..bare, -der, -ste) intelligible, comprehensible

verstand' sense, intellect, intelligence

verstan'de: *met dien* ~, provided that; **~ lik** (-e) intellectual, mental; **~lik vertraag,** mentally retarded

verstan'dig (-e; -er, -ste) intelligent, sensible, wise; *dit is ~ om,* it is wise to

verste'delik (~) urbanise; **~ing** urbanisation

versteek' (~) hide (away), stow away

versteen' (w) (~) petrify, return to stone

verste'keling (-e) stowaway

verstel' (~) mend; readjust; change gears; **~baar** (..bare) adjustable

versterk' (~) invigorate, fortify, strengthen, reinforce; **~ing** (-e, -s) support, reinforcement, fortification; **~middel** (-s) tonic, invigorator

versteur' (~) disturb, upset; *die (openbare) rus* ~, disturb the peace

verstom' (w) (~) become dumb, strike dumb

verstoot' (~) disown; cast out, repudiate

verstop' (~) plug, clog, constipate; **~ping** (-e, -s) obstruction

versto'teling (-e) outcast, pariah

verstout' (~) make bold, take courage; *jou ~ om,* make bold to

verstrek' (~) furnish, supply, provide; *besonderhede* ~, give details

verstre'ke elapsed, expired

verstrik' (~) ensnare, entrap, entangle

verstrooi' (~) scatter, disperse; **~(d)'** (-de) scattered; absent-minded

verstryk' (~) elapse, expire; terminate; **~datum** (-s) expiry date

verstuit' (~) dislocate, sprain

versuim' (s) omission, neglect; default; (w) (~) neglect; omit; *sy plig ~,* neglect one's duty

versuip' (~) drown (animal); flood (carburettor)

verswaar' (~) aggravate, encumber; *verswarende omstandighede,* aggravating circumstances

verswik' (~) sprain (ankle)

verswyg' (~) suppress, conceal, keep silent; *die feite* ~, withhold the facts

vertaal' (~) translate; *letterlik* ~, translate literally; *uit Duits in Afrikaans* ~, translate from German into Afrikaans

verta'ler (-s) translator; *beëdigde* ~, sworn translator

verta'ling (-e, -s) translation, version

ver'te (-s) distance

verteenwoor'dig (~) represent; **~end** (-e) representing; **~er** (-s) representative

verteer' (~) digest; spend (wastefully)

vertel' (~) tell, relate, narrate; **~ler** (-s) narrator, relator, storyteller; **~ing** (-e, -s) narration, narrative, tale

vertikaal' (..kale) vertical

vertoef' (~) stay, linger, tarry, abide

vertolk' (~) interpret, explain, voice; **~ing** (-e, -s) interpretation, rendering

verto'ning (-e, -s) show, display; performance (of the economy); *'n mooi/geslaagde* ~, a fine/successful display

vertoog' (..toë) treatise, discussion; *vertoë rig tot,* make representations to

vertoon' (s) show, sight; (w) (~) show; expose; perform; exhibit, display; **~kas** (-te) display cabinet, *ook* **toonkas;** **~rug-** by professional rugby

vertraag' (~) delay, slacken; held up (in traffic); retard; *~de aksie/tempo,* slow motion; *~de kinders,* retarded children

vertrek'[1] (s) (-ke) room, department

vertrek'[2] (s) departure; *dag van* ~, day of departure; (w) (~) leave, depart

vertrek'[3] (w) (~) distort; *sy gesig ~ van die pyn,* his features are twisted with pain

vertroe'tel (~) spoil, (over)indulge

vertroos' (~) console, comfort

vertrou' (~) trust, confide in, rely upon; ~ *op,* rely on; **~baar** (..bare) reliable

vertrou'e confidence, trust; *in* ~, confidentially; *die volste* ~ *geniet,* enjoy the fullest confidence; **~ling** (-e) confidant

vertrou'ensgaping credibility gap

vertrou'eswendelaar confidence trickster/conman, spiv

vertrou'lik (-e; -er, -ste) confidential, private; *streng* ~, strictly confidential

vervaar'dig (~) make; compose; manufacture; ~**er** (-s) manufacturer

verval' (s) decay, decline. maturity; (w) (~) decline, decay; fall due, expire, mature; *die wissel* ~ *(op) 21 Maart*, the bill (of exchange) matures on 21 March; ~**dag** due/expiry date

verval'le (meer ~, mees ~) dilapidated

vervals' (~) adulterate; falsify, fake; forge; ~**ing** fake; adulteration, falsification

verval'tyd due date; *op die* ~, at maturity

vervang' (~) replace, substitute

verveel' (~) bore, weary; *jou* ~, be bored

verveer' (~) moult (birds)

vervel' (~) cast the skin, slough

verve'lend (-e; -er, -ste) boring, tedious, tiresome; *'n* ~*e vent,* a regular bore

verve'lens: *tot* ~ *toe,* ad nauseam

verver'sing (-e, -s) refreshment

vervlaks'! confound it! downright! hang it!

vervloeks! damn it! dash it!

vervoeg' (~) conjugate

vervoer' (s) transport, transportation; conveyance, traffic; (w) (~) convey, carry; ~**dienste** transport services; ~**ing** enthusiasm, rapture, transport, ecstasy; *in* ~*ring raak,* go into raptures; ~**koste** transport charges; ~**toelae** (-s) transport/locomotion allowance

vervolg' (s) continuation, sequel, future; (w) (~) continue; pursue; prosecute, proceed against; *oortreders word* ~, trespassers will be prosecuted; *word* ~, to be continued; ~**ingswaan** persecution mania; ~**verhaal** (..hale) serial

vervolmaak' (w) (~) perfect; *hy het die proses* ~, he perfected the process

vervreem' (~) alienate, estrange

vervroeg' (~) fix at an earlier date, advance a date/time; antedate; expedite

verwaand' (-e; -er, -ste) conceited, pedantic, overweening, stuck up

verwaar'loos (w) (~) neglect; (b) (-de) neglected

verwag' (~) expect; look forward to

verwag'ting (-e, -s) expectation, hope; *bo* ~, beyond expectation; *die* ~ *koester,* cherish the hope

verwant' (s) (-e) relative, relation; (b) (-e) akin, allied; related; ~**skap** relationship

verwar(d) (-de) confused, disordered

verwarm' (~) warm, heat; ~**ing** heating

verwar'ring confusion, perplexity; *in* ~ *bring,* throw into confusion

verweer (s) defence; resistance; (w) (~) defend, resist

verwel'kom (~) welcome; ~**ing** (-e, -s) welcoming, welcome

verwens' (~) curse, execrate

ver'wer (-s) painter (by trade), *kyk* **skilder**

verwerf' (~) acquire, obtain, gain

verwerk' (~) work up; process; digest; revise; ~**er** (-s) processor (data, words)

verwerp' (~) reject, decline; discard; refuse, negative; *'n voorstel* ~, reject a motion

verwe'se disconcerted; dazed, stunned

verwe'senlik (~) substantiate, realise, materialise; *ambisies* ~, realise amibitions

verwester (w) Westernise

verwil'der (~) grow wild; chase away

verwis'sel (~) exchange; alternate; commute; *die tydelike met die ewige* ~, die

verwit'tig (~) acquaint, inform, notify

verwoes' (w) (~) destroy, ruin, devastate, lay waste; (b) (-te) destroyed, devastated; ~**ting** (-e, -s) destruction, devastation, havoc; ~**ting aanrig,** play havoc

verwon'der (~) astonish, amaze, surprise; *jou* ~ *oor,* be surprised at

verwurg' (~) strangle, throttle

verwy'der (~) remove, withdraw; alienate

verwyf' (w) (~) become/make effeminate; (b) (-de) womanish, effeminate

verwys' (~) refer; ~**ing** (-e, -s) reference; *met* ~*ing na,* with reference to; ~**nommer** (-s) reference number

verwyt' (s) (-e) reproach, reproof; (w) (~) reproach, blame, unbraid

very'del (~) frustrate, baffle, shatter, foil

ve'sel (-s) fibre, thread, filament; ~**glas** fibreglass

ves'tig (ge-) establish, settle, direct; found; *die aandag op iets* ~, draw attention to something; *nywerhede* ~, establish industries

vet (s) (-te) fat, lard, grease, suet; *jou lyf maar* ~ *smeer,* prepare for a good thrashing; (b) (-ter, -ste) rich, fertile; fat, corpulent; *so* ~ *soos 'n vark,* as fat as a pig

ve'te (-s) quarrel, feud

ve'ter (-s) lace, bootlace
veteraan' (..rane) veteran; ~motor vintage car; veteran car
vet: ~plant (-e) succulent; ~sug obesity
vi'a via, per
vibreer' (~, ge-) vibrate
vi'deo: ~band (-e) video tape; ~kasset= opnemer (-s) video cassette recorder; ~teek (..teke) video library, kyk bando= teek, diskoteek
vier¹ (s) (-e) four
vier² (w) (ge-) celebrate; observe, keep
vier: ~de (-s) fourth; ~dens in the fourth place
vie'ring (-e, -s) celebration
vier'kant (-e) square; ~ig (-e) square; ~ s'wortel (-s) square root
vier: ~rigtingstop(straat) fourway stop (street); ~skaar tribunal; die ~skaar span, sit in judgment
vier'uur four o'clock
vier'voud (-e) quadruple
vies (w) (ge-); jou ~, be disgusted; (b) (-er, -ste) nasty, offensive, filthy, vexed, fed-up; ~ maak, annoy, vex
vies'lik (-e; -er, -ste) dirty, filthy, loath= some; ~heid loathsomeness, filthiness
viets spruce, smart; 'n ~e nooi, a smart= looking girl
viktimiseer' (~, ge-) victimise
vilt felt; ~hoed (-e) felt hat
vin (-e) fin; geen ~ verroer nie, not lift/stir a finger
vind (ge-) find, come across, meet with
vin'dingryk (-e; -er, -ste) resourceful, inge= nious, inventive
vin'duik skindiving, findiving
vin'ger (-s) finger; ~afdruk (-ke) finger= print; ~hoed (-e) thimble; ~spraak sign language
vink (-e) finch, weaverbird
vin'kel fennel; dis ~ en koljander, it is six of the one and half a dozen of the other
vin'nig (-e; -er, -ste) quick, fast, speedy
viool' (viole) violin, fiddle; tweede ~ speel, play second fiddle; ~tjie (-s) violet
vir for, to
virtuoos' (virtuose) virtuoso
vis (s) (-se) fish
vi'se-kanselier (-s) vice-chancellor
visenteer' (ge-) search, inspect
vi'se-prinsipaal (..pale) vice-principal

vis: ~gereedskap, ~gerei fishing tackle; ~graat (..grate) fish bone; ~hoek (-e) fish hook
visier' (-e, -s) visor, elevating sight
visioen' (-e) vision
vis'ser (-s) fisher, fisherman; ~skuit (-e) fishing boat; ~y (-e) fishery
visueel' (visuele) visual
vis'terman (-ne) angler
vi'sum (-s) visa
vis'vang (w) (-ge-) catch fish; nod, doze
vit (ge-) find fault with, carp, cavil
vitaliteit' vitality
vitamien' (-e), vitami'ne (-s) vitamine
vla (-'s) custard
vlaag (vlae) sudden squall, gust (of wind)
vlag (vlae) flag; standard; vane; die ~ hys, hoist the flag; die ~ stryk, strike one's colours; ~hysing (-e, -s) flag hoisting (ceremony)
vlak (s) (-ke) plane; level, surface
vlak'te (-s) plain, flats
vlak: ~vark (-e) warthog; ~voël (-s) spike-heeled lark
vlam (s) (-me) flame, blaze; ~ vat, take fire; ene vuur en ~, very enthusiastic; (w) (ge-) blaze, burn; ~baar flammable
vlas flax; ~agtig (-e) flaxen
vlees flesh, meat; pulp, kyk vleis; ~lik (-e) carnal, sexual
vleg (w) (ge-) plait, wreathe, twine; ~sel (-s) string, tress, braid
vlei¹ (s) (-e) valley, vale, meadow; vlei
vlei² (w) (ge-) flatter, cringe, coax
vleis flesh and meat; ~braai(ery) braai, barbe= cue, braaivleis; ons is genooi vir 'n vleis= braai, we have been invited to a braai= (vleis)
vlek (s) (-ke) blot, spot, stain, smut, blem= ish; (w) (ge-) soil, blot, stain; ~vry stainless; ~vry staal, stainless steel
vlerk (-e) wing, pinion; ~sleep (w) impress; court a girl
vler'muis (-e) bat
vleu'el (-e) wing; pinion, vane; grand piano; wing threequarter; side aisle
vlie'ënd (-e) flying; ~e piering, flying saucer
vlieënier' (-s) airman, pilot, aviator
vlie'ër (-s) kite; pilot, aviator, airman
vlieg¹ (s) (vlieë) fly

vlieg² (w) (ge-) fly, aviate; ~dekskip (..skepe) aircraft carrier; ~masjien (-e) aeroplane, *kyk* vliegtuig

vlieg'tuig (..tuie) aircraft; (jet) plane; air= liner (passenger service)

vlieg'veld (-e) aerodrome

vlin'der (-s) butterfly

vloed (-e) flood, inundation; ~ramp (-e) flood disaster; ~water floodwater, storm= water

vloei (ge-) flow, stream; ~baar (..bare) fluid, liquid; ~end (-e; -er, -ste) flowing, fluent, smooth, easy; ~end *Engels praat,* be fluent in English; ~papier blotting paper; ~stof (..stowwe) liquid, fluid

vloek (s) (-e) curse, oath; (w) (ge-) swear, curse; ~ *soos 'n matroos/ketter,* swear like a trooper; ~woord (-e) swearword, curse

vloer (-e) floor; *derde* ~, third floor; ~kierie floorshift (car)

vlok (-ke) flock, flake, tuft

vlooi (-e) flea; ~byt (-e) fleabite; ~e'spel tiddlywinks; ~poeier (-s) insect powder

vloot (vlote) fleet, navy; ~eienaar fleet owner (cars); ~soldaat (..date) marine

vlos floss (silk); ~sig (-e; -er, -ste) flossy

vlot (s) (-te) raft; float (cash); (w) (ge-) suc= ceed, move easily, go smoothly; (b, bw) (-ter, -ste) fluent, facile; afloat; ~ *praat,* speak fluently; ~ *verloop,* proceed smoothly

vlug¹ (s) covey, bevy; *'n* ~ *patryse,* a covey of partridges

vlug² (s) flight; escape; *op die* ~ *slaan,* take to flight; (w) (ge-) flee; *huur*~ chartered flight

vlug³ (b) ([-ge], -ger, -ste) quick; nimble; agile; ~ *van begrip,* quick-witted

vlug: ~bal (-le) volleyball; ~heuwel (-s) traffic island; ~hou (-e) volley (tennis)

vlug: ~opnemer flight recorder (black box); ~rooster (-s) flight plan; ~skop punt(ing); ~skrif (-te) leaflet; ~sout volatile salts; ~te'ling (-e) fugitive, refugee

vlug'tig (-e; -er, -ste) hasty, cursory, fleeting; *'n* ~*e besoek,* a flying visit

vly (ge-) lay down, nestle

vlym (-e) lancet; fleam; ~skerp very sharp

vlyt diligence, industry

voed (ge-) feed, nourish

voe'ding feeding, nourishment, nutrition

voed'saam (..same; ..samer, -ste) nutri= tious, nourishing

voed'sel food, nutriment; ~vergiftiging food poisoning

voeg (s) (voeë) joint, seam; (w) (ge-) join; fit in; seam, weld; point (bricks); ~woord (-e) conjunction

voel (ge-) feel, touch, grope; *jy kan dit met 'n stok* ~, it is as plain as a pikestaff; *tuis* ~, feel at home

vo'ël (-s) bird

vo'ël: ~verskrikker (-s) scarecrow; ~vlug bird's-eye view

vo'ëlvry (-e) outlawed; free as a bird; ~ *verklaar,* outlaw a person

voer¹ (s) fodder, forage; (w) (ge-) feed

voer² (w) (ge-) conduct; wage (war); trans= port; *briefwisseling* ~, conduct corres= pondence; *samesprekings* ~, have talks; ~band (-e) conveyor belt

voe'ring (-s) lining

voer'kraal (..krale) feedlot

voer'kuil (-e) silo

voert! go! be gone! clear out!

voer'taal medium of instruction

voe(r)t'sek! get away! be off! footsack!

voer'tuig (..tuie) vehicle, carriage

voet (-e) foot; footing

voet'bal football; ~wedstryd (-e) football match

voet'brug (-ge, ..brûe(ns)) footbridge

voe'tenent (-e) foot, lower end (bed)

voet'ganger (-s) pedestrian; hopper (wing= less locust)

voe'tjie-voe'tjie slowly, cautiously

voet: ~heelkundige (-s) chiropodist; ~pad (..paaie) footpath; ~skimmel athlete's foot; ~slaan (-ge-) footslog; ~slaanpad hiking/tramping trail; ~spoor (..spore) footprint; *iem. se* ~*spore volg,* follow in another's footsteps

vog (-te) liquid, moisture; juice; ~tig (-e; -er, -ste) damp, moist

vokaal' (s) (vokale) vowel; (b) (vokale) vocal

vol (-le; -ler, -ste) full, filled; *uit* ~*le bors sing,* sing at the top of one's voice; *ten* ~*le,* completely, fully; ~bloed tho= roughbred

voldoen' (~) satisfy; pay; comply with; *aan 'n versoek* ~, comply with a request

voldo'nge accomplished; *'n ~ feit,* an accomplished fact

volg (ge-) follow, succeed; shadow; **~ens** according to; *~ens artikel 137,* under section 137; **~orde** (-s) consecutive order, sequence

volhard' (~) persevere, persist

vol'hou (-ge-) persevere, maintain, endure

volk (-e, -ere) people, nation; *die uitverkore ~,* the chosen people

vol'ke: **~kunde** anthropology, ethnology; **~reg** international law; **~re'verhoudinge** race relations

volko'me complete, quite, perfect

volks: **~etimologie** popular etymology; **~ huishouding** domestic economy; **~kunde** folklore; **~lied** (-ere) national anthem; **~mond:** *in die ~mond,* in the language of the people

volk'spele folk dances

volks'planting (-e, -s) colony, settlement

volks: **~telling** (-e, -s) census; *'n ~telling hou,* take a census; **~welsyn** social welfare

volle'dig (-e; -er, -ste) complete, entire

vol'maak (w) (vol ge-) fill

volmaak' (w) (~) perfect; (b) (-te; -ter, -ste) perfect; **~te gelukskoot** perfect fluke (golf), *kyk* **kolhou;** **~t'heid** perfection

vol'maan full moon

vol'mag (-te) power of attorney, proxy

vol'op in abundance, plentiful

volstrek' (-te) absolute; *~te meerderheid,* absolute/clear majority

vol'struis (-e) ostrich; **~skop** (-pe) flying kick, mule kick

voltal'lig (-e) complete, plenary

voltooi' (~) complete, finish; *~d teenwoordige tyd,* perfect tense

vol'treffer (-s) direct hit

voltrek' (~) execute, solemnise

vol'uit in full

volu'me (-s) volume, bulk

vol'vloertapyt (-e) wall-to-wall carpet

volwas'se adult, full-grown; **~ne** (-s) full-grown person, adult; *onderwys vir ~nes,* adult education

vomeer' (~, ge-) vomit

von'deling (-e) foundling

vonds (-te) find, discovery

vonk (-e) spark

von'kel (ge-) sparkle, emit sparks

vonk'prop (-pe) spark plug

von'nis (s) (-se) sentence, judgment; (w) (ge-) sentence, pass judgment

voog (-de) guardian; trustee

voogdy' (-e) guardianship

voor[1] (s) (vore) furrow

voor[2] (bw, vgw, vs) before; in front of; previous to; *een putjie ~,* one hole up (golf); *jou oorlosie is ~,* your watch is fast; **~aand** eve; early evening; **~af** previously, beforehand; *jy moet hom ~af waarsku,* you should warn him beforehand

voor'arm forehand (tennis)

voor'baat advance; *by ~ dank,* thank(ing) you in anticipation

voorba'rig (-e; -er, -ste) rash, premature

voor'bedag (-te) premeditated; *met ~te rade,* premeditated

voor'beeld (-e) example, instance; *by~,* for example; *'n ~ navolg,* follow an example

voorbeel'dig (-e; -er, -ste) exemplary

voor'behoedmiddel (-s) preventive, contraceptive, prophylactic

voor'behoedpil (-le) contraceptive pill

voor'behou (~) reserve; *alle regte ~,* all rights reserved

voor'belas: *~te wins,* profits before tax

voor'berei (~) prepare, coach; **~dend** (-e) preparatory; **~ding** (-e, -s) preparation; **~d'sels** arrangements

voor'beskik (~) predestinate, predestine, preordain; **~king** predestination

voor: **~bode** (-s) forerunner, precursor; omen, foreboding; **~bok** (-ke) bellwether; ringleader

voor'brand (-e) firebreak; *~ maak,* prepare, pave the way

voor'dat before

voor'deel (..dele) profit, advantage, gain, benefit; **~trekker** (-s) beneficiary, *kyk* **begunstigde**

voorde'lig (-e; -er, -ste) profitable, advantageous

voor'deur (-e) front door

voor'dra (-ge-) recite; give an item

voor'drag (-te) lecture, address, speech; delivery, recital; declamation

voor'eergister three days ago

voor: **~gee** (-ge-) pretend, profess to be; give odds; give a start, handicap; **~geewedloop** (..lope) handicap race

voor'(ge)meld (-e)   } above-mentioned
voor'(ge)noem(d) (-de) } aforesaid

voor'gereg (-te) first course, entrée

voor'geskrewe prescribed, set; ~ *boeke,* prescribed books

voor'gestel (-de) proposed; introduced

voor: ~geveg (-te) preliminary bout, curtain raiser; ~geslag (-te) ancestors, forefathers; ~gevoel presentiment, suspicion, foreboding

voor'grond foreground

voor'haker (-s) mechanical horse

voorhan'de on hand; in stock

voor'heen formerly, late; ~ *van die firma X,* formerly of X's

voor: ~hoede (-s) van, vanguard, advance guard; forward line (football); ~hoof (-de) forehead; ~huis (-e) lounge, drawing room

voor'jaar spring

voor'kant (-e) front, face

voor'keer (-ge-) prevent; bar, block; intercept

voor'keur preference; ~aandeel (..ele) preference share

voorkom' (~) forestall, prevent (accident)

voor'kome appearance, bearing, air

voorko'ming prevention; ~(s)aanval (-le) pre-emptive attack/strike

voor: ~laaier (-s) muzzleloader (rifle); front-end loader (machine); ~laaste last but one, penultimate

voor'land fate, destiny; *dis jou ~,* that is in store for you

voor'lê (-ge-) submit, lay before

voor'lees (-ge-) read to; *iem. die leviete ~,* reprimand someone

voor'legging (-s) submission (report, memorandum)

voor'letter (-s) initial (letter)

voor'liefde special liking, preference

voor'lig (-ge-) give information; ~ting(s)-beampte (-s) extension officer

voorlo'pig (b) (-e) preliminary, provisional

voorma'lig (-e) former, sometime; ~*e Eerste Minister,* former Prime Minister

voor'man (-ne) leader, foreman

voor'middag (..dae) forenoon, morning

voor'naam (..name) first name; ~-woord (-e) pronoun

voor'neem (-ge-) resolve, make up one's mind

voor'neme (-ns) intention; resolve

voornoem(d)' (-de) above-mentioned

voor'oordeel (..dele) prejudice, bias

voor: ~ouers ancestors; ~portaal (..tale) porch, hall, lobby; foyer; ~pos (-te) outpost

voor'raad (..rade) stock, provisions, supply; ~opname (-s) stocktaking

voor'rang precedence

voor: ~rede (-s) preface, foreword; ~reg (-te) privilege, prerogative; ~ruit (-e) windscreen (car)

voor'sê (-ge-) prompt, whisper to

voor'setsel (-s) preposition

voorsien' (~) provide, furnish; foresee, anticipate; *in 'n behoefte ~,* meet a need; ~ *van,* provide/supply with

Voorsie'nigheid Providence

voorsie'ning provision; ~ *maak vir,* make provision for

voor'sit (-ge-) preside, take the chair; ~ster (-s) lady chair(man), chairwoman; *Agbare ~ster,* Madam Chair; ~ter (-s) chairman

voor'skoot (..skote) apron, pinafore

voor'skot (-te) advance, accommodation; *'n ~ gee,* advance money

voor'skrif (-te) prescription, direction

voor'skyn: *te ~ bring,* produce; bring to light; *te ~ kom,* appear

voor'smaak foretaste

voor'sorg precaution, provision

voor'spel¹ (s) (-e) prelude, overture

voor'spel² (s) forward play (rugby)

voorspel'³ (w) (~) predict, prophesy, foretell, forecast

voor'speler (-s) forward (football)

voorspel'ling (-e, -s) prophecy, prediction

voor'spoed prosperity

voorspoe'dig (-e, -er, -ste) prosperous

voor'sprong start, advantage; *sy ~ behou,* retain one's lead

voor: ~stad (..stede) suburb; ~stander (-s) advocate, champion, upholder

voor'stel (s) (-le) proposal; (w) (-ge-) propose, move, introduce; ~ler (-s) proposer, mover; ~ling presentation; ~-parade (-s) passing-out parade

voort'bestaan (s) survival, continued existence

voortdu'rend (-e) continuous, incessant

voor'teken (-s) omen, augury, foretoken

voort'gaan (-ge-) continue, proceed; go on

voort'gesette: ~ *onderwys,* continuing education

voor'tou lead; *die ~ neem,* take the lead

voor'plant (-ge-) spread, multiply, propagate, transmit

voortref'lik (-e; -er, -ste) excellent, first rate; *~e diens,* meritorious service

voor'trek (-ge-) treat with favour, single out as favourite

voorts moreover, further, besides

voort'setting (-e, -s) continuation; *voortgesette onderwys,* continuing education

voort'spruit (-ge-) arise, spring from; *~ uit* arise from

voortva'rend (-e; -er, -ste) impulsive, impetuous

vooruit' beforehand, in advance; in front of, before; *~gedateerde tjek,* postdated cheque; *~betaalbaar* payable in advance; *~gang* progress, advancement, improvement

vooruit'sig (-te) prospect, outlook

vooruit'skat (-ge-) forecast; *~ting* (-s) forecast

vooruit'streef, vooruit'strewe (-ge-) forge ahead, push forward, strive forward

voorva'derlik (-e) ancestral

voor: ~val (s) (-le) incident, event; (w) (-ge-) take place, occur; *~vinger* (-s) index finger

voorwaar' indeed, truly, surely

voor'waarde (-s) condition, stipulation; *op ~ dat,* on condition that; *onder daardie ~,* on that condition

voorwaar'delik (-e) conditional

voor'waarts (-e) forward; *~ mars!* quick march!

voor'wedstryd (-e) curtain raiser

voor'wend (-ge-) pretend, profess, sham, make believe; *~sel* (-s) pretext, pretence, subterfuge

voor'werp (-e) object, thing

voor'wiel (-e) front wheel; *~aandrywing* front-wheel drive

voor'woord (-e) preface, foreword

voos (voser, -ste) spongy, pulpy; sickly

vor'der (ge-) make progress; demand, exact; *~ing* (-e, -s) progress; claim, demand; *~ing maak,* progress

vo'rentoe to the fore, forward; *~ boer,* forge ahead; *dit smaak ~,* it tastes good

vo'rige former, past, last; *die ~ dag,* the day before

vorm (s) (-e, -s) form, mould, shape; (w) (ge-) shape, form, mould; *lydende en bedrywende ~,* passive and active voice; *~brief* (..briewe) stock letter; *~drag* foundation garment

vors'telik (-e; -er, -ste) princely; *~e beloning,* princely reward

vort away, gone

vos (-se) fox

vou (s) (-e) crease, fold, ruck, pleat; (w) (ge-) fold, pleat; *~katel* (-s) stretcher; *~stoel* (-e) camp chair, folding chair

vra (ge-) ask, question, query, interrogate

vraag (vrae) question, query, request, demand; *~ en aanbod,* demand and supply; *'n groot ~ na,* a big demand for; *~bank* question bank; *~stuk* (-ke) problem, question; *~teken* (-s) question mark; query

vraat (vrate) glutton; *~sug* gluttony

vra'e: ~lys (-te) questionnaire; *~stel* (-le) (examination) paper

vrag (-te) load, cargo, freight; carriage; *~brief* (..briewe) consignment note (rail), bill of lading (boat); *~motor* (-s) motor lorry, truck; *~skip* (..skepe) cargo vessel, freighter

vrat (-te), **~jie** (-s) wart

vre'de peace, calm

vredelie'wend (-e; -er, -ste) peace-loving

vre'de: ~regter (-s) justice of the peace; *~s'naam: in ~,* for heaven's sake; *~s'voorwaardes* peace terms, conditions of peace

vreed'saam (..same; -samer, -ste) peaceful, calm; *..same naasbestaan,* peaceful coexistence

vreemd (-e; -er, -ste) strange, queer, foreign, alien; *~e: in die ~e,* in foreign parts, abroad; *~e'ling* (-e) stranger, foreigner

vrees (s) fear, apprehension; (w) (ge-) fear, dread, apprehend; *ek ~ dat ...,* I am afraid that...; *~aanja(g)end* (-e) terrifying

vrees'lik (b) (-e; -er, -ste) terrible, horrible, dreadful; (bw) terribly, awfully

vreet (ge-) eat (animals), gorge

vrek[1] (s) (-ke) miser

vrek[2] (w) (ge-) die (animals)

vrek[3] (bw) extremely; *jou ~ werk,* work oneself to death vrek'agtig, vrek'kerig, vrek'kig (-e; -er, -ste) miserly, avaricious, stingy

vreug'(de) joy, gladness

vriend (-e) friend

vrien'delik (-e; -er, -ste) kind, friendly

vriendin' (-ne) lady friend

vriend'skap friendship, favour

vriendskap'lik (-e; -er, -ste) friendly, amicable; 'n ~ ~e wedstryd/brief, a friendly match/letter

vries (ge-) freeze; ~brand frostbite; hy het ge~brand, he was frostbitten; ~punt freezing point; ~weerder (-s) anti-freeze agent

vrind ens. = vriend etc

vroed'vrou (-e, -ens) midwife

vroe'ër (b) former, late; (bw) formerly, earlier; ~ of later, sooner or later

vroeg (vroeë; vroeër, -ste) early, timely; 'n vroeë dood, an untimely death; smôrens ~, early in the morning

vroegty'dig (-e) early, in good time

vroe'tel (ge-) wallow, scratch up soil, burrow; ~vader (-s) sugardaddy

vro'lik (-e; -er, -ste) merry, gay, cheerful

vro'likheid cheerfulness, gaiety, mirth; na ~ kom olikheid, after laughter come tears

vroom (vrome; vromer, -ste) pious, devout, saintly, religious

vrot (w) (ge-) rot, putrefy, decay; (b) (-ter, -ste) rotten, decayed, putrid

vrou (-e, -ens) woman, wife

vrou'e: ~hater (-s) woman hater, misogynist; ~krag woman/fem power; ~vryheid women's lib(erty)

vrou: ~lik (-e) womanly, female; feminine; die ewig ~like, the eternal woman; ~ ~mens (-e), vrous'persoon (..sone) female

vrug result, effect; (-te) fruit; ~afdrywing abortion, ook aborsie

vrug'baar (..bare; -der, -ste) fruitful, prolific, rich, fertile

vrug'gebruik usufruct

vrug'reg (-te) royalty (mining)

vrug'te fruit; results; ~sap (-pe) fruit juice; ~slaai fruit salad, angels' food

vry¹ (w) (ge-) woo, court, flirt; hy ~ na die nooi, he is courting the girl

vry² (b) ([-e]; -er, -ste) free, bold, unconstrained; off duty; ~e markstelsel, free enterprise; dit staan jou ~, you have the option

vry'buiter (-s) privateer, freebooter, buccaneer

vry'burger (-s) free burgher

Vry'dag (..dae) Friday; Goeie ~, Good Friday

vry'er (-s) lover, suitor, wooer

vry'etyd(s)besteding recreation; utilising leisure time

vryf (ge-) rub; massage; polish

vry: ~gesèl (-le) bachelor; ~gewes (-te) dominion

vryge'wig (-e; -er, -ste) generous, liberal

vry'heid (..hede) liberty, freedom

vry: ~heidsvegter freedom fighter; ~ ~hoogte (-s) clearance; ~lating release, emancipation, liberation; ~lating van gyselaars, release of hostages

Vrymes'selaar (-s) Freemason

vrymoe'dig (-e; -er, -ste) candid, frank; ~heid frankness, candour

vry'pageiendom (-me) freehold property

vrypos'tig (-e; -er, -ste) impudent, forward

vry'skut freelance; ~werk doen, freelancing

Vrystaat'! (tw) press on regardless! well done!

vry'stel (ge-) exempt, let off; ~ling (-e, -s) exemption

vry: ~waar (ge-) protect, guard, guarantee; indemnify; iem. vry'waar van/teen siekte, safeguard someone against illness

vry'wil (w) (ge-) volunteer (for service, etc.)

vrywil'lig (-e; -er, -ste) voluntary; ~er (-s) volunteer

vuil ([-e]; -er, -ste) dirty, nasty, smutty, foul, obscene; ~ spel, foul/dirty play; ~ taal gebruik, use dirty words; ~goed dirt; rubbish; dirty person; weeds

vuis (-te) fist; in sy ~ lag, laugh up one's sleeve; uit die ~ praat, speak extempore; ~geveg (-te) boxing match; fisticuffs; ~yster (-s) knuckle duster

vul¹ (s) (-le, -lens) foal; colt (male); filly (female); (w) (ge-) foal

vul² (w) (ge-) fill, stuff

vulgêr' (-e) vulgar

vulkaan' (..kane) volcano; uitgedoofde/uitgewerkte ~, extinct volcano

vul: ~lis rubbish, refuse, trash; ~pen (-ne) fountain pen; ~stasie (-s) filling station

vu'rig (-e; -er, -ste) fiery, spirited, fervent

vurk (-e) fork; ~hyser (-s) fork lift

vuur (s) (vure) fire, flame; ardour; (w) (ge-) fire

vuur: ~**doop** baptism of fire; crucial test; ~**houtjie** (-s) match; ~**maakplek** (-ke) fireplace; comprehension; *dis bo(kant) my ~maakplek,* it is beyond me; ~**peloton** (-s) firing squad; ~**proef** crucial test, acid test, ordeal; *die ~proef deurstaan,* stand the test; ~**pyl** (-e) sky rocket; ~**pylrigter** (-s) rocket launcher; ~**slag** flint, steel and tinder; (cigarette) lighter; ~**spuwend** (-e) belching fire; volcanic; ~*spuwende berg,* volcano; ~**toring** (-s) lighthouse

vuur'vas (-te) fireproof; refractory

vuur: ~**vreter** (-s) fire-eater, hothead; ~**wapen** (-s) firearm; ~**warm** very hot; ~**werk** (-e) fireworks, pyrotechnics

vy (-e) fig

vy'and (-e) enemy, foe; *geswore ~,* sworn enemy/foe

vyan'delik (-e; -er, -ste) hostile, enemy; ~*e gebied,* enemy territory

vyan'dig (-e; -er, -ste) antagonistic, inimical; *'n ~e houding,* a hostile attitude

vyf (vywe) five; ~**de** (-s) fifth; ~*de kolonne,* fifth column; ~**kamp** pentathlon (sport); ~**tien** (-e) fifteen; ~**tig** (-s) fifty; ~**uur** five o'clock; ~**voudig** (-e) fivefold, quintuple

vy'gie (-s) several species of *Mesembryanthemum,* vygie

vyl (s) (-e) file (tool); (w) (ge-) file

vy'sel (-s) mortar; ~**stamper** (-s) pestle

vy'wer (-s) pond, pool

W

wa (-ens) wagon; carriage; truck

waag (ge-) venture, risk, hazard, stake; *'n kans ~,* take a chance; *wie nie ~ nie, wie nie wen nie,* nothing venture, nothing have; ~**arties** (-te) stuntman; ~**hals** (-e) daredevil

waaghal'sig (-e; -er, -ste) daredevilish

waag: ~**hans** (-e) chancer; ~**stuk** (-ke) hazardous undertaking

waai (w) (ge-) blow, fan; ~**er** (-s) fan; ~**erband** (-e) fanbelt

waak (ge-) watch, be awake; ~**eenheid** intensive care unit

waansin'nig (-e; -er, -ste) insane, deranged, distracted, demented

waar[1] (s) (ware) commodity, ware

waar[2] (b, bw) (ware) true, real, genuine; *die ware Jakob,* the real Mackay; *so ~ soos padda manel dra,* as true as faith

waar[3] (bw) where; ~**aan?** by what? to which? *~aan dink jy?* what are you thinking about?

waar[4] (vgw) since, seeing that

waarag'tig (b) (-e; -er, -ste) true, real, genuine; (bw) really, truly, veritably

waar'borg (s) (-e) guarantee, warranty

waarda'sie assessment, valuation

waar'de (s) (-s) worth, value

waardeer' (~, ge-) value, estimate; esteem; appreciate; assess, appraise; ~**der** (-s) valuator, appraiser

waarde'ring (-e, -s) regard, appreciation, esteem; *'n blyk van ~,* a token of appreciation

waar'de: ~**vermindering** depreciation, devaluation; ~**vol** (-le) valuable, of great value

waar'dig (-e; -er, -ste) worthy, dignified; ~**heid** dignity; *benede sy ~heid,* beneath his dignity, infra dig

waar'heen whither, where

waar'heid (..hede) truth; reality; truism

waar'in? wherein? in what/which?

waar'lik indeed, verily, truly

waar'mee? with what/which?

waar'merk (s) (-e) stamp, hallmark; (w) (ge-) stamp, certify, authenticate

waarna' after what/which, whereafter

waar'natoe? where to? whither?

waar'neem (-ge-) perceive, observe, perform; deputise; ~**vermoë** power of observation

waar'nemend (-e) acting, temporary; ~*e direkteur,* acting/deputy director

waar'om? why? wherefore?

waar'omtrent about which; whereabout

waar'onder? among which/whom? under which?

waar'oor? about what? why?

waar'op on what; ~ *staan jy?* what are you standing on?

waarop' on which, whereupon; *die stoel ~ hy sit,* the chair he is sitting on

waar'sê (-ge-) tell fortunes, foretell; **~er,** (-s) fortune teller, soothsayer

waar'sku (ge-) warn, caution; alert; **~wing** (-e, -s) warning, admonition

waarskyn'lik (-e; -er, -ste) probable, likely; **~heid** probability; *na alle ~heid,* in all probability

waar'sonder without which

waar'teen against what/which

waar'uit? out of which/what?

waar'van[1] from where? of/about what? *~ het jy gepraat?* what were you talking about?

waarvan'[2] of which, whose; *die motor ~ die band pap is,* the car whose tyre is flat

waar'voor? wherefore? why? for which?

waat'lemoen (-e) watermelon

wa'enhuis (-e) wagon house, coach house

wa'fel (-s) waffle, wafer

wag (s) (-te) watch; guard, sentry; (w) (ge-) wait, stay

wag'gel (ge-) totter, stagger, reel

wag: ~hond (-e) watchdog; **~kamer** (-s) waiting room

wag: ~lys (-te) waiting list; **~woord** (-e) watchword, password, parole

wa'kend (-e) wakeful, vigilant; *'n ~e oog hou op,* keep a watchful eye on

wak'ker (-der, -ste) awake, alive, vigilant

waks (boot) polish; (w) polish

wal (-le) bank, shore, embankment

walm (s) (-s) dense smoke, vapour

wal'rus (-se) walrus

wals (s) (-e) waltz; roller; (w) (ge-) waltz, dance; roll (steel)

wal'vis (-se) whale

wan: ~aangepas (-te) maladjusted; **~besteding** misappropriation; embezzlement; **~bestuur** mismanagement, misgovernment; **~betaling** non-payment, default

wand (-e) wall

wan'daad (..dade) misdeed, outrage

wan'del (s) walk; conduct, behaviour; *in sy handel en ~,* in his conduct of life; (w) (ge-) walk; take a walk; *gaan ~,* go for a walk/stroll; **~aar** (-s) walker, pedestrian; hiker; **~ing** (-e, -s) walk, stroll; **~laan** (..lane) (pedestrian) mall

wang (-e) cheek

wan'hoop (s) despair; (w) (ge-) despair

wan'klank (-e) dissonance, false note

wan'neer when; if

wan'orde disorder, confusion

wan'praktyk (-e) malpractice

wanska'pe monstrous, deformed

want[1] (s) rigging (ship)

want[2] (vgw) for, because

wan'trou (ge-) distrust, suspect; **~e** distrust, mistrust, suspicion; *'n mosie van ~e,* a motion of no confidence

wa'pen (s) (-s) weapon, arm(s); coat of arms, crest, badge; (w) (ge-) arm; **~gekletter** sabre rattling; **~opslagplek** (-ke) arms cache; **~stilstand** (-e) armistice, truce; **~tuig** arms, weaponry; **~wedloop** armaments race

wap'per (ge-) fly out, float, flutter

war confusion, muddle; **~boel** confusion, muddle, mixup

wa're wares, goods, commodities, *kyk* **waar**[1]

warm (w) (ge-) warm; (b) (-er, -ste) warm

warm'te heat, warmth; ardour

war'rel (ge-) whirl, swirl; reel; **~wind** (-e) whirlwind

was[1] (s) washing; (w) (ge-) wash; *iem. se kop ~,* give someone a bit of one's mind

was[2] (s) (-se) wax

was[3] (w) (ge-) grow, wax; *die ~sende maan,* the waxing moon

was[4] (w) was; *kyk* **wees**

was'bak (-ke) sink, wash basin

wa'sem (-s) vapour, steam

was'goed washing; **~mandjie** (-s) laundry basket

was'kers (-e) wax candle

was'masjien (-e) washing machine

was: ~outomaat (..mate) automatic washing machine; **~poeier** washing powder

wasseret' (-te) launderette, laundromat

was'ter (-s) washer (ring)

wat (vr. vnw.) what; *alles en nog ~,* all sorts of things; *'n stuk of ~,* a few; (betr. vnw.) who, that, which, what; (onbep. vnw.) whatever, something

wa'ter (s) dropsy; (-s) water; *te ~ laat,* launch; *~ op sy meul,* grist to his mill; (w) (ge-) water; **~bestand** water resistant; **~blommetjie** (-s) water lily; **~dig** (-te) waterproof, watertight; **~draer** (-s) drone; water carrier; **~fiskaal** (..kale) water bailiff wa'ter: ~hoof hydrocephalus; ~hoos (..hose) water spout; ~nood need/short= age of water; ~pas (s) (-se) spirit level; (b) level; ~pokkies chicken pox; ~ponie wetbike, ski-jet

wa'tersnood inundation, floods

wa'ter: ~sopnat dripping wet; ~stewel (-s) gum/rubber boot; ~stof hydrogen; ~ = stofbom (-me) hydrogen bomb; ~tand (ge-) make the mouth water; ~val (-le) waterfall, cataract

wa'terverf water colour; ~skildery (-e) watercolour painting

wa'ter: ~werend water resistant; ~wyser (-s) water diviner

wat'te wadding; cotton wool

wat'telbas wattle bark

wat'ter which; ~ een, which (one)?

watwon'ders (-e) startling, jolly good; nie 'n ~e boek nie, not a wonderful book

wa'wyd (..wye) very wide; ~ oop, ~ ope, wide open

web (-be) web

wed (ge-) wager, bet; ek ~ jou, I bet you; ~denskap (-pe) wager, bet; 'n ~denskap aangaan, lay a wager; ~der (-s) punter (horse racing), ook wedrenganger

we'derhelf (-te(s)) better half, half-section

wederke'rig (-e) mutual, reciprocal

wederom' again, anew; (tot) ~! so long! see you again!

we'(d)eropstanding resurrection

we'(d)ersyds mutual, reciprocal

wedervaar' (~-) befall, meet with, occur; reg laat ~, do justice to

wederva'ring (-e, -s) occurrence, incident

wed'loop (..lope) race (athletics)

wed'ren (-ne) race (cars, horses)

wed'stryd (-e) match, competition, contest; ~punt (-e) match point

wed'syfer (-s) odds

we'duvrou (-e, -ens) widow

we'duwee (s) widow

wed'vaart (-e) race (canoes, yachts)

wed'vlug (-te) race (aeroplanes, gliders)

wed'ywer (w) (ge-) compete, emulate, vie

weef (ge-) weave; ~masjien (-e) (power) loom; ~skool (..skole) weaving school

weeg (ge-) weigh, balance; ~skaal (..skale) balance, (pair of) scales

week[1] (s) (weke) week; oor 'n ~, this day week

week[2] (w) (ge-) soak, steep in; laat ~, leave soaking

week[3] (b) (weker, -ste) soft, tender

week'blad (..blaaie) weekly (paper)

week: ~liks (-e) weekly; ~loon weekly wages; ~s'dag (..dae) weekday

weel'de luxury; profusion; ~artikel (-s) luxury article

wee'luis (-e) (bed) bug

weemoe'dig (-e; -er, -ste) sad, melancholy

ween (ge-) weep, cry

weens (vs) on account of; ~ gebrek aan geld, for want of money

weer[1] (s) weather; swaar ~, thunder and lightning

weer[2] (w) (ge-) defend; exert oneself, strain every nerve; jy moet jou ~, you must ex= ert yourself

weer[3] (bw) again, a second time; ~ eens, (once) again; heen en ~, to and fro

weer'baar (..bare) able-bodied, fit; ~heid defensibility, preparedness

weer: ~berig (-te) weather report; ~buro (-'s) weather bureaux

weer'ga rival, match, equal; sonder ~, matchless

weergalm' (w) (~-) echo, resound

weer: ~glas (-e) barometer; ~haan (..hane) weathercock

weerhou' (~-) keep back, refrain from, re= strain; ~ van kommentaar, refrain from comment

weerkaats' (~-) reflect, re-echo; ~ing re= flection

weer'klank echo, resonance

weer'kunde meteorology

weer'lig (s) (-te) lightning

weer'loos (..lose) defenceless

weer: ~mag armed forces; defence force; ~man (-ne) private (soldier)

weer'profeet (..fete) weather prophet

weer'sien (ge-) meet again; ~s: tot ~s! so long! till we meet again!

weer'sin repugnance, antipathy, dislike

weers'kante both sides

weerspie'ël (~-) mirror, reflect; ~ing re= flection

weerspreek' (~-) contradict, gainsay

weer'stand resistance, opposition; die weg van die geringste ~, the line of least re= sistance; ~(s)beweging resistance move= ment

weers'verwagting (-e, -s) weather forecast/
expectation

weer'vas all-weather; ~te baan, all-weather
court

weer'voorspelling (-s) weather forecast

weer'wil: in ~ van, in spite of, despite

weer'wraak revenge, retribution

wees[1] (s) (wese) orphan

wees[2] (w) (is, was, ge-) to be

wees'huis (-e) orphanage

wees'kind (-ers) orphan

weet (wis, ge-) know, be conscious of, have
knowledge of

weetgie'rig (-e; -er, -ste) eager to learn

weg[1] (s) (weë) way, road

weg[2] (b, bw) away, off, gone

weg'doen (-ge-) dispose (of); ~baar disposable (e.g. syringe)

weg'kom (-ge-) get away; maak dat jy ~!
be gone

weg'kruip (-ge-) hide oneself; ~ertjie hide-
and-seek (children's game)

weg'neem (-ge-) take away; ~ete (-s) take-
away (food)

weg: ~skram (-ge-) flinch away; evade;
~'slaan (-ge-) strike/beat away, swallow
(a drink)

weg'spring (-ge-) jump away, start off; on-
gelyke ~, false start

weg: ~'steek (-ge-) hide; retain, hold up
(milk); ~'sterf, ~'sterwe (-ge-) die away

weg'wyser (-s) signpost, roadsign

wei (s) (-e) pasturage, meadow; (w) (ge-)
feed, graze; ~ding (-s) pasturage, grazing

wei'er (ge-) decline, refuse; ~ing (-e, -s) refusal

wei'fel (ge-) waver, vacillate

wei'nig (-e; minder, minste) little, few; ~ of
niks, little or nothing

wei'veld (-e) pasture land, meadow; grazing

wek (ge-) wake, rouse, stir; ~ker (-s) alarm
clock; ~roep clarion call; slogan

wel[1] (s): die ~ en wee, the weal and the woe;
(bw) (beter, bes(te)) well, all right; ~ te
ruste! good night! sleep well!

wel[2] (tw) well!

wel'behae feeling of comfort, pleasure; in
mense 'n ~, goodwill to men

wel'bekend (-e) well-known, noted

wel'daad (..dade) kindness, kind action

welda'dig (-e; -er, -ste) charitable

wel'doen (-ge-) do good, support; -er (-s)
benefactor

wele'del (-e) honourable; ~e heer, dear sir

weleerwaar'de (right) reverend

welgeluksa'lig (-e) blessed

wel: ~'geskape well-formed, well-made;
~'gesteld (-e) opulent, affluent, well-to-
do

we'lig (-e; -er, -ste) luxuriant, exuberant

wel'ke which, what, ook watter

wel'kom (-e) welcome, acceptable; ~ heet,
extend a hearty welcome; ~ in Welkom,
welcome to Welkom; ~ tuis! welcome
home!

welle'wend (-e; -er, -ste) courteous, well-
mannered, well-bred

wellui'dend (-e; -er, -ste) melodious

wel'lus (-te) delight, bliss; sensual pleasure,
lust; 'n ~ vir die oë, a feast for the
eyes

wel'opgevoed (-e) well-bred, polite

welp (-e) cub, whelp

wel'sand quicksand

wel'slae success; met ~ voltooi, complete
successfully

welspre'kend (-e; -er, -ste) eloquent, articu-
late; ~heid eloquence

wel'stand welfare, health, wellbeing; in ~
lewe, live in comfort

wel'syn wellbeing; welfare; na sy ~ verneem, enquire after his wellbeing

wel'vaart welfare, prosperity

welva'rend (-e; -er, -ste) prosperous, wealthy, thriving; affluent

welwil'lend (-e; -er, -ste) kindly disposed,
favourable; ~heids'besoek (-e) courtesy
visit

Welwil'lendheidsdag Day of Goodwill

we'mel (ge-) swarm, teem with, abound in;
dit ~ van foute, it bristles with mistakes

wen[1] (w) (ge-) accustom, make used to; ek
is daaraan gewend, I am accustomed to
that

wen[2] (w) (ge-) win, gain; outdistance; 'n
wedstryd ~, win a match

wend (ge-) turn; jou tot iem. ~ om raad,
turn to someone for advice

wen'ding (-e, -s) turn; 'n gunstige ~ neem,
take a turn for the better

wenk (-e) hint, sign, nod, tip

wen'ner (-s) winner

wens (s) (-e) wish, desire; (w) (ge-) wish, desire; ~denkery, ~dinkery wishful thinking

wens'lik (-e; -er, -ste) desirable

wens'put (-te) wishing well

wen'streep (..strepe) finish (in a race)

wen'tel (ge-) roll over; welter, wallow, revolve, rotate; orbit; ~aar orbiter; ~baan orbit; ~krediet revolving credit; ~trap (-pe) spiral/winding staircase

werd worth; nie die moeite ~ nie, not worth while

wê'reld (-e) world; ~beroemd (-e) world-famed; ~burger (-s) cosmopolitan; ~deel (..dele) continent

wêrelds (-e) worldly, secular

wê'reld: ~stad (..stede) metropolis; ~taal universal language; ~wyd world-wide; ~wys world-wise; philosophic

werf¹ (s) (werwe) farmyard; shipyard; yard

werf² (w) (ge-) enlist, enrol, recruit; stemme ~, canvass for votes

werk (s) (-e) work, labour, employment; ~ soos bossies, a mountain of work; (w) (ge-) work, labour, operate, function; ~ soos 'n esel, work like a slave; ~afbakening job reservation; ~bevrediging job satisfaction

wer'ker (-s) worker; ~skakel shop steward (in trade union)

werk: ~geleentheid job opportunity; ~gewer (-s) employer; ~gewersburo (-'s) employment agency

wer'king (-e, -s) action, efficacy, working, operation; buite ~ stel, put out of action; in volle ~, in full swing/production

werk'lik (-e) real, true, actual; ~ waar, actually; truly; ~e waarde, true/intrinsic value

werk'likheid (..hede) reality, actuality

werk'loos (..lose) unemployed; idle, inactive; ~heid unemployment

werk: ~man (-ne, ..liede, ..lui, ..mense) workman, labourer, artisan; ~nemer (-s) employee; ~olis' workaholic, ook werkslaaf

werk'saam (..same, ..samer, -ste) active, industrious, effective

werk(s)'bevrediging job satisfaction

werk'sku (-we) workshy

werk: ~slaaf (..awe) work addict; workaholic; ~soeker (-s) job seeker

werk'staking (-e, -s) strike

werk'tuig (..tuie) tool, implement

werktuigkun'dig (-e) mechanical; ~e (-s) mechanic(ian)

werk: ~verrigting performance of work; ~verskaffing (providing of) employment; ~winkel (-s) workshop; ~woord (-e) verb

werkwoor'delik (-e) verbal

werp (ge-) cast; throw; ~sel (-s) litter; ~skyf (..skywe) quoit; discuss; ~spies (-e) javelin, dart

wer'skaf (ge-) do, make, be busy; wat ~ jy? what are you busy on?

wer'wing recruiting, canvassing

wes west

we'se (-ns) being, nature, essence

we'sel (-s) weasel, mink

we'senlik (-e) essential, real, actual

wes'kus (-te) west coast

wesp (-e) wasp; ~e'nes (-te) wasp's nest

weste west; buite ~, unconscious

wes'tergrens (-e) western boundary

Wes'ters (-e) Western

wes'tewind (-e) west wind

wet¹ (s) (-te) law; act; 'n ~ oortree, contravene a law; die ~ toepas, apply the law

wet² (w) (ge-) sharpen, whet

we'te knowing, knowledge; teen jou beterwete in, against one's better judgment; buite my ~, without my knowledge

we'tenskap (-pe) science, knowledge; ~fiksie science fiction

wetenskap'lik (-e) scientific; ~e (-s) scientist

wetenswaar'dig (-e) worth knowing

wet: ~geleerde (-s) lawyer, jurist; ~gewend (-e) legislative; ~gewende liggaam, legislature; ~gewing (-e, -s) legislation; legislature

wet'lik (-e) legal; hulle is ~ geskei, they are legally divorced; ~e voorskrif, legal prescription/requirement

wets: ~gehoorsaam law abiding; ~ontwerp (-e) bill, draft act; ~toepassing law enforcement

wet'tig (w) (ge-) justify; legalise; (b) (-e) lawful, legitimate; ~e eggenoot, lawful spouse; ~e erfgenaam, heir-at-law

we'wenaar (-s) widower; blackjack

we'wer (-s) weaver; ~y (-e) weaving mill, cotton factory

wie who; whom; ~ se hoed? whose hat?

wieg (s) (wieë) cradle, cot

wie'gelied (-ere) lullaby, cradle song

wiel (-e) wheel; *iem. in die ~e ry,* put a spoke in someone's wheel; *die ~e spoor nie,* the wheels are out of alignment; *~dop* (-pe) hub cap

wiel(i)ewa'lie merry-go-round (game)

wiel'sporing wheel alignment

wier (-e) seaweed

wie'rook incense

wig (-ge, wie) wedge; quoin; key

wik (ge-) reflect, weigh, poise; *die mens ~, maar God beskik,* man proposes, God disposes

wik'kel (ge-) wrap, wind round; wobble, move from side to side; *~doedie* go-go girl

wiks (ge-) clout; beat, flog

wil[1] (s) will, wish, desire; *teen ~ en dank,* in spite of oneself; *ter ~le van,* for the sake of

wil[2] (w) (wou, ge-) wish, want to

wild (s) game; (b) (-e; -er, -ste) wild, savage, fierce; *~dief* (..diewe) poacher

wil'de (s) savage; *~bees'* (-te) wildebees, gnu; *~makou'* (-e) spur-winged goose

wil'dernis (-se) wilderness, waste

wildevy' (-e) wild fig

wildewrag'tig wild-looking/scary person

wild: *~s'vleis* venison, game; *~vreemd* (-e) quite strange

wilg (-e), **wil'ger** (-s), **wil'gerboom** (..bome), **wil'ker** (-s), **wil'kerboom** (..bome) willow tree

wil'lekeur arbitrariness; *na ~,* at will

wils'krag willpower

wim'pel (-s) pennant, pennon, streamer

wim'per (-s) eyelash

wind (-e) wind, breeze; flatulence; *deur die ~ wees,* talk airy nonsense; *die ~ van voor kry,* run into difficulties; *~buks* (-e) airgun, pellet gun; boaster; windbag; *~erig* (-e; -er, -ste) windy; *~hoos* (..hose) windspout, whirlwind; *~jekker* (-s) windbreaker; *~laaier* (-s) wind charger; *~lawaai(er)* braggart, gasbag

wind: *~meter* (-s) wind gauge; *~meul* (-e), *~meule* (-(n)s) windmill; *'n klap van die ~meul weg hê,* have bats in the belfry

wind: *~stilte* calm; *streek van ~stilte,* doldrums; *~weerstand* wind resistance

win'gerd (-s) vineyard; *~griep* hangover

wink (s) (-e) wink; (w) (ge-) wink, beckon; *~brou* (-e) eyebrow

win'kel (-s) shop, store; *~diefstal* (-le) shoplifting; *~haak* (..hake) set square, try square

winkelier' (-s) shopkeeper, dealer

win'kel: *~sentrum* shopping centre; *~slyt* shop-soiled; *~tande* dentures, false teeth; *~venster* shop window

wins (-te) profit, gain; *~ afwerp/oplewer,* yield a profit; *~drempel* break-even point

wins-en-verlies'rekening (-e, -s) profit and loss account

wins: *~ge'wend* (-e; -er, -ste) lucrative, profitable; *~grens* (-e) profit margin; *~kopie* (-s) bargain; *~verdeling(s)rekening* (-e, -s) appropriation account

win'ter (-s) winter; *in die ~,* in winter; *~hande* chilblained hands; *~slaap* hibernation

wip (s) (-pe) seesaw; snare, trap; (w) (ge-) hop; seesaw; tilt; turn cheeky; *~mat* (-te) trampoline; *~plank* (-e) seesaw; *~tuig* (tuie..) jolly-jumper

wis'kunde mathematics

wiskun'dig (-e) mathematical; *~e* (-s) mathematician

wispeltu'rig (-e; -er, -ste) fickle, inconsistent; *~heid* inconstancy, fickleness

wis'sel (s) (-s) bill, draft; points, switch (railway); *'n ~ aksepteer,* accept a bill; *'n ~ honoreer,* honour a bill; (w) (ge-) exchange, change; shed (teeth); *~aar* (-s) money changer; interchange; *~bou* crop rotation; *~fonds* cash float; *~koers* (-e) rate of exchange; *~kruising* traffic interchange; *~stroom* (..strome) alternating current; *~trofee* (..feë) floating trophy

wisselval'lig (-e; -er, -ste) uncertain, variable, unsteady, inconstant

wis'selwerking interaction, interplay

wis'ser (-s) wiper, eraser; sponge

wit (w) (ge-) whitewash; distemper; (b) (-ter, -ste) white; blank; *~blits* peach brandy, mampoer; *~gepleister* (-de) whitewashed; *~gepleisterde grafte,* whited sepulchres

Wit'man (..mense) white South African, White

wit: *~seerkeel* diphtheria; *~tebroodsdae, ~tebroodsweke* honeymoon; *~voet* whitefooted; *~voetjie soek,* curry favour

woed (ge-) rage, work havoc, rage fiercely; ~e fury, rage; ~end (-e; -er, -ste) furious, violent, infuriated

woe'fie (-s) (pet name for) dog; ~tuiste (-s) (boarding) kennels

woek'er (s) usury; interest; (w) (ge-) practice, make the most of; ~wins (-te) exorbitant profit

woel (ge-) bustle; fidget; work hard; toss about; ~water (-s) restless person, fidget, bustler

Woens'dag (..dae) Wednesday

woes (-te; -ter, -ste) desolate, waste, wild; furious, savage, fierce, ferocious

woestyn' (-e) desert, wilderness

wol wool

wolf (wolwe) wolf

wolk (-e) cloud; ~breuk (-e) cloudburst

wol'kekrabber (-s) skyscraper

wol: ~kweker (-s) woolgrower; W~raad Wool Board

wol'wegif strychnine

wond (s) (-e) wound; (w) (ge-) wound

won'der (s) (-s) wonder; (w) (ge-) wonder

won'der: ~kind (-ers) wonder child, infant prodigy; ~lik (-e; -er, -ste) marvellous, strange, curious, wonderful; ~werk (-e) miracle

wo'ning (-s) dwelling, residence

woon: ~buurt (-e) residential area; ~huis (-e) dwelling house, residence; ~stel (-le) flat, maisonette; ~wa (..waens) caravan

woord (-e) word; term; message

woor'de: ~boek (-e) dictionary; ~lik (-e) literal, verbatim; ~skat vocabulary; ~wisseling dispute, debate

woord: ~skittery verbal diarrhoea; ~speling (-e, -s) pun, quibble; ~verwerker (-s) word processor, *kyk* **teksverwerker**; ~voerder (-s) spokesman, mouthpiece

word (ge-) become, take place; *dronk* ~, get drunk; *siek* ~, take ill

wors (-e, -te) sausage; ~ *in 'n hondestal soek,* look for a needle in a haystack; ~broodjie (-s) hot dog; ~rolletjie (-s) sausage roll

wor'stel (ge-) wrestle, struggle

wor'tel (s) (-s) root; carrot

woud (-e) forest

wou'terklouter jungle-jim (play apparatus)

wraak (s) revenge, vengeance; ~ *neem,* take vengeance/revenge

wraaksug'tig (-e; -er, -ste) revengeful

wrag'gies } indeed, surely, truly; *hy is* ~
wrag'tie } *weg!* he is actually gone!

wrak (-ke) wreck, derelict; *liggaamlike* ~, physical wreck; ~werf (..werwe) scrap yard

wrang (-e; -er, -ste) acrid, astringent, acid

wreed (wrede; wreder, -ste) cruel, barbarous, truculent; ~aard (-s) cruel person

wreedaar'dig (-e; -er, -ste) cruel, inhuman

wreek (ge-) take revenge, avenge

wre'ker (-s) avenger, revenger

wre'wel resentment, rancour, spite

wrie'mel (ge-) wriggle; swarm

wring (ge-) wring, wrench, writhe; ~krag torque

wrin'tie } really, surely, truly
wrin'tig }

wroeging (-e, -s) remorse, compunction

wrok (-ke) grudge, rancour; *'n* ~ *koester,* bear a grudge

wry'wing (-e, -s) friction; rubbing

wuif, wui'we (ge-) wave, beckon; *vriende tot siens* ~, wave goodbye to friends

wulps (-e; -er, -ste) lascivious, sexy

wurg (ge-) strangle, throttle, choke; ~greep stranglehold; ~ketting choke chain; ~roof mug(ging); ~rower (-s) mugger

wurm (-s) worm, maggot, grub

wy (ge-) devote, consecrate, dedicate

wyd (wye; wyer, -ste) wide, broad, spacious, ample; ~ *en syd,* far and wide

wyds'been astraddle, astride

wyd'te (-s) width, breadth

wyf (wywe) mean woman, vixen

wy'fie (-s) female; cow (elephant); hen (birds); ~eend (-e) duck

wyk (w) (ge-) withdraw, yield, give way; *geen duimbreed* ~ *nie,* not budge an inch

wy'le late, deceased

wyn (-e) wine; ~ *in die man, wysheid in die kan,* when wine is in, wit is out; ~bou viticulture; vine growing; ~kelder (-s) wine cellar; winery

wyn: ~stok (-ke) vine; ~vaatjie (-s), ~vat (-e) wine barrel, wine cask

wys¹ (s) (-e) way, manner; mood (grammar); *by* ~e *van,* by way of

wys² (w) (ge-) show, demonstrate, indicate; direct; *iem.* ~ *waar Dawid die wortels gegrawe het,* teach someone a thing or two

wys[3] (b) ([-e]; -er, -ste) prudent, sage, wise; obstinate, impertinent
wys'begeerte philosophy
wy'se[1] (-s) wise man, sage
wy'se[2] (-s) way; mood (gram.)
wy'ser (-s) index hand (of a clock)
wys'geer (..gere) philosopher, *ook* **filosoof**
wys'heid wisdom
wy'sie (-s) melody, tune, air

wy'sig (ge-) modify, amend, alter; ~**ing** (-e, -s) amendment, modification, alteration; *die grondreëls/konstitusie* ~, amend the constitution
wys'lik wisely
wys'maak (-ge-) make believe; impose on
wys'vinger (-s) index finger, forefinger
wyt (ge-) impute, accuse, blame; *te* ~*e aan*, owing to

X

X'-bene bow/bandy legs
xenograaf' (..grawe) xenograph'
Xho'sa Xhosa

xilofoon' (..fone) xylophone
X'-strale X-rays, Röntgen rays

Y

y'del (-e; -er, -ste) idle, useless, futile; vain, conceited; ~**heid** (..hede) vanity
yk (ge-) test, adjust, assize, stamp
yl (b) (-er, -ste) thin, rarefied
ylhoof'dig (-e) delirious, light-headed
ys[1] (s) ice; *op gladde* ~ *staan,* be in danger; (w) (ge-) freeze, ice
ys[2] (w) (ge-) shudder, shiver; *ek* ~ *as ek dink . . .,* I shudder to think . . . .
ys: ~**baan** (..bane) ice/skating rink; ~**berg** (-e) iceberg; ~**ig** (-e) ice cold
ys: ~**kas** (-te) refrigerator, icebox; ~**koud** (..koue) cold as ice; *dit laat my* ~*koud,* it leaves me cold

ys'lik (-e) enormous, tremendous
ys: ~**reën** sleet; ~**sak** (-ke) coolbag
Ys'see Arctic Ocean
ys'ter (-s) iron
ys'terklou: ~ *in die grond slaan,* (i) take to one's heels; (ii) dig in one's heels
ys'ter: ~**paal** (..pale) iron standard/pole; ~**perd** (-e) bicycle; train; ~**saag** (..sae) hacksaw; ~**vark** (-e) porcupine; ~**ware** hardware, ironmongery
y'wer (s) diligence, zeal, ardour, industry

Z

ze'ro zero, naught, *kyk* **sero**
Zimbab'we Zimbabwe; *die Zimbabwiese ekonomie,* the Zimbabwe (Zimbabwean) economy
Zimbab'wiër (-s) Zimbabwean (person)
Zoe'loe (-s) Zulu; ~**impie** (-s) Zulu regiment; ~**land** Zululand

zoem (s) buzz(ing), drone; (w) (ge-) buzz, zoom, whizz, drone; ~ *in,* zoom in (fot.); ~ *weg,* zoom away; ~**er** (-s) zoom/buzz apparatus; ~**lens** (-e) zoom lens; ~**pie** (-s) blue duiker (antelope)

197

AFKORTINGS

A

Afrikaans		Engels
AA	Automobiel-Assosiasie	AA
aant.	aantekening	note
AD	*Anno Domini* (in die jaar van ons Here)	AD
ad inf.	*ad infinitum* (tot die oneindige)	ad inf.
adjt.	adjudant	adj., ADC
adj.-off.	adjudant-offisier	WO
ad lib.	*ad libitum* (na verkiesing)	ad lib.
admin.	administrateur/administrasie	adm./admin.
adm.	admiraal	Adm.
adv.	advokaat	Adv.
ad val.	*ad valorem* (volgens waarde)	ad val.
AEK	Atoomenergiekorporasie	AEC
afb.	afbeelding	illus.
afd.	afdeling	div.
afk.	afkorting	abbr.
Afr.	Afrikaans; Afrikaner	Afr.
akk.	akkusatief	acc.
alg.	algemeen	general
Angl.	Anglisisme	Angl.
antw.	antwoord	ans.
antw. asb.	antwoord asseblief	RSVP
antw. bet.	antwoord betaal	reply pd.
Apr.	April	Apr.
art.	artikel	art.
a.s.	aanstaande	prox.
asb.	asseblief	please/s.v.p.
asv.	afwesig sonder verlof	awol
asst.	assistent	asst.
Aug.	Augustus	Aug.
ATKV	Afrikaanse Taal- en Kultuurvereniging	–
AVB	Algemene (Ver)koopbelasting	GST
a.w.	aangehaalde werk	op. cit.

B

B.A.	*Baccalaureus Artium*	B.A.
bal.	balans	bal.
bat.	bataljon	bat.
BBP	baie belangrike persoon	VIP
B.Com.	*Baccalaureus Commercii*	B.Com.
B.D.	*Baccalaureus Divinitatis*	B.D.
bd.	boulevard	Bd.
B.Ed.	*Baccalaureus Educationis*	B.Ed.

Afrikaans		Engels
bet.	betaal	pd.
bg.	bogenoemd(e)	above-mentioned
bl.	bladsy(e)	p.
B.M.	*Baccalaureus Medicinae*	B.M.
B.Mus.	*Baccalaureus Musicae*	B.Mus.
BNP	Bruto Nasionale Produk	GNP
b.nw.	byvoeglike naamwoord	adj.
B.O.	bevelvoerende offisier	C.O.
b.o.	blaai om	PTO
Bpk	Beperk	Ltd
Brig.-genl.	brigadegeneraal	brig. genl.
B.Sc.	*Baccalaureus Scientiae*	B.Sc.
BSW	Buitesintuiglike Waarneming	ESP
bv.	byvoorbeeld	e.g./eg
bvp	been voor paaltjies	lbw
B.V.Sc.	*Baccalaureus Veterinariae Scientiae*	B.V.Sc.
bw	bywoord	adv.
B/W	betaalwissel	B/P
byl.	bylae	encl.

C

C	Celsius	C/Cels.
c	sent	c
cc	kubieke sentimeter	cc
cf.	*confer* (vergelyk)	cf.
cg	sentigram	cg
Ch.B	*Chirurgiae Baccalaureus*	Ch.B.
Ch.M.	*Chirurgiae Magister*	Ch.M.
CJV	Christelike Jongeliedevereniging	YMCA
cℓ	sentiliter	cℓ
cm	sentimeter	cm
CSV	Christen-Studentevereniging	SCA
CV	*Curriculum vitae*	CV

D

D	Romeinse 500	D
dat.	datief	dat.
D/N	debietnota	D/N
DBV	Dierebeskermingvereniging	SPCA
d.d.	*de dato* (gedateer)	dated
D.D.	*Doctor Divinitatis*	D.D.
deelw.	deelwoord	part.
def.	definisie	def.
dept.	departement	dept.
des.	deser	inst.
Des.	Desember	Dec.
dg	desigram	dg

Afrikaans		Engels
Dg	dekagram	Dg
dgl.	dergelike	such
d.i.	dit is	i.e./ie
di.	*domini* (predikante)	Revs.
Di.	Dinsdag	Tues.
dist.	distrik	dist.
div.	dividend	div.
dℓ	desiliter	dℓ
dl.	deel	vol.
Dℓ	dekaliter	Dℓ
D.Litt.	*Doctor Literarum*	D.Litt.
dm.	duim	in.
dm	desimeter	dm
Dm	dekameter	Dm
dnr.	dienaar	serv.
do.	*ditto* (dieselfde)	do.
Do.	Donderdag	Thurs.
dos.	dosyn	doz.
D.Phil	*Doctor Philosophiae*	D.Phil.
DPW	Departement (van) Publieke Werke	PWD
dr.	debiteur	Dr.
dr(.)	doktor/dokter	Dr
drr.	dokters/doktore	Drs
ds(.)	*dominus* (dominee)	Rev.
D.Sc.	*Doctor Scientiae*	D.Sc.
dt.	debet/debiet	Dt.
D.V.	*Deo Volente* (as God wil)	D.V.
dw.	dienswillig	obed.
d.w.s./dws	dit wil sê	i.e./ie

E

e.a.	en ander	etc.
e.d.	en dergelike	etc.
Ed.	Edele	Hon.
Ed. Agb.	Edelagbare	Hon.
e.d.m.	en dergelike/dies meer	etc.
Edms	Eiendoms	Pty
eerw.	eerwaarde	Rev.
e.g.	eersgenoemde	the former
e.k.	eerskomende	next
EKG	Elektrokardiogram	ECG
Ekon.	Ekonomie	Econ.
eks.	eksemplaar	copy
Eks.	Eksellensie	Excl.
ekskl.	eksklusief	excl.
ekv.	enkelvoud	sing.
Eng.	Engels	Engl.
ens.	ensovoorts	etc.
ere-sekr.	eresekretaris	Hon. Sec.

Afrikaans		Engels
e.s.m.	en so meer	etc.
ev.	eersvolgende	next
e.v.	en volgende	*et. seq./et. sq(q).*
EVKOM	Elektrisiteitvoorsieningskommissie	ESCOM
ex. off.	*ex officio* (ampshalwe)	ex. off.

F

F	Fahrenheit	F
FAK	Federasie van Afrikaanse Kultuurverenigings	–
fakt.	faktuur	inv.
Febr.	Februarie	Feb.
fig.	figuur(lik)	fig.
FM	frekwensiemodulasie	FM
fol.	folio	fol.
F & WU	foute en weglatings uitgesonder	E & OE

G

g	gram	g
geb.	gebore	b.
geb.	geboul	b.
gebrs.	gebroeders	Bros
geïll.	geïllustreer	illus.
gen.	genitief	gen.
genl.	generaal	Genl.
genl.-maj.	generaal-majoor	Maj. Genl.
get.	geteken	sgd.
gev.	gevang	c.
GR	Geoktrooieerde Rekenmeester	CA
gr.	grein	gr.
GRA	Genootskap van Regte Afrikaners	–

H

ha	hektaar	ha
H.d.L.	Heil die Leser	L.S.
H.Ed.	Hoogedele	Rt. Hon.
H.Eerw.	Hoogeerwaarde	Rt. Rev.
hfst.	hoofstuk	ch., cap., chap.
hg	hektogram	hg
H.K.H.	Haar Koninklike Hoogheid	H.R.H.
h*l*	hektoliter	h*l*
H.M.	Haar Majesteit	H.M.
hm	hektometer	hm
HNP	Herstigte Nasionale Party	HNP
HOD	Hoër Onderwysdiploma	HDE
HOIK	Hollands Oos-Indiese Kompanjie	DEIC

Afrikaans		Engels
hoogl.	hoogleraar	prof.
HPK	Hoofposkantoor	GPO
h/v	hoek van	cor.

I

i.e.	*id est* (dit is)	i.e./ie
I.K.	intelligensiekwosiënt	I.Q.
incog.	*incognito* (onbekend)	incog.
inf.	infinitief	inf.
infra dig.	*infra dignitatem* (benede sy waardigheid)	infra dig.
inkl.	inklusief	incl.
insl.	insluitend	incl.
i.p.v./ipv	in plaas van	instead of
i.s.	in sake	·re
i.v.m./ivm	in verband met	re

J

jr.	jaar	yr.
Jan.	Januarie	Jan.
JEB	Johannesburgse Effektebeurs	JSE
jl.	jongslede	ult.
jr.	junior	jun.
juf.	juffrou	Miss
Jul.	Julie	Jul.
Jun.	Junie	Jun.

K

kal.	kalorie	cal.
kapt.	kaptein	Capt.
k.a.v.	koste, assuransie, vrag	c.i.f.
K/B	kredietbrief	L/C
k.b.a.	kontant by aflewering	C.O.D.
kg	kilogram	kg
KI	kunsmatige inseminasie	AI
km/h	kilometer per uur	km/h
Kie.	kompanje	Co.
kℓ	kiloliter	kℓ
km	kilometer	km
k.m.b.	kontant met bestelling	C.W.O.
kmdt.	kommandant	Comdt.
kmdt.-genl.	kommandant-generaal	Comdt. Genl.
kol.	kolonel	Col.
komm.	kommissie/kommissaris	com(m).
koöp.	koöperasie	co-op.
K.P.	Kaapprovinsie/Kaapland	CP
KP	Konserwatiewe Party	CP

Afrikaans		Engels
kpl.	korporaal	cpl.
kr.	krediteur/krediteer	Cr.
KRUIK	Kaaplandse Raad vir die Uitvoerende Kunste	CAPAB
K/S	kreditsaldo/kredietsaldo	C/B
KSOK	Kleinsake-Ontwikkelingskorporasie	SBDC
kt.	krediet	Cr.
kub.	kubiek	cub.
kW	kilowatt	kW
KWV	Koöperatiewe Wynbouersvereniging	KWV

L

£	pond (geld)	£
l.	lira/links	l
ℓ	liter	ℓ
ℓ/100 km	liter per 100 km	ℓ/100 km
L	Romeinse 50	L
Lat.	Latyn	Lat.
lb.	*libra* (pond gewig)	lb.
LBS	lopende belastingstelsel	PAYE
lg.	laasgenoemde	the latter
ll.	laaslede	ult.
LL.B.	*Legum Baccalaureus*	LL.B.
l.n.r.	links na regs	l. to r.
l(oc). c(it).	*loco citato* (op die aangehaalde plek)	l.c.
log.	logaritme	log.
LPR	Lid van die Provinsiale Raad	MPC
L.S.	*Lectori Salutem* (die leser, heil)	L.S.
L.s.d.	*librae* (ponde), *solidi* (sjielings), *denarii* (pennies)	L.s.d.
lt.-genl.	luitenant-generaal	Lt. Genl.
lt.-kol.	luitenant-kolonel	Lt. Col.
luit.	luitenant	Lt.
LUK	Lid van die Uitvoerende Komitee	MEC
LV	Lid van die Volksraad	MP
lw.	lidwoord	art.
L.W.	let wel	N.B.

M

m	meter; myl	m
m.	manlik	masc.
Ma.	Maandag	Mon.
M.A.	*Magister Artium*	M.A.
maj.	majoor	Maj.
m.a.w./maw	met ander woorde	in other words
m.b.t./mbt	met betrekking tot	with reference to
M.Com.	*Magister Commercii*	M.Com.
m/d	maande na datum	m/d

Afrikaans		Engels
Me	Me(juffrou)/Me(vrou)	Ms
M.Ed.	*Magister Educationis*	M.Ed.
MEDUNSA	Mediese Universiteit van Suider-Afrika	MEDUNSA
mej(.)	mejuffrou	Miss
mejj(.)	mejuffroue	Misses
mem(o).	memorandum	memo.
mev(.)	mevrou	Mrs
mevv(.)	mevroue	Mmes
mg	milligram	mg
m.i.	myns insiens	in my view
mil.	militêr	mil.
min.	minister/minuut	Min./min.
mℓ	milliliter	mℓ
mm	millimeter	mm
MNR	Mediese Navorsingsraad	MRC
mnr(.)	meneer	Mr, Esq.
mnre(.)	menere	Messrs
M.P.	Militêre Polisie	M.P.
m.p.g.	myl per gelling	m.p.g.
m.p.u.	myl per uur	m.p.h.
Mrt.	Maart	March
m/s.	maande na sig	m/s.
ms.	manuskrip	MS.
M.Sc.	*Magister Scientiae*	M.Sc.
Mu	M(ejuffro)u/M(evro)u	Ms
mv.	meervoud	pl.
MWU	Mynwerkersunie	MWU
my.	maatskappy	Co.

N

NARUK	Natalse Raad vir die Uitvoerende Kunste	NAPAC
Nam.	Namibië	Nam.
n.a.v./nav	na aanleiding van	w.r.t.
NAVO	Noord-Atlantiese Verdragorganisasie	NATO
N.B.	*Nota Bene* (let wel)	N.B.
n.C.	na Christus	A.D.
n/d	na datum	a/d
Ndl.	Nederlands	Neth.
N(ed). G(eref).	Nederduits Gereformeerd	D.R.
N(ed). Herv.	Nederduits Hervormd	D.R.
N.G.K.	Nederduits Gereformeerde Kerk	D.R.C.
N.H.K.	Nederduits Hervormde Kerk	D.R.C.
nl.	naamlik	viz.
nm.	namiddag	pm
no.	*numero* (nommer)	No.
NOIK	Nederlands-Oos-Indiese Kompanjie	DEIC
NOK	Nywerheidontwikkelingskorporasie	IDC
nom.	nominatief	nom.
Nov.	November	Nov.

Afrikaans		Engels
NP	Nasionale Party	NP
nr.	nommer	No.
NRP	Nuwe Republiekparty	NRP
n/s	na sig	a/s.
Ns.	naskrif	P.S.
NUSAS	Nasionale Unie van Suid-Afrikaanse Studente	NUSAS
n.v.t.	nie van toepassing	n.a.
nw.	naamwoord	n.

O

o.a.	onder ander(e)	int. al.
OAE	Organisasie vir Afrika-Eenheid	OAU
ob.	*obiit* (oorlede)	ob.
obj.	objek/objektief	obj.
oef.	oefening	ex.
o.i.	onses insiens	in our view
Okt.	Oktober	Oct.
o.l.v.	onder leiding van	–
o.m.	onder meer	int. al.
ong.	ongeveer	c.
oorl.	oorlede	late
oorspr.	oorspronklik	orig.
O.P.	Oostelike Provinsie	E.P.
op.	*opus* (werk)	op.
op. cit.	*opere citato* (in die genoemde werk)	op. cit.
opm.	opmerking	rem.
o.s.	onderstaande	foll.
OVS	Oranje-Vrystaat	OFS
O/W	ontvangwissel	B/R

P

p.	*pagina* (bladsy); *per* (vir; met)	p.
p.	paaltjie (krieket)	w.
p.a.	*per annum* (per jaar)	p.a.
p.a.	per adres	c/o
par.	paragraaf	par.
P.D.	*Pro Deo* (gratis)	P.D.
pd.	pond	lb/£
per pr.	*per procurationem* (by volmag)	per pro./p.p.
Ph.D.	*Philosophiae Doctor*	Ph.D.
p.j.	per jaar	p.a.
pk.	perdekrag	h.p.
Pk.	poskantoor	P.O.
p.m.	per maand/per minuut	p.m.
p.p.	*per procurationem* (by volmag)	per pro./p.p.
pres.	president	Pres.
prof(.)	professor	Prof.

Afrikaans		**Engels**
prok.	prokureur	atty.
Prok.-Genl.	prokureur-generaal	Att. Genl./A. G.
pro tem.	*pro tempore* (tydelik)	pro tem.
prov.	provinsie	Prov.
P.R.	*poste restante*	Poste Restante
prox.	*proximo* (aanstaande)	prox.
P.S.	*post scriptum* (naskrif)	P.S.
P/S	privaat(pos)sak	P/B
PU vir CHO	Potchefstroomse Universiteit vir Christelike Hoër Onderwys	PU
P/W	poswissel	M/O

Q

q.e.	*quod est* (wat beteken)	q.e.
Q.E.D.	*quod erat demonstrandum* (wat bewys moes word)	Q.E.D.
Q.E.F.	*quod erat faciendum* (wat gedoen moes word)	Q.E.F.
q.q.	*qualitate qua* (in die hoedanigheid van)	q.q.
q.v.	*quod vide* (waarna 'n mens verwys word)	q.v.

R

R	Rand	R
RAU	Randse Afrikaanse Universiteit	RAU
red.	redakteur	ed.
rek.	rekening	a/c
RGN	Raad vir Geesteswetenskaplike Navorsing	HSRC
R.I.P.	*requiescat in pace* (rus in vrede)	R.I.P.
R.K.	Rooms-Katoliek	R.C.
rln.	rylaan	Dr.
r/min	omwentelinge per minuut	r/min
RSA	Republiek (van) Suid-Afrika	RSA
RSVP	*rèpondez s'il vous plaît* (antwoord asseblief)	RSVP

S

SA	Suid-Afrika	SA
SAL	Suid-Afrikaanse Lugdiens	SAA
SABRA	Suid-Afrikaanse Buro vir Rasseaangeleenthede	SABRA
SABS	Suid-Afrikaanse Buro vir Standaarde	SABS
SALM	Suid-Afrikaanse Lugmag	SAAF
SALU	Suid-Afrikaanse Landbou-unie	SAAU
SAP	Suid-Afrikaanse Polisie	SAP
SARK	Suid-Afrikaanse Raad van Kerke	SACC
Sa.	Saterdag	Sat.
SASOL	Suid-Afrikaanse Steenkool-, Olie- en Gaskorporasie	SASOL

Afrikaans		Engels
SAUK	Suid-Afrikaanse Uitsaaikorporasie	SABC
SAVD	Suid-Afrikaanse Vervoerdienste	SATS
SAVF	Suid-Afrikaanse Vrouefederasie	–
SDR	Streekdiensteraad	RSC
S. Ed.	Sy Edele	The Hon.
S. Ed. Agb.	Sy Edelagbare	The Hon.
S. Eerw.	Sy Eerwaarde	The Rev.
sek.	sekonde	sec.
sekr.	sekretaris	Sec.
S. Eks.	Sy Eksellensie	H.E.
sen.	senator	Sen.
Sept.	September	Sept.
sers.	sersant	Sergt.
sert.	sertifikaat	cert.
s.g.	soortlike gewig	sp. gr.
sg.	sogenaamd(e)/sogenoemd(e)	so-called
SGO	Superintendent-Generaal van Onderwys	SGE
S.H.	Sy Heiligheid/Sy Hoogheid	H.H.
S.H. Ed.	Sy Hoogedele	The Rt. Hon.
s.i.	syns insiens	in his view
S.K.H.	Sy Koninklike Hoogheid	H.R.H.
skr.	skutter	rfn.
S.M.	Sy Majesteit	H.M.
SM	Suiderkruismedalje	SM
s.nw.	selfstandige naamwoord	n.
So.	Sondag	Sun.
SOEKOR	Suidelike Olie-Eksplorasiekorporasie	SOEKOR
s.o.s.	sien ommesyde	PTO
SOS	internasionale draadlose noodsein	SOS
SP	Staatspresident	SP
spes.	spesiaal	spec.
SR	Studenteraad	SRC
sr.	senior	sen
st.	standerd	Std.
St.	*Sint* (Heilige)	St.
str.	straat	St.
subj.	subjek/subjunktief	subj.
SUKOVS	Streekraad vir die Uitvoerende Kunste OVS	PACOFS
Supt.	superintendent	Supt.
s.v.p.	*s'il vous plaît* (asseblief)	s.v.p.
s.w.	soortlike warmte	sp. ht.
SWA	Suidwes-Afrika	SWA
SWARUK	SWA Raad vir Uitvoerende Kunste	SWAPAC

T

t.	ton	t.
t.a.p.	ter aangehaalde plaatse	(in) loc. cit.
t.a.v.	ten aansien van	in respect of

Afrikaans		Engels
teenw.	teenwoordig	pres.
tel. adr.	telegramadres	tel. add.
telw.	telwoord	num.
TO	Transvaalse Onderwysersvereniging	–
TOD	Transvaalse Onderwysdepartement	TED
TOK	Transkei-Ontwikkelingskorporasie	TDC
t.o.v./tov	ten opsigte van	with regard to
TRUK	Transvaalse Raad vir die Uitvoerende Kunste	PACT
t.t.	*totus tuus* (geheel die uwe)	yours sincerely
TV	televisie	TV
Tvl.	Transvaal	Tvl.
tw.	tussenwerpsel	interj.
t.w.	te wete	viz.

U

U dw.	U dienswillige	yours obediently
U Ed.	U Edele	Your Hon.
uitbr.	uitbreiding	ext.
uitdr.	uitdrukking	expr.
UK	Universiteit (van) Kaapstad	UCT
U.K.	Uitvoerende Komitee	E.C.
UKOR	Uraanverrykingskorporasie	UCOR
UOVS	Universiteit van die OVS	UOFS
UPE	Universiteit (van) Port Elizabeth	UPE
UNISA	Universiteit van Suid-Afrika	UNISA
ult.	*ultimo* (laaste)	ult.
univ.	universiteit	Univ.
UP	Universiteit (van) Pretoria	UP
US	Universiteit (van) Stellenbosch	US
USSR	Unie van Sosialistiese Sowjet-Republieke	USSR

V

v.	*vide* (kyk, sien)	v.
v.	vroulik	f(em).
v.a.b.	vry aan boord	f.o.b.
vb.	voorbeeld	ex.
v.C.	voor Christus	B.C.
v.d.	van die; van der; van den	of the
V.D.M.	*Verbi Dei (Divini) Minister* (leraar van die goddelike Woord) (predikant)	Rev.
veldm.	veldmaarskalk	F.M.
verklw.	verkleinwoord	dim.
verl.	verlede	past
verl. dw.	verlede deelwoord	p.p.
vgl.	vergelyk	cf./cp.
vgw.	voegwoord	conj.
v/h	voorheen	late/former(ly)
vigs	verworwe immuniteitgebrek-sindroom	aids

208

Afrikaans		Engels
vk.	vierkant	sq.
VK.	Verenigde Koninkryk	UK
vlg.	volgende	seq.
v.l.s.	vry langs skip	f.a.s.
VLU	Vroue-Landbou-Unie	WAU
vm.	voormiddag	am
VN	Verenigde Nasies	UN
vnw.	voornaamwoord	pron.
v(oe)gw.	voegwoord	conj.
vol.	volume	vol.
voors.	voorsitter	Pres., −
voors.	voorsetsel	prep.
voorv.	voorvoegsel	prefix
voorw.	voorwerp	obj.
v.o.s.	vry op spoor	f.o.r.
v.o.s.	vry op skip	f.o.b.
VR	vrederegter	JP
vr.	vroulik	fem.
Vr.	Vrydag	Fri.
vs.	*versus* (teen)	v.
VSA	Verenigde State van Amerika	USA
VSR	Verteenwoordigende Studenteraad	SRC
v/t	verwys na trekker	R/D
VVO	Verenigde Volke-Organisasie (verouderde naam, *kyk* VN)	UNO
VVV	Vreemde Vlieënde Voorwerp	UFO

W

w.	woord; watt; wys	w.
wdb.	woordeboek	dict.
wed.	weduwee	widow
Wel.Ed.	Weledele	Hon.
Wel.Eerw.	Weleerwaarde	Rt. Rev.
w.g.	was geteken	sgd.
wnd.	waarnemende	actg.
WNNR	Wetenskaplike en Nywerheidnavorsingsraad	CSIR
Wo.	Woensdag	Wed.
WP	Westelike Provinsie	WP
WRK	Wêreldraad van Kerke	WCC
ww.	werkwoord	v(b).

X

x	vermenigvuldigingteken	x
X	Romeinse 10	X

Y

YSKOR	SA Yster en Staal Industriële Korporasie Bpk	ISCOR

ENGLISH – AFRIKAANS

ABBREVIATIONS

a	=	adjective
adv	=	adverb
conj	=	conjunction
interj	=	interjection
n	=	noun
pl	=	plural
prep	=	preposition
pron	=	pronoun
sing	=	singular
v	=	verb

SIGNS

..   is used where the last syllable of a word has been changed: **agency (..cies) = agencies**

~-   denotes a hyphenated word: **ill: ~-tempered = ill-tempered**

~   (separate) refers to the key word: **free: ~ burgher = free burgher**

~   (joined) means that the key word and the other word should be joined: **friend: ~less = friendless**

≠   is used, in this publication, at the end of a line to denote that the word must be written as one word

'   indicates that in pronouncing the word the accent falls on the syllable preceding the mark: **aback', ab'dicate**

/   denotes optional use: wish or want in **wish/want**

A

a, an 'n

aback' terug, agteruit; *taken ~,* oorbluf, verstom, verras

ab'acus (..ci) telraam, rekenbord

aban'don (n) oorgawe; onverskilligheid; (v) opgee; verlaat; in die steek laat; **~ed** verlate, oorgegee; losbandig, verdorwe

abate' verminder, afslaan; bedaar; **~ment** vermindering, korting

ab'attoir (-s) abattoir, slagplaas

abb'ey (-s) abdy, klooster(kerk)

abb'ot ab, kloosterhoof

abbrev'iate verkort, afkort; verklein

abbrevia'tion afkorting, verkorting

ab'dicate afstand doen (van die troon)

abdica'tion (troon)afstand, aftrede

abdom'en buik, onderbuik

abduct' ontvoer, skaak

aberra'tion afwyking, (af)dwaling

abet' (-ted, -ted) aanhits, opstook; **~tor** opstoker; handlanger

abey'ance opskorting, stilstand; *in ~,* opgeskort, oorgestaan

abide' (**abode, abode**) woon, vertoef; uithou, verdra; afwag, neerlê

abid'ing duursaam, ewig

abil'ity (..ties) bekwaamheid, vermoë, knapheid; (pl) geestesgawes, talente; *to the best of my ~,* na my beste vermoë

ablaze' aan die brand, in ligtelaaie

a'ble bekwaam, knap; bevoeg; **~ seaman** bevare/vol matroos

ablu'tion (af)wassing, reiniging; loutering, suiwering; **~ block** ablusieblok

abnorm'al onreëlmatig, abnormaal

aboard' aan boord

abol'ish afskaf, ophef, intrek; vernietig

abom'inable afskuwelik, gruwelik, walglik

abori'ginal (n) (..gines, -s) inboorling

abort' miskraam kry; **~ion** miskraam; vrugafdrywing; aborsie; misgewas

about' (adv, prep) ongeveer, omtrent; aangaande, rakende, met betrekking tot

above' (adv, prep) bo, meer; bokant; *~ all,* bowenal, veral; *~-average intelligence,* bogemiddelde intelligensie; **~-mentioned** bogenoemde; **~named** bostaande, bogemelde

abracadab'ra abrakadabra; wartaal

abra'sive (n) skaafmiddel, skuurmiddel

abreast' langs mekaar, in gelid; *~ of,* op (die) hoogte van

abridge' verkort, beperk; beknopter maak

abroad' buitekant; buitelands, oorsee

abrupt' afgebroke; plotseling, kortaf

ab'scess (-s) geswel, sweer, abses

ab'sence afwesigheid; gebrek

absent'[1] (v) (jou) verwyder, wegbly

ab'sent[2] (a) afwesig; verstrooid; **~ee** afwesige; **~eeism** absentisme, afwesigheidsyfer; **~-minded professor** verstrooide professor

ab'solute volstrek, onbeperk, volkome; absoluut, skone; heeltemal; *~ majority,* volstrekte meerderheid

absorb' opsuig, absorbeer

abstain' onthou van; afskaf; **~er** onthouer, afskaffer; *total ~er,* geheelonthouer (van drank)

absten'tion onthouding; *two ~s from voting,* twee stemonthoudings

ab'stinence afskaffing, onthouding; matigheid; *total ~,* geheelonthouding

ab'stract[1] (n) uittreksel; afkooksel; opsomming; (a) diepsinnig; abstrak

abstract'[2] (v) aftrek, abstraheer; afskei; ontleen; **~ion** abstraksie

absurd' ongerymd, verspot, absurd

abun'dance oorvloed, menigte

abun'dant oorvloedig, baie, volop, ryk

abuse' (n) mishandeling, belediging; (v) mishandel; mislei; uitskel, beledig; *~ your privileges,* jou voorregte misbruik.

abus'ive beledigend, lasterend

abyss' (-es) afgrond, poel

aca'cia (-s) akasia

academ'ic(al) akademies; onprakties

aca'demy (..mies) akademie; genootskap

accede' toestem; toestaan, instem, toegee

accel'erate versnel; verhaas; bespoedig

accel'erator versneller; dryfspier

ac'cent (n) nadruk, klemtoon; stembuiging, tongval; aksent, klemteken

accent' (v) beklemtoon; **~uate** nadruk lê op, benadruk

accept' aanneem, aanvaar, goedkeur, aksepteer (wissel); **~able** aanneemlik, aanvaarbaar; ~ed standards, aanvaarde standaarde

ac'cess toegang; ~ road toevoerpad

acces'sible toeganklik, genaakbaar

acces'sion toetrede/toetreding; aanwins; ampsaanvaarding; troonbestyging

acces'sory (n) (..ries) medepligtige; bykomstigheid; (pl) toebehore, bybehore; (a) bykomend, bykomstig; medepligtig

ac'cident toeval; ongeluk, ongeval; ~ insurance ongevalleversekering

acciden'tal toevallig; bykomend; ondergeskik

acclama'tion toejuiging; byval, akklamasie

accom'modate aanpas, skik; akkommodeer; onder dak bring, huisves, herberg

accommoda'tion skikking; huisvesting, akkommodasie; verblyf(plek)

accom'paniment begeleiding (op klavier)

accom'panist begeleier

accom'pany (..nied, ..nied) vergesel, begelei; saamgaan; ~ing bygaande

accom'plice medepligtige, handlanger

accom'plish uitvoer, tot stand bring; ~ed voltooid; bedrewe; begaaf; ~ment talent, begaafdheid; handigheid

accord' (n) ooreenstemming; verdrag; harmonie, akkoord; (v) ooreenstem; laat ooreenstem; akkordeer; ~ance ooreenstemming; in ~ance with, ooreenkomstig; ~ing volgens, na, namate, ooreenkomstig; ~ing to, volgens, ingevolge; ~ingly ooreenkomstig, gevolglik, bygevolg, dus

accor'dion akkordeon, trekklavier

account' (n) rekening; berig, verslag; rekenskap; on no ~, onder geen omstandighede nie; ~ rendered, gelewerde rekening; (v) reken, rekenskap gee, verantwoord

accoun'tancy rekeningkunde

acccoun'tant rekenmeester

accoun'ting rekeningkunde; ~ policy reken(ing)kundige beleid, boekhoubeleid

accrue' voortspruit, aangroei, toeneem; oploop; ~d interest opgeloopte rente

accum'ulate ophoop, opgaar; versamel; oploop; ~d leave opgehoopte/opgegaarde verlof

acc'uracy noukeurigheid, stiptheid, juistheid, presiesheid, akkuraatheid

acc'urate noukeurig, nougeset, akkuraat

accusa'tion beskuldiging, aanklag

accus'ative akkusatief

accuse' beskuldig, aankla; verkla; ~d' beskuldigde, aangeklaagde

accus'tom gewoon(d) maak; ~ed gewoon(d); gebruiklik

ace aas; bobaas, uitblinker; kishou (sport); within an ~, op 'n haar na

acet'ylene asetileen

ache (n) pyn; (v) pyn, seer wees, pyn ly

achieve' behaal, verrig, presteer; bereik; ~r presteerder; ~ment prestasie

a'ching seer

a'cid (n) suur; (a) suur, bitter, wrang; bitsig; ~ drop suurklontjie

a'cid test vuurproef

acknow'ledge erken, beken; berig; beantwoord; ~ receipt of, ontvangs erken van

acknow'ledgment erkenning; berig; dankbetuiging

ac'me toppunt, krisis; keerpunt

ac'ne puisie, aknee; puisiesiekte

ac'orn akker; ~ cup akkerdoppie

acous'tics geluidsleer, akoestiek

acquaint' bekend maak, berig, meedeel; ~ance bekendheid; kennis

acquire' verkry, verwerf; aanleer; aankoop; an ~d taste, 'n aangeleerde smaak

acquisi'tion verkryging, aanskaffing

acquit' (-ted, -ted) ontslaan, vryspreek, kwytskeld; ~ oneself, jou kwyt van

a'cre akker; acre (maat); ~age oppervlakte; grootte in acres

ac'robat akrobaat; ~ic/stunt fliers, kunsvlieëniers

ac'ronym letternaam (bv. YSKOR)

ac'rophobia hoogtevrees

across' (adv) dwars, oorkruis; (prep) oor; dwars; oorkruis; come ~, teëkom, ontmoet

act (n) daad, handeling; akte; wet; bedryf (toneelstuk); caught in the ~, op heter daad betrap; ~ of dedication, toewydingsformulier; (v) handel, doen, te werk gaan

act'ing (n) voordrag, spel; (a) waarnemend, agerend

act'ion handeling, verrigting; geveg, aksie; killed in ~, gesneuwel; man of ~, man v.d. daad; ~ song sangspeletjie

act'ive werksaam, bedrywig, besig

ac'tivist (n) aktivis

activ'ity (..ties) werksaamheid, bedrywig=
heid, doenigheid, aktiwiteit

ac'tor toneelspeler, akteur; bewerker

ac'tress (-es) toneelspeelster, aktrise

ac'tual werklik, wesenlik, feitlik

ac'tually regtig, werklikwaar; eintlik

ac'tuary (..ries) aktuaris; griffier

acute' skerp; fyn; vlug, gevat, skerpsinnig

ad'age spreekwoord, spreuk, gesegde

Ad'am Adam; ~'s apple adamsappel

ad'amant onwrikbaar; uiters hard

adapt' aanpas; aanwend; ~abil'ity aan=
pasbaarheid; ~able plooibaar; aanwend=
baar; ~er passtuk; aanpasser (elektrisi=
teit)

add byvoeg, optel, vermeerder

adden'dum (..denda) bylae, toevoegsel

add'er adder, pofadder

add'ict (n) verslaafde

addict' (v) toewy, oorgee aan; ~ed verslaaf,
oorgee; ~ed to drink, aan drank verslaaf;
~ion verslaafdheid

addi'tion byvoeging, optelling; in ~ to,
boonop; behalwe, benewens; ~al byko=
mend, addisioneel; ~ sum optelsom

address' (n) (-es) adres; toespraak, rede; (v)
adresseer; wend/rig (tot); ~ee' geadres=
seerde

adept' (n) ingewyde; (a) geoefen, touwys

ad'equate geskik; toereikend, afdoende

adhere' aanhang, bly by; ~ to the rules,
die reëls nakom/eerbiedig

adhes'ive vasklewend; klewerig; ~ plaster
hegpleister; ~ tape kleefband

adja'cent aangrensend, naasgeleë, naby; ~
interior aangrensende binneland

ad'jective (n) byvoeglike naamwoord; (a)
byvoeglik; ondergeskik

adjoin' aanheg; grens aan

adjourn' opskort, verdaag; ~ a meeting,
'n vergadering verdaag; ~ment verdaging

adjud'icate beoordeel, uitspraak gee

adjud'icator beoordelaar

ad'junct (n) aanhangsel, byvoegsel; (a) ad=
junk=, onder=, hulp=

adjust' in orde bring, reël, vereffen; aan=
suiwer; ~able verstelbaar; ~ment skik=
king; aansuiwering (boekhou)

ad'jutant adjudant; hulp

admin'ister bestuur, beheer

administra'tion beheer; administrasie

admin'istrative besturend, administratief

admin'istrator administrateur; admini=
streerder, administrator

ad'mirable bewonderenswaardig

ad'miral admiraal

admira'tion bewondering, verering

admire' bewonder, vereer; ~r bewonderaar,
aanbidder

admis'sible aanneemlik, toelaatbaar

admis'sion toelating, toegang; erkenning;
~ free, vry(e) toegang; ~ of guilt,
skulderkenning

admit' (-ted, -ted) toegang verleen; opneem
(hospitaal); ~tance toegang: toelating

admon'ish vermaan, teregwys

ado' ophef, gedoente, drukte, omhaal;
much ~ about nothing, veel geskree(u) en
weinig wol

adoles'cence puberteitsjare, adolessensie

adoles'cent (n) jongeling, jongmeisie, jeug=
dige; (a) jeugdig; opgroeiend, adolessent

adopt' aanneem, aanwend; ~ed aangeno=
me; ~ed child, aangenome kind; ~ion
aanneming

adore' aanbid, vereer, vurig liefhê

adorn' versier, verfraai

adren'alin(e) adrenalien, bynierstof

ad'ult (n) grootmens, volwassene; (a) vol=
wasse; ~ education, opvoeding buite
skoolverband

adul'terate verdun, vervals

adul'terer egbreker, owerspeler

adul'tery owerspel, egbreuk

advance' (n) vooruitgang; voortgang;
voorskot; (v) bevorder; voorskiet (geld);
~ money, geld voorskiet; ~ the date, die
datum vervroeg; ~d' gevorder(d); ver; ~
guard voorhoede

advan'tage (n) voordeel; nut, baat

Ad'vent Advent(tyd)

ad'ventist adventis

adven'ture (n) avontuur; waagstuk; (v)
waag, onderneem; ~r waaghals; avon=
turier, geluksoeker

adven'turous avontuurlik, ondernemend

ad'verb bywoord

adver'bial bywoordelik

ad'versary (..ries) teenstander, opponent

ad'verse teenstrydig; vyandig; ongunstig;
~ comment, ongunstige kommentaar

adver'sity teenspoed, ongeluk

ad'vertise adverteer, reklameer

adver'tisement advertensie, reklame

ad'vertiser adverteerder; aankondiger
ad'vertising adverteer, bekendstelling; ~ agency reklameburo, advertensieburo
advice' raad; berig; advies
advis'able raadsaam, gerade
advise' (v) aanraai, van raad dien, adviseer; ~r raadsman, raadgewer
advis'ory raadgewend, adviserend; ~ council adviesraad
ad'vocate (n) verdediger, advokaat; pleitbesorger; (v) bepleit, verdedig
aer'ial (n) lugdraad, antenne; ~ photograph lugfoto; ~ railway lugspoor
a'erie hoë roofvoëlnes; arendsnes
a'erobat kunsvlieënier, fratsvlieër
a'erodrome vliegveld, vliegbaan, lughawe
a'eronaut lugvaarder, ruimtevaarder
a'eroplane see aircraft
a'erosol aërosol; ~ can/container spuitkan(netjie)
aesthet'ic(al) esteties, skoonheids-
aff'able vriendelik, minsaam, inskiklik
affair' saak, aangeleentheid, besigheid, affère; (liefdes)verhouding
affect' werk op, aantas; raak, affekteer
affec'ted aangedaan, aanstellerig
affec'tionate toegeneë, liefhebbend; hartlik
affidav'it beëdigde verklaring
affilia'tion aansluiting, affiliasie
affin'ity verwantskap, affiniteit
affirm' bevestig; bekragtig; ~ative bevestigend; answer in the ~ative, bevestigend antwoord
afflict' bedroef, kwel; ~ion droefheid, leed; besoeking
af'fluence oorvloed, rykdom, weelde
af'fluent[1] (n) tak (van 'n rivier), spruit
af'fluent[2] (a) oorvloedig; ryk, welgesteld; the ~ society, die welvarende gemeenskap
afford' verskaf, gee, oplewer; bekostig, bybring; he can ~ to, hy kan dit bekostig
aflame' aan die brand, in ligtelaaie
afloat' drywend, aan die gang; in omloop
afoot' te voet; op die been; op tou
afore' (adv, prep) voor, vantevore; ~going voorgaande; ~mentioned voornoemd, voormeld; ~said voornoemd
afraid' bang, bangerig, bevrees; ~ of, bang vir; ~ to, bang om
afresh' opnuut, van voor af, weer
Af'rica Afrika

Af'rican (n) Afrikaan; (a) van Afrika; Afrikaans; ~ languages, Bantoetale, etniese tale; South ~, Suid-Afrikaner
Africa'na Africana
Afrikaans' Afrikaans
Afrika'ner (n) (-s) Afrikaner; Afrikanerbees; (a) Afrikaans
Af'ro-A'sian Afro-Asiaties
af'ter[1] (a) later; (prep) agter; naderhand; na, daarna, later; nadat; ~ all, tog, ten slotte, darem, per slot van rekening, op stuk van sake; enquire ~, vra na; look ~, kyk na, sorg vir
af'ter[2] (conj) nadat
af'ter: ~birth nageboorte; ~care nasorg; ~-dinner speech, tafelrede; ~-effect nawerking, gevolg; ~noon namiddag, agtermiddag; ~thought nagedagte; laatlammetjie, heksluiter; ~wards naderhand, daarna, later
again' weer, opnuut, nog; verder; aan die ander kant; vir die tweede maal; ~ and ~, keer op keer, herhaaldelik; now and ~, af en toe; time and ~, herhaaldelik
against' teen, strydig met
ag'ate agaat
age (n) ouderdom, leeftyd; eeu; Middle A ~ s, Middeleeue; of ~, mondig; (v) oud word, verouder; ~d oud, bejaard, afgeleef; ~ limit ouderdomsgrens
a'gency (..cies) agentskap; bemiddeling; advertising ~, reklameagentskap; employment ~, werkgewersburo; travel ~, reisburo, reisagentskap
agen'da agenda, sakelys, ter tafel
a'gent agent; rentmeester; bewerker
agg'ravate verswaar, vererger; verbitter; terg; aggravating circumstances, verswarende omstandighede
agg'regate (n) totaal, geheel; aggregaat; (v) versamel; beloop; (a) gesamentlik
aggress' aanval; ~ion aanval, aggressie; ~ive strydlustig, aggressief; ~or aggressor
aghast' ontstel(d), ontset
a'gile rats, lenig, behendig
agita'tion opskudding, agitasie
a'gitator opruier, oproermaker, agitator, onrusstoker; roerder, woelgees
agnos'tic (n) agnostikus; vrydenker
ago' gelede, terug; a week ~, 'n week gelede

ag'ony (agonies) doodstryd, doodsangs; sielsmart; kwelling, agonie

agree' ooreenstem; toestem; ~ *on*, saam= stem; ~ *with*, akkordeer met; ~**able** aangenaam, welgevallig, behaaglik; ~**d'**! top! afgespreek! ~**ment** ooreenkoms; ver= drag; vergelyk; afspraak; ~**ment** *stu= dent*, verbintenisstudent

agricul'tural landboukundig, landbou-; ~ *journal*, landboutydskrif, landboublad

agricul'ture landbou; *Department of A ~ and Fisheries*, Departemente (van) Land= bou en Visserye

agron'omy agronomie, akkerbou

ahead' vooruit, vooraan, voorwaarts

aid (n) hulp, bystand; subsidie; hulpmiddel, helper; *in ~ of*, ten bate van, ten behoewe van; (v) help, steun; bydra

ail makeer, sukkel, siek wees; ~**ing** sieklik, sukkelend; ~**ment** siekte, kwaal

aim (n) doelwit, oogmerk, doelstelling, plan; *take ~*, korrelvat op; (v) doel; korrel; beoog, mik; ~ *at*, mik op

air (n) lug, windjie; lied, melodie; *on the ~*, oor die radio, uitgesaai (word); (v) lug; ~ *one's views*, jou mening gee; (a) lugwind-; ~ *alarm* lugalarm, koe(t)stoeter; ~ **ap= prentice** lugvakleerling; ~**brick** lugroos= ter; ~**conditioning** lugversorging; *these premises are airconditioned*, hierdie win= kel is lugversorg

air'craft vliegtuig, vliegmasjien; ~ **carrier** vliegdekskip, vliegtuigdraer, abbaskip

air: ~**filter** lugsuiweraar, lugfilter; ~**force** lugmag, lugvloot

air: ~**gun** windbuks; ~ **hostess (-es)** lug= waardin; ~**lift** lugbrug; ~**line** lugredery; ~**liner** passasierstraler; ~**mail** lugpos; ~**mechanic** lugwerktuigkundige; ~ **pilot** vlieënier; ~**port** lughawe; ~ **raid** lug= aanval; ~**shelter** skuilkelder; ~**ship** lugskip; ~**tight** lugdig; ~ **traffic** lugverkeer; ~**y** lugtig, vrolik; yl

aisle vlerk, vleuel (van 'n gebou)

aitch'bone stertstuk, stuitjiestuk; ysbeen

ajar' half oop, op 'n skrefie

akim'bo: *with arms ~*, met die hande in die sye

akin' verwant, vermaagskap

al'abaster (n) albaster, albas; (a) albaster= albas=

alarm' (n) alarm, alarmsein; ~ **clock** wek= ker; ~**ing** verontrustend; onrusbarend; ~**ist** alarmis

alas'! helaas!

al'batross (-es) albatros, stormvoël

albe'it alhoewel, hoewel

albi'no (-s) albino

al'bum album; gedenkboek

al'cohol alkohol, wyngees

alcohol'ic alkoholies, bedwelmend; drank= sugtig; (n) alkoholis

al'coholism alkoholisme

al'cometer alkomete⁻, asemtoetser, *see* breathalyser

ale Engelse bier; bierfees

alert' (n) alarm(sein); (v) aansê, waarsku; (a) waaksaam, wakker

al'ga (-e) seegras, seewier, alge

al'gebra stelkunde, algebra

al'ibi alibi

al'ien (n) vreemdeling, uitlander; (a) vreemd, uitlands; ~**ate** vervreem; af= konkel; ~**ation** vervreemding

align' rig, op een lyn bring; spoor (wiel); ~**ment** linie, riglyn; sporing (van wiele)

alike' gelyk, eenders

al'imony onderhoud, versorging, *see* main= tenance

alive' lewendig; bewus, gevoelig, wemelend; wakker

al'kali (-(e)s) loogsout, alkali

all (pron) almal, algar; *not at ~*, glad nie, geensins; ~ *told*, almal ingesluit/inbe= grepe; (a) die hele; ~ *day*, heeldag; (adv) heeltemal, totaal; ~ *the better*, des te beter

allay' verlig, verminder; matig

all'-bran volsemel

all'-comers almal; iedereen

allega'tion aanklag, beskuldiging

allege' aanvoer, beweer, betoog; ~**d** *mur= derer*, beweerde/vermeende moordenaar

alle'giance getrouheid, onderdanigheid

al'legory (..ries) sinnebeeld, allegorie

all'-embracing alomvattend

allelu'ia halleluja, lofsang

aller'gic allergies

allev'iate verlig, versag

all'ey (-s) steeg, laning, gang

alli'ance verbond, bondgenootskap, al= liansie

al'ligator kaaiman, alligator

all'-in: ~ **wrestling** rofstoei
allitera'tion alliterasie, stafrym
all'-mash volmeel
all'ocate aanwys, toewys, toedeel
alloca'tion plaasaanwysing; toewysing
allot' (-ted, -ted) aanwys, toemeet, toeken; ~ment aandeel; toekenning, toewysing
all'-out uit alle mag
allow' toelaat; bewillig; ~ance toelating; toelae; *make* ~ance(s) *for,* in aanmerking neem
alloy' (n) (-s) mengsel; gehalte; allooi
all'right goed, reg, in orde
all-round (a) veelsydig; (adv) oor die algemeen
allur'ing aanloklik, verleidelik
allu'sion sinspeling, toespeling
alluv'ial uitgespoel, alluviaal, spoel~; ~ diamonds spoeldiamante
all'-weather weervas; ~ tennis court weervaste tennisbaan
al'ly (n) (allies) bondgenoot, geallieerde; (v) (allied, allied) verbind, verenig
al'manac almanak, kalender
almi'ghtiness almag
Almi'ghty: *the* ~, God, die Almagtige
alm'ond amandel
al'most amper, byna
.alms aalmoes, liefdegawe
al'oe (-s) aalwyn, aalwee
alone' (a) alleen; eensaam; (adv) net, enkel, alleen; *leave* ~, alleen laat, afbly, uitlos
along' langs, deur; met; *all* ~, die hele tyd; *get* ~, vooruitkom; ~side naas, langsaan
aloof' van ver, op 'n afstand; afsydig
aloud' hardop; *read* ~, hardop lees, luidlees
alpac'a alpakka; lamawol
al'pha alfa
al'phabet abc, alfabet
al'pine Alpe
Alps die Alpe
alread'y al, reeds, alreeds
al'so ook, eweneens
alt alt
al'tar altaar
al'ter verander, wysig; ~a'tion verandering, wysiging
alterca'tion twis, rusie, woordewisseling
alter'nate (n) plaasvervanger; (a) (af)wisselend, alternatief
al'ternate (v) (af)wissel; verwissel

al'ternating (af)wisselend; ~ *current,* wisselstroom
altern'ative (n) keuse, alternatief
although' hoewel, alhoewel
al'titude hoogte (bo seespieël); diepte; *high* ~ *tennis balls,* hoëvlak-tennisballe
altogeth'er almal; heeltemal, tesame; *in the* ~, poedelnakend
altruis'tic onselfsugtig, altruïsties
al'um aluin
alumin'ium aluminium
alum'nus (..ni) alumnus, oud-student
al'ways altyd, gedurig, aljimmers
am *see* **be**
amalgama'tion samesmelting, amalgamasie
am'ateur amateur, beginner
amaze' verbaas; ~d' verbaas, ontstel(d); ~ment verbasing, verwondering
amaz'ing verbasend, wonderlik
Am'azon Amasone; manhaftige vrou
ambass'ador ambassadeur, gesant
am'ber amber, barnsteen; ~ *traffic light,* amber/geel verkeerslig
ambidex'trous dubbelhandig; dubbelhartig
ambig'uous dubbelsinnig; duister, onduidelik
ambi'tion eersug, ambisie
ambi'tious eersugtig, eergierig, ambisieus
am'bulance ambulans
am'bush (n) hinderlaag; lokval, strik; *lay an* ~, 'n val stel; *lie in* ~, voorlê
amen' amen
amend' verbeter, wysig; ~ment wysiging; amendement (in debat)
amends' vergoeding; *make* ~, vergoed, goedmaak
amen'ity minsaamheid, innemendheid; ..ties beleefdhede; geriewe, fasiliteite
Amer'ica Amerika; ~n Amerikaner
am'iable beminlik, lief, lieftallig
am'icable vriendelik, vriendskaplik, minlik
amiss' verkeerd; kwalik; onvanpas
ammon'ia ammoniak
ammuni'tion ammunisie, skietgoed; ~ dump ammunisie-opslagplek
am'nesty vergifnis, amnestie; *grant* ~, amnestie verleen
amok' amok; *run* ~, amok maak
among' onder, tussen, by
am'orous verlief, liefdes~, minne~
amortisa'tion (skuld)delging, amortisasie

amount' (n) bedrag, opbrengs; hoeveelheid; *any ~ of money*, geld soos bossies; *expenses ~ing to*, uitgawes ten bedrae van; (v) bedra

am'pere ampere

amphib'ia tweeslagtige diere, amfibieë

am'phitheatre amfiteater; strydperk

am'ple breed, ruim; oorvloedig

am'plifier klankversterker; vergroter

am'plify (..fied, ..fied) uitbrei; toelig, vergroot, versterk

am'putate afsit, afsny

am'ulet amulet, geluksteentjie

amuse' vermaak, amuseer; ~ment vermaak, tydverdryf; ~ment park pretpark

amus'ing, amus'ive vermaaklik, onderhoudend, snaaks, amusant

an 'n

anach'ronism tydteenstrydigheid, tydverskuiwing, tydverrekening, anachronisme

anaem'ic bloedloos, bloedarm

anaesthet'ic (n) verdowingsmiddel; (ver)doofmiddel; (a) verdowend

anaes'thetist narkotiseur

an'agram anagram, letterkeer

analges'ic (a) pynstillend; (n) pynstiller

anal'ogy gelykvormigheid, analogie

analphabete' ongeletterde, analfabeet

an'alyse ontleed, oplos, analiseer

anal'ysis (..lyses) ontleding, analise

an'archist anargis, oproermaker

an'archy regeringloosheid, anargie

anat'omy ontleedkunde, anatomie

ances'tral voorvaderlik

an'cestry voorouers, afkoms, afstamming

anc'hor (n) anker (skip); steun; (v) anker; vasmaak

anchov'y ansjovis

an'cient oud, outyds; antiek

ancill'ary ondergeskik; diensbaar; ~ subjects byvakke

and en

an'ecdote anekdote, staaltjie

anem'one anemoon

anew' opnuut; weer

an'gel engel

an'ger (n) toorn, gramskap; (v) vertoorn, vererg, kwaad maak

an'gle¹ (n) hoek, vishoek; haak; (v) visvang, hengel

an'gle² (n) hoek; gesig(s)punt

an'gler hengelaar, visvanger, visterman

An'glicism Anglisisme, Engelse uitdrukking

An'glo- Engels, Anglo-; *A ~ -Boer War*, Engelse Oorlog, Tweede Vryheidsoorlog, *see* South African War

angor'a: ~ goat angorabok, sybok; ~ wool angorahaar, bokhaar

an'gry kwaad, boos; ~ about, kwaad oor; ~ with, kwaad vir

an'guish angs, foltering

an'gular hoekig, hoek=, puntig

an'imal (n) dier, bees; (a) dierlik; sinlik; ~ husbandry veeteelt; ~ king'dom die diereryk

animos'ity verbittering, wrok

an'iseed anyssaad

an'ker anker (maat)

an'kle enkel; ~ deep, tot aan die enkels

ann'als jaarboeke, annale

annex' (v) annekseer; inlyf; ~a'tion inlywing, anneksasie

ann'ex (n) aanhangsel, bylae; anneks

annex'ure aanhangsel, bylae

anni'hilate vernietig, verdelg, uitdelg

anniver'sary (..ries) verjaardag; jaarfees; gedenkdag; bestaansjaar (organisasie)

announce' aankondig, bekend maak; aanmeld; ~ment aankondiging; bekendmaking; ~r omroeper (radio); aankondiger

annoy' lastig val, erger, hinder, pla; ~ed omgekrap, vererg; ontstig; ~ing lastig, vervelig, hinderlik

ann'ual (n) jaarboek; eenjarige plant; (a) jaarliks, jaar=; eenjarig; ~ general meeting, algemene jaarvergadering

annu'ity (..ties) jaargeld, annuïteit

annul' (-led, -led) nietig verklaar, afskaf

an'odyne pynstillende middel, pynstiller

anoint' salf, smeer; ~ed (n) gesalfde; (a) gesalf; ~ment salwing

anom'aly (..lies) ongerymdheid, onreëlmatigheid, afwyking, anomalie

anon' dadelik, strakkies, netnou

anon'ymous naamloos, anoniem

anorex'ia aptytverlies, anoreksie

anoth'er 'n ander; nog een; ~ year of inflation, nog 'n inflasiejaar; one ~, mekaar

an'swer (n) antwoord, beskeid; oplossing; (v) antwoord, beantwoord; ~ the bell, die deur oopmaak; ~ the telephone, die telefoon beantwoord; ~able verantwoordelik, verantwoordbaar

ant mier

antag'onism vyandskap, antagonisme
antag'onist teenstander, teenparty
Antarc'tic suidelik; Suidpool-; ~ circle
Suidpoolsirkel; ~ ocean Suidelike Yssee;
~ pole Suidpool
Antarc'tica Suidpoolstreek, Antartika
ant: ~bear, ~eater erdvark, miervreter
an'telope wildsbok, antiloop
an'temeridian voormiddag-
anten'na (-e) voelhoring, voelspriet; lugdraad, antenne
antenup'tial van voor die huwelik, huwe-
liks-; ~ contract, voorhuwelikse kontrak
an'them koorsang; lofsang; national ~,
volkslied
ant'hill mier(s)hoop, also antheap
anthol'ogy (..gies) bloemlesing
an'thracite antrasiet
anthropol'ogist antropoloog
anthropol'ogy menskunde, antropologie
an'ti teen-, anti-, strydig met
an'ti-aircraft gun lugafweergeskut, lug-
doelkanon
antibiot'ic (n) antibiotikum; (a) antibioties
antic'ipate voorkom; verwag; voorsien
anticipa'tion voorgevoel, verwagting; voorsmaak; voorkoming; in ~, by voorbaat
anticlim'ax antiklimaks
anti-clock'wise linksom, antikloksgewys
an'tics (pl) kaskenades, manewales
an'tidote teengif, antidoot
anti-freeze agent vriesweerder
an'ti-infectious infeksiewerend
an'ti-littering campaign rommelveldtog
antip'athy (..thies) teensin, antipatie
antiquar'ian (n) oudheidkenner; (a) oud-
heidkundig, antikwaries
antique' (n) antieke kunswerk; (a) oud-
wets, antiek; ~ dealer oudhedehandelaar
antiq'uity die oudheid
anti-roll bar kanteldemper
anti-Semi'tic anti-Semities
antisep'tic bederfwerend, antisepties
an'us anus, aars, fondament
an'vil aambeeld
anxi'ety (..ties) angs, besorgdheid, onrus
an'xious besorg, beangs; verlangend; ~ to
help, gretig om te help, graag wil help
an'y elke, enige; iedereen, elkeen, enig-
iemand; applicants for the post, if any,
aansoekers om die pos, as daar is; in ~

case, at ~ rate, in alle geval; ~ person
who, enigeen/enigiemand wat
an'ybody enigeen, elkeen, iedereen
an'yhow (adv) in elk geval; hoe dan ook
an'yone enigeen, iedereen
an'ything enigiets, alles; ~ but, alles behalwe
an'ywhere oral, op enige plek
aor'ta groot slagaar, aorta
apart' afsonderlik, alleen; weg; ~ from,
afgesien van; jesting ~, gekheid op 'n
stokkie; ~heid afsonderlikheid
apart'ment vertrek, kamer
ap'athy ongevoeligheid, apatie
ape (n) aap; na-aper, koggelaar; (v) na-aap,
(uit)koggel
aph'is (aphides) plantluis
aph'orism spreuk, leenspreuk aforisme
ap'iarist byeboer
ap'iculture byeteelt
apoc'alypse openbaring, apokalips
apoc'rypha apokriewe boeke; ~l twyfelagtig, apokrief
apologet'ic verontskuldigend, apologeties
apol'ogise verontskuldig; verskoning maak
vir, ekskuus maak, apologie aanteken
apol'ogy (..gies) verskoning, apologie
apos'tle apostel, godsgesant
apostol'ic apostolies
apos'trophe afkap(pings)teken, apostroof
appal' (-led, -led) verskrik, ontstel; ~ling
vreeslik, verskriklik, ontsettend
apparat'us (-es) toestel, apparaat
appar'ent blykbaar, duidelik; skynbaar;
~ly klaarblyklik, oënskynlik
appari'tion spook, skim; gedaante
appeal' (n) appèl, hoër beroep; (v) appelleer; ~ to, 'n beroep doen op
appear' verskyn, optree; lyk, blyk
appear'ance verskyning; skyn, voorkoms
appease' bevredig; stil maak; paai; bedaar;
~ment versoening; bedaring; policy of
~ment, paaibeleid
appendicit'is blindedermontsteking, ap-
pendisitis
appen'dix (-es, ..ices) aanhangsel, bylae;
blindederm
app'etiser eetluswekker(tjie)
app'etite eetlus, aptyt; begeerte, lus
applaud' toejuig; prys, loof, approudeer
applause' toejuiging, applous

ap'ple appel; oogappel; ~ *of discord,* twis-appel

appli'ance (pl) toestelle, apparaat; *domes-tic* ~*s,* huishoudelike toestelle, huisbehore

applic'able toepaslik

app'licant aansoeker, applikant, aanvraer

applica'tion aanwending, toepassing; ap-plikasie; aansoek; ~ **form** aansoekvorm

applied' toegepas; ~ **mathematics** toege-paste wiskunde

apply' (..lied, ..lied) aanwend, oplê; toe-pas; aansoek doen; ~ *for a post,* aansoek doen om 'n betrekking

appoint' bepaal, vasstel; aanstel, benoem

appoint'ment afspraak; aanstelling, be-noeming; *keep an* ~, 'n afspraak hou/nakom; ~**s register** aanstellingregister, vakaturelys

appraise' skat, takseer, waardeer

apprais'er skatter, waardeerder; *sworn* ~, beëdigde taksateur

apprec'iable merkbaar; aansienlik

appre'ciate waardeer, op prys stel; appre-sieer

apprecia'tion waardering; waardevermeer-dering, appresiasie; *token of* ~, blyk van waardering

apprehen'sion gevangeneming; begrip; vrees; *quick of* ~, vlug van begrip

appren'tice (n) vakleerling; leerklerk; (v) inboek; ~**ship** leerskap, leerjare

approach' (n) nadering; (-es) toegang; (v) nader, naderkom; benader; ~**able** toe-ganklik, genaakbaar

approba'tion goedkeuring; *on* ~, op sig

approp'riate[1] (v) toewys, toedeel

approp'riate[2] (a) gepas, paslik; geskik

appropria'tion toewysing; ~ **account** (wins)verdelingsrekening

appro'val goedkeuring, byval; *on* ~, op sig

approve' goedkeur; bevestig; bekragtig

approx'imate (v) benader; (a) by benade-ring, naaste(n)by

ap'ricot appelkoos

Ap'ril April, Aprilmaand

Ap'ril fool Aprilgek

ap'ron voorskoot; *tied to the* ~ *strings of,* onder die plak van

apt geskik, paslik; geneig; onderhewig aan

ap'titude, apt'ness geskiktheid; bekwaam-heid, aanleg; ~ **test** aanlegtoets

a'quaplane branderplank

a'qualung duiklong

aquar'ium (..ria, -s) akwarium

aquat'ic (n) waterplant; waterdier; (pl) wa-tersport; (a) water-

a'rable ploegbaar, beboubaar

ar'bitrary willekeurig

arbitra'tion skeidsregterlike uitspraak, ar-bitrasie

ar'bitrator skeidsregter, arbiter

arc boog

arcade' deurloop, winkelgang, arkade

arch[1] (n) (-es) boog, verwulf, verwelf; (v) welf, buig, krom (rug); ~ **support** steun-sool

arch[2] (a) aarts-, opperste

archaeol'ogist oudheidkundige, argeoloog

arch'angel aartsengel

arch'bishop aartsbiskop

arch'en'emy (..mies) aartsvyand

arch'er boogskutter; ~**y** boogskiet

arch'itect argitek, boumeester

arch'itecture boukunde, argitektuur

arch'ives argief

arc'tic noordelik; noordpool

ard'ent gloeiend; ywerig; hartstogtelik

ard'uous steil; moeilik, opdraand, swaar

are *see* be

ar'ea (-s) oppervlakte; streek, wyk, gebied; area; ~ **committee** streekkomitee

aren'a (-s) strydperk, arena; kampplek

Argenti'na (n) Argentinië; **Ar'gentine** (a) Argentyns

ar'gue redetwis, stry; betoog, argumenteer

ar'gument bewysgrond; diskussie; argu-ment; debat; stelling

ar'ia aria, lied, wysie

a'rid dor, droog

arise' (arose, arisen) oprys, ontstaan; op-staan; herrys; ~ *from,* (voort)spruit uit

aristoc'racy aristokrasie, adelstand

a'ristocrat aristokraat

arith'metic rekenkunde, rekene

ark ark; *A* ~ *of the covenant,* Verbondsark; *Noah's* ~, Noag se ark

arm[1] (n) (pl) wapens; wapentuig; *take up* ~*s,* die wapens opneem; (v) wapen; ~*ed robbery,* gewapende roof; ~*s cache,* wa-penopslagplek

arm[2] (n) arm; been (van 'n hoek); tak; *in-fant/babe in* ~*s,* suigling

arm'ament bewapening, krygstoerusting; swaargeskut; ~*s race,* wapenwedloop

arm'chair leunstoel, armstoel
arm'istice wapenstilstand
arm'oured gepantser, pantser-; ~ car pantsermotor; ~ division pantserdivisie
arm'oury (..ries) arsenaal, wapenhuis, wapenkamer; magasyn
arm'y (armies) leër; heer, krygsmag; ~ pay soldy; ~ worm kommandowurm
aro'ma (-s) geur, aroma
around' om, om en om, rondom
arouse' opwek, aanspoor
arrange' skik, rangskik; reël, inrig; ~ment skikking, rangskikking; flower/floral ~ment, blommerangskikking
arrear(s)' agterstallige gelde; arrear instalments, agterstallige paaiemente
arrest' (n) inhegtenisneming, arres; under ~, onder arres; in aanhouding; (v) in hegtenis neem, arresteer; aanhou
arriv'al aankoms; aangekomene
arrive' aankom, land, arriveer; bereik
a'rrogant aanmatigend, verwaand, arrogant
a'rrow pyl
ars'enal wapenhuis, magasyn, arsenaal
ars'enic (n) arseen, rottekruid
ars'on (moedswillige) brandstigting; ~ist brandstigter
art kuns; lis, bedrog; (pl) lettere, kunste; ~s and crafts, kunsvlyt; bedryfskennis; fine ~s, skone kunste
arte'reo-sclerosis aarverkalking
art'ery (..ries) slagaar
artes'ian artesies; ~ well artesiese put
art: ~ful kunstig; listig, deurtrap; ~ gallery kunsgalery
arthri'tis gewrigsontsteking, artritis
art'icle (n) lidwoord; artikel; voorwaarde; klousule; serve one's ~s, jou leerskap uitdien; ~d clerk leerklerk, ingeskrewe klerk
artic'ulate: ~d truck gelede lorrie/vragmotor
articula'tion uitspraak, artikulasie
art'ifice streek, lis
artifi'cial kunstig; kunsmatig; vals; oneg; ~ insemination kunsmatige inseminasie/bevrugting; ~ limbs kunsledemate; ~ respiration kunsmatige asemhaling; ~ rubber kunsrubber; ~ teeth kunstande, kunsgebit; winkeltande
artill'ery geskut, artillerie
arti'san ambagsman; vakman

art'ist kunstenaar; arties
artis'tic kunsvol, artistiek, kunssinnig
as (adv. conj) as, soos; net soos; aangesien; namate; terwyl; ~ soon ~, sodra
asbes'tos gareklip, asbes; ~ cement asbessement
ascend' klim, opstyg, opvaar
Ascen'sion Day Hemelvaartdag
ascent' steilte, opdraand; bestyging
ascertain' verseker, bepaal, vasstel
ascribe' toeskryf (aan)
asep'tic (n) ontsmetmiddel; (a) ontsmettend, asepties, kiemvry
ashamed' beskaam, skaam; are you not ~ of yourself? skaam jy jou nie?
ash'es as
ash'tray (-s) asbakkie
ask vra; versoek; eis; ~ for, vra (om); ~ for trouble, moeilikheid soek, skoor soek
asleep' aan die slaap; fall ~, aan die slaap raak
aspa'ragus aspersie; wild ~, katdoring
as'pect opsig; kant; gesig(s)punt, aspek
as'pen trilpopulier, esp
as'phalt (n) asfalt; (v) asfalt lê, teer
as'pirant aspirant, kandidaat
aspire' strewe, hunker; aspireer (na)
ass (-es) esel, donkie; make an ~ of, 'n gek maak van
assail' aanval, aanrand; ~ant aanvaller
assass'in sluipmoordenaar; ~ate vermoor; ~a'tion (sluip)moord
assault' (n) aanval, aanranding; (v) aanrand; bestorm, aanval
assay' (v) toets, essaieer; beproef
ass'egai (-s) asgaai
assem'ble versamel, vergader; inmekaarsit, monteer
assem'bly (..blies) byeenkoms, vergadering; montering (masjien); Legislative A~, Wetgewende Vergadering; ~ line monteerlyn
assent' (n) toestemming, goedkeuring
assert' laat geld; handhaaf; bevestig; ~ion handhawing; bewering, stelling
assess' skat; belas, aanslaan, bepaal, evalueer; ~ment skatting, waardebepaling, evaluering; ~ment rate eiendomsbelasting, erfbelasting; ~or taksateur, waardeerder; assessor

ass'et besit, bate; aanwins; ~s bates; boe= del, nalatenskap; ~s and liabilities, bates en laste

assign'ment toewysing, opdrag; werkstuk, studiestuk, taak; bestemming

assim'ilate gelyk maak; assimileer

assist' help, bystaan, steun; ~ance hulp, bystand; ~ant (n) helper; assistent; (a) behulpsaam

asso'ciate (n) maat; assosiaat (van 'n ver= eniging); vennoot; medepligtige; (v) ver= enig; omgaan met, assosieer; ~d bybe= horende, geassosieerde

associa'tion vereniging; assosiasie; A~ of Building Societies, Genootskap van Bou= verenigings; ~ football sokkervoetbal

assort' uitsoek, sorteer; ~ment verskei= denheid

assume' aanneem; aanvaar; veronderstel; ~ responsibility, verantwoordelikheid aanvaar

assum'ing aanmatigend; ~ that, gestel dat

assump'tion veronderstelling

assur'ance versekering; assuransie

assure' verseker; verassureer; ~d verseker= de (persoon); ~r' versekeraar

as'ter aster

as'terisk sterretjie, asterisk

asth'ma asma; ~t'ic aamborstig

aston'ish verbaas, verwonder; ~ing ver= basend; ~ment verbasing, ontsetting

astound' verbaas, dronkslaan

astray' verdwaal; lead ~, verlei; op 'n dwaalspoor bring

astrol'oger sterrewiggelaar, astroloog

as'tronaut ruimtevaarder, ruimtereisiger

astron'omer sterrekundige

astronom'ical astronomies; sterrekundig

astron'omy sterrekunde

astute' skerpsinnig; geslepe; slu

asun'der vanmekaar, uitmekaar; afsonder= lik; tear ~, stukkend skeur

asyl'um (-s) toevlugsoord; skuilplek, asiel; mental ~, sielsiekegestig

at tot; te, op, in; aan, by; teen, met; na; oor; not ~ all, glad nie, heeltemal nie; ~ pre= sent, teenswoordig, nou; ~ school, col= lege and university, op skool, op/aan kollege en op/aan universiteit

ath'eist godloënaar, ateïs

ath'lete atleet, sportman; ~'s foot voet= skimmel

athlet'ic frisgebou(d), sterk, atleties

at-home' ontvangdag; ontvangs

at'las (-es) atlas

at'mosphere atmosfeer, dampkring

atmospher'ic (n, pl) lugsteuring; (a) atmos= feries

at'om atoom; ~ bomb atoombom

atom'ic atomies, atoom; ~ age, atoomeeu; ~ fission, atoomsplitsing, atoomsplyting; ~ fusion, atoomfusie

atro'city (..ties) gruweldaad, afgryslikheid

attach' vasmaak, aanheg; in beslag neem

atta'ché (gesantskaps)attaché; ~ case briewetas; aktetas, see briefcase

attack' (n) aanval; (v) aanval

attain' bereik; verkry; ~able bereikbaar; ~ment bereiking; verkryging; (pl) be= kwaamhede, talente; prestasies

attempt' (n) probeerslag, poging; aanslag; onderneming; (v) probeer, onderneem

attend' ag gee, oppas; bywoon; oplet; ~ to, aandag gee aan; let op; oppas

attend'ance bywoning, teenwoordigheid; in ~, ampshalwe teenwoordig (vergade= rings)

attend'ant (n) bediende; bediener

atten'tion aandag, oplettendheid, sorg; pay ~ to, aandag gee aan

atten'tive oplettend; beleefd

att'ic solderkamer, dakkamer

attire' (n) drag, kleding; (v) optooi

att'itude gesindheid; gestalte, houding

attor'ney (-s) prokureur; power of ~, vol= mag, prokurasie

attract' aantrek; aanlok; boei

attrac'tion aantreklikheid; aantrekkings= (krag); ~ of gravity, swaartekrag; next ~, volgende vertoning

attrac'tive aantreklik; boeiend; bekoorlik

att'ribute[1] (n) eienskap, hoedanigheid; kenmerk, attribuut

attrib'ute[2] (v) toeskryf; wyt; attributable to, toeskryfbaar aan

attri'tion wrywing, afslyting; war of ~, uitput(tings)oorlog

au'burn donkerbruin, goudbruin

auc'tion openbare verkoping; vandisie, vendusie, veiling; sell by ~, opveil

auctioneer' (vendu)afslaer

aud'ible hoorbaar

aud'ience gehoor, toehoorders; oudiënsie

aud'io-visual (a) oudiovisueel; ~ **educa-tion** oudiovisuele onderwys/onderrig
aud'it (n) oudit, ouditering; (v) oudit, ou-diteer; ~**ing** ouditkunde
aud'itor ouditeur
auditor'ium (..**ria, -s**) gehoorsaal, oudito-reum; kloosterspreekkamer
aud'itor's report oudit(eurs)verslag
augment' (v) vermeerder, vergroot, aanvul
aug'ur (n) waarsêer, voëlwiggelaar; (v) voorspel; *it ~s well*, dit beloof baie
Aug'ust[1] Augustus
august' [2] verhewe, groots, vernaam
aunt tante, tannie; tant (voor haar naam)
aus'pices bystand, beskerming; *under the ~ of*, onder beskerming van
auster'ity strengheid, hardheid; eenvou-digheid; eenvoud, soberheid
authen'tic eg, opreg, outentiek
auth'or skrywer, outeur; bewerker
autho'ritative gesaghebbend
autho'rity (..**ties**) gesag; mag; mandaat, vergunning; outoriteit; *on good ~*, uit goeie/betroubare bron
auth'orise magtig; wettig; ~*d capital*, ge-magtigde kapitaal
autobiog'raphy (..**phies**) outobiografie
autocrat'ic(al) eiemagtig, outokraties
aut'ograph (n) eie handskrif; (v) teken, outografeer; ~ **hunter** versamelaar van handtekeninge
automat'ic (n) outomatiese pistool; (a) ou-tomaties; ~ **pilot** stuuroutomaat; ~ **washing machine** wasoutomaat
automa'tion outomatisasie
auton'omous selfbesturend, outonoom
autop'sy (..**sies**) lykskouing
autosugges'tion outosuggestie
aut'umn herfs, najaar
auxil'iary (n) helper, bondgenoot; (..**ries**) hulptroepe; (a) hulp-; ~ **service** hulp-diens; ~ **verb** hulpwerkwoord

avail' (n) baat, nut; (v) baat, benut; ~ *oneself of*, iets te baat neem; ~**able** verkry(g)baar, beskikbaar
av'alanche sneeustorting, lawine
avari'cious gierig, hebsugtig, vrekkig, in-halig
avenge' wreek, wraak neem; *be ~d*, ge-wreek wees; ~**r** wreker
av'enue toegang; laning, laan
av'erage (n) gemiddelde; awery (skeeps-vaart); (pl) gemiddeldes; (a) gemid-deld
aver'sion afkeer, teensin; haat; walging
av'iary (aviaries) voëlhok
avia'tion lugvaart; vliegkuns
av'id begerig, gretig
avoca'do (-s): ~ **pear** avokado, murgpeer
avoid' vermy; weggaan; ontwyk
await' verwag, afwag, wag
awake' (v) (**awoke, awoke** or ~**ned**) wek; ontwaak, wakker word; (a) wakker; op-gewek, lewendig; *be ~ to*, besef; op die hoede wees teen
award' (n) uitspraak, beslissing; beloning; toekenning, prys, bekroning; (v) toeken; bekroon; beslis
aware' bewus; versigtig; bedag; *be ~ of*, bewus wees van
away' weg; vo(o)rt; *right ~*, dadelik, on-middellik
awe (n) ontsag, eerbied; vrees
aw'ful vreeslik; verskriklik; ontsettend, skrikwekkend
awk'ward onhandig, hinderlik; ongemak-lik
awl els
awn'ing seilkap, sonskerm; agterdek
axe byl; *have an ~ to grind*, bybedoelings ('n grief) hê; eiebelang soek
ax'le as; ~ **pin** luns, lunspen
azal'ea (-s) asalea, bergroos
az'ure hemelsblou, asuur

B

baa (n) geblêr; (v) blêr
bab'ble (n) gepraat, gebabbel, geklets; (v) babbel; murmel (water); ~**r** babbelaar, prater; verklikker
babe kindjie, babatjie; ~ *in arms*, suigling

baboon' bobbejaan
bab'y (babies) kind, baba, babatjie; ~**sit-ter** babawagter, kroostrooster; *she will be ~sitting tonight*, sy gaan vanaand kroos-troos

bach'elor vrygesel; oujongkêrel; ~ **flat** eenpersoonwoonstel; ~ **girl** selfstandige oujongnooi

back (n) rug, agterkant; agterspeler; (v) wed op; ondersteun; ~ *a horse,* op 'n perd wed; ~ *up,* ondersteun, rugsteun; (a) ag= terste; agterstallig; (adv) terug, agteruit; gelede; ~ *and forth,* heen en weer; **~fire** terugslaan, terugplof; **~ground** agter= grond; **~lash** teenreaksie; **~log** agter= stand, ophoping; **~packer** pakstapper; **~packing** pakstap; **~seat driver** bekdry= wer; **~veld** agterveld; **~ward** agterlik, lui, dom; **~wash** terugspoeling, trekking; **~yard mechanic** tjorlapper

bac'on (vark)spek; ontbytspek

bacter'ium (..ria) bakterie, kiem

bad (worse, worst) sleg; stout; nadelig; ~ **debts** dooieskuld, oninbare skuld

badge (n) kenteken, wapen; kleurteken

badg'er (n) ratel

bad'ly erg, sleg; gevaarlik

bad'minton pluimbal

baf'fle verydel, beskaam; oorbluf

bag (n) sak, tas; *in the* ~, uitgemaakte saak

bagg'age bagasie, reisgoed

bag'pipe doedelsak; *play the* ~, doedel

bail (n) borg, borgstelling, borgtog; *released on* ~, onder borgtog vrygelaat; (v) borg staan; ~ *out,* uitborg

bait (n) aas, lokaas; (v) aanhits; terg; *arti= ficial* ~, kunsaas

bake bak; hard word; **~r** bakker; **~r's** *dozen,* dertien; **~ry** (..ries) bakkery

bak'ing baksel; ~ **powder** bakpoeier

bak'kie bakkie, ligte bestelwa

bal'ance (n) balans, ewewig; saldo; (weeg)= skaal; ~ *of payments,* betalingsbalans; ~ *of power,* magsewewig; (v) weeg; veref= fen, balanseer, saldeer

bal'cony (..nies) balkon

bald kaal; kaalkop; ~ *facts,* naakte feite

bal'derdash geklets, onsin, kaf(praatjies)

bale¹ (n) baal; (v) in bale pak

bale² (v) uitskep

ball¹ dansparty, bal

ball² koeël, bal, bol; kluit; oogappel

ball'ad ballade, liedjie

ball'ast (n) ballas; (v) ballas inlaai

ball'bearing (koeël)laer

ball'et ballet, toneeldans; ~ **dancer** ballet= danser(es)

balloon' ballon, lugballon

ball'ot (n) stembriefie; stemming; *vote by* ~, per stembrief(ie) stem, met geslote briefies stem

ball'point pen bolpuntpen, bolpen

ball'room danssaal, balsaal

balm (n) balsem; **~y** balsemagtig; simpel, getik

balustrade' reling, borswering, balustrade

bamboo' (-s) bamboes

bamboo'zle bedrieg, kul, fop

ban (n) vervloeking, ban; verbod; (pl) hu= weliksgebooie; (v) (-ned, -ned) verban, ban; inperk; ~ *a book,* 'n boek verbied, in die ban doen; ~ *a person,* iem. verban/ inperk

ban'al banaal, afgesaag, alledaags

bana'na (-s) banana, piesang

band (n) bende; orkes; band

ban'dage (n) verband; (v) verbind

ban'dit voëlvryverklaarde, rower; *armed* ~, gewapende rower; dobbelmasjien

band'master kapelmeester, orkesdirigent

bandoleer' bandelier

band'saw bandsaag, lintsaag

band'wagon: *jump on the* ~, oorloop na die wenparty

ban'dy (n) hokkie; hokkiestok; (v) (..died, ..died) oor en weer slaan; **~-legged** hoe= pelbeen=

bang (n) slag, knal; *go* ~, ontplof

ban'gle armband

ban'ish verban, uitsit; **~ment** verbanning

ban'jo (-s) banjo

bank (n) bank; pot; (v) geld in die bank sit (deponeer); *commercial* ~, handelsbank; *merchant* ~, aksepbank; ~ *on,* staat= maak op; **~er** bank, bankier; ~ **exchange** bankkommissie; **~ing** bankiersake, bank= wese; ~ **rate** bankkoers

bank'rupt (n) bankrotspeler, insolvent; *go* ~, bankrot speel; **~cy** (..cies) bankrot= skap

bann'er banier, vaandel, vlag, spandoek

banns huweliksgebooie

ban'quet (n) feesmaal, banket

ban'tam kapokhoendertjie; ~ **weight** ban= tamgewig

Ban'tu Bantoe

ba'obab kremetartboom, baobab

bap'tise doop, onderdompel

bap'tism doop; ~ *of fire,* vuurdoop

bap'tist (n) doper; wederdoper

bar (n) regbank, balie; kantien, kroeg; maatstreep (mus.); *read for the ~*, in die regte studeer; (v) (-red, -red) uitsluit, be= let; *~ one*, op een na

barb (n) weerhaak; **~ed wire** doring= draad, prikkeldraad

barbar'ian (n) barbaar; wreedaard

barbar'ic barbaars

bar'barism onbeskaafdheid, woestheid, barbaarsheid; barbarisme

bar'becue braaihoek, braaiplek, braaistel

barb'el baber

barb'er barbier, haarsnyer, haarkapper

bare (v) ontbloot; (a) bloot, kaal; oop en bloot; **~faced** met onbedekte gesig; on= beskaamd; *~faced lie*, 'n onbeskaamde leuen; **~foot(ed)** kaalvoet; **~ly** ternou= ernood, skaars

bar'gain (n) winskoop, (wins)kopie, keur= koop; *into the ~*, op die koop toe; *strike a ~*, 'n slag slaan; (v) 'n koop sluit; af= ding, kwansel, knibbel; **~ing power** be= dingingsmag

barge (n) trekskuit, sloep; (v) bons

ba'ritone bariton

bark[1] (n) bas; (v) bas afmaak; 'n kors vorm

bark[2] (n) bark, skuit

bark[3] (n) geblaf; (v) blaf

bar'keeper kroegbaas, kroeghouer

bar'ley gars; *~ water* gortwater

bar'maid (-s) skinkjuffer, skinkjuffie, kroegdoedie

bar'man (..men) kroegman, kantienman, tapper

barn skuur, loods

barom'eter weerglas, barometer

ba'ron baron, vryheer

ba'rrack (n) barak; hut; leërkamp; (pl) ka= serne, barakke; (v) uitjou

ba'rrage studam, keerwal, afsluitdam

ba'rrel (n) vaatjie; geweerloop; (v) inkuip; *~ organ* draaiorrel

ba'rren bar, dor; onvrugbaar; kaal; skraal

barricade' (n) versperring; verskansing; (v) versper, verskans

ba'rrier (n) slagboom, verskansing, ver= sperring; (pl) grense; (v) afsluit; *~ line* (solid white line) sperstreep; *~ reef* (-s) koraalrif

ba'rrow burg (vark)

bart'er (n) ruilhandel; (v) ruil, verruil

base[1] (n) grondslag, basis; voetstuk; *back to (military) base*, terug na die (militêre) basis; (v) baseer, grond; *~ their opinion on*, grond hulle mening op

base[2] (a) sleg, laag; onedel; minderwaardig

base'ball bofbal

base'ment kelder(verdieping)

bash'ful skaam; verleë

bas'ic basies, grond=; *~ English*, basiese Engels; *~ principles*, grondbeginsels

bas'in kom, skottel, wasbak; hawekom

bas'is (bases) grondslag; basis

bask koester, stowe (in die son)

bas'ket mandjie, korf; **~ball** korfbal

bass (-es) basstem, bas; basviool

bast'ard (n) baster, halfnaatjie; (a) baster=; buite-egtelik; **~ise** verbaster

bat[1] (n) vlermuis

bat[2] (n) knuppel; kolfstok, krieketkolf; *off his own ~*, op eie houtjie; (v) (-ted, -ted) kolf, slaan (bal)

bat[3] (v) (-ted, -ted) knip (oog)

batch (-es) klomp; baksel (brood); broeisel (eiers); besending (goed)

bath (n) bad; badkamer; (v) bad

bathe bad, baai; besproei

bath'ing: *~ costume* badkostuum; *~ trunks* swembroek(ie)

bat'on dirigeerstok; knuppel; *~ charge* knuppelstormloop

bats'man (..men) kolwer, slaner

battal'ion bataljon

batt'ery (..ries) battery; aanranding; *~ chickens* batteryhoenders

batt'le (n) veldslag, stryd; (v) veg; **~-axe** strydbyl; kwaai vroumens

bat'tle: *~ dress* gevegstenue, vegklere; **~field** slagveld

bawl skreeu, bulk

bay[1] (n) baai; inham (see)

bay[2] (n) lourier (boom)

bay[3] (b) blaf (hond); *keep at ~*, op 'n af= stand hou; (v) blaf, aanblaf

bay[4] (n) nis; uitbousel

bay[5] (n) bruin perd; (a) bruin

bay'onet (n) bajonet

bazaar' basaar/bazaar; markwinkel

be (was, have been) wees; bestaan; *~ gone!* trap! *don't ~ long*, moenie lank wegbly nie

beach (-es) kus, strand; wal; **~buggy** dui= nebesie; **~comber** stranddief, strandjut;

strandloper, lang golf; ~**combing**, ~**rob-
bing** strandroof; ~**head** strandhoof
beac'on (n) baken; vuurtoring; (v) afbaken
bead (n) kraal; pêrel; sweetdruppel; blasie;
korrel (geweer); (pl) rosekrans; (v) inryg
bea'gle jaghond; speurhond; spioen
beak bek, snawel; kromneus; tuit (ketel)
beak'er beker
be'-all einddoel; alles; wese; *the ~ and end-
all*, die begin en die einde
beam (n) balk; juk (skaal); straal; (v) straal;
skyn; ~**ing** stralend
bean boon(tjie); (pl) pitte, geld; *full of ~s*,
op sy stukke; ~**stalk** boontjierank, boon-
tjiestingel
bear[1] (n) beer; lomperd
bear[2] (n) daalspekulant; (v) spekuleer op
daling (effektebeurs)
bear[3] (v) (**bore, born**) baar, voortbring;
(**bore, borne**) dra; verdra, duld; ~ *in
mind,* goed onthou; ~**able** draaglik, redelik
beard baard; weerhaak
bear'er draer, bringer; toonder (tjek); lyk-
draer; ~ **certificate** toondersertifikaat
bear'ing houding; draer; laer, *see* **ballbear-
ing**; peiling; ~**s** rigting
beast bees, dier; ~**ly** beesagtig, dierlik
beat (n) patrollie, rondte; slag; tik; ritme;
(v) (**beat, -en**) klop, slaan; beuk; kneus;
uitklop; oortref, wen; *that ~s me,* dit
slaan my dronk; ~ *your opponent,* jou
teenstander klop
beat'ing slanery, kloppery; pak slae
beauti'cian skoonheid(s)deskundige
beaut'iful mooi, pragtig, fraai, sierlik
beaut'y skoonheid; bevalligheid; (**..ties**)
skone; ~ **parlour** skoonheidsalon; ~ **spot**
moesie; mooi plekkie; pronkpleistertjie
beav'er bewer
because' omdat, want, daar
beck'on wink, knik, wuif
become' (**became, become**) word; betaam;
pas
becom'ing betaamlik; netjies, passend
bed bed, kooi; bedding (rivier); ~ *and
board,* kos en inwoning
bed'lam kranksinnigegestig; lawaai
bedrag'gle besmeer, betakel
bed: ~**ridden** bedlêend; ~**room** slaapkamer
bee by; vergadering
beef beesvleis; ~**steak** biefstuk

bee: ~**hive** byekorf, by(e)nes; ~**line** reguit
lyn, luglyn; ~**keeper** byeboer
beer bier; ~**hall** biersaal
beet beet
beet'le (n) kewer, tor
beet'root beet; ~ **sugar** beetsuiker
before' voor, vooruit, vantevore; vooraf,
vroeër; ~ *long,* binnekort
before'hand vantevore, vooruit, vooraf
beg (-ged, -ged) versoek; smeek; bid; bedel;
~ *pardon,* verskoning vra
begg'ar (n) bedelaar; *little ~,* klein vabond
begg'ing smekend; bedelary
begin' (**began, begun**) begin, 'n aanvang
neem; ~**ner** beginner; groentjie
begin'ning begin, aanvang; aanhef; *from
the ~,* uit die staanspoor, van meet af
begone'! voort! trap! voert!
behalf' ontwil; namens; *in/on ~ of,* ten
behoewe van, namens
behave' gedra; ~ *oneself,* jou gedra
behav'iour gedrag, houding; *behavioural
psychology,* gedragsielkunde
behead' onthoof
behind' agter; van agter, agteraan
behold' (v) (**..held, ..held**) aanskou, sien,
beskou; (interj) kyk! sien!
be'ing aansyn, bestaan; wese; skepsel; *that
~ so,* aangesien dit so is
belch wind opbreek; uitbraak
bel'fry (**belfries**) kloktoring
belief' (-s) geloof, mening
believ'able geloofbaar
believe' glo, vertrou, meen; ~ *it or not,*
raar maar waar; *make-~,* maak asof,
wysmaak; **make-~** (n) skyn, wysmakery
believ'er gelowige
belit'tle verklein, verkleineer; gering ag
bell klok, bel; *answer the ~,* oopmaak
bell' buoy klokboei, belboei
belli'gerent (n) strydende party; (a) oor-
logvoerend
bell'ow (n) geblêr; gebulk; (v) blêr; bulk
bell'ows blaasbalk; *pair of ~,* blaasbalk
bell: ~**ringer** klokluier; ~**wether** belhamel,
voorbok
bell'y (n) (**bellies**) buik, maag; holte
belong' behoort, toebehoort; *he ~s to a
church,* hy behoort tot 'n kerk; ~**ing** be-
horend; ~**ings** (pl) besittings, goed
beloved' (n) beminde, geliefde; (a) bemind
below' onder, benede, omlaag

belt (n) gordel, lyfband; dryfband; (v) om‑
gord; ~ *up!* gord/gespe vas!
bench (-es) bank, sitbank; regbank
bend (n) buiging; (v) (**bent, bent**) buig; draai
bends (n) borrelsiekte
beneath' onder, benede, onderaan
benedic'tion seëning; gebed, seënwens
ben'efactor weldoener
benefi'ciary (..ries) bedeelde; beguns‑
tigde (in 'n erflating)
ben'efit (n) voordeel; voorreg; ~ *of the
doubt,* voordeel van die twyfel; *fringe* ~,
byvoordeel; (v) bevoordeel; voordeel trek;
bevorder; ~ *society,* bystand(s)vereniging
benev'olent welwillend; goedgunstig; wel‑
dadig; ~ *fund,* bystand(s)fonds, hulp‑
fonds
benign' goed, minsaam, goedaardig
ben'zine bensien, bensine
bequeath' bemaak, nalaat
bequest' bemaking, erfporsie, erflating
bereave' (-d or **bereft, -d** or **bereft**) berowe;
ontneem; *the* ~*d parents,* die bedroefde
ouers; ~**ment** sterfgeval; verlies
be'ret baret
berg berg, ysberg; ~ **wind** bergwind
be'riberi berie-berie
ber'ry (berries) bessie; viseier
ber'serk rasend; ~**er** berserker
berth (n) ankerplek; kajuit; (v) vasmeer
(skip)
beside' langs, naas; by; behalwe, buiten;
~ *the point/question,* nie ter sake nie
besides' bowendien, behalwe, buiten
besiege' beleër
best beste; *to the* ~ *of my ability,* na my
beste vermoë; ~**seller** blitsverkoper; tref‑
fer(boek)
bes'tial dierlik, beesagtig; sinlik
best'man (..men) strooijonker
bestow' skenk, bestee, verleen
bet (n) weddenskap; (v) (**bet, bet**) wed, ver‑
wed; *you* ~*!* dit kan jy glo!
betray' verraai; mislei, bedrieg; dui op; ~**al**
verraad, troubreuk
betroth' verloof, ondertrou; toesê; ~**al**
verlowing; ~**ed'** verloofde
bet'ter (n) voordeel; oorhand; meerdere;
for ~, *for worse,* in lief en leed; (v) ver‑
beter; (a) beter; ~ *half,* wederhelf; *you
had* ~ *go,* jy moet liewer gaan
bett'ing weddery, weddenskappe sluit

between' tussen, tussenin, onder
betwixt' tussen; ~ *and between,* tussen die
boom en die bas
beware' oppas, op sy hoede wees
bewil'der verwar, verbyster; ~**ed** oorstuur,
deurmekaar
bewitch' betower; bekoor
beyond' (n) oorkant; (adv, prep) bo; oor;
buite; meer; verder; verby; oorkant; an‑
derkant; *that is* ~ *me,* dis bokant my
vuurmaakplek
bi'as (n) oorhelling; neiging; vooroordeel;
(v) (-(s)ed, -(s)ed) bevoordeel; ~**sed** be‑
vooroordeel(d), partydig
bib (n) borslappie
Bi'ble Bybel
bib'lical Bybels, Bybel-
bibliog'raphy (..phies) bibliografie
biblioman'iac boekegek, bibliomaniak
bib'liophile bibliofiel, boekversamelaar
bi'ceps (-es) biseps, armspier
bick'er (n) rusie, harwar; (v) kibbel, twis
bi'cycle (n) fiets, rywiel; (v) fiets, fiets ry
bid (n) bod; (v) (**bid** or **bad(e), bid** or -**den**)
beveel; nooi; sê; ~**ding** gebod, bevel,
bieëry (vandisie)
bide afwag, verdra; ~ *one's time,* die beste
kans afwag
bifoc'al bifokaal; ~ **spectacles,** bifocals
bifokale bril, dubbeldoorbril
big groot, swaar, dik; ~ *shot,* groot kok‑
kedoor; ~ *stick,* magsvertoon
big'amist bigamis, tweewywer
big'ot yweraar; dweper; ~**ed** skynheilig
bi'ker (n) fietser
bile gal; humeurigheid; *stir up the* ~, kwaad
maak
bilhar'zia bilharzia-parasiet, slakwurm
bilharzias'is rooiwater (siekte)
bil'iary gal‑; ~ *fever* galkoors
bilin'gual tweetalig; ~**ism** tweetaligheid
bil'ious gallerig, galagtig, mislik; oplopend
bilk bedrieg, fop; *hotel* ~**er,** glyjakkals
bill¹ (n) wetsontwerp
bill² (n) bek; snawel; (v) met die bek streel
bill³ (n) rekening, bewys; plakkaat; ~ *of
exchange,* wissel; ~ *of lading,* vragbrief;
~ *payable,* betaalwissel; skuldwissel; ~
receivable, ontvangwissel, baatwissel; ~
broker wisselmakelaar
bill'iard: ~ **cue** biljartstok; ~**s** biljartspel
bill'ion biljoen

bill'ygoat bokram
bin meelkas, kis; bak, blik
bind (bound, bound) verbind (wond); bind; verplig; ~er binder; verband; ~ery (.. ries) boekbindery
binoc'ular (pl) verkyker; toneelkyker
biochem'istry biochemie
biodegra'dable bio-afbreekbaar
biog'raphy (..phies) lewensbeskrywing, biografie
biol'ogy biologie
bi'oscope bioskoop; going to ~, bioskoop toe gaan, gaan fliek
bird voël; ~ of passage, trekvoël; ~ of prey, roofvoël; ~ie voëltjie (ook gholf); ~lime voëllym, voëlent
birth geboorte; oorsaak, ontstaan; give ~ to, die lewe skenk aan; ~ certificate geboortebewys; ~ control geboortebeperking; ~day verjaar(s)dag; ~mark moedervlek; ~rate geboortesyfer
bis'cuit soetkoekie, droëkoekie
bisect' middeldeur sny, bisekteer
bish'op biskop; raadsheer (skaak)
bis'ley (-s) prysskiet
bit¹ (n) bietjie, stukkie
bit² (n) stang; (v) (-ted, -ted) 'n toom aansit
bitch (-es) teef; hoer
bite (n) byt; hap; (v) (bit, bitten) byt, wond; kwes; vat; bedrieg
bit'ing bytend, bits, skerp; invretend
bitt'er bitter; skerp
black (n) swart; swartsel; rouklere; in ~ and white, swart op wit; (v) swart smeer, swart maak; ~ market, sluikhandel; ~ball (v) deballoteer; ~board skryfbord, skoolbord; ~jacks wewenaars, knapsekerwels; (v) (-ged, -ged) onderkruip; ~mail (n) afdreiging, afpersing; (v) afpers; ~-out verdonkering; breinfloute; ~wattle wattelboom, looibasboom
blad'der blaas; windsak; binnebal
blade lem, skeerlemmetjie; halm; blaadjie
blame (n) blaam; (v) blameer, verkwalik
blank (n) leegte, oop plek; leemte; nul; (a) wit; blank, bleek; onbeskrewe; rein; leeg; rymloos (verse)
blank'et (n) kombers; a wet ~, pretbederwer, konversasiedemper (persoon)
blare (n) gebrul; lawaai; gesketter; (v) bulk, brul; sketter

blas'phemous godslasterlik
blas'phemy (..mies) godslastering; heilig-skennis
blast (n) wind, rukwind; ontploffing; (v) uitbars, skiet (dinamiet); vervloek; ~ed fellow, vervloekste vent; ~er (dinamiet)-skieter; ~-furnace smeltoond, hoogoond; ~ing certificate skietsertifikaat; ~ing operations springwerke
blaze¹ (n) bles (van perd); (v) 'n wit streep maak; ~ a trail, die weg baan
blaze² (n) vlam, vuurgloed; gerug; in a ~, in ligtelaaie; (v) vlam, brand; skitter
blaze³ (v) rondvertel, uitbasuin; ~ forth, rondbasuin
blaze⁴ (v) skiet, losbrand
blaz'er kleurbaadjie
blaz'ing gloeiend, brandend
bleach bleik; ~ing powder bleikpoeier
bleak kaal, verlate, koud
bleat (n) geblêr; (v) blêr
bleed (bled, bled) bloedlaat; bloei; ~er bloeier
bleep'er (-s) blieper
blem'ish (n) (-es) vlek, smet; skande
blend (n) mengsel; (v) (-ed, -ed, or blent, blent) meng, vermeng
bles'bok blesbok
bless seën, loof; wy
bless'ed (n): the ~, die gesaligdes; (a) geseën, gelukkig; saliger; of ~ memory, saliger nagedagtenis
bless'ing seën, seëning; (tafel)gebed; ~ in disguise, bedekte seën
blight (n) heuningdou, roes; brand (koring); plaag, verwoesting
blind¹ (n) (rol)gordyn, blinding; skerm
blind² (v) verblind, blind maak; bedrieg; (a) blind, donker; verborge; ~ alley, blinde steeg, keerweer; doodloopstraat; ~ date, blinde afspraak/ontmoeting; ~ rise, blinde hoogte; ~ side, skeelkant; steelkant (rugby); ~fold (v) blinddoek; (a) geblinddoek; blindelings; ~ly blindelings; ~man's buff blindemannetjie, blindemolletjie (kinderspel)
blink (n) flikkering, flits; (v) knipoog, gluur
blink'ers oogklappe
bliss saligheid, geluk, heil; ~full salig
blis'ter (n) blaar, blaas; (v) afdop (verf)
blizz'ard sneeustorm, sneeujag

blob druppel; klont; blaas
block (n) blok; hindernis; (v) afsluit, ver=
sper; dwarsboom
blockade' (n) insluiting, blokkade; (v) in=
sluit, blokkeer
block: ~head domkop, uilskuiken; ~house
blokhuis; ~man (..men) blokman
blo'ke kêrel, vent, ou, *also* guy
blond blond, lig
blonde blondine, witkop
blood (n) bloed; verwantskap; *blue* ~,
aristokratiese bloed; *in cold* ~, koel=
bloedig; ~ donor bloedskenker; ~ pois=
oning bloedvergiftiging; ~ pressure
bloeddruk; ~ transfusion bloedoortap=
ping; ~y bloeddorstig, wreedaardig;
bloederig; vervloekte, vervlakste
bloom (n) bloesem, blom; fleur, bloei; blos;
(v) bloei, voorspoedig wees; blom
bloom'ers kniebroek
bloom'ing bloeiend; blosend; vervlakste
bloss'om (n) bloesem, bloeisel; (v) bloei,
blom; ~ out into, ontwikkel/ontpop
tot
blot (n) klad, vlek; skandvlek; (v) beklad
blott'er kladblok; skryfmap
blott'ing paper vloeipapier
blouse bloes(e); hempbaadjie
blow[1] (n) slag, klap; stoot; hou, raps; ramp;
come to ~s, handgemeen raak
blow[2] (blew, blown) blaas, waai; ~gun
~pipe blaaspyp
blue (n) blousel; blou, lug; (a) blou; neer=
slagtig; *out of the* ~, uit die bloute; *true*
~, volbloed; ~gum bloekom; ~stocking
bloukous, geleerde vrou
bluff[1] (n) grootpratery, bluf; (v) uitoorlê,
bangmaak, grootpraat, afsnou; oorbluf
bluff[2] (n) steil voorgebergte; (a) grof; steil
blun'der (n) flater, vergissing; blaps; fout;
~buss (-es) donderbus; ~er knoeier,
sukkelaar, domkop
blunt (v) stomp maak; ongevoelig maak;
afstomp; (a) stomp; bot; nors, kortaf
blur (n) vlek, smet; (v) (-red, -red) beklad
blurb flapteks; aanpr;sing, reklameteks
blurred gevlek, dof
blurt: ~ *out*, uitblaker, uitflap, uitklap
blush (n) (-es) blos; gloed; *without a* ~,
sonder blik (of bloos); ~ing (a) blosend
bo'a (-s) boa; ~ constric'tor luislang
boar beer; wilde swyn

board (n) plank; tafel, kas; boord (skip);
raad; kommissie; kosgeld, losies; karton;
~ *of inquiry*, ondersoekraad; ~ *and
lodging*, kos en inwoning; *sweep the* ~,
alles wen; (v) inwoon, loseer; ~er kos=
ganger, loseerder; ~ing losies, kos; lo=
siesgeld; ~ing house koshuis, losieshuis;
~ing school kosskool; ~room raad(s)=
kamer, raadsaal
boast (n) spoggery, grootpratery; (v) spog,
windmaak, roem; ~ *of*, spog met; ~er
grootprater, windmaker
boat (n) boot, skuit, skip; ~race roeiwed=
stryd
boatswain (*pron.* b'sn) bootsman
bob (v) (-bed, -bed) ruk, dobber
bobb'y (bobbies) dien(d)er, konstabel
bob'tail stompstert; *ragtag and* ~, Jan Rap
en sy maat
bod'ily liggaamlik; heeltemal; kompleet
bod'y (n) (bodies) liggaam, lyf; persoon;
bende; lyk; volheid (wyn); bak(werk)
(motor); ~ *corporate*, regspersoon(lik=
heid), beheerliggaam (deeltitels); (v)
(bodied, bodied) beliggaam; ~builder
liggaamsbouer, spierbouer; ~guard lyf=
wag; ~ language lyftaal, liggaamstaal
bof'fin uitvinder
bog (n) moeras, vlei; (v) vasval
bog'ey (-s) baansyfer (gholf)
bog'us vals, oneg; *a* ~ *collector*, 'n kam=
makollektant; *a* ~ *company*, 'n swendel=
maatskappy
bog'y (bogies) gogga, spook, skrikbeeld
boil[1] (n) pitsweer, bloedvin(t)
boil[2] (n) kook; *on the* ~, aan die kook; (v)
kook; ~er ketel, stoomketel; ~ermaker
ketelmaker; ~ing point kookpunt
bois'terous onstuimig, wild
bold vrypostig; dapper; vermetel; *make* ~,
die vryheid neem; *I make* ~ *to say*, ek
verstout my om te sê
bol'ster (n) kussing; stut; (v) ondersteun;
opvul; rugsteun; ~ *up*, steun, stut
bolt[1] (n) pyl; grendel; bout; skuif; bliksem=
straal; sprong
bolt[2] (v) weghol, op loop sit
bomb (n) bom, granaat; *atom* ~, atoom=
bom; (v) bombardeer, beskiet
bombard' bombardeer, met grofgeskut
losbrand; ~ment bombardement

bomb: ~**er** bomwerper; ~ **shelter** bomskuiling

bon'a fid'e te goeder trou, bona fide

bonan'za meevaller(tjie), gelukslag

bond (n) band; verband; verbintenis; verpligting; verbond, ooreenkoms; (v) verpand; verband, beswaar; ~**ed property** verbande eiendom, beswaarde eiendom; ~**holder** verbandhouer; ~**s** skuldbriewe, obligasies

bone (n) been; (pl) gebeente; *a ~ of contention*, 'n twisappel; *pick a ~*, 'n appeltjie skil

bon'fire vreugdevuur

bonn'et mus, kappie, hoedjie; kap (motor)

bonn'y lief, aanvallig, vrolik, dartel

bon'us (-es) beloning, bonus, premie; ~ **bond** bonusobligasie

bon'y benerig, beenagtig; vol grate

boo (v) uitjou, boe, *also* **barrack**

boob'y (**boobies**) lummel, domoor; ~ **prize** spotprys, troosprys; ~ **trap** fopmyn

book (n) boek; geskrif; Bybel; *kiss the ~*, op die Bybel sweer; ~ *of reference*, naslaanboek; bewysboek; (v) inboek; opskryf; ~**ie** beroepswedder; ~**ing office** loket, kaartjieskantoor; ~**keeping** boekhou; ~**mark** bladwyser; ~**seller** boekhandelaar; ~**token** boekbewys

boom[1] (n) sluitboom, valhek

boom[2] (n) gedreun; gebulder (kanon); (v) bulder, dreun

boom[3] (n) welvaart; oplewing, boom; hoogkonjunktuur

boom'erang boemerang, werphout

boon (n) geskenk; guns; genade; uitkoms; (a) vrolik, vriendelik; weldadig

boor lummel, lomperd; ~**ish** onbeskof

boost (v) ophemel; aanjaag; versterk; ~ *one's ego*, jou ego streel; ~**er** aanjaer; versterker; ~**er dose** skraagdosis; ~**er injection** skraaginspuiting

boot[1] (n) stewel; bagasieruim; *get the ~*, uitgeskop word; (v) skop

boot[2] (n) wins, voordeel; *to ~*, op die koop toe

booth hut, tent, kraampie, stalletjie

boot: ~**lace** skoenveter, skoenriem; ~**legger** (drank)smokkelaar; ~**polish** waks, skoensmeer; ~**s** skoenpoetser; ~ **tree** skoenlees

boot'y (**booties**) buit, roof

booze (n) drinkgoed; *on the ~*, aan die fuif/swier; (v) suip, swier, boemel

bord'er (n) rand; kant; grens (land); soom; (v) omsoom; begrens; ~ *(up)on*, grens aan; ~*line case*, grensgeval; *on the ~*, aan die grens; ~ **industry** grensnywerheid

bore[1] (n) boor; boorgat; kaliber (geweer); wydte; (v) boor; uitboor

bore[2] (n) vervelende mens of saak; (v) verveel, neul

bor'er boor; boorwurm; boorder

bor'ing vervelend, vervelig; saai

born gebore; ~ *and bred*, gebore en getoë; ~ *in the Karoo*, 'n boorling v.d. Karoo

borne gedra, *see* **bear**

bo'rough stad, dorp; munisipaliteit

bo'rrow leen (van iem.); ontleen (aan); ~**er** lener

bo'som (n) boesem, bors; ~ **friend** boesemvriend

boss (n) (-es) baas, meester; (v) bestuur, baasspeel; (a) ~**y** baasspelerig

bot'any plantkunde, botanie

both beide, albei, altwee; ~ *Ann and Mary*, sowel Ann as Mary; ~ *languages*, albei tale; ~ *of us*, ons albei

both'er (n) las, kwelling; (v) neul, lastig val, lol; moeite maak

bot'tle (n) bottel, fles; (v) bottel; inlê; ~ **neck** knelpunt; ~**store** drankwinkel

bott'om (n) boom; grond(slag); onderkant; (v) grondves; steun; (a) onderste; *a ~less pit*, 'n bodemlose put

bought *see* **buy**

boul'der rotsblok, groot klip

bounce (n) slag, opslag, hou; grootpraat; (v) huppel, spring, opspring; aanbons; ~**r** windmaker, windbuks; ligter (krieket)

bound[1] (n) grens; *out of ~s*, buite perk(e)

bound[2] (a) verbonde, verplig; bestem; ~ / *committed to*, verbind tot

boun'dary (**..ries**) grens, skeiding; grenshou (sport)

bout keer, beurt; wedstryd; ronde

bouti'que boetiek

bow[1] (n) buiging; (v) buig, buk; groet; ~ *down*, neerbuig; verpletter

bow[2] (n) boeg (van skip)

bow[3] (n) strykstok; strik; boog

bow'els ingewande; gevoel

bowl[1] (n) skaal; kom; beker

bowl[2] (n) (pl) rolbal; (v) boul; keël

bow'legged hoepelbeen
bow'ler bouler
bow'ling: ~ alley (-s) keëlbaan, kegelbaan; ~ green rolbalbaan
bowls rolbal
bow'string boogsnaar, boogpees
box[1] (n) opstopper, klap; boks; (v) boks
box[2] (n) (-es) doos, kas, kis; (pos)bus, brie= webus; ~er bokser; ~ing boks; B~ing day Tweede Kersdag, see Day of Goodwill; ~ing gloves bokshandskoene; ~ office loket; ~ office success, lokettreffer
boy (-s) jongetjie, seun, knaap
boy'cott (n) boikot; (v) boikot
boy: ~s' high school hoër seunskool; ~ scout padvinder
bra buustelyfie, buustehouer, bra
braai, braaivleis (n) vleisbraai
brace'let armband
brac'es kruisbande
brack'et (n) klamp; (v) klamp; in ~s, tussen hakies
brack'ish brak, souterig
brag (v) (-ged, -ged) spog, grootpraat, windmaak; ~gart grootprater, grootbek; ~ging (v) grootpraat
braid (n) vleg, haarvleg; koord, omboorsel
braille puntskrif, blindeskrif, Brailleskrif
brain brein, harsings; verstand; oordeel; ~= child uitvindsel, geesteskind; ~racking hoofbrekend; ~scan flikkergram; ~= washing breinspoeling; ~wave blink ge= dagte; ~y skrander, knap, slim
brake (n) remskoen, rem, briek; (v) rem, briek; ~ lining remvoering
bram'ble braam
bran semels
branch (n) (-es) tak; vertakking; takkan= toor; (v) vertak
brand (n) merk, brandmerk; handelsmerk; (v) brandmerk; kenmerk; ~ed goods merkartikels; ~ing iron brandyster
brand'-new (spik)splinternuut
bran'dy (..dies) brandewyn
brass geelkoper; geld; skaamteloosheid; ~ band blaasorkes
brass'ière buustelyfie, buustehouer, bra
brava'do grootpratery, bluf, bravade
brave (v) uitdaag; tart; (a) dapper, moedig; ~ry dapperheid
bra'vo (interj) bravo! mooi skoot! skote P(r)etoors!

brawl (n) rusie, bakleiery; (v) twis, rusie maak; lawaai opskop
brawn sult, hoofkaas; ~y gespier(d)
bray (v) skreeu soos 'n esel, balk
braze (v) sweissoldeer, braseer
braz'en-faced onbeskaamd
braz'enness astrantheid
brazil' brasielhout
breach (n) (-es) breuk, verbreking, bres, skeur; oortreding; ~ of the peace, rus= verstoring; ~ of promise, troubreuk
bread brood; quarrel with your ~ and butter, in jou eie lig staan
breadth breedte, wydte
bread'winner broodwinner
break (n) steuring; leemte; breuk; pouse; blaaskans; (v) (broke, broken) breek, ver= breek; versteur; vernietig; ~ off an engagement, 'n verlowing verbreek; ~ a rand, 'n rand kleinmaak; ~ a record, 'n rekord slaan/oortref; ~down instorting; onklaarraking; teenspoed; oponthoud; ongeluk; ontleding (van syfers); ~down lorry (..lorries) herstelwa, noodwa, hulpwa; ~down service insleepdiens
break'er brander (see)
break-even point, winsdrempel, gelyk= breekpunt
break'fast ontbyt, oggendete
break: ~through deurbraak; ~water ha= wehoof; golfbreker
breast (n) bors; boesem, skoot; make a clean ~ of, alles opbieg
breath asem; luggie, windjie; out of ~, uit= asem; take ~, asemhaal; ~alyser alko= toetser, asemtoetser
breathe asem, asemhaal; adem (fig.); ~r blaaskans
breed (n) geslag, ras, soort; (v) (bred, bred) (aan)teel; (uit)broei; voortbring; ~er teler; ~ing teelt; beskawing, verfyndheid
breeze luggie, windjie, bries
brev'ity kortheid, beknoptheid
brew (n) brousel; (v) brou, gis; ~ mischief, kwaad stig; ~ery (..ries) brouery
bri'ar wilde roos; rooshout
bribe (n) omkoping, omkoopgeld; (v) om= koop; ~ry (..ries) omkopery
bric'-a-brac snuitery, rariteite
brick (n) baksteen; staatmaker; (a) bak= steen=; ~layer messelaar
brid'al (a) bruids=; ~ couple bruidspaar

bride bruid; **~groom** bruidegom; **~s'- maid** strooimeisie; **~s'man** (..men) strooijonker, bruidsjonker

bridge[1] (n) brug (kaartspel); (v) brugspeel

bridge[2] (n) brug; vioolkam; rug (neus); (v) oorbrug; **~head** brughoof

bri'dle (n) toom, teuel; (v) beteuel

brief[1] (n) (-s) samevatting; opdrag, voorskrif, volmag, mandaat; *hold a ~ for,* as ver- dediger optree; **~case** aktetas, briewetas

brief[2] (a) kort, beknop

brigadier' brigadier; **~ general (brigadiers general)** brigade-generaal

bright helder, skitterend; skrander; **~en** verhelder, opvrolik

brikett' (-s) briket

brill'iant glinsterend, skitterend; geestig

brim (n) rand, kant

brine (n) pekel; (v) insout

bring (brought, brought) bring, saambring; veroorsaak; *~ down the house,* algemene byval vind; *~ round,* iem. weer bybring

brin'jal (n) eiervrug, brinjal

brink rand; waterkant; **~manship** waag- politiek

brin'y pekelagtig, souterig

brisk lewendig, wakker, gou; monter

bris'ket bors, borsstuk

bris'tle (n) varkhaar; borsel; *~ with,* wemel van

Brit'ain Brittanje

Brit'ish Brits

brit'tle bros, breekbaar

broach (v) ter sprake bring, opper; *~ a subject,* 'n saak aanroer

broad breed, wyd; **~bean** tuinboon, boer- boontjie

broad'cast (-ed, ..cast) uitsaai

broad'casting uitsaaiwese; **~ corporation** uitsaaikorporasie; **~ programme** radio- program; **~ station** radio-omroep

broad: ~en breed maak, verbreed; **~- minded** verlig

bro'chure brosjure, pamflet, bladskrif

broil'er braaihoender, braaikuiken

broke gebreek; platsak, bankrot

brok'en gebreek, stukkend; verslae, moe- deloos; gebroke (hart); *~ home* ge- broke gesin/huis; *~ line* stippelstreep (pad)

brok'er makelaar

bronchit'is lugpypontsteking, brongitis

bronze (n) brons; bronsfiguur; (v) (ver)- brons

brooch (-es) borsspeld

brood (n) broeisel; gespuis; (v) broei, uit- broei; **~y** broeis

brook (n) spruitjie, lopie, driffie

broom besem; veër; brem

broth dun vleissop, kragso(e)p; *too many cooks spoil the ~,* baie koks bederf die bry

broth'el bordeel, hoerhuis

broth'er (-s, brethren) broer, boet; **~hood** broe(de)rskap; **~-in-law (brothers-in-law)** swaer

brow wysbrou, winkbrou

brown bruin; donker

browse afknabbel; rondkyk, rondblaai

bruise (n) kneusplek; (v) kneus

brunette' brunet, swartkop

brunt skok, heftigheid, skerpte; *bear the ~ of,* die spit afbyt

brush (n) (-es) borsel, kwas; (v) borsel; *~- wood* (fyn)ruigte, kreupelhout

brut'al onmenslik, beesagtig

brute (n) redelose dier; onbeskofte mens; (a) dierlik, ru, onbeskof

bub'ble (n) lugbel, borrel; (v) borrel, blaas; **~gum** blaasgom

bubon'ic plague builepes

buccaneer' seerower, vrybuiter, boekanier

buck (n) bokram; modegek

buck'et emmer; bak; koker; *kick the ~,* lepel in die dak steek; *~ shop* dobbel- kantoor

buc'kle (n) gespe; (v) vasgespe

bud (n) knop, bot; ent; *nip in the ~,* in die kiem smoor; (v) (-ded, -ded) bot, uit- loop

budge wyk, verroer, beweeg

bud'ge(rigar) parkietjie, budjie

budg'et (n) begroting; leersak; (v) begroot

buff'er stootkussing, buffer

bug[1] (n) luis, weeluis; (elektroniese) klikker, luistervlooi

bug[2] (v) (-ged, -ged) meeluister, afluister; *his office was bugged,* sy kantoor was ge- klik

bug'bear skrikbeeld, paaiboelie; gogga

bu'gle beuel, glaskraal; **~r** beuelblaser

build (n) bou, vorm, liggaamsbou; (v) **(built, built)** bou; stig; oprig

buil'der bouer, boumeester

buil'ding gebou; bou, bouery; ~ **contractor** bouaannemer, boukontrakteur; ~
society (..ties) bouvereniging
built-in ingebou; ~ *resistance,* ingeboude
weerstand
built-up area beboude gebied
bulb bol; gloeilamp(ie); blombol
bulge (n) knop; (v) swel, uitsit
bulk (n) omvang, grootte, klomp; *buy in* ~,
by die grootmaat koop; ~ *posting,* mas-
saversending, massapos; ~**y** lywig
bull[1] stygspekulant (effektebeurs)
bull[2] bul; ~**calf** (..calves) bulkalf; ~**dog**
bulhond, Boeldok(hond); ~**dozer** stoot-
skraper
bull'et koeël; ~**proof** koeëlvas, koeëlvry
bull'etin daaglikse verslag, bulletin
bull'fight stiergeveg
bull'y (n) (bullies) afknouer, baasspeler,
bullebak; (v) (bullied, bullied) treiter,
baasspeel; afknou
bum agterent, agterste; skobbejak
bump (n) slag, stamp; (v) stamp
bum'per (n) stamper, buffer; ligter (krieket); (a) propvol, oorvloedig; *a* ~ *crop,* 'n
rekordoes
bump'kin lummel, lomperd, plaasjapie
bun[1] bolletjie
bun[2] bolla (hare)
bunch (-es) bos, bondel; tros
bun'dle (n) bondel, gerf; (v) saambind
bun'du gramadoelas, agterveld
bung'alow landhuis, huthuis
bun'gle (n) knoeiwerk; (v) knoei; konkel
bun'ion eelt
bunk[1] (n) slaapplek, slaapbank, kooi
bunk[2] (n) kaf, twak, onsin
bunk[3] (v) stokkies draai
bun'ker (n) kolehok; hindernis; bunker;
(sand)kuil (gholf); (v) kole laai, bunker
bunk'um onsin, bog, kafpraatjies
bun'ny troetelnaam vir hasie, konyntjie
buoy (n) (-s) baken (in see); boei
burd'en (n) las, vrag, pak; refrein; hoof-
tema; *beast of* ~, lasdier
bureau' (-x) kantoor, buro
bu'reaucrat burokraat
burg'lar inbreker, huisbreker; ~**y** (..ries)
huisbraak, inbraak; ~ **alarm** diefalarm;
~ **guard,** ~ **proofing** diefwering
bu'rial begrafnis; ~ **service** roudiens

burn (n) brandplek; (v) (burnt, burnt or -ed,
-ed) brand; gloei
burs'ar penningmeester; beurshouer; ~**y**
(..ries) studiebeurs
burst (n) bars, skeur; (v) (burst, burst) bars
bu'ry (buried, buried) begrawe
bus (-es) bus; *catch the* ~, die bus haal; *miss
the* ~, die bus mis; ~ **driver** busdrywer
bush (-es) bos, bossie; bosveld; *beat about
the* ~, uitvlugte soek; ~**baby** (..babies)
nagapie; ~**buck** bosbok; ~**fighter**
bosvegter; ~ **shrike** bokmakierie; ~**tick**
bosluis
bus'iness (-es) besigheid, bedryf, beroep,
werk; ~ **leadership** bedryfsleiding; ~ **letter** sakebrief; ~**like** prakties, metodies;
~**man** (..men) sakeman (mv sakelui,
sakemanne)
bust borsbeeld; buuste, bors
bu'stle (n) gewoel, lewe, rumoer
bus'y (a) besig, woelig, bedrywig; ~**body**
(..ies) bemoeial
but (n) maar; (prep) maar, dog, egter; behalwe; ~ *for,* was dit nie; *the last* ~ *one,*
op een na die laaste
butch'er (n) slagter; (v) slag; vermoor; ~-
bird laksman; ~**y** (..ries) slaghuis, slag-
tery
but'ler (oorspr.) bottelier; hoofbediende
butt'er (n) botter; (v) met botter smeer
butt'erfly (..flies) skoe(n)lapper, vlinder
butt'er: ~**milk** karringmelk; ~**pat** botter-
spaantjie
butt'ock boud, agterste
butt'on (n) knoop, knop; (v) toeknoop;
~**hole** knoopsgat; ruikertjie
bux'om lewendig; frisgebou; mollig
buy (bought, bought) koop, inkoop; ~**er**
koper; aankoper (vir firma)
buzz (v) gons, brom; ~ **bike** kragfiets; ~**er**
gonser; zoemer (tegn.)
by deur; tot, met; na; by, op; ~ *far the best
dictionary,* verreweg die beste woordeboek; ~ *no means,* glad nie
bye loslopie; orige speler
bye-bye! wederom! tot siens!
by'-election tussenverkiesing
by'-law munisipale verordening; reglement
by: ~**pass** (n) verbypad; omleiding (hart);
(v) verbysteek; ~**product** neweprodukt;
~**stander** omstander, toeskouer

C

cab huurrytuig; kajuit (lorrie, lokomotief); taxi
cab'aret kabaret; herberg
cabb'age (kop)kool
cab'in (n) kajuit, hut; (v) insluit
cab'inet kabinet, ministerie; kamertjie; kas; **display ~**, toonkas
ca'ble (n) kabel; kabeltou; (v) kabel; vasmaak; **~way** kabelspoor
caca'o kakao, kakaoboontjie, *see* **cocoa**
cac'kle (n) gekekkel; (v) kekkel
cac'tus (-es, ..ti) kaktus
cad gemene vent, ploert, skobbejak
cadd'ie joggie (gholf)
cadd'y (caddies) teebus
cadet' kadet
Caesa'rean opera'tion keisersnee
caf'é kafee, koffiehuis
cafeter'ia kafeteria
cage (n) koutjie, kooi, voëlhok; kooi (myne), hysbak, hyshok; (v) opsluit
cake koek
cal'abash (-es) kalbas
calam'ity (..ties) ramp, onheil
cal'cify (..fied, ..fied) verkalk
cal'culate bereken, reken; **~d** voorbedag, berekend, koelbloedig; **~d insult** berekende affront
calcula'tion berekening
cal'culator sakrekenaar, sakkomper(tjie)
cal'endar (n) kalender, almanak; rol
calen'dula gousblom
calf[1] (calves) kuit (been)
calf[2] (calves) kalf; **~ love** kalwerliefde
cal'iber deursnee; gewig, gehalte, kaliber
call (n) beroep; kuier; bevel; gefluit; oproep (foon); vraag; lokstem; bod (kaarte); signaal; beroep (predikant); **within ~**, byderhand; (v) roep; noem; beroep (predikant); besoek; kuier; troef maak (kaarte); bel, lui, skakel (foon); **~ names**, uitskel; **~ off**, afgelas; aflei; **on ~**, op/met roepdiens, op roep; **~er** roeper; besoeker; **~girl** foonsnol, loknooi
cal'ibrate (v) kalibreer
call'ing roeping; beroep; geroep
call'ous (a) ongevoelig
call'us (n) **(-es)** eelt

calm (n) kalmte, windstilte; (v) kalmeer, bedaar; stil maak; (a) kalm, rustig, stil
cal'orie warmte-eenheid, kalorie
cal'umny laster, skindertaal, agterklap
Cal'vary Kruisberg, Kalvarie
calve (v) kalf, kalwe
cam nok (aan 'n masjien)
cam'ber ronding, kromming
cam'el kameel
camell'ia japonika, kamelia
ca'meo kamee
cam'era (-s) kamera; fototoestel; kamer; **in ~**, in kamera
cam'ouflage (n) vermomming, maskering, camouflage, kamoefleerdrag; (v) vermom, masker, kamoefleer; **~ uniform**, kamoefleerpak
camp (n) laer, kamp; (v) kampeer
campaign' (n) veldtog, kampanje
campanile' kloktoring
camp: ~bed veldbed, voukatel; **~fire** kampvuur
cam'phor kanfer; **~ated** kanfer=
cam'pus kampus, (universiteits)terrein
cam'shaft nok-as
cam'wheel kamrat
can[1] (n) kan, blik; (v) **(-ned, -ned)** inmaak (in bottels); inlê, verduursaam; **~ned fruit**, ingemaakte/ingelegde vrugte; **~ned music**, blikmusiek
can[2] (v) **(could)** kan
canal' kanaal; buis; groef; **~ise** kanaliseer
canar'y (..ries) kanarie
can'cel kanselleer; herroep; skrap; **~ an appointment**, 'n afspraak afsê/afstel; **~la'tion** kansellasie; herroeping, intrekking
can'cer kanker, krap; **~ous** kankeragtig
can'did eerlik, opreg, openhartig
can'didate kandidaat; aansoeker
can'dle kers; **~stick** blaker, kandelaar
can'dour opregtheid, openhartigheid
can'dy (n) **(..dies)** kandy, sukade; suiker-klontjies; (v) **(..died, ..died)** versuiker; **~floss** spookasem; **~sugar** teesuiker
cane (n) riet, rottang, liet; suikerriet; kierie, wandelstok; (v) slaan, pak gee; mat (stoel); **~ spirits** rietblits; **~ sugar** rietsuiker

can'ine (n) hond; hoektand, oogtand; (a) honds=
can'ister trommel, blikdoos
can'ker (n) kanker; pes; sweer; hoefseer; (v) invreet, wegvreet; verpes
canned ingelê, ingemaak; ~ peaches, ingelegde/ingemaakte perskes
cann'ery inmaakfabriek
cann'ibal mensvreter, kannibaal
cann'on kanon, geskut, see gun
cann'ot kan nie
cann'y versigtig, slim, oulik
canoe' (-s) kano; ~ist kanovaarder; ~ race kano(wed)vaart
can'on kanon, kerkwet, reël
canon'ise heilig verklaar
can'opy (..pies) (troon)hemel; kap(pie)
cantank'erous vitterig, prikkelbaar, suur
canteen' kantien, kroeg; verversingslokaal; veldkombuis; winkel; ~ of cutlery, stel tafelgerei
can'ter[1] (n) huigelaar
can'ter[2] (n) kort galop, handgalop; win in a ~, fluit-fluit wen; (v) op 'n kort galop ry
can'tharis (..rides) spaansvlieg
can'tilever vrydraer, vrydraend
can'ton (n) kanton; (v) inkwartier (troepe)
can'tor kantor, voorsinger
can'vas (-es) seil(doek); skilderdoek
can'vass (v) kolporteer; (stemme) werf; ~er (stemme)werwer; ~ing klante/ stemme werf; invloedwerwing (vir 'n betrekking)
can'yon bergkloof, ravyn
cap (n) mus, hoed, pet, baret; a feather in his ~, 'n pluimpie; if the ~ fits, as die skoen pas
cap'able bekwaam, geskik, vatbaar
capa'city bekwaamheid, bevoegdheid; vermoë, lewering; bakmaat (dam); kapasiteit; in the ~ of, in die hoedanigheid van
cape[1] (n) mantel; kraag
cape[2] (n) kaap
cap'er (n) sprong, kaperjol; cut a ~, 'n flikker maak; (v) rondspring, bokspring
cap'ita: per ~, per hoof/kop/capita
cap'ital (n) hoofstad; kapitaal; hoofletter; (a) belangrik; hoof=; ~ crime/offence, halsmisdaad; ~ employed, kapitaal aangewend; employment of ~, aanwending van kapitaal; ~ punishment, doodstraf

cap'italism kapitalisme
capitula'tion kapitulasie, oorgawe
caprice' luim, gril, gier, nuk, fiemies
Cap'ricorn Steenbok; Tropic of ~, Steenbokkeerkring
capsize' omval, omslaan
cap'sule saadhuisie; kapsule; smeltkroes
cap'tain (n) kaptein; aanvoerder; (v) aanvoer
cap'tion opskrif, titel; gevangeneming
cap'tivating bekorend, betowerend; boeiend, pakkend
cap'tive (n) gevangene; (a) gevang, geboei; ~ audience, instemmende gehoor
captiv'ity gevangenskap
cap'ture (n) vangs, roof; inname; gevangeneming; buit; (v) vang; buitmaak
car kar; spoorwa; motor; by ~, per motor, met die kar; company ~, firmamotor
ca'rat karaat
ca'ravan karavaan; woonwa, kampeerwa
carb'ide karbied
carb'ine kort geweer, karabyn
carb'on koolstof; ~ paper deurslagpapier, koolpapier
carb'uncle karbonkel, nege-oog, steenpuis
carb'urettor vergasser
car'cass (-es) geraamte, romp, karkas
card (n) kaart; program; spyskaart; have a ~ up one's sleeve, 'n slag om die arm hê; ~board karton, bordpapier; ~board box kartondoos
card'iac kardiaal, hart=; ~ failure hartversaking; ~ patient hartpasiënt
card'iogram kardiogram (lesing)
card'iograph kardiograaf (apparaat)
card'inal (n) kardinaal; (a) kardinaal, vernaamste, hoof=
card'sharper valsspeler
care (n) sorg; oplettendheid, sorgvuldigheid; bekommernis; ~ of, per adres; take ~, oppas; (v) sorgdra, omgee; besorg wees
career' (n) loopbaan; beroep; voortgang; (v) rondhardloop, kerjakker; ~s adviser beroepsleier; ~s exhibition loopbaanuitstalling; ~ guidance/counselling beroepsleiding, loopbaanvoorligting; ~ path beroepsbaan
care: ~ful versigtig, oppassend; ~less natalig, agtelos
caress' (v) liefkoos, aai, streel

care: ~taker opsigter, oppasser; ~worn uitgeput, afgesloof

carg'o (-es) skeepslading, vrag

ca'ricature (n) karikatuur, spotprent

ca'rillon kariljon, klokkespel; ~ player beiaardier

carn'al vleeslik, wellustig

carna'tion angelier; vleiskleur

carn'ival karnaval

carniv'orous vleisetend

ca'rol (n) lofsang, lied; voëlsang; *Christmas -s,* Kersliedere

carp¹ (n) karp

carp² (v) vit, brom

car'penter timmerman

car'pet (n) tapyt; mat; *wall-to-wall ~,* vloertapyt

car'port motorskuiling, motorafdak

ca'rriage wa, rytuig; ~ *paid,* vragvry

ca'rrier transportryer, karweier, draer; bagasierak; posduif; kiemdraer (siekte); abbaskip; ~ pigeon posduif

ca'rrion aas, kreng

ca'rrot wortel

ca'rry (carried, carried) dra, vervoer; bring; gedra, leen; verdien (rente); ~ *on,* voortgaan; ~ *through,* voltooi; ~ *weight,* gesag hê; ~cot drawieg(ie)

cart (n) kar; voertuig; (v) vervoer, ry; ~age vraggeld; ~age contractor vervoerkontrakteur, karweier; ~el kartel

cart'ilage kraakbeen

cartog'rapher kartograaf

cartoon' spotprent; tekenprent; ~ist spotprenttekenaar

cart'ridge patroon; ~ belt bandelier

carve uitsny, houtsny, graveer; voorsny

cascade' waterval, kaskade

case¹ (n) kis, kas; doos; lekkerkas; oortreksel, dop; handkoffer; sloop; boeksak

case² (n) geval, saak; naamval; *in any ~,* in alle geval; *in every ~,* in elke geval; *in ~,* in geval; *in no ~,* onder geen omstandighede nie.

case history gevallestudie; siekteverslag

cash (n) kontant(geld); kasgeld; ~ *on delivery,* kontant by aflewering; *hard ~,* kontant; (v) (in)wissel, klein maak; trek; ~book kasboek; ~ discount kontantkorting; ~ float wisselfonds, kontantvlot; ~-and-carry koop-en-loop, haal-en-betaal; ~ flow kontantvloei

cashier¹ (n) kassier

cashier² (v) afsit, afdank, ontslaan

cash: ~ register kasregister; ~ slip kontantstrokie; ~ till kasregister

cas'ing oortreksel; voering (boorgat)

casi'no (-s) casino, dobbelhuis

cask vat, vaatjie, kuip

cask'et kissie (juwele), dosie, urn

cassette' kasset; ~ player kassetspeler

cast (n) gooi; vorm; soort; rolbesetting (drama); gietvorm; (v) (cast, cast) gooi, werp; veroordeel; uitwerp; neergooi; optel (syfers); uitbring (stem); giet (metaal); ~ *lots,* loot; ~ *a spell on,* betower

cast'away (n) (-s) skipbreukeling; verworpeling; (a) onbruikbaar, oud

caste klas, kaste

cas'tigate straf, kasty, tugtig

cast'ing vote beslissende stem

cast' iron gietyster, potyster

ca'stle kasteel; ~ *in the air,* lugkasteel

cast'-off onbruikbaar, weggegooi; afgeheg

cas'tor oil kasterolie

castrate' sny, ontman, regmaak, kastreer

ca'sual toevallig, terloops, los, kasueel; ~ labour los arbeid, geleentheidswerk; ~ wear slenterdrag

ca'sualty (..ties) ongeval, ongeluk; gesneuwelde; (pl) gesneuweldes; ~ list ongevallelys

cat kat; kats; *let the ~ out of the bag,* die aap uit die mou laat; *rain ~s and dogs,* ou vroue met knopkieries reën

cat'alogue (n) katalogus, pryslys

catamaran' tweeromper (seilboot)

cat'apult rek(ker), slingervel, katapult

cat'aract waterval; oogpêrel, katarak

catarrh' katar

catas'trophe ramp, onheil; katastrofe

cataw'ba catawba (druif)

cat: ~ burglar klouterdief, sluipdief; ~call kattegetjank; fluitroep

catch (n) (-es) vangs; buit; vanghou; voordeel; (v) (caught, caught) vang, gryp; tref; vat; inhaal; haal (trein); betrap (dief); ~ *a chill,* koue vat; ~ *a cold,* verkoue kry; ~ *fire,* aan die brand raak; ~ *up (with),* inhaal; ~ *a train,* 'n trein haal

catch'ment area opvanggebied

catch'y aantreklik, bedrieglik; aansteeklik; ~ *question,* strikvraag

cat'echism kategismus

categor'ical kategories, uitdruklik

cat'egory (..ries) kategorie, klas, soort

cat'er verskaf, voorsien; proviandeer; spy=
seneer; ~er spysenier; leweransier; ~ing
spysenering, spysverskaffing; ~ing de=
partment verversingsdepartement

cat'erpillar ruspe(r); ~ tractor kruiptrekker

cat'erwauling katmusiek, kattegeskreeu

cathed'ral domkerk, katedraal

cath'olic algemeen; katoliek; ~ taste, veel=
sydige/omvattende smaak

cat'napping indommel, 'n uiltjie knip/knap

cat-o'-nine'-tails kats

cat'tery kattery, kietsiesorg

catt'ish katterig; ~ woman, 'n snip

catt'le vee, grootvee, beeste

cauc'us (n) (-es) koukus, partyvergadering

caul net; helm; agterstuk; born with a ~,
met die helm gebore

caul'dron groot ketel, kookpot

caul'iflower blomkool

caulk (v) (toe)stop, dig(maak), kalfater

cause (n) oorsaak; beweegrede; rede; (v)
veroorsaak, laat bewerk, teweegbring; ~
damage, skade aanrig

cause'way laagwaterbrug

caus'tic bytend, skerp, brandend; ~ soda
seepsoda, bytsoda

caut'erise uitbrand, toeskroei

cau'tion (n) omsigtigheid; sekerheid; waar=
skuwing; (v) waarsku

cau'tious versigtig, behoedsaam, omsigtig

cavalcade' ruiterstoet, kavalkade

cav'alry ruitery, kavallerie

cave (n) grot; gat, spelonk; ~ in, instort;
~dweller grotbewoner, troglodiet; ~man
(..men) oermens

cavia're kaviaar

cav'ity (..ties) holte; ~ wall holmuur,
spoumuur

cay'man, cai'man kaaiman, alligator

cease ophou, laat staan, staak; ~fire (n)
skietstaking, skietstilstand

ced'ar seder

cede afstaan, opgee; sedeer; afstand doen

ceil'ing solder(ing), plafon; hoogtegrens

cel'ebrate vier, herdenk, besing

celebra'tion viering, herdenking

celeb'rity (..ties) beroemdheid

cel'ery seldery

celes'tial (n) hemelbewoner; (a) hemels; ~
bodies, hemelliggame

cel'ibacy ongetroude staat, selibaat

cell sel; kamertjie; hokkie; graf

cell'ar kelder; ~age kelderruimte

cell'ist tjellis

cell'o (-s) tjello, violonsel

cement' (n) sement; band; lym

cem'etry (..ries) kerkhof, begraafplaas

cen'otaph praalgraf, gedenksuil, senotaaf

cen'sor (n) sensor; sedemeester; (v) sensu=
reer; ~ship board sensuurraad

cen'sure (n) sensuur, berisping, bestraffing;
(v) onder sensuur sit; bestraf; afkeur

cen'sus (-es) volkstelling, sensus

cent sent; per ~, persent, per honderd

centen'ary (..ries) eeufees

cen'tigrade honderdgradig; 4 degrees ~, 4
grade Celcius

cen'timetre sentimeter

cen'tipede duisendpoot

cen'tral sentraal, middelste; vernaamste; ~
business area/district sentrale sakedeel,
sakekern

cen'tralise sentraliseer

cen'tre (n) middel(punt); sentrum; senter
(voetbal); ~ of gravity, swaartepunt; (v)
verenig; ~ punch kornael, senterpons

centrif'ugal middelpuntvliedend, sentrifu=
gaal

centrip'etal middelpuntsoekend, sentripe=
taal

cen'tury (..ries) eeu, honderd jaar; hon=
derdtal (krieket)

ceram'ics keramiek, erdeware

cer'eal (n) graan; (a) graan=;

ce'rebral harsing=, serebraal=; ~-palsied
children serebraalverlamde kinders

ce'remony (..nies) seremonie, plegtigheid;
master of ceremonies, seremoniemeester,
tafelheer; without ~, sonder pligple=
ginge

cer'tain seker, gewis; for ~, sekerlik; ~ly
sekerlik, beslis; ~ty (..ties) sekerheid

certif'icate sertifikaat, getuigskrif, diploma

cert'ify (..fied, ..fied) sertifiseer

ce'ssion afstanddoening, afstand, sessie

chafe (n) skaafplek; wrywing; (v) vryf,
skuur, skaaf; kwaad maak; irriteer

chaff (n) kaf; skerts; (v) liggies terg

cha'grin (n) verdriet, hartseer; ergernis

chain (n) ketting; reeks; (pl) boeie; (v) bind,
boei, in kettings slaan; ~ reaction ket=
ringreaksie

chair (n) stoel; setel; leerstoel; *take the ~*, die voorsitterstoel inneem; (v) voorsit; **~man** (*..men*) voorsitter; president; *Mr ~man*, Meneer die voorsitter, Agbare voorsitter

chal'ice kelk, Nagmaalsbeker

chalk (n) kryt; *by a long ~*, verreweg; (v) met kryt teken; aanteken; *~ up*, opskryf

chall'enge (n) uitdaging; aansporing; (v) uitdaag, ter verantwoording roep; eis; **~cup** uitdaagbeker; **~r** uitdager

cham'ber kamer; vertrek; grot; *~ of commerce*, kamer van koophandel, sakekamer; *~ of horrors*, gruwelgrot; *C~ of industries*, kamer van nywerhede; *C~ of mines*, Kamer van Mynwese

chamel'eon trapsoetjies, trapsuutjies, verkleurmannetjie

cham'ois gems(bok); **~ leather** seem(s)leer

champagne' sjampagne, bruiswyn, vonkelwyn

cham'pion (n) kampioen; oorwinnaar; kampvegter (vir 'n saak); (v) verdedig; bepleit; *~ player* baasspeler; **~ship** kampioenskap

chance (n) kans; toeval; waarskynlikheid; vooruitsig; *by ~*, toevallig; *on the ~*, op goeie geluk; *stand a good ~*, 'n goeie kans hê; *take a ~*, 'n kans waag; (v) waag

chan'cellor kanselier

chan'cer waaghaas; opportunis

chandelier' kandelaar, kroonlugter

change (n) verandering, kentering; ruil; kleingeld; (v) verander; ruil; verwissel; wissel, kleinmaak (geld); *~ colour*, bloos; *~ one's mind*, van plan verander

chang'ing room, changeroom kleedkamer

channel'el (n) kanaal, seestraat; (v) kanaliseer

cha'os chaos, baaierd, warboel

chao'tic chaoties, deurmekaar(spul)

chap[1] (n) bars, skeur; (v) **(-ped, -ped)** bars, skeur

chap[2] (n) kêrel; ou; *a decent ~*, 'n gawe vent/kêrel/ou; **~pie** kannetjie, tjokkertjie

cha'pel kapel, kerkie, bidhuisie

chap'eron (n) begeleidster, chaperone; (v) begelei, beskerm, chaperonneer

chap'lain kapelaan, veldprediker

chap'ter hoofstuk, kapittel; *~ and verse*, vers en kapittel

char (-red, -red) verkool, brand, skroei

cha'racter karakter; aard; kenmerk; letter; naam, reputasie; rol (toneel)

characteris'tic (n) karaktertrek; kenmerk; (a) karakteristiek; kenmerkend

char'coal houtskool

charge (n) opdrag; bewaring, beskuldiging; aanklag; *~ sheet*, klagstaat; (v) opdra; aanval; beskuldig; hef

charge' office aanklagkantoor (polisie)

chargé d'affaires' saakgelastigde

cha'riot rytuig, strydwa, triomfwa

cha'rity (*..ties*) liefdadigheid; barmhartigheid; *~ begins at home*, die hemp is nader as die rok

charl'atan kwaksalwer, boerebedrieër

charm (n) betowering; sjarme; gelukbringer; (v) betower, bekoor; verruk; toor; **~ing** betowerend, bekoorlik; sjarmant; **~ school** afrond(ing)skool, sjarmeskool

chart (see)kaart, tabel

chart'er (n) oktrooi, handves; oorkonde; (v) oktrooieer; huur; **~ed flight** huurvlug; **~ed plane** huurvliegtuig; **~ed secretary** geoktrooieerde sekretaris, oktrooisekretaris

chase (n) jag; agtervolging; (v) jag, agtervolg; jaag; *~ away*, wegjaag

chasm afgrond, kloof

chass'is (sing and pl) onderstel

chaste kuis, rein, vlekloos

chastise' kasty, tugtig

chas'tity kuisheid, reinheid, keurigheid

chat (n) praatjie; (v) **(-ted, -ted)** gesels, babbel

chatt'er (n) geklets, gebabbel; (v) babbel, klets, snater; **~box (-es)** babbelkous, babbelbek; **~ing** gesnater, gebabbel

chauffeur' motorbestuurder, chauffeur

chauv'inism nasionale eiewaan, chauvinisme

cheap goedkoop, spotkoop

cheat (n) bedrieër; (v) bedrieg, kul

check[1] (n) blokkies, geruite goed, ruitgoed

check[2] (n) kontrole, verifikasie; beperking; *internal ~*, interne kontrole; *keep in ~*, in toom hou; (v) nagaan, nareken, toets, verifieer; *~ out*, uitklaar; *~ up*, optel, vergelyk; (medies) ondersoek; **~er** laaimeester; **~up** kontrole-ondersoek

check'mate (n) skaakmat; (v) skaakmat sit

cheek[1] parmantigheid, vermetelheid

cheek[2] wang; **~bone** wangbeen, kakebeen

cheek'y parmantig, astrant, vermetel

cheer (n) onthaal; toejuiging; vrolikheid, blydskap; (v) opvrolik, toejuig; ~ful vrolik, opgeruimd; ~leader rasieleier; dirigent; ~s! gesondheid!

cheese kaas; ~ and wine reception, kaas-en-wynonthaal; ~burger kaasburger

cheet'ah jagluiperd

chef (-s) hoofkok, sjef

chem'ical skeikundig, chemies; ~ warfare, chemiese oorlogvoering; ~ weed control, chemiese onkruidbeheer; ~s chemikalieë

chem'ist apteker; skeikundige

chem'istry skeikunde, chemie

cheque tjek, wissel; blank ~, blanko tjek; ~book tjekboek

che'rish koester, liefkoos, liefhê

che'rry (n) (cherries) kersie; kersieboom

che'rub (-im, -s) gerubyn, engel(tjie)

chess (skaakspel; play at ~, skaakspeel

chest bors; kis; ~ of drawers, klerekas

chest'nut (n) kastaiing; sweetvos(perd)

chev'ron sign chevronteken

chew (n) koutjie; pruimpie; (v) kou; pruim; nadink, oordink; ~ the cud, herkou; be-peins; ~ing gum kougom

chic sjiek, elegant

chick (-ens, -s) kuiken(tjie); kind

chick'en (-s) hoender, hoendervleis; snuiter, kind; count one's ~s before they are hatched, die vel verkoop voordat die beer geskiet is; ~feed hoenderkos; kleinig-heidjie; ~-hearted lafhartig; ~ mash kuikenmeel; ~ pox waterpokkies

chic'ory sigorei

chief (n) (-s) hoof, kaptein; (a) vernaamste, hoogste, senior, opperste; ~ executive, hoofbestuursleier; ~ general manager, senior hoofbestuurder; ~ justice, hoof-regter; ~ steward, hoofkelner, hoofta-felbediende; ~ly hoofsaaklik, vernaamlik

chil'blain winterhande, wintervoete

child (-ren) kind; backward ~, geremde kind; handicapped ~, gestremde kind; retarded ~, vertraagde kind; ~birth be-valling; ~hood kinderjare; ~ish kin-deragtig; ~like kinderlik; ~ren's books kinderboeke; ~ welfare kindersorg

chill (n) koue, koudheid; kilheid; catch a ~, kou(e) vat; (v) verkoel

chill'i (n) rissie

chill'y (a) koel, natterig, kil, kouerig; kou-lik; a ~ reception, 'n kil(le) ontvangs

chime (n) klokkespel; melodie, deuntjie; welluidendheid; (v) klokke bespeel

chim'ney (-s) skoorsteen; lampglas; ope-ning; ~ piece skoorsteenmantel, kaggel; ~ sweep skoorsteenveër

chimpanzee' sjimpansee

chin ken; double ~, onderken; up to the ~, tot oor die ore

chin'a porselein, breekgoed

Chin'a China

chip (n) spaander, splinter, skyfie; a ~ of the old block, 'n aardjie na sy vaartjie; fish and ~s, vis en skyfies/flenters; (v) (-ped, -ped) afsplinter; ~ in, in die rede val; ~board spaanderbord

chirop'odist voetheelkundige

chi'ropractor chiropraktisyn

chis'el (n) beitel; cold ~, koubeitel

chit briefie, strokie

chiv'alrous ridderlik

chlor'oform (n) chloroform

chlor'ophyll bladgroen, chlorofil

choc'olate sjokolade

choice (n) keus(e); keur; ~ grade keurgraad

choir koor

choke (n) smoor(klep); demper; (v) stik, wurg, verstik; ~ chain wurgket-ting

chol'era cholera

choles'terol cholesterol, galsteenvet

choose (chose, chosen) kies, verkies

chop (n) hou, kap, slag; tjop; (v) (-ped, -ped) kap, slaan

chor'al koraal, koor; ~ist koorsanger

chord snaar; lyn, tou, koord; spinal ~, rugstring

chore werkie; ~s huispligte, sleurwerk

choreog'rapher choreograaf

chor'us (-es) koor, refrein, rei; ~ girl koor-meisie; kabaretsangeres; pronkdoedie

chos'e(n) uitverkore, see choose

Christ Christus

chri'sten (v) doop, naam gee

Chris'tian (n) Christen; (a) Christelik; ~ era Christelike jaartelling; ~ name voor-naam, also first name

Chris'tmas Kersfees, Kersmis, ~ greetings and good wishes for the New Year, Kers-en Nuwejaarsgroete; ~ box (-es) Kersge-skenk; ~ card Kerskaart(jie); ~ Day Kersdag; ~ Eve Oukersaand; ~ holiday Kersvakansie; ~ night Kersaand; ~ party

Kersparty(tjie); ~ **season** Kerstyd/Kers‑
gety; ~ **tree** Kersboom
chronolog'ical chronologies, in tydsorde
chrysan'themum (-s) krisant
chuck (n) gooi; (v) gooi; opgee, laat staan;
~*up,* in wanhoop opgee
chuck'er-out uitsmyter
chuc'kle (n) onderdrukte lag; geklok; (v)
lag; klok; ~ *with delight,* jou ver‑
kneukel
chum maat, vriend, tjom
church (-es) kerk; ~ **square** kerkplein; ~‑
yard kerkhof
chute waterval; glybaan
chut'ney blatjang
cid'er appelwyn
cigar' sigaar
cigarette' sigaret
Cinderell'a Aspoestertjie
cin'der track asbaan
cin'ema (-s) kinema, bioskoop, fliek; ~‑
goer bioskoopganger; fliekganger
cinn'amon kaneel
ciph'er (n) syfer; monogram; nul; *a mere*
~, 'n nul op 'n kontrak
cir'cle (n) sirkel; ring; kring; kroon; galery
(teater); geselskap; (v) ronddraai; omsluit;
vicious ~, bose kringloop
cir'cuit omloop, omtrek; ompad; rondreis,
rondgang; kringloop; reeks (sport);
stroombaan (elek.); *short* ~, kortsluiting;
~ **court** rondgaande hof
cir'cular (n) omsendbrief, sirkulêre; (a) sir‑
kelvormig
cir'culate in omloop bring/wees; sirku‑
leer
circula'tion sirkulasie; oplaag (koerant)
circumci'sion besnyding, besnydenis
circum'ference omtrek
circ'umflex (-es) kappie, sirkumfleks
circumlocu'tion omskrywing; breedspra‑
kigheid, omslagtigheid
circumnav'igate omvaar, rondom vaar
circ'umscribe omskryf, beperk
circumspec'tion omsigtigheid
cir'cumstance omstandigheid; *in the* ~*s,*
onder die omstandighede
circ'us (-es) sirkus
ciss'y (cissies) verwyfde mens, papbroek
cis'tern vergaarbak, spoelbak; dam; kuip
cita'tion dagvaarding; aanhaling, sitaat
cite dagvaar; siteer, aanhaal

cit'izen burger; stadsbewoner; *John C*~,
Jan Burger; ~ **band radio** burgerband‑
radio, kletsradio; ~**ship** burgerskap
cit'ric sitroen; ~ **acid** sitroensuur
cit'ron sitroen
cit'rus lemoenvrug, sitrus
cit'y (cities) stad; ~ **hall** stadhuis (gebou);
stadsaal (saal); ~ **slicker** stadskalant;
stadskoejawel
civ'et (cat) muskeljaatkat, musseljaatkat
civ'ic burgerlik, burger‑; ~ **centre** burger‑
sentrum; ~ **theatre** stadskouburg
civ'ics burgerkunde
ci'vil burgerlik; siviel; beleef; ~ **aviation**
burgerlugvaart; ~ **defence** burgerlike
beskerming; ~ **servant** staatsamptenaar;
~ **service** staatsdiens; ~ **war** burger‑
oorlog
civil'ian (n) burger, burgerlike; (a) bur‑
gerlik, burger‑; ~ **blind** burgerblindes
civilisa'tion beskawing
claim (n) eis, vordering; (v) eis, opvorder
clairvoy'ant heldersiende; fortuinverteller
clam'ber klouter
clamm'y klam, vogtig
clam'our (n) geskreeu, geroep; (v) skreeu;
~ *for,* roep om, aandring op
clamp (n) kram, klem; (v) klamp, vas‑
klem
clan stam; geslag, bende; familiegroep
clap (n) klap, slag; donderslag; knal; (v)
(-ped, -ped) klap, toeslaan
cla'rify (..fied, ..fied) ophelder; verklaar,
uiteensit
cla'rinet, clarionet' klarinet
cla'rity duidelikheid, helderheid
clash (n) (-es) stamp, skok; botsing; (v)
stamp, bots; stry
clasp (n) haak, gespe, kram; omhelsing; (v)
vashaak, toegespe; omhels; omarm
class (n) (-es) klas; orde; stand; (v) rangskik,
orden; klassifiseer; klasseer (wol); ~ **cap‑
tain** klaskaptein
class'ic (n) klassieke werk/skrywer; (a)
klassiek; ~**al** klassiek; ~**s** klassieke
classifica'tion klassifikasie, indeling
class'ify (..fied, ..fied) klassifiseer, indeel
clause sinsdeel; klousule; artikel; bysin
claustropho'bia engtevrees, noutevrees
claw (n) klou, poot; haak; (v) vasklou
clay (n) klei; (a) klei‑; ~**ey** kleierig; ~
pigeon shooting pieringskiet

clean (v) skoonmaak, reinig; ~ *up*, opruim; (a) skoon, helder; sindelik; (adv) heeltemal, totaal, glad

cleanse suiwer, reinig

clear (v) reinig; ophelder; klaarmaak; optrek (weer); (a) helder, duidelik, suiwer; (adv) skoon; totaal; duidelik; **~ance** uitverkoop; vryhoogte; **~ing** oop plek; **~ing agent** klaring(s)agent; **~ing bank** verrekeningsbank; **~ly** duidelik, onomwonde

cleave (**clove** or **cleft, cloven** or **cleft**) klowe, splits, klou; **cleft palate** gesplete verhemelte

clem'ency begenadiging; goedertierenheid; sagtheid (die weer)

clench (vuiste) bal; omklink; vasbyt

cler'gy geestelikheid; **~man** (..men) predikant, geestelike

cler'ical geestelik, klerikaal; klerklik; **~ error** skryffout; **~ work** klerklike werk

clerk klerk; winkelbediende; opsigter; **~ of works,** bouopsigter; klerk van werke

clev'er slim; handig; knap, oulik

clich'é afgesaagde uitdrukking, cliché

click (n) tik, klink; klapklank; (v) tik, klink; aankap (perd); akkordeer

cli'ent kliënt (van geleerde beroep); klant (van winkel); **~ele** klandisie, praktyk; gevolg; **~ relations** kliëntebetrekkinge

cliff (-s) klip, kliprug, krans

clim'ate klimaat

clim'ax (-es) hoogtepunt, klimaks

climb (n) klim; (v) klim, klouter; bestyg; **~ing lane** klimbaan

clinch (v) omklink; beklink; beseël; **~ a deal,** 'n transaksie beklink

cling (**clung, clung**) vashou, vasklem; **~ together,** aanmekaarklou

cling'stone taaipit

clin'ic (n) kliniek; (a) klinies

clin'ical klinies; **~ examination** kliniese ondersoek; **~ thermometer** koorspennetjie

clip (n) knipsel, skeersel; (v) (**-ped, -ped**) knip, snoei, skeer, kortwiek

clip: ~per knipper; skeermasjien; skêr; **~ping** (n) (uit)knipsel

clique kliek, aanhang

cloak (n) mantel; dekmantel; (v) bedek; bemantel; **~room** kleedkamer

clock klok, oorlosie; **~wise** kloksgewys

clod kluit, klont; domkop; **~hopper** gomtor, lummel, gaip

clog (n) blok, hindernis; klomp (houtskoen); (v) (**-ged, -ged**) belemmer; verstop

clois'ter klooster; suilegang

close (n) end, sluiting; slot; *at the ~ of play,* met/teen uitskeityd (krieket); (v) sluit, toemaak, toesluit; afsluit; (a) dig, diep (geheim); *a ~ friend,* 'n intieme vriend; **~d-circuit TV,** kringtelevisie, kabel-TV; **~fisted** inhalig; vrekkerig

clos'et (n) kabinet, studeerkamer; kleinhuisie; (v) opsluit, afsonder; verberg

close' -up (n) digby-opname, nabybeeld

clos'ing sluiting; **~ date** sluitdatum; **~ hour** sluitingsuur; **~ stage** eindstadium; **~ time** sluittyd

clot (n) klont, kluit; domkop, swaap

cloth kledingstof, laken

clothe klee, beklee, bedek; inklee

clothes klere

cloth'ing kleding, klere; inkleding; **~ industry** die klerebedryf

cloud (n) wolk; *be in the ~s,* in vervoering wees; **~burst** wolkbreuk; **~y** bewolk, dynserig

clout (n) lap, vadoek; hou; (v) 'n klap/oorveeg gee

clove (n) naeltjie

clov'er klawer; *live in ~,* lekker lewe

clown grapmaker, hanswors, harlekyn, nar

club (n) knuppel, knopkierie; klub; klawer (kaartspel); (v) (**-bed, -bed**) doodslaan; saamwerk; *~ together,* saamwerk; **~foot** klompvoet; horrelvoet; **~house** klubhuis; **~s** klawers

cluck klok, kloek (van 'n hen)

clue leidraad, spoor, aanduiding; **~d up,** gekonfyt in

clum'sy onhandig, lomp; onhanteerbaar

clus'ter tros; trop, hoop, swerm; **~ housing** korfbehuising

clutch[1] (n) (-es) greep, klou; koppeling; koppelaar (motor); (v) gryp, vashou

clutch[2] (n) (-es) broeisel

coach (n) (-es) rytuig, koets; passasierswa; afrigter, breier (sport); (v) afrig, brei

coal (n) steenkool

coali'tion verbond, samesmelting, koalisie

coarse ru; grof; lomp

coast (n) kus, strand; *the ~ is clear,* die gevaar is verby; (v) luier, vry loop (motor);

~ **battery** kusbattery; **~er** kusboot; biermatjie; **~guard** kuswag
coat (n) baadjie; jas; skil; laag (verf); ~ *of arms*, wapenskild; familiewapen; *cut your ~ according to your cloth*, sit die tering na die nering; **~ing** laag (verf), aanpaksel
coax vlei, pamperlang, mooipraat, paai
cob mieliekop; ponie; mannetjieswaan
cob'alt kobalt
cob'ble (n) straatsteen; stuk steenkool; (v) lap; saamflans; **~r** skoenmaker
cob'ra (-s) koperkapel, geelslang, kobra; *brown ~*, bruinkapel; *cape ~*, geelslang; *ringed ~*, bakkopslang
cob'web spinnerak
cocaine' kokaïen
coch'ineal cochenille (karmynkleurstof; luis)
cock[1] (n) haan; haan (geweer); mannetjie
cock[2] (v) oorhaal (geweer); spits (ore)
cockatiel' kokkatiel (voël)
cock'erel haantjie, jong haan
cock: **~-eyed** skeel; dwaas; **~-fight** hanegeveg
cock'pit stuurkajuit (vliegtuig)
cock'roach (-es) kakkerlak, kokkerot
cocks'comb hanekam; dwaas
cock'tail kewer; mengelsopie, skemerkelkie; ~ **bar** kelkiekroeg; ~ **party** (..ties) skemerparty; ~ **stick** peuselstokkie
cock'y verwaand, eiewys, hanerig
coc'oa kakao (warm sjokoladedrank)
co'conut kokosneut; klapper
cocoon' papie, kokon
cod kabeljou
code wetboek, kode; ~ *of ethics,* gedragskode; (v) (en)kodeer
cod'ling moth appelmot
cod'liver oil lewertraan, visolie
coeduca'tion koëdukasie; **~al school** koëdskool
coeffi'cient koëffisiënt
coer'cion dwang, bedwang
coff'ee koffie; boeretroos (idiom)
coff'er kis, kas, koffer; skatkis; ~ **dam** kofferdam, afsluitdam
coff'in (n) doodkis; (v) kis
cog (kam)rat, tand (van 'n wiel)
cog'nisance kennis, kennisname; erkenning; kenteken; kenmerk
cog'nitive bewyssyns~, ken~
cohab'it saamwoon, saamhuis

coher'ent samehangend, duidelik
cohe'sion samehang, verband, kohesie
coil (n) kronkeling; draai; klos; (v) inmekaarkronkel
coin (n) muntstuk; *pay one in his own ~,* iem. in sy eie munt betaal; (v) (aan)munt; versin
coin'cidence sameloop; toeval
coir klapperhaar
coke kooks
cold (n) koue; verkoudheid; *catch ~,* koue vat; (a) koud, koel; onverskillig; *in ~ blood,* koelbloedig; ~ *comfort,* skrale troos; **~-blooded** koudbloedig; **koel-bloedig**; ~ **sweat** angssweet; ~ **war** senu-oorlog, koue oorlog
cole kool; **~rape** koolraap
col'ic koliek
collab'orate saamwerk
collab'orator medewerker; meeloper (met vyand)
collapse' (n) instorting, mislukking; (v) instort, inmekaarval, inval; verslap; misluk
coll'ar (n) boordjie; kraag; halsband; (v) vang; plant; **~bone** sleutelbeen
collat'eral sydelings; bykomend, bykomstig; ~ **security** bykomende onderpand, kollaterale sekuriteit
coll'eague kollega, ampsgenoot
collect' versamel, kollekteer; ~ *money,* geld insamel/in; ~ *call* kollekteeroproep; **~ion** versameling, kollekte; **~ive bargaining** kollektiewe bedinging
coll'ege kollege; raad; ~ *of education,* onderwyskollege; *electoral ~,* kieskolle'ge
collide' bots, teen mekaar stamp
coll'iery (..ries) steenkoolmyn
colli'sion botsing
collo'quial alledaags, gemeensaam; ~ *language,* gebruikstaal, gewone omgangstaal
collude' heul, kop in een mus wees
col'on dubbelpunt (:)
colonel (*pron.* ker'nl) kolonel
colon'ial (n) kolonis; kolonialer; (a) koloniaal
colonisa'tion volksplanting; kolonisasie
col'onist nedersetter, volksplanter, kolonis
col'ony (..nies) kolonie; nedersetting, volksplanting; wingewes
coloss'al kolossaal, reusagtig, tamaai
col'our (n) kleur, tint; *C~ed relations,* Kleurlingbetrekkinge; (v) verf; kleur;

~-blind kleurblind; **~ed** gekleur; *C~ed people,* Kleurlinge, Kleurlingmense, Bruinmense; **~ful** kleurryk; **~ slide** kleurskyfie
colt jong hings; jong perd; groentjie
col'umn kolom, kolonne; suil; ry
com'a diep slaap; bedwelming, koma
comb (n) kam, haarkam; heuningkoek; (v) (v) kam; kaard (wol)
com'bat (n) geveg; *single ~,* tweegeveg; **~ unit** gevegseenheid; **~ troops** vegtroepe
combina'tion verbinding, kombinasie, vereniging; **~ harvester** stroper
combine' (n) vereniging; trust, sindikaat; stroper (graan); (v) verbind, kombineer
combus'tion verbranding; **slow ~ stove** smeulstoof
come (came, come) kom, aankom; *~ of age,* mondig word; *~ in handy,* te pas kom; *if the worst ~s to the worst,* as die ergste gebeur; **~-at'-able** toeganklik; bekombaar
comed'ian komediant, grapmaker
com'edy (..dies) komedie, blyspel
come'ly bevallig, knap, gepas
com'et komeet, stertster
com'fort (n) troos; gemak, gerief; (v) troos, opvrolik, opbeur; **~able** gemaklik, gerieflik, aangenaam, behaaglik; **~er** trooster, fopspeen
com'ic grapperig, komies, snaaks; **~s,** **~ strips** prenverhaal, strokiesprent, strokies
comm'a (-s) komma (,)
command' (n) bevel, gebod; opdrag; *be in ~,* die bevel voer; (v) beveel, gebied; beheers
commandant' kommandant, bevelvoerder; **~-general** kommandant-generaal
commandeer' kommandeer, oproep
comman'der bevelhebber; **~-in-chief** (commanders-in-chief) opperbevelhebber
command': **~ing officer** bevelvoerende offisier; **~ment** gebod, bevel; *the Ten Commandments,* die Tien Gebooie
comman'do (-s) kommando; kommandosoldaat
commem'orate herdenk, gedenk, vier
commence' begin, aanvang; **~ment** begin
commend' aanbeveel, prys, opdra; **~able** aanbevelenswaardig, prysenswaardig; **~a'tion** eervolle vermelding

commen'surate eweredig, in dieselfde verhouding; *~ with,* eweredig/gelyk aan
comm'ent (n) aanmerking, kommentaar; uitleg(ging); (v) kritiseer; verklaar; *~ on,* kommentaar lewer oor/op; **~ary** (..ries) uitlegging, kommentaar; **~ator** uitlêer, verklaarder; kommentator (radio)
comm'erce handel, verkeer; *chamber of ~,* kamer van koophandel, sakekamer
commer'cial handels-, kommersieel; **~ artist** handelskunstenaar; **~ bank** handelsbank; **~ law** kommersiële reg; handelsreg; **~ transmission** handelsender; **~ traveller** handelsreisiger
commisera'tion medelye, bejammering
commissar'iat kommissariaat
commi'ssion (n) kommissie; opdrag; (v) opdra, magtig; aanstel; **~aire'** deurwagter, portier; opsigter; **~er** kommissaris, kommissielid; opsiener; *C~ for State Administration,* Kommissie vir Staatsadministrasie; *High C~er,* hoë kommissaris
commit' (-ted, -ted) bedryf, uitvoer; *~ted to change,* verbind tot verandering; *~ to memory,* uit die hoof leer; *~ murder,* moord pleeg
commit'ment verpligting, verbondenheid (tot), verbintenis; *~ fee* bindgeld
committ'ee komitee
commod'ity (..ties) gebruiksartikel, kommoditeit; (pl) koopware, kommoditeite
comm'on (n) dorpsgrond; *have much in ~,* baie (met mekaar) gemeen hê; *~ law,* (die) gemenereg; (a) gemeenskaplik; **~age** dorpsgrond, meent; **~room** geselskap(s)kamer; personeelkamer; **~place** (n) gemeenplaas; (a) alledaags, gewoon; **~sense** gesonde verstand; **~wealth** gemenebes
commo'tion beweging; beroering, drukte
comm'une (n) gemeenskap; kommune
commun'icate meedeel, kommunikeer
communica'tion mededeling; kommunikasiekunde, kommunikasieleer (as vak); *line of ~,* verbindingslinie
commun'ion Nagmaal; gemeenskap, kommunie; *Holy C~,* Nagmaal
commun'iqué amptelike mededeling/berig
com'munist kommunis
commun'ity (..ties) gemeenskap, maatskappy; gemeente; **~ centre** gemeenskapsentrum; **~ development** gemeenskapsbou; **~ service** gemeenskap(s)diens

commute' verander, verwissel, verruil; versag (vonnis); pendel; **~r** pendelaar

com'pact[1] (n) verdrag, ooreenkoms

compact'[2] (v) saamdring, kompakteer, aaneensluit; opmaak; verkort; (a) dig; beknop; gedronge; stewig; kompak

compan'ion maat, metgesel; **~ship** geselskap

com'pany (..nies) geselskap; maatskappy, kompanjie; firma; organisasie; **~ car,** firmamotor; *holding* **~,** houermaatskappy; *subsidiary* **~,** filiaal(maatskappy)

compar'ative vergelykend; betreklik; **~** *degree,* vergrotende trap

compare' (v) vergelyk; gelyk wees

compar'ison vergelyking; *in* **~** *with,* vergeleke met, in vergelyking met, teenoor

compart'ment kompartement

com'pass (n) omtrek; omvang; (-es) kompas; *pair of* **~es,** passer

compa'ssion deernis, medelye, erbarming

compat'riot landgenoot

compel' (..led, -led) dwing, verplig, noodsaak, noop

com'pensate vergoed, kompenseer

compensa'tion (skade)vergoeding, kompensasie

compete' wedywer, meeding; kompeteer, konkurreer

com'petence bevoegdheid, bekwaamheid, geskiktheid; welgesteldheid

com'petent bevoeg, bekwaam; geskik

competi'tion mededinging, wedywer(ing); wedstryd, kompetisie, konkurrensie (besighede)

compet'itor mededinger; deelnemer (aan wedstryd/wedloop)

compile' saamstel, bymekaarmaak, versamel, kompileer; **~r** samesteller, kompilator

compla'cent voldaan, vergenoeg, tevrede

complain' kla; beklaag; **~ant** klaer, eiser

complaint' klag; kwaal, ongesteldheid; beskuldiging; *lay a* **~,** 'n klag indien

com'plement (n) aanvulling, komplement; volle getal; (v) aanvul

complete' (v) voltooi; invul ('n vorm); (a) volkome; volledig, kompleet

com'plex (n) (-es) kompleks; geheel, samestel; (a) saamgestel, ingewikkeld; **~** *sentence,* saamgestelde sin

comple'xion gelaatskleur; voorkome; aard

complex'ity (..ties) ingewikkeldheid, kompleksiteit

com'plicate (v) verwikkel, kompliseer, ingewikkeld maak; (a) ingewikkeld

complica'tion verwikkeling; komplikasie

compli'city medepligtigheid

com'pliment (n) pligpleging, kompliment; pluimpie; (pl) groete; *the* **~s** *of the season,* geseënde Kersfees en 'n voorspoedige Nuwe Jaar: *with* **~s** *of,* met (die) komplimente van; (v) gelukwens, komplimenteer

complimen'tary komplimenteus; vry**~**; **~** *ticket* komplimentêre kaartjie

comply' (..plied, ..plied) nakom, inwillig, toestem; **~** *with,* voldoen aan

compon'ent (n) bestanddeel, komponent

compose' saamstel; opstel; komponeer; **~d'** kalm, bedaard; **~r** komponis, toonsetter

composi'tion samestelling; opstel; komposisie; aard; skikking

com'post (n) kompos; mengsel

compo'sure kalmte, bedaardheid

com'pound[1] (n) kampong; mynkamp

com'pound[2] (n) samestelling; (v) verbind; berei; skik; (a) saamgestel(d); **~** *interest* saamgestelde rente; **~** *sentence* veelvoudige sin

comprehend' verstaan, begryp; omvat

comprehen'sion begrip; bevatlikheid

comprehen'sive (veel)omvattend; **~** *insurance/policy,* omvattende versekering/polis; **~** *unit,* komprehensiewe eenheid (onderwys)

com'press[1] (n) kompres; omslag, nat doek

compress'[2] (v) saamdruk, saampers; **~ed** *air* druklug

comprise' bevat, omvat, insluit

com'promise (n) skikking, kompromis; kompromie; (v) skik

comptom'eter rekenmasjien

compul'sory gedwonge, verpligtend; **~** *education,* skoolplig, verpligte onderwys; **~** *service,* diensplig

compunc'tion wroeging, spyt, berou

compute' bereken, skat, uitreken

compu'ter (n) rekenaar, komper, blikbrein; **~** *hardware* apparatuur; **~ise** rekenariseer, komp; **~** *print-out* komperdruk, komperstaat; **~** *science* rekenaarwetenskap, komperkunde; **~** *software* programmatuur; **~** *terminal* komperterminaal

com'rade maat; kameraad
con (n): *pros and ~s*, voor- en nadele
con'cave (n) holte; gewelf; (a) konkaaf
conceal' wegsteek, verberg
concede' toestem, toegee, inwillig
conceit' eiewaan, inbeelding, verwaand=
heid, trots; ~ed verwaand, eiewys
conceiv'able denkbaar, begryplik
conceive' begryp, 'n denkbeeld vorm
con'centrate (n) kragvoer; pitkos; (v) kon=
sentreer, saamtrek; ~ *on*, konsentreer/
toespits op
concentra'tion sametrekking, konsentrasie
concen'tric konsentries
con'cept denkbeeld, begrip, konsep
concern' (n) besigheid; onderneming, or=
ganisasie; besorgdheid; (v) betref, raak;
~ed' besorg; betrokke; ~ing aangaande,
betreffende, rakende, met betrekking
tot
con'cert[1] (n) ooreenstemming; konsert
concert'[2] (v) beraadslaag; skik; ~ed be=
raam; geskik; ~ed action, gesamentlike
optrede
concerti'na (-s) konsertina; donkielong,
krismiswurm (idioom)
conce'ssion toegewing, konsessie
concilia'tion versoening, konsiliasie
concise' kort, bondig, beknop, saaklik
conclude' besluit, beslis; aflei; sluit; ~d
geëindig; beslis; *to be ~d*, slot volg
conclu'sion besluit; gevolgtrekking, kon=
klusie; afloop, end; *in ~*, ten slotte
conclus'ive oortuigend, beslissend; ~ *evi=
dence/proof*, afdoende getuienis/bewys
concoct' beraam, smee; brou; versin; ~ion
fabrikasie, verdigsel; konkoksie
conc'rete (n) beton; *reinforced ~*, gewa=
pende beton
con'cubine bywyf, houvrou; handperd
concur' (-red, -red) (v) ooreenkom, oor=
eenstem, instem
concu'ssion skok, botsing, skudding; ~ *of
the brain*, harsingskudding
condemn' veroordeel; afkeur; ~ed' (n)
veroordeelde; (a) skuldig, veroordeel
condensa'tion kondensasie, verdigting
condense' kondenseer, verdik; ~d milk
blikkiesmelk, kondensmelk
condescend' verwaardig/verwerdig; ~ing
neerbuigend
con'diment kruiery

condi'tion (n) voorwaarde; kondisie; ~al
voorwaardelik, kondisioneel; ~s *of ser=
vice*, diensvoorwaardes
condole' betreur, kondoleer; ~nce roube=
klag, deelneming; letter of ~nce brief van
deelneming/meegevoel
condone' vergewe, kwytskeld, kondoneer
con'dor kondor
con'duct (n) gedrag; houding; handelwyse
conduct' (v) lei, aanvoer; bestuur; gelei; ~
an interview, 'n onderhoud lei/voer; ~ed
tour (be)geleide toer; gidsbesoek; ~or,
geleier; kondukteur (trein); dirigent
con'duit leipyp; waterleiding, buis
cone keël; dennebol; konus
confec'tion banket, suikergoed; ~er ban=
ketbakker; ~ery (..ries) soetgebak
confedera'tion konfederasie, verbond
confer' (-red, -red) beraadslaag, samespre=
king(s) voer; verleen, toeken
con'ference konferensie, byeenkoms
confess' bely, erken; bieg; ~ion belydenis;
bieg; ~*ional poetry*, biegpoësie, belyde=
nisverse
confidant', con'fident (n) vertroueling,
vertroude
con'fidence vertroue, geloof, sekerheid;
oormoedigheid; ~ trickster vertroue=
swendelaar, kulman, *also* conman
con'fident (a) vol vertroue, oortuig (van)
confiden'tial vertroulik, konfidensieel; ge=
heim; *strictly ~*, streng vertroulik
con'fine (n) grens; oorgang; (pl) grense
confine' (v) begrens, beperk; opsluit; ~
oneself to, jou bepaal/beperk tot
confined' eng, nou; gevang; *be ~*, beval, 'n
bevalling hê
confine'ment beperking; bevalling
confirm' bevestig, bekragtig; versterk; ~=
a'tion bevestiging
confirmed' beslis; verstok; *a ~ bachelor*,
'n verstokte oujongkêrel
con'fiscate konfiskeer, beslag lê op
con'flict[1] (n) botsing, stryd, konflik, geskil
conflict'[2] (v) bots, stry, worstel; ~ing
teenstrydig; ~*ing interests*, strydige/bot=
sende belange
con'fluence sameloop, samevloeiing
conform' ooreenkomstig maak; instem
met; konformeer; ~ist konformis
confound' verwar; ~ *it!* verbrands! ~ed
vervloek, verdeksels

confront' konfronteer; vergelyk; **~a'tion** konfrontasie
confuse' verwar, verbyster; **~d'** deurmekaar
confus'ion verwarring
congest' ophoop; *traffic* **~ion** verkeersophoping, verkeersdrukte
congrat'ulate gelukwens, felisiteer
congratula'tion gelukwensing; **~s!** veels geluk!
con'gregate vergader, bymekaarkom
congrega'tion vergadering; gemeente
con'gress (-es) kongres, vergadering
con'ic(al) keëlvormig, kegelvormig, konies
con'ifer naaldboom
conif'erous boldraend, keëldraend
con'jugate (v) vervoeg; saamvloei; (a) verwant; toegevoeg; ooreenkomstig
conjuga'tion vervoeging; verbinding
conjunc'tion verbinding, vereniging; voegwoord; sameloop; *in* **~** *with,* saam met
conjunc'tive (n) aanvoegende wys; (a) verbindend; konjuktief (gram.)
con'jure besweer; toor, goël; **~** *away,* wegtoor
con'jurer geesbesweerder; towenaar; goëlaar
con'man = confidence trickster
connect' verbind, in verband bring; aansluit; skakel; **~ed'** verbonde
connec'tion verbinding; aansluiting; konneksie; familie
connoisseur' kenner, fynproewer
con'quer oorwin, verower
con'queror oorwinnaar, veroweraar
con'quest oorwinning; verowering
con'science gewete, konsensie; *guilty* **~,** skuldige gewete
conscien'tious nougeset, konsensieus, pligsgetrou; **~** *objector* diensweieraar, gewetensbeswaarde, godsdiensbeswaarde
con'scious bewus; **~** *of,* bewus van
conscrip'tion konskripsie, diensplig
con'secrate (v) wy, inseën, heilig
consec'utive opeenvolgend, gereeld, volgend; **~** *number,* volgnommer; **~ly** agtereenvolgens, onafgebroke
consen'sus ooreenstemming; akkoord, konsensus
consent' (n) toestemming, konsent; (v) toestem, inwillig

con'sequence gevolg, uitwerking; *in* **~,** gevolglik; *in* **~** *of,* as gevolg van, ten gevolge van; weens; *of little* **~,** van min betekenis
conserva'tion behoud, bewaring; *nature* **~,** natuurbewaring
conserv'atism konserwatisme
conserv'ative (n) preserveermiddel; (a) konserwatief, behoudend
conserv'atoire musiekskool, konservatorium
conserv'atory (..ries) bewaarplaas; konservatorium; broeikas, glashuis
conserve' (n, pl) ingelegde vrugte; (v) bewaar, behou
consid'er oorweeg, beredeneer
consid'erable aanmerklik, aansienlik, beduidend; *a* **~** *time,* 'n geruime tyd
consid'erate sorgvuldig; omsigtig; bedagsaam; hoflik; weloorwoë
considera'tion oorweging; konsiderasie; vergoeding, teenprestasie
consign' versend; **~ee'** geadresseerde; agent; **~ment** besending
consist' bestaan; **~** *of,* bestaan uit
consist'ent duursaam, bestendig, konsekwent; **~** *with,* verenigbaar met; *she plays a* **~** *game,* sy speel bestendig
consola'tion troos, vertroosting; **~** **prize** troosprys
console' (v) troos, vertroos, bemoedig; (n) konsool
consol'idate saamgroei; konsolideer
con'sonant (n) medeklinker, konsonant
con'sort[1] (n) maat; gemaal (man), gemalin (vrou)
consort'[2] (v) omgaan met, saamlewe; ooreenstem; klaarkom met
consor'tium konsortium, groep
conspic'uous opsigtig; uitstekend; *be* **~** *by one's absence,* skitter deur afwesigheid
conspir'acy (..cies) samesweering, komplot
conspir'ator samesweerder
conspire' saamsweer, saamspan, 'n komplot smee
con'stable konstabel, polisieman
con'stant (a) standvastig, konstant; getrou
con'stantly voortdurend, onafgebroke
constella'tion gesternte, sterrebeeld; **~** *of states,* konstellasie van state
consterna'tion ontsteltenis, konsternasie

constipa'tion hardlywigheid, konstipasie
constit'uency (..cies) kiesafdeling; kiesers
con'stitute saamstel; vorm, konstitueer
constitu'tion samestelling; grondwet (van 'n
land), konstitusie; grondreëls (van 'n
klub/vereniging); gestel
constitu'tional grondwetlik, konstitusio=
neel; ~ development grondwetlike ont=
wikkeling
construct' bou, oprig, saamstel; ~ion kon=
struksie; uitleg; ~ive opbouend; ~ive
engagement, opbouende betrokkenheid
construe' verklaar, uitlê; vertaal
con'sul konsul; ~ar konsulêr; ~ate kon=
sulaat
consult' (v) raadpleeg; beraadslaag, oorleg
pleeg; ~a'tion raadpleging, konsultasie;
~ing (n) raadpleging; (a) raadplegend;
raadgewend; ~ing engineer raadgewende
ingenieur, konsult-ingenieur; ~ing hours
spreekure; ~ing room(s) spreekkamer
consume' verteer, verbruik, opgebruik
consum'er verbruiker; ~ goods verbruiks=
goedere; ~ affairs verbruikersake; ~
price index verbruikersprysindeks; ~
spending verbruiker(s)besteding
consump'tion verbruik; tering, uittering
con'tact (n) aanraking, voeling, kontak; ~
lenses kontaklense; (v) (iem.) kontak
conta'gious besmetlik (deur aanraking),
aansteeklik
contain' bevat, insluit, behels; ~er houer;
blik; ~er vessel houerskip; ~erisa'tion
behouering, houerverpakking; ~er=
vrag
contam'inate besoedel, bevlek, besmet
contem'porary (n) (..ries) tydgenoot; (a)
tydgenootlik, eietyds, kontemporêr
contempt' veragting, minagting; ~ of court,
minagting v.d. hof; ~ible veragtelik
contend' betwis, bestry; beweer; ~er aan=
spraakmaker (op 'n titel)
con'tent[1] (n) inhoud
content'[2] (n) tevredenheid; to one's heart's
~, na hartelus; (v) tevrede stel; (a) vol=
daan, vergenoeg
conten'tion stryd, twis; naywer; bewering
conten'tious kontensieus, omstrede
con'tents inhoud; omvang; table of ~, in=
houdsopgawe
con'test[1] (n) twis; stryd; wedstryd; krag=
meting

content'[2] (v) betwis, bestry; wedywer; ~ a
seat, 'n setel betwis; ~ant deelnemer,
mededinger
con'tinent (n) vasteland, kontinent
continen'tal kontinentaal, vastelands=
contin'gency (..cies) gebeurlikheid, toeval=
ligheid; ~ fund gebeurlikheidsfonds
contin'gent (a) gebeurlik, toevallig; voor=
waardelik; ~ liability, voorwaardelike
aanspreeklikheid
contin'ual voortdurend, aanhoudend
continua'tion voortsetting; vervolg; ver=
lenging
contin'ue voortsit; aanhou; vervolg; ver=
leng; to be ~d, word vervolg; continuing
education, voortgesette onderwys
continu'ity kontinuïteit, onafgebrokenheid
contin'uous aanhoudend, onafgebroke
con'tour omtrek, hoogtelyn; kontoer
contracep'tive voorbehoedmiddel
con'tract (n) verdrag, ooreenkoms, verbin=
tenis, kontrak; ~ student, verbintenis=
student
contract' (v) inkrimp, saamtrek; ~ a dis=
ease, 'n siekte kry/opdoen; ~ out, uit=
kontrakteer; ~ion sametrekking, ver=
korting; ~or kontrakteur, aannemer;
leweransier
contradict' teenspreek, weerlê; ~ion teen=
spraak; teenstrydigheid
contrapt'ion toestel, uitvindsel, kontrepsie
con'trary: on the ~, inteendeel; ~ to, in
stryd met; strydig met; (a) teenoorgestel,
strydig; koppig, eiesinnig, dwars
con'trast (n) teenstelling, kontras
contrast' (v) teenstel, kontrasteer
contraven'tion teenstand, oortreding
contrib'ute bydra, bevorder; meewerk
contribu'tion bydrae, kontribusie
contrive' uitvind; beraam, versin; prakseer;
~d bedag, gesog
control' (n) bestuur; beheer, kontrole; (v)
(-led, -led) kontroleer; beheer, beteuel;
~ler kontroleur; ~ling beherend; ~ling
body, beheerliggaam; ~ling company,
beherende maatskappy, beheermaat=
skappy
controver'sial omstrede, tendensieus, kon=
troversieel; ~ book, omstrede boek
con'troversy (..sies) geskil, dispuut; twis=
punt, strydpunt; twis, polemiek

convales'cent (n) herstellende sieke: (a) genesend; ~ **home**, hersteloord; ~ **leave**, aansterkverlof

convene' saamroep, belê; *notice convening the meeting*, byeenroepende kennisgewing; ~**r** saamroeper/sameroeper

conven'ience gemak, gerieflikheid; *for the sake of* ~, geriefshalwe

conven'ient gemaklik; geskik; gerieflik

con'vent klooster

conven'tion byeenkoms, konvensie; ~**al** gebruiklik, konvensioneel

conversa'tion gesprek, konversasie

converse'[1] (v) gesels, omgaan met, verkeer

con'verse[2] (a) teenoorgestelde, omgekeerde; ~**ly** omgekeerd

conver'sion omkering; omsetting; bekering; omrekening; doelskop (rugby)

con'vert (n) bekeerling, bekeerde

convert' (v) verdoel (rugby); bekeer

con'vex bolrond, konveks

convey' vervoer, oordra; ~**ancer** aktebesorger, transportbesorger; ~**er belt** (ver)voerband

con'vict (n) bandiet, prisonier

convict' (v) vonnis, veroordeel

convic'tion skuldigbevinding

convin'cing oortuigend

convoca'tion sameroeping, konvokasie

con'voy (n) (-s) konvooi, geleide

coo koer, kir

cook (n) kok; (v) kook; ~**ery** kookkuns, kokery; ~**ery book** resepteboek, kookboek; ~**ing utensils** kookgereedskap, kookgerei

cool (v) afkoel; bedaar; (a) koel; kalm; *a ~ hundred*, net mooi 100; ~**bag** koelsak, yssak; ~**ing tower** koeltoring

coop (n) fuik; hoenderhok; (v) opsluit; ~**er** vatmaker, kuiper

coop'erate, co-op'erate saamwerk, koöpereer

coopera'tion sameweking, koöperasie

co-op'erative (n): ~ **society** koöperasie

co-opt' byvoeg, koöpteer

coor'dinate, co-or'dinate (v) koördineer; (a) newegeskik

cope (v) hanteer; *be able to ~ with*, opgewasse wees teen/vir

copp'er (n) koper; kopergeld; (a) koper-

cop'ulate verbind; paar; koppel

cop'y (n) (**copies**) kopie, afskrif; eksemplaar (boek); (v) (**copied, copied**) afskryf, kopieer; ~**ist** kopiïs, afskrywer; ~**right** kopiereg, outeursreg

co'ral koraal; ~ **island** koraaleiland; ~ **reef** (-s) koraalrif; ~ **tree** koraalboom

cord (n) band, tou, lyn, koord; *spinal* ~, rugstring; *umbilical* ~, naelstring

cor'dial (a) hartlik; hartsterkend; ~ *relations*, hartlike betrekkinge/samewerking

cor'don kordon; muurkrans; snoer; ~ *off*, 'n kordon span/trek

cord'uroy ferweel; (pl) ferweelbroek

core kern, hart, pit; ~ **syllabus** kernsillabus

corian'der koljander

cork (n) kurk; prop; (v) toekurk; (a) kurk-; ~**screw** (n) kurketrekker

corn[1] (n) koring; graan; korrel

corn[2] (n) liddoring; *tread on one's ~s*, iem. op die tone trap

corn'ea (-s) horingvlies

cor'ner (n) hoek, hoekpunt; (v) vaskeer; vasvra; ~**stone** hoeksteen

corn: ~**flakes** koringvlokkies; ~ **weevil** kalander

cor'onary koronêr, hart-; ~ **thrombosis** koronêre trombose, kroonaarverstopping

corona'tion kroning

corp'oral[1] (n) korporaal

corp'oral[2] (a) liggaamlik; persoonlik; ~ **punishment** lyfstraf

cor'porate korporaat; *body ~*, regspersoon; ~ *strategy*, korporaatstrategie

corpora'tion stadsbestuur, korporasie; *Small Business Development C~ (SBDC)*, Kleinsake-Ontwikkelingskorporasie (KSOK)

corpse lyk

corp'ulent swaarlywig, vet, korpulent

correct' (v) verbeter; nasien; (a) presies, juis, noukeurig, korrek

correc'tion verbetering; korreksie; regstelling; *house of* ~, verbeterhuis

correla'tion korrelasie, verband

correspond' korrespondeer; ooreenstem; ~**ence** briefwisseling, korrespondensie; ~**ence college** korrespondensiekollege; ~**ent** (n) korrespondent; beriggewer

corro'sion wegvreting, korrosie

corro'sive (n) bytmiddel; (a) invretend, bytend

co'rrugate rimpel, golf; frons; **~d iron** gegolfde sinkplaat; golfyster; **~d road** sinkplaatpad

corruga'tion rimpeling, golwing; sinkplaat

corrupt' (v) bederf; omkoop; (a) bedorwe; korrup; **~ion** korrupsie; verrotting

cors'et korset, borsrok, keurslyf; **~ry** postuurdrag, vormdrag

cosmet'ic kosmetiek, skoonheidsmiddel; **~ change** kosmetiese/oppervlakkige verandering; **~ surgery** plastiese snykunde

cos'monaut ruimtevaarder, ruimteman

cosmopol'itan (n) wêreldburger; kosmopoliet; (a) kosmopolities

cos'mos[1] wêreldorde, kosmos, heelal

cos'mos[2] nooientjie-in-die-groen, kosmos (blom)

cost (n) prys; (on)koste; (pl) onkoste; *at all ~s*, tot elke prys; *~ of living allowance*, duurtetoeslag; *(v)* (cost, cost) kos

cos'ting koste(be)rekening

cost: ~ly kosbaar; **~ price** (in)koopprys

cost'ume kleredrag, kleding, kostuum; pak

cos'y (n) (cosies) teemus; (a) gesellig, behaaglik, lekker

cot kinderkateltjie, bababed; hangmat; hut

cott'age huthuis, kothuis; **~ cheese** maaskaas; **~ pie** aartappelpastei; herderspastei

cott'on katoen; garing; **~ waste** poetskatoen; **~ wool** watte

couch (n) (-es) rusbank, sofa, bed; (v) lê; inklee; uitdruk; neerdruk

cough (n, v) hoes, kug; **~ lozenge** hoesklontjie; **~ remedy** (..dies) hoesmiddel

coun'cil raad; raad(s)vergadering; **~ chamber** raadsaal; **~lor** raadslid

coun'sel (n) beraadslaging; raadgewer; (v) (-led, -led) raad gee; aanraai; **~lee** beradeling; **~ling** berading; **~lor** raadgewer; berader

count[1] (n) graaf (titel)

count[2] (n) telling; rekening; *lose ~*, die tel kwytraak; (v) tel; aftel; **~ on**, reken op; **~ out**, uittel; **~down** aftelling (ruimtelansering)

coun'ter[1] (n) toonbank; teller

coun'ter[2] (v) teenwerk; weerlê; afslaan

coun'terattack teenaanval

coun'ter: ~ claim teeneis; **~-clockwise** agteruit, teen die wysers in; links om

coun'terfeit (n) namaaksel, vervalsing; (v) namaak; vervals; (a) nagemaak, oneg; **~er** namaker, vervalser

coun'terfoil teenblad, kantstrokie

coun'terinfiltration teeninsypeling

coun'terinsurgence teeninsurgensie

countermand' (n) teenbevel; (v) herroep, afskryf; afsê; intrek

coun'termeasures teenmaatreëls

coun'teroffensive teenoffensief

coun'terproductive teenproduktief

coun'tersignature medeondertekening

coun'tess (-es) gravin

count'less talloos, ontelbaar

coun'try (..ries) land, platteland; buitedistrik; **~ club** buiteklub; **~ cousin** takhaar, plaasjapie, gomtor

coun'ty (..ties) graafskap

coup (d'état') staatsgreep, bewindoorname

coup de grâce' genadeslag

coupé' koepee

cou'ple (n) tweetal, paar; egpaar; (v) saamvoeg; koppel; paar

coup'let koeplet, tweereëlige vers

coup'ling koppeling, verbinding

coup'on koepon

cou'rage moed, dapperheid

courag'eous moedig, dapper, heldhaftig

cou'rier koerier, renbode

course (n) loop; loopbaan; baan; kursus, gang (ete); **~ of action**, gedragslyn, handelwyse

court[1] (n) (geregs)hof; landdroshof, baan; **~ of justice**, geregshof; *settle out of ~*, buite die hof skik; *supreme ~*, hooggeregshof

court[2] (v) vry, kuier; **~ a girl**, 'n meisie/nooi die hof maak, by haar vlerksleep; **~ trouble**, moeilikheid soek

court'case hofsaak, regsgeding

court'eous hoflik, beleef, beskaaf

court'esy (..sies) hoflikheid, beleefdheid; **~ visit** hoflikheid(s)besoek; geleentheid(s)besoek; *by ~ of*, met goedkeuring van; goedgunstig geleen deur; **~ bus** kliëntebus, diensbus; **~ stand** selfdienstal(letjie); **~ visit** welwillendheidsbesoek

court: ~ martial krygsraad; krygsverhoor; **~ messenger** geregsbode

court'yard binneplaas
cous'in neef, niggie; *first ~,* volle neef/ niggie; *second ~,* kleinneef, kleinniggie
cove (n) inham, baai; gewelf; (v) welf
co'venant (n) verdrag, verbond; handves; *Day of the C~,* Geloftedag, *see* Day of the Vow
co'ver (n) deksel; bedekking; dekking (assuransie); omslag (van boek); buiteblad (boek); *seek ~,* skuiling soek; (v) bedek, oordek; dek; oortrek (kussing); aflê (afstand); bestryk (kanon); *~ up,* bedek; verswyg, geheim hou; *~age* dekking (nuus); *~ charge* tafelgeld; *~ girl* voorbladnooi; *~ing* bedekking, omhulsel; *~ing bond,* dekverband; *~ing letter,* begeleidende brief
cow (n) koei; *~pea* akkerboon
cow'ard lafaard, bangbroek; *~ly* lafhartig
coy skaam, verleë, bedees
crab krap; kreef
crack (n) kraak, knak, bars; knal; doring; praatjie; (v) kraak; knak, bars; skeur; skaad; *~ jokes,* grappe verkoop; *~ up,* ophemel; (a) uitstekend, beste, uithaler; knap
crac'kle knetter, rinkel, kraak
crack'ling swoerd (gebraaide varkvel); *~s* kaiings
cra'dle (n) wieg; bakermat; (v) wieg
craft lis, sluheid; vaartuig; *~s'man* ambagsman; *~y* behendig, slu, geslepe
cram (-med, -med) volprop, opvul, vasdruk; blok, inpomp (studie)
cramp (n) kramp; (v) beperk; *~ed* nou; beperk, vasgedruk
crane (n) kraanvoël; kraan, hysmasjien; *~ operator* hys(kraan)operateur
crank¹ (n) slinger; (v) draai, slinger
crank² (n) gek; (a) gek; lendelam; los
crank: *~case* krukkas, krukhulsel; *~shaft* krukas
crape krip, floers, rouband, lanfer
crash (n) (-es) botsing; neerstorting; (v) kraak; *~ course* snelkursus, stapelkursus; *~ helmet* valhelm; *~ landing* buiklanding; *~ tackle* plettervat (rugby)
crate hok; krat; mandjie
crat'er krater
crave smeek, eis; hunker
crav'ing hunkering, begeerte

crawl (n) gekruip; kruipslag (in swem); (v) kruip, aansukkel; *~er* kruippakkie; kruiper
cray'fish (-es) varswaterkreef, rivierkreef; (see)krap
cray'on (n) tekenkryt; (v) skets
craze (n) manie, hartstog; mode; *be the ~,* hoog in die mode wees
craz'y gek, mal, kranksinnig; *~ paving,* klipplaveisel, lapbestrating
creak (n) gekraak, geknars; (v) kraak
cream (n) room; *~ of tartar,* kremetart; (v) afroom; (a) liggeel; *~ery* (..ries) melkkamer; botterfabriek; suiwelfabriek; *~ separator* roomafskeier
crease (n) vou, plooi, kreukel; streep; kolfkampie (krieket); (v) kreukel, vou; *~-resistant* kreukeltraag
create' skep; vorm; voortbring, wek; *~ the impression,* die indruk wek
crea'tion skepping, heelal
crea'tor skepper, maker; *the C~,* die Skepper
crea'ture skepsel; kreatuur; bees
crèche kinderhawe, bewaarskool, crèche
creden'tials geloofsbriewe
credibil'ity geloofwaardigheid, geloofbaarheid; *~ gap* vertrouensgaping
cred'it (n) krediet; vertroue; kredit (in boekhou); *get ~ for,* erkenning ontvang vir; (v) krediteer; *~ balance* kredietsaldo, batige saldo; *~ card* kredietkaart; *~ facilities* kredietgeriewe; *~or* krediteur, skuldeiser
cred'o (-s) geloof, geloofsbelydenis, credo
creed geloof, geloofsbelydenis
creek inham, draai, bog; spruit
creep (crept, crept) kruip, sluip; seil
creep'er klimop, slingerplant, ranker
creep'y grieselig, grillerig
cremat'e (v) veras; *I want to be ~d,* ek wil veras word
crema'tion verassing, lykverbranding
cremator'ium (-s) krematorium
crêpe krip, lanfer
crescen'do crescendo, toenemend
cres'cent (n) halfmaan; singel
cress bronkors
crest kuif; kam; maanhaar; wapen
crev'ice skeur, bars, spleet
crew skeepsbemanning; trop; *a ~ of fifteen on the island,* vyftien man op die eiland

crib (n) krip; kinderbedjie; stal; (v) **(-bed,**
-bed) opsluit; afkyk; bedrieg
crick'et[1] kriek, sonbesie
crick'et[2] krieket; *not* ~, geen eerlike spel
nie; ~ **enthusiast** krieketgeesdriftige; ~
bat kolf; ~ **match (-es)** krieketwedstryd
crime misdaad; gruweldaad; ~ *prevention,*
misdaadvoorkoming
crim'inal (n) misdadiger; *habitual* ~, ge=
woontemisdadiger; (a) misdadig, krimi=
neel; ~ *procedure,* strafprosesreg
crimp rimpel, plooi; friseer, krul
crim'son karmosyn, dieprooi
cringe ineenkrimp, kruip; ~**r** witvoetjie=
soeker, kruiper
crip'ple (n) kreupele; (a) kruppel, mank
cris'is (crises) keerpunt, toppunt, krisis
crisp (n) kroes, krul; (v) krul; (a) kroes;
bros; krakerig; ~**y** krullerig; bros
criter'ion (..teria) maatstaf, toetssteen,
kriterium; kenmerk
crit'ic beoordelaar, kritikus; ~**al** kritiek,
haglik; krities, vitterig; ~**ism** kritiek,
beoordeling; ~**ise** kritiseer, beoordeel
croak (v) kwaak, kras
cro'chet (n) hekelwerk; (v) hekel
crock (n) krukker; sukkelaar; knol; *old* ~**s,**
ou knolle; (v) seermaak
crock'ery breekgoed, erdewerk
croc'odile krokodil; ~ **tears** krokodiltrane,
bobbejaanhartseer
cron'y (..nies) tjom(mie), boesemvriend
crook (n) boef, skelm, skurk; haak, staf
croon (n) geneurie; (v) neurie; ~**er** neurie=
sanger, sniksanger
crop (n) oes; gewas, gesaaide; krop (voël);
~ *rotation,* wisselbou; ~**per** knipper;
kropduif; mislukking; val; *come a* ~**per,**
sandruiter word
cross (n) (-es) kruis; moeite; kruising; baster
(van diere); (v) kruis; *a* ~**ed cheque,** 'n
gekruiste tjek; ~ *out,* skrap; (a) dwars;
kwaad; ~**bow** kruisboog; ~**country race**
landloop, veldwedloop; ~**-examine**
kruisvra, onder kruisverhoor neem;
~**-eyed** skeel; ~**ing** kruising; oorweg;
~**kick** dwarsskop; ~**reference** kruisver=
wys(ing); ~**road** kruispad, dwarspad,
tweesprong; *at the* ~**roads,** op die keer=
punt; ~ *section* deursnee; ~ *street*
dwarsstraat; ~**word (puzzle)** blokkies=
raaisel

crouch kruip; laag buk
crow (n) kraai; koevoet; *as the* ~ *flies,* reg=
uit; (v) kraai; pronk; spog; ~**bar** koevoet,
breekyster
crowd (n) menigte, klomp
crown (n) kroon; kruin; (v) kroon; be=
kroon
crow's-foot oogrimpel, lagplooitjie
cru'cial kritiek, beslissend
cru'cible smeltkroes; vuurproef
cru'cifix (-es) kruis, kruisbeeld
crucifi'xion kruisiging, kruisdood
cru'cify (..fied, ..fied) kruisig
crude ru, kru, onafgewerk; ongesuiwer;
rou; ~ **oil** ru-olie
cru'el wreed, wreedaardig, hardvogtig; ~**ty**
wreedheid, onmenslikheid
cru'et stand sout-en-peperstel, kruiestel=
(letjie)
cruise (n) (rond)vaart; tog; (v) kruis, rond=
vaar; vaar, ry; ~**r** kruiser; ~**r weight**
ligswaargewig
cruis'ing speed togsnelheid
crumb krummel, brokkie
crum'pet plaatkoekie, flappertjie
crunch kraak, hard kou; knars
crusa'de kruistog; ~**r'** kruisvaarder
crush (-es) drukgang; (v) verpletter, saam=
pers; ~**ing** verpletterend, vernietigend
crust (n) kors, korsie; roof (van seer); aan=
paksel (in pot)
crutch (-es) kruk, stut
crux kern; groot moeilikheid, knoop
cry (n) **(cries)** skree(u), gil; *within* ~ *of,*
binne stembereik; (v) **(cried, cried)**
skree(u); uitroep; huil; ~ *for joy,* van
vreugde huil; ~**baby (..bies)** skreeubalie,
tjankbalie
crypt grafkelder; ~**ogram** geheimskrif
cry'stal kristal; ~**lise** kristalliseer, versui=
ker; ~**lised fruit,** suikervrugte
cub (n) welp; klein padvinder
cubb'yhole paneelkassie, mossienes (idiom);
(bêre)hokkie
cube (n) kubus; derde mag; ~ **root** derde=
magswortel
cub'ic kubiek, van die 3e mag
cub'icle afskorting, afskortinkie
cuck'oo (-s) koekoek; idioot
cuc'umber komkommer
cud herkoutjie
cud'dle omhels; liefkoos; lepel lê

cud'gel (n) knopkierie; knots; *take up the
~s,* die stryd aanknoop
cue[1] biljartstok
cue[2] wenk, aanwysing; wagwoord (toneel)
cuff (n) vuisslag; omslag; boei; (v) 'n klap
gee; ~ link mouskakel, mansjetknoop
cul-de-sac' (culs-de-sac) keerweer, dood=
loopstraat, keerom
cul'inary kombuis=, kook=; ~ *art,* kook=
kuns
cull (v) uitdun, uitvang, uitsoek, uitgooi;
~ing uitdun (van wild)
cul'minate 'n toppunt bereik, kulmineer
culp'able strafbaar, strafskuldig; ~ homi=
cide strafbare manslag
cul'prit skuldige, oortreder, kwaaddoener
cul'tivar (n) kultivar, cultivar
cul'tivate verbou, kweek (gewasse); teel
(diere); kultiveer; beoefen
cul'tural kultureel, beskawings=; ~ *society,*
kultuurvereniging
cul'ture (n) kultuur; beskawing; *physical
~,* liggaamsopvoeding; ~d pearls ge=
kweekte pêrels
cul'vert riool; stormsloot, duiker; deurlaat
cum'ber (n) las, hindernis; ~some lastig,
hinderlik; swaar, log, lomp
cum'quat koemkwat (vrug)
cum'ulate ophoop, opstapel, kumuleer
cum'ulative ophopend, toenemend; kumu=
latief; oplopend; ~ *preference shares,*
kumulatiewe voorkeuraandele
cum'ulus (..li) hoop; stapelwolk
cunn'ing (n) lis, sluheid; bedrewenheid; (a)
geslepe; uitgeslape, slu; behendig
cup (n) koppie; beker (sport); kelk (blom)
cup'board kas, muurkas, koskas
cura'tor voog, kurator; opsigter
curb (n) kenketting (aan toom); bedwang;
raad; randsteen; (v) beteuel; bedwing
cure (n) geneesmiddel, kuur; genesing; (v)
genees, gesond maak; ~ *skins,* velle brei
cur'few aandklokreëling, klokreël
curios'ity (..ties) nuuskierigheid, weetgie=
righeid; ~ *killed the cat,* van uitvra is die
tronk vol
cur'ious nuuskierig, sonderling
curl (n) krul, haarlok; kronkeling; (v) krul;
oprol; kronkel; ~ing iron, ~ing tongs
krulyster, krultang; ~y krullerig; ~yhead
krulkop
cu'rrant korent; *dried ~s,* korente

cu'rrency (..cies) loop; looptyd (van 'n ver=
band); koers (geld); betaalmiddel, valuta
cu'rrent (n) loop, stroom, stroming; (a)
lopend; ~ *assets* bedryfsbates; ~
liabilities bedryfslaste; ~ *price* heersende/
huidige prys
curric'ulum (-s) studiekursus, kurrikulum,
leergang
cu'rry[1] (n) (curries) kerrie
cu'rry[2] (v) (curried, curried) roskam, brei;
afransel; slaan; ~ *favour,* witvoetjie
soek; ~comb roskam
curse (n) vloek; (v) vervloek, verwens; ~d
vervloek, verwens; ~d *with,* opgeskeep/
gestraf met
curt kortaf, bits, kortweg
curtail' besnoei, verkort, verminder
curt'ain (n) gordyn; skerm; *lift the ~,* die
sluier oplig; ~ *call* buiging; ~ *fire* sper=
vuur; ~ *lecture* bedsermoen, bedpredi=
kasie; ~-raiser voorstuk; voorspel;
voorwedstryd
curt'sy (n) (..sies) kniebuiging, knieknik
curve (n) boog; kromme (stat.); kurwe
cu'shion kussing; biljartband
cus'tard vla
cus'tody bewaring, aanhouding, voogdy; *in
~,* in aanhouding; *safe ~,* veilige bewa=
ring
cus'tom gewoonte, gebruik; (pl) doeane;
invoerregte; ~ary gebruiklik; ~er klant,
koper, klandisie; ~ made, ~ised doelge=
bou; ~s duty, ~s dues doeaneregte
cut (n) sny; hou; raps; keep; *short ~,* kort=
paadjie; (v) (cut, cut) sny; afsny; kap;
kerf; raps; knip (hare); besnoei (salaris);
verlaag (pryse); ~ *back,* besnoei, inkort;
~ *and dried,* kant en klaar; ~ *short,* in
die rede val
cute skerpsinnig, skerp, fyn; oulik
cut'lery eetgerei, messeware
cut'let skaapribbetjie, karmenaadjie
cut: ~-throat (n) moordenaar; barbier=
(skeer)mes; (a) genadeloos; ~-throat
competition genadelose mededinging
cut'ting sny; uitgrawing; uitknipsel; stiggie;
~ service knipseldiens
cy'cad sikadee, broodboom
cy'cle (n) kringloop; siklus; sirkel; rywiel;
reeks; (v) fiets; ~ *racing,* naelry, naelren
cyc'list fietsryer, fietser
cyc'lone werwelstorm, sikloon

cyl'inder silinder
cym'bal simbaal
cyn'ic (n) sinikus; (a) skerp, sinies, bytend

cyp'ress (-es) sipres
czar tsaar
czarin'a tsarina

D

dachs'hund dachshund, worshond(jie)
dab (n) tikkie; vlekkie; (v) aanraak; smeer
dab'ble sprinkel; plas, bemors; liefhebber
dad, dadd'y (daddies) pa, pappie, paps
daff'odil môresterretjie, affodil
daft dwaas, mal
dagg'er dolk, kris; kruisie; *look ~s at,* iem. woedend aankyk
dahl'ia (-s) dahlia
dail'y (n) (..lies) dagblad; (a) daagliks
daint'y (n) (..ties) lekkerny; (a) lekker; kieskeurig; fyn, sierlik; netjies
dair'y (dairies) melkery; ~ **produce** sui*welprodukte
dais verhoog; troonhemel
dais'y (daisies) madeliefie
dale dal, laagte, kom, *see* dell
dall'y (dallied, dallied) stoei, speel; talm
dam[1] (n) moer (diere)
dam[2] (n) dam; (v) (-med, -med) opdam
dam'age skade; (pl) skadevergoeding; *cause ~,* skade aanrig; (v) beskadig
dame (adellike) dame; huisvrou, mevrou
damn (n) vloek; *not worth a ~,* geen flenter werd nie; (v) veroordeel, vloek, verdoem; *~ed* verdoem; vervloek; *a ~ed nuisance,* 'n vervlakste ergernis/oorlas
damp (n) damp, vogtigheid; (a) klam; neer*slagtig
dam'sel meisie, maagd
dance (n) dans(party), bal; ~ **music** dans*musiek; ~r danser(es)
dan'delion perdeblom
dan'druff skilfers
dan'dy (n) (..dies) modegek, laventelhaan, fat; (a) windmakerig, spoggerig
dan'ger gevaar, onraad; ~ous gevaarlik
dan'gle bengel, slinger, naloop; ~r mei*siegek, naloper
dapp'er agtermekaar; lewendig, fiks, viets
dap'ple (v) spikkel, bont maak; (a) bont, gespikkeld; ~-grey appelblouskimmel
dare durf, waag; uitdaag, tart; *I ~ say,* dit wil ek glo; ~devil waaghals

dar'ing (n) vermetelheid, durf, astrantheid; (a) onverskrokke, waaghalsig; vermetel
dark (n) duisterheid, duisternis; *a leap in the ~,* 'n sprong in die onbekende; (a) don*ker; somber; *D~ ages,* Middeleeue; *a ~ horse,* 'n onbekende mededinger; ~ness duisternis, donkerte; ~room donker*kamer
darl'ing (n) liefling, hartlam; skat, skatte*bol; (a) geliefde, liewe
darn (v) stop; ~ing stop(werk); ~ing need*le stopnaald
dart (n) pyl(tjie); spies; veerpyltjie; sprong; (v) gooi; wegspring, pyl; *play ~s,* (veer)* pyltjie speel; ~board pyltjiebord
dash (n) (-es) slag; aksent; aandagstreep; skeut (drank); swier, bevalligheid; (v) stoot; slaan; ~ *it!* vervlaks! ~ *off,* weg*hol; ~board spatbord; paneelbord
dat'a data, gegewe, gegewens; ~ **processing** dataverwerking
date[1] (n) dadel
date[2] (n) datum; *a blind ~,* 'n molafspraak; *out of ~,* ouderwets; *up to ~,* nuwer*wets, modern; tot datum; *what is the ~?* die hoeveelste is dit? (v) dateer; dagteken; *it dates from the 12th century,* dit dagteken van die 12e eeu
daught'er dogter; ~-in-law (daughters-in-law) skoondogter
daunt verskrik, ontmoedig; *nothing ~ed,* onvervaard
daw'dle draai, teuter, lanterfanter, talm, sloer
dawn (n) dagbreek; (v) lig word, daag; *it ~ed upon me,* dit het my bygeval
day (-s) dag; daglig; ~ *after ~,* dag na dag; *all ~ long,* die hele dag; ~s *of grace,* uitsteldae, respytdae; ~ *of the Mutt,* Brakdag; *that will be the ~!* dank jou die duiwel!; *the ~ after tomorrow,* oormôre; *the ~ before yesterday,* eergister; ~break dagbreek, rooidag; ~ **labourer** dagloner; ~ **scholar** dagskolier

Day of Goodwill Welwillendheidsdag

Day of the Vow Geloftedag

daze (n) verbystering, bedwelming; (v) ver=
byster; verblind, in verwarring bring

daz'zle verblind; verbyster

deac'on diaken, armeversorger; deken

dead (n) gesneuwelde; dooie; *in the ~ of
night,* in die holte v. d. nag; (a) dood;
dooierig; *~ as a doornail,* so dood soos 'n
mossie; *a ~ heat,* gelykop; (adv) in ergste
graad, erg; *~ sure,* so seker as wat; **~beat**
doodmoeg, boeglam; **~ drunk** stom=
dronk, smoordronk. **~ end** doodloop=
spoor; *~ end street,* doodloopstraat;
keerweer, keerom; **~line** spertyd, perk=
tyd; **~lock** (op die) dooiepunt; **~ly**
dodelik

deaf doof; *~ and blind person,* doofblinde;
~-mute doofstom

deal (n) deel; transaksie, akkoord; *make a
~,* akkoord sluit; *new ~,* nuwe bedeling;
a raw ~, slegte behandeling; (v) (**dealt,
dealt**) deel; sake doen; onderhandel; *~ in,*
handel dryf in; **~er** winkelier, handelaar,
koopman

dean deken (in Engelse kerk); dekaan (uni=
versiteit)

dear (n) hartjie; (a) lief, dierbaar; geagte;
duur; skaars; *D~ Sir/Madam,* Geagte
Heer/Dame

dearth duurte; skaarste, gebrek

death dood, uiteinde; sterfgeval. oorlye,
afsterwe; *condemn to ~,* ter dood ver=
oordeel; **~ duties** boedelbelasting, sterf=
regte; **~rate** sterftesyfer; **~ sentence**
dood(s)vonnis, doodstraf; **~ toll** dode=
tol

debar' (-red, -red) verhinder, uitsluit, belet

debat'able aanvegbaar, betwisbaar

debate' (n) debat; (v) debatteer

debat'ing society debatsvereniging

deben'ture skuldbrief, obligasie

deb'it (n) debiet/debet; (v) debiteer; belas

deb'ris puin; opdrifsels; oorskot; *nuclear
~,* kernoorskot, kernafval

debt skuld; *~ of honour* ereskuld; *the ~ of
nature,* die tol v.d. natuur; **~or** skulde=
naar, debiteur

dé'but debuut, buiging, eerste optrede

dé'butante (-s) debutante (jongdame)

dec'ade tiental, dekade

dec'adent afnemend, in verval, dekadent

decant' oorskink, afgooi (vloeistof); af=
klaar; **~er** kraffie

decap'itate onthoof

decar'bonise ontkool

decath'lon tienkamp, dekatlon

decay' (n) verval; verrotting; (v) verval;
verswak; verrot, vrot

decease' (v) sterf, doodgaan; **~d'** (n) oor=
ledene; afgestorwene; (a) oorlede; *~d
estate,* bestorwe boedel

deceit' bedrog, lis, misleiding

deceive' bedrieg, mislei; verlei

Decem'ber Desember

de'cency (..cies) fatsoenlikheid, ordentlik=
heid, betaamlikheid

de'cent fatsoenlik, ordentlik, betaamlik

decen'tralise desentraliseer

decep'tive misleidend

dec'ibel desibel (geluid-eenheid)

decide' beslis; bepaal, vasstel; besluit; oor=
deel; **~d'** beslis, nadruklik, bepaald;
~dly beslis, opsluit

decid'uous bladwisselend

de'cimal (a) tientallig; desimaal; *~ comma,*
desimaalkomma; *~ fraction,* tiendelige
breuk

deci'sion beslissing, besluit

decis'ive beslissend; deurslaggewend

deck (n) dek; (v) oortrek; bedek; versier; **~
quoits** skyfgooi

declara'tion verklaring, deklarasie; *~ of
intent,* deklarasie van voorneme

declare' verklaar; aankondig; *~ war,* oor=
log verklaar

decline' (n) verval; afname; (v) verval, ver=
buig (gram)

declutch' uitskakel; ontkoppel, loskoppel

decompose' ontbind; oplos; splits; vergaan

decompress'ion dekompressie, drukverlig=
ting

dé'cor dekor, toneelinkleding

dec'orate versier, dekoreer, optooi

decora'tion versiering; ereteken

decoy' (n) lokaas, lokmiddel; lokvink (po=
lisie); (v) aanlok; mislei; bedrieg

dec'rease (n) vermindering, afname

decrease' (v) verminder, afneem

decree' (n) dekreet; (v) verorden, dekreteer

decrep'it afgeleef, oud, gebreklik, lendelam

ded'icate toewy; opdra; *a ~d student,* 'n
toegewyde/konsensieuse student

deduct' aftrek, verminder; ~ion aftrek-
king; gevolgtrekking
deed daad; akte, dokument; ~s' office
aktekantoor
deem ag, beskou, oordeel, dink, neem
deep (n) diepte; see; (a, adv) diep, diepsinnig; grondig; ~ insight, grondige kennis;
~freeze vrieskas, hardvries(er)
deer takbok, hert
defama'tion belastering, laster, eerskennis;
~ of character, karakterskending
default' (n) versuim; gebrek; nalatigheid;
afwesigheid; wanbetaling; in~ of, by
gebrek aan: ~ of payment, wanbetaling;
win by ~, wen by verstek
defeat' (n) neerlaag; vernietiging; (v) verslaan, verydel; klop (sport)
de'fect (n) gebrek; fout; defek; tekort;
~ive gebrekkig, onklaar, defek
defect' (v) oorloop (na vyand), afvallig
word; ~or (n) oorloper, afvallige
defence' verdediging; verweer; ~ force
verdedigingsmag; weermag; ~less weer-
loos, onbeskerm
defend' verdedig, beskerm; ~ant verdediger; verweerder
defer' (-red, -red) uitstel; onderwerp aan
defi'ant uitdagend, tartend
defi'ciency gebrek, tekort; leemte
defi'cient gebrekkig; ontoereikend; mentally
~, swaksinnig
def'icit tekort, nadelige saldo
defile' (v) besmet, besoedel
define' bepaal, omskryf, definieer; omlyn
def'inite bepaald, definitief; ~ly beslis,
opsluit; ~ly not! volstrek nie!
defini'tion omskrywing, definisie
defla'tion geldskaarste, deflasie
deflect' afwyk; wegbuig; afskram, deflek-
teer
deform' mismaak, skend, vervorm; ~ed'
mismaak, wanskape; ~ity (..ties) mis-
maaktheid, wanstaltigheid, gebrek
defraud' bedrieg, kul, ontroof
defrost' ontys, ontvries (van koelkas); ontdooi (van voedsel)
defu'se (v) ontlont (krisis)
defy' (defied, defied) uitdaag, tart, trotseer
degen'erate (v) ontaard, versleg, verbaster
degrade' verneder, verlaag; ontaard; de-
gradeer
degrad'ing verlagend, vernederend

degree' graad; rang; by ~s, trapsgewyse;
to a certain ~, in sekere mate; honorary
~, eregraad
dehyd'rate (v) ontwater, droog
deject' neerslagtig maak, ontmoedig; ~ed
neerslagtig, bedruk, verslae
delay' (n) uitstel, oponthoud; without ~,
onmiddellik; oombliklik; (v) uitstel; vertraag; versuim; talm; weifel
del'egate (n) afgevaardigde, gevolmagtigde,
kursusganger, kongresganger, deputaat,
gedeputeerde; (v) afvaardig; delegeer
delega'tion afvaardiging, deputasie; ~ of
powers, delegering van magte/bevoegd-
hede
delete' uitkrap, uitwis, skrap; ~ which is
not applicable, skrap waar nodig
delib'erate (a) bedagsaam, besadig,
opsetlik; ~ly opsetlik, aspres, ekspres
delibera'tion oorlegpleging, beraadslaging
del'icacy keurigheid; (..cies) lekkerny, ver-
snapering
del'icate lekker, fyn; tinger; delikaat, swak
delicates'sen delikatesse, fynkos
deli'cious heerlik, verruklik
delight' (n) genoeë, genot, behae; (v) verheug, behaag; verruk; ~ed verruk, bly,
opgetoë; ~ed with, ingenome met; ~ful
genotvol, verruklik
delin'quency misdaad, vergryp; juvenile ~,
jeugwangedrag, jeugmisdadigheid
delin'quent (n) kwaaddoener, oortreder,
skuldige; stokkiesdraaier; juvenile ~,
jeugoortreder, jeugmisdadiger
delir'ious ylhoofdig, waansinnig, deliries
deliv'er bevry; oorlewer; aflewer
deliv'ery (..ries) aflewering; lewering; cash
on ~, kontant by aflewering; take ~ of,
in ontvangs neem; ~ man bestelbode; ~
van bestelwa, bestelmotor
demand' (n) vraag; aanvraag; ~ for, vraag
na; meet the local ~, in die plaaslike
vraag voorsien; supply and ~, vraag en
aanbod; (v) vra; eis
dement'ed kransinnig, mal
dem'i half; ~john karba
demise' (n) oordrag, bemarking; afsterwe
demist'er ontwasemer
demobilisa'tion demobilisasie
democ'racy (..cies) volksregering, demokrasie
democrat'ic demokraties

demol'ish afbreek, sloop; **~er** sloper
dem'on bose gees, duiwel, demon
dem'onstrate bewys, uitlê; betoog; de‑monstreer
demonstra'tion betoging; demonstrasie
dem'onstrator (-s), de'mo (-'s) betoger
demote' in rang verlaag, demoveer
demure' stemmig, sedig, preuts
demur'rage lêgeld, staangeld
den gat, lêplek, hol, hool; hok; kamer
deni'al ontkenning, verloëning
de'nim denim; **~s** denims, slenterdrag
denomina'tion benaming; kerkverband; klas; soort, gesindheid; *money of small ~s,* kleingeld; **~al** sektaries
denom'inator noemer
denote' aandui, aanwys, beteken
denounce' veroordeel, afkeur; betig
dense dig, dik; suf, dom, toe; **~ly popula‑ted,** digbevolk
dent (n) duik; kerf, kepie; **(v)** duik, inkeep
den'tal tand‑; **~ floss** tandegare, tan‑devlos; **~ surgeon** tandarts; **~ therap‑ist** tandterapeut
dentist tandarts
den'ture(s) (kuns)gebit, vals tande, winkel‑tande
deny' (denied, denied) ontken; weerspreek, misgun; ontsê
deod'orant reukweerder, deodorant
depart' vertrek, verlaat; afwyk van; sterf; **~ment** werkkring; departement, afdeling; *~ment of education,* onderwysdeparte‑ment
departmen'tal departementeel, afdelings‑
depar'ture vertrek, trek; afsterwe
depend' afhang; vertrou; *it ~s on,* dit hang daarvan af; *~ upon,* reken op (iemand); **~able** vertroubaar, betroubaar; **~ant (n)** afhanklike; **~ent (a)** afhanklik; **~ing** afhanklik; *~ing on,* afhangende van; na gelang van
depict' uitbeeld, afskilder, skets; beskryf
deplete' leeg maak, uitput
deplore' betreur; bejammer
deploy' ontplooi, versprei; *~ troops,* troepe ontplooi
depopula'tion ontvolking
deport' oor die grense sit, deporteer; (jou) gedra; *~ oneself,* jou gedra; *~a'tion* ver‑banning, deportasie; **~ment** houding, gedrag; houdingsleer (vak)

depos'it (n) storting, deposito; **(v)** stort, deponeer
depos'it book bankboek(ie); depositoboek
depos'itor belegger, storter, inlêer; depo‑sant (bank)
depos'it slip inlegstrokie
dep'ot bêreplek, opslagplek; depot
deprave' verslag, bederwe; **~d'** ontaard, versleg
depre'ciate depresieer; in waarde ver‑minder, minag
deprecia'tion depresiasie, waardeverminde‑ring
depress' (ter)neerdruk; neerslagtig, bedruk; **~ed'** neerslagtig, bedruk; **~ion** neer‑slagtigheid; depressie, slapte (sake); in‑sinking
deprive' ontneem; ontroof
depth diepte; diepsinnigheid; *a study in ~,* dieptestudie; *~ charge* dieptebom
deputa'tion afvaardiging, deputasie
dep'uty (..ties) plaasvervanger; adjunk‑; *~ mayor* onderburgemeester; *~ principal* adjunk‑hoof
derail' ontspoor; **~ment** ontsporing
de'relict (n) verlate skip; **(a)** verlate, op‑gegee, prysgegee
deriva'tion afleiding, afkoms, herkoms
derive' aflei, afstam; ontstaan/voorkom uit; ontleen aan
dermatol'ogist huidarts, dermatoloog
derog'atory kleinerend, neerhalend
de'rrick boortoring; hyskraan, hysbalk
desal'inate (v) ontsout; **desalination plant** ontsout(ings)aanleg
descend' (v) afklim, (af)daal; afstam; **(n) ~ant** afstammeling
descent' (n) (neer)daling; afkoms; afdraand
describe' beskryf, omskryf, aandui
descrip'tion beskrywing; aard, klas
descrip'tive beskrywend
des'ecrate ontheilig, ontwy
des'ert[1] (n) woestyn; woesteny
desert'[2] (n) verdienste; (pl) verdiende loon; *get one's ~s,* jou verdiende loon kry
desert'[3] (v) verlaat; wegloop, (weg)dros; **~er** droster
deserve' verdien; **~d'ly** na verdienste
deserv'ing verdienstelik
design' (n) ontwerp, plan; voorneme; **(v)** ontwerp, skets; beoog

des'ignate aanwys; bestem; noem; *designa=
tory title/initials,* kenletters
designa'tion betiteling; ampsbenaming
design'er ontwerper; sketstekenaar
desir'able wenslik, begeerlik
desire' (n) begeerte, verlange, wens; (v) be=
geer, verlang, wens; *leave much to be ~d,*
veel te wense oorlaat
desk lessenaar, skryftafel; skoolbank
des'olate (a) verlate, eensaam
desola'tion verwoesting; verlatenheid
despair' (n) wanhoop; vertwyfeling; (v)
wanhoop, moed opgee
despatch' *see* dispatch
des'perate wanhopig; radeloos, desperaat
despera'tion wanhoop, vertwyfeling, rade=
loosheid; *in ~,* uit wanhoop
despi'cable veragtelik, laag, gemeen
despise' verag, verfoei
despite' (prep) nieteenstaande, ondanks
despond' wanhoop; ~ency moedeloosheid,
neerslagtigheid
des'pot despoot, dwingeland, tiran
des'potism despotisme, dwingelandy
dessert' dessert, nagereg
desta'bilise (v) onbestendig maak, desta=
biliseer
destina'tion bestemming
des'tiny (..nies) lot, noodlot; bestemming,
voorland
des'titute ontbloot, behoeftig, arm; verlate
destroy' verniel, vernietig, verdelg; ~er
torpedojaer
destruc'tion vernietiging, verwoesting
destruc'tive vernielend, afbrekend; ~ *cri=
ticism,* afbrekende/neerhalende kritiek
detach' losmaak, afsonder
det'ail (n) besonderheid, detail; omstandig=
heid; uiteensetting; *in ~,* breedvoerig
detail' (v) omstandig vertel; opsom; aan=
wys, aansê
det'ailed breedvoerig, uitvoerig, omstandig
detain' terughou; aanhou, gevange hou; ~=
ee aangehoudene
detect' uitvind, betrap, ontdek; ~ive speur=
der; ~or ontdekker; opspoorder; open=
baarder; verklikker
détente' détente, ontspan(nings)politiek
deten'tion terughouding; aanhouding, ge=
vangehouding; detensie; skoolbly; ~
without trial, aanhouding sonder verhoor
deter' (-red, -red) afskrik, terughou

deter'gent (n) suiweringsmiddel, detergent
deter'iorate ontaard; agteruitgaan, versleg
determina'tion bepaling, beslissing; vasbe=
radenheid, beslistheid
deter'mine bepaal, besluit; beslis; eindig
deter'mined (a) vasberade (van aard); vas=
beslote (om iets te doen)
dete'rrent (n) afskrikmiddel
detest' verfoei, verafsku; ~able verfoeilik,
afskuwelik
de'tour omweg, ompad, (pad)verlegging
detrimen'tal nadelig, skadelik
deuce[1] twee; gelykop (tennis)
deuce[2] joos, duiwel; drommel; *what the ~?*
wat die/de drommel?
deval'uate devalueer, in waarde verminder
devasta'tion verwoesting
devel'op ontwikkel, ontvou, ontplooi; ~ed
countries, ontwikkelde lande; ~er ont=
wikkelaar; ~ment ontwikkeling, ont=
plooiing
dev'iate afwyk, afdwaal; verlê
devia'tion afwyking; syspoor; verlegging
device' oogmerk; sinspreuk; leus(e); ont=
werp, uitvindsel, apparaat; lis
dev'il duiwel; *give the ~ his due,* gee die
duiwel wat hom toekom; *between the ~
and the deep sea,* tussen twee vure; ~ish
duiwels; ~ry duiwelskunste; slegtigheid;
terglus; ~'s bones dobbelstene
devise' (v) versin, prakseer, uitdink; be=
maak
devoid' leeg, ontdaan
devote' (toe)wy; oorlewer; ~d toegewy,
toegeneê, geheg; verslaaf/verknog; *a ~d
husband,* 'n toegewyde eggenoot/man; ~
attention to, aandag wy/skenk/gee aan
devo'tion toewyding; vroomheid, gods=
vrug; (pl) godsdiensoefening, gebede
devour' verslind, verteer
devout' vroom, godsdienstig
dew (n) dou; (v) dou; ~drop doudruppel;
~lap keelvel; ~point doupunt
dexter'ity handigheid, vaardigheid
diabet'ic (n) suikersiektelyer
diabol'ic duiwelagtig, duiwels
diae'resis deelteken (¨)
di'agnose diagnoseer, vasstel
diag'onal (a) oorhoeks, diagonaal
di'agram figuur, skets, tekening, diagram
di'al (n) sonwyser; wyserplaat; (v) (-led,
-led) skakel (foon)

di'alect dialek, tongval, streekspraak
di'al(ling) tone skakeltoon
di'alogue tweegesprek; dialoog
diam'eter middellyn, deursnee
di'amond diamant; ruit; glassnyer; **~s** ruitens (kaartspel)
diarrhoe'a maagwerking, appelkoossiekte, diarree; *verbal* **~**, woordskittery
di'ary (diaries) dagboek
dice (n) dobbelsteene; (v) dobbel; uitdaag
dictate' (v) dikteer; gebied; voorskryf
dictat'or gebieder, diktator; **~ship** diktatuur, diktatorskap
dic'tion voordrag; styl, diksie
dic'tionary (..ries) woordeboek
didac'tic didakties, lerend
did'dle kul, fop, flous
die[1] (n) (dice) dobbelsteen; (-s) matrys; snymoer; muntstempel; *the* **~** *is cast*, die besluit is (onherroeplik) geneem
die[2] (v) sterf, doodgaan, sneuwel; vrek (diere); **~hard** bittereinder, kanniedood
dietic'ian dieetkundige
diff'er verskil; *I beg to* **~**, ek is dit nie daarmee eens nie; moenie glo nie
diff'erence verskil, onderskeid
diff'erent verskillend, onderskeie; **~ial** ewenaar (motor)
differentia'tion differensiëring, differensiasie
diff'icult moeilik, swaar; **~y** (..ties) moeilikheid, moeite, haakplek; beswaar
diff'ident verleë, skaam, nederig
dig (n) stoot, slag, stamp; (v) **(dug, dug)** grawe, grou, delf, spit
di'gest[1] (v) opsomming, oorsig; keurblad
digest'[2] (v) verteer; oordink; verwerk; **~ion** spysvertering
digg'er delwer
digg'ings delwery
di'git vinger; toon; syfer
di'gital (a) vinger-, toon-; syfer-; **~ watch** syferoorlosie, digitale oorlosie
dig'nified waardig, deftig; verhewe
dig'nitary (..ries) (hoog)waardigheidbekleër, dignitaris
dig'nity waardigheid, deftigheid; *beneath one's* **~**, benede jou waardigheid
digs blyplek, losies
dike damwal, dyk; gang (Aardk.)
dilap'idate verniel, laat verval; bouvallig word; **~d** bouvallig, vervalle, gehawend

dilate' uitsit, swel; uitrek; vergroot
dilemm'a (-s) dilemma, verleentheid, penarie
dilettan'te (..ti) dilettant, leek, amateur
dil'igent ywerig, fluks, vlytig, naarstig
dill dille; vinkel
dill'y-dally (..dallied, ..dallied) talm, draai, besluiteloos wees, weifel, treusel
dilute' verdun, verslap, verwater
dim (v) **(-med, -med)** donker maak; benewel; verdof, verdonker; **~** *lights*, ligte verdof/demp; ligte domp (kar); (a) donker, dof, skemerig; suf; wasig
dimen'sion afmeting, dimensie, grootte
dimini'ish verminder, verklein
dimin'utive (n) verkleinwoord; (a) klein; verkleining-; **~ form** verkleinvorm
dim'ple (wang)kuiltjie
din (n) geraas, lawaai; (v) raas, baljaar
dingh'y (dinghies) rubberbootjie
din'ing: **~ car** eetsalon, eetwa; **~ room** eetkamer
dinn'er (n) middagmaal, dinee; **~ jacket** aandbaadjie; **~ service**, **~ set** eetservies
dip (n) dip; indompeling; helling, duik; **(-ped, -ped)** dip (vee); indompel; **~** *into the future,* 'n blik in die toekoms werp
diphther'ia witseerkeel, difterie
diph'thong tweeklank, diftong
diplom'a (-s) diploma; getuigskrif
diplom'acy (..cies) diplomasie; behendigheid, takt; sluheid
dip'lomat diplomaat
diplomat'ic diplomaties; oulik, poliets
dire vreeslik, yslik, ontsettend; **~** *need,* nypende nood
direct'[1] (v) rig; bestuur; adresseer; vestig op (aandag); beveel; aanstuur
di'rect[2] (a) regstreeks, direk; dadelik; **~ speech** direkte rede
direc'tion rigting; leiding; bevel; direksie
direct'or direkteur; **~-general (directors-general)** direkteur-generaal; **~y** (..ries) adresboek
dir'igible (n) bestuurbare lugballon, lugskip; (a) bestuurbaar
dirt (n) vuilgoed, vuilis, slyk; *fling* **~**, met modder gooi; (v) vuil maak, besmeer; **~box** (-es) vullisbak; **~-cheap** spotgoedkoop; **~-track** asbaan
dirt'y (v) (..tied, ..tied) bevuil, bemors, be-

smeer; (a) vieslik; morsig, smerig; gemeen, laag; ~ **work,** vuil werk

disabil'ity gebrek; ongeskiktheid (vir werk)

disa'ble onbekwaam maak; buite geveg stel; vermink; ~**d** gestrem, gebreklik, gekwes; ~**d person,** (liggaamlik) gestremde; ~**d soldier,** invalide, verwonde soldaat

disadvan'tage nadeel; skade; verlies

disagree' nie ooreenstem nie, verskil; vassit (oor iets); *it* ~**s with me,** dit akkordeer nie met my nie

disappear' verdwyn, wegraak; ~**ance** verdwyning

disappoint' teleurstel; verydel; ~**ed** teleurgestel(d); ~**ment** teleurstelling

disapprove' afkeur, verwerp

disarm' ontwapen; paai; ~**ament** ontwapening

disas'ter ramp, ongeluk, onheil; ~ **area** rampgebied; ~ **fund** rampfonds, noodleniging(s)fonds

disas'trous noodlottig, rampspoedig

disburse' voorskiet; uitbetaal; ~**ment** voorskot, uitbetaling; uitgawe, onkoste

disc skyf; werpskyf; ~ **jockey** platejoggie; ~ **plough** skottelploeg

discard' weggooi; afdank; verwerp

discharge' (n) ontslag; loslating; kwytskelding; betaling; (v) ontslaan; afdank; vervul (plig); betaal, delg (skuld); uitmond (rivier); ~ *one's duties,* jou pligte vervul

disci'ple leerling, volgeling, dissipel

disciplinar'ian tugmeester, ordehouer

dis'ciplinary tug~, dissiplinêr; ~ **committee** tugkomitee

dis'cipline (n) tug, dissipline; (v) tugtig

disclose' onthul, openbaar (maak), blootlê

disconnect' diskonnekteer; losskakel, loskoppel; ~**ion** loskoppeling; skeiding

discontent' (n) ontevredenheid, misnoeë; (v) ontevrede maak; (a) ontevrede

discontin'ue ophou, laat staan, staak; opsê

dis'cord (n) wanklank; tweedrag, onvrede; *apple of* ~, twisappel

discord' (v) verskil, rusie maak; bots

discothéque diskoteek; *disco dancing,* diskodans

dis'count (n) korting; afslag, diskonto; *at a* ~, teen afslag; ~ **store** afslagwinkel

discou'rage ontmoedig, afskrik

dis'course (n) onderhoud; redevoering

discourt'eous onmanierlik; onbeleef

disco'ver ontdek, uitvind; onthul; ~**y** (..ries) ontdekking

discred'it (n) oneer, skande; diskrediet; (v) in diskrediet bring

discreet' beskeie, versigtig, tak(t)vol

discrep'ancy (..cies) verskil, teenstrydigheid; wanverhouding

discre'tion diskresie, goeddunke; *at* ~, na/volgens goeddunke

discrim'inate (v) onderskei, diskrimineer

discrim'inating skerpsinnig, onderskeidend

discrimina'tion verstand, oordeel; diskriminasie

dis'cus (-es, disci) werpskyf, diskus

discuss' beraadslaag, bespreek; ~**ion** sa-mespreking(s), bespreking, diskussie; ~**ion group** besprekingsgroep, diskus-siegroep

disease' siekte, kwaal

disengage' bevry, ontslaan; losmaak

disgrace' (n) skande, ongenade; (v) in on-genade bring; te skande maak; ~**ful** skandelik

disguise' (n) vermomming, masker; voorwendsel; *a blessing in* ~, 'n bedekte seën; *in* ~, vermom; (v) vermom; verklee; verbloem

disgust' (n) afkeer, walging, teensin; *be* ~*ed with,* walg van; ~**ing** walglik, stuitlik

dish (n) (-es) skottel, gereg; (pl) skottelgoed; (v); opskep; ~**cloth** vadoek

disheart'en ontmoedig, afskrik

dishon'est oneerlik, bedrieglik; ~**y** oneer-likheid, bedrog

dishon'our (n) oneer, skande; (v) onteer; ~ *a cheque,* 'n tjek dishonoreer

dish'washer skottelgoedwasser

disillu'sion ontnugter, ontgoël/ontgogel; ~**ment** ontnugtering, ontgogeling

disinfect' ontsmet; ~**ant** ontsmetmiddel; ~**ion** ontsmetting

disin'tegrate ontbind; verval; oplos; disin-tegreer, verbrokkel

disin'terested belangeloos; onpartydig

disinvest' (v) disinvesteer; ~**ment** (n) dis-investering

disjoint'ed onsamehangend

dislike' (n) afkeer, teensin; (v) 'n afkeer hê van

dis'locate verswik, verskuif, verstuit

disloy'al ontrou, dislojaal

dis'mal somber, treurig, droewig, aaklig

disman'tle afbreek, sloop; demonteer

dismay' (n) skrik, ontmoediging; ontsteltenis; (v) bang maak; ontmoedig; onthuts; ~ed' verslae, versteld

dismiss' ontslaan, afdank; ontbind (vergadering); verdaag (mil.); ~al ontslag, afdanking

dismount' afklim, afstyg

disobed'ience ongehoorsaamheid

disord'er (n) wanorde, verwarring; oproer; ongesteldheid; ~ly wanordelik

disor'ganise in die war bring, disorganiseer

dispa'rity ongelykheid, verskil, wanbalans

dispa'ssionate bedaard, kalm

dispatch' (n) afsending, versending; (v) versend; bespoedig; doodmaak; ~ rider rapportryer

dispel' (-led, -led) wegja, verban

dispen'sable (a) misbaar; wegdoenbaar

dispen'sary (..ries) apteek, mengapteek

dispensa'tion bedeling, vrystelling; beheer; stelsel; *grant ~ from*, vrystelling verleen van; *a new ~*, 'n nuwe bedeling

dispense' uitdeel; klaarmaak; sonder klaarkom; ~ *with*, daarsonder klaarkom; ~r uitdeler; apteker

disperse' verstrooi; versprei; uiteengaan

displace' verplaas; vervang; afsit (uit betrekking); ~d person ontwortelde/ontheemde persoon

display' (n) uitstalling; vertoning; (v) tentoonstel, vertoon; ~ cabinet/case (ver)toonkas; ~ diving sierduik; ~ window toonvenster

displea'sure mishae, misnoeë, ongenoeë

dispos'al beskikking, skikking; *at your ~*, tot u beskikking

dispose' beskik; reël, orden, inrig; ~ *of*, vervreem, verkoop; *disposable*, wegdoenbaar; ~d' geneig, gestem

disposi'tion skikking; gesteldheid; neiging, aard, gesindheid; opstelling (troepe)

dispossess' ontvreem, onteien

dispropor'tion onweredigheid; ~ed' oneweredig, ongelyk

dispu'table betwisbaar, aanvegbaar

dispute' (n) twis; geskil, dispuut; *the matter in ~*, die geskilpunt; *settle the ~*, die geskil besleg/bylê; (v) twis, betwis; redetwis; ~d betwis

disqualifica'tion ongeskiktheid, diskwalifikasie; uitsluiting

disqual'ify (..fied, ..fied) uitsluit; diskwalifiseer; ongeskik verklaar

disqui'et (n) onrus; (v) verontrus, ongerus maak; (a) ongerus; ~ing verontrustend

disregard' (n) veronagsaming, minagting; (v) veronagsaam, minag; geringskat

disrepair' verval, vervalle staat; lendelam

disrep'utable berug, in slegte reuk; ~ character, 'n ongure vent

disrepute' skande, berugtheid; diskrediet, oneer; *fall into ~*, 'n slegte naam kry

disrespect' oneerbiedigheid, disrespek

disrupt' uiteenspat; verbrokkel; ontwrig; ~ the class, die klas ontwrig

dissatisfac'tion ontevredenheid

dissect' ontleed; dissekteer

dissem'inate versprei; uitstrooi

dissent' verskil van opinie; ~er afgeskeidene, andersgesinde; ~ing vote teenstem

disserta'tion verhandeling, dissertasie, proefskrif, tesis

disser'vice ondiens

diss'ident (n) andersdenkende; afvallige, dissident; (a) afvallig, dissident

disso'ciate dissosieer, distansieer

diss'olute los; losbandig; liederlik

dissolve' oplos; ontbind; ~ a partnership, 'n vennootskap ontbind

diss'onance wanluidend, vals

dissuade' afraai, afskrik

dis'tance (n) afstand, distansie; (v) ver uitstof; distansieer

dis'tant ver weg; afgeleë; uit die hoogte

distaste' teensin, walging; ~ful onsmaaklik, sleg

distil' (-led, -led) distilleer, stook

distinct' onderskeie, duidelik, beslis; bepaald; eie; *keep ~*, uitmekaar hou

distinc'tion onderskeiding; aansien; eerbetoon; *with ~*, met onderskeiding, met lof

distin'guish onderskei; kenmerk; ~ed onderskeie; beroemd, vernaam; *our ~ed guests*, ons geëerde gaste

distort' verdraai; verwring; ~ion verdraaiing; ~ionist lyfwringer, slangmens

distract' aftrek; verbyster; aflei; ~ed afgetrokke; ~ion afleiding; verstrooiing

distress' (n) ellende; nood; *a damsel in ~*, 'n nooientjie in nood; ~ed behoeftig; ~ call noodroep; ~ signal noodsein

distrib'ute uitdeel, verdeel, versprei

distribu'tion verdeling, verspreiding, distribusie

distrib'utor vonkverdeler (motor)

dis'trict distrik; streek, gebied; **~ surgeon** distriksgeneesheer

distrust' (n) wantroue; argwaan; (v) wantrou; verdink

disturb' versteur, verontrus; **~ance** versteuring; opskudding; oproerigheid; (pl) onluste

ditch (n) (-es) sloot, voor; grag; (v) dreineer; oorboord gooi

ditt'y (ditties) liedjie, deuntjie

divan' sofa, divan, rusbank

dive (n) duik; (v) duik; **~ bomber** duikbomwerper; **~r** duiker

diver'sify (..fied; ..fied) afwisselend maak; verander, wysig, diversifeer

divers'ity verskeidenheid, verskil; diversiteit; **~ of opinion,** mening(s)verskil

divert' aflei; wegkeer; verlê (pad)

divide' (v) deel, verdeel; skei

divid'ed (ver)deel, afgeskei; onenig

div'idend dividend; deeltal; *cum* **~,** met dividend; *ex* **~,** sonder dividend; *interim* **~,** tussentydse dividend

divid'er deler; (pl) verdeelpasser

divine' (v) voorspel; (a) goddelik; verruklik; **~ service** godsdiensoefening, huisgodsdiens; erediens

divin'ing rod wiggelroede, waterstok

divin'ity godheid; godgeleerdheid

divis'ible deelbaar

divi'sion deling; verdeling; afdeling; verdeeldheid; onenigheid; divisie (leër)

divi'sion sum deelsom

divorce' (n) egskeiding; **~e'** geskeide vrou/persoon

div'ot sooimerk (gholf)

divulge' rugbaar maak; onthul, openbaar

dizz'y duiselig, lighoofdig; onbesonne

do (v) **(did, done)** doen, maak, verrig, werskaf; **~ for,** deug vir; *how* **~** *you* **~?** hoe gaan dit? **~ mischief,** kattekwaad aanrig

dock (n) skeepsdok; *dry* **~,** droogdok; *floating* **~,** dryfdok

dock'et dossier, uittreksel; faktuur; strook/strokie

dock'yard skeepswerf

doc'tor (n) dokter, geneesheer; arts; doktor

(in die regte, medisyne, lettere, ens.); (v) dokter; opknap

doc'torate (n) doktoraat; (v) doktoreer

doc'trine leer, leerstelling

doc'ument (n) dokument, geskrif, bewysstuk; (v) dokumenteer

documen'tary dokumentêr; **~ film,** dokumentêre film, feitefilm

documenta'tion dokumentasie

dodge (v) ontwyk, fop, uitdraai; verbyglip, ontglip, uitoorlê; **~r** ontduiker; draaijakkals

doe (-s) bokooi (wild); ree, hinde; wyfie

do'er dader, verrigter; man van die daad

doff afhaal (hoed); uittrek; wegsit

dog (n) hond; *let sleeping* **~s** *lie,* moenie slapende honde wakker maak nie; *top* **~,** uitblinker, bobaas; (v) **(-ged, -ged)** navolg, naspeur; **~fight** hondegeveg; enkelgeveg (in die lug); **~ged** stuurs, koppig

dog'kennel hondehok; (pl) hondehotel, woefietuiste

dog'ma **(-s, -ta)** leerstuk, dogma

doil'y (doilies) dolie, bekerlappie

do'ing doen, werk, doenigheid; **~s besigheid,** bedryf; gedrag; doenigheid

dol'drums (streke van) windstilte

doll pop

dol'phin dolfyn

domain' gebied; domein; heerskappy

dome koepel, dom

domes'tic (n) huisbediende; (a) huislik, huishoudelik; binnelands; **~ animal** huisdier; **~ science** huishoudkunde; **~ trade** binnelandse handel

dom'icile (n) woonplek, verblyf; (v) vestig

dom'inant (oor)heersend; dominant

dom'inate heers; oorheers; domineer

domin'ion heerskappy; gebied; gemenebes, susterstaat, vrygewes, dominium

don (n) don, hoof; *D~ Juan,* losbol, pierewaaier; opperste vryer

dona'tion skenking, gif, donasie

done (a) gedaan; gekook, gaar; klaar

don'ga (-s) spoelsloot, donga

don'key (-s) esel, donkie; domkop; *for* **~'s** *years,* jare lank, van toeka se dae af

don'or gewer; skenker, donateur

don't = do not moenie

doom (n) noodlot; ondergang; (v) vonnis, verdoem; *prophet of* **~,** doemprofeet; **~'s day** oordeelsdag

door deur, ingang; *at death's ~*, aan die
rand v.d. graf; **~keeper** portier, deur‑
wagter; **~sill** drumpel
dope (n) dwelmmiddel; (v) bedwelm
dorm'ant slapend, rustend
dorm'itory (..ries) slaapvertrek, slaapsaal
dorm'y doedoe (gholf)
dose (n) dosis; (v) doseer, medisyne ingee,
dokter; *booster ~*, skraagdosis
doss'ier dossier, lêer; strafregister
dot (n) punt, stippel; stip; (v) (**-ted, -ted**)
puntjies opsit; *~ted line*, stippellyn; stip‑
pelstreep (verkeer)
dott'y gestippel; versprei; suf, onnosel
dou'ble (n) duplikaat; dubbelganger; (pl)
dubbelspel; (v) verdubbel; vou; ombuig;
(a) dubbel; tweevoudig; *~ standards*,
dubbele standaarde/maatstawwe; **~bar‑
rel** tweeloop, dubbelloop (geweer);
~dealer bedrieër; **~faced** huigelagtig,
vals; **~storey** dubbelverdieping
doub'let doeblet, onderkleed
doubt (n) twyfel; argwaan; *give the benefit
of the ~*, die voordeel van die twyfel gee;
beyond a ~, *no ~*, *without ~*, onge‑
twyfeld; (v) twyfel, weifel; **~ful** twyfel‑
agtig, onseker; **~less** ongetwyfeld
dough deeg; **~nut** stormjaer; oliering,
oliebol
dour streng, stroef; hardnekkig
dove duif; **~tail** (n) swaelstert; (v) met 'n
swaelstert voeg
down¹ (n) dons
down² (n) teenslag; *ups and ~s*, weder‑
waardighede; (v) neergooi; neerslaan; *~
tools*, staak; (a) afdraand; neerslagtig;
(adv) neer, ondertoe; *knock ~*, platslaan;
omry; *run ~*, inhaal; sleg maak; omry;
~cast neerslagtig, mismoedig; **~fall** in‑
storting, val, ondergang; **~hearted** neer‑
slagtig, bedruk; **~hill** afdraand; berg af;
~pipe afvoerpyp; **~pour** stortbui, stort‑
reën; **~right** pure; gewoonweg; *a ~right
lie*, 'n onbeskaamde leuen
dowr'y (..ries) bruidskat; talent
do'yen doyen, oudste lid
doze (n) sluimering, dutjie; (v) sluimer, dut,
visvang
do'zen dosyn; *baker's ~*, dertien
drab vaal, ligbruin; saai, eentonig
draft (n) skets, plan; ontwerp; konsep; (v)
teken, opstel; *~ bill* konsepwetsontwerp;

~ dodger dienspligontduiker; **~ legisla‑
tion** konsepwetgewing; **~ ordinance**
konsepordonnansie; **~s'man** (skets)teke‑
naar
drag (n) rem; eg; sleepnet; blok aan die
been; (v) (**-ged, -ged**) sleep, sleur; draal,
talm; *~ factor*, sleurfaktor; **~ racing**
sleeprenne, versnelrenne; **~ster** renstel
drag'on draak
drain (n) riool; (v) dreineer; **~age** dreine‑
ring, riolering
drain'ing dreinering
drake mannetjieseend
dra'ma (-s) toneelstuk, drama
dramat'ic dramaties
dra'ma: **~tist** dramaskrywer, toneeldigter,
dramaturg; **~tise** dramatiseer
drank *see* **drink** (v)
drape drapeer, versier; **~r** handelaar in
sagte stowwe; **~ry** klerasiehandel
dras'tic kragtig, drasties
draught (n) trek, tog; teug, sluk; drankie;
afdeling; plan, skets, *see* **draft**; (v) afstuur;
ontwerp; *~ board* dambord; *~ horse*
trekperd; **~s** dambord; **~y** trekkerig
draw (n) trek; gelykopspel; loot, loting
(sport); skyfie, skuifie (rook); (v) (**drew,
drawn**) trek, sleep; span; teken; gelykop
speel; onbeslis eindig (krieket); trek
(wissel); *~ comparisons*, vergelykings
tref; *~ level*, kop aan kop; **~back**
beswaar, nadeel; **~bridge** ophaalbrug;
~ee' nemer, akseptant; **~er** trekker,
tekenaar; laaitjie; *chest of ~ers*, spieëlkas,
laaikas; **~ers** onderbroek
draw'ing tekening, skets; **~ board** teken‑
bord; **~ pin** drukspykertjie, duim‑
spykertjie; **~ room** sitkamer
drawl (n) geteem, temerige spraak; (v)
teem
drawn getrek; onbeslis (geëindig), gelykop
dread (n) skrik, vrees, ontsetting; (v) vrees;
~ful verskriklik, ontsettend
dream (n) droom; hersenskim; (v) (**-ed, -ed**,
or **-t, -t**) droom; **~er** dromer; **~y**
dromerig, vaag
drear'y treurig, aaklig, somber
dredge (n) baggermasjien; baggerboot; (v)
(uit)bagger; **~r** baggerboot
dregs (pl) moer, afsaksel; uitvaagsel, skor‑
riemorrie; *to the ~*, tot die bodem toe
drench (v) drenk; sopnat maak

dress (n) (-es) tabberd, rok; (v) aantrek; af= rig; **dresseer** (dier); verbind (wond); kap (klip); **~ed chicken,** bevrore hoender; **~ed stone,** bewerkte/gekapte klip; **~ cir= cle** eerste balkon, voorbalkon; **~coat** manel
dress'er kombuiskas, kombuisrak
dress'ing toebereiding, verband; loesing; **~ gown** kamerjapon, kamerjas; **~ room** kleedkamer; **~ table** spieëltafel
dress: **~maker** kleremaakster; modiste; **~ rehearsal** kleedrepetisie; **~ suit** aandpak; **~y** keurig gekleed; smaakvol, swierig
drew *see* **draw**
drib'ble (n) druppel; motreën; (v) dribbel (voetbal); druppel; kwyl
drift (n) neiging, drif (spruit); trek; (v) weg= dryf; aanspoel
drill (n) boor; (v) dril, oefen; boor
drink (n) drank, sopie; *stand a ~,* op 'n glasie trakteer; (v) **(drank, drunk)** drink; **~ to,** drink op; **~er** drinker, dronklap
drip (n) gedrup; indruppeling (medies); jan= dooi; (v) **(-ped, -ped)** drup, lek; **~ping** (n) braaivet; druipvet; lek; **~ping wet,** pap= nat, sopnat
drive (n) rytoertjie, ritjie; oprypad; rylaan; dryfhou (gholf); dryfkrag, stukrag; klop= jag; (v) **(drove, driven)** dryf, dwing; bestuur (motor), dryf (lorrie)
drive'-in inrit; **~ bank** inrybank; **~ bio= scope,** **~ theatre** inryteater, veldfliek
driv'el (n) kwyl; geklets; (v) kwyl; klets
dri'ver drywer; masjinis; bestuurder (motor); **~'s licence** rybewys
driz'zle motreën(tjie), stuifreën
droll (n) grapmaker; (v) skerts, gekskeer; (a) koddig, snaaks; **~ery** grappigheid
drone (n) hommel, waterdraerby; luiaard; (v) gons, brom, zoem; **~fly** (..**flies)** brom= mer
droop (v) neerhang, kwyn; sink
drop (n) druppel; skepskop; val; daling; (v) **(-ped, -ped)** drup; neerval, ophou; neerlaat; daal; **~ a hint,** 'n wenk gee; **~ a line,** 'n brief skryf; **~kick** skepskop; **~out** skoolstaker, uitsakker; vroeë skoolver= later; **~per** stutpaaltjie, hangertjie
drop'sy watersug, water (siekte)
drought droogte
drown verdrink; smoor

drow'sy vaak, soeserig, lomerig
drudge (n) slaaf, werkesel; (v) swoeg, af= sloof, ploeter; **~ry** sleurwerk
drug (n) geneeskruid; verdowingsmiddel; (medies); dwelmmiddel, verslaafmiddel; dwelms; (v) **(-ged, -ged)** verdoof; be= dwelm; vervals; **~ abuse** dwelmmisbruik; **~ addict** dwelmslaaf; **~ addiction** dwelmverslawing; **~gist** drogis, apteker; **~ pedlar/pusher** dwelmsmous
drum (n) tamboer, trom; **~ majorette** trom= poppie, tamboernooi; **~mer** tam= boerslaner
drunk (v) *see* also **drink** (v); (a) dronk, be= sope, beskonke, gekoring, getier, hoen= derkop; **~ard** dronkaard, dronklap; **~(en) driving** dronkbestuur
dry (v) **(dried, dried)** verdroog; opdroog; (a) droog, dor; **~cleaner** droogskoonmaker, droogreiniger; **~ing kiln** droogoond; **~rot** molm; houtswam
du'al (n) tweevoud, tweetal; (a) tweeledig; **~-medium,** dubbelmedium
dub **(-bed, -bed)** tot ridder slaan; verhef tot; noem; smeer; oorklank; **~bin** leervet; **~bing** ridderslag; oorklanking (TV)
dub'ious twyfelagtig; onseker
duch'ess **(-es)** hertogin
duck (n) (eend)voël; nul (krieket); liefling; (v) duik; koe(t)s; indompel; **~ling** eend= jie; **~tail** eendstert
duct pyp, geleibuis; kanaal; **~ile** rekbaar
dud (n) toiing, flenter; dowe neut; domkop; (a) dom; nikswerd, onbruikbaar
due (a) skuldig, betaalbaar; *in ~ course,* mettertyd; **~ date,** vervaldatum; *money ~ to him,* geld aan hom verskuldig
du'el (n) tweegeveg, duel
duet' duet; paar
dug (v) *see* **dig; ~out** uitgrawing, skuil= plek
duke hertog
dull (v) dof maak, verstomp; (a) dom; dof; saai, eentonig; onnosel; **~-witted** dom
du'ly behoorlik, noukeurig; op tyd
dumb stom; stemloos; stilswygend; toe; *don't be so ~,* moenie so toe wees nie; **~found** dronkslaan, verstom, oorbluf; **~ show** gebarespel
dumm'y (n) **(dummies)** figurant; fopspeen; (a) nagemaak; (v) pypkan (rugby)
dump (n) mynhoop; opslagplek; (v) stort;

dump (mark); *no ~ing,* stort(ing) ver=
bode
dump'ling kluitjie
dumps (pl) bedruktheid, somberheid, moe=
deloosheid; *down in the ~,* op moedver=
loor se vlakte
dumpy level nivelleerder
dune duin
dung (n) mis; *~ beetle* miskruier
dun'geon kerker, ondergrondse tronk
dunk (v) doop (beskuit in koffie)
dup'licate (n) duplikaat, afskrif; *in ~,* in
tweevoud, in duplo; (v) dupliseer
dup'licator afrolmasjien, dupliseerder
dur'able duursaam
duress' dwang; gevangenskap
dur'ing gedurende, tydens
dusk (n) skemering; (a) skemer, duister; *~y*
skemer; donker
dust (n) stof; gruis; saagsel; stoflike oor=
skot; (v) afstof, bestrooi; opvee; uitlooi;
~ his jacket, hom 'n pak slae gee; *~bin*

vullisblik; *~er* stofdoek, stoffer, stoflap;
~man Klaas Vakie; (..men) asryer; *~y*
stowwerig
Dutch (n, a) Nederlands, Hollands; *Cape
~,* Kaaps-Hollands; *~man* (..men)
Hollander, Nederlander; Hollands-Afri=
kaner
dut'y (duties) plig; diens; belasting; *be off
~,* van diens af wees, vry wees; *be on ~,*
diens hê; op/aan diens wees
dwarf (n) (-s) dwerg; (a) dwergagtig
dwell (**dwelt, dwelt**) woon, bly; *~ing* wo=
ning, woonhuis
dwin'dle inkrimp, verminder, wegkwyn
dye (n) kleursel, kleurstof; (v) verf, kleur
dy'ing (n) dood, (af)sterwe; (a) sterwende
dynam'ics bewegingsleer, dinamika
dyn'amite (n) dinamiet, plofstof, spring=
stof; (v) opblaas; *~r* dinamietman
dys'entery disenterie, bloedpersie
dyslex'ia leesgebrek, disleksie
dyspep'sia slegte spysvertering, dispepsie

E

each elkeen, iedereen, elk; *~ other,* me=
kaar; *R1 ~,* R1 elk
eag'er gretig, begerig; ywerig, vurig
eag'le arend, adelaar; *~t* jong arend
ear[1] (n) aar (koring); kop (mielie)
ear[2] (n) oor; *a word in your ~,* 'n woord=
jie privaat; *prick up one's ~s,* die ore
spits; *~ ache* oorpyn; *~drum* trommel=
vlies; *~ guard* oorskut, oorskerm
earl graaf; *~dom* graafskap
ear'lobe oorlel
earl'y vroeg, tydig; *the ~ bird catches the
worm,* die môrestond het goud in die
mond; *at your earliest convenience,*
spoedig, so gou moontlik; *~ bird* dou=
trapper (persoon)
ear'mark (n) merk; (v) merk (dier); afson=
der; bestem, bewillig (fondse)
earn verdien, verwerf
earn'est (n) erns; (a) ernstig, ywerig
earn'ings verdienste, loon, besoldiging
ear'ring oorbel, oorkrabbetjie
earth (n) aarde, grond; (v) aard (elektr.);
~enware breekgoed, erdewerk; *~quake*
aardbewing; *~ tremor* aardskok

ease (n) gemak; *stand at ~!* op die plek
rus! (v) gerusstel; versag
eas'el esel
eas'ily maklik; fluit-fluit
east oos; ooste; *the E~,* die Ooste; *~ coast*
ooskus; *~coast fever* ooskuskoors
Eas'ter Pase, Paasfees; *~ egg,* Paaseier;
~ show, Paasskou, Paastentoonstelling; *~
Monday,* Paasmaandag, *see* **Family Day**
eas'tern oostelik, oos=
east'ward ooswaarts
eas'y maklik; lig; *take it ~,* dit kalm op=
neem; op jou gemak doen; *~ chair* leun=
(ing)stoel
eat (**ate, eaten**) eet, opeet; *~ing house* eet=
plek, restourant
eaves dakrand, drup, dakgeut; *~dropper*
luistervink
ebb (n) eb; *~ and flow,* eb en vloed; (v) af=
loop, eb; verval; *~ away,* wegvloei
eccen'tric (n) sonderling; (a) snaaks, oor=
drewe, eksentriek, sonderling; eksentries
ec'ho (n) (-es) weerklank, eggo
eclipse' (n) verduistering; *lunar ~,* maan(s)=
verduistering; *solar ~,* son(s)verduiste=
ring

ecol'ogy ekologie, omgewingsleer; *eco sys= tem,* ekosisteem

econom'ical spaarsaam, ekonomies

econom'ics ekonomie; huishoudkunde

econ'omist ekonoom

econ'omise spaar, bespaar, besuinig

econ'omy ekonomie, staatshuishoudkunde; (..mies) spaarsaamheid; besuiniging

ec'stasy (..sies) verrukking, opgetoënheid, geesdrif, ekstase

ecumen'ical universeel, ekumenies

ec'zema uitslag, ekseem; roos

edd'y (n) (eddies) maalstroom; dwarrel= wind; (v) (eddied, eddied) dwarrel

edge (n) kant, rand; *be on ~, gespanne wees; ~ on,* aanhits

ed'ible eetbaar

ed'ict gebod, edik

ed'ifice imposante gebou/struktuur

e'dit redigeer, persklaar maak

edi'tion uitgawe, edisie, oplaag

ed'itor redakteur (koerant); redigeerder (film)

editor'ial (n) hoofartikel; (a) redaksioneel

ed'ucant (n) opvoedeling

ed'ucate opvoed; onderwys; grootmaak

educa'tion opvoeding, opleiding, onder= wys, onderrig; opvoedkunde; **~al** onder= wyskundig, opvoedkundig; **~ist** op= voeder, opvoedkundige

ed'ucator opvoeder

eel paling

effect' (n) uitwerking, gevolg; (pl) bates, besittings; *take ~,* in werking tree; *with ~ from 3 March,* met ingang 3 Maart; (v) bewerk, teweeggebring; **~ive** doeltref= fend, effektief; **~ual** doeltreffend

effem'inate verwyf, weekhartig

effervesce' opkook, gis, opbruis; **~nt** op= bruisend

effi'ciency doeltreffendheid; nuttigheids= graad

effi'cient doeltreffend; bruikbaar

eff'igy (..gies) afbeeldsel, beeld, beeltenis

eff'luent (n) afstroming; uitloop; afwater (fabriek); *factory ~ must be controlled,* fabrieke se afwater moet beheer word

eff'ort poging, inspanning, probeerslag; **~less** speel-speel, sonder inspanning

egg (n) eier; *bad ~,* vrot eier; niksnut; *newlaid ~s,* pasgelegde eiers; *scrambled*

~s, roereiers; (v) *~ on,* aanspoor, aan= hits

eg'o ek, ego; eie-ek; **~ist** egoïs; **~tis'tical** selfsugtig, egoïsties

eh hè? nè?

eid'er eidereend; **~down** veerkombers

eight ag(t); **~een** ag(t)tien; **~eenth** ag(t)= tiende; **~h** ag(t)ste; **(the) E~ies** die jare (dekade van) Tagtig, die Tagtigs, die tag= tiger jare; **~ieth** tagtigste; **~y** (..ties) tagtig

eistedd'fød (-au) kunswedstryd, eisteddfod

ei'ther (a, pron) albei; (adv, conj) of; *~ or* òf ... òf

eject' uitgooi, uitwerp; **~ion seat** (uit)= skietstoel

elab'orate (v) noukeurig uitwerk, verwerk; *~ on,* uitbrei op; (a) uitvoerig

el'and eland

elas'tic (n) rek, gomlastiek; (a) rekbaar, elasties; veerkragtig

el'bow (n) elmboog; *at your ~,* binne jou bereik; (v) stoot, stamp (met die elmboog); *~ chair* armstoel; *~ grease* spierkrag; *~ room* speling, staanplek

el'der (n) ouer persoon; ouderling; (a) ouer; **~ly** bejaard

el'dest oudste

elect' (v) uitverkies; verkies, kies; (a) uitge= kies; verkose; *the president-elect,* die ver= kose/aangewese president; *~ed to coun= cil,* tot die raad verkies/benoem; **~ion** verkiesing, eleksie

elec'toral district kiesdistrik, kiesafdeling

elec'torate kiesers

elec'tric elektries; *~ current* elektriese stroom

electri'cian elektrisiën

electri'city elektrisiteit

electrifica'tion elektrifikasie

elec'trify (..fied, ..fied) elektrifiseer

elec'trocardiogram (ECG) elektrokardio= gram (EKG), *see* **cardiograph**

elec'trocute doodskok; elektries teregstel

electro'nic (a) elektronies; *~ control* elek= troniese beheer

electron'ics elektronika, elektroneleer

el'egant sierlik, bevallig, smaakvol, elegant

el'egy (elegies) elegie, treursang, klaaglied

el'ement element; (pl) elemente, beginsels; *brave the ~s,* die elemente trotseer

elemen'tary elementêr, eenvoudig

el'ephant olifant

el'evate (v) ophef, verhef; veredel; (a) ver= hewe, hoog; ~d verhewe, lug=; ~d rail= way, lugspoor(weg)

el'evator hyser, hysbak; graansuier, silo

elev'en elf; elftal (krieket); ~th elfde

elf (elves) kaboutermannetjie, dwerg

eli'cit te voorskyn bring, uitlok

el'igible verkiesbaar, geskik; being ~ offers himself for re-election, hy is en stel hom herkiesbaar; ~ bachelor hubare/gesogte (oujong)kêrel

elim'inate weglaat, elimineer

ell el; give him an inch and he'll take an ~, gee hom 'n vinger en hy neem die hele hand

ellipse' ellips, ovaal

elm olm

elocu'tion voordrag(kuns), elokusie

elope' weglop, dros; skaak

el'oquent welsprekend; veelseggend

else anders; anyone ~? iem. anders? nog iem.? ~where êrens anders, elders

emancipa'tion vrymaking, vrywording, emansipasie

emas'culate ontman, kastreer, sny

embalm' balsem

embank' indyk, opdam; ~ment dyk; af= damming; skuinste; wal

embar'go (-es) verbod, embargo

embark' inskeep, aanvaar; aanpak

emba'rrass verleë maak; embarrasseer; you ~ me, jy bring my in die verleentheid; ~ment verleentheid

em'bassy (embassies) gesantskap

embez'zle verduister, steel; ~ment ver= duistering (geld, fondse)

embitt'er verbitter, versuur

em'blem sinnebeeld, simbool, embleem

embody' (..died, ..died) beliggaam, inlyf, omvat, insluit

embrace' (v) omhels; omvat

embroid'er borduur

em'bryo (-s) kiem, embrio

em'erald (n) smarag; (a) smaraggroen

emerge' opkom, te voorskyn kom, oprys

emer'gency (..cies) nood(geval); ~ brake noodrem; ~ exit nooddeur, nooduitgang; ~ fund (nood)hulpfonds; ~ regulations noodregulasies

em'ery paper skuurpapier

emet'ic (n) braakmiddel, vomitief

em'igrant (n) emigrant, trekker

em'inent verhewe; voortreflik

em'isary (..ries) gesant, afgesant

emit' (-ted, -ted) uitvaardig; uitstraal

emol'ument besolding, salaris, loon

emo'tion aandoening, emosie, ontroering; ~al aandoenlik, emosioneel, roerend; ~al scenes, roerende tonele

em'peror keiser

em'phasis (..ses) nadruk, klemtoon, klem

em'phasise benadruk, beklemtoon

em'pire ryk, keiserryk

employ' (n) diens; (v) gebruik; werk gee; besig; besig hou; ~ee' werknemer; ~er werkgewer; ~ing authority indiensnemer; ~ment werk, werkverband; werkverskaf= fing; besigheid, gebruik, indiensplasing, indiensneming; ~ment agency, 'werk= gewersburo; werkverskaffingburo; con= ditions of ~ment, diensvoorwaardes

emp'ty (v) (..tied, ..tied) leegmaak; (a) leeg; ydel; ~-headed dom, onnosel

em'ulate nastreef, wedywer; oortref

ena'ble in staat stel, bekwaam maak, help

enam'el (n) glasuur; emalje; erd; ~ paint glansverf

enchant' betower; ~ed betowerd, verruk; ~ing betowerend, bekoorlik

enclose' insluit; omhein, inkamp; ~d here= with, hierby ingesluit

enclo'sure omheining, hok, kamp; bylae

encode' (v) (en)kodeer; kodifiseer

encore' (n) herhaling; toegif; (v) toejuig

encoun'ter (n) ontmoeting; 'skermutseling; (v) ontmoet; aanval

encou'rage aanmoedig, aanspoor; ~ment aanmoediging, aansporing

encyclop(a)ed'ia ensiklopedie

end (n) end, einde; afloop; defeat its own ~, sy eie doel verydel; to this ~, met dié doel; be at one's wit's ~, raadop wees; (v) end, eindig

endeav'our (n) poging; (v) probeer, trag

endem'ic inheems, endemies

end'ing end, uiteinde, slot, einde

endorse' endosseer; ~ment endossement, goedkeuring

endow'ment begifting, gawe, talent; sken= king, bemaking; ~ policy uitkeerpolis

endur'ance uithouvermoë; ~ race uithou= wedren

endure' verduur; uitstaan, verdra; volhou

en'ema (-s, -ta) lawement, dermspoeling
en'emy (n) (..mies) vyand; teenstander; (a) vyandelik
energet'ic kragtig, energiek; deurtastend
en'ergy (..gies) energie; arbeidsvermoë
enforce' (af)dwing, aandring; deurdryf; ~ the law, die wet toepas/uitvoer; ~ment toepassing
engage' verloof; aanpak; huur, aanneem; be ~d in, besig wees met; ~d to, verloof aan; ~ment verlowing
en'gine enjin; motor (elektr.); ~ driver enjindrywer, masjinis; ~ revolutions enjinomwentelings
engineer' (n) ingenieur; civil ~, siviele ingenieur; electrical ~, elektrotegniese ingenieur; mechanical ~, meganiese/ werktuigkundige ingenieur; (v) bewerk; bou; genieer; ~ing ingenieurswese (vak); geniëring (proses)
Eng'land Engeland
Eng'lish Engels; ~man (..men) Engelsman
engrave' graveer; inprent; ~r graveur
engrav'ing gravure, kunsplaat
enhance' verhoog, vergroot, verhef
enig'ma (-s) raaisel, enigma
enjamb'ment enjambement, deurloop (versreël), oorvloeiing
enjoy' geniet, vermaak; ~ yourself (at the party), geniet die (partytjie); ~able aangenaam, genotvol; ~ment genot, vermaak, plesier, pret
enlarge' vergroot; ~ment vergroting
enlight'en verlig; voorlig; ~ed verlig
enorm'ous ontsaglik, enorm, tamaai
enough' genoeg, voldoende; oddly ~, vreemd genoeg
enquire' (v) navraag doen, verneem, informeer; ~ after, verneem/vra na
enquir'y (..ries) navraag; (pl) navrae; make enquiries, navraag doen, see inquiry
enrich' verryk; vrugbaar maak; ~ed uranium verrykte uraan
enrol' (-led, -led) inskryf; aansluit; in diens neem; ~ment inskrywing
enslave' slaaf maak, verslaaf
ensu'ing daaropvolgende
ensure' waarborg, verseker, seker maak
entail' (v) meebring; behels; veroorsaak
en'ter ingaan, intree; inskryf, registreer; ~ into, tree in; aangaan; sluit (kontrak); ~ for a race, inskryf vir 'n wedren

enter'ic fever, enteri'tis ingewandskoors
en'terprise onderneming; free ~, vrye ondernemerskap, vrye markstelsel, private inisiatief
en'terprising ondernemend
entertain' onthaal; vermaak; ~ guests, gaste onthaal; ~er gasheer; onthaler; ~ing onderhoudend, vermaaklik; ~ment onthaal; vermaaklikheid; ~ment tax vermaaklikheid(s)belasting
enthuse' geesdriftig raak/maak, besiel, begeester
enthu'siast entoesias; sport/sporting ~, sportliefhebber
enthusias'tic geesdriftig, entoesiasties
entice' verlok, verlei, in versoeking bring; ~ away, afrokkel
entire' heeltemal, volledig, volkome; ~ly heeltemal, geheel en al
enti'tle betitel, noem; reg gee op; ~d regtig op, gewettig; be ~d to, reg hê op, geregtig wees op
en'tity (entities) wese, entiteit
entomol'ogist entomoloog, insektekundige
en'trance (n) ingang, toegang; intrede
en'trance: ~ examination toelaateksamen; ~ fee intreegeld, inskryfgeld; ~ requirements toelaatvereistes
en'trant kandidaat, nuweling, deelnemer
entreat' smeek, bid, soebat
entrench' verskans; ~ed clauses verskanste klousules
entrepreneur' ondernemer, entrepreneur
entrust' toevertrou; opgedra
en'try (entries) ingang, intrede; inskrywing; pos; ~ form inskryfvorm
enum'erate opsom, opnoem; tel
en'velope koevert; omslag, omhulsel
en'vious afgunstig, naywerig, jaloers
envir'on omring, omsingel, insluit; ~ment omgewing, milieu; ~mental conservation, omgewingsbewaring; ~mental studies, omgewingsleer; ~mentalist omgewing(s)bewaarder
envi'sage beskou; beoog; voor die gees roep
en'voy (-s) gesant, afgesant
en'vy (n) afguns, nyd; be the ~ of, beny word deur; (v) (envied, envied) afgunstig wees, beny
ephem'eral kortstondig, eendaags
ep'ic (n) heldedig, epos; (a) epies
epidem'ic (n) epidemie; (a) epidemies

ep'igram puntdig, epigram
ep'ilepsy vallende siekte; epilepsie; *fit of* ~, toeval
epilep'tic (n) epileptikus; (a) epilepties
ep'ilogue narede, slottoespraak; oorden= king, *see* meditation
ep'isode tussenverhaal, voorval, episode
ep'och (-s) tydperk; tydstip
ep'os (-es) heldedig, epos
eq'ual (n) gelyke, weerga; (v) (-led, -led) ewenaar; (a) dieselfde, gelykvormig, gelyk; ~ *to*, gelyk aan; *on* ~ *footing*, op gelyke voet
eq'ualise gelyk maak; gelykstel; ewenaar; ~**r** gelykmaker (van punte)
equal'ity (..ties) gelykheid; ~ *of votes*, staking van stemme
eq'ually gelyk, eenders, net so
equa'tion vergelyking; ewewig
equat'or ewenaar, ekwator, sonlyn, linie
eques'trian (n) perderuiter, ruiter; ~ **sta= tue** ruiterstandbeeld
equilib'rium ewewig
eq'uinox (-es) dag- en nagewening
equip' (-ped, -ped) toerus, uitrus; voor= sien
equip'ment uitrusting, toerusting
eq'uitable billik, redelik, regverdig
eq'uity (..ties) billikheid, onpartydigheid; (pl) ekwiteite, gewone aandele; *in* ~, billikerwys
equiv'alent ekwivalent; ~ *to*, gelyk aan
er'a (-s) tydvak, jaartelling, era
erad'iate uitstraal, skitter
erad'icate ontwortel; uitroei, verdelg
erase' skrap, uitwis, uitvee, radeer; ~**r** uit= veër, wisser
ere eerder, voor, voordat
erect' (v) oprig, stig, bou; (a) regop, pen= regop, penorent; ~**ion** oprigting, stig= ting
erf (erven) erf
erm'ine hermelyn
ero'sion wegvreting, erosie, verwering, (grond)verspoeling; *combat* ~, bekamp erosie
erot'ic eroties
err fout maak, fouteer; verdwaal
e'rrand boodskap; opdrag
errat'ic wisselvallig; onbestendig (sport)
errat'um (errata) drukfout, skryffout
erron'eous verkeerd, onjuis, foutief

e'rror fout, dwaling, vergissing; *commit an* ~, 'n fout/flater begaan; ~ *of judgment*, oordeelsfout
e'rudite geleerd, grondig, belese
erupt' uitbars (vulkaan); uitbreek; ~**ion** uitbarsting; uitslag
es'calate (v) eskaleer, progressief toeneem
es'calator roltrap
escape' (n) ontsnapping; *a narrow* ~, 'n noue ontkoming; (v) ontsnap; ontkom
escarp'ment platorand; skuinste
es'cort (n) geleide, vrygeleide
escort' (v) begelei, vergesel, wegbring
espe'cial besonder; ~**ly** veral, vernaamlik
espiona'ge spioenasie, bespieding; *indus= trial* ~, nywerheidspioenasie
esplanade' (gras)plein, esplanade, wandel= baan
es'say (n) (-s) opstel, verhandeling, essay; ~**ist** essayis
ess'ence wese, essensie; grondbestanddeel
essen'tial (a) wesenlik, essensieel
essen'tially hoofsaaklik, in hoofsaak/wese
estab'lish vasstel; oprig, stig, vestig; ~**ed** gevestig, opgerig; ~**ment** saak, handels= huis
estate' besitting(s), eiendom; landgoed; boedel; ~ *duty*, boedelbelasting; *personal* ~, roerende goed; *real* ~, vaste eiendom
esteem' (n) agting; waardering; hoogagting; (v) ag, hoogag, skat; ~**ed'** geag, gesien
es'timate (n) (be)raming, skatting, waarde= ring; (v) raam, skat, waardeer, begroot, benader; *an* ~**d** *R5 million*, 'n geraamde R5 miljoen; *he* ~**s** *the cost at*, hy raam die koste op
estrange' vervreem, ontvreem
es'tuary (..ries) riviermond, monding
et cet'era ensovoort (ens.)
etch (-es) ets; ~**er** etser; ~**ing** ets
etern'al (a) ewig, ewigdurend
etern'ity ewigheid
eth'anol etanol, etielalkohol
eth'er eter; lugruim
eth'ics sedeleer, sedekunde, etiek; *code of* ~, gedragskode
eth'nic volkekunde, etnies; ~ *language*, Bantoetaal, etniese taal
e'tiquette etiket, wellewendheidsvorme
etymol'ogy woordafleiding, etimologie
eucalyp'tus (..ti) bloekom(boom)
euph'emism eufemisme, versagting

Eu'rope Europa

Europe'an (n) Europeaan, Europeër; (a) Europees

euthanas'ia genadedood, eutanasie

evac'uate ontruim, verlaat; ~ *the building,* die gebou ontruim; ~ *the inhabitants,* die inwoners na veiligheid bring

evade' ontgaan; ontwyk; ontduik

evaluat'ion evaluering, waardebepaling

evan'gel: ~ist evangelis; ~isa'tion evangelisasie

evap'orate uitwasem; verdamp, vervlieg

evas'ive ontwykend, ontduikend; vaag

eve aand; vooraand; *Christmas E~,* Oukersaand; *New Year's E~,* Oujaarsaand; *on the ~ of,* aan die vooraand van

e'ven¹ (v) gelykmaak; gelykstel; (a, adv) glad, effe, egalig, reëlmatig; *get ~ with,* iem. uitbetaal; *odd and ~,* gelyk en ongelyk; ~-tempered gelykmoedig

e'ven² (adv) selfs, ook, eweneens; ~ *if,* al was; *not ~,* nie eers/eens nie; ~ *now,* selfs nou

eve'ning aand

event' gebeurtenis, voorval; (pl) gebeure; byeenkoms; *in the ~ of,* in geval van

even'tual eventueel, moontlik, gebeurlik

even'tually ten slotte; uiteindelik

ev'er ooit; steeds, altyd; *for ~,* ewig; *thank you ~ so much,* hartlike dank; baie, baie dankie; ~ *since,* sedertdien; ~green immergroen; ~*green trees,* immergroenbome; ~last'ing ewigdurend; ~last'ings sewejaartjies; ~more vir altyd, ewig, altyd weer

ev'ery elke, ieder, alle; ~ *other day,* al om die ander dag; ~ *person who,* elkeen/ iedereen wat; ~body elkeen, iedereen; ~day daagliks; alledaags; ~one elkeen, iedereen, almal, algar; ~thing alles; ~where oral(s)

ev'idence (n) bewys, getuie; getuienis; *give ~,* getuienis aflê

ev'ident duidelik, klaarblyklik; ~ly blykbaar

ev'il (n) kwaad, euwel; (a) kwaad, sleg, sondig; ~doer boosdoener

evolu'tion ontwikkeling, evolusie

ewe ooi; ~ lamb ooilam

ex- gewese, oud~; ~pupil oudleerling

exact'¹ (v) afdwing, afpers, vorder, eis

exact'² (a) noukeurig, juis, presies, eksak

exa'ggerate oordryf, vergroot; ~d oordrewe

examina'tion eksamen, ondersoek; *sit for an ~,* eksamen doen; ~ paper eksamenvraestel

exam'ine ondersoek, eksamineer, ondervra; uitvra; verhoor; ~e' eksaminandus; geëksamineerde; ~r eksaminator

exam'ple voorbeeld; monster, proef; eksemplaar; *for ~,* byvoorbeeld; *make an ~ of,* as voorbeeld laat dien

exaspera'tion gramskap; terging; verbittering; *in ~,* tot frustrasie gedryf

excava'tion uitgrawing, opgrawing

exceed' oortref; oorskry; *losses ~ revenue,* verliese oorskry inkomste; ~ing(ly) buitengewoon, uitermate, bomatig

excel' (-led, -led) oortref, uitmunt; ~ *in tennis,* in tennis uitmunt

ex'cellence voortreflikheid, uitmuntendheid

ex'cellency (..cies) eksellensie

ex'cellent uitstekend, voortreflik, uitmuntend, puik¹

except' (v) uitsonder, uitsluit; (prep) uitgesonder(d), behalwe

excep'tion uitsondering; *take ~ to,* aanstoot neem aan; *with the ~ of,* uitgesonder(d); ~al buitengewoon, besonder, uitsonderlik

excess' (-es) oordaad, oormaat; ~ive oormatig, buitensporig

exchange' (n) wisselkoers, valuta; telefoonsentrale; *bill of ~,* (geld)wissel; ~ control valutabeheer; (v) wissel; ruil; ~ rate wisselkoers; ~ student (uit)ruilstudent

excite' aanspoor; opwind; ~d opgewonde; ~ment opwinding; opgewondenheid

excit'ing opwindend, spannend

exclama'tion uitroep, skree(u); ~ mark uitroepteken

exclude' uitsluit, uitsonder, buitesluit

exclus'ive uitsluitend, eksklusief; deftig, kieskeurig; ~ *of,* met uitsluiting van; ~ *residential area,* spog(woon)buurt; ~ *suburb,* deftige voorstad

excru'ciating martelend, folterend (pyn)

excur'sion uitstappie, ekskursie; uitweiding; ~ ticket ekskursiekaartjie

excuse' (n) verontskuldiging, verskoning,, ekskuus; (v) verontskuldig, verskoon, ekskuseer; *beg to be ~d*, vra om verskoon te word; ~ *me!* ekskuus! pardon!

ex'ecute uitvoer, voltrek; verrig, vervul; teregstel, ophang, onthoof, fusilleer

execu'tion uitvoering; voltrekking (doodstraf); teregstelling, onthoofding; beslaglegging; *sell under ~*, eksekusieverkoping; **~er** skerpregter, laksman, beul

exec'utive (n) bestuurshoof, bestuursleier; bedryfsleier; (uitvoerende) bestuur; **chief ~**, hoofbestuursleier; (a) uitvoerend; **E~ Committee** Uitvoerende Komitee; dagbestuur; **~ director** uitvoerende direkteur; **~ suite** bestuurstel

exec'utor eksekuteur; uitvoerder

exem'plar voorbeeld; toonbeeld; **~y** voorbeeldig, navolgenswaardig

exempt' (v) vrystel, ontslaan; ~ *from a subject*, van 'n vak vrystel; (a) vrygestel, uitgesonderd; **~ion** vrystelling

ex'ercise (n) oefening; (v) oefen, dril; **~book** oefenskrif, skryfboek, skrif

exert' aanwend; inspan; beywer; ~ *influence*, invloed uitoefen; ~ *oneself*, jou inspan; **~ion** inspanning

exhale' uitasem, uitdamp

exhaust'[1] (n) uitlaatpyp; knaldemper

exhaust'[2] (v) uitput, afmat, leegmaak; **~ed** gedaan, kapot, uitgeput; **~ion** uitputting, afmatting; *heat ~ion*, hitte-uitputting; **~ive** volledig, grondig

exhib'it (n) insending; uitstalling; (v) vertoon, ten toon stel, skou; uitstal; ~ *one's cattle*, jou beeste skou

exhibi'tion vertoning; tentoonstelling, skou

exhil'arating opwekkend, verfrissend

exhuma'tion opgrawing

ex'ile (n) verbanning, ballingskap; banneling; balling; (v) verban

exist' bestaan, lewe

exist'ence bestaan, lewe; aansyn, wese

exist'ing bestaande, aanwesig

ex'it (n) deur, uitgang; (v) (gaan) af (toneel); ~ **interview** vertrekgesprek

ex'odus uittog, eksodus

exorb'itant buitensporig, erg, verregaande

exot'ic uitheems, vreemd, eksoties

expand' uitsprei; uitbrei; uitsit; swel

expan'sion uitsetting; uitbreiding; swelling, ontwikkeling; toename; **~ism** ekspansionisme, uitbreidingsdrang; ~ **joint** uitsitvoeg

expat'riate (n) banneling; uitgewekene

expect' verwag; veronderstel, vermoed; **~ance, ~ancy** verwagting, hoop; *life ~ancy*, lewensverwagting; **~ant** verwagtend

expecta'tion verwagting; vooruitsig; afwagting; *contrary to ~s*, teen die verwagting in

exped'ient (n) hulpmiddel, noodhulp; (a) geskik, dienstig

ex'pedite (v) bespoedig; afstuur; verhaas

expedi'tion veldtog, ekspedisie

expel' (-led, -led) verdryf, uitsit, verban

expend' bestee, verkwis; **~able** misbaar, afskryfbaar

expen'diture uitgawe, onkoste, besteding

expense' koste, onkoste; *incidental ~s*, los/ onvoorsiene uitgawes

expen'sive duur, kosbaar; verkwistend

exper'ience (n) ondervinding, ervaring; (v) ondervind, ervaar

expe'riment (n) proefneming, eksperiment; (v) beproef, eksperimenteer

experimen'tal proefondervindelik, eksperimenteel; ~ *farm*, proefplaas

ex'pert[1] (n) deskundige, vakkundige, ekspert; **~ise** (sake)vernuf, kundigheid

ex'pert[2] (a) bedrewe, deskundig, vakkundig

expir'e uitasem, sterf; verval, verloop, verstryk, eindig; *expiry date,* verstrykdatum

explain' uitlê, verklaar, verduidelik

explana'tion uitleg(ging), verklaring, verduideliking

expli'cit uitdruklik, duidelik, stellig

explode' ontplof, bars, spring; laat ontplof

exploit' (v) uitbuit; ontgin, bewerk; ~ *the poor*, die armes uitbuit

explora'tion ondersoeking, navorsing, eksplorasie, nasporing; ontdekking

explore' ondersoek, navors, naspoor; **~r** ontdekkingsreisiger; ondersoeker, navorser

explo'sion ontploffing, uitbarsting, slag, knal; ~ *shot* plofhou (gholf)

explos'ive (n) plofstof; (pl) plofstof, springstowwe; (a) ontploffend, (ont)plofbaar; opvlieënd; ~ **cotton** skietkatoen; **~s expert** plofstofdeskundige

expon'ent eksponent, verklaarder

ex'port[1] (n) uitvoer; uitvoerartikels

export'[2] (v) uitvoer, eksporteer

ex'port: ~ duty (..ties) uitvoerreg; ~er uitvoerder; ~ trade uitvoerhandel
expose' ontbloot, blootstel; openbaar
expo'sure blootstelling; gevaar
express' (v) uitdruk; uit; betuig; (a) spoed=, opsetlik, uitdruklik; ~ion uitdrukking, gesegde; vorm; *beyond ~ion*, onbeskryflik; ~ive uitdruklik, betekenisvol; veelseggend; ~ *mail/post* spoedpos; ~ way snelpad, snelweg
expro'priate onteien
expul'sion uitsetting; verdrywing
ex'quisite (a) keurig, voortreflik; wondermooi
extend' uitstrek; uitbrei; verleng
exten'sion uitbreiding; verlenging; bylyn (telefoon), verlengstuk; *Eloff Street E~*, Eloffstraatverlenging; *Parkwood E~*, Parkwood-uitbreiding; ~ *cord* verlengkoord; ~ **ladder** skuifleer; ~ **officer** voorlig(tings)beampte, veldbeampte
exten'sive uitgestrek, uitgebrei(d)
extent' uitgestrektheid, omvang; *to the ~ of*, tot die bedrag/omvang van; *to some ~*, in sekere mate
exten'uating versagtend; ~ *circumstances*, versagtende omstandighede
exter'ior (n) uiterlik, voorkome; buitekant; (a) uitwendig; uiterlik; buite=
exterm'inate uitroei, verdelg
extern'al (n) uiterlike; (pl) uiterlikhede; bykomstighede; (a) uitwendig, ekstern, buite=; ~ *studies*, eksterne studie
extinct' dood; uitgeblus; uitgesterf; uitgedoof, uitgewerk (vulkaan); afgeskaf

exting'uish doodblaas, uitdoof, blus; ~er blusser, domper
extol' (-led, -led) prys, verhef, loof
extort' afpers, afdwing, afdreig; ~ion afpersing; uitsuiging
ex'tra (n) toegif, ekstratjie; *no ~s*, alles inbegrepe; (a) buitengewoon, ekstra; ~curricular buitekurrikulêr
ex'tract (n) uittreksel; ekstrak; aftreksel
extract' (v) uittrek; 'n uittreksel maak; ~ion afkoms, afstamming
extradi'tion uitlewering; ~ *order* uitlewerbevel
extramur'al buitemuurs
extraor'dinary buitengewoon, vreemd, sonderling; uitstekend
extrasens'ory: ~ *perception* buitesintuiglike waarneming
extrav'agance buitensporigheid; verkwisting, oordaad
extrav'agant buitensporig, oordrewe; onmatig, verkwistend, spandabel
extravagan'za musikale kykspel
extre'me (n) uiterste; ~ly uiters, uitermate
extre'mist ekstremis
exult' juig, jubel, opgetoë wees
eye (n) oog; maas (net); *turn the blind ~*, oogluikend toelaat; *see ~ to ~ with*, dit volkome eens wees met; (v) dophou, bekyk, beskou, gadeslaan; ~brow winkbrou; ~hole loerkyker(tjie) (in deur); ~lash (-es) ooghaar, wimper; ~lid ooglid; ~ opener openbaring; ~sore onooglik(heid), ~wash oogwater; kaf; ~witness (-es) ooggetuie

F

fa'ble (n) fabel, sprokie; verdigsel
fab'ric bou; maaksel, fabrikaat, stof; ~ a'tion verdigsel, versinsel
fab'ulous fabelagtig
facade' (voor)gewel, fasade
face (n) gesig, gelaat; voorkome; ~ *the facts*, feite onder oë sien; ~ *the music*, die gevolge dra; *save one's ~*, die skyn red; ~ *to ~*, onder vier oë; ~brick siersteen; ~ cream gesigsroom, pommade; ~lift ontrimpeling, gesig(s)kuur; verjongingskuur
fa'cet vlak, faset

face value nominale waarde, sigwaarde
fa'cial aangesigs=; gelaats=; gesig(s)=; ~ tissue gesigsnesie
facil'itate vergemaklik, (aan)help, verlig; ~ *matters*, sake vergemaklik
facil'ity (pl) (..ties) geriewe, fasiliteite
fa'cing (n) voorkant; (adv) teenoor
facsim'ile reproduksie, faksimilee
fact feit; daad; werklikheid; *in ~*, inderdaad; ~-*finding mission*, feitesending
fac'tion party, partyskap; faksie, kliek, (politieke) groep; ~ fight stamgeveg
fac'tor faktor, agent; oorsaak

fac'tory (..ries) fabriek; ~ **effluent** (fabrieke se) afwater; ~ **overheads** fabrieksbokoste

fac'ulty (..ties) vermoë, bekwaamheid, talent; fakulteit (van 'n universiteit)

fad gier, idee, stokperdjie

fade verwelk; verlep; kwyn, verflou

fag (n) groentjie; werkesel

fail (n) fout, feil; *without ~*, seker; (v) misluk; sak, dop, druip (eksamen)

fail'ing (n) fout, gemis; tekortkoming

fail'ure mislukking; gebrek; druipeling (in eksamen); ~ *rate*, druipsyfer

faint (n) floute; (v) flou val, verwelk; (a) swak, onduidelik; dof; *grow ~*, dof word; flou word; ~**-hearted** halfhartig

fair[1] (n) jaarmark, kermis

fair[2] (a) fraai, skoon; blond, lig; *by ~ means or foul*, tot/teen elke prys; *the ~(er) sex*, die skone geslag; ~**play** (n) eerlike spel, skoon spel; (a) regverdig, reg, eerlik; ~**way** (-s) skoonveld (gholf)

fair'y (fairies) fee; ~**land** towerland, feëland, feëryk; ~ **tale** sprokie

faith (n) geloof, vertroue; *keep ~*, woord hou; (interj) regtig, sowaar; ~**ful** getrou; ~ **healer** geloofsgeneser

fake (n) vervalsing; (a) vals; (v) vervals, namaak

fakir fakir, bedelmonnik (Indies)

fal'con valk; ~**er** valkenier

fall (n) val; daling; ondergang; skuinste; (v) (fell, fallen) val, daal, sink; ~ *due*, verval; ~ *in love*, verlief raak; ~ *through*, in duie val; deur die mat val

fall'acy (..cies) dwaalbegrip, wanopvatting

fall'ible feilbaar

fall'-out uitval; kern-as (atoombom)

fall'ow (n) braakland; (v) braak; (a) braak

false vals, skynheilig; ~**hood** valsheid; leuen, bedrog

fal'sify (..fied, ..fied) vervals, namaak

fal'ter hakkel, stamel; strompel, struikel

fame roem, faam, vermaardheid

famil'iar (a) vertroulik, eie, vrypostig; ~ *surroundings*, bekende/vertroude omgewing; ~ *with the facts*, vertroud met die feite

famil'iarise vertroud maak (met)

fam'ily (..lies) familie, gesin; geslag; stam; *be in the ~ way*, in geseënde omstandighede wees; ~ **circle** familiekring; ~

planning gesinsbeplanning; ~ **tree** stamboom

Fam'ily Day Gesinsdag

fam'ine hongersnood; gebrek

fam'ish verhonger; ~**ed** uitgehonger

fam'ous beroemd, vermaard

fan[1] (n) bewonderaar, aanhanger; entoesias; ~ **mail** bewonderaarsbriewe, dweeppos

fan[2] (n) waaier; wan; (v) (-ned, -ned) aanwakker

fanat'ic (n) dweper, fanatikus; (a) dweepsiek; ~**al** dweepsiek, fanatiek

fan'cy (n) (..cies) verbeelding, inbeelding, gril, nuk, gier; fantasie; denkbeeld; *catch the ~ of*, in die smaak val van; *take a ~ to*, aangetrokke voel tot, hou van; (v) (..cied, ..cied) verbeel, baie hou van; (interj) dink! ~ **dress** (-es) fantasiekostuum; ~**dress ball** kostuumbal, maskerbal; ~ **goods** snuisterye; fantasiegoed

fang slagtand; giftand

fan: ~**palm** waaierpalm; ~**tail** (pigeon) waaierstert, pronkduif

fantas'tic ingebeeld, grillig, fantasties

fan'tasy inbeelding; fantasie; verbeeldingskrag; gril, inval

far (n): *by ~*, verreweg; (a) ver, afgeleë, baie; (adv) baie, veel; ver, ver(re)weg; *in so ~ as*, vir sover, in soverre

farce (n) grap, klug

fare (n) reisgeld, passasiersgeld; kos

farewell' vaarwel, afskeid; ~ **dinner** afskeid(s)dinee; ~**gift/present** afskeid(s)geskenk

farm (n) plaas, boerdery; (v) boer; ~ *out*, uitbestee; ~**er** boer, landbouer

farm: ~**stall** plaaskiosk, plaasstalletjie

far-reaching verreikend, groot

far'sighted versiend(e)

farth'er (a) verder; (adv) verder

fas'cinating boeiend, bekoorlik

fa'shion (n) fatsoen; maaksel; mode; drag; *out of ~*, uit die mode; (v) fatsoeneer, vorm; ~**able** fatsoenlik; modies, modieus; ~ **designer** mode-ontwerper; ~ **parade** modeskou, modeparade; ~ **show** modeskou

fast[1] (n) vas; (v) vas

fast[2] (a, adv) vinnig; vas, standvastig, sterk; *the clock is too ~*, die klok loop voor; ~ *colour*, vaste kleur; vaskleur-; ~ *foods*, kitskos

fas'ten vasmaak; bevestig
fast'ing vas
fat (n, a) vet; (v) (-ted, -ted) vet maak
fat'al noodlottig, dodelik; ~ *accident,*
noodlottige ongeluk
fatal'ity ongeval; rampspoed; (..ties) sterf=
gevalle, dooies
fate noodlot; lot, bestemming
fat'head domkop, klipkop
fa'ther (n) vader; (v) verwek; ~-in-law
(fathers-in-law) skoonvader; ~land va=
derland; ~ly vaderlik
fath'om (n) vaam; (v) omvat, deurgrond;
I can't ~ it, ek kan dit nie kleinkry nie
fatigue' (n) moegheid, vermoeienis, afmat=
ting; *metal ~,* metaalverswakking
fat: ~ten vet maak; ~ty (n) vetsak, diksak;
potjierol (kind); (a) vetterig
fault fout, gebrek; skuld; *at ~,* verkeerd,
skuldig; ~finder foutvinder, vitter; ~less
onberispelik; foutloos; ~y gebrekkig,
foutief, defek
faun sater, bosgod, faun
faun'a (-e) dierewêreld, fauna
fav'our (n) guns; *by ~ of,* deur (vriende=
like) tussenkoms/bemiddeling van; *curry
~,* witvoetjie soek; *do one a ~,* iem. 'n
guns bewys; *in ~ of,* ten gunste van; (v)
begunstig; ~able gunstig; welwillend;
~ite (n) gunsteling; liefling; kansperd; (a)
lieflings=, geliefkoosde; *my ~ite poet,* my
gunstelingdigter; *my ~ite dog,* my lief=
lingshond; ~itism voortrekkery
fear (n) vrees, angs; *for ~ of,* uit vrees vir;
(v) bang wees, vrees; ~less onbevrees,
onverskrokke
feasibil'ity uitvoerbaarheid, lonendheid; ~
study gangbaarheidstudie, uitvoerbaar=
heidstudie, doenlikheidstudie
feast (n) fees, feesmaal; (v) feesvier, ont=
haal; geniet; fuif
feat kordaatstuk, prestasie; wapenfeit
feath'er (n) veer; *birds of a ~,* voëls van
eenderse vere; *a ~ in one's cap,* 'n pluim=
pie; ~-brained ylhoofdig; dom; ~weight
veergewig
fea'ture (n) gelaatstrek; trek; hooftrek;
kenmerk; (pl) gelaatstrekke; (v) uitbeeld;
~ programme glansprogram; hoorbeeld
(radio)
Feb'ruary Februarie
fed gevoed; ~ *up,* vies

fed'eral federaal
federa'tion verbond, federasie
fee (n) loon, geld; vergoeding; honorarium;
(v) betaal, beloon; *medical ~s,* dokters=
gelde, mediese koste
fee'ble swak, kleinmoedig, sleg; ~-minded,
swaksinnig; ~ness swakheid
feed (n) voer, kos; (v) (fed, fed) voer, voed;
insleutel (komper); ~back terugvoer(ing),
terugkoppeling; ~er pypkan, voeder; ~er
service toevoerdiens; ~ing bottle pypkan;
~lot voerkraal
feel (n) gevoel; aanvoeling; (v) (felt, felt)
voel; bevoel; ~er voelhoring, voelspriet;
~ing (n) gevoel, gedagte; opinie; (a) ge=
voelig; gevoelvol
feint (n) voorwendsel; (v) liemaak
felicita'tion gelukwensing
fel'ine kat=, katagtig
fell (v) laat val; neerval; platslaan; *see also*
fall (v)
fell'ing kap
fell'ow maat, kêrel, ou; lid(maat); genoot
(van 'n vereniging); *good/jolly ~,* 'n gawe
kêrel; ~-creature medemens; ~ship
kameraadskap, deelgenootskap; lidmaat=
skap
fel'ony (..nies) misdaad, misdryf
felt (n) vilt; (a) vilt=; ~ hat vilthoed
fem'ale (n) vroumens, vrou; wyfie; (a)
vroue=; vroulik; wyfie=; ~ doctor dok=
teres; ~ suffrage vrouestemreg
fem'inine vroulik; verwyf
fem'inist feminis
fem power vrouekrag
fence (n) heining, draad; muur; *sit on the
~,* die kat uit die boom kyk; (v) omhein;
~ *in (round, about)* inkamp, toespan
fen'cing skermkuns; ~ school skermskool
fend afweer, wegkeer; ~ *for,* sorg vir; ~er
modderskerm
fenn'el vinkel
ferment' (v) gis, fermenteer; ~a'tion gis=
ting, fermentasie
fern varing
fero'cious wild, wreed, woes
fer'rous yster=, ysterhoudend
fer'ret (n) fret (dier); snuffelaar
fer'ry (n) (ferries) veer, pont; (v) (ferried,
ferried) oorsit, oorvaar; ~boat veerboot
fert'ile vrugbaar
fert'ilise bemes; ~r kunsmis, misstof

ferv'ent vurig, warm; ywerig

fes'ter (n) sweer, verswering; (v) etter

fes'tival (n) fees, feesdag; (a) fees=, feeste= lik; *Republic* ~, Republiekfees

fes'tive feestelik, vrolik; ~ **season** feestyd/ feesgety

festiv'ity (..ties) feestelikheid, feesviering, vreugdefees, makietie

fetch (v) (gaan) haal, bring, te voorskyn bring

fête fees, kermis

feud vete, twis, rusie

feud'al leen=, feodaal; ~ **system** leenstelsel

fev'er koors; onrus; *scarlet* ~, skarlaken= koors; ~ish koorsig; koorsagtig; ~ **tree** koorsboom

few party; 'n paar; min; weinig; ~ *and far between,* dun/yl gesaai; seldsaam

fian'ce verloofde, aanstaande (manlik); ~e verloofde, aanstaande (vroulik)

fias'co (-s) mislukking, fiasko

fib (n) leuen(tjie), kluitjie; *tell* ~s, jok

fi'bre vesel; ~glass veselglas

fic'kle wispelturig, veranderlik

fiction verdigting/verdigsel; romankuns, fiksie; *science* ~, wetenskapfiksie

fid'dle (n) viool; *as fit as a* ~, so reg soos 'n roer; (v) vermors (tyd); ~ *with,* peuter aan; ~ **stick** strykstok; ~sticks! gekheid! onsin!

fidel'ity getrouheid, eerlikheid; ~ **guaran= tee** getrouheidswaarborg; **high** ~, hoë= trou, louterklank; ~ **insurance** getrou= heidsdekking

fidg'et (v) woel, vroetel; ~y rusteloos, woelig

field (n) veld, vlakte; speelveld; gebied; (v) veldwerk doen (krieket); ~ **event** veld= nommer; ~ **gun** veldgeskut, veldstuk; F~ **Marshal** veldmaarskalk

fiend bose gees, demon, besetene; ~ish ge= meen, demonies, hels

fierce wild, geweldig, woes, fel, skerp, ver= bete; verwoed

fier'y vurig; gloeiend; driftig, opvlieënd

fifteen' vyftien; ~th' vyftiende

fifth vyfde; ~ **column** vyfde kolonne; ~ly ten vyfde, in die vyfde plek, vyfdens

fif'tieth vyftigste

fif'ty (fifties) vyftig; ~-~, gelykop; half-om-half

fig vy; vyeboom; *I don't care a* ~, ek gee geen flenter om nie

fight (n) geveg, twis, rusie; (v) (**fought, fought**) veg, twis, baklei; ~er bakleier, vegter; ~er **plane** vegvliegtuig, straal= jagter

fig'ment verdigsel, versinsel; ~ *of the imagination,* hersenskim

fig'urative figuurlik, sinnebeeldig

fig'ure (n) gedaante; gestalte, vorm; figuur; syfer; *at a low* ~, teen 'n lae prys; ~ *of speech,* stylfiguur; (v) vorm, afbeeld; figure maak; syfer; ~ *out,* bereken; prakseer; uitreken; ~**head** (boeg)beeld; strooipop, skynhoof

file[1] (n) vyl; (v) vyl

file[2] (n) dossier; lêer; gelid; ry; *stand in* ~, toustaan; (v) inryg, liasseer; ~ *off,* af= marsjeer

fil'ibuster (n) vrybuiter, boekanier, kaper

fil'ing liassering; ~ **cabinet** liasseerkabinet, lêerkas; liaskabinet

fill (v) vul; versadig; beklee (pos); stop (tand); ~ *in,* invul; ~ *up,* aanvul; invul; volgooi; voltap (petrol); ~er vuller(tjie)

fill'et moot (vis); filet (beeshaas); (v) van die been sny

fill'ing aanvulling; vulsel, stopsel (tand); ~ **station** vulstasie, petrolstasie

fill'y (fillies) merrievul

film (n) velletjie, vlies; film, rolprent; (v) verfilm; ~ **library** filmoteek

fil'ter (n) filter, suiweraar; (v) filtreer

filth vuilgoed, vuilis, vullis, vuilheid; ~y vuil, vieslik, morsig

fin vin; ~ **diving** vinduik, swemduik

fin'al (n) eindeksamen; eindwedstryd; eind= ronde, finaal; (a) finaal, laaste; beslissend

fin'ally uiteindelik, ten slotte

finance', **fin'ance** (n) inkoms(te); finan= sies, geldmiddele; geldwese; (v) finansier; ~ **committee** finanskomitee

finan'cial geldelik, finansieel; ~ **year** boek= jaar, geldjaar; **annual** ~ **statements** fi= nansiële jaarstate

finch (-es) vink

find (n) vonds (mv **vondste**); ontdekking; (v) (**found, found**) vind, kry, aantref; ~ *fault with,* afkeur; ~ *one's feet,* regkom; ~ *guilty,* skuldig bevind

fine[1] (n) (geld)boete; (v) beboet

fine² (a) mooi, fyn, fraai, keurig; suiwer; helder; *the ~ arts,* die skone kunste

fing'er (n) vinger; *little ~,* pinkie; *have a ~ in the pie,* in die saak betrokke wees; *have at one's ~ tips (ends),* op jou duim ken; (v) bevoel, betas; **~print** vingerafdruk; **~tip** vingertop

fin'ical, fin'icky, fin'iking puntene(u)rig

fin'ish (n) end, voltooiing; afwerking; wenstreep (sport); (v) klaarmaak, eindig; **~ed** klaar, gereed; **~ing** (n) afwerking; **~ing school** afrond(ing)skool; **~ line** wenstreep

fiord' fjord

fire (n) brand; vuur, vlam; *the fat is in the ~,* die poppe is aan die dans; (v) aansteek, skiet; (summier) afdank; besiel; **~ alarm** brandalarm; **~arm** vuurwapen; **~ brigade** brandweer; **~ escape** brandtrap; **~ extinguisher** brandblusser; **~ fighter** brandweerman; brandslaner; **~ fighting** brandbestryding; **~fly** (..flies) vuurvlieg, gloeiwurm; **~hose** brandslang; **~ insurance** brandassuransie, brandversekering; **~man** (..men) stoker; brandweerman; **~ station** brandweerstasie; **~works** vuurwerk

fi'ring skietery, losbranding; ontsteking; **~ squad** vuurpeloton

firm¹ (n) firma; onderneming, organisasie

firm² (a, adv) standvastig, stewig, sterk, vas; *a ~ offer,* 'n vaste aanbod; **~ly** vas, stewig

firm'ament uitspansel, firmament

first (n) die eerste; begin; *from ~ to last,* van begin tot end; (a) eerste, vernaamste; *in the ~ place,* in die eerste plek, in eerste instansie; (adv) eerste, eerstens, eers; **~ come, ~ served,** eerste gesien eerste bedien; **~ aid** noodhulp, eerstehulp; **~-class** eersteklas, eersterangs, eerstegraads, uitstekend; **~ floor** eerste vloer/verdieping/vlak; **~ name** voornaam; **~-rate** eersteklas, eersterangs

fir'tree den(neboom)

fish (n) (-es, fish) vis; *~ and chips,* vis en skyfies/flenters; *neither ~ nor flesh (nor good red herring),* vis nòg vlees; (v) visvang; uitvis

fish: *~* **bait** aas; **~bone** graat; **~erman** (..men) visser; visterman

fis'hing (a) vissers=, vis=; **~ hook** (vis)hoek; **~ rod** visstok; **~ tackle** hengelgerei, visgereedskap

fish: *~* **paste** vissmeer; **~y** visagtig; visryk; verdag

fist (n) vuis; handskrif

fist'icuffs vuisslanery, boksery

fit¹ (n) vlaag, aanval; nuk, gril; *go into ~s,* dit op sy senuwees kry

fit² (v) (-ted, -ted) pas; aanpas; *the cap ~s,* die skoen pas; *~ter and turner,* passer en draaier; (a) fiks, fris; *deem ~,* goedkeur; *think ~,* dit goeddink; **~ter** monteur; passer; **~ness** geskiktheid, fiksheid; **~ting** (n) pas; (pl) benodigdhede; toebehore, onderdele, bybehore; (a) passend, gepas

five vyf; **~-course meal** vyfgang-ete; **~-speed gearbox** vyfgangratkas

fix (n) verleentheid, moeilikheid; (v) vasmaak; verrig; beslis; *in a ~,* in 'n penarie; *~ up,* op tou sit; **~ed** seker; stewig; neergelê

fix'ture vaste uitrusting; bepaling (sport); (pl) wedstrydreeks, program

flabb'ergast verbluf, oorbluf, dronkslaan

flabb'y, fac'cid slap, pap(perig), week

flag¹ (n) vlag; *hoist the ~,* die vlag hys; *lower/strike the ~,* die vlag stryk

flag² (v) (-ged, -ged) verflou; verslap

flag'hoisting vlaghysing; **~ ceremony** vlaghysseremonie

flag'rant blakend; skaamteloos, verregaand, flagrant; berug; gloeiend

flag: **~ship** vlagskip; **~staff** vlagstok

flair aanleg, instink; (goeie) neus

flake (n) vlok; vonk; skilfer; snysel; laag; (v) afskilfer; afdop

flame (n) vlam; vuur, hartstog; *burst into ~,* aan (die) brand slaan; *fan the ~s,* die vuur aanwakker/aanblaas

flaming'o (-es) flamink

flank (n) sy, flank; lies

flann'el flanel; (pl) flannelbroek; flennieonderklere; **~ graph** flenniebord

flap (n) klap; slag; slip; flap; deksel; valdeurtjie, luik

flapp'er bakvissie; vlieëplak; stert, vin

flare (n) seinfakkel (mil.); flikkerlig; (v) flikker, skitter; vertoon; *~ up* opvlam; opstuif

flash (n) (-es) blits, flits; *in a ~,* in 'n kits; *a ~ in the pan,* 'n opflikkering; 'n misluk=

king; (v) skitter; blits, uitstraal; ~ *back,*
weerkaats; ~ *up,* opstuif; ~**back** terug=
flits; ~**light** flitslig; flikkerlig
flask fles, bottel; kruithoring
flat[1] (n) woonstel
flat[2] (n) vlakte; laagte; mol (musiek); (v)
(-ted, -ted) plat maak; (a) plat; vlak; pap
(band); verslaan (bier); ~ *beer,* verslaan=
de/verskaalde bier; *at a ~ rate,* teen 'n
vaste tarief; *sing ~,* vals sing; ~**footed**
platvoet=; ~ **iron** strykyster; ~**ly** ronduit,
stompweg; plat; ~**ten** plat slaan, plet
flatt'er vlei, pamperlang, flikflooi; ~**er**
vleier, witvoetjiesoeker; ~**y** (..ries) vlei=
ery, vleitaal
flav'our (n) smaak; geur; (v) kruie, geur;
~**ing essence** geursel
flaw (n) spleet; fout, gebrek; defek; vlek
flax vlas
flea (-s) vlooi; ~**market** vlooimark
fleck (n) vlek; sproet; stippie; (v) spikkel,
vlek; ~**ed** bont, gespikkeld
fledg'ling klein voëltjie; snuiter
flee (fled, fled) vlug; ontwyk; padgee
fleece (n) vlies; vag; skeersel; *golden ~,*
gulde vlies; (v) (af)skeer; pluk; uitbuit
fleet[1] (n) vloot; see-arm; ~ **owner** vloot=
eienaar (motorkarre)
fleet[2] (v) vervlieg; (a) vinnig; ~ *of foot,*
vinnig; vlugvoetig; ~**ing** verganklik, vlug=
tig
flesh (n) vlees (menslik); vleis (dierlik); (v)
gaam; *make one's ~ creep,* hoendervleis
laat kry; ~**ly** vleeslik, sinlik; ~ **wound**
vleiswond
flex (n) elektriese koord; (v) buig; ~**time,**
flexi-time skiktyd
flex'ible buigsaam, soepel, fleksiel, lenig,
elasties; handelbaar, plooibaar
fle'xion buiging, kromming; verbuiging
flick'er (n) geflikker; getril; (v) flikker, tril;
klap (vlerke); ~ **light** flikkerlig
flick knife springmes
flight[1] (n) vlug
flight[2] vlug (groep vliegtuie); loop, vaart;
swerm; *put to ~,* op loop jaag; ~ *of
stairs,* trap; ~ **plan/schedule** vlugplan/
vlugrooster; ~ **recorder** vlugopnemer,
dataregistreerder; ~ **steward** vlugkelner
flim'sy dun; flenterig; flou
flinch aarsel, terugdeins, weifel

fling (n) gooi; dans; *have one's ~,* die lewe
geniet; (v) **(flung, flung)** gooi, slinger,
smyt
flint vuurklip, vuursteen; vuurslag
flipp'ant ligsinnig, onbesonne
flirt (n) flerrie, vryerige meisie, flirt; (v)
koketteer, flankeer; ~ *with the girls,*
flankeer met die nooiens
flit (-ted, -ted) vlieg, fladder
float (n) vlot; dobber; sierwa (optog); (v)
dryf, dobber; floteer (lening); vlot maak
(skip); oprig (maatskappy); dobber; sweef
(betaalmiddel); *cash ~,* kontantvlot
(boekhou); ~ *a company,* 'n maatskappy
oprig/stig ~ *a loan,* 'n lening uit=
skryf/aangaan; ~ **gauge** vlotter
float'ing drywend, dryf=, vlottend; ~ **dock**
dryfdok; ~ **trophy** wisseltrofee
flock (n) trop, kudde; ~ *together,* saam=
stroom, saambondel
flog (-ged, -ged) klop, pak gee, slaan; ~
oneself, jouself moor; ~**ging** pak slae,
loesing
flood (n) vloed; oorstroming; sondvloed; (v)
oorstroom; versuip (vergasser); ~**gate**
sluis; ~ **disaster** vloedramp; ~**lights**
spreiligte
floor (n) vloer; verdieping; vlak; *second ~,*
tweede vloer/vlak; ~ **shift** (car) vloer=
kierie, kieriewisselaar
flop (n) plof, bons; misoes; (v) (-ped, -ped)
fladder; neerplof; klapwiek
flor'a (-e, -s) plantegroei, flora
flor'ist bloemis, blomkweker
floss dons; vlossy; *dental ~,* tandevlos
flot'sam wrakgoed, opdrifsel
floun'der (v) worstel, spartel, kleitrap
flour fynmeel, meelblom; ~ **bag** meelsak
flou'rish (n) (-es) bloei; prag; (v)
bloei, floreer; pronk; ~**ing** bloeiend,
welvarend, voorspoedig
flow (n) vloei; stroming; *ebb and ~,* eb en
vloed; (v) vloei, stroom
flow'er (n) blom; bloeisel; (v) blom, bloei;
~ **child** blomtjom; ~ **girl** strooimeisie;
blommeverkoopster; ~**ing peach** (-es)
sierperske; ~**y** blomryk, breedsprakig
flu griep, influensa
fluc'tuate weifel, sweef, skommel; wissel;
fluctuating prices, skommelende pryse
flue skoorsteenpyp; orrelpyp
flu'ent vloeiend; glad, vlot, pront

fluff dons, pluisie; **~y** donserig, donsagtig
flu'id (n) vloeistof; (a) vloeiend, vloeibaar
fluke (n) gelukskoot, gelukslag; meevaller; *the perfect* **~**, die volmaakte gelukhou, putjie-in-een/fortuinhou (gholf)
fluores'cent light buislig
flu'rry (n) (..rries) windvlaag; opwinding
flush (v) deurspoel; aanvuur; (a) blosend; volop (geld); **~ed with wine,** deur wyn verhit
flute fluit; groef; fluitblaser; **~d** gegroef
flut'ist fluitspeler
flutt'er (n) gefladder, gejaagdheid; *have a* **~**, spekuleer; (v) fladder; opja; in die war bring
flux (n) stroming, saamvloeiing; *state of* **~**, vloeibare toestand; (v) stroom
fly[1] (n) (flies) vlieg; *a* **~** *in the ointment,* 'n vlieg in die salf
fly[2] (n) (flies) vliegwiel; onrus (oorlosie); gulp (broek); (v) (**flew, flown**) vlieg, laat waai; *let* **~** *at,* losbrand op; **~** *into a passion,* woedend word
fly[3] (a) geslepe; oulik, slim, gevat, oorlams
fly'half (..halves) losskakel (rugby)
fly'ing (a) vlieënd; **~ saucer** vlieënde piering; **~ squad** blitspatrollie
fly'leaf (..leaves) skutblad
fly'-over oorbrug
fly: **~swatter** vlieëklap; **~trap** vlieëvanger
fly'wheel vliegwiel
foal (n, v) vul
foam (n, v) skuim; **~ rubber** skuimrubber, sponsrubber
foc'al fokaal; **~ point** brandpunt, fokus
foc'us (n) (..ci, -es) brandpunt; fokus; (v) saamtrek, konsentreer, instel, fokus
fodd'er voer
foe (-s) vyand
foet'us ongebore vrug, fetus
fog (n) mis, newel; **~gy** mistig, newelig; dof, onduidelik; **~ horn** mishoring; **~ patch** miskol
foil[1] (n) bladmetaal, bladgoud; foelie
foil[2] (v) verydel, laat skipbreuk ly; teleurstel
foist: **~** *something (up)on one,* lem. iets aansmeer; iets op iem. afskuiwe
fold[1] (n) trop; kudde; kraal; (v) opsluit
fold[2] (n) vou; plooi; (v) vou; **~er** voublad; omslag; **~ing chair** voustoel; **~ing doors** voudeur

fol'iage lommer, loof, blare
fol'io (-s) bladsy; folio; foliant (boek)
folk mense; *little* **~s,** die kleinspan; *old* **~s,** ou mense; **~ dances** volksdanse; volkspele; **~lore** volksoorlewering, volkskunde, folklore; **~ medicine** boereraat; **~ song** volksliedjie; **~ tale** sprokie
foll'ow volg, navolg; **~ suit,** kleur beken; **~ up,** voortsit; opvolg; **~er** navolger, volgeling; **~ing** (n) aanhang; gevolg; (a) volgende, onderstaande; **~-on** opvolg; **~-up** opvolg(brief)
foll'y (**follies**) dwaasheid, sonde, gekheid
fond versot, verlief, gek na; dwaas
fon'dle liefkoos, streel, vertroetel
fond'ly liefkosend; liefhebbend; vurig
font doopbak(kie), doopvont
food kos, voedsel; **~** *for thought,* stof tot nadenke; pitkos; **~ poisoning** voedselvergiftiging; **~stuffs** eetgoed, eetware
fool (n) dwaas, gek; domkop, swaap; *make a* **~** *of,* vir die gek hou; **~s'** *paradise,* gekkeparadys; (v) fop, flous; vir die gek hou, liemaak; **~hardy** roekeloos, domastrant, onbesonne; **~ishness** dwaasheid, domheid, onnoselheid
foot (n) (**feet**) voet; *put one's* **~** *into it,* 'n flater begaan; (v) **~** *the bill,* opdok; **~ball** voetbal; **~ing** vastrapplek; verstandhouding; **~-and-mouth disease** beken-klouseer; **~note** voetnoot, aantekening; **~path** sypaadjie; **~print** spoor; **~slog** (**-ged, -ged**) voetslaan; **~wear** skoene, skoeisel
fop modegek, fat, ydeltuit
for (prep) vir, na, om, tot, teen; *as* **~**, wat betref; **~** *all I care,* sover dit my aangaan; *go* **~** *a walk,* 'n ent gaan loop; **~** *goodness sake,* in hemelsnaam **~** *all I know,* sover ek weet; *long* **~**, verlang na; *once* **~** *all,* eens vir altyd; **~** *my part,* wat my betref; **~** *my sake,* vir/om my ontwil; **~** *sale,* te koop; (conj) want, nieteenstaande
forbid' (**forbad or forbade, forbidden**) verbied, belet, verhinder; *Heaven* **~**, mag die Here dit verhoed; **~den** ongeoorloof, verbode
force (n) krag, mag, geweld; (pl) troepe; **~** *of circumstances,* weens omstandighede; **~** *of gravity,* swaartekrag; *in* **~**, van krag; *put in* **~**, in werking stel; (v) dwing,

dring, forseer; **~d** gemaak, onnatuurlik; **~d** *landing*, noodlanding, *see* **crash landing**

for'ceps tang, tandetrekker, knyper

fore'arm (n) onderarm; voorarm

fore'bear (n) voorvader, voorsaat

forebod'ing voorspelling; voorgevoel

fore'cast (n) vooruitskatting, projeksie; voorspelling; beraming; *weather* **~**, weervoorspelling, weersverwagting

fore'cast (v) (**forecast, forecast**) voorspel; vooruitskat, projekteer

fore'father voorvader

fore'finger voorvinger

fore'gone verby; afgedaan; **~ conclusion** uitgemaakte saak

fore: **~ground** voorgrond; **~hand** voorarm (tennis); **~head** voorhoof, voorkop

fo'reign uitheems, buitelands, vreemd; **~** *Affairs,* Buitelandse Sake; **~** *exchange,* buitelandse valuta; **~** *trade,* buitelandse handel; **~er** uitlander, vreemdeling

fore'man (..men) voorman, opsigter

fore'mentioned voornoemd

fore'most eerste, voorste, vernaamste

fore'name voornaam; **~d** voornoemd

forerunn'er voorloper, voorbode

fore'said voormeld

foresee' (..saw, ..seen) verwag, in die vooruitsig stel, voorsien, vooruitsien

foreshad'ow voorbedui, voorafskadu

fore'shore voorstrand, vloedgebied

fore'sight voorkennis, voorsorg

fore'skin voorhuid

fo'rest (n) bos, woud; (v) bebos

fo'rester bosbewoner; boswagter, houtvester

fo'restry houtvestery; bosbou, boswese

fore'taste (n) voorsmaak

fore'thought voorbedagtheid; voorsorg

forewarn' vooruit waarsku; **~ed is forearmed,** voorkoming is beter as genesing

fore'wheel voorwiel; **~ drive** voorwielaandrywing

fore'word voorwoord

forf'eit (v) verbeur, boet, verloor; **~ money** roukoop; **~ure** verbeuring; verbeurdverklaring

forge (v) smee; vervals, namaak; **~d** *money,* vervalste geld

forg'ery (..ries) vervalsing, namaking

forget' (..got, ..gotten) vergeet, in gebreke bly; afleer; **~ful** vergeetagtig

forget'-me-not vergeet-my-nietjie

forgive' (..gave, ..given) vergewe; verskoon; **~ness** vergifnis

fork (n) vurk; gaffel; mik (boom); (v) vertak; **~** *out,* opdok; opdiep; **~lift** vurkhyser

forlorn' verlore, verlate; ellendig

form (n) vorm; gedaante; formulier; *be in good* **~**, op sy stukke wees; *in great* **~**, goed op stryk; (v) vorm; maak, vervaardig

form'al vormlik, stelselmatig, styf; formeel

formal'ity (..ties) vormlikheid, formaliteit

form'at formaat

forma'tion vorming, stigting, formasie

form'er (a) vroeër; vorig; voormalig, gewese; (pron) eersgenoemde; **~** *president,* voormalige president; **~ly** (adv) voorheen, eertyds, vanmelewe, vroeër

form'idable gedug, formidabel

form'ula (-e, -s) voorskrif, formule

fornica'tion hoerery, owerspel, ontug

forsake' (..sook, -n) versaak, verlaat, in die steek laat

fort vesting, skans, fort

for'te sterkte, krag; sterk kant

forth voorwaarts, verder, vervolgens; *and so* **~**, ensovoorts; **~com'ing** naderende, eerskomende, volgende; **~with** dadelik

fort'ieth veertigste

fortifica'tion verskansing; versterking

fort'itude sielskrag, moed, sterkte

fort'night veertien dae; *this day* **~**, vandag oor veertien dae

fort'ress (-es) vesting, fort

fort'unate gelukkig, voorspoedig; gunstig

fort'une geluk; lot; fortuin; *tell one's* **~**, sy toekoms voorspel; iem. inklim; *try one's* **~**, jou geluk beproef; **~ hunter** fortuinsoeker; geluksoeker; **~ teller** waarsêer, fortuinverteller

fort'y (..ties) veertig; **~ winks**, 'n dutjie

for'ward (n) voorspeler; (v) bevorder, bespoedig; (a) voorwaarts, voorbarig; parmantig; (adv) voorwaarts; *brought* **~**, oorgebring, oorgedra; **~** *child,* 'n oulike kind, vroegryp kind; *look* **~** *to,* uitsien na

for'ward(s) vooruit, verder

foss'il (n) verstening, fossiel; (a) fossiel

fos'ter grootmaak, opkweek, voed; **~ child** pleegkind; **~ parents** pleegouers

foul 280 **Frid'ay**

foul (v) bemors; onteer; besmeer; (a) walg‑
lik, vuil; sleg; ongunstig (weer); ~ *deed*,
gemene daad; ~ *language*, vuil taal; ~
play, gemene spel, vuil spel; ~ *weather*,
slegte/gure weer; ~-**mouthed** vuilbekkig
founda'tion stigting, grondslag; fonda‑
ment; fondasie; fonds; ~ **garment** vorm‑
drag, postuurdrag; ~ **stone** hoeksteen
foun'ded gegrond, opgerig, gestig
foun'der (n) oprigter, stigter; ~ **member**
stigterslid
Foun'ders' Day Stigtingsdag
found'ling vondeling
found'ry (..ries) gietery
foun'tain fontein; bron, oorsprong; ~**head**
oorsprong; bron; ~ **pen** vulpen
four vier; *on all* ~*s*, hande-viervoet; ~**fold**
viervoudig; ~**footed** viervoetig; ~**some**
vierspel
four'teen veertien; ~**th** veertiende
fourth vierde; ~**ly** in die vierde plek, vier‑
dens
fourway stop (street) vierrigtingstop (straat)
four-wheel drive vierwielaandrywing
fowl (n) hoender; (pl) pluimvee; ~**house**
hoenderhok; ~**run** hoenderkamp
fox (n) (-es) jakkals, vos; (v) flous; ~**glove**
vingerhoedjie; ~ **hunt** jakkalsjag; ~**ter‑
rier** Foksterriër; ~**trot** jakkalsdraf (soort
dans); ~**y** slu, skelm
fo'yer foyer, voorportaal
frac'tion brokstuk; deel; breuk; fraksie;
compound ~, saamgestelde breuk; *deci‑
mal* ~, desimale breuk; *recurring* ~,
repeterende breuk; *vulgar* ~, gewone
breuk
frac'ture (n) breuk, beenbreuk; (v) breek;
~ *of the skull*, skedelbreuk
fra'gile breekbaar; bros, swak
frag'ment brokstuk, fragment
frag'mentary fragmentaries, stuksgewyse
frag'rance geurigheid
frail (a) broos; gebreklik, tingerig, swak
frame (n) raam, lys; kosyn (deur); (v) lys;
omlys, raam; ~**work** raamwerk
franc frank
France Frankryk
fran'chise stemreg, kiesreg; konsessie
frank¹ (v) frankeer
frank² (a) vrymoedig, openhartig; *quite*
~*ly*, om die waarheid te sê
fran'tic woedend, waansinnig, rasend

fratern'ity (..ties) broederskap, gilde
frat'ernise verbroeder
fraud bedrog, bedrieëry; lis; bedrieër
fraught gelaai; ryk; vol; ~ *with danger*, ge‑
vaarvol
fray (n) twis, rusie, geveg; *enter the* ~, tot
die stryd toetree
freak nuk, gril, kuur; gier; frats; ~ *acci‑
dent*, fratsongeluk; ~ *of nature*, natuur‑
gril, natuurfrats; ~ *weather*, fratsweer
frec'kle sproet, vlek
free (v) vrymaak, bevry, verlos; (a, adv) vry,
onbelemmerd; gratis; ~**booter** vrybuiter;
~ **burgher** vryburger; ~**dom** vryheid,
vrydom; ~**dom fighter** vryheidsvegter;
~**dom of the city** ereburgerskap; ~ **en‑
terprise** vrye markstelsesl, vrye onderne‑
merskap, private inisiatief; ~ **hold
property** vrypageiendom; ~**kick** straf‑
skop; ~**lance** vryskut; ~-**lance journalist**
vryskutjoernalis; ~ **Market Foundation**
Vryemarkstigting; ~ **translation** vrye ver‑
taling
Free'mason Vrymesselaar, bokryer
frees'ia (-s) fresia, kammetjie
free: ~**way** deurpad (tussenstedelik), snel‑
weg; ~**wheel** vrywiel; ~**will** (n) vrywil‑
ligheid; vrye wil; (a) vrywillig, uit eie be‑
weging
freeze (n) ryp; *deep* ~, vrieskas, hardvrie‑
ser; (v) **(froze, frozen)** vries, bevries, ys;
stol (TV-beeld); ~**r** vrieskas; ysmasjien
freez'ing point vriespunt
freight (n) vrag, lading; vragprys, vraggeld;
~**er** vragskip
French (n, a) Frans; *take* ~ *leave*, wegloop,
dros; ~ **drain** syferput; ~ **polisher** lak‑
vernisser
fren'zy waansin, kranksinnigheid
freq'uency (..cies) frekwensie; ~ *of the
pulse*, polssnelheid, polsslag; ~ **modula‑
tion (FM)** frekwensiemodulasie (FM)
frequent¹ (v) dikwels besoek; boer by
fre'quent² (a) herhaaldelik, gedurig
fre'quently dikwels, herhaaldelik
fresh vars, fris, koel; *as* ~ *as a daisy*,
springlewendig; ~**er**, ~**ette**; ~**man** (..‑
men) nuweling, groene, groentjie
fri'ar monnik
fric'tion wrywing
Frid'ay Vrydag

friend vriend, vriendin, maat; *a ~ in need is a ~ indeed,* in die nood leer 'n mens jou vriende ken; **~liness** vriendelikheid; **~ly** vriendelik, vriendskaplik; *a ~ly country,* 'n bevriende land/moondheid; *a ~ly match,*'n vriendskaplike wedstryd; **~ship** vriendskap

frig'ate fregat(skip)

fright skrik; *take ~ at,* bang word vir; *take a terrible ~,* oorhoeks skrik; **~en** bang maak, vrees aanja; **~ened** verskrik, bangerig; **~ful** verskriklik, vreeslik

frig'id yskoud; koud, koel, kil; styf

fringe (n) fraiing; soom; **~ benefits** byvoordele, *also* **perks**

friv'olous ligsinnig, kinderagtig

frizz'ly kroes

frock monnikspy; jurk; manel

frog padda

frog'man (..men) paddaman

frol'ic (n) plesier, vermaak; skerts; (v) vrolik wees, grappe maak, skerts; (a) vrolik

from van, vandaan; uit, vanuit; *apart ~,* afgesien van; behalwe, buiten; *~ childhood,* van jongs af

front (n) voorkop; voorkant, front; **~age** voorgewel; voorkant, front; **~-end loader** laaigraaf; **~-wheel drive** voorwielaandrywing

front'ier grens, grensskeiding; **~ war** grensoorlog

frost (n) ryp; (v) ryp; mat verf; versier (koek); **~-bite** (n) vriesbrand; **~bitten** gevriesbrand; **~ed glass** matglas

froth skuim; **~y** skuimagtig, skuimend

frown (n) frons; (v) frons

froz'en (v) *see* **freeze**; (a) bevries, yskoud; styf; *~ meat,* bevrore vleis

frug'al spaarsaam, matig, suinig

fruit vrugte; nut; resultaat; **~fly (..flies)** vrugtevlieg; **~ful** vrugbaar

fruit: ~ juice vrugtesap; **~ salad** vrugteslaai

frustra'tion verydeling, frustrasie

fry (v) (**fried, fried**) braai

fudge (n) borsplaat (lekkers)

fu'el (n) brandstof; **~ consumption** brandstofverbruik; **~ economy/saving** brandstofbesparing; **~ injection** brandstofinspuiting

fu'gitive (n) vlugteling; voortvlugtige; (a) voortvlugtig

fulfil' (**-led, -led**) vervul; verwesenlik; uitvoer, volbring, nakom

full (a) vol; gevul; voltallig; *~time employment,* voltydse/heeltydse werk; *in ~ swing,* in volle gang; (adv) ten volle, ruim, baie; **~back** heelagter; **~ speed** in volle vaart; **~stop** punt; **~time** voltyds, heeltyds; **~y** volkome, heeltemal, ten volle

fum'ble friemel, frommel

fume (n) rook, damp; woede; *be in a ~,* rasend wees van woede; (v) damp, rook; briesend wees; kook

fum'igate berook, ontsmet, uitrook

fun skerts, pret; *for ~,* vir die grap; *for the ~ of,* vir die aardigheid; *poke ~ at,* die gek skeer met

func'tion (n) verrigting; byeenkoms, funksie; (v) werk, fungeer, funksioneer; **~al** funksioneel

fund (n) fonds, kapitaal; (v) befonds, fundeer; **~ raising** geldinsameling, fondsinsameling

fun'eral (n) begrafnis; (a) begrafnis-, graf-, lyk-, doods-; **~ march** treurmars; **~ procession** lykstoet; **~ service** roudiens

fun' fair kermis, pretpark

fun'gicide swamdoder

fun'gus (-es, ..gi) fungus, swam

funic'ular kabel-, tou-, draad-; **~ railway** kabelspoor

funk (n) vrees; *get the ~s,* bang word

funn'el tregter; skoorsteen

funn'y grappig, snaaks, koddig

fur (n) pels, bont

fur: ~ cloak pelsmantel; **~ coat** pelsjas

fur'ious woes, woedend, rasend

fur'nace (smelt)oond; smeltkroes

furn'ish verskaf, lewer; voorsien; meubileer/meubeleer; uitrus; **~er** meubileerder/meubeleerder

fur'niture huisraad, meubelment/meubelment; *a piece of ~,* 'n meubelstuk

fu'rrow (n) voor; sloot

furth'er (v) bevorder; aanhelp; (a, adv) verder, bowendien, buitendien; *~ information,* meer/nader(e) inligting; **~more** verder, bowendien; **~most** verste, uiterste

furth'est verste, uiterste

fur'tive heimlik, skelm

fur'y (furies) woede, raserny, drif, waansin, furie, heftigheid; *in a ~,* rasend

fuse (n) lont; smeltdraadjie, sekering; *the ~ is blown,* die sekering het gesmelt
fu′sion smelting; versmelting; fusie
fuss (n) ophef, gedoente, opskudding
fut′ile vergeefs, vrugteloos, ydel

fu′ture (n) toekoms; *bright ~,* rooskleurige toekoms; *in ~,* voortaan, in vervolg; *the near ~,* die nabye/afsienbare toekoms; (a) toekomstig, aanstaande; toekomende; *~ tense,* toekomende tyd

G

gab (n) gebabbel, gekekkel; *have the gift of the ~,* goed van die tongriem gesny weees
ga′ble gewel, geweltop
gad (v) (**-ded, -ded**) ronddrentel; afdwaal; *~ about,* rondslenter
gad′get katoeter, kontrepsie
gaff (n) ysterhaak, vishaak, gaffel
gag (v) (**-ged, -ged**) muilband; woorde inlas
gag′gle (n) trop ganse; (v) snater, kekkel
gai′ety vrolikheid; pret; vertoon
gain (n) wins, profyt; voordeel; aanwins; (v) wen, verkry; verwerf; *~ the upper hand,* die oormag kry; *not for ~,* sonder winsoogmerk; *~ time,* tyd win; **~ings** winste
gal′a (-s) fees, gala; *swimming ~,* swemgala, swembyeenkoms
gal′axy melkweg, hemelstraat
gale sterk wind, stormwind, windvlaag
gall (n) gal; bitterheid; *dip one's pen in ~,* jou pen in gal doop; (v) terg; vergal
gall′ant (n) galant; (a) galant; swierig, statig
gall′ery (..ries) galery, tribune; *play to the ~,* effek soek
gall′ey (-s) galei (skip; vir drukwerk); *~ proof* galeiproef, strookproef; *~ slave* galeislaaf
gallivant′ rondjakker, jollifikasie hou
gall′op (n) galop; *at a ~,* op 'n galop
gall′ows galg
galore′ in oorvloed, volop, soos bossies
gal′vanise galvaniseer; *~d iron* (sink)plaat, (ge)galvaniseerde yster
gam′ble (n) dobbelary, dobbelspel; (v) dobbel, verkwis; *~ away,* verdobbel, verspeel; *~r* dobbelaar
gam′bling: *~ house* dobbelhuis; *~ table* dobbeltafel
gam′bol (n) bokkesprong; (v) (**-led, -led**) spring, huppel, bokspring, baljaar
game[1] (n) spel, spel(l)etjie, pot(jie), wedstryd; wild; *big ~,* grootwild; *give the ~ away,* die saak verklap; *play the ~,* eerlik handel; *the ~ is up,* die saak is verlore

game[2] (a) bereid; moedig; lam, mank
game: *~fish* sportvis; *~keeper* wildopsigter, boswagter; *~ reserve* wildtuin, wildreservaat
games′manship onsportiewe wentaktiek
gan′der gansmannetjie
gang bende; *~ leader* bendeleier
gang′er opsigter, ploegbaas
gang′rene verrotting; kouevuur, gangreen
gang′ster rampokker, straatboef
gaol (n) tronk, gevangenis; *~bird* tronkvoël; *~er* tronkbewaarder, sipier
gap gaping, opening, gat; bres; leemte; *narrow the ~,* die gaping vernou
gape (v) gaap; hunker; *~ at,* aangaap
ga′rage garage, motorhawe (publiek), motorhuis (privaat)
garb′age afval, oorskiet; vullis; *~ bin* vullisblik
gar′ble uitsoek, sif; vermink, verknoei; *a ~d message,* 'n deurmekaar boodskap
gard′en tuin, hof; *~er* tuinier, tuinman; *~ hose* tuinslang
garden′ia (-s) katjiepiering
gar′gle (n) gorreldrank; (v) gorrel
garl′ic knoffel
garm′ent kleding, kledingstuk; *~ workers* klerewerkers
ga′rrison (n) garnisoen; (v) beset
gart′er kousband
gas (n) (**-es**) gas; *~bag* gassak; bluffer, windlawaai(er)
gas: *~ cylinder* gassilinder; *~ engine* gasenjin
gash (n) (**-es**) sny, hou; (v) sny, kloof
gas′ket pakstuk; pakking, voering, vulsel
gas′ohol gasohol
gas′oline petrol, gasolien
gasp (n) snik, hyging; *the last ~,* doodsnik; (v) snik, snak, hyg; *~ for breath,* snak na asem
gas′tric maag=, gastries; *~ juice* maagsap; *~ ulcer* maagseer

gas'tronome smulpaap, lekkerbek

gate (n) hek, hekgeld; toegang; (v) insluit; hok; **~-crasher** indringer (partytjie); hekbreker; **~keeper** hekwagter, portier; **~ money** toegangsgeld, hekgeld

gath'er vergader, byeenkom; versamel; *the clouds ~*, die wolke pak saam; **~ing** versameling; vergadering, byeenkoms, saamtrek

gatsom'eter gatsometer

gaud'y (a) opsigtig, kakelbont, bont

gauge (n) spoorwydte; maat; meter; *narrow ~*, smalspoor; (v) yk; (af)meet

gaunt'let handskoen; skaapstert; *take up the ~*, die handskoen opneem

gauze gaas; wasigheid

gave see give

gav'el voorsittershamer; klophamer

gay lewendig, vrolik, los; opsigtig; (a, n) homoseksueel; (n) moffie

gaze (n) verbaasde blik; (v) (aan)staar, aangaap

gazelle' gasel

gazette' (n) staatskoerant; (v) aankondig

gear (n) gereedskap; tuig; rat, tandrat; *change ~*, oorskakel; *in ~*, ingeskakel; *low (high) ~*, laagste (hoogste) versnelling; **~box (-es)** ratkas

geiger counter geigerteller

gel'atine gelatien

geld sny, kastreer; **~ed pig**, burg

geld'ing reun (perd)

gem (n) edelsteen; juweel; briljant

gem' squash (-es) lemoenpampoentjie, skorsie

gen'der (n) geslag; (v) teel, voortbring

genealog'ical genealogies, geslags~; *~ tree*, stamboom, geslagregister

gen'eral (n) generaal; die menigte; *in ~*, oor/in die algemeen; (a) algemeen; gewoon; G~ **Assembly** Algemene Vergadering (VN); *~ practitioner* algemene praktisyn; *~ manager* hoofbestuurder; *~ meeting* algemene vergadering; *the ~ public*, die gewone/algemene publiek; **~ise** veralgemeen; *~ sales tax* algemene (ver)koopbelasting

gen'erally gewoonlik, oor die algemeen

gen'erate teel, voortplant; opwek (elektrisiteit); beskryf; ontwikkel (stoom)

genera'tion geslag, nakomelingskap; generasie; *~ gap* ouderdomsgaping, generasiegaping

gen'erator ontwikkelaar, opwekker

generos'ity grootmoediheid, vrygewigheid

gen'erous grootmoedig, vrygewig; ruim

gen'et muskeljaatkat, musseljaatkat

genet'ic geneties, geslags~; **~s** erflikheidsleer, genetika

gen'ital (n, pl) geslagsdele, geslagsorgane

gen'itive genitief

gen'ius aanleg, genie; (-es) genie; (genii) genius, gees, beskermgod

genre soort, genre

gen'tile (n) heiden, nie-Jood

gen'tle meegaande, sagsinnig, vriendelik; *~ birth*, adellike afkoms; *the ~ sex*, die skone geslag; **~man** (..men) fatsoenlike man; heer; **~man's agreement**, ereooreenkoms; ere-akkoord

gent'ly saggies, soetjies; vriendelik

gen'uine eg, opreg, onvervals; *the ~ article*, die ware Jakob, die regte ding

geog'raphy aardrykskunde, geografie

geol'ogy aardkunde, geologie

geom'etry meetkunde, geometrie

geophys'ic geofisies; **~s** geofisika

geran'ium (-s) geranium, malva

germ (n) (siekte)kiem; oorsprong

Ger'man (n) Duitser; Duits; (a) Duits; **~ measles** rooihond; **~ sausage** metwors

Ger'many Duitsland

germ'icide kiemdoder

germ'inate ontkiem, uitloop, opkom

ges'ture (n) gebaar, beweging; (v) gebare maak; deur gebare beduie

get (v) (got, got(ten) kry, verkry, bekom, verwerf; bereik; *~ along with*, met iem. klaarkom; *~ the better of*, die oorhand kry; *~ the boot*, in die pad gesteek word; *~ to business*, ter sake kom; *~ a cold*, koue vat; *~ out of hand*, hand uitruk; *~ on*, vooruitgaan; *~ ready*, klaarmaak; *~ wind of*, agterkom; **~-at'-able** genaakbaar, bekombaar; bereikbaar

gey'ser warm bron; geiser

ghast'ly afgryslik; vreeslik; aaklig

ghost spook, gees, skim; *give up the ~*, die gees gee; *Holy G~*, Heilige Gees; **~ly** spookagtig, aaklig; *~ squad* skimpatrollie; *~ story* (..ries) spookstorie

ghoul lykverslinder, grafskender

gi'ant (n) reus; (a) reuse=, reusagtig; ~ **building**, reusegebou
gidd'y duiselig, lighoofdig; ligsinnig
gift geskenk, gif, present; gawe; ~**ed** begaaf, talentvol; ~**ed child**, begaafde kind; ~ **wrap** geskenkpapier
gigan'tic reusagtig; ontsaglik
gig'gle (n) gegiggel; (v) giggel
gild verguld, verfraai; ~**ed** verguld; ryk
gill (n) kieu/kief (van 'n vis)
gilt (n) verguldsel; klatergoud; (a) verguld; ~**-edged** goudgerand (boek); doodveilig, prima (belegging)
gim'mick truuk, foefie
gin[1] (n) jenewer
gin[2] (n) pluismeul; (v) (**-ned, -ned**) afpluis (katoen)
gin'ger gemmer; rooikop; ~ **ale** gemmerlim(onade); ~**bread** (n) peperkoek; gemmerbrood; ~**ly** versigtig, behoedsaam
gip'sy (**gipsies**) Sigeuner; swartoog
giraffe' kameelperd, giraf
gird omgord, ombind
gir'dle (n) gordel, lyfband, buikgord; (v) omgord; omsluit
girl meisie, nooi; ~**hood** meisie(s)jare; ~**ish** skaam, meisiesagtig; ~**s' high school** hoër meisieskool
gist kern, hoofsaak; *the ~ of the report*, die kern van die verslag
give (**gave, given**) gee, oorgee; toegee; skenk, lewer; ~ *chase*, agternasit; ~ *someone a bit of one's mind*, iem. 'n brander gee; ~ *notice* kennis gee; ~ *offence*, aanstoot gee; ~ *up lost*, opgee as verlore; ~**n** gegewe; ~**r** gewer
gizz'ard krop; maag
gla'cier gletser
glad bly, verheug; ~ *eye*, knipogie; ~**den** bly maak, verbly
glad'iator swaardvegter, gladiator
gladiol'us (**-es, ..li**) gladiolus, swaardlelie
glad: ~ly graag; blymoedig; ~**ness** blydskap, vrolikheid
glam'orous betowerend, verleidelik
glam'our oëverblinding, betowering, aantreklikheid; ~ **girl** prikkelpop, pronkdoedie
glance (n) oogopslag; skramshou; flikkering; *at first ~*, op die eerste gesig; (v) sydelings kyk, aanblik; flikker; ~ *off*, afskram; ~ *over*, vlugtig deurkyk, glylees

gland klier
glare (n) glans, skittering; blikkering; klatergoud; (v) skitter, vonkel; flikker, blikker
glar'ing verblindend; skandelik; *a ~ omission*, 'n skandelike versuim
glass (n) (**-es**) glas; ruit; (a) glas=, glaas=; ~ = **blower** glasblaser; ~**es** bril
glaze (n) glasuur; (v) verglaas (ruite insit)
glaz'ier glasmaker; glaswerker; ruitwerker
glaz'ing glasuur; beglasing
gleam (n) flikkering; glimp; glans; (v) straal, flikker
glee vrolikheid, blydskap; ~**ful** bly, dartel
glen dal, laagte, vlei
glib beweeglik; *a ~ tongue*, 'n gladde tong
glide (v) gly, glip; sweef; kruip; laat gly; ~**r** sweeftuig
glimm'er (n) flikkering, glinstering; (v) flikker, glinster
glimpse (n) ligstraal, skyn; glimp; *catch a ~ of*, skrams raaksien
glint (n) skynsel, glinstering; glimp; (v) blink, glinster; skitter; *a ~ in his eyes*, 'n (ondeunde) kyk/flikkering in sy oë
glitt'er (n) glans, glinstering; luister; (v) blink glinster; ~**ing** skitterend
gloat gluur; hom verkneuter/verlustig
globe bol; wêreldbol; gla(a)skap (lamp)
gloom (n) somberheid; ~**y** somber, droefgeestig, neerslagtig
glor'ify (**..fies, ..fied**) verheerlik, verhef
glor'ious roemryk, heerlik, deurlugtig
glor'y (n) roem, glorie, heerlikheid; saligheid; (v) (**gloried, gloried**) roem, trots wees, koning kraai; ~ *over*, triomfeer oor
gloss[1] (n) (**-es**) kommentaar, kanttekening
gloss[2] (n) (**-es**) glans; opheldering; vals skyn; ~ *paint* glansverf
gloss'ary (**..ries**) glossarium, woordelys
glove handskoen; *be hand in ~*, kop in een mus wees
glow (n) gloed, vuur; (v) gloei, blaak; ~**worm** glimwurm, vuurvlieg
glu'cose glukose, druiwesuiker
glue (n) lym, gom; (v) vaslym, vasplak
glum somber, bedruk, droefgeestig
glut (n) oorvoorsiening; (v) (**-ted, -ted**) oorlaai; oorvoorsien (die mark); volprop
glutt'on vraat, gulsigaard
gly'cerine gliserien
gnash kners; ~ *the teeth*, op die tande kners

gnat muggie
gnaw knaag, kou, knabbel
gnome aardgees, kabouter≈
gnu (-s) wildebees
go (n) gaan; gang; energie, fut; **(v) (went, gone)** gaan; loop; ~ **bad**, bederf; ~ **halves**, gelykop deel; *the story* ~**s**, daar word gesê; *as things* ~, na omstandighede
goad (v) aanspoor, aanpor
goal grenspaal; doelpunt, doel (sport); oogmerk, doelwit; tronk; ~**keeper** doel≈ wagter, doelverdediger; ~**kick** doelskop; ~**post** doelpaal
goat bok
gob'ble gulsig eet, inlaai; ~**r** vraat
gob'elin muurtapyt, gobelin
go'-between tussenganger, bemiddelaar
gob'lin spook, spooksel; bose gees
go'-cart stootwaentjie; knortjor
God God; *for* ~**'s** *sake*, om God's wil, in God's naam; ~ *willing*, as God wil, met God's hulp
god god; ~**child (-ren)** peetkind; ~**dess (-es)** godin; ~**father** peetoom; ~**fearing** godvresend; ~**ly** godvresend; vroom; ~**s** engelebak (in teater); ~**send** uitredding, geluksdag
go'-getter deurdrywer; voorslag; inhaler
gog'gle aanstaar; uitpuil; ~**s** stofbril
go-go girl wikkeldoedie
go'ing vertrek; gaan; *the* ~ *is good*, dit gaan voor die wind; **(a)** gaande; ~ *con*≈ *cern*, gevestigde/lopende saak
goi'tre kropgeswel
gold (n) goud; **(a)** goue, goud≈
gol'den goue; gulde; ~ *age*, goue eeu; ~ *handshake*, tatatjek; *the* ~ *rule*, die gulde reël
gold: ~**leaf** bladgoud; ~ **mine** goudmyn; ~ **rush** goudstormloop
golf (n) gholf; **(v)** gholf speel; ~**ball** gholf≈ bal; ~ **club** gholfklub; gholfstok; ~ **course** gholfbaan; ~**er** gholfspeler
goll'iwog paaiboelie; spookpop
gond'ola (-s) gondel
gone gegaan; verlore
gong ghong
gonorrhoea' druiper, gonorree
good (n) die goeie; welsyn; nut; *for his own* ~, in sy eie belang; **(a, adv) (better, best)** goed, gaaf; ~ *gracious!* goeie genade! grote genugtig! ~ *heavens!* my goeie tyd!

make ~, vergoed; regkom; (tekort) aan≈ vul; (belofte) nakom; *in* ~ *spirits*, in opgewekte stemming/luim; *do a* ~ *turn*, 'n diens bewys; ~ *afternoon* (goeie)mid≈ dag; ~**bye'** tot siens, vaarwel; ~ **evening** (goeie)naand; ~ **fellowship** kameraad≈ skap; ~**for-nothing** niksnuts, deugniet
Good Friday Goeie Vrydag
good: ~**looking** mooi, aantreklik; ~ **luck** geluk; ~ **luck!** sterkte! ~ **morning** (goeie)môre; ~**natured** goedgeaard, goedaardig
good'ness goedheid, vriendelikheid; ~ *knows*, nugter weet; *for* ~' *sake*, in hemelsnaam
good night (goeie)aand; nag
goods (pl) goedere, goed; ~ **train** goedere≈ trein, vragtrein
good'will goedgesindheid; klandisie(waarde)
good'y-goody (..dies) skynheil, mamma se soet kindjie, kammapreutse persoon
goose (geese) gans; uilskuiken; ~**berry (berries)** appelliefie; ~**flesh**, ~**pimples** hoendervleis (idiom.); ~ **step** paradepas
Gord'ian Gordiaans, ingewikkeld; *cut the* ~ *knot*, die Gordiaanse knoop deurhak
gorge (n) kloof, ravyn; vretery, swelgery; **(v)** verslind; inwurg
gor'geous skitterend, pragtig, kostelik
gorill'a (-s) gorilla
go-slow' strike sloerstaking
gos'pel evangelie; ~ *truth*, heilige waarheid
goss'ip (n) skinderpraatjie; **(v)** skinder; ~**er** babbelkous, skinderbek
got *see* **get**
go-to-meet'ing kis≈, Sondagse; ~ **clothes** kisklere
gourm'et fynproewer
gout jig, pootjie, podagra; ~**y** jigtig
go'vern regeer, beheer(s), bestuur; ~**ess (-es)** goewernante
go'vernment goewerment, regering, owerheid; **(a)** regerings≈, staats≈; ~ **ga≈ zette** staatskoerant
go'vernor goewerneur; reëlaar (masjien)
gown (n) toga; tabberd; mantel; kamerjas
grab (v) (-bed, -bed) gryp, beetpak
grace (n) genade, guns, goedertierenheid; tafelgebed; swier, gepastheid; grasie, respyt; *by the* ~ *of God*, by die grasie Gods; *days of* ~, uitsteldae, respytdae; ~**ful** bekoorlik, bevallig

gra'cious bevallig, deugsaam, hoflik; *good ~! ~ me!* goeie genade! my tyd!
grade (n) graad; rang; (v) gradeer, sorteer; **~r** (pad)skraper
grad'ient helling; helling(s)hoek; gradiënt
grad'ual geleidelik; trapsgewyse; **~ly** lang= samerhand, geleidelik, trapsgewyse
grad'uate (n) gegradueerde; (v) gradeer; promoveer, gradueer
gradua'tion promosie, graduasie; **~ cere= mony** gradeplegtigheid
graft (n) ent; (v); ent; oorplant; **~er** enter
grain (n) graan, graankorrel; grein, bietjie; draad; **~ elevator** graansuier, graansilo; **~ sorghum** graansorghum
gram gram; **~ calorie** gramkalorie; *50 ~s of sugar,* 50 gram suiker
gramm'ar spraakleer, spraakkuns, gram= matika
grammat'ical grammatikaal, grammaties
gram'ophone grammofoon; **~ record** grammofoonplaat
granadill'a grenadella/granadilla
grand groot; groots; vernaam, verhewe; **~child (-ren)** kleinkind; **~ duke** groot= hertog
gran'deur grootheid, grootsheid, aansien= likheid; *illusions of ~,* grootheidswaan
grand'father oupa, grootvader; **~ clock** staanklok, staanhorlosie/staanoorlosie
grand: ~mother ouma, grootmoeder; **~ piano** vleuelklavier; **~stand** hoofpawil= joen
gran'ite graniet
grann'y (grannies) ouma, grootjie
grant (n) toekenning; skenking; (v) toeken; skenk; **~-in-aid (grants-in-aid)** hulptoe= lae; **~ee'** begiftigde, ontvanger; **~or'** skenker; begiftiger
grape druif; **~fruit** pomelo, bitterlemoen; **~juice** druiwesap; **~vine** wingerdstok; riemtelegram
graph (n) grafiek; **~ic** skilderend, duidelik, lewendig, grafies
graph'ite grafiet, potlood
grap'ple (v) gryp; vasvat; worstel
grasp (n) greep; bereik; mag; houvas; *get a good ~,* 'n goeie begrip/houvas kry; (v) gryp; begryp; vashou
grass (n) (-es) gras; weiveld; *keep off the ~,* bly weg van die gras; **~hopper** sprinkaan; **~ widow** grasweduwee

grate (n) rooster; traliewerk; vuurherd; (v) knars; raspe; *~ on the nerves,* laat gril; **~ful** dankbaar, erkentlik
grat'er rasper
gratifica'tion bevrediging, voldoening
grat'is gratis, vry, kosteloos
grat'itude dankbaarheid
gratu'ity (..ties) geskenk, vrywillige gif; beloning, toelae, gratifikasie
grave[1] (n) graf
grave[2] (a) ernstig; plegtig; swaar
grave'digger grafmaker, grafgrawer
grav'el (n) growwe sand, gruis; niersteen, graweel; (v) (-led, -led) gruis
grave: ~stone grafsteen; **~yard** kerkhof
grav'ing dock droogdok
grav'ity swaarte, gewig; *centre of ~,* swaartepunt; *specific ~,* soortlike gewig
grav'y (gravies) (vleis)sous
graze[1] (n) skaafplek; skramskoot; (v) skram
graze[2] (v) wei, laat wei, graas
graz'ing (n) weiding, weiveld
grease (n) vet; ghries; vetwol; (v) smeer, ghries, olie; omkoop; *~ the palm,* om= koop; **~ gun** ghriesspuit
greas'y olierig, vetterig; smerig; salwend
great groot; lang; beroemd, aansienlik; *a ~ deal,* baie
Great Brit'ain Groot-Brittanje
great: ~-grand-father oorgrootvader, ou= pagrootjie; **~-great-grandmother** bet= oorgrootmoeder; **~ly** grootliks; **~ness** grootte, grootheid
greed'y gulsig; inhalig, hebsugtig; snoep
green (n) grasbaan; setperk (gholf); (a) groen; fris; onryp; **~fee** baangeld; **~fly (..flies)** plantluis, bladluis; **~gage** groen= pruim; **~grocer** groentehandelaar
green'horn nuweling, groentjie
green: ~house kweekhuis; broeikas; **~ pepper** soetrissie; **~stick fracture** knak= breuk
greet groet, begroet; **~ing** groet, groetnis; groeteboodskap, groetewens(e); **~ings!** wees gegroet! dagsê!
grem'lin tokkelossie, duiweltjie
grenade' granaat
grenadel'la *see* **granadilla**
grenadier' grenadier
grew *see* **grow**
grey (a) grys, grou; wit, gespikkel, blou (perd); **~ horse,** (blou)skimmelperd;

~hound windhond; **~ish** valerig, grou=
erig
grid rooster, tralie; motorhek; bagasierak
grief droefheid, hartseer, verdriet
griev'ance grief, beswaar, ergernis
grill (n) rooster; braaigereg, braaivleis;
mixed **~**, allegaartjie; (v) braai; rooster;
~room eetkamer, (rooster)restourant
grim grimmig; nors; meedoënloos; wreed;
fel, hard; *hold on like* **~ death**, op lewe
en dood vasklou
grimace' (n) grimas, gryns; (v) skewebek
trek, gryns
grime (n) vuiligheid; roet, koolstof
grim'y vuil, morsig
grin (n) gryns, grynslag; (v) **(-ned, -ned)**
gryns
grind (ground, ground) maal, vergruis; **~**
the teeth, die tande kners; **~ing stone**
maalklip; **~stone** slypsteen
grip (n) greep; begrip; beheer; houvas; *come*
to **~s**, handgemeen raak; (v) **(-ped, -ped)**
vasgryp; gryp
gripe (n) knaging; (pl) koliek, maagpyn; (v)
gryp; knaag
gris'ly aaklig, afskuwelik; afsigtelik
grit (n) gruis; vylsel; sand; durf, pit; (v)
knars, skuur; **~ty** sanderig, korrelrig
griz'zly (n) **(..lies)** grysbeer; (a) grys; gryse=
rig, valerig
groan (n) gekreun, gesteun, sug; (v) kreun,
steun, sug
gro'cer kruidenier; **~y (..ries)** kruideniers=
winkel; (pl) kruideniersware
grog'gy aangeklam; dronkerig, bewerig
groin lies
groom staljong; bruidegom; (v) oppas, be=
dien, skoonmaak; **~ed for a senior post**,
opgelei/voorberei vir 'n senior pos; *well*
~ed, netjies uitgevat, agtermekaar
groove (n) keep, groef; roetine; (v) uithol,
ingroef; trek
grope rondtas, voel
gross¹ (n) (s, pl) gros
gross² (a) lomp; ru; bruto; **the ~ amount**
die totaal; **~ national product** bruto na=
sionale produk, bruto volksinkome; **~**
negligence growwe natlatigheid; **~ profit**
bruto wins
ground¹ (n) grond; rede; *gain* **~**, ∕eld win
ground² (n) grond; grondves, bou; belet om
te vlieg (vliegtuig); (a) gemaal, geslyp

ground: **~ floor** onderste vloer/verdieping,
grondvloer; **~ hostess** grondwaardin;
~ing grondslag; **~nut** grondboon(tjie)
group (n) groep; (v) groepeer, rangskik; **~**
dynamics groepdinamika
grouse (n) grief, klag; (v) mor, murmureer;
~r brompot, knorpot
grow (grew, grown) groei, toeneem, aanwas;
verbou, kweek (gewasse); **~ up**, groot
word; **~ vegetables**, groente kweek
growl (n) geknor, gebrul; (v) knor, brul,
brom; **~er** brompot, knorpot
grown begroei; gekweek; grootgeword; **~=**
up (s) volwassene; (a) volwasse
growth groei; gewas; **~ fund** groeifonds; **~**
point groeipunt; **~ rate** groeikoers
groyne pier
grudge (n) wrok; *bear a person a* **~**, *have*
a **~** *against one*, 'n wrok teen iem.
koester; (v) beny, misgun
gru'el gortwater, pap; loesing; **~ling** (a)
uitputtend, veeleisend
grue'some grusaam, afsigtelik
gruff nors, stuurs, suur
grum'ble mor, knor, brom; **~r** brompot
grump'y ontevrede, knorrig
grunt (n) geknor, gesteun; (v) knor, brom
G'-string deurtrekker, genadelappie
gua'na (-s) likkewaan
gua'no ghwano, voëlmis
guarantee' (n) waarborg, garansie; borg; (v)
waarborg; borg staan
guard (n) wag; sekuriteitswag; beskerming,
bewaking; brandwag; *rear* **~**, agterhoede;
(v) oppas, waghou; bewaar; bewaak
guard'ian voog, beskermer; kurator; **~**
angel beskermengel, skutpatroon
gua'va (-s) koejawel
guerrill'a guerrilla; **~ war** guerrillaoorlog
guess (n) **(-es)** gissing, vermoede; (v) gis,
raai; skat
guest gas, kuiergas; *paying* **~**, loseerder; **~**
house gastehuis; **~ speaker** geleentheid=
spreker, gasspreker
guid'ance leiding, bestuur; (beroeps)voor=
ligting
guide (n) gids, leidsman; wegwyser; raad=
gewer; handleiding; (v) lei; bestuur; raad=
gee; **~-dog** gidshond; **~d** gerig; **~d mis=**
sile, gerigte missiel; **~d tour**, begeleide
toer; **~line** riglyn, rigsnoer
guild gilde, vereniging

guil'der Hollandse gulden
guillotine' (n) guillotine, valbyl; sluiting; (v) guillotineer
guilt skuld; misdaad; ~y skuldig, strafbaar; *found ~y of,* skuldig bevind aan
guin'ea ghienie; ~-fowl tarentaal, poelpe= taan, poelpetater; ~-pig marmotjie; proefkonyn (mens in proefrol)
guise manier, voorkome; masker; *under the ~ of,* onder die skyn van
guitar' ghitaar/kitaar
gulf (-s) golf, baai; draaikolk
gull (n) seemeeu
gull'ible liggelowig, onnosel
gull'y (n) (gullies) geut, grip; riool(put); (v) (gullied, gullied) uithol, uitspoel
gulp (n) sluk; *at a ~,* in een sluk; (v) insluk; wegsluk
gum¹ (n) gom; (v) (-med, -med) gom, vas= plak; ~boot waterstewel; ~med paper gompapier
gum² (n) tandvleis
gum³ (interj): *by ~!* gits!
gun geweer; kanon; roer; vuurwapen; ~=

barrel geweerloop; ~cotton skietkatoen; ~man (..men) rampokker, gewapende boef; ~ner artilleris, kanonnier
gunn'y goiing
gun: ~powder kruit, buskruit; ~runner geweersmokkelaar; ~shot geweerskoot
gur'gle (n) borreling; gegorrel; (v) gorrel
gush (v) uitstroom, oorborrel; ~er spuit= ende petroleumbron; dweper
gust windvlaag, stroom, vloed
gut (n) derm; dermsnaar; (pl) ingewande; fut, durf; ~string dermsnaar
gutt'er (n) geut
guy (n) (-s) gek, dwaas, vent; kêrel(tjie), ou; voëlverskrikker; (v) kul; bespot
gym springjurk; gimnasium
gymkha'na (-s) ruitersport, perdesport(by= eenkoms)
gymna'sium (-s) gimnasium
gym'nast gimnas
gymnas'tics gimnastiek; ~ display gimnas= tiekvertoning
gynaecol'ogist ginekoloog, vrouespesialis
gyp'sum gips; ~ board gipsbord

H

hab'erdasher kramer; ~y kramery, snuis= tery(e), garing- en bandwinkel
hab'it (n) gewoonte; neiging; geaardheid; (ry)kleed; *force of ~,* mag van die ge= woonte
hab'itat woonplek, tuiste, habitat
habit'ual gewoonlik, gebruiklik; ~ crim= inal gewoontemisdadiger
hack'ney (-s) (n) drawwer; huurrytuig; ~ed afgesaag, holruggery
hack'saw ystersaag
had *see* have
hadd'ock skelvis
haem'orrhage bloedvloeiing, bloeding
haem'orroids aambeie
hag ou vrou, heks
hagg'ard verwilder(d), sku, maer en bleek
hag'gle (v) kibbel, kwansel, afding; twis
hail¹ (n) hael; (v) hael; ~ cover haeldek= king, haelversekering
hail² (n) heilgroet; begroeting; (v) begroet; roep; aanroep; ~ *from,* afkomstig wees van; (interj) heil! ~-fellow-well-met alle= mansvriend

hail: ~shower haelbui; ~stone haelkorrel; ~storm haelstorm
hair haar; *split ~s,* haarkloof; ~dresser haarsnyer, haarkapper; ~pin haarnaald; ~pin bend dubbele draai, s-draai; ~split= ting haarklowery, vittery; ~spray haar= sproei; ~style parade kapselparade; ~y harig
hake stokvis
hale gesond, sterk; ~ *and hearty,* gesond
half (n) (halves) helfte; halwe; (skrum)ska= kel; *better ~,* wederhelf; ~ *an hour,* 'n halfuur; ~ *past three,* halfvier; (a, adv) half; ~-baked halfgaar, onbekook; ~brother halfbroer; ~mast halfstok; ~time rustyd, pouse; ~volley lepelhou, skephou (tennis); ~-witted onnosel, simpel; ~-yearly halfjaarliks
hall saal; voorportaal, vestibule, hal; ~ stand hoedestander
hall'mark waarmerk, keurmerk
hallucina'tion hersenskim, hallusinasie
hal'o (-s) ligkrans, stralekrans
halt (n) halt; halte (spoor); stilstand

hal'ter (n) halter; strop
halve in die helfte deel, halveer
ham ham; dy; *radio* ~, radio-amateur
ham'burger hamburger, frikkadelbroodjie
ham'let dorpie, gehug(gie)
hamm'er (n) hamer; ~ *and sickle*, hamer en sekel; (v) hamer; ~ *into one's head*, instamp
hamm'ock hangmat
ham'per[1] (n) smulmandjie
ham'per[2] (v) belemmer, bemoeilik; hinder
ham'string (n) dyspier, kniesening; (v) (.. strung, ..strung) verlam, immobiel
hand (n) hand; wyser (oorlosie); *at* ~, byderhand; *by* ~, per bode; *be* ~ *in glove*, kop in een mus wees; *the matter in* ~, die onderhawige saak; *from* ~ *to mouth*, van die hand in die tand; ~*s off!* hande tuis! *second* ~, tweedehands; *under his* ~, deur hom onderteken; ~*s up!* hen(d)sop! *win* ~*s down*, fluit-fluit wen; (v) oorhandig; hand gee; ~ *in*, inlewer, indien; voorlê; ~ *in the assignment*, die taak/ werkstuk inlewer; ~ *in completed forms*, ingevulde vorms inlewer; ~**bag** handsak; ~**bill** strooibiljet; ~**book** handleiding; ~**cuff** (n) handboei; (v) boei; ~**feed** (..fed, ..fed) hans grootmaak; ~**ful** handvol; ~ **grenade** handgranaat; ~**gun** handwapen
hand'icap (n) voorgee; (v) (-ped, -ped) voorgee; gestrem; *the* ~*ped*, die gestremdes, gestremde persone
han'dicraft handwerk, kunsvlyt
han'diwork handewerk, handearbeid
hand'kerchief (-s) sakdoek
han'dle (n) handvatsel; hingsel; steel; (v) hanteer; behandel; behartig; ~**bar** stuur(stang)
hand: ~**-out** bladskrif, vlugskrif, uitgif; ~**picked** handgekeur; ~**picked staff**, handgekeurde personeel
hand'some mooi, fraai, bevallig; ~ *is that* ~ *does*, 'n mens ken 'n boom aan sy vrugte
hands'upper hensopper, oorgeër
hand'writing handskrif
han'dy handig, behendig; *come in* ~, goed te pas kom; ~**man** (..men) handlanger, janregmaak, nutsman, faktotum
hang[1] hang; helling; *get the* ~ *of a matter*, die slag kry

hang[2] (v) (**hung, hung**) hang; behang; (**-ed, -ed**) ophang
hang'ar vliegtuigloods, hangar
hang'dog boef, deugniet; ~ *face*, boewetronie, galgetronie
hang glider hangvlieër, hangswewer
hang gliding hangvlieg, hangsweef
hang'man (..men) beul, laksman
hang'out blyplek, lêplek
hang'over babalaas, babelas, wingerdgriep
hang-up inhibisie, fobia
haphaz'ard (a) bloot toevallig, lukraak
happ'en gebeur, plaasvind, voorkom; *I* ~ *to know*, toevallig weet ek
happ'ening gebeurtenis; saamtrek, kunstenaarsfees
happ'iness geluk, vreugde
happ'y gelukkig, voorspoedig; ~**-go-lucky** onbekommerd, onbesorg, sorgloos
harb'our (n) hawe; skuilplek; (v) herberg; ~ **master** hawemeester
hard (a) hard, swaar; streng; hardvogtig; *a* ~ *case*, 'n hopelose vent; *a* ~ *and fast rule*, 'n vaste reël, (adv) hard, stewig; *try* ~, hard probeer; *be* ~ *up*, platsak wees; ~**-boiled** hardgekook (eier), hardkoppig; ~ **cash** klinkende munt; ~**en** hard maak, verhard; ~**-hearted** verhard, hardvogtig; ~ **labour** dwangarbeid, hardepad; ~ **lines!** ~ **luck!** simpatie! hoe jammer! ~**ly** nouliks, skaars; ~**ship** ontbering, moeilikheid; ~**ware** hardeware, ysterware; apparatuur (komper); ~**-working** arbeidsaam, fluks; ~**y** sterk, kragtig, gehard
hare haas; ~**-brained** onbesuis, lossinnig; ~**lip** haaslip, drielip
harl'equin harlekyn, hanswors, nar
harm (a) skade, nadeel; (v) kwaad doen; benadeel; ~**ful** skadelik, nadelig; ~**less** onskadelik, onskuldig
harmon'ica (-s) mondfluitjie, harmonika
harmon'ious eensgesind, welluidend
harmon'ium harmonium, huisorrel, serfyn
harm'ony (..nies) harmonie; eendrag
harn'ess (n) (-es) tuig; wapenrusting; (v) optuig; inspan
harp (n) harp; ~ *on the same string*, op dieselfde aambeeld hamer
harpoon' (n) harpoen
ha'rrow (n) eg; (v) eg, êe; kwel; teister; ~**ing** ergerlik, kwellend

harsh ru; hard; nors; skerp; ~ *measures,* streng/strawwe maatreëls

hart takbok, hert

hart'ebees hartbees

harv'est (n) oes; (v) oes; insamel

has'-been uitgediende, ou knol

hash (n) bobotie; mengelmoes; *make a ~ of,* verknoei, verbrou

hasp (n) grendel; werwel; ~ *and staple,* kram en oorslag

hassle moeite, moeilikheid; gesukkel

haste haas, spoed; *more ~ less speed,* hoe meer haas hoe minder spoed

has'ty haastig; driftig, voortvarend

hat hoed; *talk through one's ~,* grootpraat; kaf verkoop

hatch¹ (n) (-es) luik; onderdeur; ~**back** luikrug (kar)

hatch² (n) (-es) broeisel; (v) pik; uitbroei; uitdink, beraam; ~**ery** (..ries) broeiery

hatch'et handbyl; *bury the ~,* vrede maak

hate (n) haat, afkeer; (v) haat, verafsku

hat'red haat, wrok, nyd

hat: ~ **stand** kapstok; ~ **trick** driekuns

haught'y hoogmoedig, trots

haul (n) vangs; (v) trek, sleep, hys; ~**ier** karweier, *also* **carrier**

haunch (-es) heup; dy; boud; (pl) hurke

haunt (n) boerplek (diere); (v) boer; spook; ~**ed house** spookhuis

have (v) (**had, had**) hê; besit; kry; ~ *no doubt,* nie daaraan twyfel nie; *he had no objection,* hy had geen beswaar nie (het .. gehad nie)

hav'oc (n) verwoesting

hawk¹ (n) valk; bedrieër; (v) met valke jag

hawk² (v) rondvent, smous

haw'thorn meidoring, haakdoring

hay hooi; *make ~ while the sun shines,* die yster smee terwyl dit warm is; ~**box** hooikis, prutkis(sie); ~**fever** hooikoors; ~**stack** hooimiead

haz'ard (n) gevaar; hindernis (gholf); (v) waag, riskeer; ~**ous** onseker, gevaarlik

haze (n) dynserigheid, mis

haz'el (n) haselaar; haselneut; (a) ligbruin; ~*-eyed* bruinoog∙

haz'y dynserig, mistig; nat; vaag

he (n) mansmens; mannetjie; (pron) hy

head (n) hoof, kop; koppennent; verstand; ~ *of cattle,* stuk(s) vee; ~ *over heels,* bolmakiesie; *lose one's ~,* die kluts

kwytraak; *make neither ~ nor tail of,* nie kop of stert van iets maak nie; ~*s or tails,* kruis of munt; (v) aanvoer, lei; ~**ache** hoofpyn, kopseer; ~**hunter** koppesneller; ~**line** opskrif; hooftrek; ~**master** hoof∙ onderwyser, skoolhoof, prinsipaal; ~ ∙ **mistress** (-es) hoofonderwyseres; prinsi∙ pale; ~**quarters** hoofkwartier; ~**rest** kopstut; slagkussing (motorkar); ~**strong** koppig, eiewys

heal genees, heel, gesond maak; ~**er** heler, heelmeester

health gesondheid, welstand; ~ **officer** ge∙ sondheidsbeampte; ~**y** gesond

heap (n) hoop, klomp, stapel, menigte; (v) ophoop, opstapel

hear (**heard, heard**) hoor; verneem; ~**er** toehoorder, hoorder; ~**ing** gehoor; ver∙ hoor

hear'say hoorsê, gerug

hearse roukoets, lykwa; doodsbaar

heart hart; *to one's ~'s content,* na harte∙ lus; *learn by ~,* van buite leer; ~ *and soul,* hart en siel; ~ *to ~,* openhartig; ~**ache** hartseer, sielsmart; ~ **attack** hart∙ aanval; ~**-broken** ontroosbaar; ~ **failure** hartversaking

hearth vuurherd, haard

heart: ~**ily** hartlik; ~**-rending** hartver∙ skeurend; ~**s** hartens; ~ **pacemaker** hart∙ pasaangeër; ~ **transplant** hartoorplan∙ ting; ~**y** hartlik

heat (n) hitte, warmte; gloed; loopsheid (by diere); uitdun (wedstryd); *dead ~,* gelyk∙ op; *specific ~,* soortlike warmte; (v) ver∙ hit; ~ **conductor** warmtegeleier; ~**er** ver∙ warmer; ~ **exhaustion** hitte-uitputting

heath'en (n) heiden; (a) heidens

hea'ther heide; vlakte, heideveld

heat'wave hittegolf

heave (**-d, -d or hove, hove**) hef; ophef; slaak (sug); ~ *a sign,* 'n sug slaak

hea'ven hemel; lug; *good ~s!* goeie hemel! *move ~ and earth,* hemel en aarde be∙ weeg; *for ~'s sake,* in hemelsnaam; ~**ly** hemels

hea'vy swaar; gewigtig; ~**weight** swaarge∙ wig

hec'kle hekel, roskam; ~**r** hekelaar

hec'tare hektaar

hec'tic koorsagtig; woelig, wild

hec'togram hektogram

hec'tolitre hektoliter
hec'tometre hektometer
hedge (n) laning, heining; (v); omhein; ~ ~
  hog krimpystervark, rolystervark
heed (n) aandag, sorg; hoede; (v) oppas, ag
  gee, oplet
heel (n) hakskeen; *take to one's ~s,* op loop
  sit, weghol; (v) haak (voetbal)
hef'ty fris, sterk
hei'fer vers
height hoogte; lengte
heir erfgenaam; ~loom erfstuk, familie‑
  stuk
heist (n) (bank)roof, *ook* holdup
held *see* hold
hel'icopter helikopter, hefskroefvliegtuig
hel'ipad heliblad
hel'iport helihawe
hell hel; speelhol; ~driver jaagduiwel
Hellen'ic Helleens, Grieks
hell'ish hels
helm roer, helmstok; *at the ~,* aan die roer
  (van sake)
hel'met helm; crash ~ valhelm
help (n) hulp, steun, bystand; *by the ~ of,*
  met behulp van; (v) help, steun; *a ~ing*
  push/shove, 'n hupstootjie; ~er helper,
  hulp; ~ful behulpsaam, nuttig; ~ ing (n)
  porsie, skeppie; (a) helpend; ~less hulpe‑
  loos
hem'isphere halfrond, halfbol
hemp hennep; tou; *wild ~,* dagga
hen hen, hoenderhen; ~wyfie, wyfie‑
hence van nou af, vandaar; *~ this problem,*
  vandaar hierdie probleem; *a week ~,* oor
  'n week
henchman (..men) agterryer, trawant
hen: ~house hoenderhok; ~pecked onder
  die plak/pantoffelregering
hep'tagon sewehoek
her haar
her'ald (n) voorloper, herout, bode; heral‑
  dikus; (v) aankondig, uitroep
herb kruid, bossie; (a) kruie‑; ~alist kruie‑
  kundige; bossiedokter; ~icide onkruid‑
  doder
here hier; hierso; hiernatoe; *that's neither ~*
  nor there, dit het niks met die saak te doen
  nie; ~af'ter (n) hiernamaals; (adv) hier‑
  na, later, hiernamaals; ~by' hierby,
  hiermee
hered'itary erflik, oorerflik

here: ~in' hierin; ~on hierop
he'resy (..sies) kettery, dwaalleer
he'retic (n) ketter
here: ~upon' hierop, toe; ~with' hiermee
he'ritage erf(e)nis, erfdeel
hermaph'rodite (n) trassie, hermafrodiet;
  (a) tweeslagtig, hermafrodities
herm'it kluisenaar, hermiet
hern'ia (-e, -s) breuk
her'o (-es) held; H~es' day Heldedag
hero'ic heldhaftig, heroïes; *~ poem,* hel‑
  dedig
her'oine heldin
her'on reier
her'o worship heldeverering
her'ring haring
hers hare
herself' haarself
hes'itate aarsel, weifel, draai
hes'sian goiingsak, goiingstof
hew (-ed, -n or -ed) kap, neervel
hex'agon seshoek
hib'ernate oorwinter; hiberneer
hibis'cus (-es) vuurblom, hibiskus
hic'cough (n) hik; (v) hik
hidd'en verborge
hide[1] (n) vel, huid; *dress a ~,* 'n vel looi
hide[2] (v) (hid, hidden or hid) wegkruip;
  wegsteek, verberg; *~ one's head,* jou kop
  laat sak
hid'eous afskuwelik, afsigtelik
hide'-out skuilplek, wegkruipplek
hid'ing pak, afranseling, loesing; skuilplek,
  skuiling; *be in ~,* wegkruip; *~ place*
  skuilplek, skuiling
hi'erarchy kerkregering, hiërargie
high (n) maksimum; toppunt; *~ density*
  housing hoëdigtheid(s)behuising; (a)
  hoog; verhewe; *~ level,* hoë vlak; *in ~*
  spirits, uitgelate; (adv) hoog; *~ altitude*
  hoog bo seespieël; *~altitude tennis balls*
  hoëvlaktennisballe; *~ blood pressure* hoë
  bloeddruk, hipertensie; H~ Commissio‑
  ner hoë kommissaris; *~ fidelity* hoëtrou,
  hoë klankgetrouheid; ~land hoogland
high'ly hoog, baie, besonder; *commend ~,*
  sterk aanbeveel
high: ~ness hoogheid; hoogte; *~ priest*
  hoëpriester; *~ school* hoërskool; *~ tide*
  hoogwater; *~ treason* hoogverraad; *~*
  -water mark hoogwaterlyn; hoogtepunt;
  ~way (Am.), snelweg, deurpad (tussen‑

stedelik); **~wayman (..men)** struikrower, rampokker
hi'jack skaak, kaap; **~er** skaker, kaper (vliegtuig)
hike (n) staptoer; (prys)styging; (v) voet= slaan
hik'er stapper, wandelaar, voetslaner
hi'king trail voetslaanpad
hilar'ious vrolik, opgeruimd, uitgelate
hill heuwel, bult, koppie
hilt handvatsel, greep, geves
him hom; **~self** homself
hind (a) agter=, agterste
hin'der hinder, verhinder
hin'drance hindernis, belemmering
hinge (n) skarnier; hingsel; spil
hint (n) wenk, skimp
hip heup
hippopot'amus (..mi) seekoei
hire (v) huur; verhuur; *for ~*, te huur; **~= purchase** huurkoop
his sy, syne, s'n
hiss (n) gesis; geblaas; gefluit; (v) sis, blaas; uitfluit; *~ at*, uitjou
histor'ical geskiedkundig, histories
his'tory (..ries) geskiedenis; *that is ancient ~*, dis ou nuus
hit (n) slag; treffer; (v) **(hit, hit)** slaan; mo= ker; *~ it off with one another*, met me= kaar klaarkom; *~ and run case*, tref-en-trapvoorval
hitch (n) **(-es)** lissie, haak; beletsel; (v) haak, vang; vasmaak; *~ on to*, vashaak aan; **~hike** ryloop, duimry, duimgooi; **~hiker** ryloper, duimryer, duimgooier
hith'er hiernatoe, hierheen; *~ and thither*, heen en weer; **~to** tot dusver
hit'man huurmoordenaar
hit' parade trefferparade
hive (n) byekorf, heuningnes
hoard (v) opstapel, ophoop; oppot (goud)
hoar'frost ruigryp
hoarse hees, skor; **~ness** heesheid
hoar'y grou
hoax (n)**(-es)** grap, foppery; vals alarm; *(telephone) call*, fop-oproep
hob'ble (n) strompelgang; verleentheid; (v) mank loop; strompel; *~ skirt* hobbelrok
hobb'y (hobbies) stokperdjie, liefhebbery, tydverdryf; **~horse** stokperdjie
hob'goblin kaboutermannetjie; paaiboelie
hob'nob meng (met ryker/vernamer mense)

ho'bo boemelaar; landloper
hock'ey hokkie
hodge'-podge mengelmoes
hoe (n) skoffelpik; (v) skoffel; losmaak
hog vark, swyn, burg; smeerlap; *the whole ~*, tot by oom Daantjie in die kalwerhok; **~s'back** middelmannetjie (in plaaspad)
hog'sty (..sties) varkhok
hoist (n) ligter; hystoestel; (v) hys, optrek
hold[1] (n) skeepsruim, (vrag)ruim
hold[2] (n) vat, handvatsel; (v) **(held, held)** hou; besit; behou; bevat; vier (dag); beklee (pos); *~ the line*, bly aan asseblief; (ek skakel u) deur; *~ an office*, 'n pos beklee; *~ one's tongue*, jou mond hou; **~er** houer; besitter, bekleër (pos); **~ing company** houermaatskappy; **~-up** aan= houding, ophoping (verkeer); roof; (v) beroof
hole (n) gat; putjie (gholf); *pick ~s in*, stukkend kritiseer; **~-in-one** volmaakte gelukskoot, kolhou, fortuinhou (gholf)
hol'iday (-s) vakansie, feesdag; *Christmas ~*, Kersvakansie; *on ~*, met/op vakansie; *~ resort* vakansieoord
Holl'and Holland, Nederland; **~er** Hol= lander
holl'ow (n) holte; (v) uithol, hol maak; (a) hol, leeg
hol'y heilig; *~ water* wywater
hom'age eerbetoon; hulde; *pay ~ to*, hulde betoon aan
home (n) tuiste; tehuis; *at ~*, tuis; *go ~*, huis toe gaan; *~, sweet ~*, oos, wes, tuis bes; (a) huislik, huis=; (adv) huis toe, huiswaarts; *~ comforts* huislike geriewe; *~ consumption* binnelandse verbruik; huishoudelike verbruik; **~craft** huisvlyt; *~ economics* huishoudkunde; *~ industry* tuisnywerheid; **~ly** eenvoudig; huislik; **~made** tuisberei/tuisgebak; selfgemaak; *~ management* huisbestuur
hom'eopath homeopaat, homopaat
home' perm tuiskarteling
hom'er posduif
home; **~sick**: *be ~sick*, heimwee hê; *~= stead* woonhuis, opstal; *~ stretch* pylvak; *~ work* tuiswerk, huiswerk
hom'icide manslag; moord, doodslag; *cul= pable ~*, strafbare manslag
hom'ing pigeon posduif
homoge'neous gelyksoortig, homogeen

hom'onym gelykluidend, homoniem
homosex'ual (n, a) homoseksueel
hone (n) oliesteen, slypsteen; (v) slyp
hon'est eerlik, opreg
hon'esty eerlikheid, opregtheid; ~ *is the best policy*, eerlikheid duur die langste
hon'ey heuning; skat, hartlam; ~comb heuningkoek; ~moon wittebrood(sdae), huweliksreis; ~suckle kanferfoelie
hon'ky-tonk (piano) tokkelklavier
honorar'ium (..ria), -s) honorarium
hon'orary honorêr, eervol; ere-; ~ life membership lewenslange erelidmaatskap; ~ member erelid; ~ professor ereprofessor, professor-honorêr; ~ secretary eresekretaris
hon'our (n) eer; waardigheid; *debt of* ~, ereskuld; *do the* ~s, die pligte/pligplegings waarneem; *funeral* ~s, laaste eer/eerbewys; *in* ~ *of*, ter ere van; *word of* ~, erewoord; *your H* ~, Edelagbare; (v) eer; vereer, eer bewys; ~ *a bill*, 'n wissel honoreer; ~able edel; agbaar; eervol; *The H~able the Prime Minister*, Sy Edele die Eerste Minister
hon'ours degree honneursgraad
hood (n) hoofdeksel; kap; kleurserp
hood'lum gomtor, skorriemorrie
hoo'doo (n) teenspoed, ongeluk; beswering, vloek; (v) toor
hood'wink blinddoek; fop, kul, flous
hoof (n) (-s, hooves) hoef, klou
hook (n) hoek; haak; vishoek; *by* ~ *or by crook*, eerlik of oneerlik; ~, *line and sinker*, heeltemal, volkome; (v) haak, aanhaak; ~er haker (rugby); dief, rampokker; ~worm haakwurm
hool'igan skollie, straatboef; ~ism straatboewery; ~s gespuis, skorriemorrie
hoop (n) hoepel; band
hoot (n) gejou; getoet (motor); *not care a* ~, geen flenter omgee nie; (v) uitjou; toeter; ~er toeter
hop¹ (n) hop; ~(s) beer hopbier
hop² (n) sprong; (v) (-ped, -ped) spring, huppel; wip; ~, *skip and jump*, driesprong
hope (n) hoop, verwagting; (pl) verwagtings; (v) hoop, verwag; ~ful veelbelowend; hoopvol; ~less hopeloos
horde horde, bende, swerm, trop
hori'zon gesigseinder, horison

horizon'tal (n) horisontale lyn; (a) waterpas; horisontaal; ~ bar rekstok
horn horing; voelspriet; *on the* ~s *of a dilemma*, voor 'n dilemma
horn'et perdeby, wesp
ho'roscope horoskoop
ho'rrible afskuwelik, vreeslik, gruwelik
horrif'ic ysingwekkend, afgryslik
ho'rror afsku, gruwel; afkeer; huiwering
hors d'oeuvre' (-s) voorspys, voorgereg
horse (n) perd; bok (gim.); *look a gift* ~ *in the mouth*, 'n gegewe perd in die bek kyk; ~fly (..flies) perdevlieg; ~man (..men) perderuiter; ~manship ruiterkuns, rykuns; ~play ruwe spel; ~power perdekrag; ~radish (-es) ramenas, peperwortel; ~riding competition ruiterkuns, perdesport; ~shoe (-s) hoefyster
hort'iculture tuinbou
hosann'a (-s) hosanna, lofsang
hose kous; tuinslang; brandspuit; *panty* ~, kousbroek
hos'pital hospitaal, siekehuis; *general* ~, algemene hospitaal; ~isa'tion hospitaalbehandeling; hospitalisasie
hospital'ity gasvryheid, herbergsaamheid
host¹ gasheer; *we are* ~ing *the event*, ons is gasheer vir die byeenkoms
host² trop, menigte; heer, heerskaar
hos'tage gyselaar; *release of* ~, vrylating van gyselaar
hos'tel losieshuis; koshuis; hostel' (myne)
hos'tess (-es) gasvrou; waardin; gesel-skap(s)dame, gesellin
hos'tile vyandig; vyandelik (mil.); ~ *atti-tude*, vyandige houding
hostil'ity (..ties) vyandigheid, vyandelikheid
hot warm, heet; vurig; ~bed broeines; broeikas; ~blooded warmbloedig
hot: ~cross bun paasbolletjie, kruisbolle-tjie; ~ dog worsbroodjie
hotel' hotel; ~keeper, hotelier hotelhouer, hotelier
hot: ~head drifkop, heethoof; ~house kweekhuis; broeikas; ~line rooilyn, blitslyn; ~ pursuit hakkejag, opvolgaanval; ~-tempered opvlieënd
Hott'entot (n) Hottentot; Hottentots (taal); (a) Hottentots
hound (n) jaghond; (v) (met honde) jag; agtervolg, vervolg

hour uur; ~ **glass (-es)** sandloper(tjie), uurglas; ~ **hand** uurwyser; ~**ly** elke uur

house (n) huis, woonhuis; H~ *of Assembly*, Volksraad; ~ *of God*, Godshuis; ~ *of ill fame*, bordeel; (v) huisves; herberg; woon; ~ **agent** huisagent; ~ **arrest** huisarres; ~**breaking** huisbraak, inbraak

house'hold (n) huis(houding); huisgesin; (a) huishoudelik, huis•; ~ **appliances** huis• gerei; ~ **effects** huisraad

house: ~ **journal** firmablad, lyfblad; ~• keeper huishoudstser; ~**maid** huisbe• diende, diensmeisie; ~**maid's knee** knie• water, ledewater; ~ **rent** huishuur; ~• **warming** verhuisfees; huisinwyding; ~• **wife** (..**wives**) huisvrou; werksakkie; ~• **wives' league** huisvroueliga; ~**wifery** buishoudkunde

housing huisvesting; behuising; omhulsel

hov'el pondok, strooihuis, hut; krot, hool

hov'er fladder; sweef, hang; ~ *about*, rondswerf; speel; ~**craft** skeertuig

how hoe; waarom, hoekom; ~ *are you?* hoe gaan dit? gaan dit goed? ~ *do you do*, aangenaam, aangename kennis, bly u te kenne; ~**ever** egter, nogtans, maar, nie• temin

howl (v) huil, tjank; skreeu; ~**er** huiler, tjanker, grensbalie; flater; ~**ing** (n) ge• tjank; (a) huilend, tjankend

hubb'y (**hubbies**) manlief

hub'cap wieldop, naafdop

hud'dle (n) hoop; bondel; (v) op 'n hoop gooi; *go into a* ~, beraad/koukus hou

hue[1] kleur, tint

hue[2] geskreeu; *raise a* ~ *and cry*, moord en brand skree(u)

huff (n) opvlieëndheid, drif; *be in a* ~, be• ledig voel; kwaad/opgeruk wees

hug (n) omhelsing; omknelling; (v) (**-ged, -ged**) omhels, omarm

huge reusagtig, kolossaal, tamaai, vervaar• lik; ~ *building*, reusegebou

hum (n) gegons; gemompel; (v) (**-med, -med**) gons; neurie; mompel; zoem

hum'an (n) mens; (a) menslik; ~ **relations** menseverhoudinge; ~ **resources** mense• materiaal, mensepotensiaal; arbeids• kragte; ~ **rights** menseregte; ~ **sciences** geesteswetenskappe; H~ **Sciences** Re• search Council, Raad vir Geesteswetens• skaplike Navorsing

humane' mensliewend, humaan

hum'anist humanis

humanitar'rian (n) filantroop; (a) mens• liewend, humanitêr; filantropies

human'ity mensheid, mensdom

hum'ble (v) verneder; verlaag; (a) nederig, beskeie

hum'bug (n) bluf, bog; grootpratery; swendelaar

humid'ity vogtigheid, humiditeit, nat• heid

humil'iate verneder, verlaag, (ver)kleineer

humil'ity nederigheid

hum'iture ongemak(likheid)syfer (klimaat)

humm'ing (n) gegons; ~ **bird** kolibrie

hum'orist humoris; grapmaker

hum'orous luiming, grappig, geestig

hum'our (n) luim; humeur; humor; *in a good* ~, in 'n goeie bui; (v) inwillig, sy sin gee

hump boggel; skof (dier); hobbel (spoed• breker); ~**-backed** geboggel

hum'us teelaarde, humus

hunch (-es) knop; boggel; stamp; voorge• voel; ~**back** boggelrug

hun'dred honderd, honderdtal; ~**fold** honderdvoud(ig); ~**th** honderdste

hung'er (n) honger; ~ **strike** eetstaking

hun'gry hongerig; honger; lus

hunt (n) jag; (v) jag; najaag; vervolg; ~**er** jagter, jagperd; ~**ing season** jagseisoen

hur'dle (n) hekkie; (v) oorspring; ~ **race** hekkiewedloop

hurl gooi, smyt, slinger

hu'rricane orkaan

hu'rry (n) gewoel, haastigheid; *be in a* ~, haastig wees; (v) (**hurried, hurried**) jaag; gou maak; ~ *up*, gou maak, opskud

hurt (v) (**hurt, hurt**) seer maak, beseer; be• nadeel; hinder; *feel* ~, gekrenk voel; *I* ~ *my leg*, ek het my been beseer

hus'band (n) man, eggenoot

hush (n) stilte, kalmte; (v) stil maak, bedaar; (interj) sjuut! ~ **money** omkoopgeld

husk (n) dop, skil; bas; (v) uitdop; afskil

hu'stle (n) gedrang; (v) druk, stamp, stoot; ~ *and bustle*, drukte

hut strooihuis, stroois, pondok, hut

hy'acinth naeltjie(blom), hiasint

hyb'rid (n) baster, hibried; basterwoord; (a) baster-; ~**ise** baster, kruis; ~ **maize/ mealies** bastermielies

hydran'gea hortensia, krismisroos
hyd'rant brandkraan
hydraul'ic hidroulies, water=; ~ brakes
 hidrouliese rem; ~ press waterpers
hydro-elec'tric hidroëlektries
hyd'rogen waterstof, hidrogeen; ~ bomb
 waterstofbom
hyd'roplane skeerboot; watervliegtuig
hyen'a (-s) hiëna, (strand)wolf
hygien'ic higiënies, gesondheids=
hymn gesang, kerklied, himne
hyperb'ole oordrywing, hiperbool
hyph'en (n) koppelteken; (v) ~ate koppel,
 met 'n koppelteken verbind
hyp'ermarket hipermark, alleswinkel

hyperten'sion oorspanning; hoë bloeddruk,
 hipertensie
hyp'notism hipnotisme
hyp'notise hipnotiseer
hypochon'dria verbeelsiekte, hipokondrie;
 hipokonders/ipekonders
hypochon'driac (n) hipokonder/ipekonder,
 hipokondris; (a) hipokondries
hyp'ocrite huigelaar, skynheil(ige), hipo=
 kriet
hyp'othec hipoteek, verband
hysterec'tomy histerektomie, baarmoeder=
 verwydering
hyster'ical histeries
hyster'ics senu(wee)aanval

I

I ek; ~ say, hoor ('n) bietjie
iam'bic jambies
ib'is (-es) ibis (voël)
ice (n) ys; cut no ~, nie veel uitrig nie; ~ =
 berg ysberg; ~cream roomys; ~cream
 cone roomyshorinkie
i'cing yskors; suikerkors; (ver)siersuiker
i'cy ysagtig; yskoud
ide'a (-s) idee, denkbeeld
ide'al (n) ideaal; (a) ideaal, volmaak; ~ist
 idealis; ~ise idealiseer
iden'tical identies, identiek, dieselfde
identifica'tion vereenselwiging; aanwysing;
 identifikasie; ~ parade uitkenparade
iden'tify (..fied, ..fied) vereenselwig; aan=
 wys, uitken, aantoon; identifiseer; ~
 with, vereenselwig/identifiseer met
iden'tikit identistel, identikit
iden'tity (..ties) eenselwiging, identiteit
ideol'ogy ideologie, begripsleer; dwepery
id'iom spraakwending, idioom, taaleie,
 tongval, dialek; ~a'tic idiomaties
id'iot onnosele mens, idioot, skaap(kop)
idiot'ic idioties, mal, dwaas
i'dle (v) leeglê, luier (motor); (a) ledig,
 werkloos; uitgeskakel (rat); ~ talk, kaf=
 praatjies; ~r luiaard, leeglêer
i'dling niksdoenery; leeglêery; luierspoed
 (motor)
id'ol afgod, dwaalbegrip, skynbeeld
id'olise verafgod; 'n afgod maak van
idyll'ic idillies, landelik rustig/bekoorlik

if (n) as; (conj) indien, as, so, ingeval; ~
 need be, desnoods; ~ not, so nie
igni'tion ontbranding; ontsteking (mot.)
ignoram'us (-es) domoor, domkop
ig'norance onkunde, onwetendheid; dis=
 play his ~, sy onkunde openbaar
ignore' verbysien, ignoreer, verontagsaam
igua'na likkewaan
ilk klas, soort
ill (a) siek, ongesteld; (adv) sleg, kwalik;
 skaars; ~ at ease, nie op sy gemak nie; be
 taken ~, siek word; ~-advised onver=
 standig, onbesonne
illeg'al onwettig, wederregtelik
illeg'ible onleesbaar
illegit'imate onwettig; buite-egtelik (kind)
ill: ~-feeling kwaaivriendskap; ~-fortune
 teenspoed; ongeluk; ~ health swak ge=
 sondheid
illi'cit ongeoorloof, onwettig; ~ diamond
 buying onwettige diamanthandel
illit'erate ongeletterd, analfabeties
ill: ~-mannered ongemanierd; ~ness siek=
 te, ongesteldheid
ill: ~-tempered humeurig, knorrig; ~treat
 mishandel
illum'inate verlig; versier; opluister; ~d
 address oorkonde
illu'sion sinsbedrog, illusie
illus'ive bedrieglik
ill'ustrate ophelder, verduidelik; illustreer;
 ~d verduidelik; geïllustreer

ilustra'tion illustrasie; toeligting
illus'trious beroemd, vermaard
im'age (n) beeld; afbeelding; ~ **builder** beeldbouer; **public** ~ beeld na buite
im'agery beeldspraak; beeldrykheid
ima'ginary denkbeeldig, onbestaanbaar
imagina'tion verbeelding, voorstelling
imag'ine jou verbeel, dink, jou voorstel
im'becile (n) swaksinnige, imbesiel; (a) swak, geestelik swak, idioot, imbesiel
im'itate navolg, namaak, naboots
imita'tion (n) navolging, namaaksel, nabootsing; ~ **leather** kunsleer
im'itator na-aper, nabootser
immac'ulate rein, onbevlek; onberispelik
immater'ial geestelik; onbelangrik; *that's* ~, dis om 't ewe; dit maak nie saak nie
immature' groen, onvolwasse; onryp
immed'iate onmiddellik, oombliklik; ~**ly** dadelik, subiet; ~ *past president,* pas uitgetrede president
immense' onmeetlik, onafsienbaar
immer'sion onderdompeling, indompeling; ~ **heater** dompelaar, dompelverwarmer
imm'igrant immigrant, inkomeling
immigra'tion verhuising, immigrasie
imm'inent dreigend, naby
immob'ilise onbeweeglik maak, immobiliseer, lam lê, buite geveg stel
immod'est onbeskeie, onfatsoenlik
immoral'ity onsedelikheid, sedeloosheid; ontug; ~ **act** ontugwet
immort'al onsterflik; onverganklik
immortal'ity onsterflikheid
immov'able onbeweeglik; onroerend; vas; ~ **property** vaste eiendom, vasgoed
immune' vry van, immuun
imp (n) kabouter; skelm, vabond, rakker
im'pact (n) skok, stamp, botsing, impak(t)
impal'a rooibok
impart' meedeel, gee, deelagtig maak
impar'tial onpartydig, afsydig
impass'able ontoeganklik, onbegaanbaar, onrybaar
impasse' dooiepunt; benarde toestand
impa'ssion ontroer, aanvuur; ~**ed** hartstogtelik, vurig, meeslepend
impa'tient ongeduldig, driftig, moeilik
impedi'ment hindernis, beletsel; belemmering; *speech* ~, spraakgebrek
impend' dreig, nader kom; ~**ing** dreigend, naderend

impen'etrable ondeurdringbaar, ondeurgrondelik; ongevoelig
impe'rative gebiedend; ~ **mood** gebiedende wys
imperf'ect (n) onvoltooid verlede tyd; (a) onvolmaak, onvolkome, onvoltooid
imper'ial keiserlik, imperiaal; ~**ism** imperialisme; ~**ist** imperialis
impers'onal onpersoonlik
impers'onate verpersoonlik; vertolk; uitgee vir, voorstel; ~ *a character,* 'n karakter speel/vertolk
impert'inence astrantheid; vermetelheid
impert'inent parmantig, astrant, vermetel
impet'uous voortvarend, onstuimig, heftig
im'petus (-es) beweegkrag, aandrang; *give a fresh* ~ *to,* nuwe stukrag gee aan
im'pi (-s) impie, Zoeloeregiment
im'pish ondeund, speels
im'plement (n) gereedskap, werktuig; (pl) benodigdhede; implemente (boerdery); (v) uitvoer, volbring, toepas, implementeer.
implica'tion inwikkeling; implikasie; gevolgtrekking; deelneming; *by* ~, by implikasie; stilswy(g)end
implied' stilswyend inbegrepe
implode' (v) inplof
implo'sion (n) inploffing
implore' bid, smeek
imply' (**implied, implied**) bevat; behels; te kenne gee; sinspeel op
im'port (n) invoer; inhoud; belang; gewig; betekenis; (pl) invoerartikels
import' (v) invoer, importeer; te kenne gee
import'ance belangrikheid; betekenis
import'ant belangrik, betekenisvol
im'port dues/duty invoerreg(te)
import'er invoerder, importeerder
impose' oplê; te laste lê; ~ *upon,* gebruik maak van; afsmeer aan
imposi'tion oplegging; strafwerk; bedrog
imposs'ible onmoontlik, onbegonne
im'potent magteloos, impotent
impound' (v) skut; opsluit
impov'erish verarm, uitput
imprac'ticable onuitvoerbaar, onprakties
impreg'nate bevrug, beswanger; deurtrek, vervul; ~*d with,* deurtrek van
im'press (n) (-es) stempel; merk, afdruk
impress' (v) indruk, beïndruk; stempel; indruk maak; ~ *something on a person,* iem. iets op die hart druk

impress'ion indruk; druk; uitgawe; **~ism** impressionisme; **~ist** impressionis
impress'ive indrukwekkend, treffend
im'prest voorskot (boekhouding)
im'print (n) stempel; naam; indruk
impris'on in die tronk sit; **~ment** gevangenisstraf; opsluiting
improb'able onwaarskynlik
impromp'tu (n) improvisasie; (a, adv) uit die vuis, onvoorberei(d)
improp'er onbehoorlik, onbetaamlik
improve' verbeter, veredel, verhoog; vooruitgaan (pasiënt); **~ment** verbetering, vordering
im'provise improviseer, uit die vuis lewer (toespraak); haastig prakseer/tot stand bring
im'pudent parmantig, (dom)astrant
im'pulse aandrang spoorslag; impuls
impul'sive aandrywend; impulsief
impun'ity straffoosheid; *with* **~**, straffeloos
impur'ity (..ties) onsuiwerheid; onreinheid; onkuisheid
in (adv) in, binne; (prep) in, by, op, na, tot, met; **~** *Afrikaans*, in/op Afrikaans; **~** *any case*, in elk/alle geval; **~** *cash*, kontant; **~** *fact*, inderdaad, om die waarheid te sê; **~** *honour of*, ter ere van; **~** *ink*, met ink; **~** *terms of*, ingevolge, kragtens; **~** *this way*, op hierdie manier; **~** *a week*, oor 'n week; **~** *writing*, op skrif
inabil'ity onvermoë, onbekwaamheid
inacc'urate onnoukeurig, onakkuraat
inac'tive werkloos, ledig; onaktief; traag
inad'equate onvoldoende, ontoereikend
inadvert'ent onagsaam, onoplettend, agteloos, onopsetlik; **~ly** per abuis
inapp'licable ontoepaslik, ongeskik
inapprop'riate ongeskik, onvanpas, ondienstig; misplaas, ontoepaslik
inartic'ulate onduidelik, onverstaanbaar; *he is quite* **~**, hy kan hom nie behoorlik uitdruk nie
inasmuch': **~** *as*, aangesien
iraud'ible onhoorbaar
iraug'ural intree», wydings»; **~ address** intreerede, intreepreek; openingsrede; **~ meeting** stigtingsvergadering
inaugura'tion inwyding, ingebruikneming; inhuldiging; bevestiging
in'born aangebore, ingeskape

incal'culable onberekenbaar
incandes'cent gloeiend; liggewend; **~ lamp** gloeilamp
incanta'tion towerspreuk, beswering, inkantasie
incap'able onbekwaam, onbevoeg
incapa'citate onbekwaam maak
incen'diary (a) brandstigtend; opruiend; **~ bomb** brandbom
in'cence¹ (n) wierook; bewieroking; (v) bewierook; geurig maak
incence'² (v) kwaad maak, terg, vertoorn
incen'tive (n) aansporing, spoorslag; prikkel; **~ bonus** aanspoorbonus; **~ scheme,** aanspoorskema
incep'tion begin, aanvang
incess'ant onophoudelik, aanhoudend
in'cest bloedskande
inch (-es) duim; *every* **~** *a gentleman,* 'n pure man
in'cident (n) gebeurtenis, voorval, insident; (pl) gebeure; (a) bykomstig, toevallig
inciden'tal toevallig, insidenteel, onvoorsiens; **~ly** toevallig, terloops; **~s** bykomende/onvoorsiene uitgawes
incin'erator verbrandingsoond
incis'ion insnyding, kerf, sny
incite' aanspoor; aanvuur, opstook, oprui, aanhits; **~ment** aanhitsing
inclem'ent onbarmhartig; stormagtig; wreed; **~ weather** gure weer
inclina'tion neiging, geneigdheid; helling
incline' (n) helling, afdraand, opdraand; skuinste; (v) neig; oorhang; hel
inclined' geneig; hellend; *be* **~** *to,* geneig wees om
include' insluit, bevat; meereken; *not* **~d,** nie inbegrepe nie
inclus'ive insluitend, ingeslote, inklusief
incoher'ent onsamehangend
in'come inkoms, inkome; **~ statement** inkomstestaat; **~ tax** inkomstebelasting
in'-company training indiensopleiding, interne opleiding
incompat'ible onverenigbaar, onbestaanbaar
incom'petence, incom'petency onbekwaamheid, onbevoegdheid
incom'petent onbevoeg, onbekwaam
incomplete' onvoltooi; onvolledig
incomprehen'sible onbegryplik, onverstaanbaar

inconceiv'able ondenkbaar, onbegryplik
inconclus'ive onoortuigend, onopgelos
incong'ruous ongepas, onbestaanbaar; on=
samehangend, ongelyksoortig
inconsid'erate onbesonne, agtelosig; on=
verskillig; onhoflik, onbedagsaam
inconsis'tent onbestaanbaar, teenstrydig;
ongerymd; ~ with, strydig met
inconspic'uous onmerkbaar, onopvallend
inconven'ience (n) ongerief, ongemak; *put
to* ~, ongerief veroorsaak; (v) ontrief
inconven'ient ongerieflik, ongeleë
incor'porate (v) inlyf, verenig, inkorporeer;
(a) ingelyf, verenig; ~*d association not
for gain,* ingelyfde vereniging sonder
winsoogmerk
incorpora'tion inlywing, inkorporasie
incorrect' verkeerd, foutief, onjuis
inco'rrigible onverbeterlik
in'crease (n) vermeerdering, aanwas; ver=
hoging; *on the* ~, aan die toeneem
increase' (v) vermeerder, verhoog, ver=
groot
incred'ible ongelooflik
in'crement verhoging; inkrement; aanwas
incrim'inate beskuldig, betig
in'cubator broeimasjien; kweekmasjien
in'culcate inprent, inskerp
incum'bent (n) geestelike, predikant;
amp(s)bekleër; (a) opgelê as plig; rustend;
it is ~ *on you,* dis jou plig
incur' (-red, -red) op die hals haal, blootstel
aan; ~ *debt,* skuld maak
incur'able ongeneeslik
inda'ba indaba, beraad, samespreking
indebt'ed skuldig, verskuldig, verplig; *be* ~
to, verskuldig aan; ~ness verpligting
inde'cent onbetaamlik; onfatsoenlik; on=
welvoeglik; ~ *assault* onsedelike aan=
randing
indeed' inderdaad, regtig
indefat'igable onvermoeid
indef'inite onbepaald; onbeslis; ~ *pro=
noun* onbepaalde voornaamwoord
indel'ible onuitwisbaar; ~ *pencil* inkpot=
lood
indem'nify (..fied, ..fied) skadeloos stel,
vergoed; vrywaar
indem'nity (..ties) skadeloosstelling, ver=
goeding; vrywaring
in'dent (n) kerf, keep; bestelling; ~ *agent*
invoeragent

indent' (v) inkerf, intand; bestel; inspring
(drukwerk); inboek
inden'ture (n) kontrak; verdrag, inboeking
indepen'dence onafhanklikheid; *declara=
tion of* ~, onafhanklikverklaring
indepen'dent (n) onafhanklike; (a) onaf=
hanklik, selfstandig
in'-depth study dieptestudie
indescrib'able onbeskryflik, onbepaald
indestruc'tible onvernietigbaar
indeter'minate onbepaald, onseker; onbe=
slis; vaag; ~ *sentence* onbepaalde vonnis
in'dex (n) (indices, -es) bladwyser, in=
houdsopgawe; indeks; register; wysvinger;
~ *finger* voorvinger; ~ *number* in=
deksgetal
In'dian (n) Indiër; Indiaan (Amerika);
Asiër (SA); ~ *Affairs,* Indiërsake; *Red*
~, Rooihuid; (a) Indies; Indiaans
in'diarubb'er gomlastiek, rubber
indica'tion aanduiding, aanwysing; teken
indic'ative (n) aantonende wys; (a) aan=
wysend; ~ *mood* aantonende wys
in'dicator wyser; nommerbord; aantoner;
flash ~ flikkerlig
indict' beskuldig, aankla, vervolg; ~ment
aanklag; (akte van) beskuldiging
In'dies Indië; *East* ~, Oos-Indië; *West* ~,
Wes-Indië
indiff'erent onverskillig, agtelosig; onbe=
duidend; *his health is* ~, sy gesondheid is
swak
indig'enous inheems, aangebore; ~ *trees*
inheemse bome
in'digent arm, behoeftig
indiges'tion slegte spysvertering, indigestie
indigna'tion verontwaardiging
indirect' indirek, onregstreeks, sydelings;
~ *speech,* indirekte rede
indiscreet' onverstandig, onbeskeie
indiscrim'inate voor die voet, sonder on=
derskeid; ~ly blindweg, voor die voet
indispen'sable onontbeerlik, onmisbaar
indispose' ontstem; ongesteld maak; ~d'
ongesteld, siek; ongeneë
indistinct' onduidelik, dof, vaag
individ'ual (n) individu, persoon; enkeling;
(a) individueel, afsonderlik
individ'ually persoonlik, afsonderlik, in=
dividueel, apart
indoctrina'tion indoktrinasie, indoktrine=
ring

in'dolent lui, traag, vadsig
indom'itable, ontembaar, onoorwinlik
Indone'sian (n) Indonesiër; Indonesies (taal); (a) Indonesies
in'door huis-, binne-; ~ *game,* kamerspeletjie; ~ *plants,* binnehuise plante
in'doors binnenshuis, binnehuis
induce' beweeg; oorhaal, oorreed; ~**ment** aanleiding, aansporing
induct' installeer; inwy; bevestig (dominee); ~**ion** installasie, induksie; inwyding; bevestiging
indun'a indoena, hoof, kaptein
indus'trial (a) industrieel, nywerheids-; ~ **art(s)** bedryf(s)kennis; ~ **court** nywerheidshof; ~**ist** fabrikant, nyweraar; ~**isa'tion** industrialisasie; ~ **psychologist** bedryfsielkundige; ~ **relations** arbeid(s)verhoudinge, arbeid(s)betrekkinge, bedryfsverhoudings; ~ **school** nywerheidskool; ambagskool
indus'trious werksaam, fluks, vlytig
in'dustry vlyt, werksaamheid; (..ries) nywerheid, industrie, bedryf
ineb'riate (n) dronkaard; (a) dronk
ined'ible oneetbaar
ineffi'ciency onbekwaamheid, onbevoegdheid; ondoeltreffendheid; vrugteloosheid
ineffi'cient onbekwaam; ondoeltreffend; ongeskik; onbruikbaar
inelas'tic onelasties, onrekbaar
inept' onbekwaam, ongeskik; ongepas, ongerymd; ~**itude** onbekwaamheid
inequal'ity ongelykheid; verskil
ineq'uitable onbillik, onregverdig
iner'tia traagheid, bewegingloosheid, inersie; ~ **reel seatbelt,** rukstopgordel
ines'timable onskatbaar, onberekenbaar; ~ *damage,* onberekenbare skade
inev'itable onvermydelik
inexhaus'tible onuitputlik; onvermoeid
inexpen'sive goedkoop, billik
inexper'ience onervarenheid; ~**d** onervare
infall'ible onfeilbaar, seker
in'famous verfoeilik; berug; eerloos
in'fant (n) klein kind, babatjie, kleuter, suigeling; (a) klein, jong, minderjarig; ~ *mortality rate,* kindersterftesyfer
in'fantile kinder-, kinderlik; kinderagtig, infantiel; ~ **paralysis** kinderverlamming
in'fantry infanterie, voetvolk

in'fant school kleuterskool
infat'uate versot maak, verdwaas; ~**d** versot op; smoorverlief
infect' besmet, aansteek; ~**ed** besmet, aangesteek; ~**ion** besmetting, infleksie; ~**ious** besmetlik; aansteeklik; ~**ious** *disease,* aansteeklike siekte
in'ference gevolgtrekking
infer'ior (n) ondergeskikte, mindere; (a) minderwaardig; ondergeskik
inferior'ity minderwaardigheid; ~ **complex** minderwaardigheid(s)kompleks
infer'nal hels, verfoeilik
infest' vervuil, verpes; pla; teister
infidel'ity ongeloof; ontrou
in'fighting binnegevegte, broedertwis
in'filtrate intrek, insypel, insyg, infiltreer
infiltra'tion insypeling, infiltrasie
in'finite (n) oneindigheid; (a) oneindig, grensloos
infinites'imal oneindig klein
infin'itive (n) onbepaalde wys; (a) oneindig, eindeloos; ~ **mood** onbepaalde wys
infirm' swak, gebreklik; ~**ary** (..ries) hospitaal, siekehuis; ~**ity** swakheid
inflamm'able (ont)vlambaar, brandbaar, *also* **flammable**
inflamma'tion ontsteking, inflammasie
infla'tion opblasing; inflasie
inflect' buig; verbuig (gram.)
inflex'ion verbuiging, infleksie
inflict' oplê, laat voel; toebring; ~ *punishment,* straf toedien
in'fluence (n) invloed; (v) beïnvloed
influen'tial invloedryk
influen'za influensa, griep
in'flux instroming, toevloed, toestroming; ~ **control** instroming(s)beheer
inform' meedeel, verwittig, sê
inform'al informeel
inform'ant segsman, informant
informa'tion informasie, berig, inligting; *full* ~, volledige inligting
informed' goed ingelig, saakkundig; *keep one* ~, iem. op die hoogte hou
inform'er nuusdraer, verklikker; aanklaer; verklikker, *see* **informant**
in'frastructure infrastruktuur
infreq'uent seldsaam; ~**ly** selde
infringe' oortree, verbreek, inbreuk maak op, vergryp; ~**ment,** inbreuk, oortreding
infur'iate woedend maak, vertoorn

ingen'ious vernuftig, vindingryk, knap

ingenu'ity vernuftigheid, vindingrykheid

in'grained diep (in)gewortel; verstok

ingrati'tude ondankbaarheid

ingred'ient bestanddeel, ingrediënt

inhab'it bewoon; woon; **~able** bewoonbaar; **~ant** bewoner, inwoner

inhale' inasem, intrek

inher'ent aangebore, inherent

inhe'rit erf, oorerf; **~ance** erf(e)nis, erflating, erfporsie; **~ed** geërf, oorgeërf

inhos'pitable ongasvry; onherbergsaam

inhum'an onmenslik, gevoelloos, barbaars

inhumane' onmensliewend

inim'itable onnavolgbaar

ini'tial (n) voorletter; (pl) paraaf; (v) (**-led, -led**) parafeer; (a) eerste begin=, aanvangs=; **~ investigation/exploration,** aanvang(s)ondersoek

ini'tiate (n) ingewyde; (v) inlei; inwy, insout, inisieer; ontgroen, inburger

initia'tion inwyding, inburgering; ontgroening; **~ school** inisiasieskool, bergskool

ini'tiative (n) inisiatief, voortou; *take the* **~,** die leiding neem

inject' inspuit

injec'tion inspuiting, injeksie

in'jure beseer; beskadig; benadeel, beledig

in'jury (**..ries**) besering; benadeling; letsel

injus'tice onregverdigheid, onreg

ink (n) ink; *write in* **~,** skryf met ink

ink'ling vermoede, idee; wenk, snuf

in'laid ingelê

in'land (a) binnelands; (adv) landwaarts

in-law' aangetroude familielid; *my* **~s,** my skoonfamilie

in'let inham, baai; ingang

in'mate bewoner, huisgenoot, kosganger

in'most binneste; geheimste

inn herberg, hotel

inn'er innerlik, inwendig; geheim; *the* **~ man,** die inwendige mens; **~most** binneste, innigste

inn'ings beurt; kolfbeurt

inn'keeper herbergier, waard

inn'ocence onskuld; eenvoudigheid

inn'ocent (a) onskuldig; argeloos

innova'tion nuwigheid, verandering

innum'erable ontelbaar

inoc'ulate inent, ent, okuleer

inoffen'sive onskadelik; argeloos

inop'erative buite werking; ongeldig

inopp'ortune ongeleë, ontydig

in'-patient binnepasiënt

in'put inset (produksiemiddele)

in'quest ondersoek, lykskouing

inquire' ondersoek instel; **~** *into the affairs of the company,* ondersoek instel na die maatskappy se sake

inquir'y (**..ries**) ondersoek, navorsing; *commission of* **~,** ondersoekkommissie, *see* **enquiry**

inquisi'tion ondersoek, inkwisisie

inquis'itive nuuskierig; weetgierig

in'road inval, strooptog

insane' kranksinnig, mal

inscrip'tion inskrywing, opskrif, titel; opdrag; inskripsie (op iets)

in'sect insek, gogga

insec'ticide insektedoder, insektegif

insecure' onveilig, onseker

insemina'tion bevrugting, inseminasie; *artificial* **~,** kunsmatige bevrugting, kunsmatige inseminasie (K.I.)

insep'arable onskei(d)baar; onafskeidelik (vriende)

insert' invoeg, inlas; inskakel; **~ion** invoeging; opname, plasing

in'-service: ~ training indiensopleiding, interne opleiding; **~ tuition** indiensonderrig

in'set (n) bylae,. byvoegsel; byblad; inlas, inlegsel

in'shore naby die kus (wal); **~** *fishery,* kusvissery

in'side (n) binnekant; binneste; inwendige; binnegoed; *know* **~** *out,* deur en deur ken; (a) binneste=, binne=; (adv) binnekant, binneshuis; (prep) binne

in'sight insig; begrip; blik

insignif'icant onbeduidend

insincere' onopreg, huigelagtig

insin'uate insinspeel, insinueer; inwerk

insip'id smaakloos, laf, flou

insist' aanhou, aandring; volhou; volhard by; **~** *on,* volhou, aandring op

in'solence onbeskoftheid, parmantigheid

insol'vency (**..cies**) bankrotskap, insolvensie

insol'vent (n) insolvent; bankroetier; (a) bankrot, insolvent

insom'nia slaaploosheid

inspan' (**-ned, -ned**) inspan

inspect' ondersoek; inspekteer; **~ion** inspeksie, ondersoek; **~or** inspekteur

inspira'tion besieling, inspirasie, ingewing
inspire' inasem; inboesem; besiel; inspireer, aanvuur; ~ *confidence*, vertroue inboesem; ~d' ingegee, besiel, geïnspireer, begeester(d)
inspir'ing besieling, inspirerend
instabil'ity onbestendigheid, wankelbaarheid
install' (v) installeer, aanlê, aanbring, inrig
installa'tion installasie, aanleg (fabriek)
instal'ment paaiement; aflewering; *pay in ~s*, paaiementsgewyse afbetaal
in'stance (n) voorbeeld, geval; *in the first ~,* in die eerste plek, in eerste instansie; *for ~,* byvoorbeeld
in'stant (n) oomblik, tydstip; (a, adv) onmiddellik, dadelik; dringend; kits~; *the 16th ~,* 16 deser; ~an'eous oombliklik, skielik; ~ coffee kitskoffie
instead' of in plaas van, pleks van
in'step voetboog, wreef
in'stigate aanhits, aanspoor, opstook, aanpor, aanstig
in'stigator opstoker, aanhitser
instill' (..stilled, ..stilled) inboesem, inprent, indruppel
in'stinct instink, natuurdrif
instinct'ive onwillekeurig, instinktief
in'stitute (n) instelling; wet; instituut; (pl) institute; (v) instel, stig, inrig, invoer; ~ *proceedings,* regstappe doen
institu'tion instelling; inrigting; stigting
instruct' onderrig, leer; ~ion onderrig; bevel, instruksie; ~ive leersaam; ~or leermeester, instrukteur
in'strument instrument, werktuig; speeltuig; dokument; middel
instrumen'tal bevorderlik, behulpsaam; *be ~ to,* bydra tot
insubordina'tion weerspannigheid, verset, insubordinasie
insuffi'cient ontoereikend, onvoldoende, ongenoegsaam
in'sulate afsonder, isoleer
insula'tion afsondering, isolering; ~ tape isoleerband
in'sulator isolator, nie-geleier
in'sult (n) belediging, affront, beskimping; *calculated ~,* berekende affront
insult' (v) beledig, beskimp; ~ing krenkend, beledigend, kwetsend
insu'rance versekering, assuransie; *third party ~,* derdepartyversekering, derde-

dekking; ~ agent assuransieagent; ~ company (..nies) versekering(s)maatskappy; ~ policy (..cies) versekering(s)polis, assuransiepolis
insure' verseker, verassureer; ~d' (n) die versekerde; (a) verseker, verassureer; ~r versekeraar, assuradeur
insur'gent (n) opstandeling, oproermaker; insurgent; (a) oproerig, opstandig
insurrec'tion opstand, muitery
intact' ongeskonde, onaangeroer, intak(t)
in'take inloop; inname; toevoer
in'tegral (a) heel, volledig, integraal, integrerend; ~ *calculus,* integraalrekening; ~ *part of,* integrerende deel van
integra'tion integrasie; inskakeling
integ'rity opregtheid, egtheid; eerlikheid, onkreukbaarheid, integriteit
in'tellect verstand, vernuf, gees, intellek
intellec'tual (n) intellektueel; (a) verstandelik, intellektueel; verstands-
intell'igence verstand; inligting; intelligensie; ~ *quotient* intelligensiekwosiënt
intell'igent skrander, intelligent, slim
intend' voornemens wees, wil; ~ *no harm,* geen kwaad bedoel nie; ~ed (n) aanstaande; (a) bestem(d), voorgenome
intense' hewig, kragtig, sterk, diep, fel
inten'sify (..fied, ..fied) versterk, verskerp, vererger, verhoog, verdiep; *intensified attacks,* verskerpte aanvalle
inten'sity hewigheid, intensiteit
inten'sive intensief; intens; ~ *care unit,* (intensiewe) sorgeenheid, waakeenheid
intent' (n) oogmerk, voorneme, bedoeling; *to all ~s and purposes,* vir alle praktiese doeleindes
inten'tion voorneme, bedoeling; ~al opsetlik, moedswillig
intent'ly gespanne, aandagtig
inter'[1] (v) (-red, -red) begrawe, ter aarde bestel
in'ter[2] (adv) tussen; ~ *alia,* onder andere
interact' op mekaar inwerk; ~ion wisselwerking; interaksie
intercept' onderskep, afsny; teenhou
in'terchange (n) wisseling; ruiling; verkeer; vervanging; **traffic ~** (verkeers)wisselaar, wisselkruising
interchange' (v) wissel, ruil; verwissel
in'tercourse omgang, verkeer; gemeenskap

interdenomina'tional interkerklik; inter-
sektaries; sonder/buite kerkverband
interdepend'ent onderling afhanklik
in'terdict (n) verbod, interdik
interdict' (v) verbied, skors
in'terest (n) belang; belangstelling; rente;
compound ~, saamgestelde rente; ~
bearing investment, rentedraende belegging; *rate of* ~, rentekoers; *in the* ~ *of,* in
die belang van; *simple* ~, enkelvoudige
rente; *take an* ~ *in,* belang stel in; (v)
belang stel, interesseer; *I am* ~*ed in,* ek
stel belang in; ~*ed parties,* belangstel-
lende/belanghebbende partye; ~*ing* interessant, belangwekkend
interfere' bemoei (met), inmeng (in)
in'terim (n) tussentyd; *in the* ~, intussen;
(a) voorlopig, interim-, tussentyds; ~
dividend tussentydse dividend
inter'ior (n) binneland; binneste; (a) binneste, binnelands; *Minister of the I*~,
Minister van Binnelandse Sake; ~
decorating binneversiering
interjec'tion tussenwerpsel; uitroep
interlard' deurspek
in'terlude tussenspel
intermar'ry (..married, ..married) onder
mekaar trou, ondertrou
intermed'iary (n) (..ries) tussenpersoon;
bemiddelaar; (a) tussen-, tussenliggend
intermed'iate tussenkomend, intermediêr,
tussen-; ~ **examination** intermediêre
eksamen
inter'ment begrafnis, teraardebestelling
intermi'ssion onderbreking; tussenpouse
intermitt'ent afwisselend; periodiek
intern'[1] (n) intern, inwonende (proef)arts
intern'[2] (v) interneer
inter'nal inwendig, binne; binnelands; innerlik; ~ *check,* interne kontrole; ~
combustion engine, binnebrandmotor; ~
control, interne beheer; ~ *matter,* huis-
houdelike/interne saak/aangeleentheid;
~ *student,* interne student, binnemuurse
student
interna'tional (n) internasionale speler; (a)
internasionaal; ~ *law* (die) volkereg
interplan'etary interplanetêr
inter'pret verklaar, uitlê, vertolk; ~**a'tion**
verklaring, vertolking, uitleg, interpre-
tasie; ~**er** tolk; uitlêer

interprovin'cial interprovinsiaal
interpunc'tion punktuasie, interpunksie
inte'rrogate ondervra, uitvra, kruisvra
interrupt' steur; onderbreek; ~**ion** onderbreking, steuring, interrupsie
intersect' deursny, deurkruis, sny; ~**ion**
snypunt, kruispunt; kruising (strate)
intersperse' vermeng, tussenin stel; ~*d
with,* deurvleg/deurspek met
in'terval rustyd, pouse, tussenruimte; tussentyd; afstand; *at* ~*s,* met tussenposes
intervar'sity (n) (..ties) intervarsity; (a) in-
teruniversitêr
interven'tion tussenkoms, ingryping, inter-
vensie
in'terview (n) onderhoud, gesprek; vraag-
gesprek; (v) ondervra; 'n onderhoud voer;
uithoor; *exit* ~, vertrekgesprek; ~**er**
ondervraer, rapporteur, onderhoudvoer-
der; ~**ing** onderhoudvoering
intes'tine derm; (pl) ingewande, binnegoed
in'timate[1] (v) te kenne gee, aandui
in'timate[2] (a) vertroulik, intiem; innig
intimida'tion afskrikking, vreesaanjaging,
intimidasie
in'to in, tot; ~ *the bargain,* op die koop
toe
intona'tion aanhef; intonasie, stembuiging
intox'icant (n) sterk drank; (a) dronkma-
kend, bedwelmend
intoxica'tion dronkenskap, bedwelming
intran'sitive (n) onoorganklike werkwoord;
(a) onoorganklik
intraven'ous binneaars; ~ *feeding,* binne-
aarse voeding
in'tricate ingewikkeld, verwar
intrigue' (n) intrige, komplot; gekonkel; (v)
konkel, kuip
intrin'sic innerlik, intrinsiek, wesenlik
introduce' invoer; inlei; voorstel; ~ *a bill,*
'n wetsontwerp indien
introduc'tion inleiding; voorstelling; in-
troduksie; voorspel; aanloop; ~*letter of* ~,
aanbevelingsbrief; bekendstelbrief
in'trovert (n) introvert; (a) eenselwig
intrude' indring, lastig val; opdring; inbreuk maak; steur; ~**r** indringer
intui'tion intuïsie, aanvoeling
in'undate oorstroom; oorstelp
invade' inval, aanval; indring; ~**r** inval-
ler

in'valid¹ (n) sieke, invalide; (a) swak, siek; gestrem, invalide
invalid'² (v) siek maak; siek verklaar
inval'id³ (a) ongeldig
inval'uable onskatbaar
invar'iable onveranderlik, standvastig
inva'riably gereeld, deurgaans
inva'sion inval
invent' uitvind; uitdink; ~ion uitvinding; uitvindsel; ~or uitvinder, versinner
in'ventory (n) (..ries) inventaris; voorraad= opname; (v) voorraad opneem, inventa= riseer
in'verse (n) omgekeerde; (a) omgekeer; ~ proportion/ratio, omgekeerde verhou= ding
inver'sion omkering, omsetting; woord= omsetting, inversie
invert' omkeer, omsit; ~ed commas aan= haaltekens
invest' belê, investeer (geld); gee; beves= tig
inves'tigate ondersoek, navors; ~ into, ondersoek instel na, see inquire
investiga'tion ondersoek, navorsing
invest'ment belegging, investering
inves'tor belegger
invi'gilate toesig hou oor, oppas
invi'gilator toesighouer (eksamen); opsiener
invig'orating versterkend, besielend
invin'cible onoorwinlik
invis'ible onsigbaar; ~ mending fynstop, kunsstop
invita'tion uitnodiging, beroep (vir kerklike amp)
invite' (n) uitnodiging; (v) nooi, uitnooi; ~ your friends, jou vriende nooi; ~ tenders, tenders aanvra; ~ trouble, moeilikheid soek
in'voice (n) faktuur; (v) faktureer
invol'untary onwillekeurig
invol've inwikkel; omvat; betrek; ~d in, betrokke in; ~ment betrokkenheid
in'ward (a) inwendig; innerlik; (adv) bin= newaarts; die land in
i'odine jodium, jood
io'ta jota
irate' kwaad, woedend, omgekrap
ir'is (-es) iris, reënboogvlies
i'ron (n) yster; strykyster; have too many ~s in the fire, te veel hooi op die vurk hê; cast ~ gietyster; wrought ~ smeeyster;

(a) yster=, ysteragtig; ~ foundry (..ries) ystergietery; ~ware ysterware
iron'ic(al) ironies
irrecov'erable onverhaalbaar, oninbaar (skuld); ~ debts oninbare skuld, dooie= skuld
irreg'ular (n) ongereelde; (pl) ongereelde troepe; (a) ongereeld; onreëlmatig
irregular'ity (..ties) ongereeldheid; onreël= matigheid
irrel'evant ontoepaslik, ondienstig, nie ter sake nie, irrelevant
irresis'tible onweerstaanbaar, verleidelik, bekoorlik
irrespec'tive niks ontsiende nie; ~ of, on= geag, afgesien van
irrespon'sible onverantwoordelik
irrev'erent oneerbiedig
irrev'ocable onherroeplik
i'rrigate besproei, natlei
irriga'tion besproeiing, irrigasie
i'rritable prikkelbaar, liggeraak
i'rritate vererg, prikkel, irriteer
irrita'tion irritasie, prikkeling; ergernis; wrewel
is'land eiland; ~er eilandbewoner
is'let eilandjie
is'olate afsonder, isoleer
isola'tion afsondering, isolasie; ~ hospital afsondering(s)hospitaal
Is'rael Israel; ~i (n) Israeli; (a) Israelies; ~ite Israeliet; ~itic Israelities
iss'ue (n) uitgawe (boek); kwessie, knel= punt; uitgifte (aandele, banknote); af= stammeling; without male ~, sonder manlike afstammeling; point at ~, ge= skilpunt; (v) uitreik
it dit; hy; sy; face ~, die gevolge dra; with ~, daarmee; byderwets
ital'ic (n) kursiewe letter; in ~s, kursief; (a) kursief, skuins; ~ise kursiveer
itch (n) (ge)jeuk; uitslag; hunkering; (v) jeuk, kriewel, kriebel
it'em item, nommer; artikel; pos; berig
itin'erary (n) (..ries) reisgids; reisplan
its sy, syne; haar, hare
itself' homself, haarself
iv'ory (n) ivoor, olifantstand; (ivories) dobbelsteen; biljartbal; black ~, ebbe= hout; (a) ivoor=, van ivoor
iv'y (ivies) klimop
ix'ia k(a)lossie, ixia

J

jab (n) steek, stoot; (v) steek, stoot
jabb'er (n) gebabbel, gekekkel; (v) babbel, kekkel
jacaran'da (-s) jakaranda
Jack¹ Jan; ~ *Frost*, die ryp; ~ *of all trades*, hansie-my-kneg, duiwelstoejaer; ~ *of all trades, master of none*, twaalf ambagte, dertien ongelukke
jack² (n) mannetjie (dier); boer (kaartspel); domkrag; (v) opdomkrag
jack'al jakkals
jack'ass (-es) eselhings, donkiehings; domkop
jack'boot kapstewel
jack'et baadjie; omhulsel; mantel
jack: ~-in-the-box kaartman; ~knife (.. knives) herneutermes; ~pot boerpot
jad'ed moeg, afgemat, vermoeid
jag (v) (-ged, -ged) tand, kerf, inkeep; ~ged getand, puntig, ru, skerp
jag'uar Amerikaanse luiperd, jaguar
jail (n) tronk; (v) in die tronk sit; ~bird tronkvoël; ~break ontsnapping; ~er sipier, tronkbewaarder
jam¹ (n) konfyt
jam² (n) gedrang, ophoping; verkeers= knoop; haak; (v) (-med, -med) klem, slaan; vasklem; vasknel
jamboree' samekoms, saamtrek, laer
ja'mming (n) knelling; storing (elek.); (a) knellend; ~ station steursender
jan'itor deurwagter, portier
Jan'uary Januarie
japon'ica (-s) japonika, kamelia
jar¹ (n) kruik
jar² (n) wanklank; rusie; (v) (-red, -red) kras; twis; ~ *upon the nerves*, op die senuwees werk
jarg'on brabbeltaal, koeterwaals
jas'mine jasmyn
jas'per jaspis
jaun'dice geelsug; nyd, jaloesie
jaunt (n) uitstappie; *on the* ~, op die swier
jav'elin werpspies
jaw (n) kakebeen; gepraat; (pl) bek; ~bone kakebeen; ~breaker tandpyner; tong= knoper, snelsêer
jay'walker bontloper, gansloper
jazz jazz

jeal'ous jaloers, afgunstig, naywerig; ~y jaloesie, naywer
jeans slenterbroek; jannas, jeans
jeer (n) spot, beskimping; (v) spot, uitlag
jell'y (jellies) jellie, gelei; ~ beans jellie= boontjies; ~fish seekwal; ~ powder jel= liepoeier
jeo'pardise in gevaar bring/stel; ~ *your promotion*, jou bevordering verongeluk
jeremi'ad jeremiade, klaaglied
jerk (n) ruk; stoot, stamp; *by* ~*s*, met rukke en stote; (v) ruk, pluk; smyt, stamp; ~y hortend, rukkend
je'rrybuilder knutselbouer
jers'ey (-s) trui
jest (n) skerts, grap, korswel; (v) skerts, korswel; ~ *ing apart*, alle gekheid op 'n stokkie; ~er (hof)nar, grapmaker, grap= jas, *see* joker
Je'sus Jesus
jet¹ (n) git; (a) git=
jet² (n) straal; pit; straler (vliegtuig); tuit; bek; spuit; (v) (-ted, -ted) uitspuit; straal; ~ *age* straaleeu
jet'black pikswart, gitswart
jet'fighter straaljagter, straalvegter
jet'lag straaldraal, vlugleegte; *I am suffer= ing from* ~, ek het straaldraal/tydkramp; ek is straaltam/vliegvoos/vlugflou
jet'sam strandgoed; wrakstukke, opdrifsel
jet'liner (passasier)straler
jet'set stralerkliek; ~ter stralerjakker, straaljakker
jett'y (jetties) hawehoof, pier
Jew Jood
jew'el (n) juweel, kleinood; skat; (v) versier; ~ler juwelier; ~lery juwele, juweliersware
jiff'(y) ommesientjie, kits; *in a* ~, in 'n kits, in 'n japtrap, tjop-tjop
jigg'le bar riffelstrook (teerpad)
jig'saw figuursaag; ~ puzzle legkaart
jin'gle (n) reklamedeuntjie; klingelrympie; (v) klingel, rinkel; ~ bell klingelklokkie
jit'terbug ritteldans
jit'ters ritteltit
jive (n, v) jive (dans)
job (n) werk, betrekking, pos, baantjie; taak; ~ description posbeskrywing; ~ evaluation posevaluering; ~ opportunity

(..ties) werkgeleentheid; ~ **placement** in=
diensplasing; ~ **reservation** werkafbake=
ning; ~ **seeker** werksoeker; ~ **satisfac=
tion** werk(s)bevrediging
job: ~ber makelaar; knoeier; ~ **lot** rom=
melspul
jock'ey (n) (-s) jokkie; snuiter, vent
joc'ular grapperig, grappig
jog (v) (-ged, -ged) draf, pretdraf; stamp,
stoot, sukkel; ~ **along,** aansukkel, voort=
sukkel; ~**ger** (pret)drawwer
jog'trot sukkelgang; sukkeldraffie.
johnn'y (johnnies) kêrel, vent
join (n) voeg, naat, las; verbindingslyn; (v)
verbind; saamvoeg; ~ **up,** aansluit
join'er skrynwerker
joint[1] (n) gewrig; lit; verbinding; las; *out of*
~, uit lit; (v) saamvoeg; las
joint[2] (a) mede-; gesamentlik; ~ **estate** ge=
samentlike/gemeenskaplike boedel; ~**ly**
gesamentlik; ~ **stock company** aandele=
maatskappy
joke (n) grap, frats; gekheid; *it is no* ~, dis
geen/g'n kleinigheid nie; *play a practical*
~ *on someone,* iem. 'n poets bak; (v)
grappe maak; gekskeer; speel; ~**r** grap=
maker; grapjas; asjas (kaartspel)
jollifica'tion vrolikheid, pret, plesierigheid
joll'y vrolik, plesierig; aangeklam; *you will*
~ *well have to,* jy sal eenvoudig moet
jolt stamp, stoot
jot[1] (n) jota, kleinigheid
jot[2] (v) (-ted, -ted) aanteken, aanstip; ~
down, aanstip
journ'al dagboek; dagblad; joernaal, tyd=
skrif; spil; *house* ~, firmabl**a**d; ~ **entry**
joernaalinskrywing
journalese' koeranttaal
journ'alism joernalistiek; die pers
journ'alist koerantskrywer, joernalis; ver=
slaggewer
journ'ey (n) (-s) reis; *a day's* ~, 'n dagreis
jov'ial vrolik, plesierig, opgeruimd, joviaal
jowl kakebeen; wang; krop; onderken;
keelvel; *cheek by* ~, kop in een mus
joy blydskap, vreugde; *it gives me* ~, dit
doen my genoeë; ~**ful** vrolik, bly; ~**ous**
vrolik; bly; ~**ride** plesierrit; ~**stick**
stuurstok, stuurarm
jub'ilant juigend, jubelend
jub'ilee jubileum; jubelfees; jubeljaar
judge (n) regter; beoordelaar; (v) oordeel;

vonnis; beoordeel; ~ *by,* oordeel volgens
judg'ment oordeel; vonnis; opinie; *day of*
~, oordeelsdag
judi'cial geregtelik; regterlik; ~ **manage=
ment** geregtelike bestuur
judi'cious oordeelkundig, verstandig
ju'do judo
jug kan, beker; wasbeker
jug'gle goël, wiggel; kul; ~**r** goëlaar, wig=
gelaar, jongleur
juice sop, sap
jui'cy sapperig, sappig; smaaklik
juke'box (-es) blêrkas
juk'skei: ~ **club** jukskeilaer; ~ **league**
jukskeiliga
July' Julie
jum'ble (n) verwarring; mengelmoes; alle=
gaartjie; ~ **sale** rommelverkoping
jum'bo lomperd, diksak; ~ **jet** makrostraler
jump (n) sprong; (v) spring; ~ *to a conclu=
sion,* 'n voorbarige gevolgtrekking maak
junc'tion verbinding; knoop; aansluiting
(pad, spoorweg)
junc'ture naat, voeg; tydsgewrig, tydstip
June Junie
jung'le oerwoud, ruigte, wildernis; ~**-jim**
wouterklouter (speeltuig)
jun'ior jonger, junior; ~ **clerk** onderklerk;
~ **partner** junior/jongste vennoot
junk (n) rommel, uitskot; jonk (seilboot);
~ **food** prulkos, kafkos; ~ **shop** help-
my-krapwinkel
jurisdic'tion regsgebied, jurisdiksie
jur'ist juris, regsgeleerde
jur'y (n) **(juries)** jurie
just[1] (a) regverdig, onpartydig; juis
just[2] (adv) net, presies; ~ *as,* net soos, nes;
~ *now,* netnou; ~ *as well,* net so goed
jus'tice geregtigheid; regverdigheid; justisie;
court of ~, geregshof; *do* ~ *to,* reg laat
wedervaar; ~ *of the peace,* vrederegter
justifica'tion regverdiging, wettiging
jus'tify (..fied, ..fied) regverdig, staaf
jut (n) uitsteeksel; (v) (-ted, -ted) uitsteek
jute goiing, jute
juv'enile (n) jeugdige; (a) jong, jeugdig; *J~
Affairs Board,* Jeugraad; *J~ Court,*
Kinderhof; ~ *delinquency,* jeugwange=
drag, jeugmisdadigheid; ~ *delinquent,*
jeugoortreder, jeugmisdadiger
juxtaposi'tion teenaanligging, naasme=
kaarstelling, jukstaposisie

K

kale boerkool
kaleid'oscope kaleidoskoop
kangaroo' kangaroe
Karoo' Karoo
kay'ak kajak (eskimo-bootjie)
keel (n) kiel; skip, vaartuig; (v) kiel; om=
slaan; omval; ~haul kielhaal
keen skerp; hewig; ywerig, gretig, skerpsin=
nig; as ~ as mustard, uiters gretig; ~ on,
versot op
keep (n) bewaring; onderhoud; toesig; for
~s, om te hou; (v) (kept, kept) hou; bêre;
vier; nakom; bewaar; in voorraad hou; ~
an appointment, 'n afspraak hou; ~
company, geselskap hou; ~ faith, woord
hou; ~ peace, die vrede bewaar; ~ a pro=
mise, 'n belofte nakom; ~ time, maat
hou; ~ in touch with, in voeling/aanra=
king bly met; ~ well, goed/gesond bly;
~er bewaarder, opsigter; ~sake aan=
denking, soewenier
keg vaatjie
kenn'el dierehotel; hondehotel, hondeher=
berg, hondesorg, woefietuiste
kept see keep; ~ woman houvrou, hand=
perd
kerb randsteen
kern'el pit; korrel
ketch'up blatjang, kruiesous
ket'tle ketel; a pretty ~ of fish, 'n mooi
spul; ~ drum keteltrom
key (n) (-s) sleutel (van deur); klawer; toets;
~board klawers, toetsbord; ~hole
sleutelgat; ~ industry (..ries) sleutelny=
werheid, sleutelbedryf; ~ man sleutel=
man; ~note grondtoon; ~note address,
tematoespraak; ~stone sluitsteen
kha'ki kakie; ~bos kakiebos
kibb'utz kibboets (Israel)
kick (n) skop; skok; (v) skop; ~ the bucket,
sterf, bokveld toe gaan; ~ over the traces,
oor die tou trap; ~back gunsloon; ~er
skopper; ~-off afskop
kid¹ (n) boklam; bokvel; kidleer; kind,
kannetjie, snuiter; (v) (-ded, -ded) lam
kid² (v) (-ded, -ded) kul, fop
kid'ding tergery
kid'dy (kiddies) kleintjie, kleinding
kid'nap (-ped, -ped) ontvoer, skaak, steel

('n kind); ~per kinderdief; ontvoerder;
~ping ontvoering
kid'ney (-s) nier; aard; ~ bean nierboon(tjie)
kill (v) doodmaak; slag; vermoor; ~ed in=
stantly, op slag dood (padongeluk); ~
time, tyd verdryf; ~ing (n) doodmaak;
slagting; (a) dodelik; onweerstaanbaar;
~joy suurpruim, pretbederwer, spelbreker
kiln oond, steenoond
kil'ogram kilogram
kil'ometre kilometer
kil'owatt kilowatt
kin familie, bloedverwant, maagskap
kind¹ (n) soort, geslag; aard; natuur; aan=
leg; nothing of the ~, niks daarvan nie
kind² (a) vriendelik, minsaam; lief; ~ re=
gards, vriendelike groete
kin'dergarten kleuterskool, bewaarskool
kind'hearted goedhartig
kin'dle aansteek; ontvlam; opflikker
kind'ly vriendelik, goedhartig
kind'ness vriendelikheid, goedheid
kin'dred (a) verwant; passend; gelyksoortig
king koning, vors; heer; ~'s English,
standaard-Engels; ~dom koninkryk;
~fisher visvanger; ~size bieliegrootte
kink (n) kinkel; nuk, gril; (v) 'n kinkel gee;
~y vol kinkels; eksentriek
kiosk' kiosk; tuinhuisie
kipp'er, kipp'ered herring gerookte haring,
kipper
kiss (n) (-es) soen, kus; (v) soen; ~ the dust,
in die stof byt; ~ goodbye, 'n afskeidsoen
gee; ~ curl oorkrulletjie, koketkrulletjie;
~ing (n) soenery, gesoen
kit uitrusting; ~bag knapsak
kitch'en kombuis; ~ tea: have a ~ tea,
bruidskombuis/kombuistee hou; ~ uten=
sils kombuisgerei
kite vlieër, kuikendief; haai; fly a ~, 'n
proefballon oplaat
kitt'en (n) katjie
kitt'y (kitties) katjie, kietsie
knack slag, handigheid; gewoonte
knap'sack bladsak, knapsak
knave skurk, skelm; boer (kaartspel)
knead (v) knie, knee; masseer
knee knie; ~cap knieskyf; knieskut (by
voetbal); ~ joint kniegewrig

kneel (knelt, knelt) kniel; ~ *down,* neer=
kniel
knick'erbockers, kniebroek, kuitbroek
knick'-knack snuistery
knife (n) **(knives)** mes; *have one's* ~ *into a
person,* op iem. pik; ~ **blade** lem
knight (n) ridder; perd (skaak)
knit (knit(ted), knit(ted)) brei; saamvleg; ~
the brows, die winkbroue frons; ~**ter**
breier; ~**ting** breiwerk; ~**ting machine**
breimasjien
knob knop; ~**by** knoesterig; ~**kerrie**
knopkierie
knock (n) klop; klap, raps; stamp; (v) klop,
stoot; stamp; ~ *down with a feather,*
omblaas; ~ *out,* verslaan; uitslaan; ~
spots off one, iem. opdons; ~**er** klopper;
~**-kneed** met X-bene, swak; ~**-on** aan=
slaan
knock'out uitklophou; ~ **blow** uitklop=
hou; ~ **competition** uitklopkompetisie
knot (n) knoop; kwas; knop, band; *cut the
gordian* ~, die Gordiaanse knoop deur=
hak; (v) **(-ted, -ted)** knoop; strik; ver=

bind; ~**ty** knoperig, geknoop; knoesterig;
lastig; netelig
know (n) wete; *be in the* ~, ingelig wees; (v)
(knew, known) weet, ken; verstaan; ~ *for
a fact,* seker weet; ~ *by heart,* van buite
ken; ~ *the ropes,* gekonfyt wees in iets;
~**how** kundigheid; ~**ing** kundig, ver=
nuftig; ~**ingly** opsetlik; veelbetekenend
knowl'edge kennis, kunde; wete; *to the best
of my* ~, na my beste wete; *it is common*
~, dis algemeen bekend; *first hand* ~,
eerstehandse kennis; *without my* ~,
sonder my medewete; *a working* ~,
gangbare kennis
known (v) *see* **know** (a) bekend
knuc'kle (n) kneukel; ~**-duster** vuisyster
kop'pie koppie (heuwel)
kosh'er kosjer
kraal kraal
krans krans, rotswand
ku'du koedoe
kwash'iorkor kwasjiorkor, ondervoeding=
siekte

L

lag'er (n) laer; (v) laer trek
lab'el (n) kaartjie, etiket; (v) **(-led, -led)**
merk, klassifiseer; bestempel, etiketteer
lab'ial (n) lipletter, labiaal; (a) liplabiaal
labor'atory (..ries) laboratorium
lab'our (n) arbeid, werk; *hard* ~, harde=
pad; ~ *intensive,* arbeidintensief; (v)
werk, arbei; ~ *under a mistake,* onder 'n
dwaling verkeer; ~**er** werksman, ar=
beider; ~ **relations** arbeid(s)verhou=
dings, arbeid(s)betrekkinge, bedryfsver=
houdings
lab'yrinth doolhof, labirint
lac lak
lace (n) kant, band; skoenveter, skoenriem;
(v) ryg, toeryg; met kant versier; omboor
la'cerate skeur, verskeur
lack (n) gebrek, gemis, behoefte; *for* ~ *of,*
by gebrek aan; (v) ontbreek
lacq'uer (n) lak, vernis; (v) verlak, vernis
lad seun, jongeling
ladd'er (n) leer; *go into* ~**s,** lostrek
ladd'ie knapie, kêreltjie
lad'en belaai

lad'ing lading, vrag; *bill of* ~, vragbrief
lad'le (n) potlepel, soplepel; (v) met 'n lepel
skep, opskep; ~ *out,* uitskep
lad'y (ladies) dame; ~ *of the house,* gas=
vrou, huisvrou; *our L* ~, Ons Liewe Vrou;
~**bird** skilpadjie; ~**like** damesagtig; fyn,
beskaaf, vroulik; ~**'s man** meisiesgek;
laventelhaan, ruikerridder
lag (v) **(-ged -ged)** draal, agterbly; deporteer;
~ *behind,* agterbly
lagoon' strandmeer, lagune
lair (n) lêplek, boerplek, hol; (v) lê, hou
lake meer, pan; ~ **dweller** paal(be)woner
lamb (n, v) lam
lame (a) lam, mank, kruppel, gebreklik; *a*
~ *excuse,* 'n flou ekskuus
lament' (n) weeklaag, jammerklag; (v) be=
ween, betreur
lam'inate (v) lamelleer; uitklop, plat slaan;
(a) skilferig; ~**d door** lameldeur
lamm'ergeyer lammervanger
lamp lamp; lig; ~**black** roet, lampswartsel;
~ **chimney** lampglas; ~ **post** lamppaal

lance (n) lans; harpoen; lansier; (v) deur‑
steek; oopsny; ~r lansier

lan'cet vlym, lanset

land (n) land, grond; landerye; *see how the*
~ *lies*, die kat uit die boom kyk; (v) land,
aan wal stap

land: ~**ing strip** aanloopbaan; ~**lady** lo‑
sieshoudster, hospita; ~**lord** huisbaas;
~**mine** landmyn; ~**scape gardening**
tuinargitektuur; ~ **surveyor** landmeter

lane laning, laan; deurgang; baan (verkeer)

lang'uage taal, spraak; ~ **laboratory** taal‑
laboratorium

lank skraal, maer; rank

lan'tern lantern; *chinese* ~, lampion; *magic*
~, towerlantern

lap[1] (n) skoot; klap (van saal); holte; (v)
(-ped, -ped) inwikkel; toevou; omgeef

lap[2] (n) voeg; las; rondte (sport); ~ **record**
baanrekord (motorrenne)

lap'dog skoothondjie

lapel' kraagomslag, lapel; ~ **badge** lapel‑
wapen, lapelknopie

lapse (n) verloop; ~ *of time*, tyd(s)verloop;
(v) verval; verstryk

lap'wing kiewiet

lar'board bakboord

lar'ceny (..nies) diefstal

lard (n) varkvet, reusel; (v) deurspek, lar‑
deer, met spek stop; ~**er** (voorraad)spens

large groot; breed, wyd; ruim; *as* ~ *as life*,
lewensgroot; *a gentleman at* ~, 'n rente‑
nier; ryk man sonder beroep; *the public
at* ~, die groot/breë publiek

lark[1] (n) lewerkie, leeurik

lark[2] (n) grap, gekskeerdery; (v) gekskeer,
grappe verkoop; ~**er** pretmaker

lark'spur ridderspoor

larv'a (-e) larwe, papie, maaier

laryngit'is keelontsteking, laringitis

la'rynx (-es, larynges) strottehoof

lasciv'ious weelderig, wulps, wellustig

la'ser laser; ~ **beam** laserstraal

lash (n) (-es) raps, sweepslag; voorslag;
ooghaar; (v) raps, slaan, gésel

lass (-es) meisie, nooi(e)ntjie, doedie

lasso' (n) (-s) vangriem, gooitou

last[1] lees (van 'n skoen)

last[2] (n) laaste; *the* ~ *but one*, op een na die
laaste; *the* ~ *but not the least*, les bes; *to the
very* ~, tot die bitter end; (a, adv) laaste,
vergange; eind‑; ~ *night*, gisteraand

last[3] (n) uithouvermoë; (v) duur, uithou;
aanhou; voldoende wees

last'comer heksluiter

last'ing duursaam, blywend

last'ly uiteindelik, ten laaste, ten slotte

latch (n) (-es) knip; ~**key** nagsleutel

late (a) laat; wyle, oorlede; (adv) laat; on‑
langs, vroeër

late'ly onlangs, pas, kort gelede

lat'ent verborge; latent

lathe draaibank

lath'er (n) seepsop, skuim; (v) inseep

lat'itude breedte; ruimte; beweegruimte

latrine' kleinhuisie, latrine, privaat

latt'er laasgenoemde; laaste; *the former and
the* ~, eersgenoemde en laasgenoemde;
~**ly** onlangs, in die jongste tyd

latt'ice traliewerk, rasterwerk

laud (v) prys, ophemel; ~**able** lofwaardig,
prysenswaardig

laugh (n) lag, gelag; (v) lag; ~ *at*, uitlag; ~
off, jou lag-lag daarvan afmaak; ~**able**
belaglik, snaaks

laugh'ing lag; gelag; *I could not help* ~, ek
kon nie my lag hou nie; *no* ~ *matter*, nie
iets om oor te lag nie; ~**ly** lag-lag; ~ **stock**
die spot van iedereen

laugh'ter gelag

launch[1] (n) (-es) plesierbootjie; barkas,
sloep; lansering (ruimtetuig)

launch[2] (v) van stapel laat loop (skip); loods
(skema); lanseer (ruimtetuig); gooi; slin‑
ger; aanpak; op tou sit; ~ *a project*, 'n
projek loods; ~(**ing**) **pad** lanseerblad

launderette', **laun'dromat** wasseret

laun'dry (..dries) wassery; waskamer

lau'rel (n) lourier; louerkrans; *rest on one's*
~*s*, op jou louere rus

la'va lawa

lav'atory (..ries) latrine, kleinhuisie, pri‑
vaat, toilet(kamer)

lav'ender (n) reukwater, lavental

lav'ish (a) kwistig; volop, oorvloedig

law wet; regsgeleerdheid; die reg; *common*
~, gemenereg, gewoontereg; ~ *of em‑
ployment*, arbeidsreg, diensreg; ~ *en‑
forcement*, wetstoepassing; *international*
~, volkereg; *necessity knows no* ~, nood
breek wet; *read* ~, in die regte studeer;
Roman Dutch ~, Romeins-Hollandse
reg; *statute* ~, wettereg, statutereg; *study*
~, in die regte studeer; ~ **abiding** wets‑

gehoorsaam; ordeliewend; ~ **court** ge=
regshof; ~**ful** wettig, wetlik
lawn grasperk, grasveld; ~ **mower** gras=
snyer; ~ **tennis** tennis
law'yer prokureur; regspraktisyn
lax slap, los; laks; nalatig; ~**ative** (n) lak=
seermiddel, purgeermiddel, purgasie
lay[1] (v) (**laid, laid**) lê (eier); indien ('n klag);
voorlê; dek (tafel); *see* **lie**[2]; ~ *a bet,* 'n
weddenskap aangaan; ~ *off,* tydelik af=
dank; ~ *it on thick,* met die heuningkwas
bewerk
lay[2] (a) wêreldlik; leke=; ~ **brother** leke=
broeder; ~ **preacher** lekeprediker
lay'-by spaargeld; bêrekoop
lay'er laag; loot (plant); lêhoender
lay'man (..**men**) leek, oningewyde; *for the*
~ *and the expert,* vir die leek en die ken=
ner
lay-out uiteensetting, inkleding, uitleg
laz'iness luiheid, traagheid
laz'y lui, traag; ~**bones** luisak, luilak
leach (v) uitloog; wegspoel; deursyg
lead[1] (n) lood; dieplood; koeël
lead[2] (n) leiding; leidraad; hoofrol; *play the*
~, die hoofrol vertolk; *take the* ~, die
leiding/voortou neem; (v) (**led, led**) lei,
voorgaan; aanvoer; ~ *a dog's life,* 'n
hondelewe hê/voer; ~ *the way,* die pad
wys
lead'er leier, voorman; hoofartikel (koe=
rant); ~**ship** leierskap
lead'ing leidend, vernaamste; ~ *question,*
uitlokvraag
lead: ~ **pencil** potlood; ~ **poisoning** lood=
vergiftiging
leaf (n) (**leaves**) blad; blaar; *take a* ~ *out of*
somebody's book, iem. tot voorbeeld
neem; *turn over a new* ~, 'n nuwe blaad=
jie begin; ~**let** blaartjie (boom); blad=
skrif, vlugskrif, strooibiljet, blaadjie
league (n) verbond; myl; liga; *L~ of Na=*
tions, Volke(re)bond
leak (n) lek(plek); lekkasie; (v) lek; ~ *out,*
uitlek; ~**age** lekkasie, lek
lean[1] (a) maer, skraal
lean[2] (v) (**-ed, -ed** or **-t, -t**) leun; oorhel; ge=
neig wees; ~ *on,* steun op
leap (n) sprong; *a* ~ *in the dark,* 'n sprong
in die duister; (v) (**-ed, -ed** or **-t, -t**) spring;
huppel; oorspring; ~**frog** hasieoor; ~**year**
skrikkeljaar

learn (**-ed, -ed** or **-t, -t**) leer; verneem, hoor;
~ *by heart,* uit die hoof leer; ~**ed** geleerd;
~**er** leerling; beginner; leerder; ~**er-**
driver's licence, leer(ling)rybewys; ~**ing**
geleerdheid
lease (n) huurkontrak; bruikhuur; huurtyd;
new ~ *of life,* nuwe lewensduur; (v) ver=
huur; uithuur; ~**hold** huurbesit, huurpag
leash (n) (**-es**) tou, band; *on* ~, aan 'n tou
least (n) die minste; ~ *of all,* die allermin=
ste; *at* ~, minstens (tien vrae); ten minste;
at the ~, op sy minste; *not in the* ~, glad
nie; *to say the* ~ *of it,* op sy sagste uitge=
druk; (a) kleinste, minste, geringste
leath'er leer, oorleer
leave[1] (n) verlof; vergunning; ~ *of absence,*
verlof; *on* ~, met/op verlof
leave[2] (n) afskeid; *take* ~, afskeid neem; (v)
(**left, left**) laat staan; verlaat; ~ *alone,*
met rus laat; uitlos; ~ *behind,* agterlaat;
~ *the rails,* ontspoor
lect'ern lesingstander, koorlessenaar, kna=
pie
lec'ture (n) lesing, voorlesing; (v) les gee; 'n
voorlesing hou; vermaan
lec'turer lektor, lektrise (vroulik); dosent;
~ **guide** lektorgids
lec'turing post doseerpos
led (v) *see* **lead**
ledge rand; lys; bergrand
ledg'er grootboek; dwarsbalk
leech (**-es**) bloedsuier; arts, heelmeester
leek prei; *eat the* ~, 'n belediging sluk
left[1] (n) linkerhand; *to the* ~, links, aan die
linkerkant; (a) linker-; hot; (adv) links
left[2] (v): ~**-overs** oorskietkos, *see* **leave**
left: ~**hand drive** linkerstuur; ~**handed**
links, linkshandig, hotklou; onhandig;
~**wing** linksgesind(e) (studente, werkers)
leg (n) been; poot; boud (vleis); *on one's last*
~**s,** op sy uiterste; ~ *of mutton,* skaap=
boud; *pull one's* ~, met iem. die gek
skeer; skerts, korswel; ~ *before wicket,*
been voor paaltjie
leg'acy (..**cies**) erf(e)nis; nalatenskap
leg'al wetlik, wettig; regs=; ~ **language**
regstaal; ~ **proceedings** geregtelike stap=
pe; ~ **representative** regsverteenwoor=
diger; ~ **tender** wettige betaalmiddel
leg'-bye by-loslopie
le'gend legende, sprokie; ~**ary** legendaries
legg'ing(s) kamas(te)

le'gible leesbaar
le'gion keurbende, legioen
legisla'tion wetgewing
legit'imate (v) wettig, eg verklaar; (a) wet=
tig, eg; ~ share, regmatige (aan)deel
leguan' likkewaan
leg'ume peulgewas
lei'sure ledige tyd, vrye tyd; utilising of ~,
vryetydsbesteding; ~ly op sy/haar ge=
mak, kuier-kuier
lem'on suurlemoen
lemonade' limonade
lem'ur lemur, vosaap, halfaap
lend (lent, lent) leen, uitleen; ~ itself to,
leen hom tot; ~er uitlener; ~ing rate
uitleenkoers
length lengte; duur, afstand; go to any ~,
niks ontsien nie; at some ~, taamlik uit=
voerig; ~en langer maak, verleng; ~wise
in die lengte; ~y lang, langdurig, uitgerek
len'ient versagtend, toegewend, toeskietlik
lens (-es) lens
len'til lensie
leo'pard luiperd
lep'er melaatse
lep'rosy melaatsheid
les'bian (n) lesbiër; (a) lesbies
less (n) minder; (a) minder, kleiner, gerin=
ger; in ~ than no time, in 'n kits; (adv)
minder; none the ~, nietemin; (prep)
min; for ~, goedkoper; five ~ four, vyf
min vier
lessee' huurder
less'on les, oefening; skriflesing
less'or verhuurder, huisbaas
let (v) (let, let) laat; toelaat; verhuur; ~
down, in die steek laat; ~ go, loslaat; ~
off, loslaat, vrylaat; to ~, te huur
leth'al dodelik, gevaarlik
lett'er (n) letter; brief; (pl) lettere; ~ of
attorney, volmag; by ~, per brief; capital
~, hoofletter; man of ~s, geleerde;
~box (-es) briewebus; ~card briefkaart
lett'uce slaai
leukem'ia leukemie, bloedkanker
lev'el (n) waterpas; vlak; on the same ~, op
gelyke voet; upper ~, boonste vlak; (v)
(-led, -led) gelyk maak, aanlê; (a, adv) ge=
lyk, waterpas; do one's ~ best, jou uiter=
ste bes doen; ~ crossing (spoorweg)oor=
gang; ~-headed verstandig, ewewigtig
lev'er (n) hefboom; ligter

lev'y (n) (levies) heffing, toeslag, bybelas=
ting; (v) (levied, levied) hef; lig; werf; oplê;
invorder (geld); ~ a fine, 'n boete oplê
lewd ontugtig, wellustig, hitsig
lexicog'rapher leksikograaf, woordeboek=
maker
lex'icon (-s) woordeboek, leksikon
liabil'ity (..ties) aanspreeklikheid; verant=
woordelikheid, verpligting; (pl) laste
li'able aanspreeklik; verantwoordelik; ~
for, aanspreeklik vir; hold ~, aanspreek=
lik hou
liais'on skakeling; verbinding; ~ committee
skakelkomitee, oorlegkomitee; ~ officer
skakelbeampte
li'ar leuenaar, spekskieter
lib'el (n) laster; (v) (-led, -led) belaster, be=
klad; ~ action lasteraksie; ~lous lasterlik
lib'eral (n) vrysinnige, liberaal; (a) liberaal,
vrysinnig; onbekrompe; ~ education,
vrysinnige opvoeding, veelsydige opleiding;
~ism liberalisme
lib'erate bevry, vrymaak, vrylaat
lib'ertine vrydenker, libertyn
lib'erty (..ties) vryheid; take the ~, jou die
vryheid veroorloof
librar'ian bibliotekaris
lib'rary (..ries) biblioteek, boekery
li'cence (n) lisensie, permit; rybewys
li'cense (v) toelaat, vergun; lisensieer; ~e'
lisensiehouer
licentiate lisensiaat
licen'tious losbandig, ongebonde
lick (n) lek; (v) lek; uitstof, wen, klop; ~ the
dust, die stof byt; ~ into shape, vorm gee
aan; ~ing gelek; lekkery; loesing
lid deksel; ooglid; that puts the ~ on, dit sit/
plaas die kroon op alles
lie[1] (n) leuen, kluitjie; tell a ~, lieg, jok;
white ~, noodleuen(tjie); (v) lieg, jok; ~
detector leuenverklikker
lie[2] (n) ligging; (v) (lay, lain) lê, rus; ~ in
state, in staatsie lê
lief graag
lien retensiereg, retensiegeld
lieuten'ant luitenant; ~-general (lieute=
nants-general) luitenant-generaal
life (lives) lewe; lewensduur; leefwyse; full
of ~, springlewendig; keep ~ and soul
together, liggaam en siel aanmekaarhou;
not for the ~ of him, vir geen geld ter
wêreld nie; take one's ~ in one's hands,

jou lewe waag; ~ **assurance** lewensverse=
kering; ~**belt** redgordel; reddingsboei;
~**boat** reddingsboot; ~**buoy (-s)** red=
dingsboei; ~**guard** strandwag; ~**jacket**
reddingsbaadjie; ~**less** leweloos, dooie=
rig; ~**long** lewenslank; ~ **raft** red=
(dings)vlot; ~**saver** lewensredder, strand=
wag; ~ **sentence** lewenslange gevangenis=
straf; ~-**size** lewensgrootte; ~**style** leef=
wyse

lift (n) hyser, hysbak; *give a* ~, iem. oplaai;
(v) optel, oplig; iem. oplaai; ~ **club**
saamryklub; ~-**off** lansering (ruimtetuig)

lig'ament band, ligament

light[1] (n) lig; (v) (**-ed, -ed** or **lit, lit**) lig; ver=
lig; aansteek; (a) lig, helder; blond

light[2] (v) neerkom; te lande kom; afklim;
~ *on,* gaan sit op

light[3] (a, adv) los; lig; gou, vinnig; ~ *deli=
very van,* (ligte) bestelwa, bakkie; ~
reading, ligte leesstof

light'er aansteker, vuurslag

light'-hearted lughartig, vrolik, onbesorg

light'house vuurtoring

light'ning weerlig, blits, bliksem; ~ **con=
ductor** weerligafleier, bliksemafleier

light: ~-**o-love** flerrie, ligtekooi; ~**weight**
liggewig

like (n) gelyke; ewebeeld; *his* ~*s and dis=
likes,* sy voorkeure en afkeure; (v) hou
van, lief wees vir; (a, adv) gelyk; eenders;
soortgelyk; soos; *in* ~ *manner,* op
dieselfde manier; ~**ly** waarskynlik, ver=
moedelik

lik'en vergelyk

like'ness gelykenis, ewebeeld

like'wise eweneens; desgelyks, ingelyks, net
so

lik'ing behae, smaak, welgevalle; *follow
one's own* ~, jou eie sin volg; *not to my*
~, nie na my smaak nie

lil'ac (n) sering; (a) pers, lila

lil'y (n) (**lilies**) lelie; (a) lelie=; ~-**white**
leliewit, spierwit

limb (n) ledemaat; lit; tak

lime[1] (n) kalk; voëlent; *slaked* ~, gebluste
kalk

lime[2] lemmetjie; *sweet* ~, soetlemmetjie; ~
juice lemmetjiesap

lime: ~ **kiln** kalkoond; ~**light** kalklig

lim'erick bogrympie, limerick

lim'it (n) grens, perk, limiet; *that's the* ~*!*

dis darem te erg! ~**a'tion** beperking; ~**ed**
beperk, begrens; ~**ed liability company,**
maatskappy met beperkte aanspreeklik=
heid

limp (v) mank loop, hink; (a) mank; lenig,
slap

lim'pet klipmossel; ~ **mine** kleefmyn

line (n) reël; lyn; streep; verseël; ~ *of
action,* gedragslyn; ~ *of communication,*
verbindingslyn; *drop a* ~, 'n paar reëls
skryf; *hard* ~*s!* simpatie! hoe jammer! *in*
~ *with,* op een lyn met; *read between the*
~*s,* tussen die reëls lees; ~ *of least
resistance,* weg van die geringste weer=
stand; (v) lyne trek; onderstreep; ~ *the
route,* die roete belyn

lin'eage geslag, afkoms

lin'en (n) linne; linnegoed; (a) linne=

lines'man (..**men**) vlagman, lynregter;
lynwagter

ling'er draai, draal, vertoef; kwyn, sukkel

li'ngerie linnegoed; onderklere

ling'ering talmend, dralend; *a* ~ *disease,* 'n
slepende siekte

ling'uist taalgeleerde, linguis

lin'iment smeermiddel, smeersalf

link (n) skakel; fakkel; (v) (aaneen)skakel;
~**s** gholfveld; mansjetknope

lin'seed lynsaad; ~ **oil** lynolie

lin'tel latei

li'on leeu; ~'*s den,* leeukuil; ~'*s share,*
leeueaandeel; ~**ess (-es)** leeuin, leeuwyfie;
~-**hearted** moedig, dapper; ~**ise** 'n
besoeker ophemel

lip lip; kant, rand; *keep a stiff upper* ~,
moed hou; ~ **service** lippediens; ~**stick**
lipstif(fie)

liqueur' likeur, soetsopie

liq'uid (n) vloeistof; (pl) vloeibare kos; (a)
vloeibaar; ~ **assets** likiede bates; ~**ate**
vereffen, likwideer; ~**a'tion** likwidasie;
~**iser** versapper

liq'our drank, sterk drank; *the worse for*
~, hoenderkop

liq'uorice drop, soethout

lisp (n) gelispel; (v) lispel

list (n) lys; naamlys; *stock exchange* ~**ing,**
notering op effektebeurs; (v) opskrywe;
noteer (effektebeurs); kwoteer (aandele);
lys (die vrae)

lis'ten luister; ~ *in,* (in)luister; ~**er** luiste=
raar, toehoorder; ~**ing post** luisterpos

list'less lusteloos, dooierig

li'tchi lietsjie

lit'eral letterlik, woordelik; (n) drukkers= duiwel, setsatan

lit'erary letterkundig

lit'erature letterkunde, literatuur

lit're liter; *two ~s of milk,* twee liter melk

litt'er (n) drag, werpsel; *a ~ of pups,* 'n werpsel hondjies; **~bug** morsjors, rom= melstrooier; (v) omkrap, mors; **~ing** rom= melstrooi

lit'tle (n) bietjie, min; (a) **(less, least)** klein; min, bietjie; *~ finger,* pinkie; (adv) min, weinig; *he ~ knows that,* min weet hy dat

live[1] (v) leef, woon, bly; *~ on,* teer op; *~ up to one's promise,* jou belofte gestand doen

live[2] (a) lewend, lewendig; vars; gelaai (elek.); *~ broadcast,* lewende uitsending; *a ~ wire,* 'n wakker persoon; 'n voorslag; **~lihood** bestaan; **~liness** lewendigheid; **~ly** lewendig, opgeruimd

liv'er lewer

live'stock lewende hawe, vee

liv'ing (n) bestaan, broodwinning; *make a ~,* 'n bestaan vind/voer; *the ~,* die lewendes; (a) bedrywend, lewend; lewen= dig; *within ~ memory,* binne mense= heugenis; *~ room* woonkamer; *~ wage* bestaanbare loon

liz'ard akkedis

load (n) vrag, lading; (v) laai; belas; **~ed dice** vals dobbelstene

loaf[1] (n) **(loaves)** 'n brood; *a ~ of bread,* 'n brood

loaf[2] (v) leeglê, slenter, lanterfanter; **~er** leeglêer, slenteraar, lieplapper

loan (n) lening; geldlening; (v) leen, uitleen

loathe verfoei, walg, verafsku

lobe lel; lob

lob'ster (see)kreef

loc'al lokaal, plaaslik; *~ authority* plaas= like bestuur/owerheid; *~ content* plaas= like inhoud

local'ity (..ties) lokaliteit, plek, buurt

loca'tion ligging; aanduiding; plek

loch (n) meer (Skotland)

lock[1] (n) slot (van deur); *under ~ and key,* agter slot en grendel; *~, stock and barrel,* romp en stomp; die hele boel; (v) sluit; opsluit; afsluit

lock[2] (n) krul (hare); klos (aan skape)

lock: ~er sluitkas, bewaarkas; kis; **~et**

hangertjie, medaljon; **~jaw** kaakklem, klem in die kake; **~smith** slotmaker

locomo'tion beweging, verplasing; *~ al= lowance,* vervoertoelae

locomo'tive (n) lokomotief; (a) bewegend

loc'ust sprinkaan

lodge (n) hut; jaghuis; losie (Vrymesse= laars); (v) huisves; loseer; indien (klag); inwoon; *~ a complaint,* 'n klag indien; *~ an objection,* 'n beswaar opper; **~r** loseerder, kosganger

lodg'ing huisvesting, inwoning, losies

loft solder; solderkamer; duiwehok; **~y** verhewe, hoog; trots

log (n) blok; lys, puntelys; log; logboek; (v) **(-ged, -ged)** aanteken; in blokke saag

log'arithm logaritme

log: ~book logboek, skeepsjoernaal; *~ cabin* blokhuis

logg'erhead domkop; *at ~s,* haaks, oor= hoop, aan die twis

log'ic logika, redeneerkuns; **~al** logies

loin lende; (pl) lendene; *gird up the ~s,* die lendene omgord

loit'er drentel, slenter, draai, draal, talm

loll'ipop stroopballetjie, suikerpop; stok= kielekker

Lon'don Londen

lone eensaam, verlate; **~ly** eensaam, alle= nig, verlate

long[1] (n) lang tyd; (a) lang (lank); langdu= rig; *a ~ memory,* 'n goeie geheue; *in the ~ run,* op die duur; (adv) lang, lankal; *~ ago,* lankal, vanmelewe; *don't be ~,* moenie lank wegbly nie; *so ~!* tot siens

long[2] (v) verlang

long'ing (n) verlange, hunkering, heimwee; (a) verlangend, smagtend

long: ~jump verspring; **~-playing reord** langspeelplaat, langspeler

loo (n) kleinhuisie, toilet

look (n) voorkome; uitdrukking; (pl) voor= kome, gesig; (v) kyk, sien, aanskou; *~ after,* oppas; *~ ahead,* vooruitsien; *~ forward to,* uitsien na; *~ on,* toekyk; *~ for trouble,* moeilikheid soek; *~ up,* na= slaan; besoek; **~er-on (lookers-on)** toe= skouer; **~out** uitkykpos (militêr)

loom[1] (n) weefmasjien; handvatsel; steel

loom[2] (v) oprys, opdoem, skemer

loop (n) lissie, strop; *~ the ~,* bolmakie= sievlieg; **~hole** skietgat; skuiwergat

loose (n) losspel; (v) losmaak; bevry; (a, adv) los, vry; *at a ~ end,* sonder vaste werk; **~ly** lossies; **~n** losmaak

loot (n) buit, roof; (v) plunder, buit(maak); **~er** plunderaar, buiter

Lord Here, Heer; *the ~'s prayer,* die Onse Vader; *the ~'s supper,* die Heilige Nagmaal

lord (n) heer, baas; lord; *like a ~,* soos 'n groot meneer; *~ and master,* heer en meester; (v) kommandeer, baasspeel

lo'rry (lorries) vragmotor, vragwa, lorrie; **~ driver** lorriedrywer, vragmotorbestuurder

lose (lost, lost) verloor; *~ marks,* punte verbeur; *~ one's nerve,* dit op jou senuwees kry; *~ one's temper,* kwaad word; *~ one's way,* verdwaal

los'er verloorder

loss (-es) verlies, skade; *be at a ~,* buite raad wees; *~ of memory,* geheueverlies

lost verlore; *get ~,* verdwaal; *~ in thought,* in gedagte verdiep

lot lot; aandeel; klomp; hoop; *draw ~s,* lootjies trek; *think a ~ of,* 'n hoë dunk hê van

lott'ery (..ries) lotery

loud luid; hard; luidrugtig; opsigtig; *~ hailer* luidroeper; **~speaker** luidspreker, *see* public address system

lounge (n) sofa; voorportaal; sitkamer, voorhuis; (v) luier; ronddrentel, slenter; *~ suit* dagpak

louse (lice) luis

lout lummel, gomtor

louv'er, louv're luggat, rookgat; hortjieblinding, hortjieruit

love (n) liefde, min; skat, liefling; stroop (tennis); *fall in ~ with,* verlief raak op; *there is no ~ lost between them,* hulle akkordeer nie; *make ~ to,* die hof maak; *send one's ~,* groete laat weet; (v) liefhê, bemin; **~ affair** (liefdes)verhouding; **~letter** minnebrief, vrybrief; **~liness** lieflikheid; beminlikheid; **~ly** lieflik, beminlik; **~ poem** liefdesgedig, minnedig; **~r minnaar;** **~ story** liefdesverhaal

lo'ving liefhebbend, teer; *your ~ daughter,* u liefhebbende dogter

low[1] (n) gebulk; (v) bulk

low[2] (n) laagtepunt; (a) laag, sag; nederig; *in ~ spirits,* neerslagtig; *~ profile,* lae profiel; (adv) *run ~,* opraak; *tackle ~,* laag vat; **~er** (v) verlaag, laat sak; (a) laer; swakker; minder; **~ tide** laagwater; **~veld** laeveld

loy'al getrou, lojaal; **~ist** lojalis

loz'enge tablet(jie); ruit

lub'ricant smeerolie; masjienolie

lucerne' lusern

lu'cid helder; deurskynend

luck geluk, toeval; *bad ~!* simpatie! *good ~!* die beste! beste wense!

luck'y gelukkig; *a ~ hit (shot),* 'n gelukskoot; *~bean* sierboontjie, toorboontjie; *~ dip* graaisak; *~ packet* verrassing(s)pakkie

luc'rative winsgewend, betalend, lonend

lud'icrous belaglik, bespotlik

lugg'age bagasie; *~ carrier* bagasierak

lull (n) stilte, kalmte; sussing; (v) kalmeer

lull'aby (..bies) slaapliedjie, wiegeliedjie

lumbag'o lendepyn

lum'bar punch lumbale punksie

lum'ber (n) spul, rommel; timmerhout; *~ jack* boswerker, houtkapper; *~ jacket* ritsbaadjie, bosbaadjie; *~ room* rommelkamer

lum'inous liggewend; stralend; *~ dial* glimwyserplaat; *~ paint* glimverf

lump (n) stuk, klont, brok; hoop; *a ~ sum,* 'n ronde som; (v) saamgooi; saamsmelt; *~ together,* saamgooi; **~y** klonterig

lun'ar maan~; *~ eclipse* maan(s)verduistering

lun'atic (n) kranksinnige; (a) maansiek, gek; *~ asylum* (-s) kranksinnigegestig, sielsiekegestig; malhuis

lunch (n) (-es) middagete

lunch'eon formele middagete, noenmaal

lung long

lurch (n) (-es) ruk, swaai; *leave in the ~,* in die steek laat; (v) swaai, slinger

lure (n) lokaas; (v) aanlok, weglok

lur'id (a) somber; donker

lurk (v) skuil, loer

lust (n) wellus; begeerte; (v) dors na

lus'tre glans; roem, luister

lute luit

lux'ury (..ries) luukse, weelde; oordaad; *~ bus* luuksebus; *~ car* weeldemotor

lyre lier

ly'ric (n, pl) liriese poësie; lirieke, luisterliedjies; (a) liries

M

ma ma

machine' masjien, werktuig; (v) masjineer; **~ gun** (n) masjiengeweer

machi'nery masjinerie; *plant and ~*, aanleg en masjinerie

machi'nist masjinis, bediener

mack'erel makriel

mack'intosch (-es) reënjas

mad mal, gek, dol; kranksinnig; *go ~*, gek word; *as ~ as a hatter (March hare)*, stapelgek; *~ on*, versot op

mad'am mevrou; juffrou; madam; *Madam Chair*, Agbare voorsitster

made gemaak; kunsmatig; *~ up* gemaak, kunsmatig; versonne; *a ~ up story*, 'n versinsel

mad: ~house malhuis; **~ness** malheid, gekheid

magazine' tydskrif; pakhuis; magasyn

ma'gic (n) towerkuns; *black ~*, duiwelskuns; (a) **~ lantern** towerlantern; **~ wand** towerstaf

magi'cian towenaar, goëlaar

ma'gistrate landdros, magistraat; **~'s court** landdroshof, magistraatshof

mag'net magneet

magnet'ic magneties; **~ mine** magnetiese myn; **~ needle** magneetnaald

mag'netism magnetisme, aantrekkingskrag; *terrestrial ~*, aardmagnetisme

magnif'icent pragtig, heerlik; manjifiek

mag'nifier vergrootglas

mag'nify (..fied, ..fied) vergroot, verheerlik; ophemel; **~ing glass** vergrootglas

mag'nitude grootte, omvang, trefwydte

magno'lia magnolia, tulpboom

mag'pie ekster; babbelkous, snaterbek

mahog'any mahoniehout

maid meisie, maagd; diensmeisie; vroulike (huis)bediende; *old ~*, oujongnooi

maid'en (n) meisie; nooi; maagd; leë boulbeurt; (a) maagdelik; eerste; ongetroud; **~ aunt**, ongetroude tante; **~ flight**, eerste vlug; **~ name**, nooiensvan; **~ speech**, intreerede; nuwelingstoespraak (parlement); **~hood** maagdelikheid; **~ish**, **~like**, **~ly** maagdelik, rein

maid'servant diensmeisie

mail[1] (n) harnas; pantser; (v) bepantser

mail[2] (n) pos; posbesending; (v) pos; **~bag** possak; **~boat** passasierskip, posboot; **~coach (-es)** poskar

maim (n) verminking; (v) vermink; skend

main (n) oseaan; hoofdeel; (a) hoof*; vernaamste, grootste; *the ~ point*, die hoofargument; **~ body** hoofmag; **~ entrance** hoofingang; **~land** vasteland; **~ly** hoofsaaklik, vernaamlik; **~ road** hoofweg, grootpad; **~ street** hoofstraat

maintain' handhaaf; onderhou; volhou; in stand hou; bewaar; **~er** handhawer

main'tenance instandhouding, onderhoud, handhawing; *~ costs*, instandhoukoste; *pay ~ to divorced wife*, betaal onderhoud aan geskeide vrou

maize mielies; **~ farmer** mielieboer; **~ meal** mieliemeel

majes'tic majestueus, verhewe

maj'esty (..ties) majesteit; *Your M~*, U Majesteit

maj'or[1] (n) majoor

maj'or[2] (n) meerderjarige, mondige; majeur (musiek); (a) mondig; hoof*; groot*; grootste, vernaamste

major'ity (..ties) meerderheid; mondigheid; *absolute/clear ~*, volstrekte meerderheid; **~ government** meerderheidsregering

make (n) vorm, gedaante; soort; fabrikaat; (v) **(made, made)** maak, doen; verrig; vervaardig; voer (oorlog); hou (toespraak); begaan (fout); aangaan (ooreenkoms); sluit (vrede); verdien (geld); **~ a call**, 'n besoek aflê; **~ an example of**, tot voorbeeld stel; **~a fool of**, belaglik maak; **~ good**, vergoed (vir), opmaak; vooruitgaan; **~ love**, die hof maak; **~ up one's mind**, besluit, 'n besluit neem; **~ peace**, vrede sluit; **~ a speech**, 'n toespraak afsteek; **~ sure of**, verseker, sorg dat; **~ up**, vol maak; inhaal (skade); goedmaak; aanvul; versin (verhaal); **~-believe** (n) voorwendsel; (a) voorgewend; oneg; **~shift** redmiddel, noodhulp; **~-up** grimering; vermomming

mak'ing maaksel, maak; *he has the ~ of*, hy het die aanleg vir; *his own ~*, sy eie skuld/toedoen

mal'adjusted wanaangepas

Malay' (n) Maleier, Slamaier; (a) Maleis, Slams

male (n) mannetjie; mansmens; (a) manlik; mans=; ~ **issue** manlike afstammeling; ~ **nurse** verpleër

malformed' wanskape, misvorm(d)

mal'ice boosaardigheid; (bose) opset; haat; plaagsug; *bear* ~, 'n wrok koester

malic'ious kwaadwillig, boosaardig

malign' (v) kwaadspreek, skinder, mishandel; (a) verderflik, skadelik, kwaadaardig; ~**ant** kwaadaardig; ~*ant growth/tumor,* kwaadaardige groeisel/gewas

mall wandellaan; winkelplein

mall'et houthamer

malnutri'tion ondervoeding

malprac'tice wanpraktyk, wangedrag

malt (n, v) mout

Mal'tese poodle Malteserpoedel (hond)

malt'ing plant moutery

maltreat' mishandel

mam'ba mamba

mam(m)a' mama

mamm'al soogdier

mamm'oth (n) mammoet; (a) kolossaal

man (n) (**men**) man, mansmens; eggenoot; mens; *no-~'s-land,* niemandsland; ~ *of straw,* strooiopop; *the* ~ *in the street,* die gewone man; ~ *about town,* losbol; (v) (**-ned, -ned**) beman; ~ *oneself,* moed vat; (a) manlik, man=

man'age bestuur; ~**ment** bestuur, leiding, beheer; ~**r** bestuurder; ~**ress (-es)** bestuurderes; ~**ment by objectives** doelwitbestuur; ~**ment committee** bestuurskomitee; dagbestuur

man'aging besturend; ~ **director** besturende direkteur

mand'arin[1] mandaryn (Chinese amptenaar)

mand'arin[2], **man'drine** nartjie (vrug)

man'date (n) volmag; opdrag; mandaat

man'datory (a) voorskriftelik, op die bevel

man'dolin mandolien

mane maanhaar

man: ~ **eater** mensvreter; ~**ful** manhaftig, kordaat

mang'anese mangaan

man'ger krip, trog, voerbak

man'gle mangel (vir wasgoed); (v) vermink, verskeur; radbraak

man'go (-es) mango, veselperske

mang'rove wortelboom

man: ~**handle** toetakel, mishandel, karnuffel; ~**hater** mensehater; ~**hole** skouput, inspeksieput; ~**hood** manlikheid

man'iac (n) waansinnige, maniak

man'icure (v) manikuur; ~ **set** naelstel, manikuurstel

man'ifest (n) bekendmaking, manifes; (v) bekend maak, manifesteer; ~**a'tion** openbaring, manifestasie

manifes'to (-es) manifes

man'ifold (n) spruitstuk; (v) vermenigvuldig; (a) baie, menigvuldig, herhaaldelik

man'ikin dwergie, mannetjie; model

manip'ulate behandel, bewerk, manipuleer

man: ~**kind** mensdom, mensheid; ~**liness** manlikheid; ~**ly** manlik, manmoedig

ma'nna manna

mann'equin mannekyn; modepop

mann'er manier, gewoonte, wyse; ~**ism** aanwensel; ~**liness** beleefdheid

mann'ing bemanning, personeelvoorsiening

mann'ish managtig; onhandig

manoeu'vre (n) maneuver, krygsoefening; (v) maneuvreer; bewerkstellig, manipuleer

man'-of-war (men-of-war) oorlogskip, slagskip

man'or landgoed; herehuis

man'power arbeidskrag, mannekrag; ~ **research** mannekragnavorsing; ~ **utilisa'tion** mannekragbenutting

man'rope valreep

man'sion herehuis

man'slaughter manslag, doodslag

man'telpiece skoorsteenmantel, kaggelrak

ma'ntis (mantes) hottentotsgot, bidsprinkaan

man'tle mantel; omhulsel; gloeikousie

man'ual (n) handleiding; handboek; ~ **choke** handsmoorder; ~ **labour** hand(e)=arbeid; ~**ly** handsgewys(e)

manufac'ture (n) fabrikaat; (pl) fabrikate; (v) vervaardig, fabriseer; ~**r** fabrikant, vervaardiger

manure' (n) mis; (v) mis gee, bemes

man'uscript handskrif, manuskrip

ma'ny (a) (**more, most**) baie, veel; *one too* ~, een te veel; ~ *a time,* baiemaal

map (n) kaart, landkaart; plattegrond; (v) (**-ped, -ped**) karteer; afbeeld

ma'ple esdoring, ahornboom

ma'rabou maraboe

mar'athon marathon

maraud' plunder, buit; **~er** buiter, plunderaar

mar'ble (n) marmer; albaster; (v) marmer

March[1] Maart; *as mad as a ~ hare*, stapelgek; *in die bol gepik*

march[2] (-es) (n) mars, tog; (v) mar(s)jeer; trek; opruk; *~ on*, aanruk; voortmarsjeer; *~ past*, verbymarsjeer; (n) **~-past** defileermars

mare merrie

marg'arine kunsbotter, margarien

mar'gin rand, kant; kantlyn, kantruimte; **~al** marginaal, grens=, kant=; **~al note** kantaantekening; *~ line* kantlyn

marg'rave markgraaf

marg'uerite margriet

mar'igold afrikaner; gousblom

mari'na marina, waterdorp

marine' (n) vloot; seesoldaat, vlootsoldaat; *mercantile ~*, handelsvloot; **~ cadet** adelbors; **~ insurance** seeversekering, marine-assuransie

marionette' marionet, pop

ma'rital huweliks=, egtelik; *~ state* huwelikstaat

ma'ritime maritiem; *~ law* seereg

mark[1] (n) mark (geldeenheid)

mark[2] (n) merk; teken; doel; punt (eksamen); skoonvang (rugby); *make one's ~*, naam maak; (v) merk; nasien; punte gee; *~ class tests*, klastoetse nasien; *~ time*, die pas markeer; **~er** merker, teller; nasiener (eksamenskrifte)

mark'et (n) mark; (v) bemark, verkoop; **~able** verkoopbaar, bemarkbaar; **~ indicator** markaanwyser; **~ing** bemarking; **~ing director** direkteur bemarking; **~ master** markmeester; **~ price** markprys; **~ research** marknavorsing

mark: **~ing** merk; tekening; **~ing ink** merkink, letterink; **~s'man** (..men) skerpskutter, skut

marm'alade lemoenkonfyt, marmelade

maroon' (a) bruinrooi, donkerrooi

marquee' markeetent

ma'rriage huwelik; bruilof, troue; *promise of ~*, troubelofte; **~ certificate** trousertifikaat; **~ counsellor** huwelik(s)raadgewer, huwelik(s)berader; **~ vow** huweliksgelofte

ma'rried getroud; *~ to*, getroud met; *~*

life huwelikslewe; **~ quarters** kwartiere vir getroudes

ma'rrow murg; **~ bone** murgbeen

ma'rry (married, married) trou, in die huwelik/eg tree; *~ money*, met 'n ryk vrou/man trou

marsh (-es) vlei, moeras

marsh'al (n) maarskalk; (v) (-led, -led) rangskik, versamel, orden; **~ling yard** rangeerwerf, opstelterrein (spoorweg)

marsh: **~ fever** moeraskoors; malaria; **~ mallow** malvalekker; **~y** moerassig

mart mark, verkoopsaal

mart'yr (n) martelaar

mar'vel (v) (-led, -led) verwonder, verbaas; **~lous** wonderlik, verbasend

marzipan' marsepein

mas'cot talisman, gelukbringer

mas'culine manlik; sterk, fors; kragtig

mash (n) (-es) meelkos, mengsel; (v) fynstamp; meng; **~ed** gestamp, fyngemaak; **~ed potatoes** kapokaartappels

mask (n) masker; mombakkies; (v) vermom; **~ed ball** maskerbal

mas'king tape maskeerband

mas'on (n) klipkapper; messelaar

Mas'onry[1] Vrymesselary

mas'onry[2] messelwerk

mass[1] (n) (-es) massa, menigte; massa/gewig; **~ attack** massa-aanval; **~ media** massamedia; **~ meeting** monstervergadering; **~ production** massaproduksie

mass[2] (n) mis (kerk)

mass'acre (n) bloedbad, menseslagting; moordery; (v) verdelg, uitmoor

mass'age (n) masseer; **~ parlour** masseersalon, streelperseel

masseur' masseur/masseerder

masseuse' masseuse/masseerster

mass'ive massief, dig, swaar

mast (n) mas

ma'ster (n) baas, meester; weesheer; onderwyser; jongeheer; bobaas; *~ of ceremonies*, seremoniemeester, tafelheer; *~ and servant*, werkgewer en dienaar; (v) oormeester, oorwin, baasraak; (a) hoof=; **~ builder** meesterbouer; **~ key (-s)** loper, diewesleutel; **~ly** meesterlik; **~mind** meesterbrein; **~piece** meesterstuk; **~'s degree** magister(graad); **~y** heerskappy, meesterskap

mas'tiff boel(hond), boerboel
masturba'tion selfbevlekking, masturbasie
mat¹ (n) mat; (v) (-ted, -ted) vleg
mat² (a) dof, mat
mat'ador matador, stiervegter
match¹ (n) (-es) vuurhoutjie
match² (n) (-es) paar; gelyke, portuur; wedstryd, kragmeting; *be a ~ for*, opge=
wasse wees teen; (v) paar; pas
match: ~ box (-es) vuurhoutjiedosie; ~
factory (..ries) vuurhoutjiefabriek
match: ~less weergaloos; ~maker huwe=
liksmakelaar; ~ point wedstrydpunt
(tennis)
mate¹ (n) maat, kameraad, vriend; (v) maats
maak; paar; trou
mate² (n) mat (skaak); (v) skaakmat sit
mater'ial (n) materiaal, stof, goed; (pl)
boustof; (a) stoflik, materieel; ~ism
materialisme; ~ist materialis; ~is'tic
stoflik, materialisties; ~ise verwesenlik,
verwerklik
matern'al moederlik, moeder=; ~ love
moederliefde
matern'ity moederskap; ~ home kraam=
inrigting; ~ wear kraamdrag
mathemat'ic(al) wiskundig, matematies
mathemat'ics wiskunde, matesis; *applied
~*, toegepaste wiskunde; *pure ~*, suiwer
wiskunde
mat'inee middagvertoning, middagvoor=
stelling
Matric' Matriek, Matrikulasie
matric'ulant matrikulant
matric'ulate matrikuleer
matricula'tion matrikulasie; inskrywing;
M~ Examination Matrikulasie-eksamen
matrimon'ial huweliks=, egtelik
mat'ron huismoeder, matrone
matt'er (n) stof, materie; saak; aangeleent=
heid; kwessie; *what is the ~?* wat makeer?
~ *of course*, natuurlik, vanselfsprekend;
~ *of fact*, nugter, prakties
matt'ress (-es) matras
mature' (v) ryp word; ryp maak; verval; (a)
ryp, beleë (wyn); volwasse; ~d' ryp;
volgroei, volwasse; opeisbaar
matur'ity rypheid; vervaldag; *at ~*, op (die)
vervaldag
mauve ligpers, malvapers, mauve
max'imum (n) (..ma, -s) maksimum; (a)
maksimum, grootste, maksimale

May¹ Mei
may² (might, might) mag, kan; *be that as it
~*, hoe dit ook sy; *come what ~*, wat ook
al (mag) gebeur
may'be dalk, altemit(s)
may'flower meiblom
may'or burgemeester; *lady ~*, burgemees=
teres; ~ess (-es) burgemeestersvrou; ~'s
parlour burgemeesterskamer
maze (n) doolhof; verleentheid; warboel
me my; ek; *poor ~*, arme ek
mea'gre maer, skraal; armsalig
meal¹ meel
meal² maaltyd; *at ~s*, aan tafel
meal'ie mielie; ~ grower mielieteler, mie=
lieboer; ~ meal mieliemeel, *see* maize
meal'time etenstyd
mean¹ (n) middel, middelmaat; (pl) mid=
dele; geld, vermoë; *by all ~s*, alte seker;
beyond his ~s, bokant sy vermoë; *not by
any ~s*, glad nie; *the golden ~*, die gulde
midde(l)weg; (a) gemiddeld; middel=
matig, middel=
mean² (v) (-t, -t) meen, bedoel, beteken;
what do you ~? wat bedoel jy?
mean³ (a, adv) gemeen, laag, suinig
mean'ing betekenis, bedoeling; ~ful bete=
kenisvol, sinvol; ~less betekenisloos,
niksseggend
mean: ~ness gemeenheid, laagheid; ~=
-spirited laag, gemeen
mean'time, mean'while intussen, onder=
tussen, onderwyl, inmiddels
mea'sles masels
mea'sure (n) maat; maatstaf; maatreël; *take
~s*, maatreëls tref; (v) meet, maat neem;
takseer; ~ment maat, meting
meat vleis; *minced ~*, maalvleis; ~ patty,
(..patties) frikkadel; ~ pie vleispastei
mechan'ic (n) handwerkman, ambagsman;
werktuigkundige
mechan'ical meganies; ~ engineer werk=
tuigkundige ingenieur; ~ horse voor=
haker, abbatrekker
mech'anism meganiek, meganisme
mech'anise meganiseer
med'al medalje; gedenkpenning
medal'lion gedenkpenning, medaljon
med'dle (jou) bemoei, (jou) inlaat; ~r be=
moeial, lolpot; ~some bemoeisiek
med'ia (-e) media; ~ centre mediasen=
trum; ~ users mediagebruikers

med'ian mediaan; middellyn
med'iate (v) bemiddel, tussenbei kom/tree
med'iator (be)middelaar; tussenganger
med'ical (a) medies, geneeskundig; ~ examination mediese/geneeskundige ondersoek; ~ practitioner geneesheer, dokter, arts; ~ student student in die medisyne
med'icine (n) medisyne, geneesmiddel; take ~, medisyne drink; ~ chest medisynekassie, huisapteek
mediev'al Middeleeus
med'iocre middelmatig
medita'tion oordenking; (be)peinsing, meditasie, see epilogue
med'ium (n) (..dia, -s) middel; medium, voertaal; (a) gemiddeld; middelmatig; deursnee=; language ~, voertaal
med'lar mispel
med'ley (n) (-s) allegaartjie, mengelmoes
meek sagmoedig, sagsinnig, ootmoedig
meer'cat, meer'kat meerkat
meet (v) (met, met) ontmoet, raakloop, teenkom; ~ with approval, die goedkeuring wegdra; ~ halfway, tegemoetkom; ~ one's liabilities, jou verpligtinge nakom
meet'ing vergadering, byeenkoms; ontmoeting; adjourn a ~, 'n vergadering verdaag; close a ~, 'n vergadering (af)sluit; convene a ~, 'n vergadering belê/byeenroep; ~ place vergaderplek
mell'ow (v) ryp word; saf/sag maak; laat oud word; ~ with age, skafliker word met ouderdom; (a) ryp; saf/sag; mals
melod'ious welluidend, melodies
melodramat'ic melodramaties
mel'ody (..dies) melodie, wysie, deuntjie
mel'on (waat)lemoen; honey-sweet ~, spanspek
melt (v) (melted, molten) smelt; ~ing (n) smelting; vertedering; ~ing pot smelt=kroes
mem'ber lid, lidmaat; ~ship lidmaatskap; ledetal (aantal lede); ~ship card lidkaart; ~ship fee ledegeld/lidgeld
mem'orable heuglik, gedenkwaardig
memoran'dum (..da, -s) memorandum, voorlegging, aantekening; berig
memor'ial (n) gedenkteken; (a) gedenk=, gedagtenis=, herinnerings=; ~ service gedenkdiens
mem'orise memoriseer, uit die hoof leer

mem'ory (..ries) geheue; herinnering; nagedagtenis; commit to ~, uit die hoof leer; from ~, uit die hoof; a good ~, 'n goeie geheue; in ~ of, ter gedagtenis aan
men mense; mans; manne (van daad)
men'ace (n) bedreiging; oorlas; (v) bedreig
mend (v) heelmaak, lap; verbeter; stop (kouse)
mend'ing herstelwerk; invisible ~, fyn=stop(werk)
meningit'is harsingvliesontsteking
men'opause menopouse, oorgangsleeftyd
menstrua'tion maandstonde, menstruasie
men'tal geestelik, verstandelik; ~ arith=metic hoofrekene; ~ deficiency swak=sinnigheid; ~ faculties geestesvermoë, geesvermoëns; ~ hospital kranksinnige=gestig, sielsiekegestig
mental'ity geeskrag; denkwyse, mentaliteit
men'tally geestelik, verstandelik; ~ re=tarded children, verstandvertraagde kinders
men'tion (n) melding, gewag; honourable ~, eervolle vermelding; (v) meld, noem
men'u (-s) spyskaart, spyslys
merc'antile handels=, koopmans=, kom=mersieel; ~ law handelsreg, see com=mercial law; ~ marine handelsvloot
mer'cenary (..ries) (n) huursoldaat
merch'andise negosieware, koopware
merch'ant winkelier, handelaar, koopman; ~ bank aksepbank; ~man (..men) koop=vaardyskip, handelskip
mer'ciful genadig, barmhartig
mer'ciless onbarmhartig, meedoënloos
merc'ury kwik(silwer)
mer'cy genade, barmhartigheid; have ~ upon us, wees ons genadig
mere (a, adv) (merest) eenvoudig, enkel, bloot, maar net; ~ly net, slegs, bloot
merge indompel; sink; saamsmelt; ~r sa=mesmelting; amalgamasie; oplossing
merid'ian (n) middaglyn, meridiaan
meringue' skuimpie, skuimkoekie
me'rit (n) verdienste, meriete; waarde; on its own ~s, op sigself
meritor'ious verdienstelik, voortreflik; ~ service, voortreflike diens
mer'lin steenvalk
mer'maid meermin
me'rrily vrolik, opgeruimd, lekker, pret=tig

me'rry vrolik, plesierig; *a ~ Christmas*, 'n
  geseënde Kersfees; *make ~ with*, die gek
  skeer; **~-go-round** mallemeule; **~making**
  pretmakery, feesviering, jolyt
mesh (n) (-es) netwerk, maas; strik
mess (n) gemeenskaplike tafel; deurmekaarspul; menasie (land); *make a ~ of*,
  verknoei; (v) saameet; knoei; besmeer;
  mors; *~ up*, bederf; verknoei, verongeluk
mess'age boodskap, berig
mess'enger boodskapper, bode; *~ of the*
  Court, balju, geregsbode
Messi'ah Messias
messieurs' menere, here; *~ Jones and Co.*,
  die firma Jones en Kie
mess'y vuil, smerig
mesti'zo halfbloed
met *see* meet (v)
met'al (n) metaal; *base ~*, onedele metaal;
  (a) metaal=, metaalagtig; *~ detector*
  metaalverklikker; *~ fatigue* metaalverswakking
metamorph'osis (..phoses) gedaantewisse-
  ling, metamorfose
met'aphor beeldspraak, metafoor
metapho'ric figuurlik, oordragtelik
metaphys'ical bonatuurlik, metafisies
met'eor vallende ster, meteoor
met'eorite meteoriet, meteoorsteen
meteorol'ogist weerkundige, meteoroloog
met'er meter; *~ maid* boetebessie
meth'od metode, manier; werkwyse
meth'ylated spirits brandspiritus
metic'ulous nougeset, noulettend
meton'ymy metonimia
me'tre¹ meter
me'tre² versmaat, metrum
met'ric metriek; *~ system* metrieke/tien-
  delige stelsel; **~al** metries, tiendelig
metrop'olis (-es) wêreldstad, metropolis/
  metropool
metropol'itan (a) metropolitaans; aarts-
  biskoplik; *~ area* stedelike/metropoli-
  taanse gebied
met'tle ywer, moed; fut, vuur, gees; *show*
  one's ~, toon jou staal
mews stalkompleks; winkel(binne)plein,
  winkelhof, winkelbaan
mic'a mika
mic'robe mikrobe
mic'rochip mikrovlokkie, mikroskyfie

mic'rocomputer, mic'romputer mikro-
  komper, mikromper
mic'rofilm mikrofilm
mic'rophone mikrofoon, geluidversterker
mic'roprocessor mikroverwerker
mic'roscope mikroskoop
mic'rosurgery mikrochirurgie
mic'rowave mikrogolf
mid'-air: *in ~*, tussen hemel en aarde
mid'day (n) middag; (a) middag=
mid'dle (n) middel; midde(l)weg; (v) verdeel; (a) middel, middelste; *M~ Ages*
  Middeleeue; *M~ East*, Midde-Ooste;
  ~-aged middeljarig; **~man** (..men) mid-
  delman
midge muggie; warmassie
midg'et (n) dwerg; (a) klein; *~ car* mug-
  giemotor; *~ golf* miniatuurgholf
mid: *~land* (n) middelland; (a) binnelands;
  ~night (n) middernag; (a) middernagte-
  lik; *burn the ~night oil*, laat studeer;
  ~night sun middernagson; **~riff** mid-
  delrif; **~shipman** (..men) adelbors, see-
  kadet
midst (n) middel; *in our ~*, in ons midde
mid'term break termynreses
mid'way halfpad
mid'wife (..wives) vroedvrou; **~ry** verloskunde
might¹ (n) mag, geweld; vermoë; *with all*
  one's ~, uit alle mag
might² (v) *see* may²
might'y magtig, groot, sterk; *high and ~*,
  hoog verhewe
mi'graine skeelhoofpyn
mig'rant (n) trekvoël; (a) trek=, rondtrek-
  kend; *~ labourer* trekarbeider
mig'ratory swerwend, trek=; *~ bird* trekvoël; *~ locust* treksprinkaan
mild mild, sag; koel; sagsinnig
mil'dew (n) skimmel, muf; (v) beskimmel
mile myl
mil'itant veglustig, strydend, militant
mil'itary (n) militêre diens; militêr, soldaat;
  (a) militêr, krags=; *~ court* krygshof; *~*
  force krygsmag; *~ service* diensplig;
  krygsdiens
mili'tia burgermag, milisie
milk (n) melk; *condensed ~*, blikkiesmelk;
  skimmed ~, afgeroomde melk; (v) melk;
  ~ bar melksalon, melkbuffet; **~ing strap**
  spantou; *~ jug* melkbeker; **~shake**

bruismelk; **~tooth** (..teeth) melktand; **~y** melkagtig; soetsappig; *the M~y Way,* die Melkweg

mill (n) meul(e); fabriek; spinnery; *put through the ~,* laat swaar kry; (v) maal; klop (room); ronddraai; **~ed** gemaal

mill'er meulenaar

mill'et manna; giers

mill'iard miljard

mill'igram milligram

mill'ilitre milliliter

mill'imeter millimeter

mill'iner hoedemaakster, modiste

mill'ion miljoen; **~aire'** miljoenêr

milt (n) milt; hom (vis); (v) bevrug

mime (n) gebarespel, mime; gebarespeler

mim'ic (n) na-aper, koggelaar; (v) (uit)= koggel, namaak

mimos'a mimosa

mince (n) gemaalde vleis; maalvleis; (v) maal; bewimpel, goedpraat; *do not ~ matters,* moenie daar doekies om draai nie; **~meat** maalvleis; gemaalde vleis; *make ~meat of,* kafloop; **~ pie** vleis= pastei; Kerspastei; **~r** vleismeul

mind (n) siel; gees; gemoed; verstand; me= ning; gedagte; *change one's ~,* van plan verander; *presence of ~,* teenwoordig= heid van gees; *speak one's ~,* reguit/ padlangs praat; *be in two ~s,* twyfel; (v) oppas; oplet; *~ your own business,* bemoei jou met jou eie sake; *I don't ~,* graag; *never ~!* toe maar! *would you ~?* gee jy om? wil jy asb.? **~'s eye** geestes= oog

mine¹ (n) myn; (v) delf, grawe; ontgin

mine² (pron) myne

mine: ~ captain mynkaptein; **~field** myn= veld; **~r** mynwerker, myner

min'eral (n) mineraal, delfstof; spuitwater, koeldrank; **~ baths** kruitbad(dens)

mi'ners' phthisis myntering

mine: ~ surveyor mynopmeter; **~ sweeper** mynveër

ming'le meng, deurmekaar maak

min'i (n) mini; (a) mini; **~skirt** miniromp, minirok

min'im (n) klein bietjie; halwe noot; **~al** minimaal; **~ise** verklein; verag; **~um** (..nima) (n) minste; minimum; kleinste waarde; (a) kleinste, minimum

mi'ning (n) mynbou; mynwese; (a) myn=

min'ister (n) minister; predikant, dominee, leraar; gesant; (v) bedien, versorg

mink nerts

mi'nor (n) minderjarige; mineur; (a) on= dergeskik; mineur (musiek); minder, kleiner; minderjarig; **~ offence** geringe/ mindere oortreding

minor'ity (..ties) minderheid, minderjarig= heid; **~ report** minderheid(s)verslag

mint¹ (n) kruisement

mint² (n) munt; (v) munt; (a) eersteklas, nuut

mint' sauce kruisementsous

minuet' menuet

min'us min, minus

min'ute¹ (n) minuut; brief; memorandum; (pl) notule; *in the ~s,* in die notule; *just a ~,* net 'n oomblikkie; (v) notuleer

minute'² (a) baie klein, gering, nietig

min'ute: ~ book notuleboek; **~ hand** minuutwyser

mir'acle wonderwerk, mirakel; *work ~s,* wondere verrig; **~ play (-s)** mirakelspel

mirage' lugspieëling, opgeefsel

mi'rror (n) spieël; toonbeeld; (v) weerkaats, weerspieël

mirth vrolikheid, opgeruimdheid

misappropria'tion wanbesteding, verduis= tering (geld, fondse)

miscal'culate misreken, verreken

misca'rriage mislukking; miskraam; *~ of justice,* geregtelike dwaling

miscellan'eous gemeng; diverse, allerlei

mis'chief onheil, kwaad; kattekwaad; on= nutsigheid; *be up to ~,* iets in die skild voer; *do ~,* (katte)kwaad doen

mis'chievous ondeund, onnutsig

misdeed' misdaad, wandaad

misdemean'our wangedrag, oortreding

mis'er gierigaard, vrek

mis'erable ellendig, miserabel, naar

mis'ery (..ries) ellende, nood, narigheid

misfire' (n) ketsskoot, weierskoot; (v) kets

mis'fit (n) slegpassende kledingstuk; mis= lukkeling (mens)

misformed' wanskape, mismaak

misfort'une ongeluk, teenspoed

mis'hap ongeluk, ongeval

mislaid' verlê, weg

mislead' (..led, ..led) mislei; kul; **~ing** misleidend misman'age wanbestuur; ~ment wanbestuur, wanbeheer

misnom'er verkeerde benaming

miss[1] (n) mis, newel; waas; (v) misrêen

miss[2] (n) (-es) misstoot; misskoot; gemis; (v) mis; ~ the bus, die bus mis/verpas

miss'ile missiel; projektiel, werptuig

miss'ing verlore, ontbrekend; reported ~, as vermis aangegee

mi'ssion sending; opdrag; missie; ~ary (n) (..ries) sendeling; (a) sending-; ~ work sendingwerk

miss'ive brief, sendbrief; bode

mist (n) mis, newel; waas; (v) misrêen

mistake' (n) fout, vergissing; by ~, per abuis; make a ~, 'n fout begaan; ~n verkeerd; be ~n, dit mis hê

mis'ter meneer; (die) heer

mis'tletoe mistel, voëlent

mis'tress (-es) mevrou; meesteres, nooi, ounooi; onderwyseres; houvrou, bywyf, minnares; gebiedster; the ~ of the house, die huisvrou, die gasvrou

mistrust' (v) wantrou, verdink

mist'y mistig, bewolk, dynserig

misunderstand' (..stood, ..stood) misverstaan; ~ing misverstand

misuse' (n) misbruik; verkeerde gebruik; mishandeling; (v) misbruik; mishandel

mit'igate versag, lenig, verlig; mitigating circumstances, versagtende omstandighede

mix meng, vermeng; ~ the cards, die kaarte skommel

mixed gemeng, deurmekaar; ~ grill, allegaartjie, gemengde braaigereg; ~ marriage, gemengde huwelik; be ~ up with, betrokke wees in; ~ pickles suurtjies, atjar; ~ sport mengsport

mix'ture mengsel, mikstuur

mix'-up warboel, deurmekaarspul

moan (n) gekerm; (v) kerm, steun; ~ing (n) gekerm, gejammer

mob (n) gepeupel, menigte, oproerige skare

mob'ilise mobiliseer

mock (n) bespotting; namaaksel; (v) spot, uitkoggel; bespot; ~ fight spieëlgeveg, skyngeveg; ~ing bird piet-my-vrou; ~ lobster kammakreef; ~ shutters kammahortjies; ~ trial skynverhoor, skynhof

mode metode, manier, gewoonte

mod'el (n) model, voorbeeld; (v) (-led, -led) vorm, modelleer; ~ing (n) boetseerkuns, modelleerkuns

mod'erate (n) gematigde; (v) matig; wysig; modereer (eksamen); kàlmeer; (a) matig, middelmatig

mo'derating committee modereerkomitee

mod'erator moderator; bemiddelaar

mod'ern modern, nuwerwets; ~ise moderniseer

mod'est beskeie, ingetoë; matig; ~y beskeidenheid

mod'ify (..fied, ..fied) wysig, matig

mod'ulate reël; moduleer

mod'ule eenheidsmaat, module, maatstaf

mo'hair bokhaar, angorahaar

Mohamm'ed Mohammed; ~an (n) Mohammedaan; Moslem; Slamaier

moist kalm, natterig, vogtig; ~en natmaak, bevogtig; ~ure vog, klammigheid

mol'ar kiestand, maaltand

molass'es swartstroop, triakel, melasse

mole[1] (n) mol (dier); (v) ondergrawe

mole[2] (n) moesie, moedervlek

mole[3] (n) seehoof, hawehoof, golfbreker

mol'ecule stofdceltjie, molekule

mole'hill molshoop; make a mountain out of a ~, van 'n muggie 'n olifant maak

molest' pla, lastig val, molesteer

mom'ent oomblik, rukkie, kits, moment, oogwenk; half a ~, wag 'n bietjie; in a ~, in 'n kits

mon'arch monarg, alleenheerser

mon'arch: ~ist monargis; ~y (..chies) monargie

mon'astery (..ries) klooster

Mon'day Maandag; blue ~, blou Maandag

mo'netary geldelik, monetêr, geld-, munt-; international ~ fund (IMF), internasionale monetêre fonds (IMF)

mo'ney (-s) geld, munt; betaalmiddel; ~ galore, geld soos bossies; be out of ~, platsak wees; ~box (-es) spaarpot; ~lender geldskieter; ~ market geldmark; ~ order poswissel

mon'goose muishond

mo'ngrel (n) baster; (a) baster-

mon'itor vermaner; monitor; klasleier (skool); (v) moniteer, meeluister

monk monnik, kloosterling

mo'nkey (n) (-s) aap; (v) na-aap; ~nut grondboon(tjie); ~ trick bobbejaan- streek; ~ wrench (-es) skroefhamer, bob- bejaanspanner
mon'ochrome eenkleurig, monochroom
mon'ocle oogglas, monokel
mon'ologue alleenspraak, monoloog
mon'oplane eendekker
monop'oly (..lies) monopolie, alleenhandel; kartel
mon'orail lugbus; eenspoor
monosyllab'ic eenlettergrepig
mon'otone (n) eentoon; eentonigheid; (a) vervelend, eentonig, monotoon
monot'onous eentonig, monotoon
monsoon' passaatwind, moeson
mon'ster (n) monster, gedrog; dierasie
mon'strous monsteragtig, wanskape, af- skuwelik, vreeslik
month maand; this day ~, vandag oor 'n maand
month'ly (n) (..lies) maandblad; (pl) maandstonde, menstruasie; (a) maande- liks, maand-; ~ meeting, maandverga- dering
mon'ument monument, gedenkteken
mood stemming, bui, luim; in a good ~, in 'n goeie bui; in the ~, in die stemming; ~iness humeurigheid; ~y buierig, knor- rig
moon maan; maand (poëties); once in a blue ~, 'n enkele keer
moon: ~light maanlig; ~lighting sluik- werk, privaatwerk; ~shine maanskyn; on- sin; ~shiner dranksmokkelaar; ~- struck maansiek, mal
moor¹ (n) heide; vlei, moeras
moor² (v) vasmeer, anker
moot (v) bespreek, debatteer; (a) betwis- baar; a ~ point, 'n ope vraag
mop (n) stofdoek, dweil, opvryflap; (v) (-ped, -ped) afvee, opvrywe; ~ the floor with somebody, iem. kafloop
mope (v) droom, suf; druil
mop'ed kragfiets
mor'al (n) moraal; sedeles; boodskap; (a) sedelik; moreel; ~ decay, sedelike verval; one's ~ duty, jou morele plig
morale' moed, volharding; moreel (van 'n leër); improve the ~ of his soldiers, sy soldate se moreel verstewig; ~ booster moreelkikker

moral'ity sedelikheid, sedeleer, moraliteit; (..ties) sinnespel, moraliteit
mor'als sedes
morass' (-es) moeras
mor'bid sieklik, ongesond, morbied
more meer, groter; the ~, the better, hoe meer, hoe beter; ~ or less, min of meer; the ~, the merrier, hoe meer siele, hoe meer vreugde; ~over bowendien, bui- tendien
morg'en morg
morgue lykhuis; dodehuis
morn'ing (n) môre, môreoggend, voor- middag; (a) môre-, môreoggend-; good ~, goeiemôre; this ~, vanmôre; tomor- row ~, môreoggend; ~ glory purper- winde, trompettertjie; ~ gown kamerjas; ~ paper oggendblad; ~ prayers og- gendgodsdiens
mor'on moron, volwasse swaksinnige
morph'ia, morph'ine morfien, morfine
mors'el stukkie, happie, krummel
mor'tal (n) sterfling; (a) sterflik; dodelik; menslik; ~ enemy doodsvyand; ~ re- mains stoflike oorskot
mortal'ity sterflikheid, sterfte; ~ rate sterftesyfer
mortg'age (n) verband; give in ~, onder verband plaas, verband; lend on ~, op verband leen; (v) onder verband plaas, verband; verpand; ~ bond verband- (akte); ~e' verbandhouer; ~r, mortgagor verbandgewer
mort'uary (n) (..ries) dodehuis, lykhuis
mosa'ic (n) mosaïek; (a) mosaïek-
Mos'lem (n) Mohammedaan, Moslem; Slamaier
mosque moskee
mosquit'o (-es) muskiet; ~ net muskiet- net, muskietgaas
moss (n) mos; moeras
most (a) meeste, uiterste, grootste; at the ~, hoogtens; for the ~ part, grotendeels; ~ probably, heel waarskynlik; ~ of us, die meeste van ons; (adv) hoogs, baie, uiters, besonders, aller-; ~ certainly, alte seker; ~ly mees(t)al, merendeels, hoofsaaklik
mote stofdeeltjie, stof; stipseltjie, splinter
motel' motel
moth mot; ~-eaten motgevreet
mo'ther (n) moeder; huismoeder; (v) ver- troetel, bemoeder; (a) moeder-; ~ coun-

try (..ries) vaderland; **~-in-law** (-s-in-law) skoonmoeder; **~ly** moederlik; **~ of pearl** perlemoen; **~ superior** moederowerste; **~ tongue** moedertaal

motif' motief, grondtema

mo'tion (n) beweging; mosie; **~ of no confidence,** mosie van wantroue; *of one's own* **~,** uit eie beweging; *in slow* **~,** in traagspoed/traagtempo; (v) wink; 'n teken gee; **~less** botstil, bewegingloos; **~ pictures** rolprent, bioskoop

mot'ivate (v) motiveer

motiva'tion (n) motivering

mot'ive (n) beweegrede, motief

mot'ley (a) bont, kakelbont; vreemdsoortig

mot'ocross motocross, motorfietsveldrenne

mot'or (n) motor; (a) dryf; **~ boat** motorboot; **~cade** motoroptog, motorstoet, motorkade; **~car** motor, motorkar, kar; **~coach** toerbus; **~cycle** motorfiets; **~ industry** motorbedryf, motornywerheid; **~ist** motoris; **~ rally** (..rallies) motortydren; motorbyeenkoms; **~ truck** vragmotor; **~ van** bestelwa, afleweringswa; **~ vehicle** motorvoertuig; **~way** deurpad (stedelik), motorweg

mot'tle (v) vlek, streep; (a) bont, gevlek, gemarmer; **~d** bont, gestreep

mott'o (-es) leus(e), sinspreuk, motto

mould[1] (n) vorm; gedaante; matrys; (v) vorm, giet; modelleer

mould[2] (n) skimmel; (v) skimmel, kim

moult verveer (hoender); verhaar (dier); vervel (slang)

mound (n) hoop, heuweltjie; wal, skans

mount (n) rydier; berg; (v) monteer, opplak; opklim; **~ing costs,** stygende koste; **~ed in gold,** in goud geset

moun'tain berg; *make* **~s of molehills,** van 'n muggie 'n olifant maak; **~ chain** bergreeks, bergketting; **~eer'** bergbewoner; bergenier, bergklimmer; **~eer'ing** bergklim; **~ous** bergagtig; **~ pass** (-es) bergpas, poort, nek; **~ range** bergreeks; **~ slide** bergstorting

moun'ted berede, te perd; **~ police** berede polisie

moun'ting beslag, montering

mourn rou, treur; betreur; **~er** rou(be)klaer

mouse (n) (mice) muis; **~trap** muisval

moustache' snorbaard

mouth (n) mond; bek; monding (rivier); *from hand to* **~,** van die hand in die tand; **~ful** hap, mondvol; **~ harp** trompie; **~ organ** mondfluitjie; **~piece** woordvoerder, segsman; mondstuk

mo'vable beweegbaar, verplaasbaar; **~ property** losgoed, roerende eiendom

move (n) set; beweging; (v) beweeg, roer; verhuis; **~ heaven and earth,** hemel en aarde beweeg; **~ in,** intrek; **~d** bewoë, aangedaan; **~ment** beweging; **~r** voorsteller

mo'ving bewegend, beweeg; roerend, aandoenlik; **~ violation** ry-oortreding (verkeer)

much (more, most) baie, veel; *nothing* **~,** niks besonders nie; **~ worse,** veel erger/slegter

muck mis; bog; **~ heap** mishoop; **~iness** smerigheid, vuilheid; **~ worm** miswurm

mud modder

mud'dle (n) verwarring, warboel; (v) verwar, troebel maak; verbrou; **~d** deurmekaar; **~r** knoeier

mud: **~dy** (a) modderig; troebel; **~guard** modderskerm, spatbord

muezz'in gebedsroeper (Moslem)

muf'fin roosterkoekie

muf'ti burgerdrag, siviel

mug (n) kommetjie; beker; koppie; bakkies, gevreet; domkop; (v) (-ged, -ged) volprop; opmaak, grimeer; wurgroof; **~ger** wurgrower; **~ging** wurgroof

mul'berry (mulberries) moerbei

mule muil, esel; hardekop; **~ kick** volstruisskop (by stoei)

mull'et harder

mul'ti: veel, meer, multi; **~coloured** veelkleurig; **~grade** meergraad; **~grade** *oil,* meergraad-olie; **~national** veelvolkig, multinasionaal

mul'tiparty conference veelpartykonferensie

mul'tiped duisendpoot

mul'tiple (n) veelvoud; (a) veelvoudig; **~ choice questions,** veelkeusige/meervoudige vrae

mul'tiply (..plied, ..plied) vermenigvuldig

mul'tipurpose meerdoelig, veeldoelig

mul'tiracial veelrassig, veelvolkig

mul'titude menigte, skare, massa

mum¹ (n) mams, mamma
mum² (v) (-med, -med) vermom; stilbly; (a) stil, soet; (interj) stil! st! ~'s *the word!* bly stil! hou die mond! ~ *on the issue,* swyg oor die kwessie
mum'ble (v) mompel; prewel; ~r mompelaar
mum'bling (n) gemompel; (a) mompelend
mumm'y¹ (mummies) mummie
mumm'y² (mummies) mammie, mamsie
mumps pampoentjies (siekte)
munch knabbel, oppeusel
muni'cipal munisipaal, stads•, stedelik; ~ **council** stadsraad; ~ **rates** erfbelasting
municipal'ity (..ties) munisipaliteit, stadsraad, plaaslike owerheid/bestuur
muni'tion krygsvoorraad, munisie; ~s krygstuig
mur'der (n) moord; *commit* ~, moord pleeg/begaan; (v) vermoor; ~er moordenaar; ~ess (-es) moordenares; ~ous moorddadig
murm'ur (n) gemurmel; gemompel; (v) murmel; mompel
mu'scle spier; spierkrag; *without moving a* ~, sonder om 'n spier te vertrek
muse'um (-s, ..sea) museum
mush'room paddastoel, sampioen
mus'ic musiek, toonkuns; *classical* ~, klassieke musiek; *set to* ~, toonset; ~al musikaal, welluidend; (n) musiekblyspel; ~ **centre** musieksentrum
musi'cian musikus, toonkunstenaar; musikant (speler)

musk muskus; muskusgeur; muskusdier
musk'et roer, geweer; ~eer' musketier
muss'el mossel
must (v) (**must**) moet, verplig wees; *you* ~ *not,* jy moenie
mus'tard mosterd; ~ **gas** mosterdgas
mus'ter (v) monster, oproep, versamel; ~ *up courage,* moed bymekaar skraap/skep
must'roll mosbolletjie
mus'ty muf, beskimmel; suf
mut'ilate vermink, skend
mutineer' (n) muiter, oproermaker
mut'iny (n) (..nies) muitery, oproer; (v) (..nied) opstaan, muit
mutt'er (v) mompel; brom; prewel
mutt'on skaapvleis; skaap; *as dead as* ~, so dood soos 'n mossie
mut'ual onderling, wedersyds; wederkerig; gemeenskaplik; ~ *friend,* gemeenskaplike vriend
muz'zle (n) snoet, bek; loop (van geweer); muilband; (v) muilband; besnuffel; ~ **loader** voorlaaier
my my; *oh* ~ ! goeie genade!
myop'ic bysiende, stiksienig, miopies
myself' ekself, myself; *by* ~, alleen; *I am not* ~, ek voel nie lekker nie
myster'ious geheimsinnig, misterieus; verborge, duister
mys'tery (..ries) geheim, misterie; raaisel
mys'tic (n) mistikus; (a) misties, mistiek, geheimsinnig, duister; ~ism mistiek
myth mite, fabel; ~ol'ogy mitologie, godeleer

N

naar'tjie = nartjie
nab (v) betrap, gryp, arresteer
nag (v) (-ged, -ged) pla; lol, sanik, seur
nag: ~ger plaer, sanikpot, terger; ~ging gesanik, gelol, vittery, geneul, neulery
nail (n) spyker; nael; *a* ~ *to his coffin,* 'n spyker in sy doodkis; (v) vasspyker; inslaan; ~brush (-es) naelborsel
naïve' naïef, eenvoudig, kinderlik
nak'ed nakend, naak, kaal; *with the* ~ *eye,* met die blote oog; *stark* ~, poedelnakend; ~ *truth,* die blote/naakte waar-

heid; ~ness naaktheid
name (n) naam, benaming; *first (Christian)* ~, voornaam; *make a* ~, naam maak, spore afdruk; (v) noem, naam gee; opnoem; ~ly naamlik; ~sake genant, naamgenoot; ~ **tag** kenstrokie
Namib'ia Namibië; ~n *economy,* Namibiese ekonomie; ~n Namibiër
nap¹ (n) nop (klere, setperkgras); dons (vrugte); (v) (-ped, -ped) pluis; *against the* ~, teen die nop (in)
nap² (n) dutjie, sluimering; *catch one* ~*ping,* iem. onverwags betrap; *take a* ~, 'n

uiltjie knyp/knip; (v) (**-ped, -ped**) dut, sluimer
nap'kin servet; doek; luier; ~ **service** luierdiens
narciss'ism narcisme, selfliefde
narciss'us (-es, ..cissi) narsing
narcot'ic (n) verdowingsmiddel; (a) narkoties, verdowend; ~**s bureau** narkotikaburo
narra'tion vertelling, verhaal, verslag, relaas; *minutes of* ~, notule van relaas
narrat'or verteller, verhaler
na'rrow (n) engte; (v) vernou; beperk; (a) nou, smal; *a ~ escape*, 'n noue ontkoming; ~ *views*, bekrompe idees; ~ *the wage gap*, die loongaping vernou; ~-**mind'ed** kleingeestig, benepe; bekrompe
nar'tjie (-s) nartjie, *see* **mandarin, tangerine**
nas'al (a) nasaal, neus~; ~ **cavity** neusholte; ~**ise** nasaleer
nas'tiness narigheid, vieslikheid
nastur'tium kappertjie
nas'ty naar, aaklig; gemeen, haatlik; vuil; ~ *feeling*, nare gevoel; *a ~ fellow*, 'n onaangename/skurwe vent
nat'al geboorte~
na'tion volk, nasie; moondheid; **United N**~**s** Verenigde Nasies
na'tional (n) burger, landgenoot; (a) nasionaal; vaderlands; volks~, staats~; ~ **anthem** volkslied; ~ **debt** staatskuld; N~ **Education** Nasionale Opvoeding; ~**ism** nasionalisme; ~**ist** nasionalis; ~**ity** (..**ties**) nasionaliteit; ~ **serviceman** (nasionale) dienspligtige; ~ **state** nasionale staat
Na'tive[1] Naturel, Inboorling
na'tive[2] (n) inboorling, boorling
na'tive[3] (a) aangebore; oorspronklik; eie; inheems; vry; natuurlik
nat'ural (a) natuurlik; menslik; natuur~; ~ **child** buite-egtelike kind; ~ **death** natuurlike dood; ~ **gas** aardgas; ~ **resources** natuurbronne, natuurlike hulpbronne; ~**ly** natuurlik; ~**ise** naturaliseer; ~ **science** natuurwetenskap, natuurkunde
na'ture natuur; karakter, aard, geaardheid, inbors; *freak of* ~, natuurfrats; *in* ~*'s garb*, in Adamspak; *good* ~, goeie geaardheid; ~ **resort** natuuroord
nat'urist naturis, natuurnudis
nat'uropath natuurgeneser

naught (n) niks, nul; (a) nikswerd, waardeloos
naught'y ondeund, stout; ~ *boy*, karnallie, rakker
naus'eous walglik; mislik
naut'ical see~, skeeps~; seevaart~
nav'al see~; skeeps~; vloot~; ~ **base** vlootbasis ~ **cadet** adelbors; ~ **college** vlootkollege, marineskool; ~ **term** skeepsterm
nav'el nawel, nael; ~ **orange** nawellemoen; ~ **string** naelstring
nav'igate vaar; bevaar; bestuur
naviga'tion skeepvaart; lugvaart
navi'gator seevaarder; koerspeiler (lugv.); navigator (tydrenne)
nav'y (navies) seemag, vloot; ~ **blue** marineblou
neap'tide laagwater, dooie ty/gety
near (v) nader (kom); (a) naby, digby, by, aan; *the ~ future*, die afsienbare toekoms; ~*est relative*, naaste bloedverwant/aanverwant; (adv) naby, digby, byna; ~**by** langsaan, naby; ~**ly** amper, byna; ~-**sighted** bysiende
neat (a) netjies, sindelik; keurig; handig
neat: ~**ly** netjies; keurig; ~**ness** netheid, sindelikheid
ne'cessary (a) nodig, noodsaaklik, noodwendig
necess'itate (v) noodsaak, dwing
necess'ity (..**ties**) noodsaaklikheid; behoefte; ~ *knows no law*, nood breek wet; ~ *is the mother of invention*, nood leer bid
neck nek (van diere); pas, engte (tussen berge); *escape with one's* ~, met die lewe daarvan afkom; ~**lace** halsketting, halssnoer; ~**tie** das
nec'tar nektar, godedrank
nec'tarine kaalperske
need (n) nood, behoefte; *in time of* ~, as die nood druk; (v) nodig hê, makeer; *you ~ not come*, jy hoef nie te kom nie; *you ~ not have come*, jy hoef nie te gekom het nie; (a) nodig, noodsaaklik
need'le naald; *on pins and* ~*s*, op hete kole; ~ **case** naaldekoker
need'less onnodig, nodeloos
need'lework naaldwerk, naaiwerk
needs (n) behoeftes, benodigdhede
need'y behoeftig, arm
ne'er'-do-well niksnuts

neg'ative (n) negatief; ontkenning; ~ *sign,* minusteken

neglect' (n) verwaarlosing, versuim; (v) verwaarloos, versuim; **~ful** nalatig, agtelosig

neg'ligence nalatigheid, versuim

neg'ligent nalatig, agtelosig

neg'ligible nietig, onbeduidend

nego'tiable verhandelbaar; reëlbaar; *salary* ~, salaris reëlbaar

nego'tiate onderhandel; verhandel; sluit, behartig

nego'tiator onderhandelaar

Neg'ress (-es) Negerin

Neg'ro (-es) Neger

neigh'bour (n) buurman; ~ing *countries,* naburige lande, buurlande; *next-door* ~s, naaste bure; (v) grens aan; (a) naburig; **~hood** buurt; buurskap; **~ing** naburig, aangrensend

neith'er (adv) ewemin, ook nie; (conj) nie een nie; *that's* ~ *here nor there,* dit maak geen saak nie; ~ ...*nor,* nòg ... nòg

neol'ogism nuutskepping, neologisme

neon'light neonlig

ne'phew neef/nefie, broerskind, susterskind

nerve (n) senuwee; spierkrag; moed, durf; (pl) senuwees; *get on a person's* ~s, op iem. se senuwees werk; *you have got a* ~*!* jy verbeel jou darem! **~-racking** senutergend

ner'vous senuweeagtig; skrikkerig; **~ness** senuweeagtigheid

nest (n) nes; *feather one's* ~, jou verryk; *foul one's* ~, jou nes bevuil; (v) nes maak, nestel; ~ **egg** neseier

ne'stle nestel; nes maak; ~ *close to,* aankruip teen

net[1] (n) net; spinnerak; netwerk; (v) (-ted, -ted) vang; inbring

net[2] (a) netto; skoon, suiwer; ~ **profit** netto wins

nett'ing netwerk, gaas; ~ **wire** ogiesdraad, sifdraad

nett'le (n) brandnetel; (v) vererg, prikkel; ~ **rash** netelroos

net'work netwerk

neural'gia senu(wee)pyn, gesigspyn, sinkings

neurot'ic (n) senulyer; senuweemiddel; (a) neuroties

neut'er (n) onsydige geslag; (a) onsydig; geslagloos; (v) regmaak; spei (wyfiedier)

neut'ral (a) neutraal, onpartydig, onsydig

neut'ron neutron; ~ **bomb** neutronbom

nev'er nooit, nimmer; ~ *mind,* toe maar; dit maak g'n saak nie; ~ *a word,* geen stomme woord nie; **~more** nooit meer nie; nooit weer nie; **~theless** nieteenstaande, desondanks, almiskie, nietemin, tog

new nuut, vars; *a* ~ *student,* 'n groene/ groentjie; *the* ~ *year,* die (hele) nuwe jaar; **~comer** nuweling, aankomeling; **~ly** nuut; onlangs; **~ly** *appointed,* pasaangestel(de)

news nuus, tyding; *the latest* ~, die jongste nuus; ~ **agent** nuusagent; **~cast** nuus (radio, TV); **~flash (-es)** flitsberig (radio); **~paper** koerant, nuusblad; ~ **vendor** koerantverkoper

New Year' Nuwejaar; **~'s day** Nuwejaarsdag; **~'s eve** Oujaarsaand; **~'s resolution** Nuwejaarsvoorneme

next (n) (die) volgende; (a) volgende, aanstaande; ~ *door,* langsaan; ~ *of kin,* naasbestaande(s); (prep) langsaan, naasaan

nib pen(punt)

nib'ble (n) geknaag; (v) knaag, peusel

nice lekker; gaaf, lief; oulik; *you are a* ~ *one!* jy is (ook) 'n mooie!

nick (n) kerf; stippie; kabouter; *in the very* ~ *of time,* net betyds; (v) inkerf; kul

nick'el nikkel; **~-plated** vernikkel

nick: **~name** bynaam; **~stick** kerfstok

nic'otine nikotien; pypolie

niece nig(gie), susterskind, broerskind

nigg'ard (a) vrekkerig, inhalig

nigg'le (v) neul, sanik, seur; (n) **~r** neuler, neulpot, sanikpot, seurkous

night nag, aand; *all* ~, die hele nag; *last* ~, gisteraand; ~ **adder** nagadder; **~cap** slaapmus; nagsopie, slaapdop, aandsnapsie; **~class (-es)** aandklas; **~club** nagklub; **~fall** aandskemering; ~ **fighter** nagjagter

night'ingale nagtegaal

night: **~ly** nagtelik, snags; **~mare** nagmerrie; **~shift** nagskof

nil niks, nul

nim'ble lenig, vinnig, rats

nine nege; ~ **o'clock,** nege-uur; **~teen**

negentien; ~teenth negentiende; ~tieth
negentigste; ~ty negentig
ninth negende
nip[1] (v) (-ped, -ped) byt, knyp; ~ *in the
bud*, in die kiem smoor
nip[2] (n) halfbottel; snapsie
nip'ple tepel (mens); speen (dier); nippel
(geweer)
no (n) (-es) nee, weiering; teenstem; (a)
geen, g'n; (adv) nee; *by* ~ *means*, in geen
geval nie; ~ *parking*, geen parkering
(nie); *in* ~ *time*, gou, in 'n kits/japtrap,
tjop-tjop; (adv) nee; ~ *sooner said than
done*, so gesê, so gedaan
nobil'ity adel, adeldom
no'ble (a) edel; adellik; ~man (..men)
edelman
no'body niemand
noc'turne naglied, nokturne; nagskildery
nod (n) knik, wenk; (v) (-ded, -ded) knik
noise (n) geraas, lawaai, rumoer; (v) raas;
~less stil, geruisloos
nois'y luidrugtig, rumoerig, lawaaierig
nom'ad swerwer, nomade
no-man's-land niemandsland
nom de plume' skuilnaam, skryfnaam
nom'inal in naam, nominaal; ~ value
nominale waarde
nomina'tion benoeming, nominasie
nom'inator voorsteller, benoemer
nominee' benoemde, genomineerde
non-aggress'ion pact nie-aanvalsverdrag
non-align'ed onverbonde (land)
non'chalant onverskillig, doodbedaard
non-commi'ssioned officer onderoffisier
nonconform'ist nonkonformis
none (a) niks, geen; (pron) geeneen, nie=
mand; (adv) niks; ~ *other than*, niks/
niemand anders nie as; ~ *the worse for*,
glad nie slegter nie; ~theless nietemin
non-fic'tion nie-fiksie, feiteboeke, faksie
non-pay'ment wanbetaling
non-return' ~ valve eenvloeiklep
non'sense onsin, bog, kaf, twak
non'stop deurgaande; ononderbroke: ~
dance langasemdans
noon middag, twaalfuur
noose (n) strop, galgtou; lus, strik
non'-profit undertaking onderneming son=
der winsoogmerk/winsbejag
nor ook nie, nòg; *neither* ... ~, nòg ... nòg
norm standaard, norm

nor'mal normaal; ~ **college** normaalskool,
opleidingskollege, onderwyskollege
north (n) die noorde; (a) noord; noordelik;
(adv) noordwaarts; N~ *Pole*, Noordpool;
~ward noordwaarts
nose (n) neus; *blow your* ~, snuit jou neus;
(v) ruik; snuffel; ~dive (n) duikvlug; (v)
neusduik
nos'tril neusgat
not nie; ~ *at all*, glad nie; ~ *yet*, nog nie
not'ably vernaamlik; merkbaar
not'ary (..ries) notaris
notch (n) (-es) kerf, keep; (v) kerf; aante=
ken; uitkeep; ~ **stick** kerfstok
note (n) aantekening; toon, briefie, nota;
noot (geld, musiek); ~ *of exclamation*,
uitroepteken; ~ *of interrogation*, vraag=
teken; *make* ~s, aantekeninge maak; (v)
oplet, let wel (L.W.), opmerk; ~book
aantekeningboek; ~d beroemd, ver=
maard; ~paper skryfpapier, briefpapier;
~worthy merkwaardig
no'thing niks, glad nie; ~ *at all*, glad niks
nie; *next to* ~, so goed as niks; ~ *to
speak of*, onbenullig; ~ *like trying*, aan=
houer wen
not'ice (n) kennis; kennisgewing, berig; ~
calling the meeting, byeenroepende ken=
nisgewing; *until further* ~, tot nader ken=
nisgewing; ~ *is hereby given*, geliewe ken=
nis te neem van ...; (v) opmerk, be=
merk, oplet; ~able merkbaar; ~ **board**
aanspeldbord, aanplakbord
not'ify (..fied, ..fied) meedeel, aankondig,
verwittig; *notifiable disease*, aanmeldbare
siekte
no'tion denkbeeld, idee, begrip
notor'ious berug; wêreldkundig
notwithstand'ing nieteenstaande, desnie=
teenstaande, nietemin, ondanks, tog
nought niks, nul; ~s-and-crosses tik-tak-
tol
noun selfstandige naamwoord
nou'rish voed, koester; ~ing voedsaam;
~ment voedsel, voeding
no'vel[1] (n) roman
no'vel[2] (a) nuut, modern; eienaardig
nov'el: ~ette novelle; ~ist roman=
skrywer, romansier
nov'elty (..ties) nuwigheid; (pl) fantasie=
ware
Novem'ber November

nov'ice nuweling, groentjie, beginner; leek
now (n) hede, teenswoordige; (adv) nou,
tans, teenswoordig; ~ and again, af en
toe; every ~ and then, telkens; ~ and
then, af en toe; partykeer; ~ then, toe
nou; (conj) nou; ~ that, noudat; ~adays
teenswoordig, deesdae
no'where nêrens
noz'zle nossel, spuitkop; tuit
nuc'lear kern~; ~ fall-out kern-as; ~ debris kernoorskot; ~ fission kernsplyting;
~ physics kernfisika; ~ reaction kern-
reaksie; ~ war kernoorlog; ~ warfare
kernoorlogvoering; ~ waste kernafval; ~
weapons kernwapens
nuc'leus (nuclei) kern, pit
nude (a) kaal, naak, bloot; ~ bather kaal-
(bas)swemmer
nud'ist naakloper, nudis, kaalbas
nuis'ance oorlas, plaag; laspos; a regular
~, 'n ware laspos; ~ value irritasie-
waarde, steurfaktor, lolfaktor
null nikswerd, nietig; ongeldig; ~ and void,
van nul en gener waarde; nietig
numb gevoelloos, verkluim
num'ber (n) nommer; aflewering (blad);
getal, aantal; klomp; one of our ~, een
van ons (geledere); his ~ goes up, dis

klaar met hom; (v) nommer, tel, reken; ~
among, tel onder; ~ plate nommerplaat
num'eral telwoord; syfer
numer'ical numeriek, getal~; ~ly stronger,
getalsterker; ~ order, getal(s)orde
num'erous talryk, baie; a ~ family, 'n
groot huisgesin
numismat'ics muntkunde, numismatiek
num'skull dwaas, uilskuiken
nun non; ~nery (..ries) nonneklooster
nup'tial huweliks~, bruilofs~; ~s bruilof
nurse (n) verpleegster; verpleegsuster;
plegie, kinderoppasser; (v) verpleeg, soog;
kweek (plante); ~ a grievance, 'n grief
koester; ~maid kindermeisie
nurs'ery (..ries) kinderkamer, babasaal;
kwekery; ~ rhyme kleuterversie; ~
school kleuterskool
nurs'ing verpleging, verpleegkunde; ~ sister verpleegsuster; ~ staff verpleegper-
soneel
nut neut; moertjie; ~crackers neutkraker;
~meg neutmuskaat
nutri'tion voeding, kos; voedingsleer (vak)
nut' sedge uintjie, also nut grass
nut'shell neut(e)dop; in a ~, baie beknop,
kort en saaklik
nymph nimf; ~oma'niac nimfomaan,
seksbehepte vrou

O

oak eike(hout); (a) eike~; ~ table eike-
houttafel; ~ tree eikeboom, akkerboom
oar roeispaan; roeiriem; rest on one's ~s,
op jou louere rus; ~s'man (..men) roeier
oa'sis (oases) oase
oath eed; vloek; ~ of allegiance eed van
getrouheid
oat: ~meal hawermeel; ~s hawer
obed'ient gehoorsaam, dienswillig; your ~
servant, u dienswillige dienaar
obey' gehoorsaam, luister na; ~ traffic
rules, verkeersreëls eerbiedig/gehoorsaam
obit'uary (n) (..ries) dood(s)berig
ob'ject (n) voorwerp; doel, oogmerk; bedoeling; plan; money is no ~, geld is
bysaak
object' (v) beswaar maak, teenkap, teenwerp, objekteer; ~ion beswaar, objek-
sie; raise ~ions, beware opper; ~ion-

able aanstootlik, laakbaar; ~ive (n)
doelwit, doel; (a) objektief; aims and
~ives, doelstellings; management by
~ives, doelwitbestuur
object'or teenspreker; beswaarmaker; conscientious ~, gewetensbeswaarde(r)
obliga'tion verpligting; without (any) ~,
sonder verpligting
oblige' verplig, diens bewys; feel ~d, ge-
dwonge/verplig voel; much ~d, baie
dankie
ob'long (n) reghoek; (a) langwerpig
ob'oe (-s) hobo
ob'oist hobospeler
obscene' onkuis, vuil, liederlik, obseen
obscure' (v) verduister; (a) duister, onbekend; ~ poetry, duister(e) poësie
observ'ance nakoming; Sunday ~, Son-
dagsheiliging

observ'ant oplettend; gedienstig
observa'tion opmerking; waarneming, vie=
ring; nakoming; ~ post, observasiepos
observ'atory (..ries) sterrewag
observe' bemerk, waarneem; ~ the law,
die wet eerbiedig/naleef; ~ silence, stil=
bly; ~r waarnemer
obsess'ion obsessie, kwelling, manie
obsoles'cence veroudering; planned ~, be=
plande veroudering
obs'olete verouder(d), in onbruik
ob'stacle hinderpaal, beletsel, belemme=
ring; ~ race hindernis(wed)ren
obstetri'cian verloskundige
obstet'rics verloskunde, obstetrie
ob'stinate koppig, hardkoppig, hardnekkig
obstrep'erous weerspannig, opstandig
obstruct' verhinder, belemmer, versper;
~ion belemmering, versperring
obtain' verkry, verskaf; ~able verkry(g)=
baar
ob'vious klaarblyklik; vanselfsprekend; it is
~ that, dit spreek vanself dat
occa'sion (n) geleentheid; plegtigheid; (v)
veroorsaak, teweegbring; ~al toevallig, af
en toe; geleentheids=; ~ally af en toe
occ'upant besitter; bewoner; insittende
occupa'tion beroep, ambag, besigheid, be=
dryf; ~al disease beroepsiekte; ~al
therapy arbeidsterapie
occ'upy (..pied, ..pied) besit; besig hou;
bewoon, gebruik, okkupeer; beklee
occur' (-red, -red) voorkom, voorval, ge=
beur; byval; it ~red to me, dit het my
bygeval; ~rence voorval, gebeurtenis
o'cean oseaan, wêreldsee
o'clock' op die klok; it is ten ~, dis tienuur
octag'onal agthoekig
octane' oktaan
o'ctave oktaaf
Octob'er Oktober
oc'topus (-es, ..pi) seekat, oktopus
oc'ulist oogdokter, oogarts
odd onewe, ongelyk; snaaks, koddig, son=
derling; ~ and even, gelyk en ongelyk; ~
coloured bont; ~ly snaaks, koddig;
~ments oorskietsels
odds onenigheid; waarskynlikheid; the ~
are, die kans bestaan; fight against ~,
teen die oormag stry
ode ode
od'ious haatlik, verfoeilik, walglik

od'our geur, reuk
of van, uit, aan; she ~ all people, dat dit
juis sy moet wees; the city ~ Pretoria, die
stad Pretoria
off (a) ander; regter=; the ~ season, die slap
tyd; (adv) af, weg, ver, vandaan, van;
hands ~! hande tuis! be well ~, wel=
gesteld wees; (prep) van, van ... af; ~
Church Street, uit Kerkstraat; ~ duty,
vry, van diens af; ~ the record, onoffi=
sieel
o'ffal afval (vleis); oorskiet
off'-chance moontlikheid; geluk; vir geval
off-col'our van stryk; kroes, olik
off-course (a) buitebaan (totalisator)
off'-cut afvalstuk
offence' oortreding, misdryf; give ~, aan=
stoot gee
offend' beledig; ~ed beledig, kwaad; ~er
oortreder, misdadiger
offen'sive (n) aanval, offensief; (a) beledi=
gend, aanstootlik, stuitig
off'er (n) aanbod, aanbieding; bod; (v)
aanbied, bied; offer; ~ an apology, ver=
skoning maak; ~ing offerande
off'-hand (a) kortaf, hooghartig; ongeërg
off'ice kantoor; amp, diens; ~ bearer be=
ampte, ampsdraer; amp(s)bekleër
off'icer offisier, amptenaar, beampte
offi'cial (n) amptenaar, beampte; (a) amp=
telik, offisieel, amps=; ~ car ampsmotor;
~ counterpart ampsgenoot; ~ letter
diensbrief
offi'ciate optree; ~ as, optree/fungeer as
off'ish uit die hoogte, eenkant
off'-peak afspits; ~ traffic slapverkeer,
laagverkeer
off'-ramp afrit (verkeer)
off'-road racing veldrenne (motorkarre)
off'-sales buiteverkope
off'-season buiteseisoen(s)
off'set (n) teenrekening; (v) (~, ~), ver=
reken (teen); goedmaak; neutraliseer
off'shoot loot, uitspruitsel, tak
off'-shore aflands/aflandig; ~ wind land=
wind
off'side onkant
off'spring kroos, nakomelingskap
off'-street parking buitenstraatse parkering,
terreinparkering
off'-white naaswit
oft, o'ften dikwels, baiemaal

o'gre weerwolf; paaiboelie

oil (n) olie; (v) olie (gee); ~ colour olieverf; ~ consumption olieverbruik; ~ pipeline oliepypleiding; ~ painting olieverfskildery; ~ rig olieboor; ~ slick olieslik; ~ stone oliesteen, slypsteen; ~y olieagtig; olierig

oint'ment salf, smeergoed

oka'pi (-s) boskameelperd, okapi

old oud, ou; geslepe, slim; ouderwets; ~ age, ouderdom; as ~ as the hills, so oud soos die Kaapse wapad; ~ maid, oujongnooi; of ~, vanouds, vanmelewe; ~-fashioned ouderwets, outyds; ~-aged home ouetehuis, tehuis vir bejaardes

olean'der selonsroos, oleander

o'live (n) olyf; (a) olyfkleurig; ~ oil olyfolie

olym'piad olimpiade (wisk., wetenskap)

Olym'pic Olimpies; ~ games Olimpiese spele

om'elet eierstruif, omelet

om'en (n) voorteken; (v) voorspel

om'inous onheilspellend, dreigend

omi'ssion weglating, uitlating, versuim

omit' (-ted, -ted) weglaat, uitlaat; versuim

on (a) aangeskakel; (adv) aan, deur, op; verder; off and ~, af en toe; (prep) op, in, aan, te, na, bo, met, teen; ~ account of, as gevolg van; weens; ~ an average, gemiddeld; ~ business, met/vir sake; ~ duty, op diens; ~ call, roepbaar, op/met roepdiens; ~ form, op stryk; ~ holiday, met/op vakansie; ~ my honour, op my erewoord; ~ purpose, opsetlik; ~ time, betyds; op tyd

once (n) eenmaal; (a) vroeër; (adv) eendag, een keer, eens, eenmaal; ~ again, nog 'n keer, nog eenmaal; at ~, dadelik; ~ in a blue moon, baie selde; ~ more, nog een keer; ~ upon a time, eendag; ~ or twice, een of twee maal/keer

on'coming (a) naderende; ~ traffic, aankomende verkeer, teenverkeer

one (n) een; go ~ better, iem. oortref/oortroef; I for ~, wat my betref; little ~s, die kleintjies; (a) een, enigste; ~ for the road, loopdop; (pron) een; iemand, 'n mens; ~ and all, almal; every ~, elkeen; ~-act play eenbedryf

on'ion ui

on'looker toeskouer, aanskouer

on'ly (a) enigste; the ~ of its kind, enig in sy soort; (adv) alleen, slegs, maar net; ~ too glad, maar alte bly

onomatopoe'ia klanknabootsing, onomatopee

on'-ramp oprit (verkeer)

on'slaught aanval, bestorming; total ~, totale aanslag

on'us (no pl) (bewys)las; verpligting, verantwoordelikheid; onus; the ~ rests on/ upon him, die onus rus op hom

on'ward voorwaarts, verder

on'yx (-es) oniks

ooze (n) modder, slyk, slik; sug (wond); (v) sypel, syfer

op'al opaal

op'en (n) ruimte; oopte; (v) oopmaak; open (konferensie); oopstel; bloötlê; begin; (a, adv) oop; openhartig; blootgestel; ontvanklik; with an ~ mind, met 'n oop gemoed; ~ air buitelug; ~-air museum oopelugmuseum; ~ cast oopgroef (myn); ~ day ope dag; ~er inleier (debat); oopmaker, oopsnyer; ~ ing opening, begin, kans; ~ly openlik

op'era opera; ~ glasses toneelkyker

op'erate werk; opereer; bedien (masjien)

op'erating: ~ room operasiekamer; ~ theatre operasiesaal

opera'tion operasie; bewerking; werking; verrigting; bediening; in ~, in werking; ~al area operasionele gebied

op'erative (a) werksaam; operatief; doeltreffend; become ~, in werking tree

op'erator werker, bediener; operateur

ophthal'mic (a) oog=; ~ surgeon oogarts, oogchirurg

opin'ion opinie; mening; goeddunke; sienswyse; oordeel; be of ~, van mening wees; have a high ~ of, 'n hoë dunk hê van; in my ~, na/volgens my mening; public ~, openbare mening; ~ former meningvormer; ~ poll mening(s)peiling

op'ium opium

oppon'ent teenstander, opponent

opportun'ism opportunisme

opportun'ity (..ties) geleentheid, kans

oppose' bestry; opponeer; teenwerk

opp'osite (n) die teenoorgestelde; (a) teenoorgestel; teengestel; ~ number, teëhanger; the ~ sex, die ander geslag; (adv) oorkant, anderkant; (prep) teenoor, regoor

opposi'tion teenstand, opposisie; teenparty
oppress' onderdruk, verdruk; **~ion** on=
    derdrukking, verdrukking, neerslagtig=
    heid; **~ive** onderdrukkend; benoud; **~or**
    onderdrukker, tiran
op'tical gesigs=, opties; **~ illusion** gesigs=
    bedrog
opti'cian brilmaker, optisiën, optikus
optimis'tic optimisties, hoopvol
op'tion opsie, keuse; *the ~ of a fine,*
    boetekeuse; **~al** opsioneel
op'us (no pl) werk, opus
or of; *either ... ~, òf ... òf;* **~ else,** of
    anders
o'racle godspraak, orakel
or'al mondeling; mond=; **~ examination**
    mondelinge eksamen
Orange Free State Oranje-Vrystaat
o'range lemoen, soetlemoen; oranje(kleur);
    ~ squash lemoenkwas
orang'-outang' orang-oetang
or'ator spreker, redenaar
orb'it (v) wentel; (n) wentelbaan, baan;
    ~er wentelaar; oogholte
orch'ard boord, vrugteboord
or'chestra orkes
or'chid orgidee
ord'er (n) orde, volgorde; reëlmaat; order,
    bevel, opdrag; volgorde; bestelling (van
    goedere); *by ~ of the court;* op las van die
    hof; *by ~ of management,* in opdrag van
    die bestuur; *call to ~,* tot die orde roep;
    cash with ~, kontant met bestelling; *in ~
    that,* sodat; *in ~ to (expedite delivery)* ten
    einde (aflewering te bespoedig); *out of ~,*
    buite werking, stukkend; *place an ~,*
    bestel; (v) bestel; reël; beveel, gelas; **~
    about,** rondkommandeer; **~ form** be=
    stelvorm; **~ly** (n) (..lies) lyfdienaar, or=
    donnans; (a) ordelik
ord'inal (n) rangtelwoord; (a) rangskik=
    kend; **~ number,** ranggetal
ord'inance reglement; ordinansie (kerklik);
    ordonnansie (provinsie); voorskrif
ord'inary (a) gewoon, gebruiklik; *some=
    thing out of the ~,* iets ongewoons,
    buitengewoons
ord'nance geskut, artillerie
ore erts; **~ crusher** ertsbreker, vergruiser;
    ~ deposit ertsafsetting
or'gan orgaan; orrel (mus.); blad; werk=

tuig; mondstuk; **~s of speech,** spraak=
    organe
organ'ic organies
org'anist orrelis
org'an recital orreluitvoering
organisa'tion inrigting, organisasie
org'anise organiseer; inrig; **~d** georgani=
    seer; **~r** organiseerder, organisator
org'anising committee reëlingskomitee
or'gy (orgies) swelgparty, drinkparty, orgie
orienta'tion oriëntering; ontgroening, in=
    burgering, induksie
o'rigin oorsprong, begin, bron, herkoms
ori'ginal (n) oertipe; (a) oorspronklik
orn'ament (n) sieraad, ornament; (pl) tier=
    lantyntjies; (v) versier, tooi, verfraai
ornamen'tal sierlik, versierend, sier=; fraai,
    dekoratief; **~ grid** sierrooster (kar); **~
    shrub** sierstruik
ornithol'ogist voëlkenner, ornitoloog
orph'an (n) weeskind; (a) wees=, ouerloos;
    ~age weeshuis
orthodon'tist ortodontis, tandregstelkun=
    dige
orth'odox regsinnig, ortodoks
orthog'raphy ortografie, spellingleer
orthopae'dic ortopedies; **~s** ortopedie
orthopae'dist beenheelkundige, ortopeed
osten'sibly oënskynlik, kastig
ostenta'tious ydel, opsigtig, praalsiek
os'trich (-es) volstruis; **~ farm** volstruis=
    plaas; **~ feather** volstruisveer
o'ther (n, pron, a) ander; anders; *the ~
    day,* nou die dag; *each ~,* mekaar; *every
    ~ day,* al om die ander dag; *on the ~
    hand,* aan die ander kant; **~ than,**
    behalwe
o'therwise anders, origens
ott'er otter
ought (v) behoort, moet; *you ~ to do it,* jy
    behoort dit te doen; *he ~ to have said it,*
    hy behoort dit te gesê het
ounce ons
our ons
ours ons s'n; *he likes ~ better,* hy hou meer
    van ons s'n
our'selve, our'selves ons, onsself
oust verdryf, uitstoot; uitstem
out (a) nie tuis nie; (adv, prep) uit, weg, uit,
    buite; **~ of breath,** uit-asem; **~ of date,**
    verouder; **~ of print,** uit druk; **~ of the**

question, buite die kwessie; ~ of town, uitstedig; ~ of work, werkloos
out'board buiteboords; ~ motor aan= hangmotor, buiteboordmotor
out'break uitbreking, uitbarsting
out'building buitegebou
out'burst uitbarsting
out'cast (n) balling; verstoteling
outclass' ver oortref/oorskadu; we were ~ed, hulle was veels te sterk vir ons
out'come resultaat, uitslag
out'cry lawaai, geskree(u)
outdo' (..did, -done) oortref
out'door buite=, buitelug=
out'er buite; uiterste; ~ darkness, buiten= ste duisternis
out'fit uitrusting, uitset; ~ter uitruster
outflank' omvleuel, omtrek; uitoorlê
out'flow uitvloei(ing); uitloop
out'going vertrekkende; aftredende; uit= tredende (voorsitter)
out'house buitegebou
out'ing uitstappie, kuier
outland'ish vreemd, uitlands, uitheems
outlast' oorleef, langer duur
out'law (n) balling, voëlvryverklaarde; (v) ban, voëlvry verklaar
out'lay uitgawe, koste; besteding
out'let afvoerkanaal; verkooppunt, afset= punt
out'line (n) skets, omtrek; in ~, in hoof= trekke
out'look vooruitsig; his ~ on life, sy lewensbeskouing
out'lying ver, afgeleë
outmanoeu'vre uitoorlê; die loef afsteek
outnum'ber oortref; they were ~ed, hulle was in die minderheid
out-of-date verouder; onvanpas
out'-of-doors' buite(ns)huis, buite
out-of-pock'et: ~ expenses, klein/los uit= gawes; sakgeld
out-of-way' afgeleë; ongewoon
out'-patient buitepasiënt
out'post voorpos, voorpunt, buitepos
out'put opbrengs, produksie, uitset
outra'geous skandelik, verregaande
out'right heeltemal, volkome, volstrek, openlik, onomwonde
out'room buitekamer
out'set begin, aanvang; at (from) the ~, uit die staanspoor

out'side (n) uiterlik; buitekant; (a) buite=; uiterste; (prep) buite, buitekant; ~r on= ingewyde; buitestaander; outsider (let= terk.); buiteperd
out'size buitemaat
out'skirts grens, buitewyk
out'span (n) uitspanning, uitspanplek; (v) (-ned, -ned) uitspan
outspo'ken openhartig, reguit
out'standing onbetaal, uitstaande (skulde); uitstekend, uitmuntend, treffend
out'strip (-ped, -ped) wen, verby hardloop
outvote' uitstem
out'ward (n) uiterlik; (a) uiterlik, uitwen= dig, buitekant; (adv) uitwaarts; ~ jour= ney heenreis, uitreis; ~ policy uitwaartse beleid
outwit (-ted, -ted) uitoorlê
ov'al (n) krieketveld; (a) ovaal
ov'ary (..ries) eierstok, vrugbeginsel
ova'tion hulde, ovasie, toejuiging
o'ven oond
ov'er (n) boulbeurt; (adv) oor; om, onder= stebo; hand ~, oorhandig; run ~, iem. raakry; (prep) oor, uit, bo, op; ~ and above, bo en behalwe, boonop
ov'erall (n) oorpak; (pl) oorbroek, oor= klere; (a) totaal; algeheel; ~ winner algehele wenner
overbear'ing aanmatigend, baasspelerig
overboard' oorboord
overburd'en (n) deklaag, bolaag, oordek= king; (v) oorlaai
over-cap'italise oorkapitaliseer
overcast' (a) bewolk, betrokke
over'charge (n) oorvordering; (v) he ~d me, hy het my oorvra
ov'ercoat jas, warmjas
overcome' (v) (..came, ..come) oormees= ter; oorkom, baasraak; (a) aangedaan
over-con'fident oormoedig; oorgerus
overcrowd' oorbevolk; oorlaai; ~ed oor= vol, oorbevolk
overdone' oorgaar, te gaar; oorwerk
ov'erdraft oortrokke bankrekening, oor= trekking
ov'erdrive (n) snelrat, spoedrat
overdue' agterstallig; te laat
over-es'timate oorskat, te hoog skat
over-expo'sure oorbeligting
ov'erflow (n) oorloop; oorstroming
overgrow' (..grew, -n) oorgroei, toegroei

ov'ergrowth uitwas, oorgroeisel
overhaul' (v) herstel; opknap, herkon=
  disioneer
ov'erhead (a) lug=, oorhoofs, oorkoepelend;
  bogronds; ~ camshaft bonokas; ~ ex=
  penses bokoste; ~ irrigation sprinkel=
  besproeiing; ~ projector truprojektor;
  ~ railway lugspoor; (adv) bokant die
  grond
overjoyed' verruk, opgetoë
overlap' (v) (-ped, -ped) oormekaar val,
  oorvleuel
overleaf' keersy, op die anderkant v.d.
  bladsy; see ~, blaai om
overlook' oor die hoof sien, verskoon
ov'ernight die vorige nag, oornag
overpay' (..paid, ..paid) oorbetaal
ov'er-populated oorbevolk
overpow'er oorweldig, oorstelp
over'production oorproduksie
overrate' oorskat; ~d (a) oorskat
overreact' oorreageer
overrule' verwerp (voorstel); van die hand
  wys (beswaar)
ov'erseas oorsee; ~ mail oorsese pos
ov'erseer opsigter, opsiener, toesighouer
overshad'ow oorskadu, oortref
ov'ersight vergissing, fout, versuim; toesig
oversleep' (..slept, ..slept) jou verslaap
ov'erstatement oorbeklemtoning
overstock' te groot voorraad; oorvoorsien
overstrung' (a) oorspanne
over'supply oorvoorsiening (mark); oor=
  aanbod

overtake' (..took, -n) oorval; overtaking
  cars, motors/karre verbysteek
overtax' ooreis; te swaar belas, oorbelas
overthrow' (..threw, ..thrown) omgooi,
  omverwerp; oorwin
ov'ertime (n) oortyd (diens); ~ pay oor=
  tydbetaling
ov'erture voorspel, overture; uitnodiging;
  voorstel; make ~s, toenadering soek
overturn' onderstebo keer, omkeer
overwhelm' oorstelp, oorweldig, oorrom=
  pel; ~ing oorweldigend, verpletterend
overwork' oorwerk, te veel werk
ov'um (ova) eier
owe skuld; te danke hê; ~ one a grudge, 'n
  wrok teen iem. koester
ow'ing (a) onbetaal, verskuldig; the amount
  ~, die verskuldigde bedrag; (prep) weens,
  vanweë; danksy; ~ to an error, weens 'n
  fout
owl uil; uilskuiken
own¹ (v) besit; erken, eien, toegee
own² (a) eie; of one's ~ accord, uit eie be=
  weging; ~er eienaar; baas, besitter; ~=
  ership eiendomsreg; eienaarskap (van 'n
  huis)
ox (-en) os; young ~, ossie, tollie; ~bow
  rivierdraai; boogjuk; ~braai osbraai
oxida'tion oksidasie
ox'wagon ossewa
ox'ygen suustof, oksigeen
oys'ter oester
oz'one osoon

P

pa pa
pace (n) tree, pas, skrede; gang; tempo;
  vaart; keep ~ with, tred hou met; (v) stap;
  aftree; die pas aangee; ~maker pas=
  aangeër, gangmaker (hart); ~setter pas=
  maker
paci'fic vreedsaam, stil; P~ Ocean, Stille
  Oseaan, Stille Suidsee, Groot Oseaan
pa'cifist pasifis, vrede(s)voorstander
pack (n) pak; vrag; a ~ed hall, 'n stamp=
  vol saal; ~ of rogues, 'n bende skurke; (v)
  pak, inpak; ~age pakkasie; pakket; ~age
  deal pakketakkoord, bondeltransaksie;
  ~et pakkie, pakket; ~horse pakperd;

~ing verpakking; pakgoed; pakking
pact verdrag, verbond, ooreenkoms, pakt
pad (n) kussinkie; skryfblok; beenskut; (v)
  (-ded, -ded) opvul; volstop; ~ding vulsel,
  stopsel; bladvulling
padd'le¹ (v) plas; speel; waggel
padd'le² (n) roeispaan; skepper; (v) pagaai;
  roei; ~ skiing skiroei; ~ skier skiroeier;
  ~ wheel skeprat
padd'ling pool plaspoel
pad'dock kamp; renbaanperk
pad'lock (n) hangslot; (v) toesluit
pad're kapelaan, veldprediker
paediatri'cian kinderarts, pediater

pag'an (n) heiden; (a) heidens
page¹ (n) (hotel)bode, hoteljoggie; livrei‑
kneg; (v) ontbied, spoor
page² (n) bladsy, pagina; (v) pagineer
pa'geant optog, skouspel, vertoning
page'(boy) (-s) hoteljoggie; slipdraertjie
paid betaal; voldaan; reply ~, antwoord
betaal(d) see pay
pail emmer, dopemmer
pain (n) pyn, smart, leed; (pl) moeite, in‑
spanning; for one's ~s, vir sy moeite; (v)
seer maak, pyn; kwel; bedroef; ~ful pyn‑
lik, seer, smartlik; ~killer pyndoder,
pynstiller; ~less pynloos
pains'taking (a) fluks, vlytig; presies, nou‑
geset
paint (n) verf; (v) verf; skilder; ~ the town
red, fuif, jollifikasie hou; ~ box (-es)
verfdoos; ~ brush (-es) verfkwas; ~er
verwer, huisskilder; (kuns)skilder; ~ing
skildery; skilderkuns
pair (n) paar; ~ of scissors, skêr; ~ of
spectacles, bril; ~ of trousers, broek; (v)
paar; saampas; ~ off, afpaar
pal (n) maat, makker; tjom(mie); pigeon for
~s, baantjies vir boeties; (v) (-led, -led)
omgaan met; ~ up, maats maak
pal'ace paleis; ~ of justice, paleis van jus‑
tisie
pal'ate verhemelte; cleft ~, gesplete
verhemelte
pale (v) bleek word; verbleek; (a) bleek, dof;
~ness bleekheid
pall'bearer slipdraer
pall'et pottebakkerskyf, palet; hegstrook;
laaikis, laaiplank (vir vrag)
palm¹ (n) palm(boom); segepalm; yield the
~, die veld ruim, onderdoen vir
palm² (n) palm (hand); (v) inpalm; hanteer;
streel; omkoop; ~ off upon, afsmeer aan;
~ greasing omkopery; omkoopgeld; ~ist
handkyker/handleser
palm'oil palmolie; omkoopgeld
pal'pitate klop (hart)
pal'sied verlam; geraak; cerebral ~, sere‑
braal verlam
pal'sy (n) beroerte, verlamming; (v) (palsied,
palsied) verlam
pal'try klein, onbeduidend, armsalig
pam'per vertroetel, bederf, piep
pamph'let pamflet, bladskrif, vlugskrif,
voublad, strooibiljet

pan (n) pan; (v) (-ned, -ned) was
Pan‑Af'rican Pan‑Afrikaans
pan'cake (n) pannekoek
pandemon'ium uitbarsting, hel, pande‑
monium
pane ruit; paneel; vak
pan'el (n) paneel; naamlys; strook; ~beater
paneelklopper, duikklopper; ~ling lam‑
brisering, paneelwerk; ~van paneelwa
pang angs, benoudheid; pyniging, smart;
~s of conscience, gewetenswroeging
pan'ga kapmes, panga
pan'golin jetermagô, miervreter
pan'handle pypsteel (straat)
pan'ic (n) skrik, paniek; (a) paniekerig; ~ky
paniekerig; ~ stricken verbouereerd; pa‑
niekbevange
panora'ma panorama, vergesig
pan'sy (pansies) gesiggie, viooltjie; verwyf‑
de mansmens
pant (n) gehyg; klopping; (v) hyg, snak
pantech'nicon verhuiswa, meubelwa
pan'theism panteïsme, algodedom
pan'ther panter; ~ lily tierlelie
pan'tie knapbroekie, damesbroekie
pan'tihose kousbroekie, broekiekouse
pan'try (pantries) spens
pants broek (in VSA); onderbroek (Eng.)
papa' pa, pappie
pa'paw papaja
pap'er (n) papier; vraestel; koerant; ver‑
handeling; read a ~, 'n (voor)lesing hou;
(v) plak, behang; (a) papier‑; ~ bag kar‑
does, papiersakkie; ~ chase snipperjag;
~ clip skuifspeld; papierknyper; ~ cur‑
rency papiergeld; ~ fastener papierspy;
~ hanger plakker, behanger; ~ knife
(..knives) papiermes; voubeen; ~ mill
papierfabriek; ~ money papiergeld
par pari, gelykheid; syfer (gholf)
par'able gelykenis
pa'rachute (n) valskerm; (v) valspring
pa'rachutist val(skerm)springer
parade' (n) parade, vertoon, optog; wa‑
penskou(ing); (a) paradeer
pa'radise paradys, lushof; hemel
pa'radox (-es) paradoks
pa'raffin paraffien, lampolie; ~ stove pa‑
raffienstoof, pompstofie
pa'ragon toonbeeld, model; voorbeeld
pa'ragraph (n) paragraaf; (v) paragrafeer
pa'rakeet parkiet

pa'ralans paralans (ambulans met inten=
siewe sorg)
pa'rallel (n) parallel, ewewydige lyne; *without* ~, sonder weerga; (a) parallel, ewe=
wydig; ~ **bars** brug; ~**ism** ooreenkoms,
parallelisme, vergelyking; ~ **(-medium)
school** parallel(medium)skool
parallel'ogram parallelogram
pa'ralyse verlam; magteloos maak
para'lysis verlamming, beroerte; magte=
loosheid; *infantile* ~, kinderverlamming
pa'ramedical paramedies
pa'ramount hoogste, vernaamste; ~ *chief*,
opperhoof; *of* ~ *importance*, van die al=
lergrootste belang
parapherna'lia bybehore; rommel
pa'raphrase (n) parafrase; (v) parafraseer
paraple'gic (n) parapleeg; (a) paraplegies
pa'rasite parasiet; woekerplant; klaploper
par'asol (son)sambreel, sonskerm
pa'ratroops valskermtroepe
par'cel (n) pakkie, pakket; *part and* ~ *of,*
'n onmisbare deel van; (v) (-led, -led) in=
pak; verdeel; ~ *out,* uitdeel; ~ *post*
pakketpos
parch opdroog, verseng, versmag; ~**ed**
verdroog, verskroei; ~**ment** perkament
pard'on (n) vergifnis, pardon; ekskuus; *I
beg your* ~, ekskuus, verskoon my; (v)
vergewe, kwytskeld; begenadig; verskoon
par'ent (n) ouer; vader, moeder; (a) oor=
spronklik, moeder=; ~**age** afkoms
paren'tal ouerlik; ~ **care** ouersorg
paren'thesis (..ses) parentese, hakies ( ); *in*
~, tussen hakies
parents-teachers association ouerkomitee,
ouervereniging
Pa'ris Parys; *plaster of* ~, gips
pa'rish gemeente; parogie
pa'rity gelykheid, pariteit, pari
park (n) park, wildtuin; (v) parkeer; *no*
~*ing,* geen parkering; ~**ade** parkade; ~
homes parkwonings; ~**ing area** staanplek;
~**ing attendant** parkeerbeampte
parl'iament parlement, volksraad
parl'our sitkamer, voorkamer; ontvang=
kamer, ontvanglokaal (burgemeester);
beauty ~, skoonheidsalon
pa'rody (n) (..dies) parodie; (v) (..died,
..died) parodieer
parole' erewoord, parool; wagwoord
parq'uet: ~ **floor(ing)** blokkiesvloer

pa'rrot (n) papegaai; na-aper; (v) naboots,
napraat
pars'ley pieters(i)elie
pars'nip witwortel
pars'on predikant, dominee
part (n) deel; onderdeel, aandeel; *pirate* ~,
roofonderdeel; *the* ~*s of speech,* rede=
dele; *take* ~ *in,* deelneem aan; *take
somebody's* ~, iem. se kant kies; (v) deel,
verdeel; ~ *company,* van mekaar skei; ~
with, afstand doen van
partake' (partook, -n) deelneem, deel in
par'tial gedeeltelik; partydig; *be* ~ *to,*
voortrek, partydig wees vir
parti'cipant (n) deelnemer, deelhebber; (a)
deelnemend
parti'cipate deelneem, deel
participa'tion deelneming, deelname; in=
spraak; ~ **bond** deelneemverband
par'ticiple deelwoord
part'icle deeltjie, greintjie, sprankie
partic'ular (n) besonderheid; *in* ~*s,* in be=
besonderhede; (a) kieskeurig, puntenerig;
presies, noukeurig; *a* ~ *friend,* 'n intieme
vriend
partic'ularly veral, vernaamlik
part'ing (n) deling, skeiding; ~ **meal** gal=
gemaal
partisan' (n) partyganger; volgeling, parti=
saan
parti'tion (n) afdeling; afskorting; (v) af=
skort
part'ly gedeeltelik
part'ner (n) maat; deelhebber; vennoot;
sleeping ~, stil/rustende vennoot; ~**ship**
vennootskap, deelgenootskap; *dissolve a*
~*ship,* 'n vennootskap ontbind
part'-owner deelhebber, mede-eienaar
part'-payment gedeeltelike betaling, paaie=
ment; *in* ~, op afbetaling
part'ridge patrys
part-time deeltyds; ~ **courses** deeltydse
kursusse
part'y (..ties) party, instansie; party(tjie);
makietie; *become a* ~ *to,* betrokke raak
in, medepligtig word; ~ **whip** partysweep
pass¹ (n) (-es) nek, bergpas; deurgang (by
berge)
pass² (n) (-es) paspoort; pas; aangee (voet=
bal); slaag (eksamen); (v) verbygaan;
passeer; aangee; slaag (eksamen); vel
(vonnis); ~ *away,* verdwyn; sterf; ~ *a*

bill, 'n wetsontwerp aanneem; ~ *an examination,* (in) 'n eksamen slaag; ~ *sentence on,* vonnis; ~able gangbaar; be-
gaanbaar, rybaar (pad)
pass'age gang, deurgang; oortog; reisgeld;
birds of ~, trekvoëls
pass'book bankboek, depositoboek; pas-
boek, bewysboek
pass'enger passasier
pa'sserby (passers-by) verbyganger
pa'ssing (n) verbygaan; slaag; *in* ~, terloops; (a) verbygaande; ~-out parade
voorstel(lings)parade
pa'ssion hartstog, drif, passie
pa'ssionate hartstogtelik, driftig
pa'ssion: ~ flower passieblom; ~ play (-s)
passiespel; P ~ Week Lydensweek
pass'ive (n) lydende vorm; (a) lydend; ly-
delik; ~ resistance lydelike verset; ~
voice lydende vorm
Passov'er Joodse Paasfees
pass'port paspoort
pass'word wagwoord
past (n) verlede; (a) verlede, oud-; (adv,
prep) verby, langs, oor; ~ *recovery,* on-
herstelbaar; ~ *student,* oud-student
paste (n) gom; deeg; pasta (vir tande)
pas'tel pastel, papierkryt
pas'teurise pasteuriseer
pas'time tydverdryf, ontspanning; tydkor-
ting, spel; stokperdjie
past'master meester, volleerde, bobaas
pa'stor predikant, herder, pastor (Prot.);
pastoor (R.K.)
pastorale' pastorale
pa'storal: ~ play herderspel; ~ visit huis-
besoek
pas'try (..ries) deeg; tert, soetgebak
pa'sture (n) weiveld, gras; weiding; (v) wei
pat (n) tikkie, klappie; (v) (-ted, -ted) tik,
streel; (a) toepaslik: vlot; oppervlakkig;
(adv) vanpas, toepaslik; *know off* ~, op
sy duimpie ken; ~-a-cake handjie-klap
patch (n) (-es) lap, stuk; (v) lap, heelmaak;
~ *up,* lap, saamflans; ~work lapwerk
pâté' patee (gereg)
pat'ent (n) patent, oktrooi; (a) duidelik,
vanselfsprekend; ~ee' patenthouer; ~
leather blinkleer, glansleer; ~ medicine
huismiddel
patern'al vaderlik; ~ism paternalisme
path pad, weg, baan

pathet'ic aandoenlik, pateties, roerend
pathol'ogist patoloog
pa'tience geduld, lydsaamheid
pa'tient (n) pasiënt, sieke; (a) geduldig
pat'riarch aartsvader, patriarg
pat'riotism vaderlandsliefde, patriotisme
patrol' (n) patrollie; (v) patrolleer
pat'ron beskermheer; gereelde besoeker;
(pl) klandisie; ~ saint beskermheilige,
skutpatroon; ~age beskerming; klandisie
patt'ern (n) patroon, voorbeeld; model
Paul Paulus; ~ *Pry,* nuuskierige agie
paunch (-es) pens; ~-bellied boepens-
paup'er armlastige, behoeftige
pause (n) pouse, verposing, rustyd; (v) rus,
wag, pouseer
pave plavei, bevloer; uitlê; ~ *the way for,*
die weg baan vir; ~ment plaveisel; sypaadjie
pavil'ion pawiljoen; tent
paw (n) poot, klou; (v) krap, skop; kap
pawn (n) pand; pion; *take out of* ~, inlos;
(v) verpand; ~broker pandjieshouer;
~ee' pandhouer; ~shop pandjies-
huis
pay (n) betaling, loon, soldy; (v) (paid, paid)
betaal, voldoen; beloon; vereffen; ~ *one
a compliment,* iem. 'n kompliment maak;
~ *a dividend,* 'n dividend uitbetaal/uit-
keer; ~ *off,* afbetaal; afdank; ~ *out,*
uitbetaal; ~ *up,* opdok, betaal; ~able
betaalbaar; ~-as-you-earn (PAYE)
lopende belastingstelsel (LBS); ~day (-s)
betaaldag; ~ee' ontvanger; ~er betaler;
~master betaalmeester; ~ment betaling;
~roll, ~sheet betaalstaat
pea ertjie; green ~, dop-ertjie; *sweet* ~s,
pronk-ertjies, blom-ertjies
peace vrede, rus; kalmte; *justice of the* ~,
vrederegter; *keep the* ~, die vrede bewaar; ~ful co-existence vreedsame naasbestaan; ~-loving vredeliewend; ~ offering soenoffer
peach (n) (-es) perske; *a* ~ *of a girl,* 'n beeld
van 'n nooi; ~ brandy perskebrandywyn,
perskesnaps; mampoer
pea: ~ cock pou; ~hen pouwyfie
peak (n) punt, spits; top
peak: ~ period spitstyd, spitsuur; ~ traffic
spitsverkeer
pea'nut grondboon(tjie); ~ butter grond-
boontjiebotter

pear peer
pearl (n) pêreld; (a) pêrel=; *cast ~s before (the) swine,* pêrels voor die swyne werp/gooi; ~ diver pêrelvisser
pea'sant boer, landman; ~ry boerestand
pea'soup ertjiesop
peat turf
peb'ble spoelklippie
pecan' nut pekanneut
peck (n) hap; pik; (v) pik; ~ *at,* pik na; vit op; ~ing order gesagsorde
pecul'iar besonder, eienaardig; buitengewoon, snaaks
pecun'iary geldelik, geld=
pedagog'ic opvoedkundig, pedagogies; ~s opvoedkunde, pedagogie
ped'agogy opvoedkunde, pedagogie
ped'al (n) pedaal; trapper; (v) (-led, -led) trap; fiets; ~ car trapkar
pedant'ic pedanties, verwaand
ped'estal voetstuk, onderstuk
pedes'trian (n) voetganger; (a) voet=, voetganger=; ~ mall wandellaan; ~ traffic light voetganger(verkeers)lig
ped'igree (n) stamboom; geslagsregister; afkoms; stamboek; (a) stamboek=; volbloed=, ~ cattle stamboekvee
ped'lar smous, bondeldraer, venter
peel (n) skil; dop; (v) afskil; afdop
peep[1] (n) gepiep; (v) piep (kuikens)
peep[2] (n) kykie; ~ *of dawn,* dagbreek; (v) gluur, loer; *P~ing Tom,* (af)loerder, loervink; ~hole loergat; ~show kykspel
peer (n) edelman; gelyke, eweknie, portuur; ~ group portuurgroep
peer (v) loer, gluur
peg (n) (tent)pen; kapstok; wasgoedknyper; (v) (-ged, -ged) vasslaan; afpen; vaspen; ~ *prices,* pryse vaspen
pel'ican pelikaan
pell'et (n) balletjie; pilletjie; koeëltjie; korrel; ~ gun windbuks
pel'met gordynkap
pel'vic bekken=; ~ massage bekkenmassering
pel'vis (pelves) bekken
pen[1] (n) hok, kraal; kampie
pen[2] (n) pen; (v) (-ned, -ned) neerpen, skryf/skrywe
pen'al straf=; strafbaar; ~ise straf, beboet, penaliseer

pen'alty (..ties) straf, (straf)boete; strafskop, strafpunt
pen'cil potlood; *write in ~,* skryf met potlood; ~ box (-es), ~ case potlooddoos, potloodkoker
pen'dant (n) hangkroon; hanger(tjie)
pen'dent (a) hangend; hang=; ~ watch hangoorlosie; halsoorlosie
pend'ing (a) hangende; onbeslis;
pen'dulum (-s) slinger; pendule
pen'etrate deurdring; penetreer
pen'etrating deurdringend, skerp; ~ oil penetreerolie
peng'uin pikkewyn
penicil'lin penisillien, penisilline
penin'sula skiereiland
pen'itent (n) boeteling, boetvaardige; (a) boetvaardig, berouvol
peniten'tiary (n) (..ries) verbeterhuis; strafgevangenis
pen: ~ name skuilnaam; skryfnaam; ~ = pusher pen(ne)lekker
penn'ant wimpel, driehoekvlaggie
penn'y (pence, pennies) pennie, dubbeltjie, oulap; ~ horrible sensasieverhaal; ~wise agterstevoor suinig
pen'sion (n) pensioen; jaargeld; *old-age ~,* ouderdomspensioen; *retire on ~,* met pensioen aftree; (v) pensioeneer; ~ *off,* pensioeneer; (a) pensioens=; ~ed gepensioeneer; ~er pensioentrekker, pensioenaris, gepensioeneerde; ~ fund pensioenfonds
pen'sive peinsend; swaarmoedig, droefgeestig
pen'tagon vyfhoek
pentam'eter pentameter; iambic ~ vyfvoetige jambe
pentath'lon vyfkamp (sport)
Pen'tecost Pinkster
pent'house dakwoning, dakwoonstel; skermdak; ~ suite dakstel
peo'ple (n) mense; volk; nasie; *he of all ~,* juis hy; (v) bevolk
pep fut, lewe, pit; ~ pill opkikkerpil
pepp'er (n) peper; (v) peper; inpeper; ~ = corn peperkorrel; ~mint peperment
per per, deur, deur middel van; ~ *annum,* jaarliks; ~*cent,* persent; ~ *post,* per pos, deur/oor die pos
peram'bulator kinderwaentjie; meetwiel

percent' persent; per honderd; **~age** persentasie

percep'tive waarnemings-, waarnemend; ~ *faculty*, waarneemvermoë

perch (n) (-es) stokkie (in 'n voëlkou); roede (maat); sitplek; slaapstok (hoenders); (v) gaan sit; neerstryk

per'colate deursyfer, filtreer; **~d coffee** perkoleerkoffie

percu'ssion skok, slag; ~ **band** slagorkes; ~ **cap** slagdop(pie)

perenn'ial meerjarig; standhoudend (water)

perf'ect (n) voltooid teenwoordige tyd; (a) volmaak; ideaal, volkome, perfek; ~ **fluke** volmaakte gelukhou, kolhou (gholf); ~ **nonsense** klinkklare onsin

perfect' (v) (ver)volmaak; voltooi, deurvoer; ~ *the art*, die kuns verfyn

perfect': **~ion** volmaaktheid, perfeksie, voortreflikheid; **~ionism** perfeksionisme; **~ionist** perfeksionis

perf'orate deurboor, perforeer

perform' uitvoer; opvoer, voordra

perform'ance opvoering (toneel); uitvoering (musiek); vervulling; werkverrigting, prestasie; ~ *of work*, werkverrigting; ~ **appraisal** prestasiemeting

perform'ing uitvoerend; ~ **arts** uitvoerende kunste; ~ **group/company** toneelgroep, toneelgeselskap

perf'ume (n) reukwerk, parfuum, laventel

perfume' (v) parfumeer; **~ry** reukwerk, parfumerie

perg'ola prieel

perhaps' miskien, dalk, altemit, straks

pe'ril (n) gevaar; **~ous** gevaarlik

perim'eter omtrek, buitelyn, buitekant

per'iod tydperk, tydvak, tyd, periode; punt; volsin; termyn; **~ic** periodiek

period'ical (n) tydskrif; (a) gereeld, periodiek

per'iods maandstonde

pe'riscope periskoop

pe'rish vergaan, omkom; bederf; **~able** bederfbaar

pe'ri-urban buitestedelik, omstedelik

pe'riwig pruik

pe'riwinkle alikreukel/alikruik; maagdepalm, katoog

perj'ury meineed, woordbreuk

perk orent sit; **~s** (n) byvoordele, *also* perquisites; **~y** astrant

perm'anent blywend, permanent; ~ **force** staande mag; ~ **wave** vasgolf

permiss'ible toelaatbaar, geoorloof

permiss'ion verlof, vergunning, permissie; *give* ~, toestemming gee, die jawoord gee

permiss'ive toestemmend, toelaatbaar, permissief; **~ness** permissiwiteit

perm'it (n) permit, vrybrief, pas

permit' (v) (-ted, -ted) veroorloof, vergun

perpendic'ular (n) loodlyn; (a) penregop; vertikaal, loodreg

perpet'ual onophoudelik, ewigdurend; ~ **motion** ewigdurende beweging

perpet'uate verewig, bestendig

perplex' verwar, oorbluf, verbouereer; **~ity** (..ties) verwarring, verleentheid

persecu'tion vervolging; ~ **mania** vervolgingswaan

persever'ance volharding; uithouvermoë

persevere' volhard, aanhou, deurdruk

persimm'on tamatiepruim, dadelpruim

persist' aanhou, volhard; volhou; **~ent** volhardend; hardnekkig; **~ent cough,** aanhoudende hoes

pers'on persoon, mens; persoonlikheid; *every* ~ *who,* elkeen/iedereen wat; *in* ~, persoonlik; *no* ~ *may,* niemand mag; **~age** persoon; **~al** persoonlik, self; **~al** *liability,* persoonlike aanspreeklikheid

personal'ity (..ties) persoonlikheid

pers'onally persoonlik

personifica'tion verpersoonliking, personifiëring, personifikasie

personnel' personeel; ~ **management** personeelbestuur

perspec'tive perspektief; uitsig, vergesig

perspire' sweet, perspireer

persuade' oorhaal, ompraat; oorreed; oortuig; ~ *from,* afraai

persua'sion oorreding, oortuiging, geloof

pertain': ~ *to,* behoort by; betrekking hê op

pert'inent geskik, gepas, saaklik, ter sake

perturb' versteur, verontrus

peru'sal deurlesing, ondersoek; *for* ~, ter insae

perverse' verkeerd, eiewys; befoeterd; verdorwe, sleg, pervers

perv'ert[1] (n) afgedwaalde, afvallige, pervert

pervert'[2] (v) verlei; misbruik; perverteer

pessimis'tic pessimisties

pest pes, plaag; ~ control plaagbeheer; ~icide plaagdoder, insekdoder
pes'tilence pestilensie
pe'stle stamper
pet (n) troeteldier, hansdier; (v) (-ted, -ted) vertroetel, streel; (a) geliefde; hans~; one's ~ aversion/hate, sy doodsteek, die doring in sy vlees; ~ dog, skoothondjie; ~ lamb, hanslam
pet'al blomblaar
pet'er: ~ out, doodloop, opraak
petit'ion (n) versoek; versoekskrif, petisie; ~er petisionaris
pet name lieflingsnaam, troetelnaam
pet'rel stormvoël, stormswaeltjie
pet'rify (..fied, ..fied) versteen; styf word; verlam; verstar
pe'trol petrol; ~ attendant pompjoggie; ~ consumption petrolverbruik
petrol'eum petroleum; aardolie
pet'rol: ~ pump petrolpomp; ~ station vulstasie; ~ tank petroltenk
pet'shop arkmark, dierewinkel, troetel= dierwinkel
pett'icoat onderrok; vrou; ~ government vroueregering
pett'y onbeduidend; kleingeestig; ~ cash kleinkas; ~ officer onderoffisier; boots= man (vloot)
pew kerkbank
pew'ter piouter, tingoed; tinkan
phan'tom spook, verskyning; hersenskim
pha'raoh farao
pha'risee fariseër, huigelaar
pharmaceut'ical (a) farmaseuties
pharm'acy artsenykunde, farmasie; (..cies) apteek
phase toestand, voorkome, verskynsel, sta= dium, fase; ~ out, uitfaseer
phea'sant fisant
phenom'enal buitengewoon, fenomenaal
phenom'enon (..mena) (natuur)verskynsel
phi'al botteltjie, flessie
philan'thropist filantroop, mensevriend
philat'elist posseëlversamelaar, filatelis
philharmon'ic filharmonies
philos'opher wysgeer, filosoof
philos'ophy wysbegeerte, filosofie
phone (n) telefoon; (v) (op)bel, skakel
phonet'ics klankleer, fonetiek
phon'ogram fonogram
pho'ny vals, nageboots

phos'phate fosfaat
phos'phorus fosfor
phot'o (-s) (abbrev. of photograph) foto, portret; ~copy (n) fotokopie; (v) foto= kopieer; ~-finish fotobeslissing, wen= paalfoto (wedrenne); ~gen'ic fotogenies
phot'ograph (n) portret, foto; (v) afneem, fotografeer; ~ album foto-album
photog'rapher afnemer, fotograaf
photograph'ic fotografies
photog'raphy fotografie
phot'ostat fotostaat; fotostatiese afdruk
phrase (n) frase, sinsnede; (v) fraseer; be= woord; ~ol'ogy woordkeuse, skryftrant
phthis'is longtering, myntering
phys'ical natuurkundig, fisies; liggaamlik, fisiek; ~ education liggaamsopvoeding; ~ presence fisieke teenwoordigheid; ~ science natuur- en skeikunde
physi'cian dokter, geneesheer, arts
phys'ics natuurkunde, fisika
physiol'ogy fisiologie, natuurleer
physiothe'rapy fisioterapie
physique' liggaamsbou
pi'anist pianis, klavierspeler
pian'o (-s) piano, klavier
pick[1] (n) keuse; (die) beste; the ~ of the basket (bunch), die allerbeste; (v) kies; uitsoek; ~ and choose, uitsoek
pick[2] (n) pik, tandestokkie; (v) pik; pluk; ~ a bone with, 'n appeltjie skil met; ~ and choose, te kus en te keur; ~ a quarrel with, rusie/skoor soek met; ~ up, optel, oplaai; leer; oplig (poot); ~-a-back abba=
pick'ax(e) kiel(houer)pik
pick'et (n) brandwag; stakerswag/staakwag; (v) wagstaan
pi'ckle (n) moeilikheid; pekel; (v) insout, inlê, inmaak; ~s atjar, suurtjies
pick'-me-up opknapper(tjie), sopie, ver= sterkmiddel(tjie)
pick'pocket sakkeroller, goudief
pick'-up toonopnemer (grammofoon); bakkie (motor); ~ van vangwa; bakkie, bestelwa(entjie)
pic'nic (n) piekniek, veldparty; (v) (-ked, -ked) piekniek (hou)
pic'ture (n) prent, skildery; afbeelding; (v) beskryf; afbeeld; ~ book prenteboek; ~ puzzle soekprentjie
picturesque' skilderagtig, pittoresk

pie pastei, tert; *have a finger in the ~,* in iets betrokke wees

piece (n) stuk, deel; *give a ~ of one's mind,* goed die waarheid vertel; **~meal** stuks‑ gewys(e); **~work** stukwerk

pied bont, geskakeer

pier hawehoof, seehoof, pier; pilaar

pierce deursteek, deurboor, 'n gat steek in

pi'ety vroomheid, piëteit

pif'fle bog, kaf, twak

pig (n) vark, otjie; *gelded ~,* burg; *suckling ~,* speenvark

pi'geon (n) duif; **~-hearted** bang, skrikke‑ rig; **~hole** (n) nessie, hokkie; (pos)vak‑ kie, loket

pig: **~gery** (..ries) varkboerdery, ottery; varkhok; **~gy-back** abbahart; **~- headed** eiesinnig, dom; **~-iron** ru‑yster

pig'ment kleur, verf, pigment

pig: **~sty** (..sties) varkhok; **~tail** varkstert; (pruik)stert

pike[1] spies; lans; varswatersnoek

pike[2] tol, tolhek

pil'chard sardyn, pelser

pile[1] (n) paal; pyler (brug); heipaal

pile[2] (n) hoop, massa, stapel; fortuin

piles aambeie

pil'fer steel, ontfutsel; **~ing** stelery

pil'grim pelgrim; **~age** (n) pelgrimstog

pi'ling heiwerk

pill (n) pil; *contraceptive ~,* voorbehoedpil

pill'ar (n) pilaar; steunpilaar; *from ~ to post,* van Pontius na Pilatus

pill'ion saal, kussing, agtersaaltjie

pill'ow (kop)kussing, peul; **~case,** **~slip** kussingsloop

pil'ot (n) gids; stuurman (van boot); loods, vlieër, vlieënier, bestuurder; *automatic ~,* stuuroutomaat; (v) lei, loods (vliegtuig); **~ plant** gidsaanleg, loodsaanleg; **~ scheme** proefskema

pimp koppelaar, pooier

pim'ple puisie

pin (n) speld; luns, klink; skroef; kegel; *be on ~s and needles,* op hete kole sit; (v) (-ned, -ned) vassteek, vasspeld; *~ one's faith on,* volle vertroue stel in; **~ alley** kegelbaan

pin'cers knyptang; tangetjie; knyper

pinch (n) (-es) knyp; nood, verleentheid

pine[1] (n) pyn, den; pynappel

pine[2] (v) kwyn; versmag; *~ away, weg‑ kwyn; ~ for,* smag/hunker na

pine: **~apple** pynappel; **~ cone** dennebol; **~ tree** denneboom, pynboom; **~wood** dennehout, greinhout

ping'-pong' tafeltennis, pingpong

pink[1] (n) toonbeeld; die beste; *in the ~ of condition,* in uitstekende kondisie; (a) pienk; ligrooi

pink[2] (n) gepingel, geklop; (v) pingel (motor)

pin' money sakgeld

pinn'acle top, toppunt, punt; toring

pint pint

pin'table spykertafel

pin'-up girl kalendermeisie, prikkelpop

pioneer' (n) pionier, baanbreker

pi'ous vroom, godvrugtig

pip[1] (n) vrugtepit

pip[2] (v) (-ped, -ped) kafloop; raak skiet

pipe (n) pyp; fluit; geluid; stop; (pl) doe‑ delsakke; **~line** pypleiding (olie), pyplyn; **~r** fluitspeler; **~wrench** (..-es) pypsleu‑ tel

pir'ate (n) seerower; letterdief; (v) plunder; steel; **~ part** roofonderdeel (motorhan‑ del); **~ taxi** rooftaxi

piss (n,v) water, pis

pis'tol (n) pistool; *automatic ~,* outoma‑ tiese pistool

pis'ton suier; klep; **~ ring** suierring

pit (n) put, kuil; graf; afgrond; kuip (mo‑ torwedren); *~ one's strength against,* kragte meet met

pitch[1] (n) pik; (v) met pik besmeer

pitch[2] (n) (-es) hoogte, toppunt; toonhoogte (musiek); kolfblad (krieket); (v) slinger; opslaan (tent); inplant; gooi (bal); *~ camp,* kamp opslaan; **~ed roof,** staan‑ dak

pitch'-dark pikdonker

pitch'er kruik; kan

pit'fall valstrik

pit'iful medelydend, treurig, ellendig

pit'iless onbarmhartig, meedoënloos

pitt'ance bietjie, deeltjie; liefdegawe; *work for a (mere) ~,* vir 'n karige loon werk

pit'y (n) (pities) medelye, jammer(te); *take ~ on,* medelye hê met; *what a ~,* hoe jammer tog; (v) jammer kry

piv'ot (n) spil, draaipunt

plac'ard (n) plakkaat, aanplakbiljet

place (n) plek, plaas; verblyf; *in the first ~*, in die eerste plek; *take ~*, plaasvind; (v) plaas, neersit; *~ an order*, bestel; bestelling plaas; **~kick** grondskop, stelskop; **~ment** plasing; uitplasing; **~name** pleknaam, plaasnaam

placen'ta (n) (-e) nageboorte, moederkoek

pla'cid kalm, sag, vreedsaam

pla'giarism plagiaat, letterdiefstal

plague (n) plaag, pes; (v) kwel, pla

plain (n) vlakte; vlak; (a) eenvoudig; *the ~ truth*, die naakte waarheid; (adv) duidelik; *~ly* duidelik, klaarblyklik

plain'tiff klaer, eiser

plain'tive (a) klaend

plan (n) plan; voorneme; ontwerp, skets; (v) (-ned, -ned) beplan, ontwerp

plane[1] (n) plataanboom

plane[2] (n) skaaf; (v) skaaf/skawe

plane[3] (n) vlak; hoogte, gelykte; vliegtuig; (v) vlieg; skeer oor (die water); (a) plat

plan'et planeet

planetar'ium (..ria, -s) planetarium

plank (n) plank; onderwerp; beginsel

plann'er beplanner, ontwerper

plann'ing beplanning

plant (n) plant; aanleg, installasie; uitrusting; (v) plant, beplant; *~ and machinery*, aanleg en masjinerie; **~a'tion** plantasie; **~er** planter

pla'que gedenkplaat, plakket; plaak (tande)

plas'ter (n) pleister; gips; *~ of Paris*, gips

plas'tic beeldend, plasties, plastiek; **~arts** beeldende kuns(te); **~cup** plastiekkoppie, plastiekbeker; **~frame** plastiekraam; **~surgery** plastiese snykunde

plate (n) bord; plaat; prys; **~event** (sport), plaatkompetisie

plateau' (-s, -x) plato, hoogvlakte, hoogland

plate glass spieëlglas

plat'form verhoog, platform, perron

plat'inum platina, witgoud

plat'itude platheid; gemeenplaas

platoon' peloton

play (n) vermaak; speelruimte; (-s) spel; toneelstuk; *put into ~*, in beweging stel/sit; (v) speel; bespeel; *~ the fool*, die gek skeer; *~ tricks*, poetse bak; *~ truant*, stokkies draai; **~boy** pierewaaier, swierbol; **~er** speler, toneelspeler; **~ful** spelerig, dartel, speels; **~goer** toneelganger;

~ground speelterrein, speelplek; **~ing card** speelkaart; **~mate** speelmaat; **~-off** uitspeelwedstryd; **~school** peuterskool; **~time** speeltyd, pouse; **~wright** toneelskrywer; dramaturg; **~writer** toneeldigter

plead soebat, smeek, pleit; *~ guilty*, skuldig pleit; *~ for mercy*, om genade smeek

plea'sant aangenaam, prettig

please (v) beval, behaag, belief; genoeë doen; *~ God*, as dit God behaag; *if you ~*, asseblief; (interj) asseblief; ingenome, tevrede, bly; *~d with his marks*, bly oor (ingenome met) sy punte

plea'sure (n) genot, vermaak, genoeë, plesier; *I have ~ in*, dis my 'n genoeë om; *~ resort* plesieroord

pleat plooi, vou

pledge (n) pand; borgtog; (v) verpand, borg staan; *~ one's word*, plegtig belowe; **~e'** pandhouer; **~r** pandgeër

plen'ary volkome; volledig; voltallig, vol (vergadering); *~ powers* volmag

plenipoten'tiary (..ries) gevolmagtigde

plen'tiful oorvloedig, volop

plen'ty (n) oorvloed; hele boel; *in ~*, volop; (a) genoeg, oorvloedig

ple'onasm oortolligheid (van woorde), pleonasme

pleur'isy longvliesontsteking

pli'able buigsaam, lenig, soepel; plooibaar

pli'ers draadtang, knyptang

plight (n) toestand, gesteldheid; *a sorry ~*, 'n verknorsing

plod (-ded, -ded) swoeg, ploeter; *~ along*, aansukkel; **~der** ploeteraar

plot (n) (klein)hoewe, perseel, bouperseel, erf; samewering, komplot; knoop (roman); (v) (-ted, -ted) saamsweer, saamspan; **~ter** samesweerder

plough (n) ploeg; *put one's hand to the ~*, die hand aan die ploeg slaan; (v) ploeg, braak; sak (eksamen); *~ iron*, **~share** ploegskaar

plo'ver kiewiet; strandloper(tjie)

ploy (n) voorwendsel, set, streek, slenter

pluck (n) moed, durf; (v) ruk, pluk; kul; *~ up courage/heart/spirits*, moed skep; **~y** moedig, dapper

plug (n) prop, stop; vonkprop; (v) (-ged, -ged) toestop, beskiet; dop/druip (eksamen) plum pruim; die beste

plumb'er loodgieter

plume (n) pluim; veerbos; (v) pronk

plump (a) dik, vet; mollig; *a ~ lie,* 'n on‑
beskaamde/flagrante leuen

plum'pudding rosyntjiepoeding, doekpoe‑
poeding

plun'der (n) buit, roof, plundering; (v) buit,
roof, plunder

plunge (n) indompeling; *take the ~,* die
sprong waag; (v) plons; stort; *~ into
darkness,* in duisternis hul

plur'al meervoud; *~ society,* plurale ge‑
meenskap

plus (n) plusteken; (a) ekstra; (adv) meer,
plus, daarby; **~fours** kniebroek; pof‑
broek, kardoesbroek

plush wolfluweel

plu'tocrat plutokraat

ply (n) (plies) draad (wol); laag (hout);
three‑~ wood, drielaaghout; (v) (plied,
plied) beoefen (beroep); behartig; ge‑
bruik; hanteer; *~ between,* gereeld vaar
tussen

ply'wood laaghout, plakhout

pneumat'ic lug‑, pneumaties

pneumon'ia longontsteking

poach¹ posjeer (eier)

poach² vertrap; wild steel; steel

poached' egg posjeereier, kalfsoog

poach: **~er** wildstroper, wilddief; steler;
~ing wildstelery

pock pokkie, *see* pox

pock'et (n) sak; beursie; (v) wegbêre; toe‑
eien; *~ your pride,* jou trots sluk; *~
knife* sakmes, knipmes; **~money** sakgeld

pod (n) dop, skil, peul

pod'ium (podia) verhoog, podium

po'em gedig, digstuk

po'et digter, poëet

po'etess (-es) digteres

poet'ic digterlik, poëties; *~ licence* digter‑
like vryheid

po'etry digkuns, poësie

poign'ant skerp, skrynend; pynlik

point (n) punt; onderwerp, kwessie; piek;
(pl) wissel; *in ~ of fact,* in werklikheid;
up to a ~, tot op sekere hoogte; *~ of
view,* gesig(s)punt; (v) skerp maak; wys;
~ out, aanwys; **~blank'** tromp‑op,
reguit; **~duty** puntdiens, verkeersdiens;
~ed skerp; geestig, gevat; **~er** wyser,

voorvinger; Patryshond; **~less** sinloos;
~s'man (..men) wisselwagter; verkeers‑
wagter

pois'on (n) gif, vergif, gifstof; (v) vergiftig;
~ing vergiftiging; **~ous** giftig

poke¹ (v) pook, oppor; steek; *~ fun at,*
gekskeer met

poke² sak; *buy a pig in a ~,* 'n kat in die
sak koop

pok'er vuurryster, vuurpook

pol'ar pool‑, *polêr;* *~ bear* ysbeer

polarisat'ion polarisasie

pole paal; disselboom (kar); roede

pole'cat muishond (SA)

pole'vault paalspring

police (n) polisie; *~ investigation* polisie‑
ondersoek; **~man** (..men) konstabel,
diender; *~ officer* geregsdienaar; polisie‑
man; *~ station* polisiestasie

pol'icy¹ (..cies) polis (assuransie)

pol'icy² beleid (mv beleide, beleidrigtings);
~ maker beleidmaker

pol'io(myelitis) kinderverlamming

pol'ish (-es) politoer, waks; verfyning; (v)
poleer, poets; *~ off,* kafloop; **~ed** be‑
skaaf; gepoleer

polite' beleef(d), beskaaf; hoflik, verfynd

polit'ical staatkundig, staats‑; politiek,
polities; *~ science* staatsleer

politi'cian politikus

pol'itics staatkunde, politiek

pol'ka polka

poll¹ (n) stembus; verkiesing; stemlys; *go
to the ~s,* gaan stem; (v) stem; stemme
kry

poll² (n) poenskop(dier); (v) top, snoei, af‑
knot

poll'en stuifmeel

poll'ing (n) stemmery, stem; *~ booth*
stembus; *~ officer* stemopnemer, stem‑
beampte; *~ place, ~ station* stemlokaal

poll tax (-es) hoofbelasting

pollute' besoedel, verontreinig, besmet

pollu'tion besoedeling, verontreiniging

pol'o polo

polon'y (..nies) polonie, dikwors

polyg'amist poligamis, veelwywer

pol'yglot (n) veeltalige persoon, poliglot

pol'yp poliep

polytech'nic politegnies

pomade' pomade, gesigsroom

pome'granate granaat

pomm'el (n) knop; saalknop; (v) (-(l)ed,
-(l)ed) slaan, opdons, karnuffel
pomol'ogy vrugtekunde, pomologie
pomp prag, praal, staatsie
pom'pon pompon/pompom; soort dahlia
pom'pous verwaand; hoogdrawend
pond vywer, dam, pan
pon'der peins, dink, oorweeg
pontoon' ponton, brug, pont
pon'y (ponies) ponie
poo'dle poedel
pool[1] (n) poel, vywer, kuil; (private) swembad
pool[2] (n) inset; ring; sindikaat; trust; poel;
(v) poel, kombineer; winste deel
poor (n): the ~, arm mense, armes; (a) arm,
behoeftig; a ~ show, 'n swak vertoning;
~ly armsalig; ellendig; siekerig
pop[1] (n) knal, slag; (v) (-ped, -ed) skiet; ~ a
question, 'n vraag opwerp; ~ up, opduik;
uitspring
pop[2] (n) volkskonsert; (a) populêr, pop-
pop'corn springmielies, kiepiemielies
pope pous; ~ry pousgesindheid
pop'gun speelgeweertjie; propgeweertjie
pop'lar populier
pop: ~ music popmusiek; ~ song poplied
popp'y (poppies) papawer
pop'ular populêr; bemind, gewild
popular'ity gewildheid, populariteit
popula'tion bevolking, populasie; ~ explosion bevolkingsontploffing; ~ group
volksgroep, bevolkingsgroep
porce'lain porselein
porch (-es) portaal
porc'upine ystervark
pore (n) sweetgaatjie, porie
pork varkvleis; ~er vleisvark
pornog'raphy pornografie, prikkellektuur
por'ous poreus
porp'oise seevark, tornyn, bruinvis
po'rridge pap
port[1] (n) hawe; ingang; patryspoort
(skip)
port[2] (n) bakboord; (v) na bakboord
stuur
port'able draagbaar; vervoerbaar; ~ television set draagbare televisiestel
por'ter portier; kruier, pakdraer
portfo'lio (-s) portefeulje, ministerspos;
shares ~, aandeleportefeulje
port'hole patryspoort, kajuitvenster(tjie)

por'tion (n) deel, porsie, gedeelte; erfdeel;
aandeel; (v) verdeel, uitdeel
por'trait portret; skildering, beeld
portray' afbeeld, afskilder; uitbeeld, beskryf; ~al beskrywing; uitbeelding
pose[1] (n) houding, pose; aanstellery; (v)
poseer; 'n houding aanneem; voordoen
pose[2] vasvra; ~r strikvraag
posi'tion stand; toestand, posisie; ligging;
(v) plaas, staanmaak, posisioneer
pos'itive (a) bevestigend, positief, seker; ~
sign plusteken
possess' besit, hê; bemagtig; beheers
possessed' besete, gepla; ~ by the devil,
deur die duiwel besete
posse'ssion besitting, besit, eiendom; take
~ of, besit neem van
possess'ive (n) tweede naamval; (a) besitlik
possibil'ity (..ties) moontlikheid
poss'ible (a) moontlik, doenlik; the only ~
man, die enigste (al) geskikte man
poss'ibly miskien, straks, dalk, moontlik
post[1] (n) pos; poskantoor; poswese; betrekking; by return of ~, per kerende pos;
(v) pos; oorboek; keep ~ed, op die hoogte
hou
post[2] (n) paal, stut, styl (van deur)
post[3] (voorvoegsel) na-; later
pos'tage posgeld; ~ stamp posseël
pos'tal pos-; ~ order posorder
post: ~bag possak, briewesak; ~card pos-
kaart
postdate' (v) vooruitdateer; ~d cheque
vooruitgedateerde tjek
pos'ter aanplakbiljet, plakkaat
poster'ity nageslag, nakomelingskap
postgrad'uate (n) gegradueerde; (a) na-
graads; ~ school of business nagraadse
sakeskool; ~ studies nagraadse studie
post'humous postuum, nagelate
post: ~ing box briewebus; ~man (..men)
posbesteller, briewebesteller, posbode;
~mark posmerk, posstempel; ~master
posmeester
post-mort'em (n) lykskouing; nadoodse
ondersoek; ~ examination lykskouing
post: ~ office poskantoor; ~ box (-es)
(pos)bus; ~ office savings bank pos-
spaarbank
post'paid gefrankeer, posgeld betaal
postpone' uitstel, verdaag; ~ment verdaging, uitstel, verskuiwing

post'script naskrif
pot (n) pot, kan; blompot; ~s of money, geld soos bossies
pot'ash potas, kali, potassium
potat'o (-es) ertappel, aartappel; sweet ~, patat(ta);~ chips ertappelsnippers, ert= appelskyfies
pot'belly boepens
pot'ent magtig, kragtig, potent
poten'tial (n) potensiaal; moontlikheid
pot'hole slaggat; rotsholte; maalgat
po'tion drank; gifdrank
pot'luck wat die pot verskaf
pott'er (n) pottebakker; (v) peuter, knutsel; ~'s wheel pottebakkerskyf; ~y (..ries) pottebakkery
pouch (n) (-es) sak; tabaksak; beurs; buidel; krop
poul'terer pluimveehandelaar, poelier
poul'tice (n) (warm) pap; (v) pap opsit
poul'try pluimvee; hoenders; ~ farming hoenderboerdery
pounce aanval, gryp; neerskiet; afspring op
pound[1] (n) pond (geld); massa, gewig
pound[2] (n) skut; (v) skut
pour (v) giet, uitstort; inskink; stortreën; money came ~ing in, geld het inge= stroom; ~ing rain, gietende reën
pov'erty armoede, gebrek
powd'er (n) poeier; kruit; (v) (be)poeier; fynstamp; ~ box (-es) poeierdoos; ~ ed fyn; gepoeier; ~ horn kruithoring; ~ puff poeierkwas
pow'er mag, krag; gesag; moondheid; be= voegdheid; invloed; vermoë; ~ of at= torney, volmag, prokurasie; ~ of resis= tance, weerstandsvermoë; ~ boat krag= boot; ~ brakes kragremme; ~ sharing mag(s)deling; ~ful magtig, kragtig, in= vloedryk; gepoeier; ~less magteloos, kragteloos; ~ source kragbron; ~ station kragsentrale; kragstasie
pox pokke; chicken ~, waterpokkies
prac'tical prakties; play a ~ joke, 'n poets bak; ~ experience praktiese ondervin= ding; ~ teaching praktiese onderwys, proefonderwys (vir studente)
prac'tically feitlik; prakties; ~ everyone was there, feitlik almal was daar
prac'tice (n) praktyk; uitoefening; oefening; gebruik; gewoonte; in ~, in die praktyk;

out of ~, van stryk; ~ run oefenlopie; ~ session oefensessie
prac'tise (v) oefen; instudeer, praktiseer; ~ a profession, 'n beroep beoefen
practi'tioner praktisyn; general ~, alge= mene praktisyn, geneesheer; legal ~, regspraktisyn
praise (n) lof, roem, eer; ~ be to God, die Here sy dank; (v) loof, prys, verheerlik, ophemel; ~worthy loflik, prysenswaardig
pram kinderwaentjie, stootwaentjie
prank (n) streek, kwajongstreek, grap, ka= perjol, poets; (v) pronk, uitdos, optooi
prat'tle (n) gebabbel, gekeuwel; (v) babbel
prawn steurgarnaal, (swem)krewel
pray bid, smeek, versoek
prayer gebed, versoek, smeking; the Lord's P~, die Onse Vader; say one's ~s, bid; ~ meeting biduur
pray'ing insect (mantis) hottentotsgot, bid= sprinkaan
preach preek, verkondig; ~er predikant, prediker
precau'tionary voorsorgs=; ~ measures voorsorg(s)maatreëls
precede' voorafgaan, voorgaan
prec'edent[1] (n) voorbeeld, presedent; create a ~, 'n presedent skep
prece'dent[2] (a) voorafgaande
pre'cious kosbaar, kostelik; ~ little, bloed= weinig; ~ stone edelsteen
pre'cipice afgrond, krans; steilte
préc'is opsomming, uittreksel, précis
precise' noukeurig, presies; stip, nouge= set
preci'sion noukeurigheid, presiesheid, juist= heid, presisie
pred'atory roofsugtig, roof=; ~ animal roofdier, predator
predestina'tion voorbeskikking, uitverkie= sing, predestinasie
predic'ament penarie, verknorsing, predi= kament; kategorie
pred'icate (n) gesegde, predikaat
predict' voorspel, voorsê; ~able voorspel= baar; ~ion voorspelling
predom'inant oorheersend, oorwegend
pre-empt' in opsie verkry oor; ~ive strike voorkoming(s)inval
prefab'ricated fabrieks=, monteer=; ~ house opslaanhuis, monteerhuis
pref'ace (n) voorrede, voorwoord; (v) inlei

pref'ect prefek, klasleier
prefer' (-red, -red) verkies, die voorkeur gee
  aan; ~ to, verkies bo
pref'erence voorkeur; voorrang; voorliefde;
  ~ share voorkeuraandeel
pref'ix (n) (-es) voorvoegsel
preg'nant verwagtend, swanger (mens);
  dragtig (dier); vrugbaar; veelseggend
prehistor'ic voorhistories, prehistories
pre'judice (n) vooroordeel; nadeel; (v) benadeel; without ~ to, sonder aantasting
  van
prelim'inary (a) inleidend, voorlopig, preliminêr; ~ bout/fight voorgeveg; ~
  match voorwedstryd
prel'ude (n) voorspel, prelude, inleiding
prem'ature ontydig, voortydig; voorbarig
premed'itate bepeins, oordink; ~d voorbedag; ~d murder, moord met voorbe-
  dagte rade
pre'mier (n) eerste minister, premier; (a)
  eerste, vernaamste
prem'ise (n) vooropstelling, premis; (pl)
  werf, perseel; gebou; on the ~s, op die
  plek, op die perseel
prem'ium premie; prys, beloning
premoni'tion voorgevoel, voorbode
preocc'upied afgetrokke, verstrooi(d)
prepaid' posvry, vooruitbetaal
prepara'tion voorbereiding; huiswerk, tuiswerk; bewerking; instudering
prepa'ratory voorbereidend; inleidend;
  voorbereidings=; ~ school voorberei-
  dingskool
prepare' voorberei, berei (ete), klaarmaak
prepared' klaar gereed; gewapen(d), paraat;
  ~ness weerbaarheid, paraatheid
preposi'tion voorsetsel
prepos'terous ongerymd, dwaas, onsinnig
prereq'uisite (n) voorvereiste, noodsaaklikheid; (a) noodsaaklik, voorvereis
prero'gative voorreg, prerogatief
preschool' (a) voorskools
prescribe' voorskryf; behandel; ~d voorgeskrewe; verjaar (skuld); ~d book;
  voorgeskrewe boek
prescrip'tion voorskrif, resep; preskrip-
  sie
pres'ence teenwoordigheid; in the ~ of, in
  teenwoordigheid/bysyn van; ~ of mind,
  teenwoordigheid van gees

pres'ent¹ (n) present, geskenk
pres'ent² (n) die teenwoordige, hede; at ~,
  tans, op die oomblik; (a) teenwoordig,
  aanwesig; ~ tense, teenwoordige tyd
present'³ (v) aanbied, skenk; oorhandig;
  ~ oneself, jou aanmeld; ~ prizes, pryse
  oorhandig; ~able (ver)toonbaar; pre-
  sentabel; ~a'tion voorstelling; aanbieding; oorhandiging
pres'ently netnou, nou-nou, aanstons
preserve' (n) ingelegde vrugte; konfyt; (v)
  bewaar, preserveer; inmaak, verduursaam; ~d' ingelê, ingemaak
preside' voorsit, presideer; lei, bestuur
pres'idency (..cies) presidentskap, presi-
  dentshuis; voorsitterskap
pres'ident president, voorsitter; ~'s council, presidentsraad; ~-elect verkose president
presiden'tial presidents=, voorsitters=; ~
  address voorsittersrede
press (n) pers, drukpers; drukte; drukkery;
  (v) pers, druk; dring; aanpor; hard ~ed,
  in die knyp
press: ~button telephone drukknoptele-
  foon; ~ cutting koerant(uit)knipsel; ~
  gallery (..ries) persgalery; ~ing dringend;
  dreigend; ~ release persverklaring, pers-
  mededeling
pre'ssure druk, drukking; atmospheric ~,
  lugdruk; bring ~ to bear on, druk uitoefen op; ~ burst drukbars, drukskeur; ~
  cooker drukkastrol, drukkoker; ~ group
  drukgroep; ~ stove drukstoof
prestige' invloed; prestige, aansien
presum'ably vermoedelik
pretence' voorwendsel, pretensie; on ~ of,
  onder voorwendsel van
pretend' voorgee, voorwend; ~er aanspraakmaker, pretendent; ~er to the
  throne, aanspraakmaker op die kroon/-
  koningskap
pret'ext voorwendsel; on/under the ~ of,
  onder voorwendsel/die skyn van
pre'tty (a) mooi, lief, bevallig; cost a ~
  sum, 'n mooi sommetjie kos; ~ sure,
  taamlik seker
prevail' heers; in swang wees; ~ing conditions, heersende toestand(e)
prevent' belet, verhinder; voorkom
preven'tion voorkoming, verhindering

preven'tive (n) voorbehoedmiddel; (a) voorkomend, voorbehoed=; ~ *measures,* voorkomende maatreëls

prev'iew voorskou, voorbesigtiging

prev'ious voorafgaande, vroeër, vorige

prey (n) prooi; buit; slagoffer; *bird of* ~, roofvoël; *fall a* ~ *to,* 'n slagoffer word van; (v) roof, aas; ~ *on,* teer op

price (n) prys; waarde; *at any* ~, tot elke prys; ~ **control** prysbeheer; ~ **increase** prysstyging; prysverhoging; **recom=mended** ~ rigprys; ~**less** onskatbaar; ~**list** pryslys

prick (n) steek; prikkel; ~*s of conscience,* gewetenswroeging; (v) steek, prik; ~ *up the ears,* die ore spits; ~**ly pear** turksvy

pride (n) trots, hoogmoed; (v) trots wees; ~ *oneself on,* jou (be)roem op

priest priester; geestelike

prim styf, sedig, preuts; netjies

prim'ary (a) eerste; aanvanklik; laer, pri=mêr; ~ **school** primêre skool, laerskool

prime: ~ **cost** inkoopprys; ~ **minister** eer=ste minister; ~ **lending rate** prima uit=leenkoers

prim'er eerste leesboek, abc-boek; grond=verf

primev'al oer=, oeroud, oorspronklik

prim'itive oorspronklik, primitief, vroegste

prim'rose sleutelblom, primula

prim'ula primula

prince prins; *crown* ~, kroonprins; *P~ of Peace,* Vredevors; ~**ly** vorstelik; ~*ly re=ward,* vorstelike beloning

prin'cess (-es) prinses, koningsdogter; ~ *royal,* kroonprinses

prin'cipal (n) hoof, skoolhoof, prinsipaal; opdraggewer; (a) vernaamste; ~ **debtor** hoofskuldenaar; ~ **sentence** hoofsin

prin'ciple beginsel, grondbeginsel; prinsiep

print (n) merk, spoor; druk; *out of* ~, uit= verkoop; (v) druk; merk, stempel; uitgee

print'er drukker; ~**'s devil** drukkersduiwel, setsatan

print'ing drukkuns, drukwerk; ~ **office** drukkery; ~ **press** (-es) drukpers

print-out druksel, komperstaat

pri'or (a) vroeër, eerder, voorafgaande; ~ *approval,* voorafgaande goedkeuring

prio'rity voorrang, prioriteit; *get you ..ties right,* stel jou prioriteite reg

prism prisma

pris'on gevangenis; tronk (verouder)

pris'oner gevangene, prisonier

pris'on warder bewaarder

priv'acy afsondering, privaatheid

priv'ate (n) manskap, weerman, gewone soldaat; (a) privaat; vertroulik; *in* ~ *clothes,* in burgerklere

priv'ate: ~**ly** privaat, in die geheim; ~ **lesson** privaatles; ~ **parts** geslagsdele; ~ **property** privaatbesit; ~ **secretary** pri=vaatsekretaresse (dame); privaatsekretaris (man); **:** ~ **sector** private sektor, privaat=sektor

priv'ilege (n) voorreg, privilege

priv'y (n) (privies) kleinhuisie; (a) heimlik

prize (n) prys; voordeel; (v) op prys stel; waardeer; (a) bekroon

prize: ~-**giving** prysuitdeling; ~ **ring** boks=kryt, vegplek; ~**winner** pryswenner

pro voor; ~ *and con,* voor en teen

prob'able waarskynlik

proba'tion proeftyd; *on* ~, op proef; ~ **officer** proefbeampte; ~**ary** proef=; ~*ary period,* proeftyd

prob'lem probleem, vraagstuk; raaisel

proced'ure handelwyse, werkwyse, prose=dure

proceed' aangaan, voortgaan, verder gaan

proceed'ing handelwyse, handeling, ge=dragslyn; (pl) handelinge, verslae; verrig=tinge, werksaamhede (op 'n vergadering); *institute* ~*s,* geregtelike stappe doen

pro'ceeds opbrengs/opbrings, wins

pro'cess (n) voortgang; verloop; (-es) regs=geding; proses; (v) verwerk, prosesseer

proces'sion optog, prosessie; stoet; reeks

pro'cessor verwerker; *word* ~ teksverwer=ker

proclama'tion afkondiging, proklamasie

procrastina'tion uitstel, getalm; ~ *is the thief of time,* van uitstel kom afstel

procure' verkry, verskaf, besorg; ~**r** ver=skaffer; koppelaar

prod (v) (-ded, -ded) steek; aanpor

prod'igal (a) verkwistend, roekeloos, ver=lore; *the* ~ *son,* die verlore seun

prod'igy (..gies) seldsaamheid, wonderkind

prod'uce (n) produk; oes, opbrengs

produce' (v) voortbring; oplewer, produ=seer; ~ *a play,* 'n toneelstuk opvoer; ~**r** produsent; produksieleier, regisseur

prod'uct opbrengs, produk

produc'tion vervaardiging, produksie; op=
voering
productiv'ity produktiwiteit; vrugbaarheid
profane' (a) profaan; godslasterlik; ~ *lan=*
guage, skeldtaal, vloekwoorde
profess' bely, erken; beweer
profe'ssion beroep, professie; *by* ~, van
beroep; *follow a* ~, 'n beroep beoefen
profe'ssional (n) beroepsman (pl beroeps=
lui); beroepspeler; (a) beroeps=, profes=
sioneel; ~ *code of conduct/ethics,* pro=
fessionele gedragskode; ~ **player** beroep=
speler; ~ **rugby** geldrugby, vertoonrugby;
~ **soccer** beroepsokker
profess'or professor, hoogleraar; *swinging*
~, vonkprof; **~ship** professoraat
profi'ciency bedrewenheid, bekwaamheid;
vaardigheid, kundigheid
profi'cient (a) bedrewe, bekwaam, vaardig
prof'ile (n) profiel, buitelyn
prof'it (n) wins, profyt; ~ *after tax,* (na)=
belaste wins; ~ *before tax,* voorbelaste
wins; ~ *margin,* winsgrens; (v) wins
maak; voordeel trek uit; **~able** winsge=
wend
profound' diep, diepsinnig, grondig
profuse' kwistig, oorvloedig; volop
prog'eny nageslag, nakomelingskap
prog'ramme program; **~r** programmeerder
prog'ress (n) vordering, vooruitgang; ~
report, vordering(s)verslag; *work in* ~,
onvoltooide werk (boekh.)
progress' (v) vorder, vooruitgaan
progress'ive vooruitstrewend; progressief
prohib'it belet, verbied
proj'ect (n) plan, ontwerp, projek
project' (v) ontwerp, beraam; uitsteek; **~ile**
projektiel, bom; **~ing** uitstekend; **~ion**
ontwerp, projeksie; vooruitskatting
proletar'iat proletariaat, gepeupel, Jan Rap
en sy maat
prol'ogue voorrede, voorwoord; proloog
prolong' verleng, uitrek; **~ed illness,** lang=
durige siekte
prom'inent uitstekend, opmerklik, promi=
nent; ~ *person,* vername/vooraanstaande
persoon
prom'ise (n) belofte; *keep one's* ~, jou
belofte nakom; (v) beloof
prom'ising (veel)belowend
prom'issory belowend; bindend; ~ **note**
promesse, (skuld)bewys

promote' bevorder; aanmoedig; reël; pro=
moveer; ~ *a company,* 'n maatskappy
oprig; **~r** oprigter; promotor; vegknoper,
vegventer (boks, stoei)
promo'tion bevordering, promosie
prompt (v) aanspoor; voorsê; (a) stip,vaar=
dig; ~ *payment,* stipte betaling; **~er**
voorsêer, souffleur
prong hooivurk, gaffel, tand
pron'oun voornaamwoord; *demonstrative*
~, aanwysende voornaamwoord; *indefi=*
nite ~, onbepaalde voornaamwoord; *in=*
terrogative ~, vraende voornaamwoord;
personal ~, persoonlike voornaam=
woord; *possessive* ~, besitlike voor=
naamwoord; *relative* ~, betreklike voor=
naamwoord
pronounce' uitspreek, uiter; ~ *sentence of*
death, die doodvonnis uitspreek; **~d'**
uitgesproke
pronuncia'tion uitspraak; spraak, tongval
proof (n) (-s) bewys; proef; (v) bestand
maak teen; (a) beproef, bestand; **~reader**
proefleser
prop (n) stut; steun; stutpaal; ~ *up,* onder=
skraag
propagan'da propaganda
prop'agate voortplant, verbrei, versprei
propel' (-led, -led) voortdryf, beweeg; **~ler**
skroef
prop'er reg; betaamlik, behoorlik; **~ly** be=
hoorlik, eintlik; ~ **name** eienaam
prop'erty (..ties) eiendom, besitting; eien=
skap; (pl) eienskappe; ~ *developer,* eien=
domontwikkelaar; *fixed* ~, vasgoed, vaste
eiendom; *movable* ~, losgoed, roe=
rende goed
proph'ecy (..cies) profesie, voorspelling
proph'esy (..sied, ..sied) profeteer, voorspel
proph'et profeet; **~ess** (-es) profetes; ~ *of*
doom, doemprofeet
propor'tion (n) eweredigheid, proporsie;
in ~ *to,* in verhouding tot
propor'tional eweredig, proporsioneel;
verhoudings=; ~ **representation** propor=
sionele verteenwoordiging
propo'sal voorstel, aanbod; huweliksaan=
soek
propose' voorstel, aanbied, vra; **~r** voor=
steller; aansoeker; indiener
proposi'tion voorstel, aanbod, proposisie; *a*
business ~, 'n handelstransaksie

propri'etary (n) eiendomsreg; (a) eienaars=, eiendoms=; *P~ Limited*, Eiendoms Beperk; ~ *medicines*, patente medisyne
propri'etor eienaar; besitter
prosa'ic prosaïes, alledaags
pros'aist prosaskrywer, prosaïs
prose (n) prosa; die alledaagse; (a) prosa=; prosaïes; (v) in prosa vertel
pros'ecute vervolg; uitoefen; *trespassers will be ~d*, oortreders word vervolg
pros'ecutor aanklaer; *public ~*, staatsaanklaer
prose'writer prosaskrywer, prosaïs
pros'pect (n) vooruitsig, verwagting
prospect' (v) prospekteer, ondersoek; ~**or** prospekteerder
prospec'tus (-es) prospektus
prospe'rity voorspoed, welvaart
pros'perous voorspoedig; gelukkig, welvarend, bloeiend
pros'titute (n) prostituut, straatvrou; hoer; (v) onteer, skend, ontug bedryf
prostitu'tion ontug, hoerery, prostitusie
pros'trate (v) neerwerp, neerkniel; (a) neergebuig; ootmoedig; verslaan
prot'ea suikerbos, protea
protect' beskerm, beveilig, verdedig; ~**ion** beskerming
protec'tive beskermend; ~ **clothing** skutklere, beskermkleding
protec'tor beskermer; ~**ate** protektoraat
prot'égé beskermling, protégé
prot'ein eiwitstof, proteïen, proteïne
prot'est (n) protes, verset
protest' (v) beswaar maak, protesteer
prot'ocol protokol, voorrangkode
protract' uitstel, verleng; ~**ion** uitstel, verlenging; ~**or** graadboog/gradeboog
protrude' vooruitsteek, uitpuil/uitpeul
proud trots, hoogmoedig
prove bewys; beproef; bewys lewer
prov'erb spreekwoord, spreuk, segswyse
provide' verskaf, voorsien, lewer; ~ *against*, sorg vir; ~ *with*, voorsien van; ~**d** mits, met dien verstande
Prov'idence die Voorsienigheid
prov'idence voorsorg, spaarsaamheid
prov'ident versigtig, sorgvuldig, spaarsaam; ~ **fund** voorsorgfonds, voorsiening(s)-fonds
provid'er verskaffer, leweransier, leweraar
prov'ince provinsie; afdeling; vak

provin'cial (a) provinsiaal; gewestelik; bekrompe; ~**ism** provinsialisme
provi'sion (n) voorsiening, voorsorg, voorraad; bepaling; (pl) lewensmiddele, proviand; padkos (vir 'n reis); *under the ~s of*, ooreenkomstig/kragtens die bepalings van; ~**al** voorlopig
provis'o (-s) bepaling, voorwaarde
provoc'ative (n) aanleidende oorsaak; (a) tartend, uitdagend, provokatief
prowl (n) rooftog, swerftog; *on the ~*, op roof uit; (v) rondsluip, op roof uit wees
proxim'ity nabyheid
prox'imo aanstaande (maand)
prox'y (..xies) volmag; gevolmagtigde; *marry by ~*, met die handskoen trou
prude preuts; *I am no ~*, ek is glad nie preuts nie, *see* **prudish**
pru'dence versigtigheid, verstandigheid; ~ *is the best part of valour*, versigtigheid is die moeder v.d. wysheid
pru'dent versigtig, verstandig, beleidvol
pru'dish preuts, skynsedig
prune[1] (n) pruimedant, gedroogde pruim; donkerrooi
prune[2] (v) snoei; knot; ~**r** snoeiskêr
prun'ing knife (..knives) snoeimes
pry (**pried**, **pried**) snuffel, loer; oopbreek
psalm psalm; ~**ist**, ~**odist** psalmdigter
pseud'o- vals, oneg; half=, pseudo=
pseud'onym pseudoniem, skuilnaam, skryfnaam
psychi'atrist psigiater
psycho-anal'ysis psigoanalise
psycholog'ical sielkundig, psigologies; ~ **warfare** sielkundige oorlogvoering
psychol'ogy sielkunde, psigologie
psychother'apy psigoterapie
pub kantien, kroeg; tappery; ~ **crawler** kroegloper, kroegkruiper, kroegvlieg
pub'erty puberteit, geslagsrypheid
pub'ic skaam=; ~ **hair** skaamhare
pub'lic (n) publiek; *in ~*, in die openbaar; (a) openbaar, publiek; ~ **address system** luidsprekerstelsel; ~**an** kroeghouer, kantienman; tollenaar; ~**a'tion** uitgawe, publikasie; ~ **image** openbare beeld, beeld na buite; ~ **indecency** openbare onsedelikheid; ~'**ity** openbaarmaking, publisiteit; ~ **opinion** openbare mening; ~ **relations** openbare betrekkinge; ~ **relations official/officer** (openbare) ska=

kelamptenaar; ~ **sector** owerheidsektor; ~ **service** staatsdiens; ~ **school** rege= ringskool, privaatskool (in Engeland); ~ **speaking** openbare redevoering, (die) redenaarskuns; ~ **utility company** nuts= maatskappy

pub'lish uitgee, publiseer; aankondig; **~er** uitgewer; uitgewery

puck kaboutermannetjie, elf, stouterd

pu'dding poeding; nagereg; (soort) wors

pud'dle (n) poel; gemors; warboel; (v) troebel maak, mors; pleister

puff (n) geblaas, rukwind; poeierkwas; (v) blaas, hyg, pof; ~ **adder** pofadder; **~y** kortasem

pug (n) Mopshondjie (mopar); kabouter; jakkals

pull (n) trek, ruk, pluk; *a long* ~, 'n kwaai ent; (v) trek, ruk; roei; ~ *faces,* skewebek trek; ~ *one's leg,* iem. vir die gek hou; ~ *oneself together,* jou regruk

pu'llet jong hennetjie

pu'lley (-s) katrol

pull'over langmoutrui

pul'monary long=; ~ **disease** longsiekte

pulp (n) murg; pap; pulp (papier); moes (van vrugte); (v) fynmaak; verpulp

pu'lpit preekstoel, kansel; *small* ~, knapie

pulsate' klop, tril

pulse (n) pols; *feel one's* ~, die pols voel

pum'a poema

pum'ice puimsteen

pump (n) pomp; (v) pomp; ~ **attendant** pompjoggie, petroljoggie

pump'kin pampoen

pun (n) woordspeling

punch (n) (-es) vuisslag; deurslag; knipper; (v) knip; perforeer; ~ **system** ponsstelsel

punc'tual stip, presies

punctua'tion interpunksie, punktuasie, leestekens

punc'ture (n) lek; (v) prik; ~ **proof** lek= vry

pun'ish straf, kasty; toetakel; **~able** straf= baar; **~ment** straf, boete

pun'itive straf=, straffend; ~ **measures** strafmaatreëls

punk (n) misgewas, uitvaagsel; (a) vrot, minderwaardig

punt (v) hoog skop; vlugskop; vir geld speel; **~er** beroepswedder (perde); waagspeler; vlugskopper

pup (n) jong hondjie; *a litter of* ~*s,* 'n werpsel hondjies

pup'il leerling; oogappel; kyker, pupil (oog); ~**(l)age** leertyd; minderjarigheid; ~ **teacher** kwekelingonderwyser

pupp'et speelpop, handpop, marionet; speelbal; ~ **show** poppespel, poppekas

pupp'y (puppies) jong hondjie; ~ **fat** jeug= vet; ~ **love** kalwerliefde

purch'ase (n) koop, aankoop; (pl) inkope; (v) koop; **purchasing power** koopkrag; ~ **price** inkoopprys, koopprys; **~r (aan)=** koper; klant

pure suiwer, rein, kuis; louter; ~ **nonsense** pure onsin

purge (n) (uit)suiwering, reiniging; (v) (uit)= suiwer; reinig

purifica'tion suiwering, reiniging; loutering

pur'ist taalsuiweraar, puris

pur'ity suiwerheid, reinheid

pur'ple (n) purper (kleur); (a) purper, pers

purp'ose (n) voorneme, doel, oogmerk; *for* ~*s of,* vir die doel van; *on* ~, opsetlik; (v) bedoel, beoog; **~ly** opsetlik; moeds= willig

purr spin (kat), knor

purse (n) beurs(ie); ~ **bearer** penningmees= ter; **~r** betaalmeester

pursue' vervolg; agtervolg; beoefen (be= roep)

pursuit' vervolging; (pl) werksaamhede; ~ *of knowledge,* die strewe na kennis

pus etter, vuilgoed

push (n) (-es) stamp, stoot; deursettings= vermoë; *when it comes to the* ~, in geval van nood; (v) stamp; stoot; bevorder; be= spoedig; **~bike** trapfiets

pu'ssy (pussies) katjie

put (v) (put, put) neersit, stel, plaas; ~ *out of action,* buite geveg stel; ~ *to flight,* op die vlug jaag; ~ *forward,* indien; opper; ~ *a motion,* 'n voorstel/mosie tot stem= ming bring; ~ *in order,* regmaak; ~ *up for sale,* te koop aanbied; ~ *on weight,* swaarder word; ~ *in writing,* dit op skrif stel

put'-off uitstel; uitvlug

putt (n) sethou; (v) set, put (gholf)

putt'er setyster; setter (gholf)

putt'-putt set-set

putt'y stopverf; ~ **knife** stopmes; ~ **plaster** fynpleister

puz'zle (n) raaisel; verleentheid; (v) verleë
maak; verbyster; ~d verwar(d), deurme=
kaar; ~ picture soekprentjie
pyg'my (pygmies) dwerg, pigmee
pyja'mas nagklere, slaapklere, pajamas;

slaappak
py'lon spanmas, piloon, kragmas
py'ramid piramide
pyroman'iac piromaniak (brandstigting)
pyth'on luislang, piton

Q

quack[1] (n) gekwaak; (v) kwaak
quack[2] (n) kwaksalwer; (v) kwaksalwer; ~
doctor kwaksalwer; ~ medicine kwak=
salwermiddels
quad'rangle vierkant; vierhoek; binneplaas,
binneplein
quadrille' kadriel (outydse dans)
qua'druple (n) viervoud; (a) viervoudig; (v)
verviervoudig
quadrupleg'ic (n) kwadrupleeg; (a) kwa=
druplegies
qua'druplet vierling; viertal; ~s vierling
quagg'a kwagga
quag'mire modderpoel; drilgrond; welsand
quail (n) kwartel
quaint snaaks, sonderling; vreemdsoortig;
ouderwets; ~ness snaaksheid, grilligheid
quake (n) bewing, siddering; (v) beef, tril
qualifica'tion bevoegdheid, bekwaamheid,
kwalifikasie; vereiste
qua'lified bevoeg, bekwaam, gekwalifi=
seer
qua'lify (..fied, ..fied) bevoeg maak; be=
kwaam maak; kwalifiseer, jou bekwaam;
~ for, in aanmerking kom vir, kwalifi=
seer vir
qua'lity (..ties) hoedanigheid, eienskap,
kwaliteit; aanleg; gehalte; ~ of life, le=
wenskwaliteit, lewensinhoud; ~ control
gehaltebeheer
qualm mislikheid; gewetenswroeging, angs=
gevoel; ~s of conscience, gewetenswroe=
ging; ~ish mislik, flou
quan'dary (..ries) verleentheid, penarie,
moeilikheid; be in a ~, in die knyp sit
quan'titative kwantitatief
quan'tity (..ties) hoeveelheid, kwantiteit,
menigte; in any ~, baie; ~ surveyor
bourekenaar
qua'rantine (n) kwarantyn; (v) onder kwa=
rantyn stel, afsonder, isoleer
qua'rrel (n) twis, rusie; pick a ~, rusie/
skoor soek; (v) (-led, -led) rusie maak;

skoor; ~ling getwis; ~some twissiek,
rusiemakerig
qua'rry[1] (n) (quarries) prooi; buit; wild
qua'rry[2] (n) (quarries) steengroef, gruisgat
quar'ter (n) kwartier; vierde deel; kwartaal;
kwart; (pl) kwartiere; give no ~, geen
genade betoon nie; ~ of an hour, 'n
kwartier; married ~s, kwartiere vir ge=
troudes; single ~s, enkelkwartiere; take
up one's ~s, jou intrek neem; ~ly (n)
(..lies) kwartaalblad; (a) driemaandeliks,
kwartaal=; ~ly test, kwartaaltoets;
~master kwartiermeester, betaalmeester
quartet' kwartet
quar'to (-s) kwarto, kwatryn
quartz kwarts; ~ watch kwartsoorlosie
quash verpletter, verbrysel; onderdruk
quas'i kamtig, kastig, kwansuis
quat'rain vierreëlige vers, kwatryn
quav'er (n) agtste noot; triller; (v) tril
quay (-s) hawehoof, kaai
queen (n) koningin; ~ly vorstelik, statig;
~ mother koninginmoeder
queer (n) 'n homo(seksueel); (v) verbrou,
bederf; (a) snaaks, sonderling; duiselig;
verdag; be in Q~ street, in die verknor=
sing wees; ~ness snaaksheid, sonderling=
heid
quell demp, bedwing, onderdruk
quench blus; les, bekoel; laat stilbly; ~
thirst, dors les; ~er blusser; drankie
quer'y (n) (..ries) vraag, navraag, twyfel=
vraag; vraagteken; (v) (..ried, ..ried) vra,
betwyfel, bevraagteken
quest (n) ondersoek; soektog; the ~ for,
die soeke/strewe na
ques'tion (n) vraag, kwessie; beyond ~,
sonder twyfel; out of the ~, geen sprake
van nie; (v) vra, ondervra; betwyfel; ~
the accused, die beskuldigde ondervra;
~able twyfelagtig; ~ bank vraagbank;
~er ondervraer, vraer; ~ing ondervra=
ging; ~ mark vraagteken; ~naire' vraelys

queue (n) vlegsel; ry, tou; ~ *up, form a* ~, toustaan; (v) toustaan, in 'n ry staan
quick (n) lewe; (a, adv) lewendig; vinnig, gou, rats; *be* ~ *about it!* roer jou! *a* ~ *eye,* 'n skerp oog; ~ *to take offence,* liggeraak; ~en verlewendig, versnel, aanspoor, besiel; ~**grass** kweek; ~**sand** wel= sand/wilsand, dryfsand; ~**silver** kwiksilwer; ~**-tempered** opvlieënd, kort= gebonde; ~**-witted** gevat
quid tabakpruimpie
quid pro quo' teenprestasie, quidproquo
qui'et (n) stilte, rus; bedaardheid; *on the* ~, stilletjies; (v) stilmaak; kalmeer; (a) rustig, stil, bedaard; *keep* ~, stilbly; iets stil hou; ~**en** (v) stilmaak, kalmeer
quilt (n) sprei, donskombers, veerkombers
quince kweper; ~ **jam** kweperkonfyt
quinine' kina, kinien
quin'sy mangelsweer
quint kwint
quintess'ence kern, kwintessens
quintet' kwintet; vyftal
quin'tuple (n) vyfvoud; (v) vervyfvoudig; (a) vyfvoudig

quip (n) skimpskoot; kwinkslag, geestig= heid, spitsvondigheid
quit (v) (**quit(ted), quit(ted)**) verlaat; tou opgooi; vertrek; ~ *the service,* die diens verlaat
quite heeltemal, glad, volkome; *I* ~ *like him,* ek hou nogal van hom; ~ *warm,* taamlik warm
quit'rent erfpag
quits gelyk, kiet(s); *we are* ~ *now,* nou is ons kiet(s)
quiv'er (n) pylkoker; trilling; *in a* ~, sid= derend; (v) tril, beef/bewe, ritsel
quixot'ic buitensporig, avontuurlik
quiz (n) grap; vasvrawedstryd; (v) (**-zed, -zed**) belaglik maak; ondervra, uitvra
quoit gooiskyf, gooiring
quor'um kworum
quot'a (**-s**) aandeel, kwota
quota'tion aanhaling; kwotasie; notering, prysopgawe; ~ **marks** aanhaaltekens
quote aanhaal, kwoteer, siteer; ~. . . *un= quote,* aanhaal . . . afhaal
quo'tient resultaat (van deling), kwosiënt

R

rabb'i (**-e)s**) rabbi, rabbyn
rabb'it konyn; nuweling
rabb'le gespuis, hoipolloi, gepeupel
rab'id mal, woes, onstuimig
rab'ies hondsdolheid
race[1] (n) ras, geslag; ~ **group** volksgroep; ~ **relations** volkereverhoudinge, rasse= betrekkinge
race[2] (n) wedloop, wedren, wedvaart; wed= vlug; (pl) wedlope (atletiek); wedrenne (perde, motors), wedvaarte (kano's, jag= te), wedvlugte (vlieg- en sweeftuie); (v) reisies/resies ja; jaag, hardloop; ren; ~ *course* renbaan, re(i)siesbaan
race: ~**horse** renperd, re(i)siesperd; ~ **meeting** reisies, resies, wedrenne
ra'cial ras=; ~ **discrimination** rassediskri= minasie; ~**ism** rassehaat
ra'cing renne, wedrenne, resies (ja); ~ **driver** renjaer; ~ **car** renmotor
rac'ism rassisme, rasseleer
rac'ist (n) rassis; (a) rassisties

rack (n) pynbank; rak; *go to* ~ *and ruin,* heeltemal te gronde gaan; (v) rek, strek; ~ *one's brains about,* jou hoof breek oor
rack'et[1] (n) raket, spaan (tennis)
rack'et[2] (n) geraas; rumoer; afpersbende; (v) baljaar; lawaai
racketeer' rampokker, afperser, boef, swendelaar
ra'cy geurig (wyn); pittig; ras-eg
rad'ar radar; ~ **operator** radaroperateur
rad'ial ply straallaag(band)
rad'iant (a) glansryk, glinsterend; ~ *with joy,* stralend van geluk
radia'tion (uit)straling; bestraling
rad'iator radiator, verkoeler
rad'ical (a) radikaal, ingrypend; ~ *change,* radikale verandering
rad'io (n) radio, draadloos; (v) uitsaai
rad'io-active radioaktief, uitstralend
rad'io: ~ **announcer** (radio)omroeper; ~ **drama** hoorspel, radiodrama
radiog'rapher (**-s**) radiografis

rad'io ham radio-amateur
radiol'ogist radioloog
radio play hoorspel
rad'ish (-es) radys
rad'ius (radii) straal, radius
raff'ia raffia
raf'fle (n) lotery; kantoorloting; (v) uitloot
raft (n) vlot; dryfhout; (v) dryf; op 'n vlot vaar
ra'fter kap, dakspar
rag[1] (n) vod, flard, toiing, flenter; (pl) lompe
rag[2] (n) (studente)jool; (v) (-ged, -ged) skerts
rag'amuffin skobbejak, smeerlap, skollie
rag' doll lappop
rage (n) woede, raserny; hartstog, begeerte; *all the ~*, hoog in die mode; (v) woed; tier, te kere gaan
rag' magazine joolblad
rag' procession jooloptog
rag'time sinkopasie; gesinkopeerde musiek
raid (n) rooftog, inval, strooptog; klopjag
rail (n) leuning; reling; treinspoor; spoor‑ staaf; *by ~*, per spoor; (v) spoorversend
rail'age spoorvrag, vervoerkoste
rail'ing reling, tralie; leuning
rail'road, rail'way (-s) spoorweg, treinspoor
rail'way: *~ carriage* spoorwa; *~ compart‑ ment* (spoorweg)kompartement; *~ cross‑ ing* spoororgang; *~ line* spoorlyn; *~ ticket* treinkaartjie; *~ track* spoorbaan
rain (n) reën, reent; (v) reën; *~ cats and dogs*, ou vrouens met knopkieries reën; *~bow* reënboog; *~fall* reënval; *~ gauge* reënmeter; *~proof* waterdig, reëndig; *~water* reënwater; *~y* reënagtig, reënerig
raise (n) opslag, verhoging (salaris); (v) op‑ tel, ophef, oplig; verhoog; verhef (stem); *~ a loan,* 'n lening sluit/aangaan; *~ an objection,* beswaar maak; *~ objections,* besware opper
rais'in rosyn(tjie)
rais'ing fee lening(s)kommissie, heffings‑ geld
rake (n) hark; *as lean as a ~,* so maer soos 'n kraai; (v) hark; oprakel; versamel
rall'y (n) (rallies) byeenkoms, saamtrek; tydren, sterrit (motor); (v) (rallied, rallied) herenig; houe wissel (tennis); *~ support,* steun monster; *~ to the support,* te hulp snel
ram (n) ram; stormram; stamper; (v) (-med, -med) stamp, vasstamp

ram'ble (v) rondloop; afdwaal; *~r* swerwer; klimplant; rankroos
ramifica'tion vertakking, uitvloeisel
ramp (n) helling, opdraand; laaibrug; oprit; (v) spring; klouter; stoei; steier
rampage' (n) wildheid, uitgelatenheid; *be on the ~,* woes te kere gaan
ram'rod laaistok
ram'shackle bouvallig, lendelam
ran *see* run
ranch (n) (-es) groot beesplaas; *~er* groot beesboer
ran'cid suur, rens; ransig, galsterig
ranc'our wrok, haat, wrewel
rand[1] rand (geldeenheid); *~ for ~ system,* rand-vir-randstelsel
rand[2] rant; *the R~,* die Witwatersrand, die Rand
ran'dom (n) toeval; geluk; *at ~,* blindweg, lukraak; (a) lukraak, ewekansig; toeval‑ lig; *~ test* steekproef
rang *see* ring
range (n) ry, reeks; speelruimte; omvang, bestek; afstand; *~ of vision,* gesigsveld; *within ~,* onder skoot; (v) rangskik; rond‑ dwaal; dra; *~ finder* afstandmeter
ran'ger boswagter, houtvester; swerwer
rank[1] (n) rang; ry; gelid; staanplek; (pl) ge‑ ledere; *the ~ and file,* die minderes; (v) rangskik, in gelid stel; *~ with,* gelyk staan met; *~ing* gradering, ranglys
rank[2] (a) welig, vrugbaar; galsterig; wellus‑ tig; *~ nonsense,* pure kaf, klinkklare onsin
ran'sack plunder; deursnuffel, fynkam
ran'som (n) losgeld, losprys; *hold/put to ~,* losgeld vra; (v) vrykoop, verlos
rant (v) grootpraat, spog, opskep
ranunc'ulus (-es, ..li) ranonkel
rap (n) tik; klop; knip; *I don't care a ~,* ek gee geen flenter om nie; (v) (-ped, -ped) klop, tik; uitblaker; *~ out instructions,* bevele afbyt/uitblaf
rape (n) verkragting; roof; (v) verkrag; ont‑ eer; *a ~ case,* 'n verkragtingsaak
rap'id (n) stroomversnelling; (a) gou, snel, rats; *~ fire* snelvuur
rap'ier rapier; *~ fish* swaardvis
rapt opgetoë, verruk; gespanne; *~ atten‑ tion,* die ene aandag
rap'ture verrukking; *in ~s,* verruk
rare seldsaam, skaars; buitengewoon, voor‑

treflik; yl, dun; *a ~ collection,* 'n seldsa=
me versameling
rare'bit roosterbrood met kaassous; *Welsh
~,* Walliese kaasroosterbrood
rare'ly selde
ra'scal (n) skurk, skelm, skavuit, karnallie
rash[1] (n) uitslag
rash[2] (a) onbedagsaam, voortvarend
rasp (n) rasper; gekrap; (v) raspe(r)
ra'spberry (..berries) framboos
rat (n) rot; oorloper
rat'catcher rottevanger
ratch'et (sper)rat, tandskyf
rate[1] (n) prys; graad; syfer; koers; *at any ~,*
in alle geval; *~ of exchange,* wisselkoers;
~ of interest, rentekoers; *mortality ~,*
sterftesyfer; (v) takseer, valueer; **~able**
belasbaar; **~payer** belastingbetaler (mu=
nisipaal); **~s** erfbelasting
rate[2] (v) uitskel, inklim, uitvaar
ra'ther liewer(s), taamlik; nogal; *~ not,*
liewer nie; *~ pretty,* mooierig
ra'tio (-s) verhouding
ra'tion (n) rantsoen; (v) rantsoeneer
ra'tionalise rasioneel/verstandelik verklaar
ra'tions rantsoene, kosvoorraad, proviand
rat'race rotren, rotresies, suksesjag
rattan' bamboes, rottang
ratt'le (n) geratel, gerammel; gebabbel; (v)
ratel, rammel, klater; klets; **~snake** ra=
telslang
ratt'ling (n) geratel, gerammel; (a) ratelend;
a ~ pace, 'n vinnige gang/pas
rat'trap muisval
rauc'ous hees, skor; *~ voice* rasperstem
rav'age (v) verwoes, plunder, verniel; ont=
eer
rave (v) raas, uitvaar, te kere gaan; die lof
besing; dweep met
rav'en (n) raaf; (v) verslind; roof; opvreet;
~ous roofgierig, vraatsugtig
ravine' kloof, ravyn, skeur
rav'ing (n) dwepery; yling; (a) rasend, mal,
ylend; *~ mad,* stapelgek
rav'ish ontroof; verkrag; bekoor
raw (a) ru; rou; *~ material* grondstof, ru=
materiaal; *~ recruit* baar rekruut
ray (n) (-s) straal; (v) uitstraal
ray'on rayon (soort kunssy)
raze uitkrap; sloop, afbreek
raz'or skeermes; *~ blade* skeerlemmetjie;
~ strop slypriem

re = regarding insake
reach (n) (-es) bereik; grens; *above my ~,*
bokant my vuurmaakplek; *within ~,*
binne bereik; (v) aanreik, aangee; uitstrek
react' terugwerk, reageer; **~ion** terugwer=
king, reaksie; **~ionary** (n) (..ries) op=
standeling; (a) opstandig, reaksionêr
read (read, read) lees; *~ aloud,* hardop lees,
luidlees; *~ for an examination,* vir 'n
eksamen studeer; **~able** leesbaar; **~er**
leser; proefleser; leesboek
rea'dily geredelik, graag
rea'diness bereidwilligheid, paraatheid
read'ing (n) lees; (voor)lesing, belesenheid;
vertolking; *light ~,* ligte lektuur; (a) le=
send, lees=; *~ book* leesboek; *~ desk*
lessenaar; *~ lamp* leeslamp; *~ room*
leeskamer, leessaal
rea'dy klaar, gereed; *~ cash,* kontant; *~
wit,* gevatheid; **~-made** klaargemaak(te);
~ reckoner kitsrekenaar
reaffirm' herbevestig, herbeklemtoon
re'al (a) wesenlik, regtig, reëel; eg; *in ~
terms,* in reële terme; *~ estate* vaste eien=
dom; *~ estate agent* eiendomsagent
re'alism realisme
real'ity (..ties) werklikheid, wesenlikheid
realisa'tion verwesenliking; besef; realise=
ring (van bates)
re'alise besef; realiseer (geld oplewer)
re'ally regtig, inderdaad, werklik
realm ryk, koninkryk
reap oes; insamel; win; *~ advantage,* voor=
deel trek; **~er, ~ing machine** snymasjien
rear[1] (n) agterhoede, agtergrond
rear[2] (v) kweek, teel; grootmaak; oplei;
~ children, kinders grootmaak
rear: **~-admiral** skout-by-nag; skoutadmi=
raal (S.A.); **~guard** agterhoede
rearrange' verander, verstel, herrangskik
rear'view mirror truspieël(tjie)
reas'on (n) rede, verstand; *by ~ of,* weens;
it stands to ~, dit spreek vanself; *a wo=
man's ~,* vrouelogika; (v) redeneer; be=
spreek; **~able** redelik, billik; verstandig;
~ing redenering
reassure' herverseker; gerusstel
rebate' (n) korting, afslag, rabat
reb'el (n) oproerling, rebel; (a) opstandig;
rebels
rebel' (v) (-led, -led) opstaan, rebelleer;

~lion opstand, rebellie; **~lious** oproerig, opstandig

rebound' (n) terugstuiting, terugslag; reaksie; (v) terugstuit, terugkaats

rebuff' (n) afjak; teenslag; (v) afwys, afjak

rebuke' (v) berispe, teregwys

recall' (v) herroep; terugtrek; ~ *to mind,* byval; *you will ~ that* . . ., jy sal onthou dat . . .

recapit'ulate kortliks herhaal, rekapituleer

recede' wyk, terugtrek

receipt' (n) ontvangs; bewys, kwitansie; *on ~ of,* by ontvangs van; (v) kwiteer; ~ **book** kwitansieboek

receive' ontvang; onthaal; opvang; kry

receiv'er ontvanger; gehoorbuis, hoorstuk (tel.); ontvangtoestel; ~ **of revenue** ontvanger van belastings/inkomste, belastinggaarder, Jan Taks

re'cent nuut, vars, onlangs, pas gelede; **~ly** onlangs, kort gelede

recep'tion ontvangs; onthaal; verwelkoming; aanvaarding; **~ist** ontvangklerk; ontvangdame; ~ **room** ontvangkamer

recep'tive ontvanklik, vatbaar

recess' terugtrekking; (-es) skuilplek; pouse; vakansie, reses; **~ion** insinking; slapte, resessie (handel)

recharge' herlaai, weer laai

re'cipe resep, voorskrif

recip'ient (n) ontvanger; (a) ontvangend

recip'rocal wederkerig, wedersyds

recip'rocate beantwoord, vergeld

recit'al verhaal, vertelling; voorlesing; uitvoering (musiek)

recita'tion voordrag, resitasie; opsomming

recite' opsê, voordra, resiteer

reck omgee, jou bekommer; **~less** roekeloos, onverskillig

reck'on reken, tel, skat, glo; ~ *on,* staatmaak op; **~ing** berekening; gissing; *day of ~ing,* vergeldingsdag

reclama'tion terugwinning; drooglegging

recline' leun, agteroor lê, rus, neervly

recluse' (n) kluisenaar

recogni'tion herkenning; erkenning; waardering; *in ~ of,* ter erkenning van

rec'ognise herken; erken, insien

recollec'tion herinnering, geheue

recommend' aanbeveel, aanprys, aanraai; **~ed price** aanbevole prys; rigprys

recommenda'tion aanbeveling; *letter of ~,* aanbevelingsbrief

rec'oncile versoen; herenig; bylê; ~ *oneself to,* berus in; *~ with,* rym met

reconcilia'tion versoening, rekonsiliasie

recondi'tion (v) opknap, vernuwe, opdoen, herkondisioneer

reconn'aissance verkenning, spioentog, spioenasie; ~ **flight** verken(nings)vlug

reconsid'er heroorweeg

reconstruc'tion heropbou, rekonstruksie

rec'ord (n) verslag; register; dokument, rekord; (grammofoon)plaat; *beat/break a ~,* 'n rekord slaan/oortref; *keep a ~ of,* rekord hou van (rekordhouding); *on ~,* aangeteken, op rekord

record' (v) opteken; inskryf; boekstaaf; vermeld; **~ed music** platemusiek

rec'ord book verslagboek; rekordboek

record'er argivaris; notulehouer; blokfluit

rec'ord: ~ **librarian** diskotekaris; ~ **library** diskoteek

recoup' verreken, verhaal, terugvorder; vergoed

recourse' toevlug

reco'ver herkry; terugkry; terugvorder; herstel, gesond word; verhaal (geld); ~ *consciousness,* weer bykom; ~ *damages,* skadevergoeding verhaal/kry; **~y** herstel(ling); terugvordering; (her)winning (myn)

recrea'tion tydverdryf, vermaak, vryetydbesteding, ontspanning; rekreasie; **~al facilities** ontspangeriewe

recruit' (n) rekruut; (v) werf, rekruteer; **~ing** (n) werwing; rekrutering

rectang'ular reghoekig

rec'tify (..fied, ..fied) verbeter, aansuiwer, regstel, reghelp; suiwer, distilleer

rec'tor rektor; predikant; **~ship** rektoraat, rektorskap; leraarskap; **~y** (..ries) pastorie

rec'tum (recta) endelderm, vetderm, rektum

recup'erate herstel, aansterk

recur' (-red, -red) terugkom, herhaal; repeteer (desimaal); **~rence** terugkeer, herhaling; **~ring decimal** repeterende breuk

recy'cle (v) herwin, hersikleer; herraffineer (olie)

red: *in the ~,* in die skuld; (a, adv) rooi; *R~ Cross Society,* Rooikruisvereniging; *R~*

Indian, Rooihuid; *R~ Riding Hood,* Rooikappie; **~breast** rooiborsie; **~den** rooi maak, rooi kleur; **~dish** rooierig

redeem' loskoop, vrykoop; delg; *~ing death,* soendood; *~ a promise,* 'n belofte nakom

Redeem'er Verlosser, Heiland

redemp'tion bevryding; afkoping; delging, aflossing; *~* **period** delgtermyn

red: *~-handed* op heter daad; *~-hot* gloeiend warm, vuurwarm

redirect' heradresseer, aanstuur

red'-letter gedenkwaardig, besonder; *~ day,* gedenkwaardige dag

redoubt'able gedug, gevrees

Red'skin Rooihuid, Indiaan

red' tape burokrasie, amptelike omslagtigheid; rompslomp

reduce' herlei; verminder; *in ~d circumstances,* armoedig; *~d to despair,* tot wanhoop gedryf; *~d rate,* verlaagde tarief

reduc'tion vermindering, afslag; inkorting

redun'dant oortollig, oorbodig; oorvloedig

red'water rooiwater (dier); bilharzia (mens)

reed riet; matjiesgoed, biesie; (pl) riete, fluitjiesriet; *~* **warbler** rietvink

reef (-s) rif; klipbank, rotslaag

reel[1] (n) rolletjie; garetolletjie; (v) oprol, opdraai; *~ off,* afrol (tou); aframmel (poësie)

reel[2] (v) 'n riel dans; wankel; *my head ~s,* my kop draai

re-elect' herkies; **~ion** herkiesing

re-examina'tion hereksamen

re-exam'ine hereksamineer; weer ondervra

refer' (-red, -red) verwys; *~ to,* verwys na

referee' (n) skeidsregter

ref'erence verwysing; referensie; getuigskrif; *have (bear) ~ to,* betrekking hê op; *with ~ to,* met betrekking tot; met verwysing na; *~* **book** bewysboek; *~* **guide** naslaangids; *~* **library** (..ries) naslaanbiblioteek; *~* **number** verwysnommer

referen'dum (..da, -s) referendum, volkstemming

ref'ill (n) hervulling, vulbuisie; vervanger

refine' verfyn; beskawe; raffineer (suiker, olie); *~d* verfyn; gesuiwer; *~d manners,* beskaafde maniere; *~ment* verfyning, beskawing; *~ry* (..ries) raffinadery/raffineerdery; suiweringsaanleg

reflec'tion weerkaatsing; weerspieëling; blaam, verwyt; oorweging; *cast a ~ upon,* blaam werp op

reflec'tor weerkaatser; trukaatser, kaatser; *~* **strip** glimstrook

ref'lex (n) (-es) refleks; *~* **action** refleksbeweging

reflex'ive wederkerend, refleksief; *~* **verb** wederkerende werkwoord

reform' (v) hervorm, verbeter; **~a'tion** hervorming, reformasie; **~atory** (n) (..ries) verbeterskool, verbetering(s)gestig; **~ed** hervormd, gereformeerd; **~er** hervormer; **~** **school** verbeterskool

refrain'[1] (n) refrein

refrain'[2] (v) beteuel, bedwing, terughou, weerhou; *~from,* jou weerhou van

refresh' verfris, verkwik, verkoel; **~er** **course** opknapkursus; lenteskool; **~ing** verfrissend, verkwikkend

refresh'ment verversing, verkwikking

refri'gerator koelkamer; yskas, koelkas

refu'el (-led, -led) brandstof inneem/intap

ref'uge (n) toevlug, skuilplek, toevlugsoord

refugee' vlugteling, uitgewekene

refund' (n) terugbetaling; (v) terugbetaal

refur'bish opknap, herstel

refus'al weiering, verwerping

ref'use[1] (n) afval, vullis; oorskiet, rommel; (a) vuilgoed~, vuil; *~* **bin** vullisblik

refuse'[2] (v) weier, verwerp, afwys

regain' herwin, terugkry; *~ consciousness,* bykom

reg'al koninklik

regal'ia koninklike waardigheidstekens; kroonsierade; ampsierade; *in full ~,* in volle ornaat

regard' (n) agting; opsig, betrekking; aandag; (pl) groete; *in ~ to,* met betrekking tot; *kind ~s to,* groete aan; *in this ~,* in hierdie opsig; *with ~ to,* met betrekking tot; (v) beskou, ag; *as ~s myself,* wat my betref; **~ing** aangaande, betreffende, rakende

regard'less *~ of expense,* ongeag die koste

regatt'a (-s) wedvaart, roeiwedstryd

re'gent regent; vors

regime' regering; bewind, regime; *under the old ~,* onder die ou bedeling/bewind

re'giment regiment

re'gion streek, landstreek, gebied

re'gional streek, regionaal, gewestelik; *~*

re'gister   356   remov'al

committee streekkomitee; ~ news (service) streeknuus
re'gister (n) register; rol; (v) registreer;
aanteken; inskryf; ~ a letter, 'n brief laat
aanteken/registreer; ~ed owner, geregi-
streerde/regmatige eienaar; ~ed student,
ingeskrewe/geregistreerde student
re'gistrar registrateur (universiteit); griffier
(hof)
registra'tion registrasie; inskrywing
regret' (n) spyt, berou, verdriet, hartseer;
hear with ~, met leedwese verneem; (v)
(-ted, -ted) spyt hê, betreur; I ~ to say, dit
spyt my om te sê; ~table betreurens-
waardig
reg'ular (a) gereeld, reëlmatig; ~ hours
vaste ure; ~ meetings gereelde vergaderings
reg'ulate reël, rangskik, reguleer
regula'tion reëling; voorskrif, regulasie;
reglement
reg'ulator inrigter; balans; slinger (aan
uurwerk); reëlaar (aan enjin)
rehears'al repetisie, instudering
reign (n) regering; bestuur; (v) regeer; ~ of
terror, skrikbewind
reimburse' terugbetaal, vergoed; goedmaak;
~ment terugbetaling, vergoeding
rein (n) teuel, leisel; (v) beteuel, in toom hou
rein'deer rendier
reinforce' versterk, verstewig; inskerp; ~d
concrete gewapende beton; ~ment, rein-
forcing versterking, wapening
reit'erate herhaal
rej'ect (n) afgekeurde goed; (pl) uitskot
reject' (v) verwerp, afslaan; verstoot
rejoice' verheug, juig; bly wees
rejuv'enate verjong, verlewendig
relapse' (n) verswakking, insinking
relate' (v) vertel, verhaal; ~d verwant
rela'tion betrekking; verwantskap, bloedverwant; in ~ to, met betrekking tot;
~ship verwantskap; verband (tussen)
rel'ative (n) bloedverwant, familielid; (pl)
familie; nearest ~, naaste aanverwant; (a)
betreklik, relatief
relativ'ity relatiwiteit
relax' verslap; ontspan; verlig; ~a'tion
verslapping; ontspanning
relay' (n) (-s) aflosspan; heruitsending (radio); (v) heruitsaai; ~ race afloswedloop
release' (n) loslating, ontslag; (v) loslaat;

ontslaan; vrylaat; ~ of hostages, vrylating van gyselaars; press ~, persberig
rel'evant toepaslik, ter sake, vanpas
reli'able betroubaar; vertroubaar, deeglik
relief' verligting, oplugting; ondersteuning,
noodleniging; ontset; what a ~! wat 'n
verligting! ~ fund noodleniging(s)fonds;
bystand(s)fonds; ~ train hulptrein
relieve' verlig, ondersteun; aflos; ~ the
guard, die wag aflos
reli'gion godsdiens; geloof
reli'gious godsdienstig, vroom; stip; ~ denomination kerkverband; ~ instruction
godsdiensonderrig
relinq'uish afsien van, laat vaar, opgee
rel'ish (n) smaak, geur; voorsmaak; neiging; eat with ~, smaaklik eet
reluc'tance teensin(nigheid); huiwering
reluc'tant weerstrewig, teensinnig; ~ly
teensinnig, onwillig, langtand
rely' (relied, relied) vertrou, reken op,
staatmaak op
remain' bly; oorbly; ~der oorblyfsel, oorskot; res; ~s' oorblyfsels; stoflike oorskot
remark' (n) aanmerking (ongunstig); opmerking; (v) aanmerk (ongunstig); opmerk; ~able merkwaardig, opmerklik
remed'ial genesend, remediërend; ~ education remediërende onderwys/onderrig
rem'edy (n) (..dies) geneesmiddel; regs-
middel, boereraat; (v) (..died, ..died)
regstel, herstel; genees; remedieer
remem'ber byval, onthou; ~ me to your
friends, sê groete aan jou vriende
remem'brance aandenking; gedagtenis
remind' herinner, help onthou; that ~s me,
dit laat my dink; ~er aanmaning, wenk
remit' (-ted, -ted) terugstuur; terugkeer;
terugbetaal; ~tance betaling, geld-
sending; ~tance man (uitlandige) toe-
laagtrekker
rem'nant (n) oorblyfsel, oorskot; restant,
oorskietlap; ~ sale oorskietuitverkoop,
restantverkoping
remorse' (gewetens)wroeging, berou
remote' ver, afgeleë, verwyderd; ~ control
afstand(s)beheer; not the ~st idea, nie die
flouste benul nie
remov'al verwydering; verhuising; ontslag;
~ van verhuiswa, meubelwa

remove' (v) verwyder; verplaas, verhuis; ontslaan; ~ from office, afdank

remunera'tion vergoeding, besoldiging; beloning

rend (rent, rent) verskeur; verdeel

ren'der lewer; oorgee; vertaal; account ~ed, gelewerde rekening; ~ assistance, hulp verleen; ~ a service, 'n diens bewys

ren'dering lewering; vertaling; vertolking (musiekstuk)

ren'dezvous (pl same), bymekaarkomplek, vergaderplek, versamelplek, rendezvous

ren'egade (n) renegaat, droster, hen(d)sopper

renew' vernuwe; hernu(we); herhaal; hervat; please ~ your subscription, geliewe u intekening/subskripsie te hernu; ~al vernuwing, hernuwing; ~al notice hernuwingskennisgewing

renounce' verloën, verwerp, afsweer; ~ friendship, vriendskapsbande verbreek

renova'tion vernuwing, opknapping

renown' beroemdheid, vermaardheid

rent (n) huur; huurgeld; pag; (v) huur, verhuur; ~al huur(geld)

reop'en heropen (skool)

reorganisa'tion herindeling, reorganisasie

repair' (n) herstel(ling), reparasie; out of ~, onklaar; stukkend; (v) regmaak, herstel; vergoed

repartee' gevatte antwoord; quick at ~, gevat; snedig

repay' (..paid, ..paid) terugbetaal; ~able terugbetaalbaar; ~ment terugbetaling

repeat' (n) herhaling; nabestelling; (v) herhaal, repeteer; ~edly herhaaldelik; ~er herhaler; repeteergeweer

repel' (-led, -led) verdryf, terugdryf; odour ~lent, reukweerder, deodorant

repent' spyt hê, berou hê; ~ance berou

repercu'ssion terugslag; nasleep, reperkussie; terugkaatsing

repeti'tion herhaling, repetisie; kopie

replace' verplaas, vervang; terugsit

re'play (n) trubeeld, kyk weer (TV)

replen'ish aanvul, vol maak

rep'lica ewebeeld, replika

reply' (n) (replies) antwoord; in ~ to, in antwoord op; ~ paid, antwoord betaal; (v) (replied, replied) antwoord (gee)

report' (n) berig, verslag, rapport; make a ~, 'n verslag saamstel; (v) aanmeld; berig,

verslag doen/lewer; rapporteer; ~ back, terugrapporteer; he must ~ to the trainer, hy moet hom by die afrigter aanmeld; ~er verslaggewer

represent' voorstel; verteenwoordig; ~ a'tion verteenwoordiging

represent'ative (n) verteenwoordiger; (a) verteenwoordigend; ~ committee skakelkomitee; ~ council verteenwoordigingsraad, verteenwoordigende raad

reprieve' (n) uitstel, opskorting; grant a ~, begenadig; (v) uitstel, skors

rep'rimand (n) berisping, teregwysing; (v) berispe, teregwys, bestraf

re'print herdruk; oordruk

repris'al vergelding, weerwraak

reproach' (n) (-es) verwyt, berisping, blaam; (v) verwyt, berispe; ~ onself for, jou verwyt; ~able laakbaar; ~ful verwytend, skandelik; ~less onberispelik, vlekkeloos

reproduce' kopieer, reproduseer; namaak; vermenigvuldig; voortplant

reproduc'tion reproduksie, weergawe

reprove' berispe, verwyt, bestraf

rep'tile (n) reptiel

repub'lic republiek; ~an (n) republikein; (a) republikeins

Repub'lic Day Republiekdag

repud'iate repudieer; loën, ontken

repul'sive weersinwekkend, afstootlik

rep'utable fatsoenlik, agtenswaardig, respektabel

reputa'tion aansien, eer, agting, reputasie

request' (n) versoek, vraag; by ~, op versoek; (v) versoek, vra; ~ item versoeknommer, versoekplaat (radio)

require' (ver)eis; ~d gevra, verlang; ~ment vereiste, benodigdheid, behoefte; (pl) behoeftes

requisi'tion vordering; versoek; rekwisisie; aanvraag; (v) opkommandeer

res'cue (n) redding, verlossing; (v) red, bevry; ~ attempt redpoging; ~r redder

research' (n) ondersoek, navorsing; (v) navors, naspoor, ondersoek; ~ work navorsing, bronnestudie

resed'a reseda (blomplant)

resell' (..sold, ..sold) herverkoop

resem'blance ooreenkoms, gelykenis

resent' kwalik neem, beledig voel; ~ful liggeraak, gevoelig; ~ment wrok, wrewel

reserva'tion voorbehoud; bedenking; bewaring; bespreking (plek)
reserve' (n) reserwe, noodvoorraad; terughoudendheid; wildtuin; reservaat; *without* ~, sonder voorbehoud; (v) voorbehou; agterhou, reserveer; bespreek (sitplek); ~ *the right,* behou die reg, behou hom die reg voor
reser'vist reservis (polisie)
res'ervoir reservoir, opgaardam; opgaartenk; (bêre)plek
resettle hervestig; ~ment hervestiging
reside' woon, bly; setel
res'idence woonplek; verblyf, inwoning; *board and* ~, kos en inwoning; *take up one's* ~, jou vestig
res'ident (n) bewoner; inwoner, ingesetene; (a) woonagtig; inwonend; ~ **doctor** inwonende geneesheer; ~ **engineer** resident-ingenieur; ~'s **permit** verblyfpermit
residen'tial woon-, verblyf-; inwonend; ~ area/quarter woonbuurt
resign' bedank, ontslag neem; ~ *from a committee,* uit 'n komitee bedank; ~a'tion gelatenheid; bedanking, ontslag
resil'ience veerkrag, elastisiteit
res'in gom, hars; harpuis; ~ous gomagtig
resist' weerstaan, uithou; weerstreef; ~ *temptation,* versoeking weerstaan
resis'tance weerstand, teenstand; *the line of least* ~, die weg van die geringste weerstand; *meet* ~, weerstand ondervind; *passive* ~, lydelike verset; ~ **movement** weerstand(s)beweging
resolu'tion besluit, beslissing; resolusie (vergaderings); *good* ~s, goeie voornemens
resolve' (v) voorneem; besluit, beslis
resort' (n) toevlugsoord; oord; redmiddel; *last* ~, laaste toevlug; (v) sy toevlug neem tot; ~ *to force,* geweld gebruik; **holiday** ~, vakansieoord
resound' weergalm, weerklink, skal
resource' hulpbron, redmiddel, toevlug; (pl) geldmiddele, talente; *at the end of one's* ~s, ten einde raad; **natural** ~s natuurbronne; ~**ful** slim, vindingryk, skerpsinnig
respect' (n) eerbied; agting; (pl) groete; *in all* ~s, in alle opsigte; *have* ~ *for,* eerbied hê vir; *in* ~ *of,* met betrekking tot; betreffende, rakende; uit hoofde van;

pay last ~s, die laaste eer bewys; *with* ~ *to,* met betrekking tot; ~able fatsoenlik; respektabel; ~ed geëer, geag; ~ful eerbiedig, beleef; ~ing aangaande, betreffende; ~ive betreklik, respektief; *the* ~*ive captains,* die onderskeie kapteins
respira'tion asemhaling
res'pite (n) uitstel, respyt
respond' antwoord, reageer; ~ent verweerder, respondent
response' antwoord; weerklank; *make no* ~, nie reageer nie
responsibil'ity (..ties) verantwoordelikheid; aanspreeklikheid
respon'sible verantwoordelik; betroubaar
rest[1] (n) oorskiet, res; (v) oorbly, oorskiet, rest[2] (n) rus, pouse; blaaskans; *for the* ~, origens; *set at* ~, laat bedaar, gerusstel; (v) rus; slaap; *the decision* ~s *with you,* jy moet besluit
res'taurant eethuis, restourant/restaurant
rest: ~ **camp** ruskamp; ~ **cure** ruskuur; ~ful rustig, stil; ~ **house** herberg
rest'less rusteloos, woelig
restore' teruggee; herstel; restoureer
restrain' bedwing, beteuel, beperk, inhou
restraint' bedwang, beperking; verbod; ~ *of trade,* inkorting van handelsvryheid
restrict' beperk, begrens, bepaal; inperk
restric'tion beperking, restriksie, inperking
result' (n) gevolg, uitslag, resultaat; (v) volg, ontstaan, voortspruit; **examination** ~(s) eksamenuitslag
resume' (v) hervat; saamvat; vervolg
resurrec'tion wederopstanding, verrysenis
retail' (v) verkleinhandel
ret'ail (n) kleinhandel; ~ **dealer** kleinhandelaar; ~er kleinhandelaar; ~ **price** kleinhandelprys, verbruikersprys; ~ **price maintenance** prysbinding
retain' behou; ~ing fee, ~er bindgeld, retensiegeld; ~ing wall stutmuur
retal'iate vergeld, terugbetaal, terugveg
retard' vertraag, uitstel, belemmer; ~ed child, (verstandelik) vertraagde kind
reten'tion terughouding, retensie
ret'ina (-e, -s) netvlies (oog), retina
retire' (v) (jou) terugtrek; ontslag neem; aftree; uittree; ~d chairman, uitgetrede voorsitter; ~ on a pension, met pensioen aftree; ~d oud-, gewese; stil; terugge-

trokke; gepensioeneer; ~ment aftrede, uittrede; ~ment annuity aftreeannuïteit
retir'ing stil, beskeie; ingetoë; ~ chairman uittredende voorsitter
retort' (n) berisping; gevatte antwoord; (v) teenwerp, skerp antwoord; suiwer
retrace' naspoor, weer nagaan; ~ one's steps, teruggaan
retract' terugtrek; herroep
retreat' (n) aftog, terugtog; skuilplek; sound the ~, die aftog blaas; (v) (jou) terugtrek
retrench' besnoei, afdank; ~ment besnoeiing, afdanking
retribu'tion vergelding, wraak; war of ~, vergeldingsoorlog
retrieve' (n) herstel; (v) herstel; terugkry; red; opspoor; ~ information, inligting ontsluit; ~r jaghond
ret'rospect, retrospec'tion terugblik; in ~, terugskouend
retrospec'tive terugwerkend
return' (n) terugkeer, terugkoms; opbrengs, rendement (op belegging); opgawe; many happy ~s, nog baie jare; (v) terugkom; terugstuur, teruggee; ~ a profit, wins oplewer; ~ date, ~ day keerdatum, keerdag; ~ journey (-s) terugreis; ~ match teenwedstryd; ~ ticket retoerkaartjie
reun'ion hereniging, reünie
reveal' openbaar, blootlê; vertoon
rev'el (v) (-led, -led) jolyt maak, swelg, bras; ~ in, jou verlustig in
revela'tion openbaring, onthulling
rev'eller losbol, jolytmaker, pretmaker
revenge' (n) wraak; (v) wreek; ~ful wraakgierig, wraaksugtig
rev'enue inkomste; ~ account inkomsterekening; ~ stamp inkomsteseël
rev'erence (n) eerbied, hoogagting, ontsag; hold in ~, eer; pay ~, eer betoon
rev'erend (n) eerwaarde; dominee; (a) eerwaarde
rev'erent, reveren'tial eerbiedig
rev'erie mymering, dromery, gepeins
reverse' (n) keersy, agterkant; teenspoed; neerlaag; trurat; (v) omkeer, wysig; omdraai; tru; nietig verklaar (uitspraak); ~ a judgment, 'n uitspraak omverwerp/ter syde stel; ~ gear trurat; ~ side keersy
revert' omkeer; terugkeer; terugval
review' (n) oorsig; resensie, boekbespre-

king; (v) nagaan; beoordeel, bespreek, resenseer; ~er beoordelaar, resensent
revile' beskimp, uitskel, verguis
revise' (n) hersiening; revisie; (v) hersien, bywerk; verbeter; wysig; ~d edition hersiene uitgawe
revi'sion hersiening, revisie
reviv'al herlewing; oplewing; opwekking; herstel; ~ist opwek(kings)prediker
revive' herleef; opwek; bykom; oprakel; ~ a patient, 'n pasiënt bybring
revoke' herroep, vernietig; intrek
revolt' (n) opstand, oproer; (v) opstaan, in opstand kom; ~ing weersinwekkend, stuitlik
revolu'tion revolusie; omwenteling; kringloop, wenteling, toer; ~ary (n) (..ries) opstandige, revolusionêr; (a) revolusionêr, oproerig, opstandig; ~s counter toereteller; ~ist oproerling, revolusionêr; ~ise omkeer, totaal hervorm
revol'ver rewolwer
revol'ving draai=, wentel=; ~ credit wentelkrediet; ~ tower wenteltoring
revue' musiekkomedie, revue
reward' (n) beloning, vergoeding; as a ~ of, in ~ of, ter beloning vir; due ~, verdiende loon; (v) beloon, vergeld
rhap'sody (..dies) rapsodie
rhet'oric retoriek, welsprekendheid; ~al retories, welsprekend, hoogdrawend
rheumat'ic (n) rumatieklyer; (a) rumaties; ~ fever rumatiekkoors, sinkingkoors
rheum'atism rumatiek
rhinoc'eros (-es) renoster
Rhode'sia Rhodesië (tans Zimbabwe); ~n (n) Rhodesiër; (a) Rhodesies; ~n ridgeback, rifrug(hond), pronkrughond
rhu'barb rabarber
rhyme (n) rym; rympie; poësie; without ~ or reason, sonder rede of grond; (v) rym, dig; ~d verse, berymde verse; ~r rymelaar, rymer
rhy'thm ritme, maat; ~ic(al) ritmies
rib (n) rib, ribbetjie, ribbebeen
ribb'on lint, band; flenter; tear to ~s, in flenters/flarde skeur; ~ worm lintwurm
rice rys; ~ paper ryspapier
rich ryk; kosbaar, vrugbaar (grond); voedsaam (kos); ~ food, kragtige kos; ~es rykdom; weelde; ~ness rykheid, oorvloed
rick'ets Engelse siekte, ragitis

rick'ety slap, lendelam, lutterig; ragities
rick'shaw riksja
ric'ochet (n) oplagskoot, opslagkoeël; (v)
(-(t)ed, -(t)ed) opslaan
rid, (-ded or rid, rid) vry maak, ontslaan;
verlos; verwyder; *be ~ of*, kwyt wees; *get
~ of*, ontslae raak van; **~dance** bevry=
ding, verlossing; *good ~dance*, 'n ware
oplugting, dankie bly
rid'dle (n) raaisel; (v) raai
ride (n) rit, toer; (v) (**rode, ridden**) ry, bery;
~ a winner, wen; **~r** ruiter
ridge (n) rug; nok (dak); kant; krans; mid=
delmannetjie; (v) rimpel, riffel; **~back**
rifrug(hond)
ridic'ulous belaglik, verspot
ri'ding: ~ **breeches** rybroek; ~ **habit** ry=
kostuum; ~ **school** ryskool; ~ **whip**
rysweep, karwats
riem riem; **~pie** riempie
rife oorvloedig, algemeen; *rumour is ~*, die
gerugte gaan oral rond
riff'-raff gepeupel, Jan Rap en sy maat,
uitvaagsel, gespuis, skorriemorrie, gom=
torre, hoipolloi, skollie(s)
ri'fle (n) geweer, roer; (v) roof, plunder; ~
club skietvereniging; ~ **commando** skiet=
kommando; **~man (..men)** skutter; skerp=
skutter, skut; ~ **range** skietbaan
rift (n) skeur, bars; *R~ Valley*, Slenkdal;
(v) skeur, kloof
rig (n) uitrusting; tuigasie, touwerk (skip);
boortoring; (v) (**-ged, -ged**) aantrek, op=
maak; optooi; ~ *up*, optooi; aanme=
kaartimmer; **~ger** takelaar
right (n) reg, aanspraak; (pl) regte; *by ~ of*,
kragtens; *keep to the ~*, hou regs; *might is
~*, mag is reg; (v) regstel; verbeter; (a)
regter=; billik; regverdig; *at ~ angles*,
reghoekig; *in his ~ mind*, by sy volle ver=
stand; (adv) presies, reg; ~ *about turn*,
regsomkeer; ~ *to the point*, reg op die doel
af; *~ -about* regs om; ~ **angle** regte hoek;
~eous regverdig, regskape, billik; **~ful**
regmatig, wettig; *~ -handed* regs; **~ly**
tereg, presies, juis; ~ **wing** regtervleuel
ri'gid styf; streng; strak, vas
rig'marole boel, kaf; kletsery; gedoente
rim (n) rand; lys; velling (wiel)
ring¹ (n) ring; kring; kryt; (v) (**-ed, -ed**) ring
ring² (n) klank; gelui; geluid; *have a fami=
liar ~*, bekend klink; (v) (**rang, rung**) lui;

telefoneer; bel; weerklink; ~ *in the new
year*, die nuwe jaar inlui
ring: **~finger** ringvinger, naaspink; **~leader**
belhamel, voorbok, leier; **~let** ringetjie;
~ **road** sirkelpad; **~worm** douwurm,
omloop
rink (n) baan, skaatsbaan; (v) skaats
rinse uitspoel, deurspoel, skoon spoel
ri'ot (n) oproer, onlus, muitery; ~ **police**
onluspolisie; (v) muit, oproer maak; **~er**
oproermaker; rusverstoorder; **~ous** rus=
verstorend, oproerig
ripe ryp; oud; beleë (wyn); ~ *age*, hoë ou=
derdom; **~n** ryp word; ryp maak
rip'ple (n) gekabbel, rimpeling, kabbeling;
(v) kabbel, rimpel; golf
rip'saw kloofsaag
rise (n) styging, opgang; opkoms (son);
verhoging (salaris); toename; opdraand;
give ~ to, aanleiding gee tot; ~ *of salary*,
salarisverhoging; (v) (**rose, -n**) styg; op=
kom; ontstaan; ~ *from the dead*, uit die
dode opstaan
risk (n) gevaar, risiko; *at the ~ of his life*,
met lewensgevaar; (v) waag, riskeer; **~y**
gewaag, riskant
riss'ole frikkadel(letjie)
rite plegtigheid, ritus, rite, seremonie
rit'ual (n) kerklike instelling; rituaal; ri=
tueel; (a) ritueel
riv'al (n) mededinger; teenstander; *without
a ~*, sonder weerga; (v) (**-led, -led**) mee=
ding, wedywer; (a) mededingend; **~ry**
mededinging, wedywer(ing)
riv'er rivier, stroom; ~ **basin** stroomge=
bied; **~bed** rivierbedding; **~side** rivier=
oewer; ~ **tortoise** waterskilpad
riv'et (n) klamp, kram; klinknael; (v) klink,
vasklink, vasklamp
road pad, weg; *rules of the ~*, verkeersre=
gulasies; **~block** padblokkade, padver=
sperring; **~hog** padbuffel, padvark,
jaagduiwel; **~house** padkafee; ~ **race**
padwedloop, padren; ~ **safety** padvei=
ligheid; **~sign** padteken, wegwyser, pre=
dikant; **~worthy** padwaardig; **~worthy
certificate** padwaardig(heid)sertifikaat
roam rondswerf, ronddool
roan skimmel
roan' antelope bastergemsbok
roar (n) gebrul; gebulder; (v) brul; bulder;
raas; ~ *with laughter*, skater v.d. lag

roar'ing (a) brullend; dreunend; eersteklas, uitstekend; *a ~ time,* groot pret/plesier; *~ trade,* lewendige handel, goeie sake

roast (n) braaivleis; (v) braai, bak

rob (-bed, -bed) (be)roof, steel; besteel; plunder; **~ber** rower, dief; **~bery** (..ries) roof, rowery, diefstal

robe (n) japon; toga; mantel; (pl) ampsge= waad; *~s of office,* ampsgewaad

rob'in rooiborsie

rob'ot robot; outomatiese verkeersteken

robust' sterk, gespierd, kragtig

rock[1] (n) rots, kliprots; *be on the ~s,* in die knyp sit

rock[2] (v) skud, skommel; wieg; wankel; *~ to sleep,* aan die slaap wieg

rock'-'n'-roll ruk-en-rol, ruk-en-pluk

rock'drill klipboor, diamantboor

rock'ery (..ries) rotstuin, kliptuin

rock'et vuurpyl; **~ launcher** vuurpylrigter

rock'ing: ~ chair skommelstoel, rystoel; **~ horse** hobbelperd

rock: ~pigeon bosduif, kransduif; **~rabbit** das(sie); **~y** rotsagtig, klipperig

rod stang, staaf; roede

rode *see* **ride**

rod'ent (n) knaagdier; (a) knaag=; *~ ex= terminator* rott(te)vanger

roe takbokooi; **~buck** gemsbok (Bybel)

rogue skurk, skelm, karnallie, vabond; *~ elephant* dwaalolifant

role rol, funksie

roll (n) rol, register; broodjie; gerol; *call the ~,* appèl hou; *~ of honour,* ererol; (v) rol, oprol; *~ one's R's,* bry; *~ up,* oprol; opdaag; **~call** appèl, naamlesing; **~ed gold** goudpleet

roll'er roller; rolstok; *~ blind* rolgordyn; *~ mill* walsmeule; *~ skate* rolskaats

roll'ick (n) pret, uitgelatenheid, fuif; (v) baljaar, vrolik wees

roll'ing golwend, rollend; *~ pin* deegroller; *~ press* (-es) rolpers; *~ stock* rollende materiaal (spoorweg)

rol'y-pol'y (n) rolpoeding; klein vetsak, diksak, potjierol

Rom'an (n) Romein; romein (letter); (a) Romeins; Rooms; *~ Catholic* Rooms-Katoliek

romance' (n) romanse; verdigting, versin= sel, romantiek; (v) spek skiet; oordryf

roman'tic romanties; **~ism** romantiek; **~ist** romantikus

Rome Rome; *~ was not built in a day,* Rome is nie in een dag gebou nie; *do in ~ as the Romans do,* skik jou na die om= standighede

romp (v) stoei, baljaar, jakker, ravot; *~ home,* maklik eerste kom

ronda'vel rondawel

roof (n) (-s) dak; verhemelte (van mond); gewelf; *thatched ~,* grasdak; **~carrier** dakrak, bagasierak (motor); **~clutcher** dakvink (motoris); *~ garden* daktuin; **~less** dakloos; *~ ridge* vors; **~wetting** dakviering, huisinwyding

rook (n) bedrieër; (v) bedrieg; geld afpers

room (n) kamer, vertrek, ruimte; **~y** ruim, groot

roost (n) slaapplek; stok; *go to ~,* gaan slaap; *rule the ~,* baasspeel

roos'ter hoenderhaan

root (n) wortel; stam; oorsprong; bron; *the ~ of all evil,* die wortel van alle kwaad; (v) wortelskiet; *~ up,* uitroei

rope (n) tou, lyn; *know the ~s,* goed inge= lig/touwys wees; (v) vasbind; **~ladder** touleer; **~walker** koorddanser

ros'ary (..ries) rosekrans, paternoster

rose (n) roos; rooskleur; roset; sproeier (gieter); *under the ~,* in die geheim; (a) rooskleurig; **~ apple** jamboes; **~bud** roosknop; *~ bush* (-es) roosstruik; **~mallow** stokroos

rose'mary (..ries) roosmaryn

rosette' roset, kokarde

ros'in (n) harpuis; (v) met harpuis bestryk

ros'trum (..tra, -s) snawel, bek; rostrum, podium

ros'y rooskleurig, blosend

rot (n) verrotting; onsin; *dry ~,* vermol= ming; *tommy ~,* kaf, onsin; bog; (v) (-ted, -ted) verrot, vergaan, verkwyn; terg

rot'ary ronddraaiend, rondgaand, roterend; *~ lawnmower* rotasie(gras)snyer

rotate' draai, wentel, roteer; afwissel (ge= saaides)

rota'tion rotasie, wenteling; *by ~,* rota= siegewys; *~ of crops,* wisselbou

rott'en verrot, bederf; sleg, vrotsig

rotund' rond, bolvormig; vet, omvangryk

rough (n) ruveld (gholf); (v) ru behandel; touwys maak; *~ it,* jou ongemakke ge=

troos; (a) ru, grof; ruig; *make a ~ guess,*
naastenby skat; **~-and-tumble** (n) geveg,
worsteling; (a) verward, deurmekaar,
woes; **~book** kladboek, klad; **~ draft**
konsep; **~ly** ru; naastenby, ruweg; **~**
manners onbeskaafde maniere; **~ness**
ruheid, oneffenheid, ongelykheid; **~ play**
ruwe spel; **~rider** perdetemmer; baas=
ruiter

roulette' dobbelwiel

round (n) rondte (om baan); rondgang,
rondte (polisie); kring; ronde (boks,
stoei); rondreis; rondedans; patroon;
skoot, laag; **~s** *of cartridge,* patrone; *go*
one's ~, sy rondte doen; (a) rond;
gerond; **~** *figures,* rondesyfers, globale
syfers; (adv, prep) rondom, in die rondte;
bring ~, bybring (na 'n floute); *show ~,*
rondneem; **~ed** gerond, afgerond; **~ly**
ronduit, botweg; sirkelvormig; **~ness**
rondheid, volheid; **~ robin** rondomtalie
(speelpatroon); **~ up** bymekaarmaak
(vee); klopjag

round-table conference tafelronde

rouse wakker maak; wek, opja

route (n) pad, koers, roete; *en ~,* onderweg

routine' sleur, gewoonte, roetine

row[1] (n) ry; reeks; *in ~s,* in rye

row[2] (v) roei

row[3] (n) geraas, lawaai; rusie; *kick up a ~,*
lawaai maak; **~dy** rumoerig, stormagtig

roy'al koninklik; rojaal, uitstekend; eer=
steklas; *a ~ time,* 'n heerlike tyd; **~**
game kroonwild; **~ist** rojalis, koning(s)=
gesinde; **~ty** koningskap; outeursaan=
deel; vrugreg (myn)

rub (n) wrywing; knoop, moeilikheid;
there's the ~, daar lê die knoop; (v) **(-bed,**
-bed) skaaf; blink maak; vryf; skuur; **~**
shoulders with, in aanraking kom met; **~**
one the wrong way, iem. verkeerd aanpak

rubb'er gomlastiek, rubber; wisser, uit=
veër; **~ stamp** stempel, tjap

rubb'ish vullis, vuilis; rommel; onsin, kaf;
~ removal vullisverwydering

rub'ble puin; rommel, vuilgoed

ru'by (rubies) robyn; robynkleur

ruck'sack rugsak, knapsak

ruc'tion rusie, twis, oproer

rudd'er roer, stuur

rude onbeskaaf; onbeskof; **~ness** onbe=
skoftheid

ru'diment grondslag, beginsel; (pl) grond=
beginsels, eerste beginsels

ruff'ian (n) booswig, skurk, woestaard

ruf'fle (n) plooi; verwarring; (v) frommel,
plooi, kreukel; **~d hair,** deurmekaar hare

rug (reis)deken; vloerkleed

rug'by rugbyvoetbal

rugg'ed ru; nors; stoer, gehard

ru'in (n) bouval, ruïne, murasie; (pl) bou=
val, ruïne

rule (n) reël; reglement; maatstaf; bewind;
liniaal; *the golden ~,* die gulde reël; *hard*
and fast ~s, vaste reëls; **~** *of law,* reg=
soewereiniteit; **~** *of the road,* verkeers=
reël; (v) reël, vasstel; regeer; linieer; **~** *out*
of order, buite die orde verklaar; **~** *out,*
uitskakel; **~** *the roost,* lakens uitdeel; **~r**
heerser, regeerder; bewindhebber; liniaal

ru'ling (n) beslissing; uitspraak; reëling; (a)
regerend, bewindhebbend; heersend; **~**
party bewindhebbende/regerende party;
~ price heersende prys

rum (n) rum

rum'ble (n) gerommel, geratel; (v) rommel,
ratel, dawer, dreun; **~ strip** dreunstrook
(teerpad)

rum'our (n) gerug; praatjie; *mere/false ~,*
riemtelegram

rump'steak kruisstuk, kruisskyf

rum'pus herrie, moles, opstootjie; **~ room**
jolkamer, gesinskamer

run (n) lopie (krieket); verloop; wedloop;
have a ~ for one's money, waarde vir jou
geld hê; (v) **(ran, run)** hardloop; draf;
stroom, vloei (ink); dryf (saak); laat op=
loop (rekening); **~** *up bills,* **~** *into debt,*
skuld maak; **~** *down,* omry/omloop;
opspoor; slegmaak; **~** *the risk,* die risiko
loop; **~** *a shop,* 'n winkel bestuur; **~** *the*
show, baas wees

run'away (n) **(-s)** weglopèr; (a) gevlug; op
hol; **~ victory** oorrompeling, weghol=
oorwinning

rung[1] (n) sport (van 'n leer)

rung[2] (v) *see* **ring**[1] (v)

runn'er loper, boodskapper; hardloper; **~**
bean rankboon; **~-up** naaswenner

runn'ing (a) stromend, lopend; *three days*
~, drie dae aanmekaar; **~ board** tree=
plank; **~ commentary** (deur)lopende
kommentaar; **~ costs** loopkoste (motor);
~ expenses daaglikse uitgawes; **~ shorts**

drafbroekie; ~ **stomach/tummy** loop=
maag
runt dwerg; misgewas
run'way rolbaan; aanloopbaan/stygbaan
(vliegtuig); stroombed (rivier)
rup'ture (n) breuk; skeuring; (v) breek
rur'al landelik; ~ **district** buitedistrik
rush (v) voortsnel; oorrompel, verras; ~ **at**,
bestorm; ~ **matters**, oorhaastig te werk
gaan; ~ **hour** spitsuur; ~ **time** spitstyd,
see **peak** hour
rusk (boer)beskuit
Ru'ssia Rusland; ~**n** (n) Rus; (a) Russies
rust (n) roes; (v) roes; verroes; laat roes

rus'tic (a) landelik; vreedsaam; eenvoudig,
onbedorwe; lomp, ongemanierd
ru'stle (n) geritsel; (v) ritsel, suisel; vinnig
loop; veediefstal pleeg; ~**r** veedief/vee=
stroper
rust'proofing roeswering
rus'ty roeserig, roesagtig, verroes; stram
rut[1] (n) waspoor, groef; gewoonte, roetine;
slaggat; sleur
rut[2] (n) hitsigheid, bronstyd, loopsheid
ruth medelye; verdriet; ~**less** onbarmhartig,
meedoënloos, wreed
rutt'ish hitsig/hittig, brons, loops
rye rog; ~ **bread** rogbrood

S

Sabb'ath Sabbat, rusdag; ~ **breaker** Sab=
batskender
sabbat'ic sabbat=; ~**al leave** sabbatsverlof
(vir studie/navorsing)
sa'ble antelope swartwitpens(bok)
sab'otage (n) sabotasie; (v) saboteer, on=
dermyn, rysmier, ondergrawe
saboteur' saboteur, ondermyner
sa'bre (n) sabel; (v) neersabel; ~ *rattling*,
wapengekletter
sack[1] (n) sak
sack[2] (n) ontslag; plundering; *give the* ~,
ontslaan, in die pad steek; *get the* ~, die
trekpas kry; (v) afdank, afsê, ontslaan;
plunder
sac'rament sakrament
sac'red heilig, gewyd; ~ *to the memory of*,
ter nagedagtenis aan
sac'rifice (n) offer, offerande; opoffering;
make the supreme ~, die hoogste offer
bring; (v) offer; opoffer
sac'rilege heiligskennis, ontheiliging
sad treurig, droewig, somber; ~**den** treurig
maak; bedroef; treurig word
sad'dle (n) saal; stut; (v) opsaal; belas, op=
skeep; *be* ~**d** *with*, opgeskeep sit met; ~
girth buikgord; ~ **horse** ryperd; ~**r**
saalmaker; ~**ry** (..ries) saalmakery; ~**tree**
saalboom
sadis'tic (a) sadisties
sad'ness droefheid, treurigheid, verdriet
safa'ri safari, jagtog
safe[1] (n) brandkas, kluis; geldkis; koskas
safe[2] (a) veilig, seker; ~ *and sound*, fris en
gesond; ~ **conduct** vrygeleide; ~ **custody**

versekerde/veilige bewaring; ~ **deposit**
bewaarkluis; ~**guard** (n) beskerming,
vrygeleide; beveiliging; (v) beskerm;
vrywaar
safe'ty veiligheid; sekerheid; ~ **belt** veilig=
heidsgordel, redgordel; ~ **lamp** veilig=
heidslamp; ~ **match** (-es) (Sweedse)
vuurhoutjie; ~ **pin** haakspeld; ~ **razor**
veiligheidskeermes
saff'ron (n) saffraan; saffraankleur
sag (v) (-ged, -ged) afsak, hang, sak; daal
sa'ga (-s) sage, volksverhaal, legende; saga,
heldegeskiedenis
sage (n) salie
sag'o sago
said het gesê; genoemde
sail (n) seil; (v) vaar, uitseil; ~**cloth** seildoek
sail'ing afvaart; ~ **vessel** seilskip
sail'or matroos
saint (n) heilige; (a) heilig; ~**ly** heilig,
vroom
sake: *for the* ~ *of*, ter wille van; *for your*
~, om jou ontwil; *for goodness'* ~, in
hemelsnaam
sal'ad slaai; ~ **dressing** slaaisous; ~ **oil**
slaaiolie
sal'amander koggelmander; sal(a)mander
sal'ary (n) (..ries) salaris, loon, besoldiging;
(v) (..ried, ..ried) besoldig, salarieer; ~
negotiable, salaris reëlbaar
sale verkoop, (uit)verkoping, prysfees; vei=
ling; vandisie, vendusie; *for* ~, te koop;
put up for ~, opveil; ~ **price** verkoop=
prys; ~**s'man** (..men) verkoper, verkoop=

man; ~s'manship verkoopkuns; ~s
manager verkoopbestuurder
sal'es verkope, afset
sal'ient uitstaande; treffend, opvallend
sal'ine (n) sout; soutpan; (a) soutagtig
saliv'a spoeg, spuug, speeksel
salm'on (n) salm; (a) salmkleurig
saloon' saal, salon; eetsaal, kantien
salt (n) sout; take with a grain of ~, nie te
letterlik opvat nie; (v) sout; insout, pekel;
~less soutloos, laf; ~pan soutpan
salpet're salpeter
sal'utary heilsaam, weldadig; ~ effect,
heilsame uitwerking
saluta'tion groet, begroeting, aanhef
salute' (n) saluut; take the ~, die saluut
beantwoord; (v) salueer
sal'vage (n) berging; bergloon; wrakgoe-
dere; (v) berg, red; ~ ship/vessel ber-
gingskip
salva'tion saligheid, redding, verlossing;
work out one's own ~, jou eie redding
bewerk
Salva'tion: ~ Army Heilsleër
sal'vo (-es) salvo, sarsie; uitvlug
Sama'ritan (n) Samaritaan; good ~, barm-
hartige Samaritaan; (a) Samaritaans
same dieselfde; eenders; gelyksoortig; one
and the ~, presies dieselfde
samp stampmielies
sa'mple (n) monster; steekproef; (v) mon-
sters neem; proe; toets; ~r patroon;
toetser
sa'mpling monsterneming
sanator'ium (..ria) sanatorium
sanc'tify (..fied, ..fied) heilig, heilig maak
sanctimon'ious skynheilig, skynvroom
sanc'tion (n) goedkeuring; toestemming;
(ekonomiese) strafmaatreël, sanksie; (v)
bekragtig, goedkeur
sanc'tuary (..ries) toevlugsoord, heiligdom;
bird ~, voëlreservaat
sand (n) sand; (pl) strand
san'dal sandaal
sand: ~ glass (-es) sandloper; ~man Klaas
Vakie; ~paper skuurpapier; ~stone
sandklip, sandsteen
sand'wich (n) (-es) toebroodjie; (v) inskuif,
tussenin sit; ~ man plakkaatdraer
sand'y sanderig
sane verstandig, gesond (van gees)
sang see sing

san'itary sanitêr, gesondheids-; ~ officer
gesondheidsbeampte
sank see sink² (v)
San'ta Claus Sinterklaas; Kersvader
sap (n) sap, sop, vog; lewenskrag; (v)
(-ped, -ped) tap; verswak
sap'ling jong boompie
sapp'er sappeur
sapph'ire saffier
sarcas'tic sarkasties, spottend, bytend
sardine' sardientjie; sardyn
sash¹ (-es) lyfband, serp
sash² (-es) raam; ~ window skuifraam
sat see sit
Sat'an Satan; duiwel
satch'el handsakkie; boeksak, skooltas
sat'ellite satelliet; volgeling, naloper
sat'in (n) satyn; (a) satyn-
sat'ire satire, spotskrif, hekelskrif
sati'rical satiries, spottend
satisfac'tion voldoening, bevrediging, genoeë; to the ~ of, tot bevrediging van
satisfac'tory bevredigend; voldoende, toereikend, genoegsaam
sat'isfied tevrede; versadig, bevredig; ~
with, daarvan oortuig, tevrede met
sat'isfy (..fied, ..fied) bevredig; voldoen
aan; versadig; gerusstel; ~ the examiners,
slaag
sat'urate versadig; vul; deurweek, satureer;
~d deurtrek, deurweek
Sat'urday Saterdag
sat'yr sater, bosgod; wellusteling
sauce (n) sous; hunger is the best ~, honger
is die beste kok; ~boat souskom(metjie);
~pan kastrol
sau'cer piering
saun'ter (n) drentelpas, slentergang; (v)
slenter, drentel
sau'sage wors, sosys; ~ roll worsbroodjie
sav'age (n) barbaar; (v) toetakel, mishandel; (a) barbaars
savann'ah savanne, grasvlakte
save¹ (v) red, verlos, salig maak; spaar,
bêre; bewaar, behoed; ~ one's skin,
heelhuids daarvan afkom; jou bas red
save² (prep) behalwe; uitgesonder; (conj)
tensy; the last ~ one, die voorlaaste
sav'ing (n) besparing; (pl) spaargeld; (a)
spaarsaam; ~s bank spaarbank
Sav'iour Heiland, Saligmaker, Redder
sav'our (v) proe; ruik; ~ of, ruik na; laat

dink aan; ~y (n) (..ries) soutigheid, southappie
saw¹ (n) saag; (v) (-ed, -n) saag
saw² (v) see see²
saw: ~dust saagsel; ~pit saagkuil; ~yer saer; drywende boomstam
sax'ophone saxofoon
say (n) mening, bewering; have a ~ in the matter, seggenskap in die saak hê; (v) (said, said) sê, vertel, beweer; never ~ die, moenie moed opgee nie; so to ~, as 't ware/aanware
say'ing gesegde, spreekwoord; it goes without ~, dit spreek vanself
scab roof; skurfte; brandsiek(te)
scaff'old steier; skavot; ~ing steierwerk, stellasie
scald (v) skroei, brand; opkook; uitkook
scale¹ (n) skaal; toonladder; on a large ~, grootskaals; grootskeeps; (v) opklim, beklim; ~ down, afskaal
scale² (n) skub (vis); skilfer; dopluis
scale³ (n) weegskaal; pair of ~s, (weeg)skaal; (v) weeg; trek
scall'op (n) kammossel; skulp; skulpwerk; (v) uitskulp; ~ed edge skulprand
scal'lywag vabond, bedrieër, skelm
scalp (n) skedel; kopvel; (v) skalpeer; kwaai kritiseer; ~ hunter trofeejagter
scal'pel ontleedmes, skalpeermes
scal'y skubberig, skilferig
scamp skelm, skurk, vabond
scan (-ned, -ned) skandeer; noukeurig ondersoek; vluglees, glylees; aftas; brain ~ flikkergram
scan'dal skandaal, skande; ~monger skinderbek, kwaadspreker; ~ous skandelik, skandalig
scan'sion skandering
scant (a) skraal, karig; with ~ success, met weinig sukses
scant'y karig, skraal, skraps; ~-panty amperbroekie, einabroekie, sjoebroekie
scape'goat sondebok, skuldlose
scar (n) litteken, skrap; (v) (-red, -red) skram; toegaan (seer); littekens vorm
scarce skaars, skraps; seldsaam; make oneself ~, sorg dat jy wegkom; ~ly skraps, nouliks, kwalik, ternouernood
scare (n) paniek, skrik; (v) skrik maak; afskrik; ~ away, wegjaag; ~crow voëlverskrikker

scarf (n) (scarves) serp, halsdoek
scar'let (n) skarlaken, skarlakenrooi; (a) skarlakenrooi; ~ fever skarlakenkoors
scathe (n) letsel; without ~, ongedeer(d)
scatt'er verstrooi, versprei; uitstrooi; ~-brained warhoofdig, deurmekaar
scav'enge opruim; reinig, skoonmaak; ~r straatveër; aasvoël; ~r beetle miskruier, also dung beetle
scenar'io draaiboek, filmteks
scene toneel, tafereel; skouspel; it is not my ~, dis nie vir my nie; ~ry (..ries) natuurskoon, landskap; toneeldekorasie, dekor
scen'ic toneel=; skilderagtig; ~ railway bergspoor
scent (n) geur, reuk; reukwerk, laventel
scep'tic (n) twyfelaar, skeptikus; (a) skepties, ongelowig; ~ism skeptisisme
scep'tre septer, staf
sched'ule (n) lys, skedule, opgawe, inventaris, staat, tabel; (v) skeduleer; inventariseer; lys; ~d flight roostervlug
scheme (n) skema, plan, ontwerp; skets; (v) ontwerp; planne maak; konkel
schol'ar leerling; geleerde; beurshouer; ~ly geleerd, (vak)kundig; ~ patrol skolierpatrollie; ~ship studiebeurs
school¹ (n) skool; skoolgebou; leerskool; at ~, op skool; attend ~, 'n skool besoek; dualmedium ~, dubbelmediumskool; keep after ~, laat skoolsit; (v) onderwys, leer, onderrig; skool
school² (n) skool (visse); ~ of fish, skool visse
school: ~ attendance officer skoolbesoekbeampte, lammervanger; ~board skoolraad; ~boy skoolseun; ~ holiday(s) skoolvakansie; ~ing opvoeding; onderrig; skoling; ~ inspector skoolinspekteur; ~leaver skoolverlater; ~master skoolmeester, onderwyser; ~ mistress (-es) onderwyseres; ~ principal skoolhoof, hoofonderwyser; ~room skoolkamer, klaskamer; ~teacher onderwyser(es)
schoon'er skoener
sciat'ic heup=; ~a heupjig
sci'ence natuurwetenskap; wetenskap; kennis, kunde; ~ fiction wetenskapfiksie
sci'entist wetenskaplike, natuurkundige
sci'ssors skêr; a pair of ~, 'n skêr
scoff (n) bespotting, skimp; (v) spot, skimp; ~er spotter; ~ing smalend

scold (n) feeks; rissie; neulpot; (v) uitskel, berispe, bestraf; **~ing** (n) uitbrander
scone skon, botterbroodjie
scoop (n) potlepel, skeplepel; nuustreffer, scoop (joernalistiek); *make a big* **~**, 'n groot slag slaan; (v) uitskep; uithol; wins maak; **~ wheel** skeprat
scoot'er bromponie; voetperd, skopfiets
scope gesigskring; omvang; speling; *beyond the* **~** *of*, buite die bestek van
scorch brand, skroei, verseng; blaak; **~ed earth**, versengde/verskroeide aarde; **~er** doodhou, kishou, pragstuk
score (n) kerf; rekening; rede; twintigtal; telling; partituur (musiek); *keep the* **~**, telling hou; aantekening hou; **~s of times**, baiemaal; (v) inkerf; aanteken; tel; onderstreep; **~** *a success*, sukses behaal; **~board** telbord; punteleer; **~r** teller; puntemaker
scor'ing board telbord
scorn (n) veragting, hoon; *put to* **~**, beskaam; (v) verag, versmaad; versmaai
scorp'ion skerpioen
scotch (n) (**-es**) kerf, keep; wig; (v) kerf; onskadelik maak; verydel; **~cart** skotskar; **~light** glimstrokies, glimplate
scot-free ongedeerd; ongestraf, skotvry
scoun'drel skelm, skurk, boef, skobbejak
scour[1] (n) maagwerking, buikloop; (v) skuur, vryf
scour[2] (v) rondsoek; fynkam; **~** *the area*, die omgewing fynkam
scourge gesel, plaag; (v) kasty, teister
scout (n) spioen, verkenner; padvinder; (v) spioeneer, verken
scout'master troepleier, padvinderleier
scowl (n) suur gesig; frons; (v) suur kyk
scrabb'le gekrabbel, gekrap; (v) krap
scrag (a) brandmaer; **~gy** dun, (brand)maer; verpot
scram (sl.) (v) trap; (interj) trap! siejy!
scram'ble (n) gewoel; (v) klouter; woel; grabbel; roereiers bak; **~** *for*, oormekaarval vir; **~d eggs** roereiers; **~r** veldfiets
scram'bling veldrenne
scrap[1] (n) brok, stuk; oorskot, afval, skroot; (pl) afvalstukkies, uitskot; *not care a* **~**, geen flenter omgee nie; (v) (**-ped, -ped**) skrap; weggooi; afkeur; sloop
scrap[2] (n) vegparty; (v) (**-ped, -ped**) baklei

scrap'book plakboek, knipselboek; kladboek
scrape (n) gekrap, gekras; moeilikheid; (v) skraap, kras; **~** *through*, net deurglip; **~** *together*, bymekaarskraap; **~r** krapper, krapyster; skraper
scrap'heap ashoop, afvalhoop, roeshoop
scrap'iron ysterafval, skroot; **~value** oorskotwaarde, sloopwaarde; **~yard** skrootwerf, wrakwerf
scratch (n) (**-es**) krap, skraap, skram; *start at* **~**, by nul begin; (v) krap, skraap; **~** *a horse*, 'n perd onttrek; **~** *through*, skrap, deurhaal, doodtrek
scrawl (n) slordige skrif, gekrap; (v) krap
scream (n) skree(u), gil; *a perfect* **~**, iets om jou oor slap te lag; (v) skreeu, gil; **~** *with laughter*, skater v.d. lag
scream'ing (a) skreeuend; rasend; **~ly** *funny*, vreeslik snaaks
screech (n) (**-es**) gekras, gekrys, gil; (v) kras, krys, gil; **~** *owl* steenuil, kerkuil
screen (n) skerm; doek; (v) beskerm, beskut; **~** *off*, afskort; **~** *wiper* skermveër; ruitveër
screw (n) skroef; *there is a* **~** *loose*, daar is iets nie pluis nie; (v) vasskroef; **~driver** skroewedraaier; **~jack** domkrag; **~nut** moer; **~** *propeller* skroef
scrib'ble (n) gekrap; (v) krap, krabbel; **~r** kladboek, kladskrif
scribb'ling gekrabbel; **~** *pad* kladblok
scribe skrywer, klerk; skriba; skrifgeleerde
scrimp'y suinig, vrekkerig
script geskrif; manuskrip; draaiboek (film); antwoordskrif (eksamen); **~ural** skriftuurlik; **~ure** die Heilige Skrif, die Bybel; *the (Holy) Scriptures*, die Heilige Skrif
scroll (n) rol; lys; krul; (v) oprol, opkrul
scrub (n) ruigte, struikgewas; (v) (**-bed, -bed**) skrop, skuur; **~bing board** wasplank; **~by** dwerggatig, klein; ruig; **~** *cattle* prulbeeste
scruff nekvel; *take by the* **~** *of the neck*, agter die nek beetkry
scrum (n) skrum; (v) (**-med, -med**) skrum; **~half** (..**halves**) skrumskakel
scru'ple (n) gewetensbeswaar; *a man without* **~**, 'n gewetenlose persoon
scru'pulous nougeset, sorgvuldig; noukeurig; **~ly** *clean*, silwerskoon
scrutineer' stemopnemer; ondersoeker

scru'tinise noukeurig bestudeer/bekyk
scuf'fle (n) worsteling, geharwar
scull'ery (..ries) waskombuis, waskamer
sculp beeldhou; ~tor beeldhouer; ~ture (n) beeldhoukuns; beeldhouwerk; (v) beeldhou
scum (n) skuim, afval; uitvaagsel
scurv'y skeurbuik
scut'tle[1] (n) luik; (v) kelder (skip), laat sink
scut'tle[2] (v) vlug, weghardloop
scythe sens, seis
sea see; ~ breeze seebries; ~ captain skeepskaptein; ~front strandgedeelte; ~grass seegras; wier; ~ gull seemeeu
seal[1] (n) rob, seehond
seal[2] (n) seël, stempel; *under his hand and ~,* deur hom geteken; (v) beseël; verseël, toelak; ~ed orders, verseëlde instruksies
sea'level seespieël, seevlak
seal'ing wax lak
seal'ring seëlring
seal'skin robbevel
seam (n) soom, naat; laag
sea'man (..men) seeman, matroos; able ~, bevare seeman; ~ship seemanskap
sé'ance sitting, séance
sear (v) brand, verskroei, toeskroei
search (n) soek(tog); (v) soek, ondersoek; ~ing (a) deurdringend; skerp; ~light soeklig; ~ party soekgeselskap; ~ warrant lasbrief vir visentering
sea: ~shell seeskulp; ~sick seesiek; ~side resort strandoord
seas'on (n) seisoen, jaargety; speelvak (teater); *out of ~,* ontydig; buiteseisoen; *the ~s,* die jaargetye; (v) toeberei; ~able geskik; geleë; ~al seisoengerig; seisoenaal; ~ed gekruid; beleë; ~ing toebereiding; kruie; ~ ticket seisoenkaartjie
seat (n) sitplek; setel; landgoed; sitting; sitvlak, boom (broek); ~belt (sitplek)gordel, redgordel
sea: ~weed seegras, seewier; ~worthy seewaardig
seclude' uitsluit, afsonder; ~d afgesonder(d), afgeleë
sec'ond (n) sekonde (oorlosie); tweede; ~ in command, onderbevelhebber; tweede in bevel; (v) sekondeer; ~ a motion, 'n voorstel/mosie sekondeer; (a) tweede; ~ cousin, kleinneef; *every ~ day,* al om die ander dag; ~ floor, tweede vloer/verdieping/vlak

second' (v) sekondeer (na ander plek/pos)
sec'ondary (a) sekondêr; ondergeskik; ~ school sekondêre skool, hoërskool
sec'ond class tweede klas
sec'onder sekondant
sec'ond: ~ hand (n) sekondewyser; ~hand (a) tweedehands; ~ly ten tweede, tweedens; ~rate tweederangs; minderwaardig
sec'recy geheimhouding, heimlikheid
sec'ret (n) geheim; *let out a ~,* 'n geheim verklap; (a) geheim, heimlik
secretar'ial sekretaris=, sekretarieel; ~ post sekretariële betrekking
sec'retary (..ries) sekretaris; *private ~,* privaatsekretaris; privaatsekretaresse; ~ bird sekretarisvoël; ~-general (secretaries-general) sekretaris-generaal
sec'ret: ~ly stilletjies; ~ service geheime diens
sect sekte
sectar'ian (a) sektaries
sec'tion afdeling, seksie; deursnee; ~al title deeltitel
sec'tor sektor; *private ~,* privaatsektor; *public ~,* openbare sektor, owerheidsektor
sec'ular wêreldlik, tydelik; sekulêr; ~ power wêreldlike mag; ~ school staatskool (teenoor kerkskool)
secure' (v) verseker, waarborg, beveilig; vasmaak; verkry, bereik; ~d by a bond, gedek deur 'n verband
secur'ity veiligheid, sekuriteit; beveiliging, sekerheid; (..ties) waarborg; (pl) aandele, effekte, obligasies; *collateral ~,* kollaterale sekuriteit, bykomende onderpand; *in ~ for,* as borg vir; *social ~,* bestaansbeveiliging; S~ Council Veiligheidsraad (VN); ~ guard sekerheid(s)wag, sekuriteit(s)wag; ~ police veiligheidspolisie; ~ system sekuriteitstelsel
sed'ative (n) pynstiller; (a) kalmerend
sed'iment besinksel, afsaksel, sediment
seduce' verlei, verlok; ~r verleier
seduc'tive verleidelik, verlokkend
see (v) (saw, seen) sien, kyk; ~ a doctor, 'n dokter raadpleeg; ~ the manager, die bestuurder spreek/sien; ~ off, wegsien, afsien; wegbring, begelei
seed (n) saad; (v) saai; keur (sport); *the first ~,* die eerste gekeurde (speler); ~ling saailing, saaiplant; ~ potato (-es) aartap-

pelmoer; ~y vol saad; armoedig; olik, oes, siekerig

see'ing (n) gesigsvermoë; sien; (conj) aan= gesien; daar; ~ **eye** loerkyker(tjie)

seek (**sought, sought**) soek; begeer, beoog; ~**er** soeker

seem lyk, skyn; *it ~s to me,* dit lyk vir my; ~**ing** skynbaar, oënskynlik; ~**liness** be= taamlikheid, geskiktheid; ~**ly** betaamlik, geskik

seen *see* **see**

seep lek, deursyfer

se'er siener, profeet

see-saw (n) wip(plank); (v) wipplank ry

seethe kook, borrel, sied

segrega'tion afskeiding, segregasie

seis'mograph seismograaf

seize gryp; vasvat; konfiskeer

sel'dom selde, min

select' (v) uitkies, keur, uitsoek; (a) uitge= kies, keurig; ~ **committee** gekose komi= tee; ~**ion** keuse, keur; keuring, seleksie; versameling; ~**ion board** keurraad; ~**ive** selektief; ~*ive reporting,* selektiewe beriggewing; ~**or** selektor (tegn.), keur= der (sport)

self (selves) self; *my poor ~,* arme ek; ~= **confidence** selfvertroue; ~~**conscious** selfbewus; ~**defence** selfverdediging, noodweer; ~**determination** selfbeskik= king; ~~**employed** selfgeëmplojeer, in eie diens; ~~**esteem** selfrespek, eiewaarde; ~~**evident** klaarblyklik, vanselfsprekend; ~~**interest** eiebelang; ~**ish** selfsugtig; ~ ~ **respect** selfrespek; ~~**restraint** selfbe= heersing; ~~**satisfied** selfvoldaan; ~~**ser= vice** selfbediening; ~**service shop** self= dienwinkel, selfbedienwinkel; ~**starter** aansitter; ~~**sufficient** selfgenoegsaam; ~~**supporting** selfondersteunend, self= onderhoudend

sell (v) (**sold, sold**) verkoop, van die hand sit; bedrieg, kul; ~ *by auction,* laat op= veil; ~**er** verkoper

sem'en (semina) saad

semes'ter semester, halfjaar

sem'i half=; ~~**annual** halfjaarliks; ~~**cir= cle** halfsirkel; ~**colon** kommapunt (;); ~~**conscious** halfbewus; ~**detached house** tweelinghuis, skakelhuis; ~**final** voorlaaste (wedstryd), halfeindronde, semifinaal

sem'inary (..ries) kweekskool, seminarie

sem'i-precious halfedel; ~ **stones** halfedel= stene

sem'i-rough sukkelveld (gholf)

sen'ate senaat; ~ **house** senaatsaal

sen'ator senator

send (**sent, sent**) stuur, wegstuur, versend; ~**er** versender, stuurder; afsender; ~~**off** vaarwel, uitgeleide; afskeidsfees

sen'ile kinds; ouderdoms=; afgeleef, seniel

sen'ior (n) superior; hoof; senior; (a) ouer, senior; oudste; hoogste; ~ **citizen** senior burger; ~ **partner** oudste/senior ven= noot

senior'ity voorrang, senioriteit

sensa'tion opskudding, sensasie; *cause a ~,* opskudding veroorsaak; ~**al** sensasio= neel, opspraakwekkend

sense (n) sintuig; betekenis; *common ~,* ge= sonde verstand; *in every ~,* in elke opsig; *five ~s,* vyf sintuie; ~ *of humour,* humorsin; (v) voel, besef, begryp; ~**less** bewusteloos; dwaas

sen'sible verstandig; bewus

sen'sitive fyngevoelig, liggeraak; sensitief

sen'sual sinlik, wellustig

sen'suous sinstrelend; sinlik

sent *see* **send**

sen'tence (n) sin; vonnis; (v) vonnis, veroor= deel

sen'timent gevoel; idee; sentiment

sentimen'tal oorgevoelig, sentimenteel

sen'try (..tries) skildwag

sep'arate (v) skei; afsonder; verdeel; (a) af= sonderlik, apart; ~ *development,* afson= derlike ontwikkeling; *in a ~ envelope,* af= sonderlik

separa'tion skeiding; afsondering

sep'arator afskeier; roomafskeier

Septem'ber September

sep'tic verrottend; septies; ~ **tank** septiese tenk

sep'ulchre graf

seq'uel vervolg, gevolg, resultaat

seq'uence volgorde, opeenvolging; ~ *of events,* die opeenvolging van gebeurte= nisse

sequestra'tion sekwestrasie, konfiskasie

serenade' (n) serenade; (v) serenadeer

serene' kalm, helder, bedaard, deurlugtig

serf (-s) slaaf, lyfeiene; ~**dom** lyfeiein= skap

serge'ant sersant; ~-at-arms (sergeants-at-
  arms) stafdraer; ~-major (sergeants-
  major) sersant-majoor
ser'ial (n) tydskrif; vervolgverhaal; ~
  number volgnommer
ser'ies (same pl), serie, reeks
ser'ious ernstig, plegtig; serieus; bedenk-
  lik (siektetoestand)
serm'on preek, predikasie; the S~ on the
  Mount, die Bergrede
ser'pent slang; serpent; ~ charmer slangbesweerder; ~ine slangagtig, kronkelend
ser'um (sera, -s) serum, entstof
serv'ant bediende, huisbediende, diensmeisie; dienaar; kneg, diensbode; domestic ~, huisbediende, diensmeisie, see
  maid; master and ~, werkgewer en dienaar; public ~, staatsamptenaar; ~ girl
  diensmeisie; bediende
serve dien, bedien; afslaan (tennis); ~ one's
  apprenticeship, leerskap doen; ~ its
  purpose, aan sy doel beantwoord; ~ summons on, dagvaarding bestel/beteken
  aan; ~r afslaner (tennis)
serv'ice (n) diens; kerkdiens; nut; gereg;
  afslaan (tennis); versiening (kar); servies;
  at your ~, tot u diens; (v) versorg, onderhou; versien (motor); ~able diensbaar,
  dienstig; ~ charge diensheffing; tafelgeld
  (restourant); ~ revolver diensrewolwer
serviette' servet
serv'ile slaafs, kruipend
serv'itude serwituut, beperking
se'ssion sitting, sessie; plenary ~, volle sitting
sestet' sekstet
Sesu'to Sesoetoe, Suid-Sotho
set (n) servies; stel; kliek (persone); a ~ of
  books, 'n stel boeke; (v) (set, set) sit;
  bring; plaas; skik; spalk (arm); verhard
  (sement); koers rig op; rig; dek (tafel);
  vasstel; ondergaan (son); golf (hare); ~
  an example, 'n voorbeeld stel; ~ fire to,
  aan (die) brand steek; ~-off, verreken;
  skuldverrekening, skuldvergelyking; ~
  the pace, die pas aangee; ~ the table, die
  tafel dek; (a) a ~ book, 'n voorgeskrewe
  boek; ~back teenslag, terugslag
settee' rusbank, sofa
sett'er jaghond
sett'ing toonsetting; (toneel)dekor; agtergrond

sett'le vestig; vasstel; regmaak; vereffen;
  verreken; bepaal; bylê (twis); ~ an account, 'n rekening vereffen; ~d vas;
  vasgesteld; betaal; ~ment nedersetting;
  vereffening; ~ment plan skikplan; ~r
  kolonis, nedersetter, setlaar
sev'en sewe; ~-single solus-sewe; ~teen
  sewentien; ~teenth sewentiende; ~th
  sewende; ~tieth sewentigste; ~ty (..ties)
  sewentig; ~ty four streepvis
se'ver skei, afsonder; skeur, afsny; ~ relations with, die betrekkinge verbreek met
sev'eral (a) verskeie, verskillende; (pron)
  verskeie, 'n hele paar; ~ others, baie/
  heelparty ander; ~ly afsonderlik
severe' streng; ernstig; kwaai; a ~ blow, 'n
  swaar slag; a ~ winter, 'n strawwe winter
sew (-ed, -ed or -n) werk (met naald en
  gare), naai; ~ on, aanwerk
sew'age rioolvuil, rioolwater
sew'er (n) riool; ~age riolering
sew'ing naaldwerk; ~ machine naaimas-
  jien; ~ needle naald
sex (-es) geslag; seks
sex' appeal sekstrek, seksstraling
sex: ~ drive/urge geslagsdrang; ~ education geslagsonderrig; ~ kitten seks-
  ka(a)tjie
sextett(te)' see sestet
sex'ton koster
sex'ual geslags-, seksueel
shabb'y kaal; toiingrig; skunnig; gemeen
shac'kle (n) skakel; boei, ketting; (pl) boeie,
  belemmering; (v) boei; belemmer
shadd'ock pampelmoes/pompelmoes
shade (n) skadu(wee); koelte, skakering;
  sweempie; a ~ better, 'n ietsie/rapsie
  beter
shad'ow (n) skaduwee; without a ~ of
  doubt, sonder die minste twyfel; (v) ongemerk volg
shad'y skaduryk, lommerryk; verdag
shaft pyl; skag (myn); steel (gholf); straal
  (lig); ~ sinking skagdelwing
shagg'y ruig, harig, wolhaar-
shake (n) skud; skok; in two ~s, in 'n kits;
  (v) (shook, shaken) skud, skok; uitskud;
  badly ~n, baie onthuts; ~ with fear, van
  angs bewe; ~ hands with, die hand gee;
  blad skud; ~ off, afskud; ontslae raak
  van; ~down kermisbed

shak'ing skudding, skud; *give him a good*
~, skud hom goed
shak'y bouvallig; trillerig; onvas
shale skalie
shall (should) sal; moet
shallot' salot
shall'ow (a) vlak; oppervlakkig; ~ness
vlakheid; oppervlakkigheid
sham (n) bedrog, voorwendsel; skyn; (v)
(-med, -med) bedrieg, fop, kul, veins
sham'bles slagplek, bloedbad; deurme=
kaarspul
shame (n) skande; skaamte; *put to* ~, be=
skaam; (v) skaam, beskaam; (interj) foei
tog! sies tog! ~ful skandelik; ~less
skaamteloos, onbeskaamd
sham: ~ fight spieëlgeveg, skyngeveg;
~mer aansteller, veinsaard
shamm'y seemsleer
shampoo' (n) harewas(middel), sjampoe
sham'rock klawer(blaar)
shan'dy (..dies) shandy, limonadebier
shan'ty (..ties) pondok, krot; hok; ~town
blikkiesdorp; krotbuurt, slum
shape (n) vorm; gedaante; gestalte; *take* ~,
vaste vorm aanneem; (v) vorm; maak; fat=
soeneer; *see how things* ~, kyk/sien hoe
sake ontwikkel; ~less wanstaltig, vorm=
loos; ~liness welgemaaktheid; ~ly wel=
gevorm
share¹ (n) deel, porsie; aandeel; (v) deel,
verdeel; ~ *alike,* gelykop deel
share² (n) ploegskaar
share: ~ broker aandelemakelaar, effekte=
makelaar; ~ capital aandelekapitaal;
~holder aandeelhouer; ~holding aan=
deelhouding
shark haai; skurk; uitsuier, swendelaar
sharp (n) kruis; (v) bedrieg, kul; (a) skerp;
skerpsinnig; bitsig; listig; ~ contrast,
skrille kontras; ~ practices, kullery,
knoeiery; (adv) presies; gou; *at five* ~,
klokslag vyfuur; ~en skerp maak, slyp;
~shooter skerpskutter, sluipskutter;
~-sighted skerpsiende; skerpsinnig;
~-witted geestig, gevat, skrander
shatt'er verbrysel, verpletter; verstrooi; ~=
proof splintervry
shave (n) noue ontkoming; skeer; *a close* ~,
naelskraap; (v) (-d, -d or -n) skeer; skaaf;
~ off afskeer

shav'ing krul (hout); skeerdery; (pl) krulle,
skaafsels; ~ brush (-es) skeerkwas; ~
strop skeerriem
shawl tjalie, sjaal
she sy
sheaf (n) (sheaves) gerf; (v) in gerwe bind
shear (v) (-ed, shorn) skeer; knip; pluk;
~ing time skeertyd; ~s skaapskêr; tuin=
skêr
shebeen' smokkelkroeg, sjebeen
she'-cat katwyfie
shed¹ (n) loods, skuur, afdak
shed² (v) (shed, shed) stort, vergiet; ~
blood, bloed vergiet; ~ light upon, lig
werp op; ~ a skin, vervel; ~ tears, trane
stort
sheen glans, skittering
sheep (sing. and pl.) skaap; ~fold skaap=
kraal; ~ish onnosel, dom; ~ pen skaap=
kraal, hok; ~'s eye skaapogie; ~skin
skaapvel; bokjol; ~'s trotters skaap=
pootjies
sheer (a) louter, volstrek; *by* ~ *force,* deur
brute krag; ~ nonsense, pure onsin
sheet (n) laken; vel (papier); blad; plaat
(sink); ~ iron plaatyster
she'-goat bokooi
sheikh sjeik; vroueveroweraar
shelf (shelves) plank; rak; plaat; rotslaag; *on
the* ~, afgedank, gebêre; op die bakoond
(meisie); ~ life rakleeftyd
shell (n) skil; skulp; peul; dop; uitdop (van
erte); (v) skil; bombardeer; ~fish (-es)
skulpdier; ~shock bomskok; ~y skulp=
agtig
shel'ter (n) skuilplek; ~ed occupation be=
skutte/beskermde werk/beroep; (v) be=
skut, beskerm; ~less sonder heenkome
shelve bêre, weglê, wegsit; van rakke voor=
sien; op die lang baan skuif
shel'ving (n) rakke; rakplanke; uitstel
shep'herd (n) veewagter, skaapwagter,
herder; *the good S*~, die goeie Herder; (v)
oppas; ~ess (-es) herderin
she'riff (-s) balju, geregsbode
she'rry sjerrie
shield (n) skild; beskerming; (v) beskerm
shift (n) verskuiwing, verwisseling; skof; (v)
verander, verwissel; vervang; verhuis; ~
boss (-es) ploegbaas; ~ing (n) verande=
ring; verskuiwing; (a) veranderlik; ~ing
spanner skroefsleutel

shin skeen, maermerrie
shine (n) skyn, glans; (v) (shone, shone) skyn, glinster, blink; straal; uitblink
shing'le (n) dakspaan, dakplankie; (v) met dakspane dek; stomp knip (hare)
shing'les gordelroos
shin'guard skeenskut
shin'y blink, glansend
ship (n) skip; (v) (-ped, -ped) verskeep, laai; ~broker skeepsmakelaar; ~load skeepslading, skeepsvrag; ~ment verskeping; lading; ~ping skeepvaart; verskeping; ~ping agent skeepsagent; ~ing firm/line skeepsredery; ~'s captain skeepskaptein; ~shape in orde, agtermekaar; ~hold skeepsruim; ~wreck (n) skipbreuk; (v) skipbreuk ly; ~yard skeepswerf
shirk vermy, ontduik; wegskram; ~er pligversaker, pligversuimer, ontduiker
shirt hemp; bet one's ~, wed al wat jy het; keep your ~ on, moenie kwaad word nie; ~ collar hempsboordjie; ~ sleeve hempsmou
shit kak, stront; vrotsige vent
shiv'er (n) rilling, siddering; (v) bewe, bibber; sidder, ril
shiv'ering bewend, rittelend
shoal¹ (n) klomp; skool (visse); trop; (v) wemel; skole vorm; saamskool
shoal² (n) sandbank; vlak plek; (a) vlak
shock (n) skok, botsing; (v) skok; aanstoot gee; vererg; delayed ~, vertraagde skok
shock' absorber skokbreker, skokdemper
shock'ing verskriklik, yslik; skokkend
shock' troops skoktroepe
shod see shoe
shodd'y (n) (shoddies) prulwol, bog; (a) versions, armoedig
shoe (n) skoen; hoefyster; (v) (shod, shod) beslaan; ~black skoenpoetser; ~brush (-es) skoenborsel; ~horn skoenlepel; ~lace skoenriem, skoenveter; ~last skoenlees, ysterlees; ~maker skoenmaker; ~shine skoenpoets
shone see shine
shoot¹ (n) skoot; (v) (shot, shot) skiet; verskiet (ster); ~ down, neerskiet; prices shot up, pryse het die hoogte ingeskiet
shoot² (n) spruit, loot; (v) (shot, shot) uitbot, uitloop; ~ forth buds, knoppe gee
shoot'ing (n) skiet; jag; (a) skietend, skiet=; ~ licence jaglisensie; ~ range

skietbaan; ~ season jagtyd; ~ star vallende ster
shoot' out skietery, skietgeveg
shop (n) winkel; closed ~, geslote geledere; talk ~, vakpraatjies praat/gesels; (v) (-ped, -ped) inkope doen; ~ assistant winkelbediende; ~breaking winkelinbraak; ~keeper winkelier; ~lifter winkeldief; ~lifting winkeldiefstal; ~ping inkopery; go ~ping, inkopies doen; ~ ping centre winkelsentrum; ~soiled winkelslyt; ~steward werkerskakel; fabriek(s)middelaar; ~walker klerkopsigter, winkelopsigter; ~window winkelvenster
shore¹ (n) kus, strand
shore² shorn (v) see shear (v)
short (n) tekort; kortsluiting; (a) kort, klein; beperk; a ~ cut, kortpad; ~ verhaal; fall ~ of, te kort skiet; ~ but sweet, kort maar kragtig; ~age tekort; ~bread broskoek, krummelkoek; ~ circuit kortsluiting; ~en verkort
short'hand snelskrif, stenografie; ~ typist snelskriftikster; ~ writer snelskrywer, stenograaf
short: ~ly netnou, binnekort; ~s kortbroek; ~sighted kortsigtig; bysiende, stiksienig, miopies; ~wave kortgolf; ~winded kortasem
shot (n) skut (persoon); hael; skoot (geweer); close ~, digby-opname (film); like a ~, bliksemsnel; putting the ~, gewigstoot; (v) see shoot; ~gun haelgeweer; ~put gewigstoot
should sou see shall
shoul'der (n) skouer; skof; blad (dier); give the cold ~, die rug toekeer; straight from the ~, op die man af; ~ strap skouerband
shout (n) skree(u); ~s of applause, toejuiging; (v) uitroep, skree(u); juig; ~ for joy, jubel van vreugde; ~ with laughter, skaterlag
shove (n) stoot, stamp; (v) skuif, stoot
shov'el (n) skopgraaf; (v) (-led, -led) skep
show (n) tentoonstelling, skou, vertoning; putting his chickens on ~, sy hoenders skou; Easter S~, Paastentoonstelling, Paasskou; give the ~ away, die aap uit die mou laat; (v) (-ed, -n) wys, toon, laat sien; tentoonstel, skou; ~ mercy, genade be=

toon; ~ *of force/strength* magsvertoon;
~ *off,* spog, pronk; ~*ing off,* wind=
makerig; ~ **business** verhoogkuns; ~**case**
toonkas, toonkabinet; ~**down** beslissende
stryd/stadium

show'er (n) reënbui; stortbad; (v) begiet,
besproei, reën, stort; ~ *upon,* oorlaai
met; ~ **bath** stortbad; ~**y** buierig

show: ~**girl** verhoogmeisie, pronkdoedie;
~**ground** skougrond, tentoonstellings=
terrein; ~**house** skouhuis, (ver)toonhuis;
~**-in** aandeel, seggenskap; ~ **jumping**
ruitersport, perdespringkompetisie; ~**-**
room toonlokaal, uitstalkamer; ~ **win=**
dow toonvenster, uitstalvenster

shrank *see* **shrink**

shrap'nel granaatkartets, skrapnel

shred (n) reep; snipper; *torn to* ~s, in flen=
ters; (v) (-ded, -ded) snipper, kerf

shrew feeks, wyf, teef, heks, helleveeg

shrewd slu, listig; skrander, oorlams

shrew'mouse (..mice) spitsbekmuis

shriek (n) skree(u), gil; (v) skree(u), gil; ~
with laughter, brul/gier v.d. lag

shrike janfiskaal, laksman

shrill skril, skel, skerp

shrimp garnaal, *see* **prawn;** dwerg

shrine altaar; grafteken, heilige plek

shrink (shrank, shrunk) krimp; ~ *from,*
terugdeins vir; ~ *into oneself,* in jou dop
kruip

shroud (n) lykkleed

shrub struik, bossie; ruigte; *ornamental* ~,
sierstruik; ~**bery** struikgewas, ruigte

shrug (n) skouerophaling; (v) (-ged, -ged)
die skouers optrek/ophaal

shrunk *see* **shrink**

shudd'er (n) huiwering; siddering; *it gives*
one the ~*s,* dit laat 'n mens gril; (v)
huiwer, sidder

shuf'fle (v) skuifel, skommel (kaarte); ~
along, aansukkel

shun (-ned, -ned) vermy, ontwyk

shunt regstoot, rangeer; ~**er** rangeerder;
~**ing yard** rangeerwerf, opstelterrein

shut (v) **(shut, shut)** sluit, toemaak; ~ *one's*
mouth, jou mond hou; ~**ter** luik, blin=
ding, hortjie; sluiter (kamera); *mock*
~**ter,** kammaluik, kammahortjie

shut'tle spoel(tjie); **space** ~ pendeltuig; ~
service pendeldiens

shy (a) skaam, verleë; ~**ness** skamerigheid,
bedeesdheid

sick (n) sieke; *the* ~, die siekes; (a) siek,
krank; mislik; naar; *feel* ~, naar voel;
~**bay** siekeboeg; ~**fund** siekefonds; ~**en**
siek word/maak; naar word; walg

sic'kle sekel

sick: ~ **leave** siekteverlof; ~**ness** siekte,
krankheid; mislikheid; ~**room** siekeka=
mer; ~ **visitor** sieketrooster

side (n) sy, kant; rand; *shake one's* ~, skud
van die lag; *take* ~s, party kies; kant kies;
this ~ *up,* dié kant bo; (v) party kies; ~
with, iem. se kant kies; (a) sy=; ~**board**
buffet; ~**car** syspan(wa); ~ **issue** bysaak;
~**line** byverdienste, liefhebbery; sylyn;
~**step** (n) systap; swenk; (v) (-ped, -ped)
verbyspring, swenk; liemaak; ~**track** (n)
syspoor, wisselspoor; (v) ontwyk; ~**walk**
sypaadjie; ~**-whiskers** bakbaard

sid'ing spoorweghalte; wisselspoor

siege beleg, beleëring

sieve sif

sift sif; uitvra, uitpluis

sigh (n) sug, versugting; (v) sug

sight (n) gesig; skouspel; vertoning; korrel
(geweer); besienswaardigheid; *a* ~ *for*
sore eyes, 'n verruklike gesig; *make a* ~
of oneself, jou belaglik maak; (v) sien;
korrelvat; ~**bill,** ~**draft** sigwissel; ~**ly**
mooi, fraai; ~**seeing** toer van besiens=
waardighede

sign (n) teken, merk; uithangbord; (v)
(onder)teken; 'n teken gee; ~ *on,* aan=
sluit

sig'nal (n) sein, teken, sinjaal; ~ *of*
distress, noodsein; (v) (-led, -led) sein; (a)
merkwaardig; buitengewoon; *a* ~
honour, 'n besondere eer

sig'nature handtekening, naamtekening; ~
tune kenwysie

sig'net seël; ~ **ring** seëlring

signif'icant betekenisvol, beduidend, ge=
wigtig

sign: ~ **language** vingerspraak; ~**post** pad=
teken, wegwyser, predikant; uithangbord;
~**writer** letterskilder

sil'age (n) kuilvoer; (v) inkuil

sil'ence (n) stilte; stilswye; *break* ~, die
stilswye verbreek; (v) laat swyg, laat
bedaar; ~**r** klankdemper (motor); knal=
demper (pistool)

sil'ent swygend; stil; ~ *partner,* stille/rustende vennoot; *remain* ~, stilbly
silhouette' (n) silhoeët, skadubeeld; (v) silhoeëtteer, afteken
silk (n) sy; (a) sy~; ~**en** sy~, syagtig; ~ **hat** keil; ~**worm** sywurm; ~**y** syerig, syagtig
sill drumpel, kosyn; vensterbank
sill'y onnosel, gek, dwaas, verspot, kinderagtig, laf
sil'o (n) (-s) silo, voerkuil; graansuier
silt (n) afsaksel, slik, modder; (v) versand; ~ *up,* toeslik
sil'ver (n) silwer; (v) versilwer; (a) silwer~; ~ **coin** silwermunt; ~ **foil** bladsilwer; ~ **leaf** silwerblaar, silwerblad; ~-**plated** versilwer; ~**smith** silwersmid; ~**ware** silwergoed, silwerware
sim'ilar soortgelyk; gelyksoortig; eenders
similar'ity (..ties) gelyksoortigheid gelykheid, gelykvormigheid, ooreenkoms
sim'ilarly op dieselfde manier, insgelyks, eweneens
simm'er sag kook, stoof; sing (ketel)
sim'ple eenvoudig; onnosel; ~**hearted** eenvoudig, opreg; ~ **interest** enkelvoudige rente; ~ **minded** eenvoudig (van gees)
simplic'ity eenvoud
sim'pleton swaap, dwaas, uilskuiken
sim'plify (..fied, ..fied) vereenvoudig
sim'ply eenvoudig, gewoonweg
sim'ulate veins, naboots, namaak, simuleer
sim'ulator nabootser
simultan'eous gelyktydig; ~**ly** tegelyk(ertyd)
sin (n) sonde; *as ugly as* ~, so lelik soos die nag; (v) (-ned, -ned) sondig, oortree
since (adv) gelede; daarna; (prep) sinds, sedert; (conj) nadat, sinds; omdat, daar, aangesien; vandat; *ever* ~, van toe af
sincere' opreg, suiwer, eg, eerlik; *Yours* ~*ly,* Opreg die uwe, Geheel die uwe
sincer'ity opregtheid, openhartigheid
sin'ew sening, spier; ~**y** gespierd, taai
sin'ful sondig
sing (sang, sung) sing; besing; ~ *one's praises,* iem. se lof verkondig
singe seng, skroei
sin'ger sanger, sangeres
sing'ing sang, gesing; sangkuns; ~ **bird** sangvoël; ~ **class** (-es) sangklas; ~ **lesson** sangles; ~ **master** sangonderwyser

sing'le (n) enkelspel; (v); ~ *out,* uitsoek; (a) enkelvoudig; enkel; *he lost in the* ~*s,* hy het in die enkelspel verloor; ~ **bed** enkelbed; ~ **file** agter mekaar; ~-**hearted** opreg, eerlik; ~ **medium school** enkelmediumskool; ~ **quarters** woonplek vir ongetroudes; ~**s** enkelspel
sing'ly alleen, afsonderlik; een vir een
sing'song deuntjie; sangoefening, jolsang
sing'ular (n) enkelvoud; (a) enkelvoudig; seldsaam; vreemd; sonderling
sing'ularly besonder(lik), by uitnemendheid
sin'ister onheilspellend, skrikwekkend, sinister; ~ **phiz** boewetronie
sink (n) wasbak, aanreg; (v) (sank, sunk) sink; sak; delf (skag); delg (skuld); ~ *differences,* geskille laat rus; ~ *a shaft,* 'n skag grawe; ~ *a ship,* 'n skip kelder (laat sink); ~**er** dieplood, sinklood; ~**hole** sinkgat
sink'ing (n) sink; keldering (skip); ~ **fund** delgingsfonds, amortisasiefonds
sin'us (-es) baai; kromming; (sinus)holte
sip (n) mondjievol, slukkie; (v) (-ped, -ped) slurp, proe-proe, nip
siph'on (n) hewel, sifon; (v) opsuig; hewel, oortap; ~ *petrol out of the tank,* petrol uit die tenk hewel/uitsuig
sir heer, meneer; sir
sire (n) sire; vader; vaar (dier); (v) teel, verwek
sir'en sirene, verleister; mishoring
sirl'oin lendestuk, beeslende
sis'al sisalplant; garingboom
sis'kin sysie
sis'ter suster; verpleegsuster; non; ~-**in-law** (sisters-in-law) skoonsuster; ~**ly** susterlik, teer
sit (sat, sat) sit, gaan sit, plaas neem; ~ *for an examination,* eksamen skryf/aflê; ~ *for one's portrait,* poseer; ~**down strike** sitstaking
site ligging; bouterrein; perseel
sitt'ing (n) sitting, sessie; broeisel (eiers); *at one* ~, in een slag; (a) sittend; ~ **hen** broeishen; ~ **room** sitkamer, voorkamer, voorhuis
sit'uated geleë
situa'tion ligging; plek; toestand, situasie, betrekking, pos; *the* ~ *causes concern,* die toestand wek kommer

six (-es) ses; ~ *of one and half a dozen of the other,* dis vinkel en koljander; **~fold** sesvoudig; **~teen** sestien; **~teenth** sestiende; **~th** sesde; **~th'ly** sesdens, in die sesde plek; **~tieth** sestigste; **~ty** (..ties) sestig

size (n) grootte, omvang; maat; afmeting; (v) rangskik; ~ *up a situation,* sake deurkyk; ~ **stick** maatstok

siz'zle sis, knetter, spat

sjam'bok sambok

skate (n) skaats; (v) skaats; ~ *over thin ice,* jou op gevaarlike terrein begewe; **~board** skaatsplank, skaatsbord

skat'ing rink skaatsbaan

skel'eton geraamte, skelet; *a ~ in the cupboard,* 'n pynlike geheim; ~ **key** (-s) diewesleutel, loper; ~ **map** sketskaart; ~ **staff** skadupersoneel; kernstaf (mil.)

sketch (n) (-es) uitbeelding; (v) skets

ski, skiing (n) (-s) ski, sneeuskaats; (v) (**skiid, skiid**) ski, sneeuskaats; **~boat** skiboot; **~-jet** waterponie

skid (v) (-ded, -ded) gly, rondskuif; uitgly; sleep, rem

skier skiër

skil'ful bekwaam, bedrewe, handig, knap

skill bekwaamheid, bedrewenheid; vaardigheid; **~ed labour** geskoolde arbeid

skim (v) (-med, -med) afskuim, afskep; vluglees, glylees; **~milk** afgeroomde melk

skimp'y skraal, skraps, karig, afgeskeep

skin (n) vel; vlies; bas; *save one's ~,* heelhuids daarvan afkom; *by the ~ of one's teeth,* hittete, naelskraap, ternouernood; (v) (-ned, -ned) afslag; **~deep** oppervlakkig; **~diving** vinduik, swemduik; **~ny** maer

skip[1] (n) hysbak, skip (mynbou)

skip[2] (n) sprong; (v) (-ped, -ped) spring; touspring, riemspring; oorslaan

skip[3] (n) kaptein

skip'per kaptein, skipper

skip'ping rope springtou

skirm'ish (n) (-es) skermutseling

skirt (n) romp; rok; slip, pant; kant, rand, soom; (v) omsoom, omboor

skit parodie, spotskrif, skimpskrif

skit'tle keël, kegel; ~ **alley** keëlbaan, kegelbaan; ~ **pin** keël, kegel

skol'ly skollie, leeglêer, kwaaddoener

skull skedel; doodskop; **~cap** kalotjie, mussie

skunk muishond; smeerlap, vuilis

sky (**skies**) lug, hemel(ruim); **~lark** (n) lewerkie; **~scraper** wolkekrabber; **~ - writing** rookskrif

slab plaat, steen; reep, skyf; ~ *of chocolate,* reep/plak sjokola(de)

slack (n) slapte; (pl) slenterbroek; (v) vertraag, verslap, verflou; (a, adv) slap; traag, lui; laks; *grow ~,* laks word; **~en** laat skiet, verslap; **~er** luiaard; papbroek, lamsak; **~ness** slapheid, traagheid; **~suit** broekpak

slag slak (metaal), smeltsel

slain *see* **slay**

slake les; blus; **~d lime** gebluste kalk

slam (n) harde slag; kap, slag (kaartspel); (v) toeslaan (deur); kritiseer, verdoem

slan'der (n) skinderpraatjies, laster; (v) belaster, skinder; **~er** lasteraar, kwaadspreker; **~ous** lasterlik

slang groeptaal; jargon, sleng

slant (n) skuinste, helling

slap (n) klap, slag; (v) (-ped, -ped) 'n klap gee, slaan; (adv) reg; plotseling; **~dash** (a) voortvarend; halsoorkop; (adv) onverskillig

slash (n) (-es) sny, hou; (v) sny, raps; **~ing** skerp, snydend; vernietigend

slate (n) lei; leiklip; (a) lei-, leikleurig

slate: ~ **pencil** griffie, griffel; ~ **quarry** (**quarries**) leigroef

slaught'er (n) slagting; bloedbad; (v) slag; ~ **cattle** slagbeeste, slagvee; ~ **house** slaghuis, slagplek

slave (n) slaaf; werkesel; (v) swoeg, slaaf

slav'ery slawerny

slav'ish slaafs

slay (**slew, slain**) doodmaak, vermoor

sled, sledge (n) slee; (v) met 'n slee ry

sledge'hammer voorhamer

sleek (v) blink maak; (a) glad, sag, glansend, blink; geslepe, slu, salwend

sleep (n) slaap, vaak; (v) (**slept, slept**) slaap, rus; **~er** slaper; dwarslêer (spoor)

sleep'ing slapend; ~ **accommodation** slaapplek; ~ **bag** slaapsak; ~ **draught** slaapdrank; ~ **partner** rustende vennoot; ~ **sickness** slaapsiekte

sleep: **~less** slaaploos; **~walker** slaapwandelaar; **~y** vaak, slaperig, dooierig

sleet dryfsneeu, ysreën
sleeve mou; mof; *have something up one's ~*, iets in die mou hê; *laugh in one's ~*, in jou vuis lag; *~ link* mouskakel, man= sjetknoop
sleigh slee
slen'der skraal, maer, slank, dun; gering
slept *see* **sleep** (v)
sleuth speurder; **~hound** speurhond
slew *see* **slay**
slice (n) sny, skyf; *a ~ of bread*, 'n sny brood
slick (a) handig, rats; skoon; glad, blink (diere); (adv) presies; glad, skoon
slide (n) gly; skuif; glasskyf; skyfie (foto= grafie); haarknip; (v) gly, glip; skuif; *let things ~*, sake hulle eie gang laat gaan; **~rule** rekenliniaal
slid'ing glyend, dalend; skuif=; **~ door** skuifdeur; **~ rule** rekenliniaal; **~ scale** glyskaal
slight (a) gering, min, effentjies; *not the ~est*, nie die minste nie; **~ly** effentjies, 'n rapsie
slim (v) (**-med, -med**) verslank; (a) slank, tinger, skraal; geslepe, slu
slime slyk, modder, slym
slim: **~ ming** verslanking, vermaering; **~ = ness** slankheid; tingerigheid
slim'y slymerig, glyerig, glibberig; inkrui= perig
sling (n) slingervel; draagband, hangver= band; (v) (**slung, slung**) slinger, swaai; smyt; *~ mud*, met modder gooi
slink (**slunk, slunk**) wegsluip
slip (n) vergissing, fout; stiggie, steggie; kussingsloop; onderrok; *give one the ~*, iem. ontglip; *a ~ of the pen*, 'n skryffout; (v) (**-ped, -ped**) gly, glip; 'n fout maak; *~ one's memory*, jou geheue ontgaan; **~ = cover** stoelkleed; **~ed disc** skyfletsel; **~per** pantoffel, sloffie; **~ = periness** glibberigheid, bedrieglikheid; **~ = pery** glibberig, glyerig; **~shod** slordig, on= presies; **~way** skeepshelling; glipweg (ver= keer); sleephelling
slit (n) slip, spleet; bars, skeur, groef; (v) (**slit, slit**) kloof, splits; sny; bars (hout); **~ trench** grip, skuilsloot
slobb'er (v) kwyl, teem; mors; knoei
slog (**-ged, -ged**) moker, hard slaan; swoeg

slog'an leuse, wagwoord; strydkreet; wek= roep; slagspreuk; verkoopleuse
sloop sloep
slop (n) (pl) vuil water; slap drank; (v) (**-ped, -ped**) mors, vuil maak; **~ basin** spoelkom
slope (n) skuinste, hang, helling; afdraand
slop: **~ pail** slopemmer; **~py** morsig; oor= drewe sentimenteel; **~ sink** opwasbak
slot gleuf, opening; program-item
slot machine (munt)outomaat
slouch (v) lomp loop; slof, sleep
slo'ven: **~liness** slordigheid; **~ly** slordig, morsig, vieslik
slow (v) stadiger gaan, *~ down*, vertraag, verlangsaam; (a) stadig, langsaam; traag; agter (oorlosie); *~ing down of the econ= omy*, afplatting van die ekonomie; *in ~ motion*, in traagtempo; *~ of speech*, swaar van tong; **~coach** draaikous, drentelaar; **~-combustion stove** smeulstoof; **~ motion** traagspoed, traaggang, traag= tempo
sludge modder, slyk, boorslik; rioolslyk
slug'gard luiaard; luiaard, leegloper, luilak; **~gish** lui, traag
sluice (n) sluis; watervoor; (v) uitspoel; vloei; *~ gate* sluisdeur
slum agterbuurt, krotbuurt, slum
slum'ber (n) sluimering; (v) sluimer; **~ing** (n) sluimering; (a) slapend
slump (n) in(een)storting, slapte; (v) inme= kaar sak, in(een)stort
slung *see* **sling** (v)
slur (n) vlek, smet; slordige uitspraak; (v) (**-red, -red**) sleg uitspreek; bemors, besmet
slush slyk, slik, modder; smeltende sneeu; sentimentaliteit; kletspraatjies
slut sloerie; slet; **~tish** slordig, vuil
sly (n): *on the ~*, tersluiks; (a) slu, uitge= slape, listig; slim; skelm; *~ lodger* sluip= slaper; **~ness** lis, sluheid
smack[1] (n) klap, slag; klapsoen; (v) 'n klap gee, slaan; laat klap; *~ one's lips*, met die lippe smak; (adv) vlak, pardoems; *~ up against*, reg teenaan
smack[2] (n) geur, smakie, sweem; *a ~ of pepper*, 'n knypie peper; (v) smaak
small (n): *the ~ of the back*, die kruis; (a, adv) klein; gering, weinig, min; *in the ~ hours*, na middernag; *~ arms* kleinge= were; **~holding** (landbou)hoewe, klein=

smart snout

hoewe; ~ness gierigheid, nietigheid; ~ =
pox (kinder)pokkies; ~ talk kafpraatjies,
geklets
smart¹ (v) skryn, seer maak, pynig
smart² (a) knap; vinnig; slim; modieus; le=
wendig, geestig; netjies, viets; keurig,
elegant; aardig; oulik; wakker; the ~ set,
die hoë lui
smart'ness knapheid, gevatheid; netheid;
deftigheid, swierigheid; handigheid
smash (n) (-es) botsing; breekspul; moker=
hou (tennis); (v) moker; verpletter; ~-up
botsing; in(een)storting
smear (n) vlek, kol; (v) besmeer, besoedel;
~ campaign smeerveldtog
smell (n) reuk, geur, snuf; (v) (smelt, smelt)
ruik; snuffel; ~ a rat, lont ruik
smell'ing: ~ bottle reukbottel, reukflessie;
~ salts reuksout, vlugsout
smelt smelt; see smell (v); ~ing furnace
smeltoond
smile (n) glimlag; give one a ~, vir iem.
glimlag; (v) glimlag; fortune ~s on us, die
geluk lag ons toe
smil'ing vrolik, glimlaggend; keep ~! hou
die blink kant bo!
smirch (n) (-es) klad, vlek, smet
smirk (n) grimlag, gryns; (v) grimlag
smith smid
smithereens' flenters, stukkies
smi'thy (smithies) smidswinkel
smog rookmis
smoke (n) rook, damp; (v) rook; uitrook;
~d rook=, gerook(te); ~less rookloos; ~r
roker; ~r's emporium tabakboetiek;
~screen rookskerm
smok'y rokerig; berook
smooth (v) gelyk maak, laat bedaar; versag;
~ away, glad stryk; (a) gelyk, glad; sag;
vriendelik; vloeiend (styl); a ~ tongue, 'n
gladde tong; ~-tongued vleiend
smoth'er (v) smoor, verstik; onderdruk
smoul'der (n) smeulvuur; (v) smeul
smudge (n) vlek, vuil kol; smet; (v) bevlek,
besmeer
smug (n) selfgenoegsame mens; boekwurm;
(a) selfvoldaan, selfingenome; huigelagtig;
tartend
smug'gle smokkel; ~r smokkelaar
smugg'ling smokkelary
smut (n) roet (van vuur); vuil taal; ~ty be=
smet, vuil; vol roet

snack porsie, happie, peuselhappie; snoep=
ery(e); ligte maaltyd; go ~s, deel; ~bar
peuselkroeg, snoephoekie; ~s versna=
perings
snag kwas; haakplek; I struck a ~, ek het
moeilikheid opgetel/teenspoed gekry
snail slak; go at a ~'s pace, die slakkegang
gaan
snake slang; cherish a ~ in one's bosom, 'n
adder aan jou bors koester; ~ charmer
slangbesweerder; ~ expert slangkenner,
herpatoloog
snap (n) kiekie; slag; hap, byt; pit, energie;
a cold ~, 'n skielike (vlaag) koue; (v)
(-ped, -ped) kraak; knal, klap; breek;
kiek; toeslaan; ~ at, toesnou; ~ debate
blitsdebat; ~dragon leeubekkie; ~pish
bits, driftig, snipperig; ~py vurig,
opgewerk; ~shot (n) kiekie; (v) (-ted,
-ted) kiek, afneem
snare (n) strik, wip, val; (v) vang
snarl (n) knor, snou; (v) knor, grom; ~ed
up, totaal verwar; ~er brompot
snatch (n) (-es) ruk; (v) gryp, wegruk; ~-
and-grab thief grypdief
sneak (v) sluip, verklap; ~ thief (..thieves)
goudief, sluipdief; ~y gluiperig, agter=
baks
sneer (n) spotlag, bytende skerts, hoonlag;
~ing spottend, spot=; honend
sneeze (n) nies; (v) nies; not to be ~d at, nie
te versmaai nie; ~wood nieshout
snide snedig, kwetsend; a ~ remark, 'n
snedige opmerking/aanmerking
sniff (n) gesnuffel; ruik; (v) snuffel, snuif
snigg'er (n) skelm gegiggel; (v) grinnik
snip (n) snippertjie, snytjie; knip; knipsel
snipe (n) snip (voël); domkop; (v) sluipskiet;
~r skerpskutter, sluipskutter
sniv'el (n) getjank, huigelary; (v) (-led,
-led) snotter, huil
snob ploert, flikflooier, inkruiper, snob;
~bery snobisme; ~bish snobisties
snook'er snoeker, potspel
snooze (n) dutjie, slapie; (v) dut, visvang
snore (n) gesnork; (v) snork
snort (n) snork; snuiwer, snorkel, snort (van
duikboot); (v) snuif (perd); proes
snot snot; snotneus
snout snuit, neus, snoet; ~ beetle snuitke=
wer

snow kapok, sneeu; **~ball** sneeubal; **~drop** sneeuklokkie; **~fall** sneeuval; **~flake** sneeuvlok; **~-white** sneeuwit, spierwit; **S~-White** Sneeuwitjie; **~y** spierwit

snub[1] (n) afjak, teregwysing; (v) (-bed, -bed) afsnou, afjak; bestraf; verwerp

snub[2] (a) stomp; **~nose** stompneus, platneus

snuff (n) snuif; snuitsel; *take ~,* snuif; (v) snuif; besnuffel; snuit (kers); **~box** (-es) snuifdoos; **~ers** kerssnuiter

snuf'fle (n) gesnuif; (v) deur die neus praat

snug gesellig, behaaglik, knus; *~'s the word,* geen woord daaroor nie; **~ly** knus, lekker

snugg'le warm toemaak, toedraai; *~ up to,* nader skuif

so so, dus, sodanig; *~ far ~ good,* tot sover goed; *and ~ forth,* ensovoorts; *quite ~!* presies; *~ to say,* as 't ware

soak (v) week, deurweek; drink; *~ed in,* deurtrek van; **~ing** deurdringend, deurweek

soap (n) seep; (v) inseep; *~ bubble* seepblaas, seepbel; *~ suds* seepsop; **~y** seperig, seepagtig; vleierig

soar (v) hoog vlieg, opstyg

sob (n) snik; (v) (-bed, -bed) snik

sob'er (a) matig; sober, nugter; beskeie

sob'singer sniksanger

so'-called sogenaamd, sogenoemd; kastig

socc'er sokker

so'ciable gesellig, aangenaam

so'cial (n) geselligheid, partytjie; (a) sosiaal, maatskaplik; *~ intercourse,* gesellige verkeer; *~ security,* bestaansbeveiliging; *~ worker,* maatskaplike werker/werkster; **~ism** sosialisme; **~ist** sosialis; **~ite** sosialiet

soci'ety (..ties) samelewing, maatskappy, gemeenskap; genootskap, vereniging

sociol'ogy sosiologie

sock (n) (-s) sokkie; *pull up your ~s,* roer jou riete, doen jou bes

sock'et holte; kas (van oog); potjie (heup); sok, huls; *~ joint* koeëlgewrig; *~ spanner* soksleutel

sod (n) sooi, kluit

sod'a soda; *~ fountain* bruisbron, sodapomp

sod'a water sodawater, spuitwater

sod'omy sodomie, homoseksuele omgang

sof'a sofa, rusbank

soft (a) sag, saf, week; soetsappig; gevoelig; verwyf; **~ball** sagtebal; **~drink** alkohol= vrye drank; koeldrank; **~en** sag maak, versag; *~ goods* weefstowwe, wolstowwe, tekstielware; **~-hearted** teerhartig; *~ job* maklike baantjie; *~ pedal* (-led, -led) matig; **~soap** (n) groenseep; vleiery; (v) vlei; *~ spot* teer plek; *~ware* sagteware; programmatuur (komper); **~y** (..ties) goeierd; papperd, sukkelaar

sogg'y papnat, deurweek

soil[1] (n) grond, aarde

soil[2] (n) smet; (v) vuil maak, besoedel

sol'ar son=; *~ eclipse* son(s)verduistering; *~ energy* sonenergie; *~ heating* sonver= warming, sonverhitting; *~ system* sonstelsel

sold *see* **sell**

sol'der (n) soldeersel; (v) soldeer; **~ing iron** soldeerbout

sol'dier soldaat, krygsman; *~'s pay* soldy; **~ly** soldaatagtig, soldatesk, krygshaftig

sole[1] (n) sool; (v) versool

sole[2] (n) tong(vis)

sole[3] (a) enkel, alleen, enigste; *~ rights* alleenreg

sole'ly enkel, alleenlik

sol'emn plegtig, ernstig, statig

soli'cit lok, uitlok, lastig val, onsedelike voorstelle maak; *~ support,* steun werf; **~ing** uitlokking

soli'citor prokureur

sol'id (a) solied, massief; stewig, bestendig; *for four ~ hours,* vier volle ure; **~a'rity** eensgesindheid, solidariteit; *~ contents* kubieke inhoud

sol'id measure kubieke maat

solil'oquy (..quies) alleenspraak

sol'itary (a) eensaam, verlate, allenig; *~ confinement* eensame opsluiting, alleenopsluiting

sol'itude eensaamheid, verlatenheid

solo (soli, -s) solo; **~ist** solis, solosanger

solu'tion oplossing; ontbinding; rubberlym

solve oplos, onbind; uitlê

sol'vent (n) oplosmiddel; (a) solvent

som'bre somber, duister, donker; swaarmoedig; **~ness** somberheid

some (pron) party, sommige; *~ say,* party sê; (a) party, sommige, enige; *to ~ extent,* tot op sekere hoogte; (adv) erg, danig,

baie; ~**body** iemand; ~**how** op een of ander manier; ~**one** iemand
so'mersault bolmakiesie, buiteling; *turn a ~*, bolmakiesie slaan
some'thing iets; ~ *nice*, iets lekkers
some: ~**times** soms, somtyds, partymaal; ~**where** êrens, iewers
somnam'bulist slaapwandelaar, slaaploper
son seun; ~ *of a gun*, swernoter, skobbejak
sona'ta sonate
song lied, sangstuk; poësie; *make a ~ about it*, 'n ophef maak van; *for a mere ~*, vir 'n kleinigheid/bakatel; *the same old ~*, die ou-ou liedjie
son'-in-law (sons-in-law) skoonseun
sonn'et sonnet, klinkdig
so'nny (sonnies) seuntjie, boetie
so'norous welluidend, klankryk
soon gou, gou-gou, spoedig, weldra, binnekort; *as ~ as*, sodra; *the ~er the better*, hoe eerder, hoe beter
soot roet; ~**flake** roetkorreltjie
sooth'ing versagtend; troostend
sooth'sayer waarsêer, fortuinverteller
sophis'ticate verfyn; ~**d** verfynd, kundig; gesofistikeer(d); *a ~d computer*, 'n gesofistikeerde komper/rekenaar
sopp'y nat, papnat; sentimenteel
sopra'no (..ni, -s) sopraan
sor'bit bruissuiker
sor'cerer towenaar, goëlaar
sor'did laag, gemeen, vuil; inhalig
sore (n) seer, sweer, wond; (a) seer, pynlik; *a ~ point*, 'n teer plek; *a sight for ~ eyes*, 'n verruklike gesig
sorg'hum graansorghum
so'rrel (n) suring
so'rrow (n) droefheid, smart, verdriet; ~**ful** verdrietig, droewig, treurig
so'rry (a) jammer, spyt; *be ~*, spyt wees; (interj) ekskuus, jammer
sort[1] (n) soort, aard, klas; *nothing of the ~*, niks van die aard nie
sort[2] (v) sorteer; ~ *out*, uitsoek; ~**er** sorteerder
sought *see* **seek**
soul siel, gees, wese; *not a ~*, nie 'n lewende wese nie; ~ **searching** gewetepeilend; selfondersoekend; ~ **stirring** aangrypend
sound[1] (n) geluid, klank; (v) klink, lui; ~ *the retreat*, die aftog blaas; ~**barrier**

klankgrens; ~**board** klankbord; ~ **effects** byklanke
sound[2] (a) gesond, gaaf, sterk; *a ~ beating/ thrashing*, 'n gedugte pak slae; ~ *reasons*, gegronde redes; (adv) vas; ~ *asleep*, vas aan die slaap
sound'film klankfilm
sound'proof klankdig, geluidvry
sound track klankbaan
soup sop, soep; *be in the ~*, in die verknorsing wees; ~ **kitchen** sopkombuis; ~ **plate** sopbord
sour (v) versuur; (a) suur; nors; ~ *grapes*, suur druiwe; ~**puss** suurknol
source bron, oorsprong; ~ *and application of funds*, bron/herkoms en aanwending/ besteding van fondse
sou'-sou (-s) soe-soe (rankvrug)
south (n) suide; (a) suidelik, suid; (adv) suidwaarts
South Afr'ica Suid-Afrika; ~**n** (n) Suid-Afrikaner; (a) Suid-Afrikaans; ~**n War** Tweede Vryheidsoorlog
south: ~**east'** suidoos; ~**eas'ter** suidooster, Kaapse dokter; ~**erly** suidelik; ~**ern** suidelik; ~**paw** hotklou (links); S~ **Pole** Suidpool; S~ **Seas** Stille Suidsee; ~**ward** suidwaarts; ~**wes'ter** suidwestewind; reënjas, oliejas
South'ern Afr'ica Suider-Afrika
souv'enir soewenier, aandenking; herinnering, gedagtenis
sov'ereign (n) vors, heerser; (a) oppermagtig, soewerein; vernaamste
Sov'iet Sowjet; ~ **Republics** Sowjet-unie (USSR)
sow[1] (n) sog
sow[2] (v) (-ed, -n or -ed) saai, strooi; versprei; ~**er** saaier
soy'bean sojaboon
spa badplaas, kruitbad, spa
space (n) ruimte, plek; spasie; (v) spasieer; ~ *debris* ruimterommel; ~**man** ruimtevaarder; ~**ship** ruimteskip; ~**shuttle** pendeltuig; ~ **travel** ruimtevaart
spa'cing spasiëring
spa'cious ruim, wyd, uitgestrek
spade[1] skoppens (kaarte); *ace of ~s*, skoppenaas
spade[2] graaf, spitgraaf; *call a ~ a ~*, die kind by sy naam noem; ~**work** graafwerk; aanvoorwerk

span (n) span; spanning (brug); (v) **(-ned, -ned)** span, oorspan; oorbrug
span'iel patryshond
spank (n) klap, slag; ~**ing** (n) loesing, slae; (a) groot, sterk; gaaf, uitstekend
spann'er skroefsleutel, skroefhamer
spanspek' (n) spanspek, *also* **muskmelon**
spar (n) skerm; vuisgeveg; (v) **(-red, -red)** boks; skerm; redetwis
spare[1] (n) ekstra; reserwestuk; (pl) onderdele; ~ **wheel** noodwiel
spare[2] (v) spaar, opspaar, bespaar; ~ *no expense,* geen koste ontsien nie; ~ *oneself the trouble,* jou die moeite bespaar
spare[3] (a) maer; skraal; ~ **diet** skraal kos
spare: ~ **part** onderdeel; ~ **room** vrykamer; ~ **time** vrye tyd; ~ **tyre** noodband; ~ **wheel** noodwiel
spark[1] (n) windmakerige kêrel, swierbol
spark[2] (n) vonk; sprank, greintjie; *knock* ~*s out of,* ver oortref; (v) vonk; ~**(ing) plug** vonkprop
spark'le (n) glans, vonkeling; (v) vonkel, flikker; bruis; ~**r** diamant
spark'ling vonkelend, skitterend; ~ **wine** vonkelwyn, bruiswyn, borrelwyn
spar'ring skerm, boks; ~ **partner** oefenmaat, skermmaat
spa'rrow mossie; ~ **hawk** sperwer, wit valk
sparse dun versprei, yl
spasm kramp, trekking; ~**od'ic** krampagtig; spasmodies
spas'tic (a) krampagtig, spasties
spawn (n) viseiertjies, saad, kuit; (v) eiers lê
spay (v) regmaak, spei (wyfiedier)
speak (spoke, spoken) praat, spreek; sê; ~ *one's mind,* padlangs praat; *it* ~*s volumes,* dit spreek boekdele; ~**er** spreker; *Mr S~er,* mnr. Speaker (Volksraad); ~**ing** (n) praat; (a) pratend; *not on* ~*ing terms,* kwaaivriende
spear (n) spies, speer, wig; (v) deurboor; ~**head** speerpunt; ~ **fishing** spieshengel
spe'cial (n) ekstra trein; spesiale uitgawe; (a) spesiaal, besonder; ~**ist** spesialis
special'ity (..ties) besonderheid, spesialiteit (bv. koek bak)
spe'cialise spesialiseer; wysig, beperk
spe'cies (sing and pl) soort, spesie(s)
specif'ic soortlik, spesifiek; ~**a'tion** spesifikasie; ~ **gravity** soortlike gewig
spe'cify (..fied, ..fied) spesifiseer

spe'cimen monster, proef, eksemplaar; ~ **signature** proefhandtekening
speck (n) vlek, smet, stip; deeltjie
spec'tacle skouspel, vertoning; toneel, gesig; (pl) bril; ~**d** gebril, met 'n bril
spectac'ular skouspelagtig, opsienbarend
spectat'or toeskouer, aanskouer
spec'tre spook, verskyning
spec'ulate bespiegel; spekuleer (geld, beeste); ~ *about the future,* bespiegel oor die toekoms
specula'tion spekulasie; bespiegeling
spec'ulator spekulant
speech (-es) redevoering, toespraak; spraak; *make a* ~, 'n toespraak hou/lewer/aansteek; *parts of* ~, rededele; ~ **impediment** spraakgebrek; ~**less** spraakloos, stom
speed (n) snelheid, spoed, vaart; *at full* ~, in volle vaart; (v) **(sped, sped)** spoed, haastig/gou maak; jaag; ~**boat** snelboot, kragboot; ~**cop** verkeersbeampte, verkeerskonstabel; ~ **hump** (spoed)hobbel, vaartbreker; ~**limit** snelperk, spoedperk, snelheidsgrens; ~ **merchant** jaagduiwel; ~**om'eter** snelheidsmeter; ~**ster** jaagmotor; jaagduiwel; ~**trap** snelstrik; ~**way** (-s) jaagbaan; snelweg, motorweg, deurpad; ~**way racing** (motor)fietsrenne
speed wobble spoedwaggel
spell[1] (n) towerkrag; betowering; *fall under the* ~ *of,* onder die bekoring kom van
spell[2] (n) beurt; tyd, rukkie; *a cold* ~, 'n skielike koue; *a long* ~ *of service,* 'n lang dienstermyn
spell[3] (v) **(spelt, spelt** or **(-ed, -ed)** spel; voorspel; ~ *out policy,* beleid uitstippel
spell'bound betower(d), gefassineer
spell: ~**er** speller; ~**ing** spelling
spend (n): *consumer* ~*ing,* verbruiker(s)besteding; (v) **(spent, spent)** uitgee, spandeer; bestee; ~ *time on,* tyd bestee aan; ~**thrift** deurbringer, verkwister
spent (v) *see* **spend** (v); (a) uitgeput, flou; ~ **cartridge** leë patroondop
sperm saad, sperma
sphere kring; sfeer, bol; omvang; ~ *of influence,* invloedsfeer
sphinx (-es) sfinks
spice (n) spesery, kruie; (v) krui
spick'-and-span' piekfyn, agtermekaar

spid'er spinnekop; spaider; ~line kruis=
draad (verkyker); ~'s web spinnerak
spike (n) lang spyker; spykerskoen (atle=
tiek); briefpriem; (v) vaspen; vasspyker
spik'y spits, puntig
spill (n) val; *have a nasty* ~, lelik val; (v)
(spilt, spilt or -ed) mors, uitstort, verspil
spill'way uitloop, oorloop
spin (n) draai; tolvlug (vliegtuig); toertjie,
ritjie; *go for a* ~, gaan ry; (v) (spun or
span, spun) spin, weef; draai; wentel; ~ *a
yarn*, 'n storie vertel; kluitjies bak
spin'ach spinasie
spin'al ruggraats=; ~ column ruggraat
spin'dle spil, as; ~-legged met speekbene
spin'drier toldroër
spine ruggraat, rugstring; ~less ruggraat=
loos, slapgat; papbroekig
spinn'ing spin; ~ jenny (..nnies) spinjenny;
~ mill spinfabriek, spinnery; ~ mule
spinmuil; ~ wheel spinwiel
spin'ster oujongnooi
spir'al (n) spiraal; (v) (-led, -led) kronkel,
draai; ~ staircase wenteltrap
spi'rit (n) gees; geeskrag, lewe, vuur; (pl)
bewussyn; brandewyn; brandspiritus; *in
high* ~s, opgeruimd; *the Holy S*~, die
Heilige Gees; (v) aanwakker, besiel, aan=
vuur; ~ *away*, wegtoor; ~ed lewendig,
opgeruimd; ~ lamp spirituslamp; ~ level
waterpas; ~ stove spiritusstofie, pomp=
stofie
spi'ritual geestelik, onstoflik; ~ism spiri=
tisme; ~ist spiritis
spit[1] (n) spoeg, spuug; (braai)spit; (v) (spat,
spat) spoeg, spuug; ~ *out*, uitspoeg
spit[2] (v) (-ted, -ted) deurboor; braai
spite (n) spyt, wrok; *in* ~ *of*, ten spyte van,
in weerwil van; (v) krenk, vermaak; ver=
erg; ~ful vermakerig; haatlik
spittoon' spoegbakkie, kwispedoor
spiv vertroueswendelaar
splash (n) (-es) plas, plons; spatsel; (v) be=
spat, plas, spat; ~board modderskerm;
spatbord
spleen milt; gemelikheid, ergenis
splen'did pragtig, kostelik, luisterryk; uit=
stekend, puik
splen'dour prag, glans, grootsheid
splice (n) splitsing; las (tou); (v) splits; las
splint (n) splinter; splytpen; (v) spalk

splin'ter (n) splinter, spaander; (v) ver=
splinter; splinter
split (n) skeuring, tweespalt; skeur, bars; (v)
(split, split) skeur, splits; *a* ~ *decision*,
verdeelde besluit/beslissing; ~ *persona=
lity*, geslete persoonlikheid; *in a* ~
second, oombliklik, blitsvinnig; (a) ge=
splits, verdeel; ~ infinitive verdeelde in=
finitief; ~ peas spliterte; ~pin splitpen;
~pole fence paaltjiesheining
spoil (n) buit, roof; ~s *of war*, buit; (v) (-t
or -ed, -t or -ed) bederf; verwoes, verniel;
verfomfaai (klere); ~ed, ~t bedorwe; ~er
bederwer; ~sport pretbederwer, spel=
breker
spoke[1] (n) speek; *put a* ~ *in a person's
wheel*, iem. dwarsboom
spoke[2] (v) *see* speak
spokes'man (..men) woordvoerder, segs=
man; mondstuk, spreekbuis
sponge (n) spons; klaploper; parasiet; *throw
up the* ~, tou opgooi; (v) afspons; ~ *on
one*, op iem. teer; iem. uitsuig; ~ cake
suikerbrood; ~r klaploper, parasiet, uit=
suier, inhaler; neklêer
spon'sor (n) borg; stigter; (v) borg staan vir;
borg; ~ *a tournament*, 'n toernooi borg;
~ship borgskap
spontan'eous spontaan, ongedwonge
spook spook; ~ish, ~y spookagtig
spool (n) spoel(etjie), tolletjie, klos
spoon (n) lepel; (v) skep, (op/uit)lepel
spoon'erism spoonerisme, grappige om=
setting
spoon: ~-feed (..fed, ..fed) met die lepel
voer; ~ful (-s) lepelvol
spoor (n) spoor; (v) die spoor volg
sporad'ic versprei(d), sporadies
sport (n) sport; grap, korswel; grapmaker;
(v) jou vermaak; spog met; ~ *a gold
watch*, pronk met 'n goue oorlosie; ~ing
spelend; sport=, sportief; ~s; sport;
~s'man (..men) sportman; ~s'manlike
edelmoedig, sportief; ~s'manship sport=
manskap
spot (n) kol, merk, smet, vlek; *knock* ~s
off a person, iem. deeglik op sy baadjie
gee; (v) (-ted, -ted) merk; besmet, bespat;
reg raai (vrae); ~ cash kontant; ~ check
koltoets, steekproef; ~ colour pletter=
kleur; ~fine afkoopboete; ~less vlek=

loos; ~**light** soeklig, kollig; ~ **market** kontantmark (olie); ~**ted** bont, gespikkel

spouse eggenoot, eggenote; gade

spout (n) tuit, geut; spuit; (v) spuit (walvis); hoogdrawend voordra; ~**er** volksredenaar

sprang *see* **spring** (v)

sprain (v) verrek, verstuit, verswik

spray (n) skuim; sproeireën; (v) sproei; verstuif; ~**er** spuit, sproeier; ~**can** spuitkan(netjie); ~ **paint** spuitverf

spread (n) omvang, uitgestrektheid; verspreiding; maaltyd; *prepare a* ~, 'n feestelike onthaal (voor)berei; (v) (**spread, spread**) versprei; ontplooi

spree (n) drinkparty, fuif, jool; (v) fuif, boemel, jol, rinkink

spright'ly lewendig, vrolik, dartel

spring[1] (n) lente, voorsomer; *in* ~, in die lente

spring[2] (n) bron, fontein

spring[3] (n) veer; spring, sprong; (v) (**sprang, sprung**) spring; ontspring; ~ *a surprise,* verras; ~ **balance** veerbalans, trekskaaltjie; ~**board** springplank; duikplank; afspringplek (vir aanvalle); ~**bok** springbok; ~ **chicken** piepkuiken; bakvis; ~**tide** springvloed, springty

spring'time lente, jeug

spri'nkle (v) sprinkel, besproei; (be)strooi; ~ **irrigation** sprinkelbesproeiing; ~**r** sprinkelaar

sprint (n) naelwedloop, naelren; (v) nael; sny (hardloop); ~**er** naelloper

sprite spook; kabouter, fee

sprout (n) spruit, loot; (v) uitspruit, groei; opskiet; suiwer (tabak); ~**s** spruitkool

spruce (v) opskik, mooi maak; (a) netjies, keurig; viets, piekfyn

sprung *see* **spring**[3] (v)

spry lewendig, pure perd (ou man)

spun *see* **spin**

spunk moed, fut; durf; drif, koerasie

spur (n) spoor; spoorslag; aansporing, prikkel; (v) (**-red, -red**) aanspoor; ~**gear** tandrat

spurn (n) veragting, versmading, vertrapping; (v) verag; wegskop, verstoot

spurt (v) uitspuit; spat; weglê; laat nael

spur'toed frog platanna

spur'wheel tandrat, kamwiel

spy (n) (**spies**) spioen, verspieder; bespieder; (v) (**spied, spied**) spioeneer, bespied; ~**glass** (-es) verkyker; ~**hole** kykgat, loergat; ~**ing** spioenasie

squab'ble (n) rusie, twis; (v) twis, dwarstrek, kibbel; ~**r** dwarstrekker, korrelkop

squad klomp; seksie; afdeling (soldate); ~ **car** blitsmotor

squad'ron eskadron (ruiters); eskader (vloot, lugmag)

squa'lid vuil, morsig, smerig

squa'lor morsigheid, smerigheid

squan'der verkwis, verspil, deurbring

square (n) vierkant; kwadrant; plein; winkelhaak; ouderwetse persoon; (v) vierkantig maak; vereffen; ~ *accounts with,* afreken met; ~ *up,* betaal, in orde bring; (a) vierkantig; kwadraat; reghoekig; regskape; *a* ~ *meal,* 'n stewige maal; (adv) vierkant; eerlik; *they are* ~ *now,* hulle is nou kiet(s); *treat* ~, eerlik behandel; ~ **dealing** eerlikheid; ~**d** kwadraat (x[2]); geruit; ~ **measure** oppervlaktemaat; ~**root** vierkantswortel; ~**-shouldered** breedgeskouer

squash[1] (n) kwas, suurlemoendrank; muurbal; (v) kneus; die mond snoer

squash[2] (n) (-es) skorsie; **gem** ~ lemoenpampoen(tjie)

squat (v) (**-ted, -ted**) neerhurk; plak; (a) gehurk; dik; ~**ter** plakker; ~**ting** plakkery

squeak (n) gepiep; gil; (v) piep, gil

squeal (n) gil, skreeu; (v) tjank; verklik

squeeze (n) drukking; gedrang; *it was a tight* ~, dit het naelskraap gegaan; (v) druk, vasdruk; uitpers; ~ *money out of,* geld afpers

squid pylinkvis

squint (v) skeel kyk; (a) skeel; ~**-eyed** skeeloog

squi'rrel eekhorinkie

squirt (n) spuit; straal; grootprater, windmaker; (v) (uit)spuit

stab (n) steek, dolksteek; belediging; (v) (**-bed, -bed**) deursteek; wond

stabil'ity vastheid, standvastigheid, bestendigheid, stabiliteit

stab'ilise stabiliseer, bestendig

sta'ble[1] (n) stal; renperde; (v) stal

sta'ble[2] (a) stabiel, standvastig, bestendig

stack (n) mied (voer); hoop, stapel; (v) mied pak; opstapel stad'ium (-s) stadion; *Boland* ~, Stadion Boland

staff (n) staf (militêr); personeel (skool); **editorial** ~ redaksie; ~ **officer** stafoffi=sier

stag takbok, hert; premiejaer (beurs); ~ **party** ramparty

stage (n) toneel; stadium; trek (bus); *at that* ~, in/op daardie stadium; (v) opvoer; ~ **fever** plankekoors; ~ **fright** verhoog=vrees, plankevrees; ~ **management** to=neelleiding, regie; ~ **writer** toneeldigter, toneelskrywer

stagg'er (v) waggel, wankel; steier; ~ed **hours** verspreide werkure; skiktyd; ~ing (a) wankelend; verbluffend, verbysterend

stag'nant stiltaand(e), stagnant; traag

stagna'te (v) stagneer

stain (n) vlek, klad, smet; kleur; (v) vlek, besmet, beklad; ~ed besoedel, besmet, gekleur; ~ed **glass**, kleurglas, brandskil=derglas; ~less rein, skoon; vlekvry, roesvry (staal)

stair trap; *a flight of* ~s, 'n trap; *up*~s, bo; ~ **carpet** traploper; ~case trap

stake (n) paal; inset; (pl) wedgeld; *have a* ~ *in*, belange hê in; (v) waag; wed

stal'actite (hangende) druipsteen, stalagtiet

stal'agmite (staande) druipsteen, stalagmiet

stale (a) oud, vermuf; verslete, afgesaag; bevange; ~ **beer** verslaande bier

stalk[1] (n) steel, stingel; skag (van veer)

stalk[2] (v) deftig stap; wild bekruip; ~er bekruiper; sluipjagter

stall (n) stal, hok; loket; (plaas)kiosk; (v) staak (motor); vaslê, vassit

stall'ion hings

stal'wart (n) staatmaker; (a) kragtig, stoer

stam'ina uithouvermoë, stamina

stamm'er (v) stamel, hakkel; ~er hakke=laar; ~ing (n) gehakkel

stamp (n) stempel, seël, merk, posseël, (v) merk, stempel; ~ **collector** (pos)seëlver=samelaar; ~ **duty** seëlreg

stampede' (n) oorhaaste vlug; wilde toe=loop; (v) in 'n paniek vlug (diere)

stance houding, posisie

stand (n) stand, posisie; standplaas; pawil=joen; stalletjie, kraampie; (v) (stood, stood) staan; uithou; trakteer, betaal; *I can't* ~ *the fellow*, ek kan die vent nie verdra nie; *it* ~s *to reason*, dit spreek

vanself; ~ *in good stead*, goed te pas kom; ~ *the test*, die proef deurstaan

stan'dard (n) standerd (skool); standaard, peil, gehalte; banier; maatstaf, norm; (a) standaard; ~ **bearer** vaandeldraer; ~= isa'tion standaardisering; ~ise stand=aardiseer

stand'by bystand, steun; gereedheid(s)=diens; nooddiens; *on* ~, op bystand

stan'ding (n) rang, stand; posisie, status, naam; *a man of high* ~, iem. van aansien; (a) staande; duursaam; *place a* ~ *order*, 'n vaste bestelling plaas; ~ **room** staanplek

stand'-offish eenkant, terughoudend, ge=reserveer; neusoptrekkerig

stand'point standpunt

stank *see* stink

stann'ary (..ries) tinmyn

stan'za stansa, strofe; koeplet

sta'ple[1] (n) kram; (v) kram

sta'ple[2] (n) stapel; hoofbestanddeel; (v) sorteer; (a) stapel=, vernaamste; ~ **food** stapelkos

sta'pler krammer, kramdrukker

star (n) ster; ~board stuurboord

starch (n) (-es) stysel; (v) styf

stare (v) aanstaar, aangaap

star'ing starend; *stark* ~ *mad*, stapelgek

stark (a) sterk; styf; volslae; (adv) heeltemal, gans; ~ *mad*, stapelgek; ~ *naked*, poedelnakend

starl'ing spreeu; *wattled* ~, sprinkaanvoël

start (n) begin, aanvang; voorsprong; *by fits and* ~s, met rukke en stote; (v) begin, vertrek; aansit (motor); ~er aansitter; afsit=ter (sport); begingereg

start'ing begin, wegspring; ~ **place** begin=plek; ~ **point** wegspringplek; uitgangs=punt

star'tle ontstel, skrikmaak, laat skrik

starva'tion uithongering, hongersnood

starve uithonger; gebrek ly; uitteer; van honger omkom

state[1] (n) staat; toestand; *the* ~ *of affairs*, die toedrag van sake; ~ *of emergency*, noodtoestand; *lie in* ~, in staatsie lê

state[2] (v) meld, vermeld, konstateer, vas=stel

state: ~ **aid** staatsteun; ~ **funeral** staats=begrafnis; ~ly statig, deftig, groots

state'ment opgawe, staat; berig; verklaring, bewering, stelling; formulering

state: ~ **president** staatspresident; ~ =
s'man, (..men) staatsman; ~s'manship
staatsmanskap; ~ witness staatsgetuie
sta'tic staties; vas
sta'tion (n) stasie; standplaas
sta'tionary stilstaand, vas, onbeweeglik
sta'tioner handelaar in skryfware; boek=
handelaar; ~y skryfware, skryfgoed,
skryfbehoeftes
statis'tics statistiek
stat'ue standbeeld
stat'ure gestalte, grootte, statuur
stat'us stand, rang, status; posisie, aansien
stat'ute wet, instelling, statuut; ~ law
wettereg, statutereg, (die) landswette
staunch sterk, stewig, trou, beproef
stave (n) duig (van vat); staf; notebalk
(musiek); (v) (-d, or stove, -d or stove)
verbrysel, stukkend slaan; duie insit (vat);
~ off, afwend
stay (n) verblyf; stut; (pl) korset, borsrok;
(v) (-ed or staid, -ed or staid) bly, vertoef,
loseer; ~ with, loseer/woon by; ~-at-
home huishen
stead stede, plaas; stand one in good ~,
goed te pas kom; in ~ of, in plaas van;
~fast standvastig, onwrikbaar; ~iness
deeglikheid; stewigheid
stead'y (v) (..died, ..died) tot bedaring
bring; (a) vas, gereeld; bestendig; a ~
decline, 'n geleidelike agteruitgang
steak biefstuk; moot (vis); ~house braai=
huis/braais, braairestourant
steal (stole, stolen) steel; sluip; ~ a march
on, iem. voor wees; ~ing stelery, diefstal
steam (n) stoom; (v) stoom, damp; ~ boiler
stoomketel; ~ed pudding doekpoeding;
~er ship stoomskip, stoomboot
steel (n) staal; (v) staal; (a) staal=; ~ clad
gepantser; ~ plate staalplaat
steen'bok steenbok
steen'bras steenbras
steep[1] (a) steil; kras; a ~ price, 'n hoë prys;
a ~ turn, 'n skerp draai
steep[2] (v) indoop, indompel; ~ed in alco=
hol, deurtrek van drank; ~ed in French,
gekonfyt in Frans
stee'ple kloktoring; ~chase hindernisswed=
ren, hindernisswedloop
steer[1] (n) bul; stier; jong os
steer[2] (v) stuur, rig; lei; ~ clear of, vermy,
omseil; ~ing committee reëlingskomitee;

~ing wheel stuurwiel; stuurrat; ~s'man
(..men) stuurman
stem[1] (n) stam, stingel, steel
stem[2] (v) (-med, -med) stuit, teenhou; ~ the
tide, walgooi teen
stench stank
sten'cil (n) uitgesnyde patroonplaat; was=
vel; sjabloon
stenog'apher snelskrywer, stenograaf
step (n) stap, tree; trappie; trappie; voetstap;
trapleer; maatreël; (pl) trapleer; take ~s,
stappe doen; (v) (-ped, -ped) stap, tree,
betree, loop; ~ this way, (kom) hierna=
toe; ~brother stiefbroer; ~ladder trap=
leer; ~-outs uitstapdrag; ~parents stief=
ouers
ste'reo stereo=; ~phonic stereofonies
ste'reotype (n) stereotiep(druk); (v) stereo=
tipeer; (a) stereotiep, onveranderlik; a ~d
expression, 'n stereotiepe uitdrukking
ste'rile onvrugbaar, steriel, dor
ste'rilise onvrugbaar maak; steriliseer
sterl'ing sterling; eg, suiwer, onvervals; a ~
fellow, 'n gawe/eersteklas kêrel
stern[1] (n) agterstewe (skip); stert, agterste
stern[2] (a) ernstig, streng; stug, stroef
steth'oscope stetoskoop, gehoorpyp
steve'dore stuwadoor
stew (n) bredie; be in a ~, in die knyp sit;
(v) stoof; smoor
stew'ard kelner, tafelbediende, hofmeester;
rentmeester; beampte (sport)
stick (n) stok, lat; kierie; a ~ in the mud, 'n
remskoen; (v) (stuck, stuck) steek; kleef,
vassit; ~er plakker(tjie); aanhouer; ~=
iness taaiheid, klewerigheid; ~ing plaster
kleefpleister, hegpleister; ~-in-the-mud
sukkelaar
stick'y klewerig, taai
stiff (n) niksnut(s), gomtor; (a) styf, stram,
verstyf; koppig; a ~ examination, 'n
moeilike eksamen; that's pretty ~, dis
nogal kras; scared ~, doodgeskrik; ~ness
styfheid, stramheid
stif'ling drukkend, versmorend; bedompig
stig'ma (-s, -ta) brandmerk, skandvlek,
stigma; ~tise stigmatiseer
stile oorklimtrap, trappie; steg
still[1] (n) distilleerketel, stookketel; (v)
stook, distilleer
still[2] (v) stilmaak; bedaar; (a) stil, kalm; ~
waters run deep, stille waters, diepe

grond; (adv) nog, steeds; ~ *another*, nog een

still: ~**born** doodgebore; ~ **life** stillewe

stilt (n) stelt; *on ~s*, op stelte; ~**ed** hoog-drawend, bombasties; ~**bird** steltloper

stim'ulate aanspoor, aanvuur, stimuleer

stim'ulating prikkelend, stimulerend

stim'ulus (..li) prikkel, stimulus

sting (n) prikkel; angel; steek; (v) **(stung, stung)** steek, prik; brand; ~ *to action*, tot handeling aanspoor; ~**ing** stekend, bran-dend; ~**ing nettle** brandnetel/brandnekel

stin'gy inhalig, gierig, vrekkerig, krenterig

stink (n) stank; (v) **(stank** or **stunk, stunk)** stink; ~**bomb** stinkbom; ~**wood** stink-hout

stipula'tion voorwaarde, voorskrif, stipu-lasie

stir (n) beweging, geraas, opskudding; (v) **(-red, -red)** roer, beweeg; ~ *up discon-tent*, ontevredenheid veroorsaak/aan-blaas; *not ~ a finger*, nie 'n vinger verroer nie

sti'rrup stiebeuel; ~ **strap** stiegriem

stitch (n) **(-es)** steek; (v) stik, naai; ~ *up*, toewerk

stock (n) voorraad; veestapel; aandele, ef-fekte; (pl) effekte, aandele; vilet (blom); *of good ~*, van goeie familie/afkoms; *in ~*, in voorraad; (v) voorsien van; ~ *a farm*, 'n plaas uitrus; (a) afgesaag, oud

stock: ~**breeder** veeboer; ~**broker** effek-temakelaar

stock: ~ **car** stampmotor; ~ **letter** vorm-brief; ~ **racing** stampmotor(wed)renne

stock exchange effektebeurs

stock'ing kous; windhoos (lughawe)

stock: ~**in-trade** (handels)voorraad; ~**pile** (n) opberg; oppot; ~**piling** opber-ging, voorraadvorming, oppotting

stock'taking voorraadopname, inventari-sasie; ~ **sale** opruimverkoping

stoep stoep

stoke stook; volstop; ~**r** stoker

sto'mach (n) **(-s)** maag; pens (dier); *on an empty ~*, op die nugter maag; (v) sluk, verkrop; ~ **ache** maagpyn

stone (n) klip, steen; *leave no ~ unturned*, hemel en aarde beweeg; (v) stenig; (a) klip-; steen-; (adv) totaal, heeltemal; ~ **age** steentydperk; ~ **blind** stokblind; ~ **dead** morsdood; ~ **deaf** stokdoof; ~**fruit**

pitvrugte; ~**mason** klipwerker; ~ **quarry** **(..ries)** steengroef, klipgat; ~**ware** klip-ware; erdewerk

ston'y klipperig, hard, ongevoelig

stood *see* **stand**

stooge strooipop, handlanger

stool stoel (sonder leuning); stoelgang

stoop (v) buk, buig; jou verlaag/verneder; ~**ing** krom, inmekaar

stop (n) halte (spoorweg); stilstand; end; (v) **(-ped, -ped)** ophou; teenhou, keer; stelp (bloed); staak; stop; ~ *at nothing*, vir niks stuit nie; ~ *payment*, betaling staak; ~**cock** afsluitkraan; ~ **order** aftrekor-der, *also* debit order; ~**per** prop, kurk; ~**press** nagekome berigte; ~ **street** stop-straat; ~**watch (-es)** stopoorlosie

stor'age ophoping; (op)berging; bergloon; bêreplek; pakhuisruimte

store (n) voorraad; pakhuis; winkel; stoor-(kamer); *in ~*, in voorraad; (v) bêre, opberg; opstapel; opgaar; stoor; ~ *away*, bêre, stoor; ~**house** voorraadskuur, pakhuis; stoor; ~**keeper** winkelier; ~**room** pakkamer, stoorkamer

stor'ey (-s) verdieping; *double~ (house)*, dubbelverdieping(huis); *the first ~*, die eerste verdieping/vloer

stork ooievaar; *black ~*, swart sprinkaan-voël

storm (n) storm; uitbarsting; (v) storm; ~**y** stormagtig

stor'y (..ries) storie, verhaal, vertelling; *make a long ~ short*, om kort te gaan; *tell stories*, spekskiet; ~**book** storieboek; ~**teller** verteller; leuenaar

stout (a) fris, fors, sterk, dapper; swaar-lywig; ~**hearted** moedig, dapper

stove stoof

stow bêre; wegsit; ~ *away*, wegpak; ~**age** bêreplek; opberging; ~**away (-s)** verste-keling, blinde passasier

strad'dle wydsbeen loop

strag'gle dwaal, swerf; streep-streep loop; ~**r** agterblyer; afdwaler; sukkelaar

straight (n) pylvak (in sport); (a) reguit, direk; eerlik, opreg, ruiterlik; ~ *talk*, openhartige gesprek; (adv) onmiddellik; reguit; ~ *away*, op staande voet; ~ *sets*, skoon stelle (tennis); ~**en** reguit maak; regmaak; ~**forward** reguit, rondborstig, padlangs

strain (n) inspanning; spanning; verstuiting (van enkel); trant; *in the same ~*, in dieselfde trant; (v) verrek, verstuit; *~ every nerve*, jou inspan; **~ed** gespanne; **~er** melkdoek; siffie (tee); gaatjiesbak

strait (n) seestraat; bergpas; (a) nou, eng; **~en** beperk; **~jacket** dwangbuis; **~-laced** gedwonge; preuts

strand¹ (n) string; draad; vesel; **~ed cotton** stringgare, breikatoen

strand² (n) kus, strand; (v) strand; **~ed** gestrand; verleë; in die moeilikheid

strange vreemd, onbekend; snaaks, ongewoon; eienaardig

stran'ger vreemdeling, onbekende

stra'ngle verwurg, versmoor; **~hold** wurggreep

strangula'tion wurging, verwurging

strap (n) platriem, riem, band; (v) **(-ped, -ped)** vasgord; vasmaak; **~ping** sterk, groot

strate'gic strategies

strat'egy krygskunde, strategie

strat'osphere stratosfeer

straw (n) strooi; nietigheid

straw'berry (..ries) aarbei

stray (n) verdwaalde dier; (v) **(-ed, -ed)** verdwaal; (a) afgedwaal; dakloos; *~ bullet*, 'n verdwaalde koeël; *~ dog*, losloperhond

streak (n) streep; strook; kaalhollery; *a ~ of humour*, 'n tikkie humor; (v) kaal hol/hardloop; **~er** kaalholler; stryker

stream (n) stroom; spruit; *come on ~*, begin produseer; in bedryf kom/stel; (v) stroom, vloei; **~er** wimpel, spandoek, papierlint; **~ing** stromend; **~let** stroompie; spruitjie; **~lined** vaartbelyn, gestroomlyn

street straat; *the man in the ~*, die groot publiek, Jan Publiek; *~ arab* straatkind, skollie; *~car* trem, bus; **~walker** straatmeisie, straatvlinder (prostituut)

strength sterkte, krag; *on the ~ of*, op grond van; **~en** versterk

stren'uous kragtig, energiek; veeleisend

stress (n) **(-es)** nadruk, klem(toon); inspanning; *lay ~ on*, klem/nadruk lê op; (v) beklemtoon, benadruk

stretch (n) **(-es)** uitgestrektheid; streek; *a long ~ of road*, 'n lang ent pad; (v) rek, uitrek; span; inspan; oordryf; **~er** voukateltjie, kampbed(jie); draagbaar

strew **(-ed, -ed** or **-n)** strooi, besaai

strick'en gepla, siek; geslaan

strict streng, stip; nougeset; presies; eng; *~ly confidential*, streng vertroulik

stride (n) tree, stap; *get in one's ~*, op dreef kom

strife twis, tweedrag, onenigheid

strike (n) (werk)staking; *go-slow ~*, sloerstaking; (v) **(struck, struck)** stryk (vlag); trek (vuurhoutjie); staak (werkers); **~r** staker; slaner

strik'ing treffend, opvallend

string (n) lyn, tou; seilgare; snaar (viool); vlegsel (hare); koord; snoer, string (pêrels); *a ~ of lies*, 'n rits leuens; (v) **(strung, strung)** inryg (krale); snare aansit, besnaar; *~ band* strykorkes; *~ bean* snyboon, rankboon; **~ed instrument** snaarinstrument

strip (n) strook; (v) **(-ped, -ped)** ontklee, afstroop; beroof; *~ bare*, poedelnakend uittrek; *~ off*, afruk

stripe streep, striem; **~d** gestreep

strip'per ontkleedanser(es)

strip'tease ontkleedans, lokdans, tergdans

strive (strove, striven) poog, trag, streef; *~ for*, streef na, beywer vir

stroke (n) hou, raps; slag; beroerte-aanval; streling, liefkosing; *a ~ of apoplexy*, beroerte; *a ~ of luck*, 'n gelukslag; *on the ~ of one*, op die kop (klokslag) eenuur; (v) streel, liefkoos

stroll (n) wandeling; (v) wandel, slenter

strong sterk, kragtig; *use ~ language*, jou kras uitdruk; **~headed** koppig; **~hold** vesting; **~room** brandkamer, kluis

strop (n) skeerriem; (v) **(-ped -ped)** slyp

struc'ture bou, struktuur, bouwerk

strug'gle (n) worsteling; *the ~ for existence*, die stryd om die bestaan; (v) worstel, baklei; **~r** worstelaar; sukkelaar, ploeteraar

strung *see* **string** (v)

strych'nine wolwegif, strignien

stub stomp(ie), entjie; *~ out a cigarette*, 'n sigaret dooddruk

stub'ble stoppels; **~field** stoppelland

stubb'orn hardnekkig, koppig; **~ness** koppigheid, hardnekkigheid

stuck'-up trots, verwaand

stud¹ (n) stoetery (diere); (a) stoetstud² (n) halsknopie, boordjieknoop; klinknael; stut

stud'ent student; leerling; ~ **council** leer= lingraad, studenteraad; ~**like** studenti= koos

stud'io (-s) ateljee; ~ **orchestra** ateljee= orkes

stud'ious fluks, ywerig, vlytig, leergierig

stud'y (n) (..dies) studeerkamer; studie; *take your studies seriously,* jou studie ernstig opneem; (v) (..died, ..died) studeer, bestudeer; instudeer (toneel); ~ *law/medicine,* in die regte/medisyne stu= deer

stuff (n) stof, goed; (v) opstop, stoffeer; ~*ed animals,* opgestopte diere; ~**iness** bedompigheid, benoudheid; ~**ing** op= stopsel; ~y bedompig, benoud

stum'ble (v) struikel, strompel; ~ *across (upon) someone,* iem. teen die lyf loop

stum'bling block struikelblok

stump (n) stomp; pen, paaltjie (krieket); (v) stonk (krieket); vasvra

stun (-ned, -ned) verbyster; bedwelm

stung *see* sting (v)

stunn'er: *she is a* ~, sy is 'n pragstuk

stunn'ing bedwelmend; pragtig

stunt¹ (n) toer, laai, kordaatstuk, streek; (v) toere/kunsies uithaal; ~**man** waagarties

stunt² (n) dwerg; belemmering; (v) die groei belemmer; ~**ed** dwergagtig, verpot

stup'id (n) domkop; (a) dom, onnosel; dig, toe

stupid'ity, stup'idness dwaasheid

stur'dy (a) kragtig, stoer, fors

stutt'er (n) gestotter; (v) stotter; ~**er** stot= teraar

sty¹ (sties) varkhok

sty² karkatjie (op die oog)

style (n) styl, mode, manier; benaming; *under the* ~ *of,* onder die firmanaam (van); (v) noem, betitel

styl'ish deftig, modieus, stylvol

suave vriendelik, goedig; glad, uitgeleer

sub'committee onderkomitee, subkomitee

subcon'scious onderbewus, halfbewus

subdivi'sion onderverdeling; gedeelte

subdue' (v) onderwerp, oorwin; beteuel; demp (lig)

sub-ed'itor onderredakteur, subredakteur

sub'ject (n) (studie)vak; onderdaan; on= derwerp (gram.); individu; ~ *of study,*

leervak; (a) onderworpe, onderhorig; ~ *to approval,* onderworpe aan goedkeuring

subject' (v) onderwerp, blootstel aan; ~**ive** subjektief

subjuga'tion onderwerping, onderhorigheid

subjunc'tive (n) aanvoegende wys

sublet' (..let, ..let) onderverhuur

sublime' (a) verhewe, voortreflik, subliem

sub'marine (n) duikboot; (a) ondersees; ~ **base** duikbootbasis

submerge' onderdompel, onderduik

submi'ssion onderwerping; voorlegging

submit' (-ted, -ted) voorlê, indien

subnorm'al ondernormaal, subnormaal

subord'inate (n) ondergeskikte; (a) onder= geskik, onderhorig; ~ **sentence** onder= geskikte sin

subpoen'a (n) dagvaarding; (v) dagvaar

subscribe' inteken; bydra; onderskryf; onderteken; *the loan was* ~*d,* die lening is volskryf; ~ *to a newspaper,* op 'n nuus= blad inteken; ~**r** intekenaar

subscrip'tion subskripsie, intekengeld; by= drae; ledegeld/lidgeld

sub'section onderafdeling

sub'sequent volgend, later, daaropvolgen= de, naderhand; ~**ly** daarna, vervolgens

subside' sak, bedaar, kalm word; wegsak

subsid'iary (n) (..ries) plaasvervanger, noodhulp; filiaal; (a) hulp=, aanvullend; ~ **company** filiaalmaatskappy

sub'sidise geldelik steun, subsidieer

sub'sidy (..dies) geldelike steun, subsidie

subsist'ence bestaan, broodwinning; ~ **economy** bestaansekonomie

sub'soil onderlaag, ondergrond; ~**er** kors= breker (boerdery)

sub'stance selfstandigheid; kern, inhoud; wesenlikheid; *man of* ~, 'n vermoënde man

substan'tial wesenlik; aansienlik

sub'stitute (n) plaasvervanger, substituut; (v) vervang; ~ *nylon for cotton,* katoen vervang deur nylon

subterran'ean onderaards

sub'title ondertitel

su'btle listig, subtiel, geslepe; fyn, skerp= sinnig; ~**ness**, ~**ty** (..tles) spitsvondig= heid; listigheid

subtract' aftrek, verminder; ~**ion** aftrek= king, vermindering

subtrop'ical subtropies

sub'urb voorstad; stadswyk; woonbuurt
suburb'an voorstedelik
subver'sion ondermyning, ondergrawing
subver'sive ondermynend, opruiend
sub'way duikweg; tonnel
succeed' opvolg; slaag; **~ing** volgende, opvolgende
success' (-es) sukses, welslae; **~ful** suksesvol, voorspoedig, geslaag
succe'ssion opvolging; opeenvolging; *in rapid ~,* vinnig na mekaar; **~ duty** sterfreg
success'or opvolger, erfgenaam
succ'ulent (n) vetplant; (a) sappig, sopperig; **~ plants** vetplante
succumb' beswyk, swig
such (a) sulke, sodanig; so; (pron) sulke mense, sulkes; *as ~,* (as) sodanig; *all ~ persons who,* almal wat
suck (v) suig; **~er** pypkan; suier; loot; domkop, dwaas; stokkielekker; **~ing pig** speenvark
suc'kle soog, laat drink
su'ction suiging; **~ pump** suigpomp
sudd'en(ly) plotseling, onverwags, skielik
sue vervolg (geregtelik), dagvaar, aanskryf; *~ for damages,* dagvaar vir skadevergoeding
suéde Sweedse leer
su'et niervet, harde vet; **~ dumpling** vetkoek
suff'er ly, verduur; *~ defeat,* die neerlaag ly; **~from,** ly aan; **~er** lyer, pasiënt; **~ing** (n) lyding; (a) lydend
suffice' genoeg/voldoende wees; volstaan met; *~ it to say that,* dit is voldoende om te sê dat
suffi'cient (a) genoegsaam, voldoende, toereikend
suff'ix (n) (-es) agtervoegsel
suff'ocate verstik, versmoor
suffragette' stemregvrou, stemjuffer
su'gar (n) suiker; vleitaal; mooipraatjies; (v) versuiker; *~ the pill,* die pil verguld; *~ basin* suikerpot; **~bird** suikerbekkie, jangroentjie; *~ candy* kandysuiker, teesuiker; **~cane** suikerriet; **~daddy** paaipappie, vroetelvader; *~ mill* suikerfabriek; *~ refinery* (..ries) suikerraffinadery; **~ stick** borssuiker; **~y** suikeragtig, soet

suggest' opper, aan die hand doen, suggereer, voorstel; *I ~ that,* ek doen aan die hand dat; **~ion** ingewing; voorstel, suggestie; **~ive** suggestief, veelseggend
su'icide selfmoord; *commit ~,* selfmoord pleeg
suit (n) proses, regsgeding; stel; pak klere; kleur (kaartspel); (v) pas; voldoen; bevredig, deug; *~ yourself,* soos jy verkies; **~abil'ity** geskiktheid; **~able** paslik, geskik; **~case** (hand)koffer, reistas
suite *(pron. sweet)* stel, suite; *an executive ~,* 'n bestuurstel; *a ~ of rooms,* 'n stel kamers
suit'or vryer, vryerklong
sulk pruil; **~iness** norsheid, pruilery; **~y** pruilerig; suur, nors
sul'ky (sulkies) drafkarretjie
sul'phur (n) swa(w)el, sulfer; (v) swa(w)el
sul'tan sultan
sulta'na sultana(rosyntjie); sultane
sul'try drukkend, bedompig, broeierig
sum (n) som; totaal; *~ total,* totaalbedrag; *~ up,* saamvat; optel
summ'arise opsom, saamvat
summ'ary (n) (..ries) opsomming, (kort) samevatting; *~ dismissal,* summiere ontslag
summ'er (n) somer; **~house** somerhuis, tuinhuis, prieel
summ'it toppunt, piek; *~ meeting, ~ talks* spitsberaad, leiersberaad
summ'on dagvaar; oproep; opeis; *~ up one's courage,* jou moed bymekaarskraap
summ'ons (n) (-es) dagvaarding; (v) dagvaar; *serve a ~ on someone,* 'n dagvaarding aan iem. bestel/beteken
sump oliebak; sinkput; mynput
sump'tuous weelderig, kosbaar
sun (n) son; *rise with the ~,* douvoordag opstaan; **~bath** sonbad; **~beam** sonstraal; **~blind** rolgordyn; **~bonnet** kappie; **~burnt** (son)gebruin, songebrand
sun'dae vrugteroomys
Sun'day Sondag; *his ~ best,* sy kisklere
sun'dial sonwyser
sun: **~down** sononder, son(s)ondergang; **~downer** skemerkelk(ie)
sun'dries allerlei, diverse
sun'dry allerlei, verskeie, diverse; *~ expenses* diverse uitgawes
sun'flower sonneblom

sung *see* sing
sunk *see* sink (v)
sunk'en ingeval, hol; ondergegaan (son)
sun: ~light sonlig; ~ny sonnig; opgewek, vrolik; ~rise sonop, sonsopgang; ~set sononder, sonsondergang; ~shade sambreel, sonskerm; ~shine sonskyn; ~stroke sonstraal, sonsteek, hitteslag; ~worshipper sonaanbidder
superann'uate met pensioen afdank/aftree
superb' voortreflik, pragtig, groots
superfi'cial oppervlakkig; oppervlak=
super'fluous oortollig, oorbodig
superhum'an bo(we)menslik
superimpose' bo-op lê; oorlê, superponeer
superintend' toesig hou; ~ence toesig; ~ent superintendent, toesighouer
super'ior (n) meerdere; (a) hoër, beter; *with a ~ air*, uit die hoogte; ~ *numbers*, oormag
super'lative (n) oortreffende trap; (a) oortreffend; hoogste
sup'erman (..men) oppermens, supermens
sup'ermarket supermark, alleswinkel, self=dienwinkel
superna'tural bonatuurlik
superson'ic supersonies; ~ flight supersoniese vlug
supersti'tion bygeloof
supersti'tious bygelowig
sup'ertax (-es) bybelasting, bobelasting
sup'ervise toesig hou
sup'ervisor toesighouer (fabriek); opsigter, opsiener
supp'er aandete
sup'ple lenig, buigsaam, soepel, slap
supp'lement (n) bylae, byvoegsel
supplement' (v) aanvul, byvoeg; ~ary aanvullend, aanvullings=, supplementêr; ~ary examination aanvulling(s)eksamen
suppli'er verskaffer, leweransier, leweraar
supply' (n) (..lies) voorraad; lewering; toevoer; (pl) benodigdhede; ~ *and demand*, vraag en aanbod; (v) (..lied, ..lied) verskaf, voorsien, bevoorraad, lewer; ~ dump opslagplek; ~ ship voorraadskip
support' (n) steun, bystand, hulp; onderhoud; *in ~ of*, ten bate van; (v) steun, ondersteun, onderskraag, help; onderhou; staaf; ~ *a family*, 'n gesin onderhou; ~er ondersteuner, helper; ~ price stutprys

suppose' veronderstel, vermoed; ~ *you are right*, gestel jy het gelyk
suppress' onderdruk; bedwing; demp; ~=ion onderdrukking; geheimhouding; ~=ive onderdrukkend
supp'urate etter, sweer
suprem'acy oppergesag; heerskappy
supreme' (a) oppermagtig; opperste, hoog=ste; *the ~ test*, die hoogste toets; S~ Be-ing die Allerhoogste, die Opperwese; ~ command oppergesag; S~ Court Hoog=geregshof
sur'charge (n) bybetaling; byslag, toeslag; (v) bobelas
sure (a) gewis, seker, veilig; (adv) seker(lik), waarlik; ~ly seker, sekerlik, stellig, on=getwyfeld; tog
sure'ty (..ties) borg; *stand ~ for*, borg staan vir
surf (n) branders, branding; (v) brander=plank ry, branders ry
sur'face (n) oppervlak; vlak; blad (van pad); *on the ~*, op die eerste gesig; aan die oppervlak; ~ *irrigation of crops*, op=pervlakbesproeiing van gewasse; (v) op=duik, opkom
surf: ~board branderplank; ~boat red=dingsboot; ~ skiing branderski
surge (n) golf, golwing, branding, deining; (v) dein, golf
sur'geon snydokter, chirurg
sur'gery snykunde, chirurgie; *plastic ~*, plastiese chirurgie/snykunde
sur'icate stokstertmeerkat, graatjiemeerkat
sur'ly nors, stuurs, suur; somber
surmise' (v) verbeel, vermoed, raai
surmount' oorwin, oorkom; ~able oor=koomlik, oorkombaar
sur'name van, familienaam
surpass' oortref, verbystreef
surp'lus (n) (-es) oorskot, surplus; (a) oor=tollig; ~ population oorbevolking
surprise' (n) verrassing; *take by ~*, verras, oorrompel; (v) verras; betrap; ~ *in the act*, op heter daad betrap; ~ attack ver=rassingsaanval; ~ packet verrassings=pakket; ~ party (..ties) invalparty; ~ visit onverwagte besoek
surren'der (n) oorgawe; (v) oorgee; hen=(d)sop; uitlewer; ~ *an insurance policy*, 'n assuransiepolis afkoop; ~ value af=koopwaarde

surround' omring, omsingel, insluit; **~ings** omgewing, buurt

sur'tax (-es) bybelasting; oorbelasting

surveill'ance toesig, opsig; waarneming; *under ~,* onder bewaking

surv'ey (n) (-s) opmeting; opname; **market ~,** markopname

survey' (v) (-ed, -ed) opneem; opmeet

survey'or landmeter

surviv'al oorlewing; voortbestaan; *~ of the fittest,* oorlewing van die sterkste; *~ course* oorlewing(s)kursus

survive' oorleef, in lewe bly, voortleef

surviv'or oorlewende; langslewende; **ag-** terblywende; opvarende (van gestrande skip)

suscep'tible gevoelig, vatbaar

sus'pect (n) verdagte; verdagte persoon

suspect' (v) verdink, wantrou; vermoed; (a) verdag; *~ed of arson,* verdink van brandstigting

suspend' ophang; opskort; skors; intrek; *~ a licence,* 'n lisensie intrek; *~ payment,* betalings staak; *~ed sentence,* opgeskorte vonnis; *~er* kousophouer, sokkieophouer

suspense' spanning, angs; opskorting; **~- account** afwagrekening

suspen'sion staking, skorsing, opskorting; vering (kar); *~ bridge* swaaibrug, hang- brug

suspi'cion agterdog, suspisie, argwaan; waatroue; *be under ~ of,* onder verden- king staan van

suspi'cious verdag, suspisieus, agterdogtig

swab (n) dweilap; pluisie, depper; skrop- besem

swagg'er (v) spog, grootpraat, bluf; (a) windmakerig, spoggerig; *~ cane* spog- kierietjie

swain boerekêrel; vryer, kêrel

swa'llow[1] (n) sluk; (v) sluk, verswelg

swa'llow[2] (n) swael, swa(w)eltjie; *~ tail* swaelstert

swam *see* **swim** (v)

swamp (n) moeras, vlei; (v) oorstroom; oorweldig; *~y* moerassig, drassig

swan swaan; seejuffer (vloot)

swank (v) spog, pronk; *~y* windmaker(ig), spoggerig; bakgat

swan: *~nery* (..ies) swaanboerdery; *~ song* swanesang

swarm (n) swerm; menigte; (v) swerm; wemel, krioel

swat (-ted, -ted) doodslaan

swatt'er vlieëplak, vlieëklap

sway (v) swaai, slinger; beheers; bestuur; *~ the sceptre,* die septer swaai

swear (v) (**swore, sworn**) vloek, swets; be- edig, sweer; *~ in,* beëdig, inhuldig; *~ an oath,* 'n eed aflê

sweat (n) sweet; *in the ~ of one's brow,* in die sweet van sy aanskyn; (v) sweet; swoeg; *~er* uitbuiter; oortrui, woltrui; *~ing sweet;* *~y sweet=,* natgesweet

sweep (n) veeg, slag; swaai; lotery; *make a clean ~,* skoonskip maak; (v) (**swept, swept**) vee, wegvee; *~ the board,* alles wen

sweep'ing allesomvattend; ingrypend, deurtastend; *a ~ majority,* 'n verplet- terende meerderheid; *~ statement,* wilde stelling; verregaande/oordrewe bewering

sweep'stake wedrenprys; insetgeld

sweet (n) soetigheid; skat, liefling; (pl) lek- kers, lekkergoed; (a, adv), soet, lieflik; be- vallig; aangenaam; dierbaar; lekker; *~ tooth,* lekkerbekkig wees; *~en* versoet; veraangenaam; *~ener* versoeter; *~heart* soetlief, skat, hartjie, liefste; *~ pea* pronk-ertjie; *~ potato* (-es) patat(ta); *~ tooth* lekkerbek; *~y* (..ties) hartjie, lief- ste, liefling; lekkertjie

swell (n) swelsel, swelling; geswel; deining (see); (v) (**-ed, swollen** or **-ed**) swel, op- swel; (a) puik, (piek)fyn; *~ clothes,* spog- gerige/windmakerige klere; *~ing* geswel

swel'ter (v) verdroog, smoor; *~ing* snik- warm, skroeiend (hitte)

swerve (v) swenk; opsy spring; wegswaai

swift (a, adv) vinnig, rats, gou; *~-footed* gou, vinnig; *~ness* snelheid, ratsheid

swim (v) (**swam, swum**) swem; *my head ~s,* ek word duiselig; *~mer* swemmer; *~- ming* swem, geswem; *~ming bath* swem- bad; *~ming pool* (private) swembad

swind'le (n) bedrog, swendelary; (v) swen- del, bedrieg, toetrap; *~r* bedrieër, swen- delaar, opligter

swine vark, swyn

swing (n) skoppelmaai; swaai; (v) (**swung, swung**) swaai; slinger; *~-bar* rekstok; *~ bridge* draaibrug; *~-glass, ~-mirror* draaispieël

swin'gle swingel; ~ bar, ~ tree swingel
swipe (n) mokerhou; (v) slaan, moker
swirl (n) warreling, wirwar; draaikolk; (v) draai, warrel
swish (n) geruis, ritseling; (-es) hou; (v) ransel; swiep, suis
Swiss (n) Switser; (a) Switsers; ~ roll rolkoek
switch (n) (-es) skakelaar; wisselspoor; (v) (in)skakel; aanskakel (lig); verwissel; ~ off, afdraai, afskakel; ~ on, aanskakel; ~board skakelbord; ~board operator skakelbordoperatrise, foondoedie
swiv'el draaiskyf, spil; ~ chair draaistoel
swoll'en see swell
swoon (n) beswyming, floute; (v) flou word, beswym
swoop (n) verrassingsaanval; with one ~, met een slag; (v) neerskiet, neerstryk
swop (-ped, -ped) ruil; verruil; omruil; ~ shop ruilwinkel, ruilhoekie
sword swaard, sabel; put to the ~, om die lewe bring; ~ dance swaarddans; ~s'man (..men) swaardvegter; ~s'manship skermkuns
swore see swear
sworn beëdig, geswore; kwaai; ~ enemies geswore vyande; ~ statement beëdigde verklaring
swot (v) (-ted, -ted) blok (vir eksamen); instudeer
syll'able lettergreep
syll'abus (-es) leerplan, sillabus

sym'bol sinnebeeld, simbool
symbol'ic simbolies, sinnebeeldig
symmet'ric(al) simmetries, eweredig
sympathet'ic medelydend, deelnemend; simpatiek; ~ ink simpatiese ink
sym'pathy (..thies) medely(d)e, meegevoel, simpatie
sym'phony (..nies) simfonie
symp'tom verskynsel, kenteken, simptoom
syn'agogue sinagoge
syn'chronise saamval, sinchroniseer, reguleer
syn'copate saamtrek, verkort, sinkopeer
syn'dicate sindikaat, kartel, sakegroep
syn'drome (n) sindroom, siektesimptome-groep
synec'doche sinekdogee
syn'od sinode; ~al sinodaal
syn'onym sinoniem
synop'tic sinopties, oorsigtelik; ~ chart sinoptiese kaart
syn'tax sintaksis, sinsbou; woordvoeging
syn'thesis (syntheses) samevoeging, samestelling, sintese
synthet'ic samestellend, sinteties; ~ rubber kunsrubber
syph'ilis geslagsiekte, sifilis
syph'on spuitwaterfles; sifon, hewel
syringe' (n) spuit; hypodermic ~, onderhuidse spuit; (v) spuit, inspuit
sy'rup stroop; golden ~, geelstroop
sys'tem stelsel, sisteem; metode; the solar ~, die sonnestelsel; ~at'ic stelselmatig, sistematies; ~atise sistematiseer

T

T-junction T-aansluiting
T-square winkelhaak
tabb'y (n) (tabbies) gestreepte kat; oujongnooi, kwaadspreekster; (a) gestreep; gevlam
tab'ernacle tabernakel; tent; the Feast of the T~s, die Loofhuttefees
t'able (n) tafel, dis; tabel, lys; ~ of contents, inhoudsopgawe; the ~s are turned, die bordjies is verhang; (v) ter tafel (lê); rangskik
tab'leau (-s) tablo
ta'ble: ~ boarder kosganger, dagloseerder; ~cloth tafeldoek; ~knife (..knives) tafelmes; ~land plato, hoogvlakte

Ta'ble Mountain Tafelberg
ta'ble: ~spoon tafellepel; ~ tennis tafeltennis
taboo' (n) verbod, taboe; (v) verbied, in die ban doen; (a) taboe, verbode
tab'ulate tabelleer, tabuleer; ~d getabelleer, getabuleer
tack (n) hegspyker, platkopspyker(tjie); rygsteek; (v) keer, laveer; ~ together, aanmekaarryg
tac'kle (n) takel; duikwerk (voetbal); (v) duik, plant, inspan, optuig; block and ~ katrolstel
tack'ling gereedskap; tuig; gerei; duikwerk (voetbal)

tack'y (tackies) seilskoen, tekkie; (a) kle=
werig

tact takt; **~ful** tak(t)vol; **~ical** takties,
meesterlik; **~i'cian** taktikus; **~ics**
taktiek, krygskunde

tact'less dom, tak(t)loos

tad'pole paddavis(sie)

tag (n) stif; lissie; rafel; etiket, kenstrokie;
(v) **(-ged, -ged)** aanheg; **~ end** oorskiet,
stert; **~rag:** *~rag and bobtail*, Jan Rap en
sy maat

tail (n) stert; stuitjie; keersy (munt);
~coat swaelstert (manel); **~ end** agter=
ste punt, stert; **~less** stompstert; **~light**
agterlig, stertlig

tail'or (n) kleremaker, snyer; **~made** aan=
gemeet; pasklaar; **~made suit** snyerspak

taint (n) kleur, tint; vlek; smet, besoedeling;
(v) besmet, bevlek, besoedel; **~ed** onrein,
besoedel; **~worm** miet

take (n) vangs; ontvangste; (v) **(took, taken)**
neem, vat; gryp; ontvang; *~ account of,*
rekening hou met; *~ after,* aard na; *~
aim,* korrel vat; *~ care,* oppas; pas op! *~
a chance,* 'n kans waag; *~ in consideration,* in aanmerking neem; *~ into
custody,* in hegtenis neem; *~ a degree,* 'n
graad behaal/verwerf; *~ effect,* in werking tree; *~ a fancy to,* lief word vir; *~
to heart,* ter harte neem; *~ a holiday,*
met/op vakansie gaan; *~ ill,* siek word;
~ notes, aantekeninge maak; *~ offence,*
aanstoot neem; *~ the opportunity,* van
die geleentheid gebruik maak; *~ part,*
deelneem; *~ sides,* party kies; *~ steps,*
maatreëls tref; *~n up,* ingenome, bly,
verheug; *~ a walk,* wandel, gaan stap;
~-aways wegneemetes, koop-en-loop=
happies, vat-'n-waai; **~-in** bedrog,
kullery; **~-off** wegspring; opstyging
(vliegtuig, vuurpyl); **~over** oorname

tak'ing innemend, bekoorlik; aansteeklik;
~s ontvangste

talc talk

tale storie, vertelling, verhaal, sprokie; *tell
~s,* klik; **~bearer** nuusdraer

tal'ent talent, gawe, aanleg; **~ed** begaaf,
talentvol; *a ~ed/gifted child,* 'n begaaf=
de kind

tal'isman (-s) talisman, gelukbringer

talk (n) gesprek; gerug; praatjie; onder=
houd; samespreking; *have ~s with,*

samesprekings voer met; (v) praat, gesels,
spreek; *~ nonsense,* kaf/twak praat; *~
shop,* vakpraatjies maak; **~ative** spraak=
saam, praatsiek; **~er** prater, spreker; **~ie**
klank(rol)prent, klankfilm; **~ing** (n) ge=
praat, pratery; (a) pratend, gepraat; **~-
ing-to** skrobbering

tall groot; lang/lank; hoog; *a ~ story,* 'n
ongelooflike verhaal; **~boy** laaikas

tall'ow kersvet, harde vet; talk; *~* **candle**
vetkers; **~-faced** bleek

tall'y (n) **(tallies)** kerfstok; keep; *take ~ of,*
tel; (v) **(tallied, tallied)** inkerf; ooreen=
stem; *~ with,* klop met

tam'bour (n) tamboer, trom; **~ine'** tam-
boeryn

tame (v) mak maak, tem; (a) mak; gedwee;
~r temmer

tam'pan hoenderbosluis, tampan

tam'per: *~ with,* knoei met, peuter aan

tan (n) looibas; (v) **(-ned, -ned)** looi; sonbruin; (a) geelbruin; taan (kleur); *she is
going to ~ on the beach,* sy gaan op die
strand sonbruin

tan'dem (n) tweelingfiets; tandem

tangerine' nartjie

tan'gible voelbaar, tasbaar; *~ proof of,*
tasbare bewys van

ta'ngle (n) verwikkeling, warboel

tank tenk, waterbak; tenk (vir oorlogvoering); **~ard** drinkkan; **~er** tenkskip;
tenkwa; *fill up your ~,* jou tenk voltap

tan: ~ner looier; **~nery** (..ries) looiery;
~nic acid looisuur; **~nin** looistof, looisuur, tannien; **~ning** looi; **~ning pit**
looikuip

tan'talise watertand; tantaliseer; **~r** kwel-
ler, tempteerder

tan'trum (onbeheerste) woedebui

tap¹ (n) tikkie; (v) **(-ped, -ped)** tik; klop

tap² (n) kraan; kantien; tap; *beer on ~,* bier
uit 'n vaatjie; (v) **(-ped, -ped)** aftap
(vloeistof); uittap; *~ a person,* iem. pols;
~ one's telephone, meeluister; *~ the
wires,* die telegraafdrade tap

tape (n) band, lint; maatband; *red ~,*
rompslomp; (v) vasbind, vasmaak; op=
neem; *~ aid* bandhulp (vir blindes);
~deck banddek; **~ library** bandoteek;
~line, *~* **measure** maatband, meetlint

tap'er (v) taps maak; afspits; (a) taps

tape: ~ **recorder** bandopnemer, bandmas‑
jien; ~ **recording** bandopname; ~ **slide**
sequence klankskyfiereeks

tap'ering spits, puntig, taps

tap'estry (..tries) behangsel, muurtapyt,
tapisserie; vloerkleed

tape'worm lintwurm

tap'root penwortel

tar (n) teer; matroos, janmaat; *Jack T~*,
pikbroek, matroos; (v) (-red, -red) teer; ~
and feather, teer en veer

taran'tula (-e, -s) bobbejaansspinnekop

tard'y traag, stadig, dralend, onwillig

tare eiegewig, eiemassa, tarra (massa)

targ'et skyf; mikpunt, teiken; *your* ~
readers, jou teikenlesers; ~ **practice** skyf‑
skiet

ta'riff (n) tarief; ~ **union** tolunie

tarn'ish (v) besoedel, bevlek; dof maak

tarpaul'in bokseil; matrooshoed

tart¹ (n) tert; flerrie

tart² (a) skerp; suur

tar'tar (n) wynsteen; tandsteen; *cream of*
~, kremetart

task (n) taak, werk; ~ **force** taakmag; ~ ‑
master tugmeester, leermeester

tass'el tossel, kwas, klossie

taste (n) smaak; voorsmaak; bysmaak;
voorliefde; *to my* ~, na my smaak; (v)
proe; smaak; ~**ful** smaakvol (meubile‑
ring); ~**less** laf, smaakloos; ~r proeër

tas'ty smaaklik, lekker

tatt'er flenter, toiing, flard; ~ed in toiings,
toiingrig

tat'tle (n) geklets, gebabbel; (v) babbel,
kekkel; ~r babbelaar; kekkelbek

tattoo'¹ (n) (-s) tatoeëring; (v) tatoeëer; ~
mark tatoeëermerk

tattoo'² (n) taptoe; *beat the devil's* ~, met
die vingers trommel

taught *see* **teach**

taut strak, gespanne, styf

tautol'ogy toutologie, herhaling

tav'ern kroeg, kantien; herberg; ~ **keeper**
herbergier, waard; kantienhouer

tawn'y donkergeel; taankleurig

tax (n) (-es) belasting; (v) takseer; belas;
~**able** belasbaar; ~**a'tion** belasting; ~
collector belastinggaarder, ontvanger van
belasting, Jan Taks; ~**free** belastingvry

tax'i (-s) taxi

tax'idermist diere-opstopper, taksidermis

tax'i driver taxidrywer

tax'ing (a) moeilik, veeleisend

tax'payer belastingpligtige, belastingbetaler

tea tee; ligte ete; *high* ~, teemaaltyd

teach (taught, taught) onderwys (gee), on‑
derrig, skoolhou, leer; ~**er** onderwyser‑
(es), leerkrag, (skool)meester; ~**er stu‑**
dent kwekeling; student-onderwyser; ~ ‑
ing (n) onderwys, leer; (a) onderwys‑;
~**ing experience** proefonderwys; prak‑
tiese onderwys (vir studente)

tea: ~ **cosy** (..cosies) teemus(sie); ~**cup**
teekoppie

teak kiaat(hout)

team (n) span; ~ **spirit** spangees

tear¹ (n) skeur; *fair wear and* ~, billike
slytasie; (v) (**tore, torn**) skeur, losruk; ~
one's hair, jou hare uittrek; ~ *up,* stuk‑
kend skeur; ~**off slip** skeurstrokie

tear² (n) traan; *shed* ~*s,* trane stort; ~**jer‑**
ker tranetrekker

tea'room teekamer, koffiehuis, kafee

tear'smoke traanrook

tease (n) terggees; kwelgees; (v) pla, kwel,
terg, treiter; pluiskam (hare); ~**r** plaag‑
gees, plaer

tea: ~ **service,** ~ **set** teestel, teeservies; ~
shrub teestruik

tea'spoon teelepel; ~**ful** (..fuls) teelepelsvol

teat tepel (mens); speen (dier)

tech'nical vak‑, tegnies

technic'ian tegnikus

tech'nikon (-s) technikon

technique' tegniek

ted'ious vervelig/vervelend, lastig

tee bof (gholf); pennetjie (ringspel)

teem (v) baar; wemel, krioel; ~ **with,** krioel
van, wemel van

teen'age tiender jarig, tiener‑; ~ **dress**
tienerdrag; ~ **party** tienerpartytjie; ~**r**
tienderjarige, tiener

teens tienderjarige, tiener; *in one's* ~, nog
nie twintig jaar nie, in sy tienderjare

teeth'ing tandekry; ~ **ring** bytring

teetot'aller geheelonthouer, afskaffer

teff tef

telecommunicat'ion telekommunikasie

tel'egram telegram, draadberig

tel'egraph (n) telegraaf; (v) telegrafeer

telep'athy telepatie

tel'ephone (n) telefoon; (v) bel, lui, skakel,
telefoneer; ~ **call** telefoonoproep; ~ **ex‑**

change telefoonsentrale; ~ **operator** telefonis; ~ **receiver** gehoorbuis, hoorstuk
teleph'onist telefonis(te), foondoedie
tel'escope (n) verkyker, teleskoop; (v) teleskopeer
telescop'ic teleskopies
tel'etuition afstandsonderrig
tel'evise beeldsaai, beeldsend
televi'sion televisie; beeldradio; kykkas(sie)
tel'ex (n) (-es) teleks; (v) teleks
tell (told, told) sê, vertel, meedeel, berig; ~ *that to the marines,* maak dit aan die swape wys; ~ *tales,* jok; verklik; ~**er** verteller; kassier (bank); (uit)teller
tell'ing vertel; verhaal; *you're ~ me!* weet ek dit nie! ek sou so dink!
tell'tale verklikker, klikbek, nuusdraer
tem'per (n) aard, temperament; humeur; *have a ~,* gou op sy perdjie wees; ~ *tantrum, see* **tantrum;** (v) temper, matig
tem'perament temperament, geaardheid
temperamen'tal temperamenteel
tem'perance matigheid, onthouding; ~ **society** matigheid(s)bond, afskaffersbond
tem'perate matig, gematig; bedaard; *the ~ zone,* die gematigde lugstreek
tem'perature temperatuur, warmtegraad; *have a ~,* koorsig wees
tem'pest storm, orkaan
tem'ple[1] tempel
tem'ple[2] slaap (aan kop)
tem'po (-s) tempo, maat
tem'porary tydelik, voorlopig; ~ **appointment** tydelike pos/betrekking
tempt in versoeking bring, trotseer; ~**a'tion** versoeking; *yield to the ~ation,* swig voor die versoeking
ten tien
tena'cious taai, hardnekkig
ten'ant (n) huurder, pagter; (v) huur
tend geneig wees; strek, strewe
ten'dency (..cies) strekking, neiging; aanleg; tendens
tenden'tious tendensieus, omstrede
tender[1] (n) tender, aanbod; inskrywing; *legal ~,* wettige betaalmiddel; (v) tender; ~ *one's resignation,* jou bedanking/ontslag indien
ten'der[2] (a) sag, mals; teer
ten'der: ~**-hearted** teerhartig, gevoelig; ~**ness** sagtheid, teerheid
ten'don sening, pees

ten: ~**fold** tienvoudig; ~**ner** tienrandnoot
tenn'is tennis; ~ **court** tennisbaan; ~ **tournament** tennistoernooi
ten'or gees, strekking; tenoor (stem)
ten'pins (tien)kegelspel
tense[1] (n) tyd
tense[2] (a) strak, styf, gespan(ne)
ten'sion trek; spanning; spankrag; *high ~,* hoogspanning
tent (n) tent; kap; (v) kampeer
ten'tacle voelorgaan, voelhoring; tentakel
ten'tative (a) voorlopig, tentatief
ten'terhook spanhaak; *be on ~s,* op hete kole sit
tenth tiende; ~**ly** in die tiende plek
ten'ure eiendomsreg, besit; ~ *of office,* dienstyd, ampstermyn
ter'cet terset, tersine; drieling
term (n) termyn, dienstyd; kwartaal; term; (pl) voorwaardes, bepalings; *on ~s and conditions,* onder (op) bepalings en voorwaardes; *on easy ~s,* op maklike (betaal)voorwaardes; *on equal ~s,* op gelyke voet; *in ~s of,* ingevolge, kragtens; ooreenkomstig; *not on speaking ~s,* kwaaivriende; (v) noem, benoem
term'inal (n) eindpunt, uiterste; terminaal; pool; ~ **patients** terminale pasiënte
term'inate beëindig; eindig; verstryk
terminol'ogy terminologie
term'inus (-es, ..ni) eindpunt, terminus
term'ite rysmier, termiet
te'rrace (n) terras; (v) terrasse maak
te'rrapin varswaterskilpad
terres'tial (n) aardbewoner; (a) aards, ondermaans; land~; ~ **animal** landdier
te'rrible verskriklik, yslik, vreeslik
terrif'ic verskriklik, ontsettend; wonderbaarlik
te'rrify (..fied, ..fied) verskrik, skok, bang maak, laat skrik
territor'ial territoriaal; grond~; landweer~
te'rritory (..ries, ..ries) gebied, grondgebied
te'rror skrik, ontsteltenis, angs; skrikbeeld; *reign of ~,* skrikbewind; ~**ism** skrikbewind, terrorisme, terreur; *urban ~ism,* stedelike terreur; ~**ist** terroris; ~**ise** skrik aanja, terroriseer; ~**-stricken** met skrik vervul, paniekerig
terse beknop, bondig, gedronge
ter'tiary van die derde orde, tersiêr; ~ **education** hoër/tersiêre onderwys

test (n) toets, proef; *the acid ~*, die vuur‑
proef; *stand the ~*, die toets deurstaan;
(v) toets

tes'tament testament, wilsbeskikking

testat'or erflater, testateur

testat'rix (..trices) testatrise, erflaatster

test: ~ **case** toetssaak; ~**ed** beproef; ~**ee**
toetsling

tes'ter toetser

tes'ticle teelbal

tes'tify (..fied, ..fied) getuig, plegtig ver‑
klaar; getuienis aflê

testimon'ial getuigskrif

tes'timony (..nies) getuienis, verklaring

test: ~ **match** (-es) toetswedstryd; ~ **pilot**
invlieër, toetsvlieënier; ~ **tube** proefbuis,
reageerbuis; ~*tube baby*, proefbuisbaba

tes'ty prikkelbaar, liggeraak, kortgebonde

tet'anus klem in die kaak, tetanus

text teks; onderwerp; ~**book** handboek,
handleiding

tex'tile (a) geweef(de), tekstiel‑, weef‑; ~
factory tekstielfabriek

tex'ture weefsel, tekstuur

than as

thank dank, bedank, dankie sê; ~ *you*,
dankie; ~**ful** dankbaar; ~**less** ondánk‑
baar; ~ **offering** dankoffer

thanks! dankie! *many* ~, baie dankie; ~
to Tom, we won; danksy Tom het ons
gewen

thank-you card dankkaar(tjie), dankiesê‑
kaart(jie)

that[1] (a) soveel, sodanig; *in ~ way*, op
daardie manier; (pron) dié, daardie; wat

that[2] (conj) dat, sodat

thatch (n) dekgras; strooidak; (v) dek; ~**ed
roof** grasdak, strooidak, rietdak

thaw (v) smelt (sneeu); ontdooi

the die; ~ *sooner ~ better,* hoe eerder hoe
beter

the'atre teater, skouburg; toneel; operasie‑
kamer; ~**goer** toneelganger

theat'rical (a) toneelmatig, teatraal

thee u

theft diefstal, stelery

their hulle, hul; ~**s** van hulle, hulle s'n

them hulle, hul

theme onderwerp, tema; opstel; ~ **tune**
kenwysie, *see* signature tune

themselves' hulleself

then (a) destyds, toenmalig; (adv) dan, toe;
by ~, teen daardie tyd; *every now and* ~,
kort-kort; *now and* ~, af en toe; (conj)
dan, dus

thence daarvandaan, van toe af, vandaar

theod'olite hoogtemeter, teodoliet

theol'ogy godgeleerdheid, teologie

theoret'ic teoreties

the'ory (theories) teorie; *in ~ and practice,*
in die teorie en praktyk

the'rapist terapeut

the'rapy geneeskuns, terapie; *vocational ~,*
arbeidsterapie

there daar, daarso; aldaar; daarnatoe,
soontoe; daarheen; ~**after** daarna; ~**by**
daardeur; ~**fore** daarom, dus, derhalwe;
~**from** daaruit; ~**of** daarvan; ~**upon'**
daarop, daarna

thermom'eter termometer; koorspennetjie

therm'ostat termostaat

these hierdie, dié

thes'is (theses) stelling; tesis, proefskrif,
verhandeling, dissertasie

they hulle, hul; ~ *say,* daar word gesê

thick (n) dikte; hewigste; ~**en** dik maak,
verdik

thick: ~**-headed** dom, onnosel; ~**ness**
dikte, digtheid; ~**set** dig begroei; dik,
geset; ~**-skinned** dikvellig; ~**-skulled**
hardkoppig, dom; ~**-witted** dom, bot

thief (thieves) dief; dievegge (vrou)

thieve (v) steel

thigh dy; ~ **bone** dybeen

thill disselboom

thim'ble vingerhoed

thin (v) (-ned, -ned) verdun; ~ *out,* uitdun;
(a) dun, maer; deursigtig; yl; *a ~ excuse,*
'n flou ekskuus/verskoning; ~**ner** ver‑
dunner

thine u, van u, u s'n

thing ding, goed; iets; (pl) goed, goeters;
dinge; *he knows a ~ or two,* hy is nie van‑
dag se kind nie; *poor ~,* arme drommel;
the very ~, net die regte ding

think (thought, thought) dink, nadink, be‑
dink; ~ *alike,* eenders dink; *if you ~ it
fit,* as jy dit goed vind; ~ *it over,* daaroor
nadink; ~**er** denker; filosoof; ~**ing** (n)
dink; gedagte; denke; (a) dink‑; denkend;
~**tank** dinkskrum

third (n) derde deel; terts (musiek); (a) der‑
de; ~ **degree** afdreiging van bekentenis;

~ **estate** derde stand; ~ **floor** derde vloer/vlak; ~**ly** derdens, in die derde plek; ~ **party** derde party; ~**party insu‑ rance** derdepartyversekering, derdedek‑ king; ~-**rate** derderangs, minderwaardig
thirst (n) dors; begeerte; *quench* ~, dors les; (v) verlang; *to* ~ *for knowledge*, om te dors na kennis; ~**y** dors, dorstig
thirteen' dertien; ~**th'** dertiende
thirt'ieth dertigste
thir'ty (..ties) dertig
this dit, hierdie, dié; ~ *day week,* vandag oor 'n week; ~ *month,* vandeesmaand; ~ *morning,* vanmôre; ~ *week,* vandees‑ week, hierdie week; ~ *year,* vanjaar
thi'stle distel/dissel
thong (n) riem; agterslag; (v) looi
thorn doring; *sit on* ~*s,* op hete kole sit; ~**y** doringrig, doringagtig; netelig, lastig
tho'rough grondig, deeglik; ~**bred** (n) vol‑ bloedperd, resiesperd; (a) volbloedras‑; ~**fare** deurgang; straat; ~-**going** deur‑ tastend, radikaal; ~**ly** terdeë, deur en deur
those daardie, diegene, dié
thou u
though hoewel, alhoewel, ofskoon, tog; *even* ~, selfs as
thought (n) gedagte; mening; *lost in* ~, in gedagtes verdiep; *on second* ~*s,* na ver‑ dere oorweging; (v) *see* **think**; ~**ful** be‑ dagsaam, sorgsaam, taktvol; ~**less** on‑ bedagsaam
thou'sand duisend
thrash uitlooi, afransel; oortref, verslaan; ~**ing** pak slae, loesing, *see* **thresh**
thread (n) draad; rafel; skroefdraad; (v) aan 'n draad ryg; ~ *beads,* krale inryg; ~ *one's way through,* jou weg baan deur; ~**bare** kaal, verslyt; afgesaag
threat bedreiging, dreigement
threat'en dreig, bedreig; ~**ing** (a) dreigend
three drie; *the* ~ *R's,* lees-, skryf- en re‑ kenkuns; ~**fold** drievoudig; ~**legged** drie‑ been‑; ~**ply** drielaag (hout); ~-**quarter** (n) driekwart; (a) driekwart‑
thresh dors (koring); ~**er,** ~**ing machine** dorsmasjien
thresh'old drumpel, ingang, begin
threw *see* **throw**
thrice drie maal; ~-**told** oud, afgesaag
thrift spaarsaamheid; ~**y** welvarend

thrill (n) tinteling, ontroering, sensasie; (v) ontroer, aangryp; ~**er** sensasieverhaal, spanningsboek, spanningsfilm, riller; ~-**ing** opwindend
thrips blaaspote
thriv'ing voorspoedig, florerend (besig‑ heid), bloeiend
throat keel; gorrel; *jump down one's* ~, iem. invlieg
throb (v) (**-bed, -bed**) klop, hyg, pols; ~-**bing** (n) klop, geklop; (a) kloppend
throe(s) hewige pyn, doodsangs, barensweë; ~*s of death,* doodsworsteling
thrombos'is aarverstopping, trombose
throne troon
throng (n) gedrang, gewoel; (v) toestroom
throt'tle (n) keelgorrel; strot, lugpyp; versnelklep (motor); (v) versmoor, ver‑ wurg; ~ **valve** versnelklep (motor)
through (a) deurgaande; (adv) deur; *fall* ~, deur die mat val; (prep) deur; uit; ~-**out'** dwarsdeur; deurgaans; ~**way** deurpad, deurweg
throw (n) gooi; *a stone's* ~, 'n hanetreetjie; (v) (**threw, thrown**) gooi, werp; ~ *into the bargain,* op die koop toe bygee; ~ *in one's lot with,* lief en leed deel met; ~ *in‑ to prison,* in die tronk smyt; ~ *up the sponge,* tou opgooi; ~**er** gooier
thrush[1] spru (siekte)
thrush[2] (**-es**) lyster (voël)
thrust (n) stoot, steek; dryfkrag; (v) (**thrust, thrust**) stoot, steek
thud' (n) slag, bons; (v) (**-ded, -ded**) plof
thug boef, skurk; wurger
thumb (n) duim; *hold* ~*s for a person,* vir iem. duim vashou; *Tom T*~, Klein Duim‑ pie; ~*s up,* hou moed; (v) beduimel; deurblaai; ~**latch** (**-es**) deurknip; ~**mark** duimmerk; ~**screw** duimskroef
thump (n, v) stoot, stamp; ~**ing** kolossaal
thun'der (n) donder; (v) donder, bulder; ~**bolt,** ~**clap** dondersslag; ~**cloud** don‑ derwolk; ~**ing** (a) donderend, oorverdo‑ wend; (adv) verbasend; ~**storm** donder‑ storm, onweersbui; ~-**struck** verbaas, verstom
Thurs'day Donderdag
thus dus, so, aldus; ~ *far,* tot sover
thwart dwarsboom, teenwerk
thy u, van u
thyme tiemie

thyr'oid skildvormig; ~ gland skildklier

tick¹ (n) bosluis; luis

tick² (n) tik; merk; strepie; kruisie; *in two ~s,* in 'n kits/japtrap; tjop-tjop; (v) tik; merk, afmerk

tick³ (n) krediet; *buy on ~,* op krediet koop

tick'et (n) kaartjie; *that's the ~,* mooi so; (v) beboet; ~ examiner kaartjie(s)onder= soeker; ~ office kaartjieskantoor

tick'ey (-s) trippens; trippens

tick'fever bosluiskoors (mense); ooskus= koors (beeste)

tic'kle (n) gekielie; (v) kielie; kriebel/krie= wel

tick'lish kielierig, liggeraak; netelig, deli= kaat

tid'al gety=; ~ pool getypoel; ~ wave vloedgolf

tiddlywinks' vlooiespel

tide (n) gety, eb en vloed; tyd; stroming; *high ~,* hoogwater; *low ~,* laagwater; *neap ~,* dooiety; *spring ~,* springty, springvloed; ~ gate sluisdeur

tid'iness netheid

tid'ings berig, tyding, nuus

tid'y (v) (tidied, tidied) opknap; (a) netjies, sindelik; *put things ~,* aan die kant maak

tie (n) band, knoop; das; (v) gelykop speel; bind, vasknoop; ~ up, vasbind; verbind; vassit (geld); ~ with, gelyk staan met; ~breaker valbylpot, uitkloppot (tennis)

tiff (n) slegte bui; rusie(tjie)

tig'er tier; ~ lily (..lillies) tierlelie

tight nou, eng; gierig; dronk, geswael; *be in a ~ corner,* in die knyp wees; (adv) styf; *hold ~,* hou vas; ~en nouer maak, vaster maak; ~-fisted vrekkerig, inhalig; ~-fitting nousluitend; ~s spanbroek, span= pak

tile (n) dakpan, teël; (v) teel; geteël

till¹ (n) geldlaai(tjie), kasregister

till² (v) bebou, ploeg, bewerk

till³ (prep) tot; ~ now, tot nog toe; ~ then, tot dan; *true ~ death,* getrou tot die dood; (conj) tot, totdat

tilt (n) skuinste; (v) steek, laat oorhel; ~ over, skeef staan; oorhel; ~ at windmills, teen windmeulens veg

tim'ber timmerhout, hout; ~ trade hout= handel; ~ yard timmerwerf

tim'bre timbre, toonkleur/klankkleur

time (n) tyd; maat; keer; maal; tempo; ~ *and again,* herhaaldelik; *ask the ~,* vra hoe laat dit is; *for the ~ being,* tot tyd en wyl; *keep ~,* die maat hou; ~ *and mo= tion study,* tyd-en-bewegingstudie; *in the nick of ~,* net betyds; *in no ~,* in 'n kits; *on ~,* betyds/op tyd; *at the same ~,* ter= selfdertyd; *ten ~s five,* tien maal/keer vyf; ~ *is up,* die tyd is om; *what is the ~?* hoe laat is dit? (v) maat hou; ~ *his speech,* sy toespraak klok; ~bomb tyd= bom; ~keeper tydopnemer, tydreëlaar; ~limit tydgrens; ~ly tydig, betyds; ~= piece uurwerk, klok; ~s maal/keer; ~= sharing tyddeling; ~ signal tydsein; ~ slot tydgleuf; ~ switch tydskakelaar; ~table (les)rooster, werkplan

tim'id skaam, skroomvallig, bedees

tim'ing tydreëling, tydinstelling (motor), tydopname, (tyds)berekening

tim'orous bangerig, skrikkerig

tin (n) blik; tin; (v) (-ned, -ned) vertin; in= maak, blik; ~ned meat blikkiesvleis

tin'der tontel; ~box (-es) tonteldoos

tin'foil bladtin; foelie, blinkpapier

tin'sel verguldsel; klatergoud; opskik; (v) (-led, -led) verguld; (a) oppervlakkig

tint (n, v) tint, kleur

tin'y klein, nietig, gering

tip¹ (n) tip, top; punt; *from ~ to toe,* van kop tot toon

tip² (n) fooi, bedien(ings)geld; wenk; (v) (-ped, -ped) gooi; omkantel; 'n fooi gee; 'n wenk gee; ~-off nuttige wenk/waar= skuwing

tip'sy dronk, besope, hoenderkop, lekker= lyf, aangeklam, getier; ~ cake wynkoek

tip'toe (v) op die tone loop; (adv) suutjies, katvoet, doekvoet

tip'top eersteklas, hoogste, beste, puik

tip truck wiplorrie

tip-up door wipdeur, opklapdeur

tirade' tirade, woordevloed

tire (v) vermoei, verveel; ~ out, afmat; ~d moeg, tam, mat; ~less onvermoeid; ~= some vermoeiend, vervelend

tiss'ue weefsel; sneesdoekie, snesie; *get a ~ and blow your nose,* kry 'n snesie en snuit jou neus; ~ paper sneespapier, snesie

tit tepel, tiet; ~ *for tat,* botter vir vet

titan'ic reusagtig, tamaai, groot, titanies

tit'bit lekker happie, lekkerny

tithe tiende, tiende gedeelte
tit'illate kielie; prikkel
tit'ivate opsmuk, mooi maak
ti'tle (n) titel; naam; aanspraak; (v) betitel, noem; ~d getitel; ~ deed grondbrief, transportakte, titelbewys; ~ page titelblad; ~ role titelrol
to (adv) toe; ~ and fro, heen en weer; (prep) tot, na, na . . . toe, om te; ~ the best of my ability, na my beste vermoë; ~ the best of my knowledge, na my beste wete; compared ~, in vergelyking met, vergeleke met; face ~ face, van aangesig tot aangesig; five ~ six, vyf minute voor ses; a means ~ an end, 'n middel tot 'n doel; ~ my mind, na/volgens my mening; ~ the point, ter sake; pull ~ pieces, in flenters skeur
toad padda; ~stool paddastoel; ~y (n) (.. dies) inkruiper; (a) inkruiperig
toast (n) roosterbrood; heildronk; (v) braai; 'n heildronk instel; ~er (brood)rooster; ~ed sandwich rooster(toe)broodjie
tobacc'o tabak, twak; ~nist tabakwinkel(ier), tabakboetiek; ~ pauch (-es) tabaksak
to-be' toekomstig, aanstaande
to'by blaasoppie (vis)
today' vandag; teenswoordig, deesdae
tod'dle (v) waggel, trippel; ~r kleuter, kleintjie, peuter
todd'y (to***ddies***) grok, sopie, pons
to-do' drukte, gedoente, ophef
toe (n) toon; big ~, groottoon; little ~, kleintoontjie; ~ the line, tot gehoorsaamheid dwing; ~nail toonnael
toff'ee (-s) tameletjie
tog (n) kleding(stuk); (pl) sportklere, voetbalklere; (v) (-ged, -ged) aantrek
tog'a toga, also academic gown
togeth'er saam, bymekaar, gesamentlik; all of us ~, almal saam
toil (v) swoeg; ~ and moil, swoeg en sweet; ~er werkesel
toil'et toilet; ~ paper toiletpapier; ~ set wasstel, toiletstel; ~ table kleedtafel
tok'en teken; kenteken; aandenking; ~ of appreciation, blyk van waardering; ~ism tokenisme
told see tell (v)
tol'erance verdraagsaamheid; speling, toleransie, toelaatbare afwyking

tol'erate verdra, duld, gedoog
toll[1] (n) tol, tolgeld; take ~ of, eis, verg
toll[2] (n) klokgelui; (v) lui; tamp
toll: ~bar slagboom; ~gate tolhek; ~house tolhuis; ~ money tolgeld
toll'y (tollies) jong ossie, tollie
Tom: ~, Dick and Harry, Jan Rap en sy maat; ~ Thumb, Klein Duimpie
tom'ahawk strydbyl
toma'to (-es) tamatie
tomb graftombe, graf
tom'boy (-s) rabbedoe, robbedoe, wilde meisie
tomb'stone grafsteen
tom'cat katmannetjie, kater
tomfool' gek, dwaas; ~ery gekskeerdery
tomm'y (tommies) tommie; ~rot bog, kaf, twak, absolute onsin
tomo'rrow more, môre; the day after ~, oormôre; ~ morning, môre vroeg, môre oggend
ton ton; ~s of people, hope mense
tone (n) toon, klank; ~ down, bedaar; versag; ~ up, krag gee, besiel
tongs tang
tongue tong; taal, spraak; klepel (klok); with one's ~ in one's cheek, skertsend; confusion of ~s, spraakverwarring; a slip of the ~, 'n onbedagsame woord; ~-shaped tongvormig; ~-tied spraakloos; gemuilband; ~ twister snelsêer, tongknoper
ton'ic (n) versterkmiddel, opknapper, tonikum; ~ solfa solfanotering, solfaskrif
tonight' vanaand; vannag
to'nnage tonnemaat; skeepsruimte
ton'sil mangel; ~lit'is mangelonsteking, tonsilitis
too te, alte, ook, eweeneens; only ~ true, maar alte waar
took see take
tool (n) werktuig; gereedskap; (v) bewerk; ~box (-es) gereedskapkis
toot (n) getoeter; (v) toeter
tooth (n) (teeth) tand; kam; artificial ~, vals tand, winkeltand; long in the ~, oud; fight ~ and nail, met hand en tand beveg; by the skin of the teeth, naelskraap; ~ache tandpyn; ~brush (-es) tandeborsel; ~paste (tande)pasta; ~pick tandekrapper; ~powder tandepoeier; ~some smaaklik

top¹ (n) tol (speelding); *sleep like a* ~, soos 'n klip slaap

top² (n) top; toppunt, kruin; *on ~ of this,* boonop; ~ *of one's class,* eerste in die klas; *on* ~, bo-op; (v) (**-ped, -ped**) aftop, snoei; uitmunt bo; ~ *the poll,* die meeste stemme kry; (a) boonste; beste; ~ **man-agement,** (die) topbestuur; ~ **prices,** die hoogste pryse; *at* ~ **speed,** so vinnig moontlik; (interj) goed! eersteklas!

top'az topaas

top: ~**boot** kapstewel; ~ **dog** bobaas; ~ **dressing** bolaag, bobemesting; ~ **gear** hoogste versnelling; bokerf; ~ **hat** keil; ~**heavy** topswaar

top'ic onderwerp, tema

top'ical plaaslik, aktueel; geleentheids-

top: ~ **management** topbestuur; ~**notcher** bobaas, doring, uithaler

top'ple omval, omkantel, omtuimel

top: ~ **secret** uiters geheim; ~**soil** bogrond; ~**spin** botol (van bal)

topsy-tur'vy onderstebo, bolmakiesie

torch (**-es**) toorts, fakkel, flitslig; ~**bearer** fakkeldraer; ~**light procession** fakkelloop

to'reador toreador, berede stiervegter

torment' (v) folter, pynig, kwel; ~**or** kwel-gees, plaaggees

tornad'o (**-es**) werwelstorm, tornado

torped'o (n) (**-es**) torpedo; (v) torpedeer

tor'rent stortvloed; *in* ~**s**, in strome

tor'rid dor, verskroeiend

tor'so (**-s**) romp, torso

tor'toise skilpad; ~ **shell** skilpaddop

tor'ture (v) folter, martel; ~ **chamber** fol-terkamer, martelkamer; ~**r** folteraar

toss (n) (**-es**) loot; *win the* ~, die loot wen; (v) loot; skud; ~ *aside,* opsy gooi; ~ *up,* opgooi; ~**-up** onuitgemaakte saak, gelyke kans

tot (n) klein kleuter; snaps; sopie; *a tiny* ~, 'n snuiter, kleuter

tot'al (n) volle som, totaal; (v) (**-led, -led**) optel; (a) volkome, totaal; ~ **abstinence** geheelonthouding; ~ **eclipse** algehele ver-duistering; ~ **onslaught** totale aanslag

tot'alisator totalisator; ~ **jackpot** boerpot

tot'ally heeltemal, glad, volslae

tott'er waggel, wankel; ~**ing** waggelend

touch (n) (**-es**) aanraking; tik; aanslag (mu-siek); *keep in* ~ *with,* in voeling bly met; *a* ~ *of salt,* 'n knypie sout; (v) voel, tas,

aanraak; tref; *no one can* ~ *him,* sy ma-ters is dood; ~ *down,* neerstryk (vlieg-tuig); ~ *up,* opknap; bywerk; ~**-and-go** so hittete, amper(tjies); ~**ing** (a) roerend, aandoenlik; ~ **kick** buiteskop; ~ **line** kantlyn; ~**typing** blindtik; ~**typist** blind-tikster; ~**y** liggeraak

tough taai; hard; styf; moeilik, lastig; *a* ~ **customer,** 'n lastige klant; ~**en** taai maak; ~**ness** taaiheid, hardheid

tour (n) reis, toer; rondreis; (v) toer, rond-reis; ~**ism** toerisme; ~**ist** reisiger, toeris; ~**ist attraction,** besienswaardigheid, toe-riste-aantreklikheid

tour'nament toernooi, wedstryd

tourn'iquet aarpers, skroefband, toerniket

tout (n) kliëntelokker; (v) beloer; klante/kliënte lok

tow (n) sleep; sleeptou; *take in* ~, op sleep tou neem; (v) sleep, treil; ~**-away service** insleepdiens

to'ward gewillig, volgsaam, leergierig

to'wards na, tot, teen, jeens; *his attitude* ~ *me,* sy houding teenoor my

tow'el (n) handdoek; *throw in the* ~, tou opgooi

tow'er (n) toring; ~ *of strength,* steunpi-laar; (v) toring

town dorp, stad; *man about* ~, windma-kerige niksdoener; *paint the* ~ *red,* die dorp op horings neem; ~**clerk** stadsklerk; ~ **council** stadsraad; ~ **councillor** stads-raadslid; ~ **hall** stadhuis, stadsaal; ~ **house** meenthuis; ~**'s folk** stadmense; ~**ship** dorpsgebied; woonbuurt; ~**'s man** (..men) stedeling, dorpenaar

tox'ic giftig; gif; ~**ant** (n) gif; (a) giftig

toy (n) (**-s**) speelding; (pl) speelgoed; (v) speel; ~ **dog** skoothondjie

trace¹ (n) string (van tuig); *kick over the* ~**s,** oor die tou trap

trace² (n) spoor; voetspoor; (v) opspoor; natrek; ~**r bullet** ligspoorkoeël

tra'cing paper, deurtrekpapier, natrekpa-pier, kalkeerpapier

track (n) spoor; pad; spoorlyn; (ren)baan; *be on one's* ~, op iem. se hakke wees; (v) naspeur; ~ *down,* opspoor; ~**er** spoor-snyer; speurhond; ~ **steward** baan-beampte; ~**suit** sweetpak

trac'tion trekking; trekkrag; traksie

trac'tor trekker

trade (n) handel, sake; bedryf, ambag; *a chemist by ~,* 'n apteker van beroep; (v) handel dryf, sake doen; *~ in,* inruil; *~-in value,* inruilwaarde (van 'n motor); **~ discount** handelskorting; **~ journal** vakblad; **~mark** handelsmerk; **~r** winkelier, handelaar; **~s'man** (..men) koopman, winkelier; **~s'man entrance** diensingang; **~ union** vakbond, vakunie; **~ wind** passaat(wind)

trad'ing (n) handeldryf; handel; (a) handels~; **~ company** handelsmaatskappy; **~ profit** bedryfswins

tradi'tion oorlewering, tradisie; **~al** tradisioneel

traff'ic (n) verkeer; (v) (-ked, -ked) handel dryf, smous; **~ control** verkeerbeheer; **~ hazard** verkeershindernis; **~ interchange** verkeer(s)wisselaar, wisselkruising; **~ is-land** vlugheuwel; **~ jam** verkeersknoop, verkeersophoping; **~ light** verkeerslig; **~ officer** verkeersbeampte

tra'gedy (..dies) treurspel, tragedie

tra'gic tragies

trail (n) sleep; spoor; voetpad; rank; stert (komeet); *hiking ~,* voetslaanpad; wandelpad; (v) sleep, agtervolg; **~er** rankplant; sleepwa; lokfilm; **~ net** treknet

train (n) trein; *by ~,* per spoor; *~ of thought,* gedagtegang; (v) oefen, dril; oplei; afrig; **~ed** geoefen; ervare, geskool; opgelei; gedresseer (dier)

train'bearer slipdraer

train'driver treindrywer, masjinis

trainee' kweseling, kadet, opleideling

train'er instrukteur, afrigter, breier; opleier

train'fare reisgeld, treingeld

train'ing opleiding; *be in ~,* opgelei word; geoefen wees; *go into ~,* begin oefen; **~ college** oplei(dings)kollege, onderwyskollege; **~ ship** oefenskip

train oil factory traankokery, walvisfabriek

trait (karakter)trek; eienskap; streep

trait'or verraaier

traject'ory (..ries) baan; koeëlbaan, trajek

tram trem; koolwa; **~line** tremspoor

tramp (n) landloper, rondloper; boemelaar; vragsoeker (skip)

tram'ple (n) getrap, gestamp; vertrapping; (v) trap; vertrap; *~ to death,* doodtrap

tramp'oline wipmat, trampolien

trance verrukking, geestesvervoering; beswyming, skyndood; droomtoestand

tranquill'ity rus, stilte, kalmte

tranq'uillise gerusstel, sus; **~r** kalmeermiddel; bedaarmiddel, sedatief

transact' onderhandel; verhandel; verrig; **~ion** onderhandeling, verrigting, transaksie

transcribe' oorskryf; transkribeer

trans'fer (n) transport; oordrag; oorplasing; afstand; afdruk; *deed of ~,* transportakte

transfer' (v) (-red, -red) verplaas; oordra; oorplaas; *~red to Cape Town,* na Kaapstad verplaas

transfer'able oordraagbaar; verplaasbaar

transform' vervorm, transformeer; herskep; **~a'tion** gedaanteverandering; transformasie; **~er** transformator

transfu'sion oortapping (bloed)

transgress' oortree, oorskry; **~ion** oortreding, oorskryding, sonde; **~or** oortreder

transis'tor transistor, kristalbuis

trans'it deurgang, deurtog; transito

translate' vertaal, oorsit, oorbring; *~d from Afrikaans,* uit Afrikaans vertaal

transla'tion vertaling, oorsetting

transla'tor vertaler

transmi'ssion oorsending; transmissie (motor); uitsending (draadloos)

transmit' (-ted, -ted) oorsend, oorsein (berig); oorlewer; uitsend (radio); **~ter** sender (radio)

transmuta'tion verandering, vormwisseling

transpar'ency deursigtigheid; transparant

transpar'ent deurskynend, deursigtig

transpire' uitlek; uitwasem; sweet; gebeur

transplant' verplant, oorplant; verplaas; *heart ~,* hartoorplanting

trans'port (n) transport, vervoer; **~ affairs** vervoerwese; **~ allowance** vervoertoelae; **~ and subsistence** reis en verblyf; **~ation** system vervoerstelsel; **~ services** vervoerdienste

transport' (v) vervoer, transporteer

trap (n) val, strik; slagyster; lokvink; *set a ~,* 'n val stel; (v) (-ped, -ped) vang, betrap; **~door** valdeur

trapeze' (-s) sweefstok

trap: ~per wildvanger, pelsjagter; **~pings** tooi(sel), versiersel; perdetuig

trash afval; vullis; oorskiet; bog, kletspraatjies, kaf; **~can** vullisblik

trav'el (v) (**-led, -led**) reis, bereis; **~ agent** reisagent; **~led** bereis

trav'eller reisiger; **~'s cheque** reistjek

trav'elling reis; **~ expenses** reiskoste; **~ library** (**..ries**) reisbiblioteek; **~ trunk** reiskoffer

trav'elogue reisverhaal

trawl (v) treil; **~er** treilvisser; treiler; **~ net** sleepnet

tray (**-s**) skinkbord; bakkie, (plat)kissie

trea'cherous verraderlik, vals

trea'chery verraad, verraaiery; valsheid

trea'cle triakel; swartstroop, beesstroop

tread (n) tree, tred, voetstap, skrede; loop-vlak (band); (v) (**trod, trodden**) tree, stap, betree, bewandel; **~ on thin ice,** op ge-vaarlike terrein wees

trea'dle trapper, pedaal; **~ machine** trap-masjien

tread'mill trapmeul; sleurwerk

treas'on verraad; **high ~,** hoogverraad

treas'ure (n) skat; **~ house** skatkamer; **~ hunt** skattejag; **~r** skatbewaarder; te-sourier, penningmeester, sentmeester

trea'sury (**..ries**) skatkamer, skatkis, tesou-rie; **~ bond** skatkisobligasie

treat (n) onthaal; (v) onthaal, trakteer; **~ as a joke,** as 'n grap beskou; **~ment** behan-deling

trea'tise verhandeling

treat'y (**..ties**) verdrag, traktaat; ooreen-koms

tree (n) boom; lees (vir skoene); **~ fern** boomvaring; **~ snake** boomslang

trek (n) trek; (v) (**-ked, -ked**) trek

trell'is (n) tralie(werk); prieel; **~ work** tra-liewerk, latwerk

trem'ble (n) bewing, trilling, bewerasie; (v) beef, sidder; gril; **~ with fear,** beef van angs

trem'bling (n) bewing, siddering, trilling; (a) bewend

tremen'dous verskriklik; yslik, ontsaglik, geweldig

trem'or bewing, siddering; aardskudding

trench (n) (**-es**) loopgraaf; voor; riool

trend (n) tendens; neiging, strekking; **~s in literature,** tendense in die literatuur; **~y** byderwets; **~setter** tendenser

tres'pass (n) (**-es**) oortreding, vergryp; son-de; **forgive us our ~es,** vergeef ons ons

skulde; (v) oortree, vergryp; sondig; **~er** oortreder; **~ing** betreding

tress (**-es**) haarlok, haarstring, vlegsel

tre'stle stellasie, bok

tri'al beproewing; proefneming; verhoor; hofsaak; **~ and error method,** probeer-en-tref-metode; **~ run,** oefenlopie; proef-lopie; **stand ~ for murder,** weens moord teregstaan; **~ consignment** proefsending; **~ marriage** proefhuwelik

tri'angle driehoek; triangel (mus.)

trib'al stam-; **~ war** stamoorlog

tribe stam, volkstam; ras, geslag

tribun'al regbank, geregshof, tribunaal

trib'une spreekgestoelte, tribune

trib'utary (n) (**..ries**) syrivier, takrivier; skatpligtige

trib'ute hulde, huldeblyk; **floral ~s,** kran-se; ruikers; **pay ~ to,** hulde betoon aan/teenoor

trick (n) kultoertjie, kunsie, behendigheid; skelmstreek, truuk, foefie; **play ~s,** poet-se bak; **the ~s of the trade,** fabrieksge-heime; (v) bedrieg; knoei, fop; kul; **~er,** **~ster** bedrieër, kuller; **~ery** kullery, be-drieëry, verneukery

tric'kle (v) druppel, aftap, rol; **tears ~d down her cheeks,** trane het oor haar wan-ge gerol/gebiggel

trick'y bedrieglik, vol streke, listig; oulik, gewaag; **~ question** strikvraag; **~ situa-tion** netelige situasie

tri'cycle driewiel(er)

tri'dent drietand

tried beproef, getoets

tri'fle (n) kleinigheid, bakatel; koekstruif; kits; (v) beusel; korswel, skerts; **he is not to be ~d with,** hy laat nie met hom speel nie; (adv) bietjie

trif'ling beuselagtig, onbenullig

trigg'er sneller; **~-happy** skietlustig

trigonom'etry driehoeksmeting, trigono-metrie

tril'ogy (**..gies**) trilogie, drieluik

trim (n) opskik, tooisel; (v) (**-med, -med**) tooi, versier; snoei, knip; (a) netjies; mooi, in orde; **~mer** afwerker; **~ming** opsmuk; **~park** trimpark

trin'ity drie-eenheid; drietal; **Holy T~,** Heilige Drie-eenheid

trink'et sieraad, kleinood, snuistery; **~ box** (**-es**) juweelkissie tri'o (-s) drie, trio

trip (n) uitstappie, rit; dwelmtoer; (v) (-ped, -ped) struikel, val; pootjie

tripe ingewande, binnegoed; bog, kaf

tri'plet drieling; tersine (poësie); drietal

trip'licate (n) drievoud, triplikaat

trip'od driepoot, drievoet

tripp'er plesierreisiger; trippelaar

triptique' triptiek, motorpas

trite alledaags; uitgedien; banaal

tri'umph (n) triomf, seëpraal; (v) triomfeer, seëvier; ~ over all difficulties, alle moeilikhede oorwin

trium'phant triomfantlik, seëvierend

trium'vir (-i, -s) drieman, triumvir; ~ate driemanskap

triv'ial vervelig, plat, triviaal; ~ matters, kleinighede, beuselagtighede

trocha'ic (n) trogee; (a) trogeïes

trod, tro'dden see tread

trog'lodyte grotbewoner, troglodiet

troll'y (trollies) trollie; ~bus trembus

trom'bone tromboon, skuiftrompet

troop (n) trop, hoop, menigte; afdeling; (pl) troepe, soldate; deploy ~s, troepe ontplooi; ~ carrier transportskip; troepevliegtuig; troepedraer

troph'y (..phies) trofee, beker; floating ~, wisseltrofee

trop'ic (n) keerkring; (pl) trope; T~ of Cancer, Kreefskeerkring; T~ of Capricorn, Steenbokskeerkring

trop'ical tropies; ~ diseases tropiese siektes

trot (n) draf; go for a ~, 'n entjie gaan draf; (v) (-ted, -ted) draf, op 'n draf ry; laat draf; ~ter drawwer; pootjie, afval (van vark, skaap)

troub'adour troebadoer

trou'ble (n) moeite, sorg, moeilikheid; be in ~, in die knyp sit; in real ~, kniediep in die moeilikheid; take the ~, die moeite doen; (v) moeite doen, lastig val; pla; neul; ~maker skoorsoeker; ~shooter foutspeurder; ~some lastig, neulerig, vervelig

trough trog, bak

trounce afransel, uitlooi, 'n pak gee

troupe geselskap, troep

trouss'eau (-s) (bruids)uitset, trousseau

trout forel

trow'el troffel

tru'ant (n) stokkiesdraaier; play ~, stokkies draai; (a) lui, pligversakend

truce wapenstilstand, verposing

truck (n) goederewa, trok; onderstel; vragmotor; (v) trok

tru'culent woes, wreed, barbaars

trudge (v) aansukkel, strompel, swoeg

true (n): out of the ~, nie haaks nie; (a, adv) waar; eg; opreg; suiwer; his words have come ~, sy woorde is bewaarheid; ~born eg; volbloed; ~bred raseg, opreg; ~love soetlief, hartjie, skattebol

tru'ly regtig, inderdaad; yours ~ hoogagtend

trump (n) troefkaart; (v) troef; oortroef; ~ up, uit die duim suig; ~ card troefkaart

trump'et (n) trompet; trompetgeskal; blow one's own ~, jou eie basuin blaas; (v) uitbasuin; ~ call trompetgeskal; ~er trompetblaser

trunk stomp; romp; stronk; koffer, kis; slurp (olifant); hooflyn; ~ call hooflynoproep; ~ line hooflyn; ~ road hoofweg, deurpad

trust (n) vertroue; trust; geloof; (v) vertrou; toevertrou; I ~ that, ek hoop dat; ~ company trustmaatskappy; ~ deed trustakte; ~ee' trustee, gevolmagtigde; ~eeship voogdyskap; ~ money (-s) trustgeld; ~worthy betroubaar; ~y eerlik; beproef

truth waarheid; ~ful waarheidliewend, betroubaar; ~less ontrou, vals; ~ serum waarheidserum

try (n) (tries) poging; proef; 'n drie (rugby); convert a ~, 'n drie verdoel; (v) (tried, tried) verhoor; op die proef stel, probeer, trag, beproef; ~ one's patience, jou geduld op die proef stel; ~ing lastig, moeilik, veeleisend,; ~ line doellyn; ~ square winkelhaak

tset'se fly tsetsevlieg, gifvlieg

tsot'si (-s) tsotsi

T'-square tekenhaak

tub balie, kuip, bad; tale of a ~, praatjies vir die vaak; ~by vatvormig

tube pyp, buis; binneband; ~less tyre lug(buite)band; ~ railway moltrein

tuberculos'is tuberkulose, tering

tub'erose (n) soetemaling; (a) knolvormig

tub'ing pype, pyplengte; buise

tuck (n) opnaaisel; (pl) eetgoed, snoepgoed; (v) plooi, intrek; oprol; ~ in, lekker toemaak; instop, wegslaan (kos); **~shop** snoepwinkel(tjie)

Tues'day Dinsdag

tuft (n) bos, kuif, kwas, pluim; pol (gras)

tug (n) sleepboot; **~ of war,** toutrek; (v) (**-ged, -ged**) trek, ruk; sleep

tui'tion onderwys, onderrig; **tele~** af=standsonderrig

tul'ip tulp; **~ bulb** tulpbol

tum'ble (n) val, tuimeling; warboel; (v) bolmakiesie slaan; rol; woel; val-val loop, struikel; **~ down,** instort; afrol; **~bug** miskruier, *also* **dung beetle**; **~-down** bouvallig, vervalle; **~drier** tuimeldroër; **~r** drinkglas; tuimelaar (duif); akrobaat; **~ switch** tuimelskakelaar

tumm'y (tummies) magie, pensie

tum'or geswel, gewas, groeisel, tumor

tum'ult opskudding, rumoer, lawaai

tun'dra toendra, mossteppe; moeraswêreld

tune (n) toon, klank, wysie; **out of ~,** vals; **to the ~ of,** op die wysie van; tot die be=drag van; (v) stem, instem (draadloos); **~ in to,** instem/instel op (radio); **~ful** me=lodieus, welluidend; **~r** stemmer; stem=vurk; instemmer (radio)

tun'ic uniform, skooldrag, springjurk

tun'ing (n) stem, gestem; **~ fork** stemvurk

tunn'el (n) tonnel; gang, skag; (v) (**-led, -led**) tonnel; uithol

tunn'y (tunnies) tornyn, tuna

tur'ban tulband

tur'bine turbine

turbo: ~charger turboaanjaer; **~diesel en=gine** turbodieselenjin

tur'bulence, tur'bulency onstuimigheid, oproerigheid, turbulensie

tureen' sopkom

turf (**-s**) turf, sooi; grasveld, baan; renbaan, reisiesbaan; **~ club** renbaanklub

turk'ey (n) (**-s**) kalkoen; **~ cock** kalkoen=mannetjie; **~ hen** kalkoenwyfie

turm'oil (n) onrus, gewoel, gejaagdheid

turn (n) draai, wending; beurt (by spele); **by ~s,** beurt-beurt, om die beurt; **do one a ~,** iem. 'n guns bewys; (v) draai; om=keer, verander; wend; **~ one's back on,** die rug toekeer; **~ the corner,** die hoek omgaan; **not ~ a hair,** geen spier vertrek nie; **~ hundred,** honderd jaar oud word; **~ out for practice,** vir oefening opdaag; **~ the tables,** die bordjies verhang; **~ up,**

opdaag; **~ upside down,** onderstebo keer; **~coat** manteldraaier, oorloper; **~er** draaier (ambag); **~ery** draaiwerk

turn'ing (a) draaiend; **~ point** keerpunt

turn'ip raap

turn: ~key (**-s**) tronkbewaarder, sipier; **~-out** opkoms; **~over** omset; **~pike** slag=boom, draaihek; **~stile** draaihek, draai=boom; **~table** draaitafel

turp'entine terpentyn

turq'uoise turkoois

tu'rret torinkie; skiettoring

tur'tle[1] tortelduif

tur'tle[2] waterskilpad; *turn ~,* omslaan

tusk (n) slagtand; tand; (v) oopskeur

tus'sle (n) worsteling, gestoei; (v) stoei

tut'or (n) huisonderwyser; studieleier, af=rigter; *private ~,* goewernant(e); (v) on=derrig; privaat les gee

tutor'ial (n) studieklas; breiklas; (a) groep=

tut'orship dosentskap; voogdyskap

twad'dle (n) bogpraatjies; gebasel, gebab=bel; **~r** kletser, babbelaar

twang (n) neusklank; (v) tokkel

tweedledum': **~ *and tweedledee',*** vinkel en koljander (die een is soos die ander)

tweet (n) getjilp; (v) tjilp

tweez'ers (haar)tangetjie, friseertang; pin=set; *pair of ~,* krultang

twelfth twaalfde

twelve twaalf

twen'tieth twintigste; **~ century** twintigste eeu

twen'ty (**..ties**) twintig; **~-four hours' ser=vice,** etmaaldiens

twice twee maal/keer

twid'dle (n) draaitjie, krul; (v) draai, lol; **~ one's thumbs,** met jou duime speel

twig takkie, twyg; waterwysstokkie

twi'light (aand)skemering, skemerlig, ske=meraand; **~ of the gods,** godeskemering; **~ sleep** pynlose bevalling

twin (n) tweeling; dubbelganger; **~ brother** tweelingbroer

twi'nkle (n) flikkering, vonkeling; oogknip

twi'nkling flikkering; kits; *in the ~ of an eye,* in 'n oogwink

twirl (n) draai; krul; (v) dwarrel, draai

twist (n) draai; kronkel; lok, krul; rinkhals=dans; *a moral ~,* 'n sedelike afwyking; (v) draai, verdraai; vleg; **~ evidence,** getuie=nis verdraai twitch (n) (-es) senuweetrekking; (v) losruk; trek; vertrek

twitt'er (n) gekwetter, getjilp; (v) kwetter; kweel; giggel

two (-s) twee; *cut in ~*, middeldeur sny; *put ~ and ~ together*, jou gesonde verstand gebruik; **~-engined** tweemotorig; **~fold** tweevoudig, dubbel; **~ply** tweelaag=; **~seater** tweesitplekmotor; **~some** twee= spel, dubbelspel; **~-tongued** vals

type (n) tipe, soort, setsel (drukkery); (v) tik; **~script** tikskrif; **~setter** letterset= ter; **~writer** tikmasjien; **~writing** tik= skrif

typh'oid (n) ingewandskoors; (a) tifeus; **~ fever** ingewandskoors, maagkoors

typhoon' tifoon

typh'us tifuskoors, vlektifus, luiskoors

typ'ical tipies

typ'ing tik, tikskrif, tikwerk; **~ pool** tik= poel

typ'ist tikster

typograp'ic tipografies, druk=; **~al error** drukfout

ty'ranny (..nnies) tirannie, dwingelandy

ty'rant tiran, dwingeland

tyre buiteband; *tubeless ~*, lug(buite)band; **~ lever** bandwipper

U

udd'er uier

ug'liness lelikheid, wanstaltigheid

ug'ly (a) lelik; gemeen; gevaarlik; skande= lik; *an ~ customer*, 'n nare/gevaarlike vent; *~ weather*, onaangename/gure weer

ul'cer sweer, geswel; maagseer

ulter'ior aan die ander kant; verborge, ge= heim; **~ motive** bybedoeling

ul'timate laaste, uiterste; beslissend; grond=

ultimat'um (-s, ..ta) ultimatum

ul'timo laaslede, van die vorige maand

um'ber (n) omber; (a) donkerbruin

umbil'ical nael=; **~ cord** naelstring

umbrell'a sambreel; **~ body** oorkoepelende liggaam; **~ stand** sambreelstander; **~ term** sambreelterm; **~ tree** kiepersolboom

um'pire (n) skeidsregter

una'ble onbekwaam, nie in staat nie

unaccept'able onaanneemlik

unaccus'tomed ongewoon

unaffect'ed natuurlik, ongekunstel(d), op= reg

unaligned' onverbonde (nasies)

unan'imous eenstemmig, eenparig

unans'wered onbeantwoor(d)

unarmed' ongewapen(d)

unashamed' onbeskaamd, onbeskof

unassum'ing beskeie, pretensieloos

unattached' los; alleenstaand; ongetroud

unauth'orised ongemagtig, onwettig

unavoid'able onvermydelik

unaware' onbewus, onwetend

unawares' onverwags; plotseling; *take ~*, oorval

unbal'anced ongebalanseer

unbear'able ondraaglik, onuithoubaar

unbeat'en onoorwin, onoortroffe

unbecom'ing onbetaamlik, onwelvoeglik

unbeliev'able ongelooflik

unbi'ased onbevooroordeel, onpartydig

unblem'ished onbevlek, rein, onbesmet

unbri'dled onbeteuel, losbandig, uitgelate

unbro'ken onafgebroke, deurlopend; on= getem; ongestoord; heel

unbuc'kle losgespe

unbutt'on losknoop

uncall'ed ongeroep; *~ for,* onvanpas, on= nodig; ongevra; onafgehaal (goed)

uncann'y grillerig; onwerklik, bomenslik

uncer'tain onseker, wisselvallig

unchart'ed ongekaart

unchecked' los, vry, ongedwonge

unchris'tian onchristelik

unciv'il onbeleef, ongemanierd; **~ised** on= beskaaf, barbaars

unclaimed' onopgeëis

un'cle oom; pandjiesbaas

uncom'fortable ongemaklik, ongerieflik

uncomm'on ongewoon, seldsaam

uncommun'icative stil, terughoudend, te= ruggetrokke, swygsaam

unconcern' onverskilligheid; **~ed** onbe= kommerd; doodgerus

uncondi'tional onvoorwaardelik; **~ sur= render** onvoorwaardelike oorgawe

uncon'scious bewusteloos; onwetend, on= bewus

unconstitu'tional ongrondwetlik

uncontest'ed onbetwis, onbestrede; ~ seat onbetwiste setel

unconven'tional natuurlik, informeel, vry

uncork' ontkurk, die prop uittrek

uncouth' ru, grof, onbeskaaf, onhandig

uncov'er ontdek, afdek; blootlê

uncrossed' ongekruis; onbelemmer; ~ cheque ongekruiste tjek

uncut' ongekerf; ongesny; ongeslyp (dia= mante)

undam'aged onbeskadig, heel

undat'ed ongedateer

undaunt'ed onversaag, onverskrokke

undelivered' onafgelewer; nie verlos nie

undeni'able onweerlegbaar, onbetwisbaar

undepend'able onbetroubaar

un'der (a) onderste; (adv) onder, onder= kant; (prep) onder; benede; ~ fire, onder vuur; ~ one's hand, geteken; ~ way, op weg; onderweg

under-achie'ver onderpresteerder

un'dercarriage onderstel

undercharge' te min vra; te swak laai

un'derclothes, un'derclothing onderklere

un'dercurrent onderstroom; neiging

un'dercut¹ (n) opskepskoot; opstopper (boks)

undercut'² (v) (..cut, ..cut) ondergrawe; pryse laer maak; onderbie; onderkruip

un'derdeveloped onderontwikkel, see un= developed

un'derdog verdrukte, lydende party

underdone' halfgaar (biefstuk); halfrou

underes'timate (v) onderskat

underexpose' onderbelig, te kort belig

underfed' ondervoed

undergo' (..went, ..gone) ondergaan, ly, verduur

undergrad'uate (n) ongegradueerde; (a) voorgraads

un'derground (n) moltrein; (a) ondergronds, onderaards; (adv) ondergronds, onder= aards; heimlik, stilletjies

un'dergrowth ruigte, kreupelhout, struik= gewas

underhand' (a) agterbaks, onderduims

underline' onderstreep

un'derling ondergeskikte, handlanger

underly'ing grond=; fundamenteel; ~ prin= ciples grondbeginsels

undermen'tioned ondergenoemde, onder= staande

undermine' ondermyn, benadeel; uitgrawe

underneath' benede, onder

underpaid' onderbetaal, te min betaal

underrate' onderskat, minag

undersell' (..sold, ..sold) goedkoper ver= koop as, onderbie

undersigned' ondergetekende

un'derstaffed onderbeman

understand' (..stood, ..stood) verstaan, begryp; ~ by, verstaan onder; I was given to ~, hulle het my te kenne gegee

understand'ing (n) begrip, verstandhouding; come to an ~, tot 'n skikking kom; on the ~ that, met dien verstande dat; (a) be= grypend

understate' versag, verklein; ~ment on= derbeklemtoning, onderskatting

understood' verstaan; vanselfsprekend

un'derstudy (..dies) plaasvervanger, pos= waarnemer

undertake' (..took, ..taken) onderneem, aanpak; ~r ondernemer, entrepreneur

un'dertaker lykbesorger, begrafnisonder= nemer

undertak'ing onderneming, organisasie

un'derwear onderklere

un'derwood kreupelhout, ruigte, struikge= was

un'derworld onderwêreld; doderyk; boewewêreld

un'derwriter ondertekenaar; onderskrywer, versekeraar, garandeerder

undeserved' onverdien(d)

undesir'able (a) onwenslik, ongewens; an ~ publication, 'n onsewenste publikasie

undetect'ed onopgemerk, onontdek

undeterred' onverskrokke, onvervaard

undevel'oped onontwikkel(d)

undig'nified onwaardig

undis'ciplined ongeoefend; ongedissiplineer

undisput'ed onbetwis, onbestrede

undisturbed' kalm, bedaard

undivid'ed onverdeel(d)

undo' (..did, ..done) losmaak; ongedaan maak; ~ing verderf, ondergang, vernie= tiging

undone' ongedaan, los; what is done, can= not be ~, gedane sake het geen keer nie

undoubt'ed ongetwyfeld, ontwyfelbaar, stellig, seker; ~ly ongetwyfeld, beslis

undreamt' of ongedroom, ongehoord

undress' (v) uittrek, ontklee; **~ed'** uitge-
trek, ongeklee; ongekap (klip)
undue' onbehoorlik; buitensporig
un'dulating golwend, wegdeinend
undul'y ongepas, onbehoorlik, oordrewe
undy'ing ewig, onverganklik
unearned' onverdien
unearth' opgrawe, openbaar; opdiep
uneas'y ongemaklik, onrustig; besorg
uneat'able oneetbaar
uned'ucated onopgevoed, ongeletterd
unemployed' (n, pl) werkloses; (a) werkloos; ongebruik, onaangewend
unemploy'ment werkloosheid; **~ insurance**
werkloosheid(s)versekering
unend'ing oneindig, eindeloos
unenlight'ened dom, oningelig, onkundig
unen'viable onbenydenswaardig
uneq'ual ongelykmatig; nie opgewasse nie;
~ to the task, nie teen/vir die taak opgewasse nie; **~ed** ongeëwenaard, weergaloos
une'ven ongelyk, onewe; **~ number** on-
gelyke getal
unexpect'ed onverwags, onvoorsien
unexpired' onafgeloop, onverstreke
unfail'ing onfeilbaar; seker
unfair' onbillik; oneerlik, onopreg
unfaith'ful ontrou; trouleoos; ongelowig
unfamil'iar vreemd, onbekend, onvertroud
(met)
unfa'sten losmaak; losgespe
unfav'ourable ongunstig
unfin'ished onvoltooi, onafgewerk; **~
symphony** onvoltooide simfonie
unfit' (v) (-ted, -ted) ongeskik maak; (a)
onbekwaam, ongeskik; **~ for a parson,**
nie vir predikant deug nie
unflagg'ing onverdrote, onverslap
unflinch'ing onverskrokke, onwrikbaar
unfold' ontvou, uitlê; ontplooi, uitsprei
unforeseen' onvoorsien
unforget'table onvergeetlik
unforgiv'ing onversoenlik
unfort'unate (a) ongelukkig; rampspoedig;
~ly ongelukkig
unfound'ed ongegrond, vals; **~ rumour**
riemtelegram
unfriend'ly onvriendelik; onbevriend (land)
unfulfilled' onvervul
unfurn'ished ongemeubileer
ungain'ly lomp, onhandig, onhandelbaar

ungen'tlemanly onwellewend, onhoflik
unglazed' onverglaas; sonder ruite
ungod'ly goddeloos, sondig
ungov'ernable onregeerbaar, wild, woes
ungrate'ful ondankbaar, onerkentlik
unguard'ed onbewaak; onbedagsaam
unham'pered onbelemmer(d), ongehinder
unhapp'y ongelukkig
unharmed' onbeskadig; veilig, ongedeerd
unhealth'y ongesond; onveilig
unhind'ered ongehinder
unhol'y onheilig, goddeloos
unhurt' ongedeerd, onbeseer
unhygien'ic onhigiënies, ongesond
un'icorn eenhoring
unifica'tion eenwording, unifikasie
un'iform (n) uniform, mondering; (a) eenvormig; gelyk
uniform'ity eenvormigheid, uniformiteit
unilat'eral eensydig; **~ declaration of independence (UDI)**, eensydige onafhanklikverklaring
unili'ngual eentalig
unima'ginative verbeeldingloos; fantasie-
loos
unimport'ant onbelangrik
uninhab'ited onbewoon
unini'tiated oningewy
unin'jured onbeseer, ongedeerd
uninten'tional onopsetlik
unin'terested onbelangstellend
unin'teresting oninteressant, vervelend
uninterrup'ted onafgebroke, ononderbroke, deurlopend
un'ion unie, vereniging; vakbond; samesmelting; **~ is strength**, eendrag maak
mag; **~ist** unionis
unique' enig, ongeëwenaard, uniek; **~ of
its kind**, enig in sy soort
un'isex enkelgeslag, uniseks; **~ school**.en-
kelgeslagskool, **teenoor koëdskool**
un'ison harmonie, ooreenstemming; **in ~**,
eenstemmig, eensgesind
un'it eenheid
unite' verenig; byeenvoeg; verbind, saamsmelt; **~d** verenig; eendragtig; **U~d Nations**, Verenigde Nasies; **U~d States of
America (USA)**, Verenigde State van
Amerika (VSA)
un'ity (..ties) eenheid; eensgesindheid
univer'sal algemeen, universeel
un'iverse heelal, wêreld

univer'sity (n) (..ties) universiteit, hoë=
skool; (a) universiteits=; universitêr; ~
admission universiteit(s)toelating
unjust' onregverdig, onbillik
unkempt' ongekam; slordig, onversorg
(voorkoms)
unkind' onvriendelik
unknown' (n) onbekende; (a) onbekend
unlad'ylike onvroulik, onfyn, onverfyn
unlaw'ful onwettig; buite-egtelik (kind);
ongeoorloof
unless' tensy, so nie, behalwe
unlett'ered ongeletterd(d)
unlike' ongelyk; verskillerd, anders; ~ly
onwaarskynlik
unlim'ited onbegrens, onbeperk
unload' aflaai, afpak, verkoop
unlock' oopsluit, ontsluit
unluck'y ongelukkig, rampspoedig; ~
number ongeluksgetal
unman'ageable onhandelbaar, onregeerbaar
unmann'erly ongemanierd, onhebbelik
unmarked' ongemerk; onopgemerk; onna=
gesien (opstelle)
unmarr'ied ongetroud
unmistak'able onmiskenbaar, seker
unmo'therly onmoederlik, stiefmoederlik
unmoved' onbewoë, koel; roerloos
unnamed' ongenoem; naamloos
unna'tural onnatuurlik
unne'cessary onnodig, oorbodig, oortollig
unnot'iced ongemerk, onopgemerk
unobli'ging ontegemoetkomend, ontoe=
skietlik
unobserv'ant onopmerksaam, onoplettend
unobstruct'ed onbelemmer, ongehinder
unobtain'able onverkry(g)baar
unobtrus'ive beskeie; onopvallend
unocc'upied onbeset; onbewoon, leeg
unoffi'cial nie-amptelik, onoffisieel
unopposed' onbestrede; ongehinder; ~
seat onbestrede setel
unorth'odox ketters, onortodoks
unpaid' onbetaal(d)
unpar'alleled ongeëwenaard, weergaloos
unpard'onable onvergeeflik
unperceived' onopgemerk
unperturbed' onversteur(d), houtgerus
unpleas'ant onaangenaam; onaardig
unpoet'ic ondigterlik
unpop'ular onpopulêr, ongewild
unprac'tical onprakties

unprecedent'ed ongehoord, ongekend
unprepared' onvoorberei; onklaar
unprin'cipled beginselloos
unprotect'ed onbeskerm, onbeskut
unprovid'ed onvoorsien; onversorg
unprovoked' onuitgelok, moedswillig
unpun'ished ongestraf; go ~, ongestraf bly
unqual'ified ongekwalifiseer, onbevoeg
unques'tionable onbetwisbaar, onaanveg=
baar
unreas'onable onredelik, onbillik
unrelent'ing onverbiddelik, onvermurfbaar
unreli'able onbetroubaar
un'rest onrus, angs; beroering
unrestrict'ed onbelemmer, onbeperk, on=
ingeperk
unriv'alled weergaloos, ongeëwenaar(d)
unroll' afrol; uitrol
unruf'fled kalm, bedaard, ongeërg
unrul'y wild, losbandig, onhandelbaar;
onstuimig, weerspannig
unsafe' onveilig, gevaarlik
unsaid' ongesê
unsatisfac'tory onbevredigend
unsav'oury onsmaaklik; walglik; ~ charac=
ter ongure vent
unscathed' ongedeerd, ongeskaad
unschooled' ongeskool, onkundig
unscrew' losskroef
unscrip'tural onbybels, onskriftuurlik
unscrup'ulous gewete(n)loos; beginselloos
un'seeded ongekeur; ~ player ongekeurde
speler
unseem'ly onwelvoeglik, onbetaamlik
unseen' (n) (die) ongesiene; onvoorbereide
vertaling; (a) ongesien, onsigbaar
unself'ish onselfsugtig
unserv'iceable onbruikbaar, ondienlik
unsett'le verwar, van stryk bring; ~d rus=
teloos; onbestendig (weer)
unsex' geslagloos maak; ~ed ongeseks
(kuikens)
unshrink'able krimpvry
unsight'ly onooglik, lelik
unskilled' onbedrewe, onervare; ongeskool;
~ labour ongeskoolde arbeid
unslaked' ongeblus (kalk)
unso'ciable ongesellig, onsosiaal
unsold' onverkoop
unsoli'cited ongevra; onuitgelok; ~ sup=
port, spontane steun
unsolved' onopgelos

unsophis'ticated onvervals, eg; onskuldig, onbedorwe, ongesofistikeer(d)
unsound' ongesond; bederf; swak; sieklik; onbetroubaar; *of ~ mind,* swaksinnig
unspoilt' onbedorwe
unsports'manlike onsportief
unstab'le onvas, veranderlik, onstabiel
unsuccess'ful onsuksesvol, vergeefs
unsuit'able ongeskik, onvanpas
unsurpassed' onoortroffe
unsuspect'ing argeloos, onskuldig; niksvermoedend, doodgerus
unsweet'ened onversoet
unsympathet'ic onsimpatiek
unsystemat'ic onstelselmatig, onsistematies
unthank'ful ondankbaar
unthink'ing onbedagsaam, onnadenkend
untid'y slordig, onsindelik, onnet
untie' losmaak, losbind
until' tot, totdat; *not ~ then,* eers toe
untime'ly ontydig; ongeleë
untir'ing onvermoeid
un'to tot, aan
untold' talloos; onvermeld; onberekenbaar
untouched' onaangeroer; ongedeerd
untrained' onopgelei, ongeoefen, baar
untrue' onwaar, vals; ontrou
untrust'worthy onbetroubaar
unused' ongebruik
unu'sual ongewoon, buitengewoon
unveil' onthul (standbeeld); inwy
unwant'ed onbegeer; ongewens, ongevra; *an ~ child,* 'n ongewenste kind
unwav'ering vas, onwrikbaar
unwel'come onwelkom
unwell' onwel, siek, ongesteld
unwiel'dy onhanteerbaar, swaar, log
unwill'ing onwillig; ongeneë, onbereid
unwind' (..wound, ..wound) afrol, losdraai, loswikkel, afdraai
unwise' onverstandig, dom
unwitt'ing(ly) onwetend
unworth'y onwaardig
unwrap' (-ped, -ped) oopmaak, loswikkel
unwritt'en ongeskrewe; *~ law* ongeskrewe wet
unyield'ing onversetlik, koppig, eiesinnig
up (n): *~s and downs,* voor- en teenspoed; (v) oplig; styg; (adv) op, bo, na bo, boontoe; (prep) op; *~ in arms,* in verset; *cheer ~,* opvrolik; *hurry ~,* maak gou; wikkel; *time is ~,* die tyd is om/verstreke

up'bringing opvoeding; grootmaak
up-country binneland(s)
up'date op datum bring; hersien; *an ~d edition,* 'n bygewerkte/hersiene uitgawe
upheav'al opstand, oproer; omwenteling
up'hill opdraand; swaar (werk)
uphold' (..held, ..held) handhaaf; staande hou; hooghou
uphol'ster stoffeer; ~**er** stoffeerder; ~**y** stoffering
up'keep onderhoud
up'lift (n) verheffing, opheffing
uplift' (v) oplig, ophef
upon' op, bo-op, by; aan; *once ~ a time,* eendag; op 'n goeie dag
upp'er (a) bo, hoër, boonste; *gain the ~ hand,* die oorhand kry; *~ hand* oorhand; *~ lip* bolip; ~**most** hoogste, boonste; *~ storey* boonste vloer/verdieping
up'right regop; opreg, eerlik, regskape
up'rising opstand, oproer
up'roar oproer, lawaai, herrie
uproot' uitroei, ontwortel
upset' (n) omval; verwarring; (v) (..set, ..set) omverwerp, omgooi; omkrap; verydel; *~ someone,* iem. omkrap/ontstel
up'shot gevolg, uiteinde, uitslag
up'side down' onderstebo, deurmekaar
up'stairs (a) bo, boonste; hoogmoedig; (adv) op die boonste vloer/verdieping, boontoe
up'start parvenu, gelukskind; ('n) astrant, astrante/vrypostige persoon
up'swing oplewing, opswaai (ekonomie), *see* **upturn**
up'take begrip; *slow in the ~,* traag van begrip
up-to-date byderwets, nuwerwets, op die hoogte, tot datum
up'turn oplewing (ekonomie), *see* **upswing**
up'ward opwaarts
up'wards opwaarts, boontoe; *pupils of seven and ~,* leerlinge van sewe jaar en daarbo
uran'ium uraan; *~ enrichment* uraanverryking
urb'an stedelik, stads; *~ Blacks* stedelike Swartmense; *~ terrorism* stedelike terreur; *~ transport* stedelike vervoer
ur'banise verstedelik
urge (n) aandrang; *sexual ~,* geslagsdrang; (v) aandring, aanspoor; aanpor

ur'gent dringend, spoedeisend; *an ~ mat=
ter,* 'n dringende saak
ur'ine urine, pis, water
us ons
us'age gebruik, gewoonte; behandeling
use (n) gebruik; nut; gewoonte; *it is no ~
talking,* praat help tog nie; *put to good ~,*
goed benut; (v) gebruik; aanwend; be=
handel; *get ~d to,* gewoond raak aan;
~ful nuttig, handig, diensig; ~less nut=
teloos; ~r gebruiker
ush'er (n) deurwagter; (v) aandien, binne=
lei; *~ in a new era,* 'n nuwe tydvak inlui;
~ette' plekaanwyster
u'sual gewoon(lik), gebruiklik; *as ~,* soos
gewoonlik; ~ly gewoonlik

us'ufruct vruggebruik
uten'sil werktuig, gereedskap; (kombuis)=
gerei
ut'erus (..ri) baarmoeder
util'ity nut, nuttigheid; ~ company nut(s)=
maatskappy
ut'ilise (v) benut, gebruik, aanwend
ut'most uiterste, beste; *do one's ~,* jou
uiterste (bes) doen
utt'er¹ (v) uiter; uit; in omloop bring; *forg=
ing and ~ing,* vervalsing en uitgifte
utt'er² (a) volkome, volslae, algeheel; ~
misery die diepste ellende
utt'erly heeltemal, volkome
utt'ermost verste, uiterste
uv'ula (-e) kleintongetjie, uvula

V

vac'ancy (..ies) vakature; *list of vacancies,*
vakaturelys
vac'ant vakant, leeg; oop, onbeset; *a ~
post,* 'n vakante pos; *a ~ stare,* 'n we=
senlose blik
vacate' leeg maak; afstand doen van
vaca'tion vakansie, vrye tyd; ontruiming;
~ course vakansiekursus; ~ leave vakan=
sieverlof
vac'cinate inent, vaksineer
vac'cine inent, vaksineer
vac'uum (..cua, -s) vakuum, lugleegte; ~
brake lugrem; ~ cleaner stofsuier
vag'abond (n) vagebond, swerwer
vagi'na (-e, -s) vagina, skede
vag'rant (n) rondloper, landloper; leeglêer
vague vaag, onduidelik, onseker; *not the
~st notion,* nie die flouste benul nie
vain ydel, verwaand; (te)vergeefs; *in ~,* te=
vergeefs
valedic'tory afskeids=; ~ address af=
skeidsrede
Val'entine Day Valentynsdag
val'iant dapper, moedig
val'id geldig, van krag; gegrond; *a ~ argu=
ment,* 'n geldige stelling
vall'ey (-s) laagte, vallei, dal; kloof
val'uable kosbaar, waardevol
val'uables (pl) kosbaarhede
valua'tion waardering, skatting; evaluering
val'ue (n) waarde, prys; *to the ~ of,* ter
waarde van; ten bedrae van; (v) waardeer,
skat; op prys stel

valve klep; radiolamp; ventiel (band)
vam'pire bloedsuier, vampier
van (n) bagasiewa; kondukteurswa (trein);
bestelwa, toebakkie
van'dal vandaal; ~ism vandalisme
van'guard voorhoede, voorpunt
vanill'a vanielje
van'ish verdwyn, wegraak; wegsterf
van'ity ydelheid; skyn, leegheid; ~ case
smuktassie, tooitassie; ~ mirror smuk=
spieëltjie
vanq'uish oorwin, verower
van'tage voordeel (tennis); wins
vap'our (n) damp, wasem; (v) (ver)damp
var'iable (n) veranderlike(s); (a) verander=
lik; onbestendig
varia'tion verandering; variasie
va'ricose (op)geswel; ~ veins spatare
var'ied verskeie, verskillend
var'iegated veelkleurig, bont, geskakeer
vari'ety (..ties) verskeidenheid, variëteit;
~ concert verskeidenheid(s)konsert, va=
riakonsert
var'ious verskillend; verskeie
varn'ish (n) (-es) vernis; glans; (v) vernis
vars'ity (n) (..ties) universiteit; (a) univer=
siteits=
var'y (varied, varied) verander, afwissel;
tastes ~, smaak verskil; ~ing afwisselend
vase vaas, blompot
vass'al ondergeskikte, vasal
vast (a) groot, uitgestrek, grens(e)loos

vat vat, kuip
vault (n) verwulf; grafkelder; (v) oorwelf; spring; **~ing horse** bok, perd (gimnastiek)
veal kalfsvleis
ve'getable (n) groente; (pl) groente; (a) plantaardig, plante*; **~ kingdom** plantery k; **~ marrow** murgpampoen
vegetar'ian (n) vegetariër, groente-eter
vegeta'tion plantegroei; plantwêreld
ve'hement vurig, hewig, heftig, driftig
ve'hicle voertuig; middel, medium
veil (n) sluier; masker; dekmantel; *take the ~*, non word; *under the ~ of*, onder die dekmantel van; (v) omsluier; bewimpel
vein aar; luim, gees; aanleg; trant; *in the same ~*, in dieselfde gees
veld veld; **~ school** veldskool
velo'city snelheid, vinnigheid
vel'skoen velskoen
vel'vet (n) fluweel
vendett'a bloedwraak; vete, vendetta
ven'dor verkoper, smous; inbringer (aandele)
veneer' (n) fineer; (v) fineer; **~ed brick** glasuursteen; **~ed door** fineerdeur
ven'erable eerwaardig, eerbiedwaardig
vener'eal veneries; **~ disease** geslagsiekte
Vene'tian (a) Venesiaans; **~ blind** hortjie(s)blinding, hortjie(s)blinder
ven'geance (weer)wraak; *with a ~*, kwaai
ven'ison wildbraad, wildvleis
ven'om gif, venyn; **~ous** giftig, venynig
vent (n) opening, luggat; *give ~ to*, uiting gee aan; (v) lug, uiting gee, uit
ven'til klep, ventiel; **~ate** lug gee, ventileer; **~ate a grievance**, 'n grief lug; **~a'tion** ventilasie; **~ator** ventilator
ventril'oquist buikspreker
ven'ture (n) onderneming, waagstuk; (v) waag, riskeer; **~ an opinion**, 'n mening waag
ven'ue plek, vergaderplek
veran'da veranda, (oordekte) stoep
verb werkwoord
ver'bal woordelik; werkwoordelik; mondeling, verbaal; **~ translation** letterlike vertaling
verben'a (-s) verbena, ysterkruid
verbos'ity woordrykdom, woordepraal
verd'ant groen, fris; onervare
verd'ict uitspraak, vonnis; bevinding

verge (n) rand, grens
ve'rify (..fied, ..fied) ondersoek, toets, verifieer; bekragtig
ve'ritable waaragtig, eg, werklik
vermic'ulite vermikuliet
verm'in ongedierte, goggas; gespuis
vernac'ular (n) landstaal, volkstaal, spreektaal; (a) inheems, inlands
vers'atile veelsydig; alsydig
verse (n) vers, versreël, poësie, gedig; koeplet; **blank ~** rymlose verse; **~d** bedrewe, ervare
vers'ifier rymelaar, versmaker, pruldigter
ver'sion bewerking; vertolking
vers'us teen, versus
vert'ebral werwel*, gewerwel*; **~ column** ruggraat
ver'tical (a) regop, vertikaal, loodreg
ver'vet monkey blouaap
ve'ry (a) eg, waar, opreg, werklik; *the ~ thing*, net die regte ding; (adv) baie, danig, regtig, erg, uiters; *the ~ best*, die allerbeste
ves'per aand; aandster; aandgebed
vess'el vat; vaartuig, skip; kom, kruik
vest[1] (n) onderhemp; onderbaadjie
vest[2] (v) beklee; toevertrou; **~ with power**, met mag/bevoegdheid beklee
vest'ed gevestigde, bestaande; **~ interests** gevestigde belange
ves'tibule (voor)portaal, vestibule
ves'try (..tries) sakristie; konsistoriekamer
vet'eran (n) veteraan, oudgediende, oudstryder; ringkop; (a) oud, beproef; **~ car** noagmotor, noagkar, veteraanmotor
veterinar'ian (n) veearts
vet'erinary veeartsenykundig, veeartseny*; **~ clinic** dierekliniek; **~ surgeon** veearts
vet'o (n) (-es) verbod, veto; (v) veto
vex terg, pla, kwel; **~a'tion** ergernis
vi'a oor, via
viabil'ity lewensvatbaarheid; **~ study** lewensvatbaarheidstudie, *see* **feasibility study**
vi'able lewensvatbaar, ekonomies uitvoerbaar
vibra'tion trilling; slingering; vibrasie
vic'ar vikaris; predikant; **~age** pastorie
vice[1] (n) ondeug; fout, gebrek
vice[2] (n) skroef; (v) vasdraai; vasknel; **~ grip** klemtang, kloutang
vi'ce[3] (prep) in die plek van, vise-, onder*; **~-chairman** (..men) ondervoorsitter, vise-

voorsitter; **~-principal** vise-prinsipaal, onderhoof; **~roy** (-s) onderkoning

vice vers'a vice versa, andersom, omgekeerd

vicin'ity (..ties) buurt; nabyheid, omgewing, omstreke

vi'cious boosaardig, venynig; kwaai; **~ animal** dierasie; **~ circle/spiral** bose kringloop

vic'tim slagoffer, prooi; *fall a ~ to,* die slagoffer word van; iets/iemand ten prooi val; **~ise** viktimiseer

vic'tor oorwinnaar

vic'tory (..ries) oorwinning, sege

vic'tual (n) kos, lewensmiddele; (pl) kos, lewensmiddele, proviand

vi'deo: **~ casette** videokasset; **~ library** videoteek; **~ recorder** video-opnemer; **~ tape** videoband

vie meeding, wedywer

view (n) vergesig, uitsig; mening, beskouing; *in ~ of,* met die oog op; **~ of life,** lewensbeskouing; *point of ~,* gesig(s)punt; (v) besien; kyk (TV); besigtig, beskou; **~er** (-s) kyker (TV); **~point** gesig(s)punt

vi'gil wag; (-s) nagwaak; *keep ~s,* waak

vig'orous kragtig, sterk; gespierd

vill'age dorp; **~r** dorpeling, dorpenaar

vill'ian skurk, booswig

vim fut, pit, oemf, vitaliteit, energie

vindic'tive wraakgierig, wraaksugtig

vine wingerdstok, wynstok; **~ culture** wynbou, *see* **viticulture**

vin'egar (n) asyn; (a) asyn=, asynsuur=

vine'yard wingerd

vin'tage (n) wynjaar; (a) uitstekend; oud; **~ car** veteraanmotor, toekamotor, noagkar

vio'la¹ (-s) altviool, viola

vio'la² somerviooltjie; (klein) gesiggie (blom)

vi'olate skend, oortree; verkrag; ontheilig

vi'olence geweld, geweldpleging; *die by ~,* 'n gewelddadige dood sterf

vi'olent geweldig, verskriklik; gewelddadig

vi'olet (n) viooltjie; (a) perskleurig

violin' viool; **~ist** violis, vioolspeler

violoncell'ist tjellis, tjellospeler

violoncell'o (-s) tjello, violonsel, basviool

vip'er adder

virag'o (-s) mannetjiesvrou; rissie; geitjie

vir'gin (n) maagd; (a) maagdelik; ongerep, suiwer; **~ forest** ongerepte oerwoud

vi'rile manlik, manhaftig; gespierd. viriel

virt'ual wesenlik, werklik, feitlik, eintlik; *he is ~ly broke,* hy is feitlik bankrot

virt'ue deug; krag; kuisheid; *by ~ of,* kragtens; *of easy ~,* los van sedes

vi'rulent kwaadaardig, venynig, giftig

vir'us gif, smetstof; virus; bitsigheid

vis'a (n) visum, ondertekening

viscos'ity viskositeit, taaivloeibaarheid (van olie)

visc'ount (*pron.* vi'count) burggraaf

visibil'ity sigbaarheid, sig

vis'ible sigbaar, duidelik, aanskoulik

vis'ion gesig, visioen; visie, gesigskerpte

vis'it (n) besoek, kuier; *pay a ~,* besoek; (v) besoek, (gaan) kuier; **~a'tion** beproewing, besoeking; **~ing card** naamkaartjie, visitekaartjie; **~or** besoeker; kuiermens, kuiergas

vis'ta uitsig, verskiet, vergesig

vis'ual gesigs=, visueel; **~ education** aanskouingsonderwys; **~ise** visualiseer

vit'al lewens=, lewensvatbaar, beslissend; *of ~ importance,* van die allerhoogste belang

vital'ity lewenskrag, vitaliteit; lewensduur

vit'amin vitamine, vitamien

vit'iculture wynbou

viva'cious lewendig, lewenslustig, vrolik

viv'id duidelik, helder; **~ imagination** lewendige/sterk verbeelding(s)krag

vix'en wyfiejakkals; feeks, helleveeg

vocab'ulary (..ries) woordeskat

voc'al (n) klinker, vokaal; (a) stem=; **~ chord** stemband; **~ist** sanger, sangeres

voca'tion beroep, werk, ambag; roeping

voca'tional beroeps=, vak=; **~ guidance/counselling** beroepsleiding; **~ training** beroepsopleiding

vocif'erous skreeuend, uitbundig, luidrugtig, geesdriftig

vogue swang, mode

voice (n) stem, spraak; *active ~,* bedrywende vorm; *have no ~ in,* geen seggenskap/inspraak hê nie in; *passive ~,* lydende vorm; (v) uitspreek; *~ my opinion,* my mening lug

void (n) leegte, gaping; (a) leeg; *declare ~,* nietig verklaar

vol'atile vlugtig; ongedurig; **~ oil** vlugtige olie; **~ salts** vlugsout

volcan'ic vulkanies; **~ eruption** vulkaniese uitbarsting; **~ rock** effusiegesteente

volcan'o (-es) vulkaan, vuurspuwende berg
voll'ey (n) (-s) sarsie, salvo; vlughou (tennis); ~ball vlugbal
volt volt; ~age stroomspanning
vol'uble woordryk, glad
vol'ume boekdeel, bundel; grootte, omvang, volume; speak ~s, boekdele spreek
vol'untary (a) vrywillig; spontaan
volunteer' (n) vrywilliger; (v) vrywillig onderneem; ~ one's service, jou diens aanbied; he ~ed, hy het gevrywil
vom'it (v) braak, vomeer, opgooi
vort'ex (-es, ..tices) maalstroom, draaikolk
vote (n) stem; stemreg; begrotingspos; casting ~, beslissende stem; ~ of censure,
mosie van sensuur/afkeuring; no-confi-
dence ~, mosie van wantroue; put to the
~, tot stemming bring; (v) stem, stem uit-

bring; ~ by ballot, per stembrief(ie) stem;
~ money, geld bewillig; ~r kieser, stem-
geregtigde; ~rs' roll kieser(s)lys
vot'ing stemming, stem(mery); ~ paper
stembrief(ie)
vouch bevestig; instaan vir; ~ for the truth
of, instaan vir die waarheid van; ~er
kwitansie; bewys, bewysstuk
vow (n) eed, gelofte; (v) 'n gelofte doen;
sweer, plegtig beloof; Day of the V~,
Geloftedag
vow'el klinker, vokaal
voy'age (n) seereis, vaart; ~r seereisiger
vul'gar plat, ordinêr, laag, vulgêr; ~ expression plat uitdrukking; ~ fraction gewone breuk; ~ism platheid
vul'nerable kwesbaar; wondbaar
vul'ture aasvoël; uitsuier

W

wad (n) vulsel, pluisie, prop, watte
wa'ddle waggel, strompel
wade deurwaad, deurgaan; deurworstel
waf'er wafel (koek); hostie (RK); ouel
wa'ffle wafel; (v) gorrel (in eksamen); ~
iron wafelyster
wag (v) (-ged, -ged) kwispel, swaai; the dog
~s his tail, die hond kwispel
wage¹ (n) verdienste, loon, besolding; (pl)
loon, gasie; ~ demand looneis; ~ earner
loontrekker, broodwinner; ~ gap loongaping; ~ increase loonverhoging
wage² (v) voer, maak; ~ war, oorlog voer
wa'ger (n) weddenskap; lay a ~, 'n weddenskap aangaan; (v) wed
wag'on wa, bokwa; ~ driver wadrywer; ~
house waenhuis; ~ load wavrag
wag'tail kwikstertjie
wail (v) weeklaag, huil, kerm
wail'ing gejammer; ~ wall klaagmuur
waist middel; lyfie; ~band gordel, lyfband;
~coat onderbaadjie; ~ deep tot aan die
middel
wait (n) wagtyd; (v) vertoef; wag; ~ a
minute, wag 'n bietjie; ~ one's turn, sy
beurt afwag; ~er tafelbediende, kelner;
~ing (n) wag; opwagting; bediening; (a)
wagtend; in ~ing, wagtend; bedienend;
~ing list waglys; ~ing room wagkamer;
~ress (-es) kelnerin

waive laat vaar, afstand doen van, kwytskeld
wake¹ (n) kielwater; volgstroom; in the ~
of, op die hakke van
wake² (v) (woke or -d, woken or woke or
-d) wakker word; wakker maak, wek; ~n
wakker maak, wek
walk (n) wandeling; pas, gang; voetpad; go
for a ~, gaan stap; (v) loop, wandel, stap;
~er stapper, wandelaar, voetganger;
~ie-talkie loopgeselser, tweerigtingradio;
~ing ring loopring; ~ing stick wandelstok, kierie; ~ing tour wandeltog, loop-
toer; ~out staking; ~over maklike oorwinning
wall (n) muur; wal; (v) ommuur
wall'clock hangklok
wa'llet knapsak; notetas, portefeulje
wa'llop afransel, looi; ~ing (n) loesing
wall: ~paper plakpapier; ~-to-~ carpet
volvloermat; volvloertapyt
wa'lnut okkerneut
wa'lrus (-es) walrus
waltz (n) (-es) wals; (v) wals
wand towerstaf, staf
wa'nder dwaal, swerf; ronddool; yl; his
mind ~s, hy yl; ~er swerwer; swerfling
wan'dering (a) ronddwalend, swerwend; the
W~ Jew, die Wandelende Jood
want (n) gebrek, behoefte, armoede, skaarste; for ~ of, by gebrek aan; (v) wil,

wens, verlang; *he ~s experience,* hy kom
ondervinding kort
want'ing behoeftig, gebrekkig, ontbrekend
war (n) oorlog, stryd; *civil ~,* burgeroorlog;
cold ~, senuoorlog; koue oorlog; *declare
~,* oorlog verklaar; *make ~,* oorlog voer
war'ble (v) kweel, sing; **~r** sangvoël
ward (n) wyk; saal, afdeling (hospitaal); (v)
bewaak; beskerm, beskut; *~ off,* afweer
war: *~ dance* krygsdans; *~ debt* oorlog=
skuld
war'den hoof, opsigter; voog; bewaarder
war'der bewaarder (gevangenis), wagter,
sipier
ward'robe klerekas; klere
ware (n) ware, goed; (pl) koopware
ware'house (n) pakhuis, loods; (v) (op)berg
war'like oorlogsugtig, krygshaftig
warm (v) warm maak, verwarm; (a) warm;
innig, hartlik; *have a ~ place for,* 'n teer
plekkie hê vir; *a ~ reception,* 'n hartlike
ontvangs; **~-blooded** warmbloedig; **~-
hearted** hartlik; **~ing pan** bedwarmer;
~th warmte; geesdrif
warn waarsku, vermaan; **~ing** waarsku=
wing, vermaning; aanmaning
warp (n) skering (draad); *~ and woof* ske=
ring en inslag; (v) kromtrek, skeeftrek
wa'rrant (n) volmag; lasbrief, magtiging;
(v) vrywaar; waarborg; magtig; regverdig,
wettig; **~ee'** gevolmagtigde; **~er, ~or**
borg, waarborger; volmaggewer; **~ offi=
cer** adjudant-offisier; **~ voucher** skat=
kisorder; **~y** (..ties) volmag; waarborg,
garansie
wa'rrior krygsman, soldaat, vegsman
wart vratjie; knoes, kwas
wart'hog vlakvark
wa'ry behoedsaam, versigtig
was *see* be
wash (n) wasgoed; (v) was, uitwas; spoel;
afspoel; *~ one's dirty linen in public,*
onenigheid in die openbaar uitmaak; *~ed
out,* poot-uit; **~basin** waskom; **~er** was=
ser, wasmasjien; waster; **~ing machine**
wasmasjien; **~ing powder** waspoeier;
~stand wastafel; **~tub** wasbalie
wasp wesp
wast'age verkwisting, vermorsing, verspil=
ling; afval; slytasie
waste[1] (n) verkwisting; afval; oorskiet; sly=
tasie; *atomic ~,* kernafval; (v) weggooi,

verkwis, mors; *~ time,* tyd verspil; *~
not,* want not, wie spaar, vergaar
waste[2] (a) verlate; ongebruik; *~ products*
afvalprodukte
waste: **~basket** snippermandjie; **~ful** ver=
kwistend
waste: **~paper** skeurpapier; **~paper basket**
snippermandjie; **~pipe** afvoerpyp
watch (n) (-es) oorlosie/horlosie; wag; waak=
saamheid; (v) waghou; oplet, bespied;
bewaak; **~dog** waghond; **~ful** waaksaam;
~ glass (-es) oorlosieglas; *~ hand* oorlo=
siewyser; **~maker** oorlosiemaker; **~man**
(..men) wagter; **~tower** wagtoring; **~-
word** wagwoord, leuse
wa'ter (n) water; *fish in troubled ~s,* in
troebel water visvang; (v) water gee, nat=
maak, natlei; water (oë); laat suip (dier);
~ down, verdun, verwater; *W~ Affairs*
Waterwese; *~ bailiff* waterfiskaal;
~buck waterbok; *~ chute* afglyplank; **~
closet** latrine, kleinhuisie; **~colour**
waterverf; **~-cooled** waterverkoel; **~
diviner** waterwyser; **~fall** waterval; **~ing
can** gieter; *~ level* waterpas; **~melon**
waatlemoen; **~proof** (n) reënjas; water=
digte seil; (a) waterdig; **~ rates**
waterbelasting; **~ resistant** waterwerend;
~spout waterhoos; **~shed** waterskeiding;
~tight waterdig; **~y pap,** waterig; laf
wa'ttle[1] bel, lel (pluimvee)
wa'ttle[2] looibasboom, wattelboom, Aus=
traliese akasia; **~-and-daub hut** hart=
beeshuisie
wave (n) golf, brander; wuif; golwing; *per=
manent ~,* vaste haargolf, vasgolf, per=
manente karteling; (v) golf; wiegel; waai,
wuif; **~length** golflengte
wav'er weifel, aarsel; **~er** weifelaar
wax[1] (n) was; byewas; lak
wax[2] (v) was, groei (maan); *~ing moon,*
wassende maan; *~ and wane,* toeneem/
groei en afneem
wax: **~bill** rooibekkie; *~ candle* waskers;
~ chandler waskersmaker; *~ doll* was=
pop; **~en wax=,** wasagtig
way (-s) weg, pad, rigting; manier; wyse;
by ~ of, by wyse van; *by the ~,* terloops;
in the family ~, swanger; in die ander tyd;
the ~ of all flesh, die weg van alle vlees;
get one's ~, jou sin kry; *go out of one's
~ for,* jou moeite getroos vir; *in no ~,*

glad nie; **~bill** vragbrief; **~farer** reisiger, wandelaar; **~lay** (..laid, ..laid) belaag, beloer; oorval; **~side** (n) die kant v. d. pad; (a) langs die pad; **~ward** eiewys, eiesinnig

we ons

weak swak; flou, pap; **~en** verswak; **~hearted** weekhartig; **~ling** swakkeling; **~ness** swakheid

weal welsyn, welvaart

wealth rykdom, welstand, welvarendheid, vermoë; **~y** welgesteld, bemiddeld

wean speen; afleer, afwen

wea'pon wapen; **~ry** wapentuig

wear (n) drag; slytasie; *fair ~ and tear*, billike slytasie; (v) **(wore, worn)** dra; **~away**, wegslyt; **~ to rags**, aan flenters dra; **~er** draer

wear: **~ied** vermoeid; **~iness** moegheid, vermoeidheid; **~isome** vervelig, vermoeiend; **~y** (v) (..ried, ..ried) vermoei, verveel; (a) moeg, vermoeid; vervelend

weas'el wesel

wea'ther[1] (n) weer; **~ permitting**, as die weer goed is

wea'ther[2] (v) deurstaan; verweer, verkrummel; **~ the storm**, die storm deurstaan

wea'ther: **~ bureau** weerburo; **~cock** weerhaan, windwyser; **~ forecast** weervoorspelling, weer(s)verwagting; **~ glass** (-es) weerglas

weave (wove, woven) weef; vleg; **~r** wewer; **~r bird** wewervoël, vink

weav'ing weef

web web, spinnerak; **~foot** swempoot

wed (-ded, -ded) trou, hu, verenig

wedd'ed getroud; *be ~ to*, verknog wees aan; **~ life** getroude lewe

wedd'ing bruilof, troue; huwelik; **~ cake** bruidskoek; **~ card** troukaart(jie); **~ day** troudag; **~ feast** bruilofsfees, troufees; **~ reception** huweliksonthaal; **~ ring** trouring

wedge (n) wig, keil; punt; *the thin end of the ~*, die skerp kant van die wig

wed'lock huwelik, eg; *born out of ~*, buiteegtelik gebore

Wed'nesday (pron. Wenz'de), Woensdag

wee baie klein; *a ~ bit*, 'n baie klein bietjie

weed (n) onkruid, vuilgoed; *ill ~s grow apace*, onkruid vergaan nie; (v) skoffel, skoonmaak; **~ out**, uitroei, suiwer; **~ing**

fork tuinvurk; **~killer** onkruiddoder

week week; *this day ~*, vandag oor 'n week; **~day** (-s) werkdag, weekdag; **~end** naweek; **~ly** (n) (..lies) weekblad; (a) weekliks

weep (wept, wept) huil, ween, treur; **~ for joy**, van vreugde huil; **~ing** (a) huilend, wenend; **~ing willow** treurwilg(er)

weev'il kalander

weigh weeg; oorweeg; bedink; **~ the pros and cons**, die gevolge oorweeg

weight (n) gewig/massa; swaarte; *pick up ~*, vet word; (v) beswaar; **~y** gewigtig; swaar; gesaghebbend

weir dwarswal, stuwal; studam, keerwal

weird onheilspellend, aaklig, bonatuurlik

wel'come (n) welkom, verwelkoming; *bid one ~*, iem. welkom heet; (v) verwelkom, welkom heet; (a) welkom

weld (v) sweis; **~ing rod** sweisstaaf

wel'fare welvaart, voorspoed; welsyn; **~work** maatskaplike werk; welsynswerk

well[1] (n) put, bron; fontein, koker

well[2] (n) die goeie; *wish someone ~*, iem. die beste toewens; (a) **(better, best)** goed; wel; gesond; *get ~*, beter word; (adv) goed; terdeë; *be ~ aware*, ten volle bewus wees; *~ done!* goed so! *be ~ off*, welgesteld wees; *very ~*, goed

well[3] (interj) wel

well: **~-behaved** fatsoenlik; **~being** welstand, welsyn; **~bred** goed opgevoed; goedgemanierd; **~doer** weldoener; **~-informed** goed ingelig; **~-mannered** welgemanierd; **~nigh** amper, byna, nagenoeg; **~ off** welgesteld; **~-read** belese; **~-spoken** welbespraak; **~-to-do** welgesteld, gegoed

Welsh (n) Wallies (taal); Wallieser; **~man** (..men) Wallieser; **~ rarebit** kaasroosterbrood

wel'ter (n) beroering; harwar; (v) slinger, rol, wentel; **~weight** weltergewig

wench (-es) meisie(mens), vroumens; slet

went *see* **go**

wept *see* **weep**

were'wolf (..wolves) weerwolf

west (n) in die weste; *the Far W~*, die Verre Weste; (a) weste~, westelik; (adv) na die weste, wes; *go ~*, bokveld toe gaan; **~erly** westelik; **W~ernise** (v) verwester; **~ward** weswaarts

wet (n) nattigheid, vogtigheid; (v) **(-ted, -ted)** natmaak; bevogtig; ~ *the roof,* dakfees vier; ~ *one's whistle,* 'n dop steek; (a) nat, vogtig; klam; ~ *blanket,* remskoen, pretbederwer; *dripping* ~, papnat; **~bike** waterponie; **~goods** wyn en drank

weth′er hamel

wet: **~ness** natheid, vogtigheid; **~table** be= natbaar (poeier)

whack (n) slag; deel; (v) slaan, moker; **~ing** (n) pak slae; (a) kolossaal

whale walvis; *a* ~ *of,* 'n baie groot; **~bone** balein; ~ **oil** walvistraan; **~r** walvisvaar= der

whal′ing walvisvangs

wharf (wharves, -s) (n) kaai; (v) vasmeer

what (a) wat, watter; (pron) wat; hoe; *come* ~ *may,* wat ook gebeur; ~ *if he refuses?* sê nou maar hy weier? *so* ~? en wat daar= van? (adv) hè? nè?

whatev′er wat ook al; *nothing* ~, niks hoe= genaamd nie

wheat koring; ~ **flour** koringmeel

whee′dle flikflooi, vlei, pamperlang

wheel (n) wiel, rat; (v) draai, rol; ~ *round,* swenk; ~ **alignment** wielsporing; **~bar= row** kruiwa; ~ **cap** wieldop; **~chair** rol= stoel, siekestoel; **~wright** wamaker

when (adv, conj) wanneer; toe

whence waarvandaan, vanwaar; *I take it* ~ *it comes,* van 'n esel kan jy 'n skop verwag

whene′er′, whenev′er, whensoev′er wan= neer ook al

where (n) wanneer; (pron) waarheen, waar= vandaan; (adv) waar; waarheen, waarna= toe, waarso; **~about(s)** (n) verblyfplek; adres; (a) waaromtrent, waar; **~as′** na= demaal, aangesien, daar; **~by′** waardeur, waarby; **~fore** waarom; **~of′** waarvan; **~on′** waarop; **~to′** waarby, waarnatoe; **~upon′** waarop

wher′ever waar ook al

whet (-ted, -ted) slyp; opwek (eetlus)

wheth′er (pron) watter van twee; (conj) hetsy; of; al dan nie; ~ *we go or not,* of ons gaan of nie

whet′stone slypsteen

whey wei, dikmelkwater

which watter, wie, wat; **~ever, ~soev′er** wat ook

whiff (n) asemtog, trek; luggie. sigaartjie

while[1] (n) rukkie; *after a* ~, kort daarna/ daarop; *once in a* ~, af en toe

while[2] (conj) terwyl, onderwyl, solank as

whim gril, nuk, gier, frats

whim′per (v) kerm, kreun, sanik, grens

whim′sical wispelturig, vol nukke/fiemies

whine (v) kerm, tjank, huil

whip (n) sweep, peits; karwats; sweep (par= lement); (v) **(-ped, -ped)** slaan, piets, raps; **~cord** sweepkeper, sweepkoord; ~ = **handle** sweepstok; **~lash (-es)** voorslag

whipped′ cream slagroom

whipp′et windhond

whipp′ing geslaan; pak slae, loesing; ~ **bag** slaansak; ~ **boy** sondebok

whip′round geldinsameling

whirl (v) dwarrel, draai; maal (water)

whirl: **~pool** draaikolk, maalstroom; ~ = **wind** (d)warrelwind; windhoos

whisk (n) besem, stoffer; eierklitser; (v) af= borsel; rondfladder; klits, klop

whis′ker wangbaard; bak(ke)baard

whis′per (n) gefluister; geritsel; (v) fluister

whi′stle (n) gefluit; fluitjie; *wet one's* ~, jou keel natmaak; 'n dop steek; (v) fluit

white (n) wit; blank; Blanke; (v) wit; (a) wit; bleek; blank; *a* ~ *lie,* 'n noodleuen; **~= ant** rysmier; **~-hot** witgloeiend; **~-liver= ed** lafhartig; **~wash** (n) witsel, witkalk; (v) wit, afwit

whit′low fyt; omloop

Whit′suntide Pinksterdae

whiz (v) **(-zed, -zed)** sis, gons, fluit

who wie, wat; **~ev′er, ~soev′er** wie ook (al)

whole (n) geheel; alles; totaal; *on the* ~, oor/in die algemeen; (a) heel; volkome; *go the* ~ *hog,* tot die uiterste gaan; **~-hearted** hartlik, opreg; *I agree with you* **~-heartedly,** ek stem volmondig met jou saam

whole′sale (n) groothandel; *sell by* ~, in grootmaat verkoop; (a) groothandel=; (adv) op groot skaal; ~ **dealer** groothan= delaar; ~ **prices** groothandelpryse; ~ **trade** groothandel

whole′some gesond, voedsaam

whole′wheat volgraan, volkoring

wholl′y heeltemal, volkome

whom wat, vir wie; **~ev′er, ~soev′er** wie ook (al)

whoop skree(u), roep; optrek (kinkhoes); **~ing cough** kinkhoes

whop (-ped, -ped) ransel; oorwin; verslaan; **~per** deeglike loesing; 'n groot leuen

whore hoer

whose wie s'n, wie se, van wie

why (n) die waarom; *go into the ~s and wherefores*, alle besonderhede wil weet; (adv) hoekom, waarom

wick pit (van lamp of kers)

wick'ed goddeloos, sondig, sleg, boos; onnutsig, ondeund; wys (dier)

wick'er biesie, riet; rottang; **~ chair** rottangstoel; **~ cradle** biesiewieg; **~ work** vlegwerk, rottangwerk

wick'et deurtjie; paaltjie (by krieketspel); baan; **~keeper** paaltjiewagter

wide (a, adv) wyd, breed, ruim, uitgebreid; *a ~ difference*, 'n hemelsbreë verskil; **~-awake** helder wakker; uitgeslape; **~spread** uitgebrei; wyd versprei

wid'ow weduwee, weduvrou; **~er** weewenaar; **~hood** weduweeskap; **~'s weeds** rouklere; (a) *~ed father*, beroofde vader

width wydte, breedte; uitgestrektheid

wield hanteer; swaai; ~ *the pen*, die pen voer; ~ *the sceptre*, die septer swaai

wife (wives) vrou, eggenote; **~ly** vroulik

wig vals hare, pruik

wig'wam Indiaanse tent/hut, wigwam

wild (n) wildernis, woesteny; (a, adv) wild, woes; onstuimig; *make a ~ guess*, blindweg raai; a *~-looking fellow*, 'n wildewragtig; **~ boar** wildevark; **~ cat** (n) wildekat; (a) onbesonne; **~cat strike** wilde/onwettige staking

wil'debees (-te) wildebees

wil'derness (-es) wildernis, woesteny

wild'life natuurlewe; **~ society** natuurleweereniging

wil'ful opsetlik; moedswillig; eiewys

will[1] (n) wil; wens; testament; (v) (-ed, -ed) wil, begeer; bemaak (in testament)

will[2] (v) (would) sal; **~ing** gewillig; bereid; **~lingness** gewilligheid

Will'ie Wink'ie Klaas Vakie, Sandmannetjie

will-o'-the-wisp' dwaallig; rondspringer

will'ow wilg, wilgerboom, wilker(boom)

will'power wilskrag

will'y-nill'y noodgedwonge, teen wil en dank

wilt kwyn, verwelk, verlep

wil'y listig, geslepe, slim; oorlams

win (n) oorwinning; (v) (**won, won**) wen; verdien

wince (v) terugdeins; huiwer; ineenkrimp

winch (-es) windas; slinger; hystoestel

wind[1] (v) (**wound, wound**) hys; slinger; draai, opwen; ~ *up*, opwen; likwideer

wind[2] (n) wind; lug; *find out how the ~ blows*, die kat uit die boom kyk; *take the ~ out of one's sails*, iem. die loef afsteek; (v) blaas; asem skep; **~break** windskerm; **~breaker** windjekker; **~ charger/generator** windlaaier; **~fall** afgewaaide vrugte; buitekans, meevallertjie; **~ gauge** windmeter

wind'ing (a) kronkelend, draai-; **~ staircase** wenteltrap; **~-up** likwidasie

wind'mill windmeul, windpomp

win'dow venster, raam; **~ envelope** ruitkoevert, vensterkoevert; **~ pane** vensterruit; **~ shopping** winkelwandel, loerkoop; **~ sill** vensterbank

wind: **~ resistance** windweerstand; **~screen** vooruit (kar); **~screen wiper** ruitveër; **~ surfing** seilplankry; **~y** winderig; windmakerig, ydel

wine wyn, kromhoutsap; **~bibber** wynvlieg, drinkebroer; **~glass** (-es) wynkelkie, wynglas; **~press** (-s) parsbalie, wynpers; **~ry** wynkelder; **~tub** kuipbalie; **~vault** wynkelder

wing (n) vlerk (voël); vleuel; *clip one's ~s*, iem. kortwiek

wink (n) wink, knipogie, oogwink; *forty ~s*, dutjie; (v) wink; ~ *at*, knik vir; **~ing** (n) oogknip

winn'er wenner, oorwinnaar

winn'ing (a) wen-; innemend, voorkomend; *the ~ side*, die wenkant; **~ post** wenpaal; **~ shot** kishou (sport)

win'some innemend, bevallig, bekoorlik

win'ter (n) winter; (v) oorwinter; **~ quarters** winterverblyf; **~ sports** wintersport

win'try winteragtig; koud, ysig (weer)

wipe (v) afvee, afdroog; ~ *one's eyes*, jou oë afvee/uitvee; ~ *out*, uitwis; uitvee

wire (n) draad; *barbed ~*, doringdraad; *live ~*, gelaaide draad; staatmaker; (v) bedraad; **~cutter** draadtang; **~dancer** koorddanser; **~less** draadloos; ~ **netting**

sifdraad, ogiesdraad; **~-puller** draad-trekker; konkelaar

wis'dom wysheid, verstand; **~ tooth** (**..teeth**) verstand(s)kies, verstand(s)tand

wise[1] (n) manier, wyse

wise[2] (a) verstandig, wys; raadsaam; *nobody would have been the ~r,* daar sou geen haan na gekraai het nie; **~acre** wysneus, beterweter

wish (n) (-es) wens, begeerte; *good ~es,* beste wense; (v) wens, begeer; *~ one well,* iem. die beste toewens; **~bone, ~ing bone** geluksbeentjie

wish'ful verlangend; **~ thinking** wens-denkery; wensdinkery

wish'ing well (n) wensput

wistar'ia bloureent, wistaria

wit (n) geestigheid; vernuf; verstand; *at one's ~'s end,* ten einde raad

witch (-es) (n) heks, towenares; (v) toor, beheks; **~craft** toordery, towerkuns; **~doctor** toordokter; **~weed** rooiblom, mieliegif

with met, saam met, saam, mee; *~ it,* by-derwets; *put up ~,* verdra; *~ time,* met verloop van tyd; *tremble ~ fear,* bewe van angs

withdraw' (**..drew, ..drawn**) terugtrek; herroep; *~ from the match,* hom onttrek aan die wedstryd; **~al** opvraging; terug-trekking; **~al slip** opvrastrokie; **~al symptom** onttrek(king)simptoom

with'er (v) verwelk, verlep; kwyn; uitdor

withhold' (**..held, ..held**) terughou

within' (adv) binne-in; binne; (prep) binne

with-it byderwets, modern van opvatting

without' (adv) buitekant; *do ~,* sonder klaarkom; (prep) sonder, buite; *~ doubt,* ongetwyfeld

withstand' (**..stood, ..stood**) weerstaan

wit'ness (n) (-es) getuie; getuienis; (v) sien; getuig; *~ box* (-es) getuiebank

wit: **~ticism** kwinkslag; **~tingly** opsetlik, voorbedagtelik; **~ty** geestig, gevat

wiz'ard towenaar, dolosgooier

wobb'le (v) waggel, slinger; weifel

woe wee, ellende, ramp; (pl) ellende

wolf (**wolves**) wolf; **~call** roepfluit

wo'man (n) (**..men**) vrou; vroumens; (a) vroue-; **~ doctor** dokteres; **~ hater** vrouehater; **~ish** verwyf, vroulik; **~ly** vroulik, swak; **~ power** vrouekrag, *also*

fem power; **~ soldier** soldoedie, sollie-dollie; **~ student** student(e)

womb baarmoeder, moederskoot, uterus

wom'en's: **~ lib(erty)** vrouevryheid; **~ resi-dence** dameskoshuis

won *see* **win**

wo'nder (n) wonder, wonderwerk; *work ~s,* wondere verrig; (v) wonder; **~ful** won-derlik; verbasend; **~land** towerland; **~ment** verwondering

woo (v) die hof maak; bearbei; flikflooi

wood bos, woud; hout; (pl) bosse; **~bine** kanferfoelie; **~ carving** houtsnykuns; **~cock** houtsnip; **~cut** houtsnee; **~cut-ter** houtkapper; houtgraveur; **~ed** bos-ryk; **~en** van hout, hout-; houterig; **~s'man** (**..men**) boswagter; houtkapper; **~nymph** bosnimf; **~pecker** houtkapper; **~pigeon** bosduif; **~work** houtwerk; **~y** bosryk

woof weefsel; *warp and ~,* skering en inslag

wool wol; wolgoed; *~ gathering* (n) ver-strooiheid; (a) afgetrokke; **~grower** skaapboer, wolboer; **~len** van wol, wol-; **~len blanket,** wolkombers; **~ly** wollerig; **~pack** wolbaal; **~shears** skaapskêr; **~-trade** wolhandel; wolbedryf

word (n) woord; berig; bevel; *too funny for ~s,* baie snaaks; *have ~s with,* rusie maak met; *~ of honour,* erewoord; *in other ~s,* met ander woorde; **~ing** bewoording; **~-perfect** rolvas; **~play** woordspeling; **~processor** teksverwerker; **~ splitting** haarklowery

wore *see* **wear**

work (n) werk, arbeid; (pl) fabriek, werk-plek; (v) werk, arbei; *~ together,* saam-werk; **~aholic** werkolis, werkslaaf; **~box** (-es) werkkissie; **~day** (-s) werkdag; **~er** werker, arbeider

work'ing (n) bewerking; beheer; (a) wer-kend; **~ capital** bedryfskapitaal; **~ hours** werktyd, werkure; **~ knowledge** gangbare kennis

work: **~man** (**..men**) werk(s)man; **~man-ship** vakmanskap; **~ session** werksitting, werksessie; **~shop** werkgroep, werk(s)-winkel, werklokaal; **~ shy** werksku

world wêreld; *not for the ~,* vir geen geld ter wêreld nie; *all the ~ is a stage,* die wêreld is 'n speeltoneel; **~ling** wêreldling;

~liness wêreldsgesindheid; **~ly** wêrelds; **~wide** wêreldwyd

worm (n) wurm; ruspe(r); (v) kruip; wurm; wriemel

worn afgeleef, verslyt, *see* **wear**

wo′rry (n) (**worries**) kwelling, bekommernis, sorg; (v) (**worried, worried**) kwel, pla, lol; ~ **oneself to death,** jou doodkwel; ~ **with questions,** met vrae lastig val; ~ **beads** kommerkrale

worse (n) ergste, slegste; (a, adv) *from bad to* ~, van kwaad tot erger; *for better and for* ~, in lief en leed

wor′ship (n) aanbidding, verering; godsdiens; *His W* ~ *the Mayor,* Sy Edelagbare die Burgemeester; *public* ~, erediens; *Your W* ~, Edelagbare; (v) (**-ped, -ped**) aanbid, vereer, dien; verafgo(o)d; ~ *the Lord,* die Here aanbid; **~per** aanbidder

worst (n) ergste; (a) ergste, slegste

wor′sted (n) kamstof

worth (n) waarde, prys; (a) werd; *not* ~ *while,* nie die moeite werd nie; **~less** waardeloos; **~while** waardevol, verdienstelik

wor′thy eerbaar, (agtens)waardig

would wou, sou will; **~-be** kastig, sogenaamd; aanstaande, aspirant-

wound[1] (n) wond, besering, seerplek; (v) wond, verwond, kwes; grief

wound[2] *see* **wind** (v)

wound: ~ed gekwes; verwond, gewond; **~ed soldier,** gewonde soldaat

wov′en *see* **weave**

wra′ngle (n) twis, rusie; (v) twis, rusie maak; **~r** rusiemaker, skoorsoeker

wrap (n) (om)hulsel; omslag; tjalie, serp, halsdoek; (v) (**-ped, -ped**) inwikkel, inrol; **~ped in paper,** in papier toegedraai; **~per** omslag; **~ping** omhulsel, omslag; **~ping paper** toedraaipapier; geskenkpapier

wrath gramskap, toorn; **~ful** boos, kwaad

wreath krans (begrafnis); vlegwerk

wreck (n) wrak; skipbreuk; *go to* ~ *and ruin,* te gronde gaan; (v) strand; verongeluk; **~ed goods,** wrakgoed; **~ed sailors,** skipbreukelinge; **~age** wrakstukke; **~er** verwoester

wren winterkoninkie (voël)

wrench (n) (**-es**) skroefsleutel; ~ *open,* oopbreek

wre′stle (v) worstel, stoei; **~r** stoeier

wre′stling (n) stoei, worsteling; *all-in* ~, rofstoei; *professional* ~, beroepstoei; ~ **match** (**-es**) stoeiwedstryd

wretch (**-es**) ellendeling, skurk; **~ed** ellendig; vervlakste, vervloekste

wrig′gle woel, kronkel, kriewel

wring (v) (**wrung, wrung**) wring, uitdraai; ~ *the neck of,* die nek omdraai

wri′nkle (n) rimpel, plooi; **~d** gerimpel

wrist handgewrig, pols; **~band** armband; ~ **guard** polsskerm; **~let** armband, polsband; **~watch** (**-es**) polsoorlosie

write (**wrote, written**) skryf, neerskryf, opskryf; ~ *a cheque,* 'n tjek uitskryf; **~r** skrywer, outeur; **~r's cramp** skryfkramp; **~-up** opvyseling; berig

writhe (ineen)krimp, (ver)wring; ~ *with pain,* krimp v.d. pyn

writ′ing skrif, geskrif; *in* ~, op skrif; ~ **desk** lessenaar, skryftafel; ~ **pad** skryfblok; ~ **paper** skryfpapier; ~ **table** lessenaar

writt′en geskrewe; skriftelik; *see* **write**

wrong (n) onreg, oortreding; ongelyk; (a) verkeerd; *the* ~ *side up,* onderstebo; *what is* ~ ? wat makeer? (adv) mis, verkeerd; **~doer** kwaaddoener; **~doing** oortreding; **~ful** onwettig

wrote *see* **write**

wrought gevorm, bewerk; gesmee; ~ **iron** smeeyster

wrung *see* **wring**

wry skeef, verdraai; *with a* ~ *smile,* met 'n skewe glimlag

X

Xho′sa Xhosa

X′mas Kersfees

X′-ray (n) (**-s**) X-straal, röntgenstraal

xyl′ograph houtsnede, houtgravure

xyl′ophone xilofoon, houtharmonika

xyl′ose houtsuiker

Y

yacht (n) (seil)jag; ~ **club** jagklub, seilbootklub; ~**ing** seiljagvaart; ~ **racing** seiljagwedvaart
yam broodwortel
yap (v) (-ped, -ped) blaf, kef
yard[1] agterplaas, werf; ~**sneaker** sluipslaper
yard[2] jaart, tree; ~ **measure** duimstok
yarn storie, grap; draad, garing
yawn (n) gaap; (v) gaap; ~**ing** gegaap
year jaar; *the* ~ *before last*, voorverlede jaar; ~**book** jaarboek; ~-**end** jaareinde; ~**ling** jaaroud (dier); ~**ly** jaarliks
yearn smag, hunker; ~**ing** (n) verlange; (a) verlangend, smagtend
yeast suurdeeg; gis
yell (n) gil, angskreet; (v) gil, skree(u)
yell'ow geel; jaloers; agterdogtig; lafhartig; ~ **peach** (-es) geelperske; ~ **press** sensasiepers; ~**wood** geelhout
yelp tjank, kef
yes ja: ~-**man** (..men) jabroer
yes'terday gister; *the day before* ~, eergister
yet (adv) nog; egter; nogtans, tog, darem; ~ *he comes to school,* tog kom hy skool toe

yield (n) opbrengs, lewering; (v) (op)lewer; toegee (by pad); ~ *profit,* wins oplewer/afwerp; ~ *to temptation,* vir die versoeking/verleiding swig; ~**sign** toegeeteken, voorrangteken
yod'el (-led, -led) jodel
yo'ga joga
yo'gi jogi (volgeling van joga)
yog'hurt joghurt
yoke (n) juk; band; skouerstuk
yok'el takhaar, agtervelder, javel
yolk eiergeel, dooier
you jou; jy; julle; u (beleef); ~ *never can tell,* 'n mens weet nooit nie
young·(n) kleintjie; (a) jong, jeugdig; *her* ~ *man,* haar kêrel/vryer; ~**ster** seun, jongeling, kind
your u; jou; julle
yours joue; julle s'n; van u; ~ *faithfully,* hoogagtend, hoogagtend die uwe; ~ *sincerely,* opreg die uwe
yourself' jouself, uself
youth jeug; (-s) jongkêrel; ~**ful** jeugdig; jong; ~ **hostel** jeugherberg; ~ **preparedness** jeugweerbaarheid
yo'-yo (-s) klimtol
Yule Kersfees; ~**tide** Kerstyd

Z

zeal ywer, geesdrif
zeal'ous ywerig, vurig, geesdriftig, vlytig
zeb'ra sebra, kwagga; ~ **crossing** sebraoorgang; ~ **reflector** sebrakaatser
zen'ith toppunt, senit
zeph'yr sefier, luggie, windjie
zep'pelin lugskip, zeppelin
zer'o (-es) zero, sero, nul; vriespunt
zest smaak, gretigheid, genot; geesdrif
zig'zag (n) sigsag(pad); kronkel(pad); (a) sigsag-, slingerend, kwing-kwang
Zimbab'we Zimbabwe; ~*an economy,* Zimbabwiese ekonomie; ~**an** Zimbabwiër (persoon)
zinc sink

zinn'ia jakobregop
zip gerits; pit, fut; rits; ~ **fastener,** ~**per** rits(sluiter), treksluiter
zith'er siter
zod'iac diereriem, sodiak
zone songordel; sone; landstreek
zon'ing sonering; re~ hersonering
zoo dieretuin
zoolog'ical dierkundig, diere-; ~ **garden** dieretuin
zool'ogy dierkunde, soölogie
zoom zoem; ~ *away,* zoem weg; ~ *in,* zoem in; ~ **apparatus** zoemer; ~ **lens** zoemlens
Zul'u (-s) Zoeloe; Zoeloetaal; ~ **chief** Zoeloehoof, indoena; ~**land** Zoeloeland

ABBREVIATIONS

A

English		Afrikaans
a.	adjective	b.nw.
@	at	teen
AA	Automobile Association	AA
abl.	ablative	abl.
a/c	account	rek.
acc.	accusative	akk.
a/d	after date	n/d
AD	*Anno Domini* (in the Year of our Lord)	n.C.
ADC	Aide-de-camp	adj.
ad inf.	*ad infinitum* (to the infinite)	ad inf.
adj.	adjective	b.nw.
ad lib.	*ad libitum* (at pleasure)	ad lib.
Admin.	Administration; Administrator	admin.
adv.	adverb	bw.
Adv.	Advocate	adv.
ad val.	*ad valorem* (according to value)	ad val.
advt./ad.	advertisement	advt.
AEC	Atomic Energy Corporation	AEK
Afr.	Afrikaans; Afrikaner	Afr.
AGM	Annual General Meeting	—
AI	artificial insemination	KI
AIDS	Acquired Immunodeficiency Syndrome	Vigs
alt.	altitude	hoogte
a.m.	*ante meridiem* (before noon)	vm.
amp.	ampère	amp.
amt.	amount	bedr.
ANC	African National Congress	—
Angl.	Anglicism	Angl.
anon.	anonymous	anon.
appro.	approval	op sig
Apr.	April	Apr.
arith.	arithmetic	Rek.
art.	article	art.
ass.	association	ver.
Assocom	Associated Chambers of Commerce	—
asst.	assistant	asst.
attrib.	attributive	attr.
Aug.	August	Aug.
awol	absent without leave	asv

B

b.	born; bowled	geb.
B.A.	*Baccalaureus Artium* (Bachelor of Arts)	B.A.

English		Afrikaans
B.Agr.	*Baccalaureus Agriculturae* (Bachelor of Agriculture)	B. Agric.
bal.	balance	bal.
BBC	British Broadcasting Corporation	—
B.C.	before Christ	v.C.
B.Ch.	*Baccalaureus Chirurgiae* (Bachelor of Surgery)	B.Ch.
B.Com.	*Baccalaureus Commercii* (Bachelor of Commerce)	B.Com.
Bd.	Boulevard	bd.
B.D.	*Baccalaureus Divinitatis* (Bachelor of Divinity)	B.D.
b/d	brought down	a/b
B.Econ.	*Baccalaureus Economiae* (Bachelor of Economics)	B.Econ.
B.Ed.	*Baccalaureus Educationis* (Bachelor of Education)	B.Ed.
b.f.	brought forward	o/b
biol.	biology	Biol.
B/L	Bill of Lading	L/B
B.M.	*Baccalaureus Medicinae* (Bachelor of Medicine)	B.M.
B.Mus	*Baccalaureus Musicae* (Bachelor of Music)	B.Mus.
bot.	botany	Plantk.
B/P	Bills Payable	B/W
B/R	Bills Receivable	O/W
Brig.-Genl.	Brigadier-General	brig.-genl.
Bro. in X.	Brother in Christ	Br. in X.
Bros	Brothers	gebrs.
B.Sc.	*Baccalaureus Scientiae* (Bachelor of Science)	B.Sc.
B.V.Sc.	*Baccalaureus Veterinariae Scientiae* (Bachelor of Veterinary Science)	B.V.Sc.

C

C	Celsius; Centigrade	C
c	cent	c
CA	Chartered Accountant	GR
CAPAB	Cape Performing Arts Board	KRUIK
caps.	capital letters	hfl.
C/B	Credit Balance	k.s.
cc	cubic centimetre	cc
c/d	carried down	a/b
cent	*centum* (hundred)	honderd
cert.	certificate	sert.
cf.	*confer* (compare)	vgl., cf.
cg	centigram	cg
chap.	chapter	hfst.
Ch.B.	*Chirurgiae Baccalaureus* (Bachelor of Surgery)	Ch.B.

English		Afrikaans
chem.	chemistry	Skeik.
Ch.M.	*Chirurgiae Magister* (Master of Surgery)	Ch.M.
C.I.	Christian Institute	C.I.
CID	Criminal Investigation Department	—
c.i.f.	cost, insurance, freight	k.a.v.
circ.	*circa, circiter* (about)	ca.
cit.	citation	sit.
cl	centilitre	cl
cm	centimetre	cm
C/N	Credit Note	K/N
Co	Company	Kie., My.
c/o	care of	p.a.
C.O.	Commanding Officer	B.O.
COD	cash on delivery	k.b.a.
COL	cost of living	—
Comdt.	Commandant	kmdt.
conj.	conjunction	voegw.
cons.	consignment	bes.
contd.	continued	vervolg
Co-op.	Cooperative Society	Koöp.
cor.	corner	h/v
C.P.	Cape Province	K.P.
CP	Conservative Party	KP
cp.	compare	vgl.
Cpl.	Corporal	kpl.
Cr.	Credit	kt.
Cr.	Creditor	kr.
CSA	Christian Students' Association	CSV
CSIR	Council for Scientific and Industrial Research	WNNR
cu(b).	cubic	kub.
cum div.	*cum dividendo* (with dividend)	cum div.
CV	*Curriculum Vitae*	CV
CWO	cash with order	k.m.b.

D

D	Roman 500	D
dat.	dative	dat.
dB	decibel	dB
D.Com.	*Doctor Commercii* (Doctor of Commerce)	D.Com.
D.D.	*Doctor Divinitas* (Doctor of Divinity)	D.D.
d.d.	*de dato* (dated)	d.d.
d/d	days after date	d.d.
Dec.	December	Des.
def.	definition	def., dep.
DEIC	Dutch East India Company	HOIK
dept.	department	dept.
dg	decigram	dg
Dg	decagram	Dg

English		Afrikaans
dict.	dictionary	wbk.
dim.	diminutive	verklw.
dipl.	diploma	dipl.
dist.	district	distr.
div.	division	afd.
div.	dividend	div.
DIY	Do it yourself	—
Dℓ	Decalitre	Dℓ
dℓ	decilitre	dℓ
D.Litt.	*Doctor Literarum* (Doctor of Literature)	D.Litt.
dm	decimetre	dm
Dm	Decametre	Dm
D/N	Debit Note	D/N
do.	*ditto* (the same)	do.
doz.	dozen	dos.
D.Phil.	*Doctor Philosophiae* (Doctor of Philosophy)	D.Phil.
Dr	Doctor	dr(.)
Dr.	Debtor	dr.
Dr.	drive	rln
DRC	Dutch Reformed Church	NGK, NHK, Geref.K.
Drs	Doctorandus	drs.
Dr.Theol.	*Doctor Theologiae* (Doctor of Theology)	Dr.Theol.
D.Sc.	*Doctor Scientiae* (Doctor of Science)	D.Sc.
Du.	Dutch	Holl.
D.V.	*Deo volente* (God being willing)	D.V.

E

ea.	each	elk
ECG	Electrocardiogram	EKG
econ.	economics	Ekon.
Ed.	Editor	red.
ed.	edition	dr., ed.
E & OE	errors and omissions excepted	F & WU
e.g.	*exempli gratia* (for example)	bv.
encl.	enclosure	byl.
Eng.	English	Eng.
E.P.	Eastern Province	O.P.
EPNS	electroplate on nickel silver	versilwer
ESCOM	Electric Supply Commission	EVKOM
ESP	extrasensory perception	BSW
Esq.	Esquire	mnr., Weled. Heer.
est.	established	opgerig
etc.	*et cetera* (and others)	ens., e.a., e.d.m., e.s.m.
et seq.	*et sequentes* (and the following)	e.v.
exam.	examination	eks.
ex off.	*ex officio* (by virtue of his office)	ex off., ampshalwe

English		Afrikaans
F	Fahrenheit	F
f.a.s.	free alongside ship	v.l.s.
FCIS	Fellow of the Chartered Institute of . Secretaries	FCIS
Feb.	February	Feb.
fem.	feminine	v(r).
fig.	figure	fig., afb.
(f.)l. to r.	from left to right	(v.)l.n.r.
FM	frequency modulation	FM
f.o.b.	free on board	v.a.b., v.o.s.
f.o.c.	free of charge	franko
fo.	folio	deel
foll.	following	vlg., ost.
f.o.r.	free on rail	v.o.s.
f.o.s.	free on ship	v.a.b.
Foskor	Phosphate Development Corporation	Foskor
Fr.	French	Fr.
fr.	franc	fr.
Frelimo	Front for the Liberation of Mozambique	—
Fri.	Friday	Vr.
ft.	foot, feet	vt.

G

g	gram	g
gal.	gallon	gall., gell.
G.B.	Great Britain	G.B.
GCF	greatest common factor	GGD
gen.	genitive	gen.
geogr.	geography	Aardr., Geogr.
geol.	geology	Aardk., Geol.
geom.	geometry	Meetk.
GMT	Greenwich Mean Time	—
GNP	Gross National Product	BNP
govt.	government	goewt., reg.
GPO	General Post Office	HPK
GST	General Sales Tax	AVB
gym.	gymnastics; gymnasium	gimn.

H

h.	hour	uur
ha	hectare	ha
HCF	Highest Common Factor	GGD
HDE	Higher Diploma in Education	HOD
H.E.	His Excellency	S.Eks.
hg	hectogram	hg
H.H.	Her Highness	H.H.

English		Afrikaans
His. Hon.	His Honour	S.Ed., S.Ed. Agb.
hist.	history	Gesk.
hℓ	hectolitre	hℓ
hm	hectometre	hm
H.M.	His (Her) Majesty	S. (H.) M.
HNP	Herstigte Nasionale Party	HNP
Hon.	Honourable	Agb., Ed., Ed. Agb.
Hon. Sec.	Honorary Secretary	ere-sekr.
H.Q.	Headquarters	—
HSRC	Human Sciences Research Council	RGN

I

ib(id)	*ibidem* (in the same place)	ib(id)
id.	*idem* (the same)	id.
IDB	Illicit Diamond Buying	ODH
IDC	Industrial Development Corporation	NOK
i.e.	*id est* (that is)	d.i.
illus.	illustrated	geïll.
imp.	imperative	geb. wys., imp.
imperf.	imperfect	onvolm. tyd, impf.
inc.	incorporated	geïnk./ingelyf
incl.	inclusive	insl.
inf.	infinitive	inf.
infra dig.	*infra dignitatem* (beneath one's dignity)	infra dig.
(in) loc. cit.	*(in) loco citato* (in the passage already quoted)	(in) loc. cit., t.a.p.
inst.	*instant* (this month)	deser
int. al.	*inter alia* (among other things)	o.a.
interj.	interjection	tw.
interm.	intermediate	interm.
internat.	international	internasionaal
inv.	invoice	fakt.
IOU	I owe you	skuldbewys
I.Q.	Intelligence Quotient	I.K.
Iscor	South African Iron and Steel Industrial Corporation	Yskor
ital.	italics	kurs.

J

Jan.	January	Jan.
Jap.	Japanese	Jap.
JMB	Joint Matriculation Board	GMR
JP	Justice of Peace	VR
JSE	Johannesburg Stock Exchange	JEB
jun.	*junior* (the younger)	jr.
Jul.	July	Jul.
Jun.	June	Jun.

425

K

English		Afrikaans
K.C.	King's Counsel	—
kg	kilogram	kg
kℓ	kilolitre	kℓ
km	kilometre	km
km/h	kilometre per hour	km/h
kW	kilowatt	kW

L

ℓ	litre	ℓ
ℓ/100 km	ℓ per 100 km	ℓ/100 km
L	Roman 50	L
£	*librae* (pounds)	£
lab.	laboratory	lab.
Lat.	Latin	Lat.
lb(s).	*libra(e)* (pound weight)	lb(s).
l.b.w./lbw	leg before wicket	b.v.p./bvp
l.c.	lower case	o.k.
LCM	Least Common Multiple	KGV
Lit.	literature	Letterk.
Litt.D.	*Literarum Doctor* (Doctor of Literature)	Litt.D.
LL.B.	*Legum Baccalareus* (Bachelor of Laws)	LL.B.
LL.D.	*Legum Doctor* (Doctor of Laws)	LL.D.
loc. cit.	*loco citato* (at the place quoted)	t.a.p., l(oc). c(it).
log.	logarithm	log.
L.S.	*Lectori Salutem* (the reader, hail)	L.S., H.d.L.
Lsd	*librae* (pounds), *solidi* (shillings), *denarii* (pence)	Lsd
Lt.	Lieutenant	Luit.
Ltd	Limited	Bpk.

M

m	metre	m
m.	masculine	mnl.
m.	mile	m.
M.	Monsieur	mnr(.)
M	Mark	M
M	Roman 1000	M
M.A.	*Magister Artium* (Master of Arts)	M.A.
Maj.	Major	maj.
Mar.	March	Mrt.
masc.	masculine	mnl.
maths.	mathematics	Mat.
matric.	matriculation	matriek
M.B.	*Medicinae Baccalaureus* (Bachelor of Medicine)	M.B.
MBA	Master's degree in Business Admin.	MBA/MBL

English		Afrikaans
MC	Master of Ceremonies	—
M.Com.	*Magister Commercii* (Master of Commerce)	M.Com.
m/d	months after date	m/d
M.D.	*Medicinae Doctor* (Doctor of Medicine)	M.D.
MEC	Member Executive Committee	LUK
M.Ed.	*Magister Educationis* (Master of Education)	M.Ed.
MEDUNSA	Medical University of Southern Africa	MEDUNSA
memo.	memorandum	mem(o).
Messrs	*Messieurs* (gentlemen)	mnre./firma
mg	milligram	mg
Min.	Minister	min.
min.	minute	min.
mℓ	millilitre	mℓ
mm	millimetre	mm
MOH	Medical Officer of Health	—
M(on).	Monday	Ma.
MP	Member of Parliament	LV
MPC	Member Provincial Council	LPR
Mr	Mister	mnr(.)
MRC	Medical Research Council	MNR
Mrs	Mistress	mev(.)
m/s	months after sight	m/s.
M.Sc.	*Magister Scientiae* (Master of Science)	M.Sc.
MS	manuscript	ms., hs.
Ms	Mizz	Me/Mu
Mt.	Mount	berg
Mus.Bac.	*Musicae Baccalaureus* (Bachelor of Music)	Mus.Bac.
MWU	Mine Workers' Union	MWU

N

N.	North	N.
n.	noun	s.nw.
n.a.	not applicable	n.v.t.
NAPAC	Natal Performing Arts Council	NARUK
Nat.	Nationalist; National	Nat.
NATO	North Atlantic Treaty Organisation	NAVO
N.B.	*Nota Bene* (take notice)	N.B., L.W.
NCO	non-commissioned officer	onderoffisier
No.	*numero* (number)	no., nr.
n.o.	not out	n.u.n.
nom.	nominative	nom.
Nov.	November	Nov.
NP	National Party	NP
NRP	New Republic Party	NRP
N.T.	New Testament	N.T.
NU	Natal University	NU
num.	numeral	telw.
NUSAS	National Union of South African Students	NUSAS

427

O

English		Afrikaans
o/a	on account	o.r.
OAU	Organisation for African Unity	OAE
OB	Ossewa-Brandwag	OB
o.b.	on board	a.b.
obdt.	obedient	dw.
obj.	object	voorw., obj.
O.C.	Officer Commanding	B.O.
Oct.	October	Okt.
O/D	overdraft	O/R
OFS	Orange Free State	OVS
O.K.	All Correct	goed/reg
on a/c	on account	o.r.
op.	*opus* (work)	op.
op. cit.	*opere citato* (in the named book)	op. cit., a.w.
opt.	optative	opt.
ord.	ordinance	ord.
O.T.	Old Testament	O.T.
oz.	ounce	ons

P

English		Afrikaans
p.	page	bl.
p.	*per* (for)	p.
p.a.	*per annum* (per year)	p.j., p.a.
PACOFS	Performing Arts Council O.F.S.	SUKOVS
PACT	Performing Arts Council Transvaal	TRUK
par.	paragraph	par.
part.	participle	dw.
PAYE	pay as you earn	LBS
P/B	private bag	P/S
p.c.	per cent	p.s.
pd.	paid	bet.
PEN	Poets, Editors and Novelists	—
per pro.	*per procurationem* (by proxy)	per pro., p.p.
pl.	plural	mv.
PM	Prime Minister	Premier
p.m.	*post meridiem* (after noon)	nm.
p.m.	per month	p.m.
P.O.	Post Office	Pk.
POW	Prisoner(s) of War	krygsgevangene(s)
pp.	pages	bl.
p.p.	*per procurationem* (by proxy)	p.p., per pro.
p.p.	past participle	verl. dw.
pred.	predicate	pred.
pref.	preface	voorw.
prep.	preposition	voors.
Pres.	President	pres.
priv.	private	priv.

English		Afrikaans
pro.	professional	pro.
Prof	Professor	prof., hoogl.
pron.	pronoun	vnw.
Prov.	Province	Prov.
prox.	*proximo* (next)	a.s.
P.S.	*Post Scriptum* (postscript)	Ns., P.S.
Ps.	Psalm	Ps.
pseud.	pseudonym	ps.
Pte.	Private (soldier)	manskap
P.T.O.	please turn over	b.o., s.o.s.
Pty	Proprietary	Edms
PU	Potchefstroom University	PU vir CHO
PWD	Public Works Department	DOW

Q

Q.E.D.	*quod erat demonstrandum* (that which had to be demonstrated)	Q.E.D.

R

R	Rand	R
r.	radius	r.
r.	right	r.
RAU	Randse Afrikaanse Universiteit	RAU
R.C.	Roman Catholic	RK
RD	refer to drawer	v/t
recd.	received	ontv.
Ref.	Reformed	Herv., Geref.
ref.	reference	ref.
ref.	referee	skeids.
rel. pron.	relative pronoun	betr. vnw.
resp.	respectively	resp./ondersk.
rev.	Reverend	ds., eerw., VDM, pred.
rfn.	rifleman	skr.
R.I.P.	*requiescat in pace* (may he (she) rest in peace)	R.I.V., R.I.P.
r/min	revolutions per minute	r/min
R/P	reply paid	antw. bet.
RPM	retail price maintenance	prysbinding
RSA	Republic of South Africa	RSA
RSC	Regional Services Council	SDR
RSVP	*répondez s'il vous plaît* (please answer)	antw. asb.
Rt. Hon.	Right Honourable	H.Ed., H.Ed. Gestr.
Rt. Rev.	Right Reverend	H. Eerw., Weleerw.
RU	Rhodes University	RU

S

English		Afrikaans
SA	South Africa	SA
SAA	South African Airways	SAL
SAAF	South African Air Force	SALM
SABC	South African Broadcasting Corporation	SAUK
SABRA	South African Bureau for Race Relations	SABRA
SABS	South African Bureau of Standards	SABS
SACC	South African Council of Churches	SARK
SADF	South African Defence Force	SAW
SAP	South African Police	SAP
SASOL	Suid-Afrikaanse Steenkool-, Olie- en Gaskorporasie	SASOL
Sat.	Saturday	Sa.
SATS	SA Transport Services	SAVD
SBDC	Small Business Development Corporation	KSOK
sec.	second	sek.
Sen.	Senate; Senator	sen.
sen.	*senior* (the elder)	sr.
Sept.	September	Sept.
Sergt.	Sergeant	sers.
sgd	signed	w.g., get.
SGE	Superintendent-General of Education	SGO
sing.	singular	enkv.
Soc.	Society	ver.
SOEKOR	Southern Oil Exploration Corporation	SOEKOR
SOS	wireless code-signal of extreme distress	SOS
SP	State President	SP
SPCA	Society for the Prevention of Cruelty to Animals	DBV
spec.	special	spes.
sq.	square	vk.
SRC	Students' Representative Council	SR, VSR
St.	Street	str.
St.	Saint	St.
St.	Sterling	stg.
Std.	Standard	st.
subj.	subject	onderw., subj.
subst.	substantive	substantief
S(un).	Sunday	So.
superl.	superlative	oortr., sup.
s.v.p.	*s'il vous plaît* (if you please)	asb., s.v.p.
SWA	South West Africa	SWA
SWAPO	South West African People's Organisation	SWAPO

T

TB	Tuberculosis	—
TDC	Transkei Development Corporation	TOK

English		Afrikaans
tech.	technical	tegn.
TED	Transvaal Education Department	TOD
tel.	telephone	tel.
Th.	Thursday	Do.
theol.	theology	Teol.
Thur(s).	Thursday	Do.
trans.	transitive	oorg.
transl.	translation	vert.
trig.	trigonometry	Trig.
trs.	transpose	tr.
t.t.	*totus tuus* (wholly yours)	t.t.
TTA	Transvaal Teachers Association	—
T(ues).	Tuesday	Di.
TV	television	TV
Tvl.	Transvaal	Tvl.

U

u.c.	upper case	b.k.
UCT	University of Cape Town	UK
UDI	unilateral declaration of independence	—
UFO	Unidentified Flying Object	VVV
UK	United Kingdom	VK
ult.	*ultimo* (last)	l.l., jl., ult.
UN	University of Natal	UN
UNESCO	United Nations Educational, Scientific and Cultural Organisation	UNESCO
UNISA	University of South Africa	UNISA
Univ.	University	univ.
UN	United Nations	VN
UNO	United Nations Organisation (former name, *see* UN)	VVO
UOFS	University of Orange Free State	UOVS
UP	University of Pretoria	UP
UPE	University of Port Elizabeth	UPE
US	University of Stellenbosch	US
USA	United States of America	VSA
USSR	Union of Socialist Soviet Republics	USSR

V

v.	*versus* (against)	vs.
v.	*vide* (see)	kyk, sien
V	Roman 5	V
vet.	veterinary surgeon	veearts
vid.	*vide* (see, look)	kyk, sien
VIP	very important person	BBP
viz.	*videlicet* (namely)	nl., t.w., d.w.s.

English		Afrikaans
voc.	vocative	vok.
vol.	volume	vol., dl., jg.
vs.	*versus* (against)	vs.

W

W., Wed.	Wednesday	Wo.
w.c.	water closet	privaat
WCC	World Council of Churches	WRK
W/O	warrant officer	adj.-off.
WP	Western Province	WP

X

x	multiplication sign	x
X	Roman 10	X
Xmas	Christmas	Kersfees

Y

yd.	yard	jt.
YMCA	Young Men's Christian Association	CJV
Your Hon.	Your Honour	U Ed.
yrs.	yours	U dw.
YWCA	Young Women's Christian Association	CJV

Z

Zool.	Zoology	Dierk., Soöl.

HIPPOCRENE HANDY DICTIONARIES

*For the traveler of independent spirit and curious mind, this
practical series will help you to communicate, not just to get by.*

All titles:
120 pages 5" x 7 3/4"
$6.95 paper

ARABIC
0463   ISBN 0-87052-960-9

PORTUGUESE
0735   ISBN 0-87052-053-9

CHINESE
0725   ISBN 0-87052-050-4

SERBO-CROATIAN
0728   ISBN 0-87052-051-2

DUTCH
0723   ISBN 0-87052-049-0

SWEDISH
0737   ISBN 0-87052-054-7

GREEK
0464   ISBN 0-87052-961-7

THAI
0468   ISBN 0-87052-963-3

JAPANESE
0466   ISBN 0-87052-962-5

TURKISH
0930   ISBN 0-87052-982-X

Ask for these and other Hippocrene titles at your local
booksellers!

SWAHILI PHRASEBOOK FOR TRAVELERS IN SOUTHERN AFRICA
0073   ISBN 0-87052-970-6
$6.95 paper

More Dictionaries from Hippocrene Books

Albanian-English Dictionary
0744 ISBN 0-87052-077-6 $14.95 paper

English-Albanian Dictionary
0518 ISBN 0-7818-0021-8 $16.95 cloth

English-Arabic Conversational Dictionary
0093 ISBN 0-87052-494-1 $9.95 paper

Modern Military Dictionary: English-Arabic/Arabic-English
0947 ISBN 0-87052-987-0 $30.00 cloth

Arabic For Beginners
0018 ISBN 0-87052-830-0 $7.95 paper

Elementary Modern Armenian Grammar
0172 ISBN 0-87052-811-4 $8.95 paper

Kangaroo Comments and Wallaby Words
0160 ISBN 0-87052-580-8 $7.95 paper

Bulgarian-English Dictionary
English-Bulgarian Dictionary
0331 ISBN 0-87052-154-4 $8.95 paper

Byelorussian-English/English Byelorussian Dictionary
1050 ISBN 0-87052-114-4 $9.95 paper

Cambodian-English Dictionary
0144 ISBN 0-87052-818-1 $14.95 paper

Czech-English English-Czech Concise Dictionary
0276 ISBN 0-87052-981-1 $7.95 paper

Czech Phrasebook
0599 ISBN 0-87052-967-6 $8.95 paper

Danish-English English-Danish Practical Dictioanry
0198 ISBN 0-87052-823-8 $9.95 paper

Dutch-English Concise Dictionary
0606 ISBN 0-87052-910-2 $7.95 paper

American English For Poles
0441 ISBN 83-214-0152-X $20.00 paper

American Phrasebook For Poles
0595 ISBN 0-87052-907-2 $7.95 paper

English for Poles Self-Taught
2648 ISBN 0-88254-904-9 $19.95 cloth

English Conversations for Poles
0762 ISBN 0-87052-873-4 $9.95 paper

American Phrasebook For Russians
0135 ISBN 0-7818-0054-4 $7.95 paper

Estonian-English/English-Estonian Concise Dictionary
1010 ISBN 0-87052-081-4 $11.95 paper

English-Persian Dictionary
0365 ISBN 0-7818-0056-0 $16.95 paper

Persian-English Dictionary
0350 0-7818-0055-2 $16.95 paper

Finnish-English/English-Finnish Concise Dictionary
0142 ISBN 0-87052-813-0 $9.95 paper

French-English/English-French Practical Dictionary
0199 ISBN 0-88254-815-8 $6.95 paper
2065 ISBN 0-88254-928-6 $12.95 cloth

Georgian-English English-Georgian Dictionary
1059 ISBN 0-87052-121-7 $8.95 paper

German-English/English-German Practical Dictionary
0200 ISBN 0-88254-813-1 $6.95 paper
2063 ISBN 0-88254-902-2 $12.95 cloth

English-Hebrew/Hebrew English Conversational Dictionary
0257 ISBN 0-87052-625-1 $7.95 paper

Hindi-English Standard Dictionary
0186 ISBN 0-87052-824-6 $11.95 paper

English-Hindi Standard Dictionary
0923 ISBN 0-87052-978-1 $11.95 paper

Teach Yourself Hindi
0170 ISBN 0-87052-831-9 $7.95 paper

Hungarian Basic Coursebook
0131 ISBN 0-87052-817-3 $14.95 paper

Indonesian-English/English-Indonesian Practical Dictionary
0127 ISBN 0-87052-810-6 $8.95 paper

Irish-English/English-Irish Dictionary and Phrasebook
1037 ISBN 0-87052-110-1 $7.95 paper

Italian-English/English-Italian Practical Dictionary
0201 ISBN 0-88254-816-6 $6.95 paper
2066 ISBN 0-88254-929-4 $12.95 cloth

English-Korean Korean-English Dictionary
1016 ISBN 0-87052-092-X $9.95 paper

Mexico Language and Travel Guide
0503 ISBN 0-87052-622-7 $14.95 paper

Nepali-English/English Nepali Concise Dictionary
1104   ISBN 0-87052-106-3 $8.95 paper

Norwegian-English English-Norwegian Concise Dictionary
0202 ISBN 0-88254-584-1 $7.95 paper

Pilipino-English/English-Pilipino Concise Dictionary
2040   ISBN 0-87052-491-7 $6.95 paper

Polish-English English Polish Practical Dictionary
1014 ISBN 0-87052-083-0 $9.95 paper

Polish-English English-Polish Concise Dictionary
0268 ISBN 0-87052-589-1 $6.95 paper

Polish-English English-Polish Standard Dictionary
0207 ISBN 0-87052-882-3 $14.95 paper
0665 ISBN 0-87052-908-0 $22.50 cloth

Polish Phrasebook and Dictionary
0192 ISBN 0-87052-053-9 $6.95 paper

Portugese-English/English-Portugese Dictionary
0477 ISBN 0-87052-980-3 $14.95 paper

Romanian-English/English-Romanian Dicitonary
0488 ISBN 0-87052-986-2 $19.95 paper

Romanian Conversation Guide
0153 ISBN 0-87052-803-3 $8.95 paper

English-Russian Dictionary
1025 ISBN 0-87052-100-4 $11.95 paper

A Dictionary of 1,000 Russian Verbs
1042 ISBN 0-87052-100-4 $11.95 paper

Russian-English English-Russian Dictionary
2344 ISBN 0-87052-751-7 $9.95 paper
2346 ISBN 0-87052-758-4 $14.95 cloth

Russian-English Dictionary, with Phonetics
0578 ISBN 0-87052-758-4 $11.95 paper

Russian Phrasebook and Dictionary
0597 ISBN 0-87052-965-X $9.95 paper

Slovak-English/English-Slovak Dictionary
1052 ISBN 0-87052-115-2 $8.95 paper

Spanish Verbs
0292 ISBN 07818-0024-2 $8.95

Spanish Grammar
0273 ISBN 0-87052-893-9 $8.95

Spanish-English/English-Spanish Practical Dictionary
0211 ISBN 0-88254-814-X $6.95 paper
2064 ISBN 0-88254-905-7 $12.95 cloth

Swedish-English/English-Swedish Dictioanry
0755 ISBN 0-87052-870-X $16.95 paper
0761 ISBN 0-87052-871-8 $19.95 cloth

Ukranian-English/English Ukranian Dictionary
1055 ISBN 0-87052-116-0 $8.95 paper

Vietnamese-English/English-Vietnamese Dictionary
0529 ISBN 0-87052-924-2 $19.95 paper

English-Yiddish/Yiddish-English
Concise Conversational Dictionary
1019 ISBN 0-87052-969-2 $7.95 paper

TO PURCHASE HIPPOCRENE'S BOOKS contact your local bookstore, or write to Hippocrene Books, 171 Madison Avenue, New York, NY 10016. Please enclose a check or money order, adding $3.00 shipping (UPS) for the first book, and 50 cents for each of the others.

Write also for our full catalog of maps and foreign language dictionaries and phrasebooks.